The *New York Times* Bestseller
The *Wall Street Journal* Bestseller
The *USA Today* Bestseller

'Full praise to *Eragon*, and I want more! A winner . . .
tip of the hat to young master Paolini.'
Anne McCaffrey, author of *The Dragonriders of Pern* series

'An authentic work of great talent . . .
I found myself dreaming about it at night,
and reaching for it as soon as I woke.'
The New York Times Book Review

'Christopher Paolini makes literary magic with
his precocious debut.'
People

'Unusual, powerful . . . fresh and fluid. An impressive
start to a writing career that's sure to flourish.'
Booklist

'An auspicious beginning to both career and series.'
Publishers Weekly

'Will appeal to the legions of readers who have been
captivated by the Lord of the Rings trilogy.'
School Library Journal

THE INHERITANCE CYCLE

ERAGON

and

ELDEST

BOOKS ONE AND TWO

Christopher Paolini

Corgi Books

ERAGON and ELDEST
A CORGI BOOK 978 0 552 55999 7

First published in Great Britain by Doubleday,
an imprint of Random House Children's Books

Published in the US by Alfred A Knopf,
an imprint of Random House Children's Books, a division of Random House Inc.

Eragon
Originally published, in different form, by Paolini International in 2002
Doubleday edition published 2004
Corgi edition published 2005
Text and illustrations copyright © Christopher Paolini, 2002

Eldest
Doubleday edition published 2005
Corgi edition published 2006
Text and illustrations copyright © Christopher Paolini, 2005

This omnibus edition published 2008

1 3 5 7 9 10 8 6 4 2

The Random House Group Limited supports the Forest Stewardship Council (FSC), the leading international forest certification organization. All our titles that are printed on
Greenpeace-approved FSC-certified paper carry the FSC logo. Our paper procurement policy
can be found at www.rbooks.co.uk/environment.

Corgi Books are published by Random House Children's Books,
61–63 Uxbridge Road, London W5 5SA

www.kidsatrandomhouse.co.uk
www.rbooks.co.uk

Addresses for companies within The Random House Group Limited can be found at:
www.randomhouse.co.uk/offices.htm

THE RANDOM HOUSE GROUP Limited Reg. No. 954009

A CIP catalogue record for this book is available from the British Library.

Printed in the UK by CPI Cox & Wyman, Reading, RG1 8EX

ERAGON

INHERITANCE
BOOK ONE

This book is dedicated to my mom, for showing me the magic in the world; to my dad, for revealing the man behind the curtain. And also to my sister, Angela, for helping when I'm 'blue'.

CONTENTS

PROLOGUE: SHADE OF FEAR

Wind howled through the night, carrying a scent that would change the world. A tall Shade lifted his head and sniffed the air. He looked human except for his crimson hair and maroon eyes.

He blinked in surprise. The message had been correct: they were here. Or was it a trap? He weighed the odds, then said icily, "Spread out; hide behind trees and bushes. Stop whoever is coming . . . or die."

Around him shuffled twelve Urgals with short swords and round iron shields painted with black symbols. They resembled men with bowed legs and thick, brutish arms made for crushing. A pair of twisted horns grew above their small ears. The monsters hurried into the brush, grunting as they hid. Soon the rustling quieted and the forest was silent again.

The Shade peered around a thick tree and looked up the trail. It was too dark for any human to see, but for him the faint moonlight was like sunshine streaming between the trees; every detail was clear and sharp to his searching gaze. He remained unnaturally quiet, a long pale sword in his hand. A wire-thin scratch curved down the blade. The weapon was thin enough to slip between a pair of ribs, yet stout enough to hack through the hardest armor.

The Urgals could not see as well as the Shade; they groped like blind beggars, fumbling with their weapons. An owl screeched, cutting through the silence. No one relaxed until the bird flew past. Then the monsters shivered in the cold night; one snapped a twig with his heavy boot. The Shade hissed in anger, and the Urgals shrank back, motionless. He suppressed his distaste—they smelled like fetid meat—and turned away. They were tools, nothing more.

The Shade forced back his impatience as the minutes became hours. The scent must have wafted far ahead of its owners. He did not let the Urgals get up or warm themselves. He denied himself those luxuries, too, and stayed behind the tree, watching the trail. Another gust of wind rushed through the forest. The smell was stronger this time. Excited, he lifted a thin lip in a snarl.

"Get ready," he whispered, his whole body vibrating. The tip of his sword moved in small circles. It had taken many plots and much pain to bring himself to this moment. It would not do to lose control now.

Eyes brightened under the Urgals' thick brows, and the creatures gripped their weapons tighter. Ahead of them, the Shade heard a clink as something hard struck a loose stone. Faint smudges emerged from the darkness and advanced down the trail.

Three white horses with riders cantered toward the ambush, their heads held high and proud, their coats rippling in the moonlight like liquid silver.

On the first horse was an elf with pointed ears and elegantly slanted eyebrows. His build was slim but strong, like a rapier. A powerful bow was slung on his back. A sword pressed against his side opposite a quiver of arrows fletched with swan feathers.

The last rider had the same fair face and angled features as the other. He carried a long spear in his right hand and a white dagger at his belt. A helm of extraordinary craftsmanship, wrought with amber and gold, rested on his head.

Between these two rode a raven-haired elven lady, who surveyed her surroundings with poise. Framed by long black locks, her deep eyes shone with a driving force. Her clothes were unadorned, yet her beauty was undiminished. At her side was a sword, and on her back a long bow with a quiver. She carried in her lap a pouch that she frequently looked at, as if to reassure herself that it was still there.

One of the elves spoke quietly, but the Shade could not hear what was said. The lady answered with obvious authority, and her guards switched places. The one wearing the helm took the lead, shifting his spear to a readier grip. They passed the Shade's hiding place and the first few Urgals without suspicion.

The Shade was already savoring his victory when the wind changed direction and swept toward the elves, heavy with the Urgals' stench. The horses snorted with alarm and tossed their heads. The riders stiffened, eyes flashing from side to side, then wheeled their mounts around and galloped away.

The lady's horse surged forward, leaving her guards far behind. Forsaking their hiding, the Urgals stood and released a stream of black arrows. The Shade jumped out from behind the tree, raised his right hand, and shouted, "Garjzla!"

A red bolt flashed from his palm toward the elven lady, illuminating the trees with a bloody light. It struck her steed, and the horse toppled with a high-pitched squeal, plowing into the ground chest-first. She leapt off the animal with inhuman speed, landed lightly, then glanced back for her guards.

The Urgals' deadly arrows quickly brought down the two elves. They fell from the noble horses, blood pooling in the dirt. As the Urgals rushed to the slain elves, the Shade screamed, "After her! She is the one I want!" The monsters grunted and rushed down the trail.

A cry tore from the elf's lips as she saw her dead companions. She took a step toward them, then cursed her enemies and bounded into the forest.

While the Urgals crashed through the trees, the Shade climbed a piece of granite that jutted above them. From his perch he could see all of the surrounding forest. He raised his hand and uttered, "Istalrí boetk!" and a quarter-mile section of the forest exploded into flames. Grimly he burned one section after another until there was a ring of fire, a half-league across, around the ambush site. The flames looked like a molten crown resting on the forest. Satisfied, he watched the ring carefully, in case it should falter.

3

The band of fire thickened, contracting the area the Urgals had to search. Suddenly, the Shade heard shouts and a coarse scream. Through the trees he saw three of his charges fall in a pile, mortally wounded. He caught a glimpse of the elf running from the remaining Urgals.

She fled toward the craggy piece of granite at a tremendous speed. The Shade examined the ground twenty feet below, then jumped and landed nimbly in front of her. She skidded around and sped back to the trail. Black Urgal blood dripped from her sword, staining the pouch in her hand.

The horned monsters came out of the forest and hemmed her in, blocking the only escape routes. Her head whipped around as she tried to find a way out. Seeing none, she drew herself up with regal disdain. The Shade approached her with a raised hand, allowing himself to enjoy her helplessness.

"Get her."

As the Urgals surged forward, the elf pulled open the pouch, reached into it, and then let it drop to the ground. In her hands was a large sapphire stone that reflected the angry light of the fires. She raised it over her head, lips forming frantic words. Desperate, the Shade barked, "Garjzla!"

A ball of red flame sprang from his hand and flew toward the elf, fast as an arrow. But he was too late. A flash of emerald light briefly illuminated the forest, and the stone vanished. Then the red fire smote her and she collapsed.

The Shade howled in rage and stalked forward, flinging his sword at a tree. It passed halfway through the trunk, where it stuck, quivering. He shot nine bolts of energy from his palm—which killed the Urgals instantly—then ripped his sword free and strode to the elf.

Prophecies of revenge, spoken in a wretched language only he knew, rolled from his tongue. He clenched his thin hands and glared at the sky. The cold stars stared back, unwinking, otherworldly watchers. Disgust curled his lip before he turned back to the unconscious elf.

Her beauty, which would have entranced any mortal man, held no charm for him. He confirmed that the stone was gone, then retrieved his horse from its hiding place among the trees. After tying the elf onto the saddle, he mounted the charger and made his way out of the woods.

He quenched the fires in his path but left the rest to burn.

5

DISCOVERY

Eragon knelt in a bed of trampled reed grass and scanned the tracks with a practiced eye. The prints told him that the deer had been in the meadow only a half-hour before. Soon they would bed down. His target, a small doe with a pronounced limp in her left forefoot, was still with the herd. He was amazed she had made it so far without a wolf or bear catching her.

The sky was clear and dark, and a slight breeze stirred the air. A silvery cloud drifted over the mountains that surrounded him, its edges glowing with ruddy light cast from the harvest moon cradled between two peaks. Streams flowed down the mountains from stolid glaciers and glistening snowpacks. A brooding mist crept along the valley's floor, almost thick enough to obscure his feet.

Eragon was fifteen, less than a year from manhood. Dark eyebrows rested above his intense brown eyes. His clothes were worn from work. A hunting knife with a bone handle was sheathed at his belt, and a buckskin tube protected his yew bow from the mist. He carried a wood-frame pack.

The deer had led him deep into the Spine, a range of untamed mountains that extended up and down the land of Alagaësia. Strange tales and men often came from those mountains, usually boding ill. Despite that, Eragon did not fear the Spine—he was the only hunter near Carvahall who dared track game deep into its craggy recesses.

It was the third night of the hunt, and his food was half gone. If he did not fell the doe, he would be forced to return home empty-handed. His family needed the meat for the rapidly approaching winter and could not afford to buy it in Carvahall.

Eragon stood with quiet assurance in the dusky moonlight, then strode into the forest toward a glen where he was sure the deer would rest. The trees blocked the sky from view and cast feathery shadows on the ground. He looked at the tracks only occasionally; he knew the way.

At the glen, he strung his bow with a sure touch, then drew three arrows and nocked one, holding the others in his left hand. The moonlight revealed twenty or so motionless lumps where the deer lay in the grass. The doe he wanted was at the edge of the herd, her left foreleg stretched out awkwardly.

Eragon slowly crept closer, keeping the bow ready. All his work of the past three days had led to this moment. He took a last steadying breath and—an explosion shattered the night.

The herd bolted. Eragon lunged forward, racing through the grass as a fiery wind surged past his cheek. He slid to a stop and loosed an arrow at the bounding doe. It missed by a finger's breadth and hissed into darkness. He cursed and spun around, instinctively nocking another arrow.

Behind him, where the deer had been, smoldered a large circle of grass and trees. Many of the pines stood bare of their needles. The grass outside the charring was flattened. A wisp of smoke curled in the air, carrying a burnt smell. In the center of the blast radius lay a polished blue stone. Mist snaked across the scorched area and swirled insubstantial tendrils over the stone.

Eragon watched for danger for several long minutes, but the only thing that moved was the mist. Cautiously, he released the tension from his bow and moved forward. Moonlight cast him in pale shadow as he stopped before the stone. He nudged it with an arrow, then jumped back. Nothing happened, so he warily picked it up.

Nature had never polished a stone as smooth as this one. Its flawless surface was dark blue, except for thin veins of white that spiderwebbed across it. The stone was cool and frictionless under his fingers, like hardened silk. Oval and about a foot long, it weighed several pounds, though it felt lighter than it should have.

Eragon found the stone both beautiful and frightening. *Where did it come from? Does it have a purpose?* Then a more disturbing thought came to him: *Was it sent here by accident, or am I meant to have it?* If he had learned anything from the old stories, it was to treat magic, and those who used it, with great caution.

But what should I do with the stone? It would be tiresome to carry, and there was a chance it was dangerous. It might be better to leave it behind. A flicker of indecision ran through him, and he almost dropped it, but something stayed his hand. *At the very least, it might pay for some food,* he decided with a shrug, tucking the stone into his pack.

The glen was too exposed to make a safe camp, so he slipped back into the forest and spread his bedroll beneath the upturned roots of a fallen tree. After a cold dinner of bread and cheese, he wrapped himself in blankets and fell asleep, pondering what had occurred.

PALANCAR VALLEY

The sun rose the next morning with a glorious conflagration of pink and yellow. The air was fresh, sweet, and very cold. Ice edged the streams, and small pools were completely frozen over. After a breakfast of porridge, Eragon returned to the glen and examined the charred area. The morning light revealed no new details, so he started for home.

The rough game trail was faintly worn and, in places, non-existent. Because it had been forged by animals, it often back-tracked and took long detours. Yet for all its flaws, it was still the fastest way out of the mountains.

The Spine was one of the only places that King Galbatorix could not call his own. Stories were still told about how half his army disappeared after marching into its ancient forest. A cloud of misfortune and bad luck seemed to hang over it. Though the trees grew tall and the sky shone brightly, few people could stay in the Spine for long without suffering an accident. Eragon was one of those few—not through any particular gift, it seemed to him, but because of persistent vigilance and sharp reflexes. He had hiked in the mountains for years, yet he was still wary of them. Every time he thought they had surrendered their secrets, something happened to upset his understanding of them—like the stone's appearance.

He kept up a brisk pace, and the leagues steadily disappeared. In late evening he arrived at the edge of a precipitous ravine. The Anora River rushed by far below, heading to Palancar Valley.

Gorged with hundreds of tiny streams, the river was a brute force, battling against the rocks and boulders that barred its way. A low rumble filled the air.

He camped in a thicket near the ravine and watched the moon-rise before going to bed.

It grew colder over the next day and a half. Eragon traveled quickly and saw little of the wary wildlife. A bit past noon, he heard the Igualda Falls blanketing everything with the dull sound of a thousand splashes. The trail led him onto a moist slate outcropping, which the river sped past, flinging itself into empty air and down mossy cliffs.

Before him lay Palancar Valley, exposed like an unrolled map. The base of the Igualda Falls, more than a half-mile below, was the northernmost point of the valley. A little ways from the falls was Carvahall, a cluster of brown buildings. White smoke rose from the chimneys, defiant of the wilderness around it. At this height, farms were small square patches no bigger than the end of his finger. The land around them was tan or sandy, where dead grass swayed in the wind. The Anora River wound from the falls toward Palancar's southern end, reflecting great strips of sunlight. Far in the distance it flowed past the village Therinsford and the lonely mountain Utgard. Beyond that, he knew only that it turned north and ran to the sea.

After a pause, Eragon left the outcropping and started down the trail, grimacing at the descent. When he arrived at the bottom, soft dusk was creeping over everything, blurring colors and shapes into gray masses. Carvahall's lights shimmered nearby in the twilight; the houses cast long shadows. Aside from Therinsford, Carvahall was the only village in Palancar Valley. The settlement was secluded and surrounded by harsh, beautiful land. Few traveled here except merchants and trappers.

The village was composed of stout log buildings with low roofs— some thatched, others shingled. Smoke billowed from the chimneys, giving the air a woody smell. The buildings had wide porches where people gathered to talk and conduct business. Occasionally a window brightened as a candle or lamp was lit. Eragon heard men talking loudly in the evening air while wives scurried to fetch their husbands, scolding them for being late.

Eragon wove his way between the houses to the butcher's shop, a broad, thick-beamed building. Overhead, the chimney belched black smoke.

He pushed the door open. The spacious room was warm and well lit by a fire snapping in a stone fireplace. A bare counter stretched across the far side of the room. The floor was strewn with loose straw. Everything was scrupulously clean, as if the owner spent his leisure time digging in obscure crannies for minuscule pieces of filth. Behind the counter stood the butcher Sloan. A small man, he wore a cotton shirt and a long, bloodstained smock. An impressive array of knives swung from his belt. He had a sallow, pockmarked face, and his black eyes were suspicious. He polished the counter with a ragged cloth.

Sloan's mouth twisted as Eragon entered. "Well, the mighty hunter joins the rest of us mortals. How many did you bag this time?"

"None," was Eragon's curt reply. He had never liked Sloan. The butcher always treated him with disdain, as if he were something unclean. A widower, Sloan seemed to care for only one person—his daughter, Katrina, on whom he doted.

"I'm amazed," said Sloan with affected astonishment. He turned his back on Eragon to scrape something off the wall. "And that's your reason for coming here?"

"Yes," admitted Eragon uncomfortably.

"If that's the case, let's see your money." Sloan tapped his fingers when Eragon shifted his feet and remained silent. "Come on—either you have it or you don't. Which is it?"

"I don't really have any money, but I do—"

"What, no money?" the butcher cut him off sharply. "And you expect to buy meat! Are the other merchants giving away their wares? Should I just hand you the goods without charge? Besides," he said abruptly, "it's late. Come back tomorrow with money. I'm closed for the day."

Eragon glared at him. "I can't wait until tomorrow, Sloan. It'll be worth your while, though; I found something to pay you with." He pulled out the stone with a flourish and set it gently on the scarred counter, where it gleamed with light from the dancing flames.

"Stole it is more likely," muttered Sloan, leaning forward with an interested expression.

Ignoring the comment, Eragon asked, "Will this be enough?"

Sloan picked up the stone and gauged its weight speculatively. He ran his hands over its smoothness and inspected the white veins. With a calculating look, he set it down. "It's pretty, but how much is it worth?"

"I don't know," admitted Eragon, "but no one would have gone to the trouble of shaping it unless it had some value."

"Obviously," said Sloan with exaggerated patience. "But how much value? Since you don't know, I suggest that you find a trader who does, or take my offer of three crowns."

"That's a miser's bargain! It must be worth at least ten times that," protested Eragon. Three crowns would not even buy enough meat to last a week.

Sloan shrugged. "If you don't like my offer, wait until the traders arrive. Either way, I'm tired of this conversation."

The traders were a nomadic group of merchants and entertainers who visited Carvahall every spring and winter. They bought whatever excess the villagers and local farmers had managed to grow or make, and sold what they needed to live through another year: seeds, animals, fabric, and supplies like salt and sugar.

But Eragon did not want to wait until they arrived; it could be a while, and his family needed the meat now. "Fine, I accept," he snapped.

"Good, I'll get you the meat. Not that it matters, but where did you find this?"

"Two nights ago in the Spine—"

"Get out!" demanded Sloan, pushing the stone away. He stomped furiously to the end of the counter and started scrubbing old bloodstains off a knife.

"Why?" asked Eragon. He drew the stone closer, as if to protect it from Sloan's wrath.

"I won't deal with anything you bring back from those damned mountains! Take your sorcerer's stone elsewhere." Sloan's hand suddenly slipped and he cut a finger on the knife, but he seemed not to notice. He continued to scrub, staining the blade with fresh blood.

"You refuse to sell to me!"

"Yes! Unless you pay with coins," Sloan growled, and hefted the knife, sidling away. "Go, before I make you!"

The door behind them slammed open. Eragon whirled around, ready for more trouble. In stomped Horst, a hulking man. Sloan's daughter, Katrina—a tall girl of sixteen—trailed behind him with a determined expression. Eragon was surprised to see her; she usually absented herself from any arguments involving her father. Sloan glanced at them warily, then started to accuse Eragon. "He won't—"

"Quiet," announced Horst in a rumbling voice, cracking his knuckles at the same time. He was Carvahall's smith, as his thick neck and scarred leather apron attested. His powerful arms were bare to the elbow; a great expanse of hairy muscular chest was visible through the top of his shirt. A black beard, carelessly trimmed, roiled and knotted like his jaw muscles. "Sloan, what have you done now?"

"Nothing." He gave Eragon a murderous gaze, then spat, "This . . . boy came in here and started badgering me. I asked him to leave, but he won't budge. I even threatened him and he still ignored me!" Sloan seemed to shrink as he looked at Horst.

"Is this true?" demanded the smith.

"No!" replied Eragon. "I offered this stone as payment for some meat, and he accepted it. When I told him that I'd found it in the

Spine, he refused to even touch it. What difference does it make where it came from?"

Horst looked at the stone curiously, then returned his attention to the butcher. "Why won't you trade with him, Sloan? I've no love for the Spine myself, but if it's a question of the stone's worth, I'll back it with my own money."

The question hung in the air for a moment. Then Sloan licked his lips and said, "This is my own store. I can do whatever I want."

Katrina stepped out from behind Horst and tossed back her auburn hair like a spray of molten copper. "Father, Eragon *is* willing to pay. Give him the meat, and then we can have supper."

Sloan's eyes narrowed dangerously. "Go back to the house; this is none of your business. . . . I said *go!*" Katrina's face hardened, then she marched out of the room with a stiff back.

Eragon watched with disapproval but dared not interfere. Horst tugged at his beard before saying reproachfully, "Fine, you can deal with me. What were you going to get, Eragon?" His voice reverberated through the room.

"As much as I could."

Horst pulled out a purse and counted out a pile of coins. "Give me your best roasts and steaks. Make sure that it's enough to fill Eragon's pack." The butcher hesitated, his gaze darting between Horst and Eragon. "Not selling to me would be a very bad idea," stated Horst.

Glowering venomously, Sloan slipped into the back room. A frenzy of chopping, wrapping, and low cursing reached them. After several uncomfortable minutes, he returned with an armful of wrapped meat. His face was expressionless as he accepted Horst's money, then proceeded to clean his knife, pretending that they were not there.

Horst scooped up the meat and walked outside. Eragon hurried behind him, carrying his pack and the stone. The crisp night air rolled over their faces, refreshing after the stuffy shop.

"Thank you, Horst. Uncle Garrow will be pleased."

Horst laughed quietly. "Don't thank me. I've wanted to do that for a long time. Sloan's a vicious troublemaker; it does him good to be humbled. Katrina heard what was happening and ran to fetch me. Good thing I came—the two of you were almost at blows. Unfortunately, I doubt he'll serve you or any of your family the next time you go in there, even if you do have coins."

"Why did he explode like that? We've never been friendly, but he's always taken our money. And I've never seen him treat Katrina that way," said Eragon, opening the top of the pack.

Horst shrugged. "Ask your uncle. He knows more about it than I do."

Eragon stuffed the meat into his pack. "Well, now I have one more reason to hurry home . . . to solve this mystery. Here, this is rightfully yours." He proffered the stone.

Horst chuckled. "No, you keep your strange rock. As for payment, Albriech plans to leave for Feinster next spring. He wants to become a master smith, and I'm going to need an assistant. You can come and work off the debt on your spare days."

Eragon bowed slightly, delighted. Horst had two sons, Albriech and Baldor, both of whom worked in his forge. Taking one's place was a generous offer. "Again, thank you! I look forward to working with you." He was glad that there was a way for him to pay Horst. His uncle would never accept charity. Then Eragon remembered what his cousin had told him before he had left on the hunt. "Roran wanted me to give Katrina a message, but since I can't, can you get it to her?"

"Of course."

"He wants her to know that he'll come into town as soon as the merchants arrive and that he will see her then."

"That all?"

Eragon was slightly embarrassed. "No, he also wants her to know that she is the most beautiful girl he has ever seen and that he thinks of nothing else."

Horst's face broke into a broad grin, and he winked at Eragon. "Getting serious, isn't he?"

"Yes, sir," Eragon answered with a quick smile. "Could you also give her my thanks? It was nice of her to stand up to her father for me. I hope that she isn't punished because of it. Roran would be furious if I got her into trouble."

"I wouldn't worry about it. Sloan doesn't know that she called me, so I doubt he'll be too hard on her. Before you go, will you sup with us?"

"I'm sorry, but I can't. Garrow is expecting me," said Eragon, tying off the top of the pack. He hoisted it onto his back and started down the road, raising his hand in farewell.

The meat slowed him down, but he was eager to be home, and renewed vigor filled his steps. The village ended abruptly, and he left its warm lights behind. The pearlescent moon peeked over the mountains, bathing the land in a ghostly reflection of daylight. Everything looked bleached and flat.

Near the end of his journey, he turned off the road, which continued south. A simple path led straight through waist-high grass and up a knoll, almost hidden by the shadows of protective elm trees. He crested the hill and saw a gentle light shining from his home.

The house had a shingled roof and a brick chimney. Eaves hung over the whitewashed walls, shadowing the ground below. One side of the enclosed porch was filled with split wood, ready for the fire. A jumble of farm tools cluttered the other side.

The house had been abandoned for half a century when they moved in after Garrow's wife, Marian, died. It was ten miles from Carvahall, farther than anyone else's. People considered the distance dangerous because the family could not rely on help from the village in times of trouble, but Eragon's uncle would not listen.

A hundred feet from the house, in a dull-colored barn, lived two horses—Birka and Brugh—with chickens and a cow. Sometimes there was also a pig, but they had been unable to afford one this year. A wagon sat wedged between the stalls. On the edge of their fields, a thick line of trees traced along the Anora River.

He saw a light move behind a window as he wearily reached the porch. "Uncle, it's Eragon. Let me in." A small shutter slid back for a second, then the door swung inward.

Garrow stood with his hand on the door. His worn clothes hung on him like rags on a stick frame. A lean, hungry face with intense eyes gazed out from under graying hair. He looked like a man who had been partly mummified before it was discovered that he was still alive. "Roran's sleeping," was his answer to Eragon's inquiring glance.

A lantern flickered on a wood table so old that the grain stood up in tiny ridges like a giant fingerprint. Near a woodstove were rows of cooking utensils tacked onto the wall with homemade nails. A second door opened to the rest of the house. The floor was made of boards polished smooth by years of tramping feet.

Eragon pulled off his pack and took out the meat. "What's this? Did you buy meat? Where did you get the money?" asked his uncle harshly as he saw the wrapped packages.

Eragon took a breath before answering. "No, Horst bought it for us."

"You let him pay for it? I told you before, I won't beg for our food. If we can't feed ourselves, we might as well move into town. Before you can turn around twice, they'll be sending us used clothes and asking if we'll be able to get through the winter." Garrow's face paled with anger.

"I didn't accept charity," snapped Eragon. "Horst agreed to let me work off the debt this spring. He needs someone to help him because Albriech is going away."

"And where will you get the time to work for him? Are you going to ignore all the things that need to be done here?" asked Garrow, forcing his voice down.

Eragon hung his bow and quiver on hooks beside the front door. "I don't know how I'll do it," he said irritably. "Besides, I found something that could be worth some money." He set the stone on the table.

Garrow bowed over it: the hungry look on his face became ravenous, and his fingers moved with a strange twitch. "You found this in the Spine?"

"Yes," said Eragon. He explained what had happened. "And to make matters worse, I lost my best arrow. I'll have to make more before long." They stared at the stone in the near darkness.

"How was the weather?" asked his uncle, lifting the stone. His hands tightened around it like he was afraid it would suddenly disappear.

"Cold," was Eragon's reply. "It didn't snow, but it froze each night."

Garrow looked worried by the news. "Tomorrow you'll have to help Roran finish harvesting the barley. If we can get the squash picked, too, the frost won't bother us." He passed the stone to Eragon. "Here, keep it. When the traders come, we'll find out what it's worth. Selling it is probably the best thing to do. The less we're involved with magic, the better. . . . Why did Horst pay for the meat?"

It took only a moment for Eragon to explain his argument with Sloan. "I just don't understand what angered him so."

Garrow shrugged. "Sloan's wife, Ismira, went over the Igualda Falls a year before you were brought here. He hasn't been near the Spine since, nor had anything to do with it. But that's no reason to refuse payment. I think he wanted to give you trouble."

Eragon swayed blearily and said, "It's good to be back." Garrow's eyes softened, and he nodded. Eragon stumbled to his room, pushed the stone under his bed, then fell onto the mattress. *Home.* For the first time since before the hunt, he relaxed completely as sleep overtook him.

DRAGON TALES

At dawn the sun's rays streamed through the window, warming Eragon's face. Rubbing his eyes, he sat up on the edge of the bed. The pine floor was cold under his feet. He stretched his sore legs and rubbed his back, yawning.

Beside the bed was a row of shelves covered with objects he had collected. There were twisted pieces of wood, odd bits of shells, rocks that had broken to reveal shiny interiors, and strips of dry grass tied into knots. His favorite item was a root so convoluted he never tired of looking at it. The rest of the room was bare, except for a small dresser and nightstand.

He pulled on his boots and stared at the floor, thinking. This was a special day. It was near this very hour, sixteen years ago, that his mother, Selena, had come home to Carvahall alone and pregnant. She had been gone for six years, living in the cities. When she returned, she wore expensive clothes, and her hair was bound by a net of pearls. She had sought out her brother, Garrow, and asked to stay with him until the baby arrived. Within five months her son was born. Everyone was shocked when Selena tearfully begged Garrow and Marian to raise him. When they asked why, she only wept and said, "I must." Her pleas had grown increasingly desperate until they finally agreed. She named him Eragon, then departed early the next morning and never returned.

Eragon still remembered how he had felt when Marian told him the story before she died. The realization that Garrow and Marian were not his real parents had disturbed him greatly. Things that had been permanent and unquestionable were suddenly thrown into doubt. Eventually he had learned to live with it, but he always had a nagging suspicion that he had not been good enough for his mother. *I'm sure there was a good reason for what she did; I only wish I knew what it was.*

One other thing bothered him: Who was his father? Selena had told no one, and whoever it might be had never come looking for Eragon. He wished that he knew who it was, if only to have a name. It would be nice to know his heritage.

He sighed and went to the nightstand, where he splashed his face, shivering as the water ran down his neck. Refreshed, he retrieved the stone from under the bed and set it on a shelf. The morning light caressed it, throwing a warm shadow on the wall. He touched it one more time, then hurried to the kitchen, eager to see his family. Garrow and Roran were already there, eating chicken. As Eragon greeted them, Roran stood with a grin.

Roran was two years older than Eragon, muscular, sturdy, and careful with his movements. They could not have been closer even if they had been real brothers.

Roran smiled. "I'm glad you're back. How was the trip?"

"Hard," replied Eragon. "Did Uncle tell you what happened?" He helped himself to a piece of chicken, which he devoured hungrily.

"No," said Roran, and the story was quickly told. At Roran's insistence, Eragon left his food to show him the stone. This elicited a satisfactory amount of awe, but Roran soon asked nervously, "Were you able to talk with Katrina?"

"No, there wasn't an opportunity after the argument with Sloan. But she'll expect you when the traders come. I gave the message to Horst; he will get it to her."

"You told Horst?" said Roran incredulously. "That was private. If I wanted everyone to know about it, I could have built a bonfire and used smoke signals to communicate. If Sloan finds out, he won't let me see her again."

"Horst will be discreet," assured Eragon. "He won't let anyone fall prey to Sloan, least of all you." Roran seemed unconvinced, but argued no more. They returned to their meals in the taciturn presence of Garrow. When the last bites were finished, all three went to work in the fields.

The sun was cold and pale, providing little comfort. Under its watchful eye, the last of the barley was stored in the barn. Next, they gathered prickly vined squash, then the rutabagas, beets, peas, turnips, and beans, which they packed into the root cellar. After hours of labor, they stretched their cramped muscles, pleased that the harvest was finished.

The following days were spent pickling, salting, shelling, and preparing the food for winter.

Nine days after Eragon's return, a vicious blizzard blew out of the mountains and settled over the valley. The snow came down in great sheets, blanketing the countryside in white. They only dared leave the house for firewood and to feed the animals, for they feared getting lost in the howling wind and featureless landscape. They spent their time huddled over the stove as gusts rattled the heavy window shutters. Days later the storm finally passed, revealing an alien world of soft white drifts.

"I'm afraid the traders may not come this year, with conditions this bad," said Garrow. "They're late as it is. We'll give them a chance and wait before going to Carvahall. But if they don't show soon, we'll have to buy any spare supplies from the townspeople." His countenance was resigned.

They grew anxious as the days crept by without sign of the traders. Talk was sparse, and depression hung over the house.

On the eighth morning, Roran walked to the road and confirmed that the traders had not yet passed. The day was spent readying for the trip into Carvahall, scrounging with grim expressions for saleable items. That evening, out of desperation, Eragon checked the road again. He found deep ruts cut into the snow, with numerous hoofprints between them. Elated, he ran back to the house whooping, bringing new life to their preparations.

They packed their surplus produce into the wagon before sunrise. Garrow put the year's money in a leather pouch that he carefully fastened to his belt. Eragon set the wrapped stone between bags of grain so it would not roll when the wagon hit bumps.

After a hasty breakfast, they harnessed the horses and cleared a path to the road. The traders' wagons had already broken the drifts, which sped their progress. By noon they could see Carvahall.

In daylight, it was a small earthy village filled with shouts and laughter. The traders had made camp in an empty field on the outskirts of town. Groups of wagons, tents, and fires were randomly spread across it, spots of color against the snow. The troubadours' four tents were garishly decorated. A steady stream of people linked the camp to the village.

Crowds churned around a line of bright tents and booths clogging the main street. Horses whinnied at the noise. The snow had been pounded flat, giving it a glassy surface; elsewhere, bonfires had melted it. Roasted hazelnuts added a rich aroma to the smells wafting around them.

Garrow parked the wagon and picketed the horses, then drew coins from his pouch. "Get yourselves some treats. Roran, do what you want, only be at Horst's in time for supper. Eragon, bring that stone and come with me." Eragon grinned at Roran and pocketed the money, already planning how to spend it.

Roran departed immediately with a determined expression on his face. Garrow led Eragon into the throng, shouldering his way through the bustle. Women were buying cloth, while nearby their husbands examined a new latch, hook, or tool. Children ran up and down the road, shrieking with excitement. Knives were displayed here, spices there, and pots were laid out in shiny rows next to leather harnesses.

Eragon stared at the traders curiously. They seemed less prosperous than last year. Their children had a frightened, wary look, and their clothes were patched. The gaunt men carried swords and daggers with a new familiarity, and even the women had poniards belted at their waists.

What could have happened to make them like this? And why are they so late? wondered Eragon. He remembered the traders as being full of good cheer, but there was none of that now. Garrow pushed down the street, searching for Merlock, a trader who specialized in odd trinkets and pieces of jewelry.

They found him behind a booth, displaying brooches to a group of women. As each new piece was revealed, exclamations of admiration followed. Eragon guessed that more than a few purses would soon be depleted. Merlock seemed to flourish and grow every time his wares were complimented. He wore a goatee, held himself with ease, and seemed to regard the rest of the world with slight contempt.

The excited group prevented Garrow and Eragon from getting near the trader, so they settled on a step and waited. As soon as Merlock was unoccupied, they hurried over.

"And what might you sirs want to look at?" asked Merlock. "An amulet or trinket for a lady?" With a twirl he pulled out a delicately carved silver rose of excellent workmanship. The polished metal caught Eragon's attention, and he eyed it appreciatively. The trader continued, "Not even three crowns, though it has come all the way from the famed craftsmen of Belatona."

Garrow spoke in a quiet voice. "We aren't looking to buy, but to sell." Merlock immediately covered the rose and looked at them with new interest.

"I see. Maybe, if this item is of any value, you would like to trade it for one or two of these exquisite pieces." He paused for a moment while Eragon and his uncle stood uncomfortably, then continued, "You did *bring* the object of consideration?"

"We have it, but we would rather show it to you elsewhere," said Garrow in a firm voice.

Merlock raised an eyebrow, but spoke smoothly. "In that case, let me invite you to my tent." He gathered up his wares and gently laid them in an iron-bound chest, which he locked. Then he ushered them up the street and into the temporary camp. They wound between the wagons to a tent removed from the rest of the traders'. It was crimson at the top and sable at the bottom, with thin triangles of colors stabbing into each other. Merlock untied the opening and swung the flap to one side.

Small trinkets and strange pieces of furniture, such as a round bed and three seats carved from tree stumps, filled the tent. A gnarled dagger with a ruby in the pommel rested on a white cushion.

Merlock closed the flap and turned to them. "Please, seat yourselves." When they had, he said, "Now show me why we are meeting in private." Eragon unwrapped the stone and set it between the two men. Merlock reached for it with a gleam in his eye, then stopped and asked, "May I?" When Garrow indicated his approval, Merlock picked it up.

He put the stone in his lap and reached to one side for a thin box. Opened, it revealed a large set of copper scales, which he set on the ground. After weighing the stone, he scrutinized its surface under a jeweler's glass, tapped it gently with a wooden mallet, and drew the point of a tiny clear stone over it. He measured its length and diameter, then recorded the figures on a slate. He considered the results for a while. "Do you know what this is worth?"

"No," admitted Garrow. His cheek twitched, and he shifted uncomfortably on the seat.

Merlock grimaced. "Unfortunately, neither do I. But I can tell you this much: the white veins are the same material as the blue that surrounds them, only a different color. What that material might be, though, I haven't a clue. It's harder than any rock I have seen, harder even than diamond. Whoever shaped it used tools I have never seen—or magic. Also, it's hollow."

"What?" exclaimed Garrow.

An irritated edge crept into Merlock's voice. "Did you ever hear a rock sound like this?" He grabbed the dagger from the cushion and slapped the stone with the flat of the blade. A pure note filled the air, then faded away smoothly. Eragon was alarmed, afraid that the stone had been damaged. Merlock tilted the stone toward them. "You will find no scratches or blemishes where the dagger struck. I doubt I could do anything to harm this stone, even if I took a hammer to it."

Garrow crossed his arms with a reserved expression. A wall of silence surrounded him. Eragon was puzzled. *I knew that the stone appeared in the Spine through magic, but made by magic? What for and why?* He blurted, "But what is it worth?"

"I can't tell you that," said Merlock in a pained voice. "I am sure there are people who would pay dearly to have it, but none of them are in Carvahall. You would have to go to the southern cities to find a buyer. This is a curiosity for most people—not an item to spend money on when practical things are needed."

Garrow stared at the tent ceiling like a gambler calculating the odds. "Will you buy it?"

The trader answered instantly, "It's not worth the risk. I might be able to find a wealthy buyer during my spring travels, but I can't be certain. Even if I did, you wouldn't be paid until I returned next year. No, you will have to find someone else to trade with. I am curious, however . . . Why did you insist on talking to me in private?"

Eragon put the stone away before answering. "Because," he glanced at the man, wondering if he would explode like Sloan, "I found this in the Spine, and folks around here don't like that."

Merlock gave him a startled look. "Do you know why my fellow merchants and I were late this year?"

Eragon shook his head.

"Our wanderings have been dogged with misfortune. Chaos seems to rule Alagaësia. We could not avoid illness, attacks, and the most cursed black luck. Because the Varden's attacks have increased, Galbatorix has forced cities to send more soldiers to the borders, men who are needed to combat the Urgals. The brutes have been migrating southeast, toward the Hadarac Desert. No one knows why and it wouldn't concern us, except that they're passing through populated areas. They've been spotted on roads and near cities. Worst of all are reports of a Shade, though the stories are unconfirmed. Not many people survive such an encounter."

"Why haven't we heard of this?" cried Eragon.

"Because," said Merlock grimly, "it only began a few months ago. Whole villages have been forced to move because Urgals destroyed their fields and starvation threatens."

"Nonsense," growled Garrow. "We haven't seen any Urgals; the only one around here has his horns mounted in Morn's tavern."

Merlock arched an eyebrow. "Maybe so, but this is a small village hidden by mountains. It's not surprising that you've escaped notice. However, I wouldn't expect that to last. I only mentioned this because strange things are happening here as well if you found such a stone in the Spine." With that sobering statement, he bid them farewell with a bow and slight smile.

Garrow headed back to Carvahall with Eragon trailing behind. "What do you think?" asked Eragon.

"I'm going to get more information before I make up my mind. Take the stone back to the wagon, then do what you want. I'll meet you for dinner at Horst's."

Eragon dodged through the crowd and happily dashed back to the wagon. Trading would take his uncle hours, time that he planned to enjoy fully. He hid the stone under the bags, then set out into town with a cocky stride.

He walked from one booth to another, evaluating the goods with a buyer's eye, despite his meager supply of coins. When he talked with the merchants, they confirmed what Merlock had said about the instability in Alagaësia. Over and over the message was repeated: last year's security has deserted us; new dangers have appeared, and nothing is safe.

Later in the day he bought three sticks of malt candy and a small piping-hot cherry pie. The hot food felt good after hours of standing in the snow. He licked the sticky syrup from his fingers regretfully, wishing for more, then sat on the edge of a porch and nibbled a piece of candy. Two boys from Carvahall wrestled nearby, but he felt no inclination to join them.

As the day descended into late afternoon, the traders took their business into people's homes. Eragon was impatient for evening, when the troubadours would come out to tell stories and perform tricks. He loved hearing about magic, gods, and, if they were especially lucky, the Dragon Riders. Carvahall had its own storyteller, Brom—a friend of Eragon's—but his tales grew old over the years, whereas the troubadours always had new ones that he listened to eagerly.

Eragon had just broken off an icicle from the underside of the porch when he spotted Sloan nearby. The butcher had not seen him, so Eragon ducked his head and bolted around a corner toward Morn's tavern.

The inside was hot and filled with greasy smoke from sputtering tallow candles. The shiny-black Urgal horns, their twisted span as great as his outstretched arms, were mounted over the door. The bar was long and low, with a stack of staves on one end for customers to carve. Morn tended the bar, his sleeves rolled up to his elbows. The bottom half of his face was short and mashed, as if he had rested his chin on a grinding wheel. People crowded solid oak tables and listened to two traders who had finished their business early and had come in for beer.

Morn looked up from a mug he was cleaning. "Eragon! Good to see you. Where's your uncle?"

"Buying," said Eragon with a shrug. "He's going to be a while."

"And Roran, is he here?" asked Morn as he swiped the cloth through another mug.

"Yes, no sick animals to keep him back this year."

"Good, good."

Eragon gestured at the two traders. "Who are they?"

"Grain buyers. They bought everyone's seed at ridiculously low prices, and now they're telling wild stories, expecting us to believe them."

Eragon understood why Morn was so upset. *People need that money. We can't get by without it.* "What kind of stories?"

Morn snorted. "They say the Varden have formed a pact with the Urgals and are massing an army to attack us. *Supposedly*, it's only through the grace of our king that we've been protected for so long—as if Galbatorix would care if we burned to the ground. . . . Go listen to them. I have enough on my hands without explaining their lies."

The first trader filled a chair with his enormous girth; his every movement caused it to protest loudly. There was no hint of hair on his face, his pudgy hands were baby smooth, and he had pouting lips that curled petulantly as he sipped from a flagon. The second man had a florid face. The skin around his jaw was dry and corpulent, filled with lumps of hard fat, like cold butter gone rancid. Contrasted with his neck and jowls, the rest of his body was unnaturally thin.

The first trader vainly tried to pull back his expanding borders to fit within the chair. He said, "No, no, you don't understand. It is only through the king's unceasing efforts on your behalf that you are able to argue with us in safety. If he, in all his wisdom, were to withdraw that support, woe unto you!"

Someone hollered, "Right, why don't you also tell us the Riders have returned and you've each killed a hundred elves. Do you think we're children to believe in your tales? We can take care of ourselves." The group chuckled.

The trader started to reply when his thin companion intervened with a wave of his hand. Gaudy jewels flashed on his fingers. "You misunderstand. We know the Empire cannot care for each of us personally, as you may want, but it can keep Urgals and other abominations from overrunning this," he searched vaguely for the right term, "place."

The trader continued, "You're angry with the Empire for treating people unfairly, a legitimate concern, but a government cannot please everyone. There will inevitably be arguments and conflicts.

However, the majority of us have nothing to complain about. Every country has some small group of malcontents who aren't satisfied with the balance of power."

"Yeah," called a woman, "if you're willing to call the Varden small!"

The fat man sighed. "We already explained that the Varden have no interest in helping you. That's only a falsehood perpetuated by the traitors in an attempt to disrupt the Empire and convince us that the real threat is inside—not outside—our borders. All they want to do is overthrow the king and take possession of our land. They have spies everywhere as they prepare to invade. You never know who might be working for them."

Eragon did not agree, but the traders' words were smooth, and people were nodding. He stepped forward and said, "How do you know this? I can say that clouds are green, but that doesn't mean it's true. Prove you aren't lying." The two men glared at him while the villagers waited silently for the answer.

The thin trader spoke first. He avoided Eragon's eyes. "Aren't your children taught respect? Or do you let boys challenge men whenever they want to?"

The listeners fidgeted and stared at Eragon. Then a man said, "Answer the question."

"It's only common sense," said the fat one, sweat beading on his upper lip. His reply riled the villagers, and the dispute resumed.

Eragon returned to the bar with a sour taste in his mouth. He had never before met anyone who favored the Empire and tore down its enemies. There was a deep-seated hatred of the Empire in Carvahall, almost hereditary in nature. The Empire never helped them during harsh years when they nearly starved, and its tax collectors were heartless. He felt justified in disagreeing with the traders regarding the king's mercy, but he did speculate about the Varden.

The Varden were a rebel group that constantly raided and attacked the Empire. It was a mystery who their leader was or who had formed them in the years following Galbatorix's rise to power over a century ago. The group had garnered much sympathy as they eluded Galbatorix's efforts to destroy them. Little was known about the Varden except that if you were a fugitive and had to hide, or if you hated the Empire, they would accept you. The only problem was finding them.

Morn leaned over the bar and said, "Incredible, isn't it? They're worse than vultures circling a dying animal. There's going to be trouble if they stay much longer."

"For us or for them?"

"Them," said Morn as angry voices filled the tavern. Eragon left when the argument threatened to become violent. The door thudded shut behind him, cutting off the voices. It was early evening, and the sun was sinking rapidly; the houses cast long shadows on the ground. As Eragon headed down the street, he noticed Roran and Katrina standing in an alley.

Roran said something Eragon could not hear. Katrina looked down at her hands and answered in an undertone, then leaned up on her tiptoes and kissed him before darting away. Eragon trotted to Roran and teased, "Having a good time?" Roran grunted noncommittally as he paced away.

"Have you heard the traders' news?" asked Eragon, following. Most of the villagers were indoors, talking to traders or waiting until it was dark enough for the troubadours to perform.

"Yes." Roran seemed distracted. "What do you think of Sloan?"

"I thought it was obvious."

"There'll be blood between us when he finds out about Katrina and me," stated Roran. A snowflake landed on Eragon's nose, and he looked up. The sky had turned gray. He could think of nothing appropriate to say; Roran was right. He clasped his cousin on the shoulder as they continued down the byway.

Dinner at Horst's was hearty. The room was full of conversation and laughter. Sweet cordials and heavy ales were consumed in copious amounts, adding to the boisterous atmosphere. When the plates were empty, Horst's guests left the house and strolled to the field where the traders were camped. A ring of poles topped with candles had been stuck into the ground around a large clearing. Bonfires blazed in the background, painting the ground with dancing shadows. The villagers slowly gathered around the circle and waited expectantly in the cold.

The troubadours came tumbling out of their tents, dressed in tasseled clothing, followed by older and more stately minstrels. The minstrels provided music and narration as their younger counterparts acted out the stories. The first plays were pure entertainment: bawdy and full of jokes, pratfalls, and ridiculous characters. Later, however, when the candles sputtered in their sockets and everyone was drawn together into a tight circle, the old storyteller Brom stepped forward. A knotted white beard rippled over his chest, and a long black cape was wrapped around his bent shoulders, obscuring his body. He spread his arms with hands that reached out like talons and recited thus:

"The sands of time cannot be stopped. Years pass whether we will them or not . . . but we can remember. What has been lost may yet live on in memories. That which you will hear is imperfect and fragmented, yet treasure it, for without you it does not exist. I give you now a memory that has been forgotten, hidden in the dreamy haze that lies behind us."

His keen eyes inspected their interested faces. His gaze lingered on Eragon last of all.

"Before your grandfathers' fathers were born, and yea, even before their fathers, the Dragon Riders were formed. To protect and guard was their mission, and for thousands of years they succeeded. Their prowess in battle was unmatched, for each had the strength of ten men. They were immortal unless blade or poison took them. For good only were their powers used, and under their tutelage tall cities and towers were built out of the living stone. While they kept peace, the land flourished. It was a golden time. The elves were our allies, the dwarves our friends. Wealth flowed into our cities, and men prospered. But weep . . . for it could not last."

Brom looked down silently. Infinite sadness resonated in his voice.

"Though no enemy could destroy them, they could not guard against themselves. And it came to pass at the height of their power that a boy, Galbatorix by name, was born in the province of Inzilbêth, which is no more. At ten he was tested, as was the custom, and it was found that great power resided in him. The Riders accepted him as their own.

"Through their training he passed, exceeding all others in skill. Gifted with a sharp mind and strong body, he quickly took his place among the Riders' ranks. Some saw his abrupt rise as dangerous and warned the others, but the Riders had grown arrogant in their power and ignored caution. Alas, sorrow was conceived that day.

"So it was that soon after his training was finished, Galbatorix took a reckless trip with two friends. Far north they flew, night and day, and passed into the Urgals' remaining territory, foolishly thinking their new powers would protect them. There on a thick sheet of ice, unmelted even in summer, they were ambushed in their sleep. Though his friends and their dragons were butchered and he suffered great wounds, Galbatorix slew his attackers. Tragically, during the fight a stray arrow pierced his dragon's heart. Without the arts to save her, she died in his arms. Then were the seeds of madness planted."

The storyteller clasped his hands and looked around slowly, shadows flickering across his worn face. The next words came like the mournful toll of a requiem.

"Alone, bereft of much of his strength and half mad with loss, Galbatorix wandered without hope in that desolate land, seeking death. It did not come to him, though he threw himself without fear against any living thing. Urgals and other monsters soon fled from his haunted form. During this time he came to realize that the Riders might grant him another dragon. Driven by this thought, he began the arduous journey, on foot, back through the Spine. Territory he had soared over effortlessly on a dragon's back now took him months to traverse. He could hunt with magic, but oftentimes he walked in places where animals did not travel. Thus when his feet finally left the mountains, he was close to death. A farmer found him collapsed in the mud and summoned the Riders.

"Unconscious, he was taken to their holdings, and his body healed. He slept for four days. Upon awakening he gave no sign of his fevered mind. When he was brought before a council convened to judge him, Galbatorix demanded another dragon. The desperation of the request revealed his dementia, and the council saw him for what he truly was. Denied his hope, Galbatorix, through the twisted mirror of his madness, came to believe it was the Riders' fault his dragon had died. Night after night he brooded on that and formulated a plan to exact revenge."

Brom's words dropped to a mesmerizing whisper.

"He found a sympathetic Rider, and there his insidious words took root. By persistent reasoning and the use of dark secrets learned from a Shade, he inflamed the Rider against their elders. Together they treacherously lured and killed an elder. When the foul deed was done, Galbatorix turned on his ally and slaughtered him without warning. The Riders found him, then, with blood dripping from his hands. A scream tore from his lips, and he fled into the night. As he was cunning in his madness, they could not find him.

"For years he hid in wastelands like a hunted animal, always watching for pursuers. His atrocity was not forgotten, but over time searches ceased. Then through some ill fortune he met a young Rider, Morzan—strong of body, but weak of mind. Galbatorix convinced Morzan to leave a gate unbolted in the citadel Ilirea, which is now called Urû'baen. Through this gate Galbatorix entered and stole a dragon hatchling.

"He and his new disciple hid themselves in an evil place where the Riders dared not venture. There Morzan entered into a dark apprenticeship, learning secrets and forbidden magic that should never have been revealed. When his instruction was finished and Galbatorix's black dragon, Shruikan, was fully grown, Galbatorix revealed himself to the world, with Morzan at his side. Together they fought any Rider they met. With each kill their strength grew. Twelve of the Riders joined Galbatorix out of desire for power and revenge against perceived wrongs. Those twelve, with Morzan, became the Thirteen Forsworn. The Riders were unprepared and fell beneath the onslaught. The elves, too, fought bitterly against Galbatorix, but they were overthrown and forced to flee to their secret places, from whence they come no more.

"Only Vrael, leader of the Riders, could resist Galbatorix and the Forsworn. Ancient and wise, he struggled to save what he could and keep the remaining dragons from falling to his enemies. In the last battle, before the gates of Dorú Areaba, Vrael defeated Galbatorix, but hesitated with the final blow. Galbatorix seized the moment and smote him in the side. Grievously wounded, Vrael fled to Utgard Mountain, where he hoped to gather strength. But it was not to be, for Galbatorix found him. As they fought, Galbatorix kicked Vrael in the fork of his legs. With that underhanded blow, he gained dominance over Vrael and removed his head with a blazing sword.

"Then as power rushed through his veins, Galbatorix anointed himself king over all Alagaësia.

"And from that day, he has ruled us."

With the completion of the story, Brom shuffled away with the troubadours. Eragon thought he saw a tear shining on his cheek. People murmured quietly to each other as they departed. Garrow said to Eragon and Roran, "Consider yourselves fortunate. I have heard this tale only twice in my life. If the Empire knew that Brom had recited it, he would not live to see a new month."

FATE'S GIFT

The evening after their return from Carvahall, Eragon decided to test the stone as Merlock had. Alone in his room, he set it on his bed and laid three tools next to it. He started with a wooden mallet and lightly tapped the stone. It produced a subtle ringing. Satisfied, he picked up the next tool, a heavy leather hammer. A mournful peal reverberated when it struck. Lastly, he pounded a small chisel against it. The metal did not chip or scratch the stone, but it produced the clearest sound yet. As the final note died away, he thought he heard a faint squeak.

Merlock said the stone was hollow; there could be something of value inside. I don't know how to open it, though. There must have been a good reason for someone to shape it, but whoever sent the stone into the Spine hasn't taken the trouble to retrieve it or doesn't know where it is. But I don't believe that a magician with enough power to transport the stone wouldn't be able to find it again. So was I meant to have it? He could not answer the question. Resigned to an unsolvable mystery, he picked up the tools and returned the stone to its shelf.

That night he was abruptly roused from sleep. He listened carefully. All was quiet. Uneasy, he slid his hand under the mattress and grasped his knife. He waited a few minutes, then slowly sank back to sleep.

A squeak pierced the silence, tearing him back to wakefulness. He rolled out of bed and yanked the knife from its sheath. Fumbling with a tinderbox, he lit a candle. The door to his room was closed. Though the squeak was too loud for a mouse or rat, he still checked under the bed. Nothing. He sat on the edge of the mattress and rubbed the sleep from his eyes. Another squeak filled the air, and he started violently.

Where was the noise was coming from? Nothing could be in the floor or walls; they were solid wood. The same went for his bed, and he would have noticed if anything had crawled into his straw mattress during the night. His eyes settled on the stone. He took it off the shelf and absently cradled it as he studied the room. A squeak rang in his ears and reverberated through his fingers; it came from the stone.

The stone had given him nothing but frustration and anger, and now it would not even let him sleep! It ignored his furious glare and sat solidly, occasionally peeping. Then it gave one very loud squeak and fell silent. Eragon warily put it away and got back under the sheets. Whatever secret the stone held, it would have to wait until morning.

The moon was shining through his window when he woke again. The stone was rocking rapidly on the shelf, knocking against the wall. It was bathed in cool moonlight that bleached its surface. Eragon jumped out of bed, knife in hand. The motion stopped, but he remained tense. Then the stone started squeaking and rocking faster than ever.

With an oath, he began dressing. He did not care how valuable the stone might be; he was going to take it far away and bury it. The rocking stopped; the stone became quiet. It quivered, then rolled forward and dropped onto the floor with a loud thump. He inched toward the door in alarm as the stone wobbled toward him.

Suddenly a crack appeared on the stone. Then another and another. Transfixed, Eragon leaned forward, still holding the knife. At the top of the stone, where all the cracks met, a small piece wobbled, as if it were balanced on something, then rose and toppled to the floor. After another series of squeaks, a small dark head poked out of the hole, followed by a weirdly angled body. Eragon gripped the knife tighter and held very still. Soon the creature was all the way out of the stone. It stayed in place for a moment, then skittered into the moonlight.

Eragon recoiled in shock. Standing in front of him, licking off the membrane that encased it, was a dragon.

AWAKENING

The dragon was no longer than his forearm, yet it was dignified and noble. Its scales were deep sapphire blue, the same
color as the stone. But not a stone, he realized, an egg. The
dragon fanned its wings; they were what had made it appear so contorted. The wings were several times longer than its body and
ribbed with thin fingers of bone that extended from the wing's front
edge, forming a line of widely spaced talons. The dragon's head was
roughly triangular. Two diminutive white fangs curved down out of
its upper jaw. They looked very sharp. Its claws were also white, like
polished ivory, and slightly serrated on the inside curve. A line of
small spikes ran down the creature's spine from the base of its head
to the tip of its tail. A hollow where its neck and shoulders joined
created a larger-than-normal gap between the spikes.

Eragon shifted slightly, and the dragon's head snapped around.
Hard, ice-blue eyes fixed on him. He kept very still. It might be a
formidable enemy if it decided to attack.

The dragon lost interest in Eragon and awkwardly explored the
room, squealing as it bumped into a wall or furniture. With a flutter of wings, it leapt onto the bed and crawled to his pillow,
squeaking. Its mouth was open pitifully, like a young bird's, displaying rows of pointed teeth. Eragon sat cautiously on the end of
the bed. The dragon smelled his hand, nibbled his sleeve. He
pulled his arm back.

A smile tugged at Eragon's lips as he looked at the small creature.

Tentatively, he reached out with his right hand and touched its flank. A blast of icy energy surged into his hand and raced up his arm, burning in his veins like liquid fire. He fell back with a wild cry. An iron clang filled his ears, and he heard a soundless scream of rage. Every part of his body seared with pain. He struggled to move, but was unable to. After what seemed like hours, warmth seeped back into his limbs, leaving them tingling. Shivering uncontrollably, he pushed himself upright. His hand was numb, his fingers paralyzed. Alarmed, he watched as the middle of his palm shimmered and formed a diffused white oval. The skin itched and burned like a spider bite. His heart pounded frantically.

Eragon blinked, trying to understand what had occurred. Something brushed against his consciousness, like a finger trailing over his skin. He felt it again, but this time it solidified into a tendril of thought through which he could feel a growing curiosity. It was as if an invisible wall surrounding his thoughts had fallen away, and he was now free to reach out with his mind. He was afraid that without anything to hold him back, he would float out of his body and be unable to return, becoming a spirit of the ether. Scared, he pulled away from the contact. The new sense vanished as if he had closed his eyes. He glared suspiciously at the motionless dragon.

A scaly leg scraped against his side, and he jerked back. But the energy did not shock him again. Puzzled, he rubbed the dragon's head with his right hand. A light tingling ran up his arm. The dragon nuzzled him, arching its back like a cat. He slid a finger over its thin wing membranes. They felt like old parchment, velvety and warm, but still slightly damp. Hundreds of slender veins pulsed through them.

Again the tendril touched his mind, but this time, instead of curiosity, he sensed an overpowering, ravenous hunger. He got up with a sigh. This was a dangerous animal, of that he was sure. Yet it seemed so helpless crawling on his bed, he could only wonder if there was any harm in keeping it. The dragon wailed in a reedy tone as it looked for food. Eragon quickly scratched its head to keep it quiet. *I'll think about this later,* he decided, and left the room, carefully closing the door.

Returning with two strips of dried meat, he found the dragon sitting on the windowsill, watching the moon. He cut the meat into small squares and offered one to the dragon. It smelled the square cautiously, then jabbed its head forward like a snake and snatched the meat from his fingers, swallowing it whole with a peculiar jerk. The dragon prodded Eragon's hand for more food.

He fed it, careful to keep his fingers out of the way. By the time there was only one square left, the dragon's belly was bulging. He proffered the last piece; the dragon considered it for a moment, then lazily snapped it up. Done eating, it crawled onto his arm and curled against his chest. Then it snorted, a puff of dark smoke rising from its nostrils. Eragon looked at it with wonder.

Just when he thought the dragon was asleep, a low humming came from its vibrating throat. Gently, he carried it to the bed and set it by his pillow. The dragon, eyes closed, wrapped its tail around the bedpost contentedly. Eragon lay next to it, flexing his hand in the near darkness.

He faced a painful dilemma: By raising a dragon, he could become a Rider. Myths and stories about Riders were treasured, and being one would automatically place him among those legends. However, if the Empire discovered the dragon, he and his family would be put to death unless he joined the king. No one could—or would—help them. The simplest solution was just to kill the dragon, but the idea was repugnant, and he rejected it. Dragons were too revered for him to even consider that. *Besides, what could betray us?* he thought. *We live in a remote area and have done nothing to draw attention.*

The problem was convincing Garrow and Roran to let him keep the dragon. Neither of them would care to have a dragon around. *I could raise it in secret. In a month or two it will be too large for Garrow to get rid of, but will he accept it? Even if he does, can I get enough food for the dragon while it's hiding? It's no larger than a small cat, but it ate an entire handful of meat! I suppose it'll be able to hunt for itself eventually, but how long until then? Will it be able to survive the cold outside?* All the same, he wanted the dragon. The more he thought about it, the surer he was. However things might work out with Garrow, Eragon would do everything he could to protect it. Determined, he fell asleep with the dragon cradled against him.

When dawn came, the dragon was sitting atop his bedpost, like an ancient sentinel welcoming the new day. Eragon marveled at its color. He had never seen such a clear, hard blue. Its scales were like hundreds of small gemstones. He noticed that the white oval on his palm, where he had touched the dragon, had a silvery sheen. He hoped he could hide it by keeping his hands dirty.

The dragon launched off the post and glided to the floor. Eragon gingerly picked it up and left the quiet house, pausing to grab meat, several leather strips, and as many rags as he could carry. The crisp morning was beautiful; a fresh layer of snow covered the farm. He smiled as the small creature looked around with interest from the safety of his arms.

Hurrying across the fields, he walked silently into the dark forest, searching for a safe place for the dragon to stay. Eventually he found a rowan tree standing alone on a barren knoll, its branches snow-tipped gray fingers that reached toward the sky. He set the dragon down by the base of the trunk and shook the leather onto the ground.

With a few deft movements, he made a noose and slipped it over the dragon's head as it explored the snowy clumps surrounding the tree. The leather was worn, but it would hold. He watched the dragon crawl around, then untied the noose from its neck and fashioned a makeshift harness for its legs so the dragon would not strangle itself. Next he gathered an armful of sticks and built a crude hut high in the branches, layering the inside with rags and stashing the meat. Snow fell on his face as the tree swayed. He hung more rags over the front of the shelter to keep heat inside. Pleased, he surveyed his work.

"Time to show you your new home," he said, and lifted the dragon up into the branches. It wriggled, trying to get free, then clambered into the hut, where it ate a piece of meat, curled up, and blinked coyly at him. "You'll be fine as long as you stay in here," he instructed. The dragon blinked again.

Sure that it had not understood him, Eragon groped with his mind until he felt the dragon's consciousness. Again he had the terrible feeling of *openness*—of a space so large it pressed down on him like a heavy blanket. Summoning his strength, he focused on the dragon and tried to impress on it one idea: *Stay here.* The dragon stopped moving and cocked its head at him. He pushed harder: *Stay here.* A dim acknowledgment came tentatively through the link, but Eragon wondered if it really understood. *After all, it's only an animal.* He retreated from the contact with relief and felt the safety of his own mind envelop him.

Eragon left the tree, casting glances backward. The dragon stuck its head out of the shelter and watched with large eyes as he left.

After a hurried walk home, he sneaked back into his room to dispose of the egg fragments. He was sure Garrow and Roran would not notice the egg's absence—it had faded from their thoughts after they learned it could not be sold. When his family got up, Roran mentioned that he had heard some noises during the night but, to Eragon's relief, did not pursue the issue.

Eragon's enthusiasm made the day go by quickly. The mark on his hand proved easy to hide, so he soon stopped worrying about it. Before long he headed back to the rowan, carrying sausages he had pilfered from the cellar. With apprehension, he approached the tree. *Is the dragon able to survive outside in winter?*

His fears were groundless. The dragon was perched on a branch, gnawing on something between its front legs. It started squeaking excitedly when it saw him. He was pleased to see that it had remained in the tree, above the reach of large predators. As soon as he dropped the sausages at the base of the trunk, the dragon glided down. While it voraciously tore apart the food, Eragon examined the shelter. All the meat he had left was gone, but the hut was intact, and tufts of feathers littered the floor. *Good. It can get its own food.*

It struck him that he did not know if the dragon was a he or a she. He lifted and turned it over, ignoring its squeals of displeasure, but was unable to find any distinguishing marks. *It seems like it won't give up any secrets without a struggle.*

He spent a long time with the dragon. He untied it, set it on his shoulder, and went to explore the woods. The snow-laden trees watched over them like solemn pillars of a great cathedral. In that isolation, Eragon showed the dragon what he knew about the forest, not caring if it understood his meaning. It was the simple act of sharing that mattered. He talked to it continuously. The dragon gazed back at him with bright eyes, drinking in his words. For a while he just sat with it resting in his arms and watched it with wonder, still stunned by recent events. Eragon started for home at sunset, conscious of two hard blue eyes drilling into his back, indignant at being left behind.

That night he brooded about all the things that could happen to a small and unprotected animal. Thoughts of ice storms and vicious animals tormented him. It took hours for him to find sleep. His dreams were of foxes and black wolves tearing at the dragon with bloody teeth.

In the sunrise glow, Eragon ran from the house with food and scraps of cloth—extra insulation for the shelter. He found the dragon awake and safe, watching the sunrise from high in the tree. He fervently thanked all the gods, known and unknown. The dragon came down to the ground as he approached and leapt into his arms, huddling close to his chest. The cold had not harmed it, but it seemed frightened. A puff of dark smoke blew out of its nostrils. He stroked it comfortingly and sat with his back to the rowan, murmuring softly. He kept still as the dragon buried its head in his coat. After a while it crawled out of his embrace and onto his shoulder. He fed it, then wrapped the new rags around the hut. They played together for a time, but Eragon had to return to the house before long.

A smooth routine was quickly established. Every morning Eragon ran out to the tree and gave the dragon breakfast before hurrying back. During the day he attacked his chores until they were finished and he could visit the dragon again. Both Garrow and Roran noted his behavior and asked why he spent so much time outside. Eragon just shrugged and started checking to make sure he was not followed to the tree.

After the first few days he stopped worrying that a mishap would befall the dragon. Its growth was explosive; it would soon be safe from most dangers. The dragon doubled in size in the first week. Four days later it was as high as his knee. It no longer fit inside the hut in the rowan, so Eragon was forced to build a hidden shelter on the ground. The task took him three days.

When the dragon was a fortnight old, Eragon was compelled to let it roam free because it needed so much food. The first time he untied it, only the force of his will kept it from following him back to the farm. Every time it tried, he pushed it away with his mind until it learned to avoid the house and its other inhabitants.

And he impressed on the dragon the importance of hunting only in the Spine, where there was less chance of being seen. Farmers would notice if game started disappearing from Palancar Valley. It made him feel both safer and uneasy when the dragon was so far away.

The mental contact he shared with the dragon waxed stronger each day. He found that although it did not comprehend words, he could communicate with it through images or emotions. It was an imprecise method, however, and he was often misunderstood. The range at which they could touch each other's thoughts expanded rapidly. Soon Eragon could contact the dragon anywhere within three leagues. He often did so, and the dragon, in turn, would lightly brush against his mind. These mute conversations filled his working hours. There was always a small part of him connected to the dragon, ignored at times, but never forgotten. When he talked with people, the contact was distracting, like a fly buzzing in his ear.

As the dragon matured, its squeaks deepened to a roar and the humming became a low rumble, yet the dragon did not breathe fire, which concerned him. He had seen it blow smoke when it was upset, but there was never a hint of flame.

When the month ended, Eragon's elbow was level with the dragon's shoulder. In that brief span, it had transformed from a small, weak animal into a powerful beast. Its hard scales were as tough as chain-mail armor, its teeth like daggers.

Eragon took long walks in the evening with the dragon padding beside him. When they found a clearing, he would settle against a tree and watch the dragon soar through the air. He loved to see it fly and regretted that it was not yet big enough to ride. He often sat beside the dragon and rubbed its neck, feeling sinews and corded muscles flex under his hands.

Despite Eragon's efforts, the forest around the farm filled with signs of the dragon's existence. It was impossible to erase all the huge four-clawed footprints sunk deep in the snow, and he refused even to try to hide the giant dung heaps that were becoming far too common. The dragon had rubbed against trees, stripping off the bark, and had sharpened its claws on dead logs, leaving gashes inches deep. If Garrow or Roran went too far beyond the farm's boundaries, they would discover the dragon. Eragon could imagine no worse way for the truth to come out, so he decided to preempt it by explaining everything to them.

He wanted to do two things first, though: give the dragon a suitable name and learn more about dragons in general. To that end he needed to talk with Brom, master of epics and legends—the only places where dragonlore survived.

So when Roran went to get a chisel repaired in Carvahall, Eragon volunteered to go with him.

The evening before they left, Eragon went to a small clearing in the forest and called the dragon with his mind. After a moment he saw a fast-moving speck in the dusky sky. The dragon dived toward him, pulled up sharply, then leveled off above the trees. He heard a low-pitched whistle as air rushed over its wings. It banked slowly to his left and spiraled gently down to the ground. The dragon back-flapped for balance with a deep, muffled *thwump* as it landed.

Eragon opened his mind, still uncomfortable with the strange sensation, and told the dragon that he was leaving. It snorted with unease. He attempted to soothe it with a calming mental picture, but the dragon whipped its tail, unsatisfied. He rested his hand on its shoulder and tried to radiate peace and serenity. Scales bumped under his fingers as he patted it gently.

A single word rang in his head, deep and clear.

Eragon.

It was solemn and sad, as if an unbreakable pact were being sealed. He stared at the dragon and a cold tingle ran down his arm.

Eragon.

A hard knot formed in his stomach as unfathomable sapphire eyes gazed back at him. For the first time he did not think of the dragon as an animal. It was something else, something . . . different. He raced home, trying to escape the dragon. *My dragon.*

Eragon.

TEA FOR TWO

Roran and Eragon parted at the outskirts of Carvahall. Eragon walked slowly to Brom's house, engrossed in his thoughts. He stopped at the doorstep and raised his hand to knock.

A voice rasped, "What do you want, boy?"

He whirled around. Behind him Brom leaned on a twisted staff embellished with strange carvings. He wore a brown hooded robe like a friar. A pouch hung from the scuffed leather belt clasped around his waist. Above his white beard, a proud eagle nose hooked over his mouth and dominated his face. He peered at Eragon with deep-set eyes shadowed by a gnarled brow and waited for his reply.

"To get information," Eragon said. "Roran is getting a chisel fixed and I had free time, so I came to see if you could answer a few questions."

The old man grunted and reached for the door. Eragon noticed a gold ring on his right hand. Light glinted off a sapphire, highlighting a strange symbol carved on its face. "You might as well come in; we'll be talking awhile. Your questions never seem to end." Inside, the house was darker than charcoal, an acrid smell heavy in the air. "Now, for a light." Eragon heard the old man move around, then a low curse as something crashed to the floor. "Ah, here we go." A white spark flashed; a flame wavered into existence.

Brom stood with a candle before a stone fireplace. Stacks of books surrounded a high-backed, deeply carved wooden chair that faced the mantel; the four legs were shaped like eagle claws, and the seat and back were padded with leather embossed with a swirling rose pattern. A cluster of lesser chairs held piles of scrolls. Ink pots and pens were scattered across a writing desk. "Make room for yourself, but by the lost kings, be *careful*. This stuff is valuable."

Eragon stepped over pages of parchment covered with angular runes. He gently lifted cracking scrolls off a chair and placed them on the floor. A cloud of dust flew into the air as he sat. He stifled a sneeze.

Brom bent down and lit the fire with his candle. "Good! Nothing like sitting by a fire for conversation." He threw back his hood to reveal hair that was not white, but silver, then hung a kettle over the flames and settled into the high-backed chair.

"Now, what do you want?" He addressed Eragon roughly, but not unkindly.

"Well," said Eragon, wondering how best to approach the subject, "I keep hearing about the Dragon Riders and their supposed accomplishments. Most everyone seems to want them to return, but I've never heard tell of how they were started, where the dragons came from, or what made the Riders special—aside from the dragons."

"A vast subject to tell about," grumbled Brom. He peered at Eragon alertly. "If I told you their whole story, we would still be sitting here when winter comes again. It will have to be reduced to a manageable length. But before we start properly, I need my pipe."

Eragon waited patiently as Brom tamped down the tobacco. He liked Brom. The old man was irascible at times, but he never seemed to mind taking time for Eragon. Eragon had once asked him where he came from, and Brom had laughed, saying, "A village much like Carvahall, only not quite as interesting." Curiosity aroused, Eragon asked his uncle. But Garrow could only tell him that Brom had bought a house in Carvahall nearly fifteen years ago and had lived there quietly ever since.

Brom used a tinderbox to light the pipe. He puffed a few times, then said, "There . . . we won't have to stop, except for the tea.

Now, about the Riders, or the Shur'tugal, as they are called by the elves. Where to start? They spanned countless years and, at the height of their power, held sway over twice the Empire's lands. Numerous stories have been told about them, most nonsense. If you believed everything said, you would expect them to have the powers of a lesser god. Scholars have devoted entire lives to separating these fictions from fact, but it's doubtful any of them will succeed. However, it isn't an impossible task if we confine ourselves to the three areas you specified: how the Riders began, why they were so highly regarded, and where dragons came from. I shall start with the last item." Eragon settled back and listened to the man's mesmerizing voice.

"Dragons have no beginning, unless it lies with the creation of Alagaësia itself. And if they have an end, it will be when this world perishes, for they suffer as the land does. They, the dwarves, and a few others are the true inhabitants of this land. They lived here before all others, strong and proud in their elemental glory. Their world was unchanging until the first elves sailed over the sea on their silver ships."

"Where did the elves come from?" interrupted Eragon. "And why are they called the fair folk? Do they really exist?"

Brom scowled. "Do you want your original questions answered or not? They won't be if you want to explore every obscure piece of knowledge."

"Sorry," said Eragon. He dipped his head and tried to look contrite.

"No, you're not," said Brom with some amusement. He shifted his gaze to the fire and watched it lick the underside of the kettle. "If you must know, elves are not legends, and they are called the fair folk because they are more graceful than any of the other races. They come from what they call Alalea, though none but they know what, or even where, it is.

"Now," he glared from under his bushy eyebrows to make sure there would be no more interruptions, "the elves were a proud race then, and strong in magic. At first they regarded dragons as mere

49

animals. From that belief rose a deadly mistake. A brash elven youth hunted down a dragon, as he would a stag, and killed it. Outraged, the dragons ambushed and slaughtered the elf. Unfortunately, the bloodletting did not stop there. The dragons massed together and attacked the entire elven nation. Dismayed by the terrible misunderstanding, the elves tried to end the hostilities, but couldn't find a way to communicate with the dragons.

"Thus, to greatly abbreviate a complicated series of occurrences, there was a very long and very bloody war, which both sides later regretted. At the beginning the elves fought only to defend themselves, for they were reluctant to escalate the fighting, but the dragons' ferocity eventually forced them to attack for their own survival. This lasted for five years and would have continued for much longer if an elf called Eragon hadn't found a dragon egg." Eragon blinked in surprise. "Ah, I see you didn't know of your namesake," said Brom.

"No." The teakettle whistled stridently. *Why was I named after an elf?*

50

"Then you should find this all the more interesting," said Brom. He hooked the kettle out of the fire and poured boiling water into two cups. Handing one to Eragon, he warned, "These leaves don't need to steep long, so drink it quickly before it gets too strong." Eragon tried a sip, but scalded his tongue. Brom set his own cup aside and continued smoking the pipe.

"No one knows why that egg was abandoned. Some say the parents were killed in an elven attack. Others believe the dragons purposefully left it there. Either way, Eragon saw the value of raising a friendly dragon. He cared for it secretly and, in the custom of the ancient language, named him Bid'Daum. When Bid'Daum had grown to a good size, they traveled together among the dragons and convinced them to live in peace with the elves. Treaties were formed between the two races. To ensure that war would never break out again, they decided that it was necessary to establish the Riders.

"At first the Riders were intended merely as a means of communication between the elves and dragons. However, as time passed, their worth was recognized and they were given ever more authority. Eventually they took the island Vroengard for their home and built a city on it—Dorú Areaba. Before Galbatorix overthrew them, the Riders held more power than all the kings in Alagaësia. Now I believe I have answered two of your questions."

"Yes," said Eragon absently. It seemed like an incredible coincidence that he had been named after the first Rider. For some reason his name did not feel the same anymore. "What does *Eragon* mean?"

"I don't know," said Brom. "It's very old. I doubt anyone remembers except the elves, and fortune would have to smile greatly before you talked with one. It is a good name to have, though; you should be proud of it. Not everyone has one so honorable."

Eragon brushed the matter from his mind and focused on what he had learned from Brom; there was something missing. "I don't understand. Where were we when the Riders were created?"

"We?" asked Brom, raising an eyebrow.

"You know, all of us." Eragon waved his hands vaguely. "Humans in general."

Brom laughed. "We are no more native to this land than the elves. It took our ancestors another three centuries to arrive here and join the Riders."

"That can't be," protested Eragon. "We've always lived in Palancar Valley."

"That might be true for a few generations, but beyond that, no. It isn't even true for you, Eragon," said Brom gently. "Though you consider yourself part of Garrow's family, and rightly so, your sire was not from here. Ask around and you'll find many people who haven't been here that long. This valley is old and hasn't always belonged to us."

Eragon scowled and gulped at the tea. It was still hot enough to burn his throat. This was his home, regardless of who his father was! "What happened to the dwarves after the Riders were destroyed?"

"No one really knows. They fought with the Riders through the first few battles, but when it became clear Galbatorix was going to win, they sealed all the known entrances to their tunnels and disappeared underground. As far as I know, not one has been seen since."

"And the dragons?" he asked. "What of them? Surely they weren't all killed."

Brom answered sorrowfully, "That is the greatest mystery in Alagaësia nowadays: How many dragons survived Galbatorix's murderous slaughter? He spared those who agreed to serve him, but only the twisted dragons of the Forsworn would assist his madness. If any dragons aside from Shruikan are still alive, they have hidden themselves so they will never be found by the Empire."

So where did *my dragon come from?* wondered Eragon. "Were the Urgals here when the elves came to Alagaësia?" he asked.

"No, they followed the elves across the sea, like ticks seeking blood. They were one of the reasons the Riders became valued for their battle prowess and ability to keep the peace. . . . Much can be learned from this history. It's a pity the king makes it a delicate subject," reflected Brom.

"Yes, I heard your story the last time I was in town."

"Story!" roared Brom. Lightning flashed in his eyes. "If it is a story, then the rumors of my death are true and you are speaking with a ghost! Respect the past; you never know how it may affect you."

Eragon waited until Brom's face mellowed before he dared ask, "How big were the dragons?"

A dark plume of smoke swirled above Brom like a miniature thunderstorm. "Larger than a house. Even the small ones had wingspans over a hundred feet; they never stopped growing. Some of the ancient ones, before the Empire killed them, could have passed for large hills."

Dismay swept through Eragon. *How can I hide my dragon in the years to come?* He raged silently, but kept his voice calm. "When did they mature?"

"Well," said Brom, scratching his chin, "they couldn't breathe fire until they were around five to six months old, which was about when they could mate. The older a dragon was, the longer it could breathe fire. Some of them could keep at it for minutes." Brom blew a smoke ring and watched it float up to the ceiling.

"I heard that their scales shone like gems."

Brom leaned forward and growled, "You heard right. They came in every color and shade. It was said that a group of them looked like a living rainbow, constantly shifting and shimmering. But who told you that?"

Eragon froze for a second, then lied, "A trader."

"What was his name?" asked Brom. His tangled eyebrows met in a thick white line; the wrinkles deepened on his forehead. Unnoticed, the pipe smoldered out.

Eragon pretended to think. "I don't know. He was talking in Morn's, but I never found out who he was."

"I wish you had," muttered Brom.

"He also said a Rider could hear his dragon's thoughts," said Eragon quickly, hoping that the fictitious trader would protect him from suspicion.

Brom's eyes narrowed. Slowly he took out a tinderbox and struck the flint. Smoke rose, and he took a long pull from the pipe, exhaling slowly. In a flat voice he said, "He was wrong. It isn't in any of the stories, and I know them all. Did he say anything else?"

Eragon shrugged. "No." Brom was too interested in the trader for him to continue the falsehood. Casually he inquired, "Did dragons live very long?"

Brom did not respond at once. His chin sank to his chest while his fingers tapped the pipe thoughtfully, light reflecting off his ring. "Sorry, my mind was elsewhere. Yes, a dragon will live for quite a while, forever, in fact, as long as it isn't killed and its Rider doesn't die."

"How does anyone know that?" objected Eragon. "If dragons die when their Riders do, they could only live to be sixty or seventy.

You said during your . . . narration that Riders lived for hundreds of years, but that's impossible." It troubled him to think of outliving his family and friends.

A quiet smile curled Brom's lips as he said slyly, "What is possible is subjective. Some would say that you cannot travel through the Spine and live, yet you do. It's a matter of perspective. You must be very wise to know so much at such a young age." Eragon flushed, and the old man chuckled. "Don't be angry; you can't be expected to know such things. You forget that the dragons were magical—they affected everything around them in strange ways. The Riders were closest to them and experienced this the most. The most common side effect was an extended life. Our king has lived long enough to make that apparent, but most people attribute it to his own magical abilities. There were also other, less noticeable changes. All the Riders were stronger of body, keener of mind, and truer of sight than normal men. Along with this, a human Rider would slowly acquire pointed ears, though they were never as prominent as an elf's."

Eragon had to stop his hand from reaching up to feel the tips of his ears. *How else will this dragon change my life? Not only has it gotten inside my head, but it's altering my body as well!* "Were dragons very smart?"

"Didn't you pay attention to what I told you earlier!" demanded Brom. "How could the elves form agreements and peace treaties with dumb brutes? They were as intelligent as you or I."

"But they were animals," persisted Eragon.

Brom snorted. "They were no more animals than we are. For some reason people praise everything the Riders did, yet ignore the dragons, assuming that they were nothing more than an exotic means to get from one town to another. They weren't. The Riders' great deeds were only possible because of the dragons. How many men would draw their swords if they knew a giant fire-breathing lizard—one with more natural cunning and wisdom than even a king could hope for—would soon be there to stop the violence? Hmm?" He blew another smoke ring and watched it waft away.

"Did you ever see one?"

"Nay," said Brom, "it was long before my time."

And now for a name. "I've been trying to recall the name of a certain dragon, but it keeps eluding me. I think I heard it when the traders were in Carvahall, but I'm not sure. Could you help me?"

Brom shrugged and quickly listed a stream of names. "There was Jura, Hírador, and Fundor—who fought the giant sea snake. Galzra, Briam, Ohen the Strong, Gretiem, Beroan, Roslarb . . ." He added many others. At the very end, he uttered so softly Eragon almost did not hear, ". . . and Saphira." Brom quietly emptied his pipe. "Was it any of those?"

"I'm afraid not," said Eragon. Brom had given him much to think about, and it was getting late. "Well, Roran's probably finished with Horst. I should get back, though I'd rather not."

Brom raised an eyebrow. "What, is that it? I expected to be answering your questions until he came looking for you. No queries about dragon battle tactics or requests for descriptions of breathtaking aerial combat? Are we done?"

"For now," laughed Eragon. "I learned what I wanted to and more." He stood and Brom followed.

"Very well, then." He ushered Eragon to the door. "Goodbye. Take care. And don't forget, if you remember who that trader was, tell me."

"I will. Thank you." Eragon stepped into the glaring winter sunlight, squinting. He slowly paced away, pondering what he had heard.

A NAME OF POWER

O n the way home Roran said, "There was a stranger from Therinsford at Horst's today."

"What's his name?" asked Eragon. He sidestepped a patch of ice and continued walking at a brisk pace. His cheeks and eyes burned from the cold.

"Dempton. He came here to have Horst forge him some sockets," said Roran. His stocky legs plowed through a drift, clearing the way for Eragon.

"Doesn't Therinsford have its own smith?"

"Yes," replied Roran, "but he isn't skilled enough." He glanced at Eragon. With a shrug he added, "Dempton needs the sockets for his mill. He's expanding it and offered me a job. If I accept, I'll leave with him when he picks up the sockets."

Millers worked all year. During winter they ground whatever people brought them, but in harvest season they bought grain and sold it as flour. It was hard, dangerous work; workers often lost fingers or hands to the giant millstones. "Are you going to tell Garrow?" asked Eragon.

"Yes." A grimly amused smile played across Roran's face.

"What for? You know what he thinks about us going away. It'll only cause trouble if you say anything. Forget about it so we can eat tonight's dinner in peace."

"I can't. I'm going to take the job."

Eragon halted. "Why?" They faced each other, their breath

visible in the air. "I know money is hard to come by, but we always manage to survive. You don't have to leave."

"No, I don't. But the money is for myself." Roran tried to resume walking, but Eragon refused to budge.

"What do you need it for?" he demanded.

Roran's shoulders straightened slightly. "I want to marry."

Bewilderment and astonishment overwhelmed Eragon. He remembered seeing Katrina and Roran kissing during the traders' visit, but marriage? "Katrina?" he asked weakly, just to confirm. Roran nodded. "Have you asked her?"

"Not yet, but come spring, when I can raise a house, I will."

"There's too much work on the farm for you to leave now," protested Eragon. "Wait until we're ready for planting."

"No," said Roran, laughing slightly. "Spring's the time I'll be needed the most. The ground will have to be furrowed and sown. The crops must be weeded—not to mention all the other chores. No, this is the best time for me to go, when all we really do is wait for the seasons to change. You and Garrow can make do without me. If all goes well, I'll soon be back working on the farm, with a wife."

Eragon reluctantly conceded that Roran made sense. He shook his head, but whether with amazement or anger, he knew not. "I guess I can only wish you the best of luck. But Garrow may take this with ill humor."

"We will see."

They resumed walking, the silence a barrier between them. Eragon's heart was disturbed. It would take time before he could look upon this development with favor. When they arrived home, Roran did not tell Garrow of his plans, but Eragon was sure that he soon would.

Eragon went to see the dragon for the first time since it had spoken to him. He approached apprehensively, aware now that it was an equal.

Eragon.

"Is that all you can say?" he snapped.

Yes.

His eyes widened at the unexpected reply, and he sat down roughly. *Now it has a sense of humor. What next?* Impulsively, he broke a dead branch with his foot. Roran's announcement had put him in a foul mood. A questioning thought came from the dragon, so he told it what had happened. As he talked his voice grew steadily louder until he was yelling pointlessly into the air. He ranted until his emotions were spent, then ineffectually punched the ground.

"I don't want him to go, that's all," he said helplessly. The dragon watched impassively, listening and learning. Eragon mumbled a few choice curses and rubbed his eyes. He looked at the dragon thoughtfully. "You need a name. I heard some interesting ones today; perhaps you'll like one." He mentally ran through the list Brom had given him until he found two names that struck him as heroic, noble, and pleasing to the ear. "What do you think of Vanilor or his successor, Eridor? Both were great dragons."

No, said the dragon. It sounded amused with his efforts. *Eragon.*

"That's *my* name; you can't have it," he said, rubbing his chin. "Well, if you don't like those, there are others." He continued through the list, but the dragon rejected every one he proposed. It seemed to be laughing at something Eragon did not understand, but he ignored it and kept suggesting names. "There was Ingothold, he slew the . . ." A revelation stopped him. *That's the problem! I've been choosing male names. You are a she!*

Yes. The dragon folded her wings smugly.

Now that he knew what to look for, he came up with half a dozen names. He toyed with Miremel, but that did not fit—after all, it was the name of a brown dragon. Opheila and Lenora were also discarded. He was about to give up when he remembered the last name Brom had muttered. Eragon liked it, but would the dragon?

He asked.

"Are you Saphira?" She looked at him with intelligent eyes. Deep in his mind he felt her satisfaction.

Yes. Something clicked in his head and her voice echoed, as if from a great distance. He grinned in response. Saphira started humming.

A MILLER-TO-BE

The sun had set by the time dinner was served. A blustery wind howled outside, shaking the house. Eragon eyed Roran closely and waited for the inevitable. Finally: "I was offered a job at Therinsford's mill . . . which I plan to take."

Garrow finished his mouthful of food with deliberate slowness and laid down his fork. He leaned back in his chair, then interlaced his fingers behind his head and uttered one dry word, "Why?"

Roran explained while Eragon absently picked at his food.

"I see," was Garrow's only comment. He fell silent and stared at the ceiling. No one moved as they awaited his response. "Well, when do you leave?"

"What?" asked Roran.

Garrow leaned forward with a twinkle in his eye. "Did you think I would stop you? I'd hoped you would marry soon. It will be good to see this family growing again. Katrina will be lucky to have you." Astonishment raced over Roran's face, then he settled into a relieved grin. "So when do you leave?" Garrow asked.

Roran regained his voice. "When Dempton returns to get the sockets for the mill."

Garrow nodded. "And that will be in . . . ?"

"Two weeks."

"Good. That will give us time to prepare. It'll be different to have the house to ourselves. But if nothing goes amiss, it shouldn't be for too long." He looked over the table and asked, "Eragon, did you know of this?"

He shrugged ruefully. "Not until today. . . . It's madness."

Garrow ran a hand over his face. "It's life's natural course." He pushed himself up from the chair. "All will be fine; time will settle everything. For now, though, let's clean the dishes." Eragon and Roran helped him in silence.

The next few days were trying. Eragon's temper was frayed. Except for curtly answering direct questions, he spoke with no one. There were small reminders everywhere that Roran was leaving: Garrow making him a pack, things missing from the walls, and a strange emptiness that filled the house. It was almost a week before he realized that distance had grown between Roran and him. When they spoke, the words did not come easily and their conversations were uncomfortable.

Saphira was a balm for Eragon's frustration. He could talk freely with her; his emotions were completely open to her mind, and she understood him better than anyone else. During the weeks before Roran's departure, she went through another growth spurt. She gained twelve inches at the shoulder, which was now higher than Eragon's. He found that the small hollow where her neck joined her shoulders was a perfect place to sit. He often rested there in the evenings and scratched her neck while he explained the meanings of different words. Soon she understood everything he said and frequently commented on it.

For Eragon, this part of his life was delightful. Saphira was as real and complex as any person. Her personality was eclectic and at times completely alien, yet they understood each other on a profound level. Her actions and thoughts constantly revealed new aspects of her character. Once she caught an eagle and, instead of eating it, released it, saying, *No hunter of the sky should end his days as prey. Better to die on the wing than pinned to the ground.*

Eragon's plan to let his family see Saphira was dispelled by Roran's announcement and Saphira's own cautionary words. She was reluctant to be seen, and he, partly out of selfishness, agreed. The moment her existence was divulged, he knew that shouts, accusations, and fear would be directed at him . . . so he procrastinated. He told himself to wait for a sign that it was the right time.

The night before Roran was to leave, Eragon went to talk with him. He stalked down the hallway to Roran's open door. An oil lamp rested on a nightstand, painting the walls with warm flickering light. The bedposts cast elongated shadows on empty shelves that rose to the ceiling. Roran—his eyes shaded and the back of his neck tense—was rolling blankets around his clothes and belongings. He paused, then picked up something from the pillow and bounced it in his hand. It was a polished rock Eragon had given him years ago. Roran started to tuck it into the bundle, then stopped and set it on a shelf. A hard lump formed in Eragon's throat, and he left.

STRANGERS IN CARVAHALL

Breakfast was cold, but the tea was hot. Ice inside the windows had melted with the morning fire and soaked into the wood floor, staining it with dark puddles. Eragon looked at Garrow and Roran by the kitchen stove and reflected that this would be the last time he saw them together for many months.

Roran sat in a chair, lacing his boots. His full pack rested on the floor next to him. Garrow stood between them with his hands stuck deep into his pockets. His shirt hung loosely; his skin looked drawn. Despite the young men's cajoling, he refused to go with them. When pressed for a reason, he only said that it was for the best.

"Do you have everything?" Garrow asked Roran.

"Yes."

He nodded and took a small pouch from his pocket. Coins clinked as he handed it to Roran. "I've been saving this for you. It isn't much, but if you wish to buy some bauble or trinket, it will suffice."

"Thank you, but I won't be spending my money on trifles," said Roran.

"Do what you will; it is yours," said Garrow. "I've nothing else to give you, except a father's blessing. Take it if you wish, but it is worth little."

Roran's voice was thick with emotion. "I would be honored to receive it."

"Then do, and go in peace," said Garrow, and kissed him on the forehead. He turned and said in a louder voice, "Do not think that

I have forgotten you, Eragon. I have words for both of you. It's time I said them, as you are entering the world. Heed them and they will serve you well." He bent his gaze sternly on them. "First, let no one rule your mind or body. Take special care that your thoughts remain unfettered. One may be a free man and yet be bound tighter than a slave. Give men your ear, but not your heart. Show respect for those in power, but don't follow them blindly. Judge with logic and reason, but comment not.

"Consider none your superior, whatever their rank or station in life. Treat all fairly or they will seek revenge. Be careful with your money. Hold fast to your beliefs and others will listen." He continued at a slower pace, "Of the affairs of love . . . my only advice is to be honest. That's your most powerful tool to unlock a heart or gain forgiveness. That is all I have to say." He seemed slightly self-conscious of his speech.

He hoisted Roran's pack. "Now you must go. Dawn is approaching, and Dempton will be waiting."

Roran shouldered the pack and hugged Garrow. "I will return as soon as I can," he said.

"Good!" replied Garrow. "But now go and don't worry about us."

They parted reluctantly. Eragon and Roran went outside, then turned and waved. Garrow raised a bony hand, his eyes grave, and watched as they trudged to the road. After a long moment he shut the door. As the sound carried through the morning air, Roran halted.

Eragon looked back and surveyed the land. His eyes lingered on the lone buildings. They looked pitifully small and fragile. A thin finger of smoke trailing up from the house was the only proof that the snowbound farm was inhabited.

"There is our whole world," Roran observed somberly.

Eragon shivered impatiently and grumbled, "A good one too." Roran nodded, then straightened his shoulders and headed into his new future. The house disappeared from view as they descended the hill.

It was still early when they reached Carvahall, but they found the smithy doors already open. The air inside was pleasantly warm. Baldor slowly worked two large bellows attached to the side of a stone forge filled with sparkling coals. Before the forge stood a black anvil and an iron-bound barrel filled with brine. From a line of neck-high poles protruding from the walls hung rows of items: giant tongs, pliers, hammers in every shape and weight, chisels, angles, center punches, files, rasps, lathes, bars of iron and steel waiting to be shaped, vises, shears, picks, and shovels. Horst and Dempton stood next to a long table.

Dempton approached with a smile beneath his flamboyant red mustache. "Roran! I'm glad you came. There's going to be more work than I can handle with my new grindstones. Are you ready to go?"

Roran hefted his pack. "Yes. Do we leave soon?"

"I've a few things to take care of first, but we'll be off within the hour." Eragon shifted his feet as Dempton turned to him, tugging at the corner of his mustache. "You must be Eragon. I would offer you a job too, but Roran got the only one. Maybe in a year or two, eh?"

Eragon smiled uneasily and shook his hand. The man was friendly. Under other circumstances Eragon would have liked him, but right then, he sourly wished that the miller had never come to Carvahall. Dempton huffed. "Good, very good." He returned his attention to Roran and started to explain how a mill worked.

"They're ready to go," interrupted Horst, gesturing at the table where several bundles rested. "You can take them whenever you want to." They shook hands, then Horst left the smithy, beckoning to Eragon on the way out.

Interested, Eragon followed. He found the smith standing in the street with his arms crossed. Eragon thrust his thumb back toward the miller and asked, "What do you think of him?"

Horst rumbled, "A good man. He'll do fine with Roran." He absently brushed metal filings off his apron, then put a massive hand on Eragon's shoulder. "Lad, do you remember the fight you had with Sloan?"

"If you're asking about payment for the meat, I haven't forgotten."

"No, I trust you, lad. What I wanted to know is if you still have that blue stone."

Eragon's heart fluttered. *Why does he want to know? Maybe someone saw Saphira!* Struggling not to panic, he said, "I do, but why do you ask?"

"As soon as you return home, get rid of it." Horst overrode Eragon's exclamation. "Two men arrived here yesterday. Strange fellows dressed in black and carrying swords. It made my skin crawl just to look at them. Last evening they started asking people if a stone like yours had been found. They're at it again today." Eragon blanched. "No one with any sense said anything. They know trouble when they see it, but I could name a few people who will talk."

Dread filled Eragon's heart. Whoever had sent the stone into the Spine had finally tracked it down. Or perhaps the Empire had learned of Saphira. He did not know which would be worse. *Think! Think! The egg is gone. It's impossible for them to find it now. But if they know what it was, it'll be obvious what happened. . . . Saphira might be in danger!* It took all of his self-control to retain a casual air. "Thanks for telling me. Do you know where they are?" He was proud that his voice barely trembled.

"I didn't warn you because I thought you needed to meet those men! Leave Carvahall. Go home."

"All right," said Eragon to placate the smith, "if you think I should."

"I do." Horst's face softened. "I may be overreacting, but these strangers give me a bad feeling. It would be better if you stay home until they leave. I'll try to keep them away from your farm, though it may not do any good."

Eragon looked at him gratefully. He wished he could tell him about Saphira. "I'll leave now," he said, and hurried back to Roran. Eragon clasped his cousin's arm and bade him farewell.

"Aren't you going to stay awhile?" Roran asked with surprise.

Eragon almost laughed. For some reason, the question struck him as funny. "There's nothing for me to do, and I'm not going to stand around until you go."

"Well," said Roran doubtfully, "I guess this is the last time we'll see each other for a few months."

"I'm sure it won't seem that long," said Eragon hastily. "Take care and come back soon." He hugged Roran, then left. Horst was still in the street. Aware that the smith was watching, Eragon headed to the outskirts of Carvahall. Once the smithy was out of sight, he ducked behind a house and sneaked back through the village.

Eragon kept to the shadows as he searched each street, listening for the slightest noise. His thoughts flashed to his room, where his bow hung; he wished that it was in his hand. He prowled across Carvahall, avoiding everyone until he heard a sibilant voice from around a house. Although his ears were keen, he had to strain to hear what was being said.

"When did this happen?" The words were smooth, like oiled glass, and seemed to worm their way through the air. Underlying the speech was a strange hiss that made his scalp prickle.

"About three months ago," someone else answered. Eragon identified him as Sloan.

Shade's blood, he's telling them. . . . He resolved to punch Sloan the next time they met.

A third person spoke. The voice was deep and moist. It conjured up images of creeping decay, mold, and other things best left untouched. "Are you sure? We would hate to think you had made a mistake. If that were so, it would be most . . . unpleasant." Eragon could imagine only too well what they might do. Would anyone but the Empire dare threaten people like that? Probably not, but whoever sent the egg might be powerful enough to use force with impunity.

"Yeah, I'm sure. He had it then. I'm not lying. Plenty of people know about it. Go ask them." Sloan sounded shaken. He said something else that Eragon did not catch.

"They have been . . . rather uncooperative." The words were derisive. There was a pause. "Your information has been helpful. We will not forget you." Eragon believed him.

Sloan muttered something, then Eragon heard someone hurrying away. He peered around the corner to see what was happening. Two tall men stood in the street. Both were dressed in long black cloaks that were lifted by sheaths poking past their legs. On their shirts were insignias intricately wrought with silver thread. Hoods shaded their faces, and their hands were covered by gloves. Their backs were oddly humped, as though their clothes were stuffed with padding.

Eragon shifted slightly to get a better view. One of the strangers stiffened and grunted peculiarly to his companion. They both swiveled around and sank into crouches. Eragon's breath caught. Mortal fear clenched him. His eyes locked onto their hidden faces, and a stifling power fell over his mind, keeping him in place. He struggled against it and screamed to himself, *Move!* His legs swayed, but to no avail. The strangers stalked toward him with a smooth, noiseless gait. He knew they could see his face now. They were almost to the corner, hands grasping at swords. . . .

"Eragon!" He jerked as his name was called. The strangers froze in place and hissed. Brom hurried toward him from the side, head bare and staff in hand. The strangers were blocked from the old man's view. Eragon tried to warn him, but his tongue and arms would not stir. "Eragon!" cried Brom again. The strangers gave Eragon one last look, then slipped away between the houses.

Eragon collapsed to the ground, shivering. Sweat beaded on his forehead and made his palms sticky. The old man offered Eragon a hand and pulled him up with a strong arm. "You look sick; is all well?"

Eragon gulped and nodded mutely. His eyes flickered around, searching for anything unusual. "I just got dizzy all of a sudden . . . it's passed. It was very odd—I don't know why it happened."

"You'll recover," said Brom, "but perhaps it would be better if you went home."

Yes, I have to get home! Have to get there before they do. "I think you're right. Maybe I'm getting ill."

"Then home is the best place for you. It's a long walk, but I'm sure you will feel better by the time you arrive. Let me escort you to the road." Eragon did not protest as Brom took his arm and led him away at a quick pace. Brom's staff crunched in the snow as they passed the houses.

"Why were you looking for me?"

Brom shrugged. "Simple curiosity. I learned you were in town and wondered if you had remembered the name of that trader."

Trader? What's he talking about? Eragon stared blankly; his confusion caught the attention of Brom's probing eyes. "No," he said, and then amended himself, "I'm afraid I still don't remember."

Brom sighed gruffly, as if something had been confirmed, and rubbed his eagle nose. "Well, then . . . if you do, come tell me. I am most interested in this trader who pretends to know so much about dragons." Eragon nodded with a distracted air. They walked in silence to the road, then Brom said, "Hasten home. I don't think it would be a good idea to tarry on the way." He offered a gnarled hand.

Eragon shook it, but as he let go something in Brom's hand caught on his mitt and pulled it off. It fell to the ground. The old man picked it up. "Clumsy of me," he apologized, and handed it back. As Eragon took the mitt, Brom's strong fingers wrapped around his wrist and twisted sharply. His palm briefly faced upward, revealing the silvery mark. Brom's eyes glinted, but he let Eragon yank his hand back and jam it into the mitt.

"Goodbye," Eragon forced out, perturbed, and hurried down the road. Behind him he heard Brom whistling a merry tune.

FLIGHT OF DESTINY

Eragon's mind churned as he sped on his way. He ran as fast as he could, refusing to stop even when his breath came in great gasps. As he pounded down the cold road, he cast out with his mind for Saphira, but she was too far away for him to contact. He thought about what to say to Garrow. There was no choice now; he would have to reveal Saphira.

He arrived home, panting for air and heart pounding. Garrow stood by the barn with the horses. Eragon hesitated. *Should I talk to him now? He won't believe me unless Saphira is here—I'd better find her first.* He slipped around the farm and into the forest. *Saphira!* he shouted with his thoughts.

I come, was the dim reply. Through the words he sensed her alarm. He waited impatiently, though it was not long before the sound of her wings filled the air. She landed amid a gout of smoke. *What happened?* she queried.

He touched her shoulder and closed his eyes. Calming his mind, he quickly told her what had occurred. When he mentioned the strangers, Saphira recoiled. She reared and roared deafeningly, then whipped her tail over his head. He scrambled back in surprise, ducking as her tail hit a snowdrift. Bloodlust and fear emanated from her in great sickening waves. *Fire! Enemies! Death! Murderers!*

What's wrong? He put all of his strength into the words, but an iron wall surrounded her mind, shielding her thoughts. She let out another roar and gouged the earth with her claws, tearing the frozen ground. *Stop it! Garrow will hear!*

Oaths betrayed, souls killed, eggs shattered! Blood everywhere. Murderers!

Frantic, he blocked out Saphira's emotions and watched her tail. When it flicked past him, he dashed to her side and grabbed a spike on her back. Clutching it, he pulled himself into the small hollow at the base of her neck and held on tightly as she reared again. "Enough, Saphira!" he bellowed. Her stream of thoughts ceased abruptly. He ran a hand over her scales. "Everything's going to be all right." She crouched and her wings rushed upward. They hung there for an instant, then drove down as she flung herself into the sky.

Eragon yelled as the ground dropped away and they rose above the trees. Turbulence buffeted him, snatching the breath out of his mouth. Saphira ignored his terror and banked toward the Spine. Underneath, he glimpsed the farm and the Anora River. His stomach convulsed. He tightened his arms around Saphira's neck and concentrated on the scales in front of his nose, trying not to vomit as she continued to climb. When she leveled off, he gained the courage to glance around.

The air was so cold that frost accumulated on his eyelashes. They had reached the mountains faster than he thought possible. From the air, the peaks looked like giant razor-sharp teeth waiting to slash them to ribbons. Saphira wobbled unexpectedly, and Eragon heaved over her side. He wiped his lips, tasting bile, and buried his head against her neck.

We have to go back, he pleaded. *The strangers are coming to the farm. Garrow has to be warned. Turn around!* There was no answer. He reached for her mind, but was blocked by a barrier of roiling fear and anger. Determined to make her turn around, he grimly wormed into her mental armor. He pushed at its weak places, undermined the stronger sections, and fought to make her listen, but to no avail.

Soon mountains surrounded them, forming tremendous white walls broken by granite cliffs. Blue glaciers sat between the summits like frozen rivers. Long valleys and ravines opened beneath them. He heard the dismayed screech of birds far below as Saphira soared into view. He saw a herd of woolly goats bounding from ledge to ledge on a rocky bluff.

Eragon was battered by swirling gusts from Saphira's wings, and whenever she moved her neck, he was tossed from side to side. She seemed tireless. He was afraid she was going to fly through the night. Finally, as darkness fell, she tilted into a shallow dive.

He looked ahead and saw that they were headed for a small clearing in a valley. Saphira spiraled down, leisurely drifting over the treetops. She pulled back as the ground neared, filled her wings with air, and landed on her rear legs. Her powerful muscles rippled as they absorbed the shock of impact. She dropped to all fours and skipped a step to keep her balance. Eragon slid off without waiting for her to fold her wings.

As he struck the ground, his knees buckled, and his cheek slammed against the snow. He gasped as excruciating pain seared through his legs, sending tears to his eyes. His muscles, cramped from clenching for so long, shook violently. He rolled onto his back, shivering, and stretched his limbs as best he could. Then he forced himself to look down. Two large blots darkened his wool pants on the insides of his thighs. He touched the fabric. It was wet. Alarmed, he peeled off the pants and grimaced. The insides of his legs were raw and bloody. The skin was gone, rubbed off by Saphira's hard scales. He gingerly felt the abrasions and winced. Cold bit into him as he pulled the pants back on, and he cried out as they scraped against the sensitive wounds. He tried to stand, but his legs would not support him.

The deepening night obscured his surroundings; the shaded mountains were unfamiliar. *I'm in the Spine, I don't know where, during the middle of winter, with a crazed dragon, unable to walk or find shelter. Night is falling. I have to get back to the farm tomorrow. And the only way to do that is to fly, which I can't endure anymore.* He took a deep breath. *Oh, I wish Saphira could breathe fire.* He turned his head

and saw her next to him, crouched low to the ground. He put a
hand on her side and found it trembling. The barrier in her mind
was gone. Without it, her fear scorched through him. He clamped
down on it and slowly soothed her with gentle images. *Why do the
strangers frighten you?*

Murderers, she hissed.

*Garrow is in danger and you kidnap me on this ridiculous journey!
Are you unable to protect me?* She growled deeply and snapped her
jaws. *Ah, but if you think you can, why run?*

Death is a poison.

He leaned on one elbow and stifled his frustration. *Saphira, look
where we are! The sun is down, and your flight has stripped my legs as
easily as I would scale a fish. Is that what you wanted?*

No.

Then why did you do it? he demanded. Through his link with
Saphira, he felt her regret for his pain, but not for her actions. She
looked away and refused to answer. The icy temperature deadened
Eragon's legs; although it lessened the pain, he knew that his condition was not good. He changed tack. *I'm going to freeze unless
you make me a shelter or hollow so I can stay warm. Even a pile of
pine needles and branches would do.*

She seemed relieved that he had stopped interrogating her. *There
is no need. I will curl around you and cover you with my wings—the fire
inside me will stay the cold.*

Eragon let his head thump back on the ground. *Fine, but scrape
the snow off the ground. It'll be more comfortable.* In answer, Saphira
razed a drift with her tail, clearing it with one powerful stroke. She
swept over the site again to remove the last few inches of hardened
snow. He eyed the exposed dirt with distaste. *I can't walk over there.
You'll have to help me to it.* Her head, larger than his torso, swung
over him and came to rest by his side. He stared at her large,
sapphire-colored eyes and wrapped his hands around one of her
ivory spikes. She lifted her head and slowly dragged him to the bare
spot. *Gently, gently.* Stars danced in his eyes as he slid over a rock,

but he managed to hold on. After he let go, Saphira rolled on her side, exposing her warm belly. He huddled against the smooth scales of her underside. Her right wing extended over him and enclosed him in complete darkness, forming a living tent. Almost immediately the air began to lose its frigidity.

He pulled his arms inside his coat and tied the empty sleeves around his neck. For the first time he noticed that hunger gnawed at his stomach. But it did not distract him from his main worry: Could he get back to the farm before the strangers did? And if not, what would happen? *Even if I can force myself to ride Saphira again, it'll be at least midafternoon before we get back. The strangers could be there long before that.* He closed his eyes and felt a single tear slide down his face. *What have I done?*

THE DOOM OF INNOCENCE

When Eragon opened his eyes in the morning, he thought the sky had fallen. An unbroken plane of blue stretched over his head and slanted to the ground. Still half asleep, he reached out tentatively and felt a thin membrane under his fingers. It took him a long minute to realize what he was staring at. He bent his neck slightly and glared at the scaly haunch his head rested on. Slowly he pushed his legs out from his fetal curl, scabs cracking. The pain had subsided some from yesterday, but he shrank from the thought of walking. Burning hunger reminded him of his missed meals. He summoned the energy to move and pounded weakly on Saphira's side. "Hey! Wake up!" he yelled.

She stirred and lifted her wing to admit a torrent of sunshine. He squinted as the snow momentarily blinded him. Beside him Saphira stretched like a cat and yawned, flashing rows of white teeth. When Eragon's eyes adjusted, he examined where they were. Imposing and unfamiliar mountains surrounded them, casting deep shadows on the clearing. Off to one side, he saw a trail cut through the snow and into the forest, where he could hear the muffled gurgling of a creek.

Groaning, he stood and swayed, then stiffly hobbled to a tree. He grabbed one of its branches and threw his weight against it. It held, then broke with a loud crack. He ripped off the twigs, fit one end of the branch under his arm, and planted the other firmly in the ground. With the help of his improvised crutch, he limped to the iced-over creek. He broke through the hard shell and cupped the clear, bitter water. Sated, he returned to the clearing. As he emerged from the trees, he finally recognized the mountains and the lay of the land.

This was where, amid deafening sound, Saphira's egg had first appeared. He sagged against a rough trunk. There could be no mistake, for now he saw the gray trees that had been stripped of their needles in the explosion. *How did Saphira know where this was? She was still in the egg. My memories must have given her enough information to find it.* He shook his head in silent astonishment.

Saphira was waiting patiently for him. *Will you take me home?* he asked her. She cocked her head. *I know you don't want to, but you must. Both of us carry an obligation to Garrow. He has cared for me and, through me, you. Would you ignore that debt? What will be said of us in years to come if we don't return—that we hid like cowards while my uncle was in danger? I can hear it now, the story of the Rider and his craven dragon! If there will be a fight, let's face it and not shy away. You are a dragon! Even a Shade would run from you! Yet you crouch in the mountains like a frightened rabbit.*

Eragon meant to anger her, and he succeeded. A growl rippled in her throat as her head jabbed within a few inches of his face. She bared her fangs and glared at him, smoke trailing from her nostrils. He hoped that he had not gone too far. Her thoughts reached him, red with anger. *Blood will meet blood. I will fight. Our wyrds—our fates—bind us, but try me not. I will take you because of debt owed, but into foolishness we fly.*

"Foolishness or not," he said into the air, "there is no choice—we must go." He ripped his shirt in half and stuffed a piece into each side of his pants. Gingerly, he hoisted himself onto Saphira and took a tight hold on her neck. *This time,* he told her, *fly lower and faster. Time is of the essence.*

Don't let go, she cautioned, then surged into the sky. They rose above the forest and leveled out immediately, barely staying above the branches. Eragon's stomach lurched; he was glad it was empty.

Faster, faster, he urged. She said nothing, but the beat of her wings increased. He screwed his eyes shut and hunched his shoulders. He had hoped that the extra padding of his shirt would protect him, but every movement sent pangs through his legs. Soon lines of hot blood trickled down his calves. Concern emanated from Saphira. She went even faster now, her wings straining. The land sped past, as if it were being pulled out from under them. Eragon imagined that to someone on the ground, they were just a blur.

By early afternoon, Palancar Valley lay before them. Clouds obscured his vision to the south; Carvahall was to the north. Saphira glided down while Eragon searched for the farm. When he spotted it, fear jolted him. A black plume with orange flames dancing at its base rose from the farm.

Saphira! He pointed. *Get me down there. Now!*

She locked her wings and tilted into a steep dive, hurtling groundward at a frightening rate. Then she altered her dive slightly so they sped toward the forest. He yelled over the screaming air, "Land in the fields!" He held on tighter as they plummeted. Saphira waited until they were only a hundred feet off the ground before driving her wings downward in several powerful strokes. She landed heavily, breaking his grip. He crashed to the ground, then staggered upright, gasping for breath.

The house had been blasted apart. Timbers and boards that had been walls and roof were strewn across a wide area. The wood was pulverized, as if a giant hammer had smashed it. Sooty shingles lay everywhere. A few twisted metal plates were all that remained of the stove. The snow was perforated with smashed white crockery and chunks of bricks from the chimney. Thick, oily smoke billowed from the barn, which burned fiercely. The farm animals were gone, either killed or frightened away.

"Uncle!" Eragon ran to the wreckage, hunting through the destroyed rooms for Garrow. There was no sign of him. "Uncle!" Eragon cried again. Saphira walked around the house and came to his side.

Sorrow breeds here, she said.

"This wouldn't have happened if you hadn't run away with me!" *You would not be alive if we had stayed.*

"Look at this!" he screamed. "We could've warned Garrow! It's your fault he didn't get away!" He slammed his fist against a pole, splitting the skin on his knuckles. Blood dripped down his fingers as he stalked out of the house. He stumbled to the path that led to the road and bent down to examine the snow. Several tracks were before him, but his vision was blurry and he could barely see. *Am I going blind?* he wondered. With a shaking hand, he touched his cheeks and found them wet.

A shadow fell on him as Saphira loomed overhead, sheltering him with her wings. *Take comfort; all may not be lost.* He looked up at her, searching for hope. *Examine the trail; my eyes see only two sets of prints. Garrow could not have been taken from here.*

He focused on the trampled snow. The faint imprints of two pairs of leather boots headed toward the house. On top of those were traces of the same two sets of boots leaving. And whoever had made the departing tracks had been carrying the same weight as when they arrived. *You're right, Garrow has to be here!* He leapt to his feet and hurried back to the house.

I will search around the buildings and in the forest, said Saphira.

Eragon scrambled into the remains of the kitchen and frantically started digging through a pile of rubble. Pieces of debris that he could not have moved normally now seemed to shift on their own accord. A cupboard, mostly intact, stymied him for a second, then he heaved and sent it flying. As he pulled on a board, something rattled behind him. He spun around, ready for an attack.

A hand extended from under a section of collapsed roof. It moved weakly, and he grasped it with a cry. "Uncle, can you hear me?" There was no response. Eragon tore at pieces of wood, heedless of the splinters that pierced his hands. He quickly exposed an arm and shoulder, but was barred by a heavy beam. He threw his shoulder at it and shoved with every fiber of his being, but it defied his efforts. "Saphira! I need you!"

She came immediately. Wood cracked under her feet as she crawled over the ruined walls. Without a word she nosed past him and set her side against the beam. Her claws sank into what was left of the floor; her muscles strained. With a grating sound, the beam lifted, and Eragon rushed under it. Garrow lay on his stomach, his clothes mostly torn off. Eragon pulled him out of the rubble. As soon as they were clear, Saphira released the beam, leaving it to crash to the floor.

Eragon dragged Garrow out of the destroyed house and eased him to the ground. Dismayed, he touched his uncle gently. His skin was gray, lifeless, and dry, as if a fever had burned off any sweat. His lip was split, and there was a long scrape on his cheekbone, but that was not the worst. Deep, ragged burns covered most of his body. They were chalky white and oozed clear liquid. A cloying, sickening smell hung over him—the odor of rotting fruit. His breath came in short jerks, each one sounding like a death rattle.

Murderers, hissed Saphira.

Don't say that. He can still be saved! We have to get him to Gertrude. I can't carry him to Carvahall, though.

Saphira presented an image of Garrow hanging under her while she flew.

Can you lift both of us?

I must.

Eragon dug through the rubble until he found a board and leather thongs. He had Saphira pierce a hole with a claw at each of the board's corners, then he looped a piece of leather through each hole and tied them to her forelegs. After checking to make sure the knots were secure, he rolled Garrow onto the board and lashed him down. As he did, a scrap of black cloth fell from his uncle's hand. It matched the strangers' clothing. He angrily stuffed it in a pocket, mounted Saphira, and closed his eyes as his body settled into a steady throb of pain. *Now!*

She leapt up, hind legs digging into the ground. Her wings clawed at the air as she slowly climbed. Tendons strained and popped as she battled gravity. For a long, painful second, nothing happened, but then she lunged forward powerfully and they rose higher. Once they were over the forest, Eragon told her, *Follow the road. It'll give you enough room if you have to land.*

I might be seen.

It doesn't matter anymore! She argued no further as she veered to the road and headed for Carvahall. Garrow swung wildly underneath them; only the slender leather cords kept him from falling.

The extra weight slowed Saphira. Before long her head sagged, and there was froth at her mouth. She struggled to continue, yet they were almost a league from Carvahall when she locked her wings and sank toward the road.

Her hind feet touched with a shower of snow. Eragon tumbled off her, landing heavily on his side to avoid hurting his legs. He struggled to his feet and worked to untie the leather from Saphira's legs. Her thick panting filled the air. *Find a safe place to rest,* he said. *I don't know how long I'll be gone, so you're going to have to take care of yourself for a while.*

I will wait, she said.

He gritted his teeth and began to drag Garrow down the road. The first few steps sent an explosion of agony through him. "I can't do this!" he howled at the sky, then took a few more steps. His mouth locked into a snarl. He stared at the ground between his feet as he forced himself to hold a steady pace. It was a fight against his unruly body—a fight he refused to lose. The minutes crawled by at an excruciating rate. Each yard he covered seemed many times that. With desperation he wondered if Carvahall still existed or if the strangers had burnt it down, too. After a time, through a haze of pain, he heard shouting and looked up.

Brom was running toward him—eyes large, hair awry, and one side of his head caked with dried blood. He waved his arms wildly before dropping his staff and grabbing Eragon's shoulders, saying something in a loud voice. Eragon blinked uncomprehendingly. Without warning, the ground rushed up to meet him. He tasted blood, then blacked out.

DEATHWATCH

Dreams roiled in Eragon's mind, breeding and living by their own laws. *He watched as a group of people on proud horses approached a lonely river. Many had silver hair and carried tall lances. A strange, fair ship waited for them, shining under a bright moon. The figures slowly boarded the vessel; two of them, taller than the rest, walked arm in arm. Their faces were obscured by cowls, but he could tell that one was a woman. They stood on the deck of the ship and faced the shore. A man stood alone on the pebble beach, the only one who had not boarded the ship. He threw back his head and let out a long, aching cry. As it faded, the ship glided down the river, without a breeze or oars, out into the flat, empty land. The vision clouded, but just before it disappeared, Eragon glimpsed two dragons in the sky.*

Eragon was first aware of the creaking: back and forth, back and forth. The persistent sound made him open his eyes and stare at the underside of a thatched roof. A rough blanket was draped over him, concealing his nakedness. Someone had bandaged his legs and tied a clean rag around his knuckles.

He was in a single-room hut. A mortar and pestle sat on a table with bowls and plants. Rows of dried herbs hung from the walls and suffused the air with strong, earthy aromas. Flames writhed inside a fireplace, before which sat a rotund woman in a wicker rocking chair—the town healer, Gertrude. Her head lolled, eyes closed. A pair of knitting needles and a ball of wool thread rested in her lap.

Though Eragon felt drained of willpower, he made himself sit up. That helped to clear his mind. He sifted through his memories of the last two days. His first thought was of Garrow, and his second was of Saphira. *I hope she's in a safe place.* He tried to contact her but could not. Wherever she was, it was far from Carvahall. *At least Brom got me to Carvahall. I wonder what happened to him? There was all that blood.*

Gertrude stirred and opened her sparkling eyes. "Oh," she said. "You're awake. Good!" Her voice was rich and warm. "How do you feel?"

"Well enough. Where's Garrow?"

Gertrude dragged the chair close to the bed. "Over at Horst's. There wasn't enough room to keep both of you here. And let me tell you, it's kept me on my toes, having to run back and forth, checking to see if the two of you were all right."

Eragon swallowed his worries and asked, "How is he?"

There was a long delay as she examined her hands. "Not good. He has a fever that refuses to break, and his injuries aren't healing."

"I have to see him." He tried to get up.

"Not until you eat," she said sharply, pushing him down. "I didn't spend all this time sitting by your side so you can get back up and hurt yourself. Half the skin on your legs was torn off, and your fever broke only last night. Don't worry yourself about Garrow. He'll be fine. He's a tough man." Gertrude hung a kettle over the fire, then began chopping parsnips for soup.

"How long have I been here?"

"Two full days."

Two days! That meant his last meal had been four mornings ago! Just thinking about it made Eragon feel weak. *Saphira's been on her own this entire time; I hope she's all right.*

"The whole town wants to know what happened. They sent men down to your farm and found it destroyed." Eragon nodded; he had expected that. "Your barn was burned down. . . . Is that how Garrow was injured?"

"I . . . I don't know," said Eragon. "I wasn't there when it happened."

"Well, no matter. I'm sure it'll all get untangled." Gertrude resumed knitting while the soup cooked. "That's quite a scar on your palm."

He reflexively clenched his hand. "Yes."

"How did you get it?"

Several possible answers came to mind. He chose the simplest one. "I've had it ever since I can remember. I never asked Garrow where it came from."

"Mmm." The silence remained unbroken until the soup reached a rolling boil. Gertrude poured it in a bowl and handed it to Eragon with a spoon. He accepted it gratefully and took a cautious sip. It was delicious.

When he finished, he asked, "Can I visit Garrow now?"

Gertrude sighed. "You're a determined one, aren't you? Well, if you really want to, I won't stop you. Put on your clothes and we'll go."

She turned her back as he struggled into his pants, wincing as they dragged over the bandages, and then slipped on his shirt. Gertrude helped him stand. His legs were weak, but they did not pain him like before.

"Take a few steps," she commanded, then dryly observed, "At least you won't have to crawl there."

Outside, a blustery wind blew smoke from the adjacent buildings into their faces. Storm clouds hid the Spine and covered the valley while a curtain of snow advanced toward the village, obscuring the foothills. Eragon leaned heavily on Gertrude as they made their way through Carvahall.

Horst had built his two-story house on a hill so he could enjoy a view of the mountains. He had lavished all of his skill on it. The shale roof shadowed a railed balcony that extended from a tall window on the second floor. Each water spout was a snarling gargoyle, and every window and door was framed by carvings of serpents, harts, ravens, and knotted vines.

The door was opened by Elain, Horst's wife, a small, willowy woman with refined features and silky blond hair pinned into a

bun. Her dress was demure and neat, and her movements graceful. "Please, come in," she said softly. They stepped over the
threshold into a large well-lit room. A staircase with a polished
balustrade curved down to the floor. The walls were the color of
honey. Elain gave Eragon a sad smile, but addressed Gertrude. "I
was just about to send for you. He isn't doing well. You should see
him right away."

"Elain, you'll have to help Eragon up the stairs," Gertrude said,
then hurried up them two at a time.

"It's okay, I can do it myself."

"Are you sure?" asked Elain. He nodded, but she looked doubtful. "Well . . . as soon as you're done come visit me in the kitchen.
I have a fresh-baked pie you might enjoy." As soon as she left, he
sagged against the wall, welcoming the support. Then he started up
the stairs, one painful step at a time. When he reached the top, he
looked down a long hallway dotted with doors. The last one was
open slightly. Taking a breath, he lurched toward it.

Katrina stood by a fireplace, boiling rags. She looked up, murmured a condolence, and then returned to her work. Gertrude
stood beside her, grinding herbs for a poultice. A bucket by her feet
held snow melting into ice water.

Garrow lay on a bed piled high with blankets. Sweat covered his
brow, and his eyeballs flickered blindly under their lids. The skin on
his face was shrunken like a cadaver's. He was still, save for subtle
tremors from his shallow breathing. Eragon touched his uncle's
forehead with a feeling of unreality. It burned against his hand. He
apprehensively lifted the edge of the blankets and saw that
Garrow's many wounds were bound with strips of cloth. Where the
bandages were being changed, the burns were exposed to the air.
They had not begun to heal. Eragon looked at Gertrude with hopeless eyes. "Can't you do anything about these?"

She pressed a rag into the bucket of ice water, then draped the cool
cloth over Garrow's head. "I've tried everything: salves, poultices,
tinctures, but nothing works. If the wounds closed, he would have

a better chance. Still, things may turn for the better. He's hardy and strong."

Eragon moved to a corner and sank to the floor. *This isn't the way things are supposed to be!* Silence swallowed his thoughts. He stared blankly at the bed. After a while he noticed Katrina kneeling beside him. She put an arm around him. When he did not respond, she diffidently left.

Sometime later the door opened and Horst came in. He talked to Gertrude in a low voice, then approached Eragon. "Come on. You need to get out of here." Before Eragon could protest, Horst dragged him to his feet and shepherded him out the door.

"I want to stay," he complained.

"You need a break and fresh air. Don't worry, you can go back soon enough," consoled Horst.

Eragon grudgingly let the smith help him downstairs into the kitchen. Heady smells from half a dozen dishes—rich with spices and herbs—filled the air. Albriech and Baldor were there, talking with their mother as she kneaded bread. The brothers fell silent as they saw Eragon, but he had heard enough to know that they were discussing Garrow.

"Here, sit down," said Horst, offering a chair.

Eragon sank into it gratefully. "Thank you." His hands were shaking slightly, so he clasped them in his lap. A plate, piled high with food, was set before him.

"You don't have to eat," said Elain, "but it's there if you want." She returned to her cooking as he picked up a fork. He could barely swallow a few bites.

"How do you feel?" asked Horst.

"Terrible."

The smith waited a moment. "I know this isn't the best time, but we need to know . . . what happened?"

"I don't really remember."

"Eragon," said Horst, leaning forward, "I was one of the people who went out to your farm. Your house didn't just fall apart—

something tore it to pieces. Surrounding it were tracks of a gigantic beast I've never seen nor heard of before. Others saw them too. Now, if there's a Shade or a monster roaming around, we have to know. You're the only one who can tell us."

Eragon knew he had to lie. "When I left Carvahall . . . ," he counted up the time, "four days ago, there were . . . strangers in town asking about a stone like the one I found." He gestured at Horst. "You talked to me about them, and because of that, I hurried home." All eyes were upon him. He licked his lips. "Nothing . . . nothing happened that night. The next morning I finished my chores and went walking in the forest. Before long I heard an explosion and saw smoke above the trees. I rushed back as fast as I could, but whoever did it was already gone. I dug through the wreckage and . . . found Garrow."

"So then you put him on the plank and dragged him back?" asked Albriech.

"Yes," said Eragon, "but before I left, I looked at the path to the road. There were two pairs of tracks on it, both of them men's." He dug in his pocket and pulled out the scrap of black fabric. "This was clenched in Garrow's hand. I think it matches what those strangers were wearing." He set it on the table.

"It does," said Horst. He looked both thoughtful and angry. "And what of your legs? How were they injured?"

"I'm not sure," said Eragon, shaking his head. "I think it happened when I dug Garrow out, but I don't know. It wasn't until the blood started dripping down my legs that I noticed it."

"That's horrible!" exclaimed Elain.

"We should pursue those men," stated Albriech hotly. "They can't get away with this! With a pair of horses we could catch them tomorrow and bring them back here."

"Put that foolishness out of your head," said Horst. "They could probably pick you up like a baby and throw you in a tree. Remember what happened to the house? We don't want to get in the way of those people. Besides, they have what they want now." He looked at Eragon. "They did take the stone, didn't they?"

"It wasn't in the house."

"Then there's no reason for them to return now that they have it." He gave Eragon a piercing look. "You didn't mention anything about those strange tracks. Do you know where they came from?"

Eragon shook his head. "I didn't see them."

Baldor abruptly spoke. "I don't like this. Too much of this rings of wizardry. Who are those men? Are they Shades? Why did they want the stone, and how could they have destroyed the house except with dark powers? You may be right, Father, the stone might be all they wanted, but I think we will see them again."

Silence followed his words.

Something had been overlooked, though Eragon was not sure what. Then it struck him. With a sinking heart, he voiced his suspicion. "Roran doesn't know, does he?" *How could I have forgotten him?*

Horst shook his head. "He and Dempton left a little while after you. Unless they ran into some difficulty on the road, they've been in Therinsford for a couple of days now. We were going to send a message, but the weather was too cold yesterday and the day before."

"Baldor and I were about to leave when you woke up," offered Albriech.

Horst ran a hand through his beard. "Go on, both of you. I'll help you saddle the horses."

Baldor turned to Eragon. "I'll break it to him gently," he promised, then followed Horst and Albriech out of the kitchen.

Eragon remained at the table, his eyes focused on a knot in the wood. Every excruciating detail was clear to him: the twisting grain, an asymmetrical bump, three little ridges with a fleck of color. The knot was filled with endless detail; the closer he looked, the more he saw. He searched for answers in it, but if there were any, they eluded him.

A faint call broke through his pounding thoughts. It sounded like yelling from outside. He ignored it. *Let someone else deal with it.* Several minutes later he heard it again, louder than before. Angrily, he blocked it out. *Why can't they be quiet? Garrow's resting.* He glanced at Elain, but she did not seem to be bothered by the noise.

ERAGON! The roar was so strong he almost fell out of the chair. He peered around in alarm, but nothing had changed. He suddenly realized that the shouts had been inside his head.

Saphira? he asked anxiously.

There was a pause. *Yes, stone ears.*

Relief seeped into him. *Where are you?*

She sent him an image of a small clump of trees. *I tried to contact you many times, but you were beyond reach.*

I was sick . . . but I'm better now. Why couldn't I sense you earlier?

After two nights of waiting, hunger bested me. I had to hunt.

Did you catch anything?

A young buck. He was wise enough to guard against the predators of land, but not those of sky. When I first caught him in my jaws, he kicked vigorously and tried to escape. I was stronger, though, and when defeat became unavoidable, he gave up and died. Does Garrow also fight the inevitable?

I don't know. He told her the particulars, then said, *It'll be a long time, if ever, before we can go home. I won't be able to see you for at least a couple of days. You might as well make yourself comfortable.*

Unhappily, she said, *I will do as you say. But do not take too long.*

They parted reluctantly. He looked out a window and was surprised to see that the sun had set. Feeling very tired, he limped to Elain, who was wrapping meat pies with oilcloth. "I'm going back to Gertrude's house to sleep," he said.

She finished with the packages and asked, "Why don't you stay with us? You'll be closer to your uncle, and Gertrude can have her bed back."

"Do you have enough room?" he asked, wavering.

"Of course." She wiped her hands. "Come with me; I'll get everything ready." She escorted him upstairs to an empty room. He sat on the edge of the bed. "Do you need anything else?" she asked. He shook his head. "In that case, I'll be downstairs. Call me if you need help." He listened as she descended the stairs. Then he opened the door and slipped down the hallway to Garrow's room. Gertrude gave him a small smile over her darting knitting needles.

"How is he?" whispered Eragon.

Her voice rasped with fatigue. "He's weak, but the fever's gone down a little and some of the burns look better. We'll have to wait and see, but this could mean he'll recover."

That lightened Eragon's mood, and he returned to his room. The darkness seemed unfriendly as he huddled under the blankets. Eventually he fell asleep, healing the wounds his body and soul had suffered.

THE MADNESS OF LIFE

I t was dark when Eragon jolted upright in bed, breathing hard. The room was chilly; goose bumps formed on his arms and shoulders. It was a few hours before dawn—the time when nothing moves and life waits for the first warm touches of sunlight.

His heart pounded as a terrible premonition gripped him. It felt like a shroud lay over the world, and its darkest corner was over his room. He quietly got out of bed and dressed. With apprehension he hurried down the hallway. Alarm shot through him when he saw the door to Garrow's room open and people clustered inside.

Garrow lay peacefully on the bed. He was dressed in clean clothes, his hair had been combed back, and his face was calm. He might have been sleeping if not for the silver amulet clasped around his neck and the sprig of dried hemlock on his chest, the last gifts from the living to the dead.

Katrina stood next to the bed, face pale and eyes downcast. He heard her whisper, "I had hoped to call him *Father* one day. . . ."

Call him Father, he thought bitterly, *a right even I don't have.* He felt like a ghost, drained of all vitality. Everything was insubstantial except for Garrow's face. Tears flooded Eragon's cheeks. He stood there, shoulders shaking, but did not cry out. Mother, aunt, uncle— he had lost them all. The weight of his grief was crushing, a monstrous force that left him tottering. Someone led him back to his room, uttering consolations.

He fell on the bed, wrapped his arms around his head, and

sobbed convulsively. He felt Saphira contact him, but he pushed her aside and let himself be swept away by sorrow. He could not accept that Garrow was gone. If he did, what was left to believe in? Only a merciless, uncaring world that snuffed lives like candles before a wind. Frustrated and terrified, he turned his tear-dampened face toward the heavens and shouted, "What god would do this? Show yourself!" He heard people running to his room, but no answer came from above. "He didn't deserve this!"

Comforting hands touched him, and he was aware of Elain sitting next to him. She held him as he cried, and eventually, exhausted, he slipped unwillingly into sleep.

A RIDER'S BLADE

Anguish enveloped Eragon as he awoke. Though he kept his eyes closed, they could not stop a fresh flow of tears. He searched for some idea or hope to help him keep his sanity. *I can't live with this,* he moaned.

Then don't. Saphira's words reverberated in his head.

How? Garrow is gone forever! And in time, I must meet the same fate. Love, family, accomplishments—they are all torn away, leaving nothing. What is the worth of anything we do?

The worth is in the act. Your worth halts when you surrender the will to change and experience life. But options are before you; choose one and dedicate yourself to it. The deeds will give you new hope and purpose.

But what can I do?

The only true guide is your heart. Nothing less than its supreme desire can help you.

She left him to ponder her statements. Eragon examined his emotions. It surprised him that, more than grief, he found a searing anger. *What do you want me to do . . . pursue the strangers?*

Yes.

Her frank answer confused him. He took a deep, trembling breath. *Why?*

Remember what you said in the Spine? How you reminded me of my duty as dragon, and I returned with you despite the urging of my instinct? So, too, must you control yourself. I thought long and deep the past few days, and I realized what it means to be dragon and Rider: It is our destiny to attempt the impossible, to accomplish great deeds regardless of fear. It is our responsibility to the future.

I don't care what you say; those aren't reasons to leave! cried Eragon.

Then here are others. My tracks have been seen, and people are alert to my presence. Eventually I will be exposed. Besides, there is nothing here for you. No farm, no family, and—

Roran's not dead! he said vehemently.

But if you stay, you'll have to explain what really happened. He has a right to know how and why his father died. What might he do once he knows of me?

Saphira's arguments whirled around in Eragon's head, but he shrank from the idea of forsaking Palancar Valley; it was his home. Yet the thought of enacting vengeance on the strangers was fiercely comforting. *Am I strong enough for this?*

You have me.

Doubt besieged him. It would be such a wild, desperate thing to do. Contempt for his indecision rose, and a harsh smile danced on his lips. Saphira was right. Nothing mattered anymore except the act itself. *The doing is the thing.* And what would give him more satisfaction than hunting down the strangers? A terrible energy and strength began to grow in him. It grabbed his emotions and forged them into a solid bar of anger with one word stamped on it: revenge. His head pounded as he said with conviction, *I will do it.*

He severed the contact with Saphira and rolled out of bed, his body tense like a coiled spring. It was still early morning; he had only slept a few hours. *Nothing is more dangerous than an enemy with nothing to lose,* he thought. *Which is what I have become.*

Yesterday he had had difficulty walking upright, but now he moved confidently, held in place by his iron will. The pain his body sent him was defied and ignored.

As he crept out of the house, he heard the murmur of two people talking. Curious, he stopped and listened. Elain was saying in her gentle voice, ". . . place to stay. We have room." Horst answered inaudibly in his bass rumble. "Yes, the poor boy," replied Elain.

This time Eragon could hear Horst's response. "Maybe . . ." There was a long pause. "I've been thinking about what Eragon said, and I'm not sure he told us everything."

"What do you mean?" asked Elain. There was concern in her voice.

"When we started for their farm, the road was scraped smooth by the board he dragged Garrow on. Then we reached a place where the snow was all trampled and churned up. His footprints and signs of the board stopped there, but we also saw the same giant tracks from the farm. And what about his legs? I can't believe he didn't notice losing that much skin. I didn't want to push him for answers earlier, but now I think I will."

"Maybe what he saw scared him so much that he doesn't want to talk about it," suggested Elain. "You saw how distraught he was."

"That still doesn't explain how he managed to get Garrow nearly all the way here without leaving any tracks."

Saphira was right, thought Eragon. *It's time to leave. Too many questions from too many people. Sooner or later they'll find the answers.* He continued through the house, tensing whenever the floor creaked.

The streets were clear; few people were up at this time of day. He stopped for a minute and forced himself to focus. *I don't need a horse. Saphira will be my steed, but she needs a saddle. She can hunt for both of us, so I don't have to worry about food—though I should get some anyway. Whatever else I need I can find buried in our house.*

He went to Gedric's tanning vats on the outskirts of Carvahall. The vile smell made him cringe, but he kept moving, heading for a shack set into the side of a hill where the cured hides were stored. He cut down three large ox hides from the rows of skins hanging from the ceiling. The thievery made him feel guilty, but he reasoned, *It's not really stealing. I'll pay Gedric back someday, along with Horst.* He rolled up the thick leather and took it to a stand of trees away from the village. He wedged the hides between the branches of a tree, then returned to Carvahall.

Now for food. He went to the tavern, intending to get it there, but then smiled tightly and reversed direction. If he was going to steal, it might as well be from Sloan. He sneaked up to the butcher's house. The front door was barred whenever Sloan was not there, but the side door was secured with only a thin chain, which he broke easily. The rooms inside were dark. He fumbled blindly until his hands came upon hard piles of meat wrapped in cloth. He stuffed as many of them as he could under his shirt, then hurried back to the street and furtively closed the door.

A woman shouted his name nearby. He clasped the bottom of his shirt to keep the meat from falling out and ducked behind a corner. He shivered as Horst walked between two houses not ten feet away.

Eragon ran as soon as Horst was out of sight. His legs burned as he pounded down an alley and back to the trees. He slipped between the tree trunks, then turned to see if he was being pursued. No one was there. Relieved, he let out his breath and reached into the tree for the leather. It was gone.

"Going somewhere?"

Eragon whirled around. Brom scowled angrily at him, an ugly wound on the side of his head. A short sword hung at his belt in a brown sheath. The hides were in his hands.

Eragon's eyes narrowed in irritation. How had the old man managed to sneak up on him? Everything had been so quiet, he would have sworn that no one was around. "Give them back," he snapped.

"Why? So you can run off before Garrow is even buried?" The accusation was sharp.

"It's none of your business!" he barked, temper flashing. "Why did you follow me?"

"I didn't," grunted Brom. "I've been waiting for you here. Now where are you going?"

"Nowhere." Eragon lunged for the skins and grabbed them from Brom's hands. Brom did nothing to stop him.

"I hope you have enough meat to feed your dragon."

Eragon froze. "What are you talking about?"

Brom crossed his arms. "Don't fool with me. I know where that mark on your hand, the gedwëy ignasia, the *shining palm*, comes from:

you have touched a dragon hatchling. I know why you came to me with those questions, and I know that once more the Riders live."

Eragon dropped the leather and meat. *It's finally happened . . . I have to get away! I can't run faster than him with my injured legs, but if . . . Saphira!* he called.

For a few agonizing seconds she did not answer, but then, *Yes.*

We've been discovered! I need you! He sent her a picture of where he was, and she took off immediately. Now he just had to stall Brom. "How did you find out?" he asked in a hollow voice.

Brom stared into the distance and moved his lips soundlessly as if he were talking to someone else. Then he said, "There were clues and hints everywhere; I had only to pay attention. Anyone with the right knowledge could have done the same. Tell me, how is your dragon?"

"She," said Eragon, "is fine. We weren't at the farm when the strangers came."

"Ah, your legs. You were flying?"

How did Brom figure that out? What if the strangers coerced him into doing this? Maybe they want him to discover where I'm going so they can ambush us. And where is Saphira? He reached out with his mind and found her circling far overhead. *Come!*

No, I will watch for a time.

Why!

Because of the slaughter at Dorú Areaba.

What?

Brom leaned against a tree with a slight smile. "I have talked with her, and she has agreed to stay above us until we settle our differences. As you can see, you really don't have any choice but to answer my questions. Now tell me, where are you going?"

Bewildered, Eragon put a hand to his temple. *How could Brom speak to Saphira?* The back of his head throbbed and ideas whirled through his mind, but he kept reaching the same conclusion: he had to tell the old man something. He said, "I was going to find a safe place to stay while I heal."

"And after that?"

The question could not be ignored. The throbbing in his head grew worse. It was impossible to think; nothing seemed clear anymore. All he wanted to do was tell someone about the events of the past few months. It tore at him that his secret had caused Garrow's death. He gave up and said tremulously, "I was going to hunt down the strangers and kill them."

"A mighty task for one so young," Brom said in a normal tone, as if Eragon had proposed the most obvious and suitable thing to do. "Certainly a worthy endeavor and one you are fit to carry out, yet it strikes me that help would not be unwelcome." He reached behind a bush and pulled out a large pack. His tone became gruff. "Anyway, I'm not going to stay behind while some stripling gets to run around with a dragon."

Is he really offering help, or is it a trap? Eragon was afraid of what his mysterious enemies could do. *But Brom convinced Saphira to trust him, and they've talked through the mind touch. If she isn't worried . . .* He decided to put his suspicions aside for the present. "I don't need help," said Eragon, then grudgingly added, "but you can come."

"Then we had best be going," said Brom. His face blanked for a moment. "I think you'll find that your dragon will listen to you again."

Saphira? asked Eragon.

Yes.

He resisted the urge to question her. *Will you meet us at the farm?*

Yes. So you reached an agreement?

I guess so. She broke contact and soared away. He glanced at Carvahall and saw people running from house to house. "I think they're looking for me."

Brom raised an eyebrow. "Probably. Shall we go?"

Eragon hesitated. "I'd like to leave a message for Roran. It doesn't seem right to run off without telling him why."

"It's been taken care of," assured Brom. "I left a letter for him with Gertrude, explaining a few things. I also cautioned him to be on guard for certain dangers. Is that satisfactory?"

Eragon nodded. He wrapped the leather around the meat and started off. They were careful to stay out of sight until they reached the road, then quickened their pace, eager to distance themselves from Carvahall. Eragon plowed ahead determinedly, his legs burning. The mindless rhythm of walking freed his mind to think. *Once we get home, I won't travel any farther with Brom until I get some answers*, he told himself firmly. *I hope that he can tell me more about the Riders and whom I'm fighting.*

As the wreckage of the farm came into view, Brom's eyebrows beetled with anger. Eragon was dismayed to see how swiftly nature was reclaiming the farm. Snow and dirt were already piled inside the house, concealing the violence of the strangers' attack. All that remained of the barn was a rapidly eroding rectangle of soot.

Brom's head snapped up as the sound of Saphira's wings drifted over the trees. She dived past them from behind, almost brushing their heads. They staggered as a wall of air buffeted them. Saphira's scales glittered as she wheeled over the farm and landed gracefully.

Brom stepped forward with an expression both solemn and joyous. His eyes were shining, and a tear shone on his cheek before it disappeared into his beard. He stood there for a long while, breathing heavily as he watched Saphira, and she him. Eragon heard him muttering and edged closer to listen.

"So . . . it starts again. But how and where will it end? My sight is veiled; I cannot tell if this be tragedy or farce, for the elements of both are here. . . . However it may be, my station is unchanged, and I . . ."

Whatever else he might have said faded away as Saphira proudly approached them. Eragon passed Brom, pretended he had heard nothing, and greeted her. There was something different between them now, as if they knew each other even more intimately, yet were still strangers. He rubbed her neck, and his palm tingled as their minds touched. A strong curiosity came from her.

I've seen no humans except you and Garrow, and he was badly injured, she said.

You've viewed people through my eyes.

It's not the same. She came closer and turned her long head so that she could inspect Brom with one large blue eye. *You really are queer creatures,* she said critically, and continued to stare at him. Brom held still as she sniffed the air, and then he extended a hand to her. Saphira slowly bowed her head and allowed him to touch her on the brow. With a snort, she jerked back and retreated behind Eragon. Her tail flicked over the ground.

What is it? he asked. She did not answer.

Brom turned to him and asked in an undertone, "What's her name?"

"Saphira." A peculiar expression crossed Brom's face. He ground the butt of his staff into the earth with such force his knuckles turned white. "Of all the names you gave me, it was the only one she liked. I think it fits," Eragon added quickly.

"Fit it does," said Brom. There was something in his voice Eragon could not identify. Was it loss, wonder, fear, envy? He was not sure; it could have been none of them or all. Brom raised his voice and said, "Greetings, Saphira. I am honored to meet you." He twisted his hand in a strange gesture and bowed.

I like him, said Saphira quietly.

Of course you do; everyone enjoys flattery. Eragon touched her on the shoulder and went to the ruined house. Saphira trailed behind with Brom. The old man looked vibrant and alive.

Eragon climbed into the house and crawled under a door into what was left of his room. He barely recognized it under the piles of shattered wood. Guided by memory, he searched where the inside wall had been and found his empty pack. Part of the frame was broken, but the damage could be easily repaired. He kept rummaging and eventually uncovered the end of his bow, which was still in its buckskin tube.

Though the leather was scratched and scuffed, he was pleased to see that the oiled wood was unharmed. *Finally, some luck.* He strung the bow and pulled on the sinew experimentally. It bent smoothly, without any snaps or creaks. Satisfied, he hunted for his quiver, which he found buried nearby. Many of the arrows were broken.

He unstrung the bow and handed it and the quiver to Brom, who said, "It takes a strong arm to pull that." Eragon took the compliment silently. He picked through the rest of the house for other useful items and dumped the collection next to Brom. It was a meager pile. "What now?" asked Brom. His eyes were sharp and inquisitive. Eragon looked away.

"We find a place to hide."

"Do you have somewhere in mind?"

"Yes." He wrapped all the supplies, except for his bow, into a tight bundle and tied it shut. Hefting it onto his back, he said, "This way," and headed into the forest. *Saphira, follow us in the air. Your footprints are too easily found and tracked.*

Very well. She took off behind them.

Their destination was nearby, but Eragon took a circuitous route in an effort to baffle any pursuers. It was well over an hour before he finally stopped in a well-concealed bramble.

The irregular clearing in the center was just large enough for a fire, two people, and a dragon. Red squirrels scampered into the trees, chattering in protest at their intrusion. Brom extricated himself from a vine and looked around with interest. "Does anyone else know of this?" he asked.

"No. I found it when we first moved here. It took me a week to dig into the center, and another week to clear out all the deadwood." Saphira landed beside them and folded her wings, careful to avoid the thorns. She curled up, snapping twigs with her hard scales, and rested her head on the ground. Her unreadable eyes followed them closely.

Brom leaned against his staff and fixed his gaze on her. His scrutiny made Eragon nervous.

Eragon watched them until hunger forced him to action. He built a fire, filled a pot with snow, and then set it over the flames to melt. When the water was hot, he tore off chunks of meat and dropped them into the pot with a lump of salt. *Not much of a meal,* he thought grimly, *but it'll do. I'll probably be eating this for some time to come, so I might as well get used to it.*

The stew simmered quietly, spreading a rich aroma through the clearing. The tip of Saphira's tongue snaked out and tasted the air. When the meat was tender, Brom came over and Eragon served the food. They ate silently, avoiding each other's eyes. Afterward, Brom pulled out his pipe and lit it leisurely.

"Why do you want to travel with me?" asked Eragon.

A cloud of smoke left Brom's lips and spiraled up through the trees until it disappeared. "I have a vested interest in keeping you alive," he said.

"What do you mean?" demanded Eragon.

"To put it bluntly, I'm a storyteller and I happen to think that you will make a fine story. You're the first Rider to exist outside of the king's control for over a hundred years. What will happen? Will you perish as a martyr? Will you join the Varden? Or will you kill King Galbatorix? All fascinating questions. And I will be there to see every bit of it, no matter what I have to do."

A knot formed in Eragon's stomach. He could not see himself doing any of those things, least of all becoming a martyr. *I want my vengeance, but for the rest . . . I have no ambition.* "That may be, but tell me, how can you talk with Saphira?"

Brom took his time putting more tobacco in his pipe. Once it was relit and firmly in his mouth, he said, "Very well, if it's answers you want, it's answers you'll get, but they may not be to your liking." He got up, brought his pack over to the fire, and pulled out a long object wrapped in cloth. It was about three and a half feet long and, from the way he handled it, rather heavy.

He peeled away the cloth, strip by strip, like a mummy being unswathed. Eragon gazed, transfixed, as a sword was revealed. The gold pommel was teardrop shaped with the sides cut away to reveal a ruby the size of a small egg. The hilt was wrapped in silver wire, burnished until it gleamed like starlight. The sheath was wine red and smooth as glass, adorned solely by a strange black symbol etched into it. Next to the sword was a leather belt with a heavy buckle. The last strip fell away, and Brom passed the weapon to Eragon.

The handle fit Eragon's hand as if it had been made for him. He slowly drew the sword; it slid soundlessly from the sheath. The flat blade was iridescent red and shimmered in the firelight. The keen edges curved gracefully to a sharp point. A duplicate of the black symbol was inscribed on the metal. The balance of the sword was perfect; it felt like an extension of his arm, unlike the rude farm tools he was used to. An air of power lay over it, as if an unstoppable force resided in its core. It had been created for the violent convulsions of battle, to end men's lives, yet it held a terrible beauty.

"This was once a Rider's blade," said Brom gravely. "When a Rider finished his training, the elves would present him with a sword. Their methods of forging have always remained secret.

However, their swords are eternally sharp and will never stain. The custom was to have the blade's color match that of the Rider's dragon, but I think we can make an exception in this case. This sword is named Zar'roc. I don't know what it means, probably something personal to the Rider who owned it." He watched Eragon swing the sword.

"Where did you get it?" asked Eragon. He reluctantly slipped the blade back into the sheath and attempted to hand the sword back, but Brom made no move to take it.

"It doesn't matter," said Brom. "I will only say that it took me a series of nasty and dangerous adventures to attain it. Consider it yours. You have more of a claim to it than I do, and before all is done, I think you will need it."

The offer caught Eragon off guard. "It is a princely gift, thank you." Unsure of what else to say, he slid his hand down the sheath. "What is this symbol?" he asked.

"That was the Rider's personal crest." Eragon tried to interrupt, but Brom glared at him until he was quiet. "Now, if you must know, anyone can learn how to speak to a dragon if they have the proper training. And," he raised a finger for emphasis, "it doesn't mean anything if they can. I know more about the dragons and their abilities than almost anyone else alive. On your own it might take years to learn what I can teach you. I'm offering my knowledge as a shortcut. As for how I know so much, I will keep *that* to myself."

Saphira pulled herself up as he finished speaking and prowled over to Eragon. He pulled out the blade and showed her the sword. *It has power,* she said, touching the point with her nose. The metal's iridescent color rippled like water as it met her scales. She lifted her head with a satisfied snort, and the sword resumed its normal appearance. Eragon sheathed it, troubled.

Brom raised an eyebrow. "That's the sort of thing I'm talking about. Dragons will constantly amaze you. Things . . . happen around them, mysterious things that are impossible anywhere else. Even though the Riders worked with dragons for centuries, they never completely understood their abilities. Some say that even the dragons don't know the full extent of their own powers. They are linked with this land in a way that lets them overcome great obstacles. What Saphira just did illustrates my earlier point: there is much you don't know."

There was a long pause. "That may be," said Eragon, "but I can learn. And the strangers are the most important thing I need to know about right now. Do you have any idea who they are?"

Brom took a deep breath. "They are called the Ra'zac. No one knows if that's the name of their race or what they have chosen to call themselves. Either way, if they have individual names, they keep them hidden. The Ra'zac were never seen before Galbatorix came to power. He must have found them during his travels and enlisted them in his service. Little or nothing is known about them. However, I can tell you this: they aren't human. When I glimpsed one's head, it appeared to have something resembling a beak and black eyes as large as my fist—though how they manage our speech is a mystery to me. Doubtless the rest of their bodies are just as twisted. That is why they cover themselves with cloaks at all times, regardless of the weather.

"As for their powers, they are stronger than any man and can jump incredible heights, but they cannot use magic. Be thankful for that, because if they could, you would already be in their grasp. I also know they have a strong aversion to sunlight, though it won't stop them if they're determined. Don't make the mistake of underestimating a Ra'zac, for they are cunning and full of guile."

"How many of them are there?" asked Eragon, wondering how Brom could possibly know so much.

"As far as I know, only the two you saw. There might be more, but I've never heard of them. Perhaps they're the last of a dying race. You see, they are the king's personal dragon hunters. Whenever rumors reach Galbatorix of a dragon in the land, he sends the Ra'zac to investigate. A trail of death often follows them." Brom blew a series of smoke rings and watched them float up between the brambles. Eragon ignored the rings until he noticed that they were changing color and darting around. Brom winked slyly.

Eragon was sure that no one had seen Saphira, so how could Galbatorix have heard about her? When he voiced his objections, Brom said, "You're right, it seems unlikely that anyone from Carvahall could have informed the king. Why don't you tell me where you got the egg and how you raised Saphira—that might clarify the issue."

Eragon hesitated, then recounted all the events since he had found the egg in the Spine. It felt wonderful to finally confide in someone. Brom asked a few questions, but most of the time he listened intently. The sun was about to set when Eragon finished his tale. Both of them were quiet as the clouds turned a soft pink. Eragon eventually broke the silence. "I just wish I knew where she came from. And Saphira doesn't remember."

Brom cocked his head. "I don't know. . . . You've made many things clear to me. I am sure that no one besides us has seen Saphira. The Ra'zac must have had a source of information outside of this valley, one who is probably dead by now. . . . You have had a hard time and done much. I'm impressed."

Eragon stared blankly into the distance, then asked, "What happened to your head? It looks like you were hit with a rock."

"No, but that's a good guess." He took a deep pull on the pipe. "I was sneaking around the Ra'zac's camp after dark, trying to learn what I could, when they surprised me in the shadows. It was a good trap, but they underestimated me, and I managed to drive them away. Not, however," he said wryly, "without this token of my stupidity. Stunned, I fell to the ground and didn't regain consciousness until the next day. By then they had already arrived at your farm. It was too late to stop them, but I set out after them anyway. That's when we met on the road."

Who is he to think that he could take on the Ra'zac alone? They ambushed him in the dark, and he was only stunned? Unsettled, Eragon asked hotly, "When you saw the mark, the gedwëy ignasia, on my palm, why didn't you tell me who the Ra'zac were? I would have warned Garrow instead of going to Saphira first, and the three of us could have fled."

Brom sighed. "I was unsure of what to do at the time. I thought I could keep the Ra'zac away from you and, once they had left, confront you about Saphira. But they outsmarted me. It's a mistake that I deeply regret, and one that has cost you dearly."

"Who are you?" demanded Eragon, suddenly bitter. "How come a mere village storyteller happens to have a Rider's sword? How do you know about the Ra'zac?"

Brom tapped his pipe. "I thought I made it clear I wasn't going to talk about that."

"My uncle is dead because of this. *Dead!*" exclaimed Eragon, slashing a hand through the air. "I've trusted you this far because Saphira respects you, but no more! You're not the person I've known in Carvahall for all of these years. Explain yourself!"

For a long time Brom stared at the smoke swirling between them, deep lines creasing his forehead. When he stirred, it was only to take another puff. Finally he said, "You've probably never thought about it, but most of my life has been spent outside of Palancar Valley. It was only in Carvahall that I took up the mantle of storyteller. I have played many roles to different people—I've a complicated past. It was partly through a desire to escape it that I came here. So no, I'm not the man you think I am."

"Ha!" snorted Eragon. "Then who are you?"

Brom smiled gently. "I am one who is here to help you. Do not scorn those words—they are the truest I've ever spoken. But I'm not going to answer your questions. At this point you don't need to hear my history, nor have you yet earned that right. Yes, I have knowledge Brom the storyteller wouldn't, but I'm more than he. You'll have to learn to live with that fact and the fact that I don't hand out descriptions of my life to anyone who asks!"

Eragon glared at him sullenly. "I'm going to sleep," he said, leaving the fire.

106   Brom did not seem surprised, but there was sorrow in his eyes. He spread his bedroll next to the fire as Eragon lay beside Saphira. An icy silence fell over the camp.

SADDLEMAKING

When Eragon's eyes opened, the memory of Garrow's death crashed down on him. He pulled the blankets over his head and cried quietly under their warm darkness. It felt good just to lie there . . . to hide from the world outside. Eventually the tears stopped. He cursed Brom. Then he reluctantly wiped his cheeks and got up.

Brom was making breakfast. "Good morning," he said. Eragon grunted in reply. He jammed his cold fingers in his armpits and crouched by the fire until the food was ready. They ate quickly, trying to consume the food before it lost its warmth. When he finished, Eragon washed his bowl with snow, then spread the stolen leather on the ground.

"What are you going to do with that?" asked Brom. "We can't carry it with us."

"I'm going to make a saddle for Saphira."

"Mmm," said Brom, moving forward. "Well, dragons used to have two kinds of saddles. The first was hard and molded like a horse's saddle. But those take time and tools to make, neither of which we have. The other was thin and lightly padded, nothing more than an extra layer between the Rider and dragon. Those saddles were used whenever speed and flexibility were important, though they weren't nearly as comfortable as the molded ones."

"Do you know what they looked like?" asked Eragon.

"Better, I can make one."

"Then please do," said Eragon, standing aside.

"Very well, but pay attention. Someday you may have to do this for yourself." With Saphira's permission, Brom measured her neck and chest. Then he cut five bands out of the leather and outlined a dozen or so shapes on the hides. Once the pieces had been sliced out, he cut what remained of the hides into long cords.

Brom used the cords to sew everything together, but for each stitch, two holes had to be bored through the leather. Eragon helped with that. Intricate knots were rigged in place of buckles, and every strap was made extra long so the saddle would still fit Saphira in the coming months.

The main part of the saddle was assembled from three identical sections sewn together with padding between them. Attached to the front was a thick loop that would fit snugly around one of Saphira's neck spikes, while wide bands sewn on either side would wrap around her belly and tie underneath. Taking the place of stirrups were a series of loops running down both bands. Tightened, they would hold Eragon's legs in place. A long strap was constructed to pass between Saphira's front legs, split in two, and then come up behind her front legs to rejoin with the saddle.

While Brom worked, Eragon repaired his pack and organized their supplies. The day was spent by the time their tasks were completed. Weary from his labor, Brom put the saddle on Saphira and checked to see that the straps fit. He made a few small adjustments, then took it off, satisfied.

"You did a good job," Eragon acknowledged grudgingly.

Brom inclined his head. "One tries his best. It should serve you well; the leather's sturdy enough."

Aren't you going to try it out? asked Saphira.

Maybe tomorrow, said Eragon, storing the saddle with his blankets. *It's too late now.* In truth he was not eager to fly again—not after the disastrous outcome of his last attempt.

Dinner was made quickly. It tasted good even though it was

simple. While they ate, Brom looked over the fire at Eragon and asked, "Will we leave tomorrow?"

"There isn't any reason to stay."

"I suppose not. . . ." He shifted. "Eragon, I must apologize about how events have turned out. I never wished for this to happen. Your family did not deserve such a tragedy. If there were anything I could do to reverse it, I would. This is a terrible situation for all of us." Eragon sat in silence, avoiding Brom's gaze, then Brom said, "We're going to need horses."

"Maybe you do, but I have Saphira."

Brom shook his head. "There isn't a horse alive that can outrun a flying dragon, and Saphira is too young to carry us both. Besides, it'll be safer if we stay together, and riding is faster than walking."

"But that'll make it harder to catch the Ra'zac," protested Eragon. "On Saphira, I could probably find them within a day or two. On horses, it'll take much longer—if it's even possible to overtake their lead on the ground!"

Brom said slowly, "That's a chance you'll have to take if I'm to accompany you."

Eragon thought it over. "All right," he grumbled, "we'll get horses. But you have to buy them. I don't have any money, and I don't want to steal again. It's wrong."

"That depends on your point of view," corrected Brom with a slight smile. "Before you set out on this venture, remember that your enemies, the Ra'zac, are the king's servants. They will be protected wherever they go. Laws do not stop them. In cities they'll have access to abundant resources and willing servants. Also keep in mind that nothing is more important to Galbatorix than recruiting or killing you—though word of your existence probably hasn't reached him yet. The longer you evade the Ra'zac, the more desperate he'll become. He'll know that every day you'll be growing stronger and that each passing moment will give you another chance to join his enemies. You must be very careful, as you may easily turn from the hunter into the hunted."

Eragon was subdued by the strong words. Pensive, he rolled a twig between his fingers. "Enough talk," said Brom. "It's late and my bones ache. We can say more tomorrow." Eragon nodded and banked the fire.

THERINSFORD

Dawn was gray and overcast with a cutting wind. The forest was quiet. After a light breakfast, Brom and Eragon doused the fire and shouldered their packs, preparing to leave. Eragon hung his bow and quiver on the side of his pack where he could easily reach them. Saphira wore the saddle; she would have to carry it until they got horses. Eragon carefully tied Zar'roc onto her back, too, as he did not want the extra weight. Besides, in his hands the sword would be no better than a club.

Eragon had felt safe inside the bramble, but outside, wariness crept into his movements. Saphira took off and circled overhead. The trees thinned as they returned to the farm.

I will see this place again, Eragon insisted to himself, looking at the ruined buildings. *This cannot, will not, be a permanent exile. Someday when it's safe, I'll return.* . . . Throwing back his shoulders, he faced south and the strange, barbaric lands that lay there.

As they walked, Saphira veered west toward the mountains and out of sight. Eragon felt uncomfortable as he watched her go. Even now, with no one around, they could not spend their days together. She had to stay hidden in case they met a fellow traveler.

The Ra'zac's footprints were faint on the eroding snow, but Eragon was unconcerned. It was unlikely that they had forsaken the road, which was the easiest way out of the valley, for the wilderness. Once outside the valley, however, the road divided in several places. It would be difficult to ascertain which branch the Ra'zac had taken.

They traveled in silence, concentrating on speed. Eragon's legs continued to bleed where the scabs had cracked. To take his mind off the discomfort, he asked, "So what exactly can dragons do? You said that you knew something of their abilities."

Brom laughed, his sapphire ring flashing in the air as he gestured. "Unfortunately, it's a pitiful amount compared to what I would like to know. Your question is one people have been trying to answer for centuries, so understand that what I tell you is by its very nature incomplete. Dragons have always been mysterious, though maybe not on purpose.

"Before I can truly answer your question, you need a basic education on the subject of dragons. It's hopelessly confusing to start in the middle of such a complex topic without understanding the foundation on which it stands. I'll begin with the life cycle of dragons, and if that doesn't wear you out, we can continue to another topic."

Brom explained how dragons mate and what it took for their eggs to hatch. "You see," he said, "when a dragon lays an egg, the infant inside is ready to hatch. But it waits, sometimes for years, for the right circumstances. When dragons lived in the wild, those circumstances were usually dictated by the availability of food. However, once they formed an alliance with the elves, a certain number of their eggs, usually no more than one or two, were given to the Riders each year. These eggs, or rather the infants inside, wouldn't hatch until the person destined to be its Rider came into their presence—though how they sensed that isn't known. People used to line up to touch the eggs, hoping that one of them might be picked."

"Do you mean that Saphira might not have hatched for me?" asked Eragon.

"Quite possibly, if she hadn't liked you."

He felt honored that of all the people in Alagaësia, she had chosen him. He wondered how long she had been waiting, then shuddered at the thought of being cramped inside an egg, surrounded by darkness.

Brom continued his lecture. He explained what and when dragons ate. A fully grown sedentary dragon could go for months without food, but in mating season they had to eat every week. Some plants could heal their sicknesses, while others would make them ill. There were various ways to care for their claws and clean their scales.

He explained the techniques to use when attacking from a dragon and what to do if you were fighting one, whether on foot, horseback, or with another dragon. Their bellies were armored; their armpits were not. Eragon constantly interrupted to ask questions, and Brom seemed pleased by the inquiries. Hours passed unheeded as they talked.

When evening came, they were near Therinsford. As the sky darkened and they searched for a place to camp, Eragon asked, "Who was the Rider that owned Zar'roc?"

"A mighty warrior," said Brom, "who was much feared in his time and held great power."

"What was his name?"

"I'll not say." Eragon protested, but Brom was firm. "I don't want to keep you ignorant, far from it, but certain knowledge would only prove dangerous and distracting for you right now. There isn't any reason for me to trouble you with such things until you have the time and the power to deal with them. I only wish to protect you from those who would use you for evil."

Eragon glared at him. "You know what? I think you just enjoy speaking in riddles. I've half a mind to leave you so I don't have to be bothered with them. If you're going to say something, then say it instead of dancing around with vague phrases!"

"Peace. All will be told in time," Brom said gently. Eragon grunted, unconvinced.

They found a comfortable place to spend the night and set up camp. Saphira joined them as dinner was being set on the fire. *Did you have time to hunt for food?* asked Eragon.

She snorted with amusement. *If the two of you were any slower, I would have time to fly across the sea and back without falling behind.*

You don't have to be insulting. Besides, we'll go faster once we have horses.

She let out a puff of smoke. *Maybe, but will it be enough to catch the Ra'zac? They have a lead of several days and many leagues. And I'm afraid they may suspect we're following them. Why else would they have destroyed the farm in such a spectacular manner, unless they wished to provoke you into chasing them?*

I don't know, said Eragon, disturbed. Saphira curled up beside him, and he leaned against her belly, welcoming the warmth. Brom sat on the other side of the fire, whittling two long sticks. He suddenly threw one at Eragon, who grabbed it out of reflex as it whirled over the crackling flames.

"Defend yourself!" barked Brom, standing.

Eragon looked at the stick in his hand and saw that it was shaped in the crude likeness of a sword. Brom wanted to fight him? What chance did the old man stand? *If he wants to play this game, so be it, but if he thinks to beat me, he's in for a surprise.*

He rose as Brom circled the fire. They faced each other for a moment, then Brom charged, swinging his stick. Eragon tried to block the attack but was too slow. He yelped as Brom struck him on the ribs, and stumbled backward.

Without thinking, he lunged forward, but Brom easily parried the blow. Eragon whipped the stick toward Brom's head, twisted it at the last moment, and then tried to hit his side. The solid smack of wood striking wood resounded through the camp. "Improvisation— good!" exclaimed Brom, eyes gleaming. His arm moved in a blur, and there was an explosion of pain on the side of Eragon's head. He collapsed like an empty sack, dazed.

A splash of cold water roused him to alertness, and he sat up, sputtering. His head was ringing, and there was dried blood on his face. Brom stood over him with a pan of melted snow water. "You didn't have to do that," said Eragon angrily, pushing himself up. He felt dizzy and unsteady.

Brom arched an eyebrow. "Oh? A real enemy wouldn't soften his blows, and neither will I. Should I pander to your . . . incompetence so you'll feel better? I don't think so." He picked up the stick that Eragon had dropped and held it out. "Now, defend yourself."

Eragon stared blankly at the piece of wood, then shook his head. "Forget it; I've had enough." He turned away and stumbled as he was whacked loudly across the back. He spun around, growling.

"Never turn your back to the enemy!" snapped Brom, then tossed the stick at him and attacked. Eragon retreated around the fire, beneath the onslaught. "Pull your arms in. Keep your knees bent," shouted Brom. He continued to give instructions, then paused to show Eragon exactly how to execute a certain move. "Do it again, but this time *slowly*!" They slid through the forms with exaggerated motions before returning to their furious battle. Eragon learned quickly, but no matter what he tried, he could not hold Brom off for more than a few blows.

When they finished, Eragon flopped on his blankets and groaned. He hurt everywhere—Brom had not been gentle with his stick. Saphira let out a long, coughing growl and curled her lip until a formidable row of teeth showed.

What's wrong with you? he demanded irritably.

Nothing, she replied. *It's funny to see a hatchling like you beaten by the old one.* She made the sound again, and Eragon turned red as he realized that she was laughing. Trying to preserve some dignity, he rolled onto his side and fell asleep.

He felt even worse the next day. Bruises covered his arms, and he was almost too sore to move. Brom looked up from the mush he was serving and grinned. "How do you feel?" Eragon grunted and bolted down the breakfast.

Once on the road, they traveled swiftly so as to reach Therinsford before noon. After a league, the road widened and they saw smoke in the distance. "You'd better tell Saphira to fly ahead and wait for us on the other side of Therinsford," said Brom. "She has to be careful here, otherwise people are bound to notice her."

"Why don't you tell her yourself?" challenged Eragon.

"It's considered bad manners to interfere with another's dragon."

"You didn't have a problem with it in Carvahall."

Brom's lips twitched with a smile. "I did what I had to."

Eragon eyed him darkly, then relayed the instructions. Saphira warned, *Be careful; the Empire's servants could be hiding anywhere.*

As the ruts in the road deepened, Eragon noticed more footprints. Farms signaled their approach to Therinsford. The village was larger than Carvahall, but it had been constructed haphazardly, the houses aligned in no particular order.

"What a mess," said Eragon. He could not see Dempton's mill. *Baldor and Albriech have surely fetched Roran by now.* Either way, Eragon had no wish to face his cousin.

"It's ugly, if nothing else," agreed Brom.

The Anora River flowed between them and the town, spanned by a stout bridge. As they approached it, a greasy man stepped from behind a bush and barred their way. His shirt was too short, and his dirty stomach spilled over a rope belt. Behind his cracked lips, his teeth looked like crumbling tombstones. "You c'n stop right there. This's my bridge. Gotta pay t' get over."

"How much?" asked Brom in a resigned voice. He pulled out a pouch, and the bridgekeeper brightened.

"Five crowns," he said, pulling his lips into a broad smile. Eragon's temper flared at the exorbitant price, and he started to complain hotly, but Brom silenced him with a quick look. The coins were wordlessly handed over. The man put them into a sack hanging from his belt. "Thank'ee much," he said in a mocking tone, and stood out of the way.

As Brom stepped forward, he stumbled and caught the bridgekeeper's arm to support himself. "Watch y're step," snarled the grimy man, sidling away.

"Sorry," apologized Brom, and continued over the bridge with Eragon.

"Why didn't you haggle? He skinned you alive!" exclaimed Eragon when they were out of earshot. "He probably doesn't even own the bridge. We could have pushed right past him."

"Probably," agreed Brom.

"Then why pay him?"

"Because you can't argue with all of the fools in the world. It's easier to let them have their way, then trick them when they're not paying attention." Brom opened his hand, and a pile of coins glinted in the light.

"You cut his purse!" said Eragon incredulously.

Brom pocketed the money with a wink. "And it held a surprising amount. He should know better than to keep all these coins in one place." There was a sudden howl of anguish from the other side of the river. "I'd say our friend has just discovered his loss. If you see any watchmen, tell me." He grabbed the shoulder of a young boy running between the houses and asked, "Do you know where we can buy horses?" The child stared at them with solemn eyes, then pointed to a large barn near the edge of Therinsford. "Thank you," said Brom, tossing him a small coin.

The barn's large double doors were open, revealing two long rows of stalls. The far wall was covered with saddles, harnesses, and other paraphernalia. A man with muscular arms stood at the end, brushing a white stallion. He raised a hand and beckoned for them to come over.

As they approached, Brom said, "That's a beautiful animal."

"Yes indeed. His name's Snowfire. Mine's Haberth." Haberth offered a rough palm and shook hands vigorously with Eragon and Brom. There was a polite pause as he waited for their names in return. When they were not forthcoming, he asked, "Can I help you?"

Brom nodded. "We need two horses and a full set of tack for both. The horses have to be fast and tough; we'll be doing a lot of traveling."

Haberth was thoughtful for a moment. "I don't have many

animals like that, and the ones I do aren't cheap." The stallion moved restlessly; he calmed it with a few strokes of his fingers.

"Price is no object. I'll take the best you have," said Brom. Haberth nodded and silently tied the stallion to a stall. He went to the wall and started pulling down saddles and other items. Soon he had two identical piles. Next he walked up the line of stalls and brought out two horses. One was a light bay, the other a roan. The bay tugged against his rope.

"He's a little spirited, but with a firm hand you won't have any problems," said Haberth, handing the bay's rope to Brom.

Brom let the horse smell his hand; it allowed him to rub its neck. "We'll take him," he said, then eyed the roan. "The other one, however, I'm not so sure of."

"There are some good legs on him."

"Mmm . . . What will you take for Snowfire?"

Haberth looked fondly at the stallion. "I'd rather not sell him. He's the finest I've ever bred—I'm hoping to sire a whole line from him."

"If you were willing to part with him, how much would all of this cost me?" asked Brom.

Eragon tried to put his hand on the bay like Brom had, but it shied away. He automatically reached out with his mind to reassure the horse, stiffening with surprise as he touched the animal's consciousness. The contact was not clear or sharp like it was with Saphira, but he could communicate with the bay to a limited degree. Tentatively, he made it understand that he was a friend. The horse calmed and looked at him with liquid brown eyes.

Haberth used his fingers to add up the price of the purchase. "Two hundred crowns and no less," he said with a smile, clearly confident that no one would pay that much. Brom silently opened his pouch and counted out the money.

"Will this do?" he asked.

There was a long silence as Haberth glanced between Snowfire and the coins. A sigh, then, "He is yours, though I go against my heart."

"I will treat him as if he had been sired by Gildintor, the greatest steed of legend," said Brom.

"Your words gladden me," answered Haberth, bowing his head slightly. He helped them saddle the horses. When they were ready to leave, he said, "Farewell, then. For the sake of Snowfire, I hope that misfortune does not befall you."

"Do not fear; I will guard him well," promised Brom as they departed. "Here," he said, handing Snowfire's reins to Eragon, "go to the far side of Therinsford and wait there."

"Why?" asked Eragon, but Brom had already slipped away. Annoyed, he exited Therinsford with the two horses and stationed himself beside the road. To the south he saw the hazy outline of Utgard, sitting like a giant monolith at the end of the valley. Its peak pierced the clouds and rose out of sight, towering over the lesser mountains that surrounded it. Its dark, ominous look made Eragon's scalp tingle.

Brom returned shortly and gestured for Eragon to follow. They walked until Therinsford was hidden by trees. Then Brom said, "The Ra'zac definitely passed this way. Apparently they stopped here to pick up horses, as we did. I was able to find a man who saw them. He described them with many shudders and said that they galloped out of Therinsford like demons fleeing a holy man."

"They left quite an impression."

"Quite."

Eragon patted the horses. "When we were in the barn, I touched the bay's mind by accident. I didn't know it was possible to do that."

Brom frowned. "It's unusual for one as young as you to have the ability. Most Riders had to train for years before they were strong enough to contact anything other than their dragon." His face was thoughtful as he inspected Snowfire. Then he said, "Take everything from your pack, put it into the saddlebags, and tie the pack on top." Eragon did so while Brom mounted Snowfire.

Eragon gazed doubtfully at the bay. It was so much smaller than Saphira that for an absurd moment he wondered if it could bear his weight. With a sigh, he awkwardly got into the saddle. He had only ridden horses bareback and never for any distance. "Is this going to do the same thing to my legs as riding Saphira?" he asked.

"How do they feel now?"

"Not too bad, but I think any hard riding will open them up again."

"We'll take it easy," promised Brom. He gave Eragon a few pointers, then they started off at a gentle pace. Before long the countryside began to change as cultivated fields yielded to wilder land. Brambles and tangled weeds lined the road, along with huge rosebushes that clung to their clothes. Tall rocks slanted out of the ground—gray witnesses to their presence. There was an unfriendly feel in the air, an animosity that resisted intruders.

Above them, growing larger with every step, loomed Utgard, its craggy precipices deeply furrowed with snowy canyons. The black rock of the mountain absorbed light like a sponge and dimmed the surrounding area. Between Utgard and the line of mountains that formed the east side of Palancar Valley was a deep cleft. It was the only practical way out of the valley. The road led toward it.

The horses' hooves clacked sharply over gravel, and the road dwindled to a skinny trail as it skirted the base of Utgard. Eragon glanced up at the peak looming over them and was startled to see a steepled tower perched upon it. The turret was crumbling and in disrepair, but it was still a stern sentinel over the valley. "What is that?" he asked, pointing.

Brom did not look up, but said sadly and with bitterness, "An outpost of the Riders—one that has lasted since their founding. That was where Vrael took refuge, and where, through treachery, he was found and defeated by Galbatorix. When Vrael fell, this area was tainted. Edoc'sil, 'Unconquerable,' was the name of this bastion, for the mountain is so steep none may reach the top unless they can fly. After Vrael's death the commoners called it Utgard, but it has another name, Ristvak'baen—the 'Place of Sorrow.' It was known as such to the last Riders before they were killed by the king."

Eragon stared with awe. Here was a tangible remnant of the Riders' glory, tarnished though it was by the relentless pull of time. It struck him then just how old the Riders were. A legacy of tradition and heroism that stretched back to antiquity had fallen upon him.

They traveled for long hours around Utgard. It formed a solid wall to their right as they entered the breach that divided the mountain range. Eragon stood in his stirrups; he was impatient to see what lay outside of Palancar, but it was still too far away. For a while they were in a sloped pass, winding over hill and gully, following the Anora River. Then, with the sun low behind their backs, they mounted a rise and saw over the trees.

Eragon gasped. On either side were mountains, but below them stretched a huge plain that extended to the distant horizon and fused into the sky. The plain was a uniform tan, like the color of dead grass. Long, wispy clouds swept by overhead, shaped by fierce winds.

He understood now why Brom had insisted on horses. It would have taken them weeks or months to cover that vast distance on foot. Far above he saw Saphira circling, high enough to be mistaken for a bird.

"We'll wait until tomorrow to make the descent," said Brom. "It's going to take most of the day, so we should camp now."

"How far across is the plain?" Eragon asked, still amazed.

"Two or three days to over a fortnight, depending on which direction we go. Aside from the nomad tribes that roam this section of the plains, it's almost as uninhabited as the Hadarac Desert to the east. So we aren't going to find many villages. However, to the south the plains are less arid and more heavily populated."

They left the trail and dismounted by the Anora River. As they unsaddled the horses, Brom gestured at the bay. "You should name him."

Eragon considered it as he picketed the bay. "Well, I don't have anything as noble as Snowfire, but maybe this will do." He placed his hand on the bay and said, "I name you Cadoc. It was my grandfather's name, so bear it well." Brom nodded in approval, but Eragon felt slightly foolish.

When Saphira landed, he asked, *How do the plains look?*

Dull. There's nothing but rabbits and scrub in every direction.

After dinner, Brom stood and barked, "Catch!" Eragon barely had time to raise his arm and grab the piece of wood before it hit him on the head. He groaned as he saw another makeshift sword.

"Not again," he complained. Brom just smiled and beckoned with one hand. Eragon reluctantly got to his feet. They whirled around in a flurry of smacking wood, and he backed away with a stinging arm.

The training session was shorter than the first, but it was still long enough for Eragon to amass a new collection of bruises. When they finished sparring, he threw down the stick in disgust and stalked away from the fire to nurse his injuries.

THUNDER ROAR AND
LIGHTNING CRACKLE

The next morning Eragon avoided bringing to mind any of the recent events; they were too painful for him to consider. Instead, he focused his energies on figuring out how to find and kill the Ra'zac. *I'll do it with my bow,* he decided, imagining how the cloaked figures would look with arrows sticking out of them.

He had difficulty even standing up. His muscles cramped with the slightest movement, and one of his fingers was hot and swollen. When they were ready to leave, he mounted Cadoc and said acidly, "If this keeps up, you're going to batter me to pieces."

"I wouldn't push you so hard if I didn't think you were strong enough."

"For once, I wouldn't mind being thought less of," muttered Eragon.

Cadoc pranced nervously as Saphira approached. Saphira eyed the horse with something close to disgust and said, *There's nowhere to hide on the plains, so I'm not going to bother trying to stay out of sight. I'll just fly above you from now on.*

She took off, and they began the steep descent. In many places the trail all but disappeared, leaving them to find their own way down. At times they had to dismount and lead the horses on foot, holding on to trees to keep from falling down the slope. The ground was scattered with loose rocks, which made the footing treacherous. The ordeal left them hot and irritable, despite the cold.

They stopped to rest when they reached the bottom near midday.

The Anora River veered to their left and flowed northward. A biting wind scoured the land, whipping them unmercifully. The soil was parched, and dirt flew into their eyes.

It unnerved Eragon how flat everything was; the plains were unbroken by hummocks or mounds. He had lived his entire life surrounded by mountains and hills. Without them he felt exposed and vulnerable, like a mouse under an eagle's keen eye.

The trail split in three once it reached the plains. The first branch turned north, toward Ceunon, one of the greatest northern cities; the second one led straight across the plains; and the last went south. They examined all three for traces of the Ra'zac and eventually found their tracks, heading directly into the grasslands.

"It seems they've gone to Yazuac," said Brom with a perplexed air.

"Where's that?"

"Due east and four days away, if all goes well. It's a small village situated by the Ninor River." He gestured at the Anora, which streamed away from them to the north. "Our only supply of water is here. We'll have to replenish our waterskins before attempting to cross the plains. There isn't another pool or stream between here and Yazuac."

The excitement of the hunt began to rise within Eragon. In a few days, maybe less than a week, he would use his arrows to avenge Garrow's death. *And then* . . . He refused to think about what might happen afterward.

They filled the waterskins, watered the horses, and drank as much as they could from the river. Saphira joined them and took several gulps of water. Fortified, they turned eastward and started across the plains.

Eragon decided that it would be the wind that drove him crazy first. Everything that made him miserable—his chapped lips, parched tongue, and burning eyes—stemmed from it. The ceaseless gusting followed them throughout the day. Evening only strengthened the wind, instead of subduing it.

Since there was no shelter, they were forced to camp in the open. Eragon found some scrub brush, a short tough plant that thrived on harsh conditions, and pulled it up. He made a careful pile and tried to light it, but the woody stems only smoked and gave off a pungent smell. Frustrated, he tossed the tinderbox to Brom. "I can't make it burn, especially with this blasted wind. See if you can get it going: otherwise dinner will be cold."

Brom knelt by the brush and looked at it critically. He rearranged a couple of branches, then struck the tinderbox, sending a cascade of sparks onto the plants. There was smoke, but nothing else. Brom scowled and tried again, but his luck was no better than Eragon's. "Brisingr!" he swore angrily, striking the flint again. Flames suddenly appeared, and he stepped back with a pleased expression. "There we go. It must have been smoldering inside."

They sparred with mock swords while the food cooked. Fatigue made it hard on both of them, so they kept the session short. After they had eaten, they lay next to Saphira and slept, grateful for her shelter.

The same cold wind greeted them in the morning, sweeping over the dreadful flatness. Eragon's lips had cracked during the night; every time he smiled or talked, beads of blood covered them. Licking them only made it worse. It was the same for Brom. They let the horses drink sparingly from their supply of water before mounting them. The day was a monotonous trek of endless plodding.

On the third day, Eragon woke well rested. That, coupled with the fact that the wind had stopped, put him in a cheery humor. His high spirits were dampened, however, when he saw the sky ahead of them was dark with thunderheads.

Brom looked at the clouds and grimaced. "Normally I wouldn't go into a storm like that, but we're in for a battering no matter what we do, so we might as well get some distance covered."

It was still calm when they reached the storm front. As they entered its shadow, Eragon looked up. The thundercloud had an exotic structure, forming a natural cathedral with a massive arched roof. With some imagination he could see pillars, windows, soaring tiers, and snarling gargoyles. It was a wild beauty.

As Eragon lowered his gaze, a giant ripple raced toward them through the grass, flattening it. It took him a second to realize that the wave was a tremendous blast of wind. Brom saw it too, and they hunched their shoulders, preparing for the storm.

The gale was almost upon them when Eragon had a horrible thought and twisted in his saddle, yelling, both with his voice and mind, "Saphira! Land!" Brom's face grew pale. Overhead, they saw her dive toward the ground. *She's not going to make it!*

Saphira angled back the way they had come, to gain time. As they watched, the tempest's wrath struck them like a hammer blow. Eragon gasped for breath and clenched the saddle as a frenzied howling filled his ears. Cadoc swayed and dug his hooves into the ground, mane snapping in the air. The wind tore at their clothes with invisible fingers while the air darkened with billowing clouds of dust.

Eragon squinted, searching for Saphira. He saw her land heavily and then crouch, clenching the ground with her talons. The wind reached her just as she started to fold her wings. With an angry yank, it unfurled them and dragged her into the air. For a moment she hung there, suspended by the storm's force. Then it slammed her down on her back.

With a savage wrench, Eragon yanked Cadoc around and galloped back up the trail, goading the horse with both heels and mind. *Saphira!* he shouted. *Try to stay on the ground. I'm coming!* He felt a grim acknowledgment from her. As they neared Saphira, Cadoc balked, so Eragon leapt down and ran toward her.

His bow banged against his head. A strong gust pushed him off balance and he flew forward, landing on his chest. He skidded, then got back up with a snarl, ignoring the deep scrapes in his skin.

Saphira was only three yards away, but he could get no closer because of her flailing wings. She struggled to fold them against the overpowering gale. He rushed at her right wing, intending to hold it down, but the wind caught her and she somersaulted over him. The spines on her back missed his head by inches. Saphira clawed at the ground, trying to stay down.

Her wings began to lift again, but before they could flip her, Eragon threw himself at the left one. The wing crumpled in at the joints and Saphira tucked it firmly against her body. Eragon vaulted over her back and tumbled onto the other wing. Without warning it was blown upward, sending him sliding to ground. He broke his fall with a roll, then jumped up and grabbed the wing again. Saphira started to fold it, and he pushed with all of his strength. The wind battled with them for a second, but with one last surge they overcame it.

Eragon leaned against Saphira, panting. *Are you all right?* He could feel her trembling.

She took a moment to answer. *I . . . I think so.* She sounded shaken. *Nothing's broken—I couldn't do anything; the wind wouldn't let me go. I was helpless.* With a shudder, she fell silent.

He looked at her, concerned. *Don't worry, you're safe now.* He spotted Cadoc a ways off, standing with his back to the wind. With his mind, Eragon instructed the horse to return to Brom. He then got onto Saphira. She crept up the road, fighting the gale while he clung to her back and kept his head down.

When they reached Brom, he shouted over the storm, "Is she hurt?"

Eragon shook his head and dismounted. Cadoc trotted over to him, nickering. As he stroked the horse's long cheek, Brom pointed at a dark curtain of rain sweeping toward them in rippling gray sheets. "What else?" cried Eragon, pulling his clothes tighter. He winced as the torrent reached them. The stinging rain was cold as ice; before long they were drenched and shivering.

Lightning lanced through the sky, flickering in and out of existence. Mile-high blue bolts streaked across the horizon, followed by peals of thunder that shook the ground below. It was beautiful, but dangerously so. Here and there, grass fires were ignited by strikes, only to be extinguished by the rain.

The wild elements were slow to abate, but as the day passed, they wandered elsewhere. Once again the sky was revealed, and the setting sun glowed with brilliance. As beams of light tinted the clouds with blazing colors, everything gained a sharp contrast: brightly lit on one side, deeply shadowed on the other. Objects had a unique sense of mass; grass stalks seemed sturdy as marble pillars. Ordinary things took on an unearthly beauty; Eragon felt as if he were sitting inside a painting.

The rejuvenated earth smelled fresh, clearing their minds and raising their spirits. Saphira stretched, craning her neck, and roared happily. The horses skittered away from her, but Eragon and Brom smiled at her exuberance.

Before the light faded, they stopped for the night in a shallow depression. Too exhausted to spar, they went straight to sleep.

REVELATION AT YAZUAC

Although they had managed to partially refill the waterskins during the storm, they drank the last of their water that morning. "I hope we're going in the right direction," said Eragon, crunching up the empty water bag, "because we'll be in trouble if we don't reach Yazuac today."

Brom did not seem disturbed. "I've traveled this way before. Yazuac will be in sight before dusk."

Eragon laughed doubtfully. "Perhaps you see something I don't. How can you know that when everything looks exactly the same for leagues around?"

"Because I am guided not by the land, but by the stars and sun. They will not lead us astray. Come! Let us be off. It is foolish to conjure up woe where none exists. Yazuac will be there."

His words proved true. Saphira spotted the village first, but it was not until later in the day that the rest of them saw it as a dark bump on the horizon. Yazuac was still very far away; it was only visible because of the plain's uniform flatness. As they rode closer, a dark winding line appeared on either side of the town and disappeared in the distance.

"The Ninor River," said Brom, pointing at it.

Eragon pulled Cadoc to a stop. "Saphira will be seen if she stays with us much longer. Should she hide while we go into Yazuac?"

Brom scratched his chin and looked at the town. "See that bend in the river? Have her wait there. It's far enough from Yazuac so no one should find her, but close enough that she won't be left behind. We'll go through the town, get what we need, and then meet her."

I don't like it, said Saphira when Eragon had explained the plan. *This is irritating, having to hide all the time like a criminal.*

You know what would happen if we were revealed. She grumbled but gave in and flew away low to the ground.

They kept a swift pace in anticipation of the food and drink they would soon enjoy. As they approached the small houses, they could see smoke from a dozen chimneys, but there was no one in the streets. An abnormal silence enveloped the village. By unspoken consent they stopped before the first house. Eragon abruptly said, "There aren't any dogs barking."

"No."

"Doesn't mean anything, though."

". . . No."

Eragon paused. "Someone should have seen us by now."

"Yes."

"Then why hasn't anyone come out?"

Brom squinted at the sun. "Could be afraid."

"Could be," said Eragon. He was quiet for a moment. "And if it's a trap? The Ra'zac might be waiting for us."

"We need provisions and water."

"There's the Ninor."

"Still need provisions."

"True." Eragon looked around. "So we go in?"

Brom flicked his reins. "Yes, but not like fools. This is the main entrance to Yazuac. If there's an ambush, it'll be along here. No one will expect us to arrive from a different direction."

"Around to the side, then?" asked Eragon. Brom nodded and pulled out his sword, resting the bare blade across his saddle. Eragon strung his bow and nocked an arrow.

They trotted quietly around the town and entered it cautiously. The streets were empty, except for a small fox that darted away as they came near. The houses were dark and foreboding, with shattered windows. Many of the doors swung on broken hinges. The horses rolled their eyes nervously. Eragon's palm tingled, but he resisted the urge to scratch it. As they rode into the center of town, he gripped his bow tighter, blanching. "Gods above," he whispered.

A mountain of bodies rose above them, the corpses stiff and grimacing. Their clothes were soaked in blood, and the churned ground was stained with it. Slaughtered men lay over the women they had tried to protect, mothers still clasped their children, and lovers who had tried to shield each other rested in death's cold embrace. Black arrows stuck out of them all. Neither young nor old had been spared. But worst of all was the barbed spear that rose out of the peak of the pile, impaling the white body of a baby.

Tears blurred Eragon's vision and he tried to look away, but the dead faces held his attention. He stared at their open eyes and wondered how life could have left them so easily. *What does our existence mean when it can end like this?* A wave of hopelessness overwhelmed him.

A crow dipped out of the sky, like a black shadow, and perched on the spear. It cocked its head and greedily scrutinized the infant's corpse. "Oh no you don't," snarled Eragon as he pulled back the bowstring and released it with a twang. With a puff of feathers, the crow fell over backward, the arrow protruding from its chest. Eragon fit another arrow to the string, but nausea rose from his stomach and he threw up over Cadoc's side.

Brom patted him on the back. When Eragon was done, Brom asked gently, "Do you want to wait for me outside Yazuac?"

"No . . . I'll stay," said Eragon shakily, wiping his mouth. He avoided looking at the gruesome sight before them. "Who could have done . . ." He could not force out the words.

Brom bowed his head. "Those who love the pain and suffering of others. They wear many faces and go by many disguises, but there is only one name for them: evil. There is no understanding it. All we can do is pity and honor the victims."

He dismounted Snowfire and walked around, inspecting the trampled ground carefully. "The Ra'zac passed this way," he said slowly, "but this wasn't their doing. This is Urgal work; the spear is of their make. A company of them came through here, perhaps as many as a hundred. It's odd; I know of only a few instances when they have gathered in such . . ." He knelt and examined a footprint intently. With a curse he ran back to Snowfire and leapt onto him.

"Ride!" he hissed tightly, spurring Snowfire forward. "There are still Urgals here!" Eragon jammed his heels into Cadoc. The horse jumped forward and raced after Snowfire. They dashed past the houses and were almost to the edge of Yazuac when Eragon's palm tingled again. He saw a flicker of movement to his right, then a giant fist smashed him out of the saddle. He flew back over Cadoc and crashed into a wall, holding on to his bow only by instinct. Gasping and stunned, he staggered upright, hugging his side.

An Urgal stood over him, face set in a gross leer. The monster was tall, thick, and broader than a doorway, with gray skin and yellow piggish eyes. Muscles bulged on his arms and chest, which was covered by a too small breastplate. An iron cap rested over the pair of ram's horns curling from his temples, and a roundshield was bound to one arm. His powerful hand held a short, wicked sword.

Behind him, Eragon saw Brom rein in Snowfire and start back, only to be stopped by the appearance of a second Urgal, this one with an ax. "Run, you fool!" Brom cried to Eragon, cleaving at his enemy. The Urgal in front of Eragon roared and swung his sword mightily. Eragon jerked back with a startled yelp as the weapon whistled past his cheek. He spun around and fled toward the center of Yazuac, heart pounding wildly.

The Urgal pursued him, heavy boots thudding. Eragon sent a desperate cry for help to Saphira, then forced himself to go even faster. The Urgal rapidly gained ground despite Eragon's efforts; large fangs separated in a soundless bellow. With the Urgal almost upon him, Eragon strung an arrow, spun to a stop, took aim, and released. The Urgal snapped up his arm and caught the quivering bolt on his shield. The monster collided with Eragon before he could shoot again, and they fell to the ground in a confused tangle.

Eragon sprang to his feet and rushed back to Brom, who was trading fierce blows with his opponent from Snowfire's back. *Where are the rest of the Urgals?* wondered Eragon frantically. *Are these two the only ones in Yazuac?* There was a loud smack, and Snowfire reared, whinnying. Brom doubled over in his saddle, blood streaming down his arm. The Urgal beside him howled in triumph and raised his ax for the death blow.

A deafening scream tore out of Eragon as he charged the Urgal, headfirst. The Urgal paused in astonishment, then faced him contemptuously, swinging his ax. Eragon ducked under the two-handed blow and clawed the Urgal's side, leaving bloody furrows. The Urgal's face twisted with rage. He slashed again, but missed as Eragon dived to the side and scrambled down an alley.

Eragon concentrated on leading the Urgals away from Brom. He slipped into a narrow passageway between two houses, saw it was a dead end, and slid to a stop. He tried to back out, but the Urgals had already blocked the entrance. They advanced, cursing him in their gravelly voices. Eragon swung his head from side to side, searching for a way out, but there was none.

As he faced the Urgals, images flashed in his mind: dead villagers piled around the spear and an innocent baby who would never grow to adulthood. At the thought of their fate, a burning, fiery power gathered from every part of his body. It was more than a desire for justice. It was his entire being rebelling against the fact of death— that he would cease to exist. The power grew stronger and stronger until he felt ready to burst from the contained force.

He stood tall and straight, all fear gone. He raised his bow smoothly. The Urgals laughed and lifted their shields. Eragon sighted down the shaft, as he had done hundreds of times, and aligned the arrowhead with his target. The energy inside him burned at an unbearable level. He had to release it, or it would consume him. A word suddenly leapt unbidden to his lips. He shot, yelling, "Brisingr!"

The arrow hissed through the air, glowing with a crackling blue light. It struck the lead Urgal on the forehead, and the air resounded with an explosion. A blue shock wave blasted out of the monster's head, killing the other Urgal instantly. It reached Eragon before he had time to react, and it passed through him without harm, dissipating against the houses.

Eragon stood panting, then looked at his icy palm. The gedwëy ignasia was glowing like white-hot metal, yet even as he watched, it faded back to normal. He clenched his fist, then a wave of exhaustion washed over him. He felt strange and feeble, as if he had not eaten for days. His knees buckled, and he sagged against a wall.

ADMONISHMENTS

Once a modicum of strength returned to him, Eragon staggered out of the alley, skirting the dead monsters. He did not get far before Cadoc trotted to his side. "Good, you weren't hurt," mumbled Eragon. He noticed, without particularly caring, that his hands were shaking violently and his movements were jerky. He felt detached, as if everything he saw were happening to someone else.

Eragon found Snowfire, nostrils flared and ears flat against his head, prancing by the corner of a house, ready to bolt. Brom was still slumped motionless in the saddle. Eragon reached out with his mind and soothed the horse. Once Snowfire relaxed, Eragon went to Brom.

There was a long, blood-soaked cut on the old man's right arm. The wound bled profusely, but it was neither deep nor wide. Still, Eragon knew it had to be bound before Brom lost too much blood. He stroked Snowfire for a moment, then slid Brom out of the saddle. The weight proved too much for him, and Brom dropped heavily to the ground. Eragon was shocked by his own weakness.

A scream of rage filled his head. Saphira dived out of the sky and landed fiercely in front of him, keeping her wings half raised. She hissed angrily, eyes burning. Her tail lashed, and Eragon winced as it snapped overhead. *Are you hurt?* she asked, rage boiling in her voice.

"No," he assured her as he laid Brom on his back.

She growled and exclaimed, *Where are the ones who did this? I will tear them apart!*

He wearily pointed in the direction of the alley. "It'll do no good; they're already dead."

You killed them? Saphira sounded surprised.

He nodded. "Somehow." With a few terse words, he told her what had happened while he searched his saddlebags for the rags in which Zar'roc had been wrapped.

Saphira said gravely, *You have grown.*

Eragon grunted. He found a long rag and carefully rolled back Brom's sleeve. With a few deft strokes he cleaned the cut and bandaged it tightly. *I wish we were still in Palancar Valley,* he said to Saphira. *There, at least, I knew what plants were good for healing. Here, I don't have any idea what will help him.* He retrieved Brom's sword from the ground, wiped it, then returned it to the sheath on Brom's belt.

We should leave, said Saphira. *There may be more Urgals lurking about.*

Can you carry Brom? Your saddle will hold him in place, and you can protect him.

Yes, but I'm not leaving you alone.

Fine, fly next to me, but let's get out of here. He tied the saddle onto Saphira, then put his arms around Brom and tried to lift him, but again his diminished strength failed him. *Saphira—help.*

She snaked her head past him and caught the back of Brom's robe between her teeth. Arching her neck, she lifted the old man off the ground, like a cat would a kitten, and deposited him onto her back. Then Eragon slipped Brom's legs through the saddle's straps and tightened them. He looked up when the old man moaned and shifted.

Brom blinked blearily, putting a hand to his head. He gazed down at Eragon with concern. "Did Saphira get here in time?"

Eragon shook his head. "I'll explain it later. Your arm is injured. I bandaged it as best I could, but you need a safe place to rest."

"Yes," said Brom, gingerly touching his arm. "Do you know where my sword . . . Ah, I see you found it."

Eragon finished tightening the straps. "Saphira's going to take you and follow me by air."

"Are you sure you want me to ride her?" asked Brom. "I can ride Snowfire."

"Not with that arm. This way, even if you faint, you won't fall off."

Brom nodded. "I'm honored." He wrapped his good arm around Saphira's neck, and she took off in a flurry, springing high into the sky. Eragon backed away, buffeted by the eddies from her wings, and returned to the horses.

He tied Snowfire behind Cadoc, then left Yazuac, returning to the trail and following it southward. It led through a rocky area, veered left, and continued along the bank of the Ninor River. Ferns, mosses, and small bushes dotted the side of the path. It was refreshingly cool under the trees, but Eragon did not let the soothing air lull him into a sense of security. He stopped briefly to fill the waterskins and let the horses drink. Glancing down, he saw the Ra'zac's spoor. *At least we're going in the right direction.* Saphira circled overhead, keeping a keen eye on him.

It disturbed him that they had seen only two Urgals. The villagers had been killed and Yazuac ransacked by a large horde, yet where was it? *Perhaps the ones we encountered were a rear guard or a trap left for anyone who was following the main force.*

His thoughts turned to how he had killed the Urgals. An idea, a revelation, slowly wormed its way through his mind. He, Eragon— farm boy of Palancar Valley—had used magic. *Magic!* It was the only word for what had happened. It seemed impossible, but he could not deny what he had seen. *Somehow I've become a sorcerer or wizard!* But he did not know how to use this new power again or what its limits and dangers might be. *How can I have this ability? Was it common among the Riders? And if Brom knew of it, why didn't he tell me?* He shook his head in wonder and bewilderment.

He conversed with Saphira to check on Brom's condition and to share his thoughts. She was just as puzzled as he was about the magic. *Saphira, can you find us a place to stay? I can't see very far down here.* While she searched, he continued along the Ninor.

The summons reached him just as the light was fading. *Come.* Saphira sent him an image of a secluded clearing in the trees by the river. Eragon turned the horses in the new direction and nudged them into a trot. With Saphira's help it was easy to find, but it was so well hidden that he doubted anyone else would notice it.

A small, smokeless fire was already burning when he entered the clearing. Brom sat next to it, tending his arm, which he held at an awkward angle. Saphira was crouched beside him, her body tense. She looked intently at Eragon and asked, *Are you sure you aren't hurt?*

Not on the outside . . . but I'm not sure about the rest of me.

I should have been there sooner.

Don't feel bad. We all made mistakes today. Mine was not staying closer to you. Her gratitude for that remark washed over him. He looked at Brom. "How are you?"

The old man glanced at his arm. "It's a large scratch and hurts terribly, but it should heal quickly enough. I need a fresh bandage; this one didn't last as long as I'd hoped." They boiled water to wash Brom's wound. Then Brom tied a fresh rag to his arm and said, "I must eat, and you look hungry as well. Let's have dinner first, then talk."

When their bellies were full and warm, Brom lit his pipe. "Now, I think it's time for you to tell me what transpired while I was unconscious. I am most curious." His face reflected the flickering firelight, and his bushy eyebrows stuck out fiercely.

Eragon nervously clasped his hands and told the story without embellishment. Brom remained silent throughout it, his face inscrutable. When Eragon finished, Brom looked down at the ground. For a long time the only sound was the snapping fire. Brom finally stirred. "Have you used this power before?"

"No. Do you know anything about it?"

"A little." Brom's face was thoughtful. "It seems I owe you a debt for saving my life. I hope I can return the favor someday. You should be proud; few escape unscathed from slaying their first Urgal. But the manner in which you did it was very dangerous. You could have destroyed yourself and the whole town."

"It wasn't as if I had a choice," said Eragon defensively. "The Urgals were almost upon me. If I had waited, they would have chopped me into pieces!"

Brom stamped his teeth vigorously on the pipe stem. "You didn't have any idea what you were doing."

"Then tell me," challenged Eragon. "I've been searching for answers to this mystery, but I can't make sense of it. What happened? How could I have possibly used magic? No one has ever instructed me in it or taught me spells."

Brom's eyes flashed. "This isn't something you should be taught—much less use!"

"Well, I *have* used it, and I may need it to fight again. But I won't be able to if you don't help me. What's wrong? Is there some secret I'm not supposed to learn until I'm old and wise? Or maybe you don't know anything about magic!"

"Boy!" roared Brom. "You demand answers with an insolence rarely seen. If you knew what you asked for, you would not be so quick to inquire. Do not try me." He paused, then relaxed into a kinder countenance. "The knowledge you ask for is more complex than you understand."

Eragon rose hotly in protest. "I feel as though I've been thrust into a world with strange rules that no one will explain."

"I understand," said Brom. He fiddled with a piece of grass. "It's late and we should sleep, but I will tell you a few things now, to stop your badgering. This magic—for it is magic—has rules like the rest of the world. If you break the rules, the penalty is death, without exception. Your deeds are limited by your strength, the words you know, and your imagination."

"What do you mean by words?" asked Eragon.

"More questions!" cried Brom. "For a moment I had hoped you were empty of them. But you are quite right in asking. When you shot the Urgals, didn't you say something?"

"Yes, *brisingr*." The fire flared, and a shiver ran through Eragon. Something about the word made him feel incredibly alive.

"I thought so. *Brisingr* is from an ancient language that all living things used to speak. However, it was forgotten over time and went unspoken for eons in Alagaësia, until the elves brought it back over the sea. They taught it to the other races, who used it for making and doing powerful things. The language has a name for everything, if you can find it."

"But what does that have to do with magic?" interrupted Eragon.

"Everything! It is the basis for all power. The language describes the true nature of things, not the superficial aspects that everyone sees. For example, fire is called *brisingr*. Not only is that *a* name for fire, it is *the* name for fire. If you are strong enough, you can use *brisingr* to direct fire to do whatever you will. And that is what happened today."

Eragon thought about it for a moment. "Why was the fire blue? How come it did exactly what I wanted, if all I said was *fire*?"

"The color varies from person to person. It depends on who says the word. As to why the fire did what you wanted, that's a matter of practice. Most beginners have to spell out exactly what they want to happen. As they gain more experience, it isn't as necessary. A true master could just say *water* and create something totally unrelated, like a gemstone. You wouldn't be able to understand how he had done it, but the master would have seen the connection between *water* and the gem and would have used that as the focal point for his power. The practice is more of an art than anything else. What you did was extremely difficult."

Saphira interrupted Eragon's thoughts. *Brom is a magician! That's how he was able to light the fire on the plains. He doesn't just know about magic; he can use it himself!*

Eragon's eyes widened. *You're right!*

Ask him about this power, but be careful of what you say. It is unwise to trifle with those who have such abilities. If he is a wizard or sorcerer, who knows what his motives might have been for settling in Carvahall?

Eragon kept that in mind as he said carefully, "Saphira and I just realized something. You can use this magic, can't you? That's how you started the fire our first day on the plains."

Brom inclined his head slightly. "I am proficient to some degree."

"Then why didn't you fight the Urgals with it? In fact, I can think of many times when it would have been useful—you could have shielded us from the storm and kept the dirt out of our eyes."

After refilling his pipe, Brom said, "Some simple reasons, really. I am not a Rider, which means that, even at your weakest moment, you are stronger than I. And I have outlived my youth; I'm not as strong as I used to be. Every time I reach for magic, it gets a little harder."

Eragon dropped his eyes, abashed. "I'm sorry."

"Don't be," said Brom as he shifted his arm. "It happens to everyone."

"Where did you learn to use magic?"

"That is one fact I'll keep to myself. . . . Suffice it to say, it was in a remote area and from a very good teacher. I can, at the very least, pass on his lessons." Brom snuffed his pipe with a small rock. "I know that you have more questions, and I will answer them, but they must wait until morning."

He leaned forward, eyes gleaming. "Until then, I will say this to discourage any experiments: magic takes just as much energy as if you used your arms and back. That is why you felt tired after destroying the Urgals. And that is why I was angry. It was a dreadful risk on your part. If the magic had used more energy than was in your body, it would have killed you. You should use magic only for tasks that can't be accomplished the mundane way."

"How do you know if a spell will use all your energy?" asked Eragon, frightened.

Brom raised his hands. "Most of the time you don't. That's why magicians have to know their limits well, and even then they are cautious. Once you commit to a task and release the magic, you can't pull it back, even if it's going to kill you. I mean this as a warning: don't try anything until you've learned more. Now, enough of this for tonight."

As they spread out their blankets, Saphira commented with satisfaction, *We are becoming more powerful, Eragon, both of us. Soon no one will be able to stand in our way.*

Yes, but which way shall we choose?

Whichever one we want, she said smugly, settling down for the night.

MAGIC IS THE SIMPLEST THING

"Why do you think those two Urgals were still in Yazuac?" asked Eragon, after they had been on the trail for a while. "There doesn't seem to be any reason for them to have stayed behind."

"I suspect they deserted the main group to loot the town. What makes it odd is that, as far as I know, Urgals have gathered in force only two or three times in history. It's unsettling that they are doing it now."

"Do you think the Ra'zac caused the attack?"

"I don't know. The best thing we can do is continue away from Yazuac at the fastest pace we can muster. Besides, this is the direction the Ra'zac went: south."

Eragon agreed. "We still need provisions, however. Is there another town nearby?"

Brom shook his head. "No, but Saphira can hunt for us if we must survive on meat alone. This swath of trees may look small to you, but there are plenty of animals in it. The river is the only source of water for many miles around, so most of the plains animals come here to drink. We won't starve."

Eragon remained quiet, satisfied with Brom's answer. As they rode, loud birds darted around them, and the river rushed by peacefully. It was a noisy place, full of life and energy. Eragon asked, "How did that Urgal get you? Things were happening so fast, I didn't see."

"Bad luck, really," grumbled Brom. "I was more than a match for him, so he kicked Snowfire. The idiot of a horse reared and threw me off balance. That was all the Urgal needed to give me this gash." He scratched his chin. "I suppose you're still wondering about this magic. The fact that you've discovered it presents a thorny problem. Few know it, but every Rider could use magic, though with differing strengths. They kept the ability secret, even at the height of their power, because it gave them an advantage over their enemies. Had everyone known about it, dealing with common people would have been difficult. Many think the king's magical powers come from the fact that he is a wizard or sorcerer. That's not true; it is because he's a Rider."

"What's the difference? Doesn't the fact that I used magic make me a sorcerer?"

"Not at all! A sorcerer, like a Shade, uses spirits to accomplish his will. That is totally different from your power. Nor does that make you a magician, whose powers come without the aid of spirits or a dragon. And you're certainly not a witch or wizard, who get their powers from various potions and spells.

"Which brings me back to my original point: the problem you've presented. Young Riders like yourself were put through a strict regimen designed to strengthen their bodies and increase their mental control. This regimen continued for many months, occasionally years, until the Riders were deemed responsible enough to handle magic. Up until then, not one student was told of his potential powers. If one of them discovered magic by accident, he or she was immediately taken away for private tutoring. It was rare for anyone to discover magic on his own," he inclined his head toward Eragon, "though they were never put under the same pressure you were."

"Then how were they finally trained to use magic?" asked Eragon. "I don't see how you could teach it to anyone. If you had tried to explain it to me two days ago, it wouldn't have made any sense."

"The students were presented with a series of pointless exercises designed to frustrate them. For example, they were instructed to move piles of stones using only their feet, fill ever draining tubs full of water, and other impossibilities. After a time, they would get infuriated enough to use magic. Most of the time it succeeded.

"What this means," Brom continued, "is that you will be disadvantaged if you ever meet an enemy who has received this training. There are still some alive who are that old: the king for one, not to mention the elves. Any one of those could tear you apart with ease."

"What can I do, then?"

"There isn't time for formal instruction, but we can do much while we travel," said Brom. "I know many techniques you can practice that will give you strength and control, but you cannot gain the discipline the Riders had overnight. You," he looked at Eragon humorously, "will have to amass it on the run. It will be hard in the beginning, but the rewards will be great. It may please you to know that no Rider your age ever used magic the way you did yesterday with those two Urgals."

Eragon smiled at the praise. "Thank you. Does this language have a name?"

Brom laughed. "Yes, but no one knows it. It would be a word of incredible power, something by which you could control the entire language and those who use it. People have long searched for it, but no one has ever found it."

"I still don't understand how this magic works," said Eragon. "Exactly how do I use it?"

Brom looked astonished. "I haven't made that clear?"

"No."

Brom took a deep breath and said, "To work with magic, you must have a certain innate power, which is very rare among people nowadays. You also have to be able to summon this power at will. Once it is called upon, you have to use it or let it fade away. Understood? Now, if you wish to employ the power, you must utter the word or phrase of the ancient language that describes your intent. For example, if you hadn't said *brisingr* yesterday, nothing would have happened."

"So I'm limited by my knowledge of this language?"

"Exactly," crowed Brom. "Also, while speaking it, it's impossible to practice deceit."

Eragon shook his head. "That can't be. People always lie. The sounds of the ancient words can't stop them from doing that."

Brom cocked an eyebrow and said, "Fethrblaka, eka weohnata néiat haina ono. Blaka eom iet lam." A bird suddenly flitted from a branch and landed on his hand. It trilled lightly and looked at them with beady eyes. After a moment he said, "Eitha," and it fluttered away.

"How did you do that?" asked Eragon in wonder.

"I promised not to harm him. He may not have known exactly what I meant, but in the language of power, the meaning of my words was evident. The bird trusted me because he knows what all animals do, that those who speak in that tongue are bound by their word."

"And the elves speak this language?"

"Yes."

"So they never lie?"

"Not quite," admitted Brom. "They maintain that they don't, and in a way it's true, but they have perfected the art of saying one thing and meaning another. You never know exactly what their intent is, or if you have fathomed it correctly. Many times they only reveal part of the truth and withhold the rest. It takes a refined and subtle mind to deal with their culture."

Eragon considered that. "What do personal names mean in this language? Do they give power over people?"

Brom's eyes brightened with approval. "Yes, they do. Those who speak the language have two names. The first is for everyday use and has little authority. But the second is their true name and is shared with only a few trusted people. There was a time when no one concealed his true name, but this age isn't as kind. Whoever knows your true name gains enormous power over you. It's like putting your life into another person's hands. Everyone has a hidden name, but few know what it is."

"How do you find your true name?" asked Eragon.

"Elves instinctively know theirs. No one else has that gift. The human Riders usually went on quests to discover it—or found an elf who would tell them, which was rare, for elves don't distribute that knowledge freely," replied Brom.

"I'd like to know mine," Eragon said wistfully.

Brom's brow darkened. "Be careful. It can be a terrible knowledge. To know who you are without any delusions or sympathy is a moment of revelation that no one experiences unscathed. Some have been driven to madness by that stark reality. Most try to forget it. But as much as the name will give others power, so you may gain power over yourself, if the truth doesn't break you."

And I'm sure that it would not, stated Saphira.

"I still wish to know," said Eragon, determined.

"You are not easily dissuaded. That is good, for only the resolute find their identity, but I cannot help you with this. It is a search that you will have to undertake on your own." Brom moved his injured arm and grimaced uncomfortably.

"Why can't you or I heal that with magic?" asked Eragon.

Brom blinked. "No reason—I just never considered it because it's beyond my strength. You could probably do it with the right word, but I don't want you to exhaust yourself."

"I could save you a lot of trouble and pain," protested Eragon.

"I'll live with it," said Brom flatly. "Using magic to heal a wound takes just as much energy as it would to mend on its own. I don't want you tired for the next few days. You shouldn't attempt such a difficult task yet."

"Still, if it's possible to fix your arm, could I bring someone back from the dead?"

The question surprised Brom, but he answered quickly, "Remember what I said about projects that will kill you? That is one of them. Riders were forbidden to try to resurrect the dead, for their own safety. There is an abyss beyond life where magic means nothing. If you reach into it, your strength will flee and your soul will fade into darkness. Wizards, sorcerers, and Riders—all have failed and died on that threshold. Stick with what's possible—cuts, bruises, maybe some broken bones—but definitely not dead people."

Eragon frowned. "This is a lot more complex than I thought."

"Exactly!" said Brom. "And if you don't understand what you're doing, you'll try something too big and die." He twisted in his saddle and swooped down, grabbing a handful of pebbles from the ground. With effort, he righted himself, then discarded all but one of the rocks. "See this pebble?"

"Yes."

"Take it." Eragon did and stared at the unremarkable lump. It was dull black, smooth, and as large as the end of his thumb. There were countless stones like it on the trail. "This is your training."

Eragon looked back at him, confused. "I don't understand."

"Of course you don't," said Brom impatiently. "That's why I'm teaching you and not the other way around. Now stop talking or we'll never get anywhere. What I want you to do is lift the rock off your palm and hold it in the air for as long as you can. The words you're going to use are *stenr reisa*. Say them."

"Stenr reisa."

"Good. Go ahead and try."

Eragon focused sourly on the pebble, searching his mind for any hint of the energy that had burned in him the day before. The stone remained motionless as he stared at it, sweating and frustrated. *How am I supposed to do this?* Finally, he crossed his arms and snapped, "This is impossible."

"No," said Brom gruffly. "*I'll* say when it's impossible or not. Fight for it! Don't give in this easily. Try again."

Frowning, Eragon closed his eyes, setting aside all distracting thoughts. He took a deep breath and reached into the farthest corners of his consciousness, trying to find where his power resided. Searching, he found only thoughts and memories until he felt something different—a small bump that was a part of him and yet not of him. Excited, he dug into it, seeking what it hid. He felt resistance, a barrier in his mind, but knew that the power lay on the other side. He tried to breach it, but it held firm before his efforts. Growing angry, Eragon drove into the barrier, ramming against it with all of his might until it shattered like a thin pane of glass, flooding his mind with a river of light.

"Stenr reisa," he gasped. The pebble wobbled into the air over his faintly glowing palm. He struggled to keep it floating, but the power slipped away and faded back behind the barrier. The pebble dropped to his hand with a soft plop, and his palm returned to normal. He felt a little tired, but grinned from his success.

"Not bad for your first time," said Brom.

"Why does my hand do that? It's like a little lantern."

"No one's sure," Brom admitted. "The Riders always preferred to channel their power through whichever hand bore the gedwëy ignasia. You can use your other palm, but it isn't as easy." He looked at Eragon for a minute. "I'll buy you some gloves at the next town, if it isn't gutted. You hide the mark pretty well on your own, but we don't want anyone to see it by accident. Besides, there may be times when you won't want the glow to alert an enemy."

"Do you have a mark of your own?"

"No. Only Riders have them," said Brom. "Also, you should know that magic is affected by distance, just like an arrow or a spear. If you try to lift or move something a mile away, it'll take more energy than if you were closer. So if you see enemies racing after you from a league away, let them approach before using magic. Now, back to work! Try to lift the pebble again."

"Again?" asked Eragon weakly, thinking of the effort it had taken to do it just once.

"Yes! And this time be quicker about it."

They continued with the exercises throughout most of the day. When Eragon finally stopped, he was tired and ill-tempered. In those hours, he had come to hate the pebble and everything about it. He started to throw it away, but Brom said, "Don't. Keep it." Eragon glared at him, then reluctantly tucked the stone into a pocket.

"We're not done yet," warned Brom, "so don't get comfortable." He pointed at a small plant. "This is called *delois*." From there on he instructed Eragon in the ancient language, giving him words to memorize, from *vöndr*, a thin, straight stick, to the morning star, *Aiedail*.

That evening they sparred around the fire. Though Brom fought with his left hand, his skill was undiminished.

The days followed the same pattern. First, Eragon struggled to learn the ancient words and to manipulate the pebble. Then, in the evening, he trained against Brom with the fake swords. Eragon was in constant discomfort, but he gradually began to change, almost without noticing. Soon the pebble no longer wobbled when he lifted it. He mastered the first exercises Brom gave him and undertook harder ones, and his knowledge of the ancient language grew.

In their sparring, Eragon gained confidence and speed, striking like a snake. His blows became heavier, and his arm no longer trembled when he warded off attacks. The clashes lasted longer as he learned how to fend off Brom. Now, when they went to sleep, Eragon was not the only one with bruises.

Saphira continued to grow as well, but more slowly than before. Her extended flights, along with periodic hunts, kept her fit and healthy. She was taller than the horses now, and much longer. Because of her size and the way her scales sparkled, she was altogether too visible. Brom and Eragon worried about it, but they could not convince her to allow dirt to obscure her scintillating hide.

They continued south, tracking the Ra'zac. It frustrated Eragon that no matter how fast they went, the Ra'zac always stayed a few days ahead of them. At times he was ready to give up, but then they would find some mark or print that would renew his hope.

There were no signs of habitation along the Ninor or in the plains, leaving the three companions undisturbed as the days slipped by. Finally, they neared Daret, the first village since Yazuac.

*   *   *

The night before they reached the village, Eragon's dreams were especially vivid.

He saw Garrow and Roran at home, sitting in the destroyed kitchen. They asked him for help rebuilding the farm, but he only shook his head with a pang of longing in his heart. "I'm tracking your killers," he whispered to his uncle.

Garrow looked at him askance and demanded, "Do I look dead to you?"

"I can't help you," said Eragon softly, feeling tears in his eyes.

There was a sudden roar, and Garrow transformed into the Ra'zac. "Then die," they hissed, and leapt at Eragon.

He woke up feeling ill and watched the stars slowly turn in the sky.

All will be well, little one, said Saphira gently.

DARET

Daret was on the banks of the Ninor River—as it had to be to survive. The village was small and wild-looking, without any signs of inhabitants. Eragon and Brom approached it with great caution. Saphira hid close to the town this time; if trouble arose, she would be at their sides within seconds.

They rode into Daret, striving to be silent. Brom gripped his sword with his good hand, eyes flashing everywhere. Eragon kept his bow partially drawn as they passed between the silent houses, glancing at each other with apprehension. *This doesn't look good*, commented Eragon to Saphira. She did not answer, but he felt her prepare to rush after them. He looked at the ground and was reassured to see the fresh footprints of children. *But where are they?*

Brom stiffened as they entered the center of Daret and found it empty. Wind blew through the desolate town, and dust devils swirled sporadically. Brom wheeled Snowfire about. "Let's get out of here. I don't like the feel of this." He spurred Snowfire into a gallop. Eragon followed him, urging Cadoc onward.

They advanced only a few strides before wagons toppled out from behind the houses and blocked their way. Cadoc snorted and dug in his hooves, sliding to a stop next to Snowfire. A swarthy man hopped over the wagon and planted himself before them, a broadsword slung at his side and a drawn bow in his hands. Eragon swung his own bow up and pointed it at the stranger, who commanded, "Halt! Put your weapons down. You're surrounded by sixty archers. They'll shoot if you move." As if on cue, a row of men stood up on the roofs of the surrounding houses.

Stay away, Saphira! cried Eragon. *There are too many. If you come, they'll shoot you out of the sky. Stay away!* She heard, but he was unsure if she would obey. He prepared to use magic. *I'll have to stop the arrows before they hit me or Brom.*

"What do you want?" asked Brom calmly.

"Why have you come here?" demanded the man.

"To buy supplies and hear the news. Nothing more. We're on the way to my cousin's house in Dras-Leona."

"You're armed pretty heavily."

"So are you," said Brom. "These are dangerous times."

"True." The man looked at them carefully. "I don't think you mean us ill, but we've had too many encounters with Urgals and bandits for me to trust you only on your word."

"If it doesn't matter what we say, what happens now?" countered Brom. The men on top of the houses had not moved. By their very stillness, Eragon was sure that they were either highly disciplined . . . or frightened for their lives. He hoped it was the latter.

"You say that you only want supplies. Would you agree to stay here while we bring what you need, then pay us and leave immediately?"

"Yes."

"All right," said the man, lowering his bow, though he kept it ready. He waved at one of the archers, who slid to the ground and ran over. "Tell him what you want."

Brom recited a short list and then added, "Also, if you have a spare pair of gloves that would fit my nephew, I'd like to buy those too." The archer nodded and ran off.

"The name's Trevor," said the man standing in front of them. "Normally I'd shake your hand, but under the circumstances, I think I'll keep my distance. Tell me, where are you from?"

"North," said Brom, "but we haven't lived in any place long enough to call it home. Have Urgals forced you to take these measures?"

"Yes," said Trevor, "and worse fiends. Do you have any news from other towns? We receive word from them rarely, but there have been reports that they are also beleaguered."

Brom turned grave. "I wish it wasn't our lot to bring you these tidings. Nearly a fortnight ago we passed through Yazuac and found it pillaged. The villagers had been slaughtered and piled together. We would have tried to give them a decent burial, but two Urgals attacked us."

Shocked, Trevor stepped back and looked down with tears in his eyes. "Alas, this is indeed a dark day. Still, I don't see how two Urgals could have defeated all of Yazuac. The people there were good fighters—some were my friends."

"There were signs that a band of Urgals had ravaged the town," stated Brom. "I think the ones we encountered were deserters."

"How large was the company?"

Brom fiddled with his saddlebags for a minute. "Large enough to wipe out Yazuac, but small enough to go unnoticed in the countryside. No more than a hundred, and no less than fifty. If I'm not mistaken, either number would prove fatal to you." Trevor wearily agreed. "You should consider leaving," Brom continued. "This area has become far too perilous for anyone to live in peace."

"I know, but the people here refuse to consider moving. This is their home—as well as mine, though I have only been here a couple years—and they place its worth above their own lives." Trevor looked at him seriously. "We have repulsed individual Urgals, and that has given the townspeople a confidence far beyond their abilities. I fear that we will all wake up one morning with our throats slashed."

The archer hurried out of a house with a pile of goods in his arms. He set them next to the horses, and Brom paid him. As the man left, Brom asked, "Why did they choose you to defend Daret?"

Trevor shrugged. "I was in the king's army for some years."

Brom dug through the items, handed Eragon the pair of gloves, and packed the rest of the supplies into their saddlebags. Eragon pulled the gloves on, being careful to keep his palm facing down, and flexed his hands. The leather felt good and strong, though it was scarred from use. "Well," said Brom, "as I promised, we will go now."

Trevor nodded. "When you enter Dras-Leona, would you do us this favor? Alert the Empire to our plight and that of the other towns. If word of this hasn't reached the king by now, it's cause for worry. And if it has, but he has chosen to do nothing, that too is cause for worry."

"We will carry your message. May your swords stay sharp," said Brom.

"And yours."

The wagons were pulled out of their way, and they rode from Daret into the trees along the Ninor River. Eragon sent his thoughts to Saphira. *We're on our way back. Everything turned out all right.* Her only response was simmering anger.

Brom pulled at his beard. "The Empire is in worse condition than I had imagined. When the traders visited Carvahall, they brought reports of unrest, but I never believed that it was this widespread. With all these Urgals around, it seems that the Empire itself is under attack, yet no troops or soldiers have been sent out. It's as if the king doesn't care to defend his domain."

"It is strange," agreed Eragon.

Brom ducked under a low-hanging branch. "Did you use any of your powers while we were in Daret?"

"There was no reason to."

"Wrong," corrected Brom. "You could have sensed Trevor's intentions. Even with my limited abilities, I was able to do that. If the villagers had been bent on killing us, I wouldn't have just sat there. However, I felt there was a reasonable chance of talking our way out of there, which is what I did."

"How could I know what Trevor was thinking?" asked Eragon. "Am I supposed to be able to see into people's minds?"

"Come now," chided Brom, "you should know the answer to that. You could have discovered Trevor's purpose in the same way that you communicate with Cadoc or Saphira. The minds of men are not so different from a dragon's or horse's. It's a simple thing to do, but it's a power you must use sparingly and with great caution. A person's mind is his last sanctuary. You must never violate it unless circumstances force you to. The Riders had very strict rules regarding this. If they were broken without due cause, the punishment was severe."

"And you can do this even though you aren't a Rider?" asked Eragon.

"As I said before, with the right instruction anyone can talk with their minds, but with differing amounts of success. Whether it's magic, though, is hard to tell. Magical abilities will certainly trigger the talent—or becoming linked with a dragon—but I've known plenty who learned it on their own. Think about it: you can communicate with any sentient being, though the contact may not be very clear. You could spend the entire day listening to a bird's thoughts or understanding how an earthworm feels during a rainstorm. But I've never found birds very interesting. I suggest starting with a cat; they have unusual personalities."

Eragon twisted Cadoc's reins in his hands, considering the implications of what Brom had said. "But if I can get into someone's head, doesn't that mean that others can do the same to me? How do I know if someone's prying in my mind? Is there a way to stop that?" *How do I know if Brom can tell what I'm thinking right now?*

"Why, yes. Hasn't Saphira ever blocked you from her mind?"

"Occasionally," admitted Eragon. "When she took me into the Spine, I couldn't talk to her at all. It wasn't that she was ignoring me; I don't think she could even hear me. There were walls around her mind that I couldn't get through."

Brom worked on his bandage for a moment, shifting it higher on his arm. "Only a few people can tell if someone is in their mind, and of those, only a handful could stop you from entering. It's a matter of training and of how you think. Because of your magical power, you'll always know if someone is in your mind. Once you do, blocking them is a simple matter of concentrating on one thing to the exclusion of all else. For instance, if you only think about a brick wall, that's all the enemy will find in your mind. However, it takes a huge amount of energy and discipline to block someone for any length of time. If you're distracted by even the slightest thing, your wall will waver and your opponent will slip in through the weakness."

"How can I learn to do this?" asked Eragon.

"There is only one thing for it: practice, practice, and yet more practice. Picture something in your mind and hold it there to the exclusion of all else for as long as you can. It is a very advanced ability; only a handful ever master it," said Brom.

"I don't need perfection, just safety." *If I can get into someone's mind, can I change how he thinks? Every time I learn something new about magic, I grow more wary of it.*

When they reached Saphira, she startled them by thrusting her head at them. The horses backstepped nervously. Saphira looked Eragon over carefully and gave a low hiss. Her eyes were flinty. Eragon threw a concerned look at Brom—he had never seen Saphira this angry—then asked, *What's wrong?*

You, she growled. *You are the problem.*

Eragon frowned and got off Cadoc. As soon as his feet touched the ground, Saphira swept his legs out from under him with her tail and pinned him with her talons. "What are you doing?" he yelled, struggling to get up, but she was too strong for him. Brom watched attentively from Snowfire.

Saphira swung her head over Eragon until they were eye to eye. He squirmed under her unwavering glare. *You! Every time you leave my sight you get into trouble. You're like a new hatchling, sticking your nose into everything. And what happens when you stick it into something that bites back? How will you survive then? I cannot help you when I'm miles away. I've stayed hidden so that no one would see me, but no longer! Not when it may cost you your life.*

I can understand why you're upset, said Eragon, *but I'm much older than you and can take care of myself. If anything, you're the one who needs to be protected.*

She snarled and snapped her teeth by his ear. *Do you really believe that?* she asked. *Tomorrow you will ride me—not that pitiful deer-animal you call a horse—or else I will carry you in my claws. Are you a Dragon Rider or not? Don't you care for me?*

The question burned in Eragon, and he dropped his gaze. He knew she was right, but he was scared of riding her. Their flights had been the most painful ordeal he had ever endured.

"Well?" demanded Brom.

"She wants me to ride her tomorrow," said Eragon lamely.

Brom considered it with twinkling eyes. "Well, you have the saddle. I suppose that if the two of you stay out of sight, it won't be a problem." Saphira switched her gaze to him, then returned it to Eragon.

"But what if you're attacked or there's an accident? I won't be able to get there in time and—"

Saphira pressed harder on his chest, stopping his words. *Exactly my point, little one.*

Brom seemed to hide a smile. "It's worth the risk. You need to learn how to ride her anyway. Think about it this way: with you fly-ing ahead and looking at the ground, you'll be able to spot any traps, ambushes, or other unwelcome surprises."

Eragon looked back at Saphira and said, *Okay, I'll do it. But let me up.*

Give me your word.

Is that really necessary? he demanded. She blinked. *Very well. I give you my word that I will fly with you tomorrow. Satisfied?*

I am content.

Saphira let him up and, with a push of her legs, took off. A small shiver ran through Eragon as he watched her twist through the air. Grumbling, he returned to Cadoc and followed Brom.

It was nearly sundown when they made camp. As usual, Eragon dueled with Brom before dinner. In the midst of the fight, Eragon delivered such a powerful blow that he snapped both of their sticks like twigs. The pieces whistled into the darkness in a cloud of splintered fragments. Brom tossed what remained of his stick into the fire and said, "We're done with these; throw yours in as well. You have learned well, but we've gone as far as we can with branches. There is nothing more you can gain from them. It is time for you to use the blade." He removed Zar'roc from Eragon's bag and gave it to him.

"We'll cut each other to ribbons," protested Eragon.

"Not so. Again you forget magic," said Brom. He held up his sword and turned it so that firelight glinted off the edge. He put a finger on either side of the blade and focused intensely, deepening the lines on his forehead. For a moment nothing happened, then he uttered, "Gëuloth du knífr!" and a small red spark jumped between his fingers. As it flickered back and forth, he ran his fingers down the length of the sword. Then he twirled it and did the same thing on the other side. The spark vanished the moment his fingers left the metal.

Brom held his hand out, palm up, and slashed it with the sword. Eragon jumped forward but was too slow to stop him. He was astonished when Brom raised his unharmed hand with a smile. "What did you do?" asked Eragon.

"Feel the edge," said Brom. Eragon touched it and felt an invisible surface under his fingers. The barrier was about a quarter inch wide and very slippery. "Now do the same on Zar'roc," instructed Brom. "Your block will be a bit different than mine, but it should accomplish the same thing."

He told Eragon how to pronounce the words and coached him through the process. It took Eragon a few tries, but he soon had Zar'roc's edge protected. Confident, he took his fighting stance. Before they started, Brom admonished, "These swords won't cut us, but they can still break bones. I would prefer to avoid that, so don't flail around like you normally do. A blow to the neck could prove fatal."

Eragon nodded, then struck without warning. Sparks flew off his blade, and the clash of metal filled their campsite as Brom parried. The sword felt slow and heavy to Eragon after fighting with sticks for so long. Unable to move Zar'roc fast enough, he received a sharp rap on his knee.

They both had large welts when they stopped, Eragon more so than Brom. He marveled that Zar'roc had not been scratched or dented by the vigorous pounding it had received.

THROUGH A
DRAGON'S EYE

The next morning Eragon woke with stiff limbs and purple bruises. He saw Brom carry the saddle to Saphira and tried to quell his uneasiness. By the time breakfast was ready, Brom had strapped the saddle onto Saphira and hung Eragon's bags from it.

When his bowl was empty, Eragon silently picked up his bow and went to Saphira. Brom said, "Now remember, grip with your knees, guide her with your thoughts, and stay as flat as you can on her back. Nothing will go wrong if you don't panic." Eragon nodded, sliding his unstrung bow into its leather tube, and Brom boosted him into the saddle.

Saphira waited impatiently while Eragon tightened the bands around his legs. *Are you ready?* she asked.

He sucked in the fresh morning air. *No, but let's do it!* She agreed enthusiastically. He braced himself as she crouched. Her powerful legs surged and the air whipped past him, snatching his breath away. With three smooth strokes of her wings, she was in the sky, climbing rapidly.

The last time Eragon had ridden Saphira, every flap of her wings had been strained. Now she flew steadily and effortlessly. He clenched his arms around her neck as she turned on edge, banking. The river shrank to a wispy gray line beneath them. Clouds floated around them.

When they leveled off high above the plains, the trees below were no more than specks. The air was thin, chilly, and perfectly clear. "This is wonderfu—" His words were lost as Saphira tilted and rolled completely around. The ground spun in a dizzying circle, and vertigo clutched Eragon. "Don't do that!" he cried. "I feel like I'm going to fall off."

You must become accustomed to it. If I'm attacked in the air, that's one of the simplest maneuvers I will do, she replied. He could think of no rebuttal, so he concentrated on controlling his stomach. Saphira angled into a shallow dive and slowly approached the ground.

Although Eragon's stomach lurched with every wobble, he began to enjoy himself. He relaxed his arms a bit and stretched his neck back, taking in the scenery. Saphira let him enjoy the sights awhile, then said, *Let me show you what flying is really like.*

How? he asked.

Relax and do not be afraid, she said.

Her mind tugged at his, pulling him away from his body. Eragon fought for a moment, then surrendered control. His vision blurred, and he found himself looking through Saphira's eyes. Everything was distorted: colors had weird, exotic tints; blues were more prominent now, while greens and reds were subdued. Eragon tried to turn his head and body but could not. He felt like a ghost who had slipped out of the ether.

Pure joy radiated from Saphira as she climbed into the sky. She loved this freedom to go anywhere. When they were high above the ground, she looked back at Eragon. He saw himself as she did, hanging on to her with a blank look. He could feel her body strain against the air, using updrafts to rise. All her muscles were like his own. He felt her tail swinging through the air like a giant rudder to correct her course. It surprised him how much she depended on it.

Their connection grew stronger until there was no distinction between their identities. They clasped their wings together and dived straight down, like a spear thrown from on high. No terror of falling touched Eragon, engulfed as he was in Saphira's exhilaration. The air rushed past their face. Their tail whipped in the air, and their joined minds reveled in the experience.

162

Even as they plummeted toward the ground, there was no fear of collision. They snapped open their wings at just the right moment, pulling out of the dive with their combined strength. Slanting toward the sky, they shot up and continued back over into a giant loop.

As they leveled out, their minds began to diverge, becoming distinct personalities again. For a split second, Eragon felt both his body and Saphira's. Then his vision blurred and he again sat on her back. He gasped and collapsed on the saddle. It was minutes before his heart stopped hammering and his breathing calmed. Once he had recovered, he exclaimed, *That was incredible! How can you bear to land when you enjoy flying so much?*

I must eat, she said with some amusement. *But I am glad that you took pleasure in it.*

Those are spare words for such an experience. I'm sorry I haven't flown with you more; I never thought it could be like that. Do you always see so much blue?

It is the way I am. We will fly together more often now?

Yes! Every chance we get.

Good, she replied in a contented tone.

They exchanged many thoughts as she flew, talking as they had not for weeks. Saphira showed Eragon how she used hills and trees to hide and how she could conceal herself in the shadow of a cloud. They scouted the trail for Brom, which proved to be more arduous than Eragon expected. They could not see the path unless Saphira flew very close to it, in which case she risked being detected.

Near midday, an annoying buzz filled Eragon's ears, and he became aware of a strange pressure on his mind. He shook his head, trying to get rid of it, but the tension only grew stronger. Brom's words about how people could break into others' minds flashed through Eragon's head, and he frantically tried to clear his thoughts. He concentrated on one of Saphira's scales and forced himself to ignore everything else. The pressure faded for a moment and then returned, greater than ever. A sudden gust rocked

Saphira, and Eragon's concentration slipped. Before he could marshal any defenses, the force broke through. But instead of the invasive presence of another mind, there were only the words, *What do you think you're doing? Get down here. I found something important.*

Brom? queried Eragon.

Yes, the old man said irritably. *Now get that oversized lizard of yours to land. I'm here. . . .* He sent a picture of his location. Eragon quickly told Saphira where to go, and she banked toward the river below. Meanwhile, he strung his bow and drew several arrows.

If there's trouble, I'll be ready for it.

As will I, said Saphira.

When they reached Brom, Eragon saw him standing in a clearing, waving his arms. Saphira landed, and Eragon jumped off her and looked for danger. The horses were tied to a tree on the edge of the clearing, but otherwise Brom was alone. Eragon trotted over and asked, "What's wrong?"

Brom scratched his chin and muttered a string of curses. "Don't ever block me out like that again. It's hard enough for me to reach you without having to fight to make myself heard."

"Sorry."

He snorted. "I was farther down the river when I noticed that the Ra'zac's tracks had ceased. I backtracked until I found where they had disappeared. Look at the ground and tell me what you see."

Eragon knelt and examined the dirt and found a confusion of impressions that were difficult to decipher. Numerous Ra'zac footprints overlapped each other. Eragon guessed that the tracks were only a few days old. Superimposed over them were long, thick gouges torn into the ground. They looked familiar, but Eragon could not say why.

He stood, shaking his head. "I don't have any idea what . . ." Then his eyes fell on Saphira and he realized what had made the gouges. Every time she took off, her back claws dug into the ground and ripped it in the same manner. "This doesn't make any sense, but the only thing I can think of is that the Ra'zac flew off on dragons. Or else they got onto giant birds and disappeared into the heavens. Tell me you have a better explanation."

Brom shrugged. "I've heard reports of the Ra'zac moving from place to place with incredible speed, but this is the first evidence I've had of it. It will be almost impossible to find them if they have flying steeds. They aren't dragons—I know that much. A dragon would never consent to bear a Ra'zac."

"What do we do? Saphira can't track them through the sky. Even if she could, we would leave you far behind."

"There's no easy solution to this riddle," said Brom. "Let's have lunch while we think on it. Perhaps inspiration will strike us while we eat." Eragon glumly went to his bags for food. They ate in silence, staring at the empty sky.

Once again Eragon thought of home and wondered what Roran was doing. A vision of the burnt farm appeared before him and grief threatened to overwhelm him. *What will I do if we can't find the Ra'zac? What is my purpose then? I could return to Carvahall*—he plucked a twig from the ground and snapped it between two fingers—*or just travel with Brom and continue my training.* Eragon stared out at the plains, hoping to quiet his thoughts.

When Brom finished eating, he stood and threw back his hood. "I have considered every trick I know, every word of power within my grasp, and all the skills we have, but I still don't see how we can find the Ra'zac." Eragon slumped against Saphira in despair. "Saphira could show herself at some town. That would draw the Ra'zac like flies to honey. But it would be an extremely risky thing to attempt. The Ra'zac would bring soldiers with them, and the king might be interested enough to come himself, which would spell certain death for you and me."

"So what now?" asked Eragon, throwing his hands up. *Do you have any ideas, Saphira?*

No.

"That's up to you," said Brom. "This is your crusade."

Eragon ground his teeth angrily and stalked away from Brom and

Saphira. Just as he was about to enter the trees, his foot struck something hard. Lying on the ground was a metal flask with a leather strap just long enough to hang off someone's shoulder. A silver insignia Eragon recognized as the Ra'zac's symbol was wrought into it.

Excited, he picked up the flask and unscrewed its cap. A cloying smell filled the air—the same one he had noticed when he found Garrow in the wreckage of their house. He tilted the flask, and a drop of clear, shiny liquid fell on his finger. Instantly Eragon's finger burned as if it were on fire. He yelped and scrubbed his hand on the ground. After a moment the pain subsided to a dull throbbing. A patch of skin had been eaten away.

Grimacing, he jogged back to Brom. "Look what I found." Brom took the flask and examined it, then poured a bit of the liquid into the cap. Eragon started to warn him, "Watch out, it'll burn—"

"My skin, I know," said Brom. "And I suppose you went ahead and poured it all over your hand. Your finger? Well, at least you showed sense enough not to drink it. Only a puddle would have been left of you."

"What is it?" asked Eragon.

"Oil from the petals of the Seithr plant, which grows on a small island in the frigid northern seas. In its natural state, the oil is used for preserving pearls—it makes them lustrous and strong. But when specific words are spoken over the oil, along with a blood sacrifice, it gains the property to eat any flesh. That alone wouldn't make it special—there are plenty of acids that can dissolve sinew and bone—except for the fact that it leaves everything else untouched. You can dip anything into the oil and pull it out unharmed, unless it was once part of an animal or human. This has made it a weapon of choice for torture and assassination. It can be stored in wood, slathered on the point of a spear, or dripped onto sheets so that the next person to touch them will be burned. There are myriad uses for it, limited only by your ingenuity. Any injury caused by it is always slow to heal. It's rather rare and expensive, especially this converted form."

Eragon remembered the terrible burns that had covered Garrow.

That's what they used on him, he realized with horror. "I wonder why the Ra'zac left it behind if it's so valuable."

"It must have slipped off when they flew away."

"But why didn't they come back for it? I doubt that the king will be pleased that they lost it."

"No, he won't," said Brom, "but he would be even more displeased if they delayed bringing him news of you. In fact, if the Ra'zac have reached him by now, you can be sure that the king has learned your name. And that means we will have to be much more careful when we go into towns. There will be notices and alerts about you posted throughout the Empire."

Eragon paused to think. "This oil, how rare is it exactly?"

"Like diamonds in a pig trough," said Brom. He amended himself after a second, "Actually, the normal oil is used by jewelers, but only those who can afford it."

"So there are people who trade in it?"

"Perhaps one, maybe two."

"Good," said Eragon. "Now, do the cities along the coast keep shipping records?"

Brom's eyes brightened. "Of course they do. If we could get to those records, they would tell us who brought the oil south and where it went from there."

"And the record of the Empire's purchase will tell us where the Ra'zac live!" concluded Eragon. "I don't know how many people can afford this oil, but it shouldn't be hard to figure out which ones aren't working for the Empire."

"Genius!" exclaimed Brom, smiling. "I wish I had thought of this years ago; it would have saved me many headaches. The coast is dotted with numerous cities and towns where ships can land. I suppose that Teirm would be the place to start, as it controls most of the trade." Brom paused. "The last I heard, my old friend Jeod lives there. We haven't seen each other for many years, but he might be willing to help us. And because he's a merchant, it's possible that he has access to those records."

"How do we get to Teirm?"

"We'll have to go southwest until we reach a high pass in the Spine. Once on the other side, we can head up the coast to Teirm," said Brom. A gentle wind pulled at his hair.

"Can we reach the pass within a week?"

"Easily. If we angle away from the Ninor and to our right, we might be able to see the mountains by tomorrow."

Eragon went to Saphira and mounted her. "I'll see you at dinner, then." When they were at a good height, he said, *I'm going to ride Cadoc tomorrow. Before you protest, know that I am only doing it because I want to talk with Brom.*

You should ride with him every other day. That way you can still receive your instruction, and I will have time to hunt.

You won't be troubled by it?

It is necessary.

When they landed for the day, he was pleased to discover that his legs did not hurt. The saddle had protected him well from Saphira's scales.

Eragon and Brom had their nightly fight, but it lacked energy, as both were preoccupied with the day's events. By the time they finished, Eragon's arms burned from Zar'roc's unaccustomed weight.

A SONG FOR
THE ROAD

The next day while they were riding, Eragon asked Brom,
"What is the sea like?"

"You must have heard it described before," said Brom.

"Yes, but what is it really like?"

Brom's eyes grew hazy, as if he looked upon some hidden scene.
"The sea is emotion incarnate. It loves, hates, and weeps. It defies
all attempts to capture it with words and rejects all shackles. No
matter what you say about it, there is always that which you can't.
Do you remember what I told you about how the elves came over
the sea?"

"Yes."

"Though they live far from the coast, they retain a great fascination and passion for the ocean. The sound of crashing waves, the
smell of salt air, it affects them deeply and has inspired many of
their loveliest songs. There is one that tells of this love, if you want
to hear it."

"I would," said Eragon, interested.

Brom cleared his throat and said, "I will translate it from the
ancient language as best I can. It won't be perfect, but perhaps it
will give you an idea of how the original sounds." He pulled
Snowfire to a stop and closed his eyes. He was silent for a while,
then chanted softly:

O liquid temptress 'neath the azure sky,
Your gilded expanse calls me, calls me.

For I would sail ever on,
Were it not for the elven maid,
Who calls me, calls me.
She binds my heart with a lily-white tie,
Never to be broken, save by the sea,
Ever to be torn twixt the trees and the waves.

The words echoed hauntingly in Eragon's head. "There is much more to that song, the 'Du Silbena Datia.' I have only recited one of its verses. It tells the sad tale of two lovers, Acallamh and Nuada, who were separated by longing for the sea. The elves find great meaning in the story."

"It's beautiful," said Eragon simply.

The Spine was a faint outline on the horizon when they halted that evening.

170 When they arrived at the Spine's foothills, they turned and followed the mountains south. Eragon was glad to be near the mountains again; they placed comforting boundaries on the world. Three days later they came to a wide road rutted by wagon wheels. "This is the main road between the capital, Urû'baen, and Teirm," said Brom. "It's widely used and a favorite route for merchants. We have to be more cautious. This isn't the busiest time of year, but a few people are bound to be using the road."

Days passed quickly as they continued to trek along the Spine, searching for the mountain pass. Eragon could not complain of boredom. When not learning the elven language, he was either learning how to care for Saphira or practicing magic. Eragon also learned how to kill game with magic, which saved them time hunting. He would hold a small rock on his hand and shoot it at his prey. It was impossible to miss. The results of his efforts roasted over the fire each night. And after dinner, Brom and Eragon would spar with swords and, occasionally, fists.

The long days and strenuous work stripped Eragon's body of

excess fat. His arms became corded, and his tanned skin rippled with lean muscles. *Everything about me is turning hard,* he thought dryly.

When they finally reached the pass, Eragon saw that a river rushed out of it and cut across the road. "This is the Toark," explained Brom. "We'll follow it all the way to the sea."

"How can we," laughed Eragon, "if it flows out of the Spine in *this* direction? It won't end up in the ocean unless it doubles back on itself."

Brom twisted the ring on his finger. "Because in the middle of the mountains rests the Woadark Lake. A river flows from each end of it and both are called the Toark. We see the eastward one now. It runs to the south and winds through the brush until it joins Leona Lake. The other one goes to the sea."

After two days in the Spine, they came upon a rock ledge from which they could see clearly out of the mountains. Eragon noticed how the land flattened in the distance, and he groaned at the leagues they still had to traverse. Brom pointed. "Down there and to the north lies Teirm. It is an old city. Some say it's where the elves first landed in Alagaësia. Its citadel has never fallen, nor have its warriors ever been defeated." He spurred Snowfire forward and left the ledge.

It took them until noon the next day to descend through the foothills and arrive at the other side of the Spine, where the forested land quickly leveled out. Without the mountains to hide behind, Saphira flew close to the ground, using every hollow and dip in the land to conceal herself.

Beyond the forest, they noticed a change. The countryside was covered with soft turf and heather that their feet sank into. Moss clung to every stone and branch and lined the streams that laced the ground. Pools of mud pocked the road where horses had trampled the dirt. Before long both Brom and Eragon were splattered with grime.

"Why is everything green?" asked Eragon. "Don't they have winter here?"

"Yes, but the season is mild. Mist and fog roll in from the sea and keep everything alive. Some find it to their liking, but to me it's dreary and depressing."

When evening fell, they set up camp in the driest spot they could find. As they ate, Brom commented, "You should continue to ride Cadoc until we reach Teirm. It's likely that we'll meet other travelers now that we are out of the Spine, and it will be better if you are with me. An old man traveling alone will raise suspicion. With you at my side, no one will ask questions. Besides, I don't want to show up at the city and have someone who saw me on the trail wondering where you suddenly came from."

"Will we use our own names?" asked Eragon.

Brom thought about it. "We won't be able to deceive Jeod. He already knows my name, and I think I trust him with yours. But to everyone else, I will be Neal and you will be my nephew Evan. If our tongues slip and give us away, it probably won't make a difference, but I don't want our names in anyone's heads. People have an annoying habit of remembering things they shouldn't."

A TASTE OF TEIRM

After two days of traveling north toward the ocean, Saphira sighted Teirm. A heavy fog clung to the ground, obscuring Brom's and Eragon's sight until a breeze from the west blew the mist away. Eragon gaped as Teirm was suddenly revealed before them, nestled by the edge of the shimmering sea, where proud ships were docked with furled sails. The surf's dull thunder could be heard in the distance.

The city was contained behind a white wall—a hundred feet tall and thirty feet thick—with rows of rectangular arrow slits lining it and a walkway on top for soldiers and watchmen. The wall's smooth surface was broken by two iron portcullises, one facing the western sea, the other opening south to the road. Above the wall—and set against its northeast section—rose a huge citadel built of giant stones and turrets. In the highest tower, a lighthouse lantern gleamed brilliantly. The castle was the only thing visible over the fortifications.

Soldiers guarded the southern gate but held their pikes carelessly. "This is our first test," said Brom. "Let's hope they haven't received reports of us from the Empire and won't detain us. Whatever happens, don't panic or act suspiciously."

Eragon told Saphira, *You should land somewhere now and hide. We're going in.*

Sticking your nose where it doesn't belong. Again, she said sourly.

I know. But Brom and I do have some advantages most people don't. We'll be all right.

If anything happens, I'm going to pin you to my back and never let you off.

I love you too.

Then I will bind you all the tighter.

Eragon and Brom rode toward the gate, trying to appear casual. A yellow pennant bearing the outline of a roaring lion and an arm holding a lily blossom waved over the entrance. As they neared the wall, Eragon asked in amazement, "How big is this place?"

"Larger than any city you have ever seen," said Brom.

At the entrance to Teirm, the guards stood straighter and blocked the gate with their pikes. "Wha's yer name?" asked one of them in a bored tone.

"I'm called Neal," said Brom in a wheezy voice, slouching to one side, an expression of happy idiocy on his face.

"And who's th' other one?" asked the guard.

"Well, I wus gettin' to that. This'ed be m'nephew Evan. He's m'sister's boy, not a . . ."

The guard nodded impatiently. "Yeah, yeah. And yer business here?"

"He's visitin' an old friend," supplied Eragon, dropping his voice into a thick accent. "I'm along t' make sure he don't get lost, if y' get m'meaning. He ain't as young as he used to be—had a bit too much sun when he was young'r. Touch o' the brain fever, y' know." Brom bobbed his head pleasantly.

"Right. Go on through," said the guard, waving his hand and dropping the pike. "Just make sure he doesn't cause any trouble."

"Oh, he won't," promised Eragon. He urged Cadoc forward, and they rode into Teirm. The cobblestone street clacked under the horses' hooves.

Once they were away from the guards, Brom sat up and growled, "Touch of brain fever, eh?"

"I couldn't let you have all the fun," teased Eragon.

Brom harrumphed and looked away.

The houses were grim and foreboding. Small, deep windows let in only sparse rays of light. Narrow doors were recessed into the buildings. The tops of the roofs were flat—except for metal railings—and all were covered with slate shingles. Eragon noticed that the houses closest to Teirm's outer wall were no more than one story, but the buildings got progressively higher as they went in. Those next to the citadel were tallest of all, though insignificant compared to the fortress.

"This place looks ready for war," said Eragon.

Brom nodded. "Teirm has a history of being attacked by pirates, Urgals, and other enemies. It has long been a center of commerce. There will always be conflict where riches gather in such abundance. The people here have been forced to take extraordinary measures to keep themselves from being overrun. It also helps that Galbatorix gives them soldiers to defend their city."

"Why are some houses higher than others?"

"Look at the citadel," said Brom, pointing. "It has an unobstructed view of Teirm. If the outer wall were breached, archers would be posted on all the roofs. Because the houses in the front, by the outer wall, are lower, the men farther back could shoot over them without fear of hitting their comrades. Also, if the enemy were to capture those houses and put their own archers on them, it would be an easy matter to shoot them down."

"I've never seen a city planned like this," said Eragon in wonder.

"Yes, but it was only done after Teirm was nearly burned down by a pirate raid," commented Brom. As they continued up the street, people gave them searching looks, but there was not an undue amount of interest.

Compared to our reception at Daret, we've been welcomed with open arms. Perhaps Teirm has escaped notice by the Urgals, thought Eragon. He changed his opinion when a large man shouldered past them, a sword hanging from his waist. There were other, subtler signs of adverse times: no children played in the streets, people bore hard expressions, and many houses were deserted, with weeds growing from cracks in their stone-covered yards. "It looks like they've had trouble," said Eragon.

"The same as everywhere else," said Brom grimly. "We have to find Jeod." They led their horses across the street to a tavern and tied them to the hitching post. "The Green Chestnut . . . wonderful," muttered Brom, looking at the battered sign above them as he and Eragon entered the building.

The dingy room felt unsafe. A fire smoldered in the fireplace, yet no one bothered to throw more wood on it. A few lonely people in the corners nursed their drinks with sullen expressions. A man missing two fingers sat at a far table, eyeing his twitching stumps. The bartender had a cynical twist to his lips and held a glass in his hand that he kept polishing, even though it was broken.

Brom leaned against the bar and asked, "Do you know where we can find a man called Jeod?" Eragon stood at his side, fiddling with the tip of his bow by his waist. It was slung across his back, but right then he wished that it were in his hands.

The bartender said in an overly loud voice, "Now, why would I know something like that? Do you think I keep track of the mangy louts in this forsaken place?" Eragon winced as all eyes turned toward them.

Brom kept talking smoothly. "Could you be enticed to remember?" He slid some coins onto the bar.

The man brightened and put his glass down. "Could be," he replied, lowering his voice, "but my memory takes a great deal of prodding." Brom's face soured, but he slid more coins onto the bar. The bartender sucked on one side of his cheek undecidedly. "All right," he finally said, and reached for the coins.

Before he touched them, the man missing two fingers called out from his table, "Gareth, what in th' blazes do you think you're doing? Anyone on the street could tell them where Jeod lives. What are you charging them for?"

Brom swept the coins back into his purse. Gareth shot a venomous look at the man at the table, then turned his back on them and picked up the glass again. Brom went to the stranger and said, "Thanks. The name's Neal. This is Evan."

The man raised his mug to them. "Martin, and of course you met Gareth." His voice was deep and rough. Martin gestured at some empty chairs. "Go ahead and sit down. I don't mind." Eragon took a chair and arranged it so his back was to the wall and he faced the door. Martin raised an eyebrow, but made no comment.

"You just saved me a few crowns," said Brom.

"My pleasure. Can't blame Gareth, though—business hasn't been doing so well lately." Martin scratched his chin. "Jeod lives on the west side of town, right next to Angela, the herbalist. Do you have business with him?"

"Of a sort," said Brom.

"Well, he won't be interested in buying anything; he just lost another ship a few days ago."

Brom latched onto the news with interest. "What happened? It wasn't Urgals, was it?"

"No," said Martin. "They've left the area. No one's seen 'em in almost a year. It seems they've all gone south and east. But they aren't the problem. See, most of our business is through sea trade, as I'm sure you know. Well," he stopped to drink from his mug, "starting several months ago, someone's been attacking our ships. It's not the usual piracy, because only ships that carry the goods of certain merchants are attacked. Jeod's one of 'em. It's gotten so bad that no captain will accept those merchants' goods, which makes life difficult around here. Especially because some of 'em run the largest shipping businesses in the Empire. They're being forced to send goods by land. It's driven costs painfully high, and their caravans don't always make it."

"Do you have any idea who's responsible? There must be witnesses," said Brom.

Martin shook his head. "No one survives the attacks. Ships go out, then disappear; they're never seen again." He leaned toward them and said in a confidential tone, "The sailors are saying that it's magic." He nodded and winked, then leaned back.

Brom seemed worried by his words. "What do you think?"

Martin shrugged carelessly. "I don't know. And I don't think I will unless I'm unfortunate enough to be on one of those captured ships."

"Are you a sailor?" asked Eragon.

"No," snorted Martin. "Do I look like one? The captains hire me to defend their ships against pirates. And those thieving scum haven't been very active lately. Still, it's a good job."

"But a dangerous one," said Brom. Martin shrugged again and downed the last of his beer. Brom and Eragon took their leave and headed to the west side of the city, a nicer section of Teirm. The houses were clean, ornate, and large. The people in the streets wore expensive finery and walked with authority. Eragon felt conspicuous and out of place.

AN OLD FRIEND

he herbalist's shop had a cheery sign and was easy to find. A short, curly-haired woman sat by the door. She was holding a frog in one hand and writing with the other. Eragon assumed that she was Angela, the herbalist. On either side of the store was a house. "Which one do you think is his?" he asked.

Brom deliberated, then said, "Let's find out." He approached the woman and asked politely, "Could you tell us which house Jeod lives in?"

"I could." She continued writing.

"Will you tell us?"

"Yes." She fell silent, but her pen scribbled faster than ever. The frog on her hand croaked and looked at them with baleful eyes. Brom and Eragon waited uncomfortably, but she said no more. Eragon was about to blurt something out when Angela looked up. "Of course I'll tell you! All you have to do is ask. Your first question was whether or not I *could* tell you, and the second was if I *would* tell you. But you never actually put the question to me."

"Then let me ask properly," said Brom with a smile. "Which house is Jeod's? And why are you holding a frog?"

"Now we're getting somewhere," she bantered. "Jeod is on the right. And as for the frog, he's actually a toad. I'm trying to prove that toads don't exist—that there are only frogs."

"How can toads not exist if you have one on your hand right

now?" interrupted Eragon. "Besides, what good will it do, proving that there are only frogs?"

The woman shook her head vigorously, dark curls bouncing. "No, no, you don't understand. If I prove toads don't exist, then this is a frog and never was a toad. Therefore, the toad you see now doesn't exist. And," she raised a small finger, "if I can prove there are only frogs, then toads won't be able to do anything bad—like make teeth fall out, cause warts, and poison or kill people. Also, witches won't be able to use any of their evil spells because, of course, there won't be any toads around."

"I see," said Brom delicately. "It sounds interesting, and I would like to hear more, but we have to meet Jeod."

"Of course," she said, waving her hand and returning to her writing.

Once they were out of the herbalist's hearing, Eragon said, "She's crazy!"

"It's possible," said Brom, "but you never know. She might discover something useful, so don't criticize. Who knows, toads might really be frogs!"

"And my shoes are made of gold," retorted Eragon.

They stopped before a door with a wrought-iron knocker and marble doorstep. Brom banged three times. No one answered. Eragon felt slightly foolish. "Maybe this is the wrong house. Let's try the other one," he said. Brom ignored him and knocked again, pounding loudly.

Again no one answered. Eragon turned away in exasperation, then heard someone run to the door. A young woman with a pale complexion and light blond hair cracked it open. Her eyes were puffy; it looked like she had been crying, but her voice was perfectly steady. "Yes, what do you want?"

"Does Jeod live here?" asked Brom kindly.

The woman dipped her head a little. "Yes, he is my husband. Is he expecting you?" She opened the door no farther.

"No, but we need to talk with him," said Brom.

"He is very busy."

"We have traveled far. It's very important that we see him."

Her face hardened. "He is busy."

Brom bristled, but his voice stayed pleasant. "Since he is unavailable, would you please give him a message?" Her mouth twitched, but she consented. "Tell him that a friend from Gil'ead is waiting outside."

The woman seemed suspicious, but said, "Very well." She closed the door abruptly. Eragon heard her footsteps recede.

"That wasn't very polite." he commented.

"Keep your opinions to yourself," snapped Brom. "And don't say anything. Let me do the talking." He crossed his arms and tapped his fingers. Eragon clamped his mouth shut and looked away.

The door suddenly flew open, and a tall man burst out of the house. His expensive clothes were rumpled, his gray hair wispy, and he had a mournful face with short eyebrows. A long scar stretched across his scalp to his temple.

At the sight of them, his eyes grew wide, and he sagged against the doorframe, speechless. His mouth opened and closed several times like a gasping fish. He asked softly, in an incredulous voice, "Brom . . . ?"

181

Brom put a finger to his lips and reached forward, clasping the man's arm. "It's good to see you, Jeod! I'm glad that memory has not failed you, but don't use that name. It would be unfortunate if anyone knew I was here."

Jeod looked around wildly, shock plain on his face. "I thought you were dead," he whispered. "What happened? Why haven't you contacted me before?"

"All things will be explained. Do you have a place where we can talk safely?"

Jeod hesitated, swinging his gaze between Eragon and Brom, face unreadable. Finally he said, "We can't talk here, but if you wait a moment, I'll take you somewhere we can."

"Fine," said Brom. Jeod nodded and vanished behind the door.

I hope I can learn something of Brom's past, thought Eragon.

There was a rapier at Jeod's side when he reappeared. An embroidered jacket hung loosely on his shoulders, matched by a plumed hat. Brom cast a critical eye at the finery, and Jeod shrugged self-consciously.

He took them through Teirm toward the citadel. Eragon led the horses behind the two men. Jeod gestured at their destination. "Risthart, the lord of Teirm, has decreed that all the business owners must have their headquarters in his castle. Even though most of us conduct our business elsewhere, we still have to rent rooms there. It's nonsense, but we abide by it anyway to keep him calm. We'll be free of eavesdroppers in there; the walls are thick."

They went through the fortress's main gate and into the keep. Jeod strode to a side door and pointed to an iron ring. "You can tie the horses there. No one will bother them." When Snowfire and Cadoc were safely tethered, he opened the door with an iron key and let them inside.

Within was a long, empty hallway lit by torches set into the walls. Eragon was surprised by how cold and damp it was. When he touched the wall, his fingers slid over a layer of slime. He shivered.

Jeod snatched a torch from its bracket and led them down the hall. They stopped before a heavy, wooden door. He unlocked it and ushered them into a room dominated by a bearskin rug laden with stuffed chairs. Bookshelves stacked with leather-bound tomes covered the walls.

Jeod piled wood in the fireplace, then thrust the torch under it. The fire quickly roared. "You, old man, have some explaining to do."

Brom's face crinkled with a smile. "Who are you calling an old man? The last time I saw you there was no gray in your hair. Now it looks like it's in the final stages of decomposition."

"And you look the same as you did nearly twenty years ago. Time seems to have preserved you as a crotchety old man just to inflict wisdom upon each new generation. Enough of this! Get on with the story. That's always what you were good at," said Jeod impatiently. Eragon's ears pricked up, and he waited eagerly to hear what Brom would say.

Brom relaxed into a chair and pulled out his pipe. He slowly blew a smoke ring that turned green, darted into the fireplace, then flew up the chimney. "Do you remember what we were doing in Gil'ead?"

"Yes, of course," said Jeod. "That sort of thing is hard to forget."

"An understatement, but true nevertheless," said Brom dryly. "When we were . . . separated, I couldn't find you. In the midst of the turmoil I stumbled into a small room. There wasn't anything extraordinary in it—just crates and boxes—but out of curiosity, I rummaged around anyway. Fortune smiled on me that hour, for I found what we had been searching for." An expression of shock ran over Jeod's face. "Once it was in my hands, I couldn't wait for you. At any second I might have been discovered, and all lost. Disguising myself as best I could, I fled the city and ran to the . . ." Brom hesitated and glanced at Eragon, then said, "ran to our friends. They stored it in a vault, for safekeeping, and made me promise to care for whomever received it. Until the day when my skills would be needed, I had to disappear. No one could know that I was alive—not even you—though it grieved me to pain you unnecessarily. So I went north and hid in Carvahall."

183

Eragon clenched his jaw, infuriated that Brom was deliberately keeping him in the dark.

Jeod frowned and asked, "Then our . . . friends knew that you were alive all along?"

"Yes."

He sighed. "I suppose the ruse was unavoidable, though I wish they had told me. Isn't Carvahall farther north, on the other side of the Spine?" Brom inclined his head. For the first time, Jeod inspected Eragon. His gray eyes took in every detail. He raised his eyebrows and said, "I assume, then, that you are fulfilling your duty."

Brom shook his head. "No, it's not that simple. It was stolen a while ago—at least that's what I presume, for I haven't received word from our friends, and I suspect their messengers were waylaid—so I decided to find out what I could. Eragon happened to be traveling in the same direction. We have stayed together for a time now."

Jeod looked puzzled. "But if they haven't sent any messages, how could you know that it was—"

Brom overrode him quickly, saying, "Eragon's uncle was brutally killed by the Ra'zac. They burned his home and nearly caught him in the process. He deserves revenge, but they have left us without a trail to follow, and we need help finding them."

Jeod's face cleared. "I see. . . . But why have you come here? I don't know where the Ra'zac might be hiding, and anyone who does won't tell you."

Standing, Brom reached into his robe and pulled out the Ra'zac's flask. He tossed it to Jeod. "There's Seithr oil in there—the dangerous kind. The Ra'zac were carrying it. They lost it by the trail, and we happened to find it. We need to see Teirm's shipping records so we can trace the Empire's purchases of the oil. That should tell us where the Ra'zac's lair is."

Lines appeared on Jeod's face as he thought. He pointed at the books on the shelves. "Do you see those? They are all records from my business. *One* business. You have gotten yourself into a project that could take months. There is another, greater problem. The records you seek are held in this castle, but only Brand, Risthart's administrator of trade, sees them on a regular basis. Traders such as myself aren't allowed to handle them. They fear that we will falsify the results, thus cheating the Empire of its precious taxes."

"I can deal with that when the time comes," said Brom. "But we need a few days of rest before we can think about proceeding."

Jeod smiled. "It seems that it is my turn to help you. My house is yours, of course. Do you have another name while you are here?"

"Yes," said Brom, "I'm Neal, and the boy is Evan."

"Eragon," said Jeod thoughtfully. "You have a unique name. Few have ever been named after the first Rider. In my life I've read about only three people who were called such." Eragon was startled that Jeod knew the origin of his name.

Brom looked at Eragon. "Could you go check on the horses and make sure they're all right? I don't think I tied Snowfire to the ring tightly enough."

They're trying to hide something from me. The moment I leave they're going to talk about it. Eragon shoved himself out of the chair and left the room, slamming the door shut. Snowfire had not moved; the knot that held him was fine. Scratching the horses' necks, Eragon leaned sullenly against the castle wall.

It's not fair, he complained to himself. *If only I could hear what they are saying.* He jolted upright, electrified. Brom had once taught him some words that would enhance his hearing. *Keen ears aren't exactly what I want, but I should be able to make the words work. After all, look what I could do with* brisingr!

He concentrated intensely and reached for his power. Once it was within his grasp, he said, "Thverr stenr un atra eka hórna!" and imbued the words with his will. As the power rushed out of him, he heard a faint whisper in his ears, but nothing more. Disappointed, he sank back, then started as Jeod said, "—and I've been doing that for almost eight years now."

Eragon looked around. No one was there except for a few guards standing against the far wall of the keep. Grinning, he sat on the courtyard and closed his eyes.

"I never expected you to become a merchant," said Brom. "After all the time you spent in books. And finding the passageway in that manner! What made you take up trading instead of remaining a scholar?"

"After Gil'ead, I didn't have much taste for sitting in musty rooms and reading scrolls. I decided to help Ajihad as best I could, but I'm no warrior. My father was a merchant as well—you may remember that. He helped me get started. However, the bulk of my business is nothing more than a front to get goods into Surda."

"But I take it that things have been going badly," said Brom.

"Yes, none of the shipments have gotten through lately, and Tronjheim is running low on supplies. Somehow the Empire—at least I think it's them—has discovered those of us who have been helping to support Tronjheim. But I'm still not convinced that it's the Empire. No one sees any soldiers. I don't understand it. Perhaps Galbatorix hired mercenaries to harass us."

"I heard that you lost a ship recently."

"The last one I owned," answered Jeod bitterly. "Every man on it was loyal and brave. I doubt I'll ever see them again. . . . The only option I have left is to send caravans to Surda or Gil'ead—which I know won't get there, no matter how many guards I hire—or charter someone else's ship to carry the goods. But no one will take them now."

"How many merchants have been helping you?" asked Brom.

"Oh, a good number up and down the seaboard. All of them have been plagued by the same troubles. I know what you are thinking; I've pondered it many a night myself, but I cannot bear the thought of a traitor with that much knowledge and power. If there is one, we're all in jeopardy. You should return to Tronjheim."

"And take Eragon there?" interrupted Brom. "They'd tear him apart. It's the worst place he could be right now. Maybe in a few months or, even better, a year. Can you imagine how the dwarves will react? Everyone will be trying to influence him, especially Islanzadi. He and Saphira won't be safe in Tronjheim until I at least get them through tuatha du orothrim."

Dwarves! thought Eragon excitedly. *Where is this Tronjheim? And why did he tell Jeod about Saphira? He shouldn't have done that without asking me!*

"Still, I have a feeling that they are in need of your power and wisdom."

"Wisdom," snorted Brom. "I'm just what you said earlier—a crotchety old man."

"Many would disagree."

"Let them. I've no need to explain myself. No, Ajihad will have to get along without me. What I'm doing now is much more important. But the prospect of a traitor raises troubling questions.

I wonder if that's how the Empire knew where to be. . . ." His voice trailed off.

"And I wonder why I haven't been contacted about this," said Jeod.

"Maybe they tried. But if there's a traitor . . ." Brom paused. "I have to send word to Ajihad. Do you have a messenger you can trust?"

"I think so," said Jeod. "It depends on where he would have to go."

"I don't know," said Brom. "I've been isolated so long, my contacts have probably died or forgotten me. Could you send him to whoever receives your shipments?"

"Yes, but it'll be risky."

"What isn't these days? How soon can he leave?"

"He can go in the morning. I'll send him to Gil'ead. It will be faster," said Jeod. "What can he take to convince Ajihad the message comes from you?"

"Here, give your man my ring. And tell him that if he loses it, I'll personally tear his liver out. It was given to me by the queen."

"Aren't you cheery," commented Jeod.

Brom grunted. After a long silence he said, "We'd better go out and join Eragon. I get worried when he's alone. That boy has an unnatural propensity for being wherever there's trouble."

"Are you surprised?"

"Not really."

Eragon heard chairs being pushed back. He quickly pulled his mind away and opened his eyes. "What's going on?" he muttered to himself. *Jeod and other traders are in trouble for helping people the Empire doesn't favor. Brom found something in Gil'ead and went to Carvahall to hide. What could be so important that he would let his own friend think he was dead for nearly twenty years? He mentioned a queen—when there aren't any queens in the known kingdoms—and dwarves, who, as he himself told me, disappeared underground long ago.*

He wanted answers! But he would not confront Brom now and risk jeopardizing their mission. No, he would wait until they left

Teirm, and then he would persist until the old man explained his secrets. Eragon's thoughts were still whirling when the door opened.

"Were the horses all right?" asked Brom.

"Fine," said Eragon. They untied the horses and left the castle.

As they reentered the main body of Teirm, Brom said, "So, Jeod, you finally got married. And," he winked slyly, "to a lovely young woman. Congratulations."

Jeod did not seem happy with the compliment. He hunched his shoulders and stared down at the street. "Whether congratulations are in order is debatable right now. Helen isn't very happy."

"Why? What does she want?" asked Brom.

"The usual," said Jeod with a resigned shrug. "A good home, happy children, food on the table, and pleasant company. The problem is that she comes from a wealthy family; her father has invested heavily in my business. If I keep suffering these losses, there won't be enough money for her to live the way she's used to."

Jeod continued, "But please, my troubles are not your troubles. A host should never bother his guests with his own concerns. While you are in my house, I will let nothing more than an over-full stomach disturb you."

"Thank you," said Brom. "We appreciate the hospitality. Our travels have long been without comforts of any kind. Do you happen to know where we could find an inexpensive shop? All this riding has worn out our clothes."

"Of course. That's my job," said Jeod, lightening up. He talked eagerly about prices and stores until his house was in sight. Then he asked, "Would you mind if we went somewhere else to eat? It might be awkward if you came in right now."

"Whatever makes you feel comfortable," said Brom.

Jeod looked relieved. "Thanks. Let's leave your horses in my stable."

They did as he suggested, then followed him to a large tavern. Unlike the Green Chestnut, this one was loud, clean, and full of boisterous people. When the main course arrived—a stuffed suckling pig—Eragon eagerly dug into the meat, but he especially savored the potatoes, carrots, turnips, and sweet apples that accompanied it. It had been a long time since he had eaten much more than wild game.

They lingered over the meal for hours as Brom and Jeod swapped stories. Eragon did not mind. He was warm, a lively tune jangled in the background, and there was more than enough food. The spirited tavern babble fell pleasantly on his ears.

When they finally exited the tavern, the sun was nearing the horizon. "You two go ahead; I have to check on something," Eragon said. He wanted to see Saphira and make sure that she was safely hidden.

Brom agreed absently. "Be careful. Don't take too long."

"Wait," said Jeod. "Are you going outside Teirm?" Eragon hesitated, then reluctantly nodded. "Make sure you're inside the walls before dark. The gates close then, and the guards won't let you back in until morning."

"I won't be late," promised Eragon. He turned around and loped down a side street, toward Teirm's outer wall. Once out of the city, he breathed deeply, enjoying the fresh air. *Saphira!* he called. *Where are you?* She guided him off the road, to the base of a mossy cliff surrounded by maples. He saw her head poke out of the trees on the top and waved. *How am I supposed to get up there?*

If you find a clearing, I'll come down and get you.

No, he said, eyeing the cliff, *that won't be necessary. I'll just climb up.*

It's too dangerous.

And you worry too much. Let me have some fun.

Eragon pulled off his gloves and started climbing. He relished the physical challenge. There were plenty of handholds, so the ascent was easy. He was soon high above the trees. Halfway up, he stopped on a ledge to catch his breath.

Once his strength returned, he stretched up for the next handhold, but his arm was not long enough. Stymied, he searched for another crevice or ridge to grasp. There was none. He tried backing down, but his legs could not reach his last foothold. Saphira watched with unblinking eyes. He gave up and said, *I could use some help.*

This is your own fault.

Yes! I know. Are you going to get me down or not?

If I weren't around, you would be in a very bad situation.

Eragon rolled his eyes. *You don't have to tell me.*

You're right. After all, how can a mere dragon expect to tell a man like yourself what to do? In fact, everyone should stand in awe of your brilliance of finding the only dead end. Why, if you had started a few feet in either direction, the path to the top would have been clear. She cocked her head at him, eyes bright.

All right! I made a mistake. Now can you please get me out of here? he pleaded. She pulled her head back from the edge of the cliff. After a moment he called, "Saphira?" Above him were only swaying trees. "Saphira! Come back!" he roared.

With a loud crash Saphira barreled off the top of the cliff, flipping around in midair. She floated down to Eragon like a huge bat and grabbed his shirt with her claws, scratching his back. He let go of the rocks as she yanked him up in the air. After a brief flight, she set him down gently on the top of the cliff and tugged her claws out of his shirt.

Foolishness, said Saphira gently.

Eragon looked away, studying the landscape. The cliff provided a wonderful view of their surroundings, especially the foaming sea, as well as protection against unwelcome eyes. Only birds would see Saphira here. It was an ideal location.

Is Brom's friend trustworthy? she asked.

I don't know. Eragon proceeded to recount the day's events. *There are forces circling us that we aren't aware of. Sometimes I wonder if we can ever understand the true motives of the people around us. They all seem to have secrets.*

It is the way of the world. Ignore all the schemes and trust in the nature of each person. Brom is good. He means us no harm. We don't have to fear his plans.

I hope so, he said, looking down at his hands.

This finding of the Ra'zac through writing is a strange way of tracking, she remarked. *Would there be a way to use magic to see the records without being inside the room?*

I'm not sure. You would have to combine the word for seeing with distance . . . or maybe light and distance. Either way, it seems rather difficult. I'll ask Brom.

That would be wise. They lapsed into tranquil silence.

You know, we may have to stay here awhile.

Saphira's answer held a hard edge. *And as always, I will be left to wait outside.*

That is not how I want it. Soon enough we will travel together again.

May that day come quickly.

Eragon smiled and hugged her. He noticed then how rapidly the light was fading. *I have to go now, before I'm locked out of Teirm. Hunt tomorrow, and I will see you in the evening.*

She spread her wings. *Come, I will take you down.* He got onto her scaly back and held on tightly as she launched off the cliff, glided over the trees, then landed on a knoll. Eragon thanked her and ran back to Teirm.

He came into sight of the portcullis just as it was beginning to lower. Calling for them to wait, he put on a burst of speed and slipped inside seconds before the gateway slammed closed. "Ya cut that a little close," observed one of the guards.

"It won't happen again," assured Eragon, bending over to catch his breath. He wound his way through the darkened city to Jeod's house. A lantern hung outside like a beacon.

A plump butler answered his knock and ushered him inside without a word. Tapestries covered the stone walls. Elaborate rugs dotted the polished wood floor, which glowed with the light from three gold candelabra hanging from the ceiling. Smoke drifted through the air and collected above.

"This way, sir. Your friend is in the study."

They passed scores of doorways until the butler opened one to reveal a study. Books covered the room's walls. But unlike those in Jeod's office, these came in every size and shape. A fireplace filled with blazing logs warmed the room. Brom and Jeod sat before an oval writing desk, talking amiably. Brom raised his pipe and said in a jovial voice, "Ah, here you are. We were getting worried about you. How was your walk?"

I wonder what put him in such a good mood? Why doesn't he just come out and ask how Saphira is? "Pleasant, but the guards almost locked me outside the city. And Teirm is big. I had trouble finding this house."

Jeod chuckled. "When you have seen Dras-Leona, Gil'ead, or even Kuasta, you won't be so easily impressed by this small ocean city. I like it here, though. When it's not raining, Teirm is really quite beautiful."

Eragon turned to Brom. "Do you have any idea how long we'll be here?"

Brom spread his palms upward. "That's hard to tell. It depends on whether we can get to the records and how long it will take us to find what we need. We'll all have to help; it will be a huge job. I'll talk with Brand tomorrow and see if he'll let us examine the records."

"I don't think I'll be able to help," Eragon said, shifting uneasily.

"Why not?" asked Brom. "There will be plenty of work for you."

Eragon lowered his head. "I can't read."

Brom straightened with disbelief. "You mean Garrow never taught you?"

"He knew how to read?" asked Eragon, puzzled. Jeod watched them with interest.

"Of course he did," snorted Brom. "The proud fool—what was he thinking? I should have realized that he wouldn't have taught you. He probably considered it an unnecessary luxury." Brom scowled and pulled at his beard angrily. "This sets my plans back, but not irreparably. I'll just have to teach you how to read. It won't take long if you put your mind to it."

Eragon winced. Brom's lessons were usually intense and brutally direct. *How much more can I learn at one time?* "I suppose it's necessary," he said ruefully.

"You'll enjoy it. There is much you can learn from books and scrolls," said Jeod. He gestured at the walls. "These books are my friends, my companions. They make me laugh and cry and find meaning in life."

"It sounds intriguing," admitted Eragon.

"Always the scholar, aren't you?" asked Brom.

Jeod shrugged. "Not anymore. I'm afraid I've degenerated into a bibliophile."

"A what?" asked Eragon.

"One who loves books," explained Jeod, and resumed conversing with Brom. Bored, Eragon scanned the shelves. An elegant book set with gold studs caught his attention. He pulled it off the shelf and stared at it curiously.

It was bound in black leather carved with mysterious runes. Eragon ran his fingers over the cover and savored its cool smoothness. The letters inside were printed with a reddish glossy ink. He let the pages slip past his fingers. A column of script, set off from the regular lettering, caught his eye. The words were long and flowing, full of graceful lines and sharp points.

Eragon took the book to Brom. "What is this?" he asked, pointing to the strange writing.

Brom looked at the page closely and raised his eyebrows in surprise. "Jeod, you've expanded your collection. Where did you get this? I haven't seen one in ages."

Jeod strained his neck to see the book. "Ah yes, the *Domia abr Wyrda*. A man came through here a few years ago and tried to sell it to a trader down by the wharves. Fortunately, I happened to be there and was able to save the book, along with his neck. He didn't have a clue what it was."

"It's odd, Eragon, that you should pick up this book, the *Dominance of Fate*," said Brom. "Of all the items in this house, it's probably

193

worth the most. It details a complete history of Alagaësia—starting long before the elves landed here and ending a few decades ago. The book is very rare and is the best of its kind. When it was written, the Empire decried it as blasphemy and burned the author, Heslant the Monk. I didn't think any copies still existed. The lettering you asked about is from the ancient language."

"What does it say?" asked Eragon.

It took Brom a moment to read the writing. "It's part of an elven poem that tells of the years they fought the dragons. This excerpt describes one of their kings, Ceranthor, as he rides into battle. The elves love this poem and tell it regularly—though you need three days to do it properly—so that they won't repeat the mistakes of the past. At times they sing it so beautifully it seems the very rocks will cry."

Eragon returned to his chair, holding the book gently. *It's amazing that a man who is dead can talk to people through these pages. As long as this book survives, his ideas live. I wonder if it contains any information about the Ra'zac?*

He browsed through the book while Brom and Jeod spoke. Hours passed, and Eragon began to drowse. Out of pity for his exhaustion, Jeod bid them good night. "The butler will show you to your rooms."

On the way upstairs, the servant said, "If you need assistance, use the bellpull next to the bed." He stopped before a cluster of three doors, bowed, then backed away.

As Brom entered the room on the right, Eragon asked, "Can I talk to you?"

"You just did, but come in anyway."

Eragon closed the door behind himself. "Saphira and I had an idea. Is there—"

Brom stopped him with a raised hand and pulled the curtains shut over the window. "When you talk of such things, you would do well to make sure that no unwelcome ears are present."

"Sorry," said Eragon, berating himself for the slip. "Anyway, is it possible to conjure up an image of something that you can't see?"

Brom sat on the edge of his bed. "What you are talking about is called scrying. It is quite possible and extremely helpful in some situations, but it has a major drawback. You can only observe people, places, and things that you've already seen. If you were to scry the Ra'zac, you'd see them all right, but not their surroundings. There are other problems as well. Let's say that you wanted to view a page in a book, one that you'd already seen. You could only see the page if the book were open to it. If the book were closed when you tried this, the page would appear completely black."

"Why can't you view objects that you haven't seen?" asked Eragon. Even with those limitations, he realized, scrying could be very useful. *I wonder if I could view something leagues away and use magic to affect what was happening there?*

"Because," said Brom patiently, "to scry, you have to know what you're looking at and where to direct your power. Even if a stranger was described to you, it would still be nigh impossible to view him, not to mention the ground and whatever else might be around him. You have to know *what* you're going to scry before you *can* scry it. Does that answer your question?"

Eragon thought for a moment. "But how is it done? Do you conjure up the image in thin air?"

"Not usually," said Brom, shaking his white head. "That takes more energy than projecting it onto a reflective surface like a pool of water or a mirror. Some Riders used to travel everywhere they could, trying to see as much as possible. Then, whenever war or some other calamity occurred, they would be able to view events throughout Alagaësia."

"May I try it?" asked Eragon.

Brom looked at him carefully. "No, not now. You're tired, and scrying takes lots of strength. I will tell you the words, but you must promise not to attempt it tonight. And I'd rather you wait until we leave Teirm; I have more to teach you."

Eragon smiled. "I promise."

"Very well." Brom bent over and very quietly whispered, "Draumr kópa" into Eragon's ear.

Eragon took a moment to memorize the words. "Maybe after we've left Teirm, I can scry Roran. I would like to know how he's doing. I'm afraid that the Ra'zac might go after him."

"I don't mean to frighten you, but that's a distinct possibility," said Brom. "Although Roran was gone most of the time the Ra'zac were in Carvahall, I'm sure that they asked questions about him. Who knows, they may have even met him while they were in Therinsford. Either way, I doubt their curiosity is sated. You're on the loose, after all, and the king is probably threatening them with terrible punishment if you aren't found. If they get frustrated enough, they'll go back and interrogate Roran. It's only a matter of time."

"If that's true, then the only way to keep Roran safe is to let the Ra'zac know where I am so that they'll come after me instead of him."

"No, that won't work either. You're not thinking," admonished Brom. "If you can't understand your enemies, how can you expect to anticipate them? Even if you exposed your location, the Ra'zac would *still* chase Roran. Do you know why?"

Eragon straightened and tried to consider every possibility. "Well, if I stay in hiding long enough, they might get frustrated and capture Roran to force me to reveal myself. If that didn't work, they'd kill him just to hurt me. Also, if I become a public enemy of the Empire, they might use him as bait to catch me. And if I met with Roran and they found out about it, they would torture him to find out where I was."

"Very good. You figured that out quite nicely," said Brom.

"But what's the solution? I can't let him be killed!"

Brom clasped his hands loosely. "The solution is quite obvious. Roran is going to have to learn how to defend himself. That may sound hard-hearted, but as you pointed out, you cannot risk meeting with him. You may not remember this—you were half delirious at the time—but when we left Carvahall, I told you that I had left a warning letter for Roran so he won't be totally unprepared for danger. If he has any sense at all, when the Ra'zac show up in Carvahall again, he'll take my advice and flee."

"I don't like this," said Eragon unhappily.

"Ah, but you forget something."

"What?" he demanded.

"There is some good in all of this. The king cannot afford to have a Rider roaming around that he does not control. Galbatorix is the only known Rider alive besides yourself, but he would like another one under his command. Before he tries to kill you or Roran, he will offer you the chance to serve him. Unfortunately, if he ever gets close enough to make that proposition, it will be far too late for you to refuse and still live."

"You call that some good!"

"It's all that's protecting Roran. As long as the king doesn't know which side you've chosen, he won't risk alienating you by harming your cousin. Keep that firmly in mind. The Ra'zac killed Garrow, but I think it was an ill-considered decision on their part. From what I know of Galbatorix, he would not have approved it unless he gained something from it."

"And how will I be able to deny the king's wishes when he is threatening me with death?" asked Eragon sharply.

Brom sighed. He went to his nightstand and dipped his fingers in a basin of rose water. "Galbatorix wants your willing cooperation. Without that, you're worse than useless to him. So the question becomes, If you are ever faced with this choice, are you willing to die for what you believe in? For that is the only way you will deny him."

The question hung in the air.

Brom finally said, "It's a difficult question and not one you can answer until you're faced with it. Keep in mind that many people have died for their beliefs; it's actually quite common. The real courage is in living and suffering for what you believe."

The Witch and
the Werecat

It was late in the morning when Eragon woke. He dressed, washed his face in the basin, then held the mirror up and brushed his hair into place. Something about his reflection made him stop and look closer. His face had changed since he had run out of Carvahall just a short while ago. Any baby fat was gone now, stripped away by traveling, sparring, and training. His cheekbones were more prominent, and the line of his jaw was sharper. There was a slight cast to his eyes that, when he looked closely, gave his face a wild, alien appearance. He held the mirror at arm's length, and his face resumed its normal semblance—but it still did not seem quite his own.

A little disturbed, he slung his bow and quiver across his back, then left the room. Before he had reached the end of the hall, the butler caught up with him and said, "Sir, Neal left with my master for the castle earlier. He said that you could do whatever you want today because he will not return until this evening."

Eragon thanked him for the message, then eagerly began exploring Teirm. For hours he wandered the streets, entering every shop that struck his fancy and chatting with various people. Eventually he was forced back to Jeod's by his empty stomach and lack of money.

When he reached the street where the merchant lived, he stopped at the herbalist's shop next door. It was an unusual place for a store. The other shops were down by the city wall, not crammed between expensive houses. He tried to look in the windows, but they were covered with a thick layer of crawling plants on the interior. Curious, he went inside.

At first he saw nothing because the store was so dark, but then his eyes adjusted to the faint greenish light that filtered through the windows. A colorful bird with wide tail feathers and a sharp, powerful beak looked at Eragon inquisitively from a cage near the window. The walls were covered with plants; vines clung to the ceiling, obscuring all but an old chandelier, and on the floor was a large pot with a yellow flower. A collection of mortars, pestles, metal bowls, and a clear crystal ball the size of Eragon's head rested on a long counter.

He walked to the counter, carefully stepping around complex machines, crates of rocks, piles of scrolls, and other objects he did not recognize. The wall behind the counter was covered with drawers of every size. Some of them were no larger than his smallest finger, while others were big enough for a barrel. There was a foot-wide gap in the shelves far above.

A pair of red eyes suddenly flashed from the dark space, and a large, fierce cat leapt onto the counter. It had a lean body with powerful shoulders and oversized paws. A shaggy mane surrounded its angular face; its ears were tipped with black tufts. White fangs curved down over its jaw. Altogether, it did not look like any cat Eragon had ever seen. It inspected him with shrewd eyes, then flicked its tail dismissively.

On a whim, Eragon reached out with his mind and touched the cat's consciousness. Gently, he prodded it with his thoughts, trying to make it understand that he was a friend.

You don't have to do that.

Eragon looked around in alarm. The cat ignored him and licked a paw. *Saphira? Where are you?* he asked. No one answered. Puzzled, he leaned against the counter and reached for what looked like a wood rod.

That wouldn't be wise.

Stop playing games, Saphira, he snapped, then picked up the rod.

A shock of electricity exploded through his body, and he fell to the floor, writhing. The pain slowly faded, leaving him gasping for air. The cat jumped down and looked at him.

You aren't very smart for a Dragon Rider. I did warn you.

You said that! exclaimed Eragon. The cat yawned, then stretched and sauntered across the floor, weaving its way between objects.

Who else?

But you're just a cat! he objected.

The cat yowled and stalked back to him. It jumped on his chest and crouched there, looking down at him with gleaming eyes. Eragon tried to sit up, but it growled, showing its fangs. *Do I look like other cats?*

No . . .

Then what makes you think I am one? Eragon started to say something, but the creature dug its claws into his chest. *Obviously your education has been neglected. I—to correct your mistake—am a werecat. There aren't many of us left, but I think even a farm boy should have heard of us.*

I didn't know you were real, said Eragon, fascinated. A werecat! He was indeed fortunate. They were always flitting around the edges of stories, keeping to themselves and occasionally giving advice. If the legends were true, they had magical powers, lived longer than humans, and usually knew more than they told.

The werecat blinked lazily. *Knowing is independent of being. I did not know you existed before you bumbled in here and ruined my nap. Yet that doesn't mean you weren't real before you woke me.*

Eragon was lost by its reasoning. *I'm sorry I disturbed you.*

I was getting up anyway, it said. It leapt back onto the counter and licked its paw. *If I were you, I wouldn't hold on to that rod much longer. It's going to shock you again in a few seconds.*

He hastily put the rod back where he had found it. *What is it?*

A common and boring artifact, unlike myself.

But what's it for?

Didn't you find out? The werecat finished cleaning its paw, stretched once more, then jumped back up to its sleeping place. It sat down, tucked its paws under its breast, and closed its eyes, purring.

Wait, said Eragon, *what's your name?*

One of the werecat's slanted eyes cracked open. *I go by many names. If you are looking for my proper one, you will have to seek elsewhere.* The eye closed. Eragon gave up and turned to leave. *However, you may call me Solembum.*

Thank you, said Eragon seriously. Solembum's purring grew louder.

The door to the shop swung open, letting in a beam of sunlight. Angela entered with a cloth bag full of plants. Her eyes flickered at Solembum and she looked startled. "He says you talked with him."

"You can talk with him, too?" asked Eragon.

She tossed her head. "Of course, but that doesn't mean he'll say anything back." She set her plants on the counter, then walked behind it and faced him. "He likes you. That's unusual. Most of the time Solembum doesn't show himself to customers. In fact, he says that you show some promise, given a few years of work."

"Thanks."

"It's a compliment, coming from him. You're only the third person to come in here who has been able to speak with him. The first was a woman, many years ago; the second was a blind beggar; and now you. But I don't run a store just so I can prattle on. Is there anything you want? Or did you only come in to look?"

"Just to look," said Eragon, still thinking about the werecat. "Besides, I don't really need any herbs."

"That's not all I do," said Angela with a grin. "The rich fool lords pay me for love potions and the like. I never claim that they work, but for some reason they keep coming back. But I don't think you need those chicaneries. Would you like your fortune told? I do that, too, for all the rich fool ladies."

Eragon laughed. "No, I'm afraid my fortune is pretty much unreadable. And I don't have any money."

Angela looked at Solembum curiously. "I think . . ." She gestured at the crystal ball resting on the counter. "That's only for show anyway—it doesn't do anything. But I do have . . . Wait here; I'll be right back." She hurried into a room at the back of the shop.

She came back, breathless, holding a leather pouch, which she set on the counter. "I haven't used these for so long, I almost forgot where they were. Now, sit across from me and I'll show you why I went to all this trouble." Eragon found a stool and sat. Solembum's eyes glowed from the gap in the drawers.

Angela laid a thick cloth on the counter, then poured a handful of smooth bones, each slightly longer than a finger, onto it. Runes and symbols were inscribed along their sides. "These," she said, touching them gently, "are the knucklebones of a dragon. Don't ask where I got them; it is a secret I won't reveal. But unlike tea leaves, crystal balls, or even divining cards, these have true power. They do not lie, though understanding what they say is . . . complicated. If you wish, I will cast and read them for you. But understand that to know one's fate can be a terrible thing. You must be sure of your decision."

Eragon looked at the bones with a feeling of dread. *There lies what was once one of Saphira's kin. To know one's fate . . . How can I make this decision when I don't know what lies in wait for me and whether I will like it? Ignorance is indeed bliss.* "Why do you offer this?" he asked.

"Because of Solembum. He may have been rude, but the fact that he spoke to you makes you special. He *is* a werecat, after all. I offered to do this for the other two people who talked with him. Only the woman agreed to it. Selena was her name. Ah, she regretted it, too. Her fortune was bleak and painful. I don't think she believed it—not at first."

Emotion overcame Eragon, bringing tears to his eyes. "Selena," he whispered to himself. His mother's name. *Could it have been her? Was her destiny so horrible that she had to abandon me?* "Do you remember anything about her fortune?" he asked, feeling sick.

Angela shook her head and sighed. "It was so long ago that the details have melted into the rest of my memory, which isn't as good as it used to be. Besides, I'll not tell you what I do remember. That was for her and her alone. It was sad, though; I've never forgotten the look on her face."

Eragon closed his eyes and struggled to regain control of his emotions. "Why do you complain about your memory?" he asked to distract himself. "You're not that old."

Dimples appeared on Angela's cheeks. "I'm flattered, but don't be deceived; I'm much older than I look. The appearance of youth probably comes from having to eat my own herbs when times are lean."

Smiling, Eragon took a deep breath. *If that was my mother and she could bear to have her fortune told, I can too.* "Cast the bones for me," he said solemnly.

Angela's face became grave as she grasped the bones in each hand. Her eyes closed, and her lips moved in a soundless murmur. Then she said powerfully, *"Manin! Wyrda! Hugin!"* and tossed the bones onto the cloth. They fell all jumbled together, gleaming in the faint light.

The words rang in Eragon's ears; he recognized them from the ancient language and realized with apprehension that to use them for magic, Angela must be a witch. She had not lied; this was a true fortunetelling. Minutes slowly passed as she studied the bones.

Finally, Angela leaned back and heaved a long sigh. She wiped her brow and pulled out a wineskin from under the counter. "Do you want some?" she asked. Eragon shook his head. She shrugged and drank deeply. "This," she said, wiping her mouth, "is the hardest reading I've ever done. You were right. Your future is nigh impossible to see. I've never known of anyone's fate being so tangled and clouded. I was, however, able to wrestle a few answers from it."

Solembum jumped onto the counter and settled there, watching them both. Eragon clenched his hands as Angela pointed to one of the bones. "I will start here," she said slowly, "because it is the clearest to understand."

The symbol on the bone was a long horizontal line with a circle resting on it. "Infinity or long life," said Angela quietly. "This is the first time I have ever seen it come up in someone's future. Most of the time it's the aspen or the elm, both signs that a person will live a normal span of years. Whether this means that you will live forever or that you will only have an extraordinarily long life, I'm not sure. Whatever it foretells, you may be sure that many years lie ahead of you."

No surprises there—I am a Rider, thought Eragon. Was Angela only going to tell him things he already knew?

"Now the bones grow harder to read, as the rest are in a confused pile." Angela touched three of them. "Here the wandering path, lightning bolt, and sailing ship all lie together—a pattern I've never seen, only heard of. The wandering path shows that there are many choices in your future, some of which you face even now. I see great battles raging around you, some of them fought for your sake. I see the mighty powers of this land struggling to control your will and destiny. Countless possible futures await you—all of them filled with blood and conflict—but only one will bring you happiness and peace. Beware of losing your way, for you are one of the few who are truly free to choose their own fate. That freedom is a gift, but it is also a responsibility more binding than chains."

Then her face grew sad. "And yet, as if to counteract that, here is the lightning bolt. It is a terrible omen. There is a doom upon you, but of what sort I know not. Part of it lies in a death—one that rapidly approaches and will cause you much grief. But the rest awaits in a great journey. Look closely at this bone. You can see how its end rests on that of the sailing ship. That is impossible to misunderstand. Your fate will be to leave this land forever. Where you will end up I know not, but you will never again stand in Alagaësia. This is inescapable. It will come to pass even if you try to avoid it."

Her words frightened Eragon. *Another death . . . who must I lose now?* His thoughts immediately went to Roran. Then he thought about his homeland. *What could ever force me to leave? And where would I go? If there are lands across the sea or to the east, only the elves know of them.*

Angela rubbed her temples and breathed deeply. "The next bone is easier to read and perhaps a bit more pleasant." Eragon examined it and saw a rose blossom inscribed between the horns of a crescent moon.

Angela smiled and said, "An epic romance is in your future, extraordinary, as the moon indicates—for that is a magical symbol—and strong enough to outlast empires. I cannot say if this passion will end happily, but your love is of noble birth and heritage. She is powerful, wise, and beautiful beyond compare."

Of noble birth, thought Eragon in surprise. *How could that ever happen? I have no more standing than the poorest of farmers.*

"Now for the last two bones, the tree and the hawthorn root, which cross each other strongly. I wish that this were not so—it can only mean more trouble—but betrayal is clear. And it will come from within your family."

"Roran wouldn't do that!" objected Eragon abruptly.

"I wouldn't know," said Angela carefully. "But the bones have never lied, and that is what they say."

Doubt wormed into Eragon's mind, but he tried to ignore it. What reason would there ever be for Roran to turn on him? Angela put a comforting hand on his shoulder and offered him the wineskin again. This time Eragon accepted the drink, and it made him feel better.

"After all that, death might be welcome," he joked nervously. *Betrayal from Roran? It couldn't happen! It won't!*

"It might be," said Angela solemnly, then laughed slightly. "But you shouldn't fret about what has yet to occur. The only way the future can harm us is by causing worry. I guarantee that you'll feel better once you're out in the sun."

"Perhaps." *Unfortunately,* he reflected wryly, *nothing she said will make sense until it has already happened. If it really does,* he amended himself. "You used words of power," he noted quietly.

Angela's eyes flashed. "What I wouldn't give to see how the rest of your life plays out. You can speak to werecats, know of the ancient language, and have a most interesting future. Also, few young men with empty pockets and rough traveling clothes can expect to be loved by a noblewoman. Who are you?"

Eragon realized that the werecat must not have told Angela that he was a Rider. He almost said, "Evan," but then changed his mind and simply stated, "I am Eragon."

Angela arched her eyebrows. "Is that who you are or your name?" she asked.

"Both," said Eragon with a small smile, thinking of his namesake, the first Rider.

"Now I'm all the more interested in seeing how your life will unfold. Who was the ragged man with you yesterday?"

Eragon decided that one more name couldn't hurt. "His name is Brom."

A guffaw suddenly burst out of Angela, doubling her over in mirth. She wiped her eyes and took a sip of wine, then fought off another attack of merriment. Finally, gasping for breath, she forced out, "Oh . . . that one! I had no idea!"

"What is it?" demanded Eragon.

"No, no, don't be upset," said Angela, hiding a smile. "It's only that—well, he is known by those in my profession. I'm afraid that the poor man's doom, or future if you will, is something of a joke with us."

"Don't insult him! He's a better man than any you could find!" snapped Eragon.

"Peace, peace," chided Angela with amusement. "I know that. If we meet again at the right time I'll be sure to tell you about it. But in the meantime you should—" She stopped speaking as Solembum padded between them. The werecat stared at Eragon with unblinking eyes.

Yes? Eragon asked, irritated.

Listen closely and I will tell you two things. When the time comes and you need a weapon, look under the roots of the Menoa tree. Then, when all seems lost and your power is insufficient, go to the rock of Kuthian and speak your name to open the Vault of Souls.

Before Eragon could ask what Solembum meant, the werecat walked away, waving his tail ever so gracefully. Angela tilted her head, coils of dense hair shadowing her forehead. "I don't know what he said, and I don't want to know. He spoke to you and only you. Don't tell anyone else."

"I think I have to go," said Eragon, shaken.

"If you want to," said Angela, smiling again. "You are welcome to stay here as long as you like, especially if you buy some of my goods. But go if you wish; I'm sure that we've given you enough to ponder for a while."

"Yes." Eragon quickly made his way to the door. "Thank you for reading my future." *I think.*

"You're welcome," said Angela, still smiling.

Eragon exited the shop and stood in the street, squinting until his eyes adjusted to the brightness. It was a few minutes before he could think calmly about what he had learned. He started walking, his steps unconsciously quickening until he dashed out of Teirm, feet flying as he headed to Saphira's hiding place.

He called to her from the base of the cliff. A minute later she soared down and bore him up to the cliff top. When they were both safely on the ground, Eragon told her about his day. *And so,* he concluded, *I think Brom's right; I always seem to be where there's trouble.*

You should remember what the werecat told you. It's important.

How do you know? he asked curiously.

I'm not sure, but the names he used feel powerful. Kuthian, she said, rolling the word around. *No, we should not forget what he said.*

Do you think I should tell Brom?

It's your choice, but think of this: he has no right to know your future. To tell him of Solembum and his words will only raise questions you may not want to answer. And if you decided to only ask him what those words mean, he will want to know where you learned them. Do you think you can lie convincingly to him?

No, admitted Eragon. *Maybe I won't say anything. Still, this might be too important to hide.* They talked until there was nothing more to say. Then they sat together companionably, watching the trees until dusk.

Eragon hurried back to Teirm and was soon knocking on Jeod's door. "Is Neal back?" he asked the butler.

"Yes sir. I believe he's in the study right now."

"Thank you," said Eragon. He strode to the room and peeked inside. Brom was sitting before the fire, smoking. "How did it go?" asked Eragon.

"Bloody awful!" growled Brom around his pipe.

"So you talked to Brand?"

"Not that it did any good. This *administrator* of trade is the worst sort of bureaucrat. He abides by every rule, delights in making his own whenever it can inconvenience someone, and at the same time believes that he's doing good."

"Then he won't let us see the records?" asked Eragon.

"No," snapped Brom, exasperated. "Nothing I could say would sway him. He even refused bribes! Substantial ones, too. I didn't think I would ever meet a noble who wasn't corrupt. Now that I have, I find that I prefer them when they're greedy bastards." He puffed furiously on his pipe and mumbled a steady stream of curses.

When he seemed to have calmed, Eragon asked tentatively, "So, what now?"

"I'm going to take the next week and teach you how to read."

"And after that?"

A smile split Brom's face. "After that, we're going to give Brand a nasty surprise." Eragon pestered him for details, but Brom refused to say more.

Dinner was held in a sumptuous dining room. Jeod sat at one end of the table, a hard-eyed Helen at the other. Brom and Eragon were seated between them, which Eragon felt was a dangerous place to be. Empty chairs were on either side of him, but he didn't mind the space. It helped to protect him from the glares of their hostess.

The food was served quietly, and Jeod and Helen wordlessly began eating. Eragon followed suit, thinking, *I've had cheerier meals at funerals*. And he had, in Carvahall. He remembered many burials that had been sad, yes, but not unduly so. This was different; he could feel simmering resentment pouring from Helen throughout the dinner.

OF READING AND PLOTS

Brom scratched a rune on parchment with charcoal, then showed it to Eragon. "This is the letter *a*," he said. "Learn it."

With that, Eragon began the task of becoming literate. It was difficult and strange and pushed his intellect to its limits, but he enjoyed it. Without anything else to do and with a good—if sometimes impatient—teacher, he advanced rapidly.

A routine was soon established. Every day Eragon got up, ate in the kitchen, then went to the study for his lessons, where he labored to memorize the sounds of the letters and the rules of writing. It got so that when he closed his eyes, letters and words danced in his mind. He thought of little else during that time.

Before dinner, he and Brom would go behind Jeod's house and spar. The servants, along with a small crowd of wide-eyed children, would come and watch. If there was any time afterward, Eragon would practice magic in his room, with the curtains securely closed.

His only worry was Saphira. He visited her every evening, but it was not enough time together for either of them. During the day, Saphira spent most of her time leagues away searching for food; she could not hunt near Teirm without arousing suspicion. Eragon did what he could to help her, but he knew that the only solution for both her hunger and loneliness was to leave the city far behind.

Every day more grim news poured into Teirm. Arriving merchants told of horrific attacks along the coast. There were reports of powerful people disappearing from their houses in the night and their mangled corpses being discovered in the morning. Eragon often heard Brom and Jeod discussing the events in an undertone, but they always stopped when he came near.

The days passed quickly, and soon a week had gone by. Eragon's skills were rudimentary, but he could now read whole pages without asking Brom's help. He read slowly, but he knew that speed would come with time. Brom encouraged him, "No matter, you'll do fine for what I have planned."

It was afternoon when Brom summoned both Jeod and Eragon to the study. Brom gestured at Eragon. "Now that you can help us, I think it's time to move ahead."

"What do you have in mind?" asked Eragon.

A fierce smile danced on Brom's face. Jeod groaned. "I know that look; it's what got us into trouble in the first place."

"A slight exaggeration," said Brom, "but not unwarranted. Very well, this is what we'll do. . . ."

We leave tonight or tomorrow, Eragon told Saphira from within his room.

This is unexpected. Will you be safe during this venture?

Eragon shrugged. *I don't know. We may end up fleeing Teirm with soldiers on our heels.* He felt her worry and tried to reassure her. *It'll be all right. Brom and I can use magic, and we're good fighters.*

He lay on the bed and stared at the ceiling. His hands shook slightly, and there was a lump in his throat. As sleep overcame him, he felt a wave of confusion. *I don't want to leave Teirm,* he suddenly realized. *The time I've spent here has been—almost normal. What I would give not to keep uprooting myself. To stay here and be like everyone else would be wonderful.* Then, another thought raged through him, *But I'll never be able to while Saphira is around. Never.*

Dreams owned his consciousness, twisting and directing it to their whims. At times he quaked with fear; at others he laughed with pleasure. Then something changed—it was as though his eyes had been opened for the first time—and a dream came to him that was clearer than any before.

He saw a young woman, bent over by sorrow, chained in a cold, hard cell. A beam of moonlight shone through a barred window set high in the wall and fell on her face. A single tear rolled down her cheek, like a liquid diamond.

Eragon rose with a start and found himself crying uncontrollably before sinking back into a fitful sleep.

THIEVES IN THE CASTLE

Eragon woke from his nap to a golden sunset. Red and orange beams of light streamed into the room and fell across the bed. They warmed his back pleasantly, making him reluctant to move. He dozed, but the sunlight crept off him, and he grew cold. The sun sank below the horizon, lighting the sea and sky with color. *Almost time!*

He slung his bow and quiver on his back, but left Zar'roc in the room; the sword would only slow him, and he was averse to using it. If he had to disable someone, he could use magic or an arrow. He pulled his jerkin over his shirt and laced it securely.

He waited nervously in his room until the light faded. Then he entered the hallway and shrugged so the quiver settled comfortably across his back. Brom joined him, carrying his sword and staff.

Jeod, dressed in a black doublet and hose, was waiting for them outside. From his waist swung an elegant rapier and a leather pouch. Brom eyed the rapier and observed, "That toad sticker is too thin for any real fighting. What will you do if someone comes after you with a broadsword or a flamberge?"

"Be realistic," said Jeod. "None of the guards has a flamberge. Besides, this *toad sticker* is faster than a broadsword."

Brom shrugged. "It's your neck."

They walked casually along the street, avoiding watchmen and soldiers. Eragon was tense and his heart pounded. As they passed Angela's shop, a flash of movement on the roof caught his attention,

213

but he saw no one. His palm tingled. He looked at the roof again, but it was still empty.

Brom led them along Teirm's outer wall. By the time they reached the castle, the sky was black. The sealed walls of the fortress made Eragon shiver. He would hate to be imprisoned there. Jeod silently took the lead and strode up to the gates, trying to look at ease. He pounded on the gate and waited.

A small grille slid open and a surly guard peered out. "Ya?" he grunted shortly. Eragon could smell rum on his breath.

"We need to get in," said Jeod.

The guard peered at Jeod closer. "Wha' for?"

"The boy here left something very valuable in my office. We have to retrieve it immediately." Eragon hung his head, shamefaced.

The guard frowned, clearly impatient to get back to his bottle. "Ah, wha'ever," he said, swinging his arm. "Jus' make sure 'n give 'im a good beating f'r me."

"I'll do that," assured Jeod as the guard unbolted a small door set into the gate. They entered the keep, then Brom handed the guard a few coins.

"Thank'ee," mumbled the man, tottering away. As soon as he was gone, Eragon pulled his bow from its tube and strung it. Jeod quickly let them into the main part of the castle. They hurried toward their destination, listening carefully for any soldiers on patrol. At the records room, Brom tried the door. It was locked. He put his hand against the door and muttered a word that Eragon did not recognize. It swung open with a faint click. Brom grabbed a torch from the wall, and they darted inside, closing the door quietly.

The squat room was filled with wooden racks piled high with scrolls. A barred window was set in the far wall. Jeod threaded his way between the racks, running his eyes over the scrolls. He halted at the back of the room. "Over here," he said. "These are the shipping records for the past five years. You can tell the date by the wax seals on the corner."

"So what do we do now?" asked Eragon, pleased that they had made it so far without being discovered.

"Start at the top and work down," said Jeod. "Some scrolls only deal with taxes. You can ignore those. Look for anything that mentions Seithr oil." He took a length of parchment from his pouch and stretched it out on the floor, then set a bottle of ink and a quill pen next to it. "So we can keep track of whatever we find," he explained.

Brom scooped an armful of scrolls from the top of the rack and piled them on the floor. He sat and unrolled the first one. Eragon joined him, positioning himself so he could see the door. The tedious work was especially difficult for him, as the cramped script on the scrolls was different from the printing Brom had taught him.

By looking only for the names of ships that sailed in the northern areas, they winnowed out many of the scrolls. Even so, they moved down the rack slowly, recording each shipment of Seithr oil as they located it.

It was quiet outside the room, except for the occasional watchman. Suddenly, Eragon's neck prickled. He tried to keep working, but the uneasy feeling remained. Irritated, he looked up and jerked with surprise—a small boy crouched on the windowsill. His eyes were slanted, and a sprig of holly was woven into his shaggy black hair.

Do you need help? asked a voice in Eragon's head. His eyes widened with shock. It sounded like Solembum.

Is that you? he asked incredulously.

Am I someone else?

Eragon gulped and concentrated on his scroll. *If my eyes don't deceive me, you are.*

The boy smiled slightly, revealing pointed teeth. *What I look like doesn't change who I am. You don't think I'm called a werecat for nothing, do you?*

What are you doing here? Eragon asked.

The werecat tilted his head and considered whether the question was worth an answer. *That depends on what you are doing here. If you are reading those scrolls for entertainment, then I suppose there isn't any reason for my visit. But if what you are doing is unlawful and you don't want to be discovered, I might be here to warn you that the guard whom you bribed just told his replacement about you and that this second official of the Empire has sent soldiers to search for you.*

Thank you for telling me, said Eragon.

Told you something, did I? I suppose I did. And I suggest you make use of it.

The boy stood and tossed back his wild hair. Eragon asked quickly, *What did you mean last time about the tree and the vault?*

Exactly what I said.

Eragon tried to ask more, but the werecat vanished through the window. He announced abruptly, "There are soldiers looking for us."

"How do you know?" asked Brom sharply.

"I listened in on the guard. His replacement just sent men to search for us. We have to get out of here. They've probably already discovered that Jeod's office is empty."

"Are you sure?" asked Jeod.

"Yes!" said Eragon impatiently. "They're on their way."

Brom snatched another scroll from the rack. "No matter. We have to finish this now!" They worked furiously for the next minute, scanning the records as fast as they could. As the last scroll was finished, Brom threw it back onto the rack, and Jeod jammed his parchment, ink, and pen into his pouch. Eragon grabbed the torch.

They raced from the room and shut the door, but just as it closed they heard the heavy tramp of soldiers' boots at the end of the hall. They turned to leave, but Brom hissed furiously, "Damnation! It's not locked." He put his hand against the door. The lock clicked at the same time three armed soldiers came into view.

"Hey! Get away from that door!" shouted one of them. Brom stepped back, assuming a surprised expression. The three men marched up to them. The tallest one demanded, "Why are you trying to get into the records?" Eragon gripped his bow tighter and prepared to run.

"I'm afraid we lost our way." The strain was evident in Jeod's voice. A drop of sweat rolled down his neck.

The soldier glared at them suspiciously. "Check inside the room," he ordered one of his men.

Eragon held his breath as the soldier stepped up to the door, tried to open it, then pounded on it with his mailed fist. "It's locked, sir."

The leader scratched his chin. "Ar'right, then. I don't know what you were up to, but as long as the door's locked, I guess you're free to go. Come on." The soldiers surrounded them and marched them back to the keep.

I can't believe it, thought Eragon. *They're helping us get away!*

At the main gates, the soldier pointed and said, "Now, you walk through those and don't try anything. We'll be watching. If you have to come back, wait until morning."

"Of course," promised Jeod.

Eragon could feel the guards' eyes boring into their backs as they hurried out of the castle. The moment that the gates closed behind them, a triumphant grin stretched across his face, and he jumped into the air. Brom shot him a cautioning look and growled, "Walk back to the house normally. You can celebrate there."

Chastised, Eragon adopted a staid demeanor, but inside he still bubbled with energy. Once they had hurried back to the house and into the study, Eragon exclaimed, "We did it!"

"Yes, but now we have to figure out if it was worth the trouble," said Brom. Jeod took a map of Alagaësia from the shelves and unrolled it on the desk.

On the left side of the map, the ocean extended to the unknown west. Along the coast stretched the Spine, an immense length of mountains. The Hadarac Desert filled the center of the map—the east end was blank. Somewhere in that void hid the Varden. To the south was Surda, a small country that had seceded from the Empire after the Riders' fall. Eragon had been told that Surda secretly supported the Varden.

Near Surda's eastern border was a mountain range labeled Beor

Mountains. Eragon had heard of them in many stories—they were supposed to be ten times the height of the Spine, though he privately believed that was exaggeration. The map was empty to the east of the Beors.

Five islands rested off the coast of Surda: Nía, Parlim, Uden, Illium, and Beirland. Nía was no more than an outcropping of rock, but Beirland, the largest, had a small town. Farther up, near Teirm, was a jagged island called Sharktooth. And high to the north was one more island, immense and shaped like a knobby hand. Eragon knew its name without even looking: Vroengard, the ancestral home of the Riders—once a place of glory, but now a looted, empty shell haunted by strange beasts. In the center of Vroengard was the abandoned city of Dorú Areaba.

Carvahall was a small dot at the top of Palancar Valley. Level with it, but across the plains, sprawled the forest Du Weldenvarden. Like the Beor Mountains, its eastern end was unmapped. Parts of Du Weldenvarden's western edge had been settled, but its heart lay mysterious and unexplored. The forest was wilder than the Spine; the few who braved its depths often came back raving mad, or not at all.

Eragon shivered as he saw Urû'baen in the center of the Empire. King Galbatorix ruled from there with his black dragon, Shruikan, by his side. Eragon put his finger on Urû'baen. "The Ra'zac are sure to have a hiding place here."

"You had better hope that that isn't their only sanctuary," said Brom flatly. "Otherwise you'll never get near them." He pushed the rustling map flat with his wrinkled hands.

Jeod took the parchment out of his pouch and said, "From what I saw in the records, there have been shipments of Seithr oil to every major city in the Empire over the past five years. As far as I can tell, all of them might have been ordered by wealthy jewelers. I'm not sure how we can narrow down the list without more information."

Brom swept a hand over the map. "I think we can eliminate some cities. The Ra'zac have to travel wherever the king wants, and I'm sure he keeps them busy. If they're expected to go anywhere at anytime, the only reasonable place for them to stay is at a cross-roads where they can reach every part of the country fairly easily." He was excited now and paced the room. "This crossroads has to be large enough so the Ra'zac will be inconspicuous. It also has to have enough trade so any unusual requests—special food for their mounts, for example—will go unnoticed."

"That makes sense," said Jeod, nodding. "Under those conditions, we can ignore most of the cities in the north. The only big ones are Teirm, Gil'ead, and Ceunon. I know they're not in Teirm, and I doubt that the oil has been shipped farther up the coast to Narda—it's too small. Ceunon is too isolated . . . only Gil'ead remains."

"The Ra'zac might be there," conceded Brom. "It would have a certain irony."

"It would at that," Jeod acknowledged softly.

"What about southern cities?" asked Eragon.

"Well," said Jeod. "There's obviously Urû'baen, but that's an unlikely destination. If someone were to die from Seithr oil in Galbatorix's court, it would be all too easy for an earl or some other lord to discover that the Empire had been buying large amounts of it. That still leaves many others, any one of which could be the one we want."

"Yes," said Eragon, "but the oil wasn't sent to all of them. The parchment only lists Kuasta, Dras-Leona, Aroughs, and Belatona. Kuasta wouldn't work for the Ra'zac; it's on the coast and surrounded by mountains. Aroughs is isolated like Ceunon, though it is a center of trade. That leaves Belatona and Dras-Leona, which are rather close together. Of the two, I think Dras-Leona is the likelier. It's larger and better situated."

"And that's where nearly all the goods of the Empire pass through at one time or another, including Teirm's," said Jeod. "It would be a good place for the Ra'zac to hide."

"So . . . Dras-Leona," said Brom as he sat down and lit his pipe. "What do the records show?"

Jeod looked at the parchment. "Here it is. At the beginning of the year, three shipments of Seithr oil were sent to Dras-Leona. Each shipment was only two weeks apart, and the records say they were all transported by the same merchant. The same thing happened last year and the year before that. I doubt any one jeweler, or even a group of them, has the money for so much oil."

"What about Gil'ead?" asked Brom, raising an eyebrow.

"It doesn't have the same access to the rest of the Empire. And," Jeod tapped the parchment, "they've only received the oil twice in recent years." He thought for a moment, then said, "Besides, I think we forgot something—Helgrind."

Brom nodded. "Ah yes, the Dark Gates. It's been many years since I've thought of it. You're right, that would make Dras-Leona perfect for the Ra'zac. I guess it's decided, then; that's where we'll go."

Eragon sat abruptly, too drained of emotion to even ask what Helgrind was. *I thought I would be happy to resume the hunt. Instead, I feel like an abyss has opened up before me. Dras-Leona! It's so far away. . . .*

The parchment crackled as Jeod slowly rolled up the map. He handed it to Brom and said, "You'll need this, I'm afraid. Your expeditions often take you into obscure regions." Nodding, Brom accepted the map. Jeod clapped him on the shoulder. "It doesn't feel right that you will leave without me. My heart expects to go along, but the rest of me reminds me of my age and responsibilities."

"I know," said Brom. "But you have a life in Teirm. It is time for the next generation to take up the standard. You've done your part; be happy."

"What of you?" asked Jeod. "Does the road ever end for you?"

A hollow laugh escaped Brom's lips. "I see it coming, but not for a while." He extinguished his pipe, and they left for their rooms, exhausted. Before he fell asleep, Eragon contacted Saphira to relate the night's adventures.

A COSTLY MISTAKE

I n the morning Eragon and Brom retrieved their saddlebags from the stable and prepared to depart. Jeod greeted Brom while Helen watched from the doorway. With grave looks, the two men clasped hands. "I'll miss you, old man," said Jeod.

"And you I," said Brom thickly. He bowed his white head and then turned to Helen. "Thank you for your hospitality; it was most gracious." Her face reddened. Eragon thought she was going to slap him. Brom continued, unperturbed, "You have a good husband; take care of him. There are few men as brave and as determined as he is. But even he cannot weather difficult times without support from those he loves." He bowed again and said gently, "Only a suggestion, dear lady."

Eragon watched as indignation and hurt crossed Helen's face. Her eyes flashed as she shut the door brusquely. Sighing, Jeod ran his fingers through his hair. Eragon thanked him for all his help, then mounted Cadoc. With the last farewells said, he and Brom departed.

At Teirm's south gate, the guards let them through without a second glance. As they rode under the giant outer wall, Eragon saw movement in a shadow. Solembum was crouched on the ground, tail twitching. The werecat followed them with inscrutable eyes. As the city receded into the distance, Eragon asked, "What are werecats?"

Brom looked surprised at the question. "Why the sudden curiosity?"

"I heard someone mention them in Teirm. They're not real, are they?" said Eragon, pretending ignorance.

"They are quite real. During the Riders' years of glory, they were as renowned as the dragons. Kings and elves kept them as companions—yet the werecats were free to do what they chose. Very little has ever been known about them. I'm afraid that their race has become rather scarce recently."

"Could they use magic?" asked Eragon.

"No one's sure, but they could certainly do unusual things. They always seemed to know what was going on and somehow or another manage to get themselves involved." Brom pulled his hood up to block a chill wind.

"What's Helgrind?" asked Eragon, after a moment's thought.

"You'll see when we get to Dras-Leona."

When Teirm was out of sight, Eragon reached out with his mind and called, *Saphira!* The force of his mental shout was so strong that Cadoc flicked his ears in annoyance.

Saphira answered and sped toward them with all of her strength. Eragon and Brom watched as a dark blur rushed from a cloud, then heard a dull roar as Saphira's wings flared open. The sun shone behind the thin membranes, turning them translucent and silhouetting the dark veins. She landed with a blast of air.

Eragon tossed Cadoc's reins to Brom. "I'll join you for lunch."

Brom nodded, but seemed preoccupied. "Have a good time," he said, then looked at Saphira and smiled. "It's good to see you again."

And you too.

Eragon hopped onto Saphira's shoulders and held on tightly as she bounded upward. With the wind at her tail, Saphira sliced through the air. *Hold on*, she warned Eragon, and letting out a wild bugle, she soared in a great loop. Eragon yelled with excitement as he flung his arms in the air, holding on only with his legs.

I didn't know I could stay on while you did that without being strapped into the saddle, he said, grinning fiercely.

Neither did I, admitted Saphira, laughing in her peculiar way. Eragon hugged her tightly, and they flew a level path, masters of the sky.

By noon his legs were sore from riding bareback, and his hands and face were numb from the cold air. Saphira's scales were always warm to the touch, but she could not keep him from getting chilled. When they landed for lunch, he buried his hands in his clothes and found a warm, sunny place to sit. As he and Brom ate, Eragon asked Saphira, *Do you mind if I ride Cadoc?* He had decided to question Brom further about his past.

No, but tell me what he says. Eragon was not surprised that Saphira knew his plans. It was nearly impossible to hide anything from her when they were mentally linked. When they finished eating, she flew away as he joined Brom on the trail. After a time, Eragon slowed Cadoc and said, "I need to talk to you. I wanted to do it when we first arrived in Teirm, but I decided to wait until now."

"About what?" asked Brom.

Eragon paused. "There's a lot going on that I don't understand. For instance, who are your 'friends,' and why were you hiding in Carvahall? I trust you with my life—which is why I'm still traveling with you—but I need to know more about who you are and what you are doing. What did you steal in Gil'ead, and what is the tuatha du orothrim that you're taking me through? I think that after all that's happened, I deserve an explanation."

"You eavesdropped on us."

"Only once," said Eragon.

"I see that you have yet to learn proper manners," said Brom grimly, tugging on his beard. "What makes you think that this concerns you?"

"Nothing, really," said Eragon shrugging. "Just it's an odd coincidence that you happened to be hiding in Carvahall when I found Saphira's egg *and* that you also know so much dragonlore. The more I think about it, the less likely it seems. There were other clues that I mostly ignored, but they're obvious now that I look back. Like how you knew of the Ra'zac in the first place and why they ran away when you approached. And I can't help but wonder if you had something to do with the appearance of Saphira's egg. There's a lot

223

you haven't told us, and Saphira and I can't afford to ignore anything that might be dangerous."

Dark lines appeared on Brom's forehead as he reined Snowfire to a halt. "You won't wait?" he asked. Eragon shook his head mulishly. Brom sighed. "This wouldn't be a problem if you weren't so suspicious, but I suppose that you wouldn't be worth my time if you were otherwise." Eragon was unsure if he should take that as a compliment. Brom lit his pipe and slowly blew a plume of smoke into the air. "I'll tell you," he said, "but you have to understand that I cannot reveal everything." Eragon started to protest, but Brom cut him off. "It's not out of a desire to withhold information, but because I won't give away secrets that aren't mine. There are other stories woven in with this narrative. You'll have to talk with the others involved to find out the rest."

"Very well. Explain what you can," said Eragon.

"Are you sure?" asked Brom. "There are reasons for my secretiveness. I've tried to protect you by shielding you from forces that would tear you apart. Once you know of them and their purposes, you'll never have the chance to live quietly. You will have to choose sides and make a stand. Do you really want to know?"

"I cannot live my life in ignorance," said Eragon quietly.

"A worthy goal. . . . Very well: there is a war raging in Alagaësia between the Varden and the Empire. Their conflict, however, reaches far beyond any incidental armed clashes. They are locked in a titanic power struggle . . . centered around you."

"Me?" said Eragon, disbelieving. "That's impossible. I don't have anything to do with either of them."

"Not yet," said Brom, "but your very existence is the focus of their battles. The Varden and the Empire aren't fighting to control this land or its people. Their goal is to control the next generation of Riders, of whom you are the first. Whoever controls these Riders will become the undisputed master of Alagaësia."

Eragon tried to absorb Brom's statements. It seemed incomprehensible that so many people would be interested in him and

Saphira. No one besides Brom had thought he was that important. The whole concept of the Empire and Varden fighting over him was too abstract for him to grasp fully. Objections quickly formed in his mind. "But all the Riders were killed except for the Forsworn, who joined Galbatorix. As far as I know, even those are now dead. And you told me in Carvahall that no one knows if there are still dragons in Alagaësia."

"I lied about the dragons," said Brom flatly. "Even though the Riders are gone, there are still three dragon eggs left—all of them in Galbatorix's possession. Actually there are only two now, since Saphira hatched. The king salvaged the three during his last great battle with the Riders."

"So there may soon be two new Riders, both of them loyal to the king?" asked Eragon with a sinking feeling.

"Exactly," said Brom. "There is a deadly race in progress. Galbatorix is desperately trying to find the people for whom his eggs will hatch, while the Varden are employing every means to kill his candidates or steal the eggs."

"But where did Saphira's egg come from? How could anyone have gotten it away from the king? And why do you know all of this?" asked Eragon, bewildered.

"So many questions," laughed Brom bitterly. "There is another chapter to all this, one that took place long before you were born. Back then I was a bit younger, though perhaps not as wise. I hated the Empire—for reasons I'll keep to myself—and wanted to damage it in any way I could. My fervor led me to a scholar, Jeod, who claimed to have discovered a book that showed a secret passageway into Galbatorix's castle. I eagerly brought Jeod to the Varden—who are my 'friends'—and they arranged to have the eggs stolen."

The Varden!

"However, something went amiss, and our thief got only one egg. For some reason he fled with it and didn't return to the Varden. When he wasn't found, Jeod and I were sent to bring him and the egg back." Brom's eyes grew distant, and he spoke in a curious voice. "That was the start of one of the greatest searches in history. We raced against the Ra'zac and Morzan, last of the Forsworn and the king's finest servant."

"Morzan!" interrupted Eragon. "But he was the one who betrayed the Riders to Galbatorix!" *And that happened so long ago! Morzan must have been ancient.* It disturbed him to be reminded of how long Riders lived.

"So?" asked Brom, raising an eyebrow. "Yes, he was old, but strong and cruel. He was one of the king's first followers and by far his most loyal. As there had been blood between us before, the hunt for the egg turned into a personal battle. When it was located in Gil'ead, I rushed there and fought Morzan for possession. It was a terrible contest, but in the end I slew him. During the conflict I was separated from Jeod. There was no time to search for him, so I took the egg and bore it to the Varden, who asked me to train whomever became the new Rider. I agreed and decided to hide in Carvahall—which I had been to several times before—until the Varden contacted me. I was never summoned."

"Then how did Saphira's egg appear in the Spine? Was another one stolen from the king?" asked Eragon.

Brom grunted. "Small chance of that. He has the remaining two guarded so thoroughly that it would be suicide to try and steal them. No, Saphira was taken from the Varden, and I think I know how. To protect the egg, its guardian must have tried to send it to me with magic.

"The Varden haven't contacted me to explain how they lost the egg, so I suspect that their runners were intercepted by the Empire and the Ra'zac were sent in their place. I'm sure they were quite eager to find me, as I've managed to foil many of their plans."

"Then the Ra'zac didn't know about me when they arrived in Carvahall," said Eragon with wonder.

"That's right," replied Brom. "If that ass Sloan had kept his mouth shut, they might not have found out about you. Events could have turned out quite differently. In a way I have you to thank for my life. If the Ra'zac hadn't become so preoccupied with you, they might have caught me unawares, and that would have been the end of Brom the storyteller. The only reason they ran was because I'm stronger than the two of them, especially during the day. They must have planned to drug me during the night, then question me about the egg."

"You sent a message to the Varden, telling them about me?"

"Yes. I'm sure they'll want me to bring you to them as soon as possible."

"But you're not going to, are you?"

Brom shook his head. "No, I'm not."

"Why not? Being with the Varden must be safer than chasing after the Ra'zac, especially for a new Rider."

Brom snorted and looked at Eragon with fondness. "The Varden are dangerous people. If we go to them, you will be entangled in their politics and machinations. Their leaders may send you on missions just to make a point, even though you might not be strong enough for them. I want you to be well prepared before you go anywhere near the Varden. At least while we pursue the Ra'zac, I don't have to worry about someone poisoning your water. This is the lesser of two evils. And," he said with a smile, "it keeps you happy while I train you. . . . Tuatha du orothrim is just a stage in your instruction. I *will* help you find—and perhaps even kill—the Ra'zac, for they are as much my enemies as yours. But then you will have to make a choice."

"And that would be . . . ?" asked Eragon warily.

"Whether to join the Varden," said Brom. "If you kill the Ra'zac, the only ways for you to escape Galbatorix's wrath will be to seek the Varden's protection, flee to Surda, or plead for the king's mercy and join his forces. Even if you don't kill the Ra'zac, you will still face this choice eventually."

Eragon knew the best way to gain sanctuary might be to join the Varden, but he did not want to spend his entire life fighting the Empire like they did. He mulled over Brom's comments, trying to consider them from every angle. "You still didn't explain how you know so much about dragons."

"No, I didn't, did I?" said Brom with a crooked smile. "That will have to wait for another time."

Why me? Eragon asked himself. What made him so special that he should become a Rider? "Did you ever meet my mother?" he blurted.

Brom looked grave. "Yes, I did."

"What was she like?"

The old man sighed. "She was full of dignity and pride, like Garrow. Ultimately it was her downfall, but it was one of her greatest gifts nevertheless. . . . She always helped the poor and the less fortunate, no matter what her situation."

"You knew her well?" asked Eragon, startled.

"Well enough to miss her when she was gone."

As Cadoc plodded along, Eragon tried to recall when he had thought that Brom was just a scruffy old man who told stories. For the first time Eragon understood how ignorant he had been.

He told Saphira what he had learned. She was intrigued by Brom's revelations, but recoiled from the thought of being one of Galbatorix's possessions. At last she said, *Aren't you glad that you didn't stay in Carvahall? Think of all the interesting experiences you would have missed!* Eragon groaned in mock distress.

When they stopped for the day, Eragon searched for water while Brom made dinner. He rubbed his hands together for warmth as he walked in a large circle, listening for a creek or spring. It was gloomy and damp between the trees.

He found a stream a ways from the camp, then crouched on the bank and watched the water splash over the rocks, dipping in his fingertips. The icy mountain water swirled around his skin, numbing it. *It doesn't care what happens to us, or anyone else,* thought Eragon. He shivered and stood.

An unusual print on the opposing stream bank caught his attention. It was oddly shaped and very large. Curious, he jumped across

the stream and onto a rock shelf. As he landed, his foot hit a patch
of damp moss. He grabbed a branch for support, but it broke, and
he thrust out his hand to break his fall. He felt his right wrist crack
as he hit the ground. Pain lanced up his arm.

A steady stream of curses came out from behind his clenched
teeth as he tried not to howl. Half blind with pain, he curled on the
ground, cradling his arm. *Eragon!* came Saphira's alarmed cry. *What
happened?*

Broke my wrist . . . did something stupid . . . fell.

I'm coming, said Saphira.

No—I can make it back. Don't . . . come. Trees too close for . . . wings.

She sent him a brief image of her tearing the forest apart to get
at him, then said, *Hurry.*

Groaning, he staggered upright. The print was pressed deeply
into the ground a few feet away. It was the mark of a heavy, nail-
studded boot. Eragon instantly remembered the tracks that had surrounded the pile of bodies in Yazuac. "Urgal," he spat, wishing that
Zar'roc was with him; he could not use his bow with only one hand.
His head snapped up, and he shouted with his mind, *Saphira!
Urgals! Keep Brom safe.*

Eragon leapt back over the stream and raced toward their camp,
yanking out his hunting knife. He saw potential enemies behind
every tree and bush. *I hope there's only one Urgal.* He burst into the
camp, ducking as Saphira's tail swung overhead. "Stop. It's me!" he
yelled.

Oops, said Saphira. Her wings were folded in front of her chest
like a wall.

"Oops?" growled Eragon, running to her. "You could've killed
me! Where's Brom?"

"I'm right here," snapped Brom's voice from behind Saphira's
wings. "Tell your crazy dragon to release me; she won't listen to me."

"Let him go!" said Eragon, exasperated. "Didn't you tell him?"

No, she said sheepishly. *You just said to keep him safe.* She lifted
her wings, and Brom stepped forward angrily.

"I found an Urgal footprint. And it's fresh."

Brom immediately turned serious. "Saddle the horses. We're leaving." He put out the fire, but Eragon did not move. "What's wrong with your arm?"

"My wrist is broken," he said, swaying.

Brom cursed and saddled Cadoc for him. He helped Eragon onto the horse and said, "We have to put a splint on your arm as soon as possible. Try not to move your wrist until then." Eragon gripped the reins tightly with his left hand. Brom said to Saphira, "It's almost dark; you might as well fly right overhead. If Urgals show up, they'll think twice about attacking with you nearby."

They'd better, or else they won't think again, remarked Saphira as she took off.

The light was disappearing quickly, and the horses were tired, but they spurred them on without respite. Eragon's wrist, swollen and red, continued to throb. A mile from the camp, Brom halted. "Listen," he said.

Eragon heard the faint call of a hunting horn behind them. As it fell silent, panic gripped him. "They must have found where we were," said Brom, "and probably Saphira's tracks. They will chase us now. It's not in their nature to let prey escape." Then two horns winded. They were closer. A chill ran through Eragon. "Our only chance is to run," said Brom. He raised his head to the sky, and his face blanked as he called Saphira.

She rushed out of the night sky and landed. "Leave Cadoc. Go with her. You'll be safer," commanded Brom.

"What about you?" Eragon protested.

"I'll be fine. Now go!" Unable to muster the energy to argue, Eragon climbed onto Saphira while Brom lashed Snowfire and rode away with Cadoc. Saphira flew after him, flapping above the galloping horses.

Eragon clung to Saphira as best he could; he winced whenever her movements jostled his wrist. The horns blared nearby, bringing a fresh wave of terror. Brom crashed through the underbrush, forcing the horses to their limits. The horns trumpeted in unison close behind him, then were quiet.

Minutes passed. *Where are the Urgals?* wondered Eragon. A horn sounded, this time in the distance. He sighed in relief, resting against Saphira's neck, while on the ground Brom slowed his headlong rush. *That was close,* said Eragon.

Yes, but we cannot stop until— Saphira was interrupted as a horn blasted directly underneath them. Eragon jerked in surprise, and Brom resumed his frenzied retreat. Horned Urgals, shouting with coarse voices, barreled along the trail on horses, swiftly gaining ground. They were almost in sight of Brom; the old man could not outrun them. *We have to do something!* exclaimed Eragon.

What?

Land in front of the Urgals!

Are you crazy? demanded Saphira.

Land! I know what I'm doing, said Eragon. *There isn't time for anything else. They're going to overtake Brom!*

Very well. Saphira pulled ahead of the Urgals, then turned, preparing to drop onto the trail. Eragon reached for his power and felt the familiar resistance in his mind that separated him from the magic. He did not try to breach it yet. A muscle twitched in his neck.

As the Urgals pounded up the trail, he shouted, "Now!" Saphira abruptly folded her wings and dropped straight down from above the trees, landing on the trail in a spray of dirt and rocks.

The Urgals shouted with alarm and yanked on their horses' reins. The animals went stiff-legged and collided into each other, but the Urgals quickly untangled themselves to face Saphira with bared weapons. Hate crossed their faces as they glared at her. There were twelve of them, all ugly, jeering brutes. Eragon wondered why they did not flee. He had thought that the sight of Saphira would frighten them away. *Why are they waiting? Are they going to attack us or not?*

He was shocked when the largest Urgal advanced and spat, "Our master wishes to speak with you, human!" The monster spoke in deep, rolling gutturals.

It's a trap, warned Saphira before Eragon could say anything. *Don't listen to him.*

At least let's find out what he has to say, he reasoned, curious, but extremely wary. "Who is your master?" he asked.

The Urgal sneered. "His name does not deserve to be given to one as low as yourself. He rules the sky and holds dominance over the earth. You are no more than a stray ant to him. Yet he has decreed that you shall be brought before him, *alive*. Take heart that you have become worthy of such notice!"

"I'll never go with you nor any of my enemies!" declared Eragon, thinking of Yazuac. "Whether you serve Shade, Urgal, or some twisted fiend I've not heard of, I have no wish to parley with him."

"That is a grave mistake," growled the Urgal, showing his fangs. "There is no way to escape him. Eventually you will stand before our master. If you resist, he will fill your days with agony."

Eragon wondered who had the power to bring the Urgals under one banner. Was there a third great force loose in the land—along with the Empire and the Varden? "Keep your offer and tell your master that the crows can eat his entrails for all I care!"

Rage swept through the Urgals; their leader howled, gnashing his teeth. "We'll drag you to him, then!" He waved his arm and the Urgals rushed at Saphira. Raising his right hand, Eragon barked, "Jierda!"

No! cried Saphira, but it was too late.

The monsters faltered as Eragon's palm glowed. Beams of light lanced from his hand, striking each of them in the gut. The Urgals were thrown through the air and smashed into trees, falling sense-less to the ground.

Fatigue suddenly drained Eragon of strength, and he tumbled off Saphira. His mind felt hazy and dull. As Saphira bent over him, he realized that he might have gone too far. The energy needed to lift and throw twelve Urgals was enormous. Fear engulfed him as he struggled to stay conscious.

At the edge of his vision he saw one of the Urgals stagger to his feet, sword in hand. Eragon tried to warn Saphira, but he was too weak. *No . . .* , he thought feebly. The Urgal crept toward Saphira until he was well past her tail, then raised his sword to strike her neck. *No! . . .* Saphira whirled on the monster, roaring savagely. Her talons slashed with blinding speed. Blood spurted everywhere as the Urgal was rent in two.

Saphira snapped her jaws together with finality and returned to Eragon. She gently wrapped her bloody claws around his torso, then growled and jumped into the air. The night blurred into a pain-filled streak. The hypnotic sound of Saphira's wings put him in a bleary trance: up, down; up, down; up, down. . . .

When Saphira eventually landed, Eragon was dimly aware of Brom talking with her. Eragon could not understand what they said, but a decision must have been reached because Saphira took off again.

His stupor yielded to sleep that covered him like a soft blanket.

VISION OF PERFECTION

Eragon twisted under the blankets, reluctant to open his eyes. He dozed, then a fuzzy thought entered his mind . . . *How did I get here?* Confused, he pulled the blankets tighter and felt something hard on his right arm. He tried to move his wrist. It zinged with pain. *The Urgals!* He bolted upright.

He lay in a small clearing that was empty save a small campfire heating a stew-filled pot. A squirrel chattered on a branch. His bow and quiver rested alongside the blankets. Attempting to stand made him grimace, as his muscles were feeble and sore. There was a heavy splint on his bruised right arm.

Where is everyone? he wondered forlornly. He tried to call Saphira, but to his alarm could not feel her. Ravenous hunger gripped him, so he ate the stew. Still hungry, he looked for the saddlebags, hoping to find a chunk of bread. Neither the saddlebags nor the horses were in the clearing. *I'm sure there's a good reason for this*, he thought, suppressing a surge of uneasiness.

He wandered about the clearing, then returned to his blankets and rolled them up. Without anything better to do, he sat against a tree and watched the clouds overhead. Hours passed, but Brom and Saphira did not show up. *I hope nothing's wrong.*

As the afternoon dragged on, Eragon grew bored and started to explore the surrounding forest. When he became tired, he rested under a fir tree that leaned against a boulder with a bowl-shaped depression filled with clear dew water.

Eragon stared at the water and thought about Brom's instructions for scrying. *Maybe I can see where Saphira is. Brom said that scrying takes a lot of energy, but I'm stronger than he is. . . .* He breathed deeply and closed his eyes. In his mind he formed a picture of Saphira, making it as lifelike as possible. It was more demanding than he expected. Then he said, "Draumr kópa!" and gazed at the water.

Its surface became completely flat, frozen by an invisible force. The reflections disappeared and the water became clear. On it shimmered an image of Saphira. Her surroundings were pure white, but Eragon could see that she was flying. Brom sat on her back, beard streaming, sword on his knees.

Eragon tiredly let the image fade. *At least they're safe.* He gave himself a few minutes to recuperate, then leaned back over the water. *Roran, how are you?* In his mind he saw his cousin clearly. Impulsively, he drew upon the magic and uttered the words.

The water grew still, then the image formed on its surface. Roran appeared, sitting on an invisible chair. Like Saphira, his surroundings were white. There were new lines on Roran's face—he looked more like Garrow than ever before. Eragon held the image in place as long as he could. *Is Roran in Therinsford? He's certainly nowhere I've been.*

The strain of using magic had brought beads of sweat to his forehead. He sighed and for a long time was content just to sit. Then an absurd notion struck him. *What if I tried to scry something I created with my imagination or saw in a dream?* He smiled. *Perhaps I'd be shown what my own consciousness looks like.*

It was too tempting an idea to pass by. He knelt by the water once again. *What shall I look for?* He considered a few things, but discarded them all when he remembered his dream about the woman in the cell.

After fixing the scene in his mind, he spoke the words and watched the water intently. He waited, but nothing happened. Disappointed, he was about to release the magic when inky blackness swirled across the water, covering the surface. The image of a lone candle flickered in the darkness, brightening to illuminate a

235

stone cell. The woman from his dream was curled up on a cot in one corner. She lifted her head, dark hair falling back, and stared directly at Eragon. He froze, the force of her gaze keeping him in place. Chills ran up his spine as their eyes locked. Then the woman trembled and collapsed limply.

The water cleared. Eragon rocked back on his heels, gasping. "This can't be." *She shouldn't be real; I only dreamed about her! How could she know I was looking at her? And how could I have scryed into a dungeon that I've never seen?* He shook his head, wondering if any of his other dreams had been visions.

The rhythmic thump of Saphira's wings interrupted his thoughts. He hurried back to the clearing, arriving just as Saphira landed. Brom was on her back, as Eragon had seen, but his sword was now bloody. Brom's face was contorted; the edges of his beard were stained red. "What happened?" asked Eragon, afraid that he had been wounded.

"What happened?" roared the old man. "I've been trying to clean up your mess!" He slashed the air with the sword, flinging drops of blood along its arc. "Do you know what you did with that little trick of yours? Do you?"

"I stopped the Urgals from catching you," said Eragon, a pit forming in his stomach.

"Yes," growled Brom, "but that piece of magic nearly killed you! You've been sleeping for two days. There were twelve Urgals. *Twelve!* But that didn't stop you from trying to throw them all the way to Teirm, now did it? What were you thinking? Sending a rock through each of their heads would have been the smart thing to do. But no, you had to knock them unconscious so they could run away later. I've spent the last two days trying to track them down. Even with Saphira, three escaped!"

"I didn't want to kill them," said Eragon, feeling very small.

"It wasn't a problem in Yazuac."

"There was no choice then, and I couldn't control the magic. This time it just seemed . . . extreme."

"Extreme!" cried Brom. "It's not extreme when they wouldn't show you the same mercy. And why, oh why, did you *show* yourself to them?"

"You said that they had found Saphira's footprints. It didn't make any difference if they saw me," said Eragon defensively.

Brom stabbed his sword into the dirt and snapped, "I said they had *probably* found her tracks. We didn't know for certain. They might have believed they were chasing some stray travelers. But why would they think that now? After all, *you landed right in front of them!* And since you let them live, they're scrambling around the countryside with all sorts of fantastic tales! This might even get back to the Empire!" He threw his hands up. "You don't even deserve to be called a Rider after this, *boy*." Brom yanked his sword out of the ground and stomped to the fire. He took a rag from inside his robe and angrily began to clean the blade.

Eragon was stunned. He tried to ask Saphira for advice, but all she would say was, *Speak with Brom.*

Hesitantly, Eragon made his way to the fire and asked, "Would it help if I said I was sorry?"

Brom sighed and sheathed his sword. "No, it wouldn't. Your feelings can't change what happened." He jabbed his finger at Eragon's chest. "You made some very bad choices that could have dangerous repercussions. Not the least of which is that you almost died. Died, Eragon! From now on you're going to have to think. There's a reason why we're born with brains in our heads, not rocks."

Eragon nodded, abashed. "It's not as bad as you think, though; the Urgals already knew about me. They had orders to capture me."

Astonishment widened Brom's eyes. He stuck his unlit pipe in his mouth. "No, it's not as bad as I thought. It's worse! Saphira told me you had talked with the Urgals, but she didn't mention this." The words tumbled out of Eragon's mouth as he quickly described the confrontation. "So they have some sort of leader now, eh?" questioned Brom.

Eragon nodded.

"And you just defied his wishes, insulted him, and attacked his men?" Brom shook his head. "I didn't think it could get any worse. If the Urgals had been killed, your rudeness would have gone unnoticed, but now it'll be impossible to ignore. Congratulations, you just made enemies with one of the most powerful beings in Alagaësia."

"All right, I made a mistake," said Eragon sullenly.

"Yes, you did," agreed Brom, eyes flashing. "What has me worried, though, is who this Urgal leader is."

Shivering, Eragon asked softly, "What happens now?"

There was an uncomfortable pause. "Your arm is going to take at least a couple of weeks to heal. That time would be well spent forging some sense into you. I suppose this is partially my fault. I've been teaching you *how* to do things, but not whether you *should*. It takes discretion, something you obviously lack. All the magic in Alagaësia won't help you if you don't know when to use it."

"But we're still going to Dras-Leona, right?" asked Eragon.

Brom rolled his eyes. "Yes, we can keep looking for the Ra'zac, but even if we find them, it won't do any good until you've healed." He began unsaddling Saphira. "Are you well enough to ride?"

"I think so."

"Good, then we can still cover a few miles today."

"Where are Cadoc and Snowfire?"

Brom pointed off to the side. "Over there a ways. I picketed them where there was grass." Eragon prepared to leave, then followed Brom to the horses.

Saphira said pointedly, *If you had explained what you were planning to do, none of this would have happened. I would have told you it was a bad idea not to kill the Urgals. I only agreed to do what you asked because I assumed it was halfway reasonable!*

I don't want to talk about it.

As you wish, she sniffed.

As they rode, every bump and dip in the trail made Eragon grit his teeth with discomfort. If he had been alone, he would have stopped. With Brom there, he dared not complain. Also, Brom started drilling him with difficult scenarios involving Urgals, magic, and Saphira. The imagined fights were many and varied. Sometimes a Shade or other dragons were included. Eragon discovered that it was possible to torture his body and mind at the same time. He got most of the questions wrong and became increasingly frustrated.

When they stopped for the night, Brom grumbled shortly, "It was a start." Eragon knew that he was disappointed.

MASTER OF
THE BLADE

The next day was easier on both of them. Eragon felt better and was able to answer more of Brom's questions correctly. After an especially difficult exercise, Eragon mentioned his scrying of the woman. Brom pulled on his beard. "You say she was imprisoned?"

"Yes."

"Did you see her face?" asked Brom intently.

"Not very clearly. The lighting was bad, yet I could tell that she was beautiful. It's strange; I didn't have any problem seeing her eyes. And she did look at me."

Brom shook his head. "As far as I know, it's impossible for anyone to know if they're being scryed upon."

"Do you know who she might be?" asked Eragon, surprised by the eagerness in his own voice.

"Not really," admitted Brom. "If pressed, I suppose I could come up with a few guesses, but none of them would be very likely. This dream of yours is peculiar. Somehow you managed to scry in your sleep something that you'd never seen before—without saying the words of power. Dreams do occasionally touch the spirit realm, but this is different."

"Perhaps to understand this we should search every prison and dungeon until we find the woman," bantered Eragon. He actually thought it would be a good idea. Brom laughed and rode on.

Brom's strict training filled nearly every hour as the days slowly blended into weeks. Because of his splint, Eragon was forced to use his left hand whenever they sparred. Before long he could duel as well with his left hand as he had with his right.

By the time they crossed the Spine and came to the plains, spring had crept over Alagaësia, summoning a multitude of flowers. The bare deciduous trees were russet with buds, while new blades of grass began to push up between last year's dead stalks. Birds returned from their winter absence to mate and build nests.

The travelers followed the Toark River southeast, along the edge of the Spine. It grew steadily as tributaries flowed into it from every side, feeding its bulging girth. When the river was over a league wide, Brom pointed at the silt islands that dotted the water. "We're close to Leona Lake now," he said. "It's only about two leagues away."

"Do you think we can get there before nightfall?" asked Eragon.

"We can try."

Dusk soon made the trail hard to follow, but the sound of the river at their side guided them. When the moon rose, the bright disk provided enough light to see what lay ahead.

Leona Lake looked like a thin sheet of silver beaten over the land. The water was so calm and smooth it did not even seem to be liquid. Aside from a bright strip of moonlight reflecting off the surface, it was indistinguishable from the ground. Saphira was on the rocky shore, fanning her wings to dry them. Eragon greeted her and she said, *The water is lovely—deep, cool, and clear.*

Maybe I'll go swimming tomorrow, he responded. They set up camp under a stand of trees and were soon asleep.

At dawn, Eragon eagerly rushed out to see the lake in daylight. A whitecapped expanse of water rippled with fan-shaped patterns where wind brushed it. The pure size of it delighted him. He whooped and ran to the water. *Saphira, where are you? Let's have some fun!*

The moment Eragon climbed onto her, she jumped out over the water. They soared upward, circling over the lake, but even at that height the opposing shore was not visible. *Would you like to take a bath?* Eragon casually asked Saphira.

She grinned wolfishly. *Hold on!* She locked her wings and sank to the waves, clipping the crests with her claws. The water sparkled in the sunlight as they sailed over it. Eragon whooped again. Then Saphira folded her wings and dived into the lake, her head and neck entering it like a lance.

The water hit Eragon like an icy wall, knocking out his breath and almost tearing him off Saphira. He held on tightly as she swam to the surface. With three strokes of her feet, she breached it and sent a burst of shimmering water toward the sky. Eragon gasped and shook his hair as Saphira slithered across the lake, using her tail as a rudder.

Ready?

Eragon nodded and took a deep breath, tightening his arms. This time they slid gently under the water. They could see for yards through the unclouded liquid. Saphira twisted and turned in fantastic shapes, slipping through the water like an eel. Eragon felt as if he were riding a sea serpent of legend.

Just as his lungs started to cry for air, Saphira arched her back and pointed her head upward. An explosion of droplets haloed them as she leapt into the air, wings snapping open. With two powerful flaps she gained altitude.

Wow! That was fantastic, exclaimed Eragon.

Yes, said Saphira happily. *Though it's a pity you can't hold your breath longer.*

Nothing I can do about that, he said, pressing water out of his hair. His clothes were drenched, and the wind from Saphira's wings chilled him. He pulled at his splint—his wrist itched.

Once Eragon was dry, he and Brom saddled the horses and started around Leona Lake in high spirits while Saphira playfully dived in and out of the water.

Before dinner, Eragon blocked Zar'roc's edge in preparation for their usual sparring. Neither he nor Brom moved as they waited for the other to strike first. Eragon inspected their surroundings for anything that might give him an advantage. A stick near the fire caught his attention.

Eragon swooped down, grabbed the stick, and hurled it at Brom. The splint got in his way, though, and Brom easily sidestepped the piece of wood. The old man rushed forward, swinging his sword. Eragon ducked just as the blade whistled over his head. He growled and tackled Brom ferociously.

They pitched to the ground, each struggling to stay on top. Eragon rolled to the side and swept Zar'roc over the ground at Brom's shins. Brom parried the blow with the hilt of his sword, then jumped to his feet. Twisting as he stood, Eragon attacked again, guiding Zar'roc through a complex pattern. Sparks danced from their blades as they struck again and again. Brom blocked each blow, his face tight with concentration. But Eragon could tell that he was tiring. The relentless hammering continued as each sought an opening in the other's defenses.

Then Eragon felt the battle change. Blow by blow he gained advantage; Brom's parries slowed and he lost ground. Eragon easily blocked a stab from Brom. Veins pulsed on the old man's forehead and cords bulged in his neck from the effort.

Suddenly confident, Eragon swung Zar'roc faster than ever, weaving a web of steel around Brom's sword. With a burst of speed, he smashed the flat of his blade against Brom's guard and knocked the sword to the ground. Before Brom could react, Eragon flicked Zar'roc up to his throat.

They stood panting, the red sword tip resting on Brom's collarbone. Eragon slowly lowered his arm and backed away. It was the first time he had bested Brom without resorting to trickery. Brom picked up his sword and sheathed it. Still breathing hard, he said, "We're done for today."

"But we just started," said Eragon, startled.

Brom shook his head. "I can teach you nothing more of the sword. Of all the fighters I've met, only three of them could have defeated me like that, and I doubt any of them could have done it with their left hand." He smiled ruefully. "I may not be as young as I used to be, but I can tell that you're a talented and rare swordsman."

"Does this mean we're not going to spar every night?" asked Eragon.

"Oh, you're not getting out of it," laughed Brom. "But we'll go easier now. It's not as important if we miss a night here or there." He wiped his brow. "Just remember, if you ever have the misfortune to fight an elf—trained or not, female or male—expect to lose. They, along with dragons and other creatures of magic, are many times stronger than nature intended. Even the weakest elf could easily overpower you. The same goes for the Ra'zac—they are not human and tire much more slowly than we do."

"Is there any way to become their equal?" asked Eragon. He sat cross-legged by Saphira.

You fought well, she said. He smiled.

Brom seated himself with a shrug. "There are a few, but none are available to you now. Magic will let you defeat all but the strongest enemies. For those you'll need Saphira's help, plus a great deal of luck. Remember, when creatures of magic actually use magic, they can accomplish things that could kill a human, because of their enhanced abilities."

"How do you fight with magic?" asked Eragon.

"What do you mean?"

"Well," he said, leaning on an elbow. "Suppose I was attacked by a Shade. How could I block his magic? Most spells take place instantaneously, which makes it impossible to react in time. And even if I could, how would I nullify an enemy's magic? It seems I would have to know my opponent's intention *before* he acted." He paused. "I just don't see how it can be done. Whoever attacked first would win."

Brom sighed. "What you are talking about—a 'wizards' duel,' if you will—is extremely dangerous. Haven't you ever wondered how Galbatorix was able to defeat all of the Riders with the help of only a dozen or so traitors?"

"I never thought about it," acknowledged Eragon.

"There are several ways. Some you'll learn about later, but the main one is that Galbatorix was, and still is, a master of breaking into people's minds. You see, in a wizards' duel there are strict rules that each side must observe or else both contestants will die. To begin with, no one uses magic until one of the participants gains access to the other's mind."

Saphira curled her tail comfortably around Eragon and asked, *Why wait? By the time an enemy realizes that you've attacked, it will be too late for him to act.* Eragon repeated the question out loud.

Brom shook his head. "No, it won't. If I were to suddenly use my power against you, Eragon, you would surely die, but in the brief moment before you were destroyed, there would be time for a counterattack. Therefore, unless one combatant has a death wish, neither side attacks until one of them has breached the other's defenses."

"Then what happens?" Eragon inquired.

Brom shrugged and said, "Once you're inside your enemy's mind, it's easy enough to anticipate what he will do and prevent it. Even with that advantage, it's still possible to lose if you don't know how to counteract spells."

He filled and lit his pipe. "And that requires extraordinarily quick thinking. Before you can defend yourself, you have to understand the exact nature of the forces directed at you. If you're being attacked with heat, you have to know whether it is being conveyed to you through air, fire, light, or some other medium. Only once that's known can you combat the magic by, for instance, chilling the heated material."

"It sounds difficult."

"Extremely," confirmed Brom. A plume of smoke rose from his pipe. "Seldom can people survive such a duel for more than a few seconds. The enormous amount of effort and skill required condemns anyone without the proper training to a quick death. Once you've progressed, I'll start teaching you the necessary methods. In the meantime, if you ever find yourself facing a wizards' duel, I suggest you run away as fast as you can."

THE MIRE OF
DRAS-LEONA

They lunched at Fasaloft, a bustling lakeside village. It was a charming place set on a rise overlooking the lake. As they ate in the hostel's common room, Eragon listened intently to the gossip and was relieved to hear no rumors of him and Saphira.

The trail, now a road, had grown steadily worse over the past two days. Wagon wheels and iron-shod hooves had conspired to tear up the ground, making many sections impassable. An increase in travelers forced Saphira to hide during the day and then catch up with Brom and Eragon at night.

For days they continued south along Leona Lake's vast shore. Eragon began to wonder if they would ever get around it, so he was heartened when they met men who said that Dras-Leona was an easy day's ride ahead of them.

Eragon rose early the following morning. His fingers twitched with anticipation at the thought of finally finding the Ra'zac. *The two of you must be careful*, said Saphira. *The Ra'zac could have spies watching for travelers that fit your description.*

We'll do our best to remain inconspicuous, he assured her.

She lowered her head until their eyes met. *Perhaps, but realize that I won't be able to protect you as I did with the Urgals. I will be too far away to come to your aid, nor would I survive long in the narrow streets your kind favor. Follow Brom's lead in this hunt; he is sensible.*

I know, he said somberly.

Will you go with Brom to the Varden? Once the Ra'zac are killed, he will want to take you to them. And since Galbatorix will be enraged by the Ra'zac's death, that may be the safest thing for us to do.

Eragon rubbed his arms. *I don't want to fight the Empire all the time like the Varden do. Life is more than constant war. There'll be time to consider it once the Ra'zac are gone.*

Don't be too sure, she warned, then went to hide herself until night.

The road was clogged with farmers taking their goods to market in Dras-Leona. Brom and Eragon were forced to slow their horses and wait for wagons that blocked the way.

Although they saw smoke in the distance before noon, it was another league before the city was clearly visible. Unlike Teirm, a planned city, Dras-Leona was a tangled mess that sprawled next to Leona Lake. Ramshackle buildings sat on crooked streets, and the heart of the city was surrounded by a dirty, pale yellow wall of daubed mud.

Several miles east, a mountain of bare rock speared the sky with spires and columns, a tenebrous nightmare ship. Near-vertical sides rose out of the ground like a jagged piece of the earth's bone.

Brom pointed. "*That* is Helgrind. It's the reason Dras-Leona was originally built. People are fascinated by it, even though it's an unhealthy and malevolent thing." He gestured at the buildings inside the city's wall. "We should go to the center of the city first."

As they crept along the road to Dras-Leona, Eragon saw that the highest building within the city was a cathedral that loomed behind the walls. It was strikingly similar to Helgrind, especially when its arches and flanged spires caught the light. "Who do they worship?" he asked.

Brom grimaced in distaste. "Their prayers go to Helgrind. It's a cruel religion they practice. They drink human blood and make flesh offerings. Their priests often lack body parts because they believe that the more bone and sinew you give up, the less you're attached to the mortal world. They spend much of their time arguing about which of Helgrind's three peaks is the highest and most important and whether the fourth—and lowest—should be included in their worship."

"That's horrible," said Eragon, shuddering.

"Yes," said Brom grimly, "but don't say that to a believer. You'll quickly lose a hand in 'penance.'"

At Dras-Leona's enormous gates, they led the horses through the crush of people. Ten soldiers were stationed on either side of the gates, casually scanning the crowd. Eragon and Brom passed into the city without incident.

The houses inside the city wall were tall and thin to compensate for the lack of space. Those next to the wall were braced against it. Most of the houses hung over the narrow, winding streets, covering the sky so that it was hard to tell if it was night or day. Nearly all the buildings were constructed of the same rough brown wood, which darkened the city even more. The air reeked like a sewer; the streets were filthy.

A group of ragged children ran between the houses, fighting over scraps of bread. Deformed beggars crouched next to the entrance gates, pleading for money. Their cries for help were like a chorus of the damned. *We don't even treat animals like this*, thought Eragon, eyes wide with anger. "I won't stay here," he said, rebelling against the sight.

"It gets better farther in," said Brom. "Right now we need to find an inn and form a strategy. Dras-Leona can be a dangerous place to even the most cautious. I don't want to remain on the streets any longer than necessary."

They forged deeper into Dras-Leona, leaving the squalid entrance behind. As they entered wealthier parts of the city, Eragon wondered, *How can these people live in ease when the suffering around them is so obvious?*

They found lodging at the Golden Globe, which was cheap but not decrepit. A narrow bed was crammed against one wall of the room, with a rickety table and a basin alongside it. Eragon took one look at the mattress and said, "I'm sleeping on the floor. There are probably enough bugs in that thing to eat me alive."

"Well, I wouldn't want to deprive them of a meal," said Brom, dropping his bags on the mattress. Eragon set his own on the floor and pulled off his bow.

"What now?" he asked.

"We find food and beer. After that, sleep. Tomorrow we can start looking for the Ra'zac." Before they left the room, Brom warned, "No matter what happens, make sure that your tongue doesn't loosen. We'll have to leave immediately if we're given away."

The inn's food was barely adequate, but its beer was excellent. By the time they stumbled back to the room, Eragon's head was buzzing pleasantly. He unrolled his blankets on the floor and slid under them as Brom tumbled onto the bed.

Just before Eragon fell asleep, he contacted Saphira: *We're going to be here for a few days, but this shouldn't take as long as it did at Teirm. When we discover where the Ra'zac are, you might be able to help us get them. I'll talk to you in the morning. Right now I'm not thinking too clearly.*

You've been drinking, came the accusing thought. Eragon considered it for a moment and had to agree that she was absolutely right. Her disapproval was clear, but all she said was, *I won't envy you in the morning.*

No, groaned Eragon, *but Brom will. He drank twice as much as I did.*

TRAIL OF OIL

What was I thinking? wondered Eragon in the morning. His head was pounding and his tongue felt thick and fuzzy. As a rat skittered under the floor, Eragon winced at the noise. *How are we feeling?* asked Saphira smugly.

Eragon ignored her.

A moment later, Brom rolled out of bed with a grumble. He doused his head in cold water from the basin, then left the room. Eragon followed him into the hallway. "Where are you going?" he asked.

"To recover."

"I'll come." At the bar, Eragon discovered that Brom's method of recovery involved imbibing copious amounts of hot tea and ice water and washing it all down with brandy. When they returned to the room, Eragon was able to function somewhat better.

Brom belted on his sword and smoothed the wrinkles out of his robe. "The first thing we need to do is ask some discreet questions. I want to find out where the Seithr oil was delivered in Dras-Leona and where it was taken from there. Most likely, soldiers or workmen were involved in transporting it. We have to find those men and get one to talk."

They left the Golden Globe and searched for warehouses where the Seithr oil might have been delivered. Near the center of Dras-Leona, the streets began to slant upward toward a palace of polished granite. It was built on a rise so that it towered above every building except the cathedral.

The courtyard was a mosaic of mother-of-pearl, and parts of the walls were inlaid with gold. Black statues stood in alcoves, with sticks of incense smoking in their cold hands. Soldiers stationed every four yards watched passersby keenly.

"Who lives there?" asked Eragon in awe.

"Marcus Tábor, ruler of this city. He answers only to the king and his own conscience, which hasn't been very active recently," said Brom. They walked around the palace, looking at the gated, ornate houses that surrounded it.

By midday they had learned nothing useful, so they stopped for lunch. "This city is too vast for us to comb it together," said Brom. "Search on your own. Meet me at the Golden Globe by dusk." He glowered at Eragon from under his bushy eyebrows. "I'm trusting you not to do anything stupid."

"I won't," promised Eragon. Brom handed him some coins, then strode away in the opposite direction.

Throughout the rest of the day, Eragon talked with shopkeepers and workers, trying to be as pleasant and charming as he could. His questions led him from one end of the city to the other and back again. No one seemed to know about the oil. Wherever he went, the cathedral stared down at him. It was impossible to escape its tall spires.

At last he found a man who had helped ship the Seithr oil and remembered to which warehouse it had been taken. Eragon excitedly went to look at the building, then returned to the Golden Globe. It was over an hour before Brom came back, slumped with fatigue. "Did you find anything?" asked Eragon.

Brom brushed back his white hair. "I heard a great deal of interesting things today, not the least of which is that Galbatorix will visit Dras-Leona within the week."

"What?" exclaimed Eragon.

Brom slouched against the wall, the lines on his forehead deepening. "It seems that Tábor has taken a few too many liberties with his power, so Galbatorix has decided to come teach him a lesson in humility. It's the first time the king has left Urû'baen in over ten years."

"Do you think he knows of us?" asked Eragon.

"Of course he *knows* of us, but I'm sure he hasn't been told our location. If he had, we would already be in the Ra'zac's grasp. However, this means that whatever we're going to do about the Ra'zac must be accomplished before Galbatorix arrives. We don't want to be anywhere within twenty leagues of him. The one thing in our favor is that the Ra'zac are sure to be here, preparing for his visit."

"I want to get the Ra'zac," said Eragon, his fists tightening, "but not if it means fighting the king. He could probably tear me to pieces."

That seemed to amuse Brom. "Very good: caution. And you're right; you wouldn't stand a chance against Galbatorix. Now tell me what you learned today. It might confirm what I heard."

Eragon shrugged. "It was mostly drivel, but I did talk with a man who knew where the oil was taken. It's just an old warehouse. Other than that, I didn't discover anything useful."

"My day was a little more fruitful than yours. I heard the same thing you did, so I went to the warehouse and talked with the workers. It didn't take much cajoling before they revealed that the cases of Seithr oil are always sent from the warehouse to the palace."

"And that's when you came back here," finished Eragon.

"No, it's not! Don't interrupt. After that, I went to the palace and got myself invited into the servants' quarters as a bard. For several hours I wandered about, amusing the maids and others with songs and poems—and asking questions all the while." Brom slowly filled his pipe with tobacco. "It's really amazing all the things servants find out. Did you know that one of the earls has *three* mistresses, and they all live in the same wing of the palace?" He shook his head and lit the pipe. "Aside from the fascinating tidbits, I was told, quite by accident, where the oil is taken from the palace."

"And that is . . . ?" asked Eragon impatiently.

Brom puffed on his pipe and blew a smoke ring. "Out of the city, of course. Every full moon two slaves are sent to the base of Helgrind with a month's worth of provisions. Whenever the Seithr oil arrives in Dras-Leona, they send it along with the provisions. The slaves are never seen again. And the one time someone followed them, he disappeared too."

"I thought the Riders demolished the slave trade," said Eragon.

"Unfortunately, it has flourished under the king's reign."

"So the Ra'zac are in Helgrind," said Eragon, thinking of the rock mountain.

"There or somewhere nearby."

"If they *are* in Helgrind, they'll be either at the bottom—and protected by a thick stone door—or higher up where only their flying mounts, or Saphira, can reach. Top or bottom, their shelter will no doubt be disguised." He thought for a moment. "If Saphira and I go flying around Helgrind, the Ra'zac are sure to see us—not to mention all of Dras-Leona."

"It is a problem," agreed Brom.

Eragon frowned. "What if we took the place of the two slaves? The full moon isn't far off. It would give us a perfect opportunity to get close to the Ra'zac."

Brom tugged his beard thoughtfully. "That's chancy at best. If the slaves are killed from a distance, we'll be in trouble. We can't harm the Ra'zac if they aren't in sight."

"We don't know if the slaves are killed at all," Eragon pointed out.

"I'm sure they are," said Brom, his face grave. Then his eyes sparkled, and he blew another smoke ring. "Still, it's an intriguing idea. If it were done with Saphira hidden nearby and a . . ." His voice trailed off. "It might work, but we'll have to move quickly. With the king coming, there isn't much time."

"Should we go to Helgrind and look around? It would be good to see the land in daylight so we won't be surprised by any ambushes," said Eragon.

Brom fingered his staff. "That can be done later. Tomorrow I'll return to the palace and figure out how we can replace the slaves.

I have to be careful not to arouse suspicion, though—I could easily be revealed by spies and courtiers who know about the Ra'zac."

"I can't believe it; we actually found them," said Eragon quietly. An image of his dead uncle and burned farm flashed through his mind. His jaw tightened.

"The toughest part is yet to come, but yes, we've done well," said Brom. "If fortune smiles on us, you may soon have your revenge and the Varden will be rid of a dangerous enemy. What comes after that will be up to you."

Eragon opened his mind and jubilantly told Saphira, *We found the Ra'zac's lair!*

Where? He quickly explained what they had discovered. *Helgrind,* she mused. *A fitting place for them.*

Eragon agreed. *When we're done here, maybe we could visit Carvahall.*

What is it you want? she asked, suddenly sour. *To go back to your previous life? You know that won't happen, so stop mooning after it! At a certain point you have to decide what to commit to. Will you hide for the rest of your life, or will you help the Varden? Those are the only options left to you, unless you join forces with Galbatorix, which I do not and never will accept.*

Softly, he said, *If I must choose, I cast my fate with the Varden, as you well know.*

Yes, but sometimes you have to hear yourself say it. She left him to ponder her words.

WORSHIPERS
OF HELGRIND

Eragon was alone in the room when he woke. Scrawled onto the wall with a charcoal stick was a note that read:

Eragon,

I will be gone until late tonight. Coins for food are under the mattress.
Explore the city, enjoy yourself, but <u>stay unnoticed!</u>

Brom

P.S. *Avoid the palace. Don't go anywhere without your bow! Keep it strung.*

Eragon wiped the wall clean, then retrieved the money from under the bed. He slipped the bow across his back, thinking, *I wish I didn't have to go armed all the time.*

He left the Golden Globe and ambled through the streets, stopping to observe whatever interested him. There were many intriguing stores, but none quite as exciting as Angela's herb shop in Teirm. At times he glared at the dark, claustrophobic houses and wished that he were free of the city. When he grew hungry, he bought a wedge of cheese and a loaf of bread and ate them, sitting on a curb.

Later, in a far corner of Dras-Leona, he heard an auctioneer rattling off a list of prices. Curious, he headed toward the voice and arrived at a wide opening between two buildings. Ten men stood on a waist-high platform. Arrayed before them was a richly dressed crowd that was both colorful and boisterous. *Where are the goods for sale?* wondered Eragon.

The auctioneer finished his list and motioned for a young man behind the platform to join him. The man awkwardly climbed up, chains dragging at his hands and feet. "And here we have our first item," proclaimed the auctioneer. "A healthy male from the Hadarac Desert, captured just last month, and in excellent condition. Look at those arms and legs; he's strong as a bull! He'd be perfect as a shield bearer, or, if you don't trust him for that, hard labor. But let me tell you, lords and ladies, that would be a waste. He's bright as a nail, if you can get him to talk a civilized tongue!"

The crowd laughed, and Eragon ground his teeth with fury. His lips started to form a word that would free the slave, and his arm, newly liberated from the splint, rose. The mark on his palm shimmered. He was about to release the magic when it struck him, *He'd never get away!* The slave would be caught before he reached the city walls. Eragon would only make the situation worse if he tried to help. He lowered his arm and quietly cursed. *Think! This is how you got into trouble with the Urgals.*

He watched helplessly as the slave was sold to a tall, hawk-nosed man. The next slave was a tiny girl, no more than six years old, wrenched from the arms of her crying mother. As the auctioneer started the bidding, Eragon forced himself to walk away, rigid with fury and outrage.

It was several blocks before the weeping was inaudible. *I'd like to see a thief try to cut my purse right now,* he thought grimly, almost wishing it would happen. Frustrated, he punched a nearby wall, bruising his knuckles.

That's the sort of thing I could stop by fighting the Empire, he realized. *With Saphira by my side I could free those slaves. I've been graced* with special powers; it would be selfish of me not to use them for the benefit of others. If I don't, I might as well not be a Rider at all.

It was a while before he took stock of his bearings and was surprised to find himself before the cathedral. Its twisted spires were covered with statues and scrollwork. Snarling gargoyles crouched along the eaves. Fantastic beasts writhed on the walls, and heroes and kings marched along their bottom edges, frozen in cold marble. Ribbed arches and tall stained-glass windows lined the cathedral's sides, along with columns of differing sizes. A lonely turret helmed the building like a mast.

Recessed in shadow at the cathedral's front was an iron-bound door inlaid with a row of silver script that Eragon recognized as the ancient language. As best he could tell, it read: *May thee who enter here understand thine impermanence and forget thine attachments to that which is beloved.*

The entire building sent a shiver down Eragon's spine. There was something menacing about it, as if it were a predator crouched in the city, waiting for its next victim.

A broad row of steps led to the cathedral's entrance. Eragon solemnly ascended them and stopped before the door. *I wonder if I can go in?* Almost guiltily he pushed on the door. It swung open smoothly, gliding on oiled hinges. He stepped inside.

The silence of a forgotten tomb filled the empty cathedral. The air was chill and dry. Bare walls extended to a vaulted ceiling that was so high Eragon felt no taller than an ant. Stained-glass windows depicting scenes of anger, hate, and remorse pierced the walls, while spectral beams of light washed sections of the granite pews with transparent hues, leaving the rest in shadow. His hands were shaded a deep blue.

Between the windows stood statues with rigid, pale eyes. He returned their stern gazes, then slowly trod up the center row, afraid to break the quiet. His leather boots padded noiselessly on the polished stone floor.

The altar was a great slab of stone devoid of adornment. A solitary finger of light fell upon it, illuminating motes of golden dust floating in the air. Behind the altar, the pipes of a wind organ pierced the ceiling and opened themselves to the elements. The instrument would play its music only when a gale rocked Dras-Leona.

Out of respect, Eragon knelt before the altar and bowed his head. He did not pray but paid homage to the cathedral itself. The sorrows of the lives it had witnessed, as well as the unpleasantness of the elaborate pageantry that played out between its walls, emanated from the stones. It was a forbidding place, bare and cold. In that chilling touch, though, came a glimpse of eternity and perhaps the powers that lay there.

Finally Eragon inclined his head and rose. Calm and grave, he whispered words to himself in the ancient language, then turned to leave. He froze. His heart jumped, hammering like a drum.

The Ra'zac stood at the cathedral's entrance, watching him. Their swords were drawn, keen edges bloody in a crimson light. A sibilant hiss came from the smaller Ra'zac. Neither of them moved.

Rage welled up in Eragon. He had chased the Ra'zac for so many weeks that the pain of their murderous deed had dulled within him. But his vengeance was at hand. His wrath exploded like a volcano, fueled even more by his pent-up fury at the slaves' plight. A roar broke from his lips, echoing like a thunderstorm as he snatched his bow from his back. Deftly, he fit an arrow to the string and loosed it. Two more followed an instant later.

The Ra'zac leapt away from the arrows with inhuman swiftness. They hissed as they ran up the aisle between the pews, cloaks flapping like raven wings. Eragon reached for another arrow, but caution stayed his hand. *If they knew where to find me, Brom is in danger as well! I must warn him!* Then, to Eragon's horror, a line of soldiers filed into the cathedral, and he glimpsed a field of uniforms jostling outside the doorway.

Eragon gazed hungrily at the charging Ra'zac, then swept around, searching for means of escape. A vestibule to the left of the altar caught his attention. He bounded through the archway and dashed down a corridor that led to a priory with a belfry. The patter of the Ra'zac's feet behind him made him quicken his pace until the hall abruptly ended with a closed door.

He pounded against it, trying to break it open, but the wood was too strong. The Ra'zac were nearly upon him. Frantic, he sucked in his breath and barked, "Jierda!" With a flash, the door splintered into pieces and fell to the floor. Eragon jumped into the small room and continued running.

He sped through several chambers, startling a group of priests. Shouts and curses followed him. The priory bell tolled an alarm. Eragon dodged through a kitchen, passed a pair of monks, then slipped through a side door. He skidded to stop in a garden surrounded by a high brick wall devoid of handholds. There were no other exits.

Eragon turned to leave, but there was a low hiss as the Ra'zac shouldered aside the door. Desperate, he rushed at the wall, arms pumping. Magic could not help him here—if he used it to break through the wall, he would be too tired to run.

He jumped. Even with his arms outstretched, only his fingertips cleared the edge of the wall. The rest of his body smashed against the bricks, driving out his breath. Eragon gasped and hung there, struggling not to fall. The Ra'zac prowled into the garden, swinging their heads from side to side like wolfhounds sniffing for prey.

Eragon sensed their approach and heaved with his arms. His shoulders shrieked with pain as he scrambled onto the wall and dropped to the other side. He stumbled, then regained his balance and darted down an alley just as the Ra'zac leapt over the wall. Galvanized, Eragon put on another burst of speed.

He ran for over a mile before he had to stop and catch his breath. Unsure if he had lost the Ra'zac, he found a crowded marketplace and dived under a parked wagon. *How did they find me?* he wondered, panting. *They shouldn't have known where I was . . . unless something happened to Brom!* He reached out with his mind to Saphira and said, *The Ra'zac found me. We're all in danger! Check if Brom's all right. If he is, warn him and have him meet me at the inn. And be ready to fly here as fast as you can. We may need your help to escape.*

She was silent, then said curtly, *He'll meet you at the inn. Don't stop moving; you're in great danger.*

"Don't I know it," muttered Eragon as he rolled out from under the wagon. He hurried back to the Golden Globe, quickly packed their belongings, saddled the horses, then led them to the street. Brom soon arrived, staff in hand, scowling dangerously. He swung onto Snowfire and asked, "What happened?"

"I was in the cathedral when the Ra'zac just appeared behind me," said Eragon, climbing onto Cadoc. "I ran back as fast as possible, but they could be here at any second. Saphira will join us once we're out of Dras-Leona."

"We have to get outside the city walls before they close the gates, if they haven't already," said Brom. "If they're shut, it'll be nigh impossible for us to leave. Whatever you do, don't get separated from me." Eragon stiffened as ranks of soldiers marched down one end of the street.

Brom cursed, lashed Snowfire with his reins, and galloped away. Eragon bent low over Cadoc and followed. They nearly crashed several times during the wild, hazardous ride, plunging through masses of people that clogged the streets as they neared the city wall. When the gates finally came into view, Eragon pulled on Cadoc's reins with dismay. The gates were already half closed, and a double line of pikemen blocked their way.

"They'll cut us to pieces!" he exclaimed.

"We have to try and make it," said Brom, his voice hard. "I'll deal with the men, but you have to keep the gates open for us." Eragon nodded, gritted his teeth, and dug his heels into Cadoc.

They plowed toward the line of unwavering soldiers, who lowered their pikes toward the horses' chests and braced the weapons against the ground. Though the horses snorted with fear, Eragon and Brom held them in place. Eragon heard the soldiers shout but kept his attention on the gates inching shut.

As they neared the sharp pikes, Brom raised his hand and spoke. The words struck with precision; the soldiers fell to each side as if their legs had been cut out from under them. The gap between the gates shrank by the second. Hoping that the effort would not prove too much for him, Eragon drew on his power and shouted, "Du grind huildr!"

A deep grating sound emanated from the gates as they trembled, then ground to a stop. The crowd and guards fell silent, staring with amazement. With a clatter of the horses' hooves, Brom and Eragon shot out from behind Dras-Leona's wall. The instant they were free, Eragon released the gates. They shuddered, then boomed shut.

He swayed with the expected fatigue but managed to keep riding. Brom watched him with concern. Their flight continued through the outskirts of Dras-Leona as alarm trumpets sounded on the city wall. Saphira was waiting for them by the edge of the city, hidden behind some trees. Her eyes burned; her tail whipped back and forth. "Go, ride her," said Brom. "And this time stay in the air, no matter what happens to me. I'll head south. Fly nearby; I don't care if Saphira's seen." Eragon quickly mounted Saphira. As the ground dwindled away beneath him, he watched Brom gallop along the road.

Are you all right? asked Saphira.

Yes, said Eragon. *But only because we were very lucky.*

A puff of smoke blew from her nostrils. *All the time we've spent searching for the Ra'zac was useless.*

I know, he said, letting his head sag against her scales. *If the Ra'zac had been the only enemies back there, I would have stayed and fought, but with all the soldiers on their side, it was hardly a fair match!*

You understand that there will be talk of us now? This was hardly an unobtrusive escape. Evading the Empire will be harder than ever. There was an edge to her voice that he was unaccustomed to.

I know.

They flew low and fast over the road. Leona Lake receded behind them; the land became dry and rocky and filled with tough, sharp bushes and tall cactuses. Clouds darkened the sky. Lightning flashed in the distance. As the wind began to howl, Saphira glided steeply down to Brom. He stopped the horses and asked, "What's wrong?"

"The wind's too strong."

"It's not that bad," objected Brom.

"It is up there," said Eragon, pointing at the sky.

Brom swore and handed him Cadoc's reins. They trotted away with Saphira following on foot, though on the ground she had difficulty keeping up with the horses.

The gale grew stronger, flinging dirt through the air and twisting like a dervish. They wrapped scarves around their heads to protect their eyes. Brom's robe flapped in the wind while his beard whipped about as if it had a life of its own. Though it would make them miserable, Eragon hoped it would rain so their tracks would be obliterated.

Soon darkness forced them to stop. With only the stars to guide them, they left the road and made camp behind two boulders. It was too dangerous to light a fire, so they ate cold food while Saphira sheltered them from the wind.

After the sparse dinner, Eragon asked bluntly, "How did they find us?"

Brom started to light his pipe, but thought better of it and put it away. "One of the palace servants warned me there were spies among them. Somehow word of me and my questions must have reached Tábor . . . and through him, the Ra'zac."

"We can't go back to Dras-Leona, can we?" asked Eragon.

Brom shook his head. "Not for a few years."

Eragon held his head between his hands. "Then should we draw the Ra'zac out? If we let Saphira be seen, they'll come running to wherever she is."

"And when they do, there will be fifty soldiers with them," said Brom. "At any rate, this isn't the time to discuss it. Right now we have to concentrate on staying alive. Tonight will be the most dangerous because the Ra'zac will be hunting us in the dark, when they are strongest. We'll have to trade watches until morning."

"Right," said Eragon, standing. He hesitated and squinted. His eyes had caught a flicker of movement, a small patch of color that stood out from the surrounding nightscape. He stepped toward the edge of their camp, trying to see it better.

"What is it?" asked Brom as he unrolled his blankets.

Eragon stared into the darkness, then turned back. "I don't know. I thought I saw something. It must have been a bird." Pain erupted in the back of his head, and Saphira roared. Then Eragon toppled to the ground, unconscious.

THE RA'ZAC'S REVENGE

A dull throbbing roused Eragon. Every time blood pulsed through his head it brought a fresh wave of pain. He cracked his eyes open and winced; tears rushed to his eyes as he looked directly into a bright lantern. He blinked and looked away. When he tried to sit up, he realized that his hands were tied behind his back.

264

He turned lethargically and saw Brom's arms. Eragon was relieved to see that they were bound together. Why was that? He struggled to figure it out until the thought suddenly came to him, *They wouldn't tie up a dead man!* But then who were "they"? He swiveled his head further, then stopped as a pair of black boots entered his vision.

Eragon looked up, right into the cowled face of a Ra'zac. Fear jolted through him. He reached for the magic and started to voice a word that would kill the Ra'zac, but then halted, puzzled. He could not remember the word. Frustrated, he tried again, only to feel it slip out of his grasp.

Above him the Ra'zac laughed chillingly. "The drug is working, yesss? I think you will not be bothering us again."

There was a rattle off to the left, and Eragon was appalled to see the second Ra'zac fit a muzzle over Saphira's head. Her wings were pinioned to her sides by black chains; there were shackles on her legs. Eragon tried to contact her, but felt nothing.

"She was most cooperative once we threatened to kill you," hissed the Ra'zac. Squatting by the lantern, he rummaged through

Eragon's bags, examining and discarding various items until he removed Zar'roc. "What a pretty thing for one so . . . insignificant. Maybe I will keep it." He leaned closer and sneered, "Or maybe, if you behave, our master will let you polish it." His moist breath smelled like raw meat.

Then he turned the sword over in his hands and screeched as he saw the symbol on the scabbard. His companion rushed over. They stood over the sword, hissing and clicking. At last they faced Eragon. "You will serve our master very well, yesss."

Eragon forced his thick tongue to form words: "If I do, I will kill you."

They chuckled coldly. "Oh no, we are too valuable. But you . . . you are *disposable*." A deep snarl came from Saphira; smoke roiled from her nostrils. The Ra'zac did not seem to care.

Their attention was diverted when Brom groaned and rolled onto his side. One of the Ra'zac grabbed his shirt and thrust him effortlessly into the air. "It'sss wearing off."

"Give him more."

"Let'sss just kill him," said the shorter Ra'zac. "He has caused us much grief."

The taller one ran his finger down his sword. "A good plan. But remember, the king's instructions were to keep them *alive*."

"We can sssay he was killed when we captured them."

"And what of thisss one?" the Ra'zac asked, pointing his sword at Eragon. "If he talksss?"

His companion laughed and drew a wicked dagger. "He would not dare."

There was a long silence, then, "Agreed."

They dragged Brom to the center of the camp and shoved him to his knees. Brom sagged to one side. Eragon watched with growing fear. *I have to get free!* He wrenched at the ropes, but they were too strong to break. "None of that now," said the tall Ra'zac, poking him with a sword. He nosed the air and sniffed; something seemed to trouble him.

The other Ra'zac growled, yanked Brom's head back, and swept the dagger toward his exposed throat. At that very moment a low buzz sounded, followed by the Ra'zac's howl. An arrow protruded from his shoulder. The Ra'zac nearest Eragon dropped to the ground, barely avoiding a second arrow. He scuttled to his wounded companion, and they glared into the darkness, hissing angrily. They made no move to stop Brom as he blearily staggered upright. "Get down!" cried Eragon.

Brom wavered, then tottered toward Eragon. As more arrows hissed into the camp from the unseen attackers, the Ra'zac rolled behind some boulders. There was a lull, then arrows came from the opposite direction. Caught by surprise, the Ra'zac reacted slowly. Their cloaks were pierced in several places, and a shattered arrow buried itself in one's arm.

With a wild cry, the smaller Ra'zac fled toward the road, kicking Eragon viciously in the side as he passed. His companion hesitated, then grabbed the dagger from the ground and raced after him. As he left the camp, he hurled the knife at Eragon.

A strange light suddenly burned in Brom's eyes. He threw himself in front of Eragon, his mouth open in a soundless snarl. The dagger struck him with a soft thump, and he landed heavily on his shoulder. His head lolled limply.

"No!" screamed Eragon, though he was doubled over in pain. He heard footsteps, then his eyes closed and he knew no more.

MURTAGH

For a long while, Eragon was aware only of the burning in his side. Each breath was painful. It felt as though he had been the one stabbed, not Brom. His sense of time was skewed; it was hard to tell if weeks had gone by, or only a few minutes. When consciousness finally came to him, he opened his eyes and peered curiously at a campfire several feet away. His hands were still tied together, but the drug must have worn off because he could think clearly again. *Saphira, are you injured?*

No, but you and Brom are. She was crouched over Eragon, wings spread protectively on either side.

Saphira, you didn't make that fire, did you? And you couldn't have gotten out of those chains by yourself.

No.

I didn't think so. Eragon struggled to his knees and saw a young man sitting on the far side of the fire.

The stranger, dressed in battered clothes, exuded a calm, assured air. In his hands was a bow, at his side a long hand-and-a-half sword. A white horn bound with silver fittings lay in his lap, and the hilt of a dagger protruded from his boot. His serious face and fierce eyes were framed by locks of brown hair. He appeared to be a few years older than Eragon and perhaps an inch or so taller. Behind him a gray war-horse was picketed. The stranger watched Saphira warily.

"Who are you?" asked Eragon, taking a shallow breath.

The man's hands tightened on his bow. "Murtagh." His voice was low and controlled, but curiously emotional.

Eragon pulled his hands underneath his legs so they were in front of him. He clenched his teeth as his side flared with pain. "Why did you help us?"

"You aren't the only enemies the Ra'zac have. I was tracking them."

"You know who they are?"

"Yes."

Eragon concentrated on the ropes that bound his wrists and reached for the magic. He hesitated, aware of Murtagh's eyes on him, then decided it didn't matter. "Jierda!" he grunted. The ropes snapped off his wrists. He rubbed his hands to get the blood flowing.

Murtagh sucked in his breath. Eragon braced himself and tried to stand, but his ribs seared with agony. He fell back, gasping between clenched teeth. Murtagh tried to come to his aid, but Saphira stopped him with a growl. "I would have helped you earlier, but your dragon wouldn't let me near you."

"Her name's Saphira," said Eragon tightly. *Now let him by! I can't do this alone. Besides, he saved our lives.* Saphira growled again, but folded her wings and backed away. Murtagh eyed her flatly as he stepped forward.

He grasped Eragon's arm, gently pulling him to his feet. Eragon yelped and would have fallen without support. They went to the fire, where Brom lay on his back. "How is he?" asked Eragon.

"Bad," said Murtagh, lowering him to the ground. "The knife went right between his ribs. You can look at him in a minute, but first we'd better see how much damage the Ra'zac did to you." He helped Eragon remove his shirt, then whistled. "Ouch!"

"Ouch," agreed Eragon weakly. A blotchy bruise extended down his left side. The red, swollen skin was broken in several places. Murtagh put a hand on the bruise and pressed lightly. Eragon yelled, and Saphira growled a warning.

Murtagh glanced at Saphira as he grabbed a blanket. "I think you have some broken ribs. It's hard to tell, but at least two, maybe more. You're lucky you're not coughing up blood." He tore the blanket into strips and bound Eragon's chest.

Eragon slipped the shirt back on. "Yes . . . I'm lucky." He took a shallow breath, sidled over to Brom, and saw that Murtagh had cut open the side of his robe to bandage the wound. With trembling fingers, he undid the bandage.

"I wouldn't do that," warned Murtagh. "He'll bleed to death without it."

Eragon ignored him and pulled the cloth away from Brom's side. The wound was short and thin, belying its depth. Blood streamed out of it. As he had learned when Garrow was injured, a wound inflicted by the Ra'zac was slow to heal.

He peeled off his gloves while furiously searching his mind for the healing words Brom had taught him. *Help me, Saphira,* he implored. *I am too weak to do this alone.*

Saphira crouched next to him, fixing her eyes on Brom. *I am here, Eragon.* As her mind joined his, new strength infused his body. Eragon drew upon their combined power and focused it on the words. His hand trembled as he held it over the wound. "Waíse heill!" he said. His palm glowed, and Brom's skin flowed together, as if it had never been broken. Murtagh watched the entire process.

It was over quickly. As the light vanished, Eragon sat, feeling sick. *We've never done that before,* he said.

Saphira nodded. *Together we can cast spells that are beyond either of us.*

Murtagh examined Brom's side and asked, "Is he completely healed?"

"I can only mend what is on the surface. I don't know enough to fix whatever's damaged inside. It's up to him now. I've done all I can." Eragon closed his eyes for a moment, utterly weary. "My . . . my head seems to be floating in clouds."

"You probably need to eat," said Murtagh. "I'll make soup."

While Murtagh fixed the meal, Eragon wondered who this stranger was. His sword and bow were of the finest make, as was his horn. Either he was a thief or accustomed to money—and lots of it. *Why was he hunting the Ra'zac? What have they done to make him an enemy? I wonder if he works for the Varden?*

Murtagh handed him a bowl of broth. Eragon spooned it down and asked, "How long has it been since the Ra'zac fled?"

"A few hours."

"We have to go before they return with reinforcements."

"You might be able to travel," said Murtagh, then gestured at Brom, "but he can't. You don't get up and ride away after being stabbed between the ribs."

If we make a litter, can you carry Brom with your claws like you did with Garrow? Eragon asked Saphira.

Yes, but landing will be awkward.

As long as it can be done. Eragon said to Murtagh, "Saphira can carry him, but we need a litter. Can you make one? I don't have the strength."

"Wait here." Murtagh left the camp, sword drawn. Eragon hobbled to his bags and picked up his bow from where it had been thrown by the Ra'zac. He strung it, found his quiver, then retrieved Zar'roc, which lay hidden in shadow. Last, he got a blanket for the litter.

Murtagh returned with two saplings. He laid them parallel on the ground, then lashed the blanket between the poles. After he carefully tied Brom to the makeshift litter, Saphira grasped the saplings and laboriously took flight. "I never thought I would see a sight like that," Murtagh said, an odd note in his voice.

As Saphira disappeared into the dark sky, Eragon limped to Cadoc and hoisted himself painfully into the saddle. "Thanks for helping us. You should leave now. Ride as far away from us as you can. You'll be in danger if the Empire finds you with us. We can't protect you, and I wouldn't see harm come to you on our account."

"A pretty speech," said Murtagh, grinding out the fire, "but where will you go? Is there a place nearby that you can rest in safety?"

"No," admitted Eragon.

Murtagh's eyes glinted as he fingered the hilt of his sword. "In that case, I think I'll accompany you until you're out of danger. I've no better place to be. Besides, if I stay with you, I might get another shot at the Ra'zac sooner than if I were on my own. Interesting things are bound to happen around a Rider."

Eragon wavered, unsure if he should accept help from a complete stranger. Yet he was unpleasantly aware that he was too weak to force the issue either way. *If Murtagh proves untrustworthy, Saphira can always chase him away.* "Join us if you wish." He shrugged.

Murtagh nodded and mounted his gray war-horse. Eragon grabbed Snowfire's reins and rode away from the camp, into the wilderness. An oxbow moon provided wan light, but he knew that it would only make it easier for the Ra'zac to track them.

Though Eragon wanted to question Murtagh further, he kept silent, conserving his energy for riding. Near dawn Saphira said, *I must stop. My wings are tired and Brom needs attention. I discovered a good place to stay, about two miles ahead of where you are.*

They found her sitting at the base of a broad sandstone formation that curved out of the ground like a great hill. Its sides were pocked with caves of varying sizes. Similar domes were scattered across the land. Saphira looked pleased with herself. *I found a cave that can't be seen from the ground. It's large enough for all of us, including the horses. Follow me.* She turned and climbed up the sandstone, her sharp claws digging into the rock. The horses had difficulty, as their shod hooves could not grip the sandstone. Eragon and Murtagh had to pull and shove the animals for almost an hour before they managed to reach the cave.

The cavern was a good hundred feet long and more than twenty feet wide, yet it had a small opening that would protect them from bad weather and prying eyes. Darkness swallowed the far end, clinging to the walls like mats of soft black wool.

"Impressive," said Murtagh. "I'll gather wood for a fire." Eragon hurried to Brom. Saphira had set him on a small rock ledge at the rear of the cave. Eragon clasped Brom's limp hand and anxiously watched his craggy face. After a few minutes, he sighed and went to the fire Murtagh had built.

They ate quietly, then tried to give Brom water, but the old man would not drink. Stymied, they spread out their bedrolls and slept.

LEGACY OF A RIDER

Wake up, Eragon. He stirred and groaned.

I need your help. Something is wrong! Eragon tried to ignore the voice and return to sleep.

Arise!

Go away, he grumbled.

Eragon! A bellow rang in the cave. He bolted upright, fumbling for his bow. Saphira was crouched over Brom, who had rolled off the ledge and was thrashing on the cave floor. His face was contorted in a grimace; his fists were clenched. Eragon rushed over, fearing the worst.

"Help me hold him down. He's going to hurt himself!" he cried to Murtagh, clasping Brom's arms. His side burned sharply as the old man spasmed. Together they restrained Brom until his convulsions ceased. Then they carefully returned him to the ledge.

Eragon touched Brom's forehead. The skin was so hot that the heat could be felt an inch away. "Get me water and a cloth," he said worriedly. Murtagh brought them, and Eragon gently bathed Brom's face, trying to cool him down. With the cave quiet again, he noticed the sun shining outside. *How long did we sleep?* he asked Saphira.

A good while. I've been watching Brom for most of that time. He was fine until a minute ago when he started thrashing. I woke you once he fell to the floor.

He stretched, wincing as his ribs twinged painfully. A hand suddenly gripped his shoulder. Brom's eyes snapped opened and fixed a glassy stare on Eragon. "You!" he gasped. "Bring me the wineskin!"

"Brom?" exclaimed Eragon, pleased to hear him talk. "You shouldn't drink wine; it'll only make you worse."

"Bring it, boy—just bring it . . . ," sighed Brom. His hand slipped off Eragon's shoulder.

"I'll be right back—hold on." Eragon dashed to the saddlebags and rummaged through them frantically. "I can't find it!" he cried, looking around desperately.

"Here, take mine," said Murtagh, holding out a leather skin.

Eragon grabbed it and returned to Brom. "I have the wine," he said, kneeling. Murtagh retreated to the cave's mouth so they could have privacy.

Brom's next words were faint and indistinct. "Good . . ." He moved his arm weakly. "Now . . . wash my right hand with it."

"What—" Eragon started to ask.

"No questions! I haven't time." Mystified, Eragon unstoppered the wineskin and poured the liquid onto Brom's palm. He rubbed it into the old man's skin, spreading it around the fingers and over the back of the hand. "More," croaked Brom. Eragon splashed wine onto his hand again. He scrubbed vigorously as a brown dye floated off Brom's palm, then stopped, his mouth agape with amazement. There on Brom's palm was the gedwëy ignasia.

"You're a Rider?" he asked incredulously.

A painful smile flickered on Brom's face. "Once upon a time that was true . . . but no more. When I was young . . . younger than you are now, I was chosen . . . chosen by the Riders to join their ranks. While they trained me, I became friends with another apprentice . . . Morzan, before he was a Forsworn." Eragon gasped—that had been over a hundred years ago. "But then he betrayed us to Galbatorix . . . and in the fighting at Dorú Areaba—Vroengard's city—my young dragon was killed. Her name . . . was Saphira."

"Why didn't you tell me this before?" asked Eragon softly.

Brom laughed. "Because . . . there was no need to." He stopped. His breathing was labored; his hands were clenched. "I am old, Eragon . . . so old. Though my dragon was killed, my life has been longer than most. You don't know what it is to reach my age, look back, and realize that you don't remember much of it; then to look forward and know that many years still lie ahead of you. . . . After all this time I still grieve for my Saphira . . . and hate Galbatorix for what he tore from me." His feverish eyes drilled into Eragon as he said fiercely, "Don't let that happen to you. Don't! Guard Saphira with your life, for without her it's hardly worth living."

"You shouldn't talk like this. Nothing's going to happen to her," said Eragon, worried.

Brom turned his head to the side. "Perhaps I am rambling." His gaze passed blindly over Murtagh, then he focused on Eragon. Brom's voice grew stronger. "Eragon! I cannot last much longer. This . . . this is a grievous wound; it saps my strength. I have not the energy to fight it. . . . Before I go, will you take my blessing?"

"Everything will be all right," said Eragon, tears in his eyes. "You don't have to do this."

"It is the way of things . . . I must. Will you take my blessing?" Eragon bowed his head and nodded, overcome. Brom placed a trembling hand on his brow. "Then I give it to you. May the coming years bring you great happiness." He motioned for Eragon to bend closer. Very quietly, he whispered seven words from the ancient language, then even more softly told him what they meant. "That is all I can give you. . . . Use them only in great need."

Brom blindly turned his eyes to the ceiling. "And now," he murmured, "for the greatest adventure of all. . . ."

Weeping, Eragon held his hand, comforting him as best he could. His vigil was unwavering and steadfast, unbroken by food or drink. As the long hours passed, a gray pallor crept over Brom, and his eyes slowly dimmed. His hands grew icy; the air around him took on an evil humor. Powerless to help, Eragon could only watch as the Ra'zac's wound took its toll.

The evening hours were young and the shadows long when Brom suddenly stiffened. Eragon called his name and cried for Murtagh's help, but they could do nothing. As a barren silence dampened the air, Brom locked his eyes with Eragon's. Then contentment spread across the old man's face, and a whisper of breath escaped his lips. And so it was that Brom the storyteller died.

With shaking fingers, Eragon closed Brom's eyes and stood. Saphira raised her head behind him and roared mournfully at the sky, keening her lamentation. Tears rolled down Eragon's cheeks as a sense of horrible loss bled through him. Haltingly, he said, "We have to bury him."

"We might be seen," warned Murtagh.

"I don't care!"

Murtagh hesitated, then bore Brom's body out of the cave, along with his sword and staff. Saphira followed them. "To the top," Eragon said thickly, indicating the crown of the sandstone hill.

"We can't dig a grave out of stone," objected Murtagh.

"I can do it."

Eragon climbed onto the smooth hilltop, struggling because of his ribs. There, Murtagh lay Brom on the stone.

Eragon wiped his eyes and fixed his gaze on the sandstone. Gesturing with his hand, he said, "Moi stenr!" The stone rippled. It flowed like water, forming a body-length depression in the hilltop. Molding the sandstone like wet clay, he raised waist-high walls around it.

They laid Brom inside the unfinished sandstone vault with his staff and sword. Stepping back, Eragon again shaped the stone with magic. It joined over Brom's motionless face and flowed upward into a tall faceted spire. As a final tribute, Eragon set runes into the stone:

HERE LIES BROM
Who was a Dragon Rider
And like a father
To me.
May his name live on in glory.

Then he bowed his head and mourned freely. He stood like a living statue until evening, when light faded from the land.

That night he dreamed of the imprisoned woman again.

He could tell that something was wrong with her. Her breathing was irregular, and she shook—whether from cold or pain, he did not know. In the semidarkness of the cell, the only thing clearly illuminated was her hand, which hung over the edge of the cot. A dark liquid dripped from the tips of her fingers. Eragon knew it was blood.

DIAMOND TOMB

When Eragon woke, his eyes were gritty, his body stiff. The cave was empty except for the horses. The litter was gone; no sign of Brom remained. He walked to the entrance and sat on the pitted sandstone. *So the witch Angela was correct—there was a death in my future*, he thought, staring bleakly at the land. The topaz sun brought a desert heat to the early morning.

A tear slid down his listless face and evaporated in the sunlight, leaving a salty crust on his skin. He closed his eyes and absorbed the warmth, emptying his mind. With a fingernail, he aimlessly scratched the sandstone. When he looked, he saw that he had written *Why me?*

He was still there when Murtagh climbed up to the cave, carrying a pair of rabbits. Without a word he seated himself by Eragon. "How are you?" he asked.

"Very ill."

Murtagh considered him thoughtfully. "Will you recover?" Eragon shrugged. After a few minutes of reflection, Murtagh said, "I dislike asking this at such a time, but I must know . . . Is your Brom *the* Brom? The one who helped steal a dragon egg from the king, chased it across the Empire, and killed Morzan in a duel? I heard you say his name, and I read the inscription you put on his grave, but I must know for certain, Was that he?"

"It was," said Eragon softly. A troubled expression settled on Murtagh's face. "How do you know all that? You talk about things that are secret to most, and you were trailing the Ra'zac right when we needed help. Are you one of the Varden?"

Murtagh's eyes became inscrutable orbs. "I'm running away, like you." There was restrained sorrow in his words. "I do not belong to either the Varden or the Empire. Nor do I owe allegiance to any man but myself. As for my rescuing you, I will admit that I've heard whispered tales of a new Rider and reasoned that by following the Ra'zac I might discover if they were true."

"I thought you wanted to kill the Ra'zac," said Eragon.

Murtagh smiled grimly. "I do, but if I had, I never would have met you."

But Brom would still be alive. . . . I wish he were here. He would know whether to trust Murtagh. Eragon remembered how Brom had sensed Trevor's intentions in Daret and wondered if he could do the same with Murtagh. He reached for Murtagh's consciousness, but his probe abruptly ran into an iron-hard wall, which he tried to circumvent. Murtagh's entire mind was fortified. *How did he learn to do that? Brom said that few people, if any, could keep others out of their mind without training. So who is Murtagh to have this ability?* Pensive and lonely, Eragon asked, "Where is Saphira?"

"I don't know," said Murtagh. "She followed me for a time when I went hunting, then flew off on her own. I haven't seen her since before noon." Eragon rocked onto his feet and returned to the cave. Murtagh followed. "What are you going to do now?"

"I'm not sure." *And I don't want to think about it either.* He rolled up his blankets and tied them to Cadoc's saddlebags. His ribs hurt. Murtagh went to prepare the rabbits. As Eragon shifted things in his bags, he uncovered Zar'roc. The red sheath glinted brightly. He took out the sword . . . weighed it in his hands.

He had never carried Zar'roc nor used it in combat—except when he and Brom had sparred—because he had not wanted people to see it. That concerned Eragon no more. The Ra'zac had seemed surprised and frightened by the sword; that was more than enough reason for him to wear it. With a shudder he pulled off his bow and belted on

Zar'roc. *From this moment on, I'll live by the sword. Let the whole world see what I am. I have no fear. I am a Rider now, fully and completely.*

He sorted through Brom's bags but found only clothes, a few odd items, and a small pouch of coins. Eragon took the map of Alagaësia and put the bags away, then crouched by the fire. Murtagh's eyes narrowed as he looked up from the rabbit he was skinning. "That sword. May I see it?" he asked, wiping his hands.

Eragon hesitated, reluctant to relinquish the weapon for even a moment, then nodded. Murtagh examined the symbol on the blade intently. His face darkened. "Where did you get this?"

"Brom gave it to me. Why?"

Murtagh shoved the sword back and crossed his arms angrily. He was breathing hard. "That sword," he said with emotion, "was once as well known as its owner. The last Rider to carry it was Morzan— a brutal, savage man. I thought you were a foe of the Empire, yet here I find you bearing one of the Forsworn's bloody swords!"

Eragon stared at Zar'roc with shock. He realized that Brom must have taken it from Morzan after they fought in Gil'ead. "Brom never told me where it came from," he said truthfully. "I had no idea it was Morzan's."

"He never told you?" asked Murtagh, a note of disbelief in his voice. Eragon shook his head. "That's strange. I can think of no reason for him to have concealed it."

"Neither can I. But then, he kept many secrets," said Eragon. It felt unsettling to hold the sword of the man who had betrayed the Riders to Galbatorix. *This blade probably killed many Riders in its time,* he thought with revulsion. *And worse, dragons!* "Even so, I'm going to carry it. I don't have a sword of my own. Until such time as I get one, I'll use Zar'roc."

Murtagh flinched as Eragon said the name. "It's your choice," he said. He returned to skinning, keeping his gaze focused downward.

When the meal was ready, Eragon ate slowly, though he was quite hungry. The hot food made him feel better. As they scraped out their bowls, he said, "I have to sell my horse."

"Why not Brom's?" asked Murtagh. He seemed to have gotten over his bad temper.

"Snowfire? Because Brom promised to take care of him. Since he . . . isn't around, I'll do it for him."

Murtagh set his bowl on his lap. "If that's what you want, I'm sure we can find a buyer in some town or village."

"We?" asked Eragon.

Murtagh looked at him sideways in a calculating way. "You won't want to stay here for much longer. If the Ra'zac are nearby, Brom's tomb will be like a beacon for them." Eragon had not thought of that. "And your ribs are going to take time to heal. I know you can defend yourself with magic, but you need a companion who can lift things and use a sword. I'm asking to travel with you, at least for the time being. But I must warn you, the Empire is searching for me. There'll be blood over it eventually."

Eragon laughed weakly and found himself crying because it hurt so much. Once his breath was back, he said, "I don't care if the entire army is searching for you. You're right. I do need help. I would be glad to have you along, though I have to talk to Saphira about it. But I have to warn *you*, Galbatorix just *might* send the entire army after me. You won't be any safer with Saphira and me than if you were on your own."

"I know that," said Murtagh with a quick grin. "But all the same, it won't stop me."

"Good." Eragon smiled with gratitude.

While they spoke, Saphira crawled into the cave and greeted Eragon. She was glad to see him, but there was deep sadness in her thoughts and words. She laid her big blue head on the floor and asked, *Are you well again?*

Not quite.

I miss the old one.

As do I . . . I never suspected that he was a Rider. Brom! He really was an old man—as old as the Forsworn. Everything he taught me about magic he must have learned from the Riders themselves.

Saphira shifted slightly. *I knew what he was the moment he touched me at your farm.*

And you didn't tell me? Why?

He asked me not to, she said simply.

Eragon decided not to make an issue of it. Saphira never meant to hurt him. *Brom kept more than that secret,* he told her, then explained about Zar'roc and Murtagh's reaction to it. *I understand now why Brom didn't explain Zar'roc's origins when he gave it to me. If he had, I probably would have run away from him at the first opportunity.*

You would do well to rid yourself of that sword, she said with distaste. *I know it's a peerless weapon, but you would be better off with a normal blade rather than Morzan's butchery tool.*

Perhaps. Saphira, where does our path go from here? Murtagh offered to come with us. I don't know his past, but he seems honest enough. Should we go to the Varden now? Only I don't know how to find them. Brom never told us.

He told me, said Saphira.

Eragon grew angry. *Why did he trust you, but not me, with all this knowledge?*

Her scales rustled over the dry rock as she stood above him, eyes profound. *After we left Teirm and were attacked by the Urgals, he told me many things, some of which I will not speak of unless necessary. He was concerned about his own death and what would happen to you after it. One fact he imparted to me was the name of a man, Dormnad, who lives in Gil'ead. He can help us find the Varden. Brom also wanted you to know that of all the people in Alagaësia, he believed you were the best suited to inherit the Riders' legacy.*

Tears welled in Eragon's eyes. This was the highest praise he could have ever received from Brom. *A responsibility I will bear honorably.*

Good.

We will go to Gil'ead, then, stated Eragon, strength and purpose returning to him. *And what of Murtagh? Do you think he should come with us?*

We owe him our lives, said Saphira. *But even if that weren't so, he has seen both you and me. We should keep him close so he doesn't furnish the Empire with our location and descriptions, willingly or not.*

He agreed with her, then told Saphira about his dream. *What I saw disturbed me. I feel that time is running out for her; something dreadful is going to happen soon. She's in mortal danger—I'm sure of it—but I don't know how to find her! She could be anywhere.*

What does your heart say? asked Saphira.

My heart died a while back, said Eragon with a hint of black humor. *However, I think we should go north to Gil'ead. With any luck, one of the towns or cities along our path is where this woman is being held. I'm afraid that my next dream of her will show a grave. I couldn't stand that.*

Why?

I'm not sure, he said, shrugging. *It's just that when I see her, I feel as if she's precious and shouldn't be lost. . . . It's very strange.* Saphira opened her long mouth and laughed silently, fangs gleaming. *What is it?* snapped Eragon. She shook her head and quietly padded away.

Eragon grumbled to himself, then told Murtagh what they had decided. Murtagh said, "If you find this Dormnad and then continue on to the Varden, I will leave you. Encountering the Varden would be as dangerous for me as walking unarmed into Urû'baen with a fanfare of trumpets to announce my arrival."

"We won't have to part anytime soon," said Eragon. "It's a long way to Gil'ead." His voice cracked slightly, and he squinted at the sun to distract himself. "We should leave before the day grows any older."

"Are you strong enough to travel?" asked Murtagh, frowning.

"I have to do something or I'll go crazy," said Eragon brusquely. "Sparring, practicing magic, or sitting around twiddling my thumbs aren't good options right now, so I choose to ride."

They doused the fire, packed, and led the horses out of the cave. Eragon handed Cadoc's and Snowfire's reins to Murtagh, saying, "Go on, I'll be right down." Murtagh began the slow descent from the cave.

Eragon struggled up the sandstone, resting when his side made it impossible to breathe. When he reached the top, he found Saphira already there. They stood together before Brom's grave and paid their last respects. *I can't believe he's gone . . . forever.* As Eragon turned to depart, Saphira snaked out her long neck to touch the tomb with the tip of her nose. Her sides vibrated as a low humming filled the air.

The sandstone around her nose shimmered like gilded dew, turning clear with dancing silver highlights. Eragon watched in wonder as tendrils of white diamond twisted over the tomb's surface in a web of priceless filigree. Sparkling shadows were cast on the ground, reflecting splashes of brilliant colors that shifted dazzlingly as the sandstone continued to change. With a satisfied snort, Saphira stepped back and examined her handiwork.

The sculpted sandstone mausoleum of moments before had transformed into a sparkling gemstone vault—under which Brom's untouched face was visible. Eragon gazed with yearning at the old man, who seemed to be only sleeping. "What did you do?" he asked Saphira with awe.

I gave him the only gift I could. Now time will not ravage him. He can rest in peace for eternity.

Thank you. Eragon put a hand on her side, and they left together.

CAPTURE AT GIL'EAD

Riding was extremely painful for Eragon—his broken ribs prevented them from going faster than a walk, and it was impossible for him to breathe deeply without a burst of agony. Nevertheless, he refused to stop. Saphira flew close by, her mind linked with his for solace and strength.

Murtagh rode confidently beside Cadoc, flowing smoothly with his horse's movements. Eragon watched the gray animal for a while. "You have a beautiful horse. What's his name?"

"Tornac, after the man who taught me how to fight." Murtagh patted the horse's side. "He was given to me when he was just a foal. You'd be hard pressed to find a more courageous and intelligent animal in all of Alagaësia, Saphira excepted, of course."

"He is a magnificent beast," said Eragon admiringly.

Murtagh laughed. "Yes, but Snowfire is as close to his match as I've ever seen."

They covered only a short distance that day, yet Eragon was glad to be on the move again. It kept his mind off other, more morbid matters. They were riding through unsettled land. The road to Dras-Leona was several leagues to their left. They would skirt the city by a wide margin on the way to Gil'ead, which was almost as far to the north as Carvahall.

They sold Cadoc in a small village. As the horse was led away by his new owner, Eragon regretfully pocketed the few coins he had gained from the transaction. It was difficult to relinquish Cadoc after crossing half of Alagaësia—and outracing Urgals—on him.

The days rolled by unnoticed as their small group traveled in isolation. Eragon was pleased to find that he and Murtagh shared many of the same interests; they spent hours debating the finer points of archery and hunting.

There was one subject, however, they avoided discussing by unspoken consent: their pasts. Eragon did not explain how he had found Saphira, met Brom, or where he came from. Murtagh was likewise mute as to why the Empire was chasing him. It was a simple arrangement, but it worked.

Yet because of their proximity, it was inevitable that they learned about each other. Eragon was intrigued by Murtagh's familiarity with the power struggles and politics within the Empire. He seemed to know what every noble and courtier was doing and how it affected everyone else. Eragon listened carefully, suspicions whirling through his mind.

The first week went by without any sign of the Ra'zac, which allayed some of Eragon's fears. Even so, they still kept watches at night. Eragon had expected to encounter Urgals on the way to Gil'ead, but they found no trace of them. *I thought these remote places would be teeming with monsters*, he mused. *Still, I'm not one to complain if they've gone elsewhere*.

He dreamed of the woman no more. And though he tried to scry her, he saw only an empty cell. Whenever they passed a town or city, he checked to see if it had a jail. If it did, he would disguise himself and visit it, but she was not to be found. His disguises became increasingly elaborate as he saw notices featuring his name and description—and offering a substantial reward for his capture—posted in various towns.

Their travels north forced them toward the capital, Urû'baen. It was a heavily populated area, which made it difficult to escape notice. Soldiers patrolled the roads and guarded the bridges. It took them several tense, irritable days to skirt the capital.

Once they were safely past Urû'baen, they found themselves on the edge of a vast plain. It was the same one that Eragon had crossed after leaving Palancar Valley, except now he was on the opposite side. They kept to the perimeter of the plain and continued north, following the Ramr River.

Eragon's sixteenth birthday came and went during this time. At Carvahall a celebration would have been held for his entrance into manhood, but in the wilderness he did not even mention it to Murtagh.

At nearly six months of age, Saphira was much larger. Her wings were massive; every inch of them was needed to lift her muscular body and thick bones. The fangs that jutted from her jaw were nearly as thick around as Eragon's fist, their points as sharp as Zar'roc.

The day finally came when Eragon unwrapped his side for the last time. His ribs had healed completely, leaving him with only a small scar where the Ra'zac's boot had cut his side. As Saphira watched, he stretched slowly, then with increasing vigor when there was no pain. He flexed his muscles, pleased. In an earlier time he would have smiled, but after Brom's death, such expressions did not come easily.

He tugged his tunic on and walked back to the small fire they had made. Murtagh sat next to it, whittling a piece of wood. Eragon drew Zar'roc. Murtagh tensed, though his face remained calm. "Now that I am strong enough, would you like to spar?" asked Eragon.

Murtagh tossed the wood to the side. "With sharpened swords? We could kill each other."

"Here, give me your sword," said Eragon. Murtagh hesitated, then handed over his long hand-and-a-half sword. Eragon blocked the edges with magic, the way Brom had taught him. While Murtagh examined the blade, Eragon said, "I can undo that once we're finished."

Murtagh checked the balance of his sword. Satisfied, he said, "It will do." Eragon safed Zar'roc, settled into a crouch, then swung at

Murtagh's shoulder. Their swords met in midair. Eragon disengaged with a flourish, thrust, and then riposted as Murtagh parried, dancing away.

He's fast! thought Eragon.

They struggled back and forth, trying to batter each other down. After a particularly intense series of blows, Murtagh started laughing. Not only was it impossible for either of them to gain an advantage, but they were so evenly matched that they tired at the same rate. Acknowledging with grins each other's skill, they fought on until their arms were leaden and sweat poured off their sides.

Finally Eragon called, "Enough, halt!" Murtagh stopped in midblow and sat down with a gasp. Eragon staggered to the ground, his chest heaving. None of his fights with Brom had been this fierce.

As he gulped air, Murtagh exclaimed, "You're amazing! I've studied swordplay all my life, but never have I fought one like you. You could be the king's weapon master if you wanted to."

"You're just as good," observed Eragon, still panting. "The man who taught you, Tornac, could make a fortune with a fencing school. People would come from all parts of Alagaësia to learn from him."

"He's dead," said Murtagh shortly.

"I'm sorry."

Thus it became their custom to fight in the evening, which kept them lean and fit, like a pair of matched blades. With his return to health, Eragon also resumed practicing magic. Murtagh was curious about it and soon revealed that he knew a surprising amount about how it worked, though he lacked the precise details and could not use it himself. Whenever Eragon practiced speaking in the ancient language, Murtagh would listen quietly, occasionally asking what a word meant.

On the outskirts of Gil'ead they stopped the horses side by side. It had taken them nearly a month to reach it, during which time spring had finally nudged away the remnants of winter. Eragon had felt himself changing during the trip, growing stronger and calmer.

He still thought about Brom and spoke about him with Saphira, but for the most part he tried not to awaken painful memories.

From a distance they could see the city was a rough, barbaric place, filled with log houses and yapping dogs. There was a rambling stone fortress at its center. The air was hazy with blue smoke. The place seemed more like a temporary trading post than a permanent city. Five miles beyond it was the hazy outline of Isenstar Lake.

They decided to camp two miles from the city, for safety. While their dinner simmered, Murtagh said, "I'm not sure you should be the one to go into Gil'ead."

"Why? I can disguise myself well enough," said Eragon. "And Dormnad will want to see the gedwëy ignasia as proof that I really am a Rider."

"Perhaps," said Murtagh, "but the Empire wants you much more than me. If I'm captured, I could eventually escape. But if *you* are taken, they'll drag you to the king, where you'll be in for a slow death by torture—unless you join him. Plus, Gil'ead is one of the army's major staging points. Those aren't houses out there; they're barracks. Going in there would be like handing yourself to the king on a gilded platter."

Eragon asked Saphira for her opinion. She wrapped her tail around his legs and lay next to him. *You shouldn't have to ask me; he speaks sense. There are certain words I can give him that will convince Dormnad of his truthfulness. And Murtagh's right; if anyone is to risk capture it should be him, because he would live through it.*

He grimaced. *I don't like letting him put himself in danger for us.* "All right, you can go," he said reluctantly. "But if anything goes wrong, I'm coming after you."

Murtagh laughed. "That would be fit for a legend: how a lone Rider took on the king's army single-handedly." He chuckled again and stood. "Is there anything I should know before going?"

"Shouldn't we rest and wait until tomorrow?" asked Eragon cautiously.

"Why? The longer we stay here, the greater the chance that we'll be discovered. If this Dormnad can take you to the Varden, then he needs to be found as quickly as possible. Neither of us should remain near Gil'ead longer than a few days."

Again wisdom flies from his mouth, commented Saphira dryly. She told Eragon what should be said to Dormnad, and he relayed the information to Murtagh.

"Very well," said Murtagh, adjusting his sword. "Unless there's trouble, I'll be back within a couple of hours. Make sure there's some food left for me." With a wave of his hand, he jumped onto Tornac and rode away. Eragon sat by the fire, tapping Zar'roc's pommel apprehensively.

Hours passed, but Murtagh did not return. Eragon paced around the fire, Zar'roc in hand, while Saphira watched Gil'ead attentively. Only her eyes moved. Neither of them voiced their worries, though Eragon unobtrusively prepared to leave—in case a detachment of soldiers left the city and headed toward their camp.

Look, snapped Saphira.

Eragon swiveled toward Gil'ead, alert. He saw a distant horseman exit the city and ride furiously toward their camp. *I don't like this*, he said as he climbed onto Saphira. *Be ready to fly.*

I'm prepared for more than that.

As the rider approached, Eragon recognized Murtagh bent low over Tornac. No one seemed to be pursuing him, but he did not slow his reckless pace. He galloped into the camp and jumped to the ground, drawing his sword. "What's wrong?" asked Eragon.

Murtagh scowled. "Did anyone follow me from Gil'ead?"

"We didn't see anyone."

"Good. Then let me eat before I explain. I'm starving." He seized a bowl and began eating with gusto. After a few sloppy bites, he said through a full mouth, "Dormnad has agreed to meet us outside Gil'ead at sunrise tomorrow. If he's satisfied you really are a Rider and that it's not a trap, he'll take you to the Varden."

"Where are we supposed to meet him?" asked Eragon.

Murtagh pointed west. "On a small hill across the road."

"So what happened?"

Murtagh spooned more food into his bowl. "It's a rather simple thing, but all the more deadly because of it: I was seen in the street by someone who knows me. I did the only thing I could and ran away. It was too late, though; he recognized me."

It was unfortunate, but Eragon was unsure how bad it really was. "Since I don't know your friend, I have to ask: Will he tell anyone?"

Murtagh gave a strained laugh. "If you *had* met him, that wouldn't need answering. His mouth is loosely hinged and hangs open all the time, vomiting whatever happens to be in his mind. The question isn't *whether* he will tell people, but *whom* he will tell. If word of this reaches the wrong ears, we'll be in trouble."

"I doubt that soldiers will be sent to search for you in the dark," Eragon pointed out. "We can at least count on being safe until morning, and by then, if all goes well, we'll be leaving with Dormnad."

Murtagh shook his head. "No, only you will accompany him. As I said before, I won't go to the Varden."

Eragon stared at him unhappily. He wanted Murtagh to stay. They had become friends during their travels, and he was loath to tear that apart. He started to protest, but Saphira hushed him and said gently, *Wait until tomorrow. Now is not the time.*

Very well, he said glumly. They talked until the stars were bright in the sky, then slept as Saphira took the first watch.

Eragon woke two hours before dawn, his palm tingling. Everything was still and quiet, but something sought his attention, like an itch in his mind. He buckled on Zar'roc and stood, careful not to make a sound. Saphira looked at him curiously, her large eyes bright. *What is it?* she asked.

I don't know, said Eragon. He saw nothing amiss.

Saphira sniffed the air curiously. She hissed a little and lifted her head. *I smell horses nearby, but they're not moving. They reek with an unfamiliar stench.*

Eragon crept to Murtagh and shook his shoulder. Murtagh woke with a start, yanked a dagger from under his blankets, then looked at Eragon quizzically. Eragon motioned for him to be silent, whispering, "There are horses close by."

Murtagh wordlessly drew his sword. They quietly stationed themselves on either side of Saphira, prepared for an attack. As they waited, the morning star rose in the east. A squirrel chattered.

Then an angry snarl from behind made Eragon spin around, sword held high. A broad Urgal stood at the edge of the camp, carrying a mattock with a nasty spike. *Where did he come from? We haven't seen their tracks anywhere!* thought Eragon. The Urgal roared and waved his weapon, but did not charge.

"Brisingr!" barked Eragon, stabbing out with magic. The Urgal's face contorted with terror as he exploded in a flash of blue light. Blood splattered Eragon, and a brown mass flew through the air. Behind him, Saphira bugled with alarm and reared. Eragon twisted around. While he had been occupied with the first Urgal, a group of them had run up from the side. *Of all the stupid tricks to fall for!*

Steel clashed loudly as Murtagh attacked the Urgals. Eragon tried to join him but was blocked by four of the monsters. The first one swung a sword at his shoulder. He ducked the blow and killed the Urgal with magic. He caught a second one in the throat with Zar'roc, wheeled wildly, and slashed a third through the heart. As he did, the fourth Urgal rushed at him, swinging a heavy club.

Eragon saw him coming and tried to lift his sword to block the club, but was a second too slow. As the club came down on his head, he screamed, "Fly, Saphira!" A burst of light filled his eyes and he lost consciousness.

DU SÚNDAVAR FREOHR

T
he first things Eragon noticed were that he was warm and dry, his cheek was pressed against rough fabric, and his hands were unbound. He stirred, but it was minutes before he was able to push himself upright and examine his surroundings.

He was sitting in a cell on a narrow, bumpy cot. A barred window was set high in the wall. The iron-bound door with a small window in its top half, barred like the one in the wall, was shut securely.

Dried blood cracked on Eragon's face when he moved. It took him a moment to remember that it was not his. His head hurt horribly—which was to be expected, considering the blow he had taken—and his mind was strangely fuzzy. He tried to use magic, but could not concentrate well enough to remember any of the ancient words. *They must have drugged me*, he finally decided.

With a groan he got up, missing the familiar weight of Zar'roc on his hip, and lurched to the window in the wall. He managed to see out of it by standing on his toes. It took a minute for his eyes to adjust to the bright light outside. The window was level with the ground. A street full of busy people ran past the side of his cell, beyond which were rows of identical log houses.

Feeling weak, Eragon slid to the floor and stared at it blankly. What he had seen outside disturbed him, but he was unsure why. Cursing his sluggish thinking, he leaned back his head and tried to clear his mind. A man entered the room and set a tray of food and a pitcher of water on the cot. *Wasn't that nice of him?* thought Eragon, smiling pleasantly. He took a couple of bites of the thin cabbage soup and stale bread, but was barely able to stomach it. *I wish he had brought me something better,* he complained, dropping the spoon.

He suddenly realized what was wrong. *I was captured by Urgals, not men! How did I end up here?* His befuddled brain grappled with the paradox unsuccessfully. With a mental shrug he filed the discovery away for a time when he would know what to do with it.

He sat on the cot and gazed into the distance. Hours later more food was brought in. *And I was just getting hungry,* he thought thickly. This time he was able to eat without feeling sick. When he finished, he decided it was time for a nap. After all, he was on a bed; what else was he going to do?

His mind drifted off; sleep began to envelop him. Then a gate clanged open somewhere, and the din of steel-shod boots marching on a stone floor filled the air. The noise grew louder and louder until it sounded like someone banging a pot inside Eragon's head. He grumbled to himself. *Can't they let me rest in peace?* Fuzzy curiosity slowly overcame his exhaustion, so he dragged himself to the door, blinking like an owl.

Through the window he saw a wide hallway nearly ten yards across. The opposing wall was lined with cells similar to his own. A column of soldiers marched through the hall, their swords drawn and ready. Every man was dressed in matching armor; their faces bore the same hard expression, and their feet came down on the floor with mechanical precision, never missing a beat. The sound was hypnotic. It was an impressive display of force.

Eragon watched the soldiers until he grew bored. Just then he noticed a break in the middle of the column. Carried between two burly men was an unconscious woman.

Her long midnight-black hair obscured her face, despite a leather strip bound around her head to hold the tresses back. She was dressed in dark leather pants and shirt. Wrapped around her slim waist was a shiny belt, from which hung an empty sheath on her right hip. Knee-high boots covered her calves and small feet.

Her head lolled to the side. Eragon gasped, feeling like he had been struck in the stomach. She was the woman from his dreams. Her sculpted face was as perfect as a painting. Her round chin, high cheekbones, and long eyelashes gave her an exotic look. The only mar in her beauty was a scrape along her jaw; nevertheless, she was the fairest woman he had ever seen.

Eragon's blood burned as he looked at her. Something awoke in him—something he had never felt before. It was like an obsession, except stronger, almost a fevered madness. Then the woman's hair shifted, revealing pointed ears. A chill crept over him. She was an elf.

The soldiers continued marching, taking her from his sight. Next strode a tall, proud man, a sable cape billowing behind him. His face was deathly white; his hair was red. Red like blood.

As he walked by Eragon's cell, the man turned his head and looked squarely at him with maroon eyes. His upper lip pulled back in a feral smile, revealing teeth filed to points. Eragon shrank back. He knew what the man was. A *Shade. So help me . . . a Shade*. The procession continued, and the Shade vanished from view.

Eragon sank to the floor, hugging himself. Even in his bewildered state, he knew that the presence of a Shade meant that evil was loose in the land. Whenever they appeared, rivers of blood were sure to follow. *What is a Shade doing here? The soldiers should have killed him on sight!* Then his thoughts returned to the elf-woman, and he was grasped by strange emotions again.

I have to escape. But with his mind clouded, his determination quickly faded. He returned to the cot. By the time the hallway fell silent, he was fast asleep.

As soon as Eragon opened his eyes, he knew something was different. It was easier for him to think; he realized that he was in Gil'ead. *They made a mistake; the drug's wearing off!* Hopeful, he tried to contact Saphira and use magic, but both activities were still beyond his reach. A pit of worry twisted inside him as he wondered if she and Murtagh had managed to escape. He stretched his arms and looked out the window. The city was just awakening; the street was empty except for two beggars.

He reached for the water pitcher, ruminating about the elf and Shade. As he started to drink, he noticed that the water had a faint odor, as if it contained a few drops of rancid perfume. Grimacing, he set the pitcher down. *The drug must be in there and maybe in the food as well!* He remembered that when the Ra'zac had drugged him, it had taken hours to wear off. *If I can keep from drinking and eating for long enough, I should be able to use magic. Then I can rescue the elf. . . .* The thought made him smile. He sat in a corner, dreaming about how it could be done.

The portly jailer entered the cell an hour later with a tray of food. Eragon waited until he departed, then carried the tray to the window. The meal was composed only of bread, cheese, and an onion, but the smell made his stomach grumble hungrily. Resigning himself to a miserable day, he shoved the food out the window and onto the street, hoping that no one would notice.

Eragon devoted himself to overcoming the drug's effects. He had difficulty concentrating for any length of time, but as the day progressed, his mental acuity increased. He began to remember several of the ancient words, though nothing happened when he uttered them. He wanted to scream with frustration.

When lunch was delivered, he pushed it out the window after his breakfast. His hunger was distracting, but it was the lack of water that taxed him most. The back of his throat was parched. Thoughts of drinking cool water tortured him as each breath dried his mouth and throat a bit more. Even so, he forced himself to ignore the pitcher.

He was diverted from his discomfort by a commotion in the hall. A man argued in a loud voice, "You can't go in there! The orders were clear: no one is to see him!"

"Really? Will you be the one to die stopping me, Captain?" cut in a smooth voice.

There was a subdued, "No . . . but the king—"

"*I* will handle the king," interrupted the second person. "Now, unlock the door."

After a pause, keys jangled outside Eragon's cell. He tried to adopt a languorous expression. *I have to act like I don't understand what's going on. I can't show surprise, no matter what this person says.*

The door opened. His breath caught as he looked into the Shade's face. It was like gazing at a death mask or a polished skull with skin pulled over it to give the appearance of life. "Greetings," said the Shade with a cold smile, showing his filed teeth. "I've waited a long time to meet you."

"Who—who're you?" asked Eragon, slurring his words.

"No one of consequence," answered the Shade, his maroon eyes alight with controlled menace. He sat with a flourish of his cloak. "My name does not matter to one in your position. It wouldn't mean a thing to you anyway. It's you that I'm interested in. Who are you?"

The question was posed innocently enough, but Eragon knew there had to be a catch or trap in it, though it eluded him. He pretended to struggle over the question for a while, then slowly said, frowning, "I'm not sure. . . . M'name's Eragon, but that's not all I am, is it?"

The Shade's narrow lips stretched tautly over his mouth as he laughed sharply. "No, it isn't. You have an interesting mind, my young Rider." He leaned forward. The skin on his forehead was thin and translucent. "It seems I must be more direct. What is your name?"

"Era—"

"No! Not that one." The Shade cut him off with a wave of his hand. "Don't you have another one, one that you use only rarely?"

He wants my true name so he can control me! realized Eragon. *But I can't tell him. I don't even know it myself.* He thought quickly, trying to invent a deception that would conceal his ignorance. *What if I made up a name?* He hesitated—it could easily give him away—then raced to create a name that would withstand scrutiny. As he was about to utter it, he decided to take a chance and try to scare the Shade. He deftly switched a few letters, then nodded foolishly and said, "Brom told it to me once. It was . . ." The pause stretched for a few seconds, then his face brightened as he appeared to remember. "It was Du Súndavar Freohr." Which meant almost literally "death of the shadows."

A grim chill settled over the cell as the Shade sat motionless, eyes veiled. He seemed to be deep in thought, pondering what he had learned. Eragon wondered if he had dared too much. He waited until the Shade stirred before asking ingenuously, "Why are you here?"

The Shade looked at him with contempt in his red eyes and smiled. "To gloat, of course. What use is a victory if one cannot enjoy it?" There was confidence in his voice, but he seemed uneasy, as if his plans had been disrupted. He stood suddenly. "I must attend to certain matters, but while I am gone you would do well to think on who you would rather serve: a Rider who betrayed your own order or a fellow man like me, though one skilled in arcane arts. When the time comes to choose, there will be no middle ground." He turned to leave, then glanced at Eragon's water pitcher and stopped, his face granite hard. "Captain!" he snapped.

A broad-shouldered man rushed into the cell, sword in hand. "What is it, my lord?" he asked, alarmed.

"Put that toy away," instructed the Shade. He turned to Eragon and said in a deadly quiet voice, "The boy hasn't been drinking his water. Why is that?"

"I talked with the jailer earlier. Every bowl and plate was scraped clean."

"Very well," said the Shade, mollified. "But make sure that he starts drinking again." He leaned toward the captain and murmured into his ear. Eragon caught the last few words, ". . . extra dose, just in case." The captain nodded. The Shade returned his attention to Eragon. "We will talk again tomorrow when I am not so pressed for time. You should know, I have an endless fascination for names. I will greatly enjoy discussing yours in *much* greater detail."

The way he said it gave Eragon a sinking feeling.

Once they left, he lay on the cot and closed his eyes. Brom's lessons proved their worth now; he relied on them to keep himself from panicking and to reassure himself. *Everything has been provided for me; I only have to take advantage of it.* His thoughts were interrupted by the sound of approaching soldiers.

Apprehensive, he went to the door and saw two soldiers dragging the elf down the hallway. When he could see her no more, Eragon slumped to the floor and tried to touch the magic again. Oaths flew from his lips when it eluded his grasp.

He looked out at the city and ground his teeth. It was only midafternoon. Taking a calming breath, he tried to wait patiently.

FIGHTING SHADOWS

It was dark in Eragon's cell when he sat up with a start, electrified. The wrinkle had shifted! He had felt the magic at the edge of his consciousness for hours, but every time he tried to use it, nothing happened. Eyes bright with nervous energy, he clenched his hands and said, "Nagz reisa!" With a flap, the cot's blanket flew into the air and crumpled into a ball the size of his fist. It landed on the floor with a soft thump.

Exhilarated, Eragon stood. He was weak from his enforced fast, but his excitement overcame his hunger. *Now for the real test.* He reached out with his mind and felt the lock on the door. Instead of trying to break or cut it, he simply pushed its internal mechanism into the unlocked position. With a click, the door creaked inward.

When he had first used magic to kill the Urgals in Yazuac, it had consumed nearly all of his strength, but he had grown much stronger since then. What once would have exhausted him now only tired him slightly.

He cautiously stepped into the hall. *I have to find Zar'roc and the elf. She must be in one of these cells, but there isn't time to look in them all. As for Zar'roc, the Shade might have it with him.* He realized that his thinking was still muddled. *Why am I out here? I could escape right now if I went back into the cell and opened the window with magic. But then I wouldn't be able to rescue the elf. . . . Saphira, where are you? I need your help.* He silently berated himself for not contacting her sooner. That should have been the first thing he did after getting his power back.

Her reply came with surprising alacrity. *Eragon! I'm over Gil'ead. Don't do anything. Murtagh is on the way.*

What are— Footsteps interrupted him. He spun around, crouching as a squad of six soldiers marched into the hall. They halted abruptly, eyes flicking between Eragon and the open cell door. Blood drained from their faces. *Good, they know who I am. Maybe I can scare them off so we won't have to fight.*

"Charge!" yelled one of the soldiers, running forward. The rest of the men drew their blades and pounded down the hall.

It was madness to fight six men when he was unarmed and weak, but the thought of the elf kept him in place. He could not force himself to abandon her. Uncertain if the effort would leave him standing, he pulled on his power and raised his hand, the gedwëy ignasia glowing. Fear showed in the soldiers' eyes, but they were hardened warriors and did not slow. As Eragon opened his mouth to pronounce the fatal words, there was a low buzz, a flicker of motion. One of the men crashed to the floor with an arrow in his back. Two more were struck before anyone understood what was happening.

At the end of the hall, where the soldiers had entered, stood a ragged, bearded man with a bow. A crutch lay on the floor by his feet, apparently unneeded, for he stood tall and straight.

The three remaining soldiers turned to face this new threat. Eragon took advantage of the confusion. "Thrysta!" he shouted. One of the men clutched his chest and fell. Eragon staggered as the magic took its toll. Another soldier fell, pierced through the neck with an arrow. "Don't kill him!" called Eragon, seeing his rescuer take aim at the last soldier. The bearded man lowered his bow.

Eragon concentrated on the soldier before him. The man was breathing hard; the whites of his eyes showed. He seemed to understand that his life was being spared.

"You've seen what I can do," said Eragon harshly. "If you don't answer my questions, the rest of your life will be spent in utter misery and torment. Now where's my sword—its sheath and blade are red—and what cell is the elf in?"

The man clamped his mouth shut.

Eragon's palm glowed ominously as he reached for the magic. "That was the wrong answer," he snapped. "Do you know how much pain a grain of sand can cause you when it's embedded red hot in your stomach? Especially when it doesn't cool off for the next twenty years and slowly burns its way down to your toes! By the time it gets out of you, you'll be an old man." He paused for effect. "Unless you tell me what I want."

The soldier's eyes bulged, but he remained silent. Eragon scraped some dirt off the stone floor and observed dispassionately, "This is a bit more than a piece of sand, but be comforted; it'll burn through you faster. Still, it'll leave a bigger hole." At his word, the dirt shone cherry red, though it did not burn his hand.

"All right, just don't put that in me!" yelped the soldier. "The elf's in the last cell to the left! I don't know about your sword, but it's probably in the guardroom upstairs. All the weapons are there."

Eragon nodded, then murmured, "Slytha." The soldier's eyes rolled up in his head, and he collapsed limply.

"Did you kill him?"

Eragon looked at the stranger, who was now only a few paces away. He narrowed his eyes, trying to see past the beard. "Murtagh! Is that you?" he exclaimed.

"Yes," said Murtagh, briefly lifting the beard from his shaven face. "I don't want my face seen. Did you kill him?"

"No, he's only asleep. How did you get in?"

"There's no time to explain. We have to get up to the next floor before anyone finds us. There'll be an escape route for us in a few minutes. We don't want to miss it."

"Didn't you hear what I said?" asked Eragon, gesturing at the unconscious soldier. "There's an elf in the prison. I saw her! We have to rescue her. I need your help."

"An elf . . . !" Murtagh hurried down the hall, growling, "This is a mistake. We should flee while we have the chance." He stopped before the cell the soldier had indicated and produced a ring of keys from under his ragged cloak. "I took it from one of the guards," he explained.

Eragon motioned for the keys. Murtagh shrugged and handed them to him. Eragon found the right one and swung the door open. A single beam of moonlight slanted through the window, illuminating the elf's face with cool silver.

She faced him, tense and coiled, ready for whatever would happen next. She held her head high, with a queen's demeanor. Her eyes, dark green, almost black, and slightly angled like a cat's, lifted to Eragon's. Chills shot through him.

Their gaze held for a moment, then the elf trembled and collapsed soundlessly. Eragon barely caught her before she struck the floor. She was surprisingly light. The aroma of freshly crushed pine needles surrounded her.

Murtagh entered the cell. "She's beautiful!"

"But hurt."

"We can tend to her later. Are you strong enough to carry her?" Eragon shook his head. "Then I'll do it," said Murtagh as he slung the elf across his shoulders. "Now, upstairs!" He handed Eragon a dagger, then hurried back into the hall littered with soldiers' bodies.

With heavy footsteps Murtagh led Eragon to a stone-hewn staircase at the end of the hall. As they climbed it, Eragon asked, "How are we going to get out without being noticed?"

"We're not," grunted Murtagh.

That did not allay Eragon's fears. He listened anxiously for soldiers or anyone else who might be nearby, dreading what might happen if they met the Shade. At the head of the stairs was a banquet room filled with broad wooden tables. Shields lined the walls, and the wood ceiling was trussed with curved beams. Murtagh laid the elf on a table and looked at the ceiling worriedly. "Can you talk to Saphira for me?"

"Yes."

"Tell her to wait another five minutes."

There were shouts in the distance. Soldiers marched past the entrance to the banquet room. Eragon's mouth tightened with pent-up tension. "Whatever you're planning to do, I don't think we have much time."

"Just tell her, and stay out of sight," snapped Murtagh, running off.

As Eragon relayed the message, he was alarmed to hear men coming up the stairs. Fighting hunger and exhaustion, he dragged the elf off the table and hid her underneath it. He crouched next to her, holding his breath, tightly clenching the dagger.

Ten soldiers entered the room. They swept through it hurriedly, looking under only a couple of tables, and continued on their way. Eragon leaned against a table leg, sighing. The respite made him suddenly aware of his burning stomach and parched throat. A tankard and a plate of half-eaten food on the other side of the room caught his attention.

Eragon dashed from his hiding place, grabbed the food, then scurried back to the table. There was amber beer in the tankard, which he drank in two great gulps. Relief seeped through him as the cool liquid ran down his throat, soothing the irritated tissue. He suppressed a belch before ravenously tearing into a hunk of bread.

Murtagh returned carrying Zar'roc, a strange bow, and an elegant sword without a sheath. Murtagh gave Zar'roc to Eragon. "I found the other sword and bow in the guardroom. I've never seen weapons like them before, so I assumed they were the elf's."

"Let's find out," said Eragon through a mouthful of bread. The sword—slim and light with a curved crossguard, the ends of which narrowed into sharp points—fit the elf's sheath perfectly. There was no way to tell if the bow was hers, but it was shaped so gracefully he doubted it could be anyone else's. "What now?" he asked, cramming another bite of food into his mouth. "We can't stay here forever. Sooner or later the soldiers will find us."

"Now," said Murtagh, taking out his own bow and fitting an arrow to the string, "we wait. Like I said, our escape has been arranged."

"You don't understand; there's a Shade here! If he finds us, we're doomed."

"A Shade!" exclaimed Murtagh. "In that case, tell Saphira to come immediately. We were going to wait until the watch changed, but delaying even that long is too dangerous now." Eragon relayed the message succinctly, refraining from distracting Saphira with questions. "You messed up my plans by escaping yourself," groused Murtagh, watching the room's entrances for soldiers.

Eragon smiled. "In that case, perhaps I should have waited. *Your* timing was perfect, though. I wouldn't have been able to even crawl if I had been forced to fight all those soldiers with magic."

"Glad to be of some use," remarked Murtagh. He stiffened as they heard men running nearby. "Let's just hope the Shade doesn't find us."

A cold chuckle filled the banquet room. "I'm afraid it's far too late for that."

Murtagh and Eragon spun around. The Shade stood alone at the end of the room. In his hand was a pale sword with a thin scratch on the blade. He unclasped the brooch that held his cape in place and let the garment fall to the floor. His body was like a runner's, thin and compact, but Eragon remembered Brom's warning and knew that the Shade's appearance was deceiving; he was many times stronger than a normal human.

305

"So, my young *Rider*, do you wish to test yourself against me?" sneered the Shade. "I shouldn't have trusted the captain when he said you ate all your food. I will not make that mistake again."

"I'll take care of him," said Murtagh quietly, putting down his bow and drawing his sword.

"No," said Eragon under his breath. "He wants me alive, not you. I can stall him for a short while, but then you'd better have a way out for us."

"Fine, go," said Murtagh. "You won't have to hold him off for long."

"I hope not," said Eragon grimly. He drew Zar'roc and slowly advanced. The red blade glinted with light from torches on the wall.

The Shade's maroon eyes burned like coals. He laughed softly. "Do you really think to defeat me, Du Súndavar Freohr? What a pitiful name. I would have expected something more subtle from you, but I suppose that's all you're capable of."

Eragon refused to let himself be goaded. He stared at the Shade's face, waiting for a flicker of his eyes or twitch of his lip, anything that would betray his next move. *I can't use magic for fear of provoking him to do the same. He has to think that he can win without resorting to it—which he probably can.*

Before either of them moved, the ceiling boomed and shook. Dust billowed from it and turned the air gray while pieces of wood fell around them, shattering on the floor. From the roof came screams and the sound of clashing metal. Afraid of being brained by the falling timber, Eragon flicked his eyes upward. The Shade took advantage of his distraction and attacked.

Eragon barely managed to get Zar'roc up in time to block a slash at his ribs. Their blades met with a clang that jarred his teeth and numbed his arm. *Hellfire! He's strong!* He grasped Zar'roc with both hands and swung with all of his might at the Shade's head. The Shade blocked him with ease, whipping his sword through the air faster than Eragon had thought possible.

Terrible screeches sounded above them, like iron spikes being drawn across rock. Three long cracks split the ceiling. Shingles from the slate roof fell through the fissures. Eragon ignored them, even when one smashed into the floor next to him. Though he had trained with a master of the blade, Brom, and with Murtagh, who was also a deadly swordsman, he had never been this outclassed. The Shade was *playing* with him.

Eragon retreated toward Murtagh, arms trembling as he parried the Shade's blows. Each one seemed more powerful than the last. Eragon was no longer strong enough to call upon magic for help even if he had wanted to. Then, with a contemptuous flick of his wrist, the Shade knocked Zar'roc out of Eragon's hand. The force of the blow sent him to his knees, where he stayed, panting. The screeching was louder than ever. Whatever was happening, it was getting closer.

The Shade stared down at him haughtily. "A powerful piece you may be in the game that is being played, but I'm disappointed that this is your best. If the other Riders were this weak, they must have controlled the Empire only through sheer numbers."

Eragon looked up and shook his head. He had figured out Murtagh's plan. *Saphira, now would be a good time.* "No, you forget something."

"And what might that be?" asked the Shade mockingly.

There was a thunderous reverberation as a chunk of the ceiling was torn away to reveal the night sky. "The dragons!" roared Eragon over the noise, and threw himself out of the Shade's reach. The Shade snarled in rage, swinging his sword viciously. He missed and lunged. Surprise spread across his face as one of Murtagh's arrows sprouted from his shoulder.

The Shade laughed and snapped the arrow off with two fingers. "You'll have to do better than that if you want to stop me." The next arrow caught him between the eyes. The Shade howled with agony and writhed, covering his face. His skin turned gray. Mist formed in the air around him, obscuring his figure. There was a shattering cry; then the cloud vanished.

Where the Shade had been, nothing was left but his cape and a pile of clothes. "You killed him!" exclaimed Eragon. He knew of only two heroes of legend who had survived slaying a Shade.

"I'm not so sure," said Murtagh.

A man shouted, "That's it. He failed. Go in and get them!" Soldiers with nets and spears poured into the banquet room from both ends. Eragon and Murtagh backed up against the wall, dragging the elf with them. The men formed a menacing half-circle around them. Then Saphira stuck her head through the hole in the ceiling and roared. She gripped the edge of the opening with her powerful talons and ripped off another large section of the ceiling.

Three soldiers turned and ran, but the rest held their positions.

With a resounding report, the center beam of the ceiling cracked and rained down heavy shingles. Confusion scattered the ranks as they tried to dodge the deadly barrage. Eragon and Murtagh pressed against the wall to avoid the falling debris. Saphira roared again, and the soldiers fled, some getting crushed on the way.

With a final titanic effort, Saphira tore off the rest of the ceiling before jumping into the banquet hall with her wings folded. Her weight splintered a table with a sharp crunch. Crying out with relief, Eragon threw his arms around her. She hummed contentedly. *I've missed you, little one.*

Same here. There's someone else with us. Can you carry three?

Of course, she said, kicking shingles and tables out of the way so she could take off. Murtagh and Eragon pulled the elf out of hiding. Saphira hissed in surprise as she saw her. *An elf!*

Yes, and the woman I saw in my dreams, said Eragon, picking up Zar'roc. He helped Murtagh secure the elf into the saddle, then they both climbed onto Saphira. *I heard fighting on the roof. Are there men up there?*

There were, but no more. Are you ready?

Yes.

Saphira leapt out of the banquet hall and onto the fortress's roof, where the bodies of watchmen lay scattered. "Look!" said Murtagh, pointing. A row of archers filed out of a tower on the other side of the roofless hall.

"Saphira, you have to take off. Now!" warned Eragon.

She unfurled her wings, ran toward the edge of the building, and propelled them over it with her powerful legs. The extra weight on her back made her drop alarmingly. As she struggled to gain altitude, Eragon heard the musical twang of bowstrings being released.

Arrows whizzed toward them in the dark. Saphira roared with pain as she was struck and quickly rolled to the left to avoid the next volley. More arrows perforated the sky, but the night protected them from the shafts' deadly bite. Distressed, Eragon bent over Saphira's neck. *Where are you hurt?*

My wings are pierced . . . one of the arrows didn't go all the way through. It's still there. Her breathing was labored and heavy.

How far can you take us?

Far enough. Eragon clutched the elf tightly as they skimmed over Gil'ead, then left the city behind and veered eastward, soaring upward through the night.

A WARRIOR
AND A HEALER

S aphira drifted down to a clearing, landed on the crest of a hill, and rested her outstretched wings on the ground. Eragon could feel her shaking beneath him. They were only a half-league from Gil'ead.

Picketed in the clearing were Snowfire and Tornac, who snorted nervously at Saphira's arrival. Eragon slid to the ground and immediately turned to Saphira's injuries, while Murtagh readied the horses.

Unable to see well in the darkness, Eragon ran his hands blindly over Saphira's wings. He found three places where arrows had punctured the thin membrane, leaving bloody holes as thick around as his thumb. A small piece had also been torn out of the back edge of her left wing. She shivered when his fingers brushed the injuries. He tiredly healed the wounds with words from the ancient language. Then he went to the arrow that was embedded in one of the large muscles of her flying arm. The arrowhead poked through its underside. Warm blood dripped off it.

Eragon called Murtagh over and instructed, "Hold her wing down. I have to remove this arrow." He indicated where Murtagh should grip. *This will be painful,* he warned Saphira, *but it'll be over quickly. Try not to struggle—you'll hurt us.*

She extended her neck and grabbed a tall sapling between her curved teeth. With a yank of her head, she pulled the tree out of the ground and clamped it firmly in her jaws. *I'm ready.*

Okay, said Eragon. "Hold on," he whispered to Murtagh, then broke off the head of the arrow. Trying not to cause any more damage, he swiftly pulled the shaft out of Saphira. As it left her muscle, she threw back her head and whimpered past the tree in her mouth. Her wing jerked involuntarily, clipping Murtagh under the chin and knocking him to the ground.

With a growl, Saphira shook the tree, spraying them with dirt before tossing it away. After Eragon sealed the wound, he helped Murtagh up. "She caught me by surprise," admitted Murtagh, touching his scraped jaw.

I'm sorry.

"She didn't mean to hit you," assured Eragon. He checked on the unconscious elf. *You're going to have to carry her a bit longer,* he told Saphira. *We can't take her on the horses and ride fast enough. Flying should be easier for you now that the arrow is out.*

Saphira dipped her head. *I will do it.*

Thank you, said Eragon. He hugged her fiercely. *What you did was incredible; I'll never forget it.*

311

Her eyes softened. *I will go now.* He backed away as she flew up in a flurry of air, the elf's hair streaming back. Seconds later they were gone. Eragon hurried to Snowfire, pulled himself into the saddle, and galloped away with Murtagh.

While they rode, Eragon tried to remember what he knew about elves. They had long lives—that fact was oft repeated—although he knew not how long. They spoke the ancient language, and many could use magic. After the Riders' fall, elves had retreated into seclusion. None of them had been seen in the Empire since. *So why is one here now? And how did the Empire manage to capture her? If she can use magic, she's probably drugged as I was.*

They traveled through the night, not stopping even when their flagging strength began to slow them. They continued onward despite burning eyes and clumsy movements. Behind them, lines of torch-bearing horsemen searched around Gil'ead for their trail.

After many bleary hours, dawn lightened the sky. By unspoken consent Eragon and Murtagh stopped the horses. "We have to make camp," said Eragon wearily. "I must sleep—whether they catch us or not."

"Agreed," said Murtagh, rubbing his eyes. "Have Saphira land. We'll meet her."

They followed Saphira's directions and found her drinking from a stream at the base of a small cliff, the elf still slouched on her back. Saphira greeted them with a soft bugle as Eragon dismounted.

Murtagh helped him remove the elf from Saphira's saddle and lower her to the ground. Then they sagged against the rock face, exhausted. Saphira examined the elf curiously. *I wonder why she hasn't woken. It's been hours since we left Gil'ead.*

Who knows what they did to her? said Eragon grimly.

Murtagh followed their gaze. "As far as I know, she's the first elf the king has captured. Ever since they went into hiding, he's been looking for them without success—until now. So he's either found their sanctuary, or she was captured by chance. I think it was chance. If he had found the elf haven, he would have declared war and sent his army after the elves. Since that hasn't happened, the question is, Were Galbatorix's men able to extract the elves' location before we rescued her?"

"We won't know until she regains consciousness. Tell me what happened after I was captured. How did I end up in Gil'ead?"

"The Urgals are working for the Empire," said Murtagh shortly, pushing back his hair. "And, it seems, the Shade as well. Saphira and I saw the Urgals give you to him—though I didn't know who it was at the time—and a group of soldiers. They were the ones who took you to Gil'ead."

It's true, said Saphira, curling up next to them.

Eragon's mind flashed back to the Urgals he had spoken with at Teirm and the "master" they had mentioned. *They meant the king! I insulted the most powerful man in Alagaësia!* he realized with dread. Then he remembered the horror of the slaughtered villagers in Yazuac. A sick, angry feeling welled in his stomach. *The Urgals were under Galbatorix's orders! Why would he commit such an atrocity on his own subjects?*

Because he is evil, stated Saphira flatly.

Glowering, Eragon exclaimed, "This will mean war! Once the people of the Empire learn of it, they will rebel and support the Varden."

Murtagh rested his chin in his hand. "Even if they heard of this outrage, few would make it to the Varden. With the Urgals under his command, the king has enough warriors to close the Empire's borders and remain in control, no matter how disruptive people are. With such a rule of terror, he will be able to shape the Empire however he wants. And though he is hated, people could be galvanized into joining him if they had a common enemy."

"Who would that be?" asked Eragon, confused.

"The elves and the Varden. With the right rumors they can be portrayed as the most despicable monsters in Alagaësia—fiends who are waiting to seize your land and wealth. The Empire could even say that the Urgals have been misunderstood all this time and that they are really friends and allies against such terrible enemies. I only wonder what the king promised them in return for their services."

"It wouldn't work," said Eragon, shaking his head. "No one could be deceived that easily about Galbatorix and the Urgals. Besides, why would he want to do that? He's already in power."

"But his authority is challenged by the Varden, with whom people sympathize. There's also Surda, which has defied him since it seceded from the Empire. Galbatorix is strong within the Empire, but his arm is weak outside of it. As for people seeing through his deceptions, they'll believe whatever he wants them to. It's happened before." Murtagh fell silent and gazed moodily into the distance.

His words troubled Eragon. Saphira touched him with her mind: *Where is Galbatorix sending the Urgals?*

What?

In both Carvahall and Teirm, you heard that Urgals were leaving the area and migrating southeast, as if to brave the Hadarac Desert. If the king truly does control them, why is he sending them in that direction? Maybe an Urgal army is being gathered for his private use or an Urgal city is being formed.

Eragon shuddered at the thought. *I'm too tired to figure it out. Whatever Galbatorix's plans, they'll only cause us trouble. I just wish that we knew where the Varden are. That's where we should be going, but we're lost without Dormnad. It doesn't matter what we do; the Empire will find us.*

Don't give up, she said encouragingly, then added dryly, *though you're probably right.*

Thanks. He looked at Murtagh. "You risked your life to rescue me; I owe you for that. I couldn't have escaped on my own." It was more than that, though. There was a bond between them now, welded in the brotherhood of battle and tempered by the loyalty Murtagh had shown.

"I'm just glad I could help. It . . ." Murtagh faltered and rubbed his face. "My main worry now is how we're going to travel with so many men searching for us. Gil'ead's soldiers will be hunting us tomorrow; once they find the horses' tracks, they'll know you didn't fly away with Saphira."

Eragon glumly agreed. "How did you manage to get into the castle?"

Murtagh laughed softly. "By paying a steep bribe and crawling through a filthy scullery chute. But the plan wouldn't have worked without Saphira. She," he stopped and directed his words at her, "that is, you, are the only reason we escaped alive."

Eragon solemnly put a hand on her scaly neck. As she hummed contentedly, he gazed at the elf's face, captivated. Reluctantly, he dragged himself upright. "We should make a bed for her."

Murtagh got to his feet and stretched out a blanket for the elf. When they lifted her onto it, the cuff of her sleeve tore on a branch. Eragon began to pinch the fabric together, then gasped.

The elf's arm was mottled with a layer of bruises and cuts; some were half healed, while others were fresh and oozing. Eragon shook his head with anger and pulled the sleeve up higher. The injuries continued to her shoulder. With trembling fingers, he unlaced the back of her shirt, dreading what might be under it.

As the leather slipped off, Murtagh cursed. The elf's back was strong and muscled, but it was covered with scabs that made her skin look like dry, cracked mud. She had been whipped mercilessly and branded with hot irons in the shape of claws. Where her skin was still intact, it was purple and black from numerous beatings. On her left shoulder was a tattoo inscribed with indigo ink. It was the same symbol that had been on the sapphire of Brom's ring. Eragon silently swore an oath that he would kill whoever was responsible for torturing the elf.

"Can you heal this?" asked Murtagh.

"I—I don't know," said Eragon. He swallowed back sudden queasiness. "There's so much."

Eragon! said Saphira sharply. *This is an elf. She cannot be allowed to die. Tired or not, hungry or not, you must save her. I will meld my strength with yours, but you are the one who must wield the magic.*

Yes . . . you are right, he murmured, unable to tear his eyes from the elf. Determined, he pulled off his gloves and said to Murtagh, "This is going to take some time. Can you get me food? Also, boil rags for bandages; I can't heal all her wounds."

"We can't make a fire without being seen," objected Murtagh. "You'll have to use unwashed cloths, and the food will be cold." Eragon grimaced but acquiesced. As he gently laid a hand on the elf's spine, Saphira settled next to him, her glittering eyes fixed on the elf. He took a deep breath, then reached for the magic and started working.

He spoke the ancient words, "Waíse heill!" A burn shimmered under his palm, and new, unmarked skin flowed over it, joining together without a scar. He passed over bruises or other wounds that were not life-threatening—healing them all would consume the energy he needed for more serious injuries. As Eragon toiled, he marveled that the elf was still alive. She had been repeatedly tortured to the edge of death with a precision that chilled him.

Although he tried to preserve the elf's modesty, he could not help but notice that underneath the disfiguring marks, her body was exceptionally beautiful. He was exhausted and did not dwell upon it—though his ears turned red at times, and he fervently hoped that Saphira did not know what he was thinking.

He labored through dawn, pausing only at brief intervals to eat and drink, trying to replenish himself from his fast, the escape, and now healing the elf. Saphira remained by his side, lending her strength where she could. The sun was well into the sky when he finally stood, groaning as his cramped muscles stretched. His hands were gray and his eyes felt dry and gritty. He stumbled to the saddlebags and took a long drink from the wineskin. "Is it done?" asked Murtagh.

Eragon nodded, trembling. He did not trust himself to speak. The camp spun before him; he nearly fainted. *You did well,* said Saphira soothingly.

"Will she live?"

"I don't—don't know," he said in a ravaged voice. "Elves are strong, but even they cannot endure abuse like this with impunity. If I knew more about healing, I might be able to revive her, but . . ." He gestured helplessly. His hand was shaking so badly he spilled some of the wine. Another swig helped to steady him. "We'd better start riding again."

"No! You must sleep," protested Murtagh.

"I . . . can sleep in the saddle. But we can't afford to stay here, not with the soldiers closing on us."

Murtagh reluctantly gave in. "In that case I'll lead Snowfire while you rest." They resaddled the horses, strapped the elf onto Saphira, and departed the camp. Eragon ate while he rode, trying to replace his depleted energy before he leaned forward against Snowfire and closed his eyes.

WATER FROM SAND

When they stopped for the evening, Eragon felt no better and his temper had worsened. Most of the day had been spent on long detours to avoid detection by soldiers with hunting dogs. He dismounted Snowfire and asked Saphira, *How is she?*

I think no worse than before. She stirred slightly a few times, but that was all. Saphira crouched low to the ground to let him lift the elf out of the saddle. For a moment her soft form pressed against Eragon. Then he hurriedly put her down.

He and Murtagh made a small dinner. It was difficult for them to fight off the urge to sleep. When they had eaten, Murtagh said, "We can't keep up this pace; we aren't gaining any ground on the soldiers. Another day or two of this and they'll be sure to overtake us."

"What else can we do?" snapped Eragon. "If it were just the two of us and you were willing to leave Tornac behind, Saphira could fly us out of here. But with the elf, too? Impossible."

Murtagh looked at him carefully. "If you want to go your own way, I won't stop you. I can't expect you and Saphira to stay and risk imprisonment."

"Don't insult me," Eragon muttered. "The only reason I'm free is because of you. I'm not going to abandon you to the Empire. Poor thanks that would be!"

Murtagh bowed his head. "Your words hearten me." He paused. "But they don't solve our problem."

"What can?" Eragon asked. He gestured at the elf. "I wish she could tell us where the elves are; perhaps we could seek sanctuary with them."

"Considering how they've protected themselves, I doubt she'd reveal their location. Even if she did, the others of her kind might not welcome us. Why would they want to shelter us anyway? The last Riders they had contact with were Galbatorix and the Forsworn. I doubt that left them with pleasant memories. And I don't even have the dubious honor of being a Rider like you. No, they would not want me at all."

They would accept us, said Saphira confidently as she shifted her wings to a more comfortable position.

Eragon shrugged. "Even if they would protect us, we can't find them, and it's impossible to ask the elf until she regains consciousness. We must flee, but in which direction—north, south, east, or west?"

Murtagh laced his fingers together and pressed his thumbs against his temples. "I think the only thing we can do is leave the Empire. The few safe places within it are far from here. They would be difficult to reach without being caught or followed. . . . There's nothing for us to the north except the forest Du Weldenvarden— which we might be able to hide in, but I don't relish going back past Gil'ead. Only the Empire and the sea lie westward. To the south is Surda, where you might be able to find someone to direct you to the Varden. As for going east . . ." He shrugged. "To the east, the Hadarac Desert stands between us and whatever lands exist in that direction. The Varden are somewhere across it, but without directions it might take us years to find them."

We would be safe, though, remarked Saphira. *As long as we didn't encounter any Urgals.*

Eragon knitted his brow. A headache threatened to drown his thoughts in hot throbs. "It's too dangerous to go to Surda. We would have to traverse most of the Empire, avoiding every town and village. There are too many people between us and Surda to get there unnoticed."

Murtagh raised an eyebrow. "So you want to go across the desert?"

"I don't see any other options. Besides, that way we can leave the Empire before the Ra'zac get here. With their flying steeds, they'll probably arrive in Gil'ead in a couple of days, so we don't have much time."

"Even if we do reach the desert before they get here," said Murtagh, "they could still overtake us. It'll be hard to outdistance them at all."

Eragon rubbed Saphira's side, her scales rough under his fingers. "That's assuming they can follow our trail. To catch us, though, they'll have to leave the soldiers behind, which is to our advantage. If it comes to a fight, I think the three of us can defeat them . . . as long as we aren't ambushed the way Brom and I were."

"If we reach the other side of the Hadarac safely," said Murtagh slowly, "where will we go? Those lands are well outside of the Empire. There will be few cities, if any. And then there is the desert itself. What do you know of it?"

"Only that it's hot, dry, and full of sand," confessed Eragon.

"That about sums it up," replied Murtagh. "It's filled with poisonous and inedible plants, venomous snakes, scorpions, and a blistering sun. You saw the great plain on our way to Gil'ead?"

It was a rhetorical question, but Eragon answered anyway, "Yes, and once before."

"Then you are familiar with its immense range. It fills the heart of the Empire. Now imagine something two or three times its size, and you'll understand the vastness of the Hadarac Desert. That is what you're proposing to cross."

Eragon tried to envision a piece of land that gigantic but was unable to grasp the distances involved. He retrieved the map of Alagaësia from his saddlebags. The parchment smelled musty as he unrolled it on the ground. He inspected the plains and shook his head in amazement. "No wonder the Empire ends at the desert. Everything on the other side is too far away for Galbatorix to control."

Murtagh swept his hand over the right side of the parchment. "All the land beyond the desert, which is blank on this map, was under one rule when the Riders lived. If the king were to raise up new Riders under his command, it would allow him to expand the Empire to an unprecedented size. But that wasn't the point I was trying to make. The Hadarac Desert is so huge and contains so many dangers, the chances are slim that we can cross it unscathed. It is a desperate path to take."

"We *are* desperate," said Eragon firmly. He studied the map carefully. "If we rode through the belly of the desert, it would take well over a month, perhaps even two, to cross it. But if we angle southeast, toward the Beor Mountains, we could cut through much faster. Then we can either follow the Beor Mountains farther east into the wilderness or go west to Surda. If this map is accurate, the distance between here and the Beors is roughly equal to what we covered on our way to Gil'ead."

"But that took us nearly a month!"

Eragon shook his head impatiently. "Our ride to Gil'ead was slow on account of my injuries. If we press ourselves, it'll take only a fraction of that time to reach the Beor Mountains."

"Enough. You made your point," acknowledged Murtagh. "Before I consent, however, something must be solved. As I'm sure you noticed, I bought supplies for us and the horses while I was in Gil'ead. But how can we get enough water? The roving tribes who live in the Hadarac usually disguise their wells and oases so no one can steal their water. And carrying enough for more than a day is impractical. Just think about how much Saphira drinks! She and the horses consume more water at one time than we do in a week. Unless you can make it rain whenever we need, I don't see how we can go the direction you propose."

Eragon rocked back on his heels. Making rain was well beyond his power. He suspected that not even the strongest Rider could have done it. Moving that much air was like trying to lift a mountain. He needed a solution that would not drain all of his strength.

I wonder if it's possible to convert sand into water? That would solve our problem, but only if it doesn't take too much energy.

"I have an idea," he said. "Let me experiment, then I'll give you an answer." Eragon strode out of the camp, with Saphira following closely.

What are you going to try? she asked.

"I don't know," he muttered. *Saphira, could you carry enough water for us?*

She shook her enormous head. *No, I wouldn't even be able to lift that much weight, let alone fly with it.*

Too bad. He knelt and picked up a stone with a cavity large enough for a mouthful of water. He pressed a clump of dirt into the hollow and studied it thoughtfully. Now came the hard part. Somehow he had to convert the dirt into water. *But what words should I use?* He puzzled over it for a moment, then picked two he hoped would work. The icy magic rushed through him as he breached the familiar barrier in his mind and commanded, "Deloi moi!"

321

Immediately the dirt began to absorb his strength at a prodigious rate. Eragon's mind flashed back to Brom's warning that certain tasks could consume all of his power and take his life. Panic blossomed in his chest. He tried to release the magic but could not. It was linked to him until the task was complete or he was dead. All he could do was remain motionless, growing weaker every moment.

Just as he became convinced that he would die kneeling there, the dirt shimmered and morphed into a thimbleful of water. Relieved, Eragon sat back, breathing hard. His heart pounded painfully and hunger gnawed at his innards.

What happened? asked Saphira.

Eragon shook his head, still in shock from the drain on his body's reserves. He was glad that he had not tried to transmute anything larger. *This . . . this won't work,* he said. *I don't even have the strength to give myself a drink.*

You should have been more careful, she chided. *Magic can yield unexpected results when the ancient words are combined in new ways.*

He glared at her. *I know that, but this was the only way I could test my idea. I wasn't going to wait until we were in the desert!* He reminded himself that she was only trying to help. *How did you turn Brom's grave into diamond without killing yourself? I can barely handle a bit of dirt, much less all that sandstone.*

I don't know how I did it, she stated calmly. *It just happened.*

Could you do it again, but this time make water?

Eragon, she said, looking him squarely in the face. *I've no more control over my abilities than a spider does. Things like that occur whether I will them or not. Brom told you that unusual events happen around dragons. He spoke truly. He gave no explanation for it, nor do I have one. Sometimes I can work changes just by feel, almost without thought. The rest of the time—like right now—I'm as powerless as Snowfire.*

You're never powerless, he said softly, putting a hand on her neck. For a long period they were both quiet. Eragon remembered the grave he had made and how Brom lay within it. He could still see the sandstone flowing over the old man's face. "At least we gave him a decent burial," he whispered.

He idly swirled a finger in the dirt, making twisting ridges. Two of the ridges formed a miniature valley, so he added mountains around it. With his fingernail he scratched a river down the valley, then deepened it because it seemed too shallow. He added a few more details until he found himself staring at a passable reproduction of Palancar Valley. Homesickness welled up within him, and he obliterated the valley with a swipe of his hand.

I don't want to talk about it, he muttered angrily, staving off Saphira's questions. He crossed his arms and glared at the ground. Almost against his will, his eyes flicked back to where he had gouged the earth. He straightened, surprised. Though the ground was dry, the furrow he had made was lined with moisture. Curious, he scraped away more dirt and found a damp layer a few inches under the surface. "Look at this!" he said excitedly.

Saphira lowered her nose to his discovery. *How does this help us?*

Water in the desert is sure to be buried so deeply we would have to dig for weeks to find it.

Yes, said Eragon delightedly, *but as long as it's there, I can get it. Watch!* He deepened the hole, then mentally accessed the magic. Instead of changing the dirt into water, he simply summoned forth the moisture that was already in the earth. With a faint trickle, water rushed into the hole. He smiled and sipped from it. The liquid was cool and pure, perfect for drinking. *See! We can get all we need.*

Saphira sniffed the pool. *Here, yes. But in the desert? There may not be enough water in the ground for you to bring to the surface.*

It will work, Eragon assured her. *All I'm doing is lifting the water, an easy enough task. As long as it's done slowly, my strength will hold. Even if I have to draw the water from fifty paces down, it won't be a problem. Especially if you help me.*

Saphira looked at him dubiously. *Are you sure? Think carefully upon your answer, for it will mean our lives if you are wrong.*

Eragon hesitated, then said firmly, *I'm sure.*

Then go tell Murtagh. I will keep watch while you sleep.

But you've stayed up all night like us, he objected. *You should rest.*

I'll be fine—I'm stronger than you know, she said gently. Her scales rustled as she curled up with a watchful eye turned northward, toward their pursuers. Eragon hugged her, and she hummed deeply, sides vibrating. *Go.*

He lingered, then reluctantly returned to Murtagh, who asked, "Well? Is the desert open to us?"

"It is," acknowledged Eragon. He flopped onto his blankets and explained what he had learned. When he finished, Eragon turned to the elf. Her face was the last thing he saw before falling asleep.

THE RAMR RIVER

They forced themselves to rise early in the gray predawn hours. Eragon shivered in the cool air. "How are we going to transport the elf? She can't ride on Saphira's back much longer without getting sores from her scales. Saphira can't carry her in her claws—it tires her and makes landing dangerous. A sledge won't work; it would get battered to pieces while we ride, and I don't want the horses slowed by the weight of another person."

Murtagh considered the matter as he saddled Tornac. "If you were to ride Saphira, we could lash the elf onto Snowfire, but we'd have the same problem with sores."

I have a solution, said Saphira unexpectedly. *Why don't you tie the elf to my belly? I'll still be able to move freely, and she will be safer than anywhere else. The only danger will be if soldiers shoot arrows at me, but I can easily fly above those.*

None of them could come up with a better idea, so they quickly adopted hers. Eragon folded one of his blankets in half lengthwise, secured it around the elf's petite form, then took her to Saphira. Blankets and spare clothes were sacrificed to form ropes long enough to encircle Saphira's girth. With those ropes, the elf was tied back-first against Saphira's belly, her head between Saphira's front legs. Eragon looked critically at their handiwork. "I'm afraid your scales may rub through the ropes."

"We'll have to check them occasionally for fraying," commented Murtagh.

Shall we go now? Saphira asked, and Eragon repeated the question.

Murtagh's eyes sparked dangerously, a tight smile lifting his lips. He glanced back the way they had come, where smoke from soldiers' camps was clearly visible, and said, "I always did like races."

"And now we are in one for our lives!"

Murtagh swung into Tornac's saddle and trotted out of the camp. Eragon followed close behind on Snowfire. Saphira jumped into the air with the elf. She flew low to the ground to avoid being seen by the soldiers. In this fashion, the three of them made their way southeast toward the distant Hadarac Desert.

Eragon kept a quick eye out for pursuers as he rode. His mind repeatedly wandered back to the elf. *An elf!* He had actually seen one, and she was with them! He wondered what Roran would think of that. It struck him that if he ever returned to Carvahall, he would have a hard time convincing anyone that his adventures had actually occurred.

325

For the rest of the day, Eragon and Murtagh sped through the land, ignoring discomfort and fatigue. They drove the horses as hard as they could without killing them. Sometimes they dismounted and ran on foot to give Tornac and Snowfire a rest. Only twice did they stop—both times to let the horses eat and drink.

Though the soldiers of Gil'ead were far behind now, Eragon and Murtagh found themselves having to avoid new soldiers every time they passed a town or village. Somehow the alarm had been sent ahead of them. Twice they were nearly ambushed along the trail, escaping only because Saphira happened to smell the men ahead of them. After the second incident, they avoided the trail entirely.

Dusk softened the countryside as evening drew a black cloak across the sky. Through the night they traveled, relentlessly pacing out the miles. In the deepest hours of night, the ground rose beneath them to form low cactus-dotted hills.

Murtagh pointed forward. "There's a town, Bullridge, some leagues ahead that we must bypass. They're sure to have soldiers watching for us. We should try to slip past them now while it's dark."

After three hours they saw the straw-yellow lanterns of Bullridge. A web of soldiers patrolled between watch fires scattered around the town. Eragon and Murtagh muffled their sword sheaths and carefully dismounted. They led the horses in a wide detour around Bullridge, listening attentively to avoid stumbling on an encampment.

With the town behind them, Eragon relaxed slightly. Daybreak finally flooded the sky with a delicate blush and warmed the chilly night air. They halted on the crest of a hill to observe their surroundings. The Ramr River was to their left, but it was also five miles to their right. The river continued south for several leagues, then doubled back on itself in a narrow loop before curving west. They had covered over sixteen leagues in one day.

Eragon leaned against Snowfire's neck, happy with the distance they had gone. "Let's find a gully or hollow where we can sleep undisturbed." They stopped at a small stand of juniper trees and laid their blankets beneath them. Saphira waited patiently as they untied the elf from her belly.

"I'll take the first watch and wake you at midmorning," said Murtagh, setting his bare sword across his knees. Eragon mumbled his assent and pulled the blankets over his shoulders.

Nightfall found them worn and drowsy but determined to continue. As they prepared to leave, Saphira observed to Eragon, *This is the third night since we rescued you from Gil'ead, and the elf still hasn't woken. I'm worried. And,* she continued, *she has neither drunk nor eaten in that time. I know little of elves, but she is slender, and I doubt she can survive much longer without nourishment.*

"What's wrong?" asked Murtagh over Tornac's back.

"The elf," said Eragon, looking down at her. "Saphira is troubled that she hasn't woken or eaten; it disturbs me too. I healed her wounds, at least on the surface, but it doesn't seem to have done her any good."

"Maybe the Shade tampered with her mind," suggested Murtagh.

"Then we have to help her."

Murtagh knelt by the elf. He examined her intently, then shook his head and stood. "As far as I can tell, she's only sleeping. It seems as if I could wake her with a word or a touch, yet she slumbers on. Her coma might be something elves self-induce to escape the pain of injury, but if so, why doesn't she end it? There's no danger to her now."

"But does she know that?" asked Eragon quietly.

Murtagh put a hand on his shoulder. "This must wait. We have to leave now or risk losing our hard-won lead. You can tend to her later when we stop."

"One thing first," said Eragon. He soaked a rag, then squeezed the cloth so water dripped between the elf's sculpted lips. He did that several times and dabbed above her straight, angled eyebrows, feeling oddly protective.

They headed through the hills, avoiding the tops for fear of being spotted by sentries. Saphira stayed with them on the ground for the same reason. Despite her bulk, she was stealthy; only her tail could be heard scraping over the ground, like a thick blue snake.

Eventually the sky brightened in the east. The morning star Aiedail appeared as they reached the edge of a steep bank covered with mounds of brush. Water roared below as it tore over boulders and sluiced through branches.

"The Ramr!" said Eragon over the noise.

Murtagh nodded. "Yes! We have to find a place to ford safely."

That isn't necessary, said Saphira. *I can carry you across, no matter how wide the river is.*

Eragon looked up at her blue-gray form. *What about the horses? We can't leave them behind. They're too heavy for you to lift.*

As long as you're not on them and they don't struggle too much, I'm sure that I can carry them. If I can dodge arrows with three people on my back, I can certainly fly a horse in a straight line over a river.

I believe you, but let's not attempt it unless we have to. It's too dangerous.

She clambered down the embankment. *We can't afford to squander time here.*

Eragon followed her, leading Snowfire. The bank came to an abrupt end at the Ramr, where the river ran dark and swift. White mist wafted up from the water, like blood steaming in winter. It was impossible to see the far side. Murtagh tossed a branch into the torrent and watched it race away, bobbing on the rough water.

"How deep do you think it is?" asked Eragon.

"I can't tell," said Murtagh, worry coloring his voice. "Can you see how far across it is with magic?"

"I don't think so, not without lighting up this place like a beacon."

With a gust of air, Saphira took off and soared over the Ramr. After a short time, she said, *I'm on the other bank. The river is over a half-mile wide. You couldn't have chosen a worse place to cross; the Ramr bends at this point and is at its widest.*

"A half-mile!" exclaimed Eragon. He told Murtagh about Saphira's offer to fly them.

"I'd rather not try it, for the horses' sake. Tornac isn't as accustomed to Saphira as Snowfire. He might panic and injure them both. Ask Saphira to look for shallows where we can swim over safely. If there aren't any within a mile in either direction, then I suppose she can ferry us."

At Eragon's request, Saphira agreed to search for a ford. While she explored, they hunkered next to the horses and ate dry bread. It was not long before Saphira returned, her velvet wings whispering in the early dawn sky. *The water is both deep and strong, upstream as well as downstream.*

Once he was told, Murtagh said, "I'd better go over first, so I can watch the horses." He scrambled onto Saphira's saddle. "Be careful with Tornac. I've had him for many years. I don't want anything to happen to him." Then Saphira took off.

When she returned, the unconscious elf had been untied from her belly. Eragon led Tornac to Saphira, ignoring the horse's low whinnies. Saphira reared back on her haunches to grasp the horse around the belly with her forelegs. Eragon eyed her formidable claws and said, "Wait!" He repositioned Tornac's saddle blanket, strapping it to the horse's belly so it protected his soft underside, then gestured for Saphira to proceed.

Tornac snorted in fright and tried to bolt when Saphira's forelegs clamped around his sides, but she held him tightly. The horse rolled his eyes wildly, the whites rimming his dilated pupils. Eragon tried to gentle Tornac with his mind, but the horse's panic resisted his touch. Before Tornac could try to escape again, Saphira jumped skyward, her hind legs thrusting with such force that her claws gouged the rocks underneath. Her wings strained furiously, struggling to lift the enormous load. For a moment it seemed she would fall back to the ground. Then, with a lunge, she shot into the air. Tornac screamed in terror, kicking and tossing. It was a terrible sound, like screeching metal.

Eragon swore, wondering if anyone was close enough to hear. *You'd better hurry, Saphira.* He listened for soldiers as he waited, scanning the inky landscape for the telltale flash of torches. It soon met his eye in a line of horsemen sliding down a bluff almost a league away.

As Saphira landed, Eragon brought Snowfire to her. *Murtagh's silly animal is in hysterics. He had to tie Tornac down to prevent him from running away.* She gripped Snowfire and carried him off, ignoring the horse's trumpeted protestations. Eragon watched her go, feeling lonely in the night. The horsemen were only a mile away.

Finally Saphira came for him, and they were soon on firm ground once more, with the Ramr to their backs. Once the horses were calmed and the saddles readjusted, they resumed their flight toward the Beor Mountains. The air filled with the calls of birds waking to a new day.

Eragon dozed even when walking. He was barely aware that Murtagh was just as drowsy. There were times when neither of them guided the horses, and it was only Saphira's vigilance that kept them on course.

Eventually the ground became soft and gave way under their feet, forcing them to halt. The sun was high overhead. The Ramr River was no more than a fuzzy line behind them.

They had reached the Hadarac Desert.

THE HADARAC DESERT

A vast expanse of dunes spread to the horizon like ripples on an ocean. Bursts of wind twirled the reddish gold sand into the air. Scraggly trees grew on scattered patches of solid ground—ground any farmer would have declared unfit for crops. Rising in the distance was a line of purple crags. The imposing desolation was barren of any animals except for a bird gliding on the zephyrs.

"You're sure we'll find food for the horses out there?" queried Eragon, slurring his words. The hot, dry air stung his throat.

"See those?" asked Murtagh, indicating the crags. "Grass grows around them. It's short and tough, but the horses will find it sufficient."

"I hope you're right," said Eragon, squinting at the sun. "Before we continue, let's rest. My mind is slow as a snail, and I can barely move my legs."

They untied the elf from Saphira, ate, then lay in the shadow of a dune for a nap. As Eragon settled into the sand, Saphira coiled up next to him and spread her wings over them. *This is a wondrous place*, she said. *I could spend years here and not notice the passing time*.

Eragon closed his eyes. *It would be a nice place to fly*, he agreed drowsily.

Not only that, I feel as though I was made for this desert. It has the space I need, mountains where I could roost, and camouflaged prey that I could spend days hunting. And the warmth! Cold does not disturb me, but this heat makes me feel alive and full of energy. She craned her head toward the sky, stretching happily.

You like it that much? mumbled Eragon.

Yes.

Then when this is all done, perhaps we can return. . . . He drifted into slumber even as he spoke. Saphira was pleased and hummed gently while he and Murtagh rested.

It was the morning of the fourth day since leaving Gil'ead. They had already covered thirty-five leagues.

They slept just long enough to clear their minds and rest the horses. No soldiers could be seen to the rear, but that did not lull them into slowing their pace. They knew that the Empire would keep searching until they were far beyond the king's reach. Eragon said, "Couriers must have carried news of my escape to Galbatorix. He would have alerted the Ra'zac. They're sure to be on our trail by now. It'll take them a while to catch us even by flying, but we should be ready for them at all times."

And this time they will find I am not so easily bound with chains, said Saphira.

Murtagh scratched his chin. "I hope they won't be able to follow us past Bullridge. The Ramr was an effective way to lose pursuers; there's a good chance our tracks won't be found again."

"Something to hope for indeed," said Eragon as he checked the elf. Her condition was unchanged; she still did not react to his ministrations. "I place no faith in luck right now, though. The Ra'zac could be on our trail even as we speak."

At sunset they arrived at the crags they had viewed from afar that morning. The imposing stone bluffs towered over them, casting thin shadows. The surrounding area was free of dunes for a half mile. Heat assailed Eragon like a physical blow as he dismounted Snowfire onto the baked, cracked ground. The back of his neck and his face were sunburned; his skin was hot and feverish.

After picketing the horses where they could nibble the sparse grass, Murtagh started a small fire. "How far do you think we went?" Eragon asked, releasing the elf from Saphira.

"I don't know!" snapped Murtagh. His skin was red, his eyes bloodshot. He picked up a pot and muttered a curse. "We don't have enough water. And the horses have to drink."

Eragon was just as irritated by the heat and dryness, but he held his temper in check. "Bring the horses." Saphira dug a hole for him with her claws, then he closed his eyes, releasing the spell. Though the ground was parched, there was enough moisture for the plants to live on and enough for him to fill the hole several times over.

Murtagh refilled the waterskins as water pooled in the hole, then stood aside and let the horses drink. The thirsty animals quaffed gallons. Eragon was forced to draw the liquid from ever deeper in the earth to satisfy their desire. It taxed his strength to the limit. When the horses were finally sated, he said to Saphira, *If you need a drink, take it now.* Her head snaked around him and she took two long draughts, but no more.

Before letting the water flow back into the ground, Eragon gulped down as much as he could, then watched the last drops melt back into the dirt. Holding the water on the surface was harder than he had expected. *But at least it's within my abilities,* he reflected, remembering with some amusement how he had once struggled to lift even a pebble.

It was freezing when they rose the next day. The sand had a pink hue in the morning light, and the sky was hazy, concealing the horizon. Murtagh's mood had not improved with sleep, and Eragon found his own rapidly deteriorating. During breakfast, he asked, "Do you think it'll be long before we leave the desert?"

Murtagh glowered. "We're only crossing a small section of it, so I can't imagine that it'll take us more than two or three days."

"But look how far we've already come."

"All right, maybe it won't! All I care about right now is getting out of the Hadarac as quickly as possible. What we're doing is hard enough without having to pick sand from our eyes every few minutes."

They finished eating, then Eragon went to the elf. She lay as one dead—a corpse except for her measured breathing. "Where lies your injury?" whispered Eragon, brushing a strand of hair from her face. "How can you sleep like this and yet live?" The image of her, alert and poised in the prison cell, was still vivid in his mind. Troubled, he prepared the elf for travel, then saddled and mounted Snowfire.

As they left the camp, a line of dark smudges became visible on the horizon, indistinct in the hazy air. Murtagh thought they were distant hills. Eragon was not convinced, but he could make out no details.

The elf's plight filled his thoughts. He was sure that something had to be done to help her or she would die, though he knew not what that might be. Saphira was just as concerned. They talked about it for hours, but neither of them knew enough about healing to solve the problem confronting them.

At midday they stopped for a brief rest. When they resumed their journey, Eragon noticed that the haze had thinned since morning, and the distant smudges had gained definition.

No longer were they indistinct purple-blue lumps, but rather broad, forest-covered mounds with clear outlines. The air above them was pale white, bleached of its usual hue—all color seemed to have been leached out of a horizontal band of sky that lay on top of the hills and extended to the horizon's edges.

He stared, puzzled, but the more he tried to make sense of it, the more confused he became. He blinked and shook his head, thinking that it must be some illusion of the desert air. Yet when he opened his eyes, the annoying incongruity was still there. Indeed, the whiteness blanketed half the sky before them. Sure that something was terribly wrong, he started to point this out to Murtagh and Saphira when he suddenly understood what he was seeing.

What they had taken to be hills were actually the bases of gigantic mountains, scores of miles wide. Except for the dense forest along their lower regions, the mountains were entirely covered with snow and ice. It was this that had deceived Eragon into thinking the sky white. He craned back his neck, searching for the peaks, but they were not visible. The mountains stretched up into the sky until they faded from sight. Narrow, jagged valleys with ridges that nearly touched split the mountains like deep gorges. It was like a ragged, toothy wall linking Alagaësia with the heavens.

There's no end to them! he thought, awestruck. Stories that mentioned the Beor Mountains always noted their size, but he had discounted such reports as fanciful embellishments. Now, however, he was forced to acknowledge their authenticity.

Sensing his wonder and surprise, Saphira followed his gaze with her own. Within a few seconds she recognized the mountains for what they were. *I feel like a hatchling again. Compared to them, even I feel small!*

We must be near the edge of the desert, said Eragon. *It's only taken two days and we can already see the far side and beyond!*

Saphira spiraled above the dunes. *Yes, but considering the size of those peaks, they could still be fifty leagues from here. It's hard to gauge distances against something so immense. Wouldn't they be a perfect hiding place for the elves or the Varden?*

You could hide more than the elves and Varden, he stated. *Entire nations could exist in secret there, hidden from the Empire. Imagine living with those behemoths looming over you!* He guided Snowfire to Murtagh and pointed, grinning.

"What?" grunted Murtagh, scanning the land.

"Look closely," urged Eragon.

Murtagh peered closely at the horizon. He shrugged. "What, I don't—" The words died in his mouth and gave way to slack-jawed wonder. Murtagh shook his head, muttering, "That's impossible!" He squinted so hard that the corners of his eyes crinkled. He shook his head again. "I knew the Beor Mountains were large, but not that monstrous size!"

"Let's hope the animals that live there aren't in proportion to the mountains," said Eragon lightly.

Murtagh smiled. "It will be good to find some shade and spend a few weeks in leisure. I've had enough of this forced march."

"I'm tired too," admitted Eragon, "but I don't want to stop until the elf is cured . . . or she dies."

"I don't see how continuing to travel will help her," said Murtagh gravely. "A bed will do her more good than hanging underneath Saphira all day."

Eragon shrugged. "Maybe . . . When we reach the mountains, I could take her to Surda—it's not that far. There must be a healer there who can help her; we certainly can't."

Murtagh shaded his eyes with his hand and stared at the mountains. "We can talk about it later. For now our goal is to reach the Beors. There, at least, the Ra'zac will have trouble finding us, and we will be safe from the Empire."

As the day wore on, the Beor Mountains seemed to get no closer, though the landscape changed dramatically. The sand slowly transformed from loose grains of reddish hue to hard-packed, dusky-cream dirt. In place of dunes were ragged patches of plants and deep furrows in the ground where flooding had occurred. A cool breeze wafted through the air, bringing welcome refreshment. The horses sensed the change of climate and hurried forward eagerly.

When evening subdued the sun, the mountains' foothills were a mere league away. Herds of gazelles bounded through lush fields of waving grass. Eragon caught Saphira eyeing them hungrily. They camped by a stream, relieved to be out of the punishing Hadarac Desert.

A PATH REVEALED

F atigued and haggard, but with triumphant smiles, they sat around the fire, congratulating each other. Saphira crowed jubilantly, which startled the horses. Eragon stared at the flames. He was proud that they had covered roughly sixty leagues in five days. It was an impressive feat, even for a rider able to change mounts regularly.

I am outside of the Empire. It was a strange thought. He had been born in the Empire, lived his entire life under Galbatorix's rule, lost his closest friends and family to the king's servants, and had nearly died several times within his domain. Now Eragon was free. No more would he and Saphira have to dodge soldiers, avoid towns, or hide who they were. It was a bittersweet realization, for the cost had been the loss of his entire world.

He looked at the stars in the gloaming sky. And though the thought of building a home in the safety of isolation appealed to him, he had witnessed too many wrongs committed in Galbatorix's name, from murder to slavery, to turn his back on the Empire. No longer was it just vengeance—for Brom's death as well as Garrow's—that drove him. As a Rider, it was his duty to assist those without strength to resist Galbatorix's oppression.

With a sigh he abandoned his deliberation and observed the elf stretched out by Saphira. The fire's orange light gave her face a warm cast. Smooth shadows flickered under her cheekbones. As he stared, an idea slowly came to him.

He could hear the thoughts of people and animals—and communicate with them in that manner if he chose to—but it was something he had done infrequently except with Saphira. He always remembered Brom's admonishment not to violate someone's mind unless absolutely necessary. Save for the one time he had tried to probe Murtagh's consciousness, he had refrained from doing so.

Now, however, he wondered if it were possible to contact the elf in her comatose state. *I might be able to learn from her memories why she remains like this. But if she recovers, would she forgive me for such an intrusion? . . . Whether she does or not, I must try. She's been in this condition for almost a week.* Without speaking of his intentions to Murtagh or Saphira, he knelt by the elf and placed his palm on her brow.

Eragon closed his eyes and extended a tendril of thought, like a probing finger, toward the elf's mind. He found it without difficulty. It was not fuzzy and filled with pain as he had anticipated, but lucid and clear, like a note from a crystal bell. Suddenly an icy dagger drove into his mind. Pain exploded behind his eyes with splashes of color. He recoiled from the attack but found himself held in an iron grip, unable to retreat.

Eragon fought as hard as he could and used every defense he could think of. The dagger stabbed into his mind again. He frantically threw his own barriers before it, blunting the attack. The pain was less excruciating than the first time, but it jarred his concentration. The elf took the opportunity to ruthlessly crush his defenses.

A stifling blanket pressed down on Eragon from all directions, smothering his thoughts. The overpowering force slowly contracted, squeezing the life out of him bit by bit, though he held on, unwilling to give up.

The elf tightened her relentless grip even more, so as to extinguish him like a snuffed candle. He desperately cried in the ancient language, "Eka aí fricai un Shur'tugal!" I am a Rider and friend! The deadly embrace did not loosen its hold, but its constriction halted and surprise emanated from her.

Suspicion followed a second later, but he knew she would believe him; he could not have lied in the ancient language. However, while he had said he was a friend, that did not mean he meant her no harm. For all she knew, Eragon believed himself to be her friend, making the statement true for him, though *she* might not consider him one. *The ancient language does have its limitations*, thought Eragon, hoping that the elf would be curious enough to risk freeing him.

She was. The pressure lifted, and the barriers around her mind hesitantly lowered. The elf warily let their thoughts touch, like two wild animals meeting for the first time. A cold shiver ran down Eragon's side. Her mind was alien. It felt vast and powerful, weighted with memories of uncounted years. Dark thoughts loomed out of sight and touch, artifacts of her race that made him cringe when they brushed his consciousness. Yet through all the sensations shimmered a melody of wild, haunting beauty that embodied her identity.

What is your name? she asked, speaking in the ancient language.
Her voice was weary and filled with quiet despair.

Eragon. And yours? Her consciousness lured him closer, inviting him to submerge himself in the lyric strains of her blood. He resisted the summons with difficulty, though his heart ached to accept it. For the first time he understood the fey attraction of elves. They were creatures of magic, unbound by the mortal laws of the land—as different from humans as dragons were from animals.

. . . Arya. Why have you contacted me in this manner? Am I still a captive of the Empire?

No, you are free! said Eragon. Though he knew only scattered words in the ancient language, he managed to convey: *I was imprisoned in Gil'ead, like you, but I escaped and rescued you. In the five days since then, we've crossed the edge of the Hadarac Desert and are now camped by the Beor Mountains. You've not stirred nor said a word in all that time.*

Ah . . . so it was Gil'ead. She paused. *I know that my wounds were healed. At the time I did not understand why—preparation for some new torture, I was certain. Now I realize it was you.* Softly she added, *Even so, I have not risen, and you are puzzled.*

Yes.

During my captivity, a rare poison, the Skilna Bragh, was given to me, along with the drug to suppress my power. Every morning the antidote for the previous day's poison was administered to me, by force if I refused to take it. Without it I will die within a few hours. That is why I lie in this trance—it slows the Skilna Bragh's progress, though does not stop it. . . . I contemplated waking for the purpose of ending my life and denying Galbatorix, but I refrained from doing so out of hope that you might be an ally. . . . Her voice dwindled off weakly.

How long can you remain like this? asked Eragon.

For weeks, but I'm afraid I haven't that much time. This dormancy cannot restrain death forever . . . I can feel it in my veins even now. Unless I receive the antidote, I will succumb to the poison in three or four days.

Where can the antidote be found?

It exists in only two places outside of the Empire: with my own people and with the Varden. However, my home is beyond the reach of dragonback.

What about the Varden? We would have taken you straight to them, but we don't know where they are.

I will tell you—if you give me your word that you will never reveal their location to Galbatorix or to anyone who serves him. In addition you must swear that you have not deceived me in some manner and that you intend no harm to the elves, dwarves, Varden, or the race of dragons.

What Arya asked for would have been simple enough—if they had not been conversing in the ancient language. Eragon knew she wanted oaths more binding than life itself. Once made, they could never be broken. That weighed heavily on him as he gravely pledged his word in agreement.

It is understood. . . . A series of vertigo-inducing images suddenly flashed through his mind. He found himself riding along the Beor Mountain range, traveling eastward many leagues. Eragon did his best to remember the route as craggy mountains and hills flashed past. He was heading south now, still following the mountains. Then everything wheeled abruptly, and he entered a narrow, winding valley. It snaked through the mountains to the base of a frothy waterfall that pounded into a deep lake.

The images stopped. *It is far,* said Arya, *but do not let the distance dissuade you. When you arrive at the lake Kóstha-mérna at the end of the Beartooth River, take a rock, bang on the cliff next to the waterfall, and cry, Aí varden abr du Shur'tugalar gata vanta. You will be admitted. You will be challenged, but do not falter no matter how perilous it seems.*

What should they give you for the poison? he asked.

Her voice quavered, but then she regained her strength. *Tell them—to give me Túnivor's Nectar. You must leave me now . . . I have expended too much energy already. Do not talk with me again unless there is no hope of reaching the Varden. If that is the case, there is information I must impart to you so the Varden will survive. Farewell, Eragon, rider of dragons . . . my life is in your hands.*

Arya withdrew from their contact. The unearthly strains that had echoed across their link were gone. Eragon took a shuddering breath and forced his eyes open. Murtagh and Saphira stood on either side of him, watching with concern. "Are you all right?" asked Murtagh. "You've been kneeling here for almost fifteen minutes."

"I have?" asked Eragon, blinking.

Yes, and grimacing like a pained gargoyle, commented Saphira dryly.

Eragon stood, wincing as his cramped knees stretched. "I talked with Arya!" Murtagh frowned quizzically, as if to inquire if he had gone mad. Eragon explained, "The elf—that's her name."

And what is it that ails her? asked Saphira impatiently.

Eragon swiftly told them of his entire discussion. "How far away are the Varden?" asked Murtagh.

"I'm not exactly sure," confessed Eragon. "From what she showed me, I think it's even farther than from here to Gil'ead."

"And we're supposed to cover that in three or four days?" demanded Murtagh angrily. "It took us five *long* days to get here! What do you want to do, kill the horses? They're exhausted as it is."

"But if we do nothing, she'll die! If it's too much for the horses, Saphira can fly ahead with Arya and me; at least we would get to the Varden in time. You could catch up with us in a few days."

Murtagh grunted and crossed his arms. "Of course. Murtagh the pack animal. Murtagh the horse leader. I should have remembered that's all I'm good for nowadays. Oh, and let's not forget, every soldier in the Empire is searching for me now because you couldn't defend yourself, and I had to go and *save* you. Yes, I suppose I'll just follow your instructions and bring up the horses in the rear like a good servant."

Eragon was bewildered by the sudden venom in Murtagh's voice. "What's wrong with you? I'm grateful for what you did. There's no reason to be angry with me! I didn't ask you to accompany me or to rescue me from Gil'ead. You chose that. I haven't forced you to do anything."

"Oh, not openly, no. What else could I do but help you with the Ra'zac? And then later, at Gil'ead, how could I have left with a clear conscience? The problem with you," said Murtagh, poking Eragon in the chest, "is that you're so totally helpless you force everyone to take care of you!"

The words stung Eragon's pride; he recognized a grain of truth in them. "Don't touch me," he growled.

Murtagh laughed, a harsh note in his voice. "Or what, you'll punch me? You couldn't hit a brick wall." He went to shove Eragon again, but Eragon grabbed his arm and struck him in the stomach.

"I said, don't touch me!"

Murtagh doubled over, swearing. Then he yelled and launched himself at Eragon. They fell in a tangle of arms and legs, pounding on each other. Eragon kicked at Murtagh's right hip, missed, and grazed the fire. Sparks and burning embers scattered through the air.

They scrabbled across the ground, trying to get leverage. Eragon managed to get his feet under Murtagh's chest and kicked mightily. Murtagh flew upside down over Eragon's head, landing flat on his back with a solid thump.

Murtagh's breath whooshed out. He rolled stiffly to his feet, then wheeled to face Eragon, panting heavily. They charged each other once more. Saphira's tail slapped between them, accompanied by a deafening roar. Eragon ignored her and tried to jump over her tail, but a taloned paw caught him in midair and flung him back to the ground.

Enough!

He futilely tried to push Saphira's muscled leg off his chest and saw that Murtagh was likewise pinned. Saphira roared again, snapping her jaws. She swung her head over Eragon and glared at him. *You of all people should know better! Fighting like starving dogs over a scrap of meat. What would Brom say?*

Eragon felt his cheeks burn and averted his eyes. He knew what Brom would have said. Saphira held them on the ground, letting them simmer, then said to Eragon pointedly, *Now, if you don't want to spend the night under my foot, you will politely ask Murtagh what is troubling him.* She snaked her head over to Murtagh and stared down at him with an impassive blue eye. *And tell him that I won't stand for insults from either of you.*

Won't you let us up? complained Eragon.

No.

Eragon reluctantly turned his head toward Murtagh, tasting blood in the side of his mouth. Murtagh avoided his eyes and looked up at the sky. "Well, is she going to get off us?"

"No, not unless we talk. . . . She wants me to ask you what's really the problem," said Eragon, embarrassed.

Saphira growled an affirmative and continued to stare at Murtagh. It was impossible for him to escape her piercing glare. Finally he shrugged, muttering something under his breath. Saphira's claws tightened on his chest, and her tail whistled through the air. Murtagh shot her an angry glance, then grudgingly said louder, "I told you before: I don't want to go to the Varden."

Eragon frowned. Was that all that was the matter? "Don't want to . . . or can't?"

Murtagh tried to shove Saphira's leg off him, then gave up with a curse. "Don't want to! They'll expect things from me that I can't deliver."

"Did you steal something from them?"

"I wish it were that simple."

Eragon rolled his eyes, exasperated. "Well, what is it, then? Did you kill someone important or bed the wrong woman?"

"No, I was born," said Murtagh cryptically. He pushed at Saphira again. This time she released them both. They got to their feet under her watchful eye and brushed dirt from their backs.

"You're avoiding the question," Eragon said, dabbing his split lip.

"So what?" spat Murtagh as he stomped to the edge of the camp. After a minute he sighed. "It doesn't matter why I'm in this predicament, but I can tell you that the Varden wouldn't welcome me even if I came bearing the king's head. Oh, they might greet me nicely enough and let me into their councils, but trust me? Never. And if I were to arrive under less fortuitous circumstances, like the present ones, they'd likely clap me in irons."

"Won't you tell me what this is about?" asked Eragon. "I've done things I'm not proud of, too, so it's not as if I'm going to pass judgment."

Murtagh shook his head slowly, eyes glistening. "It isn't like that. I haven't *done* anything to deserve this treatment, though it would have been easier to atone for if I had. No . . . my only wrongdoing is existing in the first place." He stopped and took a shaky breath. "You see, my father—"

A sharp hiss from Saphira cut him off abruptly. *Look!*

They followed her gaze westward. Murtagh's face paled. "Demons above and below!"

A league or so away, parallel to the mountain range, was a column of figures marching east. The line of troops, hundreds strong, stretched for nearly a mile. Dust billowed from their heels. Their weapons glinted in the dying light. A standard-bearer rode before them in a black chariot, holding aloft a crimson banner.

"It's the Empire," said Eragon tiredly. "They've found us . . . somehow." Saphira poked her head over his shoulder and gazed at the column.

"Yes . . . but those are Urgals, not men," said Murtagh.

"How can you tell?"

Murtagh pointed at the standard. "That flag bears the personal symbol of an Urgal chieftain. He's a ruthless brute, given to violent fits and insanity."

"You've met him?"

Murtagh's eyes tightened. "Once, briefly. I still have scars from that encounter. These Urgals might not have been sent here for us, but I'm sure we've been seen by now and that they will follow us. Their chieftain isn't the sort to let a dragon escape his grasp, especially if he's heard about Gil'ead."

Eragon hurried to the fire and covered it with dirt. "We have to flee! You don't want to go to the Varden, but I have to take Arya to them before she dies. Here's a compromise: come with me until I reach the lake Kóstha-mérna, then go your own way." Murtagh hesitated. Eragon added quickly, "If you leave now, in sight of the column, Urgals will follow you. And then where will you be, facing them alone?"

"Very well," said Murtagh, tossing his saddlebags over Tornac's flanks, "but when we near the Varden, I *will* leave."

Eragon burned to question Murtagh further, but not with Urgals so near. He gathered his belongings and saddled Snowfire. Saphira fanned her wings, took off in a rush, and circled above. She kept guard over Murtagh and Eragon as they left camp.

What direction shall I fly? she asked.

East, along the Beors.

Stilling her wings, Saphira rose on an updraft and teetered on the pillar of warm air, hovering in the sky over the horses. *I wonder why the Urgals are here. Maybe they were sent to attack the Varden.*

Then we should try to warn them, he said, guiding Snowfire past half-visible obstacles. As the night deepened, the Urgals faded into the gloom behind them.

A CLASH OF WILLS

When morning came, Eragon's cheek was raw from chafing against Snowfire's neck, and he was sore from his fight with Murtagh. They had alternated sleeping in their saddles throughout the night. It had allowed them to outdistance the Urgal troops, but neither of them knew if the lead could be retained. The horses were exhausted to the point of stopping, yet they still maintained a relentless pace. Whether it would be enough to escape depended on how rested the monsters were . . . and if Eragon and Murtagh's horses survived.

The Beor Mountains cast great shadows over the land, stealing the sun's warmth. To the north was the Hadarac Desert, a thin white band as bright as noonday snow.

I must eat, said Saphira. *Days have passed since I last hunted. Hunger claws my belly. If I start now, I might be able to catch enough of those bounding deer for a few mouthfuls.*

Eragon smiled at her exaggeration. *Go if you must, but leave Arya here.*

I will be swift. He untied the elf from her belly and transferred her to Snowfire's saddle. Saphira soared away, disappearing in the direction of the mountains. Eragon ran beside the horses, close enough to Snowfire to keep Arya from falling. Neither he nor Murtagh intruded on the silence. Yesterday's fight no longer seemed as important because of the Urgals, but the bruises remained.

Saphira made her kills within the hour and notified Eragon of her success. Eragon was pleased that she would soon return. Her absence made him nervous.

They stopped at a pond to let the horses drink. Eragon idly plucked a stalk of grass, twirling it while he stared at the elf. He was startled from his reverie by the steely rasp of a sword being unsheathed. He instinctively grasped Zar'roc and spun around in search of the enemy. There was only Murtagh, his long sword held ready. He pointed at a hill ahead of them, where a tall, brown-cloaked man sat on a sorrel horse, mace in hand. Behind him was a group of twenty horsemen. No one moved. "Could they be Varden?" asked Murtagh.

Eragon surreptitiously strung his bow. "According to Arya, they're still scores of leagues away. This might be one of their patrols or raiding groups."

"Assuming they're not bandits." Murtagh swung onto Tornac and readied his own bow.

"Should we try to outrun them?" asked Eragon, draping a blanket over Arya. The horsemen must have seen her, but he hoped to conceal the fact that she was an elf.

"It wouldn't do any good," said Murtagh, shaking his head. "Tornac and Snowfire are fine war-horses, but they're tired, and they aren't sprinters. Look at the horses those men have; they're meant for running. They would catch us before we had gone a half-mile. Besides, they may have something important to say. You'd better tell Saphira to hurry back."

Eragon was already doing that. He explained the situation, then warned, *Don't show yourself unless it's necessary. We're not in the Empire, but I still don't want anyone to know about you.*

Never mind that, she replied. *Remember, magic can protect you where speed and luck fail.* He felt her take off and race toward them, skimming close to the ground.

The band of men watched them from the hill.

Eragon nervously gripped Zar'roc. The wire-wrapped hilt was secure under his glove. He said in a low voice, "If they threaten us, I can frighten them away with magic. If that doesn't work, there's Saphira. I wonder how they'd react to a Rider? So many stories have been told about their powers. . . . It might be enough to avoid a fight."

"Don't count on it," said Murtagh flatly. "If there's a fight, we'll just have to kill enough of them to convince them we're not worth the effort." His face was controlled and unemotional.

The man on the sorrel horse signaled with his mace, sending the horsemen cantering toward them. The men shook javelins over their heads, whooping loudly as they neared. Battered sheaths hung from their sides. Their weapons were rusty and stained. Four of them trained arrows on Eragon and Murtagh.

Their leader swirled the mace in the air, and his men responded with yells as they wildly encircled Eragon and Murtagh. Eragon's lips twitched. He almost loosed a blast of magic into their midst, then restrained himself. *We don't know what they want yet,* he reminded himself, containing his growing apprehension.

The moment Eragon and Murtagh were thoroughly surrounded, the leader reined in his horse, then crossed his arms and examined them critically. He raised his eyebrows. "Well, these are better than the usual dregs we find! At least we got healthy ones this time. And we didn't even have to shoot them. Grieg will be pleased." The men chuckled.

At his words, a sinking sensation filled Eragon's gut. A suspicion stirred in his mind. *Saphira . . .*

"Now as for you two," said the leader, speaking to Eragon and Murtagh, "if you would be so good as to drop your weapons, you'll avoid being turned into living quivers by my men." The archers grinned suggestively; the men laughed again.

Murtagh's only movement was to shift his sword. "Who are you and what do you want? We are free men traveling through this land. You have no right to stop us."

"Oh, I have every right," said the man contemptuously. "And as for my name, *slaves* do not address their masters in that manner, unless they want to be beaten."

Eragon cursed to himself. *Slavers!* He remembered vividly the people he had seen at auction in Dras-Leona. Rage boiled within him. He glared at the men around him with new hatred and disgust.

The lines deepened on the leader's face. "Throw down your swords and surrender!" The slavers tensed, staring at them with cold eyes as neither Eragon nor Murtagh lowered his weapon. Eragon's palm tingled. He heard a rustle behind him, then a loud curse. Startled, he spun around.

One of the slavers had pulled the blanket off Arya, revealing her face. He gaped in astonishment, then shouted, "Torkenbrand, this one's an elf!" The men stirred with surprise while the leader spurred his horse over to Snowfire. He looked down at Arya and whistled.

"Well, 'ow much is she worth?" someone asked.

Torkenbrand was quiet for a moment, then spread his hands and said, "At the very least? Fortunes upon fortunes. The Empire will pay a mountain of gold for her!"

The slavers yelled with excitement and pounded each other on the back. A roar filled Eragon's mind as Saphira banked sharply far overhead. *Attack now!* he cried. *But let them escape if they run.* She immediately folded her wings and plummeted downward. Eragon caught Murtagh's attention with a sharp signal. Murtagh took the cue. He smashed his elbow into a slaver's face, knocking the man out of his saddle, and jabbed his heels into Tornac.

With a toss of his mane, the war-horse jumped forward, twirled around, and reared. Murtagh brandished his sword as Tornac plunged back down, driving his forehooves into the back of the dismounted slaver. The man screamed.

Before the slavers could gather their senses, Eragon scrambled out of the commotion and raised his hands, invoking words in the ancient language. A globule of indigo fire struck the ground in the midst of the fray, bursting into a fountain of molten drops that dissipated like sun-warmed dew. A second later, Saphira dropped from the sky and landed next to him. She parted her jaws, displaying her massive fangs, and bellowed. "Behold!" cried Eragon over the furor, "I am a Rider!" He raised Zar'roc over his head, the red blade dazzling in the sunlight, then pointed it at the slavers. "Flee if you wish to live!"

The men shouted incoherently and scrambled over each other in their haste to escape. In the confusion, Torkenbrand was struck in the temple with a javelin. He tumbled to the ground, stunned. The men ignored their fallen leader and raced away in a ragged mass, casting fearful looks at Saphira.

Torkenbrand struggled to his knees. Blood ran from his temple, branching across his cheek with crimson tendrils. Murtagh dismounted and strode over to him, sword in hand. Torkenbrand weakly raised his arm as if to ward off a blow. Murtagh gazed at him coldly, then swung his blade at Torkenbrand's neck. "No!" shouted Eragon, but it was too late.

Torkenbrand's decapitated trunk crumpled to the ground in a puff of dirt. His head landed with a hard thump. Eragon rushed to Murtagh, his jaw working furiously. "Is your brain rotten?" he yelled, enraged. "Why did you kill him?"

Murtagh wiped his sword on the back of Torkenbrand's jerkin. The steel left a dark stain. "I don't see why you're so upset—"

"Upset!" exploded Eragon. "I'm well past that! Did it even occur to you that we could just leave him here and continue on our way? No! Instead you turn into an executioner and chop off his head. He was defenseless!"

Murtagh seemed perplexed by Eragon's wrath. "Well, we couldn't keep him around—he *was* dangerous. The others ran off . . . without a horse he wouldn't have made it far. I didn't want the Urgals to find him and learn about Arya. So I thought it would—"

"But to *kill* him?" interrupted Eragon. Saphira sniffed Torkenbrand's head curiously. She opened her mouth slightly, as if to snap it up, then appeared to decide better of it and prowled to Eragon's side.

"I'm only trying to stay alive," stated Murtagh. "No stranger's life is more important than my own."

"But you can't indulge in wanton violence. Where is your empathy?" growled Eragon, pointing at the head.

"Empathy? Empathy? What empathy can I afford my enemies? Shall I dither about whether to defend myself because it will cause someone pain? If that had been the case, I would have died years ago! You must be willing to protect yourself and what you cherish, no matter what the cost."

Eragon slammed Zar'roc back into its sheath, shaking his head savagely. "You can justify any atrocity with that reasoning."

"Do you think I enjoy this?" Murtagh shouted. "My life has been threatened from the day I was born! All of my waking hours have been spent avoiding danger in one form or another. And sleep never comes easily because I always worry if I'll live to see the dawn. If there ever was a time I felt secure, it must have been in my mother's womb, though I wasn't safe even there! You don't understand—if you lived with this *fear*, you would have learned the same lesson I did: *Do not take chances*." He gestured at Torkenbrand's body. "He was a risk that I removed. I refuse to repent, and I won't plague myself over what is done and past."

Eragon shoved his face into Murtagh's. "It was still the wrong thing to do." He lashed Arya to Saphira, then climbed onto Snowfire. "Let's go." Murtagh guided Tornac around Torkenbrand's prone form in the bloodstained dust.

They rode at a rate that Eragon would have thought impossible a week ago; leagues melted away before them as if wings were attached to their feet. They turned south, between two outstretched arms of the Beor Mountains. The arms were shaped like pincers about to close, the tips a day's travel apart. Yet the distance seemed less because of the mountains' size. It was as if they were in a valley made for giants.

When they stopped for the day, Eragon and Murtagh ate dinner in silence, refusing to look up from their food. Afterward, Eragon said tersely, "I'll take the first watch." Murtagh nodded and lay on his blankets with his back to Eragon.

Do you want to talk? asked Saphira.

Not right now, murmured Eragon. *Give me some time to think; I'm . . . confused.*

She withdrew from his mind with a gentle touch and a whisper. *I love you, little one.*

And I you, he said. She curled into a ball next to him, lending him her warmth. He sat motionless in the dark, wrestling with his disquiet.

FLIGHT THROUGH
THE VALLEY

In the morning Saphira took off with both Eragon and Arya. Eragon wanted to get away from Murtagh for a time. He shivered, pulling his clothes tighter. It looked like it might snow. Saphira ascended lazily on an updraft and asked, *What are you thinking?*

Eragon contemplated the Beor Mountains, which towered above them even though Saphira flew far above the ground. *That was murder yesterday. I've no other word for it.*

Saphira banked to the left. *It was a hasty deed and ill considered, but Murtagh tried to do the right thing. The men who buy and sell other humans deserve every misfortune that befalls them. If we weren't committed to helping Arya, I would hunt down every slaver and tear them apart!*

Yes, said Eragon miserably, *but Torkenbrand was helpless. He couldn't shield himself or run. A moment more and he probably would have surrendered. Murtagh didn't give him that chance. If Torkenbrand had at least been able to fight, it wouldn't have been so bad.*

Eragon, even if Torkenbrand had fought, the results would have been the same. You know as well as I do that few can equal you or Murtagh with the blade. Torkenbrand would have still died, though you seem to think it would have been more just or honorable in a mismatched duel.

I don't know what's right! admitted Eragon, distressed. *There aren't any answers that make sense.*

Sometimes, said Saphira gently, *there are no answers. Learn what you can about Murtagh from this. Then forgive him. And if you can't* forgive, at least forget, for he meant you no harm, however rash the act was. Your head is still attached, yes?

Frowning, Eragon shifted in the saddle. He shook himself, like a horse trying to rid itself of a fly, and checked Murtagh's position over Saphira's shoulder. A patch of color farther back along their route caught his attention.

Camped by a streambed they had crossed late yesterday were the Urgals. Eragon's heartbeat quickened. How could the Urgals be on foot, yet still gain on them? Saphira saw the monsters as well and tilted her wings, brought them close to her body, and slipped into a steep dive, splitting the air. *I don't think they spotted us,* she said.

Eragon hoped not. He squinted against the blast of air as she increased the angle of their dive. *Their chieftain must be driving them at a breakneck pace,* he said.

Yes—maybe they'll all die of exhaustion.

When they landed, Murtagh asked curtly, "What now?"

"The Urgals are overtaking us," said Eragon. He pointed back toward the column's camp.

"How far do we still have to go?" asked Murtagh, putting his hands against the sky and measuring the hours until sunset.

"Normally? . . . I would guess another five days. At the speed we've been traveling, only three. But unless we get there tomorrow, the Urgals will probably catch us, and Arya will certainly die."

"She might last another day."

"We can't count on it," objected Eragon. "The only way we can get to the Varden in time is if we don't stop for anything, least of all sleep. That's our only chance."

Murtagh laughed bitterly. "How can you expect to do that? We've already gone days without adequate sleep. Unless Riders are made of different stuff than us mortals, you're as tired as I am. We've covered a staggering distance, and the horses, in case you haven't noticed, are ready to drop. Another day of this might kill us all."

Eragon shrugged. "So be it. We don't have a choice."

Murtagh gazed at the mountains. "I could leave and let you fly ahead with Saphira. . . . That would force the Urgals to divide their troops and would give you a better chance of reaching the Varden."

"It would be suicide," said Eragon, crossing his arms. "Somehow those Urgals are faster on foot than we are on horseback. They would run you down like a deer. The only way to evade them is to find sanctuary with the Varden." Despite his words, he was unsure if he wanted Murtagh to stay. *I like him,* Eragon confessed to himself, *but I'm no longer certain if that's a good thing.*

"I'll escape later," said Murtagh abruptly. "When we get to the Varden, I can disappear down a side valley and find my way to Surda, where I can hide without attracting too much attention."

"So you're staying?"

"Sleep or no sleep, I'll see you to the Varden," promised Murtagh.

With newfound determination, they struggled to distance themselves from the Urgals, yet their pursuers continued to creep nearer. At nightfall the monsters were a third closer than they had been that morning. As fatigue eroded his and Murtagh's strength, they slept in turns on the horses, while whoever was awake led the animals in the right direction.

Eragon relied heavily on Arya's memories to guide them. Because of the alien nature of her mind, he sometimes made mistakes as to the route, costing them precious time. They gradually angled toward the foothills of the eastern arm of mountains, looking for the valley that would lead them to the Varden. Midnight arrived and passed without any sign of it.

When the sun returned, they were pleased to see that the Urgals were far behind. "This is the last day," said Eragon, yawning widely. "If we're not reasonably close to the Varden by noon, I'm going to fly ahead with Arya. You'll be free to go wherever you want then, but you'll have to take Snowfire with you. I won't be able to come back for him."

"That might not be necessary; we could still get there in time," said Murtagh. He rubbed the pommel of his sword.

Eragon shrugged. "We could." He went to Arya and put a hand on her forehead. It was damp and dangerously hot. Her eyes wandered uneasily beneath her eyelids, as if she suffered a nightmare. Eragon pressed a damp rag to her brow, wishing he could do more.

Late in the morning, after they circumnavigated an especially broad mountain, Eragon saw a narrow valley tucked against its far side. The valley was so restricted it could easily be overlooked. The Beartooth River, which Arya had mentioned, flowed out of it and looped carelessly across the land. He smiled with relief; that was where they needed to go.

Looking back, Eragon was alarmed to see that the distance between them and the Urgals had shrunk to little more than a league. He pointed out the valley to Murtagh. "If we can slip in there without being seen, it might confuse them."

Murtagh looked skeptical. "It's worth a try. But they've followed us easily enough so far."

As they approached the valley, they passed under the knotted branches of the Beor Mountains' forest. The trees were tall, with creviced bark that was almost black, dull needles of the same color, and knobby roots that rose from the soil like bare knees. Cones littered the ground, each the size of a horse's head. Sable squirrels chattered from the treetops, and eyes gleamed from holes in the trunks. Green beards of tangled wolfsbane hung from the gnarled branches.

The forest gave Eragon an uneasy feeling; the hair on the back of his neck prickled. There was something hostile in the air, as if the trees resented their intrusion. *They are very old*, said Saphira, touching a trunk with her nose.

Yes, said Eragon, *but not friendly*. The forest grew denser the farther in they traveled. The lack of space forced Saphira to take off with Arya. Without a clear trail to follow, the tough underbrush slowed Eragon and Murtagh. The Beartooth River wound next to them, filling the air with the sound of gurgling water. A nearby peak obscured the sun, casting them into premature dusk.

At the valley's mouth, Eragon realized that although it looked like a slim gash between the peaks, the valley was really as wide as many of the Spine's vales. It was only the enormous size of the ridged and shadowy mountains that made it appear so confined. Waterfalls dotted its sheer sides. The sky was reduced to a thin strip winding overhead, mostly hidden by gray clouds. From the dank ground rose a clinging fog that chilled the air until their breath was visible. Wild strawberries crawled among a carpet of mosses and ferns, fighting for the meager sunlight. Sprouting on piles of rotting wood were red and yellow toadstools.

All was hushed and quiet, sounds dampened by the heavy air. Saphira landed by them in a nearby glade, the rush of her wings strangely muted. She took in the view with a swing of her head. *I just passed a flock of birds that were black and green with red markings on their wings. I've never seen birds like that before.*

Everything in these mountains seems unusual, replied Eragon. *Do you mind if I ride you awhile? I want to keep an eye on the Urgals.*

Of course.

He turned to Murtagh. "The Varden are hidden at the end of this valley. If we hurry, we might get there before nightfall."

Murtagh grunted, hands on his hips. "How am I going to get out of here? I don't see any valleys joining this one, and the Urgals are going to hem us in pretty soon. I need an escape route."

"Don't worry about it," said Eragon impatiently. "This is a long valley; there's sure to be an exit further in." He released Arya from Saphira and lifted the elf onto Snowfire. "Watch Arya—I'm going to fly with Saphira. We'll meet you up ahead." He scrambled onto Saphira's back and strapped himself onto her saddle.

"Be careful," Murtagh warned, his brow furrowed in thought, then clucked to the horses and hurried back into the forest.

As Saphira jumped toward the sky, Eragon said, *Do you think you could fly up to one of those peaks? We might be able to spot our destination,* as well as a passage for Murtagh. *I don't want to listen to him griping through the entire valley.*

We can try, agreed Saphira, *but it will get much colder.*

I'm dressed warmly.

Hold on, then! Saphira suddenly swooped straight up, throwing him back in the saddle. Her wings flapped strongly, driving their weight upward. The valley shrank to a green line below them. The Beartooth River shimmered like braided silver where light struck it.

They rose to the cloud layer, and icy moisture saturated the air. A formless gray blanket engulfed them, limiting their vision to an arm's length. Eragon hoped they would not collide with anything in the murk. He stuck out a hand experimentally, swinging it through the air. Water condensed on it and ran down his arm, soaking his sleeve.

A blurred gray mass fluttered past his head, and he glimpsed a dove, its wings pumping frantically. There was a white band around its leg. Saphira struck at the bird, tongue lashing out, jaws gaping. The dove squawked as Saphira's sharp teeth snapped together a hair's breadth behind its tail feathers. Then it darted away and disappeared into the haze, the frenzied thumping of its wings fading to silence.

When they breached the top of the clouds, Saphira's scales were covered with thousands of water droplets that reflected tiny rainbows and shimmered with the blue of her scales. Eragon shook himself, spraying water from his clothes, and shivered. He could no longer see the ground, only hills of clouds snaking between the mountains.

The trees on the mountains gave way to thick glaciers, blue and white under the sun. The glare from the snow forced Eragon to close his eyes. He tried to open them after a minute, but the light dazzled him. Irritated, he stared into the crook of his arm. *How can you stand it?* he asked Saphira.

My eyes are stronger than yours, she replied.

It was frigid. The water in Eragon's hair froze, giving him a shiny helmet. His shirt and pants were hard shells around his limbs.

Saphira's scales became slick with ice; hoarfrost laced her wings. They had never flown this high before, yet the mountaintops were still miles above them.

Saphira's flapping gradually slowed, and her breathing became labored. Eragon gasped and panted; there didn't seem to be enough air. Fighting back panic, he clutched Saphira's neck spikes for support.

We . . . have to get out of here, he said. Red dots swam before his eyes. *I can't . . . breathe.* Saphira seemed not to hear him, so he repeated the message, louder this time. Again there was no response. *She can't hear me,* he realized. He swayed, finding it hard to think, then pounded on her side and shouted, "Take us down!"

The effort made him lightheaded. His vision faded into swirling darkness.

He regained consciousness as they emerged from the bottom of the clouds. His head was pounding. *What happened?* he asked, pushing himself upright and looking around with confusion.

You blacked out, answered Saphira.

He tried to run his fingers through his hair, but stopped when he felt icicles. *Yes, I know that, but why didn't you answer me?*

My brain was confused. Your words didn't make any sense. When you lost consciousness, I knew something was wrong and descended. I didn't have to sink far before I realized what had occurred.

It's a good thing you didn't pass out as well, said Eragon with a nervous laugh. Saphira only swished her tail. He looked wistfully at where the mountain peaks were now concealed by clouds. *A pity we couldn't stand upon one of those summits. . . . Well, now we know: we can only fly out of this valley the way we came in. Why did we run out of air? How can we have it down here, but not up above?*

I don't know, but I'll never dare to fly so close to the sun again. We should remember this experience. The knowledge may be useful if we ever have to fight another Rider.

I hope that never happens, said Eragon. *Let's stay down below for now. I've had enough adventure for one day.*

They floated on the gentle air currents, drifting from one mountain to the next, until Eragon saw that the Urgal column had reached the valley's mouth. *What drives them to such speed, and how can they bear to sustain it?*

Now that we are closer to them, Saphira said, *I can see that these Urgals are bigger than the ones we've met before. They would stand chest and shoulders over a tall man. I don't know what land they march from, but it must be a fierce place to produce such brutes.*

Eragon glared at the ground below—he could not see the detail that she did. *If they keep to this pace, they'll catch Murtagh before we find the Varden.*

Have hope. The forest may hamper their progress. . . . Would it be possible to stop them with magic?

Eragon shook his head. *Stop them . . . no. There are too many.* He thought of the thin layer of mist on the valley floor and grinned. *But I might be able to delay them a bit.* He closed his eyes, selected the words he needed, stared at the mist, and then commanded, "Gath un reisa du rakr!"

There was a disturbance below. From above, it looked as if the ground was flowing together like a great sluggish river. A leaden band of mist gathered in front of the Urgals and thickened into an intimidating wall, dark as a thunderhead. The Urgals hesitated before it, then continued forward like an unstoppable battering ram. The barrier swirled around them, concealing the lead ranks from view.

The drain on Eragon's strength was sudden and massive, making his heart flutter like a dying bird. He gasped, eyes rolling. He struggled to sever the magic's hold on him—to plug the breach through which his life streamed. With a savage growl he jerked away from the magic and broke contact. Tendrils of magic snapped through his mind like decapitated snakes, then reluctantly retreated from his consciousness, clutching at the dregs of his strength. The wall of mist dissipated, and the fog sluggishly collapsed across the ground like a tower of mud sliding apart. The Urgals had not been hindered at all.

Eragon lay limply on Saphira, panting. Only now did he remember Brom saying, "Magic is affected by distance, just like an arrow or a spear. If you try to lift or move something a mile away, it'll take more energy than if you were closer." *I won't forget that again,* he thought grimly.

You shouldn't have forgotten in the first place, Saphira inserted pointedly. *First the dirt at Gil'ead and now this. Weren't you paying attention to anything Brom told you? You'll kill yourself if you keep this up.*

I paid attention, he insisted, rubbing his chin. *It's just been a while, and I haven't had an opportunity to think back on it. I've never used magic at a distance, so how could I know it would be so difficult?*

She growled. *Next thing I know you'll be trying to bring corpses back to life. Don't forget what Brom said about that, too.*

I won't, he said impatiently. Saphira dipped toward the ground, searching for Murtagh and the horses. Eragon would have helped her, but he barely had the energy to sit up.

Saphira settled in a small field with a jolt, and Eragon was puzzled to see the horses stopped and Murtagh kneeling, examining the ground. When Eragon did not dismount, Murtagh hurried over and inquired, "What's wrong?" He sounded angry, worried, and tired at the same time.

". . . I made a mistake," said Eragon truthfully. "The Urgals have entered the valley. I tried to confuse them, but I forgot one of the rules of magic, and it cost me a great deal."

Scowling, Murtagh jerked his thumb over his shoulder. "I just found some wolf tracks, but the footprints are as wide as both of my hands and an inch deep. There are animals around here that could be dangerous even to you, Saphira." He turned to her. "I know you can't enter the forest, but could you circle above me and the horses? That should keep these beasts away. Otherwise there may only be enough left of me to roast in a thimble."

"Humor, Murtagh?" asked Eragon, a quick smile coming to his face. His muscles trembled, making it hard for him to concentrate.

"Only on the gallows." Murtagh rubbed his eyes. "I can't believe that the same Urgals have been following us the whole time. They would have to be birds to catch up with us."

"Saphira said they're larger than any we've seen," remarked Eragon.

Murtagh cursed, clenching the pommel of his sword. "That explains it! Saphira, if you're right, then those are Kull, elite of the Urgals. I should have guessed that the chieftain had been put in charge of them. They don't ride because horses can't carry their weight—not one of them is under eight feet tall—and they can run for days without sleep and still be ready for battle. It can take five men to kill one. Kull never leave their caves except for war, so they must expect a great slaughter if they are out in such force."

"Can we stay ahead of them?"

"Who knows?" said Murtagh. "They're strong, determined, and large in numbers. It's possible that we may have to face them. If that happens, I only hope that the Varden have men posted nearby who'll help us. Despite our skill and Saphira, we can't hold off Kull."

Eragon swayed. "Could you get me some bread? I need to eat." Murtagh quickly brought him part of a loaf. It was old and hard, but Eragon chewed on it gratefully. Murtagh scanned the valley walls, worry in his eyes. Eragon knew he was searching for a way out. "There'll be one farther in."

"Of course," said Murtagh with forced optimism, then slapped his thigh. "We must go."

"How is Arya?" asked Eragon.

Murtagh shrugged. "The fever's worse. She's been tossing and turning. What do you expect? Her strength is failing. You should fly her to the Varden before the poison does any more damage."

"I won't leave you behind," insisted Eragon, gaining strength with each bite. "Not with the Urgals so near."

Murtagh shrugged again. "As you wish. But I'm warning you, she won't live if you stay with me."

"Don't say that," insisted Eragon, pushing himself upright in Saphira's saddle. "Help me save her. We can still do it. Consider it a life for a life—atonement for Torkenbrand's death."

Murtagh's face darkened instantly. "It's not a debt owed. You—" He stopped as a horn echoed through the dark forest. "I'll have more to say to you later," he said shortly, stomping to the horses. He grabbed their reins and trotted away, shooting an angry glare at Eragon.

Eragon closed his eyes as Saphira took flight. He wished that he could lie on a soft bed and forget all their troubles. *Saphira*, he said at last, cupping his ears to warm them, *what if we did take Arya to the Varden? Once she was safe, we could fly back to Murtagh and help him out of here.*

The Varden wouldn't let you, said Saphira. *For all they know, you might be returning to inform the Urgals of their hiding place. We aren't arriving under the best conditions to gain their trust. They'll want to know why we've brought an entire company of Kull to their very gates.*

We'll just have to tell them the truth and hope they believe us, said Eragon.

And what will we do if the Kull attack Murtagh?

Fight them, of course! I won't let him and Arya be captured or killed, said Eragon indignantly.

There was a touch of sarcasm in her words. *How noble. Oh, we would fell many of the Urgals—you with magic and blade, whilst my weapons would be tooth and claw—but it would be futile in the end. They are too numerous. . . . We cannot defeat them, only be defeated.*

What, then? he demanded. *I'll not leave Arya or Murtagh to their mercy.*

Saphira waved her tail, the tip whistling loudly. *I'm not asking you to. However, if we attack first, we may gain the advantage.*

Have you gone crazy? They'll . . . Eragon's voice trailed off as he thought about it. *They won't be able to do a thing*, he concluded, surprised.

Exactly, said Saphira. *We can inflict lots of damage from a safe height.*

Let's drop rocks on them! proposed Eragon. *That should scatter them.*

If their skulls aren't thick enough to protect them. Saphira banked to the right and quickly descended to the Beartooth River. She grasped a mid-sized boulder with her strong talons while Eragon scooped up several fist-sized rocks. Laden with the stones, Saphira glided on silent wings until they were over the Urgal host. *Now!* she exclaimed, releasing the boulder. There were muffled cracks as the missiles plummeted through the forest top, smashing branches. A second later howls echoed through the valley.

Eragon smiled tightly as he heard the Urgals scramble for cover. *Let's find more ammunition,* he suggested, bending low over Saphira. She growled in agreement and returned to the riverbed.

It was hard work, but they were able to hinder the Urgals' progress—though it was impossible to stop them altogether. The Urgals gained ground whenever Saphira went for stones. Despite that, their efforts allowed Murtagh to stay ahead of the advancing column.

The valley darkened as the hours slipped by. Without the sun to provide warmth, the sharp bite of frost crept into the air and the ground mist froze on the trees, coating them white. Night animals began to creep from their dens to peer from shadowed hideouts at the strangers trespassing on their land.

Eragon continued to examine the mountainsides, searching for the waterfall that would signify the end of their journey. He was painfully aware that every passing minute brought Arya closer to death. "Faster, faster," he muttered to himself, looking down at Murtagh. Before Saphira scooped up more rocks, he said, *Let's take a respite and check on Arya. The day is almost over, and I'm afraid her life is measured in hours, if not minutes.*

Arya's life is in Fate's hands now. You made your choice to stay with Murtagh; it's too late to change that, so stop agonizing over it. . . . You're making my scales itch. The best thing we can do right now is to keep bombarding the Urgals. Eragon knew she was right, yet her words did nothing to calm his anxiety. He resumed his search for the waterfall, but whatever lay before them was hidden by a thick mountain ridge.

True darkness began to fill the valley, settling over the trees and mountains like an inky cloud. Even with her keen hearing and delicate sense of smell, Saphira could no longer locate the Urgals through the dense forest. There was no moon to help them; it would be hours before it rose above the mountains.

Saphira made a long, gentle left turn and glided around the mountain ridge. Eragon vaguely sensed it pass by them, then squinted as he saw a faint white line ahead. *Could that be the waterfall?* he wondered.

He looked at the sky, which still held the afterglow of sunset. The mountains' dark silhouettes curved together and formed a rough bowl that closed off the valley. *The head of the valley isn't much farther!* he exclaimed, pointing at the mountains. *Do you think that the Varden know we're coming? Maybe they'll send men out to help us.*

I doubt they'll assist us until they know if we are friend or foe, Saphira said as she abruptly dropped toward the ground. *I'm returning to Murtagh—we should stay with him now. Since I can't find the Urgals, they could sneak up on him without us knowing.*

Eragon loosened Zar'roc in its sheath, wondering if he was strong enough to fight. Saphira landed to the left of the Beartooth River, then crouched expectantly. The waterfall rumbled in the distance. *He comes,* she said. Eragon strained his ears and caught the sound of pounding hooves. Murtagh ran out of the forest, driving the horses before him. He saw them but did not slow.

Eragon jumped off Saphira, stumbling a bit as he matched Murtagh's pace. Behind him Saphira went to the river so she could follow them without being hindered by the trees. Before Eragon could relay his news, Murtagh said, "I saw you dropping rocks with Saphira—ambitious. Have the Kull stopped or turned back?"

"They're still behind us, but we're almost to the head of the valley. How's Arya?"

"She hasn't died," Murtagh said harshly. His breath came in

short bursts. His next words were deceptively calm, like those of a man concealing a terrible passion. "Is there a valley or gorge ahead that I can leave through?"

Apprehensive, Eragon tried to remember if he had seen any breaks in the mountains around them; he had not thought about Murtagh's dilemma for a while. "It's dark," he began evasively, dodging a low branch, "so I might have missed something, but . . . no."

Murtagh swore explosively and came to an abrupt stop, dragging on the horses' reins until they halted as well. "Are you saying that the only place I can go is to the Varden?"

"Yes, but keep running. The Urgals are almost upon us!"

"No!" said Murtagh angrily. He stabbed a finger at Eragon. "I warned you that I wouldn't go to the Varden, but you went ahead and trapped me between a hammer and an anvil! You're the one with the elf's memories. Why didn't you tell me this was a dead end?"

Eragon bristled at the barrage and retorted, "All I knew was where we had to go, not what lay in between. Don't blame me for choosing to come."

Murtagh's breath hissed between his teeth as he furiously spun away. All Eragon could see of him was a motionless, bowed figure. His own shoulders were tense, and a vein throbbed on the side of his neck. He put his hands on his hips, impatience rising.

Why have you stopped? asked Saphira, alarmed.

Don't distract me. "What's your quarrel with the Varden? It can't be so terrible that you must keep it hidden even now. Would you rather fight the Kull than reveal it? How many times will we go through this before you trust me?"

There was a long silence.

The Urgals! reminded Saphira urgently.

I know, said Eragon, pushing back his temper. *But we have to resolve this.*

Quickly, quickly.

"Murtagh," said Eragon earnestly, "unless you wish to die, we must go to the Varden. Don't let me walk into their arms without knowing how they will react to you. It's going to be dangerous enough without unnecessary surprises."

Finally Murtagh turned to Eragon. His breathing was hard and fast, like that of a cornered wolf. He paused, then said with a tortured voice, "You have a right to know. I . . . I am the son of Morzan, first and last of the Forsworn."

THE HORNS OF
A DILEMMA

Eragon was speechless. Disbelief roared through his mind as he tried to reject Murtagh's words. *The Forsworn never had any children, least of all Morzan. Morzan! The man who betrayed the Riders to Galbatorix and remained the king's favorite servant for the rest of his life. Could it be true?*

Saphira's own shock reached him a second later. She crashed through trees and brush as she barreled from the river to his side, fangs bared, tail raised threateningly. *Be ready for anything,* she warned. *He may be able to use magic.*

"You are his heir?" asked Eragon, surreptitiously reaching for Zar'roc. *What could he want with me? Is he really working for the king?*

"I didn't choose this!" cried Murtagh, anguish twisting his face. He ripped at his clothes with a desperate air, tearing off his tunic and shirt to bare his torso. "Look!" he pleaded, and turned his back to Eragon.

Unsure, Eragon leaned forward, straining his eyes in the darkness. There, against Murtagh's tanned and muscled skin, was a knotted white scar that stretched from his right shoulder to his left hip—a testament to some terrible agony.

"See that?" demanded Murtagh bitterly. He talked quickly now, as if relieved to have his secret finally revealed. "I was only three when I got it. During one of his many drunken rages, Morzan threw his sword at me as I ran by. My back was laid open by the very sword you now carry—the only thing I expected to receive as inheritance, until Brom stole it from my father's corpse. I was lucky, I suppose—there was a healer nearby who kept me from dying. You must understand, I don't love the Empire or the king. I have no allegiance to them, nor do I mean you harm!" His pleas were almost frantic.

Eragon uneasily lifted his hand from Zar'roc's pommel. "Then your father," he said in a faltering voice, "was killed by . . ."

"Yes, Brom," said Murtagh. He pulled his tunic back on with a detached air.

A horn rang out behind them, prompting Eragon to cry, "Come, run with me." Murtagh shook the horses' reins and forced them into a tired trot, eyes fixed straight ahead, while Arya bounced limply in Snowfire's saddle. Saphira stayed by Eragon's side, easily keeping pace with her long legs. *You could walk unhindered in the riverbed,* he said as she was forced to smash through a dense web of branches.

I'll not leave you with him.

Eragon was glad for her protection. *Morzan's son!* He said between strides, "Your tale is hard to believe. How do I know you aren't lying?"

"Why would I lie?"

"You could be—"

Murtagh interrupted him quickly. "I can't prove anything to you now. Keep your doubts until we reach the Varden. They'll recognize me quickly enough."

"I must know," pressed Eragon. "Do you serve the Empire?"

"No. And if I did, what would I accomplish by traveling with you? If I were trying to capture or kill you, I would have left you in prison." Murtagh stumbled as he jumped over a fallen log.

"You could be leading the Urgals to the Varden."

"Then," said Murtagh shortly, "why am I still with you? I know where the Varden are now. What reason could I have for delivering myself to them? If I were going to attack them, I'd turn around and join the Urgals."

"Maybe you're an assassin," stated Eragon flatly.

"Maybe. You can't really know, can you?"

Saphira? Eragon asked simply.

Her tail swished over his head. *If he wanted to harm you, he could have done it long ago.*

A branch whipped Eragon's neck, causing a line of blood to appear on his skin. The waterfall was growing louder. *I want you to watch Murtagh closely when we get to the Varden. He may do something foolish, and I don't want him killed by accident.*

I'll do my best, she said as she shouldered her way between two trees, scraping off slabs of bark. The horn sounded behind them again. Eragon glanced over his shoulder, expecting Urgals to rush out of the darkness. The waterfall throbbed dully ahead of them, drowning out the sounds of the night.

The forest ended, and Murtagh pulled the horses to a stop. They were on a pebble beach directly to the left of the mouth of the Beartooth River. The deep lake Kóstha-mérna filled the valley, blocking their way. The water gleamed with flickering starlight. The mountain walls restricted passage around Kóstha-mérna to a thin strip of shore on either side of the lake, both no more than a few steps wide. At the lake's far end, a broad sheet of water tumbled down a black cliff into boiling mounds of froth.

"Do we go to the falls?" asked Murtagh tightly.

"Yes." Eragon took the lead and picked his way along the lake's left side. The pebbles underfoot were damp and slime covered. There was barely enough room for Saphira between the sheer valley wall and the lake; she had to walk with two feet in the water.

They were halfway to the waterfall when Murtagh warned, "Urgals!"

Eragon whirled around, rocks spraying from under his heel. By the shore of Kóstha-mérna, where they had been only minutes before, hulking figures streamed out of the forest. The Urgals massed before the lake. One of them gestured at Saphira; guttural words drifted over the water. Immediately the horde split and started around both sides of the lake, leaving Eragon and Murtagh without an escape route. The narrow shore forced the bulky Kull to march single file.

"Run!" barked Murtagh, drawing his sword and slapping the horses on their flanks. Saphira took off without warning and wheeled back toward the Urgals.

"No!" cried Eragon, shouting with his mind, *Come back!* but she continued, heedless to his pleas. With an agonizing effort, he tore his gaze from her and plunged forward, wrenching Zar'roc from its sheath.

Saphira dived at the Urgals, bellowing fiercely. They tried to scatter but were trapped against the mountainside. She caught a Kull between her talons and carried the screaming creature aloft, tearing at him with her fangs. The silent body crashed into the lake a moment later, an arm and a leg missing.

The Kull continued around Kóstha-mérna undeterred. With smoke streaming from her nostrils, Saphira dived at them again. She twisted and rolled as a cloud of black arrows shot toward her. Most of the darts glanced off her scaled sides, leaving no more than bruises, but she roared as the rest pierced her wings.

Eragon's arms twinged with sympathetic pain, and he had to restrain himself from rushing to her defense. Fear flooded his veins as he saw the line of Urgals closing in on them. He tried to run faster, but his muscles were too tired, the rocks too slippery.

Then, with a loud splash, Saphira plunged into Kóstha-mérna. She submerged completely, sending ripples across the lake. The Urgals nervously eyed the dark water lapping their feet. One growled something indecipherable and jabbed his spear at the lake.

The water exploded as Saphira's head shot out of the depths. Her jaws closed on the spear, breaking it like a twig as she tore it out of the Kull's hands with a vicious twist. Before she could seize the Urgal himself, his companions thrust at her with their spears, bloodying her nose.

Saphira jerked back and hissed angrily, beating the water with her tail. Keeping his spear pointed at her, the lead Kull tried to edge past, but halted when she snapped at his legs. The string of Urgals was forced to stop as she held him at bay. Meanwhile, the Kull on the other side of the lake still hurried toward the falls.

I've trapped them, she told Eragon tersely, *but hurry—I cannot hold them long.* Archers on the shore were already taking aim at her. Eragon concentrated on going faster, but a rock gave under his boot and he pitched forward. Murtagh's strong arm kept him on his feet, and clasping each other's forearms, they urged the horses forward with shouts.

They were almost to the waterfall. The noise was overwhelming, like an avalanche. A white wall of water gushed down the cliff, pounding the rocks below with a fury that sent mist spraying through the air to run down their faces. Four yards from the thunderous curtain, the beach widened, giving them room to maneuver.

Saphira roared as an Urgal spear grazed her haunch, then retreated underwater. With her withdrawal the Kull rushed forward with long strides. They were only a few hundred feet away. "What do we do now?" Murtagh demanded coldly.

"I don't know. Let me think!" cried Eragon, searching Arya's memories for her final instructions. He scanned the ground until he found a rock the size of an apple, grabbed it, then pounded on the cliff next to the falls, shouting, "Aí varden abr du Shur'tugalar gata vanta!"

Nothing happened.

He tried again, shouting louder than before, but only succeeded in bruising his hand. He turned in despair to Murtagh. "We're trap—" His words were cut off as Saphira leapt out of the lake, dousing them with icy water. She landed on the beach and crouched, ready to fight.

The horses backpedaled wildly, trying to bolt. Eragon reached out with his mind to steady them. *Behind you!* cried Saphira. He turned and glimpsed the lead Urgal running at him, heavy spear raised. Up close a Kull was as tall as a small giant, with legs and arms as thick as tree trunks.

Murtagh drew back his arm and threw his sword with incredible speed. The long weapon revolved once, then struck the Kull point first in the chest with a dull crunch. The huge Urgal toppled to the ground with a strangled gurgle. Before another Kull could attack, Murtagh dashed forward and yanked his sword out of the body.

Eragon raised his palm, shouting, "Jierda theirra kalfis!" Sharp cracks resounded off the cliff. Twenty of the charging Urgals fell into Kóstha-mérna, howling and clutching their legs where shards of bone protruded. Without breaking stride, the rest of the Urgals advanced over their fallen companions. Eragon struggled against his weariness, putting a hand on Saphira for support.

A flight of arrows, impossible to see in the darkness, brushed past them and clattered against the cliff. Eragon and Murtagh ducked, covering their heads. With a small growl, Saphira jumped over them so that her armored sides shielded them and the horses. A chorus of clinks sounded as a second volley of arrows bounced off her scales.

"What now?" shouted Murtagh. There was still no opening in the cliff. "We can't stay here!"

Eragon heard Saphira snarl as an arrow caught the edge of her wing, tearing the thin membrane. He looked around wildly, trying to understand why Arya's instructions had not worked. "I don't know! This is where we're supposed to be!"

"Why don't you ask the elf to make sure?" demanded Murtagh. He dropped his sword, snatched his bow from Tornac's saddlebags, and with a swift motion loosed an arrow from between the spikes on Saphira's back. A moment later an Urgal toppled into the water.

"Now? She's barely alive! How's she going to find the energy to say anything?"

"I don't *know*," shouted Murtagh, "but you'd better think of *something* because we can't stave off an entire army!"

Eragon, growled Saphira urgently.

What!

We're on the wrong side of the lake! I've seen Arya's memories through you, and I just realized that this isn't the right place. She tucked her head against her breast as another flight of arrows sped toward them. Her tail flicked in pain as they struck her. *I can't keep this up! They're tearing me to pieces!*

Eragon slammed Zar'roc back into its sheath and exclaimed, "The Varden are on the other side of the lake. We have to go through the waterfall!" He noted with dread that the Urgals across Kóstha-mérna were almost to the falls.

Murtagh's eyes shot toward the violent deluge blocking their way. "We'll never get the horses through there, even if we can hold our own footing."

"I'll convince them to follow us," snapped Eragon. "And Saphira can carry Arya." The Urgals' cries and bellows made Snowfire snort angrily. The elf lolled on his back, oblivious to the danger.

Murtagh shrugged. "It's better than being hacked to death." He swiftly cut Arya loose from Snowfire's saddle, and Eragon caught the elf as she slid to the ground.

I'm ready, said Saphira, rising into a half-crouch. The approaching Urgals hesitated, unsure of her intentions.

"Now!" cried Eragon. He and Murtagh heaved Arya onto Saphira, then secured her legs in the saddle's straps. The second they were finished, Saphira swept up her wings and soared over the lake. The Urgals behind her howled as they saw her escaping. Arrows clattered off her belly. The Kull on the other shore redoubled their pace so as to attain the waterfall before she landed.

Eragon reached out with his mind to force himself into the frightened thoughts of the horses. Using the ancient language, he told them that unless they swam through the waterfall, they would be killed and eaten by the Urgals. Though they did not understand everything he said, the meaning of his words was unmistakable.

Snowfire and Tornac tossed their heads, then dashed into the thundering downpour, whinnying as it struck their backs. They floundered, struggling to stay above water. Murtagh sheathed his sword and jumped after them; his head disappeared under a froth of bubbles before he bobbed up, sputtering.

The Urgals were right behind Eragon; he could hear their feet crunching on the gravel. With a fierce war cry he leapt after Murtagh, closing his eyes a second before the cold water pummeled him.

The tremendous weight of the waterfall slammed down on his shoulders with backbreaking force. The water's mindless roar filled his ears. He was driven to the bottom, where his knees gouged the rocky lakebed. He kicked off with all his strength and shot partway out of the water. Before he could take a gulp of air, the cascade rammed him back underwater.

All he could see was a white blur as foam billowed around him. He frantically tried to surface and relieve his burning lungs, but he only rose a few feet before the deluge halted his ascent. He panicked, thrashing his arms and legs, fighting the water. Weighed down by Zar'roc and his drenched clothes, he sank back to the lakebed, unable to speak the ancient words that could save him.

Suddenly a strong hand grasped the back of his tunic and dragged him through the water. His rescuer sliced through the lake with quick, short strokes; Eragon hoped it was Murtagh, not an Urgal. They surfaced and stumbled onto the pebble beach. Eragon was trembling violently; his entire body shivered in bursts.

Sounds of combat erupted to his right, and he whirled toward them, expecting an Urgal attack. The monsters on the opposite shore—where he had stood only moments before—fell beneath a withering hail of arrows from crevasses that pockmarked the cliff. Scores of Urgals already floated belly up in the water, riddled with shafts. The ones on Eragon's shore were similarly engaged. Neither group could retreat from their exposed positions, for rows of warriors had somehow appeared behind them, where the lake met the mountainsides. All that prevented the nearest Kull from rushing Eragon was the steady rain of arrows—the unseen archers seemed determined to keep the Urgals at bay.

A gruff voice next to Eragon said, "Akh Guntéraz dorzâda! What were they thinking? You would have drowned!" Eragon jerked with surprise. It was not Murtagh standing by him but a diminutive man no taller than his elbow.

The dwarf was busy wringing water out of his long braided beard. His chest was stocky, and he wore a chain-mail jacket cut off at the shoulders to reveal muscular arms. A war ax hung from a wide leather belt strapped around his waist. An iron-bound oxhide cap, bearing the symbol of a hammer surrounded by twelve stars, sat firmly on his head. Even with the cap, he barely topped four feet. He looked longingly at the fighting and said, "Barzul, but I wish I could join them!"

A *dwarf!* Eragon drew Zar'roc and looked for Saphira and Murtagh. Two twelve-foot-thick stone doors had opened in the cliff, revealing a broad tunnel nearly thirty feet tall that burrowed its way into the mysterious depths of the mountain. A line of flameless lamps filled the passageway with a pale sapphire light that spilled out onto the lake.

Saphira and Murtagh stood before the tunnel, surrounded by a grim mixture of men and dwarves. At Murtagh's elbow was a bald, beardless man dressed in purple and gold robes. He was taller than all the other humans—and he was holding a dagger to Murtagh's throat.

Eragon reached for his power, but the robed man said in a sharp, dangerous voice, "Stop! If you use magic, I'll kill your lovely friend here, who was so kind as to mention you're a Rider. Don't think I won't know if you're drawing upon it. You can't hide anything from me." Eragon tried to speak, but the man snarled and pressed the dagger harder against Murtagh's throat. "None of that! If you say or do anything I don't tell you to, he will die. Now, everyone inside." He backed into the tunnel, pulling Murtagh with him and keeping his eyes on Eragon.

Saphira, what should I do? Eragon asked quickly as the men and dwarves followed Murtagh's captor, leading the horses along with them.

Go with them, she counseled, *and hope that we live.* She entered the tunnel herself, eliciting nervous glances from those around her. Reluctantly, Eragon followed her, aware that the warriors' eyes were upon him. His rescuer, the dwarf, walked alongside him with a hand on the haft of his war ax.

Utterly exhausted, Eragon staggered into the mountain. The stone doors swung shut behind them with only a whisper of sound. He looked back and saw a seamless wall where the opening had been. They were trapped inside. But were they any safer?

HUNTING FOR ANSWERS

"This way," snapped the bald man. He stepped back, keeping the dagger pressed under Murtagh's chin, then wheeled to the right, disappearing through an arched doorway. The warriors cautiously followed him, their attention centered on Eragon and Saphira. The horses were led into a different tunnel.

Dazed by the turn of events, Eragon started after Murtagh. He glanced at Saphira to confirm that Arya was still tied to her back. *She has to get the antidote!* he thought frantically, knowing that even then the Skilna Bragh was fulfilling its deadly purpose within her flesh.

He hurried through the arched doorway and down a narrow corridor after the bald man. The warriors kept their weapons pointed at him. They swept past a sculpture of a peculiar animal with thick quills. The corridor curved sharply to the left, then to the right. A door opened and they entered a bare room large enough for Saphira to move around with ease. There was a hollow boom as the door closed, followed by a loud scrape as a bolt was secured on the outside.

Eragon slowly examined his surroundings, Zar'roc tight in his hand. The walls, floor, and ceiling were made of polished white marble that reflected a ghost image of everyone, like a mirror of veined milk. One of the unusual lanterns hung in each corner. "There's an injured—" he began, but a sharp gesture from the bald man cut him off.

"Do not speak! It must wait until you have been tested." He shoved Murtagh over to one of the warriors, who pressed a sword against Murtagh's neck. The bald man clasped his hands together softly. "Remove your weapons and slide them to me." A dwarf unbuckled Murtagh's sword and dropped it on the floor with a clank.

Loath to be parted with Zar'roc, Eragon unfastened the sheath and set it and the blade on the floor. He placed his bow and quiver next to them, then pushed the pile toward the warriors. "Now step away from your dragon and slowly approach me," commanded the bald man.

Puzzled, Eragon moved forward. When they were a yard apart, the man said, "Stop there! Now remove the defenses from around your mind and prepare to let me inspect your thoughts and memories. If you try to hide anything from me, I will take what I want by force . . . which would drive you mad. If you don't submit, your companion will be killed."

"Why?" asked Eragon, aghast.

"To be sure you aren't in Galbatorix's service and to understand why hundreds of Urgals are banging on our front door," growled the bald man. His close-set eyes shifted from point to point with cunning speed. "No one may enter Farthen Dûr without being tested."

"There isn't time. We need a healer!" protested Eragon.

"Silence!" roared the man, pressing down his robe with thin fingers. "Until you are examined, your words are meaningless!"

"But she's dying!" retorted Eragon angrily, pointing at Arya. They were in a precarious position, but he would let nothing else happen until Arya was cared for.

"It will have to wait! No one will leave this room until we have discovered the truth of this matter. Unless you wish—"

The dwarf who had saved Eragon from the lake jumped forward. "Are you blind, Egraz Carn? Can't you see that's an elf on the dragon? We cannot keep her here if she's in danger. Ajihad and the king will have our heads if she's allowed to die!"

The man's eyes tightened with anger. After a moment he relaxed and said smoothly, "Of course, Orik, we wouldn't want that to happen." He snapped his fingers and pointed at Arya. "Remove her from the dragon." Two human warriors sheathed their swords and hesitantly approached Saphira, who watched them steadily. "Quickly, quickly!"

The men unstrapped Arya from the saddle and lowered the elf to the floor. One of the men inspected her face, then said sharply, "It's the dragon-egg courier, Arya!"

"What?" exclaimed the bald man. The dwarf Orik's eyes widened with astonishment. The bald man fixed his steely gaze on Eragon and said flatly, "You have much explaining to do."

Eragon returned the intense stare with all the determination he could muster. "She was poisoned with the Skilna Bragh while in prison. Only Túnivor's Nectar can save her now."

The bald man's face became inscrutable. He stood motionless, except for his lips, which twitched occasionally. "Very well. Take her to the healers, and tell them what she needs. Guard her until the ceremony is completed. I will have new orders for you by then." The warriors nodded curtly and carried Arya out of the room. Eragon watched them go, wishing that he could accompany her. His attention snapped back to the bald man as he said, "Enough of this, we have wasted too much time already. Prepare to be examined."

Eragon did not want this hairless threatening man inside his mind, laying bare his every thought and feeling, but he knew that resistance would be useless. The air was strained. Murtagh's gaze burned into his forehead. Finally he bowed his head. "I am ready."

"Good, then—"

He was interrupted as Orik said abruptly, "You'd better not harm him, Egraz Carn, else the king will have words for you."

The bald man looked at him irritably, then faced Eragon with a small smile. "Only if he resists." He bowed his head and chanted several inaudible words.

Eragon gasped with pain and shock as a mental probe clawed its way into his mind. His eyes rolled up into his head, and he automatically began throwing up barriers around his consciousness. The attack was incredibly powerful.

Don't do that! cried Saphira. Her thoughts joined his, filling him with strength. *You're putting Murtagh at risk!* Eragon faltered, gritted his teeth, then forced himself to remove his shielding, exposing himself to the ravening probe. Disappointment emanated from the bald man. His battering intensified. The force coming from his mind felt decayed and unwholesome; there was something profoundly wrong about it.

He wants me to fight him! cried Eragon as a fresh wave of pain racked him. A second later it subsided, only to be replaced by another. Saphira did her best to suppress it, but even she could not block it entirely.

Give him what he wants, she said quickly, *but protect everything else. I'll help you. His strength is no match for mine; I'm already shielding our words from him.*

Then why does it still hurt?

The pain comes from you.

Eragon winced as the probe dug in farther, hunting for information, like a nail being driven through his skull. The bald man roughly seized his childhood memories and began sifting through them. *He doesn't need those—get him out of there!* growled Eragon angrily.

I can't, not without endangering you, said Saphira. *I can conceal things from his view, but it must be done before he reaches them. Think quickly, and tell me what you want hidden!*

Eragon tried to concentrate through the pain. He raced through his memories, starting from when he had found Saphira's egg. He hid sections of his discussions with Brom, including all the ancient words he had been taught. Their travels through Palancar Valley, Yazuac, Daret, and Teirm he left mostly untouched. But he had Saphira conceal everything he remembered of Angela's fortune-telling and Solembum. He skipped from their burglary at Teirm, to

Brom's death, to his imprisonment in Gil'ead, and lastly to Murtagh's revelation of his true identity.

Eragon wanted to hide that as well, but Saphira balked. *The Varden have a right to know who they shelter under their roof, especially if it's a son of the Forsworn!*

Just do it, he said tightly, fighting another wave of agony. *I won't be the one to unmask him, at least not to this man.*

It'll be discovered as soon as Murtagh is scanned, warned Saphira sharply.

Just do it.

With the most important information hidden, there was nothing else for Eragon to do but wait for the bald man to finish his inspection. It was like sitting still while his fingernails were extracted with rusty tongs. His entire body was rigid, jaw locked tightly. Heat radiated from his skin, and a line of sweat rolled down his neck. He was acutely aware of each second as the long minutes crept by.

The bald man wound through his experiences sluggishly, like a thorny vine pushing its way toward the sunlight. He paid keen attention to many things Eragon considered irrelevant, such as his mother, Selena, and seemed to linger on purpose so as to prolong the suffering. He spent a long time examining Eragon's recollections of the Ra'zac, and then later the Shade. It was not until his adventures had been exhaustively analyzed that the bald man began to withdraw from Eragon's mind.

The probe was extracted like a splinter being removed. Eragon shuddered, swayed, then fell toward the floor. Strong arms caught him at the last second, lowering him to the cool marble. He heard Orik exclaim from behind him, "You went too far! He wasn't strong enough for this."

"He'll live. That's all that is needed," answered the bald man curtly.

There was an angry grunt. "What did you find?"

Silence.

"Well, is he to be trusted or not?"

The words came reluctantly. "He . . . is not your enemy." There were audible sighs of relief throughout the room.

Eragon's eyes fluttered open. He gingerly pushed himself upright. "Easy now," said Orik, wrapping a thick arm around him and helping him to his feet. Eragon wove unsteadily, glaring at the bald man. A low growl rumbled in Saphira's throat.

The bald man ignored them. He turned to Murtagh, who was still being held at sword point. "It's your turn now."

Murtagh stiffened and shook his head. The sword cut his neck slightly. Blood dripped down his skin. "No."

"You will not be protected here if you refuse."

"Eragon has been declared trustworthy, so you cannot threaten to kill him to influence me. Since you can't do that, nothing you say or do will convince me to open my mind."

Sneering, the bald man cocked what would have been an eyebrow, if he had any. "What of your own life? I can still threaten that."

"It won't do any good," said Murtagh stonily and with such conviction that it was impossible to doubt his word.

The bald man's breath exploded angrily. "You don't have a choice!" He stepped forward and placed his palm on Murtagh's brow, clenching his hand to hold him in place. Murtagh stiffened, face growing as hard as iron, fists clenched, neck muscles bulging. He was obviously fighting the attack with all his strength. The bald man bared his teeth with fury and frustration at the resistance; his fingers dug mercilessly into Murtagh.

Eragon winced in sympathy, knowing the battle that raged between them. *Can't you help him?* he asked Saphira.

No, she said softly. *He will allow no one into his mind.*

Orik scowled darkly as he watched the combatants. "Ilf carnz orodüm," he muttered, then leapt forward and cried, "That is enough!" He grabbed the bald man's arm and tore him away from Murtagh with strength disproportional to his size.

The bald man stumbled back, then turned on Orik furiously. "How dare you!" he shouted. "You questioned my leadership, opened the gates without permission, and now this! You've shown nothing but insolence and treachery. Do you think your king will protect you now?"

Orik bristled. "You would have let them die! If I had waited any longer, the Urgals would have killed them." He pointed at Murtagh, whose breath came in great heaves. "We don't have any right to torture him for information! Ajihad won't sanction it. Not after you've examined the Rider and found him free of fault. *And* they've brought us Arya."

"Would you allow him to enter unchallenged? Are you so great a fool as to put us all at risk?" demanded the bald man. His eyes were feral with loosely chained rage; he looked ready to tear the dwarf into pieces.

"Can he use magic?"

"That is—"

"Can he use magic?" roared Orik, his deep voice echoing in the room. The bald man's face suddenly grew expressionless. He clasped his hands behind his back.

"No."

"Then what do you fear? It's impossible for him to escape, and he can't work any devilry with all of us here, especially if your powers are as great as you say. But don't listen to me; ask Ajihad what he wants done."

The bald man stared at Orik for a moment, his face indecipherable, then looked at the ceiling and closed his eyes. A peculiar stiffness set into his shoulders while his lips moved soundlessly. An intense frown wrinkled the pale skin above his eyes, and his fingers clenched, as if they were throttling an invisible enemy. For several minutes he stood thus, wrapped in silent communication.

When his eyes opened, he ignored Orik and snapped at the warriors, "Leave, now!" As they filed through the doorway, he addressed Eragon coldly, "Because I was unable to complete my examination, you and . . . your friend will remain here for the night. He will be killed if he attempts to leave." With those words he turned on his heel and stalked out of the room, pale scalp gleaming in the lantern light.

"Thank you," whispered Eragon to Orik.

The dwarf grunted. "I'll make sure some food is brought." He muttered a string of words under his breath, then left, shaking his head. The bolt was secured once again on the outside of the door.

Eragon sat, feeling strangely dreamy from the day's excitement and their forced march. His eyelids were heavy. Saphira settled next to him. *We must be careful. It seems we have as many enemies here as we did in the Empire.* He nodded, too tired to talk.

Murtagh, eyes glazed and empty, leaned against the far wall and slid to the shiny floor. He held his sleeve against the cut on his neck to stop the bleeding. "Are you all right?" asked Eragon. Murtagh nodded jerkily. "Did he get anything from you?"

"No."

"How were you able to keep him out? He's so strong."

"I've . . . I've been well trained." There was a bitter note to his voice.

Silence enshrouded them. Eragon's gaze drifted to one of the lanterns hanging in a corner. His thoughts meandered until he abruptly said, "I didn't let them know who you are."

Murtagh looked relieved. He bowed his head. "Thank you for not betraying me."

"They didn't recognize you."

"No."

"And you still say that you are Morzan's son?"

"Yes," he sighed.

Eragon started to speak, but stopped when he felt hot liquid splash onto his hand. He looked down and was startled to see a drop of dark blood roll off his skin. It had fallen from Saphira's wing. *I forgot. You're injured!* he exclaimed, getting up with an effort. *I'd better heal you.*

Be careful. It's easy to make mistakes when you're this tired.

I know. Saphira unfolded one of her wings and lowered it to the floor. Murtagh watched as Eragon ran his hands over the warm blue membrane, saying, "Waíse heill," whenever he found an arrow hole. Luckily, all the wounds were relatively easy to heal, even those on her nose.

Task completed, Eragon slumped against Saphira, breathing hard. He could feel her great heart beating with the steady throb of life. "I hope they bring food soon," said Murtagh.

Eragon shrugged; he was too exhausted to be hungry. He crossed his arms, missing Zar'roc's weight by his side. "Why are you here?"

"What?"

"If you really are Morzan's son, Galbatorix wouldn't let you wander around Alagaësia freely. How is it that you managed to find the Ra'zac by yourself? Why is it I've never heard of any of the Forsworn having children? And what are you doing here?" His voice rose to a near shout at the end.

Murtagh ran his hands over his face. "It's a long story."

"We're not going anywhere," rebutted Eragon.

"It's too late to talk."

"There probably won't be time for it tomorrow."

Murtagh wrapped his arms around his legs and rested his chin on his knees, rocking back and forth as he stared at the floor. "It's not a—" he said, then interrupted himself. "I don't want to stop . . . so make yourself comfortable. My story will take a while." Eragon shifted against Saphira's side and nodded. Saphira watched both of them intently.

Murtagh's first sentence was halting, but his voice gained strength and confidence as he spoke. "As far as I know . . . I am the only child of the Thirteen Servants, or the Forsworn as they're called. There may be others, for the Thirteen had the skill to hide whatever they wanted, but I doubt it, for reasons I'll explain later.

"My parents met in a small village—I never learned where—while my father was traveling on the king's business. Morzan showed my mother some small kindness, no doubt a ploy to gain her confidence, and when he left, she accompanied him. They traveled together for a time, and as is the nature of these things, she fell deeply in love with him. Morzan was delighted to discover this not only because it gave him numerous opportunities to torment her but also because he recognized the advantage of having a servant who wouldn't betray him.

"Thus, when Morzan returned to Galbatorix's court, my mother became the tool he relied upon most. He used her to carry his secret messages, and he taught her rudimentary magic, which helped her remain undiscovered and, on occasion, extract information from people. He did his best to protect her from the rest of the Thirteen—not out of any feelings for her, but because they would have used her against him, given the chance. . . . For three years things proceeded in this manner, until my mother became pregnant."

Murtagh paused for a moment, fingering a lock of his hair. He continued in a clipped tone, "My father was, if nothing else, a cunning man. He knew that the pregnancy put both him and my mother in danger, not to mention the baby—that is, me. So, in the dead of night, he spirited her away from the palace and took her to his castle. Once there, he laid down powerful spells that prevented anyone from entering his estate except for a few chosen servants. In this way the pregnancy was kept secret from everyone but Galbatorix.

"Galbatorix knew the intimate details of the Thirteen's lives: their plots, their fights—and most importantly—their thoughts. He enjoyed watching them battle each other and often helped one or the other for his own amusement. But for some reason he never revealed my existence.

"I was born in due time and given to a wet nurse so my mother could return to Morzan's side. She had no choice in the matter. Morzan allowed her to visit me every few months, but otherwise we were kept apart. Another three years passed like this, during which time he gave me the . . . scar on my back." Murtagh brooded a minute before continuing.

"I would have grown to manhood in this fashion if Morzan hadn't been summoned away to hunt for Saphira's egg. As soon as he departed, my mother, who had been left behind, vanished. No one knows where she went, or why. The king tried to hunt her down, but his men couldn't find her trail—no doubt because of Morzan's training.

"At the time of my birth, only five of the Thirteen were still alive. By the time Morzan left, that number had been reduced to three; when he finally faced Brom in Gil'ead, he was the only one remaining. The Forsworn died through various means: suicide, ambush, overuse of magic . . . but it was mostly the work of the Varden. I'm told that the king was in a terrible rage because of those losses.

"However, before word of Morzan's and the others' deaths reached us, my mother returned. Many months had passed since she had disappeared. Her health was poor, as if she had suffered a great illness, and she grew steadily worse. Within a fortnight, she died."

"What happened then?" prompted Eragon.

Murtagh shrugged. "I grew up. The king brought me to the palace and arranged for my upbringing. Aside from that, he left me alone."

"Then why did you leave?"

A hard laugh broke from Murtagh. "Escaped is more like it. At my last birthday, when I turned eighteen, the king summoned me to his quarters for a private dinner. The message surprised me because I had always distanced myself from the court and had rarely met him. We'd talked before, but always within earshot of eavesdropping nobles.

"I accepted the offer, of course, aware that it would be unwise to refuse. The meal was sumptuous, but throughout it his black eyes never left me. His gaze was disconcerting; it seemed that he was searching for something hidden in my face. I didn't know what to make of it and did my best to provide polite conversation, but he refused to talk, and I soon ceased my efforts.

"When the meal was finished, he finally began to speak. You've never heard his voice, so it's hard for me to make you understand what it was like. His words were entrancing, like a snake whispering gilded lies into my ears. A more convincing and frightening man I've never heard. He wove a vision: a fantasy of the Empire as he imagined it. There would be beautiful cities built across the country, filled with the greatest warriors, artisans, musicians, and philosophers. The Urgals would finally be eradicated. And the Empire would expand in every direction until it reached the four corners of Alagaësia. Peace and prosperity would flourish, but more wondrous yet, the Riders would be brought back to gently govern over Galbatorix's fiefdoms.

"Entranced, I listened to him for what must have been hours. When he stopped, I eagerly asked how the Riders would be reinstated, for everyone knew there were no dragon eggs left. Galbatorix grew still then and stared at me thoughtfully. For a long time he was silent, but then he extended his hand and asked, 'Will you, O son of my friend, serve me as I labor to bring about this paradise?'

"Though I knew the history behind his and my father's rise to power, the dream he had painted for me was too compelling, too seductive to ignore. Ardor for this mission filled me, and I fervently pledged myself to him. Obviously pleased, Galbatorix gave me his blessing, then dismissed me, saying, 'I shall call upon you when the need arises.'

"Several months passed before he did. When the summons came, I felt all of my old excitement return. We met in private as before, but this time he was not pleasant or charming. The Varden had just destroyed three brigades in the south, and his wrath was out in full force. He charged me in a terrible voice to take a detachment of troops and destroy Cantos, where rebels were known to hide occasionally. When I asked what we should do with the people there and how we would know if they were guilty, he shouted, 'They're all traitors! Burn them at the stake and bury their ashes with dung!' He continued to rant, cursing his enemies and describing how he would scourge the land of everyone who bore him ill will.

"His tone was so different from what I had encountered before; it made me realize he didn't possess the mercy or foresight to gain the people's loyalty, and he ruled only through brute force guided by his own passions. It was at that moment I determined to escape him and Urû'baen forever.

"As soon as I was free of his presence, I and my faithful servant, Tornac, made ready for flight. We left that very night, but somehow Galbatorix anticipated my actions, for there were soldiers waiting for us outside the gates. Ah, my sword was bloody, flashing in the dim lantern glow. We defeated the men . . . but in the process Tornac was killed.

"Alone and filled with grief, I fled to an old friend who sheltered me in his estate. While I hid, I listened carefully to every rumor, trying to predict Galbatorix's actions and plan my future. During that time, talk reached me that the Ra'zac had been sent to capture or kill someone. Remembering the king's plans for the Riders, I decided to find and follow the Ra'zac, just in case they *did* discover a dragon. And that's how I found you. . . . I have no more secrets."

We still don't know if he's telling the truth, warned Saphira.

I know, said Eragon, *but why would he lie to us?*

He might be mad.

I doubt it. Eragon ran a finger over Saphira's hard scales, watching the light reflect off them. "So why don't you join the Varden? They'll distrust you for a time, but once you prove your loyalty they'll treat you with respect. And aren't they in a sense your allies? They strive to end the king's reign. Isn't that what you want?"

"Must I spell everything out for you?" demanded Murtagh. "I don't want Galbatorix to learn where I am, which is inevitable if people start saying that I've sided with his enemies, which I've never done. These," he paused, then said with distaste, "*rebels* are trying not only to overthrow the king but to destroy the Empire . . . and I don't want that to happen. It would sow mayhem and anarchy. The king is flawed, yes, but the system itself is sound. As for earning the Varden's respect: Ha! Once I am exposed, they'll treat me like a criminal or worse. Not only that, suspicion will fall upon you because we traveled together!"

He's right, said Saphira.

Eragon ignored her. "It isn't that bad," he said, trying to sound optimistic. Murtagh snorted derisively and looked away. "I'm sure that they won't be—" His words were cut short as the door opened a hand's breadth and two bowls were pushed through the space. A loaf of bread and a hunk of raw meat followed, then the door was shut again.

"Finally!" grumbled Murtagh, going to the food. He tossed the meat to Saphira, who snapped it out of the air and swallowed it whole. Then he tore the loaf in two, gave half to Eragon, picked up his bowl, and retreated to a corner.

They ate silently. Murtagh jabbed at his food. "I'm going to sleep," he announced, putting down his bowl without another word.

"Good night," said Eragon. He lay next to Saphira, his arms under his head. She curled her long neck around him, like a cat wrapping its tail around itself, and laid her head alongside his. One of her wings extended over him like a blue tent, enveloping him in darkness.

Good night, little one.

A small smile lifted Eragon's lips, but he was already asleep.

THE GLORY
OF TRONJHEIM

Eragon jolted upright as a growl sounded in his ear. Saphira was
still asleep, her eyes wandering sightlessly under her eyelids,
and her upper lip trembled, as if she were going to snarl. He
smiled, then jerked as she growled again.

She must be dreaming, he realized. He watched her for a minute,
then carefully slid out from under her wing. He stood and stretched.
The room was cool, but not unpleasantly so. Murtagh lay on his
back in the far corner, his eyes closed.

As Eragon stepped around Saphira, Murtagh stirred. "Morning,"
he said quietly, sitting up.

"How long have you been awake?" asked Eragon in a hushed
voice.

"Awhile. I'm surprised Saphira didn't wake you sooner."

"I was tired enough to sleep through a thunderstorm," said
Eragon wryly. He sat by Murtagh and rested his head against the
wall. "Do you know what time it is?"

"No. It's impossible to tell in here."

"Has anyone come to see us?"

"Not yet."

They sat together without moving or speaking. Eragon felt oddly
bound to Murtagh. *I've been carrying his father's sword, which would
have been his . . . his inheritance. We're alike in many ways, yet our
outlook and upbringing are totally different.* He thought of Murtagh's
scar and shivered. *What man could do that to a child?*

Saphira lifted her head and blinked to clear her eyes. She sniffed the air, then yawned expansively, her rough tongue curling at the tip. *Has anything happened?* Eragon shook his head. *I hope they give me more food than that snack last night. I'm hungry enough to eat a herd of cows.*

They'll feed you, he assured her.

They'd better. She positioned herself near the door and settled down to wait, tail flicking. Eragon closed his eyes, enjoying the rest. He dozed awhile, then got up and paced around. Bored, he examined one of the lanterns. It was made of a single piece of teardrop-shaped glass, about twice the size of a lemon, and filled with soft blue light that neither wavered nor flickered. Four slim metal ribs wrapped smoothly around the glass, meeting at the top to form a small hook and again at the bottom where they melded together into three graceful legs. The whole piece was quite attractive.

Eragon's inspection was interrupted by voices outside the room. The door opened, and a dozen warriors marched inside. The first man gulped when he saw Saphira. They were followed by Orik and the bald man, who declared, "You have been summoned to Ajihad, leader of the Varden. If you must eat, do so while we march." Eragon and Murtagh stood together, watching him warily.

"Where are our horses? And can I have my sword and bow back?" asked Eragon.

The bald man looked at him with disdain. "Your weapons will be returned to you when Ajihad sees fit, not before. As for your horses, they await you in the tunnel. Now come!"

As he turned to leave, Eragon asked quickly, "How is Arya?"

The bald man hesitated. "I do not know. The healers are still with her." He exited the room, accompanied by Orik.

One of the warriors motioned. "You go first." Eragon went through the doorway, followed by Saphira and Murtagh. They returned through the corridor they had traversed the night before, passing the statue of the quilled animal. When they reached the huge tunnel through which they had first entered the mountain, the bald man was waiting with Orik, who held Tornac's and Snowfire's reins.

"You will ride single file down the center of the tunnel," instructed the bald man. "If you attempt to go anywhere else, you will be stopped." When Eragon started to climb onto Saphira, the bald man shouted, "No! Ride your horse until I tell you otherwise."

Eragon shrugged and took Snowfire's reins. He swung into the saddle, guided Snowfire in front of Saphira, and told her, *Stay close in case I need your help.*

Of course, she said.

Murtagh mounted Tornac behind Saphira. The bald man examined their small line, then gestured at the warriors, who divided in half to surround them, giving Saphira as wide a berth as possible. Orik and the bald man went to the head of the procession.

After looking them over once more, the bald man clapped twice and started walking forward. Eragon tapped Snowfire lightly on his flanks. The entire group headed toward the heart of the mountain. Echoes filled the tunnel as the horses' hooves struck the hard floor, the sounds amplified in the deserted passageway. Doors and gates occasionally disturbed the smooth walls, but they were always closed.

Eragon marveled at the sheer size of the tunnel, which had been mined with incredible skill—the walls, floor, and ceiling were crafted with flawless precision. The angles at the bases of the walls were perfectly square, and as far as he could tell, the tunnel itself did not vary from its course by even an inch.

As they proceeded, Eragon's anticipation about meeting Ajihad increased. The leader of the Varden was a shadowy figure to the people within the Empire. He had risen to power nearly twenty years ago and since then had waged a fierce war against King Galbatorix. No one knew where he came from or even what he looked like. It was rumored that he was a master strategist, a brutal fighter. With such a reputation, Eragon worried about how they would be received. Still, knowing that Brom had trusted the Varden enough to serve them helped to allay his fears.

Seeing Orik again had brought forth new questions in his mind. The tunnel was obviously dwarf work—no one else could mine with such skill—but were the dwarves part of the Varden, or were they merely sheltering them? And who was the king that Orik had mentioned? Was it Ajihad? Eragon understood now that the Varden had been able to escape discovery by hiding underground, but what about the elves? Where were they?

For nearly an hour the bald man led them through the tunnel, never straying nor turning. *We've probably already gone a league*, Eragon realized. *Maybe they're taking us all the way through the mountain!* At last a soft white glow became visible ahead of them. He strained his eyes, trying to discern its source, but it was still too far away to make out any details. The glow increased in strength as they neared it.

Now he could see thick marble pillars laced with rubies and amethysts standing in rows along the walls. Scores of lanterns hung between the pillars, suffusing the air with liquid brilliance. Gold tracery gleamed from the pillars' bases like molten thread. Arching over the ceiling were carved raven heads, their beaks open in mid-screech. At the end of the hallway rested two colossal black doors, accented by shimmering silver lines that depicted a seven-pointed crown that spanned both sides.

The bald man stopped and raised a hand. He turned to Eragon. "You will ride upon your dragon now. Do not attempt to fly away. There will be people watching, so remember who and what you are."

Eragon dismounted Snowfire, and then clambered onto Saphira's back. *I think they want to show us off*, she said as he settled into the saddle.

We'll see. I wish I had Zar'roc, he replied, tightening the straps around his legs.

It might be better that you aren't wearing Morzan's sword when the Varden first see you.

True. "I'm ready," Eragon said, squaring his shoulders.

"Good," said the bald man. He and Orik retreated to either side of Saphira, staying far enough back so she was clearly in the lead. "Now walk to the doors, and once they open, follow the path. Go slowly."

Ready? asked Eragon.

Of course. Saphira approached the doors at a measured pace. Her scales sparkled in the light, sending glints of color dancing over the pillars. Eragon took a deep breath to steady his nerves.

Without warning, the doors swung outward on hidden joints. As the rift widened between them, rays of sunlight streamed into the tunnel, falling on Saphira and Eragon. Temporarily blinded, Eragon blinked and squinted. When his eyes adjusted to the light, he gasped.

They were inside a massive volcanic crater. Its walls narrowed to a small ragged opening so high above that Eragon could not judge the distance—it might have been more than a dozen miles. A soft beam of light fell through the aperture, illuminating the crater's center, though it left the rest of the cavernous expanse in hushed twilight.

The crater's far side, hazy blue in the distance, looked to be nearly ten miles away. Giant icicles hundreds of feet thick and thousands of feet long hung leagues above them like glistening daggers. Eragon knew from his experience in the valley that no one, not even Saphira, could reach those lofty points. Farther down the crater's inner walls, dark mats of moss and lichen covered the rock.

He lowered his gaze and saw a wide cobblestone path extending from the doors' threshold. The path ran straight to the center of the crater, where it ended at the base of a snowy-white mountain that glittered like an uncut gem with thousands of colored lights. It was less than a tenth of the height of the crater that loomed over and around it, but its diminutive appearance was deceiving, for it was slightly higher than a mile.

Long as it was, the tunnel had only taken them through one side of the crater wall. As Eragon stared, he heard Orik say deeply, "Look well, human, for no Rider has set eyes upon this for nigh over a hundred years. The airy peak under which we stand is Farthen

Dûr—discovered thousands of years ago by the father of our race, Korgan, while he tunneled for gold. And in the center stands our greatest achievement: Tronjheim, the city-mountain built from the purest marble." The doors grated to a halt.

A city!

Then Eragon saw the crowd. He had been so engrossed by the sights that he had failed to notice a dense sea of people clustered around the tunnel's entrance. They lined the cobblestone pathway—dwarves and humans packed together like trees in a thicket. There were hundreds . . . thousands of them. Every eye, every face was focused on Eragon. And every one of them was silent.

Eragon gripped the base of one of Saphira's neck spikes. He saw children in dirty smocks, hardy men with scarred knuckles, women in homespun dresses, and stout, weathered dwarves who fingered their beards. All of them bore the same taut expression—that of an injured animal when a predator is nearby and escape is impossible.

A bead of sweat rolled down Eragon's face, but he dared not move to wipe it away. *What should I do?* he asked frantically.

Smile, raise your hand, anything! replied Saphira sharply.

Eragon tried to force out a smile, but his lips only twitched. Gathering his courage, he pushed a hand into the air, jerking it in a little wave. When nothing happened, he flushed with embarrassment, lowered his arm, and ducked his head.

A single cheer broke the silence. Someone clapped loudly. For a brief second the crowd hesitated, then a wild roar swept through it, and a wave of sound crashed over Eragon.

"Very good," said the bald man from behind him. "Now start walking."

Relieved, Eragon sat straighter and playfully asked Saphira, *Shall we go?* She arched her neck and stepped forward. As they passed the first row of people, she glanced to each side and exhaled a puff of smoke. The crowd quieted and shrank back, then resumed cheering, their enthusiasm only intensified.

Show-off, chided Eragon. Saphira flicked her tail and ignored him. He stared curiously at the jostling crowd as she proceeded along the path. Dwarves greatly outnumbered humans . . . and many of them glared at him resentfully. Some even turned their backs and walked away with stony faces.

The humans were hard, tough people. All the men had daggers or knives at their waists; many were armed for war. The women carried themselves proudly, but they seemed to conceal a deep-abiding weariness. The few children and babies stared at Eragon with large eyes. He felt certain that these people had experienced much hardship and that they would do whatever was necessary to defend themselves.

The Varden had found the perfect hiding place. Farthen Dûr's walls were too high for a dragon to fly over, and no army could break through the entranceway, even if it managed to find the hidden doors.

The crowd followed close behind them, giving Saphira plenty of room. Gradually the people quieted, though their attention remained on Eragon. He looked back and saw Murtagh riding stiffly, his face pale.

They neared the city-mountain, and Eragon saw that the white marble of Tronjheim was highly polished and shaped into flowing contours, as if it had been poured into place. It was dotted with countless round windows framed by elaborate carvings. A colored lantern hung in each window, casting a soft glow on the surrounding rock. No turrets or smokestacks were visible. Directly ahead, two thirty-foot-high gold griffins guarded a massive timber gate—recessed twenty yards into the base of Tronjheim—which was shadowed by thick trusses that supported an arched vault far overhead.

When they reached Tronjheim's base, Saphira paused to see if the bald man had any instructions. When none were forthcoming, she continued to the gate. The walls were lined with fluted pillars of blood-red jasper. Between the pillars hulked statues of outlandish creatures, captured forever by the sculptor's chisel.

The heavy gate rumbled open before them as hidden chains slowly raised the mammoth beams. A four-story-high passageway extended straight toward the center of Tronjheim. The top three levels were pierced by rows of archways that revealed gray tunnels curving off into the distance. Clumps of people filled the arches, eagerly watching Eragon and Saphira. On ground level, however, the archways were barred by stout doors. Rich tapestries hung between the different levels, embroidered with heroic figures and tumultuous battle scenes.

A cheer rang in their ears as Saphira stepped into the hall and paraded down it. Eragon raised his hand, eliciting another roar from the throng, though many of the dwarves did not join the welcoming shout.

The mile-long hall ended in an arch flanked by black onyx pillars. Yellow zircons three times the size of a man capped the dark columns, coruscating piercing gold beams along the hall. Saphira stepped through the opening, then stopped and craned back her neck, humming deeply in her chest.

They were in a circular room, perhaps a thousand feet across, that reached up to Tronjheim's peak a mile overhead, narrowing as it rose. The walls were lined with arches—one row for each level of the city-mountain—and the floor was made of polished carnelian, upon which was etched a hammer girdled by twelve silver pentacles, like on Orik's helm.

The room was a nexus for four hallways—including the one they had just exited—that divided Tronjheim into quarters. The halls were identical except for the one opposite Eragon. To the right and left of that hall were tall arches that opened to descending stairs, which mirrored each other as they curved underground.

The ceiling was capped by a dawn-red star sapphire of monstrous size. The jewel was twenty yards across and nearly as thick. Its face had been carved to resemble a rose in full bloom, and so skilled was the craftsmanship, the flower almost seemed to be real. A wide belt of lanterns wrapped around the edge of the sapphire, which cast striated bands of blushing light over everything below. The flashing rays of the star within the gem made it appear as if a giant eye gazed down at them.

Eragon could only gape with wonder. Nothing had prepared him for this. It seemed impossible that Tronjheim had been built by mortal beings. The city-mountain shamed everything he had seen in the Empire. He doubted if even Urû'baen could match the wealth and grandeur displayed here. Tronjheim was a stunning monument to the dwarves' power and perseverance.

The bald man walked in front of Saphira and said, "You must go on foot from here." There was scattered booing from the crowd as he spoke. A dwarf took Tornac and Snowfire away. Eragon dismounted Saphira but stayed by her side as the bald man led them across the carnelian floor to the right-hand hallway.

They followed it for several hundred feet, then entered a smaller corridor. Their guards remained despite the cramped space. After four sharp turns, they came to a massive cedar door, stained black with age. The bald man pulled it open and conducted everyone but the guards inside.

AJIHAD

E ragon entered an elegant, two-story study paneled with rows
of cedar bookshelves. A wrought-iron staircase wound up to
a small balcony with two chairs and a reading table. White
lanterns hung along the walls and ceiling so a book could be read
anywhere in the room. The stone floor was covered by an intricate
oval rug. At the far end of the room, a man stood behind a large
walnut desk.

His skin gleamed the color of oiled ebony. The dome of his head
was shaved bare, but a closely trimmed black beard covered his
chin and upper lip. Strong features shadowed his face, and grave,
intelligent eyes lurked under his brow. His shoulders were broad
and powerful, emphasized by a tapered red vest embroidered with
gold thread and clasped over a rich purple shirt. He bore himself
with great dignity, exuding an intense, commanding air.

When he spoke, his voice was strong, confident: "Welcome
to Tronjheim, Eragon and Saphira. I am Ajihad. Please, seat
yourselves."

Eragon slipped into an armchair next to Murtagh, while Saphira
settled protectively behind them. Ajihad raised his hand and
snapped his fingers. A man stepped out from behind the staircase.
He was identical to the bald man beside him. Eragon stared at the
two of them with surprise, and Murtagh stiffened. "Your confusion
is understandable; they are twin brothers," said Ajihad with a small
smile. "I would tell you their names, but they have none."

Saphira hissed with distaste. Ajihad watched her for a moment, then sat in a high-backed chair behind the desk. The Twins retreated under the stairs and stood impassively beside each other. Ajihad pressed his fingers together as he stared at Eragon and Murtagh. He studied them for a long time with an unwavering gaze.

Eragon squirmed, uncomfortable. After what seemed like several minutes, Ajihad lowered his hands and beckoned to the Twins. One of them hurried to his side. Ajihad whispered in his ear. The bald man suddenly paled and shook his head vigorously. Ajihad frowned, then nodded as if something had been confirmed.

He looked at Murtagh. "You have placed me in a difficult position by refusing to be examined. You have been allowed into Farthen Dûr because the Twins have assured me that they can control you and because of your actions on behalf of Eragon and Arya. I understand that there may be things you wish to keep hidden in your mind, but as long as you do, we cannot trust you."

"You wouldn't trust me anyway," said Murtagh defiantly.

Ajihad's face darkened as Murtagh spoke, and his eyes flashed dangerously. "Though it's been twenty and three years since it last broke upon my ear . . . I know that voice." He stood ominously, chest swelling. The Twins looked alarmed and put their heads together, whispering frantically. "It came from another man, one more beast than human. Get up."

Murtagh warily complied, his eyes darting between the Twins and Ajihad. "Remove your shirt," ordered Ajihad. With a shrug, Murtagh pulled off his tunic. "Now turn around." As he pivoted to the side, light fell upon the scar on his back.

"Murtagh," breathed Ajihad. A grunt of surprise came from Orik. Without warning, Ajihad turned on the Twins and thundered, "Did you know of this?"

The Twins bowed their heads. "We discovered his name in Eragon's mind, but we did not suspect that this *boy* was the son of one as powerful as Morzan. It never occurred—"

"And you didn't tell me?" demanded Ajihad. He raised a hand, forestalling their explanation. "We will discuss it later." He faced Murtagh again. "First I must untangle this muddle. Do you still refuse to be probed?"

"Yes," said Murtagh sharply, slipping back into his tunic. "I won't let anyone inside my head."

Ajihad leaned on his desk. "There will be unpleasant consequences if you don't. Unless the Twins can certify that you aren't a threat, we cannot give you credence, despite, and perhaps because of, the assistance you have given Eragon. Without that verification, the people here, dwarf and human alike, will tear you apart if they learn of your presence. I'll be forced to keep you confined at all times—as much for your protection as for ours. It will only get worse once the dwarf king, Hrothgar, demands custody of you. Don't force yourself into that situation when it can easily be avoided."

Murtagh shook his head stubbornly. "No . . . even if I were to submit, I would still be treated like a leper and an outcast. All I wish is to leave. If you let me do that peacefully, I'll never reveal your location to the Empire."

"What will happen if you are captured and brought before Galbatorix?" demanded Ajihad. "He will extract every secret from your mind, no matter how strong you may be. Even if you could resist him, how can we trust that you won't rejoin him in the future? I cannot take that chance."

"Will you hold me prisoner forever?" demanded Murtagh, straightening.

"No," said Ajihad, "only until you let yourself be examined. If you are found trustworthy, the Twins will remove all knowledge of Farthen Dûr's location from your mind before you leave. We won't risk someone with those memories falling into Galbatorix's hands. What is it to be, Murtagh? Decide quickly or else the path will be chosen for you."

Just give in, Eragon pleaded silently, concerned for Murtagh's safety. *It's not worth the fight.*

Finally Murtagh spoke, the words slow and distinct. "My mind is the one sanctuary that has not been stolen from me. Men have tried to breach it before, but I've learned to defend it vigorously, for I am only safe with my innermost thoughts. You have asked for the one thing I cannot give, least of all to those two." He gestured at the Twins. "Do with me what you will, but know this: death will take me before I'll expose myself to their probing."

Admiration glinted in Ajihad's eyes. "I'm not surprised by your choice, though I had hoped otherwise. . . . Guards!" The cedar door slammed open as warriors rushed in, weapons ready. Ajihad pointed at Murtagh and commanded, "Take him to a windowless room and bar the door securely. Post six men by the entrance and allow no one inside until I come to see him. Do not speak to him, either."

The warriors surrounded Murtagh, watching him suspiciously. As they left the study, Eragon caught Murtagh's attention and mouthed, "I'm sorry." Murtagh shrugged, then stared forward resolutely. He vanished into the hallway with the men. The sound of their feet faded into silence.

Ajihad said abruptly, "I want everyone out of this room but Eragon and Saphira. Now!"

Bowing, the Twins departed, but Orik said, "Sir, the king will want to know of Murtagh. And there is still the matter of my insubordination. . . ."

Ajihad frowned, then waved his hand. "I will tell Hrothgar myself. As for your actions . . . wait outside until I call for you. And don't let the Twins get away. I'm not done with them, either."

"Very well," said Orik, inclining his head. He closed the door with a solid thump.

After a long silence, Ajihad sat with a tired sigh. He ran a hand over his face and stared at the ceiling. Eragon waited impatiently for him to speak. When nothing was forthcoming, he blurted, "Is Arya all right?"

Ajihad looked down at him and said gravely, "No . . . but the healers tell me she will recover. They worked on her all through the night. The poison took a dreadful toll on her. She wouldn't have lived if not for you. For that you have the Varden's deepest thanks."

Eragon's shoulders slumped with relief. For the first time he felt that their flight from Gil'ead had been worth the effort. "So, what now?" he asked.

"I need you to tell me how you found Saphira and everything that's happened since," said Ajihad, forming a steeple with his fingers. "Some of it I know from the message Brom sent us, other parts from the Twins. But I want to hear it from you, especially the details concerning Brom's death."

Eragon was reluctant to share his experiences with a stranger, but Ajihad was patient. *Go on*, urged Saphira gently. Eragon shifted, then began his story. It was awkward at first but grew easier as he proceeded. Saphira helped him to remember things clearly with occasional comments. Ajihad listened intently the entire time.

Eragon talked for hours, often pausing between his words. He told Ajihad of Teirm, though he kept Angela's fortunetelling to himself, and how he and Brom had found the Ra'zac. He even related his dreams of Arya. When he came to Gil'ead and mentioned the Shade, Ajihad's face hardened, and he leaned back with veiled eyes.

When his narrative was complete, Eragon fell silent, brooding on all that had occurred. Ajihad stood, clasped his hands behind his back, and absently studied one of the bookshelves. After a time he returned to the desk.

"Brom's death is a terrible loss. He was a close friend of mine and a powerful ally of the Varden. He saved us from destruction many times through his bravery and intelligence. Even now, when he is gone, he's provided us with the one thing that can ensure our success—you."

"But what can you expect me to accomplish?" asked Eragon.

"I will explain it in full," said Ajihad, "but there are more urgent matters to be dealt with first. The news of the Urgals' alliance with the Empire is extremely serious. If Galbatorix is gathering an Urgal army to destroy us, the Varden will be hard pressed to survive, even though many of us are protected here in Farthen Dûr. That a Rider, even one as evil as Galbatorix, would consider a pact with such monsters is indeed proof of madness. I shudder to think of what he promised them in return for their fickle loyalty. And then there is the Shade. Can you describe him?"

Eragon nodded. "He was tall, thin, and very pale, with red eyes and hair. He was dressed all in black."

"What of his sword—did you see it?" asked Ajihad intensely. "Did it have a long scratch on the blade?"

"Yes," said Eragon, surprised. "How did you know?"

"Because I put it there while trying to cut out his heart," said Ajihad with a grim smile. "His name is Durza—one of the most vicious and cunning fiends to ever stalk this land. He is the perfect servant for Galbatorix and a dangerous enemy for us. You say that you killed him. How was it done?"

Eragon remembered it vividly. "Murtagh shot him twice. The first arrow caught him in the shoulder; the second one struck him between the eyes."

"I was afraid of that," said Ajihad, frowning. "You didn't kill him. Shades can only be destroyed by a thrust through the heart. Anything short of that will cause them to vanish and then reappear elsewhere in spirit form. It's an unpleasant process, but Durza will survive and return stronger than ever."

A moody silence settled over them like a foreboding thunderhead. Then Ajihad stated, "You are an enigma, Eragon, a quandary that no one knows how to solve. Everyone knows what the Varden want—or the Urgals, or even Galbatorix—but no one knows what *you* want. And that makes you dangerous, especially to Galbatorix. He fears you because he doesn't know what you will do next."

"Do the Varden fear me?" asked Eragon quietly.

"No," said Ajihad carefully. "We are hopeful. But if that hope proves false, then yes, we will be afraid." Eragon looked down. "You must understand the unusual nature of your position. There are factions who want you to serve their interests and no one else's. The moment you entered Farthen Dûr, their influence and power began tugging on you."

"Including yours?" asked Eragon.

Ajihad chuckled, though his eyes were sharp. "Including mine. There are certain things you should know: first is how Saphira's egg happened to appear in the Spine. Did Brom ever tell you what was done with her egg after he brought it here?"

"No," said Eragon, glancing at Saphira. She blinked and flicked her tongue at him.

Ajihad tapped his desk before beginning. "When Brom first brought the egg to the Varden, everyone was deeply interested in its fate. We had thought the dragons were exterminated. The dwarves were solely concerned with making sure that the future Rider would be an ally—though some of them were opposed to having a new Rider at all—while the elves and Varden had a more personal stake in the matter. The reason was simple enough: throughout history all the Riders have been either elven or human, with the majority being elven. There has never been a dwarf Rider.

"Because of Galbatorix's betrayals, the elves were reluctant to let any of the Varden handle the egg for fear that the dragon inside would hatch for a human with similar instabilities. It was a challenging situation, as both sides wanted the Rider for their own. The dwarves only aggravated the problem by arguing obstinately with both the elves and us whenever they had the chance. Tensions escalated, and before long, threats were made that were later regretted. It was then that Brom suggested a compromise that allowed all sides to save face.

"He proposed that the egg be ferried between the Varden and the elves every year. At each place children would parade past it, and then the bearers of the egg would wait to see if the dragon would hatch. If it didn't, they would leave and return to the other group. But if the dragon *did* hatch, the new Rider's training would be undertaken immediately. For the first year or so he or she would be instructed here, by Brom. Then the Rider would be taken to the elves, who would finish the education.

"The elves reluctantly accepted this plan . . . with the stipulation that if Brom were to die before the dragon hatched, they would be free to train the new Rider without interference. The agreement was slanted in their favor—we both knew that the dragon would likely choose an elf—but it provided a desperately needed semblance of equality."

Ajihad paused, his rich eyes somber. Shadows bit into his face under his cheekbones, making them jut out. "It was hoped that this new Rider would bring our two races closer together. We waited for well over a decade, but the egg never hatched. The matter passed from our minds, and we rarely thought about it except to lament the egg's inactivity.

"Then last year we suffered a terrible loss. Arya and the egg disappeared on her return from Tronjheim to the elven city Osilon. The elves were the first to discover she was missing. They found her steed and guards slain in Du Weldenvarden and a group of slaughtered Urgals nearby. But neither Arya nor the egg was there. When this news reached me, I feared that Urgals had both of them and would soon learn the location of Farthen Dûr and the elves' capital, Ellesméra, where their queen, Islanzadi, lives. Now I understand they were working for the Empire, which is far worse.

"We won't know exactly what occurred during that attack until Arya wakes, but I have deduced a few details from what you've said." Ajihad's vest rustled as he leaned his elbows on the desk. "The attack must have been swift and decisive, else Arya would have escaped. Without any warning, and deprived of a place to hide, she could have done only one thing—used magic to transport the egg elsewhere."

"She can use magic?" asked Eragon. Arya had mentioned that she had been given a drug to suppress her power; he wanted to confirm that she meant magic. He wondered if she could teach him more words of the ancient language.

"It was one of the reasons why she was chosen to guard the egg. Anyway, Arya couldn't have returned it to us—she was too far away—and the elves' realm is warded by arcane barriers that prevent anything from entering their borders through magical means. She must have thought of Brom and, in desperation, sent the egg toward Carvahall. Without time to prepare, I'm not surprised she missed by the margin she did. The Twins tell me it is an imprecise art."

"Why was she closer to Palancar Valley than the Varden?" asked Eragon. "Where do the elves really live? Where is this . . . Ellesméra?"

Ajihad's keen gaze bored into Eragon as he considered the question. "I don't tell you this lightly, for the elves guard the knowledge jealously. But you should know, and I do this as a display of trust. Their cities lie far to the north, in the deepest reaches of the endless forest Du Weldenvarden. Not since the Riders' time has anyone, dwarf or human, been elf-friend enough to walk in their leafy halls. I do not even know how to find Ellesméra. As for Osilon . . . based on where Arya disappeared, I suspect it is near Du Weldenvarden's western edge, toward Carvahall. You must have many other questions, but bear with me and keep them until I have finished."

He gathered his memories, then spoke at a quickened pace. "When Arya disappeared, the elves withdrew their support from the Varden. Queen Islanzadí was especially enraged and refused any further contact with us. As a result, even though I received Brom's message, the elves are still ignorant of you and Saphira. . . . Without their supplies to sustain my troops, we have fared badly these past months in skirmishes with the Empire.

"With Arya's return and your arrival, I expect the queen's hostility will abate. The fact that you rescued Arya will greatly help our case with her. Your training, however, is going to present a problem for both Varden and elves. Brom obviously had a chance to teach you, but we need to know how thorough he was. For that reason, you'll have to be tested to determine the extent of your abilities.

Also, the elves will expect you to finish your training with them, though I'm not sure if there's time for that."

"Why not?" asked Eragon.

"For several reasons. Chief among them, the tidings you brought about the Urgals," said Ajihad, his eyes straying to Saphira. "You see, Eragon, the Varden are in an extremely delicate position. On one hand, we have to comply with the elves' wishes if we want to keep them as allies. At the same time, we cannot anger the dwarves if we wish to lodge in Tronjheim."

"Aren't the dwarves part of the Varden?" asked Eragon.

Ajihad hesitated. "In a sense, yes. They allow us to live here and provide assistance in our struggle against the Empire, but they are loyal only to their king. I have no power over them except for what Hrothgar gives me, and even he often has trouble with the dwarf clans. The thirteen clans are subservient to Hrothgar, but each clan chief wields enormous power; they choose the new dwarf king when the old one dies. Hrothgar is sympathetic to our cause, but many of the chiefs aren't. He can't afford to anger them unnecessarily or he'll lose the support of his people, so his actions on our behalf have been severely circumscribed."

"These clan chiefs," said Eragon, "are they against me as well?"

"Even more so, I'm afraid," said Ajihad wearily. "There has long been enmity between dwarves and dragons—before the elves came and made peace, dragons made a regular habit of eating the dwarves' flocks and stealing their gold—and the dwarves are slow to forget past wrongs. Indeed, they never fully accepted the Riders or allowed them to police their kingdom. Galbatorix's rise to power has only served to convince many of them that it would be better never to deal with Riders or dragons ever again." He directed his last words at Saphira.

Eragon said slowly, "Why doesn't Galbatorix know where Farthen Dûr and Ellesméra are? Surely he was told of them when he was instructed by the Riders."

"Told of them, yes—shown where they are, no. It's one thing to know that Farthen Dûr lies within these mountains, quite another to find it. Galbatorix hadn't been taken to either place before his dragon was killed. After that, of course, the Riders didn't trust him. He tried to force the information out of several Riders during his rebellion, but they chose to die rather than reveal it to him. As for the dwarves, he's never managed to capture one alive, though it's only a matter of time."

"Then why doesn't he just take an army and march through Du Weldenvarden until he finds Ellesméra?" asked Eragon.

"Because the elves still have enough power to resist him," said Ajihad. "He doesn't dare test his strength against theirs, at least not yet. But his cursed sorcery grows stronger each year. With another Rider at his side, he would be unstoppable. He keeps trying to get one of his two eggs to hatch, but so far he's been unsuccessful."

Eragon was puzzled. "How can his power be increasing? The strength of his body limits his abilities—it can't build itself up forever."

412

"We don't know," said Ajihad, shrugging his broad shoulders, "and neither do the elves. We can only hope that someday he will be destroyed by one of his own spells." He reached inside his vest and somberly pulled out a battered piece of parchment. "Do you know what this is?" he asked, placing it on the desk.

Eragon bent forward and examined it. Lines of black script, written in an alien language, were inked across the page. Large sections of the writing had been destroyed by blots of blood. One edge of the parchment was charred. He shook his head. "No, I don't."

"It was taken from the leader of the Urgal host we destroyed last night. It cost us twelve men to do so—they sacrificed themselves so that you might escape safely. The writing is the king's invention, a script he uses to communicate with his servants. It took me a while, but I was able to devise its meaning, at least where it's legible. It reads:

. . . gatekeeper at Ithrö Zhâda is to let this bearer and his minions pass. They are to be bunked with the others of their kind and by . . .

*but only if the two factions refrain from fighting. Command will
be given under Tarok, under Gashz, under Durza, under Ushnark
the Mighty.*

"Ushnark is Galbatorix. It means 'father' in the Urgal tongue, an
affectation that pleases him.

*Find what they are suitable for and . . . The footmen and . . .
are to be kept separate. No weapons are to be distributed until . . .
for marching.*

"Nothing else can be read past there, except for a few vague
words," said Ajihad.

"Where's Ithrö Zhâda? I've never heard of it."

"Nor have I," confirmed Ajihad, "which makes me suspect that
Galbatorix has renamed an existing place for his own purposes.
After deciphering this, I asked myself what hundreds of Urgals were
doing by the Beor Mountains where you first saw them and where
they were going. The parchment mentions 'others of their kind,' so
I assume there are even more Urgals at their destination. There's
only one reason for the king to gather such a force—to forge a bas-
tard army of humans and monsters to destroy us.

"For now, there is nothing to do but wait and watch. Without
further information we cannot find this Ithrö Zhâda. Still, Farthen
Dûr has not yet been discovered, so there is hope. The only Urgals
to have seen it died last night."

"How did you know we were coming?" asked Eragon. "One of the
Twins was waiting for us, and there was an ambush in place for the
Kull." He was aware of Saphira listening intently. Though she kept
her own counsel, he knew she would have things to say later.

"We have sentinels placed at the entrance of the valley you traveled through—on either side of the Beartooth River. They sent a
dove to warn us," explained Ajihad.

Eragon wondered if it was the same bird Saphira had tried to eat.

413

"When the egg and Arya disappeared, did you tell Brom? He said that he hadn't heard anything from the Varden."

"We tried to alert him," said Ajihad, "but I suspect our men were intercepted and killed by the Empire. Why else would the Ra'zac have gone to Carvahall? After that, Brom was traveling with you, and it was impossible to get word to him. I was relieved when he contacted me via messenger from Teirm. It didn't surprise me that he went to Jeod; they were old friends. And Jeod could easily send us a message because he smuggles supplies to us through Surda.

"All of this has raised serious questions. How did the Empire know where to ambush Arya and, later, our messengers to Carvahall? How has Galbatorix learned which merchants help the Varden? Jeod's business has been virtually destroyed since you left him, as have those of other merchants who support us. Every time one of their ships sets sail, it disappears. The dwarves cannot give us everything we need, so the Varden are in desperate need of supplies. I'm afraid that we have a traitor, or traitors, in our midst, despite our efforts to examine people's minds for deceit."

Eragon sank deep in thought, pondering what he had learned. Ajihad waited calmly for him to speak, undisturbed by the silence. For the first time since finding Saphira's egg, Eragon felt that he understood what was going on around him. At last he knew where Saphira came from and what might lie in his future. "What do you want from me?" he asked.

"How do you mean?"

"I mean, what is expected of me in Tronjheim? You and the elves have plans for me, but what if I don't like them?" A hard note crept into his voice. "I'll fight when needed, revel when there's occasion, mourn when there is grief, and die if my time comes . . . but I won't let anyone use me against my will." He paused to let the words sink in. "The Riders of old were arbiters of justice above and beyond the leaders of their time. I don't claim that position—I doubt people would accept such oversight when they've been free of it all their lives, especially from one as young as me. But I *do* have power, and

I will wield it as I see fit. What I want to know is how *you* plan to use me. Then I will decide whether to agree to it."

Ajihad looked at him wryly. "If you were anyone else and were before another leader, you would likely have been killed for that insolent speech. What makes you think I will expose my plans just because you demand it?" Eragon flushed but did not lower his gaze. "Still, you are right. Your position gives you the privilege to say such things. You cannot escape the politics of your situation—you *will* be influenced, one way or another. I don't want to see you become a pawn of any one group or purpose any more than you do. You must retain your freedom, for in it lies your true power: the ability to make choices independent of any leader or king. My own authority over you will be limited, but I believe it's for the best. The difficulty lies in making sure that those with power include you in their deliberations.

"Also, despite your protests, the people here have certain expectations of you. They are going to bring you their problems, no matter how petty, and demand that you solve them." Ajihad leaned forward, his voice deadly serious. "There will be cases where someone's future will rest in your hands . . . with a word you can send them careening into happiness or misery. Young women will seek your opinion on whom they should marry—many will pursue you as a husband—and old men will ask which of their children should receive an inheritance. You *must* be kind and wise with them all, for they put their trust in you. Don't speak flippantly or without thought, because your words will have impact far beyond what you intend."

Ajihad leaned back, his eyes hooded. "The burden of leadership is being responsible for the well-being of the people in your charge. I have dealt with it from the day I was chosen to head the Varden, and now you must as well. Be careful. I won't tolerate injustice under my command. Don't worry about your youth and inexperience; they will pass soon enough."

Eragon was uncomfortable with the idea of people asking him for advice. "But you still haven't said what I'm to do here."

"For now, nothing. You covered over a hundred and thirty leagues in eight days, a feat to be proud of. I'm sure that you'll appreciate rest. When you've recovered, we will test your competency in arms and magic. After that—well, I will explain your options, and then you'll have to decide your course."

"And what about Murtagh?" asked Eragon bitingly.

Ajihad's face darkened. He reached beneath his desk and lifted up Zar'roc. The sword's polished sheath gleamed in the light. Ajihad slid his hand over it, lingering on the etched sigil. "He will stay here until he allows the Twins into his mind."

"You can't imprison him," argued Eragon. "He's committed no crime!"

"We can't give him his freedom without being sure that he won't turn against us. Innocent or not, he's potentially as dangerous to us as his father was," said Ajihad with a hint of sadness.

Eragon realized that Ajihad would not be convinced otherwise, and his concern *was* valid. "How were you able to recognize his voice?"

"I met his father once," said Ajihad shortly. He tapped Zar'roc's hilt. "I wish Brom had told me he had taken Morzan's sword. I suggest that you don't carry it within Farthen Dûr. Many here remember Morzan's time with hate, especially the dwarves."

"I'll remember that," promised Eragon.

Ajihad handed Zar'roc to him. "That reminds me, I have Brom's ring, which he sent as confirmation of his identity. I was keeping it for when he returned to Tronjheim. Now that he's dead, I suppose it belongs to you, and I think he would have wanted you to have it." He opened a desk drawer and took the ring from it.

Eragon accepted it with reverence. The symbol cut into the face of the sapphire was identical to the tattoo on Arya's shoulder. He fit the ring onto his index finger, admiring how it caught the light. "I . . . I am honored," he said.

Ajihad nodded gravely, then pushed back his chair and stood. He faced Saphira and spoke to her, his voice swelling in power. "Do not think that I have forgotten you, O mighty dragon. I have said these things as much for your benefit as for Eragon's. It is even more important that you know them, for to you falls the task of guarding him in these dangerous times. Do not underestimate your might nor falter at his side, because without you he will surely fail."

Saphira lowered her head until their eyes were level and stared at him through slitted black pupils. They examined each other silently, neither of them blinking. Ajihad was the first to move. He lowered his eyes and said softly, "It is indeed a privilege to meet you."

He'll do, said Saphira respectfully. She swung her head to face Eragon. *Tell him that I am impressed both with Tronjheim and with him. The Empire is right to fear him. Let him know, however, that if he had decided to kill you, I would have destroyed Tronjheim and torn him apart with my teeth.*

Eragon hesitated, surprised by the venom in her voice, then relayed the message. Ajihad looked at her seriously. "I would expect nothing less from one so noble—but I doubt you could have gotten past the Twins."

Saphira snorted with derision. *Bah!*

Knowing what she meant, Eragon said, "Then they must be much stronger than they appear. I think they would be sorely dismayed if they ever faced a dragon's wrath. The two of them might be able to defeat me, but never Saphira. You should know, a Rider's dragon strengthens his magic beyond what a normal magician might have. Brom was always weaker than me because of that. I think that in the absence of Riders, the Twins have overestimated their power."

Ajihad looked troubled. "Brom was considered one of our strongest spell weavers. Only the elves surpassed him. If what you say is true, we will have to reconsider a great many things." He bowed to Saphira. "As it is, I am glad it wasn't necessary to harm either of you." Saphira dipped her head in return.

Ajihad straightened with a lordly air and called, "Orik!" The dwarf hurried into the room and stood before the desk, crossing his arms. Ajihad frowned at him, irritated. "You've caused me a great deal of trouble, Orik. I've had to listen to one of the Twins complain all morning about your insubordination. They won't let it rest until you are punished. Unfortunately they're right. It's a serious matter that cannot be ignored. An accounting is due."

Orik's eyes flicked toward Eragon, but his face betrayed no emotion. He spoke quickly in rough tones. "The Kull were almost around Kóstha-mérna. They were shooting arrows at the dragon, Eragon, and Murtagh, but the Twins did nothing to stop it. Like . . . sheilven, they refused to open the gates even though we could see Eragon shouting the opening phrase on the other side of the waterfall. And they refused to take action when Eragon did not rise from the water. Perhaps I did wrong, but I couldn't let a Rider die."

"I wasn't strong enough to get out of the water myself," offered Eragon. "I would have drowned if he hadn't pulled me out."

Ajihad glanced at him, then asked Orik seriously, "And later, why did you oppose them?"

Orik raised his chin defiantly. "It wasn't right for them to force their way into Murtagh's mind. But I wouldn't have stopped them if I'd known who he was."

"No, you did the right thing, though it would be simpler if you hadn't. It isn't our place to force our way into people's minds, no matter who they are." Ajihad fingered his dense beard. "Your actions were honorable, but you did defy a direct order from your commander. The penalty for that has always been death." Orik's back stiffened.

"You can't kill him for that! He was only helping me," cried Eragon.

"It isn't your place to interfere," said Ajihad sternly. "Orik broke the law and must suffer the consequences." Eragon started to argue again, but Ajihad stopped him with a raised hand. "But you are right. The sentence will be mitigated because of the circumstances. As of now, Orik, you are removed from active service and forbidden to engage in any military activities under my command. Do you understand?"

Orik's face darkened, but then he only looked confused. He nodded sharply. "Yes."

"Furthermore, in the absence of your regular duties, I appoint you Eragon and Saphira's guide for the duration of their stay. You are to make sure they receive every comfort and amenity we have to offer. Saphira will stay above Isidar Mithrim. Eragon may have quarters wherever he wants. When he recovers from his trip, take him to the training fields. They're expecting him," said Ajihad, a twinkle of amusement in his eye.

Orik bowed low. "I understand."

"Very well, you all may go. Send in the Twins as you leave."

Eragon bowed and began to leave, then asked, "Where can I find Arya? I would like to see her."

"No one is allowed to visit her. You will have to wait until she comes to you." Ajihad looked down at his desk in a clear dismissal.

BLESS THE CHILD, ARGETLAM

Eragon stretched in the hall; he was stiff from sitting so long. Behind him, the Twins entered Ajihad's study and closed the door. Eragon looked at Orik. "I'm sorry that you're in trouble because of me," he apologized.

"Don't bother yourself," grunted Orik, tugging on his beard. "Ajihad gave me what I wanted."

Even Saphira was startled by the statement. "What do you mean?" said Eragon. "You can't train or fight, and you're stuck guarding me. How can that be what you wanted?"

The dwarf eyed him quietly. "Ajihad is a good leader. He understands how to keep the law yet remain just. I have been punished by his command, but I'm also one of Hrothgar's subjects. Under his rule, I'm still free to do what I wish."

Eragon realized it would be unwise to forget Orik's dual loyalty and the split nature of power within Tronjheim. "Ajihad just placed you in a powerful position, didn't he?"

Orik chuckled deeply. "That he did, and in such a way the Twins can't complain about it. This'll irritate them for sure. Ajihad's a tricky one, he is. Come, lad, I'm sure you're hungry. And we have to get your dragon settled in."

Saphira hissed. Eragon said, "Her name is Saphira."

Orik made a small bow to her. "My apologies, I'll be sure to remember that." He took an orange lamp from the wall and led them down the hallway.

"Can others in Farthen Dûr use magic?" asked Eragon, struggling to keep up with the dwarf's brisk pace. He cradled Zar'roc carefully, concealing the symbol on the sheath with his arm.

"Few enough," said Orik with a swift shrug under his mail. "And the ones we have can't do much more than heal bruises. They've all had to tend to Arya because of the strength needed to heal her."

"Except for the Twins."

"Oeí," grumbled Orik. "She wouldn't want their help anyway; their arts are not for healing. Their talents lie in scheming and plotting for power—to everyone else's detriment. Deynor, Ajihad's predecessor, allowed them to join the Varden because he needed their support . . . you can't oppose the Empire without spellcasters who can hold their own on the field of battle. They're a nasty pair, but they do have their uses."

They entered one of the four main tunnels that divided Tronjheim. Clusters of dwarves and humans strolled through it, voices echoing loudly off the polished floor. The conversations stopped abruptly as they saw Saphira; scores of eyes fixed on her. Orik ignored the spectators and turned left, heading toward one of Tronjheim's distant gates. "Where are we going?" asked Eragon.

"Out of these halls so Saphira can fly to the dragonhold above Isidar Mithrim, the Star Rose. The dragonhold doesn't have a roof—Tronjheim's peak is open to the sky, like that of Farthen Dûr—so she, that is, you, Saphira, will be able to glide straight down into the hold. It is where the Riders used to stay when they visited Tronjheim."

"Won't it be cold and damp without a roof?" asked Eragon.

"Nay." Orik shook his head. "Farthen Dûr protects us from the elements. Neither rain nor snow intrude here. Besides, the hold's walls are lined with marble caves for dragons. They provide all the shelter necessary. All you need fear are the icicles; when they fall they've been known to cleave a horse in two."

I will be fine, assured Saphira. *A marble cave is safer than any of the other places we've stayed.*

Perhaps . . . Do you think Murtagh will be all right?

Ajihad strikes me as an honorable man. Unless Murtagh tries to escape, I doubt he will be harmed.

Eragon crossed his arms, unwilling to talk further. He was dazed by the change in circumstances from the day before. Their mad race from Gil'ead was finally over, but his body expected to continue running and riding. "Where are our horses?"

"In the stables by the gate. We can visit them before leaving Tronjheim."

They exited Tronjheim through the same gate they had entered. The gold griffins gleamed with colored highlights garnered from scores of lanterns. The sun had moved during Eragon's talk with Ajihad—light no longer entered Farthen Dûr through the crater opening. Without those moted rays, the inside of the hollow mountain was velvety black. The only illumination came from Tronjheim, which sparkled brilliantly in the gloom. The city-mountain's radiance was enough to brighten the ground hundreds of feet away.

Orik pointed at Tronjheim's white pinnacle. "Fresh meat and pure mountain water await you up there," he told Saphira. "You may stay in any of the caves. Once you make your choice, bedding will be laid down in it and then no one will disturb you."

"I thought we were going to go together. I don't want to be separated," protested Eragon.

Orik turned to him. "Rider Eragon, I will do everything to accommodate you, but it would be best if Saphira waits in the dragonhold while you eat. The tunnels to the banquet halls aren't large enough for her to accompany us."

"Why can't you just bring me food in the hold?"

"Because," said Orik with a guarded expression, "the food is prepared down here, and it is a long way to the top. If you wish, a servant could be sent up to the hold with a meal for you. It will take some time, but you could eat with Saphira then."

He actually means it, Eragon thought, astonished that they would do so much for him. But the way Orik said it made him wonder if the dwarf was testing him somehow.

I'm weary, said Saphira. *And this dragonhold sounds to my liking. Go, have your meal, then come to me. It will be soothing to rest together without fear of wild animals or soldiers. We have suffered the hardships of the trail too long.*

Eragon looked at her thoughtfully, then said to Orik, "I'll eat down here." The dwarf smiled, seeming satisfied. Eragon unstrapped Saphira's saddle so she could lie down without discomfort. *Would you take Zar'roc with you?*

Yes, she said, gathering up the sword and saddle with her claws. *But keep your bow. We must trust these people, though not to the point of foolishness.*

I know, he said, disquieted.

With an explosive leap Saphira swept off the ground and into the still air. The steady whoosh of her wings was the only sound in the darkness. As she disappeared over the rim of Tronjheim's peak, Orik let out a long breath. "Ah boy, you have been blessed indeed. I find a sudden longing in my heart for open skies and soaring cliffs and the thrill of hunting like a hawk. Still, my feet are better on the ground—preferably under it."

He clapped his hands loudly. "I neglect my duties as host. I know you've not dined since that pitiful dinner the Twins saw fit to give you, so come, let's find the cooks and beg meat and bread from them!"

Eragon followed the dwarf back into Tronjheim and through a labyrinth of corridors until they came to a long room filled with rows of stone tables only high enough for dwarves. Fires blazed in soapstone ovens behind a long counter.

Orik spoke words in an unfamiliar language to a stout ruddy-faced dwarf, who promptly handed them stone platters piled with steaming mushrooms and fish. Then Orik took Eragon up several flights of stairs and into a small alcove carved out of Tronjheim's outer wall, where they sat cross-legged. Eragon wordlessly reached for his food.

When their platters were empty, Orik sighed with contentment and pulled out a long-stemmed pipe. He lit it, saying, "A worthy repast, though it needed a good draught of mead to wash it down properly."

Eragon surveyed the ground below. "Do you farm in Farthen Dûr?"

"No, there's only enough sunlight for moss, mushrooms, and mold. Tronjheim cannot survive without supplies from the surrounding valleys, which is one reason why many of us choose to live elsewhere in the Beor Mountains."

"Then there are other dwarf cities?"

"Not as many as we would like. And Tronjheim is the greatest of them." Leaning on an elbow, Orik took a deep pull on his pipe. "You have only seen the lower levels, so it hasn't been apparent, but most of Tronjheim is deserted. The farther up you go, the emptier it gets. Entire floors have remained untouched for centuries. Most dwarves prefer to dwell under Tronjheim and Farthen Dûr in the caverns and passageways that riddle the rock. Through the centuries we have tunneled extensively under the Beor Mountains. It is possible to walk from one end of the mountain range to the other without ever setting foot on the surface."

"It seems like a waste to have all that unused space in Tronjheim," commented Eragon.

Orik nodded. "Some have argued for abandoning this place because of its drain on our resources, but Tronjheim does perform one invaluable task."

"What's that?"

"In times of misfortune it can house our entire nation. There have been only three instances in our history when we have been forced to that extreme, but each time it has saved us from certain and utter destruction. That is why we always keep it garrisoned, ready for use."

"I've never seen anything as magnificent," admitted Eragon.

Orik smiled around his pipe. "I'm glad you find it so. It took generations to build Tronjheim—and our lives are much longer than those of men. Unfortunately, because of the cursed Empire, few outsiders are allowed to see its glory."

"How many Varden are here?"

"Dwarves or humans?"

"Humans—I want to know how many have fled the Empire."

Orik exhaled a long puff of smoke that coiled lazily around his head. "There are about four thousand of your kin here. But that's a poor indicator of what you want to know. Only people who wish to fight come here. The rest of them are under King Orrin's protection in Surda."

So few? thought Eragon with a sinking feeling. The royal army alone numbered nearly sixteen thousand when it was fully marshaled, not counting the Urgals. "Why doesn't Orrin fight the Empire himself?" he asked.

"If he were to show open hostility," said Orik, "Galbatorix would crush him. As it is, Galbatorix withholds that destruction because he considers Surda a minor threat, which is a mistake. It's through Orrin's assistance that the Varden have most of their weapons and supplies. Without him, there would be no resisting the Empire.

"Don't despair over the number of humans in Tronjheim. There are many dwarves here—many more than you have seen—and all will fight when the time comes. Orrin has also promised us troops for when we battle Galbatorix. The elves pledged their help as well."

Eragon absently touched Saphira's mind and found her busy eating a bloody haunch with gusto. He noticed once more the hammer and stars engraved on Orik's helm. "What does that mean? I saw it on the floor in Tronjheim."

Orik lifted the iron-bound cap off his head and brushed a rough finger over the engraving. "It is the symbol of my clan. We are the Ingietum, metalworkers and master smiths. The hammer and stars are inlaid into Tronjheim's floor because it was the personal crest of

Korgan, our founder. One clan to rule, with twelve surrounding. King Hrothgar is Dûrgrimst Ingietum as well and has brought my house much glory, much honor."

When they returned the platters to the cook, they passed a dwarf in the hall. He stopped before Eragon, bowed, and said respectfully, "Argetlam."

The dwarf left Eragon fumbling for an answer, flushed with unease, yet also strangely pleased with the gesture. No one had bowed to him before. "What did he say?" he asked, leaning closer to Orik.

Orik shrugged, embarrassed. "It's an elven word that was used to refer to the Riders. It means 'silver hand.'" Eragon glanced at his gloved hand, thinking of the gedwëy ignasia that whitened his palm. "Do you wish to return to Saphira?"

"Is there somewhere I could bathe first? I haven't been able to wash off the grime of the road for a long time. Also, my shirt is bloodstained and torn, and it stinks. I'd like to replace it, but I don't have any money to buy a new one. Is there a way I could work for one?"

"Do you seek to insult Hrothgar's hospitality, Eragon?" demanded Orik. "As long as you are in Tronjheim, you won't have to buy a thing. You'll pay for it in other ways—Ajihad and Hrothgar will see to that. Come. I'll show you where to wash, then fetch you a shirt."

He took Eragon down a long staircase until they were well below Tronjheim. The corridors were tunnels now—which cramped Eragon because they were only five feet high—and all the lanterns were red. "So the light doesn't blind you when you leave or enter a dark cavern," explained Orik.

They entered a bare room with a small door on the far side. Orik pointed. "The pools are through there, along with brushes and soap. Leave your clothes here. I'll have new ones waiting when you get out."

Eragon thanked him and started to undress. It felt oppressive being alone underground, especially with the low rock ceiling. He stripped quickly and, cold, hurried through the door, into total darkness. He inched forward until his foot touched warm water, then eased himself into it.

The pool was mildly salty, but soothing and calm. For a moment he was afraid of drifting away from the door, into deeper water, but as he waded forward, he discovered the water reached only to his waist. He groped over a slippery wall until he found the soap and brushes, then scrubbed himself. Afterward he floated with his eyes closed, enjoying the warmth.

When he emerged, dripping, into the lighted room, he found a towel, a fine linen shirt, and a pair of breeches. The clothes fit him reasonably well. Satisfied, he went out into the tunnel.

Orik was waiting for him, pipe in hand. They climbed the stairs back up into Tronjheim, then exited the city-mountain. Eragon gazed at Tronjheim's peak and called Saphira with his mind. As she flew down from the dragonhold, he asked, "How do you communicate with people at the top of Tronjheim?"

Orik chuckled. "That's a problem we solved long ago. You didn't notice, but behind the open arches that line each level is a single, unbroken staircase that spirals around the wall of Tronjheim's central chamber. The stairs climb all the way to the dragonhold above Isidar Mithrim. We call it Vol Turin, The Endless Staircase. Running up or down it isn't swift enough for an emergency, nor convenient enough for casual use. Instead, we use flashing lanterns to convey messages. There is another way too, though it is seldom used. When Vol Turin was constructed, a polished trough was cut next to it. The trough acts as a giant slide as high as a mountain."

Eragon's lips twitched with a smile. "Is it dangerous?"

"Do not think of trying it. The slide was built for dwarves and is too narrow for a man. If you slipped out of it, you could be thrown onto the stairs and against the arches, perhaps even into empty space."

Saphira landed a spear's throw away, her scales rustling dryly. As she greeted Eragon, humans and dwarves trickled out of Tronjheim, gathering around her with murmurs of interest. Eragon regarded the growing crowd uneasily. "You'd better go," said Orik, pushing him forward. "Meet me by this gate tomorrow morning. I'll be waiting."

Eragon balked. "How will I know when it's morning?"

"I'll have someone wake you. Now go!" Without further protest, Eragon slipped through the jostling group that surrounded Saphira and jumped onto her back.

Before she could take off, an old woman stepped forward and grasped Eragon's foot with a fierce grip. He tried to pull away, but her hand was like an iron talon around his ankle—he could not break her tenacious hold. The burning gray eyes she fixed on him were surrounded by a lifetime's worth of wrinkles—the skin was folded in long creases down her sunken cheeks. A tattered bundle rested in the crook of her left arm.

Frightened, Eragon asked, "What do you want?"

The woman tilted her arm, and a cloth fell from the bundle, revealing a baby's face. Hoarse and desperate, she said, "The child has no parents—there is no one to care for her but me, and I am weak. Bless her with your power, Argetlam. Bless her for luck!"

Eragon looked to Orik for help, but the dwarf only watched with a guarded expression. The small crowd fell silent, waiting for his response. The woman's eyes were still fastened on him. "Bless her, Argetlam, bless her," she insisted.

Eragon had never blessed anyone. It was not something done lightly in Alagaësia, as a blessing could easily go awry and prove to be more curse than boon—especially if it was spoken with ill intent or lack of conviction. *Do I dare take that responsibility?* he wondered.

"Bless her, Argetlam, bless her."

Suddenly decided, he searched for a phrase or expression to use. Nothing came to mind until, inspired, he thought of the ancient language. This would be a true blessing, spoken with words of power, by one of power.

He bent down and tugged the glove off his right hand. Laying his palm on the babe's brow, he intoned, "Atra gülai un ilian tauthr ono un atra ono waíse skölir frá rauthr." The words left him unexpectedly weak, as if he had used magic. He slowly pulled the glove back on and said to the woman, "That is all I can do for her. If any words have the power to forestall tragedy, it will be those."

"Thank you, Argetlam," she whispered, bowing slightly. She started to cover the baby again, but Saphira snorted and twisted until her head loomed over the child. The woman grew rigid; her breath caught in her chest. Saphira lowered her snout and brushed the baby between the eyes with the tip of her nose, then smoothly lifted away.

A gasp ran through the crowd, for on the child's forehead, where Saphira had touched her, was a star-shaped patch of skin as white and silvery as Eragon's gedwëy ignasia. The woman stared at Saphira with a feverish gaze, wordless thanks in her eyes.

Immediately Saphira took flight, battering the awestruck spectators with the wind from her powerful wing strokes. As the ground dwindled away, Eragon took a deep breath and hugged her neck tightly. *What did you do?* he asked softly.

I gave her hope. And you gave her a future.

Loneliness suddenly flowered within Eragon, despite Saphira's presence. Their surroundings were so foreign—it struck him for the first time exactly how far he was from home. A destroyed home, but still where his heart lay. *What have I become, Saphira?* he asked. *I'm only in the first year of manhood, yet I've consulted with the leader of the Varden, am pursued by Galbatorix, and have traveled with Morzan's son—and now blessings are sought from me! What wisdom can I give people that they haven't already learned? What feats can I achieve that an army couldn't do better? It's insanity! I should be back in Carvahall with Roran.*

Saphira took a long time to answer, but her words were gentle when they came. *A hatchling, that is what you are. A hatchling struggling into the world. I may be younger than you in years, but I am ancient in my thoughts. Do not worry about these things. Find peace in where and what you are. People often know what must be done. All you need do is show them the way—that is wisdom. As for feats, no army could have given the blessing you did.*

But it was nothing, he protested. *A trifle.*

Nay, it wasn't. What you saw was the beginning of another story, another legend. Do you think that child will ever be content to be a tavern keeper or a farmer when her brow is dragon-marked and your words hang over her? You underestimate our power and that of fate.

Eragon bowed his head. *It's overwhelming. I feel as if I am living in an illusion, a dream where all things are possible. Amazing things do happen, I know, but always to someone else, always in some far-off place and time. But I found your egg, was tutored by a Rider, and dueled a Shade—those can't be the actions of the farm boy I am, or was. Something is changing me.*

It is your wyrd that shapes you, said Saphira. *Every age needs an icon—perhaps that lot has fallen to you. Farm boys are not named for the first Rider without cause. Your namesake was the beginning, and now you are the continuation. Or the end.*

Ach, said Eragon, shaking his head. *It's like speaking in riddles. . . . But if all is foreordained, do our choices mean anything? Or must we just learn to accept our fate?*

Saphira said firmly, *Eragon, I chose you from within my egg. You have been given a chance most would die for. Are you unhappy with that? Clear your mind of such thoughts. They cannot be answered and will make you no happier.*

True, he said glumly. *All the same, they continue to bounce around within my skull.*

Things have been . . . unsettled . . . ever since Brom died. It has made me uneasy, acknowledged Saphira, which surprised him because she rarely seemed perturbed. They were above Tronjheim now. Eragon looked down through the opening in its peak and saw the floor of the dragonhold: Isidar Mithrim, the great star sapphire. He knew that beneath it was nothing but Tronjheim's great central chamber. Saphira descended to the dragonhold on silent wings. She slipped over its rim and dropped to Isidar Mithrim, landing with the sharp clack of claws.

Won't you scratch it? asked Eragon.

I think not. It's no ordinary gem. Eragon slid off her back and slowly turned in a circle, absorbing the unusual sight. They were in a round roofless room sixty feet high and sixty feet across. The walls were lined with the dark openings of caves, which differed in size from grottoes no larger than a man to a gaping cavern larger than a house. Shiny rungs were set into the marble walls so that people could reach the highest caves. An enormous archway led out of the dragonhold.

Eragon examined the great gem under his feet and impulsively lay down on it. He pressed his cheek against the cool sapphire, trying to see through it. Distorted lines and wavering spots of color glimmered through the stone, but its thickness made it impossible to discern anything clearly on the floor of the chamber a mile below them.

Will I have to sleep apart from you?

Saphira shook her enormous head. *No, there is a bed for you in my cave. Come see.* She turned and, without opening her wings, jumped twenty feet into the air, landing in a medium-sized cave. He clambered up after her.

The cave was dark brown on the inside and deeper than he had expected. The roughly chiseled walls gave the impression of a natural formation. Near the far wall was a thick cushion large enough for Saphira to curl up on. Beside it was a bed built into the side of the wall. The cave was lit by a single red lantern equipped with a shutter so its glow could be muted.

I like this, said Eragon. *It feels safe.*

Yes. Saphira curled up on the cushion, watching him. With a sigh he sank onto the mattress, weariness seeping through him.

Saphira, you haven't said much while we've been here. What do you think of Tronjheim and Ajihad?

We shall see. . . . It seems, Eragon, that we are embroiled in a new type of warfare here. Swords and claws are useless, but words and alliances may have the same effect. The Twins dislike us—we should be on our guard for any duplicities they might attempt. Not many of the dwarves trust us. The elves didn't want a human Rider, so there will be opposition from them as well. The best thing we can do is identify those in power and befriend them. And quickly, too.

Do you think it's possible to remain independent of the different leaders?

She shuffled her wings into a more comfortable position. *Ajihad supports our freedom, but we may be unable to survive without pledging our loyalty to one group or another. We'll soon know either way.*

MANDRAKE ROOT AND NEWT'S TONGUE

The blankets were bunched underneath Eragon when he woke, but he was still warm. Saphira was asleep on her cushion, her breath coming in steady gusts.

For the first time since entering Farthen Dûr, Eragon felt secure and hopeful. He was warm and fed and had been able to sleep as long as he liked. Tension unknotted inside him—tension that had been accumulating since Brom's death and, even before, since leaving Palancar Valley.

I don't have to be afraid anymore. But what about Murtagh? No matter the Varden's hospitality, Eragon could not accept it in good conscience, knowing that—intentionally or not—he had led Murtagh to his imprisonment. Somehow the situation had to be resolved.

His gaze roamed the cave's rough ceiling as he thought of Arya. Chiding himself for daydreaming, he tilted his head and looked out at the dragonhold. A large cat sat on the edge of the cave, licking a paw. It glanced at him, and he saw a flash of slanted red eyes.

Solembum? he asked incredulously.

Obviously. The werecat shook his rough mane and yawned languorously, displaying his long fangs. He stretched, then jumped out of the cave, landing with a solid thump on Isidar Mithrim, twenty feet below. *Coming?*

Eragon looked at Saphira. She was awake now, watching him motionlessly. *Go. I will be fine,* she murmured. Solembum was waiting for him under the arch that led to the rest of Tronjheim.

The moment Eragon's feet touched Isidar Mithrim, the werecat turned with a flick of his paws and disappeared through the arch. Eragon chased after him, rubbing the sleep from his face. He stepped through the archway and found himself standing at the top of Vol Turin, The Endless Staircase. There was nowhere else to go, so he descended to the next level.

He stood in an open arcade that curved gently to the left and encircled Tronjheim's central chamber. Between the slender columns supporting the arches, Eragon could see Isidar Mithrim sparkling brilliantly above him, as well as the city-mountain's distant base. The circumference of the central chamber increased with each successive level. The staircase cut through the arcade's floor to an identical level below and descended through scores of arcades until it disappeared in the distance. The sliding trough ran along the outside curve of the stairs. At the top of Vol Turin was a pile of leather squares to slide on. To Eragon's right, a dusty corridor led to that level's rooms and apartments. Solembum padded down the hall, flipping his tail.

Wait, said Eragon.

He tried to catch up with Solembum, but glimpsed him only fleetingly in the abandoned passageways. Then, as Eragon rounded a corner, he saw the werecat stop before a door and yowl. Seemingly of its own accord, the door slid inward. Solembum slipped inside, then the door shut. Eragon halted in front of it, perplexed. He raised his hand to knock, but before he did, the door opened once more, and warm light spilled out. After a moment's indecision he stepped inside.

He entered an earthy two-room suite, lavishly decorated with carved wood and clinging plants. The air was warm, fresh, and humid. Bright lanterns hung on the walls and from the low ceiling. Piles of intriguing items cluttered the floor, obscuring the corners. A large four-poster bed, curtained by even more plants, was in the far room.

In the center of the main room, on a plush leather chair, sat the fortuneteller and witch, Angela. She smiled brightly.

"What are you doing here?" blurted Eragon.

Angela folded her hands in her lap. "Well, why don't you sit on the floor and I'll tell you? I'd offer you a chair, but I'm sitting on the only one." Questions buzzed through Eragon's mind as he settled between two flasks of acrid bubbling green potions.

"So!" exclaimed Angela, leaning forward. "You *are* a Rider. I suspected as much, but I didn't know for certain until yesterday. I'm sure Solembum knew, but he never told me. I should have figured it out the moment you mentioned Brom. Saphira . . . I like the name—fitting for a dragon."

"Brom's dead," said Eragon abruptly. "The Ra'zac killed him."

Angela was taken aback. She twirled a lock of her dense curls. "I'm sorry. I truly am," she said softly.

Eragon smiled bitterly. "But not surprised, are you? You foretold his death, after all."

"I didn't know whose death it would be," she said, shaking her head. "But no . . . I'm not surprised. I met Brom once or twice. He didn't care for my 'frivolous' attitude toward magic. It irritated him."

Eragon frowned. "In Teirm you laughed at his fate and said that it was something of a joke. Why?"

Angela's face tightened momentarily. "In retrospect, it was in rather bad taste, but I didn't know what would befall him. How do I put this? . . . Brom was cursed in a way. It was his wyrd to fail at all of his tasks except one, although through no fault of his own. He was chosen as a Rider, but his dragon was killed. He loved a woman, but it was his affection that was her undoing. And he was chosen, I assume, to guard and train you, but in the end he failed at that as well. The only thing he succeeded at was killing Morzan, and a better deed he couldn't have done."

"Brom never mentioned a woman to me," retorted Eragon.

Angela shrugged carelessly. "I heard it from one who couldn't have lied. But enough of this talk! Life goes on, and we should not trouble the dead with our worries." She scooped a pile of reeds from the floor and deftly started plaiting them together, closing the subject to discussion.

Eragon hesitated, then gave in. "All right. So why are you in Tronjheim instead of Teirm?"

"Ah, at last an interesting question," said Angela. "After hearing Brom's name again during your visit, I sensed a return of the past in Alagaësia. People were whispering that the Empire was hunting a Rider. I knew then that the Varden's dragon egg must have hatched, so I closed my shop and set out to learn more."

"You knew about the egg?"

"Of course I did. I'm not an idiot. I've been around much longer than you would believe. Very little happens that I don't know about." She paused and concentrated on her weaving. "Anyway, I knew I had to get to the Varden as fast as possible. I've been here for nearly a month now, though I really don't care for this place— it's far too musty for my taste. And everyone in Farthen Dûr is *so* serious and noble. They're probably all doomed to tragic deaths anyway." She gave a long sigh, a mocking expression on her face. "And the dwarves are just a superstitious bunch of ninnies content to hammer rocks all their lives. The only redeeming aspect of this place is all the mushrooms and fungi that grow inside Farthen Dûr."

"Then why stay?" asked Eragon, smiling.

"Because I like to be wherever important events are occurring," said Angela, cocking her head. "Besides, if I had stayed in Teirm, Solembum would have left without me, and I enjoy his company. But tell me, what adventures have befallen you since last we talked?"

For the next hour, Eragon summarized his experiences of the last two and a half months. Angela listened quietly, but when he mentioned Murtagh's name she sputtered, "Murtagh!"

Eragon nodded. "He told me who he is. But let me finish my story before you make any judgments." He continued with his tale. When it was complete, Angela leaned back in her chair thoughtfully, her reeds forgotten. Without warning, Solembum jumped out of a hiding place and landed in her lap. He curled up, eyeing Eragon haughtily.

Angela petted the werecat. "Fascinating. Galbatorix allied with the Urgals, and Murtagh finally out in the open. . . . I'd warn you to be careful with Murtagh, but you're obviously aware of the danger."

"Murtagh has been a steadfast friend and an unwavering ally," said Eragon firmly.

"All the same, be careful." Angela paused, then said distastefully, "And then there's the matter of this Shade, Durza. I think he's the greatest threat to the Varden right now, aside from Galbatorix. I *loathe* Shades—they practice the most unholy magic, after necromancy. I'd like to dig his heart out with a dull hairpin and feed it to a pig!"

Eragon was startled by her sudden vehemence. "I don't understand. Brom told me that Shades were sorcerers who used spirits to accomplish their will, but why does that make them so evil?"

Angela shook her head. "It doesn't. Ordinary sorcerers are just that, ordinary—neither better nor worse than the rest of us. They use their magical strength to control spirits and the spirits' powers. Shades, however, relinquish that control in their search for greater power and allow their bodies to be controlled *by* spirits. Unfortunately, only the evilest spirits seek to possess humans, and once ensconced they never leave. Such possession can happen by accident if a sorcerer summons a spirit stronger than himself. The problem is, once a Shade is created, it's terribly difficult to kill. As I'm sure you know, only two people, Laetri the Elf and Irnstad the Rider, ever survived that feat."

"I've heard the stories." Eragon gestured at the room. "Why are you living so high up in Tronjheim? Isn't it inconvenient being this isolated? And how did you get all this stuff up here?"

Angela threw back her head and laughed wryly. "Truthfully? I'm in hiding. When I first came to Tronjheim, I had a few days of peace—until one of guards who let me into Farthen Dûr blabbed about who I was. Then all the magic users here, though they *barely* rate the term, pestered me to join their secret group. Especially those drajl Twins who control it. Finally, I threatened to turn the lot of them into toads, excuse me, frogs, but when that didn't deter them, I sneaked up here in the middle of the night. It was less work than you might imagine, especially for one with my skills."

"Did you have to let the Twins into your mind before you were allowed into Farthen Dûr?" asked Eragon. "I was forced to let them sift through my memories."

A cold gleam leapt into Angela's eye. "The Twins wouldn't dare probe me, for fear of what I might do to them. Oh, they'd love to, but they know the effort would leave them broken and gibbering nonsense. I've been coming here long before the Varden began examining people's minds . . . and they're not about to start on me now."

She peered into the other room and said, "Well! This has been an enlightening talk, but I'm afraid you have to go now. My brew of mandrake root and newt's tongue is about to boil, and it needs attending. Do come back again when you have the time. And *please* don't tell anyone that I'm here. I'd hate to have to move again. It would make me very . . . *irritated*. And you don't want to see me irritated!"

"I'll keep your secret," assured Eragon, getting up.

Solembum jumped off Angela's lap as she stood. "Good!" she exclaimed.

Eragon said farewell and left the room. Solembum guided him back to the dragonhold, then dismissed him with a twitch of his tail before sauntering away.

HALL OF THE
MOUNTAIN KING

A dwarf was waiting for Eragon in the dragonhold. After bowing and muttering, "Argetlam," the dwarf said with a thick accent, "Good. Awake. Knurla Orik waits for you." He bowed again and scurried away. Saphira jumped out of her cave, landing next to Eragon. Zar'roc was in her claws.

What's that for? he asked, frowning.

She tilted her head. *Wear it. You are a Rider and should bear a Rider's sword. Zar'roc may have a bloody history, but that should not shape your actions. Forge a new history for it, and carry it with pride.*

Are you sure? Remember Ajihad's counsel.

Saphira snorted, and a puff of smoke rose from her nostrils. *Wear it, Eragon. If you wish to remain above the forces here, do not let anyone's disapproval dictate your actions.*

As you wish, he said reluctantly, buckling on the sword. He clambered onto her back, and Saphira flew out of Tronjheim. There was enough light in Farthen Dûr now that the hazy mass of the crater walls—five miles away in each direction—was visible. While they spiraled down to the city-mountain's base, Eragon told Saphira about his meeting with Angela.

As soon as they landed by one of Tronjheim's gates, Orik ran to Saphira's side. "My king, Hrothgar, wishes to see both of you. Dismount quickly. We must hurry."

Eragon trotted after the dwarf into Tronjheim. Saphira easily kept pace beside them. Ignoring stares from people within the soaring corridor, Eragon asked, "Where will we meet Hrothgar?"

Without slowing, Orik said, "In the throne room beneath the city. It will be a private audience as an act of otho—of 'faith.' You do not have to address him in any special manner, but speak to him respectfully. Hrothgar is quick to anger, but he is wise and sees keenly into the minds of men, so think carefully before you speak."

Once they entered Tronjheim's central chamber, Orik led the way to one of the two descending stairways that flanked the opposite hall. They started down the right-hand staircase, which gently curved inward until it faced the direction they had come from. The other stairway merged with theirs to form a broad cascade of dimly lit steps that ended, after a hundred feet, before two granite doors. A seven-pointed crown was carved across both doors.

Seven dwarves stood guard on each side of the portal. They held burnished mattocks and wore gem-encrusted belts. As Eragon, Orik, and Saphira approached, the dwarves pounded the floor with the mattocks' hafts. A deep boom rolled back up the stairs. The doors swung inward.

A dark hall lay before them, a good bowshot long. The throne room was a natural cave; the walls were lined with stalagmites and stalactites, each thicker than a man. Sparsely hung lanterns cast a moody light. The brown floor was smooth and polished. At the far end of the hall was a black throne with a motionless figure upon it.

Orik bowed. "The king awaits you." Eragon put his hand on Saphira's side, and the two of them continued forward. The doors closed behind them, leaving them alone in the dim throne room with the king.

Their footsteps echoed through the hall as they advanced toward the throne. In the recesses between the stalagmites and stalactites rested large statues. Each sculpture depicted a dwarf king crowned and sitting on a throne; their sightless eyes gazed sternly into the distance, their lined faces set in fierce expressions. A name was chiseled in runes beneath each set of feet.

Eragon and Saphira strode solemnly between the two rows of long-dead monarchs. They passed more than forty statues, then only dark and empty alcoves awaiting future kings. They stopped before Hrothgar at the end of the hall.

The dwarf king himself sat like a statue upon a raised throne carved from a single piece of black marble. It was blocky, unadorned, and cut with unyielding precision. Strength emanated from the throne, strength that harked back to ancient times when dwarves had ruled in Alagaësia without opposition from elves or humans. A gold helm lined with rubies and diamonds rested on Hrothgar's head in place of a crown. His visage was grim, weathered, and hewn of many years' experience. Beneath a craggy brow glinted deep-set eyes, flinty and piercing. Over his powerful chest rippled a shirt of mail. His white beard was tucked under his belt, and in his lap he held a mighty war hammer with the symbol of Orik's clan embossed on its head.

Eragon bowed awkwardly and knelt. Saphira remained upright. The king stirred, as if awakening from a long sleep, and rumbled, "Rise, Rider, you need not pay tribute to me."

Straightening, Eragon met Hrothgar's impenetrable eyes. The king inspected him with a hard gaze, then said gutturally, "Âz knurl deimi lanok. 'Beware, the rock changes'—an old dictum of ours. . . . And nowadays the rock changes very fast indeed." He fingered the war hammer. "I could not meet with you earlier, as Ajihad did, because I was forced to deal with my enemies within the clans. They demanded that I deny you sanctuary and expel you from Farthen Dûr. It has taken much work on my part to convince them otherwise."

"Thank you," said Eragon. "I didn't anticipate how much strife my arrival would cause."

The king accepted his thanks, then lifted a gnarled hand and pointed. "See there, Rider Eragon, where my predecessors sit upon their graven thrones. One and forty there are, with I the forty-second. When I pass from this world into the care of the gods, my hírna will be added to their ranks. The first statue is the likeness of my ancestor Korgan, who forged this mace, Volund. For eight millennia—since the dawn of our race—dwarves have ruled under Farthen Dûr. We are the bones of the land, older than both the fair elves and the savage dragons." Saphira shifted slightly.

Hrothgar leaned forward, his voice gravelly and deep. "I am old, human—even by our reckoning—old enough to have seen the Riders in all their fleeting glory, old enough to have spoken with their last leader, Vrael, who paid tribute to me within these very walls. Few are still alive who can claim that much. I remember the Riders and how they meddled in our affairs. I also remember the peace they kept that made it possible to walk unharmed from Tronjheim to Narda.

"And now you stand before me—a lost tradition revived. Tell me, and speak truly in this, why have you come to Farthen Dûr? I know of the events that made you flee the Empire, but what is your intent now?"

"For now, Saphira and I merely want to recuperate in Tronjheim," Eragon replied. "We are not here to cause trouble, only to find sanctuary from the dangers we've faced for many months. Ajihad may send us to the elves, but until he does, we have no wish to leave."

"Then was it only the desire for safety that drove you?" asked Hrothgar. "Do you just seek to live here and forget your troubles with the Empire?"

Eragon shook his head, his pride rejecting that statement. "If Ajihad told you of my past, you should know that I have grievances enough to fight the Empire until it is nothing but scattered ashes. More than that, though . . . I want to aid those who cannot escape Galbatorix, including my cousin. I have the strength to help, so I must."

The king seemed satisfied by his answer. He turned to Saphira and asked, "Dragon, what think you in this matter? For what reason have you come?"

Saphira lifted the edge of her lip to growl. *Tell him that I thirst for the blood of our enemies and eagerly await the day when we ride to battle*

against Galbatorix. I've no love or mercy for traitors and egg breakers like
that false king. He held me for over a century and, even now, still has two
of my brethren, whom I would free if possible. And tell Hrothgar I think
you ready for this task.

Eragon grimaced at her words, but dutifully relayed them. The
corner of Hrothgar's mouth lifted in a hint of grim amusement,
deepening his wrinkles. "I see that dragons have not changed with
the centuries." He rapped the throne with a knuckle. "Do you know
why this seat was quarried so flat and angular? So that no one would
sit comfortably on it. I have not, and will relinquish it without
regret when my time comes. What is there to remind you of your
obligations, Eragon? If the Empire falls, will you take Galbatorix's
place and claim his kingship?"

"I don't seek to wear the crown or rule," said Eragon, troubled.
"Being a Rider is responsibility enough. No, I would not take the
throne in Urû'baen . . . not unless there was no one else willing or
competent enough to take it."

Hrothgar warned gravely, "Certainly you would be a kinder king
than Galbatorix, but no race should have a leader who does not age
or leave the throne. The time of the Riders has passed, Eragon.
They will never rise again—not even if Galbatorix's other eggs
were to hatch."

A shadow crossed his face as he gazed at Eragon's side. "I see that
you carry an enemy's sword; I was told of this, and that you travel
with a son of the Forsworn. It does not please me to see this
weapon." He extended a hand. "I would like to examine it."

Eragon drew Zar'roc and presented it to the king, hilt first.
Hrothgar grasped the sword and ran a practiced eye over the red
blade. The edge caught the lantern light, reflecting it sharply. The
dwarf king tested the point with his palm, then said, "A masterfully
forged blade. Elves rarely choose to make swords—they prefer bows
and spears—but when they do, the results are unmatched. This is
an ill-fated blade; I am not glad to see it within my realm. But carry
it if you will; perhaps its luck has changed." He returned Zar'roc,

and Eragon sheathed it. "Has my nephew proved helpful during your time here?"

"Who?"

Hrothgar raised a tangled eyebrow. "Orik, my youngest sister's son. He's been serving under Ajihad to show my support for the Varden. It seems that he has been returned to my command, however. I was gratified to hear that you defended him with your words."

Eragon understood that this was another sign of otho, of "faith," on Hrothgar's part. "I couldn't ask for a better guide."

"That is good," said the king, clearly pleased. "Unfortunately, I cannot speak with you much longer. My advisors wait for me, as there are matters I must deal with. I will say this, though: If you wish the support of the dwarves within my realm, you must first prove yourself to them. We have long memories and do not rush to hasty decisions. Words will decide nothing, only deeds."

"I will keep that in mind," said Eragon, bowing again.

Hrothgar nodded regally. "You may go, then."

Eragon turned with Saphira, and they proceeded out of the hall of the mountain king. Orik was waiting for them on the other side of the stone doors, an anxious expression on his face. He fell in with them as they climbed back up to Tronjheim's main chamber. "Did all go well? Were you received favorably?"

"I think so. But your king is cautious," said Eragon.

"That is how he has survived this long."

I would not want Hrothgar angry at us, observed Saphira.

Eragon glanced at her. *No, I wouldn't either. I'm not sure what he thought of you—he seems to disapprove of dragons, though he didn't say it outright.*

That seemed to amuse Saphira. *In that he is wise, especially since he's barely knee-high to me.*

In Tronjheim's center, under the sparkling Isidar Mithrim, Orik said, "Your blessing yesterday has stirred up the Varden like an overturned beehive. The child Saphira touched has been hailed as a future hero. She and her guardian have been quartered in the finest rooms. Everyone is talking about your 'miracle.' All the human mothers seem intent on finding you and getting the same for their children."

Alarmed, Eragon furtively looked around. "What should we do?"

"Aside from taking back your actions?" asked Orik dryly. "Stay out of sight as much as possible. Everyone will be kept out of the dragonhold, so you won't be disturbed there."

Eragon did not want to return to the dragonhold yet. It was early in the day, and he wanted to explore Tronjheim with Saphira. Now that they were out of the Empire, there was no reason for them to be apart. But he wanted to avoid attention, which would be impossible with her at his side. *Saphira, what do you want to do?*

She nosed him, scales brushing his arm. *I'll return to the dragonhold. There's someone there I want to meet. Wander around as long as you like.*

All right, he said, *but who do you want to meet?* Saphira only winked a large eye at him before padding down one of Tronjheim's four main tunnels.

Eragon explained to Orik where she was going, then said, "I'd like some breakfast. And then I'd like to see more of Tronjheim; it's such an incredible place. I don't want to go to the training grounds until tomorrow, as I'm still not fully recovered."

Orik nodded, his beard bobbing on his chest. "In that case, would you like to visit Tronjheim's library? It's quite old and contains many scrolls of great value. You might find it interesting to read a history of Alagaësia that hasn't been tainted by Galbatorix's hand."

With a pang, Eragon remembered how Brom had taught him to read. He wondered if he still had the skill. A long time had passed since he had seen any written words. "Yes, let's do that."

"Very well."

After they ate, Orik guided Eragon through myriad corridors to their destination. When they reached the library's carved arch, Eragon stepped through it reverently.

The room reminded him of a forest. Rows of graceful colonnades branched up to the dark, ribbed ceiling five stories above. Between the pillars, black-marble bookcases stood back to back. Racks of scrolls covered the walls, interspersed with narrow walkways reached by three twisting staircases. Placed at regular intervals around the walls were pairs of facing stone benches. Between them were small tables whose bases flowed seamlessly into the floor.

Countless books and scrolls were stored in the room. "This is the true legacy of our race," said Orik. "Here reside the writings of our greatest kings and scholars, from antiquity to the present. Also recorded are the songs and stories composed by our artisans. This library may be our most precious possession. It isn't all our work, though—there are human writings here as well. Yours is a short-lived—but prolific—race. We have little or nothing of the elves'. They guard their secrets jealously."

"How long may I stay?" asked Eragon, moving toward the shelves.

"As long as you want. Come to me if you have any questions."

Eragon browsed through the volumes with delight, reaching eagerly for those with interesting titles or covers. Surprisingly, dwarves used the same runes to write as humans. He was somewhat disheartened by how hard reading was after months of neglect. He skipped from book to book, slowly working his way deep into the vast library. Eventually he became immersed in a translation of poems by Dóndar, the tenth dwarf king.

As he scanned the graceful lines, unfamiliar footsteps approached from behind the bookcase. The sound startled him, but he berated himself for being silly—he could not be the only person in the library. Even so, he quietly replaced the book and slipped away, senses alert for danger. He had been ambushed too many times to ignore such feelings. He heard the footsteps again; only now there were two sets of them. Apprehensive, he darted across an opening, trying to remember exactly where Orik was sitting. He sidestepped around a corner and started as he found himself face to face with the Twins.

The Twins stood together, their shoulders meeting, a blank expression on their smooth faces. Their black snake eyes bored into him. Their hands, hidden within the folds of their purple robes, twitched slightly. They both bowed, but the movement was insolent and derisive.

"We have been searching for you," one said. His voice was uncomfortably like the Ra'zac's.

Eragon suppressed a shiver. "What for?" He reached out with his mind and contacted Saphira. She immediately joined thoughts with him.

"Ever since you met with Ajihad, we have wanted to . . . apologize for our actions." The words were mocking, but not in a way Eragon could challenge. "We have come to pay homage to you." Eragon flushed angrily as they bowed again.

Careful! warned Saphira.

He pushed back his rising temper. He could not afford to be riled by this confrontation. An idea came to him, and he said with a small smile, "Nay, it is I who pay homage to you. Without your approval I never could have gained entrance to Farthen Dûr." He bowed to them in turn, making the movement as insulting as he could.

There was a flicker of irritation in the Twins' eyes, but they smiled and said, "We are honored that one so . . . important . . . as yourself thinks so highly of us. We are in your debt for your kind words."

Now it was Eragon's turn to be irritated. "I will remember that when I'm in need."

Saphira intruded sharply in his thoughts. *You're overdoing it. Don't say anything you'll regret. They will remember every word they can use against you.*

This is difficult enough without you making comments! he snapped. She subsided with an exasperated grumble.

The Twins moved closer, the hems of their robes brushing softly over the floor. Their voices became more pleasant. "We have searched for you for another reason as well, Rider. The few magic users who live in Tronjheim have formed a group. We call ourselves Du Vrangr Gata, or the—"

"The Wandering Path, I know," interrupted Eragon, remembering what Angela had said about it.

"Your knowledge of the ancient language is impressive," said a Twin smoothly. "As we were saying, Du Vrangr Gata has heard of your mighty feats, and we have come to extend an invitation of membership. We would be honored to have one of your stature as a member. And I suspect that we might be able to assist you as well."

"How?"

The other Twin said, "The two of us have garnered much experience in magical matters. We could guide you . . . show you spells we've discovered and teach you words of power. Nothing would gladden us more than if we could assist, in some small way, your path to glory. No repayment would be necessary, though if you saw fit to share some scraps of your own knowledge, we would be satisfied."

Eragon's face hardened as he realized what they were asking for. "Do you think I'm a half-wit?" he demanded harshly. "I won't apprentice myself to you so you can learn the words Brom taught me! It must have angered you when you couldn't steal them from my mind."

The Twins abruptly dropped their facade of smiles. "We are not to be trifled with, boy! We are the ones who will test your abilities with magic. And that could be *most* unpleasant. Remember, it only takes one misconceived spell to kill someone. You may be a Rider, but the two of us are still stronger than you."

Eragon kept his face expressionless, even as his stomach knotted painfully. "I will consider your offer, but it may—"

"Then we will expect your answer tomorrow. Make sure that it is the right one." They smiled coldly and stalked deeper into the library.

Eragon scowled. *I'm not going to join Du Vrangr Gata, no matter what they do.*

You should talk to Angela, said Saphira. *She's dealt with the Twins before. Perhaps she could be there when they test you. That might prevent them from harming you.*

That's a good idea. Eragon wound through the bookcases until he found Orik sitting on a bench, busily polishing his war ax. "I'd like to return to the dragonhold."

The dwarf slid the haft of the ax through a leather loop at his belt, then escorted Eragon to the gate where Saphira waited. People had already gathered around her. Ignoring them, Eragon scrambled onto Saphira's back, and they escaped to the sky.

This problem must be resolved quickly. You cannot let the Twins intimidate you, Saphira said as she landed on Isidar Mithrim.

I know. But I hope we can avoid angering them. They could be dangerous enemies. He dismounted quickly, keeping a hand on Zar'roc.

So can you. Do you want them as allies?

He shook his head. *Not really . . . I'll tell them tomorrow that I won't join Du Vrangr Gata.*

Eragon left Saphira in her cave and wandered out of the dragonhold. He wanted to see Angela, but he didn't remember how to find her hiding place, and Solembum was not there to guide him. He roamed the deserted corridors, hoping to meet Angela by chance.

When he grew tired of staring at empty rooms and endless gray walls, he retraced his footsteps to the hold. As he neared it, he heard someone speaking within the room. He halted and listened, but the clear voice fell silent. *Saphira? Who's in there?*

A female . . . She has an air of command. I'll distract her while you come in. Eragon loosened Zar'roc in its sheath. *Orik said that intruders would be kept out of the dragonhold, so who could this be?* He steadied his nerves, then stepped into the hold, his hand on the sword.

A young woman stood in the center of the room, looking curiously at Saphira, who had stuck her head out of the cave. The woman appeared to be about seventeen years old. The star sapphire cast a rosy light on her, accentuating skin the same deep shade as Ajihad's. Her velvet dress was wine red and elegantly cut. A jeweled dagger, worn with use, hung from her waist in a tooled leather sheath.

Eragon crossed his arms, waiting for the woman to notice him.

She continued to look at Saphira, then curtsied and asked sweetly, "Please, could you tell me where Rider Eragon is?" Saphira's eyes sparkled with amusement.

With a small smile, Eragon said, "I am here."

The woman whirled to face him, hand flying to her dagger. Her face was striking, with almond-shaped eyes, wide lips, and round cheekbones. She relaxed and curtsied again. "I am Nasuada," she said.

Eragon inclined his head. "You obviously know who I am, but what do you want?"

Nasuada smiled charmingly. "My father, Ajihad, sent me here with a message. Would you like to hear it?"

The Varden's leader had not struck Eragon as one inclined to marriage and fatherhood. He wondered who Nasuada's mother was—she must have been an uncommon woman to have attracted Ajihad's eye. "Yes, I would."

Nasuada tossed her hair back and recited: "He is pleased that you are doing well, but he cautions you against actions like your benediction yesterday. They create more problems than they solve. Also, he urges you to proceed with the testing as soon as possible—he needs to know how capable you are before he communicates with the elves."

"Did you climb all the way up here just to tell me that?" Eragon asked, thinking of Vol Turin's length.

Nasuada shook her head. "I used the pulley system that transports goods to the upper levels. We could have sent the message with signals, but I decided to bring it myself and meet you in person."

"Would you like to sit down?" asked Eragon. He motioned toward Saphira's cave.

Nasuada laughed lightly. "No, I am expected elsewhere. You should also know, my father decreed that you may visit Murtagh, if you wish." A somber expression disturbed her previously smooth features. "I met Murtagh earlier. . . . He's anxious to speak with you. He seemed lonely; you should visit him." She gave Eragon directions to Murtagh's cell.

Eragon thanked her for the news, then asked, "What about Arya? Is she better? Can I see her? Orik wasn't able to tell me much."

She smiled mischievously. "Arya is recovering swiftly, as all elves do. No one is allowed to see her except my father, Hrothgar, and the healers. They have spent much time with her, learning all that occurred during her imprisonment." She swept her eyes over Saphira. "I must go now. Is there anything you would have me convey to Ajihad on your behalf?"

"No, except a desire to visit Arya. And give him my thanks for the hospitality he's shown us."

"I will take your words directly to him. Farewell, Rider Eragon. I hope we shall soon meet again." She curtsied and exited the dragonhold, head held high.

If she really came all the way up Tronjheim just to meet me—pulleys or no pulleys—there was more to this meeting than idle chatter, remarked Eragon.

Aye, said Saphira, withdrawing her head into the cave. Eragon climbed up to her and was surprised to see Solembum curled up in the hollow at the base of her neck. The werecat was purring deeply, his black-tipped tail flicking back and forth. The two of them looked at Eragon impudently, as if to ask, "What?"

Eragon shook his head, laughing helplessly. *Saphira, is Solembum who you wanted to meet?*

They both blinked at him and answered, *Yes*.

Just wondering, he said, mirth still bubbling inside him. It made sense that they would befriend each other—their personalities were similar, and they were both creatures of magic. He sighed, releasing some of the day's tension as he unbuckled Zar'roc. *Solembum, do you know where Angela is? I couldn't find her, and I need her advice.*

Solembum kneaded his paws against Saphira's scaled back. *She is somewhere in Tronjheim.*

When will she return?

Soon.

How soon? he asked impatiently. *I need to talk to her today.*

Not that soon.

The werecat refused to say more, despite Eragon's persistent questions. He gave up and nestled against Saphira. Solembum's purring was a low thrum above his head. *I have to visit Murtagh tomorrow*, he thought, fingering Brom's ring.

ARYA'S TEST

On the morning of their third day in Tronjheim, Eragon rolled out of bed refreshed and energized. He belted Zar'roc to his waist and slung his bow and half-full quiver across his back. After a leisurely flight inside Farthen Dûr with Saphira, he met Orik by one of Tronjheim's four main gates. Eragon asked him about Nasuada.

"An unusual girl," answered Orik, glancing disapprovingly at Zar'roc. "She's totally devoted to her father and spends all her time helping him. I think she does more for Ajihad than he knows— there have been times when she's maneuvered his enemies without ever revealing her part in it."

"Who is her mother?"

"That I don't know. Ajihad was alone when he brought Nasuada to Farthen Dûr as a newborn child. He's never said where he and Nasuada came from."

So she too grew up without knowing her mother. He shook off the thought. "I'm restless. It'll be good to use my muscles. Where should I go for this 'testing' of Ajihad's?"

Orik pointed out into Farthen Dûr. "The training field is half a mile from Tronjheim, though you can't see it from here because it's behind the city-mountain. It's a large area where both dwarves and humans practice."

I'm coming as well, stated Saphira.

Eragon told Orik, and the dwarf tugged on his beard. "That

might not be a good idea. There are many people at the training field; you will be sure to attract attention."

Saphira growled loudly. *I will come!* And that settled the matter.

The unruly clatter of fighting reached them from the field: the loud clang of steel clashing on steel, the solid thump of arrows striking padded targets, the rattle and crack of wooden staves, and the shouts of men in mock battle. The noise was confusing, yet each group had a unique rhythm and pattern.

The bulk of the training ground was occupied by a crooked block of foot soldiers struggling with shields and poleaxes nearly as tall as themselves. They drilled as a group in formations. Practicing beside them were hundreds of individual warriors outfitted with swords, maces, spears, staves, flails, shields of all shapes and sizes, and even, Eragon saw, someone with a pitchfork. Nearly all the fighters wore armor, usually chain mail and a helmet; plate armor was not as common. There were as many dwarves as humans, though the two kept mainly to themselves. Behind the sparring warriors, a broad line of archers fired steadily at gray sackcloth dummies.

Before Eragon had time to wonder what he was supposed to do, a bearded man, his head and blocky shoulders covered by a mail coif, strode over to them. The rest of him was protected by a rough oxhide suit that still had hair on it. A huge sword—almost as long as Eragon—hung across his broad back. He ran a quick eye over Saphira and Eragon, as if evaluating how dangerous they were, then said gruffly, "Knurla Orik. You've been gone too long. There's nobody left for me to spar with."

Orik smiled. "Oeí, that's because you bruise everyone from head to toe with your monster sword."

"Everyone except you," he corrected.

"That's because I'm faster than a giant like you."

The man looked at Eragon again. "I'm Fredric. I've been told to find out what you can do. How strong are you?"

"Strong enough," answered Eragon. "I have to be in order to fight with magic."

Fredric shook his head; the coif clinked like a bag of coins. "Magic has no place in what we do here. Unless you've served in an army, I doubt any fights you've been in lasted more than a few minutes. What we're concerned about is how you'll be able to hold up in a battle that may drag on for hours, or even weeks if it's a siege. Do you know how to use any weapons besides that sword and bow?"

Eragon thought about it. "Only my fists."

"Good answer!" laughed Fredric. "Well, we'll start you off with the bow and see how you do. Then once some space has cleared up on the field, we'll try—" He broke off suddenly and stared past Eragon, scowling angrily.

The Twins stalked toward them, their bald heads pale against their purple robes. Orik muttered something in his own language as he slipped his war ax out of his belt. "I told you two to stay away from the training area," said Fredric, stepping forward threateningly. The Twins seemed frail before his bulk.

They looked at him arrogantly. "We were ordered by Ajihad to test Eragon's proficiency with magic—*before* you exhaust him banging on pieces of metal."

Fredric glowered. "Why can't someone else test him?"

"No one else is powerful enough," sniffed the Twins. Saphira rumbled deeply and glared at them. A line of smoke trickled from her nostrils, but they ignored her. "Come with us," they ordered, and strode to an empty corner of the field.

Shrugging, Eragon followed with Saphira. Behind him he heard Fredric say to Orik, "We have to stop them from going too far."

"I know," answered Orik in a low voice, "but I can't interfere again. Hrothgar made it clear he won't be able to protect me the next time it happens."

Eragon forced back his growing apprehension. The Twins might know more techniques and words. . . . Still, he remembered what Brom had told him: Riders were stronger in magic than ordinary men. But would that be enough to resist the combined power of the Twins?

Don't worry so much; I will help you, said Saphira. *There are two of us as well.*

He touched her gently on the leg, relieved by her words. The Twins looked at Eragon and asked, "And how do you answer us, Eragon?"

Overlooking the puzzled expressions of his companions, he said flatly, "No."

Sharp lines appeared at the corners of the Twins' mouths. They turned so they faced Eragon obliquely and, bending at the waists, drew a large pentagram on the ground. They stepped in the middle of it, then said harshly, "We begin now. You will attempt to complete the tasks we assign you . . . that is all."

One of the Twins reached into his robe, produced a polished rock the size of Eragon's fist, and set it on the ground. "Lift it to eye level."

That's easy enough, commented Eragon to Saphira. "Stenr reisa!" The rock wobbled, then smoothly rose from the ground. Before it went more than a foot, an unexpected resistance halted it in midair. A smile touched the Twins' lips. Eragon stared at them, enraged— they were trying to make him fail! If he became exhausted now, it would be impossible to complete the harder tasks. Obviously they were confident that their combined strength could easily wear him down.

But I'm not alone either, snarled Eragon to himself. *Saphira, now!* Her mind melded with his, and the rock jerked through the air to stop, quivering, at eye level. The Twins' eyes narrowed cruelly.

"Very . . . good," they hissed. Fredric looked unnerved by the display of magic. "Now move the stone in a circle." Again Eragon struggled against their efforts to stop him, and again—to their obvious anger—he prevailed. The exercises quickly increased in complexity and difficulty until Eragon was forced to think carefully about which words to use. And each time, the Twins fought him bitterly, though the strain never showed on their faces.

It was only with Saphira's support that Eragon was able to hold his ground. In a break between two of the tasks, he asked her, *Why do they continue this testing? Our abilities were clear enough from what they saw in my mind.* She cocked her head thoughtfully. *You know what?* he said grimly as comprehension came to him. *They're using this as an opportunity to figure out what ancient words I know and perhaps learn new ones themselves.*

Speak softly then, so that they cannot hear you, and use the simplest words possible.

From then on, Eragon used only a handful of basic words to complete the tasks. But finding ways to make them perform in the same manner as a long sentence or phrase stretched his ingenuity to the limit. He was rewarded by the frustration that contorted the Twins' faces as he foiled them again and again. No matter what they tried, they could not get him to use any more words in the ancient language.

More than an hour passed, but the Twins showed no sign of stopping. Eragon was hot and thirsty, but refrained from asking for a reprieve—he would continue as long as they did. There were many tests: manipulating water, casting fire, scrying, juggling rocks, hardening leather, freezing items, controlling the flight of an arrow, and healing scratches. He wondered how long it would take for the Twins to run out of ideas.

Finally the Twins raised their hands and said, "There is only one thing left to do. It is simple enough—any *competent* user of magic should find this easy." One of them removed a silver ring from his finger and smugly handed it to Eragon. "Summon the essence of silver."

Eragon stared at the ring in confusion. What was he supposed to do? The essence of silver, what was that? And how was it to be summoned? Saphira had no idea, and the Twins were not going to help. He had never learned silver's name in the ancient language, though he knew it had to be part of *argetlam*. In desperation he combined the only word that might work, *ethgrí*, or "invoke," with *arget*.

Drawing himself upright, he gathered together what power he had left and parted his lips to deliver the invocation. Suddenly a clear, vibrant voice split the air.

"Stop!"

The word rushed over Eragon like cool water—the voice was strangely familiar, like a half-remembered melody. The back of his neck tingled. He slowly turned toward its source.

A lone figure stood behind them: Arya. A leather strip encircled her brow, restraining her voluminous black hair, which tumbled behind her shoulders in a lustrous cascade. Her slender sword was at her hip, her bow on her back. Plain black leather clothed her shapely frame, poor raiment for one so fair. She was taller than most men, and her stance was perfectly balanced and relaxed. An unmarked face reflected none of the horrific abuse she had endured.

Arya's blazing emerald eyes were fixed on the Twins, who had turned pale with fright. She approached on silent footsteps and said in soft, menacing tones, "Shame! Shame to ask of him what only a master can do. Shame that you should use such methods. Shame that you told Ajihad you didn't know Eragon's abilities. He is competent. Now leave!" Arya frowned dangerously, her slanted eyebrows meeting like lightning bolts in a sharp V, and pointed at the ring in Eragon's hand. "Arget!" she exclaimed thunderously.

The silver shimmered, and a ghostly image of the ring materialized next to it. The two were identical except that the apparition seemed purer and glowed white-hot. At the sight of it, the Twins spun on their heels and fled, robes flapping wildly. The insubstantial ring vanished from Eragon's hand, leaving the circlet of silver behind. Orik and Fredric were on their feet, eyeing Arya warily. Saphira crouched, ready for action.

The elf surveyed them all. Her angled eyes paused on Eragon. Then she turned and strode toward the heart of the training field. The warriors ceased their sparring and looked at her with wonder. Within a few moments the entire field fell silent in awe of her presence.

Eragon was inexorably dragged forward by his own fascination. Saphira spoke, but he was oblivious to her comments. A large circle formed around Arya. Looking only at Eragon, she proclaimed, "I claim the right of trial by arms. Draw your sword."

She means to duel me!

But not, I think, to harm you, replied Saphira slowly. She nudged him with her nose. *Go and acquit yourself well. I will watch.*

Eragon reluctantly stepped forward. He did not want to do this when he was exhausted from magic use and when there were so many people watching. Besides, Arya could be in no shape for sparring. It had only been two days since she had received Túnivor's Nectar. *I will soften my blows so I don't hurt her,* he decided.

They faced each other across the circle of warriors. Arya drew her sword with her left hand. The weapon was thinner than Eragon's, but just as long and sharp. He slid Zar'roc out of its polished sheath and held the red blade point-down by his side. For a long moment they stood motionless, elf and human watching each other. It flashed through Eragon's mind that this was how many of his fights with Brom had started.

He moved forward cautiously. With a blur of motion Arya jumped at him, slashing at his ribs. Eragon reflexively parried the attack, and their swords met in a shower of sparks. Zar'roc was batted aside as if it were no more than a fly. The elf did not take advantage of the opening, however, but spun to her right, hair whipping through the air, and struck at his other side. He barely stopped the blow and backpedaled frantically, stunned by her ferocity and speed.

Belatedly, Eragon remembered Brom's warning that even the weakest elf could easily overpower a human. He had about as much chance of defeating Arya as he did Durza. She attacked again, swinging at his head. He ducked under the razor-sharp edge. But then why was she . . . *toying* with him? For a few long seconds he was too busy warding her off to think about it, then he realized, *She wants to know how proficient I am.*

Understanding that, he began the most complicated series of attacks he knew. He flowed from one pose to another, recklessly combining and modifying them in every possible way. But no matter how inventive he was, Arya's sword always stopped his. She matched his actions with effortless grace.

Engaged in a fiery dance, their bodies were linked and separated by the flashing blades. At times they nearly touched, taut skin only a hair's breadth away, but then momentum would whirl them apart, and they would withdraw for a second, only to join again. Their sinuous forms wove together like twisting ropes of wind-blown smoke.

Eragon could never remember how long they fought. It was timeless, filled with nothing but action and reaction. Zar'roc grew leaden in his hand; his arm burned ferociously with each stroke. At last, as he lunged forward, Arya nimbly sidestepped, sweeping the point of her sword up to his jawbone with supernatural speed.

Eragon froze as the icy metal touched his skin. His muscles trembled from the exertion. Dimly he heard Saphira bugle and the warriors cheering raucously around them. Arya lowered her sword and sheathed it. "You have passed," she said quietly amid the noise.

Dazed, he slowly straightened. Fredric was beside him now, thumping his back enthusiastically. "That was incredible swordsmanship! I even learned some new moves from watching the two of you. And the elf—stunning!"

But I lost, he protested silently. Orik praised his performance with a broad smile, but all Eragon noticed was Arya, standing alone and silent. She motioned slightly with a finger, no more than a twitch, toward a knoll about a mile from the practice field, then turned and walked away. The crowd melted before her. A hush fell over the men and dwarves as she passed.

Eragon turned to Orik. "I have to go. I'll return to the dragon-hold soon." With a swift jab, Eragon sheathed Zar'roc and pulled himself onto Saphira. She took off over the training field, which turned into a sea of faces as everyone looked at her.

As they soared toward the knoll, Eragon saw Arya running below them with clean, easy strides. Saphira commented, *You find her form pleasing, do you not?*

Yes, he admitted, blushing.

Her face does have more character than that of most humans, she sniffed. *But it's long, like a horse's, and overall she's rather shapeless.*

Eragon looked at Saphira with amazement. *You're jealous, aren't you!*

Impossible. I never get jealous, she said, offended.

You are now, admit it! he laughed.

She snapped her jaws together loudly. *I am not!* He smiled and shook his head, but let her denial stand. She landed heavily on the knoll, jostling him roughly. He jumped down without remarking on it.

Arya was close behind them. Her fleet stride carried her faster than any runner Eragon had seen. When she reached the top of the knoll, her breathing was smooth and regular. Suddenly tongue-tied, Eragon dropped his gaze. She strode past him and said to Saphira, "Skulblaka, eka celöbra ono un mulabra ono un onr Shur'tugal né haina. Atra nosu waíse fricaya."

Eragon did not recognize most of the words, but Saphira obviously understood the message. She shuffled her wings and surveyed Arya curiously. Then she nodded, humming deeply. Arya smiled. "I am glad that you recovered," Eragon said. "We didn't know if you would live or not."

"That is why I came here today," said Arya, facing him. Her rich voice was accented and exotic. She spoke clearly, with a hint of trill, as if she were about to sing. "I owe you a debt that must be repaid. You saved my life. That can never be forgotten."

"It—it was nothing," said Eragon, fumbling with the words and knowing they were not true, even as he spoke them. Embarrassed, he changed the subject. "How did you come to be in Gil'ead?"

Pain shadowed Arya's face. She looked away into the distance. "Let us walk." They descended from the knoll and meandered toward Farthen Dûr. Eragon respected Arya's silence as they walked. Saphira padded quietly beside them. Finally Arya lifted her head and said with the grace of her kind, "Ajihad told me you were present when Saphira's egg appeared."

"Yes." For the first time, Eragon thought about the energy it must have taken to transport the egg over the dozens of leagues that separated Du Weldenvarden from the Spine. To even attempt such a feat was courting disaster, if not death.

Her next words were heavy. "Then know this: at the moment you first beheld it, I was captured by Durza." Her voice filled with bitterness and grief. "It was he who led the Urgals that ambushed and slew my companions, Faolin and Glenwing. Somehow he knew where to wait for us—we had no warning. I was drugged and transported to Gil'ead. There, Durza was charged by Galbatorix to learn where I had sent the egg and all I knew of Ellesméra."

She stared ahead icily, jaw clenched. "He tried for months without success. His methods were . . . harsh. When torture failed, he ordered his soldiers to use me as they would. Fortunately, I still had the strength to nudge their minds and make them incapable. At last Galbatorix ordered that I was to be brought to Urû'baen. Dread filled me when I learned this, as I was weary in both mind and body and had no strength to resist him. If it were not for you, I would have stood before Galbatorix in a week's time."

Eragon shuddered inwardly. It was amazing what she had survived. The memory of her injuries was still vivid in his mind. Softly, he asked, "Why do you tell me all this?"

"So that you know what I was saved from. Do not presume I can ignore your deed."

Humbled, he bowed his head. "What will you do now—return to Ellesméra?"

"No, not yet. There is much that must be done here. I cannot abandon the Varden—Ajihad needs my help. I've seen you tested in both arms and magic today. Brom taught you well. You are ready to proceed in your training."

"You mean for me to go to Ellesméra?"

"Yes."

Eragon felt a flash of irritation. Did he and Saphira have no say in the matter? "When?"

"That is yet to be decided, but not for some weeks."

At least they gave us that much time, thought Eragon. Saphira mentioned something to him, and he in turn asked Arya, "What did the Twins want me to do?"

Arya's sculpted lip curled with disgust. "Something not even they can accomplish. It is possible to speak the name of an object in the ancient language and summon its true form. It takes years of work and great discipline, but the reward is complete control over the object. That is why one's true name is always kept hidden, for if it were known by any with evil in their hearts, they could dominate you utterly."

"It's strange," said Eragon after a moment, "but before I was captured at Gil'ead, I had visions of you in my dreams. It was like scrying—and I was able to scry you later—but it was always during my sleep."

Arya pursed her lips pensively. "There were times I felt as if another presence was watching me, but I was often confused and feverish. I've never heard of anyone, either in lore or legend, being able to scry in their sleep."

"I don't understand it myself," said Eragon, looking at his hands. He twirled Brom's ring around his finger. "What does the tattoo on your shoulder mean? I didn't mean to see it, but when I was healing your wounds . . . it couldn't be helped. It's just like the symbol on this ring."

"You have a ring with the yawë on it?" she asked sharply.

"Yes. It was Brom's. See?"

He held out the ring. Arya examined the sapphire, then said, "This is a token given only to the most valued elf-friends—so valued, in fact, it has not been used in centuries. Or so I thought. I never knew that Queen Islanzadí thought so highly of Brom."

"I shouldn't wear it, then," said Eragon, afraid that he had been presumptuous.

"No, keep it. It will give you protection if you meet my people by chance, and it may help you gain favor with the queen. Tell no one of my tattoo. It should not be revealed."

"Very well."

He enjoyed talking with Arya and wished their conversation could have lasted longer. When they parted, he wandered through Farthen Dûr, conversing with Saphira. Despite his prodding, she refused to tell him what Arya had said to her. Eventually his thoughts turned to Murtagh and then to Nasuada's advice. *I'll get something to eat, then go see him,* he decided. *Will you wait for me so I can return to the dragonhold with you?*

I will wait—go, said Saphira.

With a grateful smile, Eragon dashed to Tronjheim, ate in an obscure corner of a kitchen, then followed Nasuada's instructions until he reached a small gray door guarded by a man and a dwarf. When he requested entrance, the dwarf banged on the door three times, then unbolted it. "Just holler when you want to leave," said the man with a friendly smile.

The cell was warm and well lit, with a washbasin in one corner and a writing desk—equipped with quills and ink—in another. The ceiling was extensively carved with lacquered figures; the floor was covered with a plush rug. Murtagh lay on a stout bed, reading a scroll. He looked up in surprise and exclaimed cheerily, "Eragon! I'd hoped you would come!"

"How did . . . I mean I thought—"

"You thought I was stuck in some rat hole chewing on hardtack," said Murtagh, rolling upright with a grin. "Actually, I expected the same thing, but Ajihad lets me have all this as long as I don't cause trouble. And they bring me huge meals, as well as anything I want from the library. If I'm not careful, I'll turn into a fat scholar."

Eragon laughed, and with a wondering smile seated himself next to Murtagh. "But aren't you angry? You're still a prisoner."

"Oh, I was at first," said Murtagh with a shrug. "But the more I thought about it, the more I came to realize that this is really the best place for me. Even if Ajihad gave me my freedom, I would stay in my room most of the time anyway."

"But why?"

"You know well enough. No one would be at ease around me, knowing my true identity, and there would always be people who wouldn't limit themselves to harsh looks or words. But enough of that, I'm eager to know what's new. Come, tell me."

Eragon recounted the events of the past two days, including his encounter with the Twins in the library. When he finished, Murtagh leaned back reflectively. "I suspect," he said, "that Arya is more important than either of us thought. Consider what you've learned: she is a master of the sword, powerful in magic, and, most significantly, was chosen to guard Saphira's egg. She cannot be ordinary, even among the elves."

Eragon agreed.

Murtagh stared at the ceiling. "You know, I find this imprisonment oddly peaceful. For once in my life I don't have to be afraid. I know I ought to be . . . yet something about this place puts me at ease. A good night's sleep helps, too."

"I know what you mean," said Eragon wryly. He moved to a softer place on the bed. "Nasuada said that she visited you. Did she say anything interesting?"

Murtagh's gaze shifted into the distance, and he shook his head. "No, she only wanted to meet me. Doesn't she look like a princess? And the way she carries herself! When she first entered through that doorway, I thought she was one of the great ladies of Galbatorix's court. I've seen earls and counts who had wives that, compared to her, were more fitted for life as a hog than of nobility."

Eragon listened to his praise with growing apprehension. *It may mean nothing,* he reminded himself. *You're leaping to conclusions.* Yet the foreboding would not leave him. Trying to shake off the feeling, he asked, "How long are you going to remain imprisoned, Murtagh? You can't hide forever."

Murtagh shrugged carelessly, but there was weight behind his words. "For now I'm content to stay and rest. There's no reason for me to seek shelter elsewhere nor submit myself to the Twins' examination. No doubt I'll tire of this eventually, but for now . . . I am content."

THE SHADOWS
LENGTHEN

Saphira woke Eragon with a sharp rap of her snout, bruising him with her hard jaw. "Ouch!" he exclaimed, sitting upright. The cave was dark except for a faint glow emanating from the shuttered lantern. Outside in the dragonhold, Isidar Mithrim glittered with a thousand different colors, illuminated by its girdle of lanterns.

An agitated dwarf stood in the entrance to the cave, wringing his hands. "You must come, Argetlam! Great trouble—Ajihad summons you. There is no time!"

"What's wrong?" asked Eragon.

The dwarf only shook his head, beard wagging. "Go, you must! Carkna bragha! Now!"

Eragon belted on Zar'roc, grabbed his bow and arrows, then strapped the saddle onto Saphira. *So much for a good night's sleep,* she groused, crouching low to the floor so he could clamber onto her back. He yawned loudly as Saphira launched herself from the cave.

Orik was waiting for them with a grim expression when they landed at Tronjheim's gates. "Come, the others are waiting." He led them through Tronjheim to Ajihad's study. On the way, Eragon plied him with questions, but Orik would only say, "I don't know enough myself—wait until you hear Ajihad."

The large study door was opened by a pair of burly guards. Ajihad stood behind his desk, bleakly inspecting a map. Arya and a man with wiry arms were there as well. Ajihad looked up. "Good, you're here, Eragon. Meet Jörmundur, my second in command."

They acknowledged each other, then turned their attention to Ajihad. "I roused the five of you because we are all in grave danger. About half an hour ago a dwarf ran out of an abandoned tunnel under Tronjheim. He was bleeding and nearly incoherent, but he had enough sense left to tell the dwarves what was pursuing him: an army of Urgals, maybe a day's march from here."

Shocked silence filled the study. Then Jörmundur swore explosively and began asking questions at the same time Orik did. Arya remained silent. Ajihad raised his hands. "Quiet! There is more. The Urgals aren't approaching *over* land, but *under* it. They're in the tunnels . . . we're going to be attacked from below."

Eragon raised his voice in the din that followed. "Why didn't the dwarves know about this sooner? How did the Urgals find the tunnels?"

"We're lucky to know about it this early!" bellowed Orik. Everyone stopped talking to hear him. "There are hundreds of tunnels throughout the Beor Mountains, uninhabited since the day they were mined. The only dwarves who go in them are eccentrics who don't want contact with anyone. We could have just as easily received no warning at all."

Ajihad pointed at the map, and Eragon moved closer. The map depicted the southern half of Alagaësia, but unlike Eragon's, it showed the entire Beor Mountain range in detail. Ajihad's finger was on the section of the Beor Mountains that touched Surda's eastern border. "This," he said, "is where the dwarf claimed to have come from."

"Orthíad!" exclaimed Orik. At Jörmundur's puzzled inquiry, he explained, "It's an ancient dwelling of ours that was deserted when Tronjheim was completed. During its time it was the greatest of our cities. But no one's lived there for centuries."

"And it's old enough for some of the tunnels to have collapsed," said Ajihad. "That's how we surmise it was discovered from the surface. I suspect that Orthíad is now being called Ithrö Zhâda. That's where the Urgal column that was chasing Eragon and Saphira was supposed to go, and I'm sure it's where the Urgals have been migrating all year. From Ithrö Zhâda they can travel anywhere they want in the Beor Mountains. They have the power to destroy both the Varden and the dwarves."

Jörmundur bent over the map, eyeing it carefully. "Do you know how many Urgals there are? Are Galbatorix's troops with them? We can't plan a defense without knowing how large their army is."

Ajihad replied unhappily, "We're unsure about both those things, yet our survival rests on that last question. If Galbatorix has augmented the Urgals' ranks with his own men, we don't stand a chance. But if he hasn't—because he still doesn't want his alliance with the Urgals revealed, or for some other reason—it's possible we can win. Neither Orrin nor the elves can help us at this late hour. Even so, I sent runners to both of them with news of our plight. At the very least they won't be caught by surprise if we fall."

He drew a hand across his coal-black brow. "I've already talked with Hrothgar, and we've decided on a course of action. Our only hope is to contain the Urgals in three of the larger tunnels and channel them into Farthen Dûr so they don't swarm inside Tronjheim like locusts.

"I need you, Eragon and Arya, to help the dwarves collapse extraneous tunnels. The job is too big for normal means. Two groups of dwarves are already working on it: one outside Tronjheim, the other beneath it. Eragon, you're to work with the group outside. Arya, you'll be with the one underground; Orik will guide you to them."

"Why not collapse all the tunnels instead of leaving the large ones untouched?" asked Eragon.

"Because," said Orik, "that would force the Urgals to clear away the rubble, and they might decide to go in a direction we don't want them to. Plus, if we cut ourselves off, they could attack other dwarf cities—which we wouldn't be able to assist in time."

"There's also another reason," said Ajihad. "Hrothgar warned me that Tronjheim sits on such a dense network of tunnels that if too many are weakened, sections of the city will sink into the ground under their own weight. We can't risk that."

Jörmundur listened intently, then asked, "So there won't be any fighting inside Tronjheim? You said the Urgals would be channeled outside the city, into Farthen Dûr."

Ajihad responded quickly, "That's right. We can't defend Tronjheim's entire perimeter—it's too big for our forces—so we're going to seal all the passageways and gates leading into it. That will force the Urgals out onto the flats surrounding Tronjheim, where there's plenty of maneuvering room for our armies. Since the Urgals have access to the tunnels, we cannot risk an extended battle. As long as they are here, we will be in constant danger of them quarrying up through Tronjheim's floor. If that happens, we'll be trapped, attacked from both the outside and inside. We have to prevent the Urgals from taking Tronjheim. If they secure it, it's doubtful we will have the strength to roust them."

"And what of our families?" asked Jörmundur. "I won't see my wife and son murdered by Urgals."

The lines deepened on Ajihad's face. "All the women and children are being evacuated into the surrounding valleys. If we are defeated, they have guides who will take them to Surda. That's all I can do, under the circumstances."

Jörmundur struggled to hide his relief. "Sir, is Nasuada going as well?"

"She is not pleased, but yes." All eyes were on Ajihad as he squared his shoulders and announced, "The Urgals will arrive in a matter of hours. We know their numbers are great, but we *must* hold Farthen Dûr. Failure will mean the dwarves' downfall, death to the Varden—and eventual defeat for Surda and the elves. This is one battle we cannot lose. Now go and complete your tasks! Jörmundur, ready the men to fight."

* * *

They left the study and scattered: Jörmundur to the barracks, Orik and Arya to the stairs leading underground, and Eragon and Saphira down one of Tronjheim's four main halls. Despite the early hour, the city-mountain swarmed like an anthill. People were running, shouting messages, and carrying bundles of belongings.

Eragon had fought and killed before, but the battle that awaited them sent stabs of fear into his chest. He had never had a chance to anticipate a fight. Now that he did, it filled him with dread. He was confident when facing only a few opponents—he knew he could easily defeat three or four Urgals with Zar'roc and magic—but in a large conflict, anything could happen.

They exited Tronjheim and looked for the dwarves they were supposed to help. Without the sun or moon, the inside of Farthen Dûr was dark as lampblack, punctuated by glittering lanterns bobbing jerkily in the crater. *Perhaps they're on the far side of Tronjheim,* suggested Saphira. Eragon agreed and swung onto her back.

They glided around Tronjheim until a clump of lanterns came into sight. Saphira angled toward them, then with no more than a whisper landed beside a group of startled dwarves who were busy digging with pickaxes. Eragon quickly explained why he was there. A sharp-nosed dwarf told him, "There's a tunnel about four yards directly underneath us. Any help you could give us would be appreciated."

"If you clear the area over the tunnel, I'll see what I can do." The sharp-nosed dwarf looked doubtful, but ordered the diggers off the site.

Breathing slowly, Eragon prepared to use magic. It might be possible to actually move all the dirt off the tunnel, but he needed to conserve his strength for later. Instead, he would try to collapse the tunnel by applying force to weak sections of its ceiling.

"Thrysta deloi," he whispered and sent tentacles of power into the soil. Almost immediately they encountered rock. He ignored it and reached farther down until he felt the hollow emptiness of the tunnel. Then he began searching for flaws in the rock. Every time he found one, he pushed on it, elongating and widening it. It was strenuous work, but no more than it would have been to split the stone by hand. He made no visible progress—a fact that was not lost on the impatient dwarves.

Eragon persevered. Before long he was rewarded by a resounding crack that could be heard clearly on the surface. There was a persistent screech, then the ground slid inward like water draining from a tub, leaving a gaping hole seven yards across.

As the delighted dwarves walled off the tunnel with rubble, the sharp-nosed dwarf led Eragon to the next tunnel. This one was much more difficult to collapse, but he managed to duplicate the feat. Over the next few hours, he collapsed over a half-dozen tunnels throughout Farthen Dûr, with Saphira's help.

Light crept into the small patch of sky above them as he worked. It was not enough to see by, but it bolstered Eragon's confidence. He turned away from the crumpled ruins of the latest tunnel and surveyed the land with interest.

A mass exodus of women and children, along with the Varden's elders, streamed out of Tronjheim. Everyone carried loads of provisions, clothes, and belongings. A small group of warriors, predominantly boys and old men, accompanied them.

Most of the activity, however, was at the base of Tronjheim, where the Varden and dwarves were assembling their army, which was divided into three battalions. Each section bore the Varden's standard: a white dragon holding a rose above a sword pointing downward on a purple field.

The men were silent, ironfisted. Their hair flowed loosely from under their helmets. Many warriors had only a sword and a shield, but there were several ranks of spear- and pikemen. In the rear of the battalions, archers tested their bowstrings.

The dwarves were garbed in heavy battle gear. Burnished steel hauberks hung to their knees, and thick roundshields, stamped with the crests of their clan, rested on their left arms. Short swords were sheathed at their waists, while in their right hands they carried mattocks or war axes. Their legs were covered with extra-fine mail. They wore iron caps and brass-studded boots.

A small figure detached itself from the far battalion and hurried toward Eragon and Saphira. It was Orik, clad like the other dwarves. "Ajihad wants you to join the army," he said. "There are no more tunnels to cave in. Food is waiting for both of you."

Eragon and Saphira accompanied Orik to a tent, where they found bread and water for Eragon and a pile of dried meat for Saphira. They ate it without complaint; it was better than going hungry.

When they finished, Orik told them to wait and disappeared into the battalion's ranks. He returned, leading a line of dwarves burdened with tall piles of plate armor. Orik lifted a section of it and handed it to Eragon.

"What is this?" asked Eragon, fingering the polished metal. The armor was intricately wrought with engraving and gold filigree. It was an inch thick in places and very heavy. No man could fight under that much weight. And there were far too many pieces for one person.

"A gift from Hrothgar," said Orik, looking pleased with himself. "It has lain so long among our other treasures that it was almost forgotten. It was forged in another age, before the fall of the Riders."

"But what's it *for?*" asked Eragon.

"Why, it's dragon armor, of course! You don't think that dragons went into battle unprotected? Complete sets are rare because they took so long to make and because dragons were always growing. Still, Saphira isn't too big yet, so this should fit her reasonably well."

Dragon armor! As Saphira nosed one of the pieces, Eragon asked, *What do you think?*

Let's try it on, she said, a fierce gleam in her eye.

After a good deal of struggling, Eragon and Orik stepped back to admire the result. Saphira's entire neck—except for the spikes along its ridge—was covered with triangular scales of overlapping armor. Her belly and chest were protected by the heaviest plates, while the lightest ones were on her tail. Her legs and back were completely encased. Her wings were left bare. A single molded plate lay on top of her head, leaving her lower jaw free to bite and snap.

473

Saphira arched her neck experimentally, and the armor flexed smoothly with her. *This will slow me down, but it'll help stop the arrows. How do I look?*

Very intimidating, replied Eragon truthfully. That pleased her.

Orik picked up the remaining items from the ground. "I brought you armor as well, though it took much searching to find your size. We rarely forge arms for men or elves. I don't know who this was made for, but it has never been used and should serve you well."

Over Eragon's head went a stiff shirt of leather-backed mail that fell to his knees like a skirt. It rested heavily on his shoulders and clinked when he moved. He belted Zar'roc over it, which helped keep the mail from swinging. On his head went a leather cap, then a mail coif, and finally a gold-and-silver helm. Bracers were strapped to his forearms, and greaves to his lower legs. For his hands there were mail-backed gloves. Last, Orik handed him a broad shield emblazoned with an oak tree.

Knowing that what he and Saphira had been given was worth several fortunes, Eragon bowed and said, "Thank you for these gifts. Hrothgar's presents are greatly appreciated."

"Don't give thanks now," said Orik with a chuckle. "Wait until the armor saves your life."

The warriors around them began marching away. The three battalions were repositioning themselves in different parts of Farthen Dûr. Unsure of what they should do, Eragon looked at Orik, who shrugged and said, "I suppose we should accompany them." They trailed behind a battalion as it headed toward the crater wall. Eragon asked about the Urgals, but Orik only knew that scouts had been posted underground in the tunnels and that nothing had been seen or heard yet.

The battalion halted at one of the collapsed tunnels. The dwarves had piled the rubble so that anyone inside the tunnel could easily climb out. *This must be one of the places they're going to force the Urgals to surface,* Saphira pointed out.

Hundreds of lanterns were fixed atop poles and stuck into the ground. They provided a great pool of light that glowed like an evening sun. Fires blazed along the rim of the tunnel's roof, huge cauldrons of pitch heating over them. Eragon looked away, fighting back revulsion. It was a terrible way to kill anyone, even an Urgal.

Rows of sharpened saplings were being pounded into the ground to provide a thorny barrier between the battalion and the tunnel. Eragon saw an opportunity to help and joined a group of men digging trenches between the saplings. Saphira assisted as well, scooping out the dirt with her giant claws. While they labored, Orik left to supervise the construction of a barricade to shield the archers. Eragon drank gratefully from the wineskin whenever it was passed around. After the trenches were finished and filled with pointed stakes, Saphira and Eragon rested.

Orik returned to find them seated together. He wiped his brow. "All the men and dwarves are on the battlefield. Tronjheim has been sealed off. Hrothgar has taken charge of the battalion to our left. Ajihad leads the one ahead of us."

"Who commands this one?"

"Jörmundur." Orik sat with a grunt and placed his war ax on the ground.

Saphira nudged Eragon. *Look.* His hand tightened on Zar'roc as he saw Murtagh, helmed, carrying a dwarven shield and his hand-and-a-half sword, approaching with Tornac.

Orik cursed and leapt to his feet, but Murtagh said quickly, "It's all right; Ajihad released me."

"Why would he do that?" demanded Orik.

Murtagh smiled wryly. "He said this was an opportunity to prove my good intentions. Apparently, he doesn't think I would be able to do much damage even if I did turn on the Varden."

Eragon nodded in welcome, relaxing his grip. Murtagh was an excellent and merciless fighter—exactly whom Eragon wanted by his side during battle.

"How do we know you're not lying?" asked Orik.

"Because I say so," announced a firm voice. Ajihad strode into their midst, armed for battle with a breastplate and an ivory-handled sword. He put a strong hand on Eragon's shoulder and drew him away where the others could not hear. He cast an eye over Eragon's armor. "Good, Orik outfitted you."

"Yes . . . has anything been seen in the tunnels?"

"Nothing." Ajihad leaned on his sword. "One of the Twins is staying in Tronjheim. He's going to watch the battle from the dragonhold and relay information through his brother to me. I know you can speak with your mind. I need you to tell the Twins anything, *anything*, unusual that you see while fighting. Also, I'll relay orders to you through them. Do you understand?"

The thought of being linked to the Twins filled Eragon with loathing, but he knew it was necessary. "I do."

Ajihad paused. "You're not a foot soldier or horseman, nor any other type of warrior I'm used to commanding. Battle may prove differently, but I think you and Saphira will be safer on the ground. In the air, you'll be a choice target for Urgal archers. Will you fight from Saphira's back?"

Eragon had never been in combat on horseback, much less on Saphira. "I'm not sure what we'll do. When I'm on Saphira, I'm up too high to fight all but a Kull."

"There will be plenty of Kull, I'm afraid," said Ajihad. He straightened, pulling his sword out of the ground. "The only advice I can give you is to avoid unnecessary risks. The Varden cannot afford to lose you." With that, he turned and left.

Eragon returned to Orik and Murtagh and hunkered next to Saphira, leaning his shield against his knees. The four of them waited in silence like the hundreds of warriors around them. Light from Farthen Dûr's opening waned as the sun crept below the crater rim.

Eragon turned to scan the encampment and froze, heart jolting. About thirty feet away sat Arya with her bow in her lap. Though he knew it was unreasonable, he had hoped she might accompany the other women out of Farthen Dûr. Concerned, he hastened to her. "You will fight?"

"I do what I must," Arya said calmly.

"But it's too dangerous!"

Her face darkened. "Do not pamper me, human. Elves train both their men and women to fight. I am not one of your helpless females to run away whenever there is danger. I was given the task of protecting Saphira's egg . . . which I failed. My breoal is dishonored and would be further shamed if I did not guard you and Saphira on this field. You forget that I am stronger with magic than any here, including you. If the Shade comes, who can defeat him but me? And who else has the right?"

Eragon stared at her helplessly, knowing she was right and hating the fact. "Then stay safe." Out of desperation, he added in the ancient language, "Wiol pömnuria ilian." For my happiness.

Arya turned her gaze away uneasily, the fringe of her hair obscuring her face. She ran a hand along her polished bow, then murmured, "It is my wyrd to be here. The debt must be paid."

He abruptly retreated to Saphira. Murtagh looked at him curiously. "What did she say?"

"Nothing."

Wrapped in their own thoughts, the defenders sank into a brooding silence as the hours crawled by. Farthen Dûr's crater again grew black, except for the sanguine lantern glow and the fires heating the pitch. Eragon alternated between myopically examining the links of his mail and spying on Arya. Orik repeatedly ran a whetstone over the blade of his ax, periodically eyeing the edge between strokes; the rasp of metal on stone was irritating. Murtagh just stared into the distance.

Occasionally, messengers ran through the encampment, causing the warriors to surge to their feet. But it always proved to be a false alarm. The men and dwarves became strained; angry voices were often heard. The worst part about Farthen Dûr was the lack of wind—the air was dead, motionless. Even when it grew warm and stifling and filled with smoke, there was no reprieve.

As the night dragged on, the battlefield stilled, silent as death. Muscles stiffened from the waiting. Eragon stared blankly into the darkness with heavy eyelids. He shook himself to alertness and tried to focus through his stupor.

Finally Orik said, "It's late. We should sleep. If anything happens, the others will wake us." Murtagh grumbled, but Eragon was too tired to complain. He curled up against Saphira, using his shield as a pillow. As his eyes closed, he saw that Arya was still awake, watching over them.

His dreams were confused and disturbing, full of horned beasts and unseen menaces. Over and over he heard a deep voice ask, "Are you ready?" But he never had an answer. Plagued by such visions, his sleep was shallow and uneasy until something touched his arm. He woke with a start.

BATTLE UNDER
FARTHEN DÛR

"I t has begun," Arya said with a sorrowful expression. The troops in the encampment stood alertly with their weapons drawn. Orik swung his ax to make sure he had enough room. Arya nocked an arrow and held it ready to shoot.

"A scout ran out of a tunnel a few minutes ago," said Murtagh to Eragon. "The Urgals are coming."

Together they watched the dark mouth of the tunnel through the ranks of men and sharpened stakes. A minute dragged by, then another . . . and another. Without taking his eyes from the tunnel, Eragon hoisted himself into Saphira's saddle, Zar'roc in his hand, a comfortable weight. Murtagh mounted Tornac beside him. Then a man cried, "I hear them!"

The warriors stiffened; grips tightened on weapons. No one moved . . . no one breathed. Somewhere a horse nickered.

Harsh Urgal shouts shattered the air as dark shapes boiled upward in the tunnel's opening. At a command, the cauldrons of pitch were tilted on their sides, pouring the scalding liquid into the tunnel's hungry throat. The monsters howled in pain, arms flailing. A torch was thrown onto the bubbling pitch, and an orange pillar of greasy flames roared up in the opening, engulfing the Urgals in an inferno. Sickened, Eragon looked across Farthen Dûr at the other two battalions and saw similar fires by each. He sheathed Zar'roc and strung his bow.

More Urgals soon tamped the pitch down and clambered out of

the tunnels over their burned brethren. They clumped together, presenting a solid wall to the men and dwarves. Behind the palisade Orik had helped build, the first row of archers pulled on their bows and fired. Eragon and Arya added their arrows to the deadly swarm and watched the shafts eat through the Urgals' ranks.

The Urgal line wavered, threatening to break, but they covered themselves with their shields and weathered the attack. Again the archers fired, but the Urgals continued to stream onto the surface at a ferocious rate.

Eragon was dismayed by their numbers. They were supposed to kill every single one? It seemed a madman's task. His only encouragement was that he saw none of Galbatorix's troops with the Urgals. Not yet, at least.

The opposing army formed a solid mass of bodies that seemed to stretch endlessly. Tattered and sullen standards were raised in the monsters' midst. Baleful notes echoed through Farthen Dûr as war
horns sounded. The entire group of Urgals charged with savage war cries.

They dashed against the rows of stakes, covering them with slick blood and limp corpses as the ranks at the vanguard were crushed against the posts. A cloud of black arrows flew over the barrier at the crouched defenders. Eragon ducked behind his shield, and Saphira covered her head. Arrows rattled harmlessly against her armor.

Momentarily foiled by the pickets, the Urgal horde milled with confusion. The Varden bunched together, waiting for the next attack. After a pause, the war cries were raised again as the Urgals surged forward. The assault was bitter. Its momentum carried the Urgals through the stakes, where a line of pikemen jabbed frantically at their ranks, trying to repel them. The pikemen held briefly, but the ominous tide of Urgals could not be halted, and they were overwhelmed.

The first lines of defense breached, the main bodies of the two forces collided for the first time. A deafening roar burst from the men and dwarves as they rushed into the conflict. Saphira bellowed and leapt toward the fight, diving into a whirlwind of noise and blurred action.

With her jaws and talons, Saphira tore through an Urgal. Her teeth were as lethal as any sword, her tail a giant mace. From her back, Eragon parried a hammer blow from an Urgal chief, protecting her vulnerable wings. Zar'roc's crimson blade seemed to gleam with delight as blood spurted along its length.

From the corner of his eye, Eragon saw Orik hewing Urgal necks with mighty blows of his ax. Beside the dwarf was Murtagh on Tornac, his face disfigured by a vicious snarl as he swung his sword angrily, cutting through every defense. Then Saphira spun around, and Eragon saw Arya leap past the lifeless body of an opponent.

An Urgal bowled over a wounded dwarf and hacked at Saphira's front right leg. His sword skated off her armor with a burst of sparks. Eragon smote him on the head, but Zar'roc stuck in the monster's horns and was yanked from his grasp. With a curse he dived off Saphira and tackled the Urgal, smashing his face with the shield. He jerked Zar'roc out of the horns, then dodged as another Urgal charged him.

Saphira, I need you! he shouted, but the battle's tide had separated them. Suddenly a Kull jumped at him, club raised for a blow. Unable to lift his shield in time, Eragon uttered, "Jierda!" The Kull's head snapped back with a sharp report as his neck broke. Four more Urgals succumbed to Zar'roc's thirsty bite, then Murtagh rode up beside Eragon, driving the press of Urgals backward.

"Come on!" he shouted, and reached down from Tornac, pulling Eragon onto the horse. They rushed toward Saphira, who was embroiled in a mass of enemies. Twelve spear-wielding Urgals encircled her, needling her with their lances. They had already managed to prick both of her wings. Her blood splattered the ground. Every time she rushed at one of the Urgals, they bunched together and jabbed at her eyes, forcing her to retreat. She tried to sweep the spears away with her talons, but the Urgals jumped back and evaded her.

The sight of Saphira's blood enraged Eragon. He swung off Tornac with a wild cry and stabbed the nearest Urgal through the chest, withholding nothing in his frenzied attempt to help Saphira. His attack provided the distraction she needed to break free. With a kick, she sent an Urgal flying, then barreled to him. Eragon grabbed one of her neck spikes and pulled himself back into her saddle. Murtagh raised his hand, then charged into another knot of Urgals.

By unspoken consent, Saphira took flight and rose above the struggling armies, seeking a respite from the madness. Eragon's breath trembled. His muscles were clenched, ready to ward off the next attack. Every fiber of his being thrilled with energy, making him feel more alive than ever before.

Saphira circled long enough for them to recover their strength, then descended toward the Urgals, skimming the ground to avoid detection. She approached the monsters from behind, where their archers were gathered.

Before the Urgals realized what was happening, Eragon lopped off the heads of two archers, and Saphira disemboweled three others. She took off again as alarms sounded, quickly soaring out of bow range.

They repeated the tactic on a different flank of the army. Saphira's stealth and speed, combined with the dim lighting, made it nearly impossible for the Urgals to predict where she would strike next. Eragon used his bow whenever Saphira was in the air, but he quickly ran out of arrows. Soon the only thing left in his quiver was magic, which he wanted to keep in reserve until it was desperately needed.

Saphira's flights over the combatants gave Eragon a unique understanding of how the battle was progressing. There were three separate fights raging in Farthen Dûr, one by each open tunnel. The Urgals were disadvantaged by the dispersal of their forces and their inability to get all of their army out of the tunnels at once. Even so, the Varden and dwarves could not keep the monsters from advancing and were slowly being driven back toward Tronjheim. The defenders seemed insignificant against the mass of Urgals, whose numbers continued to increase as they poured out of the tunnels.

The Urgals had organized themselves around several standards, each representing a clan, but it was unclear who commanded them overall. The clans paid no attention to each other, as if they were receiving orders from elsewhere. Eragon wished he knew who was in charge so he and Saphira could kill him.

Remembering Ajihad's orders, he began relaying information to the Twins. They were interested by what he had to say about the Urgals' apparent lack of a leader and questioned him closely. The exchange was smooth, if brief. The Twins told him, *You're ordered to assist Hrothgar; the fight goes badly for him.*

Understood, Eragon responded.

Saphira swiftly flew to the besieged dwarves, swooping low over Hrothgar. Arrayed in golden armor, the dwarf king stood at the fore of a small knot of his kin, wielding Volund, the hammer of his ancestors. His white beard caught the lantern light as he looked up at Saphira. Admiration glinted in his eyes.

Saphira landed beside the dwarves and faced the oncoming Urgals. Even the bravest Kull quailed before her ferocity, allowing the dwarves to surge forward. Eragon tried to keep Saphira safe. Her left flank was protected by the dwarves, but to her front and right raged a sea of enemies. He showed no mercy on those and took every advantage he could, using magic whenever Zar'roc could not serve him. A spear bounced off his shield, denting it and leaving him with a bruised shoulder. Shaking off the pain, he cleaved open an Urgal's skull, mixing brains with metal and bone.

He was in awe of Hrothgar—who, though he was ancient by both the standards of men and dwarves, was still undiminished on the battlefield. No Urgal, Kull or not, could stand before the dwarf king and his guards and live. Every time Volund struck, it sounded the gong of death for another enemy. After a spear downed one of his warriors, Hrothgar grabbed the spear himself and, with astounding strength, hurled it completely through its owner twenty yards away. Such heroism emboldened Eragon to ever greater risks, seeking to hold his own with the mighty king.

Eragon lunged at a giant Kull nearly out of reach and almost fell from Saphira's saddle. Before he could recover, the Kull darted past Saphira's defenses and swung his sword. The brunt of the blow caught Eragon on the side of his helm, throwing him backward and making his vision flicker and his ears ring thunderously.

Stunned, he tried to pull himself upright, but the Kull had already prepared for another blow. As the Kull's arm descended, a slim steel blade suddenly sprouted from his chest. Howling, the monster toppled to the side. In his place stood Angela.

The witch wore a long red cape over outlandish flanged armor enameled black and green. She bore a strange two-handed weapon—a long wooden shaft with a sword blade attached to each end. Angela winked at Eragon mischievously, then dashed away, spinning her staff-sword like a dervish. Close behind her was Solembum in the form of a young shaggy-haired boy. He held a small black dagger, sharp teeth bared in a feral snarl.

Still dazed from his battering, Eragon managed to straighten himself in the saddle. Saphira jumped into the air and wheeled high above, letting him recuperate. He scanned Farthen Dûr's plains and saw, to his dismay, that all three battles were going badly. Neither Ajihad, Jörmundur, nor Hrothgar could stop the Urgals. There were simply too many.

Eragon wondered how many Urgals he could kill at once with magic. He knew his limits fairly well. If he were to kill enough to make a difference . . . it would probably be suicide. That might be what it took to win.

The fighting continued for one endless hour after another. The Varden and dwarves were exhausted, but the Urgals remained fresh with reinforcements.

It was a nightmare for Eragon. Though he and Saphira fought their hardest, there was always another Urgal to take the place of the one just killed. His whole body hurt—especially his head. Every time he used magic he lost a little more energy. Saphira was in better condition, though her wings were punctured with small wounds.

As he parried a blow, the Twins contacted him urgently. *There are loud noises under Tronjheim. It sounds like Urgals are trying to dig into the city! We need you and Arya to collapse any tunnels they're excavating.*

Eragon dispatched his opponent with a sword thrust. *We'll be right there.* He looked for Arya and saw her engaged with a knot of struggling Urgals. Saphira quickly forged a path to the elf, leaving a pile of crumpled bodies in her wake. Eragon extended his hand and said, "Get on!"

Arya jumped onto Saphira's back without hesitation. She wrapped her right arm around Eragon's waist, wielding her bloodstained sword with the other. As Saphira crouched to take off, an Urgal ran at her, howling, then lifted an ax and smashed her in the chest.

Saphira roared with pain and lurched forward, feet leaving the ground. Her wings snapped open, straining to keep them from crashing as she veered wildly to one side, right wingtip scraping the ground. Below them, the Urgal pulled back his arm to throw the ax. But Arya raised her palm, shouting, and an emerald ball of energy shot from her hand, killing the Urgal. With a colossal heave of her shoulders, Saphira righted herself, barely making it over the heads of the warriors. She pulled away from the battlefield with powerful wing strokes and rasping breath.

Are you all right? asked Eragon, concerned. He could not see where she had been struck.

I'll live, she said grimly, *but the front of my armor has been crushed together. It hurts my chest, and I'm having trouble moving.*

Can you get us to the dragonhold?

. . . We'll see.

Eragon explained Saphira's condition to Arya. "I'll stay and help Saphira when we land," she offered. "Once she is free of the armor, I will join you."

"Thank you," he said. The flight was laborious for Saphira; she glided whenever she could. When they reached the dragonhold, she dropped heavily to Isidar Mithrim, where the Twins were supposed to be watching the battle, but it was empty. Eragon jumped to the floor and winced as he saw the damage the Urgal had done. Four of the metal plates on Saphira's chest had been hammered together, restricting her ability to bend and breathe. "Stay well," he said, putting a hand on her side, then ran out the archway.

He stopped and swore. He was at the top of Vol Turin, The Endless Staircase. Because of his worry for Saphira, he had not considered how he would get to Tronjheim's base—where the Urgals were breaking in. There was no time to climb down. He looked at the narrow trough to the right of the stairs, then grabbed one of the leather pads and threw himself down on it.

The stone slide was smooth as lacquered wood. With the leather underneath him, he accelerated almost instantly to a frightening speed, the walls blurring and the curve of the slide pressing him high against the wall. Eragon lay completely flat so he would go faster. The air rushed past his helm, making it vibrate like a weather vane in a gale. The trough was too confined for him, and he was perilously close to flying out, but as long as he kept his arms and legs still, he was safe.

It was a swift descent, but it still took him nearly ten minutes to reach the bottom. The slide leveled out at the end and sent him skidding halfway across the huge carnelian floor.

When he finally came to a stop, he was too dizzy to walk. His first attempt to stand made him nauseated, so he curled up, head in his hands, and waited for things to stop spinning. When he felt better, he stood and warily looked around.

The great chamber was completely deserted, the silence unsettling. Rosy light filtered down from Isidar Mithrim. He faltered—Where was he supposed to go?—and cast out his mind for the Twins. Nothing. He froze as loud knocking echoed through Tronjheim.

An explosion split the air. A long slab of the chamber floor buckled and blew thirty feet up. Needles of rocks flew outward as it crashed down. Eragon stumbled back, stunned, groping for Zar'roc. The twisted shapes of Urgals clambered out of the hole in the floor.

Eragon hesitated. Should he flee? Or should he stay and try to close the tunnel? Even if he managed to seal it before the Urgals attacked him, what if Tronjheim was already breached elsewhere? He could not find all the places in time to prevent the city-mountain from being captured. *But if I run to one of Tronjheim's gates and blast it open, the Varden could retake Tronjheim without having to siege it.* Before he could decide, a tall man garbed entirely in black armor emerged from the tunnel and looked directly at him.

It was Durza.

The Shade carried his pale blade marked with the scratch from Ajihad. A black roundshield with a crimson ensign rested on his arm. His dark helmet was richly decorated, like a general's, and a long snakeskin cloak billowed around him. Madness burned in his maroon eyes, the madness of one who enjoys power and finds himself in the position to use it.

487

Eragon knew he was neither fast enough nor strong enough to escape the fiend before him. He immediately warned Saphira, though he knew it was impossible for her to rescue him. He dropped into a crouch and quickly reviewed what Brom had told him about fighting another magic user. It was not encouraging. And Ajihad had said that Shades could only be destroyed by a thrust through the heart.

Durza gazed at him contemptuously and said, "Kaz jtierl trazhid! Otrag bagh." The Urgals eyed Eragon suspiciously and formed a circle around the perimeter of the room. Durza slowly approached Eragon with a triumphant expression. "So, my young Rider, we meet again. You were foolish to escape from me in Gil'ead. It will only make things worse for you in the end."

"You'll never capture me alive," growled Eragon.

"Is that so?" asked the Shade, raising an eyebrow. The light from the star sapphire gave his skin a ghastly tint. "I don't see your 'friend' Murtagh around to help you. You can't stop me now. No one can!"

Fear touched Eragon. *How does he know about Murtagh?* Putting all the derision he could into his voice, he jeered, "How did you like being shot?"

Durza's face tightened momentarily. "I will be repaid in blood for that. Now tell me where your dragon is hiding."

"Never."

The Shade's countenance darkened. "Then I will force it from you!" His sword whistled through the air. The moment Eragon caught the blade on his shield, a mental probe spiked deep into his thoughts. Fighting to protect his consciousness, he shoved Durza back and attacked with his own mind.

Eragon battered with all his strength against the iron-hard defenses surrounding Durza's mind, but to no avail. He swung Zar'roc, trying to catch Durza off guard. The Shade knocked the blow aside effortlessly, then stabbed in return with lightning speed.

488 The point of the sword caught Eragon in the ribs, piercing his mail and driving out his breath. The mail slipped, though, and the blade missed his side by the width of a wire. The distraction was all Durza needed to break into Eragon's mind and begin taking control.

"No!" cried Eragon, throwing himself at the Shade. His face contorted as he grappled with Durza, yanking on his sword arm. Durza tried to cut Eragon's hand, but it was protected by the mail-backed glove, which sent the blade glancing downward. As Eragon kicked his leg, Durza snarled and swept his black shield around, knocking him to the floor. Eragon tasted blood in his mouth; his neck throbbed. Ignoring his injuries, he rolled over and hurled his shield at Durza. Despite the Shade's superior speed, the heavy shield clipped him on the hip. As Durza stumbled, Eragon caught him on the upper arm with Zar'roc. A line of blood traced down the Shade's arm.

Eragon thrust at the Shade with his mind and drove through Durza's weakened defenses. A flood of images suddenly engulfed him, rushing through his consciousness—

Durza as a young boy living as a nomad with his parents on the empty plains. The tribe abandoned them and called his father "oathbreaker." Only it was not Durza then, but Carsaib—the name his mother crooned while combing his hair. . . .

The Shade reeled wildly, face twisted in pain. Eragon tried to control the torrent of memories, but the force of them was overwhelming.

Standing on a hill over the graves of his parents, weeping that the men had not killed him as well. Then turning and stumbling blindly away, into the desert. . . .

Durza faced Eragon. Terrible hatred flowed from his maroon eyes. Eragon was on one knee—almost standing—struggling to seal his mind.

How the old man looked when he first saw Carsaib lying near death on a sand dune. The days it had taken Carsaib to recover and the fear he felt upon discovering that his rescuer was a sorcerer. How he had pleaded to be taught the control of spirits. How Haeg had finally agreed. Called him "Desert Rat.". . .

489

Eragon was standing now. Durza charged . . . sword raised . . . shield ignored in his fury.

The days spent training under the scorching sun, always alert for the lizards they caught for food. How his power slowly grew, giving him pride and confidence. The weeks spent nursing his sick master after a failed spell. His joy when Haeg recovered . . .

There was not enough time to react . . . not enough time. . . .

The bandits who attacked during the night, killing Haeg. The rage Carsaib had felt and the spirits he had summoned for vengeance. But the spirits were stronger than he expected. They turned on him, possessing mind and body. He had screamed. He was—I AM DURZA!

The sword smote heavily across Eragon's back, cutting through both mail and skin. He screamed as pain blasted through him, forcing him to his knees. Agony bowed his body in half and obliterated all thought. He swayed, barely conscious, hot blood running down the small of his back. Durza said something he could not hear.

In anguish, Eragon raised his eyes to the heavens, tears streaming down his cheeks. Everything had failed. The Varden and dwarves were destroyed. He was defeated. Saphira would give herself up for his sake—she had done it before—and Arya would be recaptured or killed. Why had it ended like this? What justice could this be? All was for nothing.

As he looked at Isidar Mithrim far above his tortured frame, a flash of light erupted in his eyes, blinding him. A second later, the chamber rang with a deafening report. Then his eyes cleared, and he gaped with disbelief.

The star sapphire had shattered. An expanding torus of huge dagger-like pieces plummeted toward the distant floor—the shimmering shards near the walls. In the center of the chamber, hurtling downward headfirst, was Saphira. Her jaws were open and from between them erupted a great tongue of flame, bright yellow and tinged with blue. On her back was Arya: hair billowing wildly, arm uplifted, palm glowing with a nimbus of green magic.

Time seemed to slow as Eragon saw Durza tilt his head toward the ceiling. First shock, then anger contorted the Shade's face. Sneering defiantly, he raised his hand and pointed at Saphira, a word forming on his lips.

A hidden reserve of strength suddenly welled up inside Eragon, dredged from the deepest part of his being. His fingers curled around the hilt of his sword. He plunged through the barrier in his mind and took hold of the magic. All his pain and rage focused on one word:

"*Brisingr!*"

Zar'roc blazed with bloody light, heatless flames running along it . . .

He lunged forward . . .

And stabbed Durza in the heart.

Durza looked down with shock at the blade protruding from his breast. His mouth was open, but instead of words, an unearthly howl burst from him. His sword dropped from nerveless fingers. He grasped Zar'roc as if to pull it out, but it was lodged firmly in him.

Then Durza's skin turned transparent. Under it was neither flesh nor bone, but swirling patterns of darkness. He shrieked even louder as the darkness pulsated, splitting his skin. With one last cry, Durza was rent from head to toe, releasing the darkness, which separated into three entities who flew through Tronjheim's walls and out of Farthen Dûr. The Shade was gone.

Bereft of strength, Eragon fell back with arms outstretched. Above him, Saphira and Arya had nearly reached the floor—it looked as if they were going to smash into it with the deadly remains of Isidar Mithrim. As his sight faded, Saphira, Arya, the myriad fragments—all seemed to stop falling and hang motionless in the air.

THE MOURNING SAGE

natches of the Shade's memories continued to flash through Eragon. A whirlwind of dark events and emotions overwhelmed him, making it impossible to think. Submerged in the maelstrom, he knew neither who nor where he was. He was too weak to cleanse himself of the alien presence that clouded his mind. Violent, cruel images from the Shade's past exploded behind his eyes until his spirit cried out in anguish at the bloody sights.

A pile of bodies rose before him . . . innocents slaughtered by the Shade's orders. He saw still more corpses—whole villages of them—taken from life by the sorcerer's hand or word. There was no escape from the carnage that surrounded him. He wavered like a candle flame, unable to withstand the tide of evil. He prayed for someone to lift him out of the nightmare, but there was no one to guide him. If only he could remember what he was supposed to be: boy or man, villain or hero, Shade or Rider; all was jumbled together in a meaningless frenzy. He was lost, completely and utterly, in the roiling mass.

Suddenly a cluster of his own memories burst through the dismal cloud left by the Shade's malevolent mind. All the events since he had found Saphira's egg came to him in the cold light of revelation. His accomplishments and failures were displayed equally. He had lost much that was dear to him, yet fate had given him rare and great gifts; for the first time, he was proud of simply who he was. As if in response to his brief self-confidence, the Shade's smothering blackness assaulted him anew. His identity trailed into the void as uncertainty and fear consumed his perceptions. Who was he to think he could challenge the powers of Alagaësia and live?

He fought against the Shade's sinister thoughts, weakly at first, then more strongly. He whispered words of the ancient language and found they gave him enough strength to withstand the shadow blurring his mind. Though his defenses faltered dangerously, he slowly began to draw his shattered consciousness into a small bright shell around his core. Outside his mind he was aware of a pain so great it threatened to blot out his very life, but something—or someone—seemed to keep it at bay.

He was still too weak to clear his mind completely, but he was lucid enough to examine his experiences since Carvahall. Where would he go now . . . and who would show him the way? Without Brom, there was no one to guide or teach him.

Come to me.

He recoiled at the touch of another consciousness—one so vast and powerful it was like a mountain looming over him. This was who was blocking the pain, he realized. Like Arya's mind, music ran through this one: deep amber-gold chords that throbbed with magisterial melancholy.

Finally, he dared ask, Who . . . who are you?

One who would help. With a flicker of an unspoken thought, the Shade's influence was brushed aside like an unwanted cobweb. Freed from the oppressive weight, Eragon let his mind expand until he touched a barrier beyond which he could not pass. I have protected you as best I can, but you are so far away I can do no more than shield your sanity from the pain.

Again: Who are you to do this?

There was a low rumble. I am Osthato Chetowä, the Mourning Sage. And Togira Ikonoka, the Cripple Who Is Whole. Come to me, Eragon, for I have answers to all you ask. You will not be safe until you find me.

But how can I find you if I don't know where you are? he asked, despairing.

Trust Arya and go with her to Ellesméra—I will be there. I have waited many seasons, so do not delay or it may soon be too late. . . .

You are greater than you know, Eragon. Think of what you have done and rejoice, for you have rid the land of a great evil. You have wrought a deed no one else could. Many are in your debt.

The stranger was right; what he had accomplished was worthy of honor, of recognition. No matter what his trials might be in the future, he was no longer just a pawn in the game of power. He had transcended that and was something else, something more. He had become what Ajihad wanted: an authority independent of any king or leader.

He sensed approval as he reached that conclusion. You are learning, *said the Mourning Sage, drawing nearer. A vision passed from him to Eragon: a burst of color blossomed in his mind, resolving into a stooped figure dressed in white, standing on a sun-drenched stone cliff.* It is time for you to rest, Eragon. When you wake, do not speak of me to anyone, *said the figure kindly, face obscured by a silver nimbus.* Remember, you must go to the elves. Now, sleep. . . . *He raised a hand, as if in benediction, and peace crept through Eragon.*

His last thought was that Brom would have been proud of him.

494

"Wake," commanded the voice. "Awake, Eragon, for you have slept far too long." He stirred unwillingly, loath to listen. The warmth that surrounded him was too comfortable to leave. The voice sounded again. "Rise, Argetlam! You are needed!"

He reluctantly forced his eyes open and found himself on a long bed, swathed in soft blankets. Angela sat in a chair beside him, staring at his face intently. "How do you feel?" she asked.

Disoriented and confused, he let his eyes roam over the small room. "I . . . I don't know," he said, his mouth dry and sore.

"Then don't move. You should conserve your strength," said Angela, running a hand through her curly hair. Eragon saw that she still wore her flanged armor. Why was that? A fit of coughing made him dizzy, lightheaded, and ache all over. His feverish limbs felt heavy. Angela lifted a gilt horn from the floor and held it to his lips. "Here, drink."

Cool mead ran down his throat, refreshing him. Warmth

bloomed in his stomach and rose to his cheeks. He coughed again, which worsened his throbbing head. *How did I get here? There was a battle . . . we were losing . . . then Durza and . . .* "Saphira!" he exclaimed, sitting upright. He sagged back as his head swam and clenched his eyes, feeling sick. "What about Saphira? Is she all right? The Urgals were winning . . . she was falling. And Arya!"

"They lived," assured Angela, "and have been waiting for you to wake. Do you wish to see them?" He nodded feebly. Angela got up and threw open the door. Arya and Murtagh filed inside. Saphira snaked her head into the room after them, her body too big to fit through the doorway. Her chest vibrated as she hummed deeply, eyes sparkling.

Smiling, Eragon touched her thoughts with relief and gratitude. *It is good to see you well, little one,* she said tenderly.

And you too, but how—?

The others want to explain it, so I will let them.

You breathed fire! I saw you!

Yes, she said with pride.

He smiled weakly, still confused, then looked at Arya and Murtagh. Both of them were bandaged: Arya on her arm, Murtagh around his head. Murtagh grinned widely. "About time you were up. We've been sitting in the hall for hours."

"What . . . what happened?" asked Eragon.

Arya looked sad. But Murtagh crowed, "We won! It was incredible! When the Shade's spirits—if that's what they were—flew across Farthen Dûr, the Urgals ceased fighting to watch them go. It was as though they were released from a spell then, because their clans suddenly turned and attacked each other. Their entire army disintegrated within minutes. We routed them after that!"

"They're all dead?" asked Eragon.

Murtagh shook his head. "No, many of them escaped into the tunnels. The Varden and dwarves are busy ferreting them out right now, but it's going to take a while. I was helping until an Urgal banged me on the head and I was sent back here."

"They aren't going to lock you up again?"

His face grew sober. "No one really cares about that right now. A lot of Varden and dwarves were killed; the survivors are busy trying to recover from the battle. But at least you have cause to be happy. You're a hero! Everyone's talking about how you killed Durza. If it hadn't been for you, we would have lost."

Eragon was troubled by his words but pushed them away for later consideration. "Where were the Twins? They weren't where they were supposed to be—I couldn't contact them. I needed their help."

Murtagh shrugged. "I was told they bravely fought off a group of Urgals that broke into Tronjheim somewhere else. They were probably too busy to talk with you."

That seemed wrong for some reason, but Eragon could not decide why. He turned to Arya. Her large bright eyes had been fixed upon him the entire time. "How come you didn't crash? You and Saphira were . . ." His voice trailed off.

She said slowly, "When you warned Saphira of Durza, I was still trying to remove her damaged armor. By the time it was off, it was too late to slide down Vol Turin—you would have been captured before I reached the bottom. Besides, Durza would have killed you before letting me rescue you." Regret entered her voice, "So I did the one thing I could to distract him: I broke the star sapphire."

And I carried her down, added Saphira.

Eragon struggled to understand as another bout of lightheadedness made him close his eyes. "But why didn't any of the pieces hit you or me?"

"I didn't allow them to. When we were almost to the floor, I held them motionless in the air, then slowly lowered them to the floor—else they would have shattered into a thousand pieces and killed you," stated Arya simply. Her words betrayed the power within her.

Angela added sourly, "Yes, and it almost killed you as well. It's taken all of my skill to keep the two of you alive."

A twinge of unease shot through Eragon, matching the intensity of his throbbing head. *My back* . . . But he felt no bandages there. "How long have I been here?" he asked with trepidation.

"Only a day and a half," answered Angela. "You're lucky I was around, otherwise it would've taken you weeks to heal—if you had even lived." Alarmed, Eragon pushed the blankets off his torso and twisted around to feel his back. Angela caught his wrist with her small hand, worry reflected in her eyes. "Eragon . . . you have to understand, my power is not like yours or Arya's. It depends on the use of herbs and potions. There are limits to what I can do, especially with such a large—"

He yanked his hand out of her grip and reached back, fingers groping. The skin on his back was smooth and warm, flawless. Hard muscles flexed under his fingertips as he moved. He slid his hand toward the base of his neck and unexpectedly felt a hard bump about a half-inch wide. He followed it down his back with growing horror. Durza's blow had left him with a huge, ropy scar, stretching from his right shoulder to the opposite hip.

Pity showed on Arya's face as she murmured, "You have paid a terrible price for your deed, Eragon Shadeslayer."

Murtagh laughed harshly. "Yes. Now you're just like me."

Dismay filled Eragon, and he closed his eyes. He was disfigured. Then he remembered something from when he was unconscious . . . a figure in white who had helped him. A cripple who was whole— Togira Ikonoka. He had said, *Think of what you have done and rejoice, for you have rid the land of a great evil. You have wrought a deed no one else could. Many are in your debt. . . .*

Come to me Eragon, for I have answers to all you ask.

A measure of peace and satisfaction consoled Eragon.

I will come.

PRONUNCIATION

Ajihad—AH-zhi-hod

Alagaësia—al-uh-GAY-zee-uh

Arya—AR-ee-uh

Carvahall—CAR-vuh-hall

Dras-Leona—DRAHS-lee-OH-nuh

Du Weldenvarden—doo WELL-den-VAR-den

Eragon—EHR-uh-gahn

Farthen Dûr—FAR-then DURE (*dure* rhymes with *lure*)

Galbatorix—gal-buh-TOR-icks

Gil'ead—GILL-ee-id

Jeod—JODE (rhymes with *load*)

Murtagh—MUR-tag (*mur* rhymes with *purr*)

Ra'zac—RAA-zack

Saphira—suh-FEAR-uh

Shruikan—SHREW-kin

Teirm—TEERM

Tronjheim—TRONJ-heim

Vrael—VRAIL

Yazuac—YA-zoo-ack

Zar'roc—ZAR-rock

499

THE ANCIENT LANGUAGE

Note: As Eragon is not yet a master of the ancient language, his words and remarks were *not* translated literally, so as to save readers from his atrocious grammar. Quotations from other characters, however, have been left untouched.

Aí varden abr du Shur'tugalar gata vanta.—A warden of the Riders lacks passage.

Aiedail—the morning star

arget—silver

Argetlam—Silver Hand

Atra gülai un ilian tauthr ono un atra ono waíse skölir frá rauthr.—Let luck and happiness follow you and may you be shielded from misfortune.

500 breoal—family; house

brisingr—fire

Deloi moi!—Earth, change!

delois—a green-leafed plant with purple flowers

Domia abr Wyrda—Dominance of Fate (book)

dras—city

draumr kópa—dream stare

Du grind huildr!—Hold the gate!

"Du Silbena Datia"—"The Sighing Mists" (a poem song)

Du Súndavar Freohr—Death of the Shadows

Du Vrangr Gata—The Wandering Path

Du Weldenvarden—The Guarding Forest

Edoc'sil—Unconquerable

eitha—go; leave

Eka aí fricai un Shur'tugal!—I am a Rider and friend!

ethgrí—invoke

Fethrblaka, eka weohnata néiat haina ono. Blaka eom iet lam.—
    Bird, I will not harm you. Flap to my hand.

garjzla—light

Gath un reisa du rakr!—Unite and raise the mist!

gedwëy ignasia—shining palm

Gëuloth du knífr!—Dull the knife!

Helgrind—The Gates of Death

iet—my (informal)

Istalrí boetk!—Broad fire!

jierda—break; hit

Jierda theirra kalfis!—Break their calves!

Manin! Wyrda! Hugin!—Memory! Fate! Thought!

501

Moi stenr!—Stone, change!

Nagz reisa!—Blanket, rise!

Osthato Chetowä—the Mourning Sage

pömnuria—my (formal)

Ristvak'baen—Place of Sorrow (baen—used here and in
    Urû'baen, the capital of the Empire—is always pronounced
    bane and is an expression of great sadness/grief)

seithr—witch

Shur'tugal—Dragon Rider

Skulblaka, eka celöbra ono un mulabra ono un onr Shur'tugal né
    haina. Atra nosu waíse fricaya.—Dragon, I honor you and mean
    you and your Rider no harm. Let us be friends.

slytha—sleep

Stenr reisa!—Raise stone!

thrysta—thrust; compress

Thrysta deloi.—Compress the earth.

Thverr stenr un atra eka hórna!—Traverse stone and let me hear!

Togira Ikonoka—the Cripple Who Is Whole

tuatha du orothrim—tempering the fool's wisdom (level in Riders' training)

Varden—the Warders

vöndr—a thin, straight stick

Waíse heill!—Be healed!

Wiol pömnuria ilian.—For my happiness.

wyrda—fate

yawë—a bond of trust

THE DWARF LANGUAGE

Akh Guntéraz dorzâda!—For Guntéra's adoration!

Âz knurl deimi lanok.—Beware, the rock changes.

barzul—a curse; ill fate

Carkna bragha!—Great danger!

dûrgrimst—clan (literally, our hall/home)

Egraz Carn—Bald One

Farthen Dûr—Our Father

hírna—likeness; statue

Ilf carnz orodüm.—It is one's obligation/fate.

Ingietum—metalworkers; smiths

Isidar Mithrim—Star Sapphire

knurl—stone; rock

knurla—dwarf (literally, one of stone)

Kóstha-mérna—Foot Pool (a lake)

oeí—yes; affirmative

otho—faith

sheilven—cowards

Tronjheim—Helm of Giants

Vol Turin—The Endless Staircase

THE URGAL LANGUAGE

drajl—spawn of maggots

Ithrö Zhâda (Orthíad)—Rebel Doom

Kaz jtierl trazhid! Otrag bagh.—Do not attack! Circle him.

ushnark—father

503

ELDEST

INHERITANCE
BOOK TWO

As always, this book is for my family.
And also to my incredible fans. You made this adventure possible.
Sé onr sverdar sitja hvass!

CONTENTS

A TWIN DISASTER

The songs of the dead are the lamentations of the living.

So thought Eragon as he stepped over a twisted and hacked Urgal, listening to the keening of women who removed loved ones from the blood-muddied ground of Farthen Dûr. Behind him Saphira delicately skirted the corpse, her glittering blue scales the only color in the gloom that filled the hollow mountain.

It was three days since the Varden and dwarves had fought the Urgals for possession of Tronjheim, the mile-high, conical city nestled in the center of Farthen Dûr, but the battlefield was still strewn with carnage. The sheer number of bodies had stymied their attempts to bury the dead. In the distance, a mountainous fire glowed sullenly by Farthen Dûr's wall where the Urgals were being burned. No burial or honored resting place for them.

Since waking to find his wound healed by Angela, Eragon had tried three times to assist in the recovery effort. On each occasion he had been racked by terrible pains that seemed to explode from his spine. The healers gave him various potions to drink. Arya and Angela said that he was perfectly sound. Nevertheless, he hurt. Nor could Saphira help, only share his pain as it rebounded across their mental link.

Eragon ran a hand over his face and looked up at the stars showing through Farthen Dûr's distant top, which were smudged with sooty smoke from the pyre. *Three days.* Three days since he had killed Durza; three days since people began calling him Shadeslayer;

1

three days since the remnants of the sorcerer's consciousness had ravaged his mind and he had been saved by the mysterious Togira Ikonoka, the Cripple Who Is Whole. He had told no one about that vision but Saphira. Fighting Durza and the dark spirits that controlled him had transformed Eragon; although for better or for worse he was still unsure. He felt fragile, as if a sudden shock would shatter his reconstructed body and consciousness.

And now he had come to the site of the combat, driven by a morbid desire to see its aftermath. Upon arriving, he found nothing but the uncomfortable presence of death and decay, not the glory that heroic songs had led him to expect.

Before his uncle, Garrow, was slain by the Ra'zac months earlier, the brutality that Eragon had witnessed between the humans, dwarves, and Urgals would have destroyed him. Now it numbed him. He had realized, with Saphira's help, that the only way to stay rational amid such pain was to *do* things. Beyond that, he no longer believed that life possessed inherent meaning—not after seeing men torn apart by the Kull, a race of giant Urgals, and the ground a bed of thrashing limbs and the dirt so wet with blood it soaked through the soles of his boots. If any honor existed in war, he concluded, it was in fighting to protect others from harm.

He bent and plucked a tooth, a molar, from the dirt. Bouncing it on his palm, he and Saphira slowly made a circuit through the trampled plain. They stopped at its edge when they noticed Jörmundur—Ajihad's second in command in the Varden—hurrying toward them from Tronjheim. When he came near, Jörmundur bowed, a gesture Eragon knew he would never have made just days before.

"I'm glad I found you in time, Eragon." He clutched a parchment note in one hand. "Ajihad is returning, and he wants you to be there when he arrives. The others are already waiting for him by Tronjheim's west gate. We'll have to hurry to get there in time."

Eragon nodded and headed toward the gate, keeping a hand on Saphira. Ajihad had been gone most of the three days, hunting down Urgals who had managed to escape into the dwarf tunnels that honeycombed the stone beneath the Beor Mountains. The one time Eragon had seen him between expeditions, Ajihad was in a rage over discovering that his daughter, Nasuada, had disobeyed his orders to leave with the other women and children before the battle. Instead, she had secretly fought among the Varden's archers.

Murtagh and the Twins had accompanied Ajihad: the Twins because it was dangerous work and the Varden's leader needed the protection of their magical skills, and Murtagh because he was eager to continue proving that he bore the Varden no ill will. It surprised Eragon how much people's attitudes toward Murtagh had changed, considering that Murtagh's father was the Dragon Rider Morzan, who had betrayed the Riders to Galbatorix. Even though Murtagh despised his father and was loyal to Eragon, the Varden had not trusted him. But now, no one was willing to waste energy on a petty hate when so much work remained. Eragon missed talking with Murtagh and looked forward to discussing all that had happened, once he returned.

As Eragon and Saphira rounded Tronjheim, a small group became visible in the pool of lantern light before the timber gate. Among them were Orik—the dwarf shifting impatiently on his stout legs—and Arya. The white bandage around her upper arm gleamed in the darkness, reflecting a faint highlight onto the bottom of her hair. Eragon felt a strange thrill, as he always did when he saw the elf. She looked at him and Saphira, green eyes flashing, then continued watching for Ajihad.

By breaking Isidar Mithrim—the great star sapphire that was sixty feet across and carved in the shape of a rose—Arya had allowed Eragon to kill Durza and so win the battle. Still, the dwarves were furious with her for destroying their most prized treasure. They refused to move the sapphire's remains, leaving them in a massive circle inside Tronjheim's central chamber. Eragon had walked through the splintered wreckage and shared the dwarves' sorrow for all the lost beauty.

He and Saphira stopped by Orik and looked out at the empty

land that surrounded Tronjheim, extending to Farthen Dûr's base five miles away in each direction. "Where will Ajihad come from?" asked Eragon.

Orik pointed at a cluster of lanterns staked around a large tunnel opening a couple of miles away. "He should be here soon."

Eragon waited patiently with the others, answering comments directed at him but preferring to speak with Saphira in the peace of his mind. The quiet that filled Farthen Dûr suited him.

Half an hour passed before motion flickered in the distant tunnel. A group of ten men climbed out onto the ground, then turned and helped up as many dwarves. One of the men—Eragon assumed it was Ajihad—raised a hand, and the warriors assembled behind him in two straight lines. At a signal, the formation marched proudly toward Tronjheim.

Before they went more than five yards, the tunnel behind them swarmed with a flurry of activity as more figures jumped out. Eragon squinted, unable to see clearly from so far away.

Those are Urgals! exclaimed Saphira, her body tensing like a drawn bowstring.

Eragon did not question her. "Urgals!" he cried, and leaped onto Saphira, berating himself for leaving his sword, Zar'roc, in his room. No one had expected an attack now that the Urgal army had been driven away.

His wound twinged as Saphira lifted her azure wings, then drove them down and jumped forward, gaining speed and altitude each second. Below them, Arya ran toward the tunnel, nearly keeping apace with Saphira. Orik trailed her with several men, while Jörmundur sprinted back toward the barracks.

Eragon was forced to watch helplessly as the Urgals fell on the rear of Ajihad's warriors; he could not work magic over such a distance. The monsters had the advantage of surprise and quickly cut down four men, forcing the rest of the warriors, men and dwarves alike, to cluster around Ajihad in an attempt to protect him. Swords and axes clashed as the groups pressed together. Light

4

flashed from one of the Twins, and an Urgal fell, clutching the stump of his severed arm.

For a minute, it seemed the defenders would be able to resist the Urgals, but then a swirl of motion disturbed the air, like a faint band of mist wrapping itself around the combatants. When it cleared, only four warriors were standing: Ajihad, the Twins, and Murtagh. The Urgals converged on them, blocking Eragon's view as he stared with rising horror and fear.

No! No! No!

Before Saphira could reach the fight, the knot of Urgals streamed back to the tunnel and scrambled underground, leaving only prone forms behind.

The moment Saphira touched down, Eragon vaulted off, then faltered, overcome by grief and anger. *I can't do this*. It reminded him too much of when he had returned to the farm to find his uncle Garrow dying. Fighting back his dread with every step, he began to search for survivors.

The site was eerily similar to the battlefield he had inspected earlier, except that here the blood was fresh.

In the center of the massacre lay Ajihad, his breastplate rent with numerous gashes, surrounded by five Urgals he had slain. His breath still came in ragged gasps. Eragon knelt by him and lowered his face so his tears would not land on the leader's ruined chest. No one could heal such wounds. Running up to them, Arya paused and stopped, her face transformed with sorrow when she saw that Ajihad could not be saved.

"Eragon." The name slipped from Ajihad's lips—no more than a whisper.

"Yes, I am here."

"Listen to me, Eragon. . . . I have one last command for you." Eragon leaned closer to catch the dying man's words. "You must promise me something: promise that you . . . won't let the Varden fall into chaos. They are the only hope for resisting the Empire. . . . They must be kept strong. You must promise me."

5

"I promise."

"Then peace be with you, Eragon Shadeslayer. . . ." With his last breath, Ajihad closed his eyes, setting his noble face in repose, and died.

Eragon bowed his head. He had trouble breathing past the lump in his throat, which was so hard it hurt. Arya blessed Ajihad in a ripple of the ancient language, then said in her musical voice, "Alas, his death will cause much strife. He is right, you must do all you can to avert a struggle for power. I will assist where possible."

Unwilling to speak, Eragon gazed at the rest of the bodies. He would have given anything to be elsewhere. Saphira nosed one of the Urgals and said, *This should not have happened. It is an evil doing, and all the worse for coming when we should be safe and victorious.* She examined another body, then swung her head around. *Where are the Twins and Murtagh? They're not among the dead.*

Eragon scanned the corpses. *You're right!* Elation surged within him as he hurried to the tunnel's mouth. There pools of thickening blood filled the hollows in the worn marble steps like a series of black mirrors, glossy and oval, as if several torn bodies had been dragged down them. *The Urgals must have taken them! But why? They don't keep prisoners or hostages.* Despair instantly returned. *It doesn't matter. We can't pursue them without reinforcements; you wouldn't even fit through the opening.*

They may still be alive. Would you abandon them?

What do you expect me to do? The dwarf tunnels are an endless maze! I would only get lost. And I couldn't catch Urgals on foot, though Arya might be able to.

Then ask her to.

Arya! Eragon hesitated, torn between his desire for action and his loathing to put her in danger. Still, if any one person in the Varden could handle the Urgals, it was she. With a groan, he explained what they had found.

Arya's slanted eyebrows met in a frown. "It makes no sense."

"Will you pursue them?"

6

She stared at him for a heavy moment. "Wiol ono." For you. Then she bounded forward, sword flashing in her hand as she dove into the earth's belly.

Burning with frustration, Eragon settled cross-legged by Ajihad, keeping watch over the body. He could barely assimilate the fact that Ajihad was dead and Murtagh missing. *Murtagh*. Son of one of the Forsworn—the thirteen Riders who had helped Galbatorix destroy their order and anoint himself king of Alagaësia—and Eragon's friend. At times Eragon had wished Murtagh gone, but now that he had been forcibly removed, the loss left an unexpected void. He sat motionless as Orik approached with the men.

When Orik saw Ajihad, he stamped his feet and swore in Dwarvish, swinging his ax into the body of an Urgal. The men only stood in shock. Rubbing a pinch of dirt between his callused hands, the dwarf growled, "Ah, now a hornet's nest has broken; we'll have no peace among the Varden after this. *Barzûln*, but this makes things complicated. Were you in time to hear his last words?"

Eragon glanced at Saphira. "They must wait for the right person before I'll repeat them."

"I see. And where'd be Arya?"

Eragon pointed.

Orik swore again, then shook his head and sat on his heels.

Jörmundur soon arrived with twelve ranks of six warriors each. He motioned for them to wait outside the radius of bodies while he proceeded onward alone. He bent and touched Ajihad on the shoulder. "How can fate be this cruel, my old friend? I would have been here sooner if not for the size of this cursed mountain, and then you might have been saved. Instead, we are wounded at the height of our triumph."

Eragon softly told him about Arya and the disappearance of the Twins and Murtagh.

"She should not have gone," said Jörmundur, straightening, "but we can do naught about it now. Guards will be posted here, but it will be at least an hour before dwarf guides can be found for another expedition into the tunnels."

"I'd be willing to lead it," offered Orik.

Jörmundur looked back at Tronjheim, his gaze distant. "No, Hrothgar will need you now; someone else will have to go. I'm sorry, Eragon, but everyone important *must* stay here until Ajihad's successor is chosen. Arya will have to fend for herself. . . . We could not overtake her anyway."

Eragon nodded, accepting the inevitable.

Jörmundur swept his gaze around before saying so all could hear, "Ajihad has died a warrior's death! Look, he slew five Urgals where a lesser man might have been overwhelmed by one. We will give him every honor and hope his spirit pleases the gods. Bear him and our companions back to Tronjheim on your shields . . . and do not be ashamed to let your tears be seen, for this is a day of sorrow that all will remember. May we soon have the privilege of sheathing our blades in the monsters who have slain our leader!"

As one, the warriors knelt, baring their heads in homage to Ajihad. Then they stood and reverently lifted him on their shields so he lay between their shoulders. Already many of the Varden wept, tears flowing into beards, yet they did not disgrace their duty and allow Ajihad to fall. With solemn steps, they marched back to Tronjheim, Saphira and Eragon in the middle of the procession.

THE COUNCIL OF ELDERS

Eragon roused himself and rolled to the edge of the bed, looking about the room, which was suffused with the dim glow of a shuttered lantern. He sat and watched Saphira sleep. Her muscled sides expanded and contracted as the great bellows of her lungs forced air through her scaled nostrils. Eragon thought of the raging inferno that she could now summon at will and send roaring out of her maw. It was an awesome sight when flames hot enough to melt metal rushed past her tongue and ivory teeth without harming them. Since she first breathed fire during his fight with Durza—while plunging toward them from the top of Tronjheim—Saphira had been insufferably proud of her new talent. She was constantly releasing little jets of flame, and she took every opportunity to light objects ablaze.

Because Isidar Mithrim was shattered, Eragon and Saphira had been unable to remain in the dragonhold above it. The dwarves had given them quarters in an old guardroom on Tronjheim's bottom level. It was a large room, but with a low ceiling and dark walls.

Anguish gripped Eragon as he remembered the events of the previous day. Tears filled his eyes, spilling over, and he caught one on his hand. They had heard nothing from Arya until late that evening, when she emerged from the tunnel, weary and footsore. Despite her best efforts—and all her magic—the Urgals had escaped her. "I found these," she said. Then she revealed one of the Twins' purple robes, torn and bloodied, and Murtagh's tunic and both his leather gauntlets. "They were strewn along the edge of a black chasm, the bottom of which no tunnel reaches. The Urgals must have stolen their armor and weapons and thrown the bodies into the pit. I scryed both Murtagh and the Twins, and saw naught but the shadows of the abyss." Her eyes met Eragon's. "I'm sorry; they are gone."

Now, in the confines of his mind, Eragon mourned Murtagh. It was a dreadful, creeping feeling of loss and horror made worse by the fact that he had grown ever more familiar with it in past months.

As he stared at the tear in his hand—a small, glistening dome—he decided to scry the three men himself. He knew it was a desperate and futile prospect, but he had to try in order to convince himself that Murtagh was really gone. Even so, he was uncertain if he wanted to succeed where Arya had failed, if it would make him feel any better to catch a glimpse of Murtagh lying broken at the base of a cliff deep below Farthen Dûr.

He whispered, "Draumr kópa." Darkness enveloped the liquid, turning it into a small dot of night on his silver palm. Movement flickered through it, like the swish of a bird across a clouded moon . . . then nothing.

Another tear joined the first.

Eragon took a deep breath, leaned back, and let calm settle over him. Since recovering from Durza's wound, he had realized—humbling as it was—that he had prevailed only through sheer luck. *If I ever face another Shade, or the Ra'zac, or Galbatorix, I must be stronger if I expect to win. Brom could have taught me more, I know he could have. But without him, I have but one choice: the elves.*

Saphira's breathing quickened, and she opened her eyes, yawning expansively. *Good morning, little one.*

Is it? He looked down and leaned on his hands, compressing the mattress. *It's terrible . . . Murtagh and Ajihad . . . Why didn't sentries in the tunnels warn us of the Urgals? They shouldn't have been able to trail Ajihad's group without being noticed. . . . Arya was right, it doesn't make sense.*

We may never know the truth, said Saphira gently. She stood, wings brushing the ceiling. *You need to eat, then we must discover what the Varden are planning. We can't waste time; a new leader could be chosen within hours.*

Eragon agreed, thinking of how they had left everyone yesterday: Orik rushing off to give King Hrothgar the tidings, Jörmundur taking Ajihad's body to a place where it would rest until the funeral, and Arya, who stood alone and watched the goings-on.

Eragon rose and strapped on Zar'roc and his bow, then bent and lifted Snowfire's saddle. A line of pain sheared through his torso, driving him to the floor, where he writhed, scrabbling at his back. It felt like he was being sawed in half. Saphira growled as the ripping sensation reached her. She tried to soothe him with her own mind but was unable to alleviate his suffering. Her tail instinctually lifted, as if to fight.

It took minutes before the fit subsided and the last throb faded away, leaving Eragon gasping. Sweat drenched his face, making his hair stick and his eyes sting. He reached back and gingerly fingered the top of his scar. It was hot and inflamed and sensitive to touch. Saphira lowered her nose and touched him on the arm. *Oh, little one. . . .*

It was worse this time, he said, staggering upright. She let him lean against her as he wiped off the sweat with a rag, then he tentatively stepped toward the door.

Are you strong enough to go?

We have to. We're obliged as dragon and Rider to make a public choice regarding the next head of the Varden, and perhaps even influence the selection. I won't ignore the strength of our position; we now wield great authority within the Varden. At least the Twins aren't here to grab the position for themselves. That's the only good in the situation.

Very well, but Durza should suffer a thousand years of torture for what he did to you.

He grunted. *Just stay close to me.*

Together they made their way through Tronjheim, toward the nearest kitchen. In the corridors and hallways, people stopped and bowed to them, murmuring "Argetlam" or "Shadeslayer." Even dwarves made the motions, though not as often. Eragon was struck by the somber, haunted expressions of the humans and the dark clothing they wore to display their sadness. Many women were dressed entirely in black, lace veils covering their faces.

In the kitchen, Eragon brought a stone platter of food to a low table. Saphira watched him carefully in case he should have another attack. Several people tried to approach him, but she lifted a lip and growled, sending them scurrying away. Eragon picked at his food and pretended to ignore the disturbances. Finally, trying to divert his thoughts from Murtagh, he asked, *Who do you think has the means to take control of the Varden now that Ajihad and the Twins are gone?*

She hesitated. *It's possible you could, if Ajihad's last words were interpreted as a blessing to secure the leadership. Almost no one would oppose you. However, that does not seem a wise path to take. I see only trouble in that direction.*

I agree. Besides, Arya wouldn't approve, and she could be a dangerous enemy. Elves can't lie in the ancient language, but they have no such inhibition in ours—she could deny that Ajihad ever uttered those words if it served her purposes. No, I don't want the position. . . . What about Jörmundur?

Ajihad called him his right-hand man. Unfortunately, we know little about him or the Varden's other leaders. Such a short time has passed since we came here. We will have to make our judgment on our feelings and impressions, without the benefit of history.

Eragon pushed his fish around a lump of mashed tubers. *Don't forget Hrothgar and the dwarf clans; they won't be quiet in this. Except for Arya, the elves have no say in the succession—a decision will be made before word of this even reaches them. But the dwarves can't be—won't be—ignored. Hrothgar favors the Varden, but if enough clans oppose him, he might be maneuvered into backing someone unsuited for the command.*

And who might that be?

A person easily manipulated. He closed his eyes and leaned back. *It could be anyone in Farthen Dûr, anyone at all.*

For a long while, they both considered the issues facing them. Then Saphira said, *Eragon, there is someone here to see you. I can't scare him away.*

Eh? He cracked his eyes open, squinting as they adjusted to the light. A pale-looking youth stood by the table. The boy eyed Saphira like he was afraid she would try to eat him. "What is it?" asked Eragon, not unkindly.

The boy started, flustered, then bowed. "You have been summoned, Argetlam, to speak before the Council of Elders."

"Who are they?"

The question confused the boy even more. "The—the council is . . . are . . . people we—that is, the Varden—choose to speak on our behalf to Ajihad. They were his trusted advisers, and now they wish to see you. It is a great honor!" He finished with a quick smile.

"Are you to lead me to them?"

"Yes, I am."

Saphira looked at Eragon questioningly. He shrugged and left the uneaten food, motioning for the boy to show the way. As they walked, the boy admired Zar'roc with bright eyes, then looked down shyly.

"What are you called?" asked Eragon.

"Jarsha, sir."

"That's a good name. You carried your message well; you should be proud." Jarsha beamed and bounced forward.

They reached a convex stone door, which Jarsha pushed open. The room inside was circular, with a sky blue dome decorated with constellations. A round marble table, inlaid with the crest of Dûrgrimst Ingeitum—an upright hammer ringed by twelve stars—stood in the center of the chamber. Seated there were Jörmundur and two other men, one tall and one broad; a woman with pinched lips, close-set eyes, and elaborately painted cheeks; and a second woman with an immense pile of gray hair above a matronly face, belied by a dagger hilt peeking out of the vast hills of her bodice.

"You may go," said Jörmundur to Jarsha, who quickly bowed and left.

Conscious that he was being watched, Eragon surveyed the room, then seated himself in the middle of a swath of empty chairs, so that the council members were forced to turn in their seats in order to look at him. Saphira hunkered directly behind him; he could feel her hot breath on the top of his head.

Jörmundur got halfway up to make a slight bow, then reseated himself. "Thank you for coming, Eragon, even though you have suffered your own loss. This is Umérth," the tall man; "Falberd," the broad one; "and Sabrae and Elessari," the two women.

Eragon inclined his head, then asked, "And what of the Twins, were they part of this council?"

Sabrae shook her head sharply and tapped a long fingernail on the table. "They had naught to do with us. They were slime—worse than slime—leeches that worked only for their own benefit. They had no desire to serve the Varden. Thus, they had no place in this council." Eragon could smell her perfume all the way on the other side of the table; it was thick and oily, like a rotting flower. He hid a smile at the thought.

"Enough. We're not here to discuss the Twins," said Jörmundur. "We face a crisis that must be dealt with quickly and effectively. If we don't choose Ajihad's successor, someone else will. Hrothgar has already contacted us to convey his condolences. While he was more than courteous, he is sure to be forming his own plans even as we speak. We must also consider Du Vrangr Gata, the magic users. Most of them are loyal to the Varden, but it's difficult to predict their actions even in the best of times. They might decide to oppose our authority for their own advantage. That is why we need your assistance, Eragon, to provide the legitimacy required by whoever is to take Ajihad's place."

Falberd heaved himself up, planting his meaty hands on the

table. "The five of us have already decided whom to support. There is no doubt among us that it is the right person. But," he raised a thick finger, "before we reveal who it is, you must give us your word of honor that whether you agree or disagree with us, nothing of our discussion will leave this room."

Why would they want that? Eragon asked Saphira.

I don't know, she said, snorting. *It might be a trap. . . . It's a gamble you'll have to take. Remember, though, they haven't asked me to pledge anything. I can always tell Arya what they say, if needed. Silly of them, forgetting that I'm as intelligent as any human.*

Pleased with the thought, Eragon said, "Very well, you have my word. Now, who do you want to lead the Varden?"

"Nasuada."

Surprised, Eragon dropped his gaze, thinking quickly. He had not considered Nasuada for the succession because of her youth—she was just a few years older than Eragon. No real reason existed, of course, for her not to lead, but why would the Council of Elders want her to? How would they benefit? He remembered Brom's advice and tried to examine the issue from every angle, knowing that he had to decide swiftly.

Nasuada has steel in her, observed Saphira. *She would be like her father.*

Maybe, but what's their reason for picking her?

To gain time, Eragon asked, "Why not you, Jörmundur? Ajihad called you his right-hand man. Doesn't that mean you should take his place now that he's gone?"

A current of unease ran through the council: Sabrae sat even straighter, hands clasped before her; Umérth and Falberd glanced at each other darkly, while Elessari just smiled, the dagger hilt jiggling on her chest.

"Because," said Jörmundur, selecting his words with care, "Ajihad was speaking of military matters then, nothing more. Also, I am a member of this council, which only has power because we support one another. It would be foolish and dangerous for one of

15

us to raise himself above the rest." The council relaxed as he finished, and Elessari patted Jörmundur on the forearm.

Ha! exclaimed Saphira. *He probably would have taken power if it were possible to force the others to back him. Just look how they eye him. He's like a wolf in their midst.*

A wolf in a pack of jackals, perhaps.

"Does Nasuada have enough experience?" inquired Eragon.

Elessari pressed herself against the table's edge as she leaned forward. "I had already been here for seven years when Ajihad joined the Varden. I've watched Nasuada grow up from a darling girl to the woman she is. A trifle light-headed occasionally, but a good figure to lead the Varden. The people will love her. Now I," she patted herself affectionately on the bosom, "and my friends will be here to guide her through these troubled times. She will never be without someone to show her the way. Inexperience should be no barrier to her taking her rightful position."

Understanding flooded Eragon. *They want a puppet!*

"Ajihad's funeral will be held in two days," broke in Umérth. "Directly afterward, we plan to appoint Nasuada as our new leader. We have yet to ask her, but she will surely agree. We want you to be present at the appointing—no one, not even Hrothgar, can complain about it then—and to swear fealty to the Varden. That will give back the confidence Ajihad's death has stolen from the people, and prevent anyone from trying to splinter this organization."

Fealty!

Saphira quickly touched Eragon's mind. *Notice, they don't want you to swear to Nasuada—just to the Varden.*

Yes, and they want to be the ones to appoint Nasuada, which would indicate that the council is more powerful than she. They could have asked Arya or us to appoint her, but that would mean acknowledging whoever did it as above everyone in the Varden. This way, they assert their superiority over Nasuada, gain control over us through fealty, and also get the benefit of having a Rider endorse Nasuada in public.

16

"What happens," he asked, "if I decide not to accept your offer?"

"Offer?" Falberd asked, seeming puzzled. "Why, nothing, of course. Only it would be a terrible slight if you're not present when Nasuada is chosen. If the hero of the battle of Farthen Dûr ignores her, what can she think but that a Rider has spited her and found the Varden unworthy to serve? Who could bear such a shame?"

The message could have been no clearer. Eragon clenched Zar'roc's pommel under the table, yearning to scream that it was unnecessary to force him to support the Varden, that he would have done it anyway. Now, however, he instinctively wanted to rebel, to elude the shackles they were trying to place on him. "Since Riders are so highly thought of, I could decide that my efforts would be best spent guiding the Varden myself."

The mood in the room hardened. "That would be unwise," stated Sabrae.

Eragon combed his mind for a way to escape the situation. *With Ajihad gone,* said Saphira, *it may be impossible to remain independent of every group, as he wanted us to. We cannot anger the Varden, and if this council is to control it once Nasuada is in place, then we must appease them. Remember, they act as much out of self-preservation as we do.*

But what will they want us to do once we are in their grasp? Will they respect the Varden's pact with the elves and send us to Ellesméra for training, or command otherwise? Jörmundur strikes me as an honorable man, but the rest of the council? I can't tell.

Saphira brushed the top of his head with her jaw. *Agree to be at this ceremony with Nasuada; that much I think we must do. As for swearing fealty, see if you can avoid acquiescing. Perhaps something will occur between now and then that will change our position . . . Arya may have a solution.*

Without warning, Eragon nodded and said, "As you wish; I shall attend Nasuada's appointment."

Jörmundur looked relieved. "Good, good. Then we have only one more matter to deal with before you go: Nasuada's acceptance.

17

There's no reason to delay, with all of us here. I'll send for her immediately. And Arya too—we need the elves' approval before making this decision public. It shouldn't be difficult to procure; Arya cannot go against our council *and* you, Eragon. She will have to agree with our judgment."

"Wait," commanded Elessari, a steely glint in her eyes. "Your word, though, Rider. Will you give it in fealty at the ceremony?"

"Yes, you must do that," agreed Falberd. "The Varden would be disgraced if we couldn't provide you every protection."

A nice way to put it!

It was worth a try, said Saphira. *I fear you have no choice now.*

They wouldn't dare harm us if I refused.

No, but they could cause us no end of grief. It is not for my own sake that I say accept, but for yours. Many dangers exist that I cannot protect you from, Eragon. With Galbatorix set against us, you need allies, not enemies, around you. We cannot afford to contend with both the Empire and the Varden.

Finally, "I'll give it." All around the table were signs of relaxation—even a poorly concealed sigh from Umérth. *They're afraid of us!*

As well they should be, sniped Saphira.

Jörmundur called for Jarsha, and with a few words sent the boy scampering off for Nasuada and Arya. While he was gone, the conversation fell into an uncomfortable silence. Eragon ignored the council, focusing instead on working a way out of his dilemma. None sprang to mind.

When the door opened again, everyone turned expectantly. First came Nasuada, chin held high and eyes steady. Her embroidered gown was the deepest shade of black, deeper even than her skin, broken only by a slash of royal purple that stretched from shoulder to hip. Behind her was Arya, her stride as lithe and smooth as a cat's, and an openly awestruck Jarsha.

The boy was dismissed, then Jörmundur helped Nasuada into a seat. Eragon hastened to do the same for Arya, but she ignored the proffered chair and stood at a distance from the table. *Saphira,* he said, *let her know all that's happened. I have a feeling the council won't inform her that they've compelled me to give the Varden my loyalty.*

"Arya," acknowledged Jörmundur with a nod, then concentrated on Nasuada. "Nasuada, Daughter of Ajihad, the Council of Elders wishes to formally extend its deepest condolences for the loss you, more than anyone else, have suffered. . . ." In a lower voice, he added, "You have our personal sympathies as well. We all know what it is like to have a family member killed by the Empire."

"Thank you," murmured Nasuada, lowering her almond eyes. She sat, shy and demure, and with an air of vulnerability that made Eragon want to comfort her. Her demeanor was tragically different from that of the energetic young woman who had visited him and Saphira in the dragonhold before the battle.

"Although this is your time of mourning, a quandary exists that you must resolve. This council cannot lead the Varden. And someone must replace your father after the funeral. We ask that you receive the position. As his heir, it is rightfully yours—the Varden expect it of you."

Nasuada bowed her head with shining eyes. Grief was plain in her voice when she said, "I never thought I would be called upon to take my father's place so young. Yet . . . if you insist it is my duty . . . I will embrace the office."

Truth Among Friends

The Council of Elders beamed with triumph, pleased that Nasuada had done what they wanted. "We do insist," said Jörmundur, "for your own good and the good of the Varden." The rest of the elders added their expressions of support, which Nasuada accepted with sad smiles. Sabrae threw an angry glance at Eragon when he did not join in.

Throughout the exchange, Eragon watched Arya for any reaction to either his news or the council's announcement. Neither revelation caused her inscrutable expression to change. However, Saphira told him, *She wishes to talk with us afterward.*

Before Eragon could reply, Falberd turned to Arya. "Will the elves find this agreeable?"

She stared at Falberd until the man fidgeted under her piercing gaze, then lifted an eyebrow. "I cannot speak for my queen, but I find nothing objectionable to it. Nasuada has my blessing."

How could she find it otherwise, knowing what we've told her? thought Eragon bitterly. *We're all backed into corners.*

Arya's remark obviously pleased the council. Nasuada thanked her and asked Jörmundur, "Is there anything else that must be discussed? For I am weary."

Jörmundur shook his head. "We will make all the arrangements. I promise you won't be troubled until the funeral."

"Again, thank you. Would you leave me now? I need time to consider how best to honor my father and serve the Varden. You have given me much to ponder." Nasuada splayed her delicate fingers on the dark cloth on her lap.

Umérth looked like he was going to protest at the council being dismissed, but Falberd waved a hand, silencing him. "Of course, whatever will give you peace. If you need help, we are ready and willing to serve." Gesturing for the rest of them to follow, he swept past Arya to the door.

"Eragon, will you please stay?"

Startled, Eragon lowered himself back into his chair, ignoring alert looks from the councilors. Falberd lingered by the door, suddenly reluctant to depart, then slowly went out. Arya was the last to go. Before she closed the door, she looked at Eragon, her eyes revealing worry and apprehension that had been concealed before.

Nasuada sat partially turned away from Eragon and Saphira. "So we meet again, Rider. You haven't greeted me. Have I offended you?"

"No, Nasuada; I was reluctant to speak for fear of being rude or foolish. Current circumstances are unkind to hasty statements." Paranoia that they might be eavesdropped on gripped him. Reaching through the barrier in his mind, he delved into the magic and intoned: "Atra nosu waíse vardo fra eld hórnya. . . . There, now we may speak without being overheard by man, dwarf, or elf."

Nasuada's posture softened. "Thank you, Eragon. You don't know what a gift that is." Her words were stronger and more self-assured than before.

Behind Eragon's chair, Saphira stirred, then carefully made her way around the table to stand before Nasuada. She lowered her great head until one sapphire eye met Nasuada's black ones. The dragon stared at her for a full minute before snorting softly and straightening. *Tell her,* said Saphira, *that I grieve for her and her loss. Also that her strength must become the Varden's when she assumes Ajihad's mantle. They will need a sure guide.*

Eragon repeated the words, adding, "Ajihad was a great man— his name will always be remembered. . . . There is something I must

21

tell you. Before Ajihad died, he charged me, commanded me, to keep the Varden from falling into chaos. Those were his last words. Arya heard them as well.

"I was going to keep what he said a secret because of the implications, but you have a right to know. I'm not sure what Ajihad meant, nor exactly what he wanted, but I am certain of this: I will always defend the Varden with my powers. I wanted you to understand that, and that I've no desire to usurp the Varden's leadership."

Nasuada laughed brittlely. "But that leadership isn't to be me, is it?" Her reserve had vanished, leaving behind only composure and determination. "I know why you were here before me and what the council is trying to do. Do you think that in the years I served my father, we never planned for this eventuality? I expected the council to do exactly what it did. And now everything is in place for me to take command of the Varden."

"You have no intention of letting them rule you," said Eragon with wonder.

"No. Continue to keep Ajihad's instruction secret. It would be unwise to bandy it about, as people might take it to mean that he wanted you to succeed him, and that would undermine my authority and destabilize the Varden. He said what he thought he had to in order to protect the Varden. I would have done the same. My father . . ." She faltered briefly. "My father's work will not go unfinished, even if it takes me to the grave. That is what *I* want you, as a Rider, to understand. All of Ajihad's plans, all his strategies and goals, they are mine now. I will not fail him by being weak. The Empire *will* be brought down, Galbatorix *will* be dethroned, and the rightful government *will* be raised."

By the time she finished, a tear ran down her cheek. Eragon stared, appreciating how difficult her position was and recognizing a depth of character he had not perceived before. "And what of me, Nasuada? What shall I do in the Varden?"

She looked directly into his eyes. "You can do whatever you want. The council members are fools if they think to control you.

You are a hero to the Varden and the dwarves, and even the elves will hail your victory over Durza when they hear of it. If you go against the council or me, we will be forced to yield, for the people will support you wholeheartedly. Right now, you are the most powerful person in the Varden. However, if you accept my leadership, I will continue the path laid down by Ajihad: you will go with Arya to the elves, be instructed there, then return to the Varden."

Why is she so honest with us? wondered Eragon. *If she's right, could we have refused the council's demands?*

Saphira took a moment to answer. *Either way, it's too late. You have already agreed to their requests. I think Nasuada is honest because your spell lets her be, and also because she hopes to win our loyalty from the elders.*

An idea suddenly came to Eragon, but before sharing it, he asked, *Can we trust her to hold to what she's said? This is very important.*

Yes, said Saphira. *She spoke with her heart.*

Then Eragon shared his proposal with Saphira. She consented, so he drew Zar'roc and walked to Nasuada. He saw a flash of fear as he approached; her gaze darted toward the door, and she slipped a hand into a fold in her dress and grasped something. Eragon stopped before her, then knelt, Zar'roc flat in his hands.

"Nasuada, Saphira and I have been here for only a short while. But in that time we came to respect Ajihad, and now, in turn, you. You fought under Farthen Dûr when others fled, including the two women of the council, and have treated us openly instead of with deception. Therefore, I offer you my blade . . . and my fealty as a Rider."

Eragon uttered the pronouncement with a sense of finality, knowing he would never have mouthed it before the battle. Seeing so many men fall and die around him had altered his perspective. Resisting the Empire was no longer something he did for himself, but for the Varden and all the people still trapped under Galbatorix's rule. However long it would take, he had dedicated himself to that task. For the time being, the best thing he could do was serve.

Still, he and Saphira were taking a terrible risk in pledging themselves to Nasuada. The council could not object because all Eragon had said was that he would swear fealty, but not to whom. Even so, he and Saphira had no guarantee that Nasuada would make a good leader. *It's better to be sworn to an honest fool than to a lying scholar,* decided Eragon.

Surprise flitted across Nasuada's face. She grasped Zar'roc's hilt and lifted it—staring at its crimson blade—then placed the tip on Eragon's head. "I do accept your fealty with honor, Rider, as you accept all the responsibilities accompanying the station. Rise as my vassal and take your sword."

Eragon did as he was bidden. He said, "Now I can tell you openly as my master, the council made me agree to swear to the Varden once you were appointed. This was the only way Saphira and I could circumvent them."

Nasuada laughed with genuine delight. "Ah, I see you have already learned how to play our game. Very well, as my newest and only vassal, will you agree to give your fealty to me again—in public, when the council expects your vow?"

"Of course."

"Good, that will take care of the council. Now, until then, leave me. I have much planning to do, and I must prepare for the funeral. . . . Remember, Eragon, the bond we have just created is equally binding; I am as responsible for your actions as you are required to serve me. Do not dishonor me."

"Nor you I."

Nasuada paused, then gazed into his eyes and added in a gentler tone: "You have my condolences, Eragon. I realize that others beside myself have cause for sorrow; while I have lost my father, you have also lost a friend. I liked Murtagh a great deal and it saddens me that he is gone. . . . Goodbye, Eragon."

Eragon nodded, a bitter taste in his mouth, and left the room with Saphira. The hallway outside was empty along its gray length.

Eragon put his hands on his hips, tilted back his head, and exhaled. The day had barely begun, yet he was already exhausted by all the emotions that had flooded through him.

Saphira nosed him and said, *This way.* Without further explanation, she headed down the right side of the tunnel. Her polished claws clicked on the hard floor.

Eragon frowned, but followed her. *Where are we going?* No answer. *Saphira, please.* She just flicked her tail. Resigned to wait, he said instead, *Things have certainly changed for us. I never know what to expect from one day to the next—except sorrow and bloodshed.*

All is not bad, she reproached. *We have won a great victory. It should be celebrated, not mourned.*

It doesn't help, having to deal with this other nonsense.

She snorted angrily. A thin line of fire shot from her nostrils, singeing Eragon's shoulder. He jumped back with a yelp, biting back a string of curses. *Oops,* said Saphira, shaking her head to clear the smoke.

Oops! You nearly roasted my side!

I didn't expect it to happen. I keep forgetting that fire will come out if I'm not careful. Imagine that every time you raised your arm, lightning struck the ground. It would be easy to make a careless motion and destroy something unintentionally.

You're right. . . . Sorry I growled at you.

Her bony eyelid clicked as she winked at him. *No matter. The point I was trying to make is that even Nasuada can't force you to do anything.*

But I gave my word as a Rider!

Maybe so, but if I must break it to keep you safe, or to do the right thing, I will not hesitate. It is a burden I could easily carry. Because I'm joined to you, my honor is inherent in your pledge, but as an individual, I'm not bound by it. If I must, I will kidnap you. Any disobedience then would be no fault of your own.

It should never come to that. If we have to use such tricks to do what's right, then Nasuada and the Varden will have lost all integrity.

Saphira stopped. They stood before the carved archway of

Tronjheim's library. The vast, silent room seemed empty, though the ranks of back-to-back bookshelves interspersed with columns could conceal many people. Lanterns poured soft light across the scroll-covered walls, illuminating the reading alcoves along their bases.

Weaving through the shelves, Saphira led him to one alcove, where Arya sat. Eragon paused as he studied her. She seemed more agitated than he had ever seen her, though it manifested itself only in the tension of her movements. Unlike before, she wore her sword with the graceful crossguard. One hand rested on the hilt.

Eragon sat at the opposite side of the marble table. Saphira positioned herself between them, where neither could escape her gaze.

"What have you done?" asked Arya with unexpected hostility.

"How so?"

She lifted her chin. "What have you promised the Varden? *What have you done?*"

The last part even reached Eragon mentally. He realized just how close the elf was to losing control. A bit of fear touched him. "We only did what we had to. I'm ignorant of elves' customs, so if our actions upset you, I apologize. There's no cause to be angry."

"Fool! You know nothing about me. I have spent seven decades representing my queen here—fifteen years of which I bore Saphira's egg between the Varden and the elves. In all that time, I struggled to ensure the Varden had wise, strong leaders who could resist Galbatorix and respect our wishes. Brom helped me by forging the agreement concerning the new Rider—you. Ajihad was committed to your remaining independent so that the balance of power would not be upset. Now I see you siding with the Council of Elders, willingly or not, to control Nasuada! You have overturned a lifetime of work! *What have you done?*"

Dismayed, Eragon dropped all pretenses. With short, clear words, he explained why he had agreed to the council's demands and how he and Saphira had attempted to undermine them.

When he finished, Arya stated, "So."

"So." *Seventy years.* Though he knew elves' lives were extraordinarily long, he had never suspected that Arya was that old, and older, for she appeared to be a woman in her early twenties. The only sign of age on her unlined face was her emerald eyes—deep, knowing, and most often solemn.

Arya leaned back, studying him. "Your position is not what I would wish, but better than I had hoped. I was impolite; Saphira . . . and you . . . understand more than I thought. Your compromise will be accepted by the elves, though you must never forget your debt to us for Saphira. There would be no Riders without our efforts."

"The debt is burned into my blood and my palm," said Eragon. In the silence that followed, he cast about for a new topic, eager to prolong their conversation and perhaps learn more about her. "You have been gone for such a long time; do you miss Ellesméra? Or did you live elsewhere?"

"Ellesméra was, and always shall be, my home," she said, looking beyond him. "I have not lived in my family's house since I left for the Varden, when the walls and windows were draped with spring's first flowers. The times I've returned were only fleeting stays, vanishing flecks of memory by our measurement."

He noticed, once again, that she smelled like crushed pine needles. It was a faint, spicy odor that opened his senses and refreshed his mind. "It must be hard to live among all these dwarves and humans without any of your kind."

She cocked her head. "You speak of humans as if you weren't one."

"Perhaps . . . ," he hesitated, "perhaps I am something else—a mixture of two races. Saphira lives inside me as much as I live in her. We share feelings, senses, thoughts, even to the point where we are more one mind than two." Saphira dipped her head in agreement, nearly bumping the table with her snout.

"That is how it should be," said Arya. "A pact more ancient and powerful than you can imagine links you. You won't truly understand what it means to be a Rider until your training is completed. But that must wait until after the funeral. In the meantime, may the stars watch over you."

With that she departed, slipping into the library's shadowed depths. Eragon blinked. *Is it me, or is everyone on edge today? Like Arya—one moment she's angry, the next she's giving me a blessing!*

No one will be comfortable until things return to normal.

Define normal.

✦　　✦　　✦

RORAN

Roran trudged up the hill.

He stopped and squinted at the sun through his shaggy hair. *Five hours till sunset. I won't be able to stay long.* With a sigh, he continued along the row of elm trees, each of which stood in a pool of uncut grass.

This was his first visit to the farm since he, Horst, and six other men from Carvahall had removed everything worth salvaging from the destroyed house and burned barn. It had been nearly five months before he could consider returning.

Once on the hilltop, Roran halted and crossed his arms. Before him lay the remains of his childhood home. A corner of the house still stood—crumbling and charred—but the rest had been flattened and was already covered with grass and weeds. Nothing could be seen of the barn. The few acres they had managed to cultivate each year were now filled with dandelions, wild mustard, and more grass. Here and there, stray beets or turnips had survived, but that was all. Just beyond the farm, a thick belt of trees obscured the Anora River.

Roran clenched a fist, jaw muscles knotting painfully as he fought back a combination of rage and grief. He stayed rooted to the spot for many long minutes, trembling whenever a pleasant memory rushed through him. This place had been his entire life and more. It had been his past . . . and his future. His father, Garrow, once said, "The land is a special thing. Care for it, and it'll care for you. Not many things will do that." Roran had intended to do exactly that up until the moment his world was ruptured by a quiet message from Baldor.

With a groan, he spun away and stalked back toward the road. The shock of that moment still resonated within him. Having everyone he loved torn away in an instant was a soul-changing event from which he would never recover. It had seeped into every aspect of his behavior and outlook.

It also forced Roran to think more than ever before. It was as if bands had been cinched around his mind, and those bands had snapped, allowing him to ponder ideas that were previously unimaginable. Such as the fact that he might not become a farmer, or that justice—the greatest standby in songs and legends—had little hold in reality. At times these thoughts filled his consciousness to the point where he could barely rise in the morning, feeling bloated with their heaviness.

Turning on the road, he headed north through Palancar Valley, back to Carvahall. The notched mountains on either side were laden with snow, despite the spring greenery that had crept over the valley floor in past weeks. Overhead, a single gray cloud drifted toward the peaks.

Roran ran a hand across his chin, feeling the stubble. *Eragon caused all this—him and his blasted curiosity—by bringing that stone out of the Spine.* It had taken Roran weeks to reach that conclusion. He had listened to everyone's accounts. Several times he had Gertrude, the town healer, read aloud the letter Brom had left him. And there was no other explanation. *Whatever that stone was, it must have attracted the strangers.* For that alone, he blamed Garrow's death on Eragon, though not in anger; he knew that Eragon had intended no harm. No, what roused his fury was that Eragon had left Garrow unburied and fled Palancar Valley, abandoning his responsibilities to gallop off with the old storyteller on some harebrained journey. *How could Eragon have so little regard for those left behind? Did he run because he felt guilty? Afraid? Did Brom mislead him with wild tales of adventure? And why would Eragon listen to such things at a time like that? . . . I don't even know if he's dead or alive right now.*

Roran scowled and rolled his shoulders, trying to clear his mind. *Brom's letter . . . Bah!* He had never heard a more ridiculous collection of insinuations and ominous hints. The only thing it made clear was to avoid the strangers, which was common sense to begin with. *The old man was crazy,* he decided.

A flicker of movement caused Roran to turn, and he saw twelve deer—including a young buck with velvet horns—trotting back into the trees. He made sure to note their location so he could find them tomorrow. He was proud that he could hunt well enough to support himself in Horst's house, though he had never been as skilled as Eragon.

As he walked, he continued to order his thoughts. After Garrow's death, Roran had abandoned his job at Dempton's mill in Therinsford and returned to Carvahall. Horst had agreed to house him and, in the following months, had provided him with work in the forge. Grief had delayed Roran's decisions about the future until two days ago, when he finally settled upon a course of action.

He wanted to marry Katrina, the butcher's daughter. The reason he went to Therinsford in the first place was to earn money to ensure a smooth beginning to their life together. But now, without a farm, a home, or means to support her, Roran could not in good conscience ask for Katrina's hand. His pride would not allow it. Nor did Roran think Sloan, her father, would tolerate a suitor with such poor prospects. Even under the best of circumstances, Roran had expected to have a hard time convincing Sloan to give up Katrina; the two of them had never been friendly. And it was impossible for Roran to wed Katrina without her father's consent, not unless they wished to divide her family, anger the village by defying tradition, and, most likely, start a blood feud with Sloan.

Considering the situation, it seemed to Roran that the only option available to him was to rebuild his farm, even if he had to raise the house and barn himself. It would be hard, starting from nothing, but once his position was secured, he could approach Sloan with his head held high. *Next spring is the soonest we might talk,* thought Roran, grimacing.

He knew Katrina would wait—for a time, at least.

He continued at a steady pace until evening, when the village came into view. Within the small huddle of buildings, wash hung on lines strung from window to window. Men filed back toward the houses from surrounding fields thick with winter wheat. Behind Carvahall, the half-mile-high Igualda Falls gleamed in the sunset as it tumbled down the Spine into the Anora. The sight warmed Roran because it was so ordinary. Nothing was more comforting than having everything where it should be.

Leaving the road, he made his way up the rise to where Horst's house sat with a view of the Spine. The door was already open. Roran tromped inside, following the sounds of conversation into the kitchen.

Horst was there, leaning on the rough table pushed into one corner of the room, his arms bare to the elbow. Next to him was his wife, Elain, who was nearly five months pregnant and smiling with quiet contentment. Their sons, Albriech and Baldor, faced them.

As Roran entered, Albriech said, ". . . and I still hadn't left the forge yet! Thane swears he saw me, but I was on the other side of town."

"What's going on?" asked Roran, slipping off his pack.

Elain exchanged a glance with Horst. "Here, let me get you something to eat." She set bread and a bowl of cold stew before him. Then she looked him in the eye, as if searching for a particular expression. "How was it?"

Roran shrugged. "All of the wood is either burnt or rotting—nothing worth using. The well is still intact, and that's something to be grateful for, I suppose. I'll have to cut timber for the house as soon as possible if I'm going to have a roof over my head by planting season. Now tell me, what's happened?"

"Ha!" exclaimed Horst. "There's been quite a row, there has. Thane is missing a scythe and he thinks Albriech took it."

"He probably dropped it in the grass and forgot where he left it," snorted Albriech.

"Probably," agreed Horst, smiling.

Roran bit into the bread. "It doesn't make much sense, accusing you. If you needed a scythe, you could just forge one."

"I know," said Albriech, dropping into a chair, "but instead of looking for his, he starts grousing that he saw someone leaving his field and that it looked a bit like me . . . and since no one else looks like me, I must have stolen the scythe."

It was true that no one looked like him. Albriech had inherited both his father's size and Elain's honey-blond hair, which made him an oddity in Carvahall, where brown was the predominant hair color. In contrast, Baldor was both thinner and dark-haired.

"I'm sure it'll turn up," said Baldor quietly. "Try not to get too angry over it in the meantime."

"Easy for you to say."

As Roran finished the last of the bread and started on the stew, he asked Horst, "Do you need me for anything tomorrow?"

"Not especially. I'll just be working on Quimby's wagon. The blasted frame still won't sit square."

Roran nodded, pleased. "Good. Then I'll take the day and go hunting. There are a few deer farther down the valley that don't look too scrawny. Their ribs weren't showing, at least."

Baldor suddenly brightened. "Do you want some company?"

"Sure. We can leave at dawn."

When he finished eating, Roran scrubbed his face and hands clean, then wandered outside to clear his head. Stretching leisurely, he strolled toward the center of town.

Halfway there, the chatter of excited voices outside the Seven Sheaves caught his attention. He turned, curious, and made his way to the tavern, where an odd sight met him. Sitting on the porch was a middle-aged man draped in a patchwork leather coat. Beside him was a pack festooned with the steel jaws of the trappers' trade. Several dozen villagers listened as he gestured expansively and said,

"So when I arrived at Therinsford, I went to this man, Neil. Good, honest man; I help in his fields during the spring and summer."

Roran nodded. Trappers spent the winter squirreled away in the mountains, returning in the spring to sell their skins to tanners like Gedric and then to take up work, usually as farmhands. Since Carvahall was the northernmost village in the Spine, many trappers passed through it, which was one of the reasons Carvahall had its own tavern, blacksmith, and tanner.

"After a few steins of ale—to lubricate my speaking, you understand, after a 'alf year with nary a word uttered, except perhaps for blaspheming the world and all beyond when losing a bear-biter—I come to Neil, the froth still fresh on my beard, and start exchanging gossip. As our transaction proceeds, I ask him all gregarious-like, what news of the Empire or the king—may he rot with gangrene and trench mouth. Was anyone born or died or banished that I should know of? And then guess what? Neil leaned forward, going all serious 'bout the mouth, and said that word is going around, there is, from Dras-Leona and Gil'ead of strange happenings here, there, and everywhere in Alagaësia. The Urgals have fair disappeared from civilized lands, and good riddance, but not one man can tell why or where. 'Alf the trade in the Empire has dried up as a result of raids and attacks and, from what I heard, it isn't the work of mere brigands, for the attacks are too widespread, too calculated. No goods are stolen, only burned or soiled. But that's not the end of it, oh no, not by the tip of your blessed grandmother's whiskers."

The trapper shook his head and took a sip from his wineskin before continuing: "There be mutterings of a Shade haunting the northern territories. He's been seen along the edge of Du Weldenvarden and near Gil'ead. They say his teeth are filed to points, his eyes are as red as wine, and his hair is as red as the blood he drinks. Worse, something seems to have gotten our fine, mad monarch's dander up, so it has. Five days past, a juggler from the south stopped in Therinsford on his lonesome way to Ceunon, and he said that troops have been moving and gathering, though for *what* was beyond him." He shrugged. "As my pap taught me when I was a suckling babe, where there's smoke, there's fire. Perhaps it's the Varden. They've caused old Iron Bones enough pain in the arse over the years. Or perhaps Galbatorix finally decided he's had enough of tolerating Surda. At least he knows where to find it, unlike those rebels. He'll crush Surda like a bear crushes an ant, he will."

Roran blinked as a babble of questions exploded around the trapper. He was inclined to doubt the report of a Shade—it sounded too much like a story a drunk woodsman might invent—but the rest of it all sounded bad enough to be true. *Surda* . . . Little information reached Carvahall about that distant country, but Roran at least knew that, although Surda and the Empire were ostensibly at peace, Surdans lived in constant fear that their more powerful neighbor to the north would invade them. For that reason, it was said that Orrin, their king, supported the Varden.

If the trapper was right about Galbatorix, then it could mean ugly war crouched in the future, accompanied by the hardships of increased taxes and forced conscription. *I would rather live in an age devoid of momentous events. Upheaval makes already difficult lives, such as ours, nigh impossible.*

"What's more, there have even been tales of . . ." Here the trapper paused and, with a knowing expression, tapped the side of his nose with his forefinger. "Tales of a new Rider in Alagaësia." He laughed then, a big, hearty laugh, slapping his belly as he rocked back on the porch.

Roran laughed as well. Stories of Riders appeared every few years. They had excited his interest the first two or three times, but he soon learned not to trust such accounts, for they all came to naught. The rumors were nothing more than wishful thinking on the part of those who longed for a brighter future.

He was about to head off when he noticed Katrina standing by the corner of the tavern, garbed in a long russet dress decorated with green ribbon. She gazed at him with the same intensity with which he gazed at her. Going over, he touched her on the shoulder and, together, they slipped away.

They walked to the edge of Carvahall, where they stood looking at the stars. The heavens were brilliant, shimmering with thousands of celestial fires. And arching above them, from north to south, was the glorious pearly band that streamed from horizon to horizon, like diamond dust tossed from a pitcher.

Without looking at him, Katrina rested her head on Roran's shoulder and asked, "How was your day?"

"I returned home." He felt her stiffen against him.

"What was it like?"

"Terrible." His voice caught and he fell silent, holding her tightly. The scent of her copper hair on his cheek was like an elixir of wine and spice and perfume. It seeped deep inside him, warm and comforting. "The house, the barn, the fields, they're all being overrun. . . . I wouldn't have found them if I didn't know where to look."

She finally turned to face him, stars flashing in her eyes, sorrow on her face. "Oh, Roran." She kissed him, lips brushing his for a brief moment. "You have endured so much loss, and yet your strength has never failed you. Will you return to your farm now?"

"Aye. Farming is all I know."

"And what shall become of me?"

He hesitated. From the moment he began to court her, an unspoken assumption that they would marry had existed between them. There had been no need to discuss his intentions; they were as plain as the day was long, and so her question unsettled him. It also felt improper to address the issue in such an open manner when he was not ready to tender an offer. It was *his* place to make the overtures—first to Sloan and then to Katrina—not hers. Still, he had to deal with her concern now that it had been expressed. "Katrina . . . I cannot approach your father as I had planned. He would laugh at me, and rightly so. We have to wait. Once I have a place for us to live and I've collected my first harvest, then he will listen to me."

She faced the sky once more and whispered something so faint, he could not make it out. "What?"

"I said, are you afraid of him?"

"Of course not! I—"

"Then you must get his permission, tomorrow, and set the engagement. Make him understand that, though you have nothing now, you will give me a good home and be a son-in-law he can be proud of. There's no reason we should waste our years living apart when we feel like this."

"I can't do that," he said with a note of despair, willing her to understand. "I can't provide for you, I can't—"

"Don't you *understand?*" She stepped away, her voice strained with urgency. "I love you, Roran, and I want to be with you, but Father has other plans for me. There are far more eligible men than you, and the longer you delay, the more he presses me to consent to a match of which he approves. He fears I will become an old maid, and I fear that too. I have only so much time or choice in Carvahall. . . . If I must take another, I will." Tears glistened in her eyes as she gave him a searching glance, waiting for his response, then gathered up her dress and rushed back to the houses.

Roran stood there, motionless with shock. Her absence was as acute for him as losing the farm—the world suddenly gone cold and unfriendly. It was as if part of himself had been torn away.

It was hours before he could return to Horst's and slip into bed.

THE HUNTED HUNTERS

Dirt crunched under Roran's boots as he led the way down the valley, which was cool and pale in the early hours of the overcast morning. Baldor followed close behind, both of them carrying strung bows. Neither spoke as they studied their surroundings for signs of the deer.

"There," said Baldor in a low voice, pointing at a set of tracks leading toward a bramble on the edge of the Anora.

Roran nodded and started after the spoor. It looked about a day old, so he risked speaking. "Could I have your advice, Baldor? You seem to have a good understanding of people."

"Of course. What is it?"

For a long time, the pad of their feet was the only noise. "Sloan wants to marry off Katrina, and not to me. Every day that passes increases the chance he will arrange a union to his liking."

"What does Katrina say of this?"

Roran shrugged. "He is her father. She cannot continue to defy his will when no one she *does* want has stepped forward to claim her."

"That is, you."

"Aye."

"And that's why you were up so early." It was no question.

In fact, Roran had been too worried to sleep at all. He had spent the entire night thinking about Katrina, trying to find a solution to their predicament. "I can't bear to lose her. But I don't think Sloan will give us his blessing, what with my position and all."

"No, I don't think he would," agreed Baldor. He glanced at Roran out of the corner of his eye. "What is it you want my advice on, though?"

A snort of laughter escaped Roran. "How can I convince Sloan otherwise? How can I resolve this dilemma without starting a blood feud?" He threw his hands up. "What should I do?"

"Have you no ideas?"

"I do, but not of a sort I find pleasing. It occurred to me that Katrina and I could simply announce we were engaged—not that we are yet—and hang the consequences. That would force Sloan to accept our betrothal."

A frown creased Baldor's brow. He said carefully, "Maybe, but it would also create a slew of bad feelings throughout Carvahall. Few would approve of your actions. Nor would it be wise to force Katrina to choose between you or her family; she might resent you for it in years to come."

"I know, but what alternative do I have?"

"Before you take such a drastic step, I recommend you try to win Sloan over as an ally. There's a chance you might succeed, after all, if it's made clear to him that no one else will want to marry an angry Katrina. Especially when you're around to cuckold the husband." Roran grimaced and kept his gaze on the ground. Baldor laughed. "If you fail, well then, you can proceed with confidence, knowing that you have indeed exhausted all other routes. And people will be less likely to spit upon you for breaking tradition and more likely to say Sloan's bullheaded ways brought it upon himself."

"Neither course is easy."

"You knew that to begin with." Baldor grew somber again. "No doubt there'll be harsh words if you challenge Sloan, but things will settle down in the end—perhaps not comfortably, but at least bearably. Aside from Sloan, the only people you'll really offend are prudes like Quimby, though how Quimby can brew such a hale drink yet be so starched and bitter himself is beyond me."

Roran nodded, understanding. Grudges could simmer for years in Carvahall. "I'm glad we could talk. It's been . . ." He faltered, thinking of all the discussions he and Eragon used to share. They had been, as Eragon once said, brothers in all but blood. It had been deeply comforting to know that someone existed who would listen to him, no matter the time or circumstances. And to know that person would always help him, no matter the cost.

The absence of such a bond left Roran feeling empty.

Baldor did not press him to finish his sentence, but instead stopped to drink from his waterskin. Roran continued for a few yards, then halted as a scent intruded on his thoughts.

It was the heavy odor of seared meat and charred pine boughs. *Who would be here besides us?* Breathing deeply, he turned in a circle, trying to determine the source of the fire. A slight gust brushed past him from farther down the road, carrying a hot, smoky wave. The aroma of food was intense enough to make his mouth water.

He beckoned to Baldor, who hurried to his side. "Smell that?"

Baldor nodded. Together they returned to the road and followed it south. About a hundred feet away, it bent around a copse of cottonwoods and curved out of view. As they approached the turn, the rise and fall of voices reached them, muffled by the thick layer of morning fog over the valley.

At the copse's fringe, Roran slowed to a stop. It was foolish to surprise people when they too might be out hunting. Still, something bothered him. Perhaps it was the number of voices; the group seemed bigger than any family in the valley. Without thinking, he stepped off the road and slipped behind the underbrush lining the copse.

"What are you doing?" whispered Baldor.

Roran put a finger to his lips, then crept along, parallel to the road, keeping his footsteps as quiet as possible. As they rounded the bend, he froze.

On the grass by the road was a camp of soldiers. Thirty helmets gleamed in a shaft of morning light as their owners devoured fowl

40

and stew cooked over several fires. The men were mud splattered and travel stained, but Galbatorix's symbol was still visible on their red tunics, a twisting flame outlined in gold thread. Underneath the tunics, they wore leather brigandines—heavy with riveted squares of steel—mail shirts, and then padded gambesons. Most of the soldiers bore broadswords, though half a dozen were archers and another half-dozen carried wicked-looking halberds.

And hunched in their midst were two twisted black forms that Roran recognized from the numerous descriptions the villagers provided upon his return from Therinsford: the strangers who had destroyed his farm. His blood chilled. *They're servants of the Empire!* He began to step forward, fingers already reaching for an arrow, when Baldor grabbed his jerkin and dragged him to the ground.

"Don't. You'll get us both killed."

Roran glared at him, then snarled. "That's . . . they're the bastards . . ." He stopped, noticing that his hands were shaking. *"They've returned!"*

"Roran," whispered Baldor intently, "you can't do anything. Look, they work for the king. Even if you managed to escape, you'd be an outlaw everywhere, and you'd bring disaster on Carvahall."

"What do they want? What *can* they want?" *The king. Why did Galbatorix countenance my father's torture?*

"If they didn't get what they needed from Garrow, and Eragon fled with Brom, then they must want you." Baldor paused, letting the words sink in. "We have to get back and warn everyone. Then you have to hide. The strangers are the only ones with horses. We can get there first if we run."

Roran stared through the brush at the oblivious soldiers. His heart pounded fiercely for revenge, clamoring to attack and fight, to see those two agents of misfortune pierced with arrows and brought to their own justice. It mattered not that he would die as long as he could wash clean his pain and sorrow in one fell moment. All he had to do was break cover. The rest would take care of itself.

Just one small step.

With a choked sob, he clenched his fist and dropped his head. *I can't leave Katrina.* He remained rigid—eyes squeezed shut—then with agonizing slowness dragged himself back. "Home then."

Without waiting for Baldor's reaction, Roran slipped through the trees as fast as he dared. Once the camp was out of sight, he broke out onto the road and ran down the dirt track, channeling his frustration, anger, and even fear into speed.

Baldor scrambled behind him, gaining on the open stretches. Roran slowed to a comfortable trot and waited for him to draw level before saying, "You spread the word. I'll talk with Horst." Baldor nodded, and they pushed on.

After two miles, they stopped to drink and rest briefly. When their panting subsided, they continued through the low hills preceding Carvahall. The rolling ground slowed them considerably, but even so, the village soon burst into view.

Roran immediately broke for the forge, leaving Baldor to make his way to the center of town. As he pounded past the houses, Roran wildly considered schemes to evade or kill the strangers without incurring the wrath of the Empire.

He burst into the forge to catch Horst tapping a peg into the side of Quimby's wagon, singing:

> . . . hey O!
> *And a ringing and a dinging*
> *Rang from old iron! Wily old iron.*
> *With a beat and a bang on the bones of the land,*
> *I conquered wily old iron!*

Horst stopped his mallet in midblow when he saw Roran. "What's the matter, lad? Is Baldor hurt?"

Roran shook his head and leaned over, gasping for air. In short bursts, he reiterated all they had seen and its possible implications, most importantly that it was now clear the strangers were agents of the Empire.

Horst fingered his beard. "You have to leave Carvahall. Fetch some food from the house, then take my mare—Ivor's pulling stumps with her—and ride into the foothills. Once we know what the soldiers want, I'll send Albriech or Baldor with word."

"What will you say if they ask for me?"

"That you're out hunting and we don't know when you'll return. It's true enough, and I doubt they'll chance blundering around in the trees for fear of missing you. Assuming it's you they're really after."

Roran nodded, then turned and ran to Horst's house. Inside, he grabbed the mare's tack and bags from the wall, quickly tied turnips, beets, jerky, and a loaf of bread in a knot of blankets, snatched up a tin pot, and dashed out, pausing only long enough to explain the situation to Elain.

The supplies were an awkward bundle in his arms as he jogged east from Carvahall to Ivor's farm. Ivor himself stood behind the farmhouse, flicking the mare with a willow wand as she strained to tear the hairy roots of an elm tree from the ground.

"Come on now!" shouted the farmer. "Put your back into it!" The horse shuddered with effort, her bit lathered, then with a final surge tilted the stump on its side so the roots reached toward the sky like a cluster of gnarled fingers. Ivor stopped her exertion with a twitch of the reins and patted her good-naturedly. "All right. . . . There we go."

Roran hailed him from a distance and, when they were close, pointed to the horse. "I need to borrow her." He gave his reasons.

Ivor swore and began unhitching the mare, grumbling, "Always the moment I get a bit of work done, that's when the interruption comes. Never before." He crossed his arms and frowned as Roran cinched the saddle, intent on his work.

When he was ready, Roran swung onto the horse, bow in hand. "I am sorry for the trouble, but it can't be helped."

"Well, don't worry about it. Just make sure you aren't caught."

"I'll do that."

As he set heels to the mare's sides, Roran heard Ivor call, "And don't be hiding up my creek!"

Roran grinned and shook his head, bending low over the horse's neck. He soon reached the foothills of the Spine and worked his way up to the mountains that formed the north end of Palancar Valley. From there he climbed to a point on the mountainside where he could observe Carvahall without being seen. Then he picketed his steed and settled down to wait.

Roran shivered, eyeing the dark pines. He disliked being this close to the Spine. Hardly anyone from Carvahall dared set foot in the mountain range, and those who did often failed to return.

Before long Roran saw the soldiers march up the road in a double line, two ominous black figures at their head. They were stopped at the edge of Carvahall by a ragged group of men, some of them with picks in hand. The two sides spoke, then simply faced each other, like growling dogs waiting to see who would strike first. After a long moment, the men of Carvahall moved aside and let the intruders pass.

What happens now? wondered Roran, rocking back on his heels.

By evening the soldiers had set up camp in a field adjacent to the village. Their tents formed a low gray block that flickered with weird shadows as sentries patrolled the perimeter. In the center of the block, a large fire sent billows of smoke into the air.

Roran had made his own camp, and now he simply watched and thought. He always assumed that when the strangers destroyed his home, they got what they wanted, which was the stone Eragon brought from the Spine. *They must not have found it,* he decided. *Perhaps Eragon managed to escape with the stone. . . . Perhaps he felt that he had to leave in order to protect it.* He frowned. That would go a long way toward explaining why Eragon fled, but it still seemed far-fetched to Roran. *Whatever the reason, that stone must be a fantastic treasure for the king to send so many men to retrieve it. I can't understand what would make it so valuable. Maybe it's magic.*

He breathed deeply of the cool air, listening to the hoot of an owl. A flicker of movement caught his attention. Glancing down the mountain, he saw a man approaching in the forest below. Roran ducked behind a boulder, bow drawn. He waited until he was sure it was Albriech, then whistled softly.

Albriech soon arrived at the boulder. On his back was an overfull pack, which he dropped to the ground with a grunt. "I thought I'd never find you."

"I'm surprised you did."

"Can't say I enjoyed wandering through the forest after sundown. I kept expecting to walk into a bear, or worse. The Spine isn't a fit place for men, if you ask me."

Roran looked back out at Carvahall. "So why are they here?"

"To take you into custody. They're willing to wait as long as they have to for you to return from 'hunting.'"

Roran sat with a hard thump, his gut clenched with cold anticipation. "Did they give a reason? Did they mention the stone?"

Albriech shook his head. "All they would say is that it's the king's business. The whole day they've been asking questions about you and Eragon—it's all they're interested in." He hesitated. "I'd stay, but they'll notice if I am missing tomorrow. I brought plenty of food and blankets, plus some of Gertrude's salves in case you injure yourself. You should be fine up here."

Summoning his energy, Roran smiled. "Thanks for the help."

"Anyone would do it," said Albriech with an embarrassed shrug. He started to leave, then tossed over his shoulder, "By the way, the two strangers . . . they're called the Ra'zac."

❖ ❖ ❖

45

SAPHIRA'S PROMISE

The morning after meeting with the Council of Elders, Eragon was cleaning and oiling Saphira's saddle—careful not to overexert himself—when Orik came to visit. The dwarf waited until Eragon finished with a strap, then asked, "Are you better today?"

"A little."

"Good, we all need our strength. I came partly to see to your health and also because Hrothgar wishes to speak with you, if you are free."

Eragon gave the dwarf a wry smile. "I'm always free for him. He must know that."

Orik laughed. "Ah, but it's polite to ask nicely." As Eragon put down the saddle, Saphira uncoiled from her padded corner and greeted Orik with a friendly growl. "Morning to you as well," he said with a bow.

Orik led them through one of Tronjheim's four main corridors, toward its central chamber and the two mirroring staircases that curved underground to the dwarf king's throne room. Before they reached the chamber, however, he turned down a small flight of stairs. It took Eragon a moment to realize that Orik had taken a side passageway to avoid seeing the wreckage of Isidar Mithrim.

They came to a stop before the granite doors engraved with a seven-pointed crown. Seven armored dwarves on each side of the entrance pounded the floor simultaneously with the hafts of their mattocks. With the echoing thud of wood on stone, the doors swung inward.

Eragon nodded to Orik, then entered the dim room with Saphira. They advanced toward the distant throne, passing the rigid statues, hírna, of past dwarf kings. At the foot of the heavy black throne, Eragon bowed. The dwarf king inclined his silver-maned head in return, the rubies wrought into his golden helm glowing dully in the light like flecks of hot iron. Volund, the war hammer, lay across his mail-sheathed legs.

Hrothgar spoke: "Shadeslayer, welcome to my hall. You have done much since last we met. And, so it seems, I have been proved wrong about Zar'roc. Morzan's blade will be welcome in Tronjheim so long as you bear it."

"Thank you," said Eragon, rising.

"Also," rumbled the dwarf, "we wish you to keep the armor you wore in the battle of Farthen Dûr. Even now our most skilled smiths are repairing it. The dragon armor is being treated likewise, and when it is restored, Saphira may use it as long as she wishes, or until she outgrows it. This is the least we can do to show our gratitude. If it weren't for the war with Galbatorix, there would be feasts and celebrations in your name . . . but those must wait until a more appropriate time."

Voicing both his and Saphira's sentiment, Eragon said, "You are generous beyond all expectations. We will cherish such noble gifts."

Clearly pleased, Hrothgar nevertheless scowled, bringing his snarled eyebrows together. "We cannot linger on pleasantries, though. I am besieged by the clans with demands that I do one thing or another about Ajihad's successor. When the Council of Elders proclaimed yesterday that they would support Nasuada, it created an uproar the likes of which I haven't seen since I ascended to the throne. The chiefs had to decide whether to accept Nasuada or look for another candidate. Most have concluded that Nasuada should lead the Varden, but I wish to know where you stand on this, Eragon, before I lend my word to either side. The worst thing a king can do is look foolish."

How much can we tell him? Eragon asked Saphira, thinking quickly.

He's always treated us fairly, but we can't know what he may have promised other people. We'd best be cautious until Nasuada actually takes power.

Very well.

"Saphira and I have agreed to help her. We won't oppose her ascension. And"—Eragon wondered if he was going too far—"I plead that you do the same; the Varden can't afford to fight among themselves. They need unity."

"Oeí," said Hrothgar, leaning back, "you speak with new authority. Your suggestion is a good one, but it will cost a question: Do you think Nasuada will be a wise leader, or are there other motives in choosing her?"

It's a test, warned Saphira. *He wants to know why we've backed her.*

Eragon felt his lips twitch in a half-smile. "I think her wise and canny beyond her years. She will be good for the Varden."

"And that is why you support her?"

"Yes."

Hrothgar nodded, dipping his long, snowy beard. "That relieves me. There has been too little concern lately with what is right and good, and more about what will bring individual power. It is hard to watch such idiocy and not be angry."

An uncomfortable silence fell between them, stifling in the long throne room. To break it, Eragon asked, "What will be done with the dragonhold? Will a new floor be laid down?"

For the first time, the king's eyes grew mournful, deepening the surrounding lines that splayed like spokes on a wagon wheel. It was the closest Eragon had ever seen a dwarf come to weeping. "Much talk is needed before that step can be taken. It was a terrible deed, what Saphira and Arya did. Maybe necessary, but terrible. Ah, it might have been better if the Urgals had overrun us before Isidar

Mithrim was ever broken. The heart of Tronjheim has been shattered, and so has ours." Hrothgar placed his fist over his breast, then slowly unclenched his hand and reached down to grasp Volund's leather-wrapped handle.

Saphira touched Eragon's mind. He sensed several emotions in her, but what surprised him the most was her remorse and guilt. She truly regretted the Star Rose's demise, despite the fact that it had been required. *Little one*, she said, *help me. I need to speak with Hrothgar. Ask him: Do the dwarves have the ability to reconstruct Isidar Mithrim out of the shards?*

As he repeated the words, Hrothgar muttered something in his own language, then said, "The skill we have, but what of it? The task would take months or years, and the end result would be a ruined mockery of the beauty that once graced Tronjheim! It is an abomination I will not sanction."

Saphira continued to stare unblinkingly at the king. *Now tell him: If Isidar Mithrim were put together again, with not one piece missing, I believe I could make it whole once more.*

Eragon gaped at her, forgetting Hrothgar in his astonishment. *Saphira! The energy that would require! You told me yourself that you can't use magic at will, so what makes you sure you can do this?*

I can do it if the need is great enough. It will be my gift to the dwarves. Remember Brom's tomb; let that wash your doubt away. And close your mouth—it's unbecoming and the king is watching.

When Eragon conveyed Saphira's offer, Hrothgar straightened with an exclamation. "Is it possible? Not even the elves might attempt such a feat."

"She is confident in her abilities."

"Then we will rebuild Isidar Mithrim, no matter if it takes a hundred years. We will assemble a frame for the gem and set each piece into its original place. Not a single chip will be forgotten. Even if we must break the larger pieces to move them, it will be done with all our skill in working stone, so that no dust or flecks are lost. You will come then, when we are finished, and heal the Star Rose."

"We will come," agreed Eragon, bowing.

Hrothgar smiled, and it was like the cracking of a granite wall. "Such joy you have given me, Saphira. I feel once more a reason to rule and live. If you do this, dwarves everywhere will honor your name for uncounted generations. Go now with my blessings while I spread the tidings among the clans. And do not feel bound to wait upon my announcement, for no dwarf should be denied this news; convey it to all whom you meet. May the halls echo with the jubilation of our race."

With one more bow, Eragon and Saphira departed, leaving the dwarf king still smiling on his throne. Out of the hall, Eragon told Orik what had transpired. The dwarf immediately bent and kissed the floor before Saphira. He rose with a grin and clasped Eragon's arm, saying, "A wonder indeed. You have given us exactly the hope we needed to combat recent events. There will be drinking tonight, I wager!"

"And tomorrow is the funeral."

Orik sobered for a moment. "Tomorrow, yes. But until then we shall not let unhappy thoughts disturb us! Come!"

Taking Eragon's hand, the dwarf pulled him through Tronjheim to a great feast hall where many dwarves sat at stone tables. Orik leaped onto one, scattering dishes across the floor, and in a booming voice proclaimed the news of Isidar Mithrim. Eragon was nearly deafened by the cheers and shouts that followed. Each of the dwarves insisted on coming to Saphira and kissing the floor as Orik had. When that was finished, they abandoned their food and filled their stone tankards with beer and mead.

Eragon joined the revelry with an abandon that surprised him. It helped to ease the melancholy gathered in his heart. However, he did try to resist complete debauchery, for he was conscious of the duties that awaited them the following day and he wanted to have a clear head.

Even Saphira took a sip of mead, and finding that she liked it, the dwarves rolled out a whole barrel for her. Delicately lowering her mighty jaws through the cask's open end, she drained it with three long draughts, then tilted her head toward the ceiling and belched a giant tongue of flame. It took several minutes for Eragon to convince the dwarves that it was safe to approach her again, but once he did, they brought her another barrel—overriding the cook's protests—and watched with amazement as she emptied it as well.

As Saphira became increasingly inebriated, her emotions and thoughts washed through Eragon with more and more force. It became difficult for him to rely upon the input of his own senses: her vision began to slip over his own, blurring movement and changing colors. Even the odors he smelled shifted at times, becoming sharper, more pungent.

The dwarves began to sing together. Weaving as she stood, Saphira hummed along, punctuating each line with a roar. Eragon opened his mouth to join in and was shocked when, instead of words, out came the snarling rasp of a dragon's voice. *That,* he thought, shaking his head, *is going too far. . . . Or am I just drunk?* He decided it did not matter and proceeded to sing boisterously, dragon's voice or not.

Dwarves continued to stream into the hall as word of Isidar Mithrim spread. Hundreds soon packed the tables, with a thick ring around Eragon and Saphira. Orik called in musicians who arranged themselves in a corner, where they pulled slipcovers of green velvet off their instruments. Soon harps, lutes, and silver flutes floated their gilded melodies over the throng.

Many hours passed before the noise and excitement began to calm. When it did, Orik once more climbed onto the table. He stood there, legs spread wide for balance, tankard in hand, iron-bound cap awry, and cried, "Hear, hear! At last we have celebrated as is proper. The Urgals are gone, the Shade is dead, and we have won!" The dwarves all pounded their tables in approval. It was a good speech—short and to the point. But Orik was not finished. "To Eragon and Saphira!" he roared, lifting the tankard. This too was well received.

Eragon stood and bowed, which brought more cheers. Beside him, Saphira reared and swung a foreleg across her chest, attempting to duplicate his move. She tottered, and the dwarves, realizing their danger, scrambled away from her. They were barely in time. With a loud whoosh, Saphira fell backward, landing flat on a banquet table.

Pain shot through Eragon's back and he collapsed insensate by her tail.

REQUIEM

"**W**ake, Knurlhiem! You cannot sleep now. We are needed at the gate—they won't start without us."

Eragon forced his eyes open, conscious of an aching head and sore body. He was lying on a cold stone table. "What?" He grimaced at the sick taste on his tongue.

Orik tugged on his brown beard. "Ajihad's procession. We must be present for it!"

"No, what did you call me?" They were still in the banquet hall, but it was empty except for him, Orik, and Saphira, who lay on her side between two tables. She stirred and lifted her head, looking around with bleary eyes.

"Stonehead! I called you Stonehead because I've been trying to wake you for almost an hour."

Eragon pushed himself upright and slid off the table. Flashes of memory from the night before jumped through his mind. *Saphira, how are you?* he asked, stumbling to her.

She swiveled her head, running her crimson tongue in and out over her teeth, like a cat that ate something unpleasant. *Whole . . . I think. My left wing feels a bit strange; I think it's the one I landed on. And my head is filled with a thousand hot arrows.*

"Was anyone hurt when she fell?" asked Eragon, concerned.

A hearty chuckle exploded from the dwarf's thick chest. "Only those who dropped off their seats from laughing so hard. A dragon getting drunk and bowing at that! I'm sure lays will be sung about it for decades." Saphira shuffled her wings and looked away primly. "We thought it best to leave you here, since we couldn't move you, Saphira. It upset the head cook terribly—he feared you would drink more of his best stock than the four barrels you already did."

And you chastised me once for drinking! If I consumed four barrels, it would kill me!

That's why you're not a dragon.

Orik thrust a bundle of clothes into Eragon's arms. "Here, put these on. They are more appropriate for a funeral than your own attire. But hurry, we have little time." Eragon struggled into the items—a billowy white shirt with ties at the cuffs, a red vest decorated with gold braiding and embroidery, dark pants, shiny black boots that clacked on the floor, and a swirling cape that fastened under his throat with a studded brooch. In place of the usual plain leather band, Zar'roc was fastened to an ornate belt.

Eragon splashed his face with water and tried to arrange his hair neatly. Then Orik rushed him and Saphira out of the hall and toward Tronjheim's south gate. "We must start from there," he explained, moving with surprising speed on his stocky legs, "because that is where the procession with Ajihad's body stopped three days ago. His journey to the grave cannot be interrupted, or else his spirit will find no rest."

An odd custom, remarked Saphira.

Eragon agreed, noting a slight unsteadiness in her gait. In Carvahall, people were usually buried on their farm, or if they lived in the village, in a small graveyard. The only rituals that accompanied the process were lines recited from certain ballads and a death feast held afterward for relatives and friends. *Can you make it through the whole funeral?* he asked as Saphira staggered again.

She grimaced briefly. *That and Nasuada's appointment, but then I'll need to sleep. A pox on all mead!*

Returning to his conversation with Orik, Eragon asked, "Where will Ajihad be buried?"

Orik slowed and glanced at Eragon with caution. "That has been a matter of contention among the clans. When a dwarf dies, we believe he must be sealed in stone or else he will never join his ancestors. . . . It is complex and I cannot say more to an outsider . . . but we go to great lengths to assure such a burial. Shame falls on a family or clan if they allow any of their own to lie in a lesser element.

"Under Farthen Dûr exists a chamber that is the home of all knurlan, all dwarves, who have died here. It is there Ajihad will be taken. He cannot be entombed with us, as he is human, but a hallowed alcove has been set aside for him. There the Varden may visit him without disturbing our sacred grottos, and Ajihad will receive the respect he is due."

"Your king has done much for the Varden," commented Eragon.

"Some think too much."

Before the thick gate—drawn up on its hidden chains to reveal faint daylight drifting into Farthen Dûr—they found a carefully arranged column. Ajihad lay at the front, cold and pale on a white marble bier borne by six men in black armor. Upon his head was a helm strewn with precious stones. His hands were clasped beneath his collarbone, over the ivory hilt of his bare sword, which extended from underneath the shield covering his chest and legs. Silver mail, like circlets of moonbeams, weighed down his limbs and fell onto the bier.

Close behind the body stood Nasuada—grave, sable-cloaked, and strong in stature, though tears adorned her countenance. To the side was Hrothgar in dark robes; then Arya; the Council of Elders, all with suitably remorseful expressions; and finally a stream of mourners that extended a mile from Tronjheim.

Every door and archway of the four-story-high hall that led to the central chamber of Tronjheim, half a mile away, was thrown open and crowded with humans and dwarves alike. Between the gray bands of faces, the long tapestries swayed as they were brushed with hundreds of sighs and whispers when Saphira and Eragon came into view.

Jörmundur beckoned for them to join him. Trying not to disturb the formation, Eragon and Saphira picked through the column to the space by his side, earning a disapproving glare from Sabrae. Orik went to stand behind Hrothgar.

Together they waited, though for what, Eragon knew not.

All the lanterns were shuttered halfway so that a cool twilight suffused the air, lending an ethereal feel to the event. No one seemed to move or breathe: for a brief moment, Eragon fancied that they were all statues frozen for eternity. A single plume of incense drifted from the bier, winding toward the hazy ceiling as it spread the scent of cedar and juniper. It was the only motion in the hall, a whiplash line undulating sinuously from side to side.

Deep in Tronjheim, a drum gonged. *Boom.* The sonorous bass note resonated through their bones, vibrating the city-mountain and causing it to echo like a great stone bell.

They stepped forward.

Boom. On the second note, another, lower drum melded with the first, each beat rolling inexorably through the hall. The force of the sound propelled them along at a majestic pace. It gave each step significance, a purpose and gravity suited to the occasion. No thought could exist in the throbbing that surrounded them, only an upwelling of emotion that the drums expertly beguiled, summoning tears and bittersweet joy at the same time.

Boom.

When the tunnel ended, Ajihad's bearers paused between the onyx pillars before gliding into the central chamber. There Eragon saw the dwarves grow even more solemn upon beholding Isidar Mithrim.

Boom.

They walked through a crystal graveyard. A circle of towering shards lay in the center of the great chamber, surrounding the inlaid hammer and pentacles. Many pieces were larger than Saphira.

The rays of the star sapphire still shimmered in the fragments, and on some, petals of the carved rose were visible.

Boom.

The bearers continued forward, between the countless razor edges. Then the procession turned and descended broad flights of stairs to the tunnels below. Through many caverns they marched, passing stone huts where dwarven children clutched their mothers and stared with wide eyes.

Boom.

And with that final crescendo, they halted under ribbed stalactites that branched over a great catacomb lined with alcoves. In each alcove lay a tomb carved with a name and clan crest. Thousands—hundreds of thousands—were buried here. The only light came from sparsely placed red lanterns, pale in the shadows.

After a moment, the bearers strode to a small room annexed to the main chamber. In the center, on a raised platform, was a great crypt open to waiting darkness. On the top was carved in runes:

> *May all, Knurlan, Humans, and Elves,*
> *Remember*
> *This Man.*
> *For he was Noble, Strong, and Wise.*
>
> *Gûntera Arûna*

When the mourners were gathered around, Ajihad was lowered into the crypt, and those who had known him personally were allowed to approach. Eragon and Saphira were fifth in line, behind Arya. As they ascended the marble steps to view the body, Eragon was gripped by an overwhelming sense of sorrow, his anguish compounded by the fact that he considered this as much Murtagh's funeral as Ajihad's.

Stopping alongside the tomb, Eragon gazed down at Ajihad. He appeared far more calm and tranquil than he ever did in life, as if death had recognized his greatness and honored him by removing all traces of his worldly cares. Eragon had known Ajihad only a short while, but in that time he had come to respect him both as a person and for what he represented: freedom from tyranny. Also, Ajihad was the first person to grant safe haven to Eragon and Saphira since they left Palancar Valley.

Stricken, Eragon tried to think of the greatest praise he could give. In the end, he whispered past the lump in his throat, "You will be remembered, Ajihad. I swear it. Rest easy knowing that Nasuada shall continue your work and the Empire will be overthrown because of what you accomplished." Conscious of Saphira's touch on his arm, Eragon stepped off the platform with her and allowed Jörmundur to take his place.

When at last everyone had paid their respects, Nasuada bowed over Ajihad and touched her father's hand, holding it with gentle urgency. Uttering a pained groan, she began to sing in a strange, wailing language, filling the cavern with her lamentations.

Then came twelve dwarves, who slid a marble slab over Ajihad's upturned face. And he was no more.

FEALTY

ragon yawned and covered his mouth as people filed into the underground amphitheater. The spacious arena echoed with a babble of voices discussing the funeral that had just concluded.

Eragon sat on the lowest tier, level with the podium. With him were Orik, Arya, Hrothgar, Nasuada, and the Council of Elders. Saphira stood on the row of stairs that cut upward through the tiers. Leaning over, Orik said, "Ever since Korgan, each of our kings has been chosen here. It's fitting that the Varden should do likewise."

It's yet to be seen, thought Eragon, *if this transfer of power will remain peaceful*. He rubbed an eye, brushing away fresh tears; the funeral ceremony had left him shaken.

Lathered over the remnants of his grief, anxiety now twisted his gut. He worried about his own role in the upcoming events. Even if all went well, he and Saphira were about to make potent enemies. His hand dropped to Zar'roc and tightened on the pommel.

It took several minutes for the amphitheater to fill. Then Jörmundur stepped up to the podium. "People of the Varden, we last stood here fifteen years ago, at Deynor's death. His successor, Ajihad, did more to oppose the Empire and Galbatorix than any before. He won countless battles against superior forces. He nearly killed Durza, putting a scratch on the Shade's blade. And greatest of all, he welcomed Rider Eragon and Saphira into Tronjheim. However, a new leader must be chosen, one who will win us even more glory."

Someone high above shouted, "Shadeslayer!"

Eragon tried not to react—he was pleased to see that Jörmundur did not even blink. He said, "Perhaps in years to come, but he has other duties and responsibilities now. No, the Council of Elders has thought long on this: we need one who understands our needs and wants, one who has lived and suffered alongside us. One who refused to flee, even when battle was imminent."

At that moment, Eragon sensed comprehension rush through the listeners. The name came as a whisper from a thousand throats and was uttered by Jörmundur himself: "Nasuada." With a bow, Jörmundur stepped aside.

Next was Arya. She surveyed the waiting audience, then said, "The elves honor Ajihad tonight. . . . And on behalf of Queen Islanzadí, I recognize Nasuada's ascension and offer her the same support and friendship we extended to her father. May the stars watch over her."

Hrothgar took the podium and stated gruffly, "I too support Nasuada, as do the clans." He moved aside.

Then it was Eragon's turn. Standing before the crowd, with all eyes upon him and Saphira, he said, "We support Nasuada as well." Saphira growled in affirmation.

Pledges spoken, the Council of Elders lined themselves on either side of the podium, Jörmundur at their head. Bearing herself proudly, Nasuada approached and knelt before him, her dress splayed in raven billows. Raising his voice, Jörmundur said, "By the right of inheritance and succession, we have chosen Nasuada. By merit of her father's achievements and the blessings of her peers, we have chosen Nasuada. I now ask you: Have we chosen well?"

The roar was overwhelming. "Yes!"

Jörmundur nodded. "Then by the power granted to this council, we pass the privileges and responsibilities accorded to Ajihad to his only descendant, Nasuada." He gently placed a circlet of silver on Nasuada's brow. Taking her hand, he lifted her upright and pronounced, "I give you our new leader!"

For ten minutes, the Varden and dwarves cheered, thundering their approbation until the hall rang with the clamor. Once their cries subsided, Sabrae motioned to Eragon, whispering, "Now is the time to fulfill your promise."

At that moment, all noise seemed to cease for Eragon. His nervousness disappeared too, swallowed in the tide of the moment. Steeling himself with a breath, he and Saphira started toward Jörmundur and Nasuada, each step an eternity. As they walked, he stared at Sabrae, Elessari, Umérth, and Falberd—noting their half-smiles, smugness, and on Sabrae's part, outright disdain. Behind the council members stood Arya. She nodded in support.

We are about to change history, said Saphira.

We're throwing ourselves off a cliff without knowing how deep the water below is.

Ah, but what a glorious flight!

With a brief look at Nasuada's serene face, Eragon bowed and kneeled. Slipping Zar'roc from its sheath, he placed the sword flat on his palms, then lifted it, as if to proffer it to Jörmundur. For a moment, the sword hovered between Jörmundur and Nasuada, teetering on the wire edge of two different destinies. Eragon felt his breath catch—such a simple choice to balance a life on. And more than a life—a dragon, a king, an Empire!

Then his breath rushed in, filling his lungs with time once again, and he swung to face Nasuada. "Out of deep respect . . . and appreciation of the difficulties facing you . . . I, Eragon, first Rider of the Varden, Shadeslayer and Argetlam, give you my blade and my fealty, Nasuada."

The Varden and dwarves stared, dumbstruck. In that same instant, the Council of Elders flashed from triumphant gloating to enraged impotence. Their glares burned with the strength and venom of those betrayed. Even Elessari let outrage burst through her pleasant demeanor. Only Jörmundur—after a brief jolt of surprise—seemed to accept the announcement with equanimity.

Nasuada smiled and grasped Zar'roc, placing the sword's tip on

Eragon's forehead, just as before. "I am honored that you choose to serve me, Rider Eragon. I accept, as you accept all the responsibilities accompanying the station. Rise as my vassal and take your sword."

Eragon did so, then stepped back with Saphira. With shouts of approval, the crowd rose to their feet, the dwarves stamping in rhythm with their hobnail boots while human warriors banged swords across shields.

Turning to the podium, Nasuada gripped it on either side and looked up at all the people in the amphitheater. She beamed at them, pure joy shining from her face. "People of the Varden!"

Silence.

"As my father did before me, I give my life to you and our cause. I will never cease fighting until the Urgals are vanquished, Galbatorix is dead, and Alagaësia is free once more!"

More cheering and applause.

"Therefore, I say to you, now is the time to prepare. Here in Farthen Dûr—after endless skirmishes—we won our greatest battle. It is our turn to strike back. Galbatorix is weak after losing so many forces, and there will never again be such an opportunity.

"Therefore, I say again, now is the time to prepare so that we may once more stand victorious!"

After more speeches by various personages—including a still-glowering Falberd—the amphitheater began to empty. As Eragon stood to leave, Orik grasped his arm, stopping him. The dwarf was wide-eyed. "Eragon, did you plan all that beforehand?"

Eragon briefly considered the wisdom of telling him, then nodded. "Yes."

Orik exhaled, shaking his head. "That was a bold stroke, it was. You've given Nasuada a strong position to begin with. It was dangerous, though, if the reactions of the Council of Elders are anything to judge by. Did Arya approve of this?"

"She agreed it was necessary."

The dwarf studied him thoughtfully. "I'm sure it was. You just altered the balance of power, Eragon. No one will underestimate you again because of it. . . . Beware the rotten stone. You have earned some powerful enemies today." He slapped Eragon on the side and continued past.

Saphira watched him go, then said, *We should prepare to leave Farthen Dûr. The council will be thirsty for revenge. The sooner we're out of their reach, the better.*

A SORCERESS, A SNAKE,
AND A SCROLL

That evening, as Eragon returned to his quarters from bathing, he was surprised to find a tall woman waiting for him in the hall. She had dark hair, startling blue eyes, and a wry mouth. Wound around her wrist was a gold bracelet shaped like a hissing snake. Eragon hoped that she wasn't there to ask him for advice, like so many of the Varden.

"Argetlam." She curtsied gracefully.

He inclined his head in return. "Can I help you?"

"I hope so. I'm Trianna, sorceress of Du Vrangr Gata."

"Really? A sorceress?" he asked, intrigued.

"And battle mage and spy and anything else the Varden deem necessary. There aren't enough magic users, so we each end up with a half-dozen tasks." She smiled, displaying even, white teeth. "That's why I came today. We would be honored to have you take charge of our group. You're the only one who can replace the Twins."

Almost without realizing it, he smiled back. She was so friendly and charming, he hated to say no. "I'm afraid I can't; Saphira and I are leaving Tronjheim soon. Besides, I'd have to consult with Nasuada first anyway." *And I don't want to be entangled in any more politics . . . especially not where the Twins used to lead.*

Trianna bit her lip. "I'm sorry to hear that." She moved a step closer. "Perhaps we can spend some time together before you have to go. I could show you how to summon and control spirits. . . . It would be *educational* for both of us."

64

Eragon felt a hot flush warm his face. "I appreciate the offer, but I'm really too busy at the moment."

A spark of anger flared within Trianna's eyes, then vanished so quickly, he wondered whether he had seen it at all. She sighed delicately. "I understand."

She sounded so disappointed—and looked so forlorn—Eragon felt guilty for rebuffing her. *It can't hurt to talk with her for a few minutes*, he told himself. "I'm curious; how did you learn magic?"

Trianna brightened. "My mother was a healer in Surda. She had a bit of power and was able to instruct me in the old ways. Of course, I'm nowhere near as powerful as a Rider. None of Du Vrangr Gata could have defeated Durza alone, like you did. That was a heroic deed."

Embarrassed, Eragon scuffed his boots against the ground. "I wouldn't have survived if not for Arya."

"You are too modest, Argetlam," she admonished. "It was *you* who struck the final blow. You should be proud of your accomplishment. It's a feat worthy of Vrael himself." She leaned toward him. His heart quickened as he smelled her perfume, which was rich and musky, with a hint of an exotic spice. "Have you heard the songs composed about you? The Varden sing them every night around their fires. They say you've come to take the throne from Galbatorix!"

"No," said Eragon, quick and sharp. That was one rumor he would not tolerate. "They might, but I don't. Whatever my fate may be, I don't aspire to rule."

"And it's wise of you not to. What is a king, after all, but a man imprisoned by his duties? That would be a poor reward indeed for the last free Rider and his dragon. No, for you the ability to go and do what you will and, by extension, to shape the future of Alagaësia." She paused. "Do you have any family left in the Empire?"

What? "Only a cousin."

"Then you're not betrothed?"

The question caught him off guard. He had never been asked that before. "No, I'm not betrothed."

"Surely there must be someone you care about." She came another step closer, and her ribboned sleeve brushed his arm.

"I wasn't close to anyone in Carvahall," he faltered, "and I've been traveling since then."

Trianna drew back slightly, then lifted her wrist so the serpent bracelet was at eye level. "Do you like him?" she inquired. Eragon blinked and nodded, though it was actually rather disconcerting. "I call him Lorga. He's my familiar and protector." Bending forward, she blew upon the bracelet, then murmured, "Sé orúm thornessa hávr sharjalví lífs."

With a dry rustle, the snake stirred to life. Eragon watched, fascinated, as the creature writhed around Trianna's pale arm, then lifted itself and fixed its whirling ruby eyes upon him, wire tongue whipping in and out. Its eyes seemed to expand until they were each as large as Eragon's fist. He felt as if he were tumbling into their fiery depths; he could not look away no matter how hard he tried.

Then at a short command, the serpent stiffened and resumed its former position. With a tired sigh, Trianna leaned against the wall. "Not many people understand what we magic users do. But I wanted you to know that there are others like you, and we will help if we can."

Impulsively, Eragon put his hand on hers. He had never attempted to approach a woman this way before, but instinct urged him onward, daring him to take the chance. It was frightening, exhilarating. "If you want, we could go and eat. There's a kitchen not far from here."

She slipped her other hand over his, fingers smooth and cool, so different from the rough grips he was accustomed to. "I'd like that. Shall we—" Trianna stumbled forward as the door burst open behind her. The sorceress whirled around, only to yelp as she found herself face to face with Saphira.

Saphira remained motionless, except for one lip that slowly lifted to reveal a line of jagged teeth. Then she growled. It was a marvelous growl—richly layered with scorn and menace—that rose and fell through the hall for more than a minute. Listening to it was like enduring a blistering, hackle-raising tirade.

Eragon glared at her the whole time.

When it was over, Trianna was clenching her dress with both fists, twisting the fabric. Her face was white and scared. She quickly curtsied to Saphira, then, with a barely controlled motion, turned and fled. Acting as if nothing had happened, Saphira lifted a leg and licked a claw. *It was nearly impossible to get the door open,* she sniffed.

Eragon could not contain himself any longer. *Why did you do that?* he exploded. *You had no reason to interfere!*

You needed my help, she continued, unperturbed.

If I'd needed your help, I would have called!

Don't yell at me, she snapped, letting her jaws click together. He could sense her emotions boiling with as much turmoil as his. *I'll not have you run around with a slattern who cares more for Eragon as Rider than you as a person.*

She wasn't a slattern, roared Eragon. He pounded the wall in frustration. *I'm a man now, Saphira, not a hermit. You can't expect me to ignore . . . ignore women just because of who I am. And it's certainly not your decision to make. At the very least, I might have enjoyed a conversation with her, anything other than the tragedies we've dealt with lately. You're in my head enough to know how I feel. Why couldn't you leave me alone? Where was the harm?*

You don't understand. She refused to meet his eyes.

Don't understand! Will you prevent me from ever having a wife and children? What of a family?

Eragon. She finally fixed one great eye on him. *We are intimately linked.*

Obviously!

And if you pursue a relationship, with or without my blessing, and become . . . attached . . . to someone, my feelings will become engaged as well. You should know that. Therefore—and I warn you only once—be careful who you choose, because it will involve both of us.

He briefly considered her words. Our bond works both ways, however. If you hate someone, I will be influenced likewise. . . . I understand your concern. So you weren't just jealous?

She licked the claw once more. Perhaps a little.

Eragon was the one who growled this time. He brushed past her into the room, grabbed Zar'roc, then stalked away, belting on the sword.

He wandered through Tronjheim for hours, avoiding contact with everyone. What had occurred pained him, though he could not deny the truth of Saphira's words. Of all the matters they shared, this was the most delicate and the one they agreed upon least. That night—for the first time since he was captured at Gil'ead—he slept away from Saphira, in one of the dwarves' barracks.

Eragon returned to their quarters the following morning. By unspoken consent, he and Saphira avoided discussing what had transpired; further argument was pointless when neither party was willing to yield ground. Besides, they were both so relieved to be reunited, they did not want to risk endangering their friendship again.

They were eating lunch—Saphira tearing at a bloody haunch—when Jarsha trotted up. Like before, he stared wide-eyed at Saphira, following her movements as she nibbled off the end of a leg bone. "Yes?" asked Eragon, wiping his chin and wondering if the Council of Elders had sent for them. He had heard nothing from them since the funeral.

Jarsha turned away from Saphira long enough to say, "Nasuada would like to see you, sir. She's waiting in her father's study."

Sir! Eragon almost laughed. Only a little while ago, he would have been calling people sir, not the other way around. He glanced at Saphira. "Are you done, or should we wait a few minutes?"

Rolling her eyes, she fit the rest of the meat into her mouth and split the bone with a loud crack. I'm done.

"All right," said Eragon, standing, "you can go, Jarsha. We know the way."

It took almost half an hour to reach the study because of the city-mountain's size. As during Ajihad's rule, the door was guarded, but instead of two men, an entire squad of battle-hardened warriors now stood before it, alert for the slightest hint of danger. They would clearly sacrifice themselves to protect their new leader from ambush or attack. Though the men could not have failed to recognize Eragon and Saphira, they barred the way while Nasuada was alerted of her visitors. Only then were the two allowed to enter.

Eragon immediately noticed a change: a vase of flowers in the study. The small purple blossoms were unobtrusive, but they suffused the air with a warm fragrance that—for Eragon—evoked summers of fresh-picked raspberries and scythed fields turning bronze under the sun. He inhaled, appreciating the skill with which Nasuada had asserted her individuality without obliterating Ajihad's memory.

She sat behind the broad desk, still cloaked in the black of mourning. As Eragon seated himself, Saphira beside him, she said, "Eragon." It was a simple statement, neither friendly nor hostile. She turned away briefly, then focused on him, her gaze steely and intent. "I have spent the last few days reviewing the Varden's affairs, such as they are. It was a dismal exercise. We are poor, over-extended, and low on supplies, and few recruits are joining us from the Empire. I mean to change that.

"The dwarves cannot support us much longer, as it's been a lean year for farming and they've suffered losses of their own. Considering this, I have decided to move the Varden to Surda. It's a difficult proposition, but one I believe necessary to keep us safe. Once in Surda, we will finally be close enough to engage the Empire directly."

Even Saphira stirred with surprise. *The work that would involve!* said Eragon. *It could take months to get everyone's belongings to Surda, not to mention all the people. And they'd probably be attacked along the way.* "I thought King Orrin didn't dare openly oppose Galbatorix," he protested.

Nasuada smiled grimly. "His stance has changed since we defeated the Urgals. He will shelter and feed us and fight by our side. Many Varden are already in Surda, mainly women and children who couldn't or wouldn't fight. They will also support us, else I will strip our name from them."

"How," asked Eragon, "did you communicate with King Orrin so quickly?"

"The dwarves use a system of mirrors and lanterns to relay messages through their tunnels. They can send a dispatch from here to the western edge of the Beor Mountains in less than a day. Couriers then transport it to Aberon, capital of Surda. Fast as it is, that method is still too slow when Galbatorix can surprise us with an Urgal army and give us less than a day's notice. I intend to arrange something far more expedient between Du Vrangr Gata and Hrothgar's magicians before we go."

Opening the desk drawer, Nasuada removed a thick scroll. "The Varden will depart Farthen Dûr within the month. Hrothgar has agreed to provide us with safe passage through the tunnels. Moreover, he sent a force to Orthíad to remove the last vestiges of Urgals and seal the tunnels so no one can invade the dwarves by that route again. As this may not be enough to guarantee the Varden's survival, I have a favor to ask of you."

Eragon nodded. He had expected a request or order. That was the only reason for her to have summoned them. "I am yours to command."

"Perhaps." Her eyes flicked to Saphira for a second. "In any case, this is not a command, and I want you to think carefully before replying. To help rally support for the Varden, I wish to spread word throughout the Empire that a new Rider—named Eragon Shadeslayer—and his dragon, Saphira, have joined our cause. I would like your permission before doing so, however."

It's too dangerous, objected Saphira.

Word of our presence here will reach the Empire anyway, pointed out Eragon. *The Varden will want to brag about their victory and Durza's death. Since it'll happen with or without our approval, we should agree to help.*

She snorted softly. *I'm worried about Galbatorix. Until now we haven't made it public where our sympathies lie.*

Our actions have been clear enough.

Yes, but even when Durza fought you in Tronjheim, he wasn't trying to kill you. If we become outspoken in our opposition to the Empire, Galbatorix won't be so lenient again. Who knows what forces or plots he may have kept in abeyance while he tried to gain hold of us? As long as we remain ambiguous, he won't know what to do.

The time for ambiguity has passed, asserted Eragon. *We fought the Urgals, killed Durza, and I have sworn fealty to the leader of the Varden. No ambiguity exists. No, with your permission, I will agree to her proposal.*

She was silent for a long while, then dipped her head. *As you wish.*

He put a hand on her side before returning his attention to Nasuada and saying, "Do what you see fit. If this is how we can best assist the Varden, so be it."

"Thank you. I know it is a lot to ask. Now, as we discussed before the funeral, I expect you to travel to Ellesméra and complete your training."

"With Arya?"

"Of course. The elves have refused contact with both humans and dwarves ever since she was captured. Arya is the only being who can convince them to emerge from seclusion."

"Couldn't she use magic to tell them of her rescue?"

"Unfortunately not. When the elves retreated into Du Weldenvarden after the fall of the Riders, they placed wards around the forest that prevent any thought, item, or being from entering it through arcane means, though not from exiting it, if I understood Arya's explanation. Thus, Arya must physically visit Du Weldenvarden before Queen Islanzadí will know that she is alive, that you and Saphira exist, and of the numerous events that have befallen the Varden these past months." Nasuada handed him the scroll. It was stamped with a wax sigil. "This is a missive for Queen Islanzadí, telling her about the Varden's situation and my own plans. Guard it with your life; it would cause a great deal of harm in the wrong hands. I hope that after all that's happened, Islanzadí will feel kindly enough toward us to reinitiate diplomatic ties. Her assistance could mean the difference between victory and defeat. Arya knows this and has agreed to press our case, but I wanted you aware of the situation too, so you could take advantage of any opportunities that might arise."

Eragon tucked the scroll into his jerkin. "When will we leave?"

"Tomorrow morning . . . unless you have something already planned?"

"No."

"Good." She clasped her hands. "You should know, one other person will be traveling with you." He looked at her quizzically. "King Hrothgar insisted that in the interest of fairness there should be a dwarf representative present at your training, since it affects their race as well. So he's sending Orik along."

Eragon's first reaction was irritation. Saphira could have flown Arya and him to Du Weldenvarden, thereby eliminating weeks of unnecessary travel. Three passengers, however, were too many to fit on Saphira's shoulders. Orik's presence would confine them to the ground.

Upon further reflection, Eragon acknowledged the wisdom of Hrothgar's request. It was important for Eragon and Saphira to maintain a semblance of equality in their dealings with the different races. He smiled. "Ah, well, it'll slow us down, but I suppose we have to placate Hrothgar. To tell the truth, I'm glad Orik is coming. Crossing Alagaësia with only Arya was a rather daunting prospect. She's . . ."

Nasuada smiled too. "She's different."

"Aye." He grew serious again. "Do you really mean to attack the Empire? You said yourself that the Varden are weak. It doesn't seem like the wisest course. If we wait—"

"If we wait," she said sternly, "Galbatorix will only get stronger. This is the first time since Morzan was slain that we have even the slightest opportunity of catching him unprepared. He had no reason to suspect we could defeat the Urgals—which we did thanks to you—so he won't have readied the Empire for invasion."

Invasion! exclaimed Saphira. *And how does she plan to kill Galbatorix when he flies out to obliterate their army with magic?*

Nasuada shook her head in response when Eragon restated the objection. "From what we know of him, he won't fight until Urû'baen itself is threatened. It doesn't matter to Galbatorix if we destroy half the Empire, so long as we come to him, not the other way around. Why should he bother anyway? If we do manage to reach him, our troops will be battered and depleted, making it all the easier for him to destroy us."

"You still haven't answered Saphira," protested Eragon.

"That's because I can't yet. This will be a long campaign. By its end you might be powerful enough to defeat Galbatorix, or the elves may have joined us . . . and their spellcasters are the strongest in Alagaësia. No matter what happens, we cannot afford to delay. Now is the time to gamble and dare what no one thinks we can accomplish. The Varden have lived in the shadows for too long—we must either challenge Galbatorix or submit and pass away."

The scope of what Nasuada was suggesting disturbed Eragon. So many risks and unknown dangers were involved, it was almost absurd to consider such a venture. However, it was not his place to make the decision, and he accepted that. Nor would he dispute it further. *We have to trust in her judgment now.*

"But what of you, Nasuada? Will you be safe while we're gone? I must think of my vow. It's become my responsibility to ensure that you won't have your own funeral soon."

Her jaw tightened as she gestured at the door and the warriors beyond. "You needn't fear, I am well defended." She looked down. "I will admit . . . one reason for going to Surda is that Orrin knows me of old and will offer his protection. I cannot tarry here with you and Arya gone and the Council of Elders still with power. They won't accept me as their leader until I prove beyond doubt that the Varden are under *my* control, not theirs."

Then she seemed to draw on some inner strength, squaring her shoulders and lifting her chin so she was distant and aloof. "Go now, Eragon. Ready your horse, gather supplies, and be at the north gate by dawn."

He bowed low, respecting her return to formality, then left with Saphira.

After dinner, Eragon and Saphira flew together. They sailed high above Tronjheim, where crenulated icicles hung from the sides of Farthen Dûr, forming a great white band around them. Though it was still hours until night, it was already nearly dark within the mountain.

Eragon threw back his head, savoring the air on his face. He missed the wind—wind that would rush through the grass and stir the clouds until everything was tousled and fresh. Wind that would bring rain and storms and lash the trees so they bent. *For that matter, I miss trees as well,* he thought. *Farthen Dûr is an incredible place, but it's as empty of plants and animals as Ajihad's tomb.*

Saphira agreed. *The dwarves seem to think that gems take the place of flowers.* She was silent as the light continued to fade. When it was too dark for Eragon to see comfortably, she said, *It's late. We should return.*

All right.

She drifted toward the ground in great, lazy spirals, drawing nearer to Tronjheim—which glowed like a beacon in the center of Farthen Dûr. They were still far from the city-mountain when she swung her head, saying, *Look.*

He followed her gaze, but all he could see was the gray, featureless plain below them. *What?*

Instead of answering, she tilted her wings and glided to their left, slipping down to one of the four roads that radiated from Tronjheim along the cardinal compass points. As they landed, he noticed a patch of white on a small hill nearby. The patch wavered strangely in the dusk, like a floating candle, then resolved into Angela, who was wearing a pale wool tunic.

The witch carried a wicker basket nearly four feet across and filled with a wild assortment of mushrooms, most of which Eragon did not recognize. As she approached, he gestured at them and said, "You've been gathering toadstools?"

"Hello," laughed Angela, putting her load down. "Oh no, *toadstool* is far too general a term. And anyway, they really ought to be called frogstools, not toadstools." She spread them with her hand. "*This* one is sulphur tuft, and *this* is an inkcap, and here's navelcap, and dwarf shield, russet tough-shank, blood ring, and *that* is a spotted deceiver. Delightful, isn't it!" She pointed to each in turn, ending on a mushroom with pink, lavender, and yellow splashed in rivulets across its cap.

"And that one?" he asked, indicating a mushroom with a lightning-blue stem, molten-orange gills, and a glossy black two-tiered cap.

She looked at it fondly. "Fricai Andlát, as the elves might say. The stalk is instant death, while the cap can cure most poisons. It's what Tunivor's Nectar is extracted from. Fricai Andlát only grows in caves in Du Weldenvarden and Farthen Dûr, and it would die out here if the dwarves started carting their dung elsewhere."

Eragon looked back at the hill and realized that was exactly what it was, a dung heap.

"Hello, Saphira," said Angela, reaching past him to pat Saphira on the nose. Saphira blinked and looked pleased, tail twitching. At the same time, Solembum padded into sight, his mouth clamped firmly around a limp rat. Without so much as a flick of his whiskers, the werecat settled on the ground and began to nibble on the rodent, studiously ignoring the three of them.

"So," said Angela, tucking back a curl of her enormous hair, "off to Ellesméra?" Eragon nodded. He did not bother asking how she had found out; she always seemed to know what was going on. When he remained silent, she scowled. "Well, don't act so morose. It's not as if it's your execution!"

"I know."

"Then *smile*, because if it's not your execution, you should be happy! You're as flaccid as Solembum's rat. *Flaccid*. What a wonderful word, don't you think?"

That wrung a grin out of him, and Saphira chortled with amusement deep in her throat. "I'm not sure it's quite as wonderful as you think, but yes, I understand your point."

"I'm glad you understand. Understanding is good." With arched eyebrows, she hooked a fingernail underneath a mushroom and flipped it over, inspecting its gills as she said, "It's fortuitous we met tonight, as you are about to leave and I . . . I will accompany the Varden to Surda. As I told you before, I like to be where things are happening, and that's the place."

Eragon grinned even more. "Well then, that must mean we'll have a safe journey, else you'd be with us."

Angela shrugged, then said seriously, "Be careful in Du Weldenvarden. Just because elves do not display their emotions doesn't mean they aren't subject to rage and passion like the rest of us mortals. What can make them so deadly, though, is how they conceal it, sometimes for years."

"You've been there?"

"Once upon a time."

After a pause, he asked, "What do you think of Nasuada's plans?"

"Mmm . . . she's doomed! You're doomed! They're all doomed!" She cackled, doubling over, then straightened abruptly. "Notice I didn't specify what kind of doom, so no matter what happens, I predicted it. How very *wise* of me." She lifted the basket again, setting it on one hip. "I suppose I won't see you for a while, so farewell, best of luck, avoid roasted cabbage, don't eat earwax, and look on the bright side of life!" And with a cheery wink, she strolled off, leaving Eragon blinking and nonplussed.

After an appropriate pause, Solembum picked up his dinner and followed, ever so dignified.

HROTHGAR'S GIFT

awn was a half hour away when Eragon and Saphira arrived at Tronjheim's north gate. The gate was raised just enough to let Saphira pass, so they hurried underneath it, then waited in the recessed area beyond, where red jasper pillars loomed above and carved beasts snarled between the bloody piers. Past those, at the very edge of Tronjheim, sat two thirty-foot-high gold griffins. Identical pairs guarded each of the city-mountain's gates. No one was in sight.

Eragon held Snowfire's reins. The stallion was brushed, reshod, and saddled, his saddlebags bulging with goods. He pawed the floor impatiently; Eragon had not ridden him for over a week.

Before long Orik ambled up, bearing a large pack on his back and a bundle in his arms. "No horse?" asked Eragon, somewhat surprised. *Are we supposed to walk all the way to Du Weldenvarden?*

Orik grunted. "We'll be stopping at Tarnag, just north of here. From there we take rafts along the Az Ragni to Hedarth, an outpost for trading with the elves. We won't need steeds before Hedarth, so I'll use my own feet till then."

He set the bundle down with a clang, then unwrapped it, revealing Eragon's armor. The shield had been repainted—so the oak tree stood clearly in the center—and all the dings and scrapes removed. Beneath it was the long mail shirt, burnished and oiled until the steel gleamed brilliantly. No sign existed of where it had been rent when Durza cut Eragon's back. The coif, gloves, bracers, greaves, and helmet were likewise repaired.

"Our greatest smiths worked on these," said Orik, "as well as your armor, Saphira. However, since we can't take dragon armor with us, it was given to the Varden, who will guard it against our return."

Please thank him for me, said Saphira.

Eragon obliged, then laced on the greaves and bracers, storing the other items in his bags. Last of all, he reached for his helm, only to find Orik holding it. The dwarf rolled the piece between his hands, then said, "Do not be so quick to don this, Eragon. There is a choice you must make first."

"What choice is that?"

Raising the helmet, Orik uncovered its polished brow, which, Eragon now saw, had been altered: etched in the steel were the hammer and stars of Hrothgar and Orik's clan, the Ingeitum. Orik scowled, looking both pleased and troubled, and said in a formal voice, "Mine king, Hrothgar, desires that I present this helm as a symbol of the friendship he bears for you. And with it Hrothgar extends an offer to adopt you as one of Dûrgrimst Ingeitum, as a member of his own family."

Eragon stared at the helm, amazed that Hrothgar would make such a gesture. *Does this mean I'd be subjected to his rule? . . . If I continue to accrue loyalties and allegiances at this pace, I'll be incapacitated before long—unable to do anything without breaking some oath!*

You don't have to put it on, pointed out Saphira.

And risk insulting Hrothgar? Once again, we're trapped.

It may be intended as a gift, though, another sign of otho, not a trap. I would guess he's thanking us for my offer to repair Isidar Mithrim.

That had not occurred to Eragon, for he had been too busy trying to figure out how the dwarf king might gain advantage over them. *True. But I think it's also an attempt to correct the imbalance of power created when I swore fealty to Nasuada. The dwarves couldn't have been pleased with that turn of events.* He looked back at Orik, who was waiting anxiously. "How often has this been done?"

"For a human? Never. Hrothgar argued with the Ingeitum families for a day and a night before they agreed to accept you. If you consent to bear our crest, you will have full rights as clan member. You may attend our councils and give voice on every issue. And," he grew very somber, "if you so wish, you will have the right to be buried with our dead."

For the first time, the enormity of Hrothgar's action struck Eragon. The dwarves could offer no higher honor. With a swift motion, he took the helm from Orik and pressed it down upon his head. "I am privileged to join Dûrgrimst Ingeitum."

Orik nodded with approval and said, "Then take this Knurlnien, this Heart of Stone, and cup it between your hands—yes, like so. You must steel yourself now and prick open a vein to wet the stone. A few drops will suffice. . . . To finish, repeat after me: Os il dom qirânû carn dûr thargen, zeitmen, oen grimst vor formv edaris rak skilfz. Narho is belgond . . ." It was a lengthy recitation and all the longer because Orik stopped to translate every few sentences. Afterward, Eragon healed his wrist with a quick spell.

"Whatever else the clans may say about this business," observed Orik, "you have behaved with integrity and respect. They cannot ignore that." He grinned. "We are of the same clan now, eh? You are my foster brother! Under more normal circumstances, Hrothgar would have presented your helm himself and we would have held a lengthy ceremony to commemorate your induction into Dûrgrimst Ingeitum, but events move too swiftly for us to tarry. Fear not that you are being slighted, though! Your adoption shall be celebrated with the proper rituals when you and Saphira next return to Farthen Dûr. You shall feast and dance and have many pieces of paper to sign in order to formalize your new position."

"I look forward to the day," said Eragon. He was still preoccupied with sifting through the numerous possible ramifications of belonging to Dûrgrimst Ingeitum.

Sitting against a pillar, Orik shrugged off his pack and drew his ax, which he proceeded to twirl between his palms. After several minutes, he leaned forward, glaring back into Tronjheim. "Barzûl knurlar! Where are they? Arya said she would be right here. Ha! Elves' only concept of time is late and even later."

"Have you dealt with them much?" asked Eragon, crouching. Saphira watched with interest.

The dwarf laughed suddenly. "Eta. Only Arya, and then sporadically because she traveled so often. In seven decades, I've learned but one thing about her: You can't rush an elf. Trying is like hammering a file—it might break, but it'll never bend."

"Aren't dwarves the same?"

"Ah, but stone will shift, given enough time." Orik sighed and shook his head. "Of all the races, elves change the least, which is one reason I'm reluctant to go."

"But we'll get to meet Queen Islanzadí and see Ellesméra and who knows what else? When was the last time a dwarf was invited into Du Weldenvarden?"

Orik frowned at him. "Scenery means nothing. Urgent tasks remain in Tronjheim and our other cities, yet I must tramp across Alagaësia to exchange pleasantries and sit and grow fat as you are tutored. It could take years!"

Years! . . . Still, if that's what is required to defeat Shades and the Ra'zac, I'll do it.

Saphira touched his mind: *I doubt Nasuada will let us stay in Ellesméra for more than a few months. With what she told us, we'll be needed fairly soon.*

"At last!" said Orik, pushing himself upright.

Approaching were Nasuada—slippers flashing beneath her dress, like mice darting from a hole—Jörmundur, and Arya, who bore a pack like Orik's. She wore the same black leather outfit Eragon had first seen her in, as well as her sword.

At that moment, it struck Eragon that Arya and Nasuada might not approve of him joining the Ingeitum. Guilt and trepidation shot through him as he realized that it had been his duty to consult Nasuada first. *And Arya!* He cringed, remembering how angry she had been after his first meeting with the Council of Elders.

Thus, when Nasuada stopped before him, he averted his eyes, ashamed. But she only said, "You accepted." Her voice was gentle, restrained.

He nodded, still looking down.

"I wondered if you would. Now once again, all three races have a hold on you. The dwarves can claim your allegiance as a member of Dûrgrimst Ingeitum, the elves will train and shape you—and their influence may be the strongest, for you and Saphira are bound by their magic—and you have sworn fealty to me, a human.... Perhaps it is best that we share your loyalty." She met his surprise with an odd smile, then pressed a small bag of coins into his palm and stepped away.

Jörmundur extended a hand, which Eragon shook, feeling a bit dazed. "Have a good trip, Eragon. Guard yourself well."

"Come," said Arya, gliding past them into the darkness of Farthen Dûr. "It is time to leave. Aiedail has set, and we have far to go."

"Aye," Orik agreed. He pulled out a red lantern from the side of his pack.

Nasuada looked them over once more. "Very well. Eragon and Saphira, you have the Varden's blessings, as well as mine. May your journey be safe. Remember, you carry the weight of our hopes and expectations, so acquit yourselves honorably."

"We will do our best," promised Eragon.

Gripping Snowfire's reins firmly, he started after Arya, who was already several yards away. Orik followed, then Saphira. As Saphira passed Nasuada, Eragon saw her pause and lightly lick Nasuada on the cheek. Then she lengthened her stride, catching up with him.

As they continued north along the road, the gate behind them shrank smaller and smaller until it was reduced to a pinprick of light—with two lonely silhouettes where Nasuada and Jörmundur remained watching.

When they finally reached Farthen Dûr's base, they found a pair of gigantic doors—thirty feet tall—open and waiting. Three dwarf guards bowed and moved away from the aperture. Through the doors was a tunnel of matching proportions, lined with columns and lanterns for the first fifty feet. After that it was as empty and silent as a mausoleum.

It looked exactly like Farthen Dûr's western entrance, but Eragon knew that this tunnel was different. Instead of burrowing through the mile-thick base to emerge outside, it proceeded underneath mountain after mountain, all the way to the dwarf city Tarnag.

"Here is our path," said Orik, lifting the lantern.

He and Arya crossed over the threshold, but Eragon held back, suddenly uncertain. While he did not fear the dark, neither did he welcome being surrounded by eternal night until they arrived at Tarnag. And once he entered the barren tunnel, he would again be hurling himself into the unknown, abandoning the few things he had grown accustomed to among the Varden in exchange for an uncertain destiny.

What is it? asked Saphira.

Nothing.

He took a breath, then strode forward, allowing the mountain to swallow him in its depths.

◆　　◆　　◆

HAMMER AND TONGS

Three days after the Ra'zac's arrival, Roran found himself pacing uncontrollably along the edge of his camp in the Spine. He had heard nothing since Albriech's visit, nor was it possible to glean information by observing Carvahall. He glared at the distant tents where the soldiers slept, then continued pacing.

At midday Roran had a small, dry lunch. Wiping his mouth with the back of his hand, he wondered, *How long are the Ra'zac willing to wait?* If it was a test of patience, he was determined to win.

To pass the time, he practiced his archery on a rotting log, stopping only when an arrow shattered on a rock embedded in the trunk. After that nothing else remained to do, except to resume striding back and forth along the bare track that stretched from a boulder to where he slept.

He was still pacing when footsteps sounded in the forest below. Grabbing his bow, Roran hid and waited. Relief rushed through him when Baldor's face bobbed into view. Roran waved him over.

As they sat, Roran asked, "Why hasn't anyone come?"

"We couldn't," said Baldor, wiping sweat off his brow. "The soldiers have been watching us too closely. This was the first opportunity we had to get away. I can't stay long either." He turned his face toward the peak above them and shuddered. "You're braver than I, staying here. Have you had any trouble with wolves, bears, mountain cats?"

"No, no, I'm fine. Did the soldiers say anything new?"

"One of them bragged to Morn last night that their squad was handpicked for this mission." Roran frowned. "They haven't been too quiet. . . . At least two or three of them get drunk each night. A group of them tore up Morn's common room the first day."

"Did they pay for the damage?"

" 'Course not."

Roran shifted, staring down at the village. "I still have trouble believing that the Empire would go to these lengths to capture me. What could I give them? What do they *think* I can give them?"

Baldor followed his gaze. "The Ra'zac questioned Katrina today. Someone mentioned that the two of you are close, and the Ra'zac were curious if she knew where you'd gone."

Roran refocused on Baldor's open face. "Is she all right?"

"It would take more than those two to scare her," reassured Baldor. His next sentence was cautious and probing. "Perhaps you should consider turning yourself in."

"I'd sooner hang myself and them with me!" Roran started up and stalked over his usual route, still tapping his leg. "How can you say that, knowing how they tortured my father?"

Catching his arm, Baldor said, "What happens if you remain in hiding and the soldiers don't give up and leave? They'll assume we lied to help you escape. The Empire doesn't forgive traitors."

Roran shrugged off Baldor. He spun around, tapping his leg, then abruptly sat. *If I don't show myself, the Ra'zac will blame the people at hand. If I attempt to lead the Ra'zac away . . .* Roran was not a skilled enough woodsman to evade thirty men and the Ra'zac. *Eragon could do it, but not me.* Still, unless the situation changed, it might be the only choice available to him.

He looked at Baldor. "I don't want anyone to be hurt on my behalf. I'll wait for now, and if the Ra'zac grow impatient and threaten someone . . . Well then, I'll think of something else to do."

"It's a nasty situation all around," offered Baldor.

"One I intend to survive."

Baldor departed soon afterward, leaving Roran alone with his thoughts on his endless path. He covered mile after mile, grinding a rut into the earth under the weight of his ruminations. When chill dusk arrived, he removed his boots—for fear of wearing them out—and proceeded to pad barefoot.

Just as the waxing moon rose and subsumed the night shadows in beams of marble light, Roran noticed a disturbance in Carvahall. Scores of lanterns bobbed through the darkened village, winking in and out as they floated behind houses. The yellow specks clustered in the center of Carvahall, like a cloud of fireflies, then streamed haphazardly toward the edge of town, where they were met by a hard line of torches from the soldiers' camp.

For two hours, Roran watched the opposing sides face each other—the agitated lanterns milling helplessly against the stolid torches. Finally, the lambent groups dispersed and filtered back into the tents and houses.

When nothing else of interest occurred, Roran untied his bedroll and slipped under the blankets.

Throughout the next day, Carvahall was consumed with unusual activity. Figures strode between houses and even, Roran was surprised to see, rode out into Palancar Valley toward various farms. At noon he saw two men enter the soldiers' camp and disappear into the Ra'zac's tent for almost an hour.

So involved was he with the proceedings, Roran barely moved the entire day.

He was in the middle of dinner when, as he had hoped, Baldor reappeared. "Hungry?" asked Roran, gesturing.

Baldor shook his head and sat with an air of exhaustion. Dark lines under his eyes made his skin look thin and bruised. "Quimby's dead."

Roran's bowl clattered as it struck the ground. He cursed, wiping cold stew off his leg, then asked, "How?"

"A couple of soldiers started bothering Tara last night." Tara was Morn's wife. "She didn't really mind, except the men got in a fight over who she was supposed to serve next. Quimby was there—checking a cask Morn said had turned—and he tried to break them up." Roran nodded. That was Quimby, always interfering to make sure others behaved properly. "Only thing is, a soldier threw a pitcher and hit him on the temple. Killed him instantly."

Roran stared at the ground with his hands on his hips, struggling to regain control over his ragged breathing. He felt as if Baldor had knocked the wind out of him. *It doesn't seem possible. . . . Quimby, gone?* The farmer and part-time brewer was as much a part of the landscape as the mountains surrounding Carvahall, an unquestioned presence that shaped the fabric of the village. "Will the men be punished?"

Baldor held up his hand. "Right after Quimby died, the Ra'zac stole his body from the tavern and hauled it out to their tents. We tried to get it back last night, but they wouldn't talk with us."

"I saw."

Baldor grunted, rubbing his face. "Dad and Loring met with the Ra'zac today and managed to convince them to release the body. The soldiers, however, won't face any consequences." He paused. "I was about to leave when Quimby was handed over. You know what his wife got? Bones."

"Bones!"

"Every one of them was nibbled clean—you could see the bite marks—and most had been cracked open for the marrow."

Disgust gripped Roran, as well as profound horror for Quimby's fate. It was well known that a person's spirit could never rest until his body was given a proper burial. Revolted by the desecration, he asked, "What, *who*, ate him then?"

"The soldiers were just as appalled. It must have been the Ra'zac."

"Why? To what end?"

"I don't think," said Baldor, "that the Ra'zac are human. You've never seen them up close, but their breath is foul, and they always cover their faces with black scarves. Their backs are humped and twisted, and they speak to each other with clicks. Even their men seem to fear them."

"If they aren't human, then what kind of creatures can they be?" demanded Roran. "They're not Urgals."

"Who knows?"

Fear now joined Roran's revulsion—fear of the supernatural. He saw it echoed on Baldor's face as the young man clasped his hands. For all the stories of Galbatorix's misdeeds, it was still a shock to have the king's evil roosted among their homes. A sense of history settled on Roran as he realized he was involved with forces he had previously been acquainted with only through songs and stories. "Something should be done," he muttered.

The air grew warmer through the night, until by afternoon Palancar Valley shimmered and sweltered with the unexpected spring heat. Carvahall looked peaceful under the bald blue sky, yet Roran could feel the sour resentment that clenched its inhabitants with malicious intensity. The calm was like a sheet stretched taut in the wind.

Despite the aura of expectation, the day proved to be utterly boring; Roran spent most of his time brushing Horst's mare. At last he lay to sleep, looking up past the towering pines at the haze of stars that adorned the night sky. They seemed so close, it felt as if he hurtled among them, falling toward the blackest void.

The moon was setting when Roran woke, his throat raw from smoke. He coughed and rolled upright, blinking as his eyes burned and watered. The noxious fumes made it difficult to breathe.

Roran grabbed his blankets and saddled the frightened mare, then spurred her farther up the mountain, hoping to find clear air. It quickly became apparent that the smoke was ascending with him, so he turned and cut sideways through the forest.

After several minutes spent maneuvering in the dark, they finally broke free and rode onto a ledge swept clean by a breeze. Purging his lungs with long breaths, Roran scanned the valley for the fire. He spotted it in an instant.

Carvahall's hay barn glowed white in a cyclone of flames, transforming its precious contents into a fountain of amber motes. Roran trembled as he watched the destruction of the town's feed. He wanted to scream and run through the forest to help with the bucket brigade, yet he could not force himself to abandon his own safety.

Now a molten spark landed on Delwin's house. Within seconds, the thatched roof exploded in a wave of fire.

Roran cursed and tore his hair, tears streaming down his face. This was why mishandling fire was a hanging offense in Carvahall. *Was it an accident? Was it the soldiers? Are the Ra'zac punishing the villagers for shielding me? . . . Am I somehow responsible for this?*

Fisk's house joined the conflagration next. Aghast, Roran could only avert his face, hating himself for his cowardice.

By dawn all the fires had been extinguished or burned out on their own. Only sheer luck and a calm night saved the rest of Carvahall from being consumed.

Roran waited until he was sure of the outcome, then retreated to his old camp and threw himself down to rest. From morning through evening, he was oblivious to the world, except through the lens of his troubled dreams.

Upon his return to awareness, Roran simply waited for the visitor he was sure would appear. This time it was Albriech. He arrived at dusk with a grim, worn expression. "Come with me," he said.

Roran tensed. "Why?" *Have they decided to give me up?* If he *was* the cause of the fire, he could understand the villagers wanting him gone. He might even agree it was necessary. It was unreasonable to expect everyone in Carvahall to sacrifice themselves for him. Still, that did not mean he would allow them to just hand him over to the Ra'zac. After what the two monsters had done to Quimby, Roran would fight to the death to avoid being their prisoner.

"Because," said Albriech, clenching his jaw muscles, "it was the soldiers who started the fire. Morn banned them from the Seven Sheaves, but they still got drunk on their own beer. One of them dropped a torch against the hay barn on his way to bed."

"Was anyone hurt?" asked Roran.

"A few burns. Gertrude was able to handle them. We tried to negotiate with the Ra'zac. They spat on our requests that the Empire replace our losses and the guilty face justice. They even refused to confine the soldiers to the tents."

"So why should I return?"

Albriech chuckled hollowly. "For hammer and tongs. We need your help to . . . *remove* the Ra'zac."

"You would do that for me?"

"We're not risking ourselves for your sake alone. This concerns the entire village now. At least come talk to Father and the others and hear their thoughts . . . I'd think you would be glad to get out of these cursed mountains."

Roran considered Albriech's proposition long and hard before deciding to accompany him. *It's this or run for it, and I can always run later.* He fetched the mare, tied his bags to the saddle, then followed Albriech toward the valley floor.

Their progress slowed as they neared Carvahall, using trees and brush for cover. Slipping behind a rain barrel, Albriech checked to see if the streets were clear, then signaled to Roran. Together they crept from shadow to shade, constantly on guard for the Empire's servants. At Horst's forge, Albriech opened one of the double doors just far enough for Roran and the mare to quietly enter.

Inside, the workshop was lit by a single candle, which cast a trembling glow over the ring of faces that hovered about it in the surrounding darkness. Horst was there—his thick beard protruded like a shelf into the light—flanked by the hard visages of Delwin, Gedric, and then Loring. The rest of the group was composed of younger men: Baldor, Loring's three sons, Parr, and Quimby's boy, Nolfavrell, who was only thirteen.

They all turned to look as Roran entered the assembly. Horst said, "Ah, you made it. You escaped misfortune while in the Spine?"

"I was lucky."

"Then we can proceed."

"With what, exactly?" Roran hitched the mare to an anvil as he spoke.

Loring answered, the shoemaker's parchment face a mass of contorting lines and grooves. "We have attempted reason with these Ra'zac . . . these *invaders*." He stopped, his thin frame racked with an unpleasant, metallic wheeze deep in his chest. "They have refused *reason*. They have endangered us all with no sign of remorse or *contrition*." He made a noise in his throat, then said with pronounced deliberation, "They . . . must . . . go. Such creatures—"

"No," said Roran. "Not creatures. Desecrators."

The faces scowled and bobbed in agreement. Delwin picked up the thread of conversation: "The point is, everyone's life is at stake. If that fire had spread any farther, dozens of people would have been killed and those who escaped would have lost everything they own. As a result, we've agreed to drive the Ra'zac away from Carvahall. Will you join us?"

Roran hesitated. "What if they return or send for reinforcements? We can't defeat the entire Empire."

"No," said Horst, grave and solemn, "but neither can we stand silent and allow the soldiers to kill us and to destroy our property. A man can endure only so much abuse before he must strike back."

Loring laughed, throwing back his head so the flame gilded the stumps of his teeth. "First we fortify," he whispered with glee, "then we fight. We'll make them regret they ever clapped their festering eyes on Carvahall! Ha ha!"

RETALIATION

Roran hefted a pick, then set it aside. Though he had never cared for Brom's stories, one of them, the "Song of Gerand," resonated with him whenever he heard it. It told of Gerand, the greatest warrior of his time, who relinquished his sword for a wife and farm. He found no peace, however, as a jealous lord initiated a blood feud against Gerand's family, which forced Gerand to kill once more. Yet he did not fight with his blade, but with a simple hammer.

Going to the wall, Roran removed a medium-sized hammer with a long handle and a rounded blade on one side of the head. He tossed it from hand to hand, then went to Horst and asked, "May I have this?"

Horst eyed the tool and Roran. "Use it wisely." Then he said to the rest of the group, "Listen. We want to scare, not kill. Break a few bones if you want, but don't get carried away. And whatever you do, don't stand and fight. No matter how brave or heroic you feel, remember that they are trained soldiers."

When everyone was equipped, they left the forge and wound their way through Carvahall to the edge of the Ra'zac's camp. The soldiers had already gone to bed, except for four sentries who patrolled the perimeter of the gray tents. The Ra'zac's two horses were picketed by a smoldering fire.

Horst quietly issued orders, sending Albriech and Delwin to ambush two of the sentries, and Parr and Roran to ambush the other two.

Roran held his breath as he stalked the oblivious soldier. His heart began to shudder as energy spiked through his limbs. He hid behind the corner of a house, quivering, and waited for Horst's signal. *Wait.*

Wait.

With a roar, Horst burst from hiding, leading the charge into the tents. Roran darted forward and swung his hammer, catching the sentry on the shoulder with a grisly crunch.

The man howled and dropped his halberd. He staggered as Roran struck his ribs and back. Roran raised the hammer again and the man retreated, screaming for help.

Roran ran after him, shouting incoherently. He knocked in the side of a wool tent, trampling whatever was inside, then smashed the top of a helmet he saw emerging from another tent. The metal rang like a bell. Roran barely noticed as Loring danced past—the old man cackled and hooted in the night as he jabbed the soldiers with a pitchfork. Everywhere was a confusion of struggling bodies.

Whirling around, Roran saw a soldier attempting to string his bow. He rushed forward and hit the back of the bow with his steel mallet, breaking the wood in two. The soldier fled.

The Ra'zac scrambled free of their tent with terrible screeches, swords in hand. Before they could attack, Baldor untethered the horses and sent them galloping toward the two scarecrow figures. The Ra'zac separated, then regrouped, only to be swept away as the soldiers' morale broke and they ran.

Then it was over.

Roran panted in the silence, his hand cramped around the hammer's handle. After a moment, he picked his way through the crumpled mounds of tents and blankets to Horst. The smith was grinning under his beard. "That's the best brawl I've had in years."

Behind them, Carvahall jumped to life as people tried to discover the source of the commotion. Roran watched lamps flare up behind shuttered windows, then turned as he heard soft sobbing.

The boy, Nolfavrell, was kneeling by the body of a soldier, methodically stabbing him in the chest as tears slid down his chin. Gedric and Albriech hurried over and pulled Nolfavrell away from the corpse.

"He shouldn't have come," said Roran.

Horst shrugged. "It was his right."

All the same, killing one of the Ra'zac's men will only make it harder to rid ourselves of the desecrators. "We should barricade the road and between the houses so they won't catch us by surprise." Studying the men for any injuries, Roran saw that Delwin had received a long cut on his forearm, which the farmer bandaged with a strip torn from his ruined shirt.

With a few shouts, Horst organized their group. He dispatched Albriech and Baldor to retrieve Quimby's wagon from the forge and had Loring's sons and Parr scour Carvahall for items that could be used to secure the village.

Even as he spoke, people congregated on the edge of the field, staring at what was left of the Ra'zac's camp and the dead soldier. "What happened?" cried Fisk.

Loring scuttled forward and stared the carpenter in the eye. "What happened? I'll tell you what *happened*. We routed the dung-beardlings . . . caught them with their boots off and whipped them like dogs!"

"I am glad." The strong voice came from Birgit, an auburn-haired woman who clasped Nolfavrell against her bosom, ignoring the blood smeared across his face. "They deserve to die like cowards for my husband's death."

The villagers murmured in agreement, but then Thane spoke: "Have you gone mad, Horst? Even if you frightened off the Ra'zac and their soldiers, Galbatorix will just send more men. The Empire will never give up until they get Roran."

"We should hand him over," snarled Sloan.

Horst raised his hands. "I agree; no one is worth more than all of Carvahall. But if we surrender Roran, do you really think Galbatorix will let us escape punishment for our resistance? In his eyes, we're no better than the Varden."

"Then *why* did you attack?" demanded Thane. "Who gave you the authority to make this decision? You've doomed us all!"

This time Birgit answered. "Would you let them kill your wife?" She pressed her hands on either side of her son's face, then showed Thane her bloody palms, like an accusation. "Would you let them burn us? . . . Where is your manhood, loam breaker?"

He lowered his gaze, unable to face her stark expression.

"They burned my farm," said Roran, "devoured Quimby, and nearly destroyed Carvahall. Such crimes cannot go unpunished. Are we frightened rabbits to cower down and accept our fate? No! We have a right to defend ourselves." He stopped as Albriech and Baldor trudged up the street, dragging the wagon. "We can debate later. Now we have to prepare. Who will help us?"

Forty or more men volunteered. Together they set about the difficult task of making Carvahall impenetrable. Roran worked incessantly, nailing fence slats between houses, piling barrels full of rocks for makeshift walls, and dragging logs across the main road, which they blocked with two wagons tipped on their sides.

As Roran hurried from one chore to another, Katrina waylaid him in an alley. She hugged him, then said, "I'm glad you're back, and that you're safe."

He kissed her lightly. "Katrina . . . I have to speak with you as soon as we're finished." She smiled uncertainly, but with a spark of hope. "You were right; it was foolish of me to delay. Every moment we spend together is precious, and I have no desire to squander what time we have when a whim of fate could tear us apart."

Roran was tossing water on the thatching of Kiselt's house—so it could not catch fire—when Parr shouted, "Ra'zac!"

Dropping the bucket, Roran ran to the wagons, where he had left his hammer. As he grabbed the weapon, he saw a single Ra'zac sitting on a horse far down the road, almost out of bowshot. The creature was illuminated by a torch in its left hand, while its right was drawn back, as if to throw something.

Roran laughed. "Is he going to toss rocks at us? He's too far away to even hit—" He was cut off as the Ra'zac whipped down its arm and a glass vial arched across the distance between them and shattered against the wagon to his right. An instant later, a fireball launched the wagon into the air while a fist of burning air flung Roran against a wall.

Dazed, he fell to his hands and knees, gasping for breath. Through the roaring in his ears came the tattoo of galloping horses. He forced himself upright and faced the sound, only to dive aside as the Ra'zac raced into Carvahall through the burning gap in the wagons.

The Ra'zac reined in their steeds, blades flashing as they hacked at the people strewn around them. Roran saw three men die, then Horst and Loring reached the Ra'zac and began pressing them back with pitchforks. Before the villagers could rally, soldiers poured through the breach, killing indiscriminately in the darkness.

Roran knew they had to be stopped, else Carvahall would be taken. He jumped at a soldier, catching him by surprise, and hit him in the face with the hammer's blade. The soldier crumpled without a sound. As the man's compatriots rushed toward him, Roran wrestled the corpse's shield off his limp arm. He barely managed to get it free in time to block the first strike.

Backstepping toward the Ra'zac, Roran parried a sword thrust, then swung his hammer up under the man's chin, sending him to the ground. "To me!" shouted Roran. "Defend your homes!" He sidestepped a jab as five men attempted to encircle him. "To me!"

Baldor answered his call first, then Albriech. A few seconds later, Loring's sons joined him, followed by a score of others. From the side streets, women and children pelted the soldiers with rocks. "Stay together," ordered Roran, standing his ground. "There are more of us."

The soldiers halted as the line of villagers before them continued to thicken. With more than a hundred men at his back, Roran slowly advanced.

"Attack, you foolsss," screamed a Ra'zac, dodging Loring's pitchfork.

A single arrow whizzed toward Roran. He caught it on his shield and laughed. The Ra'zac were level with the soldiers now, hissing with frustration. They glared at the villagers from under their inky cowls. Suddenly Roran felt himself become lethargic and powerless to move; it was hard to even think. Fatigue seemed to chain his arms and legs in place.

Then from farther in Carvahall, Roran heard a raw shout from Birgit. A second later, a rock hurtled over his head and bored toward the lead Ra'zac, who twitched with supernatural speed to avoid the missile. The distraction, slight though it was, freed Roran's mind from the soporific influence. *Was that magic?* he wondered.

He dropped the shield, grasped his hammer with both hands, and raised it far above his head—just like Horst did when spreading metal. Roran went up on tiptoe, his entire body bowed backward, then whipped his arms down with a *huh!* The hammer cartwheeled through the air and bounced off the Ra'zac's shield, leaving a formidable dent.

The two attacks were enough to disrupt the last of the Ra'zac's strange power. They clicked rapidly to each other as the villagers roared and marched forward, then the Ra'zac yanked on their reins, wheeling around.

"Retreat," they growled, riding past the soldiers. The crimson-clad warriors sullenly backed out of Carvahall, stabbing at anyone who came too close. Only when they were a good distance from the burning wagons did they dare turn their backs.

Roran sighed and retrieved his hammer, feeling the bruises on his side and back where he had hit the wall. He bowed his head as he saw that the explosion had killed Parr. Nine other men had died. Already wives and mothers rent the night with their wails of grief.

How could this happen here?

"Everyone, come!" called Baldor.

Roran blinked and stumbled to the middle of the road, where Baldor stood. A Ra'zac sat beetle-like on a horse only twenty yards away. The creature crooked a finger at Roran and said, "You . . . you sssmell like your cousin. We never forget a sssmell."

"What do you want?" he shouted. "Why are you here?"

The Ra'zac chuckled in a horrible, insectile way. "We want . . . *information.*" It glanced over its shoulder, where its companions had disappeared, then cried, "Release Roran and you ssshall be sold as ssslaves. Protect him, and we will eat you all. We ssshall have your answer when next we come. Be sssure it is the right one."

◆   ◆   ◆

AZ SWELDN RAK ANHÛIN

Light burst into the tunnel as the doors dragged open. Eragon winced, his eyes sorely unaccustomed to daylight after so long underground. Beside him, Saphira hissed and arched her neck to get a better view of their surroundings.

It had taken them two days to traverse the subterranean passage from Farthen Dûr, though it felt longer to Eragon, due to the never-ending dusk that surrounded them and the silence it had imposed upon their group. In all, he could recall only a handful of words being exchanged during their journey.

Eragon had hoped to learn more about Arya while they traveled together, but the only information he had gleaned came simply as a result of observation. He had not supped with her before and was startled to see that she brought her own food and ate no meat. When he asked her why, she said, "You will never again consume an animal's flesh after you have been trained, or if you do, it will be only on the rarest of occasions."

"Why should I give up meat?" he scoffed.

"I cannot explain with words, but you will understand once we reach Ellesméra."

All that was forgotten now as he hurried to the threshold, eager to see their destination. He found himself standing on a granite outcropping, more than a hundred feet above a purple-hued lake, brilliant under the eastern sun. Like Kóstha-mérna, the water reached from mountain to mountain, filling the valley's end. From the lake's far side, the Az Ragni flowed north, winding between the peaks until—in the far distance—it rushed out onto the eastern plains.

To his right, the mountains were bare, save for a few trails, but to his left . . . to his left was the dwarf city Tarnag. Here the dwarves had reworked the seemingly immutable Beors into a series of terraces. The lower terraces were mainly farms—dark curves of land waiting to be planted—dotted with squat halls, which as best he could tell were built entirely of stone. Above those empty levels rose tier upon tier of interlocking buildings until they culminated in a giant dome of gold and white. It was as if the entire city was nothing more than a line of steps leading to the dome. The cupola glistened like polished moonstone, a milky bead floating atop a pyramid of gray slate.

Orik anticipated Eragon's question, saying, "That is Celbedeil, the greatest temple of dwarfdom and home of Dûrgrimst Quan—the Quan clan—who act as servants and messengers to the gods."

Do they rule Tarnag? asked Saphira. Eragon repeated the query.

"Nay," said Arya, stepping past them. "Though the Quan are strong, they are small in numbers, despite their power over the afterlife . . . and gold. It is the Ragni Hefthyn—the River Guard—who control Tarnag. We will stay with their clan chief, Ûndin, while here."

As they followed the elf off the outcropping and through the gnarled forest that blanketed the mountain, Orik whispered to Eragon, "Mind her not. She has been arguing with the Quan for many a year. Every time she visits Tarnag and speaks with a priest, it produces a quarrel fierce enough to scare a Kull."

"Arya?"

Orik nodded grimly. "I know little of it, but I've heard she disagrees strongly with much that the Quan practice. It seems that elves do not hold with 'muttering into the air for help.'"

Eragon stared at Arya's back as they descended, wondering if Orik's words were true, and if so, what Arya herself believed. He took a deep breath, pushing the matter from his mind. It felt wonderful to be back in the open, where he could smell the moss and ferns and trees of the forest, where the sun was warm on his face and bees and other insects swarmed pleasantly.

The path took them down to the edge of the lake before rising back toward Tarnag and its open gates. "How have you hidden Tarnag from Galbatorix?" asked Eragon. "Farthen Dûr I understand, but this . . . I've never seen anything like it."

Orik laughed softly. "Hide it? That would be impossible. No, after the Riders fell, we were forced to abandon all our cities aboveground and retreat into our tunnels in order to escape Galbatorix and the Forsworn. They would often fly through the Beors, killing anyone who they encountered."

"I thought that dwarves always lived underground."

Orik's thick eyebrows met in a frown. "Why should we? We may have an affinity for stone, but we like the open air as much as elves or humans. However, it has only been in the last decade and a half, ever since Morzan died, that we have dared return to Tarnag and other of our ancient dwellings. Galbatorix may be unnaturally powerful, but even he would not attack an entire city alone. Of course, he and his dragon could cause us no end of trouble if they wanted, but these days they rarely leave Urû'baen, even for short trips. Nor could Galbatorix bring an army here without first defeating Buragh or Farthen Dûr."

Which he nearly did, commented Saphira.

Cresting a small mound, Eragon jolted with surprise as an animal crashed through the underbrush and onto the path. The scraggly creature looked like a mountain goat from the Spine, except that it was a third larger and had giant ribbed horns that curled around its cheeks, making an Urgal's seem no bigger than a swallow nest. Odder still was the saddle lashed across the goat's back and the dwarf seated firmly on it, aiming a half-drawn bow into the air.

"Hert dûrgrimst? Fild rastn?" shouted the strange dwarf.

"Orik Thrifkz menthiv oen Hrethcarach Eragon rak Dûrgrimst

100

Ingeitum," answered Orik. "Wharn, az vanyali-carharûg Arya. Né oc Ûndinz grimstbelardn." The goat stared warily at Saphira. Eragon noted how bright and intelligent its eyes were, though its face was rather droll with its frosty beard and somber expression. It reminded him of Hrothgar, and he almost laughed, thinking how very dwarfish the animal was.

"Azt jok jordn rast," came the reply.

With no discernible command on the dwarf's part, the goat leaped forward, covering such an extraordinary distance it seemed to take flight for a moment. Then rider and steed vanished between the trees.

"What was that?" asked Eragon, amazed.

Orik resumed walking. "A Feldûnost, one of the five animals unique to these mountains. A clan is named after each one. However, Dûrgrimst Feldûnost is perhaps the bravest and most revered of the clans."

"Why so?"

"We depend upon Feldûnost for milk, wool, and meat. Without their sustenance, we could not live in the Beors. When Galbatorix and his traitorous Riders were terrorizing us, it was Dûrgrimst Feldûnost who risked themselves—and still do—to tend the herds and fields. As such, we are all in their debt."

"Do all dwarves ride Feldûnost?" He stumbled slightly over the unusual word.

"Only in the mountains. Feldûnost are hardy and sure-footed, but they are better suited for cliffs than open plains."

Saphira nudged Eragon with her nose, causing Snowfire to shy away. *Now those would be good hunting, better than any I had in the Spine or hence! If I have time in Tarnag—*

No, he said. *We can't afford to offend the dwarves.*

She snorted, irritated. *I could ask permission first.*

Now the path that had concealed them for so long under dark boughs entered the great clearing that surrounded Tarnag. Groups of observers had already begun to gather in the fields when seven

Feldûnost with jeweled harnesses bounded out from the city. Their riders bore lances tipped with pennants that snapped like whips in the air. Reining in his strange beast, the lead dwarf said, "Thou art well-come to this city of Tarnag. By otho of Ûndin and Gannel, I, Thorv, son of Brokk, offer in peace the shelter of our halls." His accent grumbled and rasped with a rough burr quite unlike Orik's.

"And by Hrothgar's otho, we of the Ingeitum accept your hospitality," responded Orik.

"As do I, in Islanzadí's stead," added Arya.

Appearing satisfied, Thorv motioned to his fellow riders, who spurred their Feldûnost into formation around the four of them. With a flourish, the dwarves rode off, guiding them to Tarnag and through the city gates.

The outer wall was forty feet thick and formed a shadowed tunnel to the first of the many farms that belted Tarnag. Five more tiers—each of which was defended by a fortified gate—carried them past the fields and into the city proper.

In contrast to Tarnag's thickly built ramparts, the buildings within, though of stone, were shaped with such cunning as to give the impression of grace and lightness. Strong, bold carvings, usually of animals, adorned the houses and shops. But even more striking was the stone itself: vibrant hues, from bright scarlet to the subtlest of greens, glazed the rock in translucent layers.

And hung throughout the city were the dwarves' flameless lanterns, their multicolored sparks harbingers of the Beors' long dusk and night.

Unlike Tronjheim, Tarnag had been constructed in proportion to the dwarves, with no concession for human, elf, or dragon visitors. At the most, doorways were five feet high, and they were often only four and a half. Eragon was of middling height, but now he felt like a giant transported onto a puppet stage.

The streets were wide and crammed. Dwarves of various clans hurried about their business or stood haggling in and around shops. Many were garbed in strange, exotic costumes, such as a block of fierce black-haired dwarves who wore silver helmets forged in the likeness of wolf heads.

Eragon stared at the dwarf women the most, as he had only caught brief glimpses of them while in Tronjheim. They were broader than the men, and their faces were heavyset, yet their eyes sparkled and their hair was lustrous and their hands were gentle on their diminutive children. They eschewed frippery, except for small, intricate brooches of iron and stone.

At the Feldûnost's piercing footsteps, the dwarves turned to look at the new arrivals. They did not cheer as Eragon had expected, but rather bowed and murmured, "Shadeslayer." As they saw the hammer and stars upon Eragon's helm, admiration was replaced by shock and, in many cases, outrage. A number of the angrier dwarves contracted around the Feldûnost, glaring between the animals at Eragon and shouting imprecations.

The back of Eragon's neck prickled. *It seems that adopting me wasn't the most popular decision Hrothgar could make.*

Aye, agreed Saphira. *He may have strengthened his hold on you, but at the cost of alienating many of the dwarves. . . . We'd better get out of sight before blood is shed.*

Thorv and the other guards rode forward as if the crowd was nonexistent, clearing the way through seven additional tiers until only a single gate separated them from the mass of Celbedeil. Then Thorv turned left, toward a great hall pressed against the side of the mountain and protected in fore by a barbican with two machicolated towers.

As they neared the hall, a group of armed dwarves streamed out from between the houses and formed a thick line, blocking the street. Long purple veils covered their faces and draped over their shoulders, like mail coifs.

The guards immediately reined in their Feldûnost, faces hard. "What is it?" Eragon asked Orik, but the dwarf only shook his head and strode forward, a hand on his ax.

"Etzil nithgech!" cried a veiled dwarf, raising a fist. "Formv

103

Hrethcarach . . . formv Jurgencarmeitder nos eta goroth bahst Tarnag, dûr encesti rak kythn! Jok is warrev az barzûlegûr dûr dûrgrimst, Az Sweldn rak Anhûin, môgh tor rak Jurgenvren? Né ûdim etal os rast knurlag. Knurlag ana . . ." For a long minute, he continued to rant with growing spleen.

"Vrron!" barked Thorv, cutting him off, then the two dwarves began arguing. Despite the harsh exchange, Eragon saw that Thorv seemed to respect the other dwarf.

Eragon shifted to the side—trying to get a better view past Thorv's Feldûnost—and the veiled dwarf abruptly fell silent, jabbing at Eragon's helm with an expression of horror.

"Knurlag qana qirânû Dûrgrimst Ingeitum!" he screamed. "Qarzûl ana Hrothgar oen volfild—"

"Jok is frekk dûrgrimstvren?" interrupted Orik quietly, drawing his ax. Worried, Eragon glanced at Arya, but she was too intent on the confrontation to notice him. He surreptitiously slid his hand down and around Zar'roc's wire-wrapped hilt.

The strange dwarf stared hard at Orik, then removed an iron ring from his pocket, plucked three hairs from his beard, twined them around the ring, and threw it onto the street with an impervious clink, spitting after it. Without a word, the purple-shrouded dwarves filed away.

Thorv, Orik, and the other warriors flinched as the ring bounced across the granite pavement. Even Arya seemed taken aback. Two of the younger dwarves blanched and reached for their blades, then dropped their hands as Thorv barked, "Eta!"

Their reactions unsettled Eragon far more than the raucous exchange had. As Orik strode forward alone and deposited the ring in a pouch, Eragon asked, "What does it mean?"

"It means," said Thorv, "that you have enemies."

They hurried through the barbican to a wide courtyard arrayed with three banquet tables, decorated with lanterns and banners. Before the tables stood a group of dwarves, foremost among them a gray-bearded dwarf swathed in wolfskin. He spread his arms, saying, "Welcome to Tarnag, home of Dûrgrimst Ragni Hefthyn. We have heard much praise of you, Eragon Shadeslayer. I am Ûndin, son of Derûnd and clan chief."

Another dwarf stepped forward. He had the shoulders and chest of a warrior, topped with hooded black eyes that never left Eragon's face. "And I, Gannel, son of Orm Blood-ax and clan chief of Dûrgrimst Quan."

"It is an honor to be your guests," said Eragon, inclining his head. He felt Saphira's irritation at being ignored. *Patience*, he murmured, forcing a smile.

She snorted.

The clan chiefs greeted Arya and Orik in turn, but their hospitality was lost on Orik, whose only response was to extend his hand, the iron ring on his palm.

Ûndin's eyes widened, and he gingerly lifted the ring, pinching it between his thumb and forefinger as if it were a venomous snake. "Who gave this to you?"

"It was Az Sweldn rak Anhûin. And not to me, but to Eragon."

As alarm spread across their faces, Eragon's earlier apprehension returned. He had seen lone dwarves face an entire group of Kull without shirking. The ring must symbolize something dreadful indeed if it could undermine their courage.

Ûndin frowned as he listened to the muttering of his advisers, then said, "We must consult on this issue. Shadeslayer, a feast is prepared in your honor. If you would allow my servants to guide you to your quarters, you can refresh yourself, and then we might begin."

"Of course." Eragon handed Snowfire's reins to a waiting dwarf and followed a guide into the hall. As he passed through the doorway, he glanced back and saw Arya and Orik bustling away with the clan chiefs, their heads pressed close together. *I won't be long,* he promised Saphira.

After crouching through dwarf-sized corridors, he was relieved that the room assigned to him was spacious enough to stand freely. The servant bowed and said, "I will return when Grimstborith Ûndin is ready."

Once the dwarf was gone, Eragon paused and took a deep breath, grateful for the silence. The encounter with the veiled dwarves hovered in his mind, making it difficult for him to relax. *At least we won't be in Tarnag long. That should prevent them from hindering us.*

Peeling off his gloves, Eragon went to a marble basin set on the floor next to the low bed. He put his hands in the water, then jerked them out with an involuntary yelp. The water was almost boiling. *It must be a dwarf custom*, he realized. He waited until it cooled a bit, then doused his face and neck, rubbing them clean as steam swirled off his skin.

Rejuvenated, he stripped out of his breeches and tunic and out-fitted himself in the clothes he had worn to Ajihad's funeral. He touched Zar'roc, but decided it would only insult Ûndin's table and instead belted on his hunting knife.

Then, from his pack, he took the scroll Nasuada had charged him with delivering to Islanzadí and weighed it in his hand, wondering where to hide it. The missive was too important to leave out in the open, where it could be read or stolen. Unable to think of a better place, he slipped the scroll up his sleeve. *It'll be safe there unless I get into a fight, in which case I'll have bigger problems to worry about.*

When at last the servant returned for Eragon, it was only an hour or so past noon, but the sun had already vanished behind the looming mountains, plunging Tarnag into dusk. Exiting the hall, Eragon was struck by the city's transformation. With the premature advent of night, the dwarves' lanterns revealed their true strength, flooding the streets with pure, unwavering light that made the entire valley glow.

Ûndin and the other dwarves were gathered in the courtyard, along with Saphira, who had situated herself at the head of a table. No one appeared interested in disputing her choice.

Has anything happened? asked Eragon, hurrying toward her.

Ûndin summoned extra warriors, then had the gates barred.

Does he expect an attack?

At the very least, he's concerned about the possibility.

106

"Eragon, please join me," said Ûndin, gesturing at the chair to his right. The clan chief seated himself as Eragon did, and the rest of the company hurriedly followed suit.

Eragon was happy when Orik ended up beside him with Arya directly across the table, although both looked grim. Before he could ask Orik about the ring, Ûndin slapped the table and roared, "Ignh az voth!"

Servants streamed out of the hall, bearing platters of beaten gold piled high with meats, pies, and fruit. They divided into three columns—one for each table—and deposited the dishes with a flourish.

Before them were soups and stews filled with various tubers, roasted venison, long hot loaves of sourdough bread, and rows of honeycakes dripped with raspberry preserve. In a bed of greens lay filleted trout garnished with parsley, and on the side, pickled eel stared forlornly at an urn of cheese, as if hoping to somehow escape back into a river. A swan sat on each table, surrounded by a flock of stuffed partridges, geese, and ducks.

Mushrooms were everywhere: broiled in juicy strips, placed atop a bird's head like a bonnet, or carved in the shape of castles amid moats of gravy. An incredible variety was on display, from puffy white mushrooms the size of Eragon's fist, to ones he could have mistaken for gnarled bark, to delicate toadstools sliced neatly in half to showcase their blue flesh.

Then the centerpiece of the feast was revealed: a gigantic roasted boar, glistening with sauce. At least Eragon thought it was a boar, for the carcass was as large as Snowfire and took six dwarves to carry. The tusks were longer than his forearms, the snout as wide as his head. And the smell, it overwhelmed all others in pungent waves that made his eyes water from their strength.

"Nagra," whispered Orik. "Giant boar. Ûndin truly honors you tonight, Eragon. Only the bravest dwarves dare hunt Nagran, and it is only served to those who have great valor. Also, I think he makes a gesture that he will support you over Dûrgrimst Nagra."

Eragon leaned toward him so no one else could hear. "Then this is another animal native to the Beors? What are the rest?"

"Forest wolves big enough to prey on a Nagra and nimble enough to catch Feldûnost. Cave bears, which we call Urzhadn and the elves call Beorn and for which they dubbed these peaks, though we do not call them such ourselves. The mountains' name is a secret that we share with no race. And—"

"Smer voth," commanded Ûndin, smiling at his guests. The servants immediately drew small curved knives and cut portions of the Nagra, which they set on everyone's plates—except for Arya's—including a weighty piece for Saphira. Ûndin smiled again, took a dagger, and sliced off a bit of his meat.

Eragon reached for his own knife, but Orik grabbed his arm. "Wait."

Ûndin chewed slowly, rolling his eyes and nodding in an exaggerated fashion, then swallowed and proclaimed, "Ilf gauhnith!"

"Now," said Orik, turning to the meal as conversation erupted along the tables.

Eragon had never tasted anything like the boar. It was juicy, soft, and oddly spicy—as if the meat had been soaked in honey and cider—which was enhanced by the mint used to flavor the pork. *I wonder how they managed to cook something so large.*

Very slowly, commented Saphira, nibbling on her Nagra.

Between bites, Orik explained, "It is custom, from days when poisoning was rampant among clans, for the host to taste the food first and declare it safe for his guests."

During the banquet, Eragon divided his time between sampling the multitude of dishes and conversing with Orik, Arya, and dwarves farther down the table. In that manner, the hours hastened by, for the feast was so large, it was late afternoon before the last course had been served, the last bite consumed, and the last chalice drained. As servants removed the tableware, Ûndin turned to Eragon and said, "The meal pleased you, yes?"

"It was delicious."

Ûndin nodded. "I'm glad you enjoyed it. I had the tables moved outside yesterday so the dragon might dine with us." He remained intently focused on Eragon all the while he spoke.

Eragon went cold inside. Intentionally or not, Ûndin had treated Saphira as no more than a beast. Eragon had intended to ask about the veiled dwarves in private, but now—out of a desire to unsettle Ûndin—he said, "Saphira and I thank you." Then, "Sir, why was the ring thrown at us?"

A painful silence crept over the courtyard. Out of the corner of his eye, Eragon saw Orik wince. Arya, however, smiled as if she understood what he was doing.

Ûndin put down his dagger, scowling thickly. "The knurlagn you met are of a tragic clan. Before the Riders' fall, they were among the oldest, richest families of our kingdom. Their doom was sealed, though, by two mistakes: they lived on the western edge of the Beor Mountains, and they volunteered their greatest warriors in Vrael's service."

Anger broke through his voice with sharp cracks. "Galbatorix and his ever-cursed Forsworn slaughtered them in your city of Urû'baen. Then they flew on us, killing many. Of that clan, only Grimstcarvlorss Anhûin and her guards survived. Anhûin soon died of grief, and her men took the name Az Sweldn rak Anhûin, The Tears of Anhûin, covering their faces to remind themselves of their loss and their desire for revenge."

Eragon's cheeks stung with shame as he fought to keep his face expressionless. "So," said Ûndin, glowering at a pastry, "they rebuilt the clan over the decades, waiting and hunting for recompense. And now you come, bearing Hrothgar's mark. It is the ultimate insult to them, no matter your service in Farthen Dûr. Thus the ring, the ultimate challenge. It means Dûrgrimst Az Sweldn rak Anhûin will oppose you with all their resources, in every matter, big or small. They have set themselves against you utterly, declared themselves blood enemies."

"Do they mean me bodily harm?" asked Eragon stiffly.

Ûndin's gaze faltered for a moment as he cast a look at Gannel, then he shook his head and uttered a gruff laugh that was, perhaps, louder than the occasion warranted. "No, Shadeslayer! Not even they would dare hurt a guest. It is forbidden. They only want you gone, gone, gone." Yet Eragon still wondered. Then Ûndin said, "Please, let us talk no more of these unpleasant matters. Gannel and I have offered our food and mead in friendship; is that not what matters?" The priest murmured in concordance.

"It is appreciated," Eragon finally relented.

Saphira looked at him with solemn eyes and said, *They are afraid, Eragon. Afraid and resentful because they have been forced to accept a Rider's assistance.*

Aye. They may fight with us, but they don't fight for us.

CELBEDEIL

The dawnless morning found Eragon in Ûndin's main hall, listening as the clan chief spoke to Orik in Dwarvish. Ûndin broke off as Eragon approached, then said, "Ah, Shadeslayer. You slept well?"

"Yes."

"Good." He gestured at Orik. "We have been considering your departure. I had hoped you'd be able to spend some time with us. But under the circumstances, it seems best if you resume your journey early tomorrow morning, when few are in the streets who might trouble you. Supplies and transportation are being readied even as I speak. It was Hrothgar's orders that guards should accompany you as far as Ceris. I have increased their numbers from three to seven."

"And in the meantime?"

Ûndin shrugged his fur-bound shoulders. "I had intended to show you the wonders of Tarnag, but it would be foolish now for you to wander mine city. However, Grimstborith Gannel has invited you to Celbedeil for the day. Accept if you wish. You'll be safe with him." The clan chief seemed to have forgotten his earlier assertion that Az Sweldn rak Anhûin would not harm a guest.

"Thank you, I might at that." As Eragon left the hall, he pulled Orik aside and asked, "How serious is this feud, really? I need to know the truth."

Orik answered with obvious reluctance: "In the past, it was not uncommon for blood feuds to endure for generations. Entire families were driven extinct because of them. It was rash of Az Sweldn rak Anhûin to invoke the old ways; such a thing has not been done since the last of the clan wars. . . . Until they rescind their oath, you must guard against their treachery, whether it be for a year or a century. I'm sorry that your friendship with Hrothgar has brought this upon you, Eragon. But you are not alone. Dûrgrimst Ingeitum stands with you in this."

Once outside, Eragon hurried to Saphira, who had spent the night coiled in the courtyard. *Do you mind if I visit Celbedeil?*

Go if you must. But take Zar'roc. He followed her advice, also tucking Nasuada's scroll into his tunic.

When Eragon approached the gates to the hall's enclosure, five dwarves pushed the rough-hewn timbers aside, then closed in around him, hands on their axes and swords as they inspected the street. The guards remained as Eragon retraced yesterday's path to the barred entrance of Tarnag's foremost tier.

Eragon shivered. The city seemed unnaturally empty. Doors were closed, windows were shuttered, and the few pedestrians in evidence averted their faces and turned down alleys to avoid walking past him. *They're scared to be seen near me,* he realized. *Perhaps because they know Az Sweldn rak Anhûin will retaliate against anyone who helps me.* Eager to escape the open street, Eragon raised his hand to knock, but before he could, one door grated outward, and a black-robed dwarf beckoned from within. Tightening his sword belt, Eragon entered, leaving his guards outside.

His first impression was of color. A burning-green sward splayed around the pillared mass of Celbedeil, like a mantle dropped over the symmetrical hill that upheld the temple. Ivy strangled the building's ancient walls in foot after foot of hairy ropes, dew still glittering on the pointed leaves. And curving above all but the mountains was the great white cupola ribbed with chiseled gold.

His next impression was of smell. Flowers and incense mixed

their perfumes into an aroma so ethereal, Eragon felt as if he could live on the scent alone.

Last was sound, for despite clumps of priests strolling along mosaic pathways and spacious grounds, the only noise Eragon could discern was the soft thump of a rook flying overhead.

The dwarf beckoned again and strode down the main avenue toward Celbedeil. As they passed under its eaves, Eragon could only marvel at the wealth and craftsmanship displayed around him. The walls were spotted with gems of every color and cut—though all flawless—and red gold had been hammered into the veins lacing the stone ceilings, walls, and floor. Pearls and silver provided accents. Occasionally, they passed a screen partition carved entirely of jade.

The temple was devoid of cloth decorations. In their absence, the dwarves had carved a profusion of statues, many depicting monsters and deities locked in epic battles.

After climbing several floors, they passed through a copper door waxy with verdigris and embossed with intricate, patterned knots into a bare room floored with wood. Armor hung thickly on the walls, along with racks of staff-swords identical to the one Angela had fought with in Farthen Dûr.

Gannel was there, sparring with three younger dwarves. The clan chief's robe was rucked up over his thighs so he could move freely, his face a fierce scowl as the wood shaft spun in his hands, unsharpened blades darting like riled hornets.

Two dwarves lunged at Gannel, only to be stymied in a clatter of wood and metal as he spun past them, rapping their knees and heads and sending them to the floor. Eragon grinned as he watched Gannel disarm his last opponent in a brilliant flurry of blows.

At last the clan chief noticed Eragon and dismissed the other dwarves. As Gannel set his weapon on a rack, Eragon said, "Are all Quan so proficient with the blade? It seems an odd skill for priests."

Gannel faced him. "We must be able to defend ourselves, no? Many enemies stalk this land."

Eragon nodded. "Those are unique swords. I've never seen their like, except for one an herbalist used in the battle of Farthen Dûr."

The dwarf sucked in his breath, then let it hiss out between his teeth. "Angela." His expression soured. "She won her staff from a priest in a game of riddles. It was a nasty trick, as we are the only ones allowed to use hûthvírn. She and Arya . . ." He shrugged and went to a small table, where he filled two mugs with ale. Handing one to Eragon, he said, "I invited you here today at Hrothgar's request. He told me that if you accepted his offer to become Ingeitum, I was to acquaint you with dwarf traditions."

Eragon sipped the ale and kept silent, eyeing how Gannel's thick brow caught the light, shadows dripping down his cheeks from the bony ridge.

The clan chief continued: "Never before has an outsider been taught our secret beliefs, nor may you speak of them to human or elf. Yet without this knowledge, you cannot uphold what it means to be knurla. You are Ingeitum now: our blood, our flesh, our honor. You understand?"

"I do."

"Come." Keeping his ale in hand, Gannel took Eragon from the sparring room and conveyed him through five grand corridors, stopping in the archway to a dim chamber hazy with incense. Facing them, the squat outline of a statue swelled ponderously from floor to ceiling, a faint light cast across the brooding dwarf face hacked with uncharacteristic crudeness from brown granite.

"Who is he?" asked Eragon, intimidated.

"Gûntera, King of the Gods. He is a warrior and a scholar, though fickle in his moods, so we burn offerings to assure his affection at the solstices, before sowing, and at deaths and births." Gannel twisted his hand in a strange gesture and bowed to the statue. "It is to him we pray before battles, for he molded this land from the bones of a giant and gives the world its order. All realms are Gûntera's."

Then Gannel instructed Eragon how to properly venerate the

god, explaining the signs and words that were used for homage. He elucidated the meaning of the incense—how it symbolized life and happiness—and spent long minutes recounting legends about Gûntera, how the god was born fully formed to a she-wolf at the dawn of stars, how he had battled monsters and giants to win a place for his kin in Alagaësia, and how he had taken Kílf, the goddess of rivers and the sea, as his mate.

Next they went to Kílf's statue, which was carved with exquisite delicacy out of pale blue stone. Her hair flew back in liquid ripples, rolling down her neck and framing merry amethyst eyes. In her hands, she cupped a water lily and a chunk of porous red rock that Eragon did not recognize.

"What is that?" he asked, pointing.

"Coral taken from deep within the sea that borders the Beors."

"Coral?"

Gannel took a draught of ale, then said, "Our divers found it while searching for pearls. It seems that, in brine, certain stones grow like plants."

Eragon stared with wonder. He had never thought of pebbles or boulders as alive, yet here was proof that all they needed was water and salt to flourish. It finally explained how rocks had continued to appear in their fields in Palancar Valley, even after the soil had been combed clean each spring. *They grew!*

They proceeded to Urûr, master of the air and heavens, and his brother Morgothal, god of fire. At the carmine statue of Morgothal, the priest told how the brothers loved each other so much, neither could exist independently. Thus, Morgothal's burning palace in the sky during the day, and the sparks from his forge that appeared overhead every night. And also thus, how Urûr constantly fed his sibling so he would not die.

Only two more gods were left after that: Sindri—mother of the earth—and Helzvog.

Helzvog's statue was different from the rest. The nude god was bowed in half over a dwarf-sized lump of gray flint, caressing it with the tip of his forefinger. The muscles of his back bunched and knotted with inhuman strain, yet his expression was incredibly tender, as if a newborn child lay before him.

Gannel's voice dropped to a low rasp: "Gûntera may be King of the Gods, but it is Helzvog who holds our hearts. It was he who felt that the land should be peopled after the giants were vanquished. The other gods disagreed, but Helzvog ignored them and, in secret, formed the first dwarf from the roots of a mountain.

"When his deed was discovered, jealousy swept the gods and Gûntera created elves to control Alagaësia for himself. Then Sindri brought forth humans from the soil, and Urûr and Morgothal combined their knowledge and released dragons into the land. Only Kílf restrained herself. So the first races entered this world."

Eragon absorbed Gannel's words, accepting the clan chief's sincerity but unable to quell a simple question: *How does he know?* Eragon sensed that it would be an awkward query, however, and merely nodded as he listened.

"This," said Gannel, finishing the last of his ale, "leads to our most important rite, which I know Orik has discussed with you. . . . All dwarves must be buried in stone, else our spirits will never join Helzvog in his hall. We are not of earth, air, or fire, but of *stone*. And as Ingeitum, it is your responsibility to assure a proper resting place for any dwarf who may die in your company. If you fail—in the absence of injury or enemies—Hrothgar will exile you, and no dwarf will acknowledge your presence until after your death." He straightened his shoulders, staring hard at Eragon. "You have much more to learn, yet uphold the customs I outlined today and you will do well."

"I won't forget," said Eragon.

Satisfied, Gannel led him away from the statues and up a winding staircase. As they climbed, the clan chief dipped a hand into his robe and withdrew a simple necklace, a chain threaded through the pommel of a miniature silver hammer. He gave it to Eragon.

"This is another favor Hrothgar asked of me," Gannel explained.

"He worries that Galbatorix may have gleaned an image of you from the minds of Durza, the Ra'zac, or any number of soldiers who saw you throughout the Empire."

"Why should I fear that?"

"Because then Galbatorix could scry you. Perhaps he already has."

A shiver of apprehension wormed down Eragon's side, like an icy snake. *I should have thought of that,* he berated himself.

"The necklace will prevent anyone from scrying you or your dragon, as long as you wear it. I placed the spell myself, so it should hold before even the strongest mind. But be forewarned, when activated, the necklace will draw upon your strength until you either take it off or the danger has passed."

"What if I'm asleep? Could the necklace consume all my energy before I was aware of it?"

"Nay. It will wake you."

Eragon rolled the hammer between his fingers. It was difficult to avert another's spells, least of all Galbatorix's. *If Gannel is so accomplished, what other enchantments might be hidden in his gift?* He noticed a line of runes cut along the hammer's haft. They spelled *Astim Hefthyn.* The stairs ended as he asked, "Why do dwarves write with the same runes as humans?"

For the first time since they met, Gannel laughed, his voice booming through the temple as his large shoulders shook. "It is the other way around; humans write with *our* runes. When your ancestors landed in Alagaësia, they were as illiterate as rabbits. However, they soon adopted our alphabet and matched it to *this* language. Some of your words even come from us, like *father,* which was originally *farthen.*"

"So then Farthen Dûr means . . . ?" Eragon slipped the necklace over his head and tucked it under his tunic.

"Our Father."

Stopping at a door, Gannel ushered Eragon through to a curved gallery located directly below the cupola. The passageway banded

Celbedeil, providing a view through the open archways of the mountains behind Tarnag, as well as the terraced city far below.

Eragon barely glanced at the landscape, for the gallery's inner wall was covered with a single continuous painting, a gigantic narrative band that began with a depiction of the dwarves' creation under Helzvog's hand. The figures and objects stood in relief from the surface, giving the panorama a feeling of hyperrealism with its saturated, glowing colors and minute detail.

Captivated, Eragon asked, "How was this made?"

"Each scene is carved out of small plates of marble, which are fired with enamel, then fitted into a single piece."

"Wouldn't it be easier to use regular paint?"

"It would," said Gannel, "but not if we wanted it to endure centuries—millennia—without change. Enamel never fades or loses its brilliancy, unlike oil paint. This first section was carved only a decade after the discovery of Farthen Dûr, well before elves set foot on Alagaësia."

The priest took Eragon by the arm and guided him along the tableau. Each step carried them through uncounted years of history.

Eragon saw how the dwarves were once nomads on a seemingly endless plain, until the land grew so hot and desolate they were forced to migrate south to the Beor Mountains. *That was how the Hadarac Desert was formed*, he realized, amazed.

As they proceeded down the mural, heading toward the back of Celbedeil, Eragon witnessed everything from the domestication of Feldûnost to the carving of Isidar Mithrim, the first meeting between dwarves and elves, and the coronation of each new dwarf king. Dragons frequently appeared, burning and slaughtering. Eragon had difficulty restraining comment during those sections.

His steps slowed as the painting shifted to the event he had hoped to find: the war between elves and dragons. Here the dwarves had devoted a vast amount of space to the destruction wreaked upon Alagaësia by the two races. Eragon shuddered with horror at the sight of elves and dragons killing each other. The battles continued for yards, each image more bloody than the last, until the darkness lifted and a young elf was shown kneeling on the edge of a cliff, holding a white dragon egg.

"Is that . . . ?" whispered Eragon.

"Aye, it's Eragon, the First Rider. It's a good likeness too, as he agreed to sit for our artisans."

Drawn forward by his fascination, Eragon studied the face of his namesake. *I always imagined him older.* The elf had angled eyes that peered down a hooked nose and narrow chin, giving him a fierce appearance. It was an alien face, completely different from his own . . . and yet the set of his shoulders, high and tense, reminded Eragon of how he had felt upon finding Saphira's egg. *We're not so different, you and I,* he thought, touching the cool enamel. *And once my ears match yours, we shall truly be brothers through time. . . . I wonder, would you approve of my actions?* He knew they had made at least one identical choice; they had both kept the egg.

He heard a door open and close and turned to see Arya approaching from the far end of the gallery. She scanned the wall with the same blank expression Eragon had seen her use when confronting the Council of Elders. Whatever her specific emotions, he sensed that she found the situation distasteful.

Arya inclined her head. "Grimstborith."

"Arya."

"You have been educating Eragon in your mythology?"

Gannel smiled flatly. "One should always understand the faith of the society that one belongs to."

"Yet comprehension does not imply belief." She fingered the pillar of an archway. "Nor does it mean that those who purvey such beliefs do so for more than . . . material gain."

"You would deny the sacrifices my clan makes to bring comfort to our brethren?"

"I deny nothing, only ask what good might be accomplished if your wealth were spread among the needy, the starving, the homeless, or even to buy supplies for the Varden. Instead, you've piled it into a monument to your own wishful thinking."

"Enough!" The dwarf clenched his fists, his face mottled.

"Without us, the crops would wither in drought. Rivers and lakes would flood. Our flocks would give birth to one-eyed beasts. The very heavens would shatter under the gods' rage!" Arya smiled. "Only *our* prayers and service prevent that from happening. If not for Helzvog, where—"

Eragon soon lost track of the argument. He did not understand Arya's vague criticisms of Dûrgrimst Quan, but he gathered from Gannel's responses that, in some indirect way, she had implied that the dwarf gods did not exist, questioned the mental capacity of every dwarf who entered a temple, and pointed out what she took to be flaws in their reasoning—all in a pleasant and polite voice.

After a few minutes, Arya raised her hand, stopping Gannel, and said, "That is the difference between us, Grimstborith. You devote yourself to that which you believe to be true but cannot prove. There, we must agree to disagree." She turned to Eragon then. "Az Sweldn rak Anhûin has inflamed Tarnag's citizens against you. Ûndin believes, as do I, that it would be best for you to remain behind his walls until we leave."

Eragon hesitated. He wanted to see more of Celbedeil, but if there was to be trouble, then his place was by Saphira's side. He bowed to Gannel and begged to be excused. "You need not apologize, Shadeslayer," said the clan chief. He glared at Arya. "Do what you must, and may the blessings of Gûntera be upon you."

Together Eragon and Arya departed the temple and, surrounded by a dozen warriors, trotted through the city. As they did, Eragon heard shouts from an angry mob on a lower tier. A stone skipped over a nearby roof. The motion drew his eye to a dark plume of smoke rising from the city's edge.

Once in the hall, Eragon hurried to his room. There he slipped on his mail hauberk; strapped the greaves to his shins and the bracers to his forearms; jammed the leather cap, coif, and then helm over his head; and grabbed his shield. Scooping up his pack and saddlebags, he ran back to the courtyard, where he sat against Saphira's right foreleg.

Tarnag is like an overturned anthill, she observed.

Let's hope we don't get bitten.

Arya joined them before long, as did a group of fifty heavily armed dwarves who settled in the middle of the courtyard. The dwarves waited impassively, talking in low grunts as they eyed the barred gate and the mountain that rose up behind them.

"They fear," said Arya, seating herself by Eragon, "that the crowds may prevent us from reaching the rafts."

"Saphira can always fly us out."

"Snowfire as well? And Ûndin's guards? No, if we are stopped, we shall have to wait until the dwarves' outrage subsides." She studied the darkening sky. "It's unfortunate that you managed to offend so many dwarves, but perhaps inevitable. The clans have ever been contentious; what pleases one infuriates another."

He fingered the edge of his mail. "I wish now I hadn't accepted Hrothgar's offer."

"Ah, yes. As with Nasuada, I think you made the only viable choice. You are not to blame. The fault, if any, lies with Hrothgar for making the offer in the first place. He must have been well aware of the repercussions."

Silence reigned for several minutes. A half-dozen dwarves marched around the courtyard, stretching their legs. Finally, Eragon asked, "Do you have any family in Du Weldenvarden?"

It was a long time before Arya answered. "None that I'm close to."

"Why . . . why is that?"

She hesitated again. "They disliked my choice to become the Queen's envoy and ambassador; it seemed inappropriate. When I ignored their objections and still had the yawë tattooed on my shoulder—which indicates that I have devoted myself to the greater good of our race, as is the case with your ring from Brom—my family refused to see me again."

"But that was over seventy years ago," he protested.

Arya looked away, concealing her face behind a veil of hair.

Eragon tried to imagine what it must have been like for her—ostracized from her family and sent to live among two completely different races. *No wonder she's so withdrawn*, he realized. "Are there any other elves outside of Du Weldenvarden?"

Still keeping her face covered, she said, "Three of us were sent forth from Ellesméra. Fäolin and Glenwing always traveled with me when we transported Saphira's egg between Du Weldenvarden and Tronjheim. Only I survived Durza's ambush."

"What were they like?"

"Proud warriors. Glenwing loved speaking to birds with his mind. He would stand in the forest surrounded by a flock of songbirds and listen to their music for hours. Afterward, he might sing us the prettiest melodies."

"And Fäolin?" This time Arya refused to answer, though her hands tightened on her bow. Undaunted, Eragon cast around for another subject. "Why do you dislike Gannel so much?"

She faced him suddenly and touched his cheek with soft fingers. Eragon flinched with surprise. "That," she said, "is a discussion for another time." Then she stood and calmly relocated herself across the courtyard.

Confused, Eragon stared at her back. *I don't understand*, he said, leaning against Saphira's belly. She snorted, amused, then curled her neck and tail around him and promptly fell asleep.

As the valley darkened, Eragon struggled to stay alert. He pulled out Gannel's necklace and examined it several times with magic, but found only the priest's guarding spell. Giving up, he replaced the necklace under his tunic, pulled his shield over him, and settled down to wait through the night.

At the first hint of light in the sky overhead—though the valley itself was still in shadow and would remain so until almost midday—Eragon roused Saphira. The dwarves were already up, busy muffling their weapons so they could creep through Tarnag with utter secrecy. Ûndin even had Eragon tie rags around Saphira's claws and Snowfire's hooves.

When all was ready, Ûndin and his warriors assembled in a large block around Eragon, Saphira, and Arya. The gates were carefully opened—no sound came from the oiled hinges—and then they set out for the lake.

Tarnag seemed deserted, the vacant streets lined with houses where its inhabitants lay oblivious and dreaming. The few dwarves they encountered gazed at them silently, then padded away like ghosts in the twilight.

At the gate to each tier, a guard waved them through without comment. They soon left the buildings and found themselves crossing the barren fields at Tarnag's base. Beyond those, they reached the stone quay that edged the still, gray water.

Waiting for them were two wide rafts tied alongside a pier. Three dwarves squatted on the first raft, four on the second. They stood as Ûndin came into view.

Eragon helped the dwarves hobble and blindfold Snowfire, then coax the reluctant horse onto the second raft, where he was forced to his knees and tied down. Meanwhile, Saphira slipped off the pier into the lake. Only her head remained above the surface as she paddled through the water.

Ûndin grasped Eragon's arm. "Here is where we part. You have my best men; they will protect you until you reach Du Welden-varden." Eragon tried to thank him, but Ûndin shook his head. "No, it is not a matter for gratitude. It is my duty. I am only shamed that your stay was darkened by the hatred of Az Sweldn rak Anhûin."

Eragon bowed, then boarded the first raft with Orik and Arya. The mooring ropes were unknotted, and the dwarves pushed away from shore with long poles. As dawn approached, the two rafts drifted toward the mouth of the Az Ragni, Saphira swimming between them.

✦   ✦   ✦

DIAMONDS IN THE NIGHT

he Empire has violated my home.

So thought Roran as he listened to the anguished moans of the men injured during the previous night's battle with the Ra'zac and soldiers. Roran shuddered with fear and rage until his whole body was consumed with feverish chills that left his cheeks burning and his breath short. And he was sad, so very sad . . . as if the Ra'zac's deeds had destroyed the innocence of his childhood haunts.

Leaving the healer, Gertrude, tending to the wounded, Roran continued toward Horst's house, noting the makeshift barriers that filled the gaps between buildings: the boards, the barrels, the piles of rocks, and the splintered frames of the two wagons destroyed by the Ra'zac's explosives. It all seemed pitifully fragile.

The few people who moved through Carvahall were glassy-eyed with shock, grief, and exhaustion. Roran was tired too, more than he could ever remember being. He had not slept since the night before last, and his arms and back ached from the fighting.

He entered Horst's house and saw Elain standing by the open doorway to the dining room, listening to the steady burn of conversation that emanated from within. She beckoned him over.

After they had foiled the Ra'zac's counterattack, the prominent members of Carvahall had sequestered themselves in an attempt to decide what action the village should take and if Horst and his allies should be punished for initiating the hostilities. The group had been in deliberation most of the morning.

Roran peeked into the room. Seated around the long table were Birgit, Loring, Sloan, Gedric, Delwin, Fisk, Morn, and a number of others. Horst presided at the head of the table.

". . . and I say that it was stupid and reckless!" exclaimed Kiselt, propping himself upright on his bony elbows. "You had no cause to endanger—"

Morn waved a hand. "We've been over this before. Whether what *has* been done *should* have been done is beside the point. I happen to agree with it—Quimby was my friend as much as anyone's, and I shudder to think what those monsters would do with Roran—but . . . but what I want to know is how we can escape this predicament."

"Easy, kill the soldiers," barked Sloan.

"And then what? More men will follow until we drown in a sea of crimson tunics. Even if we surrender Roran, it'll do no good; you heard what the Ra'zac said—they'll kill us if we protect Roran and enslave us if we don't. You may feel differently, but, as for myself, I would rather die than spend my life as a slave." Morn shook his head, his mouth set in a flat grim line. "We cannot survive."

Fisk leaned forward. "We could leave."

"There's nowhere to go," retorted Kiselt. "We're backed against the Spine, the soldiers have blocked the road, and beyond them is the rest of the Empire."

"It's all your fault," cried Thane, stabbing a shaking finger at Horst. "They will torch our houses and murder our children because of you. You!"

Horst stood so quickly, his chair toppled over backward. "Where is your honor, man? Will you let them eat us without fighting back?"

"*Yes*, if it means suicide otherwise." Thane glared around the table, then stormed out past Roran. His face was contorted by pure, unadulterated fear.

Gedric spotted Roran then and waved him in. "Come, come, we've been waiting for you."

Roran clasped his hands in the small of his back as scores of hard eyes inspected him. "How can I help?"

"I think," said Gedric, "we've all agreed that it would accomplish nothing to give you to the Empire at this point. Whether we would if that wasn't the case is neither here nor there. The only thing we can do is prepare for another attack. Horst will make spearheads—and other weapons if he has time—and Fisk has agreed to construct shields. Fortunately, his carpentry shop didn't burn. And someone needs to oversee our defenses. We would like it to be you. You'll have plenty of assistance."

Roran nodded. "I'll do my best."

Beside Morn, Tara stood, towering over her husband. She was a large woman, with gray-streaked black hair and strong hands that were just as capable of twisting off a chicken's head as separating a pair of brawlers. She said, "Make sure you do, Roran, else we'll have more funerals." Then she turned to Horst. "Before we go any further, there are men to bury. And there are children who should be sent to safety, maybe to Cawley's farm on Nost Creek. You should go as well, Elain."

"I won't leave Horst," said Elain calmly.

Tara bristled. "This is no place for a woman five months pregnant. You'll lose the child running around like you have."

"It would do me far more harm to worry in ignorance than remain here. I have borne my sons; I will stay, as I know you and every other wife in Carvahall will."

Horst came around the table and, with a tender expression, took Elain's hand. "Nor would I have you anywhere but at my side. The children should go, though. Cawley will care for them well, but we must make sure that the route to his farm is clear."

"Not only that," rasped Loring, "none of us, not one blasted man jack can have a thing to do with the families down the valley, 'side from Cawley, of course. They can't help us, and we don't want those *desecrators* to trouble 'em."

Everyone agreed that he was right, then the meeting ended and the attendees dispersed throughout Carvahall. Before long, however, they recongregated—along with most of the village—in the small cemetery behind Gertrude's house. Ten white-swathed corpses were arranged beside their graves, a sprig of hemlock on each of their cold chests and a silver amulet around each of their necks.

Gertrude stood forth and recited the men's names: "Parr, Wyglif, Ged, Bardrick, Farold, Hale, Garner, Kelby, Melkolf, and Albem." She placed black pebbles over their eyes, then raised her arms, lifted her face to the sky, and began the quavering death lay. Tears seeped from the corners of her closed eyes as her voice rose and fell with the immemorial phrases, sighing and moaning with the village's sorrow. She sang of the earth and the night and of humanity's ageless sorrow from which none escape.

After the last mournful note faded into silence, family members praised the feats and traits of those they had lost. Then the bodies were buried.

As Roran listened, his gaze lit upon the anonymous mound where the three soldiers had been interred. *One killed by Nolfavrell, and two by me.* He could still feel the visceral shock of muscle and bone giving . . . crunching . . . pulping under his hammer. His bile rose and he had to struggle not to be sick in full view of the village. *I am the one who destroyed them.* Roran had never expected or wanted to kill, and yet he had taken more lives than anyone else in Carvahall. It felt as if his brow was marked with blood.

He left as soon as possible—not even stopping to speak with Katrina—and climbed to a point where he could survey Carvahall and consider how best to protect it. Unfortunately, the houses were too far apart to form a defensive perimeter by just fortifying the spaces between buildings. Nor did Roran think it would be a good idea to have soldiers fighting up against the walls of people's houses and trampling their gardens. *The Anora River guards our western flank,* he thought, *but as for the rest of Carvahall, we couldn't even keep a child out of it. . . . What can we build in a few hours that will be a strong enough barrier?*

He jogged into the middle of the village and shouted, "I need everyone who is free to help cut down trees!" After a minute, men began to trickle out of the houses and through the streets. "Come on, more! We all have to help!" Roran waited as the group around him continued to grow.

One of Loring's sons, Darmmen, shouldered to his side. "What's your plan?"

Roran raised his voice so they could all hear. "We need a wall around Carvahall; the thicker the better. I figure if we get some big trees, lay them on their sides, and sharpen the branches, the Ra'zac will have a pretty hard time getting over them."

"How many trees do you think it'll take?" asked Orval.

Roran hesitated, trying to gauge Carvahall's circumference. "At least fifty. Maybe sixty to do it properly." The men swore and began to argue. "Wait!" Roran counted the number of people in the crowd. He arrived at forty-eight. "If you each fell a tree in the next hour, we'll be almost done. Can you do that?"

"What do you take us for?" retorted Orval. "The last time I took an hour on a tree, I was ten!"

Darmmen spoke up: "What about brambles? We could drape them over the trees. I don't know anyone who can climb through a knot of thorny vines."

Roran grinned. "That's a great idea. Also, those of you with sons, have them harness your horses so we can drag the trees back." The men agreed and scattered through Carvahall to gather axes and saws for the job. Roran stopped Darmmen and said, "Make sure that the trees have branches all along the trunk or else they won't work."

"Where will you be?" asked Darmmen.

"Working on another line of defense." Roran left him then and ran to Quimby's house, where he found Birgit busy boarding up the windows.

"Yes?" she said, looking at him.

He quickly explained his plan with the trees. "I want to dig a trench inside the ring of trees, to slow down anyone who gets

128

through. We could even put pointed stakes in the bottom of it and—"

"What is your point, Roran?"

"I'd like you to organize every woman and child, and everyone else you can, to dig. It's too much for me to handle by myself, and we don't have long. . . ." Roran looked her straight in the eyes. "Please."

Birgit frowned. "Why ask me?"

"Because, like me, you hate the Ra'zac, and I know you will do everything possible to stop them."

"Aye," whispered Birgit, then clapped her hands briskly. "Very well, as you wish. But I will never forget, Roran Garrowsson, that it was you and your family who brought about my husband's doom." She strode away before Roran could respond.

He accepted her animosity with equanimity; it was to be expected, considering her loss. He was only lucky she had not started a blood feud. Then he shook himself and ran to where the main road entered Carvahall. It was the weakest spot in the village and had to be doubly protected. *The Ra'zac can't be allowed to just blast their way in again.*

Roran recruited Baldor, and together they began excavating a ditch across the road. "I'll have to go soon," warned Baldor between strokes of his pickax. "Dad needs me in the forge."

Roran grunted an acknowledgment without looking up. As he worked, his mind once again filled with memories of the soldiers: how they had looked as he struck them, and the feeling, the horrible *feeling* of smashing a body as if it were a rotten stump. He paused, nauseated, and noted the commotion throughout Carvahall as people readied themselves for the next assault.

After Baldor left, Roran completed the thigh-deep ditch himself, then went to Fisk's workshop. With the carpenter's permission, he had five logs from the stockpile of seasoned wood pulled by horses back to the main road. There Roran tipped the logs on end into the trench so that they formed an impenetrable barrier into Carvahall.

As he tamped down the earth around the logs, Darmmen trotted up. "We got the trees. They're just being put into place now." Roran accompanied him to Carvahall's northern edge, where twelve men wrestled four lush green pines into alignment while a team of draft horses under the whip of a young boy returned to the foothills. "Most of us are helping to retrieve the trees. The others got inspired; they seemed determined to chop down the rest of the forest when I left."

"Good, we can use the extra timber."

Darmmen pointed to a pile of dense brambles that sat on the edge of Kiselt's fields. "I cut those along the Anora. Use them however you want. I'm going to find more."

Roran clapped him on the arm, then turned toward the eastern side of Carvahall, where a long, curved line of women, children, and men labored in the dirt. He went to them and found Birgit issuing orders like a general and distributing water among the diggers. The trench was already five feet wide and two feet deep. When Birgit paused for breath, he said, "I'm impressed."

She brushed back a lock of hair without looking at him. "We plowed the ground to begin with. It made things easier."

"Do you have a shovel I can use?" he asked. Birgit pointed to a mound of tools at the other end of the trench. As Roran walked toward it, he spied the copper gleam of Katrina's hair in the midst of the bobbing backs. Beside her, Sloan hacked at the soft loam with a furious, obsessive energy, as if he were attempting to tear open the earth's skin, to peel back its clay hide and expose the muscle beneath. His eyes were wild, and his teeth were bared in a knotted grimace, despite the flecks of dirt and filth that spotted his lips.

Roran shuddered at Sloan's expression and hurried past, averting his face so as to avoid meeting his bloodshot gaze. He grabbed a shovel and immediately plunged it into the soil, doing his best to forget his worries in the heat of physical exertion.

The day progressed in a continuous rush of activity, without breaks for meals or rest. The trench grew longer and deeper, until it cupped two-thirds of the village and reached the banks of the Anora River. All the loose dirt was piled on the inside edge of the trench in an attempt to prevent anyone from jumping over it . . . and to make it difficult to climb out.

The wall of trees was finished in early afternoon. Roran stopped digging then to help sharpen the innumerable branches—which were overlapped and interlocked as much as possible—and affix the nets of brambles. Occasionally, they had to pull out a tree so farmers like Ivor could drive their livestock into the safety of Carvahall.

By evening the fortifications were stronger and more extensive than Roran had dared hope, though they still required several more hours of work to complete to his satisfaction.

He sat on the ground, gnawing a hunk of sourdough bread and staring at the stars through a haze of exhaustion. A hand dropped on his shoulder, and he looked up to see Albriech. "Here." Albriech extended a rough shield—made of sawed boards pegged together—and a six-foot-long spear. Roran accepted them gratefully, then Albriech proceeded onward, distributing spears and shields to whomever he encountered.

Roran dragged himself upright, got his hammer from Horst's house, and thus armed, went to the entrance to the main road, where Baldor and two others kept watch. "Wake me when you need to rest," Roran said, then lay on the soft grass underneath the eaves of a nearby house. He arranged his weapons so he could find them in the dark and closed his eyes in eager anticipation.

"Roran."

The whisper came from by his right ear. "Katrina?" He struggled into a sitting position, blinking as she unshuttered a lantern so a key of light struck his thigh. "What are you doing here?"

"I wanted to see you." Her eyes, large and mysterious against her pale face, pooled with the night's shadows. She took his arm and led him to a deserted porch far out of earshot of Baldor and the other guards. There she placed her hands on his cheeks and softly kissed him, but he was too tired and troubled to respond to her affection. She drew away and studied him. "What is wrong, Roran?"

A bark of humorless laughter escaped him. "What's wrong? The world is wrong; it's as askew as a picture frame knocked on its side." He jammed his fist against his gut. "And I am wrong. Every time I allow myself to relax, I see the soldiers bleeding under my hammer. Men I *killed*, Katrina. And their eyes . . . their *eyes*! They knew they were about to die and that they could nothing do about it." He trembled in the darkness. "They knew . . . I knew . . . and I still had to do it. It couldn't—" Words failed him as he felt hot tears roll down his cheeks.

Katrina cradled his head as Roran cried from the shock of the past few days. He wept for Garrow and Eragon; he wept for Parr, Quimby, and the other dead; he wept for himself; and he wept for the fate of Carvahall. He sobbed until his emotions ebbed and left him as dry and hollow as an old barley husk.

Forcing himself to take a long breath, Roran looked at Katrina and noticed her own tears. He brushed them away with his thumb, like diamonds in the night. "Katrina . . . my love." He said it again, tasting the words: "My love. I have naught to give you but my love. Still . . . I must ask. Will you marry me?"

In the dim lantern light, he saw pure joy and wonder leap across her face. Then she hesitated and troubled doubt appeared. It was wrong for him to ask, or for her to accept, without Sloan's permission. But Roran no longer cared; he had to know now if he and Katrina would spend their lives together.

Then, softly: "Yes, Roran, I will."

UNDER A DARKLING SKY

That night it rained.

Layer upon layer of pregnant clouds blanketed Palancar Valley, clinging to the mountains with tenacious arms and filling the air with heavy, cold mist. From inside, Roran watched as cords of gray water pelted the trees with their frothing leaves, muddied the trench around Carvahall, and scrabbled with blunt fingers against the thatched roofs and eaves as the clouds disgorged their load. Everything was streaked, blurred, and hidden behind the torrent's inexorable streamers.

By midmorning the storm had abated, although a continuous drizzle still percolated through the mist. It quickly soaked Roran's hair and clothes when he took his watch at the barricade to the main road. He squatted by the upright logs, shook his cloak, then pulled the hood farther over his face and tried to ignore the cold.

Despite the weather, Roran soared and exulted with his joy at Katrina's acceptance. They were engaged! In his mind, it was as if a missing piece of the world had dropped into place, as if he had been granted the confidence of an invulnerable warrior. What did the soldiers matter, or the Ra'zac, or the Empire itself, before love such as theirs? They were nothing but tinder to the blaze.

For all his new bliss, however, his mind was entirely focused on what had become the most important conundrum of his existence: how to assure that Katrina would survive Galbatorix's wrath. He had thought of nothing else since waking. *The best thing would be for*

Katrina to go to Cawley's, he decided, staring down the hazy road, *but she would never agree to leave . . . unless Sloan told her to. I might be able to convince him; I'm sure he wants her out of danger as much as I do.*

As he considered ways to approach the butcher, the clouds thickened again and the rain renewed its assault on the village, arching down in stinging waves. Around Roran, the puddles jumped to life as pellets of water drummed their surfaces, bouncing back up like startled grasshoppers.

When Roran grew hungry, he passed his watch to Larne—Loring's youngest son—and went to find lunch, darting from the shelter of one eave to another. As he rounded a corner, he was surprised to see Albriech on the house's porch, arguing violently with a group of men.

Ridley shouted, ". . . you're blind—follow the cottonwoods and they'll never see! You took the addle-brain's route."

"Try it if you want," retorted Albriech.

"I will!"

"Then you can tell me how you like the taste of arrows."

"Maybe," said Thane, "we aren't as clubfooted as you are."

Albriech turned on him with a snarl. "Your words are as thick as your wits. I'm not stupid enough to risk my family on the cover of a few leaves that I've never seen before." Thane's eyes bulged and his face turned a deep mottled crimson. "What?" taunted Albriech. "Have you no tongue?"

Thane roared and struck Albriech on the cheek with his fist. Albriech laughed. "Your arm is as weak as a woman's." Then he grabbed Thane's shoulder and threw him off the porch and into the mud, where he lay on his side, stunned.

Holding his spear like a staff, Roran jumped beside Albriech, preventing Ridley and the others from laying hands on him. "No more," growled Roran, furious. "We have other enemies. An assembly can be called and arbitrators will decide whether compensation is due to either Albriech or Thane. But until then, we *can't* fight ourselves."

"Easy for you to say," spat Ridley. "You have no wife or children." Then he helped Thane to his feet and departed with the group of men.

Roran stared hard at Albriech and the purple bruise that was spreading beneath his right eye. "What started it?" he asked.

"I—" Albriech stopped with a grimace and felt his jaw. "I went scouting with Darmmen. The Ra'zac have posted soldiers on several hills. They can see across the Anora and up and down the valley. One or two of us might, *might,* be able to creep past them without notice, but we'll never get the children to Cawley without killing the soldiers, and then we might as well tell the Ra'zac where we're going."

Dread clutched at Roran, flooding like poison through his heart and veins. *What can I do?* Sick with a sense of impending doom, he put an arm around Albriech's shoulders. "Come on; Gertrude should have a look at you."

"No," said Albriech, shrugging him off. "She has more pressing cases than me." He took a preparatory breath—as if he were about to dive into a lake—and lumbered off through the downpour in the direction of the forge.

Roran watched him go, then shook his head and went inside. He found Elain sitting on the floor with a row of children, sharpening a pile of spearheads with files and whetstones. Roran gestured to Elain. Once they were in another room, he told her what had just occurred.

Elain swore harshly—startling him, for he had never heard her use such language—then asked, "Is there cause for Thane to declare a feud?"

"Possibly," admitted Roran. "They both insulted each other, but Albriech's oaths were the strongest. . . . However, Thane did strike first. You could declare a feud yourself."

"Nonsense," asserted Elain, wrapping a shawl around her shoulders. "This is a dispute for arbitrators to resolve. If we must pay a fine, so be it, as long as bloodshed is avoided." She headed out the front door, a finished spear in hand.

Troubled, Roran located bread and meat in the kitchen, then helped the children sharpen spearheads. Once Felda, one of the mothers, arrived, Roran left the children in her care and slogged back through Carvahall to the main road.

As he squatted in the mud, a shaft of sunlight burst underneath the clouds and illuminated the folds of rain so each drop flashed with crystalline fire. Roran stared, awestruck, ignoring the water streaming down his face. The rift in the clouds widened until a shelf of massive thunderheads hung over the western three-quarters of Palancar Valley, facing a strip of pure blue sky. Because of the billowy roof above and the angle of the sun, the rain-drenched landscape was lit brilliantly on one side and painted with rich shadows on the other, giving the fields, bushes, trees, river, and mountains the most extraordinary colors. It was as if the entire world had been transformed into a sculpture of burnished metal.

Just then, movement caught Roran's eye, and he looked down to see a soldier standing on the road, his mail shining like ice. The man gaped with amazement at Carvahall's new fortifications, then turned and fled back into the golden mist.

"Soldiers!" shouted Roran, jolting to his feet. He wished that he had his bow, but he had left it inside to protect it from the elements. His only comfort was that the soldiers would have an even harder time keeping their weapons dry.

Men and women ran from their houses, gathered along the trench, and peered out through the wall of overlapping pines. The long branches wept beads of moisture, translucent cabochons that reflected the rows of anxious eyes.

Roran found himself standing beside Sloan. The butcher held one of Fisk's makeshift shields in his left hand, and in his right a cleaver curved like a half-moon. His belt was festooned with at least a dozen knives, all of them large and honed to a razor edge. He and Roran exchanged brisk nods, then refocused on where the soldier had disappeared.

Less than a minute later, the disembodied voice of a Ra'zac slithered out of the mist: "By continuing to defend Carvahall, you proclaim your choice and ssseal your doom. You ssshall die!"

Loring responded: "Show your maggot-riddled faces if you dare, you lily-livered, bandy-legged, snake-eyed *wretches*! We'll crack your skulls open and fatten our hogs on your blood!"

A dark shape floated toward them, followed by the dull thump of a spear embedding itself in a door an inch from Gedric's left arm.

"Take cover!" shouted Horst from the middle of the line. Roran knelt behind his shield and peered through a hairline gap between two of the boards. He was just in time, for a half-dozen spears hurtled over the wall of trees and buried themselves among the cowering villagers.

From somewhere in the mist came an agonized scream.

Roran's heart jumped with a painful flutter. He panted for breath, though he had not moved, and his hands were slick with sweat. He heard the faint sound of shattering glass on the northern edge of Carvahall . . . then the bellow of an explosion and crashing timbers.

Spinning around, he and Sloan sped through Carvahall, where they found a team of six soldiers dragging away the splintered remains of several trees. Beyond them, pale and wraithlike in the glittering shards of rain, sat the Ra'zac on their black horses. Without slowing, Roran fell upon the first man, jabbing his spear. His first and second stabs were deflected by an upraised arm, then Roran caught the soldier on the hip, and when he stumbled, in his throat.

Sloan howled like an enraged beast, threw his cleaver, and split one of the men's helms, crushing his skull. Two soldiers charged him with drawn swords. Sloan sidestepped, laughing now, and blocked their attacks with his shield. One soldier swung so hard, his blade stuck in the shield's rim. Sloan yanked him closer and gored him through the eye with a carving knife from his belt. Drawing a second cleaver, the butcher circled his other opponent with a maniacal grin. "Shall I gut and hamstring you?" he demanded, almost prancing with a terrible, bloody glee.

Roran lost his spear to the next two men he faced. He barely managed to drag out his hammer in time to stop a sword from shearing off his leg. The soldier who had torn the spear from Roran's grip now cast the weapon at him, aiming for his breast. Roran dropped his hammer, caught the shaft in midair—which astounded him as much as the soldiers—spun it around, and drove the spear through the armor and ribs of the man who had launched it. Left weaponless, Roran was forced to retreat before the remaining soldier. He stumbled over a corpse, cutting his calf on a sword as he fell, and rolled to avoid a two-handed blow from the soldier, scrabbling frantically in the ankle-deep mud for something, *anything* he could use for a weapon. A hilt bruised his fingers, and he ripped it from the muck and slashed at the soldier's sword hand, severing his thumb.

The man stared dumbly at the glistening stump, then said, "This is what comes from not shielding myself."

"Aye," agreed Roran, and beheaded him.

The last soldier panicked and fled toward the impassive specters of the Ra'zac while Sloan bombarded him with a stream of insults and foul names. When the soldier finally pierced the shining curtain of rain, Roran watched with a thrill of horror as the two black figures bent down from their steeds on either side of the man and gripped the nape of his neck with twisted hands. The cruel fingers tightened, and the man shrieked desperately and convulsed, then went limp. The Ra'zac placed the corpse behind one of their saddles before turning their horses and riding away.

Roran shuddered and looked at Sloan, who was cleaning his blades. "You fought well." He had never suspected that the butcher contained such ferocity.

Sloan said in a low voice, "They'll never get Katrina. Never, even if I must skin the lot of them, or fight a thousand Urgals and the king to boot. I'd tear the sky itself down and let the Empire drown in its own blood before she suffers so much as a scratch." He clamped his mouth shut then, jammed the last of his knives into his belt, and began dragging the three broken trees back into position.

While he did, Roran rolled the dead soldiers through the trampled mud, away from the fortifications. *Now I have killed five*. At the completion of his labor, he straightened and glanced around, puzzled, for all he heard was silence and the hissing rain. *Why has no one come to help us?*

Wondering what else might have occurred, he returned with Sloan to the scene of the first attack. Two soldiers hung lifelessly on the slick branches of the tree wall, but that was not what held their attention. Horst and the other villagers knelt in a circle around a small body. Roran caught his breath. It was Elmund, son of Delwin. The ten-year-old boy had been struck in his side by a spear. His parents sat in the mud beside him, their faces as blank as stone.

Something has to be done, thought Roran, dropping to his knees and leaning against his spear. Few children survived their first five or six years. But to lose your firstborn son *now*, when everything indicated that he should grow tall and strong to take his father's place in Carvahall—it was enough to crush you. *Katrina . . . the children . . . they all have to be protected.*

But where? . . . Where? . . . Where? . . . Where!

✦   ✦   ✦

DOWN THE RUSHING
MERE-WASH

On the first day from Tarnag, Eragon made an effort to learn the names of Ûndin's guards. They were Ama, Trîhga, Hedin, Ekksvar, Shrrgnien—which Eragon found unpronounceable, though he was told it meant Wolfheart—Dûthmér, and Thorv.

Each raft had a small cabin in the center. Eragon preferred to spend his time seated on the edge of the logs, watching the Beor Mountains scroll by. Kingfishers and jackdaws flitted along the clear river, while blue herons stood stiltlike on the marshy bank, which was planked with splotches of light that fell through the boughs of hazel, beech, and willow. Occasionally, a bullfrog would croak from a bed of ferns.

When Orik settled beside him, Eragon said, "It's beautiful."

"That it is." The dwarf quietly lit his pipe, then leaned back and puffed.

Eragon listened to the creak of wood and rope as Trîhga steered the raft with the long paddle at the aft. "Orik, can you tell me why Brom joined the Varden? I know so little about him. For most of my life, he was just the town storyteller."

"He never *joined* the Varden; he helped found it." Orik paused to tap some ashes into the water. "After Galbatorix became king, Brom was the only Rider still alive, outside of the Forsworn."

"But he wasn't a Rider, not then. His dragon was killed in the fighting at Doru Araeba."

"Well, a Rider by training. Brom was the first to organize the

140

friends and allies of the Riders who had been forced into exile. It was he who convinced Hrothgar to allow the Varden to live in Farthen Dûr, and he who obtained the elves' assistance."

They were silent for a while. "Why did Brom relinquish the leadership?" asked Eragon.

Orik smiled wryly. "Perhaps he never wanted it. It was before Hrothgar adopted me, so I saw little of Brom in Tronjheim. . . . He was always off fighting the Forsworn or engaged in one plot or another."

"Your parents are dead?"

"Aye. The pox took them when I was young, and Hrothgar was kind enough to welcome me into his hall and, since he has no children of his own, to make me his heir."

Eragon thought of his helm, marked with the Ingeitum symbol. *Hrothgar has been kind to me as well.*

When the afternoon twilight arrived, the dwarves hung a round lantern at each corner of the rafts. The lanterns were red, which Eragon remembered was to preserve night vision. He stood by Arya and studied the lanterns' pure, motionless depths. "Do you know how these are made?" he asked.

"It was a spell we gave the dwarves long ago. They use it with great skill."

Eragon reached up and scratched his chin and cheeks, feeling the patches of stubble that had begun to appear. "Could you teach me more magic while we travel?"

She looked at him, her balance perfect on the undulating logs. "It is not my place. A teacher is waiting for you."

"Then tell me this, at least," he said. "What does the name of my sword mean?"

Arya's voice was very soft. "*Misery* is your sword. And so it was until you wielded it."

Eragon stared with aversion at Zar'roc. The more he learned about his weapon, the more malevolent it seemed, as if the blade could cause misfortune of its own free will. *Not only did Morzan kill*

Riders with it, but Zar'roc's very name is evil. If Brom had not given it to him, and if not for the fact that Zar'roc never dulled and could not be broken, Eragon would have thrown it into the river at that very moment.

Before it grew any darker, Eragon swam out to Saphira. They flew together for the first time since leaving Tronjheim and soared high above the Az Ragni, where the air was thin and the water below was only a purple streak.

Without the saddle, Eragon gripped Saphira tightly with his knees, feeling her hard scales rub the scars from their first flight.

As Saphira tilted to the left, rising on an updraft, he saw three brown specks launch themselves from the mountainside below and ascend rapidly. At first Eragon took them to be falcons, but as they neared, he realized that the animals were almost twenty feet long, with attenuated tails and leathery wings. In fact, they looked like dragons, though their bodies were smaller, thinner, and more serpentine than Saphira's. Nor did their scales glitter, but were dappled green and brown.

Excited, Eragon pointed them out to Saphira. *Could they be dragons?* he asked.

I don't know. She floated in place, inspecting the newcomers as they spiraled around them. The creatures seemed puzzled by Saphira. They darted toward her, only to hiss and swoop overhead at the last moment.

Eragon grinned and reached out with his mind, trying to touch their thoughts. As he did, the three recoiled and shrieked, opening their maws like hungry snakes. Their piercing keen was mental as well as physical. It tore through Eragon with a savage strength, seeking to incapacitate him. Saphira felt it too. Continuing the racking cry, the creatures attacked with razor claws.

Hold on, warned Saphira. She folded her left wing and spun halfway around, avoiding two of the animals, then flapped quickly, rising above the other. At the same time, Eragon worked furiously to block the shriek. The instant his mind was clear, he reached for the magic. *Don't kill them,* said Saphira. *I want the experience.*

Though the creatures were more agile than Saphira, she had the advantage of bulk and strength. One of the creatures dove at her. She flipped upside down—falling backward—and kicked the animal in the chest.

The shriek dropped in intensity as her injured foe retreated.

Saphira flared her wings, looping right side up so she faced the other two as they converged on her. She arched her neck, Eragon heard a deep rumble between her ribs, and then a jet of flame roared from her jaws. A molten-blue halo engulfed Saphira's head, flashing through her gemlike scales until she sparkled gloriously and seemed to be lit from within.

The two dragon-beasts squawked in dismay and veered to either side. The mental assault ceased as they sped away, sinking back toward the mountainside.

You almost threw me off, said Eragon, loosening his cramped arms from around her neck.

She looked at him smugly. *Almost, but not quite.*

That's true, he laughed.

Flushed with the thrill of victory, they returned to the rafts. As Saphira landed amid two great fins of water, Orik shouted, "Are you hurt?"

"No," called Eragon. The icy water whirled around his legs as Saphira swam to the side of the raft. "Were they another race unique to the Beors?"

Orik pulled him onto the raft. "We call them Fanghur. They're not as intelligent as dragons and they can't breathe fire, but they are still formidable foes."

"So we discovered." Eragon massaged his temples in an attempt to alleviate the headache the Fanghur's attack had brought on. "Saphira was more than a match for them, however."

Of course, she said.

"It's how they hunt," explained Orik. "They use their minds to immobilize their prey while they kill it."

Saphira flicked water at Eragon with her tail. *It's a good idea. Maybe I'll try it next time I go hunting.*

He nodded. *It could come in handy in a fight too.*

Arya came to the edge of the raft. "I'm glad you did not kill them. Fanghur are rare enough that those three would have been sorely missed."

"They still manage to eat enough of our herds," growled Thorv from inside the cabin. The dwarf marched out to Eragon, champing irritably under the twisted knots of his beard. "Do not fly anymore while in these Beor Mountains, Shadeslayer. It is difficult enough to keep you unharmed without you and thine dragon fighting wind-vipers."

"We'll stay on the ground until we reach the plains," promised Eragon.

"Good."

When they stopped for the night, the dwarves moored the rafts to aspen trees along the mouth of a small stream. Ama started a fire while Eragon helped Ekksvar pull Snowfire onto land. They pick-eted the stallion on a strip of grass.

Thorv oversaw the erection of six large tents. Hedin gathered firewood to last until morning, and Dûthmér carried supplies off the second raft and began making dinner. Arya took up watch on the edge of camp, where she was soon joined by Ekksvar, Ama, and Tríhga when they finished their tasks.

When Eragon realized he had nothing to do, he squatted by the fire with Orik and Shrrgnien. As Shrrgnien pulled off his gloves and held his scarred hands over the flames, Eragon noticed that a polished steel stud—perhaps a quarter of an inch long—protruded from each of the dwarf's knuckles, except for on his thumbs.

"What are those?" he asked.

Shrrgnien looked at Orik and laughed. "These are mine Ascûdgamln . . . mine 'fists of steel.' " Without standing, he twisted and punched the bole of an aspen, leaving four symmetrical holes in the bark. Shrrgnien laughed again. "They are good for hitting things, eh?"

Eragon's curiosity and envy were aroused. "How are they made? I mean, how are the spikes attached to your hands?"

Shrrgnien hesitated, trying to find the right words. "A healer puts you in a deep sleep, so you feel no pain. Then a hole is—is *drilled*, yes?—is drilled down through the joints . . ." He broke off and spoke quickly to Orik in the dwarf language.

"A metal socket is embedded in each hole," explained Orik. "Magic is used to seal it in place, and when the warrior has fully recovered, various-sized spikes can be threaded into the sockets."

"Yes, see," said Shrrgnien, grinning. He gripped the stud above his left index finger, carefully twisted it free of his knuckle, and then handed it to Eragon.

Eragon smiled as he rolled the sharp lump around his palm. "I wouldn't mind having 'fists of steel' myself." He returned the stud to Shrrgnien.

"It's a dangerous operation," warned Orik. "Few knurlan get Ascûdgamln because you can easily lose the use of your hands if the drill goes too deep." He raised his fist and showed it to Eragon. "Our bones are thicker than yours. It might not work for a human."

"I'll remember that." Still, Eragon could not help but imagine what it would be like to fight with Ascûdgamln, to be able to strike anything he wanted with impunity, including armored Urgals. He loved the idea.

After eating, Eragon retired to his tent. The fire provided enough light that he could see the silhouette of Saphira nestled alongside the tent, like a figure cut from black paper and pasted against the canvas wall.

Eragon sat with the blankets pulled over his legs and stared at his lap, drowsy but unwilling to sleep quite yet. Unbidden, his mind turned to thoughts of home. He wondered how Roran, Horst, and everyone else from Carvahall was doing, and if the weather in Palancar Valley was warm enough for the farmers to start planting their crops. Longing and sadness suddenly gripped Eragon.

He removed a wood bowl from his pack and, taking his waterskin, filled it to the brim with liquid. Then he focused on an image of Roran and whispered, "Draumr kópa."

As always, the water went black before brightening to reveal the object being scryed. Eragon saw Roran sitting alone in a candlelit bedroom he recognized from Horst's house. *Roran must have given up his job in Therinsford,* realized Eragon. His cousin leaned on his knees and clasped his hands, staring at the far wall with an expression that Eragon knew meant Roran was grappling with some difficult problem. Still, Roran seemed well enough, if a bit drawn, which comforted Eragon. After a minute, he released the magic, ending the spell and clearing the surface of the water.

Reassured, Eragon emptied the bowl, then lay down, pulling the blankets up to his chin. He closed his eyes and sank into the warm dusk that separates consciousness and sleep, where reality bends and sways to the wind of thought, and where creativity blossoms in its freedom from boundaries and all things are possible.

Slumber soon took him. Most of his rest was uneventful, but right before he woke, the usual night phantasms were replaced with a vision as clear and vibrant as any waking experience.

He saw a tortured sky, black and crimson with smoke. Crows and eagles swirled high above flights of arrows that arched from one side to another of a great battle. A man sprawled in the clotted mud with a dented helm and bloody mail—his face concealed behind an upthrown arm.

An armored hand entered Eragon's view. The gauntlet was so near it blotted out half the world with polished steel. Like an inexorable machine, the thumb and last three fingers curled into a fist, leaving the trunk of the index finger to point at the downed man with all the authority of fate itself.

The vision still filled Eragon's mind when he crawled out of the tent. He found Saphira some distance from the camp, gnawing on a furry lump. When he told her what he had seen, she paused in midbite, then jerked her neck and swallowed a strip of meat.

The last time this occurred, she said, *it proved to be a true prediction of events elsewhere. Do you think a battle is in progress in Alagaësia?*

He kicked a loose branch. *I'm not sure. . . . Brom said you could only scry people, places, and things that you had already seen. Yet I've never seen this place. Nor had I seen Arya when I first dreamt about her in Teirm.*

Perhaps Togira Ikonoka will be able to explain it.

As they prepared to leave, the dwarves seemed much more relaxed now that they were a good distance from Tarnag. When they started poling down the Az Ragni, Ekksvar—who was steering Snowfire's raft—began chanting in his rough bass:

Down the rushing mere-wash
Of Kílf's welling blood,
We ride the twisting timbers,
For hearth, clan, and honor.

Under the ernes' sky-vat,
Through the ice-wolves' forest bowls,
We ride the gory wood,
For iron, gold, and diamond.

Let hand-ringer and bearded gaper fill my grip
And battle-leaf guard my stone
As I leave the halls of my fathers
For the empty land beyond.

The other dwarves joined Ekksvar, slipping into Dwarvish as they continued on to other verses. The low throb of their voices accompanied Eragon as he carefully made his way to the head of the raft, where Arya sat cross-legged.

"I had a . . . vision during my sleep," said Eragon. Arya looked at him with interest, and he recounted the images he had seen. "If it's scrying, then—"

"It's not scrying," said Arya. She spoke with deliberate slowness, as if to prevent any misunderstanding. "I thought for a long time about how you saw me imprisoned in Gil'ead, and I believe that as I lay unconscious, my spirit was searching for help, wherever I might find it."

"But why me?"

Arya nodded toward where Saphira undulated through the water. "I grew accustomed to Saphira's presence during the fifteen years I guarded her egg. I was reaching out for anything that felt familiar when I touched your dreams."

"Are you really strong enough to contact someone in Teirm from Gil'ead? Especially if you were drugged."

A ghost of a smile touched Arya's lips. "I could stand on the very gates of Vroengard and still speak with you as clearly as I am now." She paused. "If you did not scry me in Teirm, then you could not have scryed this new dream. It must be a premonition. They have been known to occur throughout the sentient races, but especially among magic users."

Eragon clutched the netting around a bundle of supplies as the raft lurched. "If what I saw *will* come to pass, then how can we change anything that happens? Do our choices matter? What if I threw myself off the raft right now and drowned?"

"But you won't." Arya dipped her left forefinger in the river and stared at the single drop that clung to her skin, like a quivering lens. "Once, long ago, the elf Maerzadí had a premonition that he would accidentally kill his son in battle. Rather than live to see it happen, he committed suicide, saving his son, and at the same time proving that the future isn't set. Short of killing yourself, however, you can do little to change your destiny, since you don't know what choices will lead you to the particular point of time that you saw." She flipped her hand and the drop splattered against the log between them. "We know that it's possible to retrieve information from the future—fortunetellers can often sense the paths a person's life may take—but we've been unable to refine the process to the point where you can choose what, where, or when you want to see."

Eragon found the entire concept of funneling knowledge through time profoundly disturbing. It raised too many questions about the nature of reality. *Whether fate and destiny really exist, the only thing I can do is enjoy the present and live as honorably as possible.*

Yet he could not help asking, "What's to stop me, though, from scrying one of my memories? I've seen everything in them . . . so I should be able to view them with magic."

Arya's gaze darted to meet his. "If you value your life, never attempt it. Many years ago, several of our spellweavers devoted themselves to defeating time's enigmas. When they tried to summon up the past, they only succeeded in creating a blurred image on their mirror before the spell consumed their energy and killed them. We made no more experiments on the subject. It is argued that the spell would work if more magicians participated, but no one is willing to accept the risk and the theory remains unproven. Even if one could scry the past, it would be of limited use. And to scry the future, one would have to know exactly what was going to happen and where and when, which defeats the purpose.

"It's a mystery, then, how people can have premonitions while sleeping, how they can do something unconsciously that has defeated our greatest sages. Premonitions may be linked to the very nature and fabric of magic . . . or they may function in a similar way to the dragons' ancestral memories. We don't know. Many avenues of magic have yet to be explored." She stood in a single fluid movement. "Take care not to lose yourself among them."

DRIFTING

The valley widened throughout the morning as the rafts swept toward a bright gap between two mountains. They reached the opening at midday and found themselves looking out of shadow upon a sunny prairie that faded into the north.

Then the current pushed them beyond the frosted crags and the walls of the world dropped away to reveal a gigantic sky and flat horizon. Almost immediately, the air grew warmer. The Az Ragni curved to the east, edging the foothills of the mountain range on one side and the plains on the other.

The amount of open space seemed to unsettle the dwarves. They muttered among themselves and glanced longingly at the cavernous rift behind them.

Eragon found the sunlight invigorating. It was hard to ever really feel awake when three-quarters of the day was spent in twilight. Behind his raft, Saphira launched herself out of the water and flew up over the prairie until she dwindled to a winking speck in the azure dome above.

What do you see? he asked.

I see vast herds of gazelles to the north and east. To the west, the Hadarac Desert. That is all.

No one else? No Urgals, slavers, or nomads?

We are alone.

That evening, Thorv chose a small cove for their camp. While Dûthmér fixed dinner, Eragon cleared a space beside his tent, then drew Zar'roc and settled into the ready stance Brom had taught him when they first sparred. Eragon knew he was at a disadvantage compared to the elves, and he had no intention of arriving in Ellesméra out of practice.

With excruciating slowness, he looped Zar'roc over his head and brought it back down with both hands, as if to cleave an enemy's helm. He held the pose for a second. Keeping his motion under complete control, he pivoted to the right—twisting Zar'roc's point to parry an imaginary blow—then stopped with rigid arms.

Out of the corner of his eye, Eragon noticed Orik, Arya, and Thorv watching. He ignored them and focused only on the ruby blade in his hands; he held it as if it were a snake that could writhe out of his grip and bite his arm.

Turning again, he commenced a series of forms, flowing from one to another with disciplined ease as he gradually increased his speed. In his mind, he was no longer in the shadowy cove, but surrounded by a knot of ferocious Urgals and Kull. He ducked and slashed, parried, riposted, jumped to the side, and stabbed in a whirl of activity. He fought with mindless energy, as he had in Farthen Dûr, with no thought for the safety of his own flesh, dashing and tearing aside his imagined enemies.

He spun Zar'roc around—in an attempt to flip the hilt from one palm to another—then dropped the sword as a jagged line of pain bisected his back. He staggered and fell. Above him, he could hear Arya and the dwarves babbling, but all he saw was a constellation of sparkling red haze, like a bloody veil dropped over the world. No sensation existed other than pain. It blotted out thought and reason, leaving only a feral animal that screamed for release.

When Eragon recovered enough to notice his whereabouts, he found that he had been placed inside his tent and wrapped tightly with blankets. Arya sat beside him, while Saphira's head stuck through the entrance flaps.

Was I out long? asked Eragon.

A while. You slept a little at the end. I tried to draw you from your

body into mine and shield you from the pain, but I could do little with
you unconscious.

Eragon nodded and closed his eyes. His entire body throbbed. Taking a deep breath, he looked up at Arya and quietly asked, "How can I train? . . . How can I fight, or use magic? . . . I am a broken vessel." His face felt heavy with age as he spoke.

She answered just as softly: "You can sit and watch. You can listen. You can read. And you can learn."

Despite her words, he heard a hitch of uncertainty, even fear, in her voice. He rolled onto his side to avoid meeting her eyes. It shamed him to appear so helpless before her. "How did the Shade do this to me?"

"I have no answers, Eragon. I am neither the wisest nor the strongest elf. We all do our best, and you cannot be blamed for it. Perhaps time will heal your wound." Arya pressed her fingers to his brow and murmured, "Sé mor'ranr ono finna," then left the tent.

Eragon sat and winced as his cramped back muscles stretched. He stared at his hands without seeing them. *I wonder if Murtagh's scar ever pained him like mine does.*

I don't know, said Saphira.

A dead silence followed. Then: *I'm afraid.*

Why?

Because . . . He hesitated. *Because nothing I do will prevent another attack. I don't know when or where it will happen, but I do know that it's inevitable. So I wait, and every moment I fear that if I lift something too heavy or stretch in the wrong way, the pain will return. My own body has become the enemy.*

Saphira hummed deep in her throat. *I have no answers either. Life is both pain and pleasure. If this is the price you must pay for the hours you enjoy, is it too much?*

Yes, he snapped. He pulled off the blankets and shoved past her, stumbling into the center of the camp, where Arya and the dwarves sat around a fire. "Is there food left?" asked Eragon.

Dûthmér wordlessly filled a bowl and handed it to him. With a deferential expression, Thorv asked, "Are you better now, Shadeslayer?" He and the other dwarves seemed awed by what they had seen.

"I'm fine."

"You bear a heavy burden, Shadeslayer."

Eragon scowled and abruptly walked to the edge of the tents, where he seated himself in darkness. He could sense Saphira nearby, but she left him in peace. He swore under his breath and jabbed Dûthmér's stew with dull anger.

Just as he took a bite, Orik said from beside him, "You should not treat them so."

Eragon glared at Orik's shadowed face. "What?"

"Thorv and his men were sent to protect you and Saphira. They will die for you if need be, and trust their sacred burial to you. You should remember that."

Eragon bit back a sharp retort and gazed at the black surface of the river—always moving, never stopping—in an attempt to calm his mind. "You're right. I let my temper get away from me."

Orik's teeth gleamed in the night as he smiled. "It's a lesson that every commander must learn. I had it beaten into me by Hrothgar after I threw my boot at a dwarf who left his halberd where someone could step on it."

"Did you hit him?"

"I broke his nose," chuckled Orik.

Despite himself, Eragon laughed as well. "I'll remember not to do that." He held the bowl with both hands to keep them warm.

Eragon heard the jangle of metal as Orik extracted something from a pouch. "Here," said the dwarf, dropping a knot of intertwined gold rings on Eragon's palm. "It's a puzzle we use to test cleverness and dexterity. There are eight bands. If you arrange them properly, they form a single ring. I've found it useful for distracting myself when I'm troubled."

"Thank you," murmured Eragon, already entranced by the complexity of the gleaming nest.

"You can keep it if you can put it together."

When he returned to his tent, Eragon lay on his stomach and inspected the rings in the dim firelight that seeped past the entrance flaps. Four bands looped through four bands. Each was smooth on the bottom half and an asymmetrical wriggling mass on the top, where it would weave through the other pieces.

As Eragon experimented with various configurations, he quickly became frustrated by a simple fact: it seemed impossible to get the two sets of bands parallel so they would lie flat together.

Absorbed by the challenge, he forgot the terror he had just endured.

Eragon woke right before dawn. Scrubbing the sleep from his eyes, he exited the tent and stretched. His breath turned white in the brisk morning air. He nodded to Shrrgnien, who was keeping guard by the fire, then strolled to the edge of the river and washed his face, blinking from the shock of the cold water.

He located Saphira with a flick of his mind, belted on Zar'roc, and headed toward her through the beech trees that lined the Az Ragni. Before long Eragon's hands and face were slick with dew from a tangled wall of chokecherry bushes that obstructed his way. With an effort, he pushed through the net of branches and escaped onto the silent plains. A round hill rose before him. On its crest—like two ancient statues—stood Saphira and Arya. They faced east, where a molten glow crept into the sky and burnished the prairie amber.

As the clear light struck the two figures, Eragon was reminded of how Saphira had watched the sunrise from his bedpost only a few hours after she hatched. She was like a hawk or falcon with her hard, sparkling eyes under their bony ridges, the fierce arch of her neck, and the lean strength etched into every line of her body. She was a huntress, and endowed with all the savage beauty that the term implied. Arya's angled features and panther grace perfectly matched the dragon beside her. No discrepancy existed between their demeanors as they stood bathed in dawn's first rays.

A tingle of awe and joy shuddered along Eragon's spine. *This* was where he belonged, as a Rider. Of all the things in Alagaësia, he had been lucky enough to be joined with *this*. The wonder of it brought tears to his eyes and a smile of wild exultation that dispelled all his doubts and fears in a surge of pure emotion.

Still smiling, he mounted the hill and took his place by Saphira as they surveyed the new day.

Arya looked at him. Eragon met her gaze, and something lurched within him. He flushed without knowing why, feeling a sudden connection with her, a sense that she understood him better than anyone other than Saphira. His reaction confused him, for no one had affected him in that manner before.

Throughout the rest of the day, all Eragon had to do was think back on that moment to make himself smile and set his insides churning with a mixture of odd sensations he could not identify. He spent most of his time seated against the raft's cabin, working on Orik's ring and watching the changing landscape.

Around midday they passed the mouth of a valley, and another river melded into the Az Ragni, doubling its size and speed until the shores were over a mile apart. It was all the dwarves could do to keep the rafts from being tossed like flotsam before the inexorable current and to avoid smashing into the trees that occasionally floated by.

A mile after the rivers joined, the Az Ragni turned north and flowed past a lonely cloud-wreathed peak that stood separate from the main body of the Beor range, like a gigantic watchtower built to keep vigil over the plains.

The dwarves bowed to the peak when they saw it, and Orik told Eragon, "There is Moldûn the Proud. He is the last true mountain we shall see on this journey."

When the rafts were moored for the evening, Eragon saw Orik unwrap a long black box inlaid with mother-of-pearl, rubies, and curved lines of silver. Orik flicked a clasp, then raised the lid to reveal an unstrung bow nestled in red velvet. The bow's reflexed limbs were ebony, which formed the background for intricate patterns of vines, flowers, animals, and runes, all executed in the finest gold. It was such a luxurious weapon, Eragon wondered how anyone dared use it.

Orik strung the bow—it was nearly as tall as he was, but still no bigger than a child's bow by Eragon's standards—put the box away, and said, "I'm going to find some fresh meat. I'll be back in an hour." With that he disappeared into the brush. Thorv grunted disapprovingly, but made no move to stop him.

True to his word, Orik returned with a brace of long-necked geese. "I found a flock of them perched in a tree," he said, tossing the birds to Dûthmér.

As Orik retrieved the bejeweled case, Eragon asked, "What kind of wood is your bow made of?"

"Wood?" Orik laughed, shaking his head. "You can't make a bow this short out of wood and cast an arrow more than twenty yards; it breaks, or follows the string after a few shots. No, this is an Urgal horn bow!"

Eragon eyed him suspiciously, sure that the dwarf was trying to fool him. "Horn isn't flexible or springy enough to make a bow."

"Ah," chortled Orik, "that's because you have to know how to treat it right. We first learned to do it with Feldûnost horns, but it works just as well with an Urgal's. It's done by cutting the horn in half lengthwise, then trimming the outside coil until it's the right thickness. The strip is boiled flat and sanded into the final shape before being fixed to the belly of an ash stave with glue made from fish scales and the skin from the roof of trout's mouths. Then the back of the stave is covered with multiple layers of sinew; they give the bow its *snap*. The last step is decoration. The entire process can take almost a decade."

"I've never heard of a bow built like that before," said Eragon. It made his own weapon seem no more than a crudely hacked branch. "How far does it shoot?"

"See for yourself," said Orik. He let Eragon take the bow, which he held gingerly, for fear of scuffing its finish. Orik removed an arrow from his quiver and handed it to him. "You'll owe me an arrow, though."

Eragon fit shaft to string, aimed over the Az Ragni, and pulled back. The bow's draw length was less than two feet, but he was surprised to find that its weight far exceeded that of his own bow; he was barely strong enough to hold the string. He released the arrow and it vanished with a *twang*, only to reappear far above the river. Eragon watched with amazement as the arrow landed in a spray of water halfway across the Az Ragni.

He immediately reached through the barrier in his mind so that the magic's power suffused him and said, "Gath sem oro un lam iet." After a few seconds, the arrow darted back through the air to land on his outstretched palm. "And there," he said, "is the arrow I owe you."

Orik clapped his fist to his chest and then embraced the arrow and bow with obvious delight. "Wonderful! Now I still have an even two dozen. Otherwise, I would have had to wait until Hedarth to replenish my stock." He deftly unstrung the bow and stored it away, wrapping the case in soft rags to protect it.

Eragon saw Arya watching. He asked her, "Do elves use horn bows as well? You're so strong, a wood bow would shatter if it was made heavy enough for you."

"We sing our bows from trees that do not grow." And then she walked away.

For days, they drifted through fields of spring grass while the Beor Mountains faded into a hazy white wall behind them. The banks were often covered with vast herds of gazelles and small red deer that watched them with liquid eyes.

Now that the Fanghur were no longer a threat, Eragon flew almost constantly with Saphira. It was their first opportunity since before Gil'ead to spend so much time together in the air, and they took full advantage of it. Also, Eragon welcomed the chance to escape the cramped deck of the raft, where he felt awkward and unsettled with Arya so near.

ARYA SVIT-KONA

E ragon and his company followed the Az Ragni until it joined the Edda River, which then drifted into the unknown east. At the juncture between the rivers, they visited the dwarves' trading outpost, Hedarth, and exchanged their rafts for donkeys. Dwarves never used horses on account of their size.

Arya refused the steed offered to her, saying, "I will *not* return to the land of my ancestors on the back of a donkey."

Thorv frowned. "How will you keep pace with us?"

"I will run." And run she did, outstripping Snowfire and the donkeys, only to sit waiting for them at the next hill or copse. Despite her exertions, she displayed no sign of weariness when they stopped for the night, nor any inclination to utter more than a few words between breakfast and supper. With every step, she seemed to grow tenser.

From Hedarth, they trekked north, going up the Edda River toward its point of origin at Eldor Lake.

Du Weldenvarden came into view within three days. The forest first appeared as a hazy ridge on the horizon, then quickly expanded into an emerald sea of ancient oaks, beeches, and maples. From Saphira's back, Eragon saw that the woods reached unbroken to the horizon both north and west, and he knew they extended far beyond that, stretching the entire length of Alagaësia.

To him, the shadows underneath the trees' arching boughs seemed mysterious and enticing, as well as dangerous, for there lived the elves. Hidden somewhere in the dappled heart of Du Welden-varden lay Ellesméra—where he would complete his training—as well as Osilon, and other elven cities few outsiders had visited since the fall of the Riders. The forest was a perilous place for mortals, Eragon felt, certain to be riddled with strange magic and stranger creatures.

It's like another world, he observed. A pair of butterflies spiraled around each other as they rose from the dark interior of the forest.

I hope, said Saphira, *there will be room for me within the trees on whatever path the elves use. I cannot fly the whole time.*

I'm sure they found ways to accommodate dragons during the time of the Riders.

Mmm.

That night, just as Eragon was about to seek his blankets, Arya appeared by his shoulder, like a spirit materializing out of the air. Her stealth made him jump; he could never understand how she moved so quietly. Before he could ask what she wanted, her mind touched his and she said, *Follow me as silently as you can.*

The contact surprised him as much as the request. They had shared thoughts during the flight to Farthen Dûr—it had been the only way Eragon could speak to her through her self-induced coma—but since Arya's recovery, he had made no attempt to touch her mind again. It was a profoundly personal experience. Whenever he reached out to another person's consciousness, it felt as if a facet of his bare soul rubbed against theirs. It seemed boorish and rude to initiate something so private without an invitation, as well as a betrayal of Arya's trust, slender as it was. Also, Eragon was afraid that such a link would reveal his new and confused feelings for Arya, and he had no desire to be ridiculed for them.

He accompanied her as she slipped out from the ring of tents, carefully evaded Tríhga, who had taken the first watch, and passed beyond the dwarves' hearing. Within him, Saphira kept a close watch on his progress, ready to leap to his side if need be.

Arya squatted on a moss-eaten log and wrapped her arms around her knees without looking at him. "There are things you must know before we reach Ceris and Ellesméra so that you do not shame yourself or me through your ignorance."

"Such as?" He crouched opposite her, curious.

Arya hesitated. "During my years as Islanzadí's ambassador, it was my observation that humans and dwarves are quite similar. You share many of the same beliefs and passions. More than one human has lived comfortably among the dwarves because he or she can understand their culture, as they understand yours. You both love, lust, hate, fight, and create in much the same manner. Your friendship with Orik and your acceptance into Dûrgrimst Ingeitum are examples of this." Eragon nodded, although their differences seemed greater to him than that. "Elves, though, are not like other races."

"You speak as though you weren't one," he said, echoing her words from Farthen Dûr.

"I have lived with the Varden for enough years to become accustomed to their traditions," replied Arya in a brittle tone.

"Ah . . . So then do you mean to say that elves don't have the same emotions as dwarves and humans? I find that hard to believe. All living things have the same basic needs and desires."

"That is not what I mean to say!" Eragon recoiled, then frowned and studied her. It was unusual for her to be so brusque. Arya closed her eyes and placed her fingers on her temples, taking a long breath. "Because elves live for so many years, we consider courtesy to be the highest social virtue. You cannot afford to give offense when a grudge can be held for decades or centuries. Courtesy is the only way to prevent such hostility from accumulating. It doesn't always succeed, but we adhere to our rituals rigorously, for they protect us from extremes. Nor are elves fecund, so it is vital that we avoid conflict among ourselves. If we shared the same rate of crime as you or the dwarves, we would soon be extinct.

"There is a proper way to greet the sentinels in Ceris, certain

160

patterns and forms that you must observe when presented to Queen Islanzadí, and a hundred different manners in which to greet those around you, if it's not better to just remain quiet."

"With all your customs," Eragon risked saying, "it seems as though you've only made it easier to offend people."

A smile flickered across her lips. "Perhaps. You know as well as I that you will be judged by the highest standards. If you make a mistake, the elves will think you did it on purpose. And only harm will come if they discover that it was born of ignorance. Far better to be thought rude and capable than rude and incapable, else you risk being manipulated like The Serpent in a match of Runes. Our politics move in cycles that are both subtle and lengthy. What you see or hear of an elf one day may only be a slight move in a strategy that reaches back millennia, and may have no bearing on how that elf will behave tomorrow. It is a game that we all play but few control, a game that you are about to enter.

"Now perhaps you realize why I say elves are not like other races. The dwarves are also long-lived, yet they are more prolific than us and do not share our restraint or our taste for intrigue. And humans . . ." She let her voice fade into a tactful silence.

"Humans," said Eragon, "do the best they can with what they are given."

"Even so."

"Why don't you tell Orik all this as well? He'll be staying in Ellesméra, same as me."

An edge crept into Arya's voice. "He is already somewhat familiar with our etiquette. However, as a Rider, you would do well to appear better educated than him."

Eragon accepted her rebuke without protest. "What must I learn?"

So Arya began to tutor him and, through him, Saphira in the niceties of elven society. First she explained that when one elf meets another, they stop and touch their first two fingers to their lips to indicate that "we shall not distort the truth during our "conversation." This is followed by the phrase "Atra esterní ono thelduin" to which one replies "Atra du evarínya ono varda."

"And," said Arya, "if you are being especially formal, a third response is made: 'Un atra mor'ranr lífa unin hjarta onr,' which means, 'And may peace live in your heart.' These lines were adopted from a blessing that was made by a dragon when our pact with them was finalized. It goes:

Atra esterní ono thelduin,
Mor'ranr lífa unin hjarta onr,
Un du evarínya ono varda.

"Or: 'May good fortune rule over you, peace live in your heart, and the stars watch over you.'"

"How do you know who is supposed to speak first?"

"If you greet someone with greater status than yourself or if you wish to honor a subordinate, then speak first. If you greet someone with less status than yourself, speak last. But if you are uncertain of your position, give your counterpart a chance to speak, and if they are silent, speak first. Such is the rule."

Does it apply to me as well? asked Saphira.

Arya plucked a dry leaf from the ground and crumpled it between her fingers. Behind her, the camp faded into shadow as the dwarves banked the fire, dampening the flames with a layer of dirt so that the coals and embers would survive until morning. "As a dragon, none are higher than you in our culture. Not even the queen would claim authority over you. You may do and say as you wish. We do not expect dragons to be bound by our laws."

Next she showed Eragon how to twist his right hand and place it over his sternum in a curious gesture. "This," she said, "you will use when you meet Islanzadí. By it you indicate that you offer her your loyalty and obedience."

"Is it binding, like my oath of fealty to Nasuada?"

"No, only a courtesy, and a small one at that."

162

Eragon struggled to remember the sundry modes of address that Arya instructed them in. The salutations varied from man to woman, adults to children, boys to girls, as well as by rank and prestige. It was a daunting list, but one that Eragon knew he had to memorize perfectly.

When he had absorbed all he could, Arya stood and dusted her hands. "So long as you do not forget, you'll do well enough." She turned to leave.

"Wait," said Eragon. He reached out to stop her, then snatched back his hand before she noticed his presumption. She looked over her shoulder with a query in her dark eyes, and his stomach clenched as he tried to find a way to voice his thoughts. Despite his best efforts, he ended up just saying, "Are you well, Arya? . . . You've seemed distracted and out of sorts ever since we left Hedarth."

As Arya's face hardened into a blank mask, he winced inwardly, knowing that he had chosen the wrong approach, although he could not fathom why the question should offend her.

"When we are in Du Weldenvarden," she informed him, "I expect that you will not speak to me in such a familiar way, unless you wish to cause affront." She stalked away.

Run after her! exclaimed Saphira.

What?

We can't afford to have her angry with you. Go apologize.

His pride rebelled. *No! It's her fault, not mine.*

Go apologize, Eragon, or I'll fill your tent with carrion. It was no idle threat.

How?

Saphira thought for a second, then told him what to do. Without arguing, he jumped to his feet and darted in front of Arya, forcing her to stop. She regarded him with a haughty expression.

He touched his fingers to his lips and said, "Arya Svit-kona," using the honorific he had just learned for a woman of great wisdom. "I spoke badly, and for that I cry your pardon. Saphira and I were concerned for your welfare. After all you've done for us, it seemed the least we could do was offer our help in return, if you need it."

Finally, Arya relented and said, "Your concern is appreciated. And I too spoke badly." She looked down. In the dark, the outline of her limbs and torso was painfully rigid. "You ask what troubles me, Eragon? Do you truly wish to know? Then I will tell you." Her voice was as soft as thistledown floating on the wind. "I am afraid."

Dumbfounded, Eragon made no response, and she stepped past, leaving him alone in the night.

CERIS

On the morning of the fourth day, when Eragon rode alongside Shrrgnien, the dwarf said, "So tell me, do men really have ten toes, as is said? For truly I have never traveled beyond our borders before."

"Of course we have ten toes!" said Eragon, astonished. He shifted in Snowfire's saddle, lifted his foot, removed his right boot and sock, and wiggled his toes under Shrrgnien's amazed eyes. "Don't you?"

Shrrgnien shook his head. "Nay, we have seven on each foot. It is how Helzvog made us. Five is too few and six is the wrong number, but seven . . . seven is just right." He glanced at Eragon's foot again, then spurred his donkey ahead and began speaking animatedly to Ama and Hedin, who eventually handed him several silver coins.

I think, said Eragon as he pulled the boot back on, *that I was just the source of a bet.* For some reason, Saphira found that immensely amusing.

As dusk fell and the full moon rose, the Edda River drew ever closer to the fringe of Du Weldenvarden. They rode down a narrow trail through tangled dogwood and rosebushes in full bloom, which filled the evening air with the flowers' warm scent.

Eager anticipation swelled within Eragon as he gazed into the dark forest, knowing they had already entered the elves' domain and were close to Ceris. He leaned forward in Snowfire's saddle, the reins pulled tight between his hands. Saphira's excitement was as great as his own; she ranged overhead, flicking her tail back and forth with impatience.

Eragon felt as if they had wandered into a dream. *It doesn't seem real,* he said.

Aye. Here the legends of old still bestride the earth.

At last they came upon a small meadow set between the river and forest. "Stop here," said Arya in a low voice. She walked forward until she stood alone in the midst of the lush grass, then cried in the ancient language, "Come forth, my brethren! You have nothing to fear. 'Tis I, Arya of Ellesméra. My companions are friends and allies; they mean us no harm." She added other words as well, ones alien to Eragon.

For several minutes, the only sound was the river rushing behind them, until from underneath the still leaves came a line of Elvish, so quick and fleeting that Eragon missed the meaning. Arya responded: "I do."

With a rustle, two elves stood on the edge of the forest and two ran lightly out on the boughs of a gnarled oak. Those on the ground bore long spears with white blades, while the others held bows. All were garbed in tunics the color of moss and bark underneath flowing cloaks clasped at the shoulder with ivory brooches. One had tresses as black as Arya's. Three had hair like starlight.

The elves dropped from the trees and embraced Arya, laughing in their clear, pure voices. They joined hands and danced in a circle around her like children, singing merrily as they spun through the grass.

Eragon watched in amazement. Arya had never given him reason to suspect that elves liked to—or even *could*—laugh. It was a wondrous sound, like flutes and harps trilling with delight at their own music. He wished that he could listen to it forever.

Then Saphira drifted over the river and settled beside Eragon. At her approach, the elves cried out in alarm and aimed their weapons toward her. Arya spoke quickly in soothing tones, motioning first at Saphira, then at Eragon. When she paused for breath, Eragon drew back the glove on his right hand, tilted his palm so that the gedwëy ignasia caught the moonlight, and said, as he once had to Arya so long ago, "Eka fricai un Shur'tugal." I am a Rider and friend. Remembering his lesson from yesterday, he touched his lips, adding, "Atra esterní ono thelduin."

The elves lowered their weapons as their angled faces lit up with radiant joy. They pressed their forefingers to their lips and bowed to Saphira and him, murmuring their reply in the ancient language.

Then they rose, pointed at the dwarves, and laughed as if at a hidden joke. Drifting back into the forest, they waved their hands and called, "Come, come!"

Eragon followed Arya with Saphira and the dwarves, who were grumbling among themselves. As they passed between the trees, the canopy overhead plunged them into velvet darkness, except where fragments of moonlight gleamed through chinks in the shell of overlapping leaves. Eragon could hear the elves whispering and laughing all around, though he could not see them. Occasionally, they would call directions when he or the dwarves blundered.

Ahead, a fire glowed through the trees, sending shadows racing like sprites across the leafy ground. As Eragon entered the radius of light, he saw three small huts clustered together around the base of a large oak. High in the tree was a roofed platform where a watchman could observe the river and forest. A pole had been lashed between two of the huts: from it hung bundles of drying plants.

The four elves vanished into the huts, then returned with their arms piled high with fruits and vegetables—but no meat—and began preparing a meal for their guests. They hummed as they worked, flitting from one tune to another as the fancy took them. When Orik asked their names, the dark-haired elf pointed to himself and said, "I am Lifaen of House Rílvenar. And my companions are Edurna, Celdin, and Narí."

Eragon sat beside Saphira, happy for an opportunity to rest and to watch the elves. Though all four were male, their faces resembled Arya's, with delicate lips, thin noses, and large slanted eyes that shone under their brows. The rest of their bodies matched, with narrow shoulders and slender arms and legs. Each was more fair and noble than any human Eragon had seen, albeit in a rarefied, exotic manner.

Who ever thought I would get to visit the elves' homeland? Eragon asked himself. He grinned and leaned against the corner of a hut, drowsy with the fire's warmth. Above him, Saphira's dancing blue eyes tracked the elves with unwavering precision.

More magic is in this race, she finally remarked, *than either humans or dwarves. They do not feel as if they come from the earth or the stone, but rather from another realm, half in, half out, like reflections seen through water.*

They certainly are graceful, he said. The elves moved like dancers, their every action smooth and lithe.

Brom had told Eragon that it was rude for someone to speak with their mind to a Rider's dragon without permission, and the elves adhered to that custom, voicing aloud their comments to Saphira, who would then answer the elves directly. Saphira usually refrained from touching the thoughts of humans and dwarves and allowed Eragon to relay her words, since few members of those races had the training to guard their minds if they wished for privacy. It also seemed an imposition to use such an intimate form of contact for casual exchanges. The elves had no such inhibitions, though; they welcomed Saphira into their minds, reveling in her presence.

At last the food was ready and served on carved plates that felt like dense bone, although wood grain wandered through the flowers and vines decorating the rim. Eragon was also supplied with a flagon of gooseberry wine—made of the same unusual material—with a sculpted dragon wrapped around its stem.

As they ate, Lifaen produced a set of reed pipes and began to play a flowing melody, his fingers running along the various holes. Soon the tallest silver-haired elf, Narí, raised his voice and sang:

O!

The day is done; the stars are bright;
The leaves are still; the moon is white!

Laugh at woe and laugh at foe,
Menoa's scion now is safe this night!

A forest child we lost to strife;
A sylvan daughter caught by life!
Freed of fear and freed of flame,
She tore a Rider from the shadows rife!

Again the dragons rise on wing,
And we avenge their suffering!
Strong of blade and strong of arm,
The time is ripe for us to kill a king!

O!

The wind is soft; the river deep;
The trees are tall; the birds do sleep!
Laugh at woe and laugh at foe,
The hour has arrived for joy to reap!

When Narí finished, Eragon released his pent-up breath. He had never heard such a voice before; it felt as if the elf had revealed his essence, his very soul. "That was beautiful, Narí-vodhr."

"A rough composition, Argetlam," demurred Narí. "But I thank you, nevertheless."

Thorv grunted. "Very pretty, Master Elf. However, there are matters more serious than reciting verse that we must attend to. Are we to accompany Eragon farther?"

"No," said Arya quickly, drawing looks from the other elves. "You may return home in the morning. We will assure that Eragon reaches Ellesméra."

Thorv dipped his head. "Then our task is complete."

As Eragon lay on the bedding the elves had arranged for him, he strained his ears to catch Arya's speech, which drifted from one of the huts. Though she used many unfamiliar words in the ancient language, he deduced that she was explaining to their hosts how she had lost Saphira's egg and the events since. A long silence followed after she stopped, then an elf said, "It is good that you have returned, Arya Dröttningu. Islanzadí was sorely wounded by grief when you were captured and the egg was stolen, and by Urgals no less! She was—and is—sick at heart."

"Hush, Edurna . . . hush," chided another. "Dvergar are small, but they have sharp ears, and I am sure these will report to Hrothgar."

Then their voices dropped and Eragon could discern no more from the murmur of voices, which melded into the whisper of leaves as he drifted to sleep, the elf's song repeating endlessly through his dreams.

The scent of flowers was heavy in the air when Eragon woke to behold a sun-drenched Du Weldenvarden. Above him arched a mottled panoply of drifting leaves, supported by the thick trunks that buried themselves in the dry, bare ground. Only moss, lichen, and a few low shrubs survived in the pervasive green shade. The scarcity of underbrush made it possible to see for great distances between the knotted pillars and to walk about freely beneath the dappled ceiling.

Rolling to his feet, Eragon found Thorv and his guards packed and ready to leave. Orik's donkey was tied behind Ekksvar's steed. Eragon approached Thorv and said, "Thank you, all of you, for protecting me and Saphira. Please convey our gratitude to Ûndin."

Thorv pressed his fist to his chest. "I will carry your words." He hesitated and looked back at the huts. "Elves are a queer race, full of light and dark. In the morning, they drink with you; in the evening, they stab you. Keep thine back to a wall, Shadeslayer. Capricious, they are."

"I will remember that."

"Mmm." Thorv gestured toward the river. "They plan to travel up Eldor Lake in boats. What will you do with thine horse? We could return him to Tarnag with us, and from there, to Tronjheim."

"Boats!" cried Eragon with dismay. He had always planned to bring Snowfire to Ellesméra. It was convenient to have a horse whenever Saphira was away, or in places too confined for her bulk. He fingered the sparse bristles along his jaw. "That is a kind offer. Will you make sure Snowfire is well cared for? I couldn't bear it if anything were to happen to him."

"On mine honor," pledged Thorv, "you will return to find him fat and sleek."

Eragon fetched Snowfire and transferred the stallion, his saddle, and his grooming supplies into Thorv's care. He bade each of the warriors farewell, then he, Saphira, and Orik watched the dwarves ride back along the trail they had arrived on.

Returning to the huts, Eragon and the remainder of his party followed the elves to a thicket on the edge of the Edda River. There, docked on either side of a boulder, were two white canoes with vines carved along their sides.

Eragon boarded the nearest boat and stowed his pack beneath his feet. He was amazed by how light the craft was; he could have lifted it with a single hand. Even more astounding, the hulls appeared to be composed of birch-bark panels melded into a seamless whole. Curious, he touched the side. The bark was hard and taut, like stretched parchment, and cool from its contact with the water. He rapped it with a knuckle. The fibrous shell reverberated like a muted drum.

"Are all your boats made this way?" he asked.

"All except the very largest," answered Narí, seating himself at the prow of Eragon's vessel. "For those, we sing the finest cedar and oak into shape."

Before Eragon could ask what he meant, Orik joined their canoe while Arya and Lifaen appropriated the second one. Arya turned to Edurna and Celdin—who stood on the bank—and said, "Guard this way so that none may follow us, and tell no one of our presence.

The queen must be the first to know. I will send reinforcements as soon as we reach Sílthrim."

"Arya Dröttningu."

"May the stars watch over you!" she answered.

Bending forward, Narí and Lifaen drew spiked poles ten feet long from inside the boats and began propelling the vessels upstream. Saphira slid into the water behind them and clawed her way along the riverbed until they were level. When Eragon looked at her, she winked lazily, then submerged, forcing the river to swell into a mound over her jagged back. The elves laughed as she did so and made many compliments about her size and strength.

After an hour, they reached Eldor Lake, which was rough with small, jagged waves. Birds and flies swarmed by a wall of trees edging the western shore, while the eastern shore sloped up into the plains. On that side meandered hundreds of deer.

Once they escaped the river's current, Narí and Lifaen stowed their poles, then distributed leaf-bladed paddles. Orik and Arya already knew how to steer a boat, but Narí had to explain the process to Eragon. "We turn toward whichever side you paddle on," said the elf. "So if I paddle on the right and Orik paddles on the left, then you must paddle first on one side, then the other, else we will drift off course." In the daylight, Narí's hair shimmered like the finest wire, each strand a fiery line.

Eragon soon mastered the ability, and as the motion became habitual, his mind was freed to daydream. Thus, he floated up the cool lake, lost in the fantastic worlds hidden behind his eyes. When he paused to rest his arms, he once again pulled Orik's puzzle ring from his belt and struggled to arrange the obstinate gold bands into the correct pattern.

Narí noticed what he was doing. "May I see that ring?"

Eragon passed it to the elf, who turned his back. For a few moments, Eragon and Orik maneuvered the canoe alone as Narí picked at the entwined bands. Then, with a pleased exclamation, Narí raised his hand, and the completed ring flashed on his middle finger. "A delightful riddle," said Narí. He slipped off the ring and shook it, so that it was in its original state when he returned it to Eragon.

"How did you solve it?" demanded Eragon, dismayed and envious that Narí had been able to master the puzzle so easily. "Wait . . . Don't tell me. I want to figure it out on my own."

"Of course," said Narí, smiling.

◆ ◆ ◆

WOUNDS OF THE PAST

For three and a half days, the citizens of Carvahall discussed the latest attack, the tragedy of young Elmund's death, and what could possibly be done to escape their thrice-blasted situation. The debate raged with bitter fury through every room of every home. In the space of a word, friends turned against friends, husbands against wives, children against parents, only to reconcile moments later in their frantic attempt to discover a means of survival.

Some said that since Carvahall was doomed anyway, they might as well kill the Ra'zac and remaining soldiers so as to at least have their vengeance. Others said that if Carvahall really was doomed, then the only logical course was to surrender and trust themselves to the king's mercy, even if it did mean torture and death for Roran and enslavement for everyone else. And still others sided with neither opinion, but rather descended into a sullen black anger directed at everyone who had brought about this calamity. Many did their best to hide their panic in the depths of a tankard.

The Ra'zac themselves had apparently realized that with eleven soldiers dead they no longer had a large enough force to attack Carvahall, and thus had retreated farther down the road, where they were content to post sentinels across Palancar Valley and wait. "Wait for flea-bitten troops from Ceunon or Gil'ead, if you ask me," Loring said at one meeting. Roran listened to that and more, kept his own council, and silently judged the various schemes. They all seemed dangerously risky.

Roran still had not told Sloan that he and Katrina were engaged. He knew it was foolish to wait, but he feared how the butcher would react when he learned that Roran and Katrina had flouted tradition and, in doing so, undermined Sloan's authority. Besides, there was plenty of work to divert Roran's attention; he convinced himself that strengthening the fortifications around Carvahall was his most important task at the moment.

Getting people to help was easier than Roran anticipated. After the last fight, the villagers were more apt to listen and to obey him—that is, those who did not blame him for causing their predicament. He was mystified by his new authority, until he realized that it was the result of the awe, respect, and perhaps even fear his kills had elicited. They called him Stronghammer. Roran Stronghammer.

The name pleased him.

As night engulfed the valley, Roran leaned against a corner of Horst's dining room, his eyes closed. Conversation flowed from the men and women seated around the candlelit table. Kiselt was in the middle of explaining the state of Carvahall's supplies. "We won't starve," he concluded, "but if we can't tend to our fields and our flocks soon, we might as well cut our own throats before next winter. It would be a kinder fate."

Horst scowled. "Dog tripe!"

"Dog tripe or not," said Gertrude, "I doubt we'll have a chance to find out. We outnumbered the soldiers ten to one when they arrived. They lost eleven men; we lost twelve, and I'm caring for another nine wounded. What happens, Horst, when they outnumber us ten to one?"

"We will give the bards a reason to remember our names," retorted the smith. Gertrude shook her head sadly.

Loring banged a fist on the table. "And I say it's our turn to strike, before we *are* outnumbered. All we need are a few men, shields, and spears, and we can wipe out their *infestation*. It could be done tonight!"

Roran shifted restlessly. He had heard all this before, and like before, Loring's proposal ignited an argument that consumed the group. After an hour, the debate still showed no sign of being resolved, nor had any new ideas been presented, except for Thane's suggestion that Gedric should go tan his own hide, which nearly resulted in a fistfight.

Finally, when the conversation lulled, Roran limped to the table as quickly as his injured calf would allow. "I have something to say." For him it was the equivalent of stepping on a long thorn and then yanking it out without stopping to consider the pain; it had to be done, and the faster the better.

All eyes—hard, soft, angry, kind, indifferent, and curious—turned to him, and Roran took a deep breath. "Indecision will kill us just as surely as a sword or an arrow." Orval rolled his eyes, but the rest still listened. "I don't know if we should attack or flee—"

"Where?" snorted Kiselt.

"—but I do know one thing: our children, our mothers, and our infirm must be protected from danger. The Ra'zac have barred us from Cawley and the other farms down the valley. So what? We know this land better than any in Alagaësia, and there is a place . . . there is a place where our loved ones will be safe: the Spine."

Roran winced as a barrage of outraged voices assaulted him. Sloan was the loudest, shouting, "I'll be hanged before I set foot in those cursed mountains!"

"Roran," said Horst, overriding the commotion. "You of all people should know that the Spine is too dangerous—it's where Eragon found the stone that brought the Ra'zac! The mountains are cold, and filled with wolves, bears, and other monsters. Why even mention them?"

To keep Katrina safe! Roran wanted to scream. Instead, he said, "Because no matter how many soldiers the Ra'zac summon, they will never dare enter the Spine. Not after Galbatorix lost half his army in it."

"That was a long time ago," said Morn doubtfully.

Roran jumped on his statement. "And the stories have grown all the more frightening in the telling! A trail already exists to the top of Igualda Falls. All we have to do is send the children and others up there. They'll only be on the fringe of the mountains, but they'll still be safe. If Carvahall is taken, they can wait until the soldiers leave, then find refuge in Therinsford."

"It is too dangerous," growled Sloan. The butcher gripped the edge of the table so hard that the tips of his fingers turned white. "The cold, the beasts. No sane man would send his family among those."

"But . . ." Roran faltered, put off-balance by Sloan's response. Though he knew the butcher hated the Spine more than most—because his wife had plummeted to her death from the cliffs beside Igualda Falls—he had hoped that Sloan's rabid desire to protect Katrina would be strong enough to overcome his aversion. Roran now understood he would have to win over Sloan just like everyone else. Adopting a placating tone, Roran said, "It's not that bad. The snow is already melting off the peaks. It's no colder in the Spine than it was down here a few months ago. And I doubt that wolves or bears would bother such a large group."

Sloan grimaced, twisting his lips up over his teeth, and shook his head. "You will find nothing but death in the Spine."

The others seemed to agree, which only strengthened Roran's determination, for he was convinced that Katrina would die unless he could sway them. He scanned the long oval of faces, searching for a sympathetic expression. "Delwin, I know it's cruel of me to say it, but if Elmund hadn't been in Carvahall, he would still be alive. Surely you must agree that this is the right thing to do! You have an opportunity to save other parents from your suffering."

No one responded. "And Birgit!" Roran dragged himself toward her, clutching the backs of chairs to keep himself from falling. "Do you want Nolfavrell to share his father's fate? He has to leave. Can't you see, that is the only way he'll be safe. . . ." Though Roran did his best to fight it, he could feel tears flood his eyes. "It's for the children!" he shouted angrily.

The room was silent as Roran stared at the wood beneath his hands, struggling to control himself. Delwin was the first to stir. "I will never leave Carvahall so long as my son's killers remain here. However," he paused, then continued with painful slowness, "I cannot deny the truth of your words; the children must be protected."

"As I said from the beginning," declared Tara.

Then Baldor spoke: "Roran is right. We can't allow ourselves to be blinded by fear. Most of us have climbed to the top of the falls at one time or another. It's safe enough."

"I too," Birgit finally added, "must agree."

Horst nodded. "I would rather not do it, but considering the circumstances. . . . I don't think we have any other choice." After a minute, the various men and women began to reluctantly acquiesce to the proposal.

"Nonsense!" exploded Sloan. He stood and stabbed an accusing finger at Roran. "How will they get enough food to wait for weeks on end? They can't carry it. How will they stay warm? If they light fires, they'll be seen! How, how, how? If they don't starve, they'll freeze. If they don't freeze, they'll be eaten. If they're not eaten . . . Who knows? They may fall!"

Roran spread his hands. "If we all help, they will have plenty of food. Fire won't be a problem if they move farther back into the forest, which they must anyway, since there isn't room to camp right by the falls."

"Excuses! Justifications!"

"What would you have us do, Sloan?" asked Morn, eyeing him with curiosity.

Sloan laughed bitterly. "Not this."

"Then what?"

"It doesn't matter. Only this is the wrong choice."

"You don't have to participate," pointed out Horst.

"Nor will I," said the butcher. "Proceed if you want, but neither I nor my blood shall enter the Spine while I still have marrow in my bones." He grabbed his cap and left with a venomous glare at Roran, who returned the scowl in kind.

As Roran saw it, Sloan was endangering Katrina through his own pigheaded stubbornness. *If he can't bring himself to accept the Spine as a place of refuge*, decided Roran, *then he's become my enemy and I have to take matters into my own hands*.

Horst leaned forward on his elbows and interlaced his thick fingers. "So . . . If we are going to use Roran's plan, what preparations will be needed?" The group exchanged wary glances, then gradually began to discuss the topic.

Roran waited until he was convinced that he had achieved his goal before slipping out of the dining room. Loping through the dusky village, he searched for Sloan along the inner perimeter of the tree wall. Eventually, he spotted the butcher hunched underneath a torch, his shield clasped around his knees. Roran spun around on one foot and ran to Sloan's shop, where he hurried to the kitchen in the back.

Katrina paused in the middle of setting their table and stared at him with amazement. "Roran! Why are you here? Did you tell Father?"

"No." He came forward and took her arm, savoring the touch. Just being in the same room with her filled him with joy. "I have a great favor to ask of you. It's been decided to send the children and a few others into the Spine above Igualda Falls." Katrina gasped. "I want you to accompany them."

With a shocked expression, Katrina pulled free of his grasp and turned to the open fireplace, where she hugged herself and stared at the bed of throbbing embers. For a long time, she said nothing. Then: "Father forbade me to go near the falls after Mother died. Albem's farm is the closest I've been to the Spine in over ten years." She shivered, and her voice grew accusing. "How can you suggest that I abandon both you and my father? This is my home as much as yours. And why should I leave when Elain, Tara, and Birgit will remain?"

"Katrina, please." He tentatively put his hands on her shoulders. "The Ra'zac are here for me, and I would not have you harmed because of that. As long as you're in danger, I can't concentrate on what has to be done: defending Carvahall."

"Who would respect me for fleeing like a coward?" She lifted her chin. "I would be ashamed to stand before the women of Carvahall and call myself your wife."

"Coward? There is no cowardice in guarding and protecting the children in the Spine. If anything, it requires greater courage to enter the mountains than to stay."

"What horror is this?" whispered Katrina. She twisted in his arms, eyes shining and mouth set firmly. "The man who would be my husband no longer wants me by his side."

He shook his head. "That's not true. I—"

"It *is* true! What if you are killed while I'm gone?"

"Don't say—"

"No! Carvahall has little hope of survival, and if we must die, I would rather die together than huddle in the Spine without life or heart. Let those with children tend to their own. As will I." A tear rolled down her cheek.

Gratitude and wonder surged through Roran at the strength of her devotion. He looked deep into her eyes. "It is for that love that I would have you go. I know how you feel. I know that this is the hardest sacrifice either of us could make, and I ask it of you now."

Katrina shuddered, her entire body rigid, her white hands clenched around her muslin sash. "If I do this," she said with a shaking voice, "you must promise me, here and now, that you will never make such a request again. You must promise that even if we faced Galbatorix himself and only one of us could escape, you would not ask me to leave."

Roran looked at her helplessly. "I can't."

"Then how can you expect me to do what you won't!" she cried. "That is my price, and neither gold nor jewels nor pretty words can replace your oath. If you don't care enough for me to make your own sacrifice, Roran *Stronghammer*, then be gone and I never wish to see your face again!"

I cannot lose her. Though it pained him almost beyond endurance, he bowed his head and said, "You have my word."

Katrina nodded and sank into a chair—her back stiff and upright—and blotted her tears on the cuff of her sleeve. In a quiet voice, she said, "Father will hate me for going."

"How will you tell him?"

"I won't," she said defiantly. "He would never let me enter the Spine, but he has to realize that this is my decision. Anyway, he won't dare pursue me into the mountains; he fears them more than death itself."

"He may fear losing you even more."

"We shall see. If—when—the time comes to return, I expect you to have already spoken to him about our engagement. That should give him enough time to reconcile himself to the fact."

Roran found himself nodding in agreement, all the while thinking that they would be lucky if events worked out so well.

WOUNDS OF THE PRESENT

When dawn arrived, Roran woke and lay staring at the whitewashed ceiling while he listened to the slow rasp of his own breathing. After a minute, he rolled off the bed, dressed, and proceeded to the kitchen, where he procured a chunk of bread, smeared it with soft cheese, then stepped out onto the front porch to eat and admire the sunrise.

His tranquility was soon disrupted when a herd of unruly children dashed through the garden of a nearby house, shrieking with delight at their game of Catch-the-Cat, followed by a number of adults intent on snaring their respective charges. Roran watched the cacophonous parade vanish around a corner, then placed the last of the bread in his mouth and returned to the kitchen, which had filled with the rest of the household.

Elain greeted him. "Good morning, Roran." She pushed open the window shutters and gazed up at the sky. "It looks like it may rain again."

"The more the better," asserted Horst. "It'll help keep us hidden while we climb Narnmor Mountain."

"Us?" inquired Roran. He sat at the table beside Albriech, who was rubbing the sleep from his eyes.

Horst nodded. "Sloan was right about the food and supplies; we have to help carry them up the falls, or else there won't be enough."

"Will there still be men to defend Carvahall?"

"Of course, of course."

✳   ✳   ✳

Once they all had breakfast, Roran helped Baldor and Albriech wrap spare food, blankets, and supplies into three large bundles that they slung across their shoulders and hauled to the north end of the village. Roran's calf pained him, but not unbearably. Along the way, they met the three brothers Darmmen, Larne, and Hamund, who were similarly burdened.

Just inside the trench that circumnavigated the houses, Roran and his companions found a large gathering of children, parents, and grandparents all busy organizing for the expedition. Several families had volunteered their donkeys to carry goods and the younger children; the animals were picketed in an impatient, braying line that added to the overall confusion.

Roran set his bundle on the ground and scanned the group. He saw Svart—Ivor's uncle and, at nearly sixty, the oldest man in Carvahall—seated on a bale of clothes, teasing a baby with the tip of his long white beard; Nolfavrell, who was guarded over by Birgit; Felda, Nolla, Calitha, and a number of other mothers with worried expressions; and a great many reluctant people, both men and women. Roran also saw Katrina among the crowd. She glanced up from a knot she was tying on a pack and smiled at him, then returned to her task.

Since no one seemed to be in charge, Roran did his best to sort out the chaos by overseeing the arranging and packaging of the various supplies. He discovered a shortage of waterskins, but when he asked for more, he ended up with thirteen too many. Delays such as those consumed the early-morning hours.

In the middle of discussing with Loring the possible need for extra shoes, Roran stopped as he noticed Sloan standing at the entrance to an alleyway.

The butcher surveyed the mass of activity before him. Contempt cut into the lines along his downturned mouth. His sneer hardened into enraged incredulity as he spotted Katrina, who had shouldered her pack, removing any possibility that she was there only to help. A vein throbbed down the middle of Sloan's forehead.

Roran hurried toward Katrina, but Sloan reached her first. He grabbed the top of the pack and shook it violently, shouting, "Who made you do this?" Katrina said something about the children and tried to pull free, but Sloan yanked at the pack—twisting her arms as the straps slid off her shoulders—and threw it on the ground so that the contents scattered. Still shouting, Sloan grabbed Katrina's arm and began to drag her away. She dug in her heels and fought, her copper hair swirling over her face like a dust storm.

Furious, Roran threw himself at Sloan and tore him from Katrina, shoving the butcher in the chest so that he stumbled backward several yards. "Stop! I'm the one who wanted her to go."

Sloan glared at Roran and snarled, "You have no right!"

"I have every right." Roran looked at the ring of spectators who had gathered around and then declared so that all could hear: "Katrina and I are engaged to be married, and I would not have my future wife treated so!" For the first time that day, the villagers fell completely silent; even the donkeys were quiet.

Surprise and a deep, inconsolable pain sprang onto Sloan's vulnerable face, along with the glimmer of tears. For a moment, Roran felt sympathy for him, then a series of contortions distorted Sloan's visage, each more extreme than the last, until his skin turned beet red. He cursed and said, "You two-faced coward! How could you look me in the eye and speak to me like an honest man while, at the same time, courting my daughter without permission? I dealt with you in good faith, and here I find you plundering my house while my back is turned."

"I had hoped to do this properly," said Roran, "but events have conspired against me. It was never my intention to cause you grief. Even though this hasn't gone the way either of us wanted, I still want your blessing, if you are willing."

"I would rather have a maggot-riddled pig for a son than you! You have no farm. You have no family. And you will have naught to do with my daughter!" The butcher cursed again. "And she'll have naught to do with the Spine!"

Sloan reached for Katrina, but Roran blocked the way, his face as

184

hard as his clenched fists. Only a handsbreadth apart, they stared directly at each other, trembling from the strength of their emotions. Sloan's red-rimmed eyes shone with manic intensity.

"Katrina, come here," Sloan commanded.

Roran withdrew from Sloan—so that the three of them formed a triangle—and looked at Katrina. Tears streamed down her face as she glanced between him and her father. She stepped forward, hesitated, then with a long, anguished cry, tore at her hair in a frenzy of indecision.

"Katrina!" exclaimed Sloan with a burr of fear.

"Katrina," murmured Roran.

At the sound of his voice, Katrina's tears ceased and she stood straight and tall with a calm expression. She said, "I'm sorry, Father, but I have decided to marry Roran," and stepped to his side.

Sloan turned bone white. He bit his lip so hard that a bead of ruby blood appeared. "You can't leave me! You're my daughter!" He lunged at her with crooked hands. In that instant, Roran bellowed and struck the butcher with all his strength, knocking him sprawling in the dirt before the entire village.

Sloan rose slowly, his face and neck flushed with humiliation. When he saw Katrina again, the butcher seemed to crumple inward, losing height and stature until Roran felt as if he were looking at a specter of the original man. In a low whisper, he said, "It is always so; those closest to the heart cause the most pain. Thou will have no dowry from me, snake, nor your mother's inheritance." Weeping bitterly, Sloan turned and fled toward his shop.

Katrina leaned against Roran, and he put an arm around her. Together they clung to each other as people crowded against them offering condolences, advice, congratulations, and disapproval. Despite the commotion, Roran was aware of nothing but the woman whom he held, and who held him.

Just then, Elain bustled up as fast as her pregnancy would allow. "Oh, you poor dear!" she cried, and embraced Katrina, drawing her from Roran's arms. "Is it true you are engaged?" Katrina nodded and smiled, then erupted into hysterical tears against Elain's shoulder. "There now, there now." Elain cradled Katrina gently, petting her and trying to soothe her, but without avail—every time Roran thought she was about to recover, Katrina began to cry with renewed intensity. Finally, Elain peered over Katrina's quaking shoulder and said, "I'm taking her back to the house."

"I'll come."

"No, you won't," retorted Elain. "She needs time to calm down, and you have work to do. Do you want my advice?" Roran nodded dumbly. "Stay away until evening. I guarantee that she will be as right as rain by then. She can join the others tomorrow." Without waiting for his response, Elain escorted the sobbing Katrina away from the wall of sharpened trees.

Roran stood with his hands hanging limply by his sides, feeling dazed and helpless. *What have we done?* He regretted that he had not revealed their engagement to Sloan sooner. He regretted that he and Sloan could not work together to shield Katrina from the Empire. And he regretted that Katrina had been forced to relinquish her only family for him. He was now doubly responsible for her welfare. They had no choice *but* to get married. *I've made a terrible mess of this.* He sighed and clenched his fist, wincing as his bruised knuckles stretched.

"How are you?" asked Baldor, coming alongside him.

Roran forced a smile. "It didn't turn out quite how I hoped. Sloan's beyond reason when it comes to the Spine."

"And Katrina."

"That too. I—" Roran fell silent as Loring stopped before them.

"That was a blasted *fool* thing to do!" growled the shoemaker, wrinkling his nose. Then he stuck out his chin, grinned, and bared his stumps of teeth. "But I 'ope you and the girl have the best of luck." He shook his head. "Heh, you're going to need it, Stronghammer!"

"We're all going to need it," snapped Thane as he walked past.

Loring waved a hand. "Bah, sourpuss. Listen, Roran; I've lived in Carvahall for many, many years, and in my experience, it's better that this happened *now*, instead of when we're all warm and cozy."

Baldor nodded, but Roran asked, "Why so?"

"Isn't it obvious? Normally, you and Katrina would be the meat of gossip for the next nine months." Loring put a finger on the side of his nose. "Ah, but this way, you'll soon be forgotten amid everything else that's going on, and then the two of you might even have some peace."

Roran frowned. "I'd rather be talked about than have those desecrators camped on the road."

"So would we all. Still, it's something to be grateful for, and we all need something to be grateful for—'specially once you're married!" Loring cackled and pointed at Roran. "Your face just turned purple, boy!"

Roran grunted and set about gathering Katrina's possessions off the ground. As he did, he was interrupted by comments from whoever happened to be nearby, none of which helped to settle his nerves. "Rotgut," he muttered to himself after a particularly invidious remark.

Although the expedition into the Spine was delayed by the unusual scene the villagers had just witnessed, it was only slightly after midmorning when the caravan of people and donkeys began to ascend the bare trail scratched into the side of Narnmor Mountain to the crest of the Igualda Falls. It was a steep climb and had to be taken slowly, on account of the children and the size of the burdens everyone carried.

Roran spent most of his time caught behind Calitha—Thane's wife—and her five children. He did not mind, as it gave him an opportunity to indulge his injured calf and to consider recent events at length. He was disturbed by his confrontation with Sloan. *At least*, he consoled himself, *Katrina won't remain in Carvahall much longer.* For Roran was convinced, in his heart of hearts, that the village would soon be defeated. It was a sobering, yet unavoidable, realization.

He paused to rest three-quarters of the way up the mountain and leaned against a tree as he admired the elevated view of Palancar Valley. He tried to spot the Ra'zac's camp—which he knew was just to the left of the Anora River and the road south—but was unable to discern even a wisp of smoke.

Roran heard the roar of the Igualda Falls long before they came into sight. The falls appeared for all the world like a great snowy mane that billowed and drifted off Narnmor's craggy head to the valley floor a half mile below. The massive stream curved in several directions as it fell, the result of different layers of wind.

Past the slate ledge where the Anora River became airborne, down a glen filled with thimbleberries, and then finally into a large clearing guarded on one side by a pile of boulders, Roran found that those at the head of the procession had already begun setting up camp. The forest rang with the children's shouts and cries.

Removing his pack, Roran untied an ax from the top, then set about clearing the underbrush from the site along with several other men. When they finished, they began chopping down enough trees to encircle the camp. The aroma of pine sap filled the air. Roran worked quickly, the wood chips flying in unison with his rhythmic swings.

By the time the fortifications were complete, the camp had already been erected with seventeen wool tents, four small cookfires, and glum expressions from people and donkeys alike. No one wanted to leave, and no one wanted to stay.

Roran surveyed the assortment of boys and old men clutching spears, and thought, *Too much experience and too little. The grandfathers know how to deal with bears and the like, but will the grandsons have the strength to actually do it?* Then he noticed the hard glint in the women's eyes and realized that while they might hold a babe or be busy tending a scraped arm, their own shields and spears were never far from reach. Roran smiled. *Perhaps . . . perhaps we still have hope.*

He saw Nolfavrell sitting alone on a log—staring back toward Palancar Valley—and joined the boy, who looked at him seriously. "Are you leaving soon?" asked Nolfavrell. Roran nodded, impressed by his poise and determination. "You will do your best, won't you, to kill the Ra'zac and avenge my father? I would do it, except that Mama says I must guard my brothers and sisters."

"I'll bring you their heads myself, if I can," promised Roran.

The boy's chin trembled. "That is good!"

"Nolfavrell . . ." Roran paused as he searched for the right words. "You are the only one here, besides me, who has killed a man. It doesn't mean that we are better or worse than anyone else, but it means that I can trust you to fight well if you are attacked. When Katrina comes here tomorrow, will you make sure that she's well protected?"

Nolfavrell's chest swelled with pride. "I'll guard her wherever she goes!" Then he looked regretful. "That is . . . when I don't have to look after—"

Roran understood. "Oh, your family comes first. But maybe Katrina can stay in the tent with your brothers and sisters."

"Yes," said Nolfavrell slowly. "Yes, I think that would work. You can rely on me."

"Thank you." Roran clapped him on the shoulder. He could have asked an older and more capable person, but the adults were too busy with their own responsibilities to defend Katrina as he hoped. Nolfavrell, however, would have the opportunity and inclination to assure that she remained safe. *He can hold my place while we are apart.* Roran stood as Birgit approached.

Eyeing him flatly, she said, "Come, it is time." Then she hugged her son and continued toward the falls with Roran and the other villagers who were returning to Carvahall. Behind them, everyone in the small camp clustered against the felled trees and stared forlornly out through their wooden bars.

HIS ENEMY'S FACE

As Roran proceeded about his work throughout the rest of the day, he felt Carvahall's emptiness deep inside. It was as if part of himself had been extracted and hidden in the Spine. And with the children gone, the village now felt like an armed camp. The change seemed to have made everyone grim and grave.

When the sun finally sank into the waiting teeth of the Spine, Roran climbed the hill to Horst's house. He stopped before the front door and placed a hand on the knob, but remained there, unable to enter. *Why does this frighten me as much as fighting?*

In the end, he forsook the front door entirely and went to the side of the house, where he slipped into the kitchen and, to his dismay, saw Elain knitting on one side of the table, speaking to Katrina, who was opposite her. They both turned toward him, and Roran blurted, "Are . . . are you all right?"

Katrina came to his side. "I'm fine." She smiled softly. "It just was a terrible shock when Father . . . when . . ." She ducked her head for a moment. "Elain has been wonderfully kind to me. She agreed to lend me Baldor's room for the night."

"I'm glad you are better," said Roran. He hugged her, trying to convey all of his love and adoration through that simple touch.

Elain wrapped up her knitting. "Come now. The sun has set, and it's time you were off to bed, Katrina."

Roran reluctantly let go of Katrina, who kissed him on the cheek and said, "I'll see you in the morning."

He started to follow her out, but stopped when Elain said with a barbed tone, "Roran." Her delicate face was hard and stern.

"Yes?"

Elain waited until they heard the creak of stairs that indicated Katrina was out of earshot. "I hope that you meant every promise you gave that girl, because if you didn't, I'll call an assembly and have you exiled within a week."

Roran was dumbfounded. "Of course I meant them. I love her."

"Katrina just surrendered everything she owned or cared about for you." Elain stared up at him with unwavering eyes. "I've seen men who throw their affection at young maids, like grain tossed at chickens. The maids sigh and weep and believe that they are special, yet for the man, it's only a trifling amusement. You have always been honorable, Roran, but one's loins can turn even the most sensible person into a prancing booby or a sly, wicked fox. Are you one? For Katrina requires neither a fool, a trickster, nor even love; what she requires above all else is a man who will provide for her. If you abandon her, she will be the meanest person in Carvahall, forced to live off her friends, our first and only beggar. By the blood in my veins, I won't let that happen."

"Nor would I," protested Roran. "I would have to be heartless, or worse, to do so."

Elain jerked her chin. "Exactly. Don't forget that you intend to marry a woman who has lost both her dowry and her mother's inheritance. Do you understand what it means for Katrina to lose her inheritance? She has no silver, no linens, no lace, nor any of the things needed for a well-run home. Such items are all we own, passed from mother to daughter since the day we first settled Alagaësia. They determine our worth. A woman without her inheritance is like . . . is like—"

"Is like a man without a farm or a trade," said Roran.

"Just so. It was cruel of Sloan to deny Katrina her inheritance, but that can't be helped now. Both you and she have no money or resources. Life is difficult enough without that added hardship.

191

You'll be starting from nothing and with nothing. Does the prospect frighten you or seem unbearable? So I ask you once again—and don't lie or the two of you will regret it for the rest of your lives—will you care for her without grudge or resentment?"

"Yes."

Elain sighed and filled two earthen cups with cider from a jug hanging among the rafters. She handed one to Roran as she seated herself back at the table. "Then I suggest that you devote yourself to replacing Katrina's home and inheritance so that she and any daughters you may have can stand without shame among the wives of Carvahall."

Roran sipped the cool cider. "If we live that long."

"Aye." She brushed back a strand of her blond hair and shook her head. "You've chosen a hard path, Roran."

"I had to make sure that Katrina would leave Carvahall."

Elain lifted an eyebrow. "So that was it. Well, I won't argue about it, but why on earth didn't you speak to Sloan about your engagement before this morning? When Horst asked my father, he gave our family twelve sheep, a sow, and eight pairs of wrought-iron candlesticks before he even knew if my parents would agree. That's how it should be done. Surely you could have thought of a better strategy than striking your father-in-law-to-be."

A painful laugh escaped Roran. "I could have, but it never seemed the right time with all the attacks."

"The Ra'zac haven't attacked for almost six days now."

He scowled. "No, but . . . it was . . . Oh, I don't know!" He banged his fist on the table with frustration.

Elain put down her cup and wrapped her tiny hands around his. "If you can mend this rift between you and Sloan *now*, before years of resentment accumulate, your life with Katrina will be much, much easier. Tomorrow morning you should go to his house and beg his forgiveness."

"I won't beg! Not to him."

"Roran, listen to me. It's worth a month of begging to have peace in your family. I know from experience; strife does naught but make you miserable."

"Sloan hates the Spine. He'll have nothing to do with me."

"You have to try, though," said Elain earnestly. "Even if he spurns your apology, at least you can't be blamed for not making the effort. If you love Katrina, then swallow your pride and do what's right for her. Don't make her suffer for your mistake." She finished her cider, used a tin hat to snuff the candles, and left Roran sitting alone in the dark.

Several minutes elapsed before Roran could bring himself to stir. He stretched out an arm and traced along the counter's edge until he felt the doorway, then proceeded upstairs, all the while running the tips of his fingers over the carved walls to keep his balance. In his room, he disrobed and threw himself lengthwise on the bed.

Wrapping his arms around his wool-stuffed pillow, Roran listened to the faint sounds that drifted through the house at night: the scrabble of a mouse in the attic and its intermittent squeaks, the groan of wood beams cooling in the night, the whisper and caress of wind at the lintel of his window, and . . . and the rustle of slippers in the hall outside his room.

He watched as the latch above the doorknob was pulled free of its hook, then the door inched forward with a rasp of protest. It paused. A dark form slipped inside, the door closed, and Roran felt a curtain of hair brush his face along with lips like rose petals. He sighed.

Katrina.

A thunderclap tore Roran from sleep.

Light flared on his face as he struggled to regain awareness, like a diver desperate to reach the surface. He opened his eyes and saw a jagged hole blasted through his door. Six soldiers rushed through the yawning cleft, followed by the two Ra'zac, who seemed to fill the room with their ghastly presence. A sword was pressed against

Roran's neck. Beside him, Katrina screamed and pulled the blankets around her.

"*Up*," ordered the Ra'zac. Roran cautiously got to his feet. His heart felt like it was about to explode in his chest. "Tie his handsss and bring him."

As a soldier approached Roran with rope, Katrina screamed again and jumped on the men, biting and clawing furiously. Her sharp nails furrowed their faces, drawing streams of blood that blinded the cursing soldiers.

Roran dropped to one knee and grabbed his hammer from the floor, then planted his feet, swinging the hammer over his head and roaring like a bear. The soldiers threw themselves at him in an attempt to subdue him through sheer numbers, but to no avail: Katrina was in danger, and he was invincible. Shields crumpled beneath his blows, brigandines and mail split under his merciless weapon, and helmets caved in. Two men were wounded, and three fell to rise no more.

The clang and clamor had roused the household; Roran dimly heard Horst and his sons shouting in the hall. The Ra'zac hissed to one another, then scuttled forward and grasped Katrina with inhuman strength, lifting her off the floor as they fled the room.

"*Roran!*" she shrieked.

Summoning his energy, Roran bowled past the two remaining men. He stumbled into the hall and saw the Ra'zac climbing out a window. Roran dashed toward them and struck at the last Ra'zac, just as it was about to descend below the windowsill. Jerking upward, the Ra'zac caught Roran's wrist in midair and chittered with delight, blowing its fetid breath onto his face. "Yesss! You are the one we want!"

Roran tried to twist free, but the Ra'zac did not budge. With his free hand, Roran buffeted the creature's head and shoulders— which were as hard as iron. Desperate and enraged, he seized the edge of the Ra'zac's hood and wrenched it back, exposing its features.

A hideous, tortured face screamed at him. The skin was shiny black, like a beetle carapace. The head was bald. Each lidless eye was the size of his fist and gleamed like an orb of polished hematite; no iris or pupil existed. In place of a nose, mouth, and chin, a thick beak hooked to a sharp point that clacked over a barbed purple tongue.

Roran yelled and jammed his heels against the sides of the window frame, struggling to free himself from the monstrosity, but the Ra'zac inexorably drew him out of the house. He could see Katrina on the ground, still screaming and fighting.

Just as Roran's knees buckled, Horst appeared by his side and wrapped a knotted arm around his chest, locking him in place. "Someone get a spear!" shouted the smith. He snarled, veins bulging on his neck from the strain of holding Roran. "It'll take more than this demon spawn to best us!"

The Ra'zac gave a final yank, then, when it failed to dislodge Roran, cocked its head and said, "You are *oursss!*" It lunged forward with blinding speed, and Roran howled as he felt the Ra'zac's beak close on his right shoulder, snipping through the front of the muscle. His wrist cracked at the same time. With a malicious cackle, the Ra'zac released him and fell backward into the night.

Horst and Roran sprawled against each other in the hallway. "They have Katrina," groaned Roran. His vision flickered and went black around the edges as he pushed himself upright on his left arm—his right hung useless. Albriech and Baldor emerged from his room, splattered with gore. Only corpses remained behind them. *Now I have killed eight.* Roran retrieved his hammer and staggered down the hall, finding his way blocked by Elain in her white sleeping shift.

She looked at him with wide eyes, then took his arm and pushed him down onto a wood chest set against the wall. "You have to see Gertrude."

"But—"

"You'll pass out if this bleeding isn't stopped."

He looked down at his right side; it was drenched in crimson. "We have to rescue Katrina before"—he clenched his teeth as the pain surged—"before they do anything to her."

"He's right; we can't wait," said Horst, looming over them. "Bind him up as best you can, then we'll go." Elain pursed her lips and hurried to the linen closet. She returned with several rags, which she wrapped tightly around Roran's torn shoulder and his fractured wrist. Meanwhile, Albriech and Baldor scavenged armor and swords from the soldiers. Horst contented himself with just a spear.

Elain put her hands on Horst's chest and said, "Be careful." She looked at her sons. "All of you."

"We'll be fine, Mother," promised Albriech. She forced a smile and kissed them on the cheek.

They left the house and ran to the edge of Carvahall, where they found that the wall of trees had been pulled open and the watchman, Byrd, slain. Baldor knelt and examined the body, then said with a choked voice, "He was stabbed from behind." Roran barely heard him through the pounding in his ears. Dizzy, he leaned against a house and panted for breath.

"Ho! Who goes?"

From their stations along Carvahall's perimeter, the other watchmen congregated around their murdered compatriot, forming a huddle of shuttered lanterns. In hushed tones, Horst described the attack and Katrina's plight. "Who will help us?" he asked. After a quick discussion, five men agreed to accompany them; the rest would remain to guard the breach in the wall and rouse the villagers.

Pushing himself off the house, Roran trotted to the head of the group as it slipped through the fields and down the valley toward the Ra'zac's camp. Every step was agony, yet it did not matter; nothing mattered except Katrina. He stumbled once and Horst wordlessly caught him.

Half a mile from Carvahall, Ivor spotted a sentry on a hillock, which compelled them to make a wide detour. A few hundred yards beyond, the ruddy glow of torches became visible. Roran raised his good arm to slow their advance, then began to dodge and crawl through the tangled grass, startling a jackrabbit. The men followed Roran's lead as he worked his way to the edge of a grove of cattails, where he stopped and parted the curtain of stalks to observe the thirteen remaining soldiers.

Where is she?

In contrast to when they had first arrived, the soldiers appeared sullen and haggard, their weapons nicked and their armor dented. Most of them wore bandages that were rusty with splotches of dried blood. The men were clumped together, facing the two Ra'zac—both of whom were now hooded—across a low fire.

One man was shouting: ". . . over half of us killed by a bunch of inbred, cockle-brained woodrats that can't tell a pike from a poleax or find the point of a sword even if it's lodged in their gut, because *you* don't have half the sense my banner boy does! I don't care if Galbatorix himself licks your boots clean, we won't do a thing until we have a new commander." The men nodded. "One who's *human*."

"Really?" demanded the Ra'zac softly.

"We've had enough taking orders from hunchbacks like you, with all your clicking and teapot whistling—makes us sick! And I don't know what you did with Sardson, but if you stay another night, we'll put steel in you and find out if you bleed like us. You can leave the girl, though, she'll be—"

The man did not get a chance to continue, for the largest Ra'zac jumped across the fire and landed on his shoulders, like a giant crow. Screaming, the soldier collapsed under the weight. He tried to draw his sword, but the Ra'zac pecked twice at his neck with its hidden beak, and he was still.

"We have to fight *that*?" muttered Ivor behind Roran.

The soldiers remained frozen with shock as the two Ra'zac lapped from the neck of the corpse. When the black creatures rose, they rubbed their knobby hands together, as if they were washing, and said, "Yesss. We will go. Stay if you wisssh; reinforsssements are only daysss away." The Ra'zac threw back their heads and began to shriek at the sky, the wail becoming increasingly shrill until it passed from hearing.

Roran looked up as well. At first he saw nothing, but then a nameless terror gripped him as two barbed shadows appeared high over the Spine, eclipsing the stars. They advanced quickly, growing larger and larger until they obscured half the sky with their ominous presence. A foul wind rushed across the land, bringing with it a sulfurous miasma that made Roran cough and gag.

The soldiers were likewise afflicted; their curses echoed as they pressed sleeves and scarves over their noses.

Above them, the shadows paused and then began to drift downward, enclosing the camp in a dome of menacing darkness. The sickly torches flickered and threatened to extinguish themselves, yet they still provided sufficient light to reveal the two beasts descending among the tents.

Their bodies were naked and hairless—like newborn mice—with leathery gray skin pulled tight across their corded chests and bellies. In form they resembled starved dogs, except that their hind legs bulged with enough muscle to crush a boulder. A narrow crest extended from the back of each of their attenuated heads, opposite a long, straight, ebony beak made for spearing prey, and cold, bulbous eyes identical to the Ra'zac's. From their shoulders and backs sprang huge wings that made the air moan under their weight.

Flinging themselves to the ground, the soldiers cowered and hid their faces from the monsters. A terrible, alien intelligence emanated from the creatures, bespeaking a race far older and far more powerful than humans. Roran was suddenly afraid that his mission might fail. Behind him, Horst whispered to the men, urging them to hold their ground and remain hidden, else they would be slain.

The Ra'zac bowed to the beasts, then slipped into a tent and returned carrying Katrina—who was bound with ropes—and leading Sloan. The butcher walked freely.

Roran stared, unable to comprehend how Sloan had been captured. *His house isn't anywhere near Horst's.* Then it struck him. "He betrayed us," said Roran with wonder. His fist slowly tightened on his hammer as the true horror of the situation exploded within him. *"He killed Byrd and he betrayed us!"* Tears of rage streamed down his face.

"Roran," murmured Horst, crouching beside him. "We can't attack now; they'd slaughter us. Roran . . . do you hear me?"

He heard but a whisper in the distance as he watched the smaller Ra'zac jump onto one beast above the shoulders, then catch Katrina as the other Ra'zac tossed her up. Sloan seemed upset and frightened now. He began arguing with the Ra'zac, shaking his head and pointing at the ground. Finally, the Ra'zac struck him across the mouth, knocking him unconscious. Mounting the second beast, with the butcher slung over its shoulder, the largest Ra'zac declared, "We will return once it isss sssafe again. Kill the boy, and your livesss are forfeit." Then the steeds flexed their massive thighs and leaped into the sky, once again shadows upon the field of stars.

No words or emotions were left to Roran. He was utterly destroyed. All that remained was to kill the soldiers. He stood and raised his hammer in preparation to charge, but as he stepped forward, his head throbbed in unison with his wounded shoulder, the ground vanished in a burst of light, and he toppled into oblivion.

✦ ✦ ✦

ARROW TO THE HEART

Every day since leaving the outpost of Ceris was a hazy dream of warm afternoons spent paddling up Eldor Lake and then the Gaena River. All around them, water gurgled through the tunnel of verdant pines that wound ever deeper into Du Weldenvarden.

Eragon found traveling with the elves delightful. Narí and Lifaen were perpetually smiling, laughing, and singing songs, especially when Saphira was around. They rarely looked elsewhere or spoke of another subject but her in her presence.

However, the elves were not human, no matter the similarity of appearance. They moved too quickly, too fluidly, for creatures born of simple flesh and blood. And when they spoke, they often used roundabout expressions and aphorisms that left Eragon more confused than when they began. In between their bursts of merriment, Lifaen and Narí would remain silent for hours, observing their surroundings with a glow of peaceful rapture on their faces. If Eragon or Orik attempted to talk with them during their contemplation, they would receive only a word or two in response.

It made Eragon appreciate how direct and forthright Arya was by comparison. In fact, she seemed uneasy around Lifaen and Narí, as if she were no longer sure how to behave with her own kind.

From the prow of the canoe, Lifaen looked over his shoulder and said, "Tell me, Eragon-finiarel. . . . What do your people sing about in these dark days? I remember the epics and lays I heard in Ilirea—sagas of your proud kings and earls—but it was long, long ago and the memories are like withered flowers in my mind. What new works have your people created?" Eragon frowned as he tried to recall the names of stories Brom had recited. When Lifaen heard them, he shook his head sorrowfully and said, "So much has been lost. No court ballads survive, and, if you speak truly, nor does most of your history or art, except for fanciful tales Galbatorix has allowed to thrive."

"Brom once told us about the fall of the Riders," said Eragon defensively. An image of a deer bounding over rotting logs flashed behind his eyes from Saphira, who was off hunting.

"Ah, a brave man." For a minute, Lifaen paddled silently. "We too sing about the Fall . . . but rarely. Most of us were alive when Vrael entered the void, and we still grieve for our burned cities—the red lilies of Éwayëna, the crystals of Luthivíra—and for our slain families. Time cannot dull the pain of those wounds, not if a thousand thousand years pass and the sun itself dies, leaving the world to float in eternal night."

Orik grunted in the back. "As it is with the dwarves. Remember, elf, we lost an entire clan to Galbatorix."

"And we lost our king, Evandar."

"I never heard that," said Eragon, surprised.

Lifaen nodded as he guided them around a submerged rock. "Few have. Brom could have told you about it; he was there when the fatal blow was struck. Before Vrael's death, the elves faced Galbatorix on the plains of Ilirea in our final attempt to defeat him. There Evandar—"

"Where is Ilirea?" asked Eragon.

"It's Urû'baen, boy," said Orik. "Used to be an elf city."

Unperturbed by the interruption, Lifaen continued: "As you say, Ilirea was one of our cities. We abandoned it during our war with the dragons, and then, centuries later, humans adopted it as their capital after King Palancar was exiled."

Eragon said, "King Palancar? Who was he? Is that how Palancar Valley got its name?"

This time the elf turned and looked at him with amusement. "You have as many questions as leaves on a tree, Argetlam."

"Brom was of the same opinion."

Lifaen smiled, then paused, as if to gather his thoughts. "When your ancestors arrived in Alagaësia eight hundred years ago, they roamed far across it, seeking a suitable place to live. Eventually, they settled in Palancar Valley—though it was not called such then—as it was one of the few defendable locations that we or the dwarves had not claimed. There your king, Palancar, began to build a mighty state.

"In an attempt to expand his borders, he declared war against us, though we had offered no provocation. Three times he attacked, and three times we prevailed. Our strength frightened Palancar's nobles and they pled with their liege for peace. He ignored their counsel. Then the lords approached us with a treaty, which we signed without the king's knowledge.

"With our help, Palancar was usurped and banished, but he, his family, and their vassals refused to leave the valley. Since we had no wish to murder them, we constructed the tower of Ristvak'baen so the Riders could watch over Palancar and ensure he would never again rise to power or attack anyone else in Alagaësia.

"Before long Palancar was killed by a son who did not wish to wait for nature to take its course. Thereafter, family politics consisted of assassination, betrayal, and other depravities, reducing Palancar's house to a shadow of its former grandeur. However, his descendants never left, and the blood of kings still runs in Therinsford and Carvahall."

"I see," said Eragon.

Lifaen lifted one dark eyebrow. "Do you? It has more significance than you may think. It was this event that convinced Anurin—Vrael's predecessor as head Rider—to allow humans to become Riders, in order to prevent similar disputes."

Orik emitted a bark of laughter. "That must have caused some argument."

"It was an unpopular decision," admitted Lifaen. "Even now some question the wisdom of it. It caused such a disagreement between Anurin and Queen Dellanir that Anurin seceded from our government and established the Riders on Vroengard as an independent entity."

"But if the Riders were separated from your government, then how could they keep the peace, as they were supposed to?" asked Eragon.

"They couldn't," said Lifaen. "Not until Queen Dellanir saw the wisdom of having the Riders free of any lord or king and restored their access to Du Weldenvarden. Still, it never pleased her that any authority could supersede her own."

Eragon frowned. "Wasn't that the whole point, though?"

"Yes . . . and no. The Riders were supposed to guard against the failings of the different governments and races, yet who watched the watchers? It was that very problem that caused the Fall. No one existed who could descry the flaws within the Riders' own system, for they were above scrutiny, and thus, they perished."

Eragon stroked the water—first on one side and then the other—while he considered Lifaen's words. His paddle fluttered in his hands as it cut diagonally across the current. "Who succeeded Dellanir as king or queen?"

"Evandar did. He took the knotted throne five hundred years ago—when Dellanir abdicated in order to study the mysteries of magic—and held it until his death. Now his mate, Islanzadí, rules us."

"That's—" Eragon stopped with his mouth open. He was going to say *impossible*, but then realized how ridiculous the statement would sound. Instead, he asked, "Are elves immortal?"

In a soft voice, Lifaen said, "Once we were like you, bright, fleeting, and as ephemeral as the morning dew. Now our lives stretch endlessly through the dusty years. Aye, we are immortal, although we are still vulnerable to injuries of the flesh."

"You *became* immortal? How?" The elf refused to elaborate,

though Eragon pressed him for details. Finally, Eragon asked, "How old is Arya?"

Lifaen turned his glittering eyes on him, probing Eragon with disconcerting acuteness. "Arya? What is your interest in her?"

"I . . ." Eragon faltered, suddenly unsure of his intentions. His attraction to Arya was complicated by the fact that she was an elf, and that her age, whatever it might be, was so much greater than his own. *She must view me as a child.* "I don't know," he said honestly. "But she saved both my life and Saphira's, and I'm curious to know more about her."

"I feel ashamed," said Lifaen, pronouncing each word carefully, "for asking such a question. Among our kind, it is rude to pry into one's affairs. . . . Only, I must say, and I believe that Orik agrees with me, that you would do well to guard your heart, Argetlam. Now is not the time to lose it, nor would it be well placed in this instance."

"Aye," grunted Orik.

Heat suffused Eragon as blood rushed to his face, like hot tallow melting through him. Before he could utter a retort, Saphira entered his mind and said, *And now is the time to guard your tongue. They mean well. Don't insult them.*

He took a deep breath and tried to let his embarrassment drain away. *Do you agree with them?*

I believe, Eragon, that you are full of love and that you are looking for one who will reciprocate your affection. No shame exists in that.

He struggled to digest her words, then finally said, *Will you be back soon?*

I'm on my way now.

Returning his attention to his surroundings, Eragon found that both the elf and the dwarf were watching him. "I understand your concern . . . and I'd still like my question answered."

Lifaen hesitated briefly. "Arya is quite young. She was born a year before the destruction of the Riders."

A hundred! Though he had expected such a figure, Eragon was still shocked. He concealed it behind a blank face, thinking, *She could have great-grandchildren older than me!* He brooded on the subject for several minutes and then, to distract himself, said, "You mentioned that humans discovered Alagaësia eight hundred years ago. Yet Brom said that we arrived three centuries after the Riders were formed, which was thousands of years ago."

"Two thousand, seven hundred, and four years, by our reckoning," declared Orik. "Brom was right, if you consider a single ship with twenty warriors the 'arrival' of humans in Alagaësia. They landed in the south, where Surda is now. We met while they were exploring and exchanged gifts, but then they departed and we didn't see another human for almost two millennia, or until King Palancar arrived with a fleet in tow. The humans had completely forgotten us by then, except for vague stories about hairy men-of-the-mountains that preyed on children in the night. Bah!"

"Do you know where Palancar came from?" asked Eragon.

Orik frowned and gnawed the tip of his mustache, then shook his head. "Our histories only say that his homeland was far to the south, beyond the Beors, and that his exodus was the result of war and famine."

Excited by an idea, Eragon blurted, "So there might be countries elsewhere that could help us against Galbatorix."

"Possibly," said Orik. "But they would be difficult to find, even on dragonback, and I doubt that you'd speak the same language. Who would want to help us, though? The Varden have little to offer another country, and it's hard enough to get an army from Farthen Dûr to Urû'baen, much less bring forces from hundreds, if not thousands, of miles away."

"We could not spare you anyway," said Lifaen to Eragon.

"I still—" Eragon broke off as Saphira soared over the river, followed by a furious crowd of sparrows and blackbirds intent on driving her away from their nests. At the same time, a chorus of squeaks and chatters burst from the armies of squirrels hidden among the branches.

Lifaen beamed and cried, "Isn't she glorious? See how her scales catch the light! No treasure in the world can match this sight." Similar exclamations floated across the river from Narí.

"Bloody unbearable, that's what it is," muttered Orik into his beard. Eragon hid a smile, though he agreed with the dwarf. The elves never seemed to tire of praising Saphira.

Nothing's wrong with a few compliments, said Saphira. She landed with a gigantic splash and submerged her head to escape a diving sparrow.

Of course not, said Eragon.

Saphira eyed him from underwater. *Was that sarcasm?*

He chuckled and let it pass. Glancing at the other boat, Eragon watched Arya paddle, her back perfectly straight, her face inscrutable as she floated through webs of mottled light beneath the mossy trees. She seemed so dark and somber, it made him want to comfort her. "Lifaen," he asked softly so that Orik would not hear, "why is Arya so . . . unhappy? You and—"

Lifaen's shoulders stiffened underneath his russet tunic and he whispered, so low that Eragon could barely hear, "We are honored to serve Arya Dröttningu. She has suffered more than you can imagine for our people. We celebrate out of joy for what she has achieved with Saphira, and we weep in our dreams for her sacrifice . . . and her loss. Her sorrows are her own, though, and I cannot reveal them without her permission."

As Eragon sat by their nightly campfire, petting a swatch of moss that felt like rabbit fur, he heard a commotion deeper in the forest. Exchanging glances with Saphira and Orik, he crept toward the sound, drawing Zar'roc.

Eragon stopped at the lip of a small ravine and looked across to the other side, where a gyrfalcon with a broken wing thrashed in a bed of snowberries. The raptor froze when it saw him, then opened its beak and uttered a piercing screech.

What a terrible fate, to be unable to fly, said Saphira.

When Arya arrived, she eyed the gyrfalcon, then strung her bow and, with unerring aim, shot it through the breast. At first Eragon thought that she had done it for food, but she made no move to retrieve either the bird or her arrow.

"Why?" he asked.

With a hard expression, Arya unstrung her bow. "It was too injured for me to heal and would have died tonight or tomorrow. Such is the nature of things. I saved it hours of suffering."

Saphira lowered her head and touched Arya on the shoulder with her snout, then returned to their camp, her tail scraping bark off the trees. As Eragon started to follow, he felt Orik tug his sleeve and bent down to hear the dwarf say in an undertone, "Never ask an elf for help; they might decide that you're better off dead, eh?"

THE DAGSHELGR
INVOCATION

Though he was tired from the previous day, Eragon forced himself to rise before dawn in an attempt to catch one of the elves asleep. It had become a game with him to discover when the elves got up—or if they slept at all—as he had yet to see any of them with their eyes closed. Today was no exception.

"Good morning," said Narí and Lifaen from above him. Eragon craned back his head and saw that they each stood on the bough of a pine tree, over fifty feet in the air. Jumping from branch to branch with feline grace, the elves dropped to the ground alongside him.

"We have been keeping watch," explained Lifaen.

"For what?"

Arya stepped around a tree and said, "For my fears. Du Weldenvarden has many mysteries and dangers, especially for a Rider. We have lived here for thousands of years, and old spells still linger in unexpected places; magic permeates the air, the water, and the earth. In places it has affected the animals. Sometimes strange creatures are found roaming the forest, and not all of them friendly."

"Are they—" Eragon stopped as his gedwëy ignasia tingled. The silver hammer on the necklace Gannel had given him grew hot on his chest, and he felt the amulet's spell draw upon his strength.

Someone was trying to scry him.

Is it Galbatorix? he wondered, frightened. He clutched the necklace and pulled it out of his tunic, ready to yank it off should he become too weak. From the other side of the camp, Saphira rushed to his side, bolstering him with her own reserves of energy.

A moment later, the heat leached out of the hammer, leaving it cold against Eragon's skin. He bounced it on his palm, then tucked it back under his clothes, whereupon Saphira said, *Our enemies are searching for us.*

Enemies? Could not it be someone in Du Vrangr Gata?

I think Hrothgar would have told Nasuada that he ordered Gannel to enchant you this necklace. . . . She might have even come up with the idea in the first place.

Arya frowned when Eragon explained what had occurred. "This makes it all the more important we reach Ellesméra quickly so your training can resume. Events in Alagaësia move apace, and I fear you won't have adequate time for your studies."

Eragon wanted to discuss it further, but lost the opportunity in the rush to leave camp. Once the canoes were loaded and the fire tamped out, they continued to forge up the Gaena River.

They had only been on the water for an hour when Eragon noticed that the river was growing wider and deeper. A few minutes later, they came upon a waterfall that filled Du Weldenvarden with its throbbing rumble. The cataract was about a hundred feet tall, and streamed down a stone face with an overhang that made it impossible to climb. "How do we get past that?" He could already feel cool spray on his face.

Lifaen pointed at the left shore, some distance from the falls, where a trail had been worn up the steep ridge. "We have to portage our canoes and supplies for half a league before the river clears."

The five of them untied the bundles wedged between the seats of the canoes and divided the supplies into piles that they stuffed into their packs. "Ugh," said Eragon, hefting his load. It was twice as heavy as what he usually carried when traveling on foot.

I could fly it upstream for you . . . all of it, offered Saphira, crawling onto the muddy bank and shaking herself dry.

When Eragon repeated her suggestion, Lifaen looked horrified. "We would never dream of using a dragon as a beast of burden. It would dishonor you, Saphira—and Eragon as Shur'tugal—and it would shame our hospitality."

Saphira snorted, and a plume of flame erupted from her nostrils, vaporizing the surface of the river and creating a cloud of steam. *This is nonsense.* Reaching past Eragon with one scaly leg, she hooked her talons through the packs' shoulder straps, then took off over their heads. *Catch me if you can!*

A peal of clear laughter broke the silence, like the trill of a mockingbird. Amazed, Eragon turned and looked at Arya. It was the first time he had ever heard her laugh; he loved the sound. She smiled at Lifaen. "You have much to learn if you presume to tell a dragon what she may or may not do."

"But the dishonor—"

"It is no dishonor if Saphira does it of her free will," asserted Arya. "Now, let us go before we waste any more time."

Hoping that the strain would not trigger the pain in his back, Eragon picked up his canoe with Lifaen and fit it over his shoulders. He was forced to rely on the elf to guide him along the trail, as he could only see the ground beneath his feet.

An hour later, they had topped the ridge and hiked beyond the dangerous white water to where the Gaena River was once again calm and glassy. Waiting for them was Saphira, who was busy catching fish in the shallows, jabbing her triangular head into the water like a heron.

Arya called her over and said to both her and Eragon, "Beyond the next curve lies Ardwen Lake and, upon its western shore, Sílthrim, one of our greatest cities. Past that, a vast expanse of forest still separates us from Ellesméra. We will encounter many elves close to Sílthrim. However, I don't want either of you to be seen until we speak with Queen Islanzadí."

Why? asked Saphira, echoing Eragon's thoughts.

In her musical accent, Arya answered: "Your presence represents a great and terrible change for our kingdom, and such shifts are dangerous unless handled with care. The queen must be the first to meet with you. Only she has the authority and wisdom to oversee this transition."

"You speak highly of her," commented Eragon.

At his words, Narí and Lifaen stopped and watched Arya with guarded eyes. Her face went blank, then she drew herself up proudly. "She has led us well. . . . Eragon, I know you carry a hooded cape from Tronjheim. Until we are free of possible observers, will you wear it and keep your head covered so that none can see your rounded ears and know that you are human?" He nodded. "And, Saphira, you must hide during the day and catch up with us at night. Ajihad told me that is what you did in the Empire."

And I hated every moment of it, she growled.

"It's only for today and tomorrow. After that we will be far enough away from Sílthrim that we won't have to worry about encountering anyone of consequence," promised Arya.

Saphira turned her azure eyes on Eragon. *When we escaped the Empire, I swore that I would always stay close enough to protect you. Every time I leave, bad things happen: Yazuac, Daret, Dras-Leona, the slavers.*

Not in Teirm.

You know what I mean! I'm especially loath to leave since you can't defend yourself with your crippled back.

I trust that Arya and the others will keep me safe. Don't you?

Saphira hesitated. *I trust Arya.* She twisted away and padded up the riverbank, sat for a minute, then returned. *Very well.* She broadcast her acceptance to Arya, adding, *But I won't wait any longer than tomorrow night, even if you're in the middle of Sílthrim at the time.*

"I understand," said Arya. "You will still have to be careful when flying after dark, as elves can see clearly on all but the blackest nights. If you are sighted by chance, you could be attacked by magic."

Wonderful, commented Saphira.

While Orik and the elves repacked the boats, Eragon and Saphira explored the dim forest, searching for a suitable hiding place. They settled on a dry hollow rimmed by crumbling rocks and blanketed with a bed of pine needles that were pleasantly soft underfoot. Saphira curled up on the ground and nodded her head. *Go now. I will be fine.*

Eragon hugged her neck—careful to avoid her sharp spines—and then reluctantly departed, glancing backward. At the river, he donned his cape before they resumed their journey.

The air was motionless when Ardwen Lake came into view, and as a result, the vast mantle of water was smooth and flat, a perfect mirror for the trees and clouds. The illusion was so flawless, Eragon felt as if he were looking through a window at another world and that if they continued forward, the canoes would fall endlessly into the reflected sky. He shivered at the thought.

In the hazy distance, numerous white birch-bark boats darted like water striders along both shores, propelled to incredible speeds by the elves' strength. Eragon ducked his head and tugged on the edge of his hood to ensure that it covered his face.

His link with Saphira grew ever more tenuous the farther apart they became, until only a wisp of thought connected them. By evening he could no longer feel her presence, even if he strained his mind to its limits. All of a sudden, Du Weldenvarden seemed much more lonely and desolate.

As the gloom deepened, a cluster of white lights—placed at every conceivable height among the trees—sprang into existence a mile ahead. The sparks glowed with the silver radiance of the full moon, eerie and mysterious in the night.

"There lies Sílthrim," said Lifaen.

With a faint splash, a dark boat passed them from the opposite direction, accompanied by a murmur of "Kvetha Fricai" from the elf steering.

Arya brought her canoe alongside Eragon's. "We will stop here tonight."

They made camp a ways from Ardwen Lake, where the ground was dry enough to sleep on. The ferocious droves of mosquitoes forced Arya to cast a protective spell so that they could eat dinner in relative comfort.

Afterward, the five of them sat around the fire, staring at the gold flames. Eragon leaned his head against a tree and watched a meteor streak across the sky. His eyelids were about to sink shut when a woman's voice drifted through the woods from Sílthrim, a faint susurration that brushed the inside of his ear like a down feather. He frowned and straightened, trying to better hear the tenuous whisper.

Like a thread of smoke that thickens as a newborn fire blazes to life, so the voice rose in strength until the forest sighed with a teasing, twisting melody that leaped and fell with wild abandon. More voices joined the unearthly song, embroidering the original theme with a hundred variations. The air itself seemed to shimmer with the fabric of the tempestuous music.

The fey strains sent jolts of elation and fear down Eragon's spine; they clouded his senses, drawing him into the velvet night. Seduced by the haunting notes, he jumped to his feet, ready to dash through the forest until he found the source of the voices, ready to dance among the trees and moss, anything so that he could join the elves' revels. But before he could move, Arya caught his arm and yanked him around to face her.

"Eragon! Clear your mind!" He struggled in a futile attempt to break her grip. "Eyddr eyreya onr!" Empty your ears! Everything fell silent then, as if he had gone deaf. He stopped fighting and looked around, wondering what had just occurred. On the other side of the fire, Lifaen and Narí wrestled noiselessly with Orik.

Eragon watched Arya's mouth move as she spoke, then sound returned to the world with a *pop*, though he could no longer hear the music. "What . . . ?" he asked, dazed.

"Gerr'off me," growled Orik. Lifaen and Narí lifted their hands and backed away.

"Your pardon, Orik-vodhr," said Lifaen.

Arya gazed toward Sílthrim. "I miscounted the days; I didn't want to be anywhere near a city during Dagshelgr. Our saturnalias, our celebrations, are perilous for mortals. We sing in the ancient language, and the lyrics weave spells of passion and longing that are difficult to resist, even for us."

Narí stirred restlessly. "We should be at a grove."

"We should," agreed Arya, "but we will do our duty and wait."

Shaken, Eragon sat closer to the fire, wishing for Saphira; he was sure she could have protected his mind from the music's influence. "What is the point of Dagshelgr?" he asked.

Arya joined him on the ground, crossing her long legs. "It is to keep the forest healthy and fertile. Every spring we sing for the trees, we sing for the plants, and we sing for the animals. Without us, Du Weldenvarden would be half its size." As if to emphasize her point, birds, deer, squirrels—red and gray—striped badgers, foxes, rabbits, wolves, frogs, toads, tortoises, and every other nearby animal forsook their hiding and began to rush madly about with a cacophony of yelps and cries. "They are searching for mates," explained Arya. "All across Du Weldenvarden, in each of our cities, elves are singing this song. The more who participate, the stronger the spell, and the greater Du Weldenvarden will be this year."

Eragon snatched back his hand as a trio of hedgehogs trundled past his thigh. The entire forest yammered with noise. *I've stepped into fairyland,* he thought, hugging himself.

Orik came around the fire and raised his voice above the clamor: "By my beard and my ax, I'll not be controlled against my will by magic. If it happens again, Arya, I swear on Helzvog's stone girdle that I'll return to Farthen Dûr and you will have the wrath of Dûrgrimst Ingeitum to deal with."

"It was not my intention for you to experience Dagshelgr," said Arya. "I apologize for my mistake. However, though I am shielding you from this spell, you cannot escape magic in Du Weldenvarden; it permeates everything."

"So long as it doesn't befoul my mind." Orik shook his head and fingered the haft of his ax while eyeing the shadowy beasts that lumbered in the gloom beyond the pool of firelight.

No one slept that night. Eragon and Orik remained awake because of the frightful din and the animals that kept crashing by their tents, the elves because they still listened to the song. Lifaen and Narí took to pacing in endless circles, while Arya stared toward Sílthrim with a hungry expression, her tawny skin drawn thin and taut over her cheekbones.

Four hours into the riot of sound and motion, Saphira dove out of the sky, her eyes sparkling with a queer aspect. She shivered and arched her neck, panting between her open jaws. *The forest,* she said, *is alive. And I am alive. My blood burns like never before. It burns as yours burns when you think of Arya. I . . . understand!*

Eragon put his hand on her shoulder, feeling the tremors that racked her frame; her sides vibrated as she hummed along with the music. She gripped the ground with her ivory claws, her muscles coiled and clenched in a supreme effort to remain motionless. The tip of her tail twitched like she was about to pounce.

Arya stood and joined Eragon on the opposite side of Saphira. The elf also put a hand on Saphira's shoulder, and the three of them faced the darkness, united into a living chain.

When dawn broke, the first thing Eragon noticed was that all the trees now had buds of bright green needles at the ends of their branches. He bent and examined the snowberries at his feet and found that every plant, large or small, had acquired new growth during the night. The forest vibrated with the ripeness of its colors; everything was lush and fresh and clean. The air smelled like it had just rained.

Saphira shook herself beside Eragon and said, *The fever has passed; I am myself again. Such things I felt . . . It was as if the world were being born anew and I was helping to create it with the fire in my limbs.*

How are you? On the inside, I mean.

I will need some time to understand what I experienced.

Since the music had ceased, Arya removed her spell from Eragon and Orik. She said, "Lifaen. Narí. Go to Sílthrim and get horses for the five of us. We cannot walk all the way from here to Ellesméra. Also, alert Captain Damítha that Ceris requires reinforcements."

Narí bowed. "And what shall we say when she asks why we have deserted our post?"

"Tell her that that which she once hoped for—and feared—has occurred; the wyrm has bitten its own tail. She will understand."

The two elves departed for Sílthrim after the boats were emptied of supplies. Three hours later, Eragon heard a stick snap and looked up to see them returning through the forest on proud white stallions, leading four other identical horses. The magnificent beasts moved among the trees with uncanny stealth, their coats shimmering in the emerald twilight. None of them wore saddles or harnesses.

"Blöthr, blöthr," murmured Lifaen, and his steed halted, pawing the ground with its dark hooves.

"Are all your horses as noble as these?" asked Eragon. He cautiously approached one, amazed by its beauty. The animals were only a few inches taller than ponies, which made it easy for them to navigate among the closely placed trunks. They did not seem frightened by Saphira.

"Not all," laughed Narí, tossing his silver hair, "but most. We have bred them for many centuries."

"How am I supposed to ride?"

Arya said, "An elf horse responds instantly to commands in the ancient language; tell it where you wish to go and it will take you. However, do not mistreat them with blows or harsh words, for they are not our slaves, but our friends and partners. They bear you only so long as they consent to; it is a great privilege to ride one. I was only able to save Saphira's egg from Durza because our horses sensed that something was amiss and stopped us from riding into his ambush. . . . They won't let you fall unless you deliberately throw yourself off, and they are skilled in choosing the safest, quickest path through treacherous ground. The dwarves' Feldûnost are like that."

"Right you are," grunted Orik. "A Feldûnost can run you up a cliff and down without a single bruise. But how can we carry food and whatnot without saddles? I won't ride while wearing a full pack."

Lifaen tossed a pile of leather bags at Orik's feet and indicated the sixth horse. "Nor will you have to."

It took half an hour to arrange their supplies in the bags and heap them into a lumpy mound on the horse's back. Afterward, Narí told Eragon and Orik the words they could use to direct the horses: "*Gánga fram* to go forward, *blöthr* to stop, *hlaupa* if needs you must run, and *gánga aptr* to go back. You can give more precise instructions if you know more of the ancient language." He led Eragon to a horse and said, "This is Folkvír. Hold out your hand."

Eragon did, and the stallion snorted, flaring his nostrils. Folkvír sniffed Eragon's palm, then touched it with his muzzle and allowed Eragon to stroke his thick neck. "Good," said Narí, appearing satisfied. The elf had Orik do the same with the next horse.

As Eragon mounted Folkvír, Saphira drew closer. He looked up at her, noting how troubled she still seemed from the night. *One more day*, he said.

Eragon . . . She paused. *I thought of something while I was under the influence of the elves' spell, something that I have always considered of little consequence, but now looms within me like a mountain of black dread: Every creature, no matter how pure or monstrous, has a mate of their own kind. Yet I have none.* She shuddered and closed her eyes. *In this regard, I am alone.*

Her statements reminded Eragon that she was barely more than eight months old. On most occasions, her youth did not show—due to the influence of her hereditary instincts and memories—but, in this arena, she was even more inexperienced than he was with his feeble stabs at romance in Carvahall and Tronjheim. Pity welled inside Eragon, but he suppressed it before it could seep across their mental link. Saphira would have only contempt for the emotion: it could neither solve her problem nor make her feel better. Instead, he said, *Galbatorix still has two dragon eggs. During our first audience with Hrothgar, you mentioned that you would like to rescue them. If we can—*

Saphira snorted bitterly. *It could take years, and even if we did retrieve the eggs, I have no guarantee that they would hatch, nor that they would be male, nor that we would be fit mates. Fate has abandoned my race to extinction.* She lashed her tail with frustration, breaking a sapling in two. She seemed perilously close to tears.

What can I say? he asked, disturbed by her distress. *You can't give up hope. You still have a chance to find a mate, but you have to be patient. Even if Galbatorix's eggs don't work, dragons must exist elsewhere in the world, just like humans, elves, and Urgals do. The moment we are free of our obligations, I'll help you search for them. All right?*

All right, she sniffed. She craned back her head and released a puff of white smoke that dispersed among the branches overhead. *I should know better than to let my emotions get the best of me.*

Nonsense. You would have to be made of stone not to feel this way. It's perfectly normal. . . . But promise you won't dwell on it while you're alone.

She fixed one giant sapphire eye on him. *I won't.* He turned warm inside as he felt her gratitude for his reassurances and companionship. Leaning out from Folkvír, he put a hand on her rough cheek and held it there for a moment. *Go on, little one,* she murmured. *I will see you later.*

Eragon hated to leave her in such a state. He reluctantly entered the forest with Orik and the elves, heading west toward the heart of Du Weldenvarden. After an hour spent pondering Saphira's plight, he mentioned it to Arya.

Faint lines creased Arya's forehead as she frowned. "It is one of Galbatorix's greatest crimes. I do not know if a solution exists, but we can hope. We must hope."

THE PINEWOOD CITY

Eragon had been in Du Weldenvarden for so long that he had begun to long for clearings, fields, or even a mountain, instead of the endless tree trunks and meager underbrush. His flights with Saphira provided no respite as they only revealed hills of prickly green that rolled unbroken into the distance like a verdant sea.

Oftentimes, the branches were so thick overhead, it was impossible to tell from what direction the sun rose and set. That, combined with the repetitive scenery, made Eragon hopelessly lost, no matter how many times Arya or Lifaen troubled to show him the points of the compass. If not for the elves, he knew that he could wander in Du Weldenvarden for the rest of his life without ever finding his way free.

When it rained, the clouds and the forest canopy plunged them into profound darkness, as if they were entombed deep underground. The falling water would collect on the black pine needles above, then trickle through and pour a hundred feet or more down onto their heads, like a thousand little waterfalls. At such times, Arya would summon a glowing orb of green magic that floated over her right hand and provided the only light in the cavernous forest. They would stop and huddle underneath a tree until the storm abated, but even then water cached in the myriad branches would, at the slightest provocation, shower them with droplets for hours afterward.

As they rode deeper into the heart of Du Weldenvarden, the trees grew thicker and taller, as well as farther apart to accommodate the increased span of their branches. The trunks—bare brown shafts that towered up into the overarching ribbed ceiling, which was smudged and obscured by shadow—were over two hundred feet tall, higher than any tree in the Spine or the Beors. Eragon paced out the girth of one tree and measured it at seventy feet.

He mentioned this to Arya, and she nodded, saying, "It means that we are near Ellesméra." She reached out and rested her hand lightly on the gnarled root beside her, as if touching, with consummate delicacy, the shoulder of a friend or lover. "These trees are among the oldest living creatures in Alagaësia. Elves have loved them since first we saw Du Weldenvarden, and we have done everything within our power to help them flourish." A faint blade of light pierced the dusty emerald branches overhead and limned her arm and face with liquid gold, dazzlingly bright against the murky background. "We have traveled far together, Eragon, but now you are about to enter my world. Tread softly, for the earth and air are heavy with memories and naught is as it seems. . . . Do not fly with Saphira today, as we have already triggered certain wards that protect Ellesméra. It would be unwise to stray from the path."

Eragon bowed his head and retreated to Saphira, who lay curled on a bed of moss, amusing herself by releasing plumes of smoke from her nostrils and watching them roil out of sight. Without preamble, she said, *There is plenty of room for me on the ground now. I will have no difficulty.*

Good. He mounted Folkvír and followed Orik and the elves farther into the empty, silent forest. Saphira crawled beside him. She and the white horses gleamed in the somber half light.

Eragon paused, overcome by the solemn beauty of his surroundings. Everything had a feeling of wintry age, as if nothing had changed under the thatched needles for a thousand years and nothing ever would; time itself seemed to have fallen into a slumber from which it would never wake.

In late afternoon, the gloom lifted to reveal an elf standing before them, sheathed in a brilliant ray of light that slanted down from the ceiling. He was garbed in flowing robes, with a circlet of silver upon his brow. His face was old, noble, and serene.

"Eragon," murmured Arya. "Show him your palm and your ring."

Baring his right hand, Eragon raised it so that first Brom's ring and then the gedwëy ignasia was visible. The elf smiled, closed his eyes, and spread his arms in a gesture of welcome. He held the posture.

"The way is clear," said Arya. At a soft command, her steed moved forward. They rode around the elf—like water parting at the base of a weathered boulder—and when they had all passed, he straightened, clasped his hands, and vanished as the light that illuminated him ceased to exist.

Who is he? asked Saphira.

Arya said, "He is Gilderien the Wise, Prince of House Miolandra, wielder of the White Flame of Vándil, and guardian of Ellesméra since the days of Du Fyrn Skulblaka, our war with the dragons. None may enter the city unless he permits it."

A quarter of a mile beyond, the forest thinned and breaks appeared within the canopy, allowing planks of mottled sunlight to bar the way. Then they passed underneath two burled trees that leaned against each other and stopped at the edge of an empty glade.

The ground was strewn with dense patches of flowers. From pink roses to bluebells and lilies, spring's fleeting treasure was heaped about like piles of rubies, sapphires, and opals. Their intoxicating aromas attracted hordes of bumblebees. To the right, a stream chuckled behind a row of bushes, while a pair of squirrels chased each other around a rock.

At first it looked to Eragon like a place where deer might bed for the night. But as he continued to stare, he began to pick out paths hidden among the brush and trees; soft warm light where normally there would be auburn shadows; an odd pattern in the shapes of the twigs and branches and flowers, so subtle that it nearly escaped detection—clues that what he saw was not entirely natural. He blinked, and his vision suddenly shifted as if a lens had been placed over his eyes, resolving everything into recognizable shapes. Those were paths, aye. And those were flowers, aye. But what he had taken to be clusters of lumpy, twisted trees were in fact graceful buildings that grew directly out of the pines.

One tree bulged at the base to form a two-story house before sinking its roots into the loam. Both stories were hexagonal, although the upper level was half as small as the first, which gave the house a tiered appearance. The roofs and walls were made of webbed sheets of wood draped over six thick ridges. Moss and yellow lichen bearded the eaves and hung over jeweled windows set into each side. The front door was a mysterious black silhouette recessed under an archway wrought with symbols.

Another house was nestled between three pines, which were joined to it through a series of curved branches. Reinforced by those flying buttresses, the house rose five levels, light and airy. Beside it sat a bower woven out of willow and dogwood and hung with flameless lanterns disguised as galls.

Each unique building enhanced and complemented its surroundings, blending seamlessly with the rest of the forest until it was impossible to tell where artifice ended and nature resumed. The two were in perfect balance. Instead of mastering their environment, the elves had chosen to accept the world as it was and adapt themselves to it.

The inhabitants of Ellesméra eventually revealed themselves as a flicker of movement at the fringe of Eragon's sight, no more than needles stirring in the breeze. Then he caught glimpses of hands, a pale face, a sandaled foot, an upraised arm. One by one, the wary elves stepped into view, their almond eyes fixed upon Saphira, Arya, and Eragon.

The women wore their hair unbound. It rippled down their backs in waves of silver and sable braided with fresh blossoms, like a garden waterfall. They all possessed a delicate, ethereal beauty that belied their unbreakable strength; to Eragon, they seemed flawless. The men were just as striking, with high cheekbones, finely sculpted noses, and heavy eyelids. Both sexes were garbed in rustic tunics of green and brown, fringed with dusky colors of orange, russet, and gold.

The Fair Folk indeed, thought Eragon. He touched his lips in greeting.

As one, the elves bowed from the waist. Then they smiled and laughed with unrestrained happiness. From within their midst, a woman sang:

Gala O Wyrda brunhvitr,
Abr Berundal vandr-fódhr,
Burthro laufsblädar ekar undir,
Eom kona dauthleikr . . .

Eragon clapped his hands over his ears, fearing that the melody was a spell like the one he had heard at Sílthrim, but Arya shook her head and lifted his hands. "It is not magic." Then she spoke to her horse, saying, "Gánga." The stallion nickered and trotted away. "Release your steeds as well. We have no further need of them and they deserve to rest in our stables."

The song waxed stronger as Arya proceeded along a cobblestone path set with bits of green tourmaline, which looped among the hollyhocks and the houses and the trees before finally crossing a stream. The elves danced around their party as they walked, flitting here and there as the fancy struck them, laughing, and occasionally leaping up onto a branch to run over their heads. They praised Saphira with names like "Longclaws" and "Daughter of Air and Fire" and "Strong One."

Eragon smiled, delighted and enchanted. *I could live here,* he thought with a sense of peace. Tucked away in Du Weldenvarden, as much outdoors as in, safe from the rest of the world . . . Yes, he liked Ellesméra very much indeed, more than any of the dwarf cities. He pointed to a dwelling situated within a pine tree and asked Arya, "How is that done?

"We sing to the forest in the old tongue and give it our strength to grow in the shape that we desire. All our buildings and tools are made in that manner."

The path ended at a net of roots that formed steps, like bare pools of earth. They climbed to a door embedded within a wall of saplings. Eragon's heart quickened as the door swung open, seemingly of its own accord, and revealed a hall of trees. Hundreds of branches melded together to form the honeycombed ceiling. Below, twelve chairs were arrayed along each wall.

In them reposed four-and-twenty elf lords and ladies.

Wise and handsome were they, with smooth faces unmarked by age and keen eyes that gleamed with excitement. They leaned forward, gripping the arms of their chairs, and stared at Eragon's group with open wonder and hope. Unlike the other elves, they had swords belted at their waists—hilts studded with beryls and garnets—and circlets that adorned their brows.

And at the head of the assembly stood a white pavilion that sheltered a throne of knotted roots. Queen Islanzadí sat upon it. She was as beautiful as an autumn sunset, proud and imperious, with two dark eyebrows slanted like upraised wings, lips as bright and red as holly berries, and midnight hair bound under a diamond diadem. Her tunic was crimson. Round her hips hung a girdle of braided gold. And clasped at the hollow of her neck was a velvet cloak that fell to the ground in languid folds. Despite her imposing countenance, the queen seemed fragile, as if she concealed a great pain.

By her left hand was a curved rod with a chased crosspiece. A brilliant-white raven perched on it, shuffling impatiently from foot to foot. He cocked his head and surveyed Eragon with uncanny intelligence, then gave a long, low croak and shrieked, *"Wyrda!"* Eragon shivered from the force of that single cracked word.

The door closed behind the six of them as they entered the hall and approached the queen. Arya knelt on the moss-covered ground and bowed first, then Eragon, Orik, Lifaen, and Narí. Even Saphira, who had never bowed to anyone, not even Ajihad or Hrothgar, lowered her head.

Islanzadí stood and descended from the throne, her cloak trailing behind her. She stopped before Arya, placed trembling hands on her shoulders, and said in a rich vibrato, "Rise." Arya did, and the queen scrutinized her face with increasing intensity, until it seemed as if she were trying to decipher an obscure text.

At last Islanzadí cried out and embraced Arya, saying, "O my daughter, I have wronged you!"

QUEEN ISLANZADÍ

Eragon knelt before the queen of the elves and her councilors in a fantastic room made from the boles of living trees in a near-mythic land, and the only thing that filled his mind was shock. *Arya is a princess!* It was fitting in a way—she had always possessed an air of command—but he bitterly regretted the fact, for it placed another barrier between them when he would have torn them all away. The knowledge filled his mouth with the taste of ashes. He remembered Angela's prophecy that he would love one of noble birth . . . and her warning that she could not see if it would end for good or for ill.

He could feel Saphira's own surprise, then her amusement. She said, *It appears that we have been traveling in the presence of royalty without knowing it.*

Why didn't she tell us?

Perhaps it would have placed her in greater danger.

"Islanzadí Dröttning," said Arya formally.

The queen withdrew as if she had been stung and then repeated in the ancient language, "O my daughter, I have wronged you." She covered her face. "Ever since you disappeared, I've barely slept or eaten. I was haunted by your fate, and feared that I would never see you again. Banning you from my presence was the greatest mistake I have ever made. . . . Can you forgive me?"

The gathered elves stirred with amazement.

Arya's response was long in coming, but at last she said, "For seventy years, I have lived and loved, fought and killed without ever speaking to you, my mother. Our lives are long, but even so, that is no small span."

Islanzadí drew herself upright, lifting her chin. A tremor ran her length. "I cannot undo the past, Arya, no matter how much I might desire to."

"And I cannot forget what I endured."

"Nor should you." Islanzadí clasped her daughter's hands. "Arya, I love you. You are my only family. Go if you must, but unless you wish to renounce me, I would be reconciled with you."

For a terrible moment, it seemed as if Arya would not answer, or worse, would reject the offer. Eragon saw her hesitate and quickly look at her audience. Then she lowered her eyes and said, "No, Mother. I could not leave." Islanzadí smiled uncertainly and embraced her daughter again. This time Arya returned the gesture, and smiles broke out among the assembled elves.

The white raven hopped on his stand, cackling, "And on the door was graven evermore, what now became the family lore, *Let us never do but to adore!*"

"Hush, Blagden," said Islanzadí to the raven. "Keep your doggerel to yourself." Breaking free, the queen turned to Eragon and Saphira. "You must excuse me for being discourteous and ignoring you, our most important guests."

Eragon touched his lips and then twisted his right hand over his sternum, as Arya had taught him. "Islanzadí Dröttning. Atra esterní ono thelduin." He had no doubt that he was supposed to speak first.

Islanzadí's dark eyes widened. "Atra du evarínya ono varda."

"Un atra mor'ranr lífa unin hjarta onr," replied Eragon, completing the ritual. He could tell that the elves were caught off guard by his knowledge of their customs. In his mind, he listened as Saphira repeated his greeting to the queen.

When she finished, Islanzadí asked, "Dragon, what is your name?"

Saphira.

A flash of recognition appeared in the queen's expression, but she made no comment on it. "Welcome to Ellesméra, Saphira. And yours, Rider?"

"Eragon Shadeslayer, Your Majesty." This time an audible stir rippled among the elves seated behind them; even Islanzadí appeared startled.

"You carry a powerful name," she said softly, "one that we rarely bestow upon our children. . . . Welcome to Ellesméra, Eragon Shadeslayer. We have waited long for you." She moved on to Orik, greeted him, then returned to her throne and draped her velvet cloak over her arm. "I assume by your presence here, Eragon, so soon after Saphira's egg was captured, and by the ring on your hand and the sword on your hip, that Brom is dead and that your training with him was incomplete. I wish to hear your full story, including how Brom fell and how you came to meet my daughter, or how she met you, as it may be. Then I will hear of your mission here, dwarf, and of your adventures, Arya, since your ambush in Du Weldenvarden."

Eragon had narrated his experiences before, so he had no trouble reiterating them now for the queen. The few occasions where his memory faltered, Saphira was able to provide an accurate description of events. In several places, he simply left the telling to her. When they finished, Eragon retrieved Nasuada's scroll from his pack and presented it to Islanzadí.

She took the roll of parchment, broke the red wax seal, and, upon completing the missive, sighed and briefly closed her eyes. "I see now the true depth of my folly. My grief would have ended so much sooner if I had not withdrawn our warriors and ignored Ajihad's messengers after learning that Arya had been ambushed. I should have never blamed the Varden for her death. For one so old, I am still far too foolish. . . ."

A long silence followed, as no one dared to agree or disagree. Summoning his courage, Eragon said, "Since Arya has returned alive, will you agree to help the Varden, like before? Nasuada cannot succeed otherwise, and I am pledged to her cause."

"My quarrel with the Varden is as dust in the wind," said Islanzadí. "Fear not; we will assist them as we once did, and more, because of you and their victory over the Urgals." She leaned forward on one arm. "Will you give me Brom's ring, Eragon?" Without hesitation, he pulled it off his finger and offered it to the queen, who plucked it from his palm with her slim fingers. "You should not have worn this, Eragon, as it was not meant for you. However, because of the aid you have rendered the Varden and my family, I now name you Elf Friend and bestow this ring, Aren, upon you, so that all elves, wherever you go, will know that you are to be trusted and helped."

Eragon thanked her and returned the ring to his finger, acutely aware of the queen's gaze, which remained upon him with disturbing perception, studying and analyzing. He felt as if she knew everything that he might say or do. She said, "Such tidings as yours, we have not heard the like of in Du Weldenvarden for many a year. We are accustomed to a slower way of life here than the rest of Alagaësia, and it troubles me that so much could occur so swiftly without word of it reaching my ear."

"And what of my training?" Eragon snatched a furtive glance at the seated elves, wondering if any of them could be Togira Ikonoka, the being who had reached into his mind and freed him of Durza's foul influence after the battle in Farthen Dûr—and who had also encouraged Eragon to travel to Ellesméra.

"It will begin in the fullness of time. Yet I fear that instructing you is futile so long as your infirmity persists. Unless you can overcome the Shade's magic, you will be reduced to no more than a figurehead. You may still be useful, but only as a shadow of the hope that we have nurtured for over a century." Islanzadí spoke without reproach, yet her words struck Eragon like hammer blows. He knew that she was right. "Your situation is not your fault, and it pains me to voice such things, but you must understand the gravity of your disability. . . . I am sorry."

Then Islanzadí addressed Orik: "It has been long since one of your race entered our halls, dwarf. Eragon-finiarel has explained your presence, but do you have aught to add?"

"Only royal greetings from my king, Hrothgar, and a plea, now unneeded, for you to resume contact with the Varden. Beyond that, I am here to see that the pact that Brom forged between you and the humans is honored."

"We keep our promises whether we utter them in this language or in the ancient language. I accept Hrothgar's greetings and return them in kind." Finally, as Eragon was sure she had longed to do since they first arrived, Islanzadí looked at Arya and asked, "Now, daughter, what befell you?"

Arya began to speak in a slow monotone, first of her capture and then of her long imprisonment and torture in Gil'ead. Saphira and Eragon had deliberately avoided the details of her abuse, but Arya herself seemed to have no difficulty recounting what she had been subjected to. Her emotionless descriptions roused the same rage within Eragon as when he first saw her wounds. The elves remained completely silent throughout Arya's tale, although they gripped their swords and their faces hardened into razor lines of cold anger. A single tear rolled down Islanzadí's cheek.

Afterward, a lithe elf lord paced along the mossy sward between the chairs. "I know that I speak for us all, Arya Dröttningu, when I say that my heart burns with sorrow for your ordeal. It is a crime beyond apology, mitigation, or reparation, and Galbatorix must be punished for it. Also, we are in your debt for keeping the locations of our cities hidden from the Shade. Few of us could have withstood him for so long."

"Thank you, Däthedr-vor."

Now Islanzadí spoke, and her voice rang like a bell among the trees. "Enough. Our guests wait tired on their feet, and we have spoken of evil things for far too long. I will not have this occasion marred by lingering on past injuries." A glorious smile brightened her expression. "My daughter has returned, a dragon and her Rider have appeared, and I will see us celebrate in the proper fashion!" She stood, tall and magnificent in her crimson tunic, and clapped her hands. At the sound, the chairs and pavilion were showered with hundreds of lilies and roses that appeared twenty feet above their heads and drifted down like colorful snowflakes, suffusing the air with their heady fragrance.

She didn't use the ancient language, observed Eragon.

He noticed that, while everyone was occupied by the flowers, Islanzadí touched Arya gently on the shoulder and murmured, almost too softly to hear, "You never would have suffered so if you had taken my counsel. I was right to oppose your decision to accept the yawë."

"It was my decision to make."

The queen paused, then nodded and extended her arm. "Blagden." With a flutter of wings, the raven flew from his perch and landed on her left shoulder. The entire assembly bowed as Islanzadí proceeded to the end of the hall and threw open the door to the hundreds of elves outside, whereupon she made a brief declaration in the ancient language that Eragon did not understand. The elves burst into cheers and began to rush about.

"What did she say?" whispered Eragon to Narí.

Narí smiled. "To break open our finest casks and light the cook-fires, for tonight shall be a night of feast and song. Come!" He grabbed Eragon's hand and pulled him after the queen as she threaded her way between the shaggy pines and through banks of cool ferns. During their time indoors, the sun had dropped low in the sky, drenching the forest with an amber light that clung to the trees and plants like a layer of glistering oil.

You do realize, don't you, said Saphira, *that the king Lifaen mentioned, Evandar, must be Arya's father?*

Eragon almost stumbled. *You're right. . . . And that means he was killed by either Galbatorix or the Forsworn.*

Circles within circles.

They stopped on the crest of a small hill, where a team of elves had set out a long trestle table and chairs. All around them, the forest hummed with activity. As evening approached, the cheery glow of fires appeared scattered throughout Ellesméra, including a bonfire near the table.

Someone handed Eragon a goblet made of the same odd wood

that he had noticed in Ceris. He drank the cup's clear liqueur and gasped as it blazed down his throat. It tasted like mulled cider mixed with mead. The potion made the tips of his fingers and ears tingle and gave him a marvelous sense of clarity. "What is this?" he asked Narí.

Narí laughed. "Faelnirv? We distill it from crushed elderberries and spun moonbeams. If he needs must, a strong man can travel for three days on naught else."

Saphira, you have to taste this. She sniffed the goblet, then opened her mouth and allowed him to pour the rest of the faelnirv down her throat. Her eyes widened and her tail twitched.

Now that's a treat! Is there more?

Before Eragon could reply, Orik stomped over to them. "Daughter to the queen," he grumbled, shaking his head. "I wish that I could tell Hrothgar and Nasuada. They'd want to know."

Islanzadí seated herself in a high-backed chair and clapped her hands once again. From within the city came a quartet of elves bearing musical instruments. Two had harps of cherrywood, the third a set of reed pipes, and the fourth nothing but her voice, which she immediately put to use with a playful song that danced about their ears.

Eragon caught only every third word or so, but what he did understand made him grin. It was the story of a stag who could not drink at a pond because a magpie kept harassing him.

As Eragon listened, his gaze wandered and alighted upon a small girl prowling behind the queen. When he looked again, he saw that her shaggy hair was not silver, like many of the elves, but bleached white with age, and that her face was creased and lined like a dry, withered apple. She was no elf, nor dwarf, nor—Eragon felt—even human. She smiled at him, and he glimpsed rows of sharp teeth.

When the singer finished, and the pipes and lutes filled the silence, Eragon found himself approached by scores of elves who wished to meet him and—more importantly, he sensed—Saphira. The elves presented themselves by bowing softly and touching their lips with their first and middle fingers, to which Eragon responded in kind, along with endless repetitions of their greeting in the ancient language. They plied Eragon with polite questions about his exploits, but they reserved the bulk of their conversation for Saphira.

At first Eragon was content to let Saphira talk, since this was the first place where anyone was interested in having a discussion just with her. But he soon grew annoyed at being ignored; he had become used to having people listen when he spoke. He grinned ruefully, dismayed that he had come to rely on people's attention so much since he had joined the Varden, and forced himself to relax and enjoy the celebration.

Before long the scent of food permeated the glade and elves appeared carrying platters piled with delicacies. Aside from loaves of warm bread and stacks of small, round honeycakes, the dishes were made entirely of fruit, vegetables, and berries. The berries predominated; they were in everything from blueberry soup to raspberry sauce to thimbleberry jelly. A bowl of sliced apples dripped with syrup and sprinkled with wild strawberries sat beside a mushroom pie stuffed with spinach, thyme, and currants.

No meat was to be found, not even fish or fowl, which still puzzled Eragon. In Carvahall and elsewhere in the Empire, meat was a symbol of status and luxury. The more gold you had, the more often you could afford steak and veal. Even the minor nobility ate meat with every meal. To do otherwise would indicate a deficit in their coffers. And yet the elves did not subscribe to this philosophy, despite their obvious wealth and the ease with which they could hunt with magic.

The elves rushed to the table with an enthusiasm that surprised Eragon. Soon all were seated: Islanzadí at the head of the table with Blagden, the raven; Däthedr to her left; Arya and Eragon by her right hand; Orik across from them; and then all the rest of the elves, including Narí and Lifaen. No chair was at the far end of the table, only a huge carved plate for Saphira.

As the meal progressed, everything dissolved around Eragon into a blur of talk and mirth. He was so caught up in the festivities, he lost track of time, aware of only the laughter and the foreign words swirling over his head and the warm glow left in his stomach by the faelnirv. The elusive harp music sighed and whispered at the edges of his hearing and sent shivers of excitement down his side. Occasionally, he found himself distracted by the lazy slit-eyed stare of the woman-child, which she kept focused on him with single-minded intensity, even when eating.

During a lull in the conversation, Eragon turned toward Arya, who had uttered no more than a dozen words. He said nothing, only looked and wondered who she really was.

Arya stirred. "Not even Ajihad knew."

"What?"

"Outside of Du Weldenvarden, I told no one of my identity. Brom was aware of it—he first met me here—but he kept it a secret at my request."

Eragon wondered if she was explaining to him out of a sense of duty or because she felt guilty for deceiving him and Saphira. "Brom once said that what elves *didn't* say was often more important that what they did."

"He understood us well."

"Why, though? Did it matter if anyone knew?"

This time Arya hesitated. "When I left Ellesméra, I had no desire to be reminded of my position. Nor did it seem relevant to my task with the Varden and dwarves. It had nothing to do with who I became . . . with who I am." She glanced at the queen.

"You could have told Saphira and me."

Arya seemed to bridle at the reproach in his voice. "I had no reason to suspect that my standing with Islanzadí had improved, and telling you that would have changed nothing. My thoughts are my own, Eragon." He flushed at her implied meaning: Why should *she*—who was a diplomat, a princess, an elf, and older than both his father and grandfather, whoever they were—confide in him, a sixteen-year-old human?

"At least," he muttered, "you made up with your mother."

She smiled oddly. "Did I have a choice?"

At that moment, Blagden jumped from Islanzadí's shoulder and strutted down the middle of the table, bobbing his head left and right in a mocking bow. He stopped before Saphira, uttered a hoarse cough, and then croaked:

> Dragons, like wagons,
> Have tongues.
> Dragons, like flagons,
> Have necks.
> But while two hold beer,
> The other eats deer!

The elves froze with mortified expressions while they waited for Saphira's reaction. After a long silence, Saphira looked up from her quince pie and released a puff of smoke that enveloped Blagden. *And little birds too*, she said, projecting her thoughts so that everyone could hear. The elves finally laughed as Blagden staggered back, cawing indignantly and flapping his wings to clear the air.

"I must apologize for Blagden's wretched verses," said Islanzadí. "He has ever had a saucy tongue, despite our attempts to tame it."

Apology accepted, said Saphira calmly, and returned to her pie.

"Where does he come from?" Eragon asked, eager to return to more cordial footing with Arya but also genuinely curious.

"Blagden," said Arya, "once saved my father's life. Evandar was fighting an Urgal when he stumbled and lost his sword. Before the Urgal could strike, a raven flew at him and pecked out his eyes. No one knows why the bird did it, but the distraction allowed Evandar to regain his balance and so win the battle. My father was always generous, so he thanked the raven by blessing him with spells for intelligence and long life. However, the magic had two effects that he did not foresee: Blagden lost all color in his feathers and he gained the ability to predict certain events."

"He can see into the future?" asked Eragon, startled.

"See? No. But perhaps he can sense what is to come. In any case, he always speaks in riddles, most of which are a fair bit of nonsense. Just remember that if Blagden ever comes to you and tells you something that is not a joke or a pun, you would do well to heed his words."

Once the meal had concluded, Islanzadí stood—causing a flurry of activity as everyone hastened to do likewise—and said, "It is late, I am tired, and I would return to my bower. Accompany me, Saphira and Eragon, and I will show you where you may sleep tonight." The queen motioned with one hand to Arya, then left the table. Arya followed.

As Eragon stepped around the table with Saphira, he paused by the woman-child, caught by her feral eyes. All the elements of her appearance, from her eyes to her shaggy hair to her white fangs, triggered Eragon's memory. "You're a werecat, aren't you?" She blinked once and then bared her teeth in a dangerous smile. "I met one of your kin, Solembum, in Teirm and in Farthen Dûr."

Her grin widened. "Aye. A good one he is. Humans bore me, but *he* finds it amusing to travel with the witch Angela." Then her gaze switched to Saphira and she uttered a throaty half-growl, half-purr of appreciation.

What is your name? asked Saphira.

"Names be powerful things in the heart of Du Weldenvarden, dragon, yes they are. However . . . among the elves, I am known as The Watcher and as Quickpaw and as The Dream Dancer, but you may know me as Maud." She tossed her mane of stiff white bangs. "You'd better catch up with the queen, younglings; she does not take lightly to fools or laggards."

"It was a pleasure meeting you, Maud," said Eragon. He bowed, and Saphira inclined her head. Eragon glanced at Orik, wondering where the dwarf would be taken, and then pursued Islanzadí.

They overtook the queen just as she reached the base of a tree. The trunk was ridged by a delicate staircase that spiraled up to a series of globular rooms cupped and suspended in the tree's crown by a spray of branches.

Islanzadí lifted an elegant hand and pointed at the eyrie. "You needs must fly there, Saphira. Our stairs were not grown with dragons in mind." Then she spoke to Eragon: "This is where the leader of the Dragon Riders would dwell while in Ellesméra. I give it to you now, for you are the rightful heir to that title. . . . It is your inheritance." Before Eragon could thank her, the queen swept past and departed with Arya, who held his gaze for a long moment before vanishing deeper into the city.

Shall we see what accommodations they've provided us with? asked Saphira. She jumped into the air and sailed around the tree in a tight circle, balancing on one wing tip, perpendicular to the ground.

As Eragon took the first step, he saw that Islanzadí had spoken true; the stairs were one with the tree. The bark beneath his feet was smooth and flat from the many elves who had traversed it, but it was still part of the trunk, as were the twisting cobweb banisters by his side and the curved railing that slid under his right hand.

Because the stairs had been designed with the elves' strength in mind, they were steeper than Eragon was used to, and his calves and thighs soon began to burn. He was breathing so hard when he reached the top—after climbing through a trapdoor in the floor of one of the rooms—he had to put his hands on his knees and bend over to pant. Once recovered, he straightened and examined his surroundings.

He stood in a circular vestibule with a pedestal in the center, out of which spiraled a sculpture of two pale hands and forearms that twined around each other without touching. Three screen doors led from the vestibule—one to an austere dining room that might hold ten people at the most, one to a closet with an empty hollow in the floor that Eragon could think of no discernible use for, and the last to a bedroom overlooking, and open to, the wide expanse of Du Weldenvarden.

Taking a lantern from its hook in the ceiling, Eragon entered the bedroom, creating a host of shadows that jumped and swirled like madcap dancers. A teardrop gap large enough for a dragon pierced the outer wall. Inside the room was a bed, situated so that he could watch the sky and the moon while lying on his back; a fireplace made of gray wood that felt as hard and cold as steel when he touched it, as if the timber had been compressed to unsurpassed density; and a huge low-rimmed bowl set in the floor and lined with soft blankets where Saphira could sleep.

Even as he watched, she swooped down and landed on the edge of the opening, her scales twinkling like a constellation of blue stars. Behind her, the last rays of the sun streaked across the forest, painting the various ridges and hills with a hazy amber that made the needles glow like hot iron and chased the shadows back toward the violet horizon. From their height, the city appeared as a series of gaps in the voluminous canopy, islands of calm in a restless ocean. Ellesméra's true scope was now revealed; it extended for several miles to the west and to the north.

I respect the Riders even more if this is how Vrael normally lived, said Eragon. *It's much simpler than I expected.* The entire structure rocked slightly in response to a breath of wind.

Saphira sniffed her blankets. *We have yet to see Vroengard,* she cautioned, although he sensed that she agreed with him.

As Eragon closed the screen to the bedroom, he saw something in the corner that he had missed during his first inspection: a spiral staircase that wound up a dark wood chimney. Thrusting the lantern before him, he cautiously ascended, one step at a time. After about twenty feet, he emerged in a study furnished with a writing desk—stocked with quills, ink, and paper, but no parchment—and another padded roost for a dragon to curl up on. The far wall also had an opening to fly through.

Saphira, come see this.

How? she asked.

Through the outside. Eragon winced as layers of bark splintered and cracked under Saphira's claws while she crawled out of the bedroom and up the side of the compound to the study. *Satisfied?* he asked when she arrived. Saphira raked him with her sapphire eyes, then proceeded to scrutinize the walls and furniture.

I wonder, she said, *how you are supposed to stay warm when the rooms are open to the elements?*

I don't know. Eragon examined the walls on either side of the breach, running his hands over abstract patterns that had been coaxed from the tree by the elves' songs. He stopped when he felt a vertical ridge embedded in the bark. He tugged on it, and a diaphanous membrane unspooled from within the wall. Pulling it across the portal, he found a second groove to hold the hem of the cloth. As soon as it was fastened, the air thickened and became noticeably hotter. *There's your answer,* he said. He released the cloth and it lashed back and forth as it rewound itself.

When they returned to the bedroom, Eragon unpacked while Saphira coiled upon her dais. He carefully arranged his shield, bracers, greaves, coif, and helm, then stripped off his tunic and removed his shirt of leather-backed mail. He sat bare-chested on the bed and studied the oiled links, struck by their similarity to Saphira's scales.

We made it, he said, bemused.

A long journey . . . but yes, we made it. We're lucky that misfortune did not strike upon the road.

He nodded. *Now we'll find out if it was worth it. Sometimes I wonder if our time would have been better spent helping the Varden.*

Eragon! You know that we need further instruction. Brom would have wanted it. Besides, Ellesméra and Islanzadí were certainly worth coming all this way to see.

Maybe. Finally, he asked, *What do you make of all this?*

Saphira parted her jaws slightly to show her teeth. *I don't know. The elves keep more secrets than even Brom, and they can do things with magic that I never thought possible. I have no idea what methods they use to grow their trees into such shapes, nor how Islanzadí summoned those flowers. It is beyond my ken.*

Eragon was relieved that he was not the only one who felt overwhelmed. *And Arya?*

What about her?

You know, who she really is.

She hasn't changed, only your perception of her. Saphira chuckled deep in her throat, where it sounded like stones grinding against each other, and rested her head on her two front feet.

The stars were bright in the sky now, and the soft hoots of owls drifted through Ellesméra. All the world was calm and silent as it slumbered away the liquid night.

Eragon clambered underneath his downy sheets and reached to shutter the lantern, then stopped, his hand an inch from the latch. Here he was in the elves' capital, over a hundred feet in the air, lying in what used to be Vrael's bed.

The thought was too much for him.

Rolling upright, he grabbed the lantern with one hand, Zar'roc with the other, and surprised Saphira by crawling onto her dais and snuggling against her warm side. She hummed and dropped a velvet wing over him as he extinguished the light and closed his eyes.

Together they slept long and deep in Ellesméra.

Out of the Past

ragon woke at dawn well rested. He tapped Saphira's ribs, and she lifted her wing. Running his hands through his hair, he walked to the room's precipice and leaned against one side, bark rough against his shoulder. Below, the forest sparkled like a field of diamonds as each tree reflected the morning light with a thousand thousand drops of dew.

He jumped with surprise as Saphira dove past him, twisting like an auger toward the canopy before she pulled up and circled through the sky, roaring with joy. *Morning, little one.* He smiled, happy that she was happy.

He opened the screen to their bedroom, where he found two trays of food—mostly fruit—that had been placed by the lintel during the night. By the trays was a bundle of clothes with a paper note pinned to it. Eragon had difficulty deciphering the flowing script, since he had not read for over a month and had forgotten some of the letters, but at last he understood that it said:

Greetings, Saphira Bjartskular and Eragon Shadeslayer.

I, Bellaen of House Miolandra, do humble myself and apologize to you, Saphira, for this unsatisfactory meal. Elves do not hunt, and no meat is to be had in Ellesméra, nor in any of our cities. If you wish, you can do as the dragons of old were wont, and catch what you may in Du Weldenvarden. We only ask that you leave your kills in the forest so that our air and water remain untainted by blood.

241

Eragon, these clothes are for you. They were woven by Niduen of Islanzadí's house and are her gift to you.

> *May good fortune rule over you,*
> *Peace live in your heart,*
> *And the stars watch over you.*

Bellaen du Hljödhr

When Eragon told Saphira the message, she said, *It does not matter; I won't need to eat for a while after yesterday's meal.* However, she did snap up a few seed cakes. *Just so that I don't appear rude*, she explained.

After Eragon finished breakfast, he hauled the bundle of clothes onto his bed and carefully unfolded them, finding two full-length tunics of russet trimmed with thimbleberry green, a set of creamy leggings to wrap his calves in, and three pairs of socks so soft, they felt like liquid when he pulled them through his hands. The quality of the fabric shamed the weaving of the women of Carvahall as well as the dwarf clothes he wore now.

Eragon was grateful for the new raiment. His own tunic and breeches were sadly travel-worn from their weeks exposed to the rain and sun since Farthen Dûr. Stripping, he donned one of the luxurious tunics, savoring its downy texture.

He had just laced on his boots when someone knocked on the screen to the bedroom. "Come in," he said, reaching for Zar'roc.

Orik poked his head inside, then cautiously entered, testing the floor with his feet. He eyed the ceiling. "Give me a cave any day instead of a bird's nest like this. How fared your night, Eragon? Saphira?"

"Well enough. And yours?" said Eragon.

"I slept like a rock." The dwarf chuckled at his own jest, then his chin sank into his beard and he fingered the head of his ax. "I see you've eaten, so I'll ask you to accompany me. Arya, the queen, and

242

a host of other elves await you at the base of the tree." He fixed Eragon with a testy gaze. "Something is going on that they haven't told us about. I'm not sure what they want from you, but it's important. Islanzadí's as tense as a cornered wolf . . . I thought I'd warn you beforehand."

Eragon thanked him, then the two of them descended by way of the stairs, while Saphira glided to earth. They were met on the ground by Islanzadí arrayed in a mantle of ruffled swan feathers, which were like winter snow heaped upon a cardinal's breast. She greeted them and said, "Follow me."

Her wending course took the group to the edge of Ellesméra, where the buildings were few and the paths were faint from disuse. At the base of a wooded knoll, Islanzadí stopped and said in a terrible voice, "Before we go any farther, the three of you must swear in the ancient language that you will never speak to outsiders of what you are about to see, not without permission from me, my daughter, or whoever may succeed us to the throne."

"Why should I gag myself?" demanded Orik.

Why indeed? asked Saphira. *Do you not trust us?*

"It is not a matter of trust, but of safety. We must protect this knowledge at all costs—it's our greatest advantage over Galbatorix—and if you are bound by the ancient language, you will never willingly reveal our secret. You came to supervise Eragon's training, Orik-vodhr. Unless you give me your word, you may as well return to Farthen Dûr."

At last Orik said, "I believe that you mean no harm to dwarves or to the Varden, else I would never agree. And I hold you to the honor of your hall and clan that this isn't a ploy to deceive us. Tell me what to say."

While the queen tutored Orik in the correct pronunciation of the desired phrase, Eragon asked Saphira, *Should I do it?*

Do we have a choice? Eragon remembered that Arya had asked the same question yesterday, and he began to have an inkling of what she had meant: the queen left no room to maneuver.

When Orik finished, Islanzadí looked expectantly at Eragon. He hesitated, then delivered the oath, as did Saphira. "Thank you," said Islanzadí. "Now we may proceed."

At the top of the knoll, the trees were replaced by a bed of red clover that ran several yards to the edge of a stone cliff. The cliff extended a league in either direction and dropped a thousand feet to the forest below, which pooled outward until it merged with the sky. It felt as if they stood on the edge of the world, staring across an endless expanse of forest.

I know this place, realized Eragon, remembering his vision of Togira Ikonoka.

Thud. The air shivered from the strength of the concussion. *Thud*. Another dull blow made Eragon's teeth chatter. *Thud*. He jammed his fingers in his ears, trying to protect them from the painful spikes in pressure. The elves stood motionless. *Thud*. The clover bent under a sudden gust of wind.

Thud. From below the edge of the cliff rose a huge gold dragon with a Rider on its back.

◆　◆　◆

CONVICTION

Roran glared at Horst.

They were in Baldor's room. Roran was propped upright in bed, listening as the smith said, "What did you expect me to do? We couldn't attack once you fainted. Besides, the men were in no state to fight. Can't blame them either. I nearly bit off my tongue when I saw those monsters." Horst shook his wild mane of hair. "We've been dragged into one of the old tales, Roran, and I don't like it one bit." Roran retained his stony expression. "Look, you can kill the soldiers if you want, but you have to get your strength back first. You'll have plenty of volunteers; people trust you in battle, especially after you defeated the soldiers here last night." When Roran remained silent, Horst sighed, patted him on his good shoulder, and left the room, closing the door behind him.

Roran did not even blink. So far in his life, he had only truly cared about three things: his family, his home in Palancar Valley, and Katrina. His family had been annihilated last year. His farm had been smashed and burned, though the land remained, which was all that really mattered.

But now Katrina was gone.

A choked sob escaped past the iron lump in his throat. He was faced with a quandary that tore at his very essence: the only way to rescue Katrina would be to somehow pursue the Ra'zac and leave Palancar Valley, yet he could not abandon Carvahall to the soldiers. Nor could he forget Katrina.

My heart or my home, he thought bitterly. They were worthless without each other. If he killed the soldiers it would only prevent the Ra'zac—and perhaps Katrina—from returning. Anyway, the slaughter would be pointless if reinforcements were nearby, for their arrival would surely signal Carvahall's demise.

Roran clenched his teeth as a fresh burst of pain emanated from his bound shoulder. He closed his eyes. *I hope Sloan gets eaten like Quimby.* No fate could be too terrible for that traitor. Roran cursed him with the blackest oaths he knew.

Even if I were free to leave Carvahall, how could I find the Ra'zac? Who would know where they live? Who would dare inform on Galbatorix's servants? Despair rolled over him as he wrestled with the problem. He imagined himself in one of the great cities of the Empire, searching aimlessly among dirty buildings and hordes of strangers for a hint, a glimpse, a taste of his love.

It was hopeless.

A river of tears followed as he doubled over, groaning from the strength of his agony and fear. He rocked back and forth, blind to anything but the desolation of the world.

An endless amount of time reduced Roran's sobs to weak gasps of protest. He wiped his eyes and forced himself to take a long, shuddering breath. He winced. His lungs felt like they were filled with shards of glass.

I have to think, he told himself.

He leaned against the wall and—through the sheer strength of his will—began to gradually subdue each of his unruly emotions, wrestling them into submission to the one thing that could save him from insanity: reason. His neck and shoulders trembled from the violence of his efforts.

Once he regained control, Roran carefully arranged his thoughts, like a master craftsman organizing his tools into precise rows. *There must be a solution hidden amid my knowledge, if only I'm creative enough.*

He could not track the Ra'zac through the air. That much was clear. Someone would have to tell him where to find them, and of all the people he could ask, the Varden probably knew the most. However, they would be just as hard to find as the desecrators, and he could not waste time searching for them. *Although* . . . A small voice in his head reminded him of the rumors he had heard from trappers and traders that Surda secretly supported the Varden.

Surda. The country lay at the bottom of the Empire, or so Roran had been told, as he had never seen a map of Alagaësia. Under ideal conditions, it would take several weeks to reach on horse, longer if he had to evade soldiers. Of course, the swiftest mode of transportation would be to sail south along the coast, but that would mean having to travel all the way to the Toark River and then to Teirm to find a ship. It would take far too long. And he still might be apprehended by soldiers.

"If, could, would, *might*," he muttered, repeatedly clenching his left hand. North of Teirm, the only port he knew of was Narda, but to reach it, he would have to cross the entire width of the Spine— a feat unheard of, even for the trappers.

Roran swore quietly. The conjecture was pointless. *I should be trying to save Carvahall, not desert it.* The problem was, he had already determined that the village and all who remained in it were doomed. Tears gathered at the corners of his eyes again. *All who remain* . . .

What . . . what if everyone in Carvahall accompanied me to Narda and then to Surda? He would achieve both his desires simultaneously.

The audacity of the idea stunned him.

It was heresy, blasphemy, to think that he could convince the farmers to abandon their fields and the merchants their shops . . . and yet . . . and yet what was the alternative but slavery or death? The Varden were the only group that would harbor fugitives of the Empire, and Roran was sure that the rebels would be delighted to have a village's worth of recruits, especially ones who had proved

247

themselves in battle. Also, by bringing the villagers to them, he would earn the Varden's confidence, so that they would trust him with the location of the Ra'zac. *Maybe they can explain why Galbatorix is so desperate to capture me.*

If the plan were to succeed, though, it would have to be implemented before the new troops reached Carvahall, which left only a few days—if that—to arrange the departure of some three hundred people. The logistics were frightening to consider.

Roran knew that mere reason could not persuade anyone to leave; it would require messianic zeal to stir people's emotions, to make them *feel* in the depths of their hearts the need to relinquish the trappings of their identities and lives. Nor would it be enough to simply instill fear—for he knew that fear often made those in peril fight harder. Rather, he had to instill a sense of purpose and destiny, to make the villagers believe, as he did, that joining the Varden and resisting Galbatorix's tyranny was the noblest action in the world.

It required passion that could not be intimidated by hardship, deterred by suffering, or quenched by death.

In his mind, Roran saw Katrina standing before him, pale and ghostly with solemn amber eyes. He remembered the heat of her skin, the mulled scent of her hair, and what it felt like to be with her under the cover of darkness. Then in a long line behind her appeared his family, friends, and everyone he had known in Carvahall, both dead and alive. *If not for Eragon . . . and me . . . the Ra'zac would have never come here. I must rescue the village from the Empire as surely as I must rescue Katrina from those desecrators.*

Drawing upon the strength of his vision, Roran rose from bed, causing his maimed shoulder to burn and sting. He staggered and leaned against a wall. *Will I ever regain the use of my right arm?* He waited for the pain to subside. When it did not, he bared his teeth, shoved himself upright, and marched from the room.

Elain was folding towels in the hallway. She cried out with amazement. "Roran! What are you—"

"Come," he growled, lurching past.

With a worried expression, Baldor stepped out of a doorway. "Roran, you shouldn't be walking around. You lost too much blood. I'll help—"

"Come."

Roran heard them follow as he descended the curved stairs toward the entrance of the house, where Horst and Albriech stood talking. They looked up with astonishment.

"Come."

He ignored the babble of questions, opened the front door, and stepped into the evening's faded light. Above, an imposing plume of clouds was laced with gold and purple.

Leading the small group, Roran stomped to the edge of Carvahall—repeating his monosyllabic message whenever he passed a man or woman—pulled a torch mounted on a pole from the grasping mud, wheeled about, and retraced his path to the center of town. There he stabbed the pole between his feet, then raised his left arm and roared, "COME!"

The village rang with his voice. He continued the summons as people drifted from the houses and shadowed alleyways and began to gather around him. Many were curious, others sympathetic, some awed, and some angry. Again and again, Roran's chant echoed in the valley. Loring arrived with his sons in tow. From the opposite direction came Birgit, Delwin, and Fisk with his wife, Isold. Morn and Tara left the tavern together and joined the crush of spectators.

When most of Carvahall stood before him, Roran fell silent, tightening his left fist until his fingernails cut into his palm. *Katrina.* Raising his hand, he opened it and showed everyone the crimson tears that dripped down his arm. "This," he said, "is my pain. Look well, for it will be yours unless we defeat the curse wanton fate has set upon us. Your friends and family will be bound in chains, destined for slavery in foreign lands, or slain before your eyes, hewn open by soldiers' merciless blades. Galbatorix will sow

249

our land with salt so that it lies forever fallow. This I have seen. This I know." He paced like a caged wolf, glowering and swinging his head. He had their attention. Now he had to stoke them into a frenzy to match his own.

"My father was killed by the desecrators. My cousin has fled. My farm was razed. And my bride-to-be was kidnapped by her own father, who murdered Byrd and betrayed us all! Quimby eaten, the hay barn burned along with Fisk's and Delwin's houses. Parr, Wyglif, Ged, Bardrick, Farold, Hale, Garner, Kelby, Melkolf, Albem, and Elmund: all slain. Many of you have been injured, like me, so that you can no longer support your family. Isn't it enough that we toil every day of our lives to eke a living from the earth, subjected to the whims of nature? Isn't it enough that we are forced to pay Galbatorix's iron taxes, without also having to endure these senseless torments?" Roran laughed maniacally, howling at the sky and hearing the madness in his own voice. No one stirred in the crowd.

"I know now the true nature of the Empire and of Galbatorix; they are *evil*. Galbatorix is an unnatural blight on the world. He destroyed the Riders and the greatest peace and prosperity we ever had. His servants are foul demons birthed in some ancient pit. But is Galbatorix content to grind us beneath his heel? No! He seeks to poison all of Alagaësia, to suffocate us with his cloak of misery. Our children and their descendants shall live in the shadow of his darkness until the end of time, reduced to slaves, worms, *vermin* for him to torture at his pleasure. Unless . . ."

Roran stared into the villagers' wide eyes, conscious of his control over them. No one had ever dared say what he was about to. He let his voice rasp low in his throat: "Unless we have the courage to resist evil.

"We've fought the soldiers and the Ra'zac, but it means nothing if we die alone and forgotten—or are carted away as chattel. We cannot stay here, and I won't allow Galbatorix to obliterate everything that's worth living for. I would rather have my eyes plucked out and my hands chopped off than see him triumph! I choose to fight! I choose to step from my grave and let my enemies bury themselves in it!

"I choose to leave Carvahall.

"I will cross the Spine and take a ship from Narda down to Surda, where I will join the Varden, who have struggled for decades to free us of this oppression." The villagers looked shocked at the idea. "But I do not wish to go alone. Come with me. Come with me and seize this chance to forge a better life for yourselves. Throw off the shackles that bind you here." Roran pointed at his listeners, moving his finger from one target to the next. "A hundred years from now, what names shall drop from the bards' lips? Horst . . . Birgit . . . Kiselt . . . Thane; they will recite our sagas. They will sing "The Epic of Carvahall," for we were the only village brave enough to defy the Empire."

Tears of pride flooded Roran's eyes. "What could be more noble than cleansing Galbatorix's stain from Alagaësia? No more would we live in fear of having our farms destroyed, or being killed and eaten. The grain we harvest would be ours to keep, save for any extra that we might send as a gift to the rightful king. The rivers and streams would run thick with gold. We would be safe and happy and fat!

"It is our destiny."

Roran held his hand before his face and slowly closed his fingers over the bleeding wounds. He stood hunched over his injured arm—crucified by the scores of gazes—and waited for a response to his speech. None came. At last he realized that they *wanted* him to continue; they wanted to hear more about the cause and the future he had portrayed.

Katrina.

Then as darkness gathered around the radius of his torch, Roran drew himself upright and resumed speaking. He hid nothing, only labored to make them understand his thoughts and feelings, so they too could share the sense of purpose that drove him. "Our age is at an end. We must step forward and cast our lot with the Varden if we and our children are to live free." He spoke with rage and hon-eyed tones in equal amount, but always with a fervid conviction that kept his audience entranced.

When his store of images was exhausted, Roran looked into the faces of his friends and neighbors and said, "I march in two days. Accompany me if you wish, but I go regardless." He bowed his head and stepped out of the light.

Overhead, the waning moon glowed behind a lens of clouds. A slight breeze wafted through Carvahall. An iron weather vane creaked on a roof as it swung in the direction of the current.

From within the crowd, Birgit picked her way into the light, clutching the folds of her dress to avoid tripping. With a subdued expression, she adjusted her shawl. "Today we saw an . . ." She stopped, shook her head, and laughed in an embarrassed way. "I find it hard to speak after Roran. I don't like his plan, but I believe that it's necessary, although for a different reason: I would hunt down the Ra'zac and avenge my husband's death. I will go with him. And I will take my children." She too stepped away from the torch.

A silent minute passed, then Delwin and his wife, Lenna, ad-vanced with their arms around each other. Lenna looked at Birgit and said, "I understand your need, Sister. We want our vengeance as well, but more than that, we want the rest of our children to be safe. For that reason, we too will go." Several women whose hus-bands had been slain came forward and agreed with her.

The villagers murmured among themselves, then fell silent and motionless. No one else seemed willing to address the subject; it was too momentous. Roran understood. He was still trying to digest the implications himself.

Finally, Horst strode to the torch and stared with a drawn face into the flame. "It's no good talking any more. . . . We need time to think. Every man must decide for himself. Tomorrow . . . tomorrow will be another day. Perhaps things will be clearer then." He shook his head and lifted the torch, then inverted it and extinguished it against the ground, leaving everyone to find their way home in the moonlight.

Roran joined Albriech and Baldor, who walked behind their parents at a discreet distance, giving them privacy to talk. Neither of the brothers would look at Roran. Unsettled by their lack of expression, Roran asked, "Do you think anyone else will go? Was I good enough?"

Albriech emitted a bark of laughter. "Good enough!"

"Roran," said Baldor in an odd voice, "you could have convinced an Urgal to become a farmer tonight."

"No!"

"When you finished, I was ready to grab my spear and dash into the Spine after you. I wouldn't have been alone either. The question isn't who *will* leave, it's who *won't*. What you said . . . I've never heard anything like it before."

Roran frowned. His goal had been to persuade people to accept his plan, not to get them to follow him personally. *If that's what it takes*, he thought with a shrug. Still, the prospect had caught him unawares. At an earlier time, it would have disturbed him, but now he was just thankful for anything that could help him to rescue Katrina and save the villagers.

Baldor leaned toward his brother. "Father would lose most of his tools." Albriech nodded solemnly.

Roran knew that smiths made whatever implement was required by the task at hand, and that these custom tools formed a legacy that was bequeathed from father to son, or from master to journeyman. One measure of a smith's wealth and skill was the number of tools he owned. For Horst to surrender his would be . . . *Would be no harder than what anyone else has to do*, thought Roran. He only regretted that it would entail depriving Albriech and Baldor of their rightful inheritance.

When they reached the house, Roran retreated to Baldor's room and lay in bed. Through the walls, he could still hear the faint sound of Horst and Elain talking. He fell asleep imagining similar discussions taking place throughout Carvahall, deciding his—and their—fate.

REPERCUSSIONS

The morning after his speech, Roran looked out his window and saw twelve men leaving Carvahall, heading toward Igualda Falls. He yawned and limped downstairs to the kitchen.

Horst sat alone at the table, twisting a mug of ale in his hands. "Morning," he said.

Roran grunted, tore a heel of bread off the loaf on the counter, then seated himself at the opposite end of the table. As he ate, he noted Horst's bloodshot eyes and unkempt beard. Roran guessed that the smith had been awake the entire night. "Do you know why a group is going up—"

"Have to talk with their families," said Horst abruptly. "They've been running into the Spine since dawn." He put the mug down with a *crack*. "You have no idea what you did, Roran, by asking us to leave. The whole village is in turmoil. You backed us into a corner with only one way out: your way. Some people hate you for it. Of course a fair number of them already hated you for bringing this upon us."

The bread in Roran's mouth tasted like sawdust as resentment flared inside him. *Eragon was the one who brought back the stone, not me.* "And the others?"

Horst sipped his ale and grimaced. "The others adore you. I never thought I would see the day when Garrow's son would stir my heart with words, but you did it, boy, you did it." He swung a gnarled

254

hand over his head. "All this? I built it for Elain and my sons. It took me seven years to finish! See that beam over the door right there? I broke three toes getting that into place. And you know what? I'm going to give it up because of what you said last night."

Roran remained silent; it was what he wanted. Leaving Carvahall was the right thing to do, and since he had committed himself to that course, he saw no reason to torment himself with guilt and regret. *The decision is made. I will accept the outcome without complaint, no matter how dire, for this is our only escape from the Empire.*

"But," said Horst, and leaned forward on one elbow, his black eyes burning beneath his brow, "just you remember that if reality falls short of the airy dreams you conjured, there'll be debts to pay. Give people a hope and then take it away, and they'll destroy you."

The prospect was of no concern to Roran. *If we make it to Surda, we will be greeted as heroes by the rebels. If we don't, our deaths will fulfill all debts.* When it was clear that the smith had finished, Roran asked, "Where is Elain?"

Horst scowled at the change of topic. "Out back." He stood and straightened his tunic over his heavy shoulders. "I have to go clear out the smithy and decide what tools I'm going to take. I'll hide or destroy the rest. The Empire won't benefit from *my* work."

"I'll help." Roran pushed back his chair.

"No," said Horst roughly. "This is a task I can only do with Albriech and Baldor. That forge has been my entire life, and theirs. . . . You wouldn't be much help with that arm of yours anyway. Stay here. Elain can use you."

After the smith left, Roran opened the side door and found Elain talking with Gertrude by the large pile of firewood Horst maintained year-round. The healer went up to Roran and put a hand on his forehead. "Ah, I was afraid that you might have a fever after yesterday's excitement. Your family heals at the most extraordinary rate. I could barely believe my eyes when Eragon started walking about after having his legs skinned and spending two days in bed."

Roran stiffened at the mention of his cousin, but she did not seem to notice. "Let's see how your shoulder is doing, shall we?"

Roran bowed his neck so that Gertrude could reach behind him and untie the knot to the wool sling. When it was undone, he carefully lowered his right forearm—which was immobilized in a splint—until his arm was straight. Gertrude slid her fingers under the poultice packed on his wound and peeled it off.

"Oh my," she said.

A thick, rancid smell clogged the air. Roran clenched his teeth as his gorge rose, then looked down. The skin under the poultice had turned white and spongy, like a giant birthmark of maggot flesh. The bite itself had been stitched up while he was unconscious, so all he saw was a jagged pink line caked with blood on the front of his shoulder. Swelling and inflammation had forced the twisted catgut threads to cut deep into his flesh, while beads of clear liquid oozed from the wound.

Gertrude clucked her tongue as she inspected him, then refastened the bandages and looked Roran in the eye. "You're doing well enough, but the tissue may become diseased. I can't tell yet. If it does, we'll have to cauterize your shoulder."

Roran nodded. "Will my arm work once it heals?"

"As long as the muscle knits together properly. It also depends on how you want to use it. You—"

"Will I be able to fight?"

"If you want to fight," said Gertrude slowly, "I suggest that you learn to use your left hand." She patted his cheek, then hurried back toward her hut.

My *arm.* Roran stared at his bound limb as if it no longer belonged to him. Until that moment, he had not realized how closely his sense of identity was linked to the condition of his body. Injuring his flesh caused injury to his psyche, as well as the other way around. Roran was proud of his body, and seeing it mutilated sent a jolt of panic through him, especially since the damage was permanent. Even if he regained the use of his arm, he would always bear a thick scar as a memento of his injury.

Taking his hand, Elain led Roran back into the house, where she crumbled mint into a kettle, then set it on the stove to boil. "You really love her, don't you?"

"What?" He looked at her, startled.

Elain rested a hand on her belly. "Katrina." She smiled. "I'm not blind. I know what you've done for her, and I'm proud of you. Not every man would go as far."

"It won't matter, if I can't free her."

The kettle began to whistle stridently. "You will, I'm sure of it— one way or another." Elain poured the tea. "We had better start preparing for the trip. I'm going to sort through the kitchen first. While I do, can you go upstairs and bring me all the clothes, bedding, and anything else you think might be useful?"

"Where should I put it?" asked Roran.

"The dining room will be fine."

Since the mountains were too steep—and the forest too dense—for wagons, Roran realized that their supplies were limited to however much they could carry themselves, as well as what they could pile onto Horst's two horses, although one of those had to be left partially unburdened so that Elain could ride whenever the trail proved too strenuous for her pregnancy.

Compounding the issue was the fact that some families in Carvahall did not have enough steeds for both provisions and the young, old, and infirm who would be unable to keep pace on foot. Everyone would have to share resources. The question, though, was with whom? They still did not know who else was going, besides Birgit and Delwin.

Thus, when Elain finished packing the items she deemed essential—mainly food and shelter—she sent Roran to find out if anyone needed extra storage space and, if not, if she could borrow some in turn, for there were plenty of nonessential items she wanted to bring but would otherwise abandon.

Despite the people hurrying through the streets, Carvahall was heavy with a forced stillness, an unnatural calm that belied the feverish activity hidden within the houses. Almost everyone was silent and walked with downturned faces, engrossed in their own thoughts.

When Roran arrived at Orval's house, he had to pound on the knocker for almost a minute before the farmer answered the door. "Oh, it's you, Stronghammer." Orval stepped out on the porch. "Sorry for the wait, but I was busy. How can I help you?" He tapped a long black pipe against his palm, then began to roll it nervously between his fingers. Inside the house, Roran heard chairs being shoved across the floor and pots and pans banging together.

Roran quickly explained Elain's offer and request. Orval squinted up at the sky. "I reckon I've got enough room for my own stuff. Ask around, an' if you still need space, I have a pair of oxen that could hold a bit more."

"So you *are* going?"

Orval shifted uncomfortably. "Well, I wouldn't say that. We're just . . . getting ready in case of another attack."

"Ah." Puzzled, Roran trudged on to Kiselt's house. He soon discovered that no one was willing to reveal whether they had decided to leave—even when evidence of their preparations was in plain sight.

And they all treated Roran with a deference that he found unsettling. It manifested itself in small gestures: offers of condolences for his misfortune, respectful silence whenever he spoke, and murmurs of assent when he made a statement. It was as if his deeds had inflated his stature and intimidated the people he had known since childhood, distancing him from them.

I am branded, thought Roran, limping through the mud. He stopped at the edge of a puddle and bent to examine his reflection, curious if he could discern what made him so different.

He saw a man in ragged, blood-stained clothes, with a humped back and a crooked arm tied across his chest. His neck and cheeks were scumbled with an impending beard, while his hair was matted into snarled ropes that writhed in a halo around his head. Most frightening of all, though, were his eyes, which had sunk deep into the sockets, giving him a haunted appearance. From within those two morbid caverns, his gaze boiled like molten steel, full of loss, rage, and an obsessive craving.

A lopsided smile crept across Roran's face, rendering his visage even more shocking. He liked how he looked. It matched his feelings. Now he understood how he had managed to influence the villagers. He bared his teeth. *I can use this image. I can use it to destroy the Ra'zac.*

Lifting his head, he slouched up the street, pleased with himself. Just then, Thane approached him and grasped his left forearm in a hearty grip. "Stronghammer! You don't know how glad I am to see you."

"You are?" Roran wondered if the whole world had been turned inside out during the night.

Thane nodded vigorously. "Ever since we attacked the soldiers, everything has seemed hopeless to me. It pains me to admit it, but so it was. My heart pounded all the time, like I was about to fall down a well; my hands shook; and I felt dreadfully ill. I thought someone had poisoned me! It was worse than death. But what you said yesterday healed me instantly and let me see purpose and meaning in the world again! I . . . I can't even explain the horror you saved me from. I am in your debt. If you need or want anything, just ask and I'll help."

Moved, Roran gripped the farmer's forearm in return and said, "Thank you, Thane. Thank you." Thane bowed his head, tears in his eyes, then released Roran and left him standing alone in the middle of the street.

What have I done?

EXODUS

A wall of thick, smoky air engulfed Roran as he entered the Seven Sheaves, Morn's tavern. He stopped beneath the Urgal horns pegged over the door and let his eyes adjust to the dim interior. "Hello?" he called.

The door to the back rooms banged open as Tara plowed forward, trailed by Morn. They both glared sullenly at Roran. Tara planted her meaty fists on her hips and demanded, "What do you want here?"

Roran stared at her for a moment, trying to determine the source of her animosity. "Have you decided whether to accompany me into the Spine?"

"That's none of your business," snapped Tara.

Oh yes, it is. He restrained himself, though, and instead said, "Whatever your intentions are, if you *were* to go, Elain would like to know if you have room in your bags for a few more items, or if you need extra room yourself. She has—"

"Extra room!" burst out Morn. He waved at the wall behind the bar, which was lined with oak casks. "I have, packed in straw, twelve barrels of the clearest winter ale, which have been kept at the perfect temperature for the past five months. They were Quimby's last batch! What am I supposed to do with them? Or my hogsheads of lager and stout? If I leave them, the soldiers will dispose of it in a week, or they'll spike the barrels and pour the beer into the ground, where the only creatures who'll enjoy it will be grubs and worms. Oh!" Morn sat and wrung his hands, shaking his head. "Twelve years of work! Ever since Father died I ran the tavern the same way he did, day in and day out. And then you and Eragon had to cause this trouble. It . . ." He stopped, breathing with difficulty, and wiped his mashed face with the edge of his sleeve.

"There, there now," said Tara. She put her arm around Morn and jabbed a finger at Roran. "Who gave you leave to stir up Carvahall with your fancy words? If we go, how will my poor husband make a living? He can't take his trade with him like Horst or Gedric. He can't squat in an empty field and farm it like you! Impossible! Everyone will go and we will starve. Or we will go and we will *still* starve. You have ruined us!"

Roran looked from her flushed, angry face to Morn's distraught one, then turned and opened the door. He paused on the threshold and said in a low voice, "I have always counted you among my friends. I would not have you killed by the Empire." Stepping outside, he pulled his vest tight around himself and paced away from the tavern, ruminating the whole way.

At Fisk's well, he stopped for a drink and found himself joined by Birgit. She watched him struggle to turn the crank with only one hand, then took it from him and brought up the water bucket, which she passed to him without drinking. He sipped the cool liquid, then said, "I'm glad that you are coming." He handed the bucket back.

Birgit eyed him. "I recognize the force that drives you, Roran, for it propels me as well; we both wish to find the Ra'zac. Once we do, though, I will have my compensation from you for Quimby's death. Never forget that." She pushed the full bucket back into the well and let it fall unchecked, the crank spinning wildly. A second later, the well echoed with a hollow splash.

Roran smiled as he watched her walk away. He was more pleased than upset by her declaration; he knew that even if everyone else in Carvahall were to forsake the cause or die, Birgit would still help him to hunt the Ra'zac. Afterward, though—if an afterward existed—he would have to pay her price or kill her. That was the only way to resolve such matters.

By evening Horst and his sons had returned to the house, bearing two small bundles wrapped in oilcloth. "Is that all?" asked Elain. Horst nodded curtly, lay the bundles on the kitchen table, and unwrapped them to expose four hammers, three tongs, a clamp, a medium-sized bellows, and a three-pound anvil.

As the five of them sat to dinner, Albriech and Baldor discussed the various people they had seen making covert preparations. Roran listened intently, trying to keep track of who had lent donkeys to whom, who showed no signs of departing, and who might need help to leave.

"The biggest problem," said Baldor, "is food. We can only carry so much, and it'll be difficult to hunt enough in the Spine to feed two or three hundred people."

"Mmm." Horst shook his finger, his mouth full of beans, then swallowed. "No, hunting won't work. We have to bring our flocks with us. Combined, we own enough sheep and goats to feed the lot of us for a month or more."

Roran raised his knife. "Wolves."

"I'm more worried about keeping the animals from wandering off into the forest," replied Horst. "Herding them will be a chore."

Roran spent the following day assisting whomever he could, saying little, and generally allowing people to see him working for the good of the village. Late that night, he tumbled into bed exhausted but hopeful.

The advent of dawn pierced Roran's dreams and woke him with a sense of momentous expectation. He stood and tiptoed downstairs, then went outside and stared at the misty mountains, absorbed by the morning's silence. His breath formed a white plume in the air, but he felt warm, for his heart throbbed with fear and eagerness.

After a subdued breakfast, Horst brought the horses to the front of the house, where Roran helped Albriech and Baldor load them with saddlebags and other bundles of supplies. Next Roran took up his own pack, hissing as the leather shoulder strap pressed down on his injury.

Horst closed the door to the house. He lingered for a moment with his fingers on the steel doorknob, then took Elain's hand and said, "Let's go."

As they walked through Carvahall, Roran saw somber families gathering by their houses with their piles of possessions and yammering livestock. He saw sheep and dogs with bags tied on their backs, teary-eyed children on donkeys, and makeshift sledges hitched to horses with crates of fluttering chickens hung on each side. He saw the fruits of his success, and he knew not whether to laugh or to cry.

They stopped at Carvahall's north end and waited to see who would join them. A minute passed, then Birgit approached from the side, accompanied by Nolfavrell and his younger siblings. Birgit greeted Horst and Elain and stationed herself nearby.

Ridley and his family arrived outside the wall of trees, driving over a hundred sheep from the east side of Palancar Valley. "I figured that it would be better to keep them out of Carvahall," shouted Ridley over the animals.

"Good thinking!" replied Horst.

Next came Delwin, Lenna, and their five children; Orval and his family; Loring with his sons; Calitha and Thane—who gave Roran a large smile; and then Kiselt's clan. Those women who had been recently widowed, like Nolla, clustered around Birgit. Before the sun had cleared the mountain peaks, most of the village had assembled along the wall. But not all.

Morn, Tara, and several others had yet to show themselves, and when Ivor arrived, it was without any supplies. "You're staying," observed Roran. He sidestepped a knot of testy goats that Gertrude was attempting to restrain.

"Aye," said Ivor, drawing out the word into a weary admission. He shivered, crossed his bony arms for warmth, and faced the rising sun, lifting his head so as to catch the transparent rays. "Svart refused to leave. Heh! It was like carving against the grain to get him into the Spine in the first place. Someone has to look after him, an' I don't have any children, so . . ." He shrugged. "Doubt I could give up the farm anyway."

"What will you do when the soldiers arrive?"

"Give them a fight that they'll remember."

Roran laughed hoarsely and clapped Ivor on the arm, doing his best to ignore the unspoken fate that they both knew awaited anyone who remained.

A thin, middle-aged man, Ethlbert, marched to the edge of the congregation and shouted, "You're all fools!" With an ominous rustle, people turned to look at their accuser. "I've held my peace through this madness, but I'll not follow a nattering lunatic! If you weren't blinded by his words, you'd see that he's leading you to destruction! Well, I won't go! I'll take my chances sneaking past the soldiers and finding refuge in Therinsford. They're our own people at least, not the barbarians you'll find in Surda." He spat on the ground, then spun on his heel and stomped away.

Afraid that Ethlbert might convince others to defect, Roran scanned the crowd and was relieved to see nothing more than restless muttering. Still, he did not want to dawdle and give people a chance to change their minds. He asked Horst under his breath, "How long should we wait?"

"Albriech, you and Baldor run around as fast as you can and check if anyone else is coming. Otherwise, we'll leave." The brothers dashed off in opposite directions.

Half an hour later, Baldor returned with Fisk, Isold, and their borrowed horse. Leaving her husband, Isold hurried toward Horst, shooing her hands at anyone who got in her way, oblivious to the fact that most of her hair had escaped imprisonment in its bun and stuck out in odd tufts. She stopped, wheezing for breath. "I *am* sorry we're so late, but Fisk had trouble closing up the shop. He couldn't pick which planers or chisels to bring." She laughed in a shrill tone, almost hysterical. "It was like watching a cat surrounded by mice trying to decide which one to chase. First this one, then that one."

A wry smile tugged at Horst's lips. "I understand perfectly."

Roran strained for a glimpse of Albriech, but to no avail. He gritted his teeth. "Where *is* he?"

Horst tapped his shoulder. "Right over there, I do believe."

Albriech advanced between the houses with three beer casks tied to his back and an aggrieved look that was comic enough to make Baldor and several others laugh. On either side of Albriech walked Morn and Tara, who staggered under the weight of their enormous packs, as did the donkey and two goats that they towed behind them. To Roran's astonishment, the animals were burdened with even more casks.

"They won't last a mile," said Roran, growing angry at the couple's foolishness. "And they don't have enough food. Do they expect us to feed them or—"

With a chuckle, Horst cut him off. "I wouldn't worry about the food. Morn's beer will be good for morale, and that's worth more than a few extra meals. You'll see."

As soon as Albriech had freed himself of the casks, Roran asked him and his brother, "Is that everyone?" When they answered in the affirmative, Roran swore and struck his thigh with a clenched fist. Excluding Ivor, three families were determined to remain in Palancar Valley: Ethlbert's, Parr's, and Knute's. *I can't force them to come.* He sighed. "All right. There's no sense in waiting longer."

Excitement rippled through the villagers; the moment had finally arrived. Horst and five other men pulled open the wall of trees, then laid planks across the trench so that the people and animals could walk over.

Horst gestured. "I think that you should go first, Roran."

"Wait!" Fisk ran up and, with evident pride, handed Roran a blackened six-foot-long staff of hawthorn wood with a knot of polished roots at the top, and a blued-steel ferrule that tapered into a blunt spike at the base. "I made it last night," said the carpenter. "I thought that you might have need of it."

Roran ran his left hand over the wood, marveling at its smoothness. "I couldn't have asked for anything better. Your skill is masterful. . . . Thank you." Fisk grinned and backed away.

Conscious of the fact that the entire crowd was watching, Roran faced the mountains and the Igualda Falls. His shoulder throbbed beneath the leather strap. Behind him lay his father's bones and everything he had known in life. Before him the jagged peaks piled high into the pale sky and blocked his way and his will. But he would not be denied. And he would not look back.

Katrina.

Lifting his chin, Roran strode forward. His staff knocked against the hard planks as he crossed the trench and passed out of Carvahall, leading the villagers into the wilderness.

◆　◆　◆

ON THE CRAGS OF TEL'NAEÍR

T *hud.*

Bright as a flaming sun, the dragon hung before Eragon and everyone clustered along the Crags of Tel'naeír, buffeting them with gusts from its mighty wings. The dragon's body appeared to be on fire as the brilliant dawn illuminated its golden scales and sprayed the ground and trees with dazzling chips of light. It was far larger than Saphira, large enough to be several hundred years old, and proportionally thicker in its neck, limbs, and tail. Upon its back sat the Rider, robes startling white against the brilliance of the scales.

Eragon fell to his knees, his face upturned. *I'm not alone. . . .* Awe and relief coursed through him. No more would he have to bear the responsibility of the Varden and of Galbatorix by himself. Here was one of the guardians of old resurrected from the depths of time to guide him, a living symbol, and a testament to the legends he had been raised with. Here was his master. Here *was* a legend!

As the dragon turned to land, Eragon gasped; the creature's left foreleg had been severed by a terrible blow, leaving a helpless white stump in place of the once mighty limb. Tears filled his eyes.

A whirlwind of dry twigs and leaves enveloped the hilltop as the dragon settled on the sweet clover and folded its wings. The Rider carefully descended from his steed along the dragon's intact front right leg, then approached Eragon, his hands clasped before him. He was an elf with silver hair, old beyond measure, though the only sign of age was the expression of great compassion and sadness upon his face.

"Osthato Chetowä," said Eragon. "The Mourning Sage . . . As you asked, I have come." With a jolt, he remembered his manners and touched his lips. "Atra esterní ono thelduin."

The Rider smiled. He took Eragon by the shoulders and lifted him upright, staring at him with such kindness that Eragon could look at nothing else; he was consumed by the endless depths within the elf's eyes. "Oromis is my proper name, Eragon Shadeslayer."

"You knew," whispered Islanzadí with a hurt expression that quickly transformed into a storm of rage. "You knew of Eragon's existence and yet you did not tell me? Why have you betrayed me, Shur'tugal?"

Oromis released Eragon from his gaze and transferred it onto the queen. "I kept my peace because it was uncertain if Eragon or Arya would live long enough to come here; I had no wish to give you a fragile hope that might have been torn away at any moment."

Islanzadí spun about, her cape of swan feathers billowing like wings. "You had no right to withhold such information from me! I could have sent warriors to protect Arya, Eragon, and Saphira in Farthen Dûr and to escort them safely here."

Oromis smiled sadly. "I hid nothing from you, Islanzadí, but what you had already chosen not to see. If you had scryed the land, as is your duty, you would have discerned the source of the chaos that has swept Alagaësia and learned the truth of Arya and Eragon. That you might forget the Varden and the dwarves in your grief is understandable, but Brom? Vinr Älfakyn? The last of the Elf Friends? You have been blind to the world, Islanzadí, and lax upon your throne. I could not risk driving you further away by subjecting you to another loss."

Islanzadí's anger drained away, leaving her face pale and her shoulders slumped. "I am diminished," she whispered.

A cloud of hot, moist air pressed against Eragon as the gold dragon bent to examine him with eyes that glittered and sparked.

We are well met, Eragon Shadeslayer. I am Glaedr. His voice—for it was unmistakably male—rumbled and shook through Eragon's mind, like the growl of a mountain avalanche.

All Eragon could do was touch his lips and say, "I am honored."

Then Glaedr brought his attention to bear on Saphira. She remained perfectly still, her neck arched stiffly as Glaedr sniffed her cheek and along the line of her wing. Eragon saw Saphira's clenched leg muscles flutter with an involuntary tremor. *You smell of humans,* said Glaedr, *and all you know of your own race is what your instincts have taught you, but you have the heart of a true dragon.*

During this silent exchange, Orik presented himself to Oromis. "Truly, this is beyond anything that I dared hope or expect. You are a pleasant surprise in these dark times, Rider." He clapped his fist over his heart. "If it is not too presumptuous, I would ask a boon on behalf of my king and my clan, as was the custom between our people."

Oromis nodded. "And I will grant it if it is within my power."

"Then tell me: Why have you remained hidden for all these years? You were sorely needed, Argetlam."

"Ah," said Oromis. "Many sorrows exist in this world, and one of the greatest is being unable to help those in pain. I could not risk leaving this sanctuary, for if I had died before one of Galbatorix's eggs had hatched, then there would have been no one to pass on our secrets to the new Rider, and it would have been even harder to defeat Galbatorix."

"*That* was your reason?" spat Orik. "Those are the words of a coward! The eggs might have never hatched."

Everyone went deathly quiet, except for a faint growl that emanated from between Glaedr's teeth. "If you were not my guest here," said Islanzadí, "I would strike you down myself for that insult."

Oromis spread his hands. "Nay, I am not offended. It is an apt reaction. Understand, Orik, that Glaedr and I cannot fight. Glaedr has his disability, and I," he touched the side of his head, "I am also

269

maimed. The Forsworn broke something within me when I was their captive, and while I can still teach and learn, I can no longer control magic, except for the smallest of spells. The power escapes me, no matter how much I struggle. I would be worse than useless in battle, I would be a weakness and a liability, one who could easily be captured and used against you. So I removed myself from Galbatorix's influence for the good of the many, even though I yearned to openly oppose him."

"The Cripple Who Is Whole," murmured Eragon.

"Forgive me," said Orik. He appeared stricken.

"It is of no consequence." Oromis placed a hand on Eragon's shoulder. "Islanzadí Dröttning, by your leave?"

"Go," she said wearily. "Go and be done with you."

Glaedr crouched low to the ground, and Oromis nimbly climbed up his leg and into the saddle on his back. "Come, Eragon and Saphira. We have much to talk about." The gold dragon leaped off the cliff and circled overhead, rising on an updraft.

Eragon and Orik solemnly clasped arms. "Bring honor to your clan," said the dwarf.

As Eragon mounted Saphira, he felt as if he were about to embark on a long journey and that he should say farewell to those who remained behind. Instead, he just looked at Arya and smiled, letting his wonder and joy show. She half frowned, appearing troubled, but then he was gone, swept into the sky by the eagerness of Saphira's flight.

Together the two dragons followed the white cliff northward for several miles, accompanied only by the sound of their wings. Saphira flew abreast of Glaedr. Her enthusiasm boiled over into Eragon's mind, heightening his own emotions.

They landed in another clearing situated on the edge of the cliff, just before the wall of exposed stone crumbled back into the earth. A bare path led from the precipice to the doorstep of a low hut grown between the trunks of four trees, one of which straddled a stream that emerged from the moody depths of the forest.

Glaedr would not fit inside; the hut could have easily sat between his ribs.

"Welcome to my home," said Oromis as he alighted on the ground with uncommon ease. "I live here, on the brink of the Crags of Tel'naeír, because it provides me the opportunity to think and study in peace. My mind works better away from Ellesméra and the distractions of other people."

He disappeared inside the hut, then returned with two stools and flagons of clear, cold water for both himself and Eragon. Eragon sipped his drink and admired the spacious view of Du Weldenvarden in an attempt to conceal his awe and nervousness while he waited for the elf to speak. *I'm in the presence of another Rider!* Beside him, Saphira crouched with her eyes fixed on Glaedr, slowly kneading the dirt between her claws.

The gap in their conversation stretched longer and longer. Ten minutes passed . . . half an hour . . . then an hour. It reached the point where Eragon began to measure the elapsed time by the sun's progress. At first his mind buzzed with questions and thoughts, but those eventually subsided into calm acceptance. He enjoyed just observing the day.

Only then did Oromis say, "You have learned the value of patience well. That is good."

It took Eragon a moment to find his voice. "You can't stalk a deer if you are in a hurry."

Oromis lowered his flagon. "True enough. Let me see your hands. I find that they tell me much about a person." Eragon removed his gloves and allowed the elf to grip his wrists with thin, dry fingers. He examined Eragon's calluses, then said, "Correct me if I am wrong. You have wielded a scythe and plow more often than a sword, though you are accustomed to a bow."

"Aye."

"And you have done little writing or drawing, maybe none at all."

"Brom taught me my letters in Teirm."

"Mmm. Beyond your choice of tools, it seems obvious that you tend to be reckless and disregard your own safety."

"What makes you say that, Oromis-elda?" asked Eragon, using the most respectful and formal honorific that he could think of.

"Not *elda*," corrected Oromis. "You may call me master in this tongue and ebrithil in the ancient language, nothing else. You will extend the same courtesy to Glaedr. We are your teachers; you are our students; and you will act with proper respect and deference." Oromis spoke gently, but with the authority of one who expects absolute obedience.

"Yes, Master Oromis."

"As will you, Saphira."

Eragon could sense how hard it was for Saphira to unbend her pride enough to say, *Yes, Master.*

Oromis nodded. "Now. Anyone with such a collection of scars has either been hopelessly unfortunate, fights like a berserker, or deliberately pursues danger. Do you fight like a berserker?"

"No."

"Nor do you seem unfortunate; quite the opposite. That leaves only one explanation. Unless you think differently?"

Eragon cast his mind over his experiences at home and on the road, in an attempt to categorize his behavior. "I would say, rather, that once I dedicate myself to a certain project or path, I see it through, no matter the cost . . . especially if someone I love is in danger." His gaze flicked toward Saphira.

"And do you undertake challenging projects?"

"I like to be challenged."

"So you feel the need to pit yourself against adversity in order to test your abilities."

"I enjoy overcoming challenges, but I've faced enough hardship to know that it's foolish to make things more difficult than they are. It's all I can do to survive as it is."

"Yet you chose to follow the Ra'zac when it would have been easier to remain in Palancar Valley. And you came here."

"It was the right thing to do . . . Master."

For several minutes, no one spoke. Eragon tried to guess what the elf was thinking, but could glean no information from his masklike visage. Finally, Oromis stirred. "Were you, perchance, given a trinket of some kind in Tarnag, Eragon? A piece of jewelry, armor, or even a coin?"

"Aye." Eragon reached inside of his tunic and fished out the necklace with the tiny silver hammer. "Gannel made this for me on Hrothgar's orders, to prevent anyone from scrying Saphira or me. They were afraid that Galbatorix might have discovered what I look like. . . . How did you know?"

"Because," said Oromis, "I could no longer sense you."

"Someone tried to scry me by Sílthrim about a week ago. Was that you?"

Oromis shook his head. "After I first scryed you with Arya, I had no need to use such crude methods to find you. I could reach out and touch your mind with mine, as I did when you were injured in Farthen Dûr." Lifting the amulet, he murmured several lines in the ancient language, then released it. "It contains no other spells I can detect. Keep it with you at all times; it is a valuable gift." He pressed the tips of his long fingers together, his nails as round and bright as fish scales, and stared between the arches they formed toward the white horizon. "Why are you here, Eragon?"

"To complete my training."

"And what do you think that process entails?"

Eragon shifted uncomfortably. "Learning more about magic and fighting. Brom wasn't able to finish teaching me everything that he knew."

"Magic, swordsmanship, and other such skills are useless unless you know how and when to apply them. This I will teach you. However, as Galbatorix has demonstrated, power without moral direction is the most dangerous force in the world. My main task, then, is to help you, Eragon and Saphira, to understand what principles guide you, so that you do not make the right choices for the wrong reasons. You must learn more about yourself, who you are and what you are capable of doing. That is why you are here."

When do we begin? asked Saphira.

Oromis began to answer when he stiffened and dropped his flagon. His face went crimson and his fingers tightened into hooked claws that dragged at his robe like cockleburs. The change was frightening and instantaneous. Before Eragon could do more than flinch, the elf had relaxed again, although his entire body now bespoke weariness.

Concerned, Eragon dared to ask, "Are you well?"

A trace of amusement lifted the corner of Oromis's mouth. "Less so than I might wish. We elves fancy ourselves immortal, but not even we can escape certain maladies of the flesh, which are beyond our knowledge of magic to do more than delay. No, do not worry . . . it isn't contagious, but neither can I rid myself of it." He sighed. "I have spent decades binding myself with hundreds of small, weak spells that, layered one upon another, duplicate the effect of enchantments that are now beyond my reach. I bound myself with them so that I might live long enough to witness the birth of the last dragons and to foster the Riders' resurrection from the ruin of our mistakes."

"How long until . . ."

Oromis lifted a sharp eyebrow. "How long until I die? We have time, but precious little for you or me, especially if the Varden decide to call upon your help. As a result—to answer your question, Saphira—we will begin your instruction immediately, and we will train faster than any Rider ever has or ever will, for I must condense decades of knowledge into months and weeks."

"You do know," said Eragon, struggling against the embarrassment and shame that made his cheeks burn, "about my . . . my own *infirmity*." He ground out the last word, hating the sound of it. "I am as crippled as you are."

Sympathy tempered Oromis's gaze, though his voice was firm. "Eragon, you are only a cripple if you consider yourself one. I understand how you feel, but you must remain optimistic, for a negative outlook is more of a handicap than any physical injury. I speak from personal experience. Pitying yourself serves neither you nor Saphira. I and the other spellweavers will study your malady to see if we might devise a way to alleviate it, but in the meantime, your training will proceed as if nothing were amiss."

Eragon's gut clenched and he tasted bile as he considered the implications. *Surely Oromis wouldn't make me endure that torment again!* "The pain is unbearable," he said frantically. "It would kill me. I—"

"No, Eragon. It will not kill you. That much I know about your curse. However, we both have our duty; you to the Varden, and I to you. We cannot shirk it for the sake of mere pain. Far too much is at risk, and we can ill afford to fail." All Eragon could do was shake his head as panic threatened to overwhelm him. He tried to deny Oromis's words, but their truth was inescapable. "Eragon. You must accept this burden freely. Have you no one or nothing that you are willing to sacrifice yourself for?"

His first thought was of Saphira, but he was not doing this for her. Nor for Nasuada. Nor even for Arya. What drove him, then? When he had pledged fealty to Nasuada, he had done so for the good of Roran and the other people trapped within the Empire. But did they mean enough to him to put himself through such anguish? *Yes*, he decided. *Yes, they do, because I am the only one who has a chance to help them, and because I won't be free of Galbatorix's shadow until they are as well. And because this is my only purpose in life. What else would I do?* He shuddered as he mouthed the ghastly phrase, "I accept on behalf of those I fight for: the people of Alagaësia—of all races—who have suffered from Galbatorix's brutality. No matter the pain, I swear that I will study harder than any student you've had before."

Oromis nodded gravely. "I ask for nothing less." He looked at Glaedr for a moment, then said, "Stand and remove your tunic. Let me see what you are made of."

Wait, said Saphira. *Was Brom aware of your existence here, Master?* Eragon paused, struck by the possibility.

"Of course," said Oromis. "He was my pupil as a boy in Ilirea. I

275

am glad that you gave him a proper burial, for he had a hard life and few enough ever showed him kindness. I hope that he found peace before he entered the void."

Eragon slowly frowned. "Did you know Morzan as well?"

"He was my apprentice before Brom."

"And Galbatorix?"

"I was one of the Elders who denied him another dragon after his first was killed, but no, I never had the misfortune to teach him. He made sure to personally hunt down and kill each of his mentors."

Eragon wanted to inquire further, but he knew that it would be better to wait, so he stood and unlaced the top of his tunic. *It seems,* he said to Saphira, *that we will never learn all of Brom's secrets.* He shivered as he pulled off the tunic in the cool air, then squared his shoulders and lifted his chest.

Oromis circled him, stopping with an astonished exclamation as he saw the scar that crossed Eragon's back. "Did not Arya or one of the Varden's healers offer to remove this weal? You should not have to carry it."

"Arya did offer, but . . ." Eragon stopped, unable to articulate his feelings. Finally, he just said, "It's part of me now, just as Murtagh's scar is part of him."

"Murtagh's scar?"

"Murtagh bore a similar mark. It was inflicted when his father, Morzan, threw Zar'roc at him while he was only a child."

Oromis stared at him seriously for a long time before he nodded and moved on. "You have a fair amount of muscle, and you are not as lopsided as most swordsmen. Are you ambidextrous?"

"Not really, but I had to teach myself to fight with my left hand after I broke my wrist by Teirm."

"Good. That will save some time. Clasp your hands behind your back and lift them as high as possible." Eragon did as he was told, but the posture hurt his shoulders and he could barely make his hands meet. "Now bend forward while keeping your knees straight. Try to touch the ground." This was even harder for Eragon; he ended up bowed like a hunchback, with his arms hanging uselessly by his head while his hamstrings twinged and burned. His fingers were still nine or ten inches from the ground. "At least you can stretch without hurting yourself. I had not hoped for so much. You can perform a number of exercises for flexibility without overexerting. Yes."

Then Oromis addressed Saphira: "I would know your capabilities as well, dragon." He gave her a number of complex poses that had her contort every foot of her sinuous length in fantastic ways, culminating in a series of aerial acrobatics the likes of which Eragon had never seen before. Only a few things exceeded her ability, such as executing a backward loop while corkscrewing through the air.

When she landed, it was Glaedr who said, *I fear that we coddled the Riders. If our hatchlings had been forced to care for themselves in the wild—as you were, and so our ancestors were—then perhaps they would have possessed your skill.*

"No," said Oromis, "even if Saphira had been raised on Vroengard using the established methods, she would still be an extraordinary flier. I've rarely seen a dragon so naturally suited to the sky." Saphira blinked, then shuffled her wings and busied herself cleaning one of her claws in a manner that hid her head from view. "You have room to improve, as do we all, but little, very little." The elf reseated himself, his back perfectly straight.

For the next five hours, by Eragon's reckoning, Oromis delved into every aspect of his and Saphira's knowledge, from botany to woodworking to metallurgy and medicine, although he mainly concentrated on their grasp of history and the ancient language. The interrogation comforted Eragon, as it reminded him of how Brom used to quiz him during their long treks to Teirm and Dras-Leona.

When they broke for lunch, Oromis invited Eragon into his house, leaving the two dragons alone. The elf's quarters were barren except for those few essentials necessary for food, hygiene, and the pursuit of an intellectual life. Two entire walls were dotted with cubbyholes that held hundreds of scrolls. Next to the table hung a golden sheath—the same color as Glaedr's scales—and a matching sword with a blade the color of iridescent bronze.

On the inner pane of the door, set within the heart of the wood, was a flat panel one span high and two wide. It depicted a beautiful, towering city built against an escarpment and caught in the ruddy light of a rising harvest moon. The pitted lunar face was bisected by the horizon and appeared to sit on the ground like a maculated dome as large as a mountain. The picture was so clear and perfectly detailed, Eragon at first took it to be a magical window; it was only when he saw that the image was indeed static that he could accept it as a piece of art.

"Where is this?" he asked.

Oromis's slanted features tightened for an instant. "You would do well to memorize that landscape, Eragon, for there lies the heart of your misery. You see what was once our city of Ilirea. It was burned and abandoned during Du Fyrn Skulblaka and became the capital of the Broddring Kingdom and now is the black city of Urû'baen. I made that fairth on the night that I and others were forced to flee our home before Galbatorix arrived."

"You painted this . . . fairth?"

"No, no such thing. A fairth is an image fixed by magic upon a square of polished slate that is prepared beforehand with layers of pigments. The landscape upon that door is exactly how Ilirea presented itself to me at the moment I uttered my spell."

"And," said Eragon, unable to stop the flow of questions, "what was the Broddring Kingdom?"

Oromis's eyes widened with dismay. "You don't know?" Eragon shook his head. "How can you not? Considering your circumstances and the fear that Galbatorix wields among your people, I might understand that you were raised in darkness, ignorant of your heritage. But I cannot credit Brom with being so lax with your instruction as to neglect subjects that even the youngest elf or dwarf knows. The children of your Varden could tell me more about the past."

"Brom was more concerned with keeping me alive than teaching me about people who are already dead," retorted Eragon.

This drew silence from Oromis. Finally, he said, "Forgive me. I did not mean to impugn Brom's judgment, only I am impatient beyond reason; we have so little time, and each new thing you must learn reduces that which you can master during your tenure here." He opened a series of cupboards hidden within the curved wall and removed bread rolls and bowls of fruit, which he rowed out on the table. He paused for a moment over the food with his eyes closed before beginning to eat. "The Broddring Kingdom was the human's country before the Riders fell. After Galbatorix killed Vrael, he flew on Ilirea with the Forsworn and deposed King Angrenost, taking his throne and titles for his own. The Broddring Kingdom then formed the core of Galbatorix's conquests. He added Vroengard and other lands to the east and south to his holdings, creating the empire you are familiar with. Technically, the Broddring Kingdom still exists, though, at this point, I doubt that it is much more than a name on royal decrees."

Afraid to pester the elf with further inquiries, Eragon concentrated on his food. His face must have betrayed him, though, because Oromis said, "You remind me of Brom when I chose him as my apprentice. He was younger than you, only ten, but his curiosity was just as great. I doubt I heard aught from him for a year but *how, what, when,* and, above all else, *why.* Do not be shy to ask what lies in your heart."

"I want to know so much," whispered Eragon. "Who are you? Where do you come from? . . . Where did Brom come from? What was Morzan like? How, what, when, *why*? And I want to know everything about Vroengard and the Riders. Maybe then my own path will be clearer."

Silence fell between them as Oromis meticulously disassembled a blackberry, prying out one plump segment at a time. When the last corpuscle vanished between his port-red lips, he rubbed his hands flat together—"polishing his palms," as Garrow used to say—and said, "Know this about me, then: I was born some centuries past in our city of Luthivíra, which stood in the woods by Lake Tüdosten. At the age of twenty, like all elf children, I was presented

279

to the eggs that the dragons had given the Riders, and Glaedr hatched for me. We were trained as Riders, and for near a century, we traveled the world over, doing Vrael's will. Eventually, the day arrived when it was deemed appropriate for us to retire and pass on our experience to the next generation, so we took a position in Ilirea and taught new Riders, one or two at a time, until Galbatorix destroyed us."

"And Brom?"

"Brom came from a family of illuminators in Kuasta. His mother was Nelda and his father Holcomb. Kuasta is so isolated by the Spine from the rest of Alagaësia, it has become a peculiar place, full of strange customs and superstitions. When he was still new to Ilirea, Brom would knock on a door frame three times before entering or leaving a room. The human students teased him about it until he abandoned the practice along with some of his other habits.

"Morzan was my greatest failure. Brom idolized him. He never left his side, never contradicted him, and never believed that he could best Morzan in any venture. Morzan, I'm ashamed to admit— for it was within my power to stop—was aware of this and took advantage of Brom's devotion in a hundred different ways. He grew so proud and cruel that I considered separating him from Brom. But before I could, Morzan helped Galbatorix to steal a dragon hatchling, Shruikan, to replace the one Galbatorix had lost, killing the dragon's original Rider in the process. Morzan and Galbatorix then fled together, sealing our doom.

"You cannot begin to fathom the effect Morzan's betrayal had on Brom until you understand the depth of Brom's affection for him. And when Galbatorix at last revealed himself and the Forsworn killed Brom's dragon, Brom focused all of his anger and pain on the one who he felt was responsible for the destruction of his world: Morzan."

Oromis paused, his face grave. "Do you know why losing your dragon, or vice versa, usually kills the survivor?"

"I can imagine," said Eragon. He quailed at the thought.

"The pain is shock enough—although it isn't always a factor—but what really causes the damage is feeling part of your mind, part of your identity, die. When it happened to Brom, I fear that he went mad for a time. After I was captured and escaped, I brought him to Ellesméra for safety, but he refused to stay, instead marching with our army to the plains of Ilirea, where King Evandar was slain.

"The confusion then was indescribable. Galbatorix was busy consolidating his power, the dwarves were in retreat, the southwest was a mass of war as the humans rebelled and fought to create Surda, and we had just lost our king. Driven by his desire for vengeance, Brom sought to use the turmoil to his advantage. He gathered together many of those who had been exiled, freed some who had been imprisoned, and with them he formed the Varden. He led them for a few years, then surrendered the position to another so that he was free to pursue his true passion, which was Morzan's downfall. Brom personally killed three of the Forsworn, including Morzan, and he was responsible for the deaths of five others. He was rarely happy during his life, but he was a good Rider and a good man, and I am honored to have known him."

"I never heard his name mentioned in connection to the Forsworn's deaths," objected Eragon.

"Galbatorix did not want to publicize the fact that any still existed who could defeat his servants. Much of his power resides in the appearance of invulnerability."

Once again, Eragon was forced to revise his conception of Brom, from the village storyteller that Eragon had first taken him to be, to the warrior and magician he had traveled with, to the Rider he was at last revealed as, and now firebrand, revolutionary leader, and assassin. It was hard to reconcile all of those roles. *I feel as if I barely knew him. I wish that we had had a chance to talk about all of this at least once.* "He was a good man," agreed Eragon.

He looked out one of the round windows that faced the edge of the cliff and allowed the afternoon warmth to suffuse the room. He watched Saphira, noting how she acted with Glaedr, seeming both shy and coy. One moment she would twist around to examine some feature of the clearing, the next she would shuffle her wings and make small advances on the larger dragon, weaving her head from side to side, the tip of her tail twitching as if she were about to pounce on a deer. She reminded Eragon of a kitten trying to bait an old tomcat into playing with her, only Glaedr remained impassive throughout her machinations.

Saphira, he said. She responded with a distracted flicker of her thoughts, barely acknowledging him. *Saphira, answer me.*

What?

I know you're excited, but don't make a fool of yourself.

You've made a fool of yourself plenty of times, she snapped.

Her reply was so unexpected, it stunned him. It was the sort of casually cruel remark that humans often make, but that he had never thought to hear from her. He finally managed to say, *That doesn't make it any better.* She grunted and closed her mind to his, although he could still feel the thread of her emotions connecting them.

Eragon returned to himself to find Oromis's gray eyes heavy upon him. The elf's gaze was so perceptive, Eragon was sure that Oromis understood what had transpired. Eragon forced a smile and motioned toward Saphira. "Even though we're linked, I can never predict what she's going to do. The more I learn about her, the more I realize how different we are."

Then Oromis made his first statement that Eragon thought was truly wise: "Those whom we love are often the most alien to us." The elf paused. "She is very young, as are you. It took Glaedr and I decades before we fully understood each other. A Rider's bond with his dragon is like any relationship—that is, a work in progress. Do you trust her?"

"With my life."

"And does she trust you?"

"Yes."

"Then humor her. You were brought up as an orphan. She was brought up to believe that she was the last sane individual of her entire race. And now she has been proved wrong. Don't be surprised if it takes some months before she stops pestering Glaedr and returns her attention to you."

Eragon rolled a blueberry between his thumb and forefinger; his appetite had vanished. "Why don't elves eat meat?"

"Why should we?" Oromis held up a strawberry and rotated it so that the light reflected off its dimpled skin and illuminated the tiny hairs that bearded the fruit. "Everything that we need or want we sing from the plants, including our food. It would be barbaric to make animals suffer that we might have additional courses on the table. . . . Our choice will make greater sense to you before long."

Eragon frowned. He had always eaten meat and did not look forward to living solely on fruit and vegetables while in Ellesméra. "Don't you miss the taste?"

"You cannot miss that which you have never had."

"What about Glaedr, though? He can't live off grass."

"No, but neither does he needlessly inflict pain. We each do the best we can with what we are given. You cannot help who or what you are born as."

"And Islanzadí? Her cape was made of swan feathers."

"Loose feathers gathered over the course of many years. No birds were killed to make her garment."

They finished the meal, and Eragon helped Oromis to scour the dishes clean with sand. As the elf stacked them in the cupboard, he asked, "Did you bathe this morning?" The question startled Eragon, but he answered that no, he had not. "Please do so tomorrow then, and every day following."

"Every day! The water's too cold for that. I'll catch the ague."

Oromis eyed him oddly. "Then make it warmer."

Now it was Eragon's turn to look askance. "I'm not strong enough to heat an entire stream with magic," he protested.

The house echoed as Oromis laughed. Outside, Glaedr swung his head toward the window and inspected the elf, then returned to his earlier position. "I assume that you explored your quarters last night." Eragon nodded. "And you saw a small room with a depression in the floor?"

"I thought that it might be for washing clothes or linens."

"It is for washing *you*. Two nozzles are concealed in the side of the wall above the hollow. Open them and you can bathe in water of any temperature. Also," he gestured at Eragon's chin, "while you are my student, I expect you to keep yourself clean-shaven until you can grow a full beard—if you so choose—and not look like a tree with half its leaves blown off. Elves do not shave, but I will have a razor and mirror found and sent to you."

Wincing at the blow to his pride, Eragon agreed. They returned outside, whereupon Oromis looked at Glaedr and the dragon said, *We have decided upon a curriculum for Saphira and you.*

The elf said, "You will start—"

—an hour after sunrise tomorrow, in the time of the Red Lily. Return here then.

"And bring the saddle that Brom made for you, Saphira," continued Oromis. "Do what you wish in the meantime; Ellesméra holds many wonders for a foreigner, if you care to see them."

"I'll keep that in mind," said Eragon, bowing his head. "Before I go, Master, I want to thank you for helping me in Tronjheim after I killed Durza. I doubt that I would have survived without your assistance. I am in your debt."

We are both in your debt, added Saphira.

Oromis smiled slightly and inclined his head.

THE SECRET LIVES OF ANTS

The moment that Oromis and Glaedr were out of sight, Saphira said, *Eragon, another dragon! Can you believe it?*

He patted her shoulder. *It's wonderful.* High above Du Weldenvarden, the only sign of habitation in the forest was an occasional ghostly plume of smoke that rose from the crown of a tree and soon faded into clear air.

I never expected to encounter another dragon, except for Shruikan. Maybe rescue the eggs from Galbatorix, yes, but that was the extent of my hopes. And now this! She wriggled underneath him with joy. *Glaedr is incredible, isn't he? He's so old and strong and his scales are so bright. He must be two, no, three times bigger than me. Did you see his claws? They . . .*

She continued on in that manner for several minutes, waxing eloquent about Glaedr's attributes. But stronger than her words were the emotions Eragon sensed roiling within her: eagerness and enthusiasm, twined over what he could only identify as a longing adoration.

Eragon tried to tell Saphira what he had learned from Oromis— since he knew that she had not paid attention—but he found it impossible to change the subject of conversation. He sat silently on her back, the world an emerald ocean below, and felt himself the loneliest man in existence.

Back at their quarters, Eragon decided against any sightseeing; he was far too tired from the day's events and the weeks of traveling.

And Saphira was more than content to sit on her bed and chatter about Glaedr while he examined the mysteries of the elves' wash closet.

Morning came, and with it a package wrapped in onionskin paper containing the razor and mirror that Oromis had promised. The blade was of elvish make, so it needed no sharpening or stropping. Grimacing, Eragon first bathed in steaming hot water, then held up the mirror and confronted his visage.

I look older. Older and worn. Not only that, but his features had become far more angled, giving him an ascetic, hawklike appearance. He was no elf, but neither would anyone take him to be a purebred human if they inspected him closely. Pulling back his hair, he bared his ears, which now tapered to slight points, more evidence of how his bond with Saphira had changed him. He touched one ear, letting his fingers wander over the unfamiliar shape.

It was difficult for him to accept the transformation of his flesh. Even though he had known it would occur—and occasionally welcomed the prospect as the last confirmation that he was a Rider—the reality of it filled him with confusion. He resented the fact that he had no say in how his body was being altered, yet at the same time he was curious where the process would take him. Also, he was aware that he was still in the midst of his own, human adolescence, and its attendant realm of mysteries and difficulties.

When will I finally know who and what I am?

He placed the edge of the razor against his cheek, as he had seen Garrow do, and dragged it across his skin. The hairs came free, but they were cut long and ragged. He altered the angle of the blade and tried again with a bit more success.

When he reached his chin, though, the razor slipped in his hand and cut him from the corner of his mouth to the underside of his jaw. He howled and dropped the razor, clapping his hand over the incision, which poured blood down his neck. Spitting the words past bared teeth, he said, "Waíse heill." The pain quickly receded as magic knitted his flesh back together, though his heart still pounded from the shock.

Eragon! cried Saphira. She forced her head and shoulders into the vestibule and nosed open the door to the closet, flaring her nostrils at the scent of blood.

I'll live, he assured her.

She eyed the sanguine water. *Be more careful. I'd rather you were as ragged as a molting deer than have you decapitate yourself for the sake of a close shave.*

So would I. Go on, I'm fine.

Saphira grunted and reluctantly withdrew.

Eragon sat, glaring at the razor. Finally, he muttered, "Forget this." Composing himself, he reviewed his store of words from the ancient language, selected those that he needed, and then allowed his invented spell to roll off his tongue. A faint stream of black powder fell from his face as his stubble crumbled into dust, leaving his cheeks perfectly smooth.

Satisfied, Eragon went and saddled Saphira, who immediately took to the air, aiming their course toward the Crags of Tel'naeír. They landed before the hut and were met by Oromis and Glaedr.

Oromis examined Saphira's saddle. He traced each strap with his fingers, pausing on the stitching and buckles, and then pronounced it passable handiwork considering how and when it had been constructed. "Brom was always clever with his hands. Use this saddle when you must travel with great speed. But when comfort is allowed—" He stepped into his hut for a moment and reappeared carrying a thick, molded saddle decorated with gilt designs along the seat and leg pieces. "—use this. It was crafted in Vroengard and imbued with many spells so that it will never fail you in time of need."

Eragon staggered under the weight of the saddle as he received it from Oromis. It had the same general shape as Brom's, with a row of buckles—intended to immobilize his legs—hanging from each side. The deep seat was sculpted out of the leather in such a way that he could fly for hours with ease, both sitting upright and lying flat against Saphira's neck. Also, the straps encircling Saphira's chest were rigged with slips and knots so that they could extend to accommodate years of growth. A series of broad ties on either side of the head of the saddle caught Eragon's attention. He asked their purpose.

Glaedr rumbled, *Those secure your wrists and arms so that you are not killed like a rat shaken to death when Saphira performs a complex maneuver.*

Oromis helped Eragon relieve Saphira of her current saddle. "Saphira, you will go with Glaedr today, and I will work with Eragon here."

As you wish, she said, and crowed with excitement. Heaving his golden bulk off the ground, Glaedr soared off to the north, Saphira close behind.

Oromis did not give Eragon long to ponder Saphira's departure; the elf marched him to a square of hard-packed dirt beneath a willow tree at the far side of the clearing. Standing opposite him in the square, Oromis said, "What I am about to show you is called the Rimgar, or the Dance of Snake and Crane. It is a series of poses that we developed to prepare our warriors for combat, although all elves use it now to maintain their health and fitness. The Rimgar consists of four levels, each more difficult than the last. We will start with the first."

Apprehension for the coming ordeal sickened Eragon to the point where he could barely move. He clenched his fists and hunched his shoulders, his scar tugging at the skin of his back as he glared between his feet.

"Relax," advised Oromis. Eragon jerked open his hands and let them hang limply at the end of his rigid arms. "I asked you to relax, Eragon. You can't do the Rimgar if you are as stiff as a piece of rawhide."

"Yes, Master." Eragon grimaced and reluctantly loosened his muscles and joints, although a knot of tension remained coiled in his belly.

"Place your feet together and your arms at your sides. Look straight ahead. Now take a deep breath and lift your arms over your head so that your palms meet. . . . Yes, like that. Exhale and bend down as far as you can, put your palms on the ground, take another breath . . . and jump back. Good. Breathe in and bend up, looking toward the sky . . . and exhale, lifting your hips until you form a triangle. Breathe in through the back of your throat . . . and out. In . . . and out. In . . ."

To Eragon's utter relief, the stances proved gentle enough to hold without igniting the pain in his back, yet challenging enough that sweat beaded his forehead and he panted for breath. He found himself grinning with joy at his reprieve. His wariness evaporated and he flowed through the postures—most of which far exceeded his flexibility—with more energy and confidence than he had possessed since before the battle in Farthen Dûr. *Maybe I've healed!*

Oromis performed the Rimgar with him, displaying a level of strength and flexibility that astounded Eragon, especially for one so old. The elf could touch his forehead to his toes. Throughout the exercise, Oromis remained impeccably composed, as if he were doing no more than strolling down a garden path. His instruction was calmer and more patient than Brom's, yet completely unyielding. No deviation was allowed from the correct path.

"Let us wash the sweat from our limbs," said Oromis when they finished.

Going to the stream by the house, they quickly disrobed. Eragon surreptitiously watched the elf, curious as to what he looked like without his clothes. Oromis was very thin, yet his muscles were perfectly defined, etched under his skin with the hard lines of a woodcut. No hair grew upon his chest or legs, not even around his groin. His body seemed almost freakish to Eragon, compared to the men he was used to seeing in Carvahall—although it had a certain refined elegance to it, like that of a wildcat.

When they were clean, Oromis took Eragon deep into Du Weldenvarden to a hollow where the dark trees leaned inward, obscuring the sky behind branches and veils of snarled lichen. Their feet sank into the moss above their ankles. All was silent about them.

Pointing to a white stump with a flat, polished top three yards across that rested in the center of the hollow, Oromis said, "Sit here." Eragon did as he was told. "Cross your legs and close your eyes." The world went dark around him. From his right, he heard Oromis whisper, "Open your mind, Eragon. Open your mind and listen to the world around you, to the thoughts of every being in this glade, from the ants in the trees to the worms in the ground. Listen until you can hear them all and you understand their purpose and nature. Listen, and when you hear no more, come tell me what you have learned."

Then the forest was quiet.

Unsure if Oromis had left, Eragon tentatively lowered the barriers around his mind and reached out with his consciousness, like he did when trying to contact Saphira at a great distance. Initially only a void surrounded him, but then pricks of light and warmth began to appear in the darkness, strengthening until he sat in the midst of a galaxy of swirling constellations, each bright point representing a life. Whenever he had contacted other beings with his mind, like Cadoc, Snowfire, or Solembum, the focus had always been on the one he wanted to communicate with. But this . . . this was as if he had been standing deaf in the midst of a crowd and now he could hear the rivers of conversation whirling around him.

He felt suddenly vulnerable; he was completely exposed to the world. Anyone or anything that might want to leap into his mind and control him could now do so. He tensed unconsciously, withdrawing back into himself, and his awareness of the hollow vanished. Remembering one of Oromis's lessons, Eragon slowed his breathing and monitored the sweep of his lungs until he had relaxed enough to reopen his mind.

Of all the lives he could sense, the majority were, by far, insects. Their sheer number astounded him. Tens of thousands dwelled in a square foot of moss, teeming millions throughout the rest of the small hollow, and uncounted masses beyond. Their abundance actually frightened Eragon. He had always known that humans were scarce and beleaguered in Alagaësia, but he had never imagined that they were so outnumbered by even *beetles*.

Since they were one of the few insects that he was familiar with, and Oromis had mentioned them, Eragon concentrated his attention on the columns of red ants marching across the ground and up the stems of a wild rosebush. What he gleaned from them were not so much thoughts—their brains were too primitive—but urges: the urge to find food and avoid injury, the urge to defend one's territory, the urge to mate. By examining the ants' instincts, he could begin to puzzle out their behavior.

It fascinated him to discover that—except for the few individuals exploring outside the borders of their province—the ants knew exactly where they were going. He was unable to ascertain what mechanism guided them, but they followed clearly defined paths from their nest to food and back. Their source of food was another surprise. As he had expected, the ants killed and scavenged other insects, but most of their efforts were directed toward the cultivation of . . . of *something* that dotted the rosebush. Whatever the lifeform was, it was barely large enough for him to sense. He focused all of his strength on it in an attempt to identify it and satisfy his curiosity.

The answer was so simple, he laughed out loud when he comprehended it: *aphids*. The ants were acting as shepherds for aphids, driving and protecting them, as well as extracting sustenance from them by massaging the aphids' bellies with the tips of their antennae. Eragon could hardly believe it, but the longer he watched, the more he became convinced that he was correct.

He traced the ants underground into their complex matrix of warrens and studied how they cared for a certain member of their species that was several times bigger than a normal ant. However, he was unable to determine the insect's purpose; all he could see were servants swarming around it, rotating it, and removing the specks of matter it produced at regular intervals.

After a time, Eragon decided that he had gleaned all the information from the ants that he could—unless he was willing to sit there for the rest of the day—and was about to return to his body when a squirrel jumped into the glade. Its appearance was like a blast of light to him, attuned as he was to the insects. Stunned, he was overwhelmed by a rush of sensations and feelings from the animal. He smelled the forest with its nose, felt the bark give under his hooked claws and the air swish through his upraised plume of a tail. Compared to an ant, the squirrel burned with energy and possessed unquestionable intelligence.

Then it leaped to another branch and faded from his awareness.

The forest seemed much darker and quieter than before when Eragon opened his eyes. He took a deep breath and looked about, appreciating for the first time how much life existed in the world. Unfolding his cramped legs, he walked over to the rosebush.

He bent down and examined the branches and twigs. Sure enough, aphids and their crimson guardians clung to them. And near the base of the plant was the mound of pine needles that marked the entrance to the ants' lair. It was strange to see with his own eyes; none of it betrayed the numerous and subtle interactions that he was now aware of.

Engrossed in his thoughts, Eragon returned to the clearing, wondering what he might be crushing under his feet with every step. When he emerged from under the trees' shelter, he was startled by how far the sun had fallen. *I must have been sitting there for at least three hours.*

He found Oromis in his hut, writing with a goose-feather quill. The elf finished his line, then wiped the nib of the quill clean, stoppered his ink, and asked, "And what did you hear, Eragon?"

Eragon was eager to share. As he described his experience, he heard his voice rise with enthusiasm over the details of the ants' society. He recounted everything that he could recall, down to the minutest and most inconsequential observation, proud of the information that he had gathered.

When he finished, Oromis raised an eyebrow. "Is that all?"

"I . . ." Dismay gripped Eragon as he understood that he had somehow missed the point of the exercise. "Yes, Ebrithil."

"And what about the other organisms in the earth and the air? Can you tell me what they were doing while your ants tended their droves?"

"No, Ebrithil."

"Therein lies your mistake. You must become aware of all things equally and not blinker yourself in order to concentrate on a particular subject. This is an essential lesson, and until you master it, you will meditate on the stump for an hour each day."

"How will I know when I have mastered it?"

"When you can watch one and know all."

Oromis motioned for Eragon to join him at the table, then set a fresh sheet of paper before him, along with a quill and a bottle of ink. "So far you have made do with an incomplete knowledge of the ancient language. Not that any of us knows all the words in the language, but you must be familiar with its grammar and structure so that you do not kill yourself through an incorrectly placed verb or similar mistake. I do not expect you to speak our language like an elf—that would take a lifetime—but I do expect you to achieve unconscious competence. That is, you must be able to use it without thinking.

"In addition, you must learn to read and write the ancient language. Not only will this help you to memorize words, it is an essential skill if you need to compose an especially long spell and you don't trust your memory, or if you find such a spell recorded and you want to use it.

"Every race has evolved their own system of writing the ancient language. The dwarves use their runic alphabet, as do humans. They are only makeshift techniques, though, and are incapable of expressing the language's true subtleties as well as our Liduen

Kvaedhí, the Poetic Script. The Liduen Kvaedhí was designed to be as elegant, beautiful, and precise as possible. It is composed of forty-two different shapes that represent various sounds. These shapes can be combined in a nearly infinite range of glyphs that represent both individual words and entire phrases. The symbol on your ring is one such glyph. The symbol on Zar'roc is another. . . . Let us start: What are the basic vowel sounds of the ancient language?"

"What?"

Eragon's ignorance of the underpinnings of the ancient language quickly became apparent. When he had traveled with Brom, the old storyteller had concentrated on having Eragon memorize lists of words that he might need to survive, as well as perfecting his pronunciation. In those two areas, he excelled, but he could not even explain the difference between a definite and indefinite article. If the gaps in his education frustrated Oromis, the elf did not betray it through word or action, but labored persistently to mend them.

At a certain point during the lesson, Eragon commented, "I've never needed very many words in my spells; Brom said it was a gift that I could do so much with just *brisingr*. I think the most I ever said in the ancient language was when I spoke to Arya in her mind and when I blessed an orphan in Farthen Dûr."

"You blessed a child in the ancient language?" asked Oromis, suddenly alert. "Do you remember how you worded this blessing?"

"Aye."

"Recite it for me." Eragon did so, and a look of pure horror engulfed Oromis. He exclaimed, "You used *skölir*! Are you sure? Wasn't it *sköliro*?"

Eragon frowned. "No, *skölir*. Why shouldn't I have used it? *Skölir* means *shielded*. '. . . and may you be shielded from misfortune.' It was a good blessing."

"That was no blessing, but a curse." Oromis was more agitated than Eragon had ever seen him. "The suffix *o* forms the past tense of verbs ending with *r* and *i*. *Sköliro* means *shielded*, but *skölir* means *shield*. What you said was 'May luck and happiness follow you and may you be a *shield* from misfortune.' Instead of protecting this

294

child from the vagaries of fate, you condemned her to be a sacrifice for others, to absorb their misery and suffering so that they might live in peace."

No, no! It can't be! Eragon recoiled from the possibility. "The effect a spell has isn't only determined by the word's sense, but also by your intent, and I didn't intend to harm—"

"You cannot gainsay a word's inherent nature. Twist it, yes. Guide it, yes. But not contravene its definition to imply the very opposite." Oromis pressed his fingers together and stared at the table, his lips reduced to a flat white line. "I will trust that you did *not* mean harm, else I would refuse to teach you further. If you were honest and your heart was pure, then this blessing may cause less evil than I fear, though it will still be the nucleus of more pain than either of us could wish."

Violent trembling overtook Eragon as he realized what he had done to the child's life. "It may not undo my mistake," he said, "but perhaps it will alleviate it; Saphira marked the girl on the brow, just like she marked my palm with the gedwëy ignasia."

For the first time in his life, Eragon witnessed an elf dumbstruck. Oromis's gray eyes widened, his mouth opened, and he clutched the arms of his chair until the wood groaned with protest. "One who bears the sign of the Riders, and yet is not a Rider," he murmured. "In all my years, I have never met anyone such as the two of you. Every decision you make seems to have an impact far beyond what anyone could anticipate. You change the world with your whims."

"Is that good or bad?"

"Neither, it just is. Where is the babe now?"

It took a moment for Eragon to compose his thoughts. "With the Varden, either in Farthen Dûr or Surda. Do you think that Saphira's mark will help her?"

"I know not," said Oromis. "No precedent exists to draw upon for wisdom."

"There must be ways to remove the blessing, to negate a spell." Eragon was almost pleading.

"There are. But for them to be most effective, you should be the one to apply them, and you cannot be spared here. Even under the best of circumstances, remnants of your magic will haunt this girl evermore. Such is the power of the ancient language." He paused. "I see that you understand the gravity of the situation, so I will say this only once: you bear full responsibility for this girl's doom, and, because of the wrong you did her, it is incumbent upon you to help her if ever the opportunity should arise. By the Riders' law, she is your shame as surely as if you had begotten her out of wedlock, a disgrace among humans, if I remember correctly."

"Aye," whispered Eragon. "I understand." *I understand that I forced a defenseless baby to pursue a certain destiny without ever giving her a choice in the matter. Can someone be truly good if they never have the opportunity to act badly? I made her a slave.* He also knew that if he had been bound in that manner without permission, he would hate his jailer with every fiber of his being.

"Then we will speak of this no more."

"Yes, Ebrithil."

Eragon was still subdued, even depressed, by the end of the day. He barely looked up when they went outside to meet Saphira and Glaedr upon their return. The trees shook from the fury of the gale that the two dragons created with their wings. Saphira seemed proud of herself; she arched her neck and pranced toward Eragon, opening her chops in a lupine grin.

A stone cracked under Glaedr's weight as the ancient dragon turned a giant eye—as large as a dinner platter—on Eragon and asked, *What are the rules three to spotting downdrafts, and the rules five for escaping them?*

Startled out of his reverie, Eragon could only blink dumbly. "I don't know."

Then Oromis confronted Saphira and asked, "What creatures do ants farm, and how do they extract food from them?"

I wouldn't know, declared Saphira. She sounded affronted.

A gleam of anger leaped into Oromis's eyes and he crossed his arms, though his expression remained calm. "After all the two of you have done together, I would think that you had learned the most basic lesson of being Shur'tugal: Share everything with your partner. Would you cut off your right arm? Would you fly with only one wing? Never. Then why would you ignore the bond that links you? By doing so, you reject your greatest gift and your advantage over any single opponent. Nor should you just talk to each other with your minds, but rather mingle your consciousnesses until you act and think as one. I expect both of you to know what either one of you is taught."

"What about our privacy?" objected Eragon.

Privacy? said Glaedr. *Keep your thoughts to thyself when you leave here, if it pleases you, but while we tutor you, you have no privacy.*

Eragon looked at Saphira, feeling even worse than before. She avoided his gaze, then stamped a foot and faced him directly. *What?*

They're right. We have been negligent.

It's not my fault.

I didn't say that it was. She had guessed his opinion, though. He resented the attention she lavished on Glaedr and how it drew her away from him. *We'll do better, won't we?*

Of course! she snapped.

She declined to offer Oromis and Glaedr an apology, though, leaving the task to Eragon. "We won't disappoint you again."

"See that you don't. You will be tested tomorrow on what the other learned." Oromis revealed a round wood bauble nestled in the middle of his palm. "So long as you take care to wind it regularly, this device will wake you at the proper time each morning. Return here as soon as you have bathed and eaten."

The bauble was surprisingly heavy when Eragon took it. The size of a walnut, it had been carved with deep whorls around a knob wrought in the likeness of a moss-rose blossom. He turned the knob experimentally and heard three clicks as a hidden ratchet advanced. "Thank you," he said.

UNDER THE MENOA TREE

After Eragon and Saphira had said their farewells, they flew back to their tree house with Saphira's new saddle dangling between her front claws. Without acknowledging the fact, they gradually opened their minds and allowed their connection to widen and deepen, though neither of them consciously reached for the other. Eragon's tumultuous emotions must have been strong enough for Saphira to sense anyway, though, for she asked, *What happened, then?*

A throbbing pain built up behind his eyes as he explained the terrible crime he had committed in Farthen Dûr. Saphira was as appalled by it as he was. He said, *Your gift may help that girl, but what I did is inexcusable and will only hurt her.*

The blame isn't all yours. I share your knowledge of the ancient language, and I didn't spot the error any more than you did. When Eragon remained silent, she added, *At least your back didn't cause any trouble today. Be grateful for that.*

He grunted, unwilling to be tempted out of his black mood. *And what did you learn this fine day?*

How to identify and avoid dangerous weather patterns. She paused, apparently ready to share the memories with him, but he was too busy worrying about his distorted blessing to inquire further. Nor could he bear the thought of being so intimate right then. When he did not pursue the matter, Saphira withdrew into a taciturn silence.

Back in their bedroom, he found a tray of food by the screen door, as he had the previous night. Carrying the tray to his bed—which had been remade with fresh linens—he settled down to eat, cursing the lack of meat. Already sore from the Rimgar, he propped himself up with pillows and was about to take his first bite when there came a gentle rapping at the opening to his chamber. "Enter," he growled. He took a drink of water.

Eragon nearly choked as Arya stepped through the doorway. She had abandoned the leather clothes she usually wore in favor of a soft green tunic cinched at the waist with a girdle adorned with moonstones. She had also removed her customary headband, allowing her hair to tumble around her face and over her shoulders. The biggest change, however, was not so much in her dress but her bearing; the brittle tension that had permeated her demeanor ever since Eragon first met her was now gone.

She seemed to have finally relaxed.

He scrambled to his feet, noticing that her own were bare. "Arya! Why are you here?"

Touching her first two fingers to her lips, she said, "Do you plan on spending another evening inside?"

"I—"

"You have been in Ellesméra for three days now, and yet you have seen nothing of our city. I know that you always wished to explore it. Set aside your weariness this once and accompany me." Gliding toward him, she took Zar'roc from where it lay by his side and beckoned to him.

He rose from the bed and followed her into the vestibule, where they descended through the trapdoor and down the precipitous staircase that wound around the rough tree trunk. Overhead, the gathering clouds glowed with the sun's last rays before it was extinguished behind the edge of the world.

A piece of bark fell on Eragon's head and he looked up to see Saphira leaning out of their bedroom, gripping the wood with her claws. Without opening her wings, she sprang into the air and dropped the hundred or so feet to the ground, landing in a thunderous cloud of dirt. *I'm coming.*

"Of course," said Arya, as if she expected nothing less. Eragon scowled; he had wanted to be alone with her, but he knew better than to complain.

They walked under the trees, where dusk already extended its tendrils from inside hollow logs, dark crevices in boulders, and the underside of knobby eaves. Here and there, a gemlike lantern twinkled within the side of a tree or at the end of a branch, casting gentle pools of light on either side of the path.

Elves worked on various projects in and around the lanterns' radius, solitary except for a few, rare couples. Several elves sat high in the trees, playing mellifluous tunes on their reed pipes, while others stared at the sky with peaceful expressions—neither awake nor asleep. One elf sat cross-legged before a pottery wheel that whirled round and round with a steady rhythm while a delicate urn took form beneath his hands. The werecat, Maud, crouched beside him in the shadows, watching his progress. Her eyes flared silver as she looked at Eragon and Saphira. The elf followed her gaze and nodded to them without halting his work.

Through the trees, Eragon glimpsed an elf—man or woman, he could not tell—squatting on a rock in the middle of a stream, muttering a spell over the orb of glass clutched in its hands. He twisted his neck in an attempt to get an unobstructed view, but the spectacle had already vanished into the dark.

"What," asked Eragon, keeping his voice low so as to not disturb anyone, "do most elves do for a living or profession?"

Arya answered just as quietly. "Our strength with magic grants us as much leisure as we desire. We neither hunt nor farm, and, as a result, we spend our days working to master our interests, whatever they might be. Very little exists that we must strive for."

Through a tunnel of dogwood draped with creepers, they entered the enclosed atrium of a house grown out of a ring of trees. An open-walled hut occupied the center of the atrium, which sheltered a forge and an assortment of tools that Eragon knew even Horst would covet.

An elf woman held a pair of small tongs in a nest of molten coals, working bellows with her right hand. With uncanny speed, she pulled the tongs from the fire—revealing a ring of white-hot steel clamped in the pincers' jaws—looped the ring through the edge of an incomplete mail corselet hung over the anvil, grasped a hammer, and welded shut the open ends of the ring with a blow and a burst of sparks.

Only then did Arya approach. "Atra esterní ono thelduin."

The elf faced them, her neck and cheek lit from underneath by the coals' bloody light. Like taut wires embedded in her skin, her face was scribed with a delicate pattern of lines—the greatest display of age Eragon had seen in an elf. She gave no response to Arya, which he knew was offensive and discourteous, especially since the queen's daughter had honored her by speaking first.

"Rhunön-elda, I have brought you the newest Rider, Eragon Shadeslayer."

"I heard you were dead," said Rhunön to Arya. Rhunön's voice guttered and rasped unlike any other elf's. It reminded Eragon of the old men of Carvahall who sat on the porches outside their houses, smoking pipes and telling stories.

Arya smiled. "When did you last leave your house, Rhunön?"

"You should know. It was that Midsummer's Feast you forced me to attend."

"That was three years ago."

"Was it?" Rhunön frowned as she banked the coals and covered them with a grated lid. "Well, what of it? I find company trying. A gaggle of meaningless chatter that . . ." She glared at Arya. "Why are we speaking this foul language? I suppose you want me to forge a sword for him? You know I swore to never create instruments of death again, not after that traitor of a Rider and the destruction he wreaked with my blade."

"Eragon already has a sword," said Arya. She raised her arm and presented Zar'roc to the smith.

Rhunön took Zar'roc with a look of wonder. She caressed the wine-red sheath, lingered on the black symbol etched into it, rubbed a bit of dirt from the hilt, then wrapped her fingers around the handle and drew the sword with all the authority of a warrior. She sighted down each of Zar'roc's edges and flexed the blade between her hands until Eragon feared it might break. Then, in a single movement, Rhunön swung Zar'roc over her head and brought it down upon the tongs on her anvil, riving them in half with a resounding ring.

"Zar'roc," said Rhunön. "I remember thee." She cradled the weapon like a mother would her firstborn. "As perfect as the day you were finished." Turning her back, she looked up at the knotted branches while she traced the curves of the pommel. "My entire life I spent hammering these swords out of ore. Then *he* came and destroyed them. Centuries of effort obliterated in an instant. So far as I knew, only four examples of my art still existed. *His* sword, Oromis's, and two others guarded by families who managed to rescue them from the Wyrdfell."

Wyrdfell? Eragon dared ask Arya with his mind.

Another name for the Forsworn.

Rhunön turned on Eragon. "Now Zar'roc has returned to me. Of all my creations, this I least expected to hold again, save for *his*. How came you to possess Morzan's sword?"

"It was given to me by Brom."

"Brom?" She hefted Zar'roc. "Brom . . . I remember Brom. He begged me to replace the sword he had lost. Truly, I wished to help him, but I had already taken my oath. My refusal angered him beyond reason. Oromis had to knock him unconscious before he would leave."

Eragon seized on the information with interest. "Your handiwork has served me well, Rhunön-elda. I would be long dead were it not for Zar'roc. I killed the Shade Durza with it."

"Did you now? Then some good has come of it." Sheathing Zar'roc, Rhunön returned it to him, though not without reluctance, then looked past him to Saphira. "Ah. Well met, Skulblaka."

Well met, Rhunön-elda.

Without bothering to ask permission, Rhunön went up to Saphira's shoulder and tapped a scale with one of her blunt fingernails, twisting her head from side to side in an attempt to peer into the translucent pebble. "Good color. Not like those brown dragons, all muddy and dark. Properly speaking, a Rider's sword should match the hue of his dragon, and this blue would have made a gorgeous blade. . . ." The thought seemed to drain the energy from her. She returned to the anvil and stared at the wrecked tongs, as if the will to replace them had deserted her.

Eragon felt that it would be wrong to end the conversation on such a depressing note, but he could not think of a tactful way to change the subject. The glimmering corselet caught his attention and, as he studied it, he was astonished to see that every ring was welded shut. Because the tiny links cooled so quickly, they usually had to be welded before being attached to the main piece of mail, which meant that the finest mail—such as Eragon's hauberk—was composed of links that were alternately welded and riveted closed. Unless, it seemed, the smith possessed an elf's speed and precision.

Eragon said, "I've never seen the equal of your mail, not even among the dwarves. How do you have the patience to weld every link? Why don't you just use magic and save yourself the work?"

He hardly expected the burst of passion that animated Rhunön. She tossed her short-cropped hair and said, "And rob myself of all pleasure in this task? Aye, every other elf and I could use magic to satisfy our desires—and some do—but then what meaning is there in life? How would you fill your time? Tell me."

"I don't know," he confessed.

"By pursuing that which you love the most. When you can have anything you want by uttering a few words, the goal matters not, only the journey to it. A lesson for you. You'll face the same dilemma one day, if you live long enough. . . . Now begone! I am weary of this talk." With that Rhunön plucked the lid off the forge, retrieved a new pair of tongs, and immersed a ring in the coals while she worked the bellows with single-minded intensity.

"Rhunön-elda," said Arya, "remember, I will return for you on the eve of the Agaetí Blödhren." A grunt was her only reply.

The rhythmic peal of steel on steel, as lonely as the cry of a death bird in the night, accompanied them back through the dogwood tunnel and onto the path. Behind them, Rhunön was no more than a black figure bowed over the sullen glow of her forge.

"She made all the Riders' swords?" asked Eragon. "Every last one?"

"That and more. She's the greatest smith who has ever lived. I thought that you should meet her, for her sake and yours."

"Thank you."

Is she always so brusque? asked Saphira.

Arya laughed. "Always. For her, nothing matters except her craft, and she's famously impatient with anything—or anyone—that interferes with it. Her eccentricities are well tolerated, though, because of her incredible skill and accomplishments."

While she spoke, Eragon tried to work out the meaning of *Agaetí Blödhren*. He was fairly sure that *blödh* stood for *blood* and, as a result, that *blödhren* was *blood-oath*, but he had never heard of *agaetí*.

"*Celebration*," explained Arya when he asked. "We hold the Blood-oath Celebration once every century to honor our pact with the dragons. Both of you are fortunate to be here now, for it is nigh upon us. . . ." Her slanted eyebrows met as she frowned. "Fate has indeed arranged a most auspicious coincidence."

She surprised Eragon by leading them deeper into Du Welden-varden, down paths tangled with nettles and currant bushes, until the lights around them vanished and they entered the restless wilderness. In the darkness, Eragon had to rely on Saphira's keen night vision so as to not lose his way. The craggy trees increased in width, crowding closer and closer together and threatening to form an impenetrable barrier. Just when it appeared that they could go no farther, the forest ended and they entered a clearing washed with moonlight from the bright sickle low in the eastern sky.

A lone pine tree stood in the middle of the clearing. No taller than the rest of its brethren, it was thicker than a hundred regular trees combined; in comparison, they looked as puny as windblown saplings. A blanket of roots radiated from the tree's massive trunk, covering the ground with bark-sheathed veins that made it seem as if the entire forest flowed out from the tree, as if it were the heart of Du Weldenvarden itself. The tree presided over the woods like a benevolent matriarch, protecting its inhabitants under the shelter of her branches.

"Behold the Menoa tree," whispered Arya. "We observe the Agaetí Blödhren in her shade."

A cold tingle crawled down Eragon's side as he recognized the name. After Angela told his fortune in Teirm, Solembum had come up to him and said, *When the time comes and you need a weapon, look under the roots of the Menoa tree. Then, when all seems lost and your power is insufficient, go to the rock of Kuthian and speak your name to open the Vault of Souls.* Eragon could not imagine what kind of weapon might be buried under the tree, nor how he would go about finding it.

Do you see anything? he asked Saphira.

No, but then I doubt that Solembum's words will make sense until our need is clear.

Eragon told Arya about both parts of the werecat's counsel, although—as he had with Ajihad and Islanzadí—he kept Angela's prophecy a secret because of its personal nature, and because he feared that it might lead Arya to guess his attraction to her.

When he finished, Arya said, "Werecats rarely offer help, and when they do, it's not to be ignored. So far as I know, no weapon is hidden here, not even in song or legend. As for the Rock of Kuthian . . . the name echoes in my head like a voice from a half-forgotten dream, familiar yet strange. I've heard it before, though I cannot recall where."

As they approached the Menoa tree, Eragon's attention was caught by the multitude of ants crawling over the roots. Faint black smudges were all he could see of the insects, but Oromis's

305

assignment had sensitized him to the currents of life around him, and he could feel the ants' primitive consciousness with his mind. He lowered his defenses and allowed his awareness to flood outward, lightly touching Saphira and Arya and then expanding beyond them to see what else lived in the clearing.

With unexpected suddenness, he encountered an immense entity, a sentient being of such a colossal nature, he could not grasp the limits of its psyche. Even Oromis's vast intellect, which Eragon had been in contact with in Farthen Dûr, was dwarfed in comparison to this presence. The very air seemed to thrum with the energy and strength that emanated from . . . *the tree?*

The source was unmistakable.

Deliberate and inexorable, the tree's thoughts moved at a measured pace as slow as the creep of ice over granite. It took no notice of Eragon nor, he was sure, of any single individual. It was entirely concerned with the affairs of things that grow and flourish in the bright sunlight, with the dogbane and the lily, the evening primrose and the silky foxglove and the yellow mustard tall beside the crabapple with its purple blossoms.

"It's awake!" exclaimed Eragon, shocked into speaking. "I mean . . . it's intelligent." He knew that Saphira felt it too; she cocked her head toward the Menoa tree, as if listening, then flew to one of its branches, which were as thick as the road from Carvahall to Therinsford. There she perched with her tail hanging free, waving the tip of it back and forth, ever so gracefully. It was such an odd sight, a dragon in a tree, that Eragon almost laughed.

"Of course she's awake," said Arya. Her voice was low and mellow in the night air. "Shall I tell you the story of the Menoa tree?"

"I'd like that."

A flash of white streaked across the sky, like a banished specter, and resolved itself beside Saphira in the form of Blagden. The raven's narrow shoulders and crooked neck gave him the appearance of a miser basking in the radiance of a pile of gold. The raven lifted his pallid head and uttered his ominous cry, *"Wyrda!"*

"This is what happened. Once there lived a woman, Linnëa, in the years of spice and wine before our war with the dragons and before we became as immortal as any beings still composed of vulnerable flesh can be. Linnëa had grown old without the comfort of a mate or children, nor did she feel the need to seek them out, preferring to occupy herself with the art of singing to plants, of which she was a master. That is, she did until a young man came to her door and beguiled her with words of love. His affections woke a part of Linnëa that she had never suspected existed, a craving to experience the things that she had unknowingly sacrificed. The offer of a second chance was too great an opportunity for her to ignore. She deserted her work and devoted herself to the young man and, for a time, they were happy.

"But the young man was young, and he began to long for a mate closer to his own age. His eye fell upon a young woman, and he wooed and won her. And for a time, they too were happy.

"When Linnëa discovered that she had been spurned, scorned, and abandoned, she went mad with grief. The young man had done the worst possible thing; he had given her a taste of the fullness of life, then torn it away with no more thought than a rooster flitting from one hen to the next. She found him with the woman and, in her fury, she stabbed him to death.

"Linnëa knew that what she had done was evil. She also knew that even if she was exonerated of the murder, she could not return to her previous existence. Life had lost all joy for her. So she went to the oldest tree in Du Weldenvarden, pressed herself against it, and sang herself into the tree, abandoning all allegiance to her own race. For three days and three nights she sang, and when she finished, she had become one with her beloved plants. And through all the millennia since has she kept watch over the forest. . . . Thus was the Menoa tree created."

At the conclusion of her tale, Arya and Eragon sat side by side on the crest of a huge root, twelve feet off the ground. Eragon bounced his heels against the tree and wondered if Arya had intended the story as a warning to him or if it was merely an innocent piece of history.

His doubt hardened into certainty when she asked, "Do you think that the young man was to blame for the tragedy?"

"I think," he said, knowing that a clumsy reply could turn her against him, "that what he did was cruel . . . and that Linnëa overreacted. They were both at fault."

Arya stared at him until he was forced to avert his gaze. "They weren't suited for each other."

Eragon began to deny it but then stopped himself. She was right. And she had maneuvered him so that he had to say it out loud, so that he had to say it to *her*. "Perhaps," he admitted.

Silence accumulated between them like sand piling into a wall that neither of them was willing to breach. The high-pitched hum of cicadas echoed from the edge of the clearing. At last he said, "Being home seems to agree with you."

"It does." With unconscious ease, she leaned over and picked up a thin branch that had fallen from the Menoa tree and began to weave the clumps of needles into a small basket.

Hot blood rushed to Eragon's face as he watched her. He hoped that the moon was not bright enough to reveal that his cheeks had turned mottled red. "Where . . . where do you live? Do you and Islanzadí have a palace or castle . . . ?"

"We live in Tialdarí Hall, our family's ancestral buildings, in the western part of Ellesméra. I would enjoy showing our home to you."

"Ah." A practical question suddenly intruded in Eragon's muddled thoughts, driving away his embarrassment. "Arya, do you have any siblings?" She shook her head. "Then you are the sole heir to the elven throne?"

"Of course. Why do you ask?" She sounded bemused by his curiosity.

"I don't understand why you were allowed to become an ambassador to the Varden and dwarves, as well as ferry Saphira's egg from here to Tronjheim. It's too dangerous an errand for a princess, much less the queen-in-waiting."

"You mean it's too dangerous for a *human* woman. I told you before that I am not one of your helpless females. What you fail to realize is that we view our monarchs differently than you or the dwarves. To us, a king or queen's highest responsibility is to serve their people however and wherever possible. If that means forfeiting our lives in the process, we welcome the opportunity to prove our devotion to—as the dwarves say—hearth, hall, and honor. If I had died in the course of my duty, then a replacement successor would have been chosen from among our various Houses. Even now I would not be required to become queen if I found the prospect distasteful. We do not choose leaders who are unwilling to devote themselves wholeheartedly to their obligation." She hesitated, then hugged her knees against her chest and propped her chin on them. "I had many years to perfect those arguments with my mother." For a minute, the *wheet-wheet* of the cicadas went undisturbed in the clearing. Then she asked, "How go your studies with Oromis?"

Eragon grunted as his foul temper returned on a wave of unpleasant memories, souring his pleasure at being with Arya. All he wanted to do was crawl into bed, go to sleep, and forget the day. "Oromis-elda," he said, working each word around his mouth before letting it escape, "is quite thorough."

He winced as she gripped his upper arm with bruising strength. "What has gone amiss?"

He tried to shrug her hand off. "Nothing."

"I've traveled with you long enough to know when you're happy, angry . . . or in pain. Did something happen between you and Oromis? If so, you have to tell me so that it can be rectified as soon as possible. Or was it your back? We could—"

"It's not my training!" Despite his pique, Eragon noticed that she seemed genuinely concerned, which pleased him. "Ask Saphira. She can tell you."

"I want to hear it from you," she said quietly.

The muscles in Eragon's jaw spasmed as he clenched his teeth. In a low voice, no more than a whisper, he first described how he had failed at his meditation in the glade, then the incident that poisoned his heart like a viper coiled in his chest: his blessing.

Arya released his arm and clutched at the root of the Menoa tree, as if to steady herself. "Barzûl." The dwarf curse alarmed him; he had never heard her use profanity before, and this one was particularly apt, for it meant *ill fate*. "I knew of your act in Farthen Dûr, for sure, but I never thought . . . I never *suspected* that such a thing could occur. I cry your pardon, Eragon, for forcing you to leave your rooms tonight. I did not comprehend your discomfort. You must want to be alone."

"No," he said. "No, I appreciate the company and the things you've shown me." He smiled at her, and after a moment, she smiled back. Together they sat small and still at the base of the ancient tree and watched the moon arch high over the peaceful forest before it hid behind the gathering clouds. "I only wonder what will become of the child."

High above their heads, Blagden ruffled his bone-white feathers and shrieked, *"Wyrda!"*

◆   ◆   ◆

A MAZE OF OPPOSITION

Nasuada crossed her arms without bothering to conceal her impatience as she examined the two men before her.

The one on the right had a neck so thick, it forced his head to jut forward at nearly right angles to his shoulders, giving him a stubborn, dim-witted appearance. This was intensified by his heavy brow with its two cliffs of matted hair—almost long enough to pull over his eyes—and bulbous lips that remained puckered into a pink mushroom, even when he spoke. She knew better than to put stock in his repulsive looks, though. No matter its rough housing, his tongue was as clever as a jester's.

The only identifying feature of the second man was his pale skin, which refused to darken under Surda's relentless sun, even though the Varden had been in Aberon, the capital, for some weeks now. From his coloring, Nasuada guessed he had been born in the northern reaches of the Empire. He held a knit wool cap that he wrung into a hard rope between his hands.

"You," she said, pointing at him. "How many of your chickens did he kill again?"

"Thirteen, Ma'am."

Nasuada returned her attention to the ugly man. "An unlucky number, by all accounts, Master Gamble. And so it has proved for you. You are guilty of both theft and destroying someone else's property without offering proper recompense."

"I never denied it."

"I only wonder how you ate thirteen chickens in four days. Are you *ever* full, Master Gamble?"

He gave her a jocular grin and scratched the side of his face. The rasp of his untrimmed fingernails over his stubble annoyed her, and it was only with an effort of will that she kept from asking him to stop. "Well, not to be disrespectful, Ma'am, but filling my stomach wouldn't be a problem if you fed us properly, what with all the work we do. I'm a large man, an' I need a bit o' meat in my belly after half a day breaking rocks with a mattock. I did my best to resist temptation, I did. But three weeks of short rations and watching these farmers drive around fat livestock they wouldn't share even if a body were starving . . . Well, I'll admit, it broke me. I'm not a strong man when it comes to food. I like it hot and I like plenty of it. An' I don't fancy I'm the only one willing to help himself."

And that's the heart of the problem, reflected Nasuada. The Varden could not afford to feed its members, not even with Surda's king, Orrin, helping. Orrin had opened his treasury to them, but he had refused to behave as Galbatorix was wont to do when moving his army across the Empire, which was to appropriate supplies from his countrymen without paying for them. *A noble sentiment, but one that only makes my task harder*. Still, she knew that acts like those were what separated her, Orrin, Hrothgar, and Islanzadí from Galbatorix's despotism. *It would be so easy to cross that divide without noticing it*.

"I understand your reasons, Master Gamble. However, although the Varden aren't a country and we answer to no one's authority but our own, that does *not* give you or anyone else leave to ignore the rule of law as laid down by my predecessors or as it's observed here in Surda. Therefore, I order you to pay a copper for each chicken you stole."

Gamble surprised her by acceding without protest. "As you wish, Ma'am," he said.

"That's it?" exclaimed the pale man. He wrung his cap even tighter. "That's no fair price. If I sold them in any market, they'd—"

She could not contain herself any longer. "Yes! You'd get more. But I happen to know that Master Gamble cannot afford to give you the chickens' full price, as I'm the one who provides his salary! As I do yours. You forget that if I decided to acquire your poultry for the good of the Varden, you'd get no more than a copper a chicken and be lucky at that. Am I understood?"

"He can't—"

"Am I understood?"

After a moment, the pale man subsided and muttered, "Yes, Ma'am."

"Very well. You're both dismissed." With an expression of sardonic admiration, Gamble touched his brow and bowed to Nasuada before backing out of the stone room with his sullen opponent. "You too," she said to the guards on either side of the door.

As soon as they were gone, she slumped in her chair with an exhausted sigh and reached for her fan, batting it over her face in a futile attempt to dissipate the pinpricks of sweat that accumulated on her forehead. The constant heat drained her strength and made even the smallest task arduous.

She suspected she would feel tired even if it were winter. Familiar as she was with the innermost secrets of the Varden, it still had taken more work than she expected to transport the entire organization from Farthen Dûr, through the Beor Mountains, and deliver them to Surda and Aberon. She shuddered, remembering long, uncomfortable days spent in the saddle. Planning and executing their departure had been exceedingly difficult, as was integrating the Varden into their new surroundings while simultaneously preparing for an attack on the Empire. *I don't have enough time each day to solve all these problems*, she lamented.

Finally, she dropped the fan and rang the bellpull, summoning her handmaid, Farica. The banner hanging to the right of the cherrywood desk rippled as the door hidden behind it opened. Farica slipped out to stand with downcast eyes by Nasuada's elbow.

"Are there any more?" asked Nasuada.

"No, Ma'am."

She tried not to let her relief show. Once a week, she held an open court to resolve the Varden's various disputes. Anyone who felt that they had been wronged could seek an audience with her and ask for her judgment. She could not imagine a more difficult and thankless chore. As her father had often said after negotiating with Hrothgar, "A good compromise leaves everyone angry." And so it seemed.

Returning her attention to the matter at hand, she told Farica, "I want that Gamble reassigned. Give him a job where his talent with words will be of some use. Quartermaster, perhaps, just so long as it's a job where he'll get full rations. I don't want to see him before me for stealing again."

Farica nodded and went to the desk, where she recorded Nasuada's instructions on a parchment scroll. That skill alone made her invaluable. Farica asked, "Where can I find him?"

"One of the work gangs in the quarry."

"Yes, Ma'am. Oh, while you were occupied, King Orrin asked that you join him in his laboratory."

"What has he done in there now, blind himself?" Nasuada washed her wrists and neck with lavender water, then checked her hair in the mirror of polished silver that Orrin had given her and tugged on her overgown until the sleeves were straight.

Satisfied with her appearance, she swept out of her chambers with Farica in tow. The sun was so bright today that no torches were needed to illuminate the inside of Borromeo Castle, nor could their added warmth have been tolerated. Shafts of light fell through the crossletted arrow slits and glowed upon the inner wall of the corridor, striping the air with bars of golden dust at regular intervals. Nasuada looked out one embrasure toward the barbican, where thirty or so of Orrin's orange-clad cavalry soldiers were setting forth on another of their ceaseless rounds of patrols in the countryside surrounding Aberon.

Not that they could do much good if Galbatorix decided to attack us himself, she thought bitterly. Their only protection against that was

Galbatorix's pride and, she hoped, his fear of Eragon. All leaders were aware of the risk of usurpation, but usurpers themselves were doubly afraid of the threat that a single determined individual could pose. Nasuada knew that she was playing an exceedingly dangerous game with the most powerful madman in Alagaësia. If she misjudged how far she could push him, she and the rest of the Varden would be destroyed, along with any hope of ending Galbatorix's reign.

The clean smell of the castle reminded her of the times she had stayed there as a child, back when Orrin's father, King Larkin, still ruled. She never saw much of Orrin then. He was five years older than her and already occupied with his duties as a prince. Nowadays, though, she often felt as if she were the elder one.

At the door to Orrin's laboratory, she had to stop and wait for his bodyguards, who were always posted outside, to announce her presence to the king. Soon Orrin's voice boomed out into the stairwell: "Lady Nasuada! I'm so glad you came. I have something to show you."

Mentally bracing herself, she entered the laboratory with Farica. A maze of tables laden with a fantastic array of alembics, beakers, and retorts confronted them, like a glass thicket waiting to snag their dresses on any one of its myriad fragile branches. The heavy odor of metallic vapors made Nasuada's eyes water. Lifting their hems off the floor, she and Farica wended their way in single file toward the back of the room, past hourglasses and scales, arcane tomes bound with black iron, dwarven astrolabes, and piles of phosphorescent crystal prisms that produced fitful blue flashes.

They met Orrin by a marble-topped bench, where he stirred a crucible of quicksilver with a glass tube that was closed at one end, open at the other, and must have measured at least three feet in length, although it was only a quarter of an inch thick.

"Sire," said Nasuada. As befitted one of equal rank to the king, she remained upright while Farica curtsied. "You seem to have recovered from the explosion last week."

Orrin grimaced good-naturedly. "I learned that it's not wise to combine phosphorus and water in an enclosed space. The result can be quite violent."

"Has all of your hearing returned?"

"Not entirely, but . . ." Grinning like a boy with his first dagger, he lit a taper with the coals from a brazier, which she could not fathom how he endured in the stifling weather, carried the flaming brand back to the bench, and used it to start a pipe packed with cardus weed.

"I didn't know that you smoked."

"I don't really," he confessed, "except that I found that since my eardrum hasn't completely sealed up yet, I can do this. . . ." Drawing on the pipe, he puffed out his cheeks until a tendril of smoke issued from his left ear, like a snake leaving its den, and coiled up the side of his head. It was so unexpected, Nasuada burst out laughing, and after a moment, Orrin joined her, releasing a plume of smoke from his mouth. "It's the most peculiar sensation," he confided. "Tickles like crazy on the way out."

Growing serious again, Nasuada asked, "Was there something else that you wished to discuss with me, Sire?"

He snapped his fingers. "Of course." Dipping his long glass tube in the crucible, he filled it with quicksilver, then capped the open end with one finger and showed it to her. "Would you agree that the only thing in this tube is quicksilver?"

"I would." *Is this why he wanted to see me?*

"And what about now?" With a quick movement, he inverted the tube and planted the open end inside the crucible, removing his finger. Instead of all pouring out, as Nasuada expected, the quicksilver in the tube dropped about halfway, then stopped and held its position. Orrin pointed to the empty section above the suspended metal. He asked, "What occupies that space?"

"It must be air," asserted Nasuada.

Orrin grinned and shook his head. "If that were true, how would the air bypass the quicksilver or diffuse through the glass? No routes are available by which the atmosphere can gain admission." He gestured at Farica. "What's your opinion, maid?"

Farica stared at the tube, then shrugged and said, "It can't be nothing, Sire."

"Ah, but that's exactly what I think it is: *nothing*. I believe that I've solved one of the oldest conundrums of natural philosophy by creating and proving the existence of a vacuum! It completely invalidates Vacher's theories and means that Ládin was actually a genius. Blasted elves always seem to be right."

Nasuada struggled to remain cordial as she asked, "What purpose does it serve, though?"

"Purpose?" Orrin looked at her with genuine astonishment. "None, of course. At least not that I can think of. However, this will help us to understand the mechanics of our world, how and why things happen. It's a wondrous discovery. Who knows what else it might lead to?" While he spoke, he emptied the tube and carefully placed it in a velvet-padded box that held similar delicate instruments. "The prospect that truly excites me, though, is of using magic to ferret out nature's secrets. Why, just yesterday, with a single spell, Trianna helped me to discover two entirely new gases. Imagine what could be learned if magic were systematically applied to the disciplines of natural philosophy. I'm considering learning magic myself, if I have the talent for it, and if I can convince some magic users to divulge their knowledge. It's a pity that your Dragon Rider, Eragon, didn't accompany you here; I'm sure that he could help me."

Looking at Farica, Nasuada said, "Wait for me outside." The woman curtsied and then departed. Once Nasuada heard the door to the laboratory close, she said, "Orrin. Have you taken leave of your senses?"

"Whatever do you mean?"

"While you spend your time locked in here conducting experiments that no one understands—endangering your well-being in the process—your country totters on the brink of war. A myriad issues await your decision, and you stand here blowing smoke and playing with quicksilver?"

His face hardened. "I am quite aware of my duties, Nasuada. You may lead the Varden, but I'm still king of Surda, and you would do well to recall that before you speak so disrespectfully. Need I remind you that your sanctuary here depends on my continued goodwill?"

She knew it was an idle threat; many of the Surdan people had relatives in the Varden, and vice versa. They were too closely linked for either of them to abandon the other. No, the real reason that Orrin had taken offense was the question of authority. Since it was nigh impossible to keep large groups of armed warriors at the ready over extended periods of time—as Nasuada had learned, feeding that many inactive people was a logistical nightmare—the Varden had begun taking jobs, starting farms, and otherwise assimilating into their host country. *Where will that leave me eventually? As the leader of a nonexistent army? A general or councilor under Orrin?* Her position was precarious. If she moved too quickly or with too much initiative, Orrin would perceive it as a threat and turn against her, especially now that she was cloaked in the glamour of the Varden's victory in Farthen Dûr. But if she waited too long, they would lose their chance to exploit Galbatorix's momentary weakness. Her only advantage over the maze of opposition was her command of the one element that had instigated this act of the play: Eragon and Saphira.

She said, "I don't seek to undermine your command, Orrin. That was never my intention, and I apologize if it appeared that way." He bowed his neck with a stiff bob. Unsure of how to continue, she leaned on her fingertips against the lip of the bench. "It's only . . . so many things must be done. I work night and day—I keep a tablet beside my bed for notes—and yet I never catch up; I feel as if we are always balanced on the brink of disaster."

Orrin picked up a pestle stained black from use and rolled it between his palms with a steady, hypnotic rhythm. "Before you came here . . . No, that's not right. Before your Rider materialized fully formed from the ethers like Moratensis from his fountain, I expected to live my life as my father and grandfather before me. That is, opposing Galbatorix in secret. You must excuse me if it takes a while to accustom myself to this new reality."

It was as much contrition as she could expect in return. "I understand."

He stopped the pestle in its path for a brief moment. "You are newly come to your power, whereas I have held mine for a number of years. If I may be arrogant enough to offer advice, I've found that it's essential for my sanity to allocate a certain portion of the day for my own interests."

"I couldn't do that," objected Nasuada. "Every moment I waste might be the moment of effort that's needed to defeat Galbatorix."

The pestle paused again. "You do the Varden a disservice if you insist on overworking yourself. No one can function properly without occasional peace and quiet. They don't have to be long breaks, just five or ten minutes. You could even practice your archery, and then you would still serve your goals, albeit in a different manner. . . . That's why I had this laboratory constructed in the first place. That's why I blow smoke and play with quicksilver, as you put it—so that I don't scream with frustration throughout the rest of the day."

Despite her reluctance to surrender her view of Orrin as a feckless layabout, Nasuada could not help but acknowledge the validity of his argument. "I will keep your recommendation in mind."

Some of his former levity returned as he smiled. "That's all I ask."

Walking to the window, she pushed the shutters farther open and gazed down upon Aberon, with its cries of quick-fingered merchants hawking their wares to unsuspecting customers, the clotted yellow dust blowing from the western road as a caravan approached the city gates, the air that shimmered over clay tile roofs and carried the scent of cardus weed and incense from the marble temples, and the fields that surrounded Aberon like the outstretched petals of a flower.

Without turning around, she asked, "Have you received copies of our latest reports from the Empire?"

"I have." He joined her at the window.

"What's your opinion of them?

"That they're too meager and incomplete to extract any meaningful conclusions."

"They're the best we have, though. Give me your suspicions and your hunches. Extrapolate from the known facts like you would if this were one of your experiments." She smiled to herself. "I promise that I won't attach meaning to what you say."

She had to wait for his reply, and when it came, it was with the dolorous weight of a doomsday prophecy. "Increased taxes, emptied garrisons, horses and oxen confiscated throughout the Empire . . . It seems that Galbatorix gathers his forces in preparation to confront us, though I cannot tell whether he means to do it in offense or defense." Revolving shadows cooled their faces as a cloud of starlings whirled across the sun. "The question that weighs upon my mind now is, how long will it take him to mobilize? For that will determine the course of our strategies."

"Weeks. Months. Years. I cannot predict his actions."

He nodded. "Have your agents continued to spread tidings of Eragon?"

"It has become increasingly dangerous, but yes. My hope is that if we inundate cities like Dras-Leona with rumors of Eragon's prowess, when we actually reach the city and they see him, they will join us of their own accord and we can avoid a siege."

"War is rarely so easy."

She let the comment pass uncontested. "And how fares the mobilization of your own army? The Varden, as always, are ready to fight."

Orrin spread his hands in a placating gesture. "It's difficult to rouse a nation, Nasuada. There are nobles who I must convince to back me, armor and weapons to be constructed, supplies to be gathered. . . ."

"And in the meantime, how do I feed my people? We need more land than you allotted us—"

"Well, I know it," he said.

"—and we'll only get it by invading the Empire, unless you fancy making the Varden a permanent addition to Surda. If so, you'll have to find homes for the thousands of people I brought from

Farthen Dûr, which won't please your existing citizens. Whatever your choice, choose quickly, because I fear that if you continue to procrastinate, the Varden will disintegrate into an uncontrollable horde." She tried not to make it sound like a threat.

Nevertheless, Orrin obviously did not appreciate the insinuation. His upper lip curled and he said, "Your father never let his men get out of hand. I trust you won't either, if you expect to remain leader of the Varden. As for our preparations, there's a limit to what we can do in so short a time; you'll just have to wait until we are ready."

She gripped the windowsill until veins stood out on her wrists and her fingernails sank into the crevices between the stones, yet she allowed none of her anger to color her voice: "In that case, will you lend the Varden more gold for food?"

"No. I've given you all the money I can spare."

"How will we eat, then?"

"I would suggest that you raise the funds yourself."

Furious, she gave him her widest, brightest smile—holding it long enough to make him shift with unease—and then curtsied as deeply as a servant, never letting her demented grimace waver. "Farewell then, Sire. I hope that the rest of your day is as enjoyable as our conversation was."

Orrin muttered an unintelligible response as she swept back to the laboratory's entrance. In her anger, Nasuada caught her right sleeve on a jade bottle and knocked it over, cracking the stone and releasing a flood of yellow liquid that splattered her sleeve and soaked her skirt. She flicked her wrist in annoyance without stopping.

Farica rejoined her in the stairwell, and together they traversed the warren of passageways to Nasuada's chambers.

HANGING BY A THREAD

Throwing open the doors to her rooms, Nasuada strode to her desk, then dropped into a chair, blind to her surroundings. Her spine was so rigid that her shoulders did not touch the back. She felt frozen by the insoluble quandary the Varden faced. The rise and fall of her chest slowed until it was imperceptible. *I have failed*, was all she could think.

"Ma'am, your sleeve!"

Jolted from her reverie, Nasuada looked down to find Farica beating at her right arm with a cleaning rag. A wisp of smoke rose from the embroidered sleeve. Alarmed, Nasuada pushed herself out of the chair and twisted her arm, trying to find the cause of the smoke. Her sleeve and skirt were disintegrating into chalky cobwebs that emitted acrid fumes.

"Get me out of this," she said.

She held her contaminated arm away from her body and forced herself to remain still as Farica unlaced her overgown. The handmaid's fingers scrabbled against Nasuada's back with frantic haste, fumbling with the knots, and then finally loosening the wool shell that encased Nasuada's torso. As soon as the overgown sagged, Nasuada yanked her arms out of the sleeves and clawed her way free of the robe.

Panting, she stood by the desk, clad only in her slippers and linen chemise. To her relief, the expensive chainsil had escaped harm, although it had acquired a foul reek.

"Did it burn you?" asked Farica. Nasuada shook her head, not trusting her tongue to respond. Farica nudged the overgown with the tip of her shoe. "What evil is this?"

"One of Orrin's foul concoctions," croaked Nasuada. "I spilled it in his laboratory." Calming herself with long breaths, she examined the ruined gown with dismay. It had been woven by the dwarf women of Dûrgrimst Ingeitum as a gift for her last birthday and was one of the finest pieces in her wardrobe. She had nothing to replace it, nor could she justify commissioning a new dress, considering the Varden's financial difficulties. *Somehow I will have to make do without.*

Farica shook her head. "It's a shame to lose such a pretty dress." She went round the desk to a sewing basket and returned with a pair of etched scissors. "We might as well save as much of the cloth as we can. I'll cut off the ruined parts and have them burned."

Nasuada scowled and paced the length of the room, seething with anger at her own clumsiness and at having another problem added to her already overwhelming list of worries. "What am I going to wear to court now?" she demanded.

The scissors bit into the soft wool with brisk authority. "Mayhap your linen dress."

"It's too casual to appear in before Orrin and his nobles."

"Give me a chance with it, Ma'am. I'm sure that I can alter it so it's serviceable. By the time I'm done, it'll look twice as grand as this one ever did."

"No, no. It won't work. They'll just laugh at me. It's hard enough to command their respect when I'm dressed properly, much less if I'm wearing patched gowns that advertise our poverty."

The older woman fixed Nasuada with a stern gaze. "It *will* work, so long as you don't apologize for your appearance. Not only that, I guarantee that the other ladies will be so taken with your new fashion that they'll imitate you. Just you wait and see." Going to the door, she cracked it open and handed the damaged fabric to one of the guards outside. "Your mistress wants this burned. Do it in secret and breathe not a word of this to another soul or you'll have me to answer to." The guard saluted.

Nasuada could not help smiling. "How would I function without you, Farica?"

"Quite well, I should think."

After donning her green hunting frock—which, with its light skirt, provided some respite from the day's heat—Nasuada decided that even though she was ill disposed toward Orrin, she would take his advice and break with her regular schedule to do nothing more important than help Farica rip out stitches from the overgown. She found the repetitive task an excellent way to focus her thoughts. While she pulled on the threads, she discussed the Varden's predicament with Farica, in the hope that she might perceive a solution that had escaped Nasuada.

In the end, Farica's only assistance was to observe, "Seems most matters in this world have their root in gold. If we had enough of it, we could buy Galbatorix right off his black throne . . . might not even have to fight his men."

Did I really expect that someone else would do my job for me? Nasuada asked herself. *I led us into this blind and I have to lead us out.*

Intending to cut open a seam, she extended her arm and snagged the tip of her knife on a fringe of bobbin lace, slicing it in half. She stared at the ragged wound in the lace, at the frayed ends of the parchment-colored strands that wriggled across the overgown like so many contorted worms, stared and felt a hysterical laugh claw at her throat even as a tear formed in her eye. Could her luck be any worse?

The bobbin lace was the most valuable part of the dress. Even though lace required skill to make, its rarity and expense were mainly due to its central ingredient: vast, copious, mind-numbing, and deadening amounts of time. It took so long to produce that if you attempted to create a lace veil by yourself, your progress would be measured not in weeks but in months. Ounce for ounce, lace was worth more than gold or silver.

She ran her fingers over the band of threads, pausing on the rift that she had created. *It's not as if lace takes that much energy, just time*. She hated making it herself. *Energy . . . energy . . .* At that moment, a series of images flashed through her mind: Orrin talking about using magic for research; Trianna, the woman who had helmed Du Vrangr Gata since the Twins' deaths; looking up at one of the Varden's healers while he explained the principles of magic to Nasuada when she was only five or six years old. The disparate experiences formed a chain of reasoning that was so outrageous and unlikely, it finally released the laugh imprisoned in her throat.

Farica gave her an odd look and waited for an explanation. Standing, Nasuada tumbled half the overgown off her lap and onto the floor. "Fetch me Trianna this instant," she said. "I don't care what she's doing; bring her here."

The skin around Farica's eyes tightened, but she curtsied and said, "As you wish, Ma'am." She departed through the hidden servants' door.

"Thank you," Nasuada whispered in the empty room.

She understood her maid's reluctance; she too felt uncomfortable whenever she had to interact with magic users. Indeed, she only trusted Eragon because he was a Rider—although that was no proof of virtue, as Galbatorix had shown—and because of his oath of fealty, which Nasuada knew he would never break. It scared her to consider magicians' and sorcerers' powers. The thought that a seemingly ordinary person could kill with a word; invade your mind if he or she wished; cheat, lie, and steal without being caught; and otherwise defy society with near impunity . . .

Her heart quickened.

How did you enforce the law when a certain segment of the population possessed special powers? At its most basic level, the Varden's war against the Empire was nothing more than an attempt to bring to justice a man who had abused his magical abilities and to prevent him from committing further crimes. *All this pain and destruction because no one had the strength to defeat Galbatorix. He won't even die after a normal span of years!*

Although she disliked magic, she knew that it would play a

crucial role in removing Galbatorix and that she could not afford to alienate its practitioners until victory was assured. Once that occurred, she intended to resolve the problem that they presented.

A brazen knock on her chamber door disturbed her thoughts. Fixing a pleasant smile on her face and guarding her mind as she had been trained, Nasuada said, "Enter!" It was important that she appear polite after summoning Trianna in such a rude manner.

The door thrust open and the brunette sorceress strode into the room, her tousled locks piled high above her head with obvious haste. She looked as if she had just been roused from bed. Bowing in the dwarven fashion, she said, "You asked for me, Lady?"

"I did." Relaxing into a chair, Nasuada let her gaze slowly drift up and down Trianna. The sorceress lifted her chin under Nasuada's examination. "I need to know: What is the most important rule of magic?"

Trianna frowned. "That whatever you do with magic requires the same amount of energy as it would to do otherwise."

"And what you *can* do is only limited by your ingenuity and by your knowledge of the ancient language?"

"Other strictures apply, but in general, yes. Lady, why do you ask? These are basic principles of magic that, while not commonly bandied about, I am sure you are familiar with."

"I am. I wished to ensure that I understood them properly." Without moving from her chair, Nasuada reached down and lifted the overgown so that Trianna could see the mutilated lace. "So then, within those limits, you should be able to devise a spell that will allow you to manufacture lace with magic."

A condescending sneer distorted the sorceress's dark lips. "Du Vrangr Gata has more important duties than repairing your clothes, Lady. Our art is not so common as to be employed for mere whims. I'm sure that you will find your seamstresses and tailors more than capable of fulfilling your request. Now, if you will excuse me, I—"

"Be quiet, woman," said Nasuada in a flat voice. Astonishment muted Trianna in midsentence. "I see that I must teach Du Vrangr

Gata the same lesson that I taught the Council of Elders: I may be young, but I am no child to be patronized. I ask about lace because if you can manufacture it quickly and easily with magic, then we can support the Varden by selling inexpensive bobbin and needle lace throughout the Empire. Galbatorix's own people will provide the funds we need to survive."

"But that's ridiculous," protested Trianna. Even Farica looked skeptical. "You can't pay for a war with *lace*."

Nasuada raised an eyebrow. "Why not? Women who otherwise could never afford to own lace will leap at the chance to buy ours. Every farmer's wife who longs to appear richer than she is will want it. Even wealthy merchants and nobles will give us their gold because our lace will be finer than any thrown or stitched by human hands. We'll garner a fortune to rival the dwarves'. That is, *if* you are skilled enough in magic to do what I want."

Trianna tossed her hair. "You doubt my abilities?"

"Can it be done!"

Trianna hesitated, then took the overgown from Nasuada and studied the lace strip for a long while. At last she said, "It should be possible, but I'll have to conduct some tests before I know for certain."

"Do so immediately. From now on, this is your most important assignment. And find an experienced lace maker to advise you on the patterns."

"Yes, Lady Nasuada."

Nasuada allowed her voice to soften. "Good. I also want you to select the brightest members of Du Vrangr Gata and work with them to invent other magical techniques that will help the Varden. That's your responsibility, not mine."

"Yes, Lady Nasuada."

"*Now* you are excused. Report back to me tomorrow morning."

"Yes, Lady Nasuada."

Satisfied, Nasuada watched the sorceress depart, then closed her eyes and allowed herself to enjoy a moment of pride for what she had accomplished. She knew that no man, not even her father, would have thought of her solution. "This is *my* contribution to the Varden," she told herself, wishing that Ajihad could witness it. Louder, she asked, "Did I surprise you, Farica?"

"You always do, Ma'am."

ELVA

"Ma'am? . . . You're needed, Ma'am."

"What?" Reluctant to move, Nasuada opened her eyes and saw Jörmundur enter the room. The wiry veteran pulled off his helm, tucked it in the crook of his right arm, and made his way to her with his left hand planted on the pommel of his sword.

The links of his hauberk clinked as he bowed. "My Lady."

"Welcome, Jörmundur. How is your son today?" She was pleased that he had come. Of all the members of the Council of Elders, he had accepted her leadership the most easily, serving her with the same dogged loyalty and determination as he had Ajihad. *If all my warriors were like him, no one could stop us.*

"His cough has subsided."

"I'm glad to hear it. Now, what brings you?"

Lines appeared on Jörmundur's forehead. He ran his free hand over his hair, which was tied back in a ponytail, then caught himself and pushed his hand back down to his side. "Magic, of the strangest kind."

"Oh?"

"Do you remember the babe that Eragon blessed?"

"Aye." Nasuada had seen her only once, but she was well aware of the exaggerated tales about the child that circulated among the Varden, as well as the Varden's hopes for what the girl might achieve once she grew up. Nasuada was more pragmatic about the

329

subject. Whatever the infant became, it would not be for many years, by which time the battle with Galbatorix would already be won or lost.

"I've been asked to take you to her."

"Asked? By whom? And why?"

"A boy on the practice field told me that you should visit the child. Said that you would find it interesting. He refused to give me his name, but he looked like what that witch's werecat is supposed to turn into, so I thought . . . Well, I thought you should know." Jörmundur looked embarrassed. "I asked my men questions about the girl, and I heard things . . . that she's *different*."

"In what way?"

He shrugged. "Enough to believe that you should do what the werecat says."

Nasuada frowned. She knew from the old stories that ignoring a werecat was the height of folly and often led to one's doom. However, his companion—Angela the herbalist—was another magic user that Nasuada did not entirely trust; she was too independent and unpredictable. "Magic," she said, making it a curse.

"Magic," agreed Jörmundur, though he used it as a word of awe and fear.

"Very well, let us go visit this child. Is she within the castle?"

"Orrin gave her and her caretaker rooms on the west side of the keep."

"Take me to her."

Gathering up her skirts, Nasuada ordered Farica to postpone the rest of the day's appointments, then left the chambers. Behind her, she heard Jörmundur snap his fingers as he directed four guards to take up positions around her. A moment later, he joined her side, pointing out their course.

The heat within Borromeo Castle had increased to the point where they felt as if they were trapped within a giant bread oven. The air shimmered like liquid glass along the windowsills.

Though she was uncomfortable, Nasuada knew that she dealt

with the heat better than most people because of her swarthy skin. The ones who had the hardest time enduring the high temperatures were men like Jörmundur and her guards, who had to wear their armor all day long, even if they were stationed out under the lidless gaze of the sun.

Nasuada kept close watch on the five men as sweat gathered on their exposed skin and their breathing became ever more ragged. Since they had arrived in Aberon, a number of the Varden had fainted from heatstroke—two of whom died an hour or two later—and she had no intention of losing more of her subjects by driving them beyond their physical limits.

When she deemed they needed to rest, she bade them to stop—overriding their objections—and get drinks of water from a servant. "I can't have you toppling like ninepins."

They had to break twice more before they reached their destination, a nondescript door recessed in the inner wall of the corridor. The floor around it was littered with gifts.

Jörmundur knocked, and a quavering voice from inside asked, "Who is it?"

"Lady Nasuada, come to see the child," he said.

"Be you of true heart and steadfast resolve?"

This time Nasuada answered, "My heart is pure and my resolve is as iron."

"Cross the threshold, then, and be welcome."

The door swung open to an entryway lit by a single red dwarf lantern. No one was at the door. Proceeding inward, Nasuada saw that the walls and ceiling were swathed with layers of dark fabric, giving the place the appearance of a cave or lair. To her surprise, the air was quite cold, almost chilly, like a brisk autumn night. Apprehension sank its poisonous claws into her belly. *Magic*.

A black mesh curtain blocked her way. Brushing it aside, she found herself in what was once a sitting room. The furniture had been removed, except for a line of chairs pushed against the shrouded walls. A cluster of faint dwarf lanterns were hung in a dimple of the sagging fabric overhead, casting weird multicolored shadows in every direction.

A bent crone watched her from the depths of one corner, bracketed by Angela the herbalist and the werecat, who stood with his hackles raised. In the center of the room knelt a pale girl that Nasuada took to be three or four years old. The girl picked at a platter of food on her lap. No one spoke.

Confused, Nasuada asked, "Where is the baby?"

The girl looked up.

Nasuada gasped as she saw the dragon mark bright upon the child's brow and as she peered deep into her violet eyes. The girl quirked her lips with a terrible, knowing smile. "I am Elva."

Nasuada recoiled without thinking, clutching at the dagger she kept strapped to her left forearm. It was an adult's voice and filled with an adult's experience and cynicism. It sounded profane coming from the mouth of a child.

"Don't run," said Elva. "I'm your friend." She put the platter aside; it was empty now. To the crone, she said, "More food." The old woman hurried from the room. Then Elva patted the floor beside her. "Please, sit. I have been waiting for you ever since I learned to talk."

Keeping her grip on her dagger, Nasuada lowered herself to the stones. "When was that?"

"Last week." Elva folded her hands in her lap. She fixed her ghastly eyes on Nasuada, pinning her in place through the unnatural strength of her gaze. Nasuada felt as if a violet lance had pierced her skull and was twisting inside her mind, tearing apart her thoughts and memories. She fought the desire to scream.

Leaning forward, Elva reached out and cupped Nasuada's cheek with one soft hand. "You know, Ajihad could not have led the Varden better than you have. You chose the correct path. Your name will be praised for centuries for having the courage and foresight to move the Varden to Surda and attack the Empire when everyone else thought it was insane to do so."

Nasuada gaped at the girl, stunned. Like a key matched to a lock, Elva's words perfectly addressed Nasuada's primal fears, the doubts that kept her awake at night, sweating in the darkness. An involuntary surge of emotion rushed through her, bolstering her with a sense of confidence and peace that she had not possessed since before Ajihad's death. Tears of relief burst from her eyes and rolled down her face. It was as if Elva had known exactly what to say in order to comfort her.

Nasuada loathed her for it.

Her euphoria warred against her distaste for how this moment of weakness had been induced and by whom. Nor did she trust the girl's motivation.

"What *are* you?" she demanded.

"I am what Eragon made me."

"He blessed you."

The dreadful, ancient eyes were obscured for a moment as Elva blinked. "He did not understand his actions. Since Eragon ensorcelled me, whenever I see a person, I sense all the hurts that beset him and are about to beset him. When I was smaller, I could do nothing about it. So I grew bigger."

"Why would—"

"The magic in my blood drives me to protect people from pain . . . no matter the injury to myself or whether I want to help or not." Her smile acquired a bitter twist. "It costs me dearly if I resist the urge."

As Nasuada digested the implications, she realized that Elva's unsettling aspect was a by-product of the suffering that she had been exposed to. Nasuada shivered at the thought of what the girl had endured. *It must have torn her apart to have this compulsion and yet be unable to act on it.* Against her better judgment, she began to feel a measure of sympathy for Elva.

"Why have you told me this?"

"I thought that you should know who and what I am." Elva paused, and the fire in her gaze strengthened. "And that I will fight

333

for you however I can. Use me as you would an assassin—in hiding, in the dark, and without mercy." She laughed with a high, chilling voice. "You wonder why; I see you do. Because unless this war ends, and sooner rather than later, it will drive me insane. I find it hard enough to deal with the agonies of everyday life without also having to confront the atrocities of battle. Use me to end it and I'll ensure that your life is as happy as any human has had the privilege to experience."

At that moment, the crone scurried back into the room, bowed to Elva, and handed her a new platter of food. It was a physical relief to Nasuada as Elva looked down and attacked a leg of mutton, cramming the meat into her mouth with both hands. She ate with the ravenous intensity of a gorging wolf, displaying a complete lack of decorum. With her violet eyes hidden and her dragon mark covered by black bangs, she once again appeared to be nothing more than an innocent child.

Nasuada waited until it became apparent that Elva had said all she was going to. Then—at a gesture from Angela—she accompanied the herbalist through a side door, leaving the pale girl sitting alone in the center of the dark, cloth-bound room, like a dire fetus nestled in its womb, waiting for the right moment to emerge.

Angela made sure that the door was closed and whispered, "All she does is eat and eat. We can't sate her appetite with the current rations. Can you—"

"She'll be fed. You needn't worry about it." Nasuada rubbed her arms, trying to eradicate the memory of those awful, horrible eyes. . . .

"Thank you."

"Has this ever happened to anyone else?"

Angela shook her head until her curly hair bounced on her shoulders. "Not in the entire history of magic. I tried to cast her future, but it's a hopeless quagmire—lovely word, *quagmire*—because her life interacts with so many others."

"Is she dangerous?"

"We're all dangerous."

"You know what I mean."

Angela shrugged. "She's more dangerous than some and less than others. The one she's most likely to kill, though, is herself. If she meets someone who's about to be hurt and Eragon's spell catches her unawares, then she'll take the doomed person's place. That's why she stays inside most of the time."

"How far in advance can she foretell events?"

"Two or three hours at the most."

Leaning against the wall, Nasuada considered the newest complication in her life. Elva could be a potent weapon if she were applied correctly. *Through her, I can discern my opponents' troubles and weaknesses, as well as what will please them and make them amenable to my wishes.* In an emergency, the girl could also act as an infallible guard if one of the Varden, like Eragon or Saphira, had to be protected.

She can't be left unsupervised. I need someone to watch her. Someone who understands magic and is comfortable enough with their own identity to resist Elva's influence . . . and who I can trust to be reliable and honest. She immediately discounted Trianna.

Nasuada looked at Angela. Though she was wary of the herbalist, she knew that Angela had helped the Varden with matters of the utmost delicacy and importance—like healing Eragon—and had asked for nothing in return. Nasuada could think of no one else who had the time, inclination, and expertise to look after Elva.

"I realize," said Nasuada, "that this is presumptuous of me, as you aren't under my command and I know little of your life or duties, but I have a favor to ask of you."

"Proceed." Angela waved a hand.

Nasuada faltered, disconcerted, then forged ahead. "Would you be willing to keep an eye on Elva for me? I need—"

"Of course! And I'll keep two eyes on her, if I can spare them. I relish the opportunity to study her."

"You'll have to report to me," warned Nasuada.

"The poison dart hidden in the raisin tart. Ah, well, I suppose I can manage."

"I have your word, then?"

"You have my word."

Relieved, Nasuada groaned and sank into a nearby chair. "Oh, what a mess. What a *quagmire*. As Eragon's liegelord, I'm responsible for his deeds, but I never imagined that he would do anything as dreadful as this. It's a blight on my honor as much as his."

A ripple of sharp pops filled the room as Angela cracked her knuckles. "Yes. I intend to speak to him about it once he returns from Ellesméra."

Her expression was so fierce, it alarmed Nasuada. "Well, don't hurt him. We need him."

"I won't . . . permanently."

◆　　◆　　◆

RESURGENCE

A blast of ravening wind tore Eragon from his sleep.

Blankets flapped over him as a tempest clawed at his room, hurling his possessions into the air and knocking the lanterns against the walls. Outside, the sky was black with thunderheads.

Saphira watched as Eragon staggered upright and fought to keep his balance as the tree swayed like a ship at sea. He lowered his head against the gale and made his way around the room, clutching at the wall until he reached the teardrop portal through which the storm howled.

Eragon looked past the heaving floor to the ground below. It appeared to rock back and forth. He swallowed and tried to ignore the churning in his stomach.

By touch he found the edge of the cloth membrane that could be pulled out of the wood to cover the opening. He prepared to launch himself from one side of the gap to the next. If he slipped, nothing would stop him from falling onto the roots of the tree.

Wait, said Saphira.

She backed off the low pedestal where she slept and laid her tail alongside him so that he could use it as a handrail.

Holding the cloth with just his right hand, which took all his strength, Eragon used the line of spikes on Saphira's tail to pull himself across the portal. As soon as he reached the far side, he grabbed the cloth with both hands and pressed its edge into the groove that locked it in place.

The room went silent.

The membrane bulged inward under the force of the angry elements but showed no sign of giving. Eragon poked it with his finger. The fabric was as taut as a drum.

It's amazing what the elves can do, he said.

Saphira cocked her head, then lifted it so that her head was flat against the ceiling while she listened. *You'd better close up the study; it's being wrecked.*

As he headed toward the stairs, the tree jolted and his leg buckled, sending him down hard on one knee.

"Blast it," he growled.

The study was a whirlwind of paper and quills, darting about as if they had a mind of their own. He dove into the flurry with his arms wrapped around his head. It felt like he was being pelted with stones when the tips of the quills struck him.

Eragon struggled to close the upper portal without Saphira's help. The moment he did, pain—endless, mind-numbing *pain*—ripped open his back.

He screamed once and went hoarse from the strength of his cry. His vision flashed with red and yellow, then faded to black as he toppled to his side. Below, he heard Saphira howl with frustration; the staircase was too small and, outside, the wind was too ferocious for her to reach him. His connection with her receded. He surrendered to the waiting darkness as a release from his agony.

A sour taste filled Eragon's mouth when he woke. He did not know how long he had been lying on the floor, but the muscles in his arms and legs were knotted from being curled into a tight ball. The storm still assailed the tree, accompanied by a thudding rain that matched the pounding in his head.

Saphira . . . ?

I'm here. Can you come down?

I'll try.

He was too weak to stand on the pitching floor, so he crawled to the stairs and slid down one at a time, wincing with each impact. Halfway down, he encountered Saphira, who had jammed her head and neck as far up the stairs as she could, gouging the wood in her frenzy.

Little one. She flicked out her tongue and caught him on the hand with its rough tip. He smiled. Then she arched her neck and tried to pull back, but to no avail.

What's wrong?

I'm stuck.

You're . . . He could not help it; he laughed even though it hurt. The situation was too absurd.

She snarled and heaved her entire body, shaking the tree with her efforts and knocking him over. Then she collapsed, panting. *Well, don't just sit there grinning like an idiot fox. Help me!*

Fighting the urge to giggle, he put his foot on her nose and pushed as hard as he dared while Saphira twisted and squirmed in an attempt to free herself.

It took more than ten minutes before she succeeded. Only then did Eragon see the full extent of the damage to the stairwell. He groaned. Her scales had cut through the bark and obliterated the delicate patterns grown out from the wood.

Oops, said Saphira.

At least you did it, not me. The elves might forgive you. They'd sing dwarf love ballads night and day if you asked them to.

He joined Saphira on her dais and huddled against the flat scales of her belly, listening as the storm roared about them. The wide membrane became translucent whenever lightning pulsed in jagged shards of light.

What time do you think it is?

Several hours before we must meet Oromis. Go on, sleep and recover. I will keep guard.

He did just that, despite the tree's churning.

WHY DO YOU FIGHT?

O romis's timepiece buzzed like a giant hornet, blaring in
Eragon's ears until he retrieved the bauble and wound the
mechanism.

His bashed knee had turned purple, he was sore both from his attack and the elves' Dance of Snake and Crane, and he could do no
more than croak with his ragged throat. The worst injury, though,
was his sense of foreboding that this would not be the last time
Durza's wound would trouble him. The prospect sickened him,
draining his strength and will.

So many weeks passed between attacks, he said, *I began to hope that
maybe, just maybe, I was healed. . . . I suppose sheer luck is the only
reason I was spared that long.*

Extending her neck, Saphira nuzzled him on the arm. *You know
you aren't alone, little one. I'll do everything I can to help.* He responded with a weak smile. Then she licked his face and added, *You
should get ready to leave.*

I know. He stared at the floor, unwilling to move, then dragged
himself to the wash closet, where he scrubbed himself clean and
used magic to shave.

He was in the middle of drying himself when he felt a presence
touch his mind. Without pausing to think, Eragon began to fortify
his mind, concentrating on an image of his big toe to the exclusion
of all else. Then he heard Oromis say, *Admirable, but unnecessary.
Bring Zar'roc with you today.* The presence vanished.

Eragon released a shaky breath. *I need to be more alert,* he told Saphira. *I would have been at his mercy if he were an enemy.*

Not with me around.

When his ablutions were complete, Eragon unhooked the membrane from the wall and mounted Saphira, cradling Zar'roc in the crook of his arm.

Saphira took flight with a rush of air, angling toward the Crags of Tel'naeír. From their high vantage point, they could see the damage that the storm had wreaked on Du Weldenvarden. No trees had fallen in Ellesméra, but farther away, where the elves' magic was weaker, numerous pines had been knocked over. The remaining wind made the crossed branches and trees rub together, producing a brittle chorus of creaks and groans. Clouds of golden pollen, as thick as dust, streamed out from the trees and flowers.

While they flew, Eragon and Saphira exchanged memories of their separate lessons from the day before. He told her what he had learned about ants and the ancient language, and she told him about downdrafts and other dangerous weather patterns and how to avoid them.

Thus, when they landed and Oromis interrogated Eragon about Saphira's lessons and Glaedr interrogated Saphira about Eragon's, they were able to answer every question.

"Very good, Eragon-vodhr."

Aye. Well played, Bjartskular, added Glaedr to Saphira.

As before, Saphira was sent off with Glaedr while Eragon remained on the cliffs, although this time he and Saphira were careful to maintain their link so as to absorb each other's instruction.

As the dragons departed, Oromis observed, "Your voice is rougher today, Eragon. Are you sick?"

"My back hurt again this morning."

"Ah. You have my sympathy." He motioned with one finger. "Wait here."

Eragon watched as Oromis strode into his hut and then reappeared, looking fierce and warlike with his silver mane rippling in the wind and his bronze sword in hand. "Today," he said, "we shall forgo the Rimgar and instead cross our two blades, Naegling and Zar'roc. Draw thy sword and guard its edge as your first master taught you."

Eragon wanted nothing more than to refuse. However, he had no intention of breaking his vow or letting his resolve waver in front of Oromis. He swallowed his trepidation. *This is what it means to be a Rider*, he thought.

Drawing upon his reserves, he located the nub deep within his mind that connected him to the wild flow of magic. He delved into it, and the energy suffused him. "Gëuloth du knífr," he said, and a winking blue star popped into existence between his thumb and forefinger, jumping from one to the next as he ran it down Zar'roc's perilous length.

The instant their swords met, Eragon knew that he was as outmatched by Oromis as by Durza and Arya. Eragon was an exemplary human swordsman, but he could not compete with warriors whose blood ran thick with magic. His arm was too weak and his reflexes too slow. Still, that did not stop him from trying to win. He fought to the limits of his abilities, even if, in the end, it was a futile prospect.

Oromis tested him in every conceivable manner, forcing Eragon to utilize his entire arsenal of blows, counterblows, and underhand tricks. It was all for naught. He could not touch the elf. As a last resort, he tried altering his style of fighting, which could unsettle even the most hardened veteran. All it got him was a welt on his thigh.

"Move your feet faster," cried Oromis. "He who stands like a pillar dies in battle. He who bends like a reed is triumphant!"

The elf was glorious in action, a perfect blend of control and untamed violence. He pounced like a cat, struck like a heron, and bobbed and wove with the grace of a weasel.

They had been sparring for almost twenty minutes when Oromis faltered, his narrow features clamped in a brief grimace. Eragon recognized the symptoms of Oromis's mysterious illness and lashed out with Zar'roc. It was a low thing to do, but Eragon was so frustrated, he was willing to take advantage of any opening, no matter how unfair, just to have the satisfaction of marking Oromis at least once.

Zar'roc never reached its target. As Eragon twisted, he over-extended and strained his back.

The pain was upon him without warning.

The last thing he heard was Saphira shouting, *Eragon!*

Despite the intensity of the fit, Eragon remained conscious throughout his ordeal. Not that he was aware of his surroundings, only the fire that burned in his flesh and prolonged each second into an eternity. The worst part was that he could do nothing to end his suffering but wait . . .

 . . . and wait . . .

Eragon lay panting in the cold mud. He blinked as his vision came into focus and he saw Oromis sitting on a stool next to him. Pushing himself onto his knees, Eragon surveyed his new tunic with a mixture of regret and disgust. The fine russet cloth was caked with dirt from his convulsions on the ground. Muck filled his hair as well.

He could sense Saphira in his mind, radiating concern as she waited for him to notice her. *How can you continue like this?* she fretted. *It'll destroy you.*

Her misgivings undermined Eragon's remaining fortitude. Saphira had never before expressed doubt that he would prevail, not at Dras-Leona, Gil'ead, or Farthen Dûr, nor with any of the dangers they had encountered. Her confidence had given him courage. Without it he was truly afraid.

You should concentrate on your lesson, he said.

I should concentrate on you.

Leave me alone! He snapped at her like a wounded animal that wants to nurse its injuries in silence and in dark. She fell silent, leaving just enough of their connection intact so that he was vaguely aware of Glaedr teaching her about fireweed, which she could chew to help her digestion.

Eragon combed the mud from his hair with his fingers, then spat out a globule of blood. "Bit my tongue."

Oromis nodded as if it were to be expected. "Do you require healing?"

"No."

"Very well. Tend to your sword, then bathe and go to the stump in the glade and listen to the thoughts of the forest. Listen, and when you hear no more, come tell me what you have learned."

"Yes, Master."

As he sat on the stump, Eragon found that his turbulent thoughts and emotions prevented him from mustering the concentration to open his mind and sense the creatures in the hollow. Nor was he interested in doing so.

Still, the peaceful quality of his surroundings gradually ameliorated his resentment, confusion, and stubborn anger. It did not make him happy, but it did bring him a certain fatalistic acceptance. *This is my lot in life, and I'd better get used to it because it's not about to improve in the foreseeable future.*

After a quarter of an hour, his faculties had regained their usual acuity, so he resumed studying the colony of red ants that he had discovered the day before. He also tried to be aware of everything else that was happening in the glade, as Oromis had instructed.

Eragon met with limited success. If he relaxed and allowed himself to absorb input from all the consciousnesses nearby, thousands of images and feelings rushed into his head, piling on top of one another in quick flashes of sound and color, touch and smell, pain and pleasure. The amount of information was overwhelming. Out of pure habit, his mind would snatch one subject or another from the torrent, excluding all the rest before he noticed his lapse and wrenched himself back into a state of passive receptivity. The cycle repeated itself every few seconds.

Despite that, he was able to improve his understanding of the ants' world. He got his first clue as to their genders when he deduced that the huge ant in the heart of their underground lair was laying eggs, one every minute or so, which made it—her—a female. And when he accompanied a group of the red ants up the stem of their rosebush, he got a vivid demonstration of the kind of enemies they faced: some *thing* darted out from underneath a leaf and killed one of the ants he was bound to. It was hard for him to guess exactly what the creature was, since the ants only saw fragments of it and, in any case, they placed more emphasis on smell than vision. If they had been people, he would have said that they were attacked by a terrifying monster the size of a dragon, which had jaws as powerful as the spiked portcullis at Teirm and could move with whiplash speed.

The ants ringed in the monster like grooms working to capture a runaway horse. They darted at it with a total lack of fear, nipping at its knobbed legs and withdrawing an instant before they were caught in the monster's iron pincers. More and more ants joined the throng. They worked together to overpower the intruder, never faltering, even when two were caught and killed and when several of their brethren fell off the stem to the ground below.

It was a desperate battle, with neither side willing to give quarter. Only escape or victory would save the combatants from a horrible death. Eragon followed the fray with breathless anticipation, awed by the ants' bravery and how they continued to fight in spite of injuries that would incapacitate a human. Their feats were heroic enough to be sung about by bards throughout the land.

Eragon was so engrossed by the contest that when the ants finally prevailed, he loosed an elated cry so loud, it roused the birds from their roosts among the trees.

Out of curiosity, he returned his attention to his own body, then walked to the rosebush to view the dead monster for himself. What he saw was an ordinary brown spider with its legs curled into a fist being transported by the ants down to their nest for food.

Amazing.

He started to leave, but then realized that once again he had neglected to keep watch over the myriad other insects and animals in the glade. He closed his eyes and whirled through the minds of several dozen beings, doing his best to memorize as many interesting details as he could. It was a poor substitute for prolonged observation, but he was hungry and he had already exhausted his assigned hour.

When Eragon rejoined Oromis in his hut, the elf asked, "How went it?"

"Master, I could listen night and day for the next twenty years and still not know everything that goes on in the forest."

Oromis raised an eyebrow. "You have made progress." After Eragon described what he had witnessed, Oromis said, "But still not enough, I fear. You must work harder, Eragon. I know you can. You are intelligent and persistent, and you have the potential to be a great Rider. As difficult as it is, you have to learn to put aside your troubles and concentrate entirely on the task at hand. Find peace within yourself and let your actions flow from there."

"I'm doing my best."

"No, this isn't your best. We shall recognize your best when it appears." He paused thoughtfully. "Perhaps it would help if you had a fellow student to compete with. Then we might see your best. . . . I will think on the matter."

From his cupboards, Oromis produced a loaf of freshly baked bread, a wood jar of hazelnut butter—which the elves used in place of actual butter—and a pair of bowls that he ladled full of a vegetable stew that had been simmering in a pot hung over a bed of coals in the corner fireplace.

Eragon looked at the stew with distaste; he was sick of the elves' fare. He longed for meat, fish, or fowl, something hearty that he could sink his teeth into, not this endless parade of plants. "Master," he asked to distract himself, "why do you have me meditate? Is it so that I will understand the doings of the animals and insects, or is there more to it than that?"

"Can you think of no other motive?" Oromis sighed when Eragon shook his head. "Always it is thus with my new students, and especially with the human ones; the mind is the last muscle they train or use, and the one that they regard the least. Ask them about swordplay and they can list every blow from a duel a month old, but ask them to solve a problem or make a coherent statement and . . . well, I would be lucky to get more than a blank stare in return. You are still new to the world of gramarye—as magic is properly called—but you must begin to consider its full implications."

"How so?"

"Imagine for a moment that you are Galbatorix, with all of his vast resources at your command. The Varden have destroyed your Urgal army with the help of a rival Dragon Rider, who you know was educated—at least in part—by one of your most dangerous and implacable foes, Brom. You are also aware that your enemies are massing in Surda for a possible invasion. Given that, what would be the easiest way to deal with these various threats, short of flying into battle yourself?"

Eragon stirred his stew to cool it while he examined the issue. "It seems to me," he said slowly, "that the easiest thing would be to train a corps of magicians—they wouldn't even have to be that powerful—force them to swear loyalty to me in the ancient language, then have them infiltrate Surda to sabotage the Varden's efforts, poison wells, and assassinate Nasuada, King Orrin, and other key members of the resistance."

"And why hasn't Galbatorix done this yet?"

"Because until now, Surda was of negligible interest to him, and because the Varden have dwelled in Farthen Dûr for decades, where they were able to examine every newcomer's mind for duplicity, which they can't do in Surda since its border and population are so large."

"Those are my very conclusions," said Oromis. "Unless Galbatorix forsakes his lair in Urû'baen, the greatest danger you're likely to encounter during the Varden's campaign will come from fellow magicians. You know as well as I how difficult it is to guard against magic, especially if your opponent has sworn in the ancient language to kill you, no matter the cost. Instead of attempting to first conquer your mind, such a foe will simply cast a spell to obliterate you, even though—in the instant before you are destroyed—you will still be free to retaliate. However, you cannot fell your murderer if you don't know who or where he is."

"So sometimes you don't have to bother taking control of your opponent's mind?"

"Sometimes, but it's a risk to avoid." Oromis paused to consume a few spoonfuls of stew. "Now, to address the heart of this issue, how do you defend yourself against anonymous enemies who can contravene any physical precautions and slay with a muttered word?"

"I don't see how, unless . . ." Eragon hesitated, then smiled. "Unless I was aware of the consciousnesses of all the people around me. Then I could sense if they meant me harm."

Oromis appeared pleased by his answer. "Even so, Eragon-finiarel. And that's the answer to your question. Your meditations condition your mind to find and exploit flaws in your enemies' mental armor, no matter how small."

"But won't another magic user know if I touch their mind?"

"Aye, they will know, but most people won't. And as for the magicians, they will know, they will be afraid, and they will shield their minds from you out of their fear, and you will know them because of it."

"Isn't it dangerous to leave your consciousness unguarded? If you're attacked mentally, you could easily be overwhelmed."

"It's less dangerous than being blind to the world."

Eragon nodded. He tapped his spoon against his bowl in a measured meter of time, engrossed in his thoughts, then said, "It feels wrong."

"Oh? Explain yourself."

"What about people's privacy? Brom taught me to never intrude in someone's mind unless it was absolutely necessary. . . . I guess I'm uncomfortable with the idea of prying into people's secrets . . . secrets that they have every right to keep to themselves." He cocked his head. "Why didn't Brom tell me about this if it's so important? Why didn't he train me in it himself?"

"Brom told you," said Oromis, "what was appropriate to tell you under the circumstances. Dipping into the pool of minds can prove addictive to those with a malicious personality or a taste for power. It was not taught to prospective Riders—though we had them meditate as you do throughout their training—until we were convinced that they were mature enough to resist temptation.

"It *is* an invasion of privacy, and you will learn many things from it that you never wanted to. However, this is for your own good and the good of the Varden. I can say from experience, and from watching other Riders experience the same, that this, above all else, will help you to understand what drives people. And understanding begets empathy and compassion, even for the meanest beggar in the meanest city of Alagaësia."

They were quiet for a while, eating, then Oromis asked, "Can you tell me, What is the most important mental tool a person can possess?"

It was a serious question, and Eragon considered it for a reasonable span before he ventured to say, "Determination."

Oromis tore the loaf in half with his long white fingers. "I can understand why you arrived at that conclusion—determination has served you well in your adventures—but no. I meant the tool most necessary to choose the best course of action in any given situation. Determination is as common among men who are dull and foolish as it is among those who are brilliant intellects. So, no, determination cannot be what we're looking for."

This time Eragon treated the question as he would a riddle, counting the number of words, whispering them out loud to establish whether they rhymed, and otherwise examining them for hidden meaning. The problem was, he was no more than a mediocre riddler and had never placed very high in Carvahall's annual riddle contest. He thought too literally to work out the answers to riddles that he had not heard before, a legacy of Garrow's practical upbringing.

"Wisdom," he finally said. "Wisdom is the most important tool for a person to possess."

"A fair guess, but, again, no. The answer is logic. Or, to put it another way, the ability to reason analytically. Applied properly, it can overcome any lack of wisdom, which one only gains through age and experience."

Eragon frowned. "Yes, but isn't having a good heart more important than logic? Pure logic can lead you to conclusions that are ethically wrong, whereas if you are moral and righteous, that will ensure that you don't act shamefully."

A razor-thin smile curled Oromis's lips. "You confuse the issue. All I wanted to know was the most useful *tool* a person can have, regardless of whether that person is good or evil. I agree that it's important to be of a virtuous nature, but I would also contend that if you had to choose between giving a man a noble disposition or teaching him to think clearly, you'd do better to teach him to think clearly. Too many problems in this world are caused by men with noble dispositions and clouded minds.

"History provides us with numerous examples of people who were convinced that they were doing the right thing and committed terrible crimes because of it. Keep in mind, Eragon, that no one thinks of himself as a villain, and few make decisions they think are wrong. A person may dislike his choice, but he will stand by it because, even in the worst circumstances, he believes that it was the best option available to him at the time.

"On its own, being a decent person is no guarantee that you will act well, which brings us back to the one protection we have against demagogues, tricksters, and the madness of crowds, and our surest guide through the uncertain shoals of life: clear and reasoned thinking. Logic will never fail you, unless you're unaware of—or deliberately ignore—the consequences of your deeds."

"If elves are so logical," said Eragon, "then you must all agree on what to do."

"Hardly," averred Oromis. "Like every race, we adhere to a wide range of tenets, and, as a result, we often arrive at differing conclusions, even in identical situations. Conclusions, I might add, that make logical sense from each person's point of view. And although I wish it were otherwise, not all elves have trained their minds properly."

"How do you intend to teach me this logic?"

Oromis's smile broadened. "By the oldest and most effective method: debating. I will ask you a question, then you will answer and defend your position." He waited while Eragon refilled his bowl with stew. "For example, why do you fight the Empire?"

The sudden change of topic caught Eragon off guard. He had a feeling that Oromis had just reached the subject that he had been driving toward all along. "As I said before, to help those who suffer from Galbatorix's rule and, to a lesser extent, for personal vengeance."

"Then you fight for humanitarian reasons?"

"What do you mean?"

"That you fight to help the people who Galbatorix has harmed and to stop him from hurting any more."

"Exactly," said Eragon.

"Ah, but answer me this, my young Rider: Won't your war with Galbatorix cause more pain than it will ever prevent? The majority of people in the Empire live normal, productive lives untouched by their king's madness. How can you justify invading their land, destroying their homes, and killing their sons and daughters?"

Eragon gaped, stunned that Oromis could ask such a question—Galbatorix was *evil*—and stunned because no easy reply presented itself. He knew that he was in the right, but how could he prove it? "Don't you believe that Galbatorix should be overthrown?"

"That is not the question."

"You *must* believe it, though," persisted Eragon. "Look what he did to the Riders."

Dunking his bread in his stew, Oromis resumed eating, letting Eragon fume in silence. When he finished, Oromis folded his hands in his lap and asked, "Have I upset you?"

"Yes, you have."

"I see. Well then, continue to ponder the matter until you find an answer. I expect it to be a convincing one."

BLACK MORNING GLORY

hey cleared the table and took the dishes outside, where they
cleaned them with sand. Oromis crumbled what remained of
the bread around his house for the birds to eat, then they returned inside.

Oromis brought out pens and ink for Eragon, and they resumed
his education of the Liduen Kvaedhí, the written form of the ancient language, which was so much more elegant than the humans'
or dwarves' runes. Eragon lost himself in the arcàne glyphs, happy
to have a task that required nothing more strenuous than rote
memorization.

After hours spent bent over the paper sheets, Oromis waved a
hand and said, "Enough. We will continue this tomorrow." Eragon
leaned back and rolled his shoulders while Oromis selected five
scrolls from their nooks in the wall. "Two of these are in the ancient
language, three are in your native tongue. They will help you to
master both alphabets, as well as give you valuable information that
would be tedious for me to vocalize."

"Vocalize?"

With unerring accuracy, Oromis's hand darted out and plucked a
massive sixth scroll from the wall, which he added to the pyramid
in Eragon's arms. "This is a dictionary. I doubt you can, but try to
read it all."

When the elf opened the door for him to leave, Eragon said,
"Master?"

"Yes, Eragon?"

"When will we start working with magic?"

Oromis leaned on one arm against the doorway, caving in on himself as if he no longer possessed the will to remain upright. Then he sighed and said, "You must trust me to guide your training, Eragon. Still, I suppose it would be foolish of me to delay any longer. Come, leave the scrolls on the table, and let us go explore the mysteries of gramarye."

On the greensward before the hut, Oromis stood looking out over the Crags of Tel'naeír, his back to Eragon, his feet shoulder width apart, and his hands clasped in the small of his back. Without turning around, he asked, "What is magic?"

"The manipulation of energy through the use of the ancient language."

There was a pause before Oromis responded. "Technically, you are correct, and many spellcasters never understand more than that. However, your description fails to capture the essence of magic. Magic is the art of *thinking*, not strength or language—you already know that a limited vocabulary is no obstacle to using magic. As with everything else you must master, magic relies on having a disciplined intellect.

"Brom bypassed the normal training regimen and ignored the subtleties of gramarye to ensure that you had the skills you needed to remain alive. I too must distort the regimen in order to focus on the skills that you will likely require in the coming battles. However, whereas Brom taught you the crude mechanics of magic, I will teach you its finer applications, the secrets that were reserved for the wisest of the Riders: how you can kill with no more energy than moving your finger, the method by which you can instantaneously transport an item from one point to another, a spell that will allow you to identify poisons in your food and drink, a variation on scrying that allows you to hear as well as to see, how you can draw energy from your surroundings and thus preserve your own strength, and how you can maximize your strength in every possible way.

"These techniques are so potent and dangerous, they were never shared with novice Riders such as yourself, but circumstances demand that I divulge them and trust that you won't abuse them." Raising his right arm to his side, his hand a hooked claw, Oromis proclaimed, "Adurna!"

Eragon watched as a sphere of water coalesced from the brook by the hut and floated through the air until it hovered between Oromis's outstretched fingers.

The brook was dark and brown under the branches of the forest, but the sphere, removed from it, was as colorless as glass. Flecks of moss, dirt, and other bits of detritus floated inside the orb.

Still gazing toward the horizon, Oromis said, "Catch." He tossed the sphere back over his shoulder toward Eragon.

Eragon tried to grab the ball, but as soon as it touched his skin, the water lost cohesion and splashed across his chest.

"Catch it with magic," said Oromis. Again, he cried, "Adurna!" and a sphere of water gathered itself from the surface of the brook and leaped into his hand like a trained hawk obeying its master.

This time Oromis threw the ball without warning. Eragon was prepared, though, and said, "Reisa du adurna," even as he reached for the ball. It slowed to a halt a hairsbreadth from the skin of his palm.

"An awkward word choice," said Oromis, "but workable, nevertheless."

Eragon grinned and whispered, "Thrysta."

The ball reversed its course and sped toward the base of Oromis's silver head. However, the sphere did not land where Eragon had intended, but rather shot past the elf, whipped around, and flew back at Eragon with increased velocity.

The water remained as hard and solid as polished marble when it struck Eragon, producing a dull *thunk* as it collided with his skull. The blow knocked him sprawling on the turf, where he lay stunned, blinking as pulsing lights swam across the sky.

"Yes," said Oromis. "A better word might be *letta* or *kodthr*." He finally turned to look at Eragon and raised an eyebrow with apparent surprise. "Whatever are you doing? Get up. We can't lay about all day."

"Yes, Master," groaned Eragon.

When Eragon got back on his feet, Oromis had him manipulate the water in various ways—shaping it into complex knots, changing the color of light that it absorbed or reflected, and freezing it in certain prescribed sequences—none of which proved difficult for him.

The exercises continued for so long that Eragon's initial interest faded and was replaced by impatience and puzzlement. He was chary of offending Oromis, but he saw no point to what the elf was doing; it was as if Oromis were avoiding any spells that would require him to use more than a minimal amount of strength. *I've already demonstrated the extent of my skills. Why does he persist in reviewing these fundamentals?* He said, "Master, I know all of this. Can we not move on?"

The muscles in Oromis's neck hardened, and his shoulders were like chiseled granite for all they moved; even the elf's breathing halted before he said, "Will you never learn respect, Eragon-vodhr? So be it!" Then he uttered four words from the ancient language in a voice so deep that their meaning escaped Eragon.

Eragon yelped as he felt each of his legs enveloped by pressure up to the knee, squeezing and constricting his calves in such a way that made it impossible for him to walk. His thighs and upper body were free to move, but other than that, it was as if he had been cast in lime mortar.

"Free yourself," said Oromis.

Here now was a challenge that Eragon had never dealt with before: how to counter someone else's spells. He could sever his invisible bonds using one of two different methods. The most effective would be if he knew *how* Oromis had immobilized him—whether by affecting his body directly or using an external source—for then he could redirect the element or force to disperse Oromis's power. Or he could use a generic, vague spell to block whatever

Oromis was doing. The downside to the tactic was that it would lead to a direct contest of strength between them. *It had to happen sometime*, thought Eragon. He entertained no hope of prevailing against an elf.

Assembling the required phrase, he said, "Losna kalfya iet." Release my calves.

The surge of energy that deserted Eragon was greater than he had anticipated; he went from being moderately tired from the day's pains and exertions to feeling as if he had hiked over rough terrain since morn. Then the pressure vanished from his legs, causing him to stagger as he regained his balance.

Oromis shook his head. "Foolish," he said, "very foolish. If I had committed more to maintaining my spell, that would have killed you. Never use absolutes."

"Absolutes?"

"Never word your spells so that only two outcomes are possible: success or death. If an enemy had trapped your legs and if he were stronger than you, then you would have expended all of your energy trying to break his spell. You would have died with no chance to abort the attempt once you realized that it was futile."

"How do I avoid that?" asked Eragon.

"It's safer to make the spell a *process* that you can terminate at your discretion. Instead of saying *release my calves*, which is an absolute, you could say *reduce the magic imprisoning my calves*. A bit wordy, but you could then decide how much you wanted your opponent's spell decreased and if it were safe to remove it entirely. We will try again."

The pressure returned to Eragon's legs as soon as Oromis mouthed his inaudible invocation. Eragon was so tired, he doubted that he could provide much opposition. Nevertheless, he reached for the magic.

Before the ancient language left Eragon's mouth, he became aware of a curious sensation as the weight constraining his legs lessened at a steady rate. It tickled and felt like he was being pulled out of a mire of cold, slick mud. He glanced at Oromis and saw the elf's face scribed by passion, as if he clung to something precious that he could not bear to lose. A vein throbbed at one of Oromis's temples.

When Eragon's arcane fetters ceased to exist, Oromis recoiled as if he had been pricked by a wasp and stood with his gaze fixed on his two hands, his thin chest heaving. For perhaps a minute, he remained thus, then he drew himself upright and walked to the very edge of the Crags of Tel'naeír, a lone figure outlined against the pale sky.

Regret and sorrow welled in Eragon—the same emotions that had gripped him when he first saw Glaedr's mutilated foreleg. He cursed himself for being so arrogant with Oromis, so oblivious to his infirmities, and for not placing more confidence in the elf's judgment. *I'm not the only one who must deal with past injuries*. Eragon had not fully comprehended what it meant when Oromis said that all but the slightest magic escaped his grasp. Now he appreciated the depths of Oromis's situation and the pain that it must cause him, especially for one of his race, who was born and bred with magic.

Eragon went to Oromis, knelt, and bowed in the fashion of the dwarves, pressing his bruised forehead against the ground. "Ebrithil, I beg your pardon."

The elf gave no indication that he had heard.

The two of them lingered in their respective positions while the sun declined before them, the birds sang their evening songs, and the air grew cool and moist. From the north came the faint offbeat thumps of Saphira and Glaedr's wing strokes as they returned for the day.

In a low, distant voice, Oromis said, "We will begin anew tomorrow, with this and other subjects." From his profile, Eragon could tell that Oromis had regained his customary expression of impassive reserve. "Is that agreeable to you?"

"Yes, Master," said Eragon, grateful for the question.

"I think it best if, from now on, you endeavor to speak only in the ancient language. We have little time at our disposal, and this is the fastest way for you to learn."

"Even when I talk to Saphira?"

"Even then."

Adopting the elven tongue, Eragon vowed, "Then I will work ceaselessly until I not only think, but dream, in your language."

"If you achieve that," said Oromis, replying in kind, "our venture may yet succeed." He paused. "Instead of flying directly here in the morning, you will accompany the elf I send to guide you. He will take you to where those of Ellesméra practice swordplay. Stay for an hour, then continue on as normal."

"Won't you teach me yourself?" asked Eragon, feeling slighted.

"I have naught to teach. You are as good a swordsman as ever I have met. I know no more of fighting than you, and that which I possess and you do not, I cannot give you. All that remains for you is to preserve your current level of skill."

"Why can't I do that with you . . . Master?"

"Because I do not appreciate beginning the day with alarum and conflict." He looked at Eragon, then relented and added, "And because it will be good for you to become acquainted with others who live here. I am not representative of my race. But enough of that. Look, they approach."

The two dragons glided across the flat disk of the sun. First came Glaedr with a roar of wind, blotting out the sky with his massive bulk before he settled on the grass and folded his golden wings, then Saphira, as quick and agile as a sparrow beside an eagle.

As they had that morning, Oromis and Glaedr asked a number of questions to ensure that Eragon and Saphira had paid attention to each other's lessons. They had not always, but by cooperating and sharing information between themselves, they were able to answer all of the questions. Their only stumbling block was the foreign language they were required to communicate in.

Better, rumbled Glaedr afterward. *Much better*. He bent his gaze toward Eragon. *You and I will have to train together soon*.

"Of course, Skulblaka."

The old dragon snorted and crawled alongside Oromis, half hopping with his front leg to compensate for his missing limb. Darting forward, Saphira nipped at the end of Glaedr's tail, tossing it into the air with a flip of her head, like she would to break the neck of a deer. She recoiled as Glaedr twisted round and snapped at her neck, exposing his enormous fangs.

Eragon winced and, too late, covered his ears to protect them from Glaedr's roar. The speed and intensity of Glaedr's response suggested to Eragon that this was not the first time Saphira had annoyed him throughout the day. Instead of remorse, Eragon detected an excited playfulness in her—like a child with a new toy—and a near-blind devotion to the other dragon.

"Contain yourself, Saphira!" said Oromis. Saphira pranced backward and settled on her haunches, though nothing in her demeanor expressed contrition. Eragon muttered a feeble excuse, and Oromis waved a hand and said, "Begone, both of you."

Without arguing, Eragon scrambled onto Saphira. He had to urge her to take flight, and once she did, she insisted on circling over the clearing three times before he got her to angle toward Ellesméra.

What possessed you to bite him? he demanded. He thought he knew, but he wanted her to confirm it.

I was only playing.

It was the truth, since they spoke in the ancient language, yet he suspected that it was but a piece of a larger truth. *Yes, and at what game?* She tensed underneath him. *You forget your duty. By . . .* He searched for the right word. Unable to find it, he reverted to his native speech, *By provoking Glaedr, you distract him, Oromis, and me—and hinder what we must accomplish. You've never been so thoughtless before.*

Do not presume to be my conscience.

He laughed then, heedless for a moment of where he sat among the clouds, rolling to his side until he almost dropped from the peak of her shoulders. *Oh, rich irony that, after the times you've told me what to do. I am your conscience, Saphira, as much as you are mine. You've had good reason to chastise and warn me in the past, and now I must do the same for you: stop pestering Glaedr with your attentions.*

She remained silent.

Saphira?

I hear you.

I hope so.

After a minute of peaceful flying, she said, *Two seizures in one day. How are you now?*

Sore and ill. He grimaced. *Some of it's from the Rimgar and sparring, but mostly it's the aftereffects of the pain. It's like a poison, weakening my muscles and clouding my mind. I just hope that I can remain sane long enough to reach the end of this training. Afterward, though . . . I don't know what I'll do. I certainly can't fight for the Varden like this.*

Don't think about it, she counseled. *You can do nothing about your condition, and you'll only make yourself feel worse. Live in the present, remember the past, and fear not the future, for it doesn't exist and never shall. There is only now.*

He patted her shoulder and smiled with resigned gratitude. To their right, a goshawk rode a warm air current while it patrolled the broken forest for signs of furred or feathered quarry. Eragon watched it, pondering the question that Oromis had given him: How could he justify fighting the Empire when it would cause so much grief and agony?

I have an answer, said Saphira.

What is it?

That Galbatorix has . . . She hesitated, then said, *No, I won't tell you. You should figure this out for yourself.*

Saphira! Be reasonable.

I am. If you don't know why what we do is the right thing, you might as well surrender to Galbatorix for all the good you'll do. No matter how eloquent his pleas, he could extract nothing more from her, for she blocked him from that part of her mind.

Back in their eyrie, Eragon ate a light supper and was just about to open one of Oromis's scrolls when a knock on the screen door disturbed his quiet.

"Enter," he said, hoping that Arya had returned to see him.

She had.

Arya greeted Eragon and Saphira, then said, "I thought that you might appreciate an opportunity to visit Tialdarí Hall and the adjacent gardens, since you expressed interest in them yesterday. That is, if you aren't too tired." She wore a flowing red kirtle trimmed and decorated with intricate designs wrought in black thread. The color scheme echoed the queen's robes and emphasized the strong resemblance between mother and daughter.

Eragon pushed aside the scrolls. "I'd be delighted to see them."

He means we'd *be delighted,* added Saphira.

Arya looked surprised when both of them spoke in the ancient language, so Eragon explained Oromis's command. "An excellent idea," said Arya, joining them in the same language. "And it is more appropriate to speak thus while you stay here."

When all three of them had descended from the tree, Arya directed them westward toward an unfamiliar quadrant of Ellesméra. They encountered many elves on the path, all of whom stopped to bow to Saphira.

Eragon noticed once again that no elf children were to be seen. He mentioned this to Arya, and she said, "Aye, we have few children. Only two are in Ellesméra at the present, Dusan and Alanna. We treasure children above all else because they are so rare. To have a child is the greatest honor and responsibility that can be bestowed upon any living being."

At last they arrived at a ribbed lancet arch—grown between two trees—which served as the entrance for a wide compound. Still in the ancient language, Arya chanted, "Root of tree, fruit of vine, let me pass by this blood of mine."

The two archway doors trembled, then swung outward, releasing five monarch butterflies that fluttered toward the dusky sky. Through the archway lay a vast flower garden arranged to look as pristine and natural as a wild meadow. The one element that betrayed artifice was the sheer variety of plants; many of the species were blooming out of season, or came from hotter or colder climates and would never have flourished without the elves' magic. The scene was lit with the gemlike flameless lanterns, augmented by constellations of swirling fireflies.

To Saphira, Arya said, "Mind your tail, that it does not sweep across the beds."

Advancing, they crossed the garden and pressed deep into a line of scattered trees. Before Eragon quite knew where he was, the trees became more numerous and then thickened into a wall. He found himself standing on the threshold of a burnished wood hall without ever being conscious of having gone inside.

The hall was warm and homey—a place of peace, reflection, and comfort. Its shape was determined by the tree trunks, which on the inside of the hall had been stripped of their bark, polished, and rubbed with oil until the wood gleamed like amber. Regular gaps between the trunks acted as windows. The scent of crushed pine needles perfumed the air. A number of elves occupied the hall, reading, writing, and, in one dark corner, playing a set of reed pipes. They all paused and inclined their heads to acknowledge Saphira's presence.

"Here you would stay," said Arya, "were you not Rider and dragon."

"It's magnificent," replied Eragon.

Arya guided him and Saphira everywhere in the compound that was accessible to dragons. Each new room was a surprise; no two were alike, and each chamber found different ways to incorporate the forest in its construction. In one room, a silver brook trickled down the gnarled wall and flowed across the floor on a vein of pebbles and back out under the sky. In another, creepers blanketed the entire room, except for the floor, in a leafy green pelt adorned with trumpet-shaped flowers with the most delicate pink and white colors. Arya called it the Lianí Vine.

They saw many great works of art, from fairths and paintings to sculptures and radiant mosaics of stained glass—all based on the curved shapes of plants and animals.

Islanzadí met with them for a short time in an open pavilion joined to two other buildings by covered pathways. She inquired about the progress of Eragon's training and the state of his back, both of which he described with brief, polite phrases. This seemed to satisfy the queen, who exchanged a few words with Saphira and then departed.

In the end, they returned to the garden. Eragon walked beside Arya—Saphira trailing behind—entranced by the sound of her voice as she told him about the different varieties of flowers, where they originated, how they were maintained, and, in many instances, how they had been altered with magic. She also pointed out the flowers that only opened their petals during the night, like a white datura.

"Which one is your favorite?" he asked.

Arya smiled and escorted him to a tree on the edge of the garden, by a pond lined with rushes. Around the tree's lowest branch coiled a morning glory with three velvety black blossoms that were clenched shut.

Blowing on them, Arya whispered, "Open."

The petals rustled as they unfurled, fanning their inky robes to expose the hoard of nectar in their centers. A starburst of royal blue filled the flowers' throats, diffusing into the sable corolla like the vestiges of day into night.

"Is it not the most perfect and lovely flower?" asked Arya.

Eragon gazed at her, exquisitely aware of how close they were, and said, "Yes . . . it is." Before his courage deserted him, he added, "As are you."

Eragon! exclaimed Saphira.

Arya fixed her eyes upon him, studying him until he was forced to look away. When he dared face her again, he was mortified to see her wearing a faint smile, as if amused by his reaction. "You are too kind," she murmured. Reaching up, she touched the rim of a blossom and glanced from it to him. "Fäolin created this especially for me one summer solstice, long ago."

He shuffled his feet and responded with a few unintelligible words, hurt and offended that she did not take his compliment more seriously. He wished he could turn invisible, and even considered trying to cast a spell that would allow him to do just that.

In the end, he drew himself upright and said, "Please excuse us, Arya Svit-kona, but it is late, and we must return to our tree."

Her smile deepened. "Of course, Eragon. I understand." She accompanied them to the main archway, opened the doors for them, and said, "Good night, Saphira. Good night, Eragon."

Good night, replied Saphira.

Despite his embarrassment, Eragon could not help asking, "Will we see you tomorrow?"

Arya tilted her head. "I think I shall be busy tomorrow." Then the doors closed, cutting off his view of her as she returned to the main compound.

Crouching low on the path, Saphira nudged Eragon in the side. *Stop daydreaming and get on my back.* Climbing up her left foreleg, he took his usual place, then clutched the neck spike in front of him as Saphira rose to her full height. After a few steps: *How can you criticize my behavior with Glaedr and then go and do something like that? What were you thinking?*

You know how I feel about her, he grumbled.

Pah! If you are my conscience and I am yours, then it's my duty to tell you when you're acting like a deluded popinjay. You're not using logic, like Oromis keeps telling us to. What do you really expect to happen between you and Arya? She's a princess!

And I'm a Rider.

She's an elf; you're a human!

I look more like an elf every day.

Eragon, she's over a hundred years old!

I'll live as long as her or any elf.

Ah, but you haven't yet, and that's the problem. You can't overcome such a vast difference. She's a grown woman with a century of experience, while you're—

365

What? What am I? he snarled. *A child? Is that what you mean?*

No, not a child. Not after what you have seen and done since we were joined. But you are young, even by the reckoning of your short-lived race—much less by that of the dwarves, dragons, and elves.

As are you.

His retort silenced her for a minute. Then: *I'm just trying to protect you, Eragon. That's all. I want you to be happy, and I'm afraid you won't be if you insist on pursuing Arya.*

The two of them were about to retire when they heard the trapdoor in the vestibule bang open and the jingle of mail as someone climbed inside. Zar'roc in hand, Eragon threw back the screen door, ready to confront the intruder.

His hand dropped as he saw Orik on the floor. The dwarf took a hearty draught from the bottle he wielded in his left hand, then squinted at Eragon. "Bricks and bones, where be you? Ah, there you shtand. I wondered where you were. Couldn't find you, so I thought that given this fine dolorous night, I might go find you . . . and here you are! What shall we talk about, you and I, now that we're together in this delectable bird's nest?"

Taking hold of the dwarf's free arm, Eragon pulled him upright, surprised, as he always was, by how dense Orik was, like a miniature boulder. When Eragon removed his support, Orik swayed from one side to the other, achieving such precarious angles that he threatened to topple at the slightest provocation.

"Come on in," said Eragon in his own language. He closed the trapdoor. "You'll catch cold out here."

Orik blinked his round, deep-set eyes at Eragon. "I've not sheen you round my leafy exile, no I haven't. You've abandoned me to the company of elves . . . and misherable, dull company they are, yesh indeed."

A touch of guilt made Eragon disguise himself with an awkward smile. He *had* forgotten the dwarf amid the goings-on. "I'm sorry I haven't visited you, Orik, but my studies have kept me busy. Here, give me your cloak." As he helped the dwarf out of his brown mantle, he asked, "What are you drinking?"

"Faelnirv," declared Orik. "A mosht wonderful, ticklish potion. The besht and greatest of the elves' tricksty inventions; it gives you the gift of loquacion. Words float from your tongue like shoals of flapping minnows, like flocks of breathlessh hummingbirds, like rivers of writhing shnakes." He paused, apparently taken by the unique magnificence of his similes. As Eragon ushered him into the bedroom, Orik saluted Saphira with his bottle and said, "Greetings, O Irontooth. May your shcales shine as bright as the coals of Morgothal's forge."

Greetings, Orik, said Saphira, laying her head on the rim of her bed. *What has put you in this state? It is not like you.* Eragon repeated her question.

"What has put me in mine shtate?" repeated Orik. He dropped into the chair that Eragon provided—his feet dangling several inches above the ground—and began to shake his head. "Red cap, green cap, elves here and elves there. I drown in elvesh and their thrice-damned courtesy. Bloodless they be. Taciturn they are. Yesh sir, no shir, three bagsh full, sir, yet nary a pip more can I extract." He looked at Eragon with a mournful expression. "What am I to do while you meander through your instruction? Am I to sit and twiddle mine thumbs while I turn to shtone and join the shpirits of mine anshestors? Tell me, O sagacious Rider."

Have you no skills or hobbies that you might occupy yourself with? asked Saphira.

"Aye," said Orik. "I'm a fair enough smith by any who'd care to judge. But why should I craft bright armsh and armor for those who treasure them not? I'm usheless here. As usheless as a three-legged Feldûnost."

Eragon extended a hand toward the bottle. "May I?" Orik glanced between him and the bottle, then grimaced and gave it up. The faelnirv was cold as ice as it ran down Eragon's throat, stinging and smarting. He blinked as his eyes watered. After he indulged in a second quaff, he passed the bottle back to Orik, who seemed disappointed by how little of the concoction remained.

"And what mischief," asked Orik, "have you two managed to ferret out of Oromis and yon bucolic woods?"

The dwarf alternately chuckled and groaned as Eragon described his training, his misplaced blessing in Farthen Dûr, the Menoa tree, his back, and all else that had filled the past few days. Eragon ended with the topic that was dearest to him at the moment: Arya. Emboldened by the liqueur, he confessed his affection for her and described how she had dismissed his advance.

Wagging a finger, Orik said, "The rock beneath you is flawed, Eragon. Don't tempt fate. Arya . . ." He stopped, then growled and took another gulp of faelnirv. "Ah, it's too late for thish. Who am I to say what is wisdom and what isn't?"

Saphira had closed her eyes a while ago. Without opening them, she asked, *Are you married, Orik?* The question surprised Eragon; he had never stopped to wonder about Orik's personal life.

"Eta," said Orik. "Although I'm promised to fair Hvedra, daughter of Thorgerd One-eye and Himinglada. We were to be wed thish spring, until the Urgals attacked and Hrothgar sent me on this accursed trip."

"Is she of Dûrgrimst Ingeitum?" asked Eragon.

"Of coursh!" roared Orik, pounding his fist on the side of the chair. "Thinkest thou I would marry outside my clan? She's the granddaughter of mine aunt Vardrûn, Hrothgar's coushin twice removed, with white, round calves as smooth as satin, cheeks as red as apples, and the prettiesht dwarf maid who ever did exist."

Undoubtedly, said Saphira.

"I'm sure it won't be long before you see her again," said Eragon.

"Hmph." Orik squinted at Eragon. "Do you believe in giants? Tall giants, shtrong giants, thick and bearded giants with fingers like spadeses?"

"I've never seen nor heard of them," said Eragon, "except in stories. If they do exist, it's not in Alagaësia."

"Ah, but they do! They do!" exclaimed Orik, waving the bottle about his head. "Tell me, O Rider, if a fearshome giant were to meet you on the garden path, what might he call you, if not dinner?"

"Eragon, I would presume."

"No, no. He'd call you a dwarf, for dwarf you'd be to him." Orik guffawed and nudged Eragon in the ribs with his hard elbow. "See you now? Humans and elvesh are the giants. The land's full of them, here, there, and everywhere, stomping about with their big feet and casting us in endless shadowses." He continued laughing, rocking back in his chair until it tipped over and he fell to the floor with a solid thump.

Helping him upright, Eragon said, "I think you'd better stay here for the night. You're in no condition to go down those stairs in the dark."

Orik agreed with cheery indifference. He allowed Eragon to remove his mail and bundle him onto one side of the bed. Afterward, Eragon sighed, covered the lights, and lay on his side of the mattress.

He fell asleep hearing the dwarf mutter, ". . . Hvedra . . . Hvedra . . . Hvedra . . ."

THE NATURE OF EVIL

Bright morning arrived all too soon.

Jolted to awareness by the buzz of the vibrating timepiece, Eragon grabbed his hunting knife and sprang out of bed, expecting an attack. He gasped as his body shrieked with protest from the abuse of the past two days.

Blinking away tears, Eragon rewound the timepiece. Orik was gone; the dwarf must have slipped away in the wee hours of the morning. With a groan, Eragon hobbled to the wash closet for his daily ablutions, like an old man afflicted by rheumatism.

He and Saphira waited by the tree for ten minutes before they were met by a solemn, black-haired elf. The elf bowed, touched two fingers to his lips—which Eragon mirrored—and then preempted Eragon by saying, "May good fortune rule over you."

"And may the stars watch over you," replied Eragon. "Did Oromis send you?"

The elf ignored him and said to Saphira, "Well met, dragon. I am Vanir of House Haldthin." Eragon scowled with annoyance.

Well met, Vanir.

Only then did the elf address Eragon: "I will show you where you may practice with your blade." He strode away, not waiting for Eragon to catch up.

The sparring yard was dotted with elves of both sexes fighting in pairs and groups. Their extraordinary physical gifts resulted in flurries of blows so quick and fast, they sounded like bursts of hail striking an iron bell. Under the trees that fringed the yard, individual elves performed the Rimgar with more grace and flexibility than Eragon thought he would ever achieve.

After everyone on the field stopped and bowed to Saphira, Vanir unsheathed his narrow blade. "If you will guard your sword, Silver Hand, we can begin."

Eragon eyed the inhuman swordsmanship of the other elves with trepidation. *Why do I have to do this?* he asked. *I'll just be humiliated.*

You'll be fine, said Saphira, yet he could sense her concern for him.

Right.

As he prepared Zar'roc, Eragon's hands trembled with dread. Instead of throwing himself into the fray, he fought Vanir from a distance, dodging, sidestepping, and doing everything possible to avoid triggering another fit. Despite Eragon's evasions, Vanir touched him four times in rapid succession—once each on his ribs, shin, and both shoulders.

Vanir's initial expression of stoic impassivity soon devolved into open contempt. Dancing forward, he slid his blade up Zar'roc's length while at the same time twirling Zar'roc in a circle, wrenching Eragon's wrist. Eragon allowed Zar'roc to fly out of his hand rather than resist the elf's superior strength.

Vanir dropped his sword onto Eragon's neck and said, "Dead." Shrugging off the sword, Eragon trudged over to retrieve Zar'roc. "Dead," said Vanir. "How do you expect to defeat Galbatorix like this? I expected better, even from a weakling human."

"Then why don't you fight Galbatorix yourself instead of hiding in Du Weldenvarden?"

Vanir stiffened with outrage. "Because," he said, cool and haughty, "I'm not a Rider. And if I were, I would not be such a coward as you."

No one moved or spoke on the field.

His back to Vanir, Eragon leaned on Zar'roc and craned his neck toward the sky, snarling to himself. *He knows nothing. This is just one more test to overcome.*

"Coward, I say. Your blood is as thin as the rest of your race's. I think that Saphira was confused by Galbatorix's wiles and made the wrong choice of Rider." The spectating elves gasped at Vanir's words and muttered among themselves with open disapproval for his atrocious breach of etiquette.

Eragon ground his teeth. He could stand insults to himself, but not to Saphira. She was already moving when his pent-up frustration, fear, and pain burst within him and he whirled around, the tip of Zar'roc whistling through the air.

The blow would have killed Vanir had he not blocked it at the last second. He looked surprised by the ferocity of the attack. Holding nothing in reserve, Eragon drove Vanir to the center of the field, jabbing and slashing like a madman—determined to hurt the elf however he could. He nicked Vanir on the hip with enough force to draw blood, even with Zar'roc's blunted edge.

At that instant, Eragon's back ruptured in an explosion of agony so intense, he experienced it with all five senses: as a deafening, crashing waterfall of sound; a metallic taste that coated his tongue; an acrid, eye-watering stench in his nostrils, redolent of vinegar; pulsing colors; and, above all, the feeling that Durza had just laid open his back.

He could see Vanir standing over him with a derisive sneer. It occurred to Eragon that Vanir was very young.

After the seizure, Eragon wiped the blood from his mouth with his hand and showed it to Vanir, asking, "Thin enough?" Vanir did not deign to respond, but rather sheathed his sword and walked away.

"Where are you going?" demanded Eragon. "We have unfinished business, you and I."

"You are in no fit condition to spar," scoffed the elf.

"Try me." Eragon might be inferior to the elves, but he refused to give them the satisfaction of fulfilling their low expectations of him. He would earn their respect through sheer persistence, if nothing else.

He insisted on completing Oromis's assigned hour, after which

Saphira marched up to Vanir and touched him on the chest with the point of one of her ivory talons. *Dead,* she said. Vanir paled. The other elves edged away from him.

Once they were in the air, Saphira said, *Oromis was right.*

About what?

You give more of yourself when you have an opponent.

At Oromis's hut, the day resumed its usual pattern: Saphira accompanied Glaedr for her instruction while Eragon remained with Oromis.

Eragon was horrified when he discovered that Oromis expected him to do the Rimgar in addition to his earlier exercises. It took all of his courage to obey. His apprehension proved groundless, though, for the Dance of Snake and Crane was too gentle to injure him.

That, coupled with his meditation in the secluded glade, provided Eragon with his first opportunity since the previous day to order his thoughts and consider the question that Oromis had posed him.

While he did, he observed his red ants invade a smaller, rival anthill, overrunning the inhabitants and stealing their resources. By the end of the massacre, only a handful of the rival ants were left alive, alone and purposeless in the vast and hostile pine-needle barrens.

Like the dragons in Alagaësia, thought Eragon. His connection to the ants vanished as he considered the dragons' unhappy fate. Bit by bit, an answer to his problem revealed itself to him, an answer that he could live with and believe in.

He finished his meditations and returned to the hut. This time Oromis seemed reasonably satisfied with what Eragon had accomplished.

As Oromis served the midday meal, Eragon said, "I know why fighting Galbatorix is worth it, though thousands of people may die."

"Oh?" Oromis seated himself. "Do tell me."

"Because Galbatorix has already caused more suffering over the past hundred years than we ever could in a single generation. And unlike a normal tyrant, we cannot wait for him to die. He could rule for centuries or millennia—persecuting and tormenting people the entire time—unless we stop him. If he became strong enough, he would march on the dwarves and you here in Du Weldenvarden and kill or enslave both races. And . . . ," Eragon rubbed the heel of his palm against the edge of the table, ". . . because rescuing the two eggs from Galbatorix is the only way to save the dragons."

The strident warble of Oromis's teakettle intruded, escalating in volume until Eragon's ears rang. Standing, Oromis hooked the kettle off the cookfire and poured the water for blueberry tea. The creases around his eyes softened. "Now," he said, "you understand."

"I understand, but I take no pleasure in it."

"Nor should you. But now we can be confident that you won't shrink from the path when you are confronted by the injustices and atrocities that the Varden will inevitably commit. We cannot afford to have you consumed by doubts when your strength and focus are most needed." Oromis steepled his fingers and gazed into the dark mirror of his tea, contemplating whatever he saw in its tenebrous reflection. "Do you believe that Galbatorix is evil?"

"Of course!"

"Do you believe that he considers himself evil?"

"No, I doubt it."

Oromis tapped his forefingers against each other. "Then you must also believe that Durza was evil?"

The fragmented memories Eragon had gleaned from Durza when they fought in Tronjheim returned to him now, reminding him how the young Shade—Carsaib, then—had been enslaved by the wraiths he had summoned to avenge the death of his mentor, Haeg. "He wasn't evil himself, but the spirits that controlled him were."

"And what of the Urgals?" asked Oromis, sipping his tea. "Are they evil?"

Eragon's knuckles whitened as he gripped his spoon. "When I

think of death, I see an Urgal's face. They're worse than beasts. The things they have done . . ." He shook his head, unable to continue.

"Eragon, what kind of opinion would you form of humans if all you knew of them were the actions of your warriors on the field of battle?"

"That's not . . ." He took a deep breath. "It's different. Urgals deserve to be wiped out, every last one of them."

"Even their females and children? The ones who haven't harmed you and likely never will? The innocents? Would you kill them and condemn an entire race to the void?"

"They wouldn't spare us, given the chance."

"Eragon!" exclaimed Oromis in biting tones. "I never want to hear you use that excuse again, that because someone else has done—or would do—something means that you should too. It's lazy, repugnant, and indicative of an inferior mind. Am I clear?"

"Yes, Master."

The elf raised his mug to his lips and drank, his bright eyes fixed on Eragon the entire time. "What do you actually know of Urgals?"

"I know their strengths, weaknesses, and how to kill them. It's all I need to know."

"Why do they hate and fight humans, though? What about their history and legends, or the way in which they live?"

"Does it matter?"

Oromis sighed. "Just remember," he said gently, "that at a certain point, your enemies may have to become your allies. Such is the nature of life."

Eragon resisted the urge to argue. He swirled his own tea in its mug, accelerating the liquid into a black whirlpool with a white lens of foam at the bottom of the vortex. "Is that why Galbatorix enlisted the Urgals?"

"That is not an example I would have chosen, but yes."

"It seems strange that he befriended them. After all, they were the ones who killed his dragon. Look what he did to us, the Riders, and we weren't even responsible for his loss."

"Ah," said Oromis, "mad Galbatorix may be, but he's still as cunning as a fox. I guess that he intended to use the Urgals to destroy the Varden and the dwarves—and others, if he had triumphed in Farthen Dûr—thereby removing two of his enemies while simultaneously weakening the Urgals so that he could dispose of them at his leisure."

Study of the ancient language devoured the afternoon, whereupon they took up the practice of magic. Much of Oromis's lectures concerned the proper way in which to control various forms of energy, such as light, heat, electricity, and even gravity. He explained that since these forces consumed strength faster than any other type of spell, it was safer to find them already in existence in nature and then shape them with gramarye, instead of trying to create them from nothing.

Abandoning the subject, Oromis asked, "How would you kill with magic?"

"I've done it many ways," said Eragon. "I've hunted with a pebble—moving and aiming it with magic—as well as using the word *jierda* to break Urgals' legs and necks. Once, with *thrysta*, I stopped a man's heart."

"There are more efficient methods," revealed Oromis. "What does it take to kill a man, Eragon? A sword through the chest? A broken neck? The loss of blood? All it takes is for a single artery in the brain to be pinched off, or for certain nerves to be severed. With the right spell, you could obliterate an army."

"I should have thought of that in Farthen Dûr," said Eragon, disgusted with himself. *Not just Farthen Dûr either, but also when the Kull chased us from the Hadarac Desert.* "Again, why didn't Brom teach me this?"

"Because he did not expect you to face an army for months or years to come; it is not a tool given to untested Riders."

"If it's so easy to kill people, though, what's the point of us or Galbatorix raising an army?"

"To be succinct, *tactics*. Magicians are vulnerable to physical attack when they are embroiled in their mental struggles. Therefore, they need warriors to protect them. And the warriors must be shielded, at least in part, from magical attacks, else they would be slain within minutes. These limitations mean that when armies confront one another, their magicians are scattered throughout the bulk of their forces, close to the edge but not so close as to be in danger. The magicians on both sides open their minds and attempt to sense if anyone is using or is about to use magic. Since their enemies might be beyond their mental reach, magicians also erect wards around themselves and their warriors to stop or lessen long-range attacks, such as a pebble sent flying toward their head from a mile away."

"Surely one man can't defend an entire army," said Eragon.

"Not alone, but with enough magicians, you can provide a reasonable amount of protection. The greatest danger in this sort of conflict is that a clever magician may think of a unique attack that can bypass your wards without tripping them. That itself could be enough to decide a battle.

"Also," said Oromis, "you must keep in mind that the ability to use magic is exceedingly rare among the races. We elves are no exception, although we have a greater allotment of spellweavers than most, as a result of oaths we bound ourselves with centuries ago. The majority of those blessed with magic have little or no appreciable talent; they struggle to heal even so much as a bruise."

Eragon nodded. He had encountered magicians like that in the Varden. "But it still takes the same amount of energy to accomplish a task."

"Energy, yes, but lesser magicians find it harder than you or I do to feel the flow of magic and immerse themselves in it. Few magicians are strong enough to pose a threat to an entire army. And those who are usually spend the bulk of their time during battles evading, tracking, or fighting their opposites, which is fortunate from the standpoint of ordinary warriors, else they would all soon be killed."

Troubled, Eragon said, "The Varden don't have many magicians."

"That is one reason why you are so important."

A moment passed as Eragon reflected on what Oromis had told him. "These wards, do they only drain energy from you when they are activated?"

"Aye."

"Then, given enough time, you could acquire countless layers of wards. You could make yourself . . ." He struggled with the ancient language as he attempted to express himself. ". . . untouchable? . . . impregnable? . . . impregnable to any assault, magical or physical."

"Wards," said Oromis, "rely upon the strength of your body. If that strength is exceeded, you die. No matter how many wards you have, you will only be able to block attacks so long as your body can sustain the output of energy."

"And Galbatorix's strength has been increasing each year. . . . How is that possible?"

It was a rhetorical question, yet when Oromis remained silent, his almond eyes fixed on a trio of swallows pirouetting overhead, Eragon realized that the elf was considering how best to answer him. The birds chased each other for several minutes. When they flitted from view, Oromis said, "It is not appropriate to have this discussion at the present."

"Then you know?" exclaimed Eragon, astonished.

"I do. But that information must wait until later in your training. You are not ready for it." Oromis looked at Eragon, as if expecting him to object.

Eragon bowed. "As you wish, Master." He could never prize the information out of Oromis until the elf was willing to share it, so why try? Still, he wondered what could be so dangerous that Oromis dared not tell him, and why the elves had kept it secret from the Varden. Another thought presented itself to him, and he said, "If battles with magicians are conducted like you said, then why did Ajihad let me fight without wards in Farthen Dûr? I didn't even know that I needed to keep my mind open for enemies. And why didn't Arya kill most or all of the Urgals? No magicians were there to oppose her except for Durza, and he couldn't have defended his troops when he was underground."

"Did not Ajihad have Arya or one of Du Vrangr Gata set defenses around you?" demanded Oromis.

"No, Master."

"And you fought thus?"

"Yes, Master."

Oromis's eyes unfocused, withdrawing into himself as he stood motionless on the greensward. He spoke without warning: "I have consulted Arya, and she says that the Twins of the Varden were ordered to assess your abilities. They told Ajihad you were competent in all magic, including wards. Neither Ajihad nor Arya doubted their judgment on that matter."

"Those smooth-tongued, bald-pated, tick-infested, treacherous dogs," swore Eragon. "They tried to get me killed!" Reverting to his own language, he indulged in several more pungent oaths.

"Do not befoul the air," said Oromis mildly. "It ill becomes you. . . . In any case, I suspect the Twins allowed you into battle unprotected *not* so you would be killed, but so that Durza could capture you."

"What?"

"By your own account, Ajihad suspected that the Varden had been betrayed when Galbatorix began persecuting their allies in the Empire with near-perfect accuracy. The Twins were privy to the identities of the Varden's collaborators. Also, the Twins lured you to the heart of Tronjheim, thereby separating you from Saphira and placing you within Durza's reach. That they were traitors is the logical explanation."

"If they *were* traitors," said Eragon, "it doesn't matter now; they're long dead."

Oromis inclined his head. "Even so. Arya said that the Urgals did have magicians in Farthen Dûr and that she fought many of them. None of them attacked you?"

"No, Master."

"More evidence that you and Saphira were left for Durza to capture and take to Galbatorix. The trap was well laid."

Over the next hour, Oromis taught Eragon twelve methods to kill, none of which took more energy than lifting an ink-laden pen. As he finished memorizing the last one, a thought struck Eragon that caused him to grin. "The Ra'zac won't stand a chance the next time they cross my path."

"You must still be wary of them," cautioned Oromis.

"Why? Three words and they'll be dead."

"What do ospreys eat?"

Eragon blinked. "Fish, of course."

"And if a fish were slightly faster and more intelligent than its brethren, would it be able to escape a hunting osprey?"

"I doubt it," said Eragon. "At least not for very long."

"Just as ospreys are designed to be the best possible hunters of fish, wolves are designed to be the best hunters of deer and other large game, and every animal is gifted to best suit its purpose. So too are the Ra'zac designed to prey upon humans. They are the monsters in the dark, the dripping nightmares that haunt your race."

The back of Eragon's neck prickled with horror. "What manner of creatures are they?"

"Neither elf; man; dwarf; dragon; furred, finned, or feathered beast; reptile; insect; nor any other category of animal."

Eragon forced a laugh. "Are they plants, then?"

"Nor that either. They reproduce by laying eggs, like dragons. When they hatch, the young—or pupae—grow black exoskeletons that mimic the human form. It's a grotesque imitation, but convincing enough to let the Ra'zac approach their victims without undo alarm. All areas where humans are weak, the Ra'zac are strong. They can see on a cloudy night, track a scent like a bloodhound, jump higher, and move faster. However, bright light pains them and they have a morbid fear of deep water, for they cannot swim. Their greatest weapon is their evil breath, which fogs the minds of humans—incapacitating many—though it is less potent on dwarves, and elves are immune altogether."

Eragon shivered as he remembered his first sight of the Ra'zac in Carvahall and how he had been unable to flee once they noticed him. "It felt like a dream where I wanted to run but I couldn't move, no matter how hard I tried."

"As good a description as any," said Oromis. "Though the Ra'zac cannot use magic, they are not to be underestimated. If they know that you hunt them, they will not reveal themselves but keep to the shadows, where they are strong, and plot to ambush you as they did by Dras-Leona. Even Brom's experience could not protect him from them. Never grow overconfident, Eragon. Never grow arrogant, for then you will be careless and your enemies will exploit your weakness."

"Yes, Master."

Oromis fixed Eragon with a steady gaze. "The Ra'zac remain pupae for twenty years while they mature. On the first full moon of their twentieth year, they shed their exoskeletons, spread their wings, and emerge as adults ready to hunt all creatures, not just humans."

"Then the Ra'zac's mounts, the ones they fly on, are really . . ."

"Aye, their parents."

IMAGE OF PERFECTION

At last I understand the nature of my enemies, thought Eragon. He had feared the Ra'zac ever since they first appeared in Carvahall, not only because of their villainous deeds but because he knew so little about the creatures. In his ignorance, he credited the Ra'zac with more powers than they actually possessed and regarded them with an almost superstitious dread. *Nightmares indeed.* But now that Oromis's explanation had stripped away the Ra'zac's aura of mystery, they no longer seemed quite so formidable. The fact that they were vulnerable to light and water strengthened Eragon's conviction that when next they met, he would destroy the monsters that had killed Garrow and Brom.

"Are their parents called Ra'zac as well?" he asked.

Oromis shook his head. "Lethrblaka, we named them. And whereas their offspring are narrow-minded, if cunning, Lethrblaka have all the intelligence of a dragon. A cruel, vicious, and twisted dragon."

"Where do they come from?"

"From whatever land your ancestors abandoned. Their depredations may have been what forced King Palancar to emigrate. When we, the Riders, became aware of the Ra'zac's foul presence in Alagaësia, we did our best to eradicate them, as we would leaf blight. Unfortunately, we were only partially successful. Two Lethrblaka escaped, and they along with their pupae are the ones who have caused you so much grief. After he killed Vrael,

Galbatorix sought them out and bargained for their services in return for his protection and a guaranteed amount of their favorite food. That is why Galbatorix allows them to live by Dras-Leona, one of the Empire's largest cities."

Eragon's jaw tightened. "They have much to answer for." *And they will, if I have my way.*

"That they do," Oromis agreed. Returning to the hut, he stepped through the black shadow of the doorway, then reappeared carrying a half-dozen slate tablets about a half-foot wide and a foot high. He presented one to Eragon. "Let us abandon such unpleasant topics for a time. I thought you might enjoy learning how to make a fairth. It is an excellent device for focusing your thoughts. The slate is impregnated with enough ink to cover it with any combination of colors. All you need do is concentrate upon the image that you wish to capture and then say, 'Let that which I see in my mind's eye be replicated on the surface of this tablet.' " As Eragon examined the clay-smooth slate, Oromis gestured at the clearing. "Look about you, Eragon, and find something worth preserving."

The first objects that Eragon noticed seemed too obvious, too banal to him: a yellow lily by his feet, Oromis's overgrown hut, the white stream, and the landscape itself. None were unique. None would give an observer an insight into the subject of the fairth or he who had created it. *Things that change and are lost, that is what's worth preserving,* he thought. His eye alighted upon the pale green nubs of spring growth at the tip of a tree's branches and then the deep, narrow wound that seamed the trunk where a storm had broken a bough, tearing off a rope of bark with it. Translucent orbs of sap encrusted the seam, catching and refracting the light.

Eragon positioned himself alongside the trunk so that the rotund galls of the tree's congealed blood bulged out in silhouette and were framed by a cluster of shiny new needles. Then he fixed the scene in his mind as best he could and uttered the spell.

The surface of the gray tablet brightened as splashes of color bloomed across it, blending and mixing to produce the proper array of hues. When the pigments at last stopped moving, Eragon found himself looking at a strange copy of what he had wanted to reproduce. The sap and needles were rendered with vibrant, razor-sharp detail, while all else was slurred and bleary, as if seen through half-opened eyes. It was far removed from the universal clarity of Oromis's fairth of Ilirea.

At a sign from Oromis, Eragon handed the tablet to him. The elf studied it for a minute, then said, "You have an unusual way of thinking, Eragon-finiarel. Most humans have difficulty achieving the proper concentration to create a recognizable image. You, on the other hand, seem to observe nearly everything about whatever interests you. It's a narrow focus, though. You have the same problem here that you do with your meditation. You must relax, broaden your field of vision, and allow yourself to absorb everything around you without judging what is important or not." Setting aside the picture, Oromis took a second, blank tablet from the grass and gave it to Eragon. "Try again with what I—"

"Hail, Rider!"

Startled, Eragon turned and saw Orik and Arya emerge side by side from the forest. The dwarf raised his arm in greeting. His beard was freshly trimmed and braided, his hair was pulled back into a neat ponytail, and he wore a new tunic—courtesy of the elves—that was red and brown and embroidered with gold thread. His appearance gave no indication of his condition the previous night.

Eragon, Oromis, and Arya exchanged the traditional greeting, then, abandoning the ancient language, Oromis asked, "To what may I attribute this visit? You are both welcome to my hut, but as you can see, I am in the midst of working with Eragon, and that is of paramount importance."

"I apologize for disturbing you, Oromis-elda," said Arya, "but—"

"The fault is mine," said Orik. He glanced at Eragon before continuing: "I was sent here by Hrothgar to ensure that Eragon receives the instruction he is due. I have no doubt that he is, but I am obliged to see his training with my own eyes so that when I return to Tronjheim, I may give my king a true account of events."

Oromis said, "That which I teach Eragon is not to be shared with anyone else. The secrets of the Riders are for him alone."

"And I understand that. However, we live in uncertain times; the stone that once was fixed and solid is now unstable. We must adapt to survive. So much depends on Eragon, we dwarves have a right to verify that his training proceeds as promised. Do you believe our request is an unreasonable one?"

"Well spoken, Master Dwarf," said Oromis. He tapped his fingers together, inscrutable as always. "May I assume, then, that this is a matter of duty for you?"

"Duty and honor."

"And neither will allow you to yield on this point?"

"I fear not, Oromis-elda," said Orik.

"Very well. You may stay and watch for the duration of this lesson. Will that satisfy you?"

Orik frowned. "Are you near the end of the lesson?"

"We have just begun."

"Then yes, I will be satisfied. For the moment, at least."

While they spoke, Eragon tried to catch Arya's eye, but she kept her attention centered on Oromis.

". . . Eragon!"

He blinked, jolted out of his reverie. "Yes, Master?"

"Don't wander, Eragon. I want you to make another fairth. Keep your mind open, like I told you before."

"Yes, Master." Eragon hefted the tablet, his hands slightly damp at the thought of having Orik and Arya there to judge his performance. He wanted to do well in order to prove that Oromis was a good teacher. Even so, he could not concentrate on the pine needles and sap; Arya tugged at him like a lodestone, drawing his attention back to her whenever he thought of something else.

At last he realized that it was futile for him to resist the attraction. He composed an image of her in his head—which took but a heartbeat, since he knew her features better than his own—and voiced the spell in the ancient language, pouring all of his adoration, love, and fear of her into the currents of fey magic.

The result left him speechless.

The fairth depicted Arya's head and shoulders against a dark, indistinct background. She was bathed in firelight on her right side and gazed out at the viewer with knowing eyes, appearing not just as she was but as he thought of her: mysterious, exotic, and the most beautiful woman he had ever seen. It was a flawed, imperfect picture, but it possessed such intensity and passion that it evoked a visceral response from Eragon. *Is this how I really see her?* Whoever this woman was, she was so wise, so powerful, and so hypnotic, she could consume any lesser man.

From a great distance, he heard Saphira whisper, *Be careful. . . .*

"What have you wrought, Eragon?" demanded Oromis.

"I . . . I don't know." Eragon hesitated as Oromis extended his hand for the fairth, reluctant to let the others examine his work, especially Arya. After a long, terrifying pause, Eragon pried his fingers off the tablet and released it to Oromis.

The elf's expression grew stern as he looked at the fairth, then back at Eragon, who quailed under the weight of his stare. Without a word, Oromis handed the tablet to Arya.

Her hair obscured her face as she bowed over the tablet, but Eragon saw cords and veins ridge her hands as she clenched the slate. It shook in her grip.

"Well, what is it?" asked Orik.

Raising the fairth over her head, Arya hurled it against the ground, shattering the picture into a thousand pieces. Then she drew herself upright and, with great dignity, walked past Eragon, across the clearing, and into the tangled depths of Du Weldenvarden.

Orik picked up one of the fragments of slate. It was blank. The image had vanished when the tablet broke. He tugged his beard. "In all the decades I've known her, Arya has never lost her temper like that. Never. What did you do, Eragon?"

Dazed, Eragon said, "A portrait of her."

Orik frowned, obviously puzzled. "A portrait? Why would that—"

"I think it would be best if you left now," said Oromis. "The lesson is over, in any case. Come back tomorrow or the day after if you want a better idea of Eragon's progress."

The dwarf squinted at Eragon, then nodded and brushed the dirt from his palms. "Yes, I believe I'll do that. Thank you for your time, Oromis-elda. I appreciate it." As he headed back toward Ellesméra, he said over his shoulder to Eragon, "I'll be in the common room of Tialdarí Hall, if you want to talk."

When Orik was gone, Oromis lifted the hem of his tunic, knelt, and began to gather up the remains of the tablet. Eragon watched him, unable to move.

"Why?" he asked in the ancient language.

"Perhaps," said Oromis, "Arya was frightened by you."

"Frightened? She never gets frightened." Even as he said it, Eragon knew that it was not true. She just concealed her fear better than most. Dropping to one knee, he took a piece of the fairth and pressed it into Oromis's palm. "Why would I frighten her?" he asked. "Please, tell me."

Oromis stood and walked to the edge of the stream, where he scattered the fragments of slate over the bank, letting the gray flakes trickle through his fingers. "Fairths only show what you want them to. It's possible to lie with them, to create a false image, but to do so requires more skill than you yet have. Arya knows this. She also knows, then, that your fairth was an accurate representation of your feelings for her."

"But why would that frighten her?"

Oromis smiled sadly. "Because it revealed the depth of your infatuation." He pressed his fingertips together, forming a series of arches. "Let us analyze the situation, Eragon. While you are old enough to be considered a man among your people, in our eyes, you are no more than a child." Eragon frowned, hearing echoes of Saphira's words from the previous night. "Normally, I would not compare a human's age to an elf's, but since you share our longevity, you must also be judged by our standards.

"And you are a Rider. We rely upon you to help us defeat

Galbatorix; it could be disastrous for everyone in Alagaësia if you are distracted from your studies.

"Now then," said Oromis, "how should Arya have responded to your fairth? It's clear that you see her in a romantic light, yet— while I have no doubt Arya is fond of you—a union between the two of you is impossible due to your own youth, culture, race, and responsibilities. Your interest has placed Arya in an uncomfortable position. She dare not confront you, for fear of disrupting your training. But, as the queen's daughter, she cannot ignore you and risk offending a Rider—especially one upon which so much depends. . . . Even if you were a fit match, Arya would refrain from encouraging you so that you could devote all of your energy to the task at hand. She would sacrifice her happiness for the greater good." Oromis's voice thickened: "You must understand, Eragon, that slaying Galbatorix is more important than any one person. Nothing else matters." He paused, his gaze gentle, then added, "Given the circumstances, is it so strange Arya was frightened that your feelings for her could endanger everything we have worked for?"

Eragon shook his head. He was ashamed that his behavior had caused Arya distress, and dismayed by how reckless and juvenile he had been. *I could have avoided this entire mess if I'd just kept better control of myself.*

Touching him on the shoulder, Oromis guided him back inside the hut. "Think not that I am devoid of sympathy, Eragon. Everyone experiences ardor like yours at one point or another during their lives. It's part of growing up. I also know how hard it is for you to deny yourself the usual comforts of life, but it's necessary if we are to prevail."

"Yes, Master."

They sat at the kitchen table, and Oromis began to lay out writing materials for Eragon to practice the Liduen Kvaedhí. "It would be unreasonable of me to expect you to forget your fascination with Arya, but I do expect you to prevent it from interfering with my instruction again. Can you promise me that?"

"Yes, Master. I promise."

"And Arya? What would be the honorable thing to do about her predicament?"

Eragon hesitated. "I don't want to lose her friendship."

"No."

"Therefore . . . I will go to her, I will apologize, and I will reassure her that I never intend to cause her such hardship again." It was difficult for him to say, but once he did, he felt a sense of relief, as if acknowledging his mistake cleansed him of it.

Oromis appeared pleased. "By that alone, you prove that you have matured."

The sheets of paper were smooth underneath Eragon's hands as he pressed them flat against the tabletop. He stared at the blank white expanse for a moment, then dipped a quill in ink and began to transcribe a column of glyphs. Each barbed line was like a streak of night against the paper, an abyss into which he could lose himself and try to forget his confused feelings.

THE OBLITERATOR

The following morn, Eragon went looking for Arya in order to apologize. He searched for over an hour without success. It seemed as if she had vanished among the many hidden nooks within Ellesméra. He caught a glimpse of her once as he paused by the entrance to Tialdarí Hall and called out to her, but she slipped away before he could reach her side. *She's avoiding me*, he finally realized.

As the days rolled by, Eragon embraced Oromis's training with a zeal that the elder Rider praised, devoting himself to his studies in order to distract himself from thoughts of Arya.

Night and day, Eragon strove to master his lessons. He memorized the words of making, binding, and summoning; learned the true names of plants and animals; and studied the perils of transmutation, how to call upon the wind and the sea, and the myriad skills needed to understand the forces of the world. At spells that dealt with the great energies—such as light, heat, and magnetism—he excelled, for he possessed the talent to judge nigh exactly how much strength a task required and whether it would exceed that of his body.

Occasionally, Orik would come and watch, standing without comment by the edge of the clearing while Oromis tutored Eragon, or while Eragon struggled alone with a particularly difficult spell.

Oromis set many challenges before him. He had Eragon cook meals with magic, in order to teach him finer control of his gramarye;

Eragon's first attempts resulted in a blackened mess. The elf showed Eragon how to detect and neutralize poisons of every sort and, from then on, Eragon had to inspect his food for the different venoms Oromis was liable to slip into it. More than once Eragon went hungry when he could not find the poison or was unable to counteract it. Twice he became so sick, Oromis had to heal him. And Oromis had Eragon cast multiple spells simultaneously, which required tremendous concentration to keep the spells directed at their intended targets and prevent them from shifting among the items Eragon wanted to affect.

Oromis devoted long hours to the craft of imbuing matter with energy, either to be released at a later time or to give an object certain attributes. He said, "This is how Rhunön charmed the Riders' swords so they never break or dull; how we sing plants into growing as we desire; how a trap might be set in a box, only to be triggered when the box is opened; how we and the dwarves make the Erisdar, our lanterns; and how you may heal one who is injured, to name but a few uses. These are the most potent of spells, for they can lie dormant for a thousand years or more and are difficult to perceive or avert. They permeate much of Alagaësia, shaping the land and the destiny of those who live here."

Eragon asked, "You could use this technique to alter your body, couldn't you? Or is that too dangerous?"

Oromis's lips quirked in a faint smile. "Alas, you have stumbled upon elves' greatest weakness: our vanity. We love beauty in all its forms, and we seek to represent that ideal in our appearance. That is why we are known as the Fair Folk. Every elf looks exactly as he or she wishes to. When elves learn the spells for growing and molding living things, they often choose to modify their appearance to better reflect their personalities. A few elves have gone beyond mere aesthetic changes and altered their anatomy to adapt to various environments, as you will see during the Blood-oath Celebration. Oftentimes, they are more animal than elf.

"However, transferring power to a living creature is different from transferring power to an inanimate object. Very few materials are suitable for storing energy; most either allow it to dissipate or become so charged with force that when you touch the object, a bolt of lightning drives through you. The best materials we have found for this purpose are gemstones. Quartz, agates, and other lesser stones are not as efficient as, say, a diamond, but any gem will suffice. That is why Riders' swords always have a jewel set in their pommels. It is also why your dwarf necklace—which is entirely metal—must sap your strength to fuel its spell, since it can hold no energy of its own."

When not with Oromis, Eragon supplemented his education by reading the many scrolls the elf gave him, a habit he soon became addicted to. Eragon's rearing—limited as it was by Garrow's scant tutelage—had exposed him only to the knowledge needed to run a farm. The information he discovered on the miles of paper flooded into him like rain on parched desert, sating a previously unknown thirst. He devoured texts on geography, biology, anatomy, philosophy, and mathematics, as well as memoirs, biographies, and histories. More important than mere facts was his introduction to alternative ways of thinking. They challenged his beliefs and forced him to reexamine his assumptions about everything from the rights of an individual within society to what caused the sun to move across the sky.

He noticed that a number of scrolls concerned Urgals and their culture. Eragon read them and made no mention of it, nor did Oromis broach the topic.

From his studies, Eragon learned much about the elves, a subject that he avidly pursued, hoping that it would help him to better understand Arya. To his surprise, he discovered that the elves did not practice marriage, but rather took mates for however long they wanted, whether it be for a day or a century. Children were rare, and having a child was considered by the elves to be the ultimate vow of love.

Eragon also learned that since their two races had first met, only a handful of elf-human couples had existed: mainly human Riders who found appropriate mates among the elves. However, as best he could tell from the cryptic records, most such relationships ended in tragedy, either because the lovers were unable to relate to one another or because the humans aged and died while the elves escaped the ravages of time.

In addition to nonfiction, Oromis presented Eragon with copies of the elves' greatest songs, poems, and epics, which captured Eragon's imagination, for the only stories he was familiar with were the ones Brom had recited in Carvahall. He savored the epics as he might a well-cooked meal, lingering over *The Deed of Gëda* or *The Lay of Umhodan* so as to prolong his enjoyment of the tales.

Saphira's own training proceeded apace. Linked as he was to her mind, Eragon got to watch as Glaedr put her through an exercise regimen every bit as strenuous as his. She practiced hovering in the air while lifting boulders, as well as sprints, dives, and other acrobatics. To increase her endurance, Glaedr had her breathe fire for hours upon a natural stone pillar in an attempt to melt it. At first Saphira could only maintain the flames for a few minutes at a time, but before long the blistering torch roared from her maw for over a half hour uninterrupted, heating the pillar white-hot. Eragon was also privy to the dragon lore Glaedr imparted to Saphira, details about the dragons' lives and history that complemented her instinctual knowledge. Much of it was incomprehensible to Eragon, and he suspected that Saphira concealed even more from him, secrets of her race that dragons shared with no one but themselves. One thing he did glean, and that Saphira treasured, was the name of her sire, Iormúngr, and her dam, Vervada, which meant Stormcleaver in the old speech. While Iormúngr had been bound to a Rider, Vervada was a wild dragon who had laid many eggs but entrusted only one to the Riders: Saphira. Both dragons perished in the Fall.

Some days Eragon and Saphira would fly with Oromis and Glaedr, practicing aerial combat or visiting crumbling ruins hidden within Du Weldenvarden. Other days they would reverse the usual order of things, and Eragon would accompany Glaedr while Saphira remained on the Crags of Tel'naeír with Oromis.

Each morning Eragon sparred with Vanir, which, without exception, ignited one or more of Eragon's seizures. To make matters worse, the elf continued to treat Eragon with haughty condescension. He delivered oblique slights that, on the surface, never exceeded the bounds of politeness, and he refused to be drawn to anger no matter how Eragon needled him. Eragon hated him and his cool, mannered bearing. It seemed as if Vanir was insulting him with every movement. And Vanir's companions—who, as best Eragon could tell, were of a younger generation of elves—shared his veiled distaste for Eragon, though they never displayed aught but respect for Saphira.

Their rivalry came to a head when, after defeating Eragon six times in a row, Vanir lowered his sword and said, "Dead yet again, Shadeslayer. How repetitive. Do you wish to continue?" His tone indicated that he thought it would be pointless.

"Aye," grunted Eragon. He had already suffered an episode with his back and was in no mood to bandy words.

Still, when Vanir said, "Tell me, as I am curious: How did you kill Durza when you are so slow? I cannot fathom how you managed it," Eragon felt compelled to reply: "I caught him by surprise."

"Forgive me; I should have guessed trickery was involved."

Eragon fought the impulse to grind his teeth. "If I were an elf or you a human, you would not be able to match my blade."

"Perhaps," said Vanir. He assumed his ready position and, within the span of three seconds and two blows, disarmed Eragon. "But I think not. You should not boast to a better swordsman, else he may decide to punish your temerity."

Eragon's temper broke then, and he reached deep within himself and into the torrent of magic. He released the pent-up energy with one of the twelve minor words of binding, crying "Malthinae!" to chain Vanir's legs and arms in place and hold his jaw shut so that he could not utter a counterspell. The elf's eyes bulged with outrage.

Eragon said, "And you should not boast to one who is more skilled in magic than you."

Vanir's dark eyebrows met.

Without warning or a whisper of a sound, an invisible force clouted Eragon on the chest and threw him ten yards across the grass, where he landed upon his side, driving the wind from his lungs. The impact disrupted Eragon's control of the magic and freed Vanir.

How did he do that?

Advancing upon him, Vanir said, "Your ignorance betrays you, human. You do not know whereof you speak. To think that you were chosen to succeed Vrael, that you were given his quarters, that you have had the honor to serve the Mourning Sage . . ." He shook his head. "It sickens me that such gifts are bestowed upon one so unworthy. You do not even understand what magic is or how it works."

Eragon's anger resurged like a crimson tide. "What," he said, "have I ever done to wrong you? Why do you despise me so? Would you prefer it if no Rider existed to oppose Galbatorix?"

"My opinions are of little consequence."

"I agree, but I would hear them."

"Listening, as Nuala wrote in *Convocations*, is the path to wisdom only when the result of a conscious decision and not a void of perception."

"Straighten your tongue, Vanir, and give me an honest answer!"

Vanir smiled coldly. "As you command, O Rider." Drawing near so that only Eragon could hear his soft voice, the elf said, "For eighty years after the fall of the Riders, we held no hope of victory. We survived by hiding ourselves through deceit and magic, which is but a temporary measure, for eventually Galbatorix will be strong enough to march upon us and sweep aside our defenses. Then, long after we had resigned ourselves to our fate, Brom and Jeod rescued

Saphira's egg, and once again a chance existed to defeat the foul usurper. Imagine our joy and celebration. We knew that in order to withstand Galbatorix, the new Rider had to be more powerful than any of his predecessors, more powerful than even Vrael. Yet how was our patience rewarded? With another human like Galbatorix. Worse . . . a cripple. You doomed us all, Eragon, the instant you touched Saphira's egg. Do not expect us to welcome your presence." Vanir touched his lips with his first and second finger, then sidestepped Eragon and walked off the sparring field, leaving Eragon rooted in place.

He's right, thought Eragon. *I'm ill suited for this task. Any of these elves, even Vanir, would make a better Rider than me.*

Emanating outrage, Saphira broadened the contact between them. *Do you think so little of my judgment, Eragon? You forget that when I was in my egg, Arya exposed me to each and every one of these elves—as well as many of the Varden's children—and that I rejected them all. I wouldn't have chosen someone to be my Rider unless they could help your race, mine, and the elves, for the three of us share an intertwined fate. You were the right person, at the right place, at the right time. Never forget that.*

If ever that were true, he said, *it was before Durza injured me. Now I see naught but darkness and evil in our future. I won't give up, but I despair that we may not prevail. Perhaps our task is not to overthrow Galbatorix but to prepare the way for the next Rider chosen by the remaining eggs.*

At the Crags of Tel'naeír, Eragon found Oromis at the table in his hut, painting a landscape with black ink along the bottom edge of a scroll he had finished writing.

Eragon bowed and knelt. "Master."

Fifteen minutes elapsed before Oromis finished limning the tufts of needles on a gnarled juniper tree, laid aside his ink, cleaned his sable brush with water from a clay pot, and then addressed Eragon, saying, "Why have you come so early?"

"I apologize for disturbing you, but Vanir abandoned our contest partway through and I did not know what to do with myself."

"Why did Vanir leave, Eragon-vodhr?"

Oromis folded his hands in his lap while Eragon described the encounter, ending with: "I should not have lost control, but I did, and I looked all the more foolish because of it. I have failed you, Master."

"You have," agreed Oromis. "Vanir may have goaded you, but that was no reason to respond in kind. You must keep a better hold over your emotions, Eragon. It could cost you your life if you allow your temper to sway your judgment during battle. Also, such childish displays do nothing but vindicate those elves who are opposed to you. Our machinations are subtle and allow little room for such errors."

"I am sorry, Master. It won't happen again."

As Oromis seemed content to wait in his chair until the time when they normally performed the Rimgar, Eragon seized the opportunity to ask, "How could Vanir have worked magic without speaking?"

"Did he? Perhaps another elf decided to assist him."

Eragon shook his head. "During my first day in Ellesméra, I also saw Islanzadí summon a downpour of flowers by clapping her hands, nothing more. And Vanir said that I didn't understand how magic works. What did he mean?"

"Once again," said Oromis, resigned, "you grasp at knowledge that you are not prepared for. Yet, because of our circumstances, I cannot deny it to you. Only know this: that which you ask for was not taught to Riders—and is not taught to our magicians—until they had, and have, mastered every other aspect of magic, for this is the secret to the true nature of magic and the ancient language. Those who know it may acquire great power, yes, but at a terrible risk." He paused for a moment. "How is the ancient language bound to magic, Eragon-vodhr?"

"The words of the ancient language can release the energy stored within your body and thus activate a spell."

"Ah. Then you mean that certain sounds, certain vibrations in the air, somehow tap into this energy? Sounds that might be produced at random by any creature or thing?"

"Yes, Master."

"Does not that seem absurd?"

Confused, Eragon said, "It doesn't matter if it seems absurd, Master; it just is. Should I think it absurd that the moon wanes and waxes, or that the seasons turn, or that birds fly south in the winter?"

"Of course not. But how could mere sound do so much? Can particular patterns of pitch and volume really trigger reactions that allow us to manipulate energy?"

"But they do."

"Sound has no control over magic. Saying a word or phrase in this language is not what's important, it's *thinking* them in this language." With a flick of his wrist, a golden flame appeared over Oromis's palm, then disappeared. "However, unless the need is dire, we still utter our spells out loud to prevent stray thoughts from disrupting them, which is a danger to even the most experienced magic user."

The implications staggered Eragon. He thought back to when he almost drowned under the waterfall of the lake Kóstha-mérna and how he had been unable to access magic because of the water surrounding him. *If I had known this then, I could have saved myself,* he thought. "Master," he said, "if sound does not affect magic, why, then, do thoughts?"

Now Oromis smiled. "Why indeed? I must point out that we ourselves are not the source of magic. Magic can exist on its own, independent of any spell, such as the werelights in the bogs by Aroughs, the dream well in Mani's Caves in the Beor Mountains, and the floating crystal on Eoam. Wild magic such as this is treacherous, unpredictable, and often stronger than any we can cast.

"Eons ago, all magic was thus. To use it required nothing but the ability to sense magic with your mind—which every magician must possess—and the desire and strength to use it. Without the structure of the ancient language, magicians could not govern their talent and, as a result, loosed many evils upon the land, killing thousands. Over time they discovered that stating their intentions in their language helped them to order their thoughts and avoid costly errors. But it was no foolproof method. Eventually, an accident occurred so horrific that it almost destroyed every living being in the world. We know of the event from fragments of manuscripts that survived the era, but who or what cast the fatal spell is hidden from us. The manuscripts say that, afterward, a race called the Grey Folk—not elves, for we were young then—gathered their resources and wrought an enchantment, perhaps the greatest that was or ever shall be. Together the Grey Folk changed the nature of magic itself. They made it so that their language, the ancient language, could control what a spell does . . . could actually limit the magic so that if you said *burn that door* and by chance looked at me and thought of me, the magic would still burn the door, not me. And they gave the ancient language its two unique traits, the ability to prevent those who speak it from lying and the ability to describe the true nature of things. How they did this remains a mystery.

"The manuscripts differ on what happened to the Grey Folk when they completed their work, but it seems that the enchantment drained them of their power and left them but a shadow of themselves. They faded away, choosing to live in their cities until the stones crumbled to dust or to take mates among the younger races and so pass into darkness."

"Then," said Eragon, "it is still possible to use magic without the ancient language?"

"How do you think Saphira breathes fire? And, by your own account, she used no word when she turned Brom's tomb to diamond nor when she blessed the child in Farthen Dûr. Dragons' minds are different from ours; they need no protection from magic. They cannot use it consciously, aside from their fire, but when the gift touches them, their strength is unparalleled. . . . You look troubled, Eragon. Why?"

Eragon stared down at his hands. "What does this mean for me, Master?"

"It means that you will continue to study the ancient language, for you can accomplish much with it that would be too complex or too dangerous otherwise. It means that if you are captured and gagged, you can still call upon magic to free yourself, as Vanir did. It means that if you are captured and drugged and cannot recall the ancient language, yes, even then, you may cast a spell, though only in the gravest circumstances. And it means that if you would cast a spell for that which has no name in the ancient language, you can." He paused. "But beware the temptation to use these powers. Even the wisest among us hesitate to trifle with them for fear of death or worse."

The next morning, and every morning thereafter so long as he stayed in Ellesméra, Eragon dueled with Vanir, but he never lost his temper again, no matter what the elf did or said.

Nor did Eragon feel like devoting energy to their rivalry. His back pained him more and more frequently, driving him to the limits of his endurance. The debilitating attacks sensitized him; actions that previously had caused him no trouble could now leave him writhing on the ground. Even the Rimgar began to trigger the seizures as he advanced to more strenuous poses. It was not uncommon for him to suffer three or four such episodes in one day.

Eragon's face grew haggard. He walked with a shuffle, his movements slow and careful as he tried to preserve his strength. It became hard for him to think clearly or to pay attention to Oromis's lessons, and gaps began to appear in his memory that he could not account for. In his spare time, he took up Orik's puzzle ring again, preferring to concentrate upon the baffling interlocked rings rather than his condition. When she was with him, Saphira insisted that he ride upon her back and did everything that she could to make him comfortable and to save him effort.

One morning, as he clung to a spike on her neck, Eragon said, *I have a new name for pain.*

What's that?

The Obliterator. Because when you're in pain, nothing else can exist. Not thought. Not emotion. Only the drive to escape the pain. When it's strong enough, the Obliterator strips us of everything that makes us who we are, until we're reduced to creatures less than animals, creatures with a single desire and goal: escape.

A good name, then.

I'm falling apart, Saphira, like an old horse that's plowed too many fields. Keep hold of me with your mind, or I may drift apart and forget who I am.

I will never let go of you.

Soon afterward, Eragon fell victim to three bouts of agony while fighting Vanir and then two more during the Rimgar. As he uncurled from the clenched ball he had rolled into, Oromis said, "Again, Eragon. You must perfect your balance."

Eragon shook his head and growled in an undertone, "No." He crossed his arms to hide his tremors.

"What?"

"No."

"Get up, Eragon, and try again."

"No! Do the pose yourself; I won't."

Oromis knelt beside Eragon and placed a cool hand on his cheek. Holding it there, he gazed at Eragon with such kindness, Eragon understood the depth of the elf's compassion for him, and that, if it were possible, Oromis would willingly assume Eragon's pain to relieve his suffering. "Don't abandon hope," said Oromis. "Never that." A measure of strength seemed to flow from him to Eragon. "We are the Riders. We stand between the light and the dark, and keep the balance between the two. Ignorance, fear, hate: these are our enemies. Deny them with all your might, Eragon, or we will surely fail." He stood and extended a hand toward Eragon. "Now rise, Shadeslayer, and prove you can conquer the instincts of your flesh!"

Eragon took a deep breath and pushed himself upright on one arm, wincing from the effort. He got his feet underneath himself, paused for a moment, then straightened to his full height and looked Oromis in the eye.

The elf nodded with approval.

Eragon remained silent until they finished the Rimgar and went to bathe in the stream, whereupon he said, "Master."

"Yes, Eragon?"

"Why must I endure this torture? You could use magic to give me the skills I need, to shape my body as you do the trees and plants."

"I could, but if I did, you would not understand how you got the body you had, your own abilities, nor how to maintain them. No shortcuts exist for the path you walk, Eragon."

Cold water rushed over the length of Eragon's body as he lowered himself into the stream. He ducked his head under the surface, holding a rock so that he would not float away, and lay stretched out along the streambed, feeling like an arrow flying through the water.

◆　　◆　　◆

NARDA

Roran leaned on one knee and scratched his new beard as he looked down at Narda.

The small town was dark and compact, like a crust of rye bread tamped into a crevasse along the coast. Beyond it, the wine-red sea glimmered with the last rays of the dying sunset. The water fascinated him; it was utterly different from the landscape he was accustomed to.

We made it.

Leaving the promontory, Roran walked back to his makeshift tent, enjoying deep breaths of the salty air. They had camped high in the foothills of the Spine in order to avoid detection by anyone who might alert the Empire as to their whereabouts.

As he strode among the clumps of villagers huddled beneath the trees, Roran surveyed their condition with sorrow and anger. The trek from Palancar Valley had left people sick, battered, and exhausted; their faces gaunt from lack of food; their clothes tattered. Most everyone wore rags tied around their hands to ward off frostbite during the frigid mountain nights. Weeks of carrying heavy packs had bowed once-proud shoulders. The worst sight was the children: thin and unnaturally still.

They deserve better, thought Roran. *I'd be in the clutches of the Ra'zac right now if they hadn't protected me.*

Numerous people approached Roran, most of whom wanted nothing more than a touch on the shoulder or a word of comfort.

Some offered him bits of food, which he refused or, when they insisted, gave to someone else. Those who remained at a distance watched with round, pale eyes. He knew what they said about him, that he was mad, that spirits possessed him, that not even the Ra'zac could defeat him in battle.

Crossing the Spine had been even harder than Roran expected. The only paths in the forest were game trails, which were too narrow, steep, and meandering for their group. As a result, the villagers were often forced to chop their way through the trees and underbrush, a painstaking task that everyone despised, not least because it made it easy for the Empire to track them. The one advantage to the situation was that the exercise restored Roran's injured shoulder to its previous level of strength, although he still had trouble lifting his arm at certain angles.

Other hardships took their toll. A sudden storm trapped them on a bare pass high above the timberline. Three people froze in the snow: Hida, Brenna, and Nesbit, all of whom were quite old. That night was the first time Roran was convinced that the entire village would die because they had followed him. Soon after, a boy broke his arm in a fall, and then Southwell drowned in a glacier stream. Wolves and bears preyed upon their livestock on a regular basis, ignoring the watchfires that the villagers lit once they were concealed from Palancar Valley and Galbatorix's hated soldiers. Hunger clung to them like a relentless parasite, gnawing at their bellies, devouring their strength, and sapping their will to continue.

And yet they survived, displaying the same obstinacy and fortitude that kept their ancestors in Palancar Valley despite famine, war, and pestilence. The people of Carvahall might take an age and a half to reach a decision, but once they did, nothing could deter them from their course.

Now that they had reached Narda, a sense of hope and accomplishment permeated the camp. No one knew what would happen next, but the fact that they had gotten so far gave them confidence.

We won't be safe until we leave the Empire, thought Roran. *And it's up to me to ensure that we aren't caught. I've become responsible for everyone here. . . .* A responsibility that he had embraced whole-heartedly because it allowed him to both protect the villagers from Galbatorix and pursue his goal of rescuing Katrina. *It's been so long since she was captured. How can she still be alive?* He shuddered and pushed the thoughts away. True madness awaited him if he allowed himself to brood over Katrina's fate.

At dawn Roran, Horst, Baldor, Loring's three sons, and Gertrude set out for Narda. They descended from the foothills to the town's main road, careful to stay hidden until they emerged onto the lane. Here in the lowlands, the air seemed thick to Roran; it felt as if he were trying to breathe underwater.

Roran gripped the hammer at his belt as they approached Narda's gate. Two soldiers guarded the opening. They examined Roran's group with hard eyes, lingering on their ragged clothes, then lowered their poleaxes and barred the entrance.

"Where'd you be from?" asked the man on the right. He could not have been older than twenty-five, but his hair was already pure white.

Swelling his chest, Horst crossed his arms and said, "Roundabouts Teirm, if it please you."

"What brings you here?"

"Trade. We were sent by shopkeepers who want to buy goods directly from Narda, instead of through the usual merchants."

"That so, eh? What goods?"

When Horst faltered, Gertrude said, "Herbs and medicine on my part. The plants I've received from here have either been too old or moldy and spoiled. I have to procure a fresh supply."

"And my brothers and I," said Darmmen, "came to bargain with your cobblers. Shoes made in the northern style are fashionable in Dras-Leona and Urû'baen." He grimaced. "At least they were when we set out."

Horst nodded with renewed confidence. "Aye. And I'm here to collect a shipment of ironwork for my master."

"So you say. What about that one? What does he do?" asked the soldier, motioning toward Roran with his ax.

"Pottery," said Roran.

"Pottery?"

"Pottery."

"Why the hammer, then?"

"How do you think the glaze on a bottle or jar gets cracked? It doesn't happen by itself, you know. You have to hit it." Roran returned the white-haired man's stare of disbelief with a blank expression, daring him to challenge the statement.

The soldier grunted and ran his gaze over them again. "Be as that may, you don't look like tradesmen to me. Starved alley cats is more like it."

"We had difficulty on the road," said Gertrude.

"That I'd believe. If you came from Teirm, where be your horses?"

"We left them at our camp," supplied Hamund. He pointed south, opposite where the rest of the villagers were actually hidden.

"Don't have the coin to stay in town, eh?" With a scornful chuckle, the soldier raised his ax and gestured for his companion to do likewise. "All right, you can pass, but don't cause trouble or you'll be off to the stocks or worse."

Once through the gate, Horst pulled Roran to the side of the street and growled in his ear, "That was a fool thing to do, making up something as ridiculous as that. Cracking the glaze! Do you *want* a fight? We can't—" He stopped as Gertrude plucked at his sleeve.

"Look," murmured the healer.

To the left of the entrance stood a six-foot-wide message board with a narrow shingle roof to protect the yellowing parchment underneath. Half the board was devoted to official notices and proclamations. On the other half hung a block of posters displaying sketches of various criminals. Foremost among them was a drawing of Roran without a beard.

Startled, Roran glanced around to make sure that no one in the street was close enough to compare his face to the illustration, then devoted his attention to the poster. He had expected the Empire to pursue them, but it was still a shock to encounter proof of it. *Galbatorix must be expending an enormous amount of resources trying to catch us.* When they were in the Spine, it was easy to forget that the outside world existed. *I bet posters of me are nailed up throughout the Empire.* He grinned, glad that he had stopped shaving and that he and the others had agreed to use false names while in Narda.

A reward was inked at the bottom of the poster. Garrow never taught Roran and Eragon to read, but he did teach them their figures because, as he said, "You have to know how much you own, what it's worth, and what you're paid for it so you don't get rooked by some two-faced knave." Thus, Roran could see that the Empire had offered ten thousand crowns for him, enough to live in comfort for several decades. In a perverse way, the size of the reward pleased him, giving him a sense of importance.

Then his gaze drifted to the next poster in line.

It was Eragon.

Roran's gut clenched as if he had been struck, and for a few seconds he forgot to breathe.

He's alive!

After his initial relief subsided, Roran felt his old anger about Eragon's role in Garrow's death and the destruction of their farm take its place, accompanied by a burning desire to know why the Empire was hunting Eragon. *It must have something to do with that blue stone and the Ra'zac's first visit to Carvahall.* Once again, Roran wondered what kind of fiendish machinations he and the rest of Carvahall had become entangled in.

Instead of a reward, Eragon's poster bore two lines of runes. "What crime is he accused of?" Roran asked Gertrude.

The skin around Gertrude's eyes wrinkled as she squinted at the board. "Treason, the both of you. It says Galbatorix will bestow an earldom on whoever captures Eragon, but that those who try should take care because he's extremely dangerous."

Roran blinked with astonishment. *Eragon?* It seemed inconceivable until Roran considered how he himself had changed in the past few weeks. *The same blood runs in our veins. Who knows, Eragon may have accomplished as much or more than I have since he left.*

In a low voice, Baldor said, "If killing Galbatorix's men and defying the Ra'zac only earns you ten thousand crowns—large as that is—what makes you worth an earldom?"

"Buggering the king himself," suggested Larne.

"That's enough of that," said Horst. "Guard your tongue better, Baldor, or we'll end up in irons. And, Roran, don't draw attention to yourself again. With a reward like that, people are bound to be watching strangers for anyone who matches your description." Running a hand through his hair, Horst pulled up his belt and said, "Right. We all have jobs to do. Return here at noon to report on your progress."

With that their party split into three. Darmmen, Larne, and Hamund set out together to purchase food for the villagers, both to meet present needs and to sustain them through the next stage of their journey. Gertrude—as she had told the guard—went to replenish her stock of herbs, unguents, and tinctures. And Roran, Horst, and Baldor headed down the sloping streets to the docks, where they hoped to charter a ship that could transport the villagers to Surda or, at the very least, Teirm.

When they reached the weathered boardwalk that covered the beach, Roran halted and stared out at the ocean, which was gray from low clouds and dotted with whitecaps from erratic wind. He had never imagined that the horizon could be so perfectly flat. The hollow boom of water knocking against the piles beneath his feet made it feel as if he stood upon the surface of a huge drum. The odor of fish—fresh, gutted, and rotting—overwhelmed every other smell.

Glancing from Roran to Baldor, who was likewise entranced, Horst said, "Quite a sight, isn't it?"

"Aye," said Roran.

"Makes you feel rather small, doesn't it?"

"Aye," said Baldor.

Horst nodded. "I remember when I first saw the ocean, it had a similar effect on me."

"When was that?" asked Roran. In addition to the flocks of seagulls whirling over the cove, he noticed an odd type of bird perched upon the piers. The animal had an ungainly body with a striped beak that it kept tucked against its breast like a pompous old man, a white head and neck, and a sooty torso. One of the birds lifted its beak, revealing a leathery pouch underneath.

"Bartram, the smith who came before me," said Horst, "died when I was fifteen, a year before the end of my apprenticeship. I had to find a smith who was willing to finish another man's work, so I traveled to Ceunon, which is built along the North Sea. There I met Kelton, a vile old man but good at what he did. He agreed to teach me." Horst laughed. "By the time we were done, I wasn't sure if I should thank him or curse him."

"Thank him, I should think," said Baldor. "You never would have married Mother otherwise."

Roran scowled as he studied the waterfront. "There aren't many ships," he observed. Two craft were berthed at the south end of the port and a third at the opposite side with nothing but fishing boats and dinghies in between. Of the southern pair, one had a broken mast. Roran had no experience with ships but, to him, none of the vessels appeared large enough to carry almost three hundred passengers.

Going from one ship to the next, Roran, Horst, and Baldor soon discovered that they were all otherwise engaged. It would take a month or more to repair the ship with the broken mast. The vessel beside it, the *Waverunner*, was rigged with leather sails and was about to venture north to the treacherous islands where the Seithr plant grew. And the *Albatross*, the last ship, had just arrived from distant Feinster and was getting its seams recaulked before departing with its cargo of wool.

A dockworker laughed at Horst's questions. "You're too late and too early at the same time. Most of the spring ships came and left two, three weeks ago. An' another month, the nor'westers will start gusting, an' then the seal and walrus hunters will return and we'll get ships from Teirm and the rest of the Empire to take the hides, meat, and oil. Then you might have a chance of hiring a captain with an empty hold. Meanwhile, we don't see much more traffic than this."

Desperate, Roran asked, "Is there no other way to get goods from here to Teirm? It doesn't have to be fast or comfortable."

"Well," said the man, hefting the box on his shoulder, "if it doesn't have to be fast an' you're only going to Teirm, then you might try Clovis over there." He pointed to a line of sheds that floated between two piers where boats could be stored. "He owns some barges that he ships grain on in the fall. The rest of the year, Clovis fishes for a living, like most everybody in Narda." Then he frowned. "What kind of goods do you have? The sheep have already been shorn, an' no crops are in as of yet."

"This and that," said Horst. He tossed the man a copper.

The dockworker pocketed it with a wink and a nudge. "Right you are, sir. This an' that. I know a dodge when I see one. But no need to fear old Ulric; mum's th' word, it is. Be seeing you, then, sir." He strolled off, whistling.

As it turned out, Clovis was absent from the docks. After getting directions, it took them a half hour to walk to his house on the other side of Narda, where they found Clovis planting iris bulbs along the path to his front door. He was a stout man with sun-burned cheeks and a salt-and-pepper beard. An additional hour passed before they could convince the mariner that they really were interested in his barges, despite the season, and then troop back to the sheds, which he unlocked to reveal three identical barges, the *Merrybell*, *Edeline*, and *Red Boar*.

Each barge was seventy-five feet long, twenty feet wide, and painted rust red. They had open holds that could be covered with tarpaulins, a mast that could be erected in the center for a single square sail, and a block of above-decks cabins at the rear—or aft, as Clovis called it—of the craft.

"Their draft be deeper than that of an inland scow," explained

Clovis, "so you needn't fear them capsizing in rough weather, though you'd do well to avoid being caught in a real tempest. These barges aren't meant for the open sea. They're meant to stay within sight of land. And now be the worst time to launch them. By my honor, we've had nothing but thunderstorms every afternoon for a month."

"Do you have crews for all three?" asked Roran.

"Well now . . . see, there's a problem. Most of the men I employ left weeks ago to hunt seals, as they're wont to do. Since I need them only after the harvest, they're free to come and go as they please for the rest of the year. . . . I'm sure you fine gentlemen understand my position." Clovis tried to smile, then glanced between Roran, Horst, and Baldor as if uncertain whom to address.

Roran walked the length of the *Edeline*, examining it for damage. The barge looked old, but the wood was sound and the paint was fresh. "If we replace the missing men in your crews, how much would it cost to go to Teirm with all three barges?"

"That depends," said Clovis. "The sailors earn fifteen coppers per day, plus as much good food as they can eat and a dram of whisky besides. What your men earn be your own business. I won't put them on my payroll. Normally, we also hire guards for each barge, but they're—"

"They're off hunting, yes," said Roran. "We'll provide guards as well."

The knob in Clovis's tanned throat jumped as he swallowed. "That'd be more than reasonable . . . so it would. In addition to the crew's wages, I charge a fee of two hundred crowns, plus recompense for any damage to the barges on account of your men, plus— as both owner and captain—twelve percent of the total profit from sale of the cargo."

"Our trip will have no profit."

That, more than anything, seemed to unnerve Clovis. He rubbed the dimple in his chin with his left thumb, began to talk twice, stopped, then finally said, "If that be the case, another four hundred crowns upon completion of the voyage. What—if I may make so bold as to inquire—do you wish to transport?"

We frighten him, thought Roran. "Livestock."

"Be it sheep, cattle, horses, goats, oxen . . . ?"

"Our herds contain an assortment of animals."

"And why do you want to take them to Teirm?"

"We have our reasons." Roran almost smiled at Clovis's confusion. "Would you consider sailing past Teirm?"

"No! Teirm's my limit, it is. I don't know the waters beyond, nor would I want to be gone any longer from my wife and daughter."

"When could you be ready?"

Clovis hesitated and executed two little steps. "Mayhap five or six days. No . . . no, you'd better make it a week; I have affairs that I must attend to before departing."

"We'd pay an additional ten crowns to leave day after tomorrow."

"I don't—"

"Twelve crowns."

"Day after tomorrow it is," vowed Clovis. "One way or another, I'll be ready by then."

Trailing his hand along the barge's gunwale, Roran nodded without looking back at Clovis and said, "May I have a minute alone to confer with my associates?"

"As you wish, sir. I'll just go for a turn about the docks until you're done." Clovis hurried to the door. Just as he exited the shed, he asked, "I'm sorry, but what'd be your name again? I fear I missed it earlier, an' my memory can be something dreadful."

"Stronghammer. My name is Stronghammer."

"Ah, of course. A good name, that."

When the door closed, Horst and Baldor converged on Roran. Baldor said, "We can't afford to hire him."

"We can't afford *not* to," replied Roran. "We don't have the gold to buy the barges, nor do I fancy teaching myself to handle them when everyone's lives depend on it. It'll be faster and safer to pay for a crew."

"It's still too expensive," said Horst.

Roran drummed his fingers against the gunwale. "We can pay

412

Clovis's initial fee of two hundred crowns. Once we reach Teirm, though, I suggest that we either steal the barges using the skills we learn during the trip or incapacitate Clovis and his men until we can escape through other means. That way, we avoid paying the extra four hundred crowns, as well as the sailors' wages."

"I don't like cheating a man out of honest work," said Horst. "It goes against my fiber."

"I don't like it either, but can you think of an alternative?"

"How would you get everyone onto the barges?"

"Have them meet Clovis a league or so down the coast, out of sight of Narda."

Horst sighed. "Very well, we'll do it, but it leaves a bad taste in my mouth. Call Clovis back in, Baldor, and we'll seal this pact."

That evening, the villagers gathered around a small banked fire in order to hear what had transpired in Narda. From where he knelt on the ground, Roran stared at the pulsing coals while he listened to Gertrude and the three brothers describe their separate adventures. The news about Roran's and Eragon's posters caused murmurs of unease among the audience.

When Darmmen finished, Horst took his place and, with short, brisk sentences, related the lack of proper ships in Narda, how the dockworker recommended Clovis, and the deal that was brokered thereafter. However, the moment Horst mentioned the word *barges*, the villagers' cries of ire and discontent blotted out his voice.

Marching to the forefront of the group, Loring raised his arms for attention. "Barges?" said the cobbler. "Barges? We don't want no *stinking* barges!" He spat by his foot as people clamored with agreement.

"Everyone, be quiet!" said Delwin. "We'll be heard if we keep this up." When the crackling fire was the loudest noise, he continued at a slower pace: "I agree with Loring. Barges are unacceptable. They're slow and vulnerable. And we'd be crammed together with a complete lack of privacy and no shelter to speak of for who knows how long. Horst, Elain is six months pregnant. You can't expect her and others who are sick and infirm to sit under the blazing sun for weeks on end."

"We can lash tarpaulins over the holds," replied Horst. "It's not much, but it'll shield us from the sun and the rain."

Birgit's voice cut through the crowd's low babble: "I have another concern." People moved aside as she walked to the fire. "What with the two hundred crowns Clovis is due and the money Darmmen and his brothers spent, we've used up most of our coin. Unlike those in cities, our wealth lies not in gold but in animals and property. Our property is gone and few animals are left. Even if we turn pirate and steal these barges, how can we buy supplies at Teirm or passage farther south?"

"The important thing," rumbled Horst, "is to get to Teirm in the first place. Once we're there, then we can worry about what to do next. . . . It's possible that we may have to resort to more drastic measures."

Loring's bony face crumpled into a mass of wrinkles. "Drastic? What do you mean, *drastic?* We've already done drastic. This whole *venture* is drastic. I don't care what you say; I won't use those confounded barges, not after what we've gone through in the Spine. Barges are for grain and animals. What we want is a ship with cabins and bunks where we can sleep in comfort. Why not wait another week or so and see if a ship arrives that we can bargain passage on? Where's the harm in that, eh? Or why not—" He continued to rail for over fifteen minutes, amassing a mountain of objections before ceding to Thane and Ridley, who built upon his arguments.

The conversation halted as Roran unfolded his legs and rose to his full height, silencing the villagers through his presence. They waited, breathless, hoping for another of his visionary speeches.

"It's this or walk," he said.

Then he went to bed.

THE HAMMER FALLS

The moon floated high among the stars when Roran left the makeshift tent he shared with Baldor, padded to the edge of the camp, and replaced Albriech on watch.

"Nothing to report," whispered Albriech, then slipped off.

Roran strung his bow and planted three goose-feather arrows upright in the loam, within easy reach, then wrapped himself in a blanket and curled against the rockface to his left. His position afforded him a good view down and across the dark foothills.

As was his habit, Roran divided the landscape into quadrants, examining each one for a full minute, always alert for the flash of movement or the hint of light that might betray the approach of enemies. His mind soon began to wander, drifting from subject to subject with the hazy logic of dreams, distracting him from his task. He bit the inside of his cheek to force himself to concentrate. Staying awake was difficult in such mild weather. . . .

Roran was just glad that he had escaped drawing lots for the two watches preceding dawn, because they gave you no opportunity to catch up on lost sleep afterward and you felt tired for the rest of the day.

A breath of wind ghosted past him, tickling his ear and making the skin on the back of his neck prickle with an apprehension of evil. The intrusive touch frightened Roran, obliterating everything but the conviction that he and the rest of the villagers were in mortal danger. He quaked as if with the ague, his heart pounded, and he had to struggle to resist the urge to break cover and flee.

What's wrong with me? It required an effort for him to even nock an arrow.

To the east, a shadow detached itself from the horizon. Visible only as a void among the stars, it drifted like a torn veil across the sky until it covered the moon, where it remained, hovering. Illuminated from behind, Roran could see the translucent wings of one of the Ra'zac's mounts.

The black creature opened its beak and uttered a long, piercing shriek. Roran grimaced with pain at the cry's pitch and frequency. It stabbed at his eardrums, turned his blood to ice, and replaced hope and joy with despair. The ululation woke the entire forest. Birds and beasts for miles around exploded into a yammering chorus of panic, including, to Roran's alarm, what remained of the villagers' herds.

Staggering from tree to tree, Roran returned to the camp, whispering, "The Ra'zac are here. Be quiet and stay where you are," to everyone he encountered. He saw the other sentries moving among the frightened villagers, spreading the same message.

Fisk emerged from his tent with a spear in hand and roared, "Are we under attack? What's set off those blasted—" Roran tackled the carpenter to silence him, uttering a muffled bellow as he landed on his right shoulder and pained his old injury.

"Ra'zac," Roran groaned to Fisk.

Fisk went still and in an undertone asked, "What should I do?"

"Help me to calm the animals."

Together they picked their way through the camp to the adjacent meadow where the goats, sheep, donkeys, and horses were bedded. The farmers who owned the bulk of the herds slept with their charges and were already awake and working to soothe the beasts. Roran thanked his paranoia that he had insisted on having the animals scattered along the edge of the meadow, where the trees and brush helped to camouflage them from unfriendly eyes.

As he tried to pacify a clump of sheep, Roran glanced up at the terrible black shadow that still obscured the moon, like a giant bat.

To his horror, it began to move toward their hiding place. *If that creature screams again, we're doomed.*

By the time the Ra'zac circled overhead, most of the animals had quieted, except for one donkey, who insisted upon loosing a grating *hee-haw*. Without hesitation, Roran dropped to one knee, fit arrow to string, and shot the ass between the ribs. His aim was true, and the animal dropped without a sound.

He was too late, though; the braying had already alerted the Ra'zac. The monster swung its head in the direction of the clearing and descended toward it with outstretched claws, preceded by its fetid stench.

Now the time has come to see if we can slay a nightmare, thought Roran. Fisk, who was crouched beside him in the grass, hefted his spear, preparing to hurl it once the brute was in range.

Just as Roran drew his bow—in an attempt to begin and end the battle with a well-placed shaft—he was distracted by a commotion in the forest.

A mass of deer burst through the underbrush and stampeded across the meadow, ignoring villagers and livestock alike in their frantic desire to escape the Ra'zac. For almost a minute, the deer bounded past Roran, mincing the loam with their sharp hooves and catching the moonlight with their white-rimmed eyes. They came so close, he heard the soft gasps of their labored breathing.

The multitude of deer must have hidden the villagers because, after one last circuit over the meadow, the winged monster turned to the south and glided farther down the Spine, melding into the night.

Roran and his companions remained frozen in place, like hunted rabbits, afraid that the Ra'zac's departure might be a ruse to flush them into the open or that the creature's twin might be close behind. They waited for hours, tense and anxious, barely moving except to string a bow.

When the moon was about to set, the Ra'zac's bone-chilling shriek echoed far in the distance . . . then nothing.

⁂   *⁂*   *⁂*

We were lucky, decided Roran when he woke the next morning. *And we can't count on luck to save us the next time.*

After the Ra'zac's appearance, none of the villagers objected to traveling by barge. On the contrary, they were so eager to be off, many of them asked Roran if it was possible to set sail that day instead of the next.

"I wish we could," he said, "but too much has to be done."

Forgoing breakfast, he, Horst, and a group of other men hiked into Narda. Roran knew that he risked being recognized by accompanying them, but their mission was too important for him to neglect. Besides, he was confident that his current appearance was different enough from his portrait on the Empire's poster that no one would equate one with the other.

They had no difficulty gaining entrance, as a different set of soldiers guarded the town gate, whereupon they went to the docks and delivered the two hundred crowns to Clovis, who was busy overseeing a gang of men as they readied the barges for sea.

"Thank'ee, Stronghammer," he said, tying the bag of coins to his belt. "There be nothing like yellow gold to brighten a man's day." He led them to a worktable and unrolled a chart of the waters surrounding Narda, complete with notations on the strength of various currents; locations of rocks, sandbars, and other hazards; and decades' worth of sounding measurements. Drawing a line with his finger from Narda to a small cove directly south of it, Clovis said, "Here's where we'll meet your livestock. The tides are gentle this time o' year, but we still don't want to fight them an' no bones about it, so we'll have to be on our way directly after the high tide."

"High tide?" said Roran. "Wouldn't it be easier to wait until low tide and let it carry us out?"

Clovis tapped his nose with a twinkle in his eye. "Aye, it would, an' so I've begun many a cruise. What I don't want, though, is to be slung up on the beach, loading your animals, when the tide comes a-rushing back in and pushes us farther inland. There be no danger of that this way, but we'll have to move smart so as we're not left high an' dry when the waters recede. Assuming we do, the sea'll work for us, eh?"

Roran nodded. He trusted Clovis's experience. "And how many men will you need to fill out your crews?"

"Well, I managed to dig up seven lads—strong, true, an' good seamen all—who have agreed to this venture, odd as it is. Mind you, most of the boys were at the bottom of their tankards when I cornered them last night, drinking off the pay from their last voyage, but they'll be sober as spinsters come morn; that I promise you. Seeing as seven were all I could find, I'd like four more."

"Four it is," said Roran. "My men don't know much about sailing, but they're able-bodied and willing to learn."

Clovis grunted. "I usually take on a brace of new lads each trip anyway. So long as they follow orders, they'll do fine; otherwise, they'll get a belaying pin upsides the head, mark my words. As for guards, I'd like to have nine—three per boat. An' they'd better not be as green as your sailors, or I won't budge from the dock, not for all the whisky in the world."

Roran allowed himself a grim smile. "Every man who rides with me has proved himself in battle many times over."

"An' they all answer to you, eh, young Stronghammer?" said Clovis. He scratched his chin, eyeing Gedric, Delwin, and the others who were new to Narda. "How many are with you?"

"Enough."

"Enough, you say. I wonder." He waved a hand. "Never you mind me; my tongue runs a league before my own common sense, or so my father used to tell me. My first mate, Torson, is at the chandler's now, overseeing the purchase of goods and equipment. I understand you have feed for your livestock?"

"Among other things."

"Then you'd best fetch them. We can load them into the holds once the masts are up."

Throughout the rest of the morning and afternoon, Roran and

the villagers with him labored to ferry the supplies—which Loring's sons had procured—from the warehouse where it was stored into the sheds with the barges.

As Roran trudged across the gangplank to the *Edeline* and lowered his bag of flour to the sailor waiting in the hold, Clovis observed, "Most of this t'aint feed, Stronghammer."

"No," said Roran. "But it's needed." He was pleased that Clovis had the sense not to inquire further.

When the last item had been stored away, Clovis beckoned to Roran. "You might as well go. Me and the boys will handle the rest. Just you remember to be at the docks three hours after dawn with every man jack you promised me, or we'll lose the tide."

"We'll be there."

Back in the foothills, Roran helped Elain and the others prepare for departure. It did not take long, as they were accustomed to breaking camp each morning. Then he picked twelve men to accompany him to Narda the next day. They were all good fighters, but he asked the best, like Horst and Delwin, to remain with the rest of the villagers in case soldiers found them or the Ra'zac returned.

Once night fell, the two groups parted. Roran crouched on a boulder and watched Horst lead the column of people down through the foothills toward the cove where they would wait for the barges.

Orval came up beside him and crossed his arms. "Do you think they'll be safe, Stronghammer?" Anxiety ran through his voice like a taut bowstring.

Though he too was worried, Roran said, "I do. I'd bet you a barrel of cider that they'll still be asleep when we put ashore tomorrow. You can have the pleasure of waking up Nolla. How does that sound?" Orval smiled at the mention of his wife and nodded, appearing reassured.

I hope I'm right. Roran remained on the boulder, hunched like a bleak gargoyle, until the dark line of villagers vanished from his sight.

*　*　*

They woke an hour before sunrise, when the sky had just begun to brighten with pale green and the damp night air numbed their fingers. Roran splashed his face with water and then outfitted himself with his bow and quiver, his ever-present hammer, one of Fisk's shields, and one of Horst's spears. The others did likewise, with the addition of swords obtained during the skirmishes in Carvahall.

Running as fast as they dared down the hummocky hills, the thirteen men soon arrived at the road to Narda and, shortly after that, the town's main gate. To Roran's dismay, the same two soldiers who had troubled them earlier stood guard by the entrance. As before, the soldiers lowered their poleaxes to block the way.

"There be quite a bit more of you this time," observed the white-haired man. "And not all the same ones either. Except for you." He focused on Roran. "I suppose you expect me to believe that the spear and shield be for pottery as well?"

"No. We've been hired by Clovis to protect his barges from attack on the way to Teirm."

"You? Mercenaries?" The soldiers burst out laughing. "You said you were tradesmen."

"This pays better."

The white-haired man scowled. "You lie. I tried my hand at being a gentleman of fortune once. I spent more nights hungry than not. How large be your company of *tradesmen* anyway? Seven yesterday and twelve today—thirteen counting you. It seems too large for an expedition from a bunch of shopkeepers." His eyes narrowed as he scrutinized Roran's face. "You look familiar. What'd be your name, eh?"

"Stronghammer."

"It wouldn't happen to be *Roran*, would—"

Roran jabbed forward with his spear, catching the white-haired soldier in the throat. Scarlet blood fountained. Releasing the spear, Roran drew his hammer and twisted round as he blocked the second soldier's poleax with his shield. Swinging his hammer up and around, Roran crushed the man's helm.

He stood panting between the two corpses. *Now I have killed ten.*

Orval and the other men stared at Roran with shock. Unable to bear their gazes, Roran turned his back on them and gestured at the culvert that ran beneath the road. "Hide the bodies before anyone sees," he ordered, brusque and harsh. As they hurried to obey, he examined the parapet on top of the wall for sentries. Fortunately, no one was visible there or in the street through the gate. He bent and pulled his spear free, wiping the blade clean on a tuft of grass.

"Done," said Mandel, clambering out of the ditch. Despite his beard, the young man appeared pale.

Roran nodded and, steeling himself, faced his band. "Listen. We will walk to the docks at a quick but reasonable pace. We will not run. When the alarm is sounded—and someone may have heard the clash just now—act surprised and interested but not afraid. Whatever you do, give people no reason to suspect us. The lives of your families and friends depend on it. If we are attacked, your only duty is to see the barges launched. Nothing else matters. Am I clear?"

"Aye, Stronghammer," they answered.

"Then follow me."

As he strode through Narda, Roran felt so tense, he feared he might snap and explode into a thousand pieces. *What have I made of myself?* he wondered. He glanced from man to woman, child to man, man to dog in an effort to identify potential enemies. Everything around him appeared unnaturally bright and filled with detail; it seemed as if he could see the individual threads in people's clothing.

They reached the docks without incident, whereupon Clovis said, "You be early, Stronghammer. I like that in a man. It'll give us the opportunity to put things nice an' shipshape before we head out."

"Can we leave now?" asked Roran.

"You should know better'n that. Have to wait till the tide's finished coming in, so we do." Clovis paused then, taking his first good look at the thirteen of them, and said, "Why, what'd be the matter, Stronghammer? The lot of you look as if you saw the ghost of old Galbatorix himself."

"Nothing a few hours of sea air won't cure," said Roran. In his current state, he could not smile, but he did let his features assume a more pleasant expression in order to reassure the captain.

With a whistle, Clovis summoned two sailors from the boats. Both men were tanned the color of hazelnuts. "This'd be Torson, my first mate," said Clovis, indicating the man to his right. Torson's bare shoulder was decorated with a coiled tattoo of a flying dragon. "He'll be skipper of the *Merrybell*. And this black dog is Flint. He's in command of the *Edeline*. While you are on board, their word is law, as is mine on the *Red Boar*. You'll answer to them and me, not Stronghammer. . . . Well, give me a proper *aye, aye* if you heard me."

"Aye, aye," said the men.

"Now, which of you be my hands and which be my men-at-arms? For the life of me, I can't tell you apart."

Ignoring Clovis's admonishment that he was their commander, not Roran, the villagers looked at Roran to see if they should obey. He nodded his approval, and they divided into two factions, which Clovis proceeded to partition into even smaller groups as he assigned a certain number of villagers to each barge.

For the next half hour, Roran worked alongside the sailors to finish preparing the *Red Boar* for departure, ears open for the first hint of alarm. *We're going to be captured or killed if we stay much longer*, he thought, checking the height of the water against the piers. He mopped sweat from his brow.

Roran started as Clovis gripped his forearm.

Before he could stop himself, Roran pulled his hammer halfway out of his belt. The thick air clogged his throat.

Clovis raised an eyebrow at his reaction. "I've been watching you, Stronghammer, and I'd be interested to know how you won such loyalty from your men. I've served with more captains than I care to recall, an' not one commanded the level of obedience you do without raising his pipes."

Roran could not help it; he laughed. "I'll tell you how I did it; I saved them from slavery and from being eaten."

Clovis's eyebrows rose almost to his hairline. "Did you now? There's a story I'd like to hear."

"No, you wouldn't."

After a minute, Clovis said, "No, maybe I wouldn't at that." He glanced overboard. "Why, I'll be hanged. I do believe we can be on our way. Ah, and here's my little Galina, punctual as ever."

The burly man sprang onto the gangplank and, from there, onto the docks, where he embraced a dark-haired girl of perhaps thirteen and a woman who Roran guessed was her mother. Clovis ruffled the girl's hair and said, "Now, you'll be good while I'm gone, won't you, Galina?"

"Yes, Father."

As he watched Clovis bid his family farewell, Roran thought of the two soldiers dead by the gate. *They might have had families as well. Wives and children who loved them and a home they returned to each day . . .* He tasted bile and had to wrench his thoughts back to the pier to avoid being sick.

On the barges, the men appeared anxious. Afraid that they might lose their nerve, Roran made a show of walking about the deck, stretching, and doing whatever he could to seem relaxed. At last Clovis jumped back onto the *Red Boar* and cried, "Cast off, me lads! It's the briny deep for us."

In short order, the gangplanks were pulled aboard, the mooring ropes untied, and the sails raised on the three barges. The air rang with shouted orders and chants of heave-ho as the sailors pulled on ropes.

Behind them, Galina and her mother remained watching as the barges drew away, still and silent, hooded and grave.

"We're lucky, Stronghammer," said Clovis, clapping him on the shoulder. "We've a bit o' wind to push us along today. We may not have to row in order to reach the cove before the tide changes, eh!"

When the *Red Boar* was in the middle of Narda's bay and still ten minutes from the freedom of the open sea, that which Roran dreaded occurred: the sound of bells and trumpets floated across the water from among the stone buildings.

"What's that?" he asked.

"I don't rightly know," said Clovis. He frowned as he stared at the town, his hands planted on his hips. "It could be a fire, but no smoke is in the air. Maybe some Urgals were discovered in the area. . . ." Concern grew upon his face. "Did you perchance spy anyone on the road this morning?"

Roran shook his head, not trusting himself to speak.

Flint drew alongside them and shouted from the deck of the *Edeline*, "Should we turn back, sir?" Roran gripped the gunwale so hard that he drove splinters under his nails, ready to intercede but afraid to appear too anxious.

Tearing his gaze from Narda, Clovis bellowed in return, "No. We'd miss the tide then."

"Aye, aye, sir! But I'd give a day's pay to find out what caused that clamor."

"So would I," muttered Clovis.

As the houses and buildings shrank behind them, Roran crouched at the rear port of the barge, wrapped his arms around his knees, and leaned against the cabins. He looked at the sky, struck by its depth, clarity, and color, then into the *Red Boar*'s roiling green wake, where ribbons of seaweed fluttered. The pitch of the barge lulled him like the rock of a cradle. *What a beautiful day it is,* he thought, grateful he was there to observe it.

After they escaped the cove—to his relief—Roran climbed the ladder to the poop deck behind the cabins, where Clovis stood with his hand on the tiller, guiding their course. The captain said, "Ah, there's something exhilarating about the first day of a voyage, before you realize how bad the food is an' start longing for home."

Mindful of his need to learn what he could about the barge, Roran asked Clovis the names and functions of various objects on board, at which point he was treated to an enthusiastic lecture on the workings of barges, ships, and the art of sailing in general.

Two hours later, Clovis pointed at a narrow peninsula that lay before them. "The cove be on the far side of that." Roran straightened off the railing and craned his neck, eager to confirm that the villagers were safe.

As the *Red Boar* rounded the rocky spit of land, a white beach was revealed at the apex of the cove, upon which were assembled the refugees from Palancar Valley. The crowd cheered and waved as the barges emerged from behind the rocks.

Roran relaxed.

Beside him, Clovis uttered a dreadful oath. "I knew something were amiss the moment I clapped eyes upon you, Stronghammer. Livestock indeed. Bah! You played me like a fool, you did."

"You wrong me," replied Roran. "I did not lie; this is my flock and I am their shepherd. Is it not within my right to call them 'livestock' if I want?"

"Call them what you will, I didn't agree to haul people to Teirm. *Why* you didn't tell me the true nature of your cargo, I might wonder, an' the only answer on the horizon is that whatever venture you're engaged in means trouble . . . trouble for you an' trouble for me. I should toss the lot of you overboard an' return to Narda."

"But you won't," said Roran, deadly quiet.

"Oh? An' why not?"

"Because I need these barges, Clovis, and I'll do anything to keep them. Anything. Honor our bargain and you'll have a peaceful trip and you'll get to see Galina again. If not . . ." The threat sounded worse than it was; Roran had no intention of killing Clovis, though if he had to, he would abandon him somewhere along the coast.

Clovis's face reddened, but he surprised Roran by grunting and saying, "Fair enough, Stronghammer." Pleased with himself, Roran returned his attention to the beach.

Behind him, he heard a *snick*.

Acting on instinct, Roran recoiled, crouching, twisting, and covering his head with his shield. His arm vibrated as a belaying pin broke across the shield. He lowered the shield and gazed at a dismayed Clovis, who retreated across the deck.

Roran shook his head, never taking his eyes off his opponent. "You can't defeat me, Clovis. I'll ask you again: Will you honor our bargain? If you don't, I'll put you ashore, commandeer the barges, and press your crew into service. I don't want to ruin your livelihood, but I will if you force me. . . . Come now. This can be a normal, uneventful voyage if you choose to help us. Remember, you've already been paid."

Drawing himself up with great dignity, Clovis said, "If I agree, then you must do me the courtesy of explaining why this ruse were necessary, an' why these people are here an' where they're from. No matter how much gold you offer me, I won't assist an undertaking that contradicts my principles; no, I won't. Are you bandits? Or do you serve the blasted king?"

"The knowledge may place you in greater danger."

"I insist."

"Have you heard of Carvahall in Palancar Valley?" asked Roran.

Clovis waved a hand. "Once or twice. What of it?"

"You see it now on the beach. Galbatorix's soldiers attacked us without provocation. We fought back and, when our position became untenable, we crossed the Spine and followed the coast to Narda. Galbatorix has promised that every man, woman, and child from Carvahall will be killed or enslaved. Reaching Surda is our only hope of survival." Roran left out mention of the Ra'zac; he did not want to frighten Clovis too badly.

The weathered seaman had gone gray. "Are you still pursued?"

"Aye, but the Empire has yet to discover us."

"An' are you why the alarm was sounded?"

Very softly, Roran said, "I killed two soldiers who recognized me." The revelation startled Clovis: his eyes widened, he stepped back, and the muscles in his forearms rippled as he clenched his fists. "Make your choice, Clovis; the shore draws near."

He knew he had won when the captain's shoulders drooped and the bravado faded from his bearing. "Ah, the plague take you,

Stronghammer. I'm no friend of the king; I'll get you to Teirm. But then I want nothing more to do with you."

"Will you give me your word that you won't attempt to slip away in the night or any similar deception?"

"Aye. You have it."

Sand and rocks grated across the bottom of the *Red Boar*'s hull as the barge drove itself up onto the beach, followed on either side by its two companions. The relentless, rhythmic surge of water dashing itself against the land sounded like the breathing of a gigantic monster. Once the sails were furled and the gangplanks extended, Torson and Flint both strode over to the *Red Boar* and accosted Clovis, demanding to know what was going on.

"There's been a change of plans," said Clovis.

Roran left him to explain the situation—skirting the exact reasons why the villagers left Palancar Valley—and jumped onto the sand, whereupon he set out to find Horst among the milling knots of people. When he spotted the smith, Roran pulled him aside and told him about the deaths in Narda. "If it's discovered that I left with Clovis, they may send soldiers on horses after us. We have to get everyone onto the barges as fast as possible."

Horst met his eye for a long minute. "You've become a hard man, Roran, harder than I'll ever be."

"I've had to."

"Mind that you don't forget who you are."

Roran spent the next three hours moving and packing the villagers' belongings in the *Red Boar* until Clovis expressed his satisfaction. The bundles had to be secured so that they would not shift unexpectedly and injure someone, as well as distributed so that the barge rode level in the water, which was no easy task as the bundles were of irregular size and density. Then the animals were coaxed on board—much to their displeasure—and immobilized by tethers lashed to iron rings in the hold.

Last of all came the people, who, like the rest of the cargo, had to be organized into a symmetrical pattern within the barge to keep it from capsizing. Clovis, Torson, and Flint each ended up standing at the fore of their barges, shouting directions to the mass of villagers below.

What now? thought Roran as he heard an argument break out on the beach. Pushing his way to the source of the disturbance, he saw Calitha kneeling beside her stepfather, Wayland, trying to calm the old man.

"No! I won't go on that *beast!* You can't make me," cried Wayland. He thrashed his withered arms and beat his heels in an attempt to free himself from Calitha's embrace. Spittle flew from his lips. "Let me *go*, I say. Let me go!"

Wincing from his blows, Calitha said, "He's been unreasonable ever since we made camp last night."

It would have been better for all concerned if he had died in the Spine, what with the trouble he's caused, thought Roran. He joined Calitha, and together they managed to soothe Wayland so that he no longer screamed and hit. As a reward for his good behavior, Calitha gave him a piece of jerky, which occupied his entire attention. While Wayland concentrated on gumming the meat, she and Roran were able to guide him onto the *Edeline* and get him settled in a deserted corner where he would not be a nuisance.

"Move your backsides, you lubbers," shouted Clovis. "The tide's about to turn. Hop to, hop to."

After a final flurry of activity, the gangplanks were withdrawn, leaving a cluster of twenty men standing on the beach before each barge. The three groups gathered around the prows and prepared to push them back into the water.

Roran led the effort on the *Red Boar*. Chanting in unison, he and his men strained against the weight of the huge barge, the gray sand giving beneath their feet, the timbers and cables creaking, and the smell of sweat in the air. For a moment, their efforts seemed to be in vain, then the *Red Boar* lurched and slid back a foot.

"Again!" shouted Roran. Foot by foot, they advanced into the sea, until the frigid water surged about their waists. A breaker crashed over Roran, filling his mouth with seawater, which he spat out vigorously, disgusted by the taste of salt; it was far more intense than he expected.

When the barge lifted free of the seabed, Roran swam alongside the *Red Boar* and pulled himself up with one of the ropes draped over the gunwale. Meanwhile, the sailors deployed long poles that they used to propel the *Red Boar* into ever deeper water, as did the crews of the *Merrybell* and *Edeline*.

The instant they were a reasonable distance from shore, Clovis ordered the poles stowed away and oars broken out, with which the sailors aimed the *Red Boar*'s prow toward the cove's entrance. They hoisted the sail, aligned it to catch the light wind, and, at the vanguard of the trio of barges, set forth for Teirm upon the uncertain expanse of the bounding main.

◆ ◆ ◆

THE BEGINNING OF WISDOM

The days Eragon spent in Ellesméra blended together without distinction; time seemed to have no hold in the pinewood city. The season aged not, even as the afternoons and evenings lengthened, barring the forest with rich shadows. Flowers of all months bloomed at the urging of the elves' magic, nourished by the enchantments spun through the air.

Eragon came to love Ellesméra with its beauty and its quiet, the graceful buildings that flowed out of the trees, the haunting songs that echoed at twilight, the works of art hidden within the mysterious dwellings, and the introspection of the elves themselves, which they mixed with outbursts of merriment.

The wild animals of Du Weldenvarden had no fear of hunters. Often Eragon would look from his eyrie to see an elf petting a stag or a gray fox or murmuring to a shy bear that trundled along the edge of a clearing, reluctant to expose himself. Some animals had no recognizable form. They appeared at night, moving and grunting in the bushes and fleeing if Eragon dared approach. Once he glimpsed a creature like a furred snake and once a white-robed woman whose body wavered and disappeared to reveal a grinning she-wolf in her place.

Eragon and Saphira continued to explore Ellesméra when they had the chance. They went alone or with Orik, for Arya no longer accompanied them, nor had Eragon spoken to her since she broke his fairth. He saw her now and then, flitting between the trees, but whenever he approached—intending to apologize—she withdrew, leaving him alone among the ancient pines. At last Eragon realized that he had to take the initiative if he were to ever have a chance of mending his relationship with her. So one evening, he picked a bouquet from the flowers along the path by his tree and hobbled to Tialdarí Hall, where he asked directions to Arya's quarters from an elf in the common room.

The screen door was open when he reached her chambers. No one answered when he knocked. He stepped inside, listening for approaching footsteps as he glanced around the spacious vine-covered living room, which opened to a small bedroom on one side and a study on the other. Two fairths decorated the walls: a portrait of a stern, proud elf with silver hair, who Eragon guessed was King Evandar, and that of a younger male elf whom he did not recognize.

Eragon wandered through the apartment, looking but not touching, savoring his glimpse into Arya's life, gleaning what he could about her interests and hobbies. By her bed, he saw a glass sphere with a preserved blossom of the black morning glory embedded within it; on her desk, neat rows of scrolls with titles like *Osilon: Harvest Report* and *Activity Noted by Gil'ead Watchtower*; on the sill of an open bay window, three miniature trees grown in the shape of glyphs from the ancient language, the glyphs for *peace*, *strength*, and *wisdom*; and by the trees, a scrap of paper with an unfinished poem, covered with crossed-out words and scribbled marks. It read:

> *Under the moon, the bright white moon,*
> *Lies a pool, a flat silver pool,*
> *Among the brakes and brambles,*
> *And black-heart pines.*
>
> *Falls a stone, a living stone,*
> *Cracks the moon, the bright white moon,*
> *Among the brakes and brambles,*
> *And black-heart pines.*

Shards of light, swords of light,
Ripple 'cross the pool,
The quiet mere, the still tarn,
The lonely lake there.

In the night, the dark and heavy night,
Flutter shadows, confused shadows,
Where once . . .

Going to the small table by the entrance, Eragon laid his bouquet upon it and turned to leave. He froze as he saw Arya standing in the doorway. She looked startled by his presence, then concealed her emotions behind an impassive expression.

They stared at each other in silence.

He lifted the bouquet, half offering it to her. "I don't know how to make a blossom for you, like Fäolin did, but these are honest flowers and the best I could find."

"I cannot accept them, Eragon."

"They're not . . . they're not that sort of gift." He paused. "It's no excuse, but I didn't realize beforehand that my fairth would put you in such a difficult situation. For that, I'm sorry, and I cry your pardon. . . . I was just trying to make a fairth, not cause trouble. I understand the importance of my studies, Arya, and you needn't fear I will neglect them in order to moon after you." He swayed and leaned against the wall, too dizzy to remain on his feet without support. "That's all."

She regarded him for a long moment, then slowly reached out and took the bouquet, which she held beneath her nose. Her eyes never left his. "They are honest flowers," she conceded. Her gaze flickered down to his feet and back up again. "Have you been ill?"

"No. My back."

"I had heard, but I did not think . . ."

He pushed himself away from the wall. "I should go."

"Wait." Arya hesitated, then guided him to the bay window,

where he sat on the padded bench that curved from the wall. Removing two goblets from a cupboard, Arya crumbled dried nettle leaves into them, then filled the goblets with water and—saying "Boil"—heated the water for tea.

She gave a goblet to Eragon, who held it with both hands so the warmth seeped into him. He glanced out the window to the ground twenty feet below, where elves walked among the royal gardens, talking and singing, and fireflies floated through the dusky air.

"I wish . . . ," said Eragon, "I wish it could always be like this. It's so perfect and quiet."

Arya stirred her tea. "How fares Saphira?"

"The same. And you?"

"I have been preparing to return to the Varden."

Alarm shot through him. "When?"

"After the Blood-oath Celebration. I have tarried here far too long as it is, but I have been loath to leave and Islanzadí wished me to stay. Also . . . I have never attended a Blood-oath Celebration and it is the most important of our observances." She considered him over the rim of her goblet. "Is there nothing Oromis can do for you?"

Eragon forced a weary shrug. "He tried everything he knows."

They sipped their tea and watched the groups and couples meander along the garden paths. "Your studies go well, though?" she asked.

"They do." In the lull that followed, Eragon picked up the scrap of paper from between the trees and examined her stanzas, as if reading them for the first time. "Do you often write poetry?"

Arya extended her hand for the paper and, when he gave it to her, rolled it into a tube so that the words were no longer visible. "It is custom that everyone who attends the Blood-oath Celebration should bring a poem, a song, or some other piece of art that they have made and share it with those assembled. I have but begun to work on mine."

"I think it's quite good."

"If you had read much poetry—"

"I have."

Arya paused, then dipped her head and said, "Forgive me. You are not the person I first met in Gil'ead."

"No. I . . ." He stopped and twisted the goblet between his hands while he searched for the right words. "Arya . . . you'll be leaving soon enough. I would count it a shame if this is the last I see of you between now and then. Could we not meet occasionally, as we did before, and you could show Saphira and me more of Ellesméra?"

"It would not be wise," she said in a gentle but firm voice.

He looked up at her. "Must the price of my indiscretion be our friendship? I cannot help how I feel toward you, but I would rather suffer another wound from Durza than allow my foolishness to destroy the companionship that existed between us. I value it too highly."

Lifting her goblet, Arya finished the last of her tea before responding. "Our friendship shall endure, Eragon. As for us spending time together . . ." Her lips curved with a hint of a smile. "Perhaps. However, we shall have to wait and see what the future brings, for I am busy and can promise nothing."

He knew her words were the closest thing to a conciliation he was likely to receive, and he was grateful for them. "Of course, Arya Svit-kona," he said, and bowed his head.

They exchanged a few more pleasantries, but it was clear that Arya had gone as far as she was willing to go that day, so Eragon returned to Saphira, his hope restored by what he had accomplished. *Now it's up to fate to decide the outcome,* he thought as he settled before Oromis's latest scroll.

Reaching into the pouch at his belt, Eragon withdrew a soapstone container of nalgask—beeswax melted with hazelnut oil—and smeared it over his lips to protect them against the cold wind that scoured his face. He closed the pouch, then wrapped his arms around Saphira's neck and buried his face in the crook of his elbow to reduce the glare from the wimpled clouds beneath them. The tireless beat of Saphira's wings dominated his hearing, higher and faster than that of Glaedr's, whom she followed.

They flew southwest from dawn until early afternoon, often pausing for enthusiastic sparring bouts between Saphira and Glaedr, during which Eragon had to strap his arms onto the saddle to prevent himself from being thrown off by the stomach-turning acrobatics. He then would free himself by pulling on slipknots with his teeth.

The trip ended at a cluster of four mountains that towered over the forest, the first mountains Eragon had seen in Du Weldenvarden. White-capped and windswept, they pierced the veil of clouds and bared their crevassed brows to the beating sun, which was heatless at such altitude.

They look so small compared to the Beors, said Saphira.

As had become his habit during weeks of meditation, Eragon extended his mind in every direction, touching upon the consciousnesses around him in search of any who might mean him harm. He felt a marmot warm in her burrow, ravens, nuthatches, and hawks, numerous squirrels running among the trees, and, farther down the mountain, rock snakes undulating through the brush in search of the mice that were their prey, as well as the hordes of ubiquitous insects.

When Glaedr descended to a bare ridge on the first mountain, Saphira had to wait until he folded his massive wings before there was enough room for her to land. The field of boulder-strewn talus they alighted upon was brilliant yellow from a coating of hard, crenulated lichen. Above them loomed a sheer black cliff. It acted as buttress and dam for a cornice of blue ice that groaned and split under the wind, loosing jagged slabs that shattered on the granite below.

This peak is known as Fionula, said Glaedr. *And her brothers are Ethrundr, Merogoven, and Griminsmal. Each has its own tale, which I shall recount on the flight back. But for now, I shall address the purpose of this trip, namely the nature of the bond forged between dragons and elves and, later, humans. You both know something of it—and I have hinted at its full implications to Saphira—but the time has come to learn the solemn and profound meaning of your partnership so that you may uphold it when Oromis and I are no more.*

"Master?" asked Eragon, wrapping his cloak around himself to stay warm.

Yes, Eragon.

"Why is Oromis not here with us?"

Because, rumbled Glaedr, *it is my duty—as was always the duty of an elder dragon in centuries past—to ensure that the newest generation of Riders understands the true importance of the station they have assumed. And because Oromis is not as well as he appears.*

The rocks cracked with muffled reports as Glaedr coiled up, nestling himself among the scree and placing his majestic head upon the ground lengthwise to Eragon and Saphira. He examined them with one gold eye as large as a polished roundshield and twice as brilliant. A gray smudge of smoke drifted from his nostrils and was blown to tatters by the wind. *Parts of what I am about to reveal were common knowledge among the elves, Riders, and learned humans, but much of it was known only to the leader of the Riders, a mere handful of elves, the humans' current potentate, and, of course, the dragons.*

Listen now, my hatchlings. When peace was made between dragons and elves at the end of our war, the Riders were created to ensure that such conflict would never again arise between our two races. Queen Tarmunora of the elves and the dragon who had been selected to represent us, whose name—he paused and conveyed a series of impressions to Eragon: long tooth, white tooth, chipped tooth; fights won, fights lost; countless eaten Shrrg and Nagra; seven-and-twenty eggs sired and nineteen offspring grown to maturity—*cannot be expressed in any language, decided that a common treaty would not suffice. Signed paper means nothing to a dragon. Our blood runs hot and thick and, given enough time, it was inevitable that we would clash with the elves again, as we had with the dwarves over the millennia. But unlike with* the dwarves, neither we nor the elves could afford another war. We were both too powerful, and we would have destroyed each other. The one way to prevent that and to forge a meaningful accord was to link our two races with magic.

Eragon shivered, and with a touch of amusement, Glaedr said, *Saphira, if you are wise, you will heat one of these rocks with the fire from your belly so that your Rider does not freeze.*

Thereupon Saphira arched her neck, and a jet of blue flame emanated from between her serrated fangs and splashed against the scree, blackening the lichen, which released a bitter smell as it burned. The air grew so hot that Eragon was forced to turn away. He felt the insects underneath the rocks being crisped in the inferno. After a minute, Saphira clapped shut her jaws, leaving a circle of stones five feet across glowing cherry red.

Thank you, Eragon said to her. He hunched by the edge of the scorched rocks and warmed his hands over them.

Remember, Saphira, to use your tongue to direct the stream, admonished Glaedr. *Now . . . it took nine years for the elves' wisest magicians to devise the needed spell. When they had, they and the dragons gathered together at Ilirea. The elves provided the structure of the enchantment, the dragons provided the strength, and together they melded the souls of elves and dragons.*

*The joining changed us. We dragons gained the use of language and other trappings of civilization, while the elves shared in our longevity, since before that moment, their lives were as short as humans'. In the end, the elves were the most affected. Our magic, dragons' magic—which permeates every fiber of our being—was transmitted to the elves and, in time, gave them their much-vaunted strength and grace. Humans have never been influenced as strongly, since you were added to the spell after its completion and it has not had as much time to work upon you as with the elves. Still—*and here Glaedr's eye gleamed—*it has already gentled your race from the rough barbarians who first landed in Alagaësia, though you have begun to regress since the Fall.*

"Were dwarves ever part of this spell?" asked Eragon.

No, and that is why there has never been a dwarf Rider. They do not care for dragons, nor we for them, and they found the idea of being joined with us repellent. Perhaps it is fortunate that they did not enter into our pact, for they have escaped the decline of humans and elves.

Decline, Master? queried Saphira in what Eragon would have sworn was a teasing tone of voice.

Aye, decline. If one or another of our three races suffer, so do they all. By killing dragons, Galbatorix harmed his own race as well as the elves. The two of you have not seen this, for you are new to Ellesméra, but the elves are on the wane; their power is not what it once was. And humans have lost much of their culture and been consumed by chaos and corruption. Only by righting the imbalance between our three races shall order return to the world.

The old dragon kneaded the scree with his talons, crumbling it into gravel so that he was more comfortable. *Layered within the enchantment Queen Tarmunora oversaw was the mechanism that allows a hatchling to be linked with his or her Rider. When a dragon decides to give an egg to the Riders, certain words are said over the egg—which I shall teach you later—that prevent the dragon inside from hatching until it is brought into contact with the person with whom it decides to bond. As dragons can remain in their eggs indefinitely, time is of no concern, nor is the infant harmed. You yourself are an example of this, Saphira.*

The bond that forms between a Rider and dragon is but an enhanced version of the bond that already exists between our races. The human or elf becomes stronger and fairer, while some of the dragon's fiercer traits are tempered by a more reasoned outlook. . . . I see a thought biting at your tongue, Eragon. What is it?

"It's just . . ." He hesitated. "I have a hard time imagining you or Saphira being any fiercer. Not," he added anxiously, "that that's a bad thing."

The ground shook as if with an avalanche as Glaedr chuckled, rolling his great big staring eye behind its horny lid and back again. *If ever you met an unbonded dragon, you would not say so. A dragon alone answers to no one and no thing, takes whatever pleases it, and* bears no thought of kindness for aught but its kith and kin. Fierce and proud were the wild dragons, even arrogant. . . . The females were so formidable, it was accounted a great accomplishment among the Riders' dragons to mate with one.

The lack of this bond is why Galbatorix's partnership with Shruikan, his second dragon, is such a perverted union. Shruikan did not choose Galbatorix as his partner; he was twisted by certain black magics into serving Galbatorix's madness. Galbatorix has constructed a depraved imitation of the relationship that you, Eragon, and you, Saphira, possess and that he lost when the Urgals murdered his original dragon.

Glaedr paused and looked between the two of them. His eye was all that moved. *That which links you exceeds any simple connection between minds. Your very souls, your identities—call it what you will— have been welded on a primal level.* His eye flicked to Eragon. *Do you believe that a person's soul is separate from his body?*

"I don't know," said Eragon. "Saphira once took me out of my body and let me see the world through her eyes. . . . It *seemed* like I was no longer connected to my body. And if the wraiths that a sorcerer calls upon can exist, then maybe our consciousness is independent of flesh as well."

Extending the needle-sharp tip of his foreclaw, Glaedr flipped over a rock to expose a woodrat cowering in its nest. He snapped up the rat with a flash of his red tongue; Eragon winced as he felt the animal's life extinguished.

When the flesh is destroyed, so is the soul, said Glaedr.

"But an animal isn't a person," protested Eragon.

After your meditations, do you truly believe that any of us are so different from a woodrat? That we are gifted with a miraculous quality that other creatures do not enjoy and that somehow preserves our beings after death?

"No," muttered Eragon.

I thought not. Because we are so closely joined, when a dragon or Rider is injured, they must harden their hearts and sever the connection between them in order to protect each other from unnecessary suffering,

440

even insanity. And since the soul cannot be torn from the flesh, you must resist the temptation to try to take your partner's soul into your own body and shelter it there, as that will result in both your deaths. Even if it were possible, it would be an abomination to have multiple consciousnesses in one body.

"How terrible," said Eragon, "to die alone, separate even from the one who is closest to you."

Everyone dies alone, Eragon. Whether you are a king on a battlefield or a lowly peasant lying in bed among your family, no one can accompany you into the void. . . . Now I will have you practice separating your consciousnesses. Start by . . .

Eragon stared at the tray of dinner left in the anteroom of the tree house. He cataloged the contents: bread with hazelnut butter, berries, beans, a bowl of leafy greens, two hard-boiled eggs—which, in accordance with the elves' beliefs, were unfertilized—and a stoppered jug of fresh spring water. He knew that each dish was prepared with the utmost care, that the elves lavished all of their culinary skill upon his meals, and that not even Islanzadí ate better than him.

He could not bear the sight of the tray.

I want meat, he growled, stomping back into the bedroom. Saphira looked up at him from her dais. *I'd even settle for fish or fowl, anything besides this never-ending stream of vegetables. They don't fill up my stomach. I'm not a horse; why should I be fed like one?*

Saphira unfolded her legs, walked to the edge of the teardrop gap overlooking Ellesméra, and said, *I have needed to eat these past few days. Would you like to join me? You can cook as much meat as you like and the elves will never know.*

That I would, he said, brightening. *Should I get the saddle?*

We won't go that far.

Eragon fetched his supply of salt, herbs, and other seasonings from his bags and then, careful not to overexert himself, climbed into the gap between the spikes along Saphira's spine.

Launching herself off the ground, Saphira let an updraft waft her high above the city, whereupon she glided off the column of warm air, slipping down and sideways as she followed a braided stream through Du Weldenvarden to a pond some miles thence. She landed and hunched low to the ground, making it easier for Eragon to dismount.

She said, *There are rabbits in the grass by the edge of the water. See if you can catch them. In the meantime, I go to hunt deer.*

What, you don't want to share your own prey?

No, I don't, she replied grumpily. *Though I will if those oversized mice elude you.*

He grinned as she took off, then faced the tangled clumps of grass and cow parsnip that surrounded the pond and set about procuring his dinner.

Less than a minute later, Eragon collected a brace of dead rabbits from their nest. It had taken him but an instant to locate the rabbits with his mind and then kill them with one of the twelve death words. What he had learned from Oromis had drained the challenge and excitement from the chase. *I didn't even have to stalk them,* he thought, remembering the years he had spent honing his tracking abilities. He grimaced with sour amusement. *I can finally bag any game I want and it seems meaningless to me. At least when I hunted with a pebble with Brom, it was still a challenge, but this . . . this is slaughter.*

The warning of the sword-shaper Rhunön returned to him then: "When you can have anything you want by uttering a few words, the goal matters not, only the journey to it."

I should have paid more attention to her, realized Eragon.

With practiced movements, he drew his old hunting knife, skinned and gutted the rabbits, and then—putting aside the hearts, lungs, kidneys, and livers—buried the viscera so that the scent would not attract scavengers. Next he dug a pit, filled it with wood, and lit a small blaze with magic, since he had not thought to bring his flint and steel. He tended the fire until he had a bed of coals. Cutting a wand of dogwood, he stripped the bark and seared the wood over the coals to burn off the bitter sap, then spitted the carcasses on the wand and suspended them between two forked branches pounded into the ground. For the organs, he placed a flat stone upon a section of the coals and greased it with fat for a makeshift frying pan.

Saphira found him crouched by the fire, slowly turning the wand to cook the meat evenly. She landed with a limp deer hanging from her jaws and the remains of a second deer clutched in her talons. Measuring her length out in the fragrant grass, she proceeded to gorge upon her prey, eating the entire deer, including the hide. Bones cracked between her razor teeth, like branches snapping in a gale.

When the rabbits were ready, Eragon waved them in the air to cool them, then stared at the glistening, golden meat, the smell of which he found almost unbearably enticing.

As he opened his mouth to take the first bite, his thoughts turned unbidden to his meditations. He remembered his excursions into the minds of birds and squirrels and mice, how full of energy they felt and how vigorously they fought for the right to exist in the face of danger. *And if this life is all they have . . .*

Gripped by revulsion, Eragon thrust the meat away, as appalled by the fact that he had killed the rabbits as if he had murdered two people. His stomach churned and threatened to make him purge himself.

Saphira paused in her feast to eye him with concern.

Taking a long breath, Eragon pressed his fists against his knees in an attempt to master himself and understand why he was so strongly affected. His entire life he had eaten meat, fish, and fowl. He *enjoyed* it. And yet it now made him physically ill to consider dining upon the rabbits. He looked at Saphira. *I can't do it,* he said.

It is the way of the world that everything eats everything else. Why do you resist the order of things?

He pondered her question. He did not condemn those who did partake of flesh—he knew that it was the only means of survival for many a poor farmer. But he could no longer do so himself unless faced with starvation. Having been inside of a rabbit and having felt what a rabbit feels . . . eating one would be akin to eating himself. *Because we can better ourselves*, he answered Saphira. *Should we give in to our impulses to hurt or kill any who anger us, to take whatever we want from those who are weaker, and, in general, to disregard the feelings of others? We are made imperfect and must guard against our flaws lest they destroy us.* He gestured at the rabbits. *As Oromis said, why should we cause unnecessary suffering?*

Would you deny all of your desires, then?

I would deny those that are destructive.

You are adamant on this?

Aye.

In that case, said Saphira, advancing upon him, *these will make a fine dessert.* In a blink, she gulped down the rabbits and then licked clean the stone with the organs, abrading the slate with the barbs on her tongue. *I, at least, cannot live on plants alone—that is food for prey, not a dragon. I refuse to be ashamed about how I must sustain myself. Everything has its place in the world. Even a rabbit knows that.*

I'm not trying to make you feel guilty, he said, patting her on the leg. *This is a personal decision. I won't force my choice upon anyone.*

Very wise, she said with a touch of sarcasm.

BROKEN EGG AND
SCATTERED NEST

"**C**oncentrate, Eragon," said Oromis, though not unkindly.

Eragon blinked and rubbed his eyes in an attempt to focus on the glyphs that decorated the curling parchment paper before him. "Sorry, Master." Weariness dragged upon him like lead weights tied to his limbs. He squinted at the curved and spiked glyphs, raised his goose-feather quill, and began to copy them again.

Through the window behind Oromis, the green shelf on top of the Crags of Tel'naeír was streaked with shadows from the descending sun. Beyond, feathery clouds banded the sky.

Eragon's hand jerked as a line of pain shot up his leg, and he broke the nib of the quill and sprayed ink across the paper, ruining it. Across from him, Oromis also started, clutching his right arm.

Saphira! cried Eragon. He reached for her with his mind and, to his bewilderment, was deflected by impenetrable barriers that she had erected around herself. He could barely feel her. It was as if he were trying to grasp an orb of polished granite coated with oil. She kept slipping away from him.

He looked at Oromis. "Something's happened to them, hasn't it?"

"I know not. Glaedr returns, but he refuses to talk to me." Taking his blade, Naegling, from the wall, Oromis strode outside and stood upon the edge of the crags, head uplifted as he waited for the gold dragon to appear.

Eragon joined him, thinking of everything—probable and

445

improbable—that might have befallen Saphira. The two dragons had left at noon, flying north to a place called the Stone of Broken Eggs, where the wild dragons had nested in ages past. It was an easy trip. *It couldn't be Urgals; the elves don't allow them into Du Weldenvarden,* he told himself.

At last Glaedr came into view high above as a winking speck among the darkening clouds. As he descended to land, Eragon saw a wound on the back of the dragon's right foreleg, a tear in his lapped scales as wide as Eragon's hand. Scarlet blood laced the grooves between the surrounding scales.

The moment Glaedr touched the ground, Oromis rushed toward him, only to stop when the dragon growled at him. Hopping on his injured leg, Glaedr crawled to the edge of the forest, where he curled up beneath the outstretched boughs, his back to Eragon, and set about licking clean his wound.

Oromis went and knelt in the clover by Glaedr, keeping his distance with calm patience. It was obvious that he would wait as long as need be. Eragon fidgeted as the minutes elapsed. Finally, by some unspoken signal, Glaedr allowed Oromis to draw near and inspect his leg. Magic glowed from Oromis's gedwëy ignasia as he placed his hand over the rent in Glaedr's scales.

"How is he?" asked Eragon when Oromis withdrew.

"It looks a fearsome wound, but it is no more than a scratch for one so large as Glaedr."

"What about Saphira, though? I still can't contact her."

"You must go to her," said Oromis. "She is hurt, in more ways than one. Glaedr said little of what transpired, but I have guessed much, and you would do well to hurry."

Eragon glanced about for any means of transportation and groaned with anguish when he confirmed that none existed. "How can I reach her? It's too far to run, there's no trail, and I can't—"

"Calm thyself, Eragon. What was the name of the steed who bore you hence from Sílthrim?"

It took Eragon a moment to recall. "Folkvír."

"Then summon him with your skill at gramarye. Name him and your need in this, the most powerful of languages, and he will come to your assistance."

Letting the magic suffuse his voice, Eragon cried out for Folkvír, sending his plea echoing over the forested hills toward Ellesméra with all the urgency he could muster.

Oromis nodded, satisfied. "Well done."

Twelve minutes later, Folkvír emerged like a silver ghost from the dark shadows among the trees, tossing his mane and snorting with excitement. The stallion's sides heaved from the speed of his journey.

Throwing a leg over the small elven horse, Eragon said, "I'll return as soon as I can."

"Do what you must," said Oromis.

Then Eragon touched his heels to Folkvír's ribs and shouted, "Run, Folkvír! Run!" The horse leaped forward and bounded into Du Weldenvarden, threading his way with incredible dexterity between the gnarled pines. Eragon guided him toward Saphira with images from his mind.

Lacking a trail through the underbrush, a horse like Snowfire would have taken three or four hours to reach the Stone of Broken Eggs. Folkvír managed the trip in a bit over an hour.

At the base of the basalt monolith—which ascended from the forest floor like a mottled green pillar and stood a good hundred feet higher than the trees—Eragon murmured, "Halt," then slid to the ground. He looked at the distant top of the Stone of Broken Eggs. Saphira was up there.

He walked around the perimeter, searching for a means to achieve the pinnacle, but in vain, for the weathered formation was impregnable. It possessed no fissures, crevices, or other faults near enough to the ground that he could use to climb its sides.

This might hurt, he thought.

"Stay here," he told Folkvír. The horse looked at him with intelligent eyes. "Graze if you want, but *stay here*, okay?" Folkvír

447

nickered and, with his velvet muzzle, nudged Eragon's arm. "Yes, good boy. You've done well."

Fixing his gaze on the crest of the monolith, Eragon gathered his strength, then said in the ancient language, "Up!"

He realized later that if he had not been accustomed to flying with Saphira, the experience might have proved unsettling enough to cause him to lose control of the spell and plunge to his death. The ground dropped away beneath his feet at a swift clip, while the tree trunks narrowed as he floated toward the underside of the canopy and the fading evening sky beyond. Branches clung like grasping fingers to his face and shoulders as he pushed through into the open. Unlike during one of Saphira's dives, he retained his sense of weight, as if he still stood upon the loam below.

Rising above the edge of the Stone of Broken Eggs, Eragon moved himself forward and released his grip on the magic, alighting upon a mossy patch. He sagged with exhaustion and waited to see if the exertion would pain his back, then sighed with relief when it did not.

The top of the monolith was composed of jagged towers divided by deep and wide gullies where naught but a few scattered wildflowers grew. Black caves dotted the towers, some natural, others clawed out of the basalt by talons as thick as Eragon's leg. Their floors were blanketed with a deep layer of lichen-ridden bones, remnants of the dragons' ancient kills. Birds now nested where dragons once had—hawks and falcons and eagles, who watched him from their perches, ready to attack if he should threaten their eggs.

Eragon picked his way across the forbidding landscape, careful not to twist an ankle on the loose flakes of stone or to get too close to the occasional rifts that split the column. If he fell down one, it would send him tumbling out into empty space. Several times he had to climb over high ridges, and twice more he had to lift himself with magic.

Evidence of the dragons' habitation was visible everywhere, from deep scratches in the basalt to puddles of melted rock to a number of dull, colorless scales caught in nooks, along with other detritus. He even stepped upon a sharp object that, when he bent to examine it, proved to be a fragment of a green dragon egg.

On the eastern face of the monolith stood the tallest tower, in the center of which, like a black pit turned on its side, was the largest cave. It was there that Eragon finally beheld Saphira, curled in a hollow against the far wall, her back to the opening. Tremors ran her length. The walls of the cave bore fresh scorch marks, and the piles of brittle bones were scattered about as if from a fight.

"Saphira," said Eragon, speaking out loud since her mind was closed to him.

Her head whipped up, and she stared at him as if he were a stranger, her pupils contracting to thin black slits as her eyes adjusted to the light from the setting sun behind him. She snarled once, like a feral dog, and then twisted away. As she did, she lifted her left wing and exposed a long, ragged gash along her upper thigh. His heart caught at the sight.

Eragon knew that she would not let him approach, so he did as Oromis had with Glaedr; he knelt among the crushed bones and waited. He waited without word or motion until his legs were numb and his hands were stiff with cold. Yet he did not resent the discomfort. He paid the price gladly if it meant he could help Saphira.

After a time, she said, *I have been a fool.*

We are all fools sometimes.

That makes it no easier when it is your turn to play dunce.

I suppose not.

I have always known what to do. When Garrow died, I knew it was the right thing to pursue the Ra'zac. When Brom died, I knew that we should go to Gil'ead and thence to the Varden. And when Ajihad died, I knew that you should pledge yourself to Nasuada. The path has always been clear to me. Except now. In this issue alone, I am lost.

What is it, Saphira?

Instead of answering, she turned the subject and said, *Do you know why this is called the Stone of Broken Eggs?*

No.

Because during the war between dragons and elves, the elves tracked us to this location and killed us while we slept. They tore apart our nests, then shattered our eggs with their magic. That day, it rained blood in the forest below. No dragon has lived here since.

Eragon remained silent. That was not why he was here. He would wait until she could bring herself to address the situation at hand.

Say something! demanded Saphira.

Will you let me heal your leg?

Leave well enough alone.

Then I shall remain as mute as a statue and sit here until I turn to dust, for I have the patience of a dragon from you.

When they came, her words were halting, bitter, and self-mocking: *It shames me to admit it. When we first came here and I saw Glaedr, I felt such joy that another member of my race survived besides Shruikan. I had never even seen another dragon before, except in Brom's memories. And I thought . . . I thought that Glaedr would be as pleased by my existence as I was by his.*

But he was.

You don't understand. I thought that he would be the mate I never expected to have and that together we could rebuild our race. She snorted, and a burst of flame escaped her nostrils. *I was mistaken. He does not want me.*

Eragon chose his response with care to avoid offending her and to provide a modicum of comfort. *That's because he knows you are destined for someone else: one of the two remaining eggs. Nor would it be proper for him to mate with you when he is your mentor.*

Or perhaps he does not find me comely enough.

Saphira, no dragon is ugly, and you are the fairest of dragons.

I am a fool, she said. But she raised her left wing and kept it in the air as permission for him to tend to her injury.

Eragon limped to Saphira's side, where he examined the crimson wound, glad that Oromis had given him so many scrolls on anatomy to read. The blow—by claw or tooth, he was not sure—

had torn the quadriceps muscle beneath Saphira's hide, but not so much as to bare the bone. Merely closing the surface of the wound, as Eragon had done so many times, would not be enough. The muscle had to be knitted back together.

The spell Eragon used was long and complex, and even he did not understand all its parts, for he had memorized it from an ancient text that offered little explanation beyond the statement that, given no bones were broken and the internal organs were whole, "this charm will heal any ailment of violent origins, excepting that of grim death." Once he uttered it, Eragon watched with fascination as Saphira's muscle writhed beneath his hand—veins, nerves, and fibers weaving together—and became whole once more. The wound was big enough that, in his weakened state, he dared not heal it with just the energy from his body, so he drew upon Saphira's strength as well.

It itches, said Saphira when he finished.

Eragon sighed and leaned his back against the rough basalt, looking at the sunset through his eyelashes. *I fear that you will have to carry me off this rock. I'm too tired to move.*

With a dry rustle, she twisted in place and laid her head on the bones beside him. *I have treated you poorly ever since we came to Ellesméra. I ignored your advice when I should have listened. You warned me about Glaedr, but I was too proud to see the truth in your words. . . . I have failed to be a good companion for you, betrayed what it means to be a dragon, and tarnished the honor of the Riders.*

No, never that, he said vehemently. *Saphira, you haven't failed your duty. You may have made a mistake, but it was an honest one, and one that anyone might have committed in your position.*

That does not excuse my behavior toward you.

He tried to meet her eye, but she avoided his gaze until he touched her upon the neck and said, *Saphira, family members forgive one another, even if they don't always understand why someone acts in a certain way. . . . You are as much my family as Roran—more. Nothing you can do will ever change that. Nothing.* When she did not

451

respond, he reached behind her jaw and tickled the patch of leathery skin below one of her ears. *Do you hear me, eh? Nothing!*

She coughed low in her throat with reluctant amusement, then arched her neck and lifted her head to escape his dancing fingers. *How can I face Glaedr again? He was in a terrible rage. . . . The entire stone shook with the force of his anger.*

At least you held your own when he attacked you.

It was the other way around.

Caught by surprise, Eragon raised his eyebrows. *Well, in any case, the only thing to do is to apologize.*

Apologize!

Aye. Go tell him that you are sorry, that this won't happen again, and that you want to continue your training with him. I'm sure he will be sympathetic if you give him the chance.

Very well, she said in a low voice.

You'll feel better once you do. He grinned. *I know from experience.*

She grunted and padded to the edge of the cave, where she crouched and surveyed the rolling forest. *We should go. Soon it will be dark.* Gritting his teeth, he forced himself upright—every movement costing him effort—and climbed onto her back, taking twice the time he usually did. *Eragon? . . . Thank you for coming. I know what you risked with your back.*

He patted her on the shoulder. *Are we one again?*

We are one.

452

THE GIFT OF DRAGONS

The days leading up to the Agaetí Blödhren were the best and worst of times for Eragon. His back troubled him more than ever, battering down his health and endurance and destroying his calm of mind; he lived in constant fear of triggering an episode. Yet, in contrast, he and Saphira had never been so close. They lived as much in each other's minds as in their own. And every now and then Arya would visit the tree house and walk through Ellesméra with Eragon and Saphira. She never came alone, though, always bringing either Orik or Maud the werecat.

Over the course of their wanderings, Arya introduced Eragon and Saphira to elves of distinction: great warriors, poets, and artists. She took them to concerts held under the thatched pines. And she showed them many hidden wonders of Ellesméra.

Eragon seized every opportunity to talk with her. He told her about his upbringing in Palancar Valley, about Roran, Garrow, and his aunt Marian, stories of Sloan, Ethlbert, and the other villagers, and his love of the mountains surrounding Carvahall and the flaming sheets of light that adorned the winter sky at night. He told her about the time a vixen fell into Gedric's tanning vats and had to be fished out with a net. He told her about the joy he found in planting a crop, weeding and nurturing it, and watching the tender green shoots grow under his care—a joy that he knew she, of all people, could appreciate.

In turn, Eragon gleaned occasional insights into her own life. He heard mentions of her childhood, her friends and family, and her experiences among the Varden, which she spoke about most freely, describing raids and battles she participated in, treaties she helped to negotiate, her disputes with the dwarves, and the momentous events she witnessed during her tenure as ambassador.

Between her and Saphira, a measure of peace entered Eragon's heart, but it was a precarious balance that the slightest influence might disrupt. Time itself was an enemy, for Arya was destined to leave Du Weldenvarden after the Agaetí Blödhren. Thus, Eragon treasured his moments with her and dreaded the arrival of the forthcoming celebration.

The entire city bustled with activity as the elves prepared for the Agaetí Blödhren. Eragon had never seen them so excited before. They decorated the forest with colored bunting and lanterns, especially around the Menoa tree, while the tree itself was adorned with a lantern upon the tip of each branch, where they hung like glowing teardrops. Even the plants, Eragon noticed, took on a festive appearance with a collection of bright new flowers. He often heard the elves singing to them late at night.

Each day hundreds of elves arrived in Ellesméra from their cities scattered throughout the woods, for no elf would willingly miss the centennial observance of their treaty with the dragons. Eragon guessed that many of them also came to meet Saphira. *It seems as if I do nothing but repeat their greeting,* he thought. The elves who were absent because of their responsibilities would hold their own festivities simultaneously and would participate in the ceremonies at Ellesméra by scrying through enchanted mirrors that displayed the likeness of those watching, so that no one felt as if they were being spied upon.

A week before the Agaetí Blödhren, when Eragon and Saphira were about to return to their quarters from the Crags of Tel'naeír, Oromis said, "You should both think about what you can bring to the Blood-oath Celebration. Unless your creations require magic to make or to function, I suggest that you avoid using gramarye. No one will respect your work if it's the product of a spell and not of your own hands. I also suggest you each make a separate piece. That too is custom."

In the air, Eragon asked Saphira, *Do you have any ideas?*

I might have one. But if you don't mind, I'd like to see if it works before I tell you. He caught part of an image from her of a bare knuckle of stone protruding from the forest floor before she concealed it from him.

He grinned. *Won't you give me a hint?*

Fire. Lots of fire.

Back in their tree house, Eragon cataloged his skills and thought, *I know more about farming than anything else, but I don't see how I can turn that to my advantage. Nor can I hope to compete with the elves with magic or match their accomplishments with the crafts I am familiar with. Their talent exceeds that of the finest artisans in the Empire.*

But you possess one quality that no one else does, said Saphira.

Oh?

Your identity. Your history, deeds, and situation. Use those to shape your creation and you will produce something unique. Whatever you make, base it upon that which is most important to you. Only then will it have depth and meaning, and only then will it resonate with others.

He looked at her with surprise. *I never realized that you knew so much about art.*

I don't, she said. *You forget I spent an afternoon watching Oromis paint his scrolls while you flew with Glaedr. Oromis discussed the topic quite a bit.*

Ah, yes. I had forgotten.

After Saphira left to pursue her project, Eragon paced along the edge of the open portal in the bedroom, pondering what she had said. *What's important to me?* he asked himself. *Saphira and Arya, of course, and being a good Rider, but what can I say about those subjects that isn't blindingly obvious? I appreciate beauty in nature, but, again, the elves have already expressed everything possible on that topic. Ellesméra itself is a monument to their devotion.* He turned his gaze

455

inward and scrutinized himself to determine what struck the deepest, darkest chords within him. What stirred him with enough passion—of either love or hate—that he burned to share it with others?

Three things presented themselves to him: his injury at the hands of Durza, his fear of one day fighting Galbatorix, and the elves' epics that so engrossed him.

A rush of excitement flared within Eragon as a story combining those elements took form in his mind. Light on his feet, he ran up the twisting stairs—two at a time—to the study, where he sat before the writing desk, dipped quill in ink, and held it trembling over a pale sheet of paper.

The nib rasped as he made the first stroke:

In the kingdom by the sea,
In the mountains mantled blue . . .

The words flowed from his pen seemingly of their own accord. He felt as if he were not inventing his tale, but merely acting as a conduit to transport it fully formed into the world. Having never composed a work of his own before, Eragon was gripped by the thrill of discovery that accompanies new ventures—especially since, previously, he had not suspected that he might enjoy being a bard.

He labored in a frenzy, not stopping for bread or drink, his tunic sleeves rolled past his elbows to protect them from the ink flicked from his quill by the wild force of his writing. So intense was his concentration, he heard nothing but the beat of his poem, saw nothing but the empty paper, and thought of nothing but the phrases etched in lines of fire behind his eyes.

An hour and a half later, he dropped the quill from his cramped hand, pushed his chair away from the desk, and stood. Fourteen pages lay before him. It was the most he had ever written at one time. Eragon knew that his poem could not match those of the elves' and dwarves' great authors, but he hoped it was honest enough that the elves would not laugh at his effort.

He recited the poem to Saphira when she returned. Afterward, she said, *Ah, Eragon, you have changed much since we left Palancar Valley. You would not recognize the untested boy who first set out for vengeance, I think. That Eragon could not have written a lay after the style of the elves. I look forward to seeing who you become in the next fifty or a hundred years.*

He smiled. *If I live that long.*

"Rough but true," was what Oromis said when Eragon read him the poem.

"Then you like it?"

"'Tis a good portrait of your mental state at the present and an engaging read, but no masterpiece. Did you expect it to be?"

"I suppose not."

"However, I am surprised that you can give voice to it in this tongue. No barrier exists to *writing* fiction in the ancient language. The difficulty arises when one attempts to speak it, for that would require you to tell untruths, which the magic will not allow."

"I can say it," replied Eragon, "because I believe it's true."

"And that gives your writing far more power. . . . I am impressed, Eragon-finiarel. Your poem will be a worthy addition to the Blood-oath Celebration." Raising a finger, Oromis reached within his robe and gave Eragon a scroll tied shut with ribbon. "Inscribed on that paper are nine wards I want you to place about yourself and the dwarf Orik. As you discovered at Sílthrim, our festivities are potent and not for those with constitutions weaker than ours. Unprotected, you risk losing yourself in the web of our magic. I have seen it happen. Even with these precautions, you must take care you are not swayed by fancies wafted on the breeze. Be on your guard, for during this time, we elves are apt to go mad—wonderfully, gloriously mad, but mad all the same."

✳ ✳ ✳

On the eve of the Agaetí Blödhren—which was to last three days—Eragon, Saphira, and Orik accompanied Arya to the Menoa tree, where a host of elves were assembled, their black and silver hair flickering in the lamplight. Islanzadí stood upon a raised root at the base of the trunk, as tall, pale, and fair as a birch tree. Blagden roosted on the queen's left shoulder, while Maud, the werecat, lurked behind her. Glaedr was there, as well as Oromis garbed in red and black, and other elves Eragon recognized, such as Lifaen and Narí and, to his distaste, Vanir. Overhead, the stars glittered in the velvet sky.

"Wait here," said Arya. She slipped through the crowd and returned leading Rhunön. The smith blinked like an owl at her surroundings. Eragon greeted her, and she nodded to him and Saphira. "Well met, Brightscales and Shadeslayer." Then she spied Orik and addressed him in Dwarvish, to which Orik replied with enthusiasm, obviously delighted to converse with someone in the rough speech of his native land.

"What did she say?" asked Eragon, bending down.

"She invited me to her home to view her work and discuss metal working." Awe crossed Orik's face. "Eragon, she first learned her craft from Fûthark himself, one of the legendary grimstborithn of Dûrgrimst Ingeitum! What I would give to have met him."

Together they waited until the stroke of midnight, when Islanzadí raised her bare left arm so that it pointed toward the new moon like a marble spear. A soft white orb gathered itself above her palm from the light emitted by the lanterns that dotted the Menoa tree. Then Islanzadí walked along the root to the massive trunk and placed the orb in a hollow in the bark, where it remained, pulsing.

Eragon turned to Arya. "Is it begun?"

"It is begun!" She laughed. "And it will end when the werelight expends itself."

The elves divided themselves into informal camps throughout the forest and clearing that encircled the Menoa tree. Seemingly out of nowhere, they produced tables laden high with fantastic

dishes, which from their unearthly appearance were as much the result of the spellweavers' handiwork as the cooks'.

Then the elves began to sing in their clear, flutelike voices. They
sang many songs, yet each was but part of a larger melody that wove
an enchantment over the dreamy night, heightening senses, removing inhibitions, and burnishing the revels with fey magic.
Their verses concerned heroic deeds and quests by ship and horse
to forgotten lands and the sorrow of lost beauty. The throbbing music enveloped Eragon, and he felt a wild abandon take hold of him,
a desire to run free of his life and dance through elven glades forever more. Beside him, Saphira hummed along with the tune, her
glazed eyes lidded halfway.

What transpired afterward, Eragon was never able to adequately
recall. It was as if he had a fever and faded in and out of consciousness. He could remember certain incidents with vivid clarity—
bright, pungent flashes filled with merriment—but it was beyond
him to reconstruct the order in which they occurred. He lost track
of whether it was day or night, for no matter the time, dusk seemed
to pervade the forest. Nor could he ever say if he had slumbered, or
needed sleep, during the celebration. . . .

He remembered spinning in circles while holding the hands of an
elf-maid with cherry lips, the taste of honey on his tongue and the
smell of juniper in the air. . . .

He remembered elves perched on the outstretched branches of the
Menoa tree, like a flock of starlings. They strummed golden harps
and called riddles to Glaedr below and, now and then, pointed a
finger at the sky, whereupon a burst of colored embers would appear
in various shapes before fading away. . . .

He remembered sitting in a dell, propped against Saphira, and
watching the same elf-maid sway before a rapt audience while she
sang:

Away, away, you shall fly away,
O'er the peaks and vales
To the lands beyond.
Away, away, you shall fly away,
And never return to me.

Gone! Gone you shall be from me,
And I will never see you again.
Gone! Gone you shall be from me,
Though I wait for you evermore.

He remembered endless poems, some mournful, others joyful—most both. He heard Arya's poem in full and thought it fine indeed, and Islanzadí's, which was longer but of equal merit. All the elves gathered to listen to those two works. . . .

He remembered the wonders the elves had made for the celebration, many of which he would have deemed impossible beforehand, even with the assistance of magic. Puzzles and toys, art and weapons, and items whose function escaped him. One elf had charmed a glass ball so that every few seconds a different flower bloomed within its heart. Another elf had spent decades traveling Du Weldenvarden and memorizing the sounds of the elements, the most beautiful of which he now played from the throats of a hundred white lilies.

Rhunön contributed a shield that would not break, a pair of gloves woven from steel thread that allowed the wearer to handle molten lead and other such items without harm, and a delicate sculpture of a wren in flight chiseled from a solid block of metal and painted with such skill that the bird seemed alive.

A tiered wood pyramid eight inches high and constructed of fifty-eight interlocking pieces was Orik's offering, much to the elves' delight, who insisted upon disassembling and reassembling the pyramid as often as he would allow. "Master Longbeard," they called him, and said, "Clever fingers mean a clever mind." . . .

He remembered Oromis pulling him aside, away from the music, and asking the elf, "What's wrong?"

"You need to clear your mind." Oromis guided him to a fallen log and had him sit. "Stay here for a few minutes. You will feel better."

"I'm fine. I don't need to rest," protested Eragon.

"You are in no position to judge yourself right now. Stay here until you can list the spells of changing, great and minor, and then you may rejoin us. Promise me this." . . .

He remembered creatures dark and strange, drifting in from the depths of the forest. The majority were animals who had been altered by the accumulated spells in Du Weldenvarden and were now drawn to the Agaetí Blödhren as a starving man is drawn to food. They seemed to find nourishment in the presence of the elves' magic. Most dared reveal themselves only as pairs of glowing eyes on the outskirts of the lantern light. One animal that did expose itself was the she-wolf—in the form of a white-robed woman—that Eragon had encountered before. She lurked behind a dogwood bush, dagger teeth bared in an amused grin, her yellow eyes darting from point to point.

But not all the creatures were animals. Some few were elves who had altered their original forms for functionality or in pursuit of a different ideal of beauty. An elf covered in brindled fur leaped over Eragon and continued to gambol about, as often on all fours as on his feet. His head was narrow and elongated with ears like a cat, his arms hung to his knees, and his long-fingered hands had rough pads on the palm.

Later, two identical elf women presented themselves to Saphira. They moved with languid grace and, when they touched their hands to their lips in the traditional greeting, Eragon saw that their fingers were joined by translucent webbing. "We have come far," they whispered. As they spoke, three rows of gills pulsed on each side of their slender necks, exposing pink flesh underneath. Their skin glistened as if with oil. Their lank hair hung past their narrow shoulders.

He met an elf armored in imbricated scales like a dragon, with a bony crest upon his head, a line of spikes that ran down his back, and two pallid flames that ever flickered in the pits of his flared nostrils.

And he met others who were not so recognizable: elves whose outlines wavered as if seen through water; elves who, when motionless, were indistinguishable from trees; tall elves with eyes of black, even where the whites should have been, who possessed an awful beauty that frightened Eragon and, when they chanced to touch something, passed through it like shadows.

The ultimate example of this phenomenon was the Menoa tree, which was once the elf Linnëa. The tree seemed to quicken with life at the activity in the clearing. Its branches stirred, though no breeze touched them, at times the creaks of its trunk could be heard to match the flow of music, and an air of gentle benevolence emanated from the tree and lay upon those in the vicinity. . . .

And he remembered two attacks from his back, screaming and groaning in the shadows while the mad elves continued their revels around him and only Saphira came to guard over him. . . .

On the third day of the Agaetí Blödhren, or so Eragon later learned, he delivered his verses to the elves. He stood and said, "I am no smith, nor skilled at carving or weaving or pottery or painting or any of the arts. Nor can I rival your accomplishments with spells. Thus, all that remains to me are my own experiences, which I have attempted to interpret through the lens of a story, though I am also no bard." Then, in the manner that Brom had performed lays in Carvahall, Eragon chanted:

In the kingdom by the sea,
In the mountains mantled blue,

On frigid winter's final day
Was born a man with but one task:

To kill the foe in Durza,
In the land of shadows.

Nurtured by the kind and wise
Under oaks as old as time,
He ran with deer and wrestled bears,
And from his elders learned the skills,

To kill the foe in Durza,
In the land of shadows.

Taught to spy the thief in black
When he grabs the weak and strong;
To block his blows and fight the fiend
With rag and rock and plant and bone;

And kill the foe in Durza,
In the land of shadows.

Quick as thought, the years did turn,
'Til the man had come of age,
His body burned with fevered rage,
While youth's impatience seared his veins.

Then he met a maiden fair,
Who was tall and strong and wise,
Her brow adorned with Gëda's Light,
Which shone upon her trailing gown.

In her eyes of midnight blue,
In those enigmatic pools,

463

Appeared to him a future bright,
Together, where they would not have

To fear the foe in Durza,
In the land of shadows.

So Eragon told of how the man voyaged to the land of Durza, where he found and fought the foe, despite the cold terror within his heart. Yet though at last he triumphed, the man withheld the fatal blow, for now that he had defeated his enemy, he did not fear the doom of mortals. He did not need to kill the foe in Durza. Then the man sheathed his sword and returned home and wed his love on summer's eve. With her, he spent his many days content until his beard was long and white. But:

In the dark before the dawn,
In the room where slept the man,
The foe, he crept and loomed above
His mighty rival now so weak.

From his pillow did the man
Raise his head and gaze upon
The cold and empty face of Death,
The king of everlasting night.

Calm acceptance filled the man's
Aged heart; for long ago,
He'd lost all fear of Death's embrace,
The last embrace a man will know.

Gentle as a morning breeze,
Bent the foe and from the man
His glowing, pulsing spirit took,
And thence in peace they went to dwell,

Forevermore in Durza,
In the land of shadows.

Eragon fell quiet and, conscious of the eyes upon him, ducked his head and quickly found his seat. He felt embarrassed that he had revealed so much of himself.

The elf lord, Däthedr, said, "You underestimate yourself, Shade-slayer. It seems that you have discovered a new talent."

Islanzadí raised one pale hand. "Your work shall be added to the great library in Tialdarí Hall, Eragon-finiarel, so that all who wish can appreciate it. Though your poem is allegory, I believe that it has helped many of us to better understand the hardships you have faced since Saphira's egg appeared to you, for which we are, in no small way, responsible. You must read it to us again so we may think upon this further."

Pleased, Eragon bowed his head and did as she commanded. Afterward was time for Saphira to present her work to the elves. She flew off into the night and returned with a black stone thrice the size of a large man clutched in her talons. Landing on her hind legs, she placed the stone upright in the middle of the bare greensward, in full view of everyone. The glossy rock had been melted and somehow molded into intricate curves that wound about each other, like frozen waves. The striated tongues of rock twisted in such convoluted patterns that the eye had difficulty following a single piece from base to tip, but rather flitted from one coil to the next.

As it was his first time seeing the sculpture, Eragon gazed at it with as much interest as the elves. *How did you make this?*

Saphira's eyes twinkled with amusement. *By licking the molten rock.* Then she bent and breathed fire long upon the stone, bathing it in a golden pillar that ascended toward the stars and clawed at them with lucent fingers. When Saphira closed her jaws, the paper-thin edges of the sculpture glowed cherry red, while small flames flickered in the dark hollows and recesses throughout the rock. The flowing strands of rock seemed to move under the hypnotic light.

The elves exclaimed with wonder, clapping their hands and dancing about the piece. An elf cried, "Well wrought, Bright-scales!"

It's beautiful, said Eragon.

Saphira touched him on the arm with her nose. *Thank you, little one.*

Then Glaedr brought out his offering: a slab of red oak that he had carved with the point of one talon into a likeness of Ellesméra as seen from high above. And Oromis revealed his contribution: the completed scroll that Eragon had often watched him illustrate during their lessons. Along the top half of the scroll marched columns of glyphs—a copy of "The Lay of Vestarí the Mariner"—while along the bottom half ran a panorama of a fantastic land-scape, rendered with breathtaking artistry, detail, and skill.

Arya took Eragon's hand then and drew him through the forest and toward the Menoa tree, where she said, "Look how the were-light dims. We have but a few hours left to us before dawn arrives and we must return to the world of cold reason."

Around the tree, the host of elves gathered, their faces bright with eager anticipation. With great dignity, Islanzadí emerged from within their midst and walked along a root as wide as a pathway un-til it angled upward and doubled back on itself. She stood upon the gnarled shelf overlooking the slender, waiting elves. "As is our cus-tom, and as was agreed upon at the end of The Dragon War by Queen Tarmunora, the first Eragon, and the white dragon who rep-resented his race—he whose name cannot be uttered in this or any language—when they bound the fates of elves and dragons to-gether, we have met to honor our blood-oath with song and dance and the fruits of our labor. Last this celebration occurred, many long years ago, our situation was desperate indeed. It has improved somewhat since, the result of our efforts, the dwarves', and the Varden's, though Alagaësia still lies under the black shadow of the Wyrdfell and we must still live with our shame of how we have failed the dragons.

"Of the Riders of eld, only Oromis and Glaedr remain. Brom and many others entered the void this past century. However, new hope has been granted to us in the form of Eragon and Saphira, and it is only right and proper that they should be here now, as we reaffirm the oath between our races three."

At the queen's signal, the elves cleared a wide expanse at the base of the Menoa tree. Around the perimeter, they staked a ring of lanterns mounted upon carved poles, while musicians with flutes, harps, and drums assembled along the ridge of one long root. Guided by Arya to the edge of the circle, Eragon found himself seated between her and Oromis, while Saphira and Glaedr crouched on either side of them like gem-studded bluffs.

To Eragon and Saphira, Oromis said, "Watch you carefully, for this is of great importance to your heritage as Riders."

When all the elves were settled, two elf-maids walked to the center of the space in the host and stood with their backs to each other. They were exceedingly beautiful and identical in every respect, except for their hair: one had tresses as black as a forgotten pool, while the other's hair gleamed like burnished silver wire.

"The Caretakers, Iduna and Nëya," whispered Oromis.

From Islanzadí's shoulder, Blagden shrieked, *"Wyrda!"*

Moving in unison, the two elves raised their hands to the brooches at their throats, unclasped them, and allowed their white robes to fall away. Though they wore no garments, the women were clad in an iridescent tattoo of a dragon. The tattoo began with the dragon's tail wrapped around the left ankle of Iduna, continued up her leg and thigh, over her torso, and then across Nëya's back, ending with the dragon's head on Nëya's chest. Every scale on the dragon was inked a different color; the vibrant hues gave the tattoo the appearance of a rainbow.

The elf-maids twined their hands and arms together so that the dragon appeared to be a continuous whole, rippling from one body to the next without interruption. Then they each lifted a bare foot and brought it down on the packed ground with a soft *thump*.

And again: *thump*.

On the third *thump,* the musicians struck their drums in rhythm. A *thump* later, the harpists plucked the strings of their gilt instruments, and a moment after that, those elves with flutes joined the throbbing melody.

Slowly at first, but with gathering speed, Iduna and Nëya began to dance, marking time with the stamp of their feet on the dirt and undulating so that it was not they who seemed to move but the dragon upon them. Round and round they went, and the dragon flew endless circles across their skin.

Then the twins added their voices to the music, building upon the pounding beat with their fierce cries, their lyrics verses of a spell so complex that its meaning escaped Eragon. Like the rising wind that precedes a storm, the elves accompanied the incantation, singing with one tongue and one mind and one intent. Eragon did not know the words but found himself mouthing them along with the elves, swept along by the inexorable cadence. He heard Saphira and Glaedr hum in concordance, a deep pulse so strong that it vibrated within his bones and made his skin tingle and the air shimmer.

Faster and faster spun Iduna and Nëya until their feet were a dusty blur and their hair fanned about them and they glistened with a film of sweat. The elf-maids accelerated to an inhuman speed and the music climaxed in a frenzy of chanted phrases. Then a flare of light ran the length of the dragon tattoo, from head to tail, and the dragon stirred. At first Eragon thought his eyes had deceived him, until the creature blinked, raised his wings, and clenched his talons.

A burst of flame erupted from the dragon's maw and he lunged forward and pulled himself free of the elves' skin, climbing into the air, where he hovered, flapping his wings. The tip of his tail remained connected to the twins below, like a glowing umbilical cord. The giant beast strained toward the black moon and loosed an untamed roar of ages past, then turned and surveyed the assembled elves.

As the dragon's baleful eye fell upon him, Eragon knew that the creature was no mere apparition but a conscious being bound and sustained by magic. Saphira and Glaedr's humming grew ever louder until it blocked all other sound from Eragon's ears. Above, the specter of their race looped down over the elves, brushing them with an insubstantial wing. It came to a stop before Eragon, engulfing him in an endless, whirling gaze. Bidden by some instinct, Eragon raised his right hand, his palm tingling.

In his mind echoed a voice of fire: *Our gift so you may do what you must.*

The dragon bent his neck and, with his snout, touched the heart of Eragon's gedwëy ignasia. A spark jumped between them, and Eragon went rigid as incandescent heat poured through his body, consuming his insides. His vision flashed red and black, and the scar on his back burned as if branded. Fleeing to safety, he fell deep within himself, where darkness grasped him and he had not the strength to resist it.

Last, he again heard the voice of fire say, *Our gift to you.*

IN A STARRY GLADE

Eragon was alone when he woke.

He opened his eyes to stare at the carved ceiling in the tree house he and Saphira shared. Outside, night still reigned and the sounds of the elves' revels drifted from the glittering city below.

Before he noticed more than that, Saphira leaped into his mind, radiating concern and anxiety. An image passed to him of her standing beside Islanzadí at the Menoa tree, then she asked, *How are you?*

I feel . . . good. Better than I've felt in a long time. How long have I—

Only an hour. I would have stayed with you, but they needed Oromis, Glaedr, and me to complete the ceremony. You should have seen the elves' reaction when you fainted. Nothing like this has occurred before.

Did you cause this, Saphira?

It was not my work alone, nor Glaedr's. The memories of our race, which were given form and substance by the elves' magic, anointed you with what skill we dragons possess, for you are our best hope to avoid extinction.

I don't understand.

Look in a mirror, she suggested. *Then rest and recover and I shall re-join you at dawn.*

She left, and Eragon got to his feet and stretched, amazed by the sense of well-being that pervaded him. Going to the wash closet, he retrieved the mirror he used for shaving and brought it into the light of a nearby lantern.

Eragon froze with surprise.

It was as if the numerous physical changes that, over time, alter the appearance of a human Rider—and which Eragon had already begun to experience since bonding with Saphira—had been completed while he was unconscious. His face was now as smooth and angled as an elf's, with ears tapered like theirs and eyes slanted like theirs, and his skin was as pale as alabaster and seemed to emit a faint glow, as if with the sheen of magic. *I look like a princeling.* Eragon had never before applied the term to a man, least of all himself, but the only word that described him now was *beautiful*. Yet he was not entirely an elf. His jaw was stronger, his brow thicker, his face broader. He was fairer than any human and more rugged than any elf.

With trembling fingers, Eragon reached around the nape of his neck in search of his scar.

He felt nothing.

Eragon tore off his tunic and twisted in front of the mirror to examine his back. It was as smooth as it had been before the battle of Farthen Dûr. Tears sprang to Eragon's eyes as he slid his hand over the place where Durza had maimed him. He knew that his back would never trouble him again.

Not only was the savage blight he had elected to keep gone, but every other scar and blemish had vanished from his body, leaving him as unmarked as a newborn babe. Eragon traced a line upon his wrist where he had cut himself while sharpening Garrow's scythe. No evidence of the wound remained. The blotchy scars on the insides of his thighs, remnants from his first flight with Saphira, had also disappeared. For a moment, he missed them as a record of his life, but his regret was short-lived as he realized that the damage from every injury he had ever suffered, no matter how small, had been repaired.

I have become what I was meant to be, he thought, and took a deep breath of the intoxicating air.

He dropped the mirror on the bed and garbed himself in his finest clothes: a crimson tunic stitched with gold thread; a belt studded with white jade; warm, felted leggings; a pair of the cloth boots favored by the elves; and upon his forearms, leather vambraces the dwarves had given him.

Descending from the tree, Eragon wandered the shadows of Ellesméra and observed the elves carousing in the fever of the night. None of them recognized him, though they greeted him as one of their own and invited him to share in their saturnalias.

Eragon floated in a state of heightened awareness, his senses thrumming with the multitude of new sights, sounds, smells, and feelings that assailed him. He could see in darkness that would have blinded him before. He could touch a leaf and, by touch alone, count the individual hairs that grew upon it. He could identify the odors wafting about him as well as a wolf or a dragon. And he could hear the patter of mice in the underbrush and the noise a flake of bark makes as it falls to earth; the beating of his heart was as a drum to him.

His aimless path led him past the Menoa tree, where he paused to watch Saphira among the festivities, though he did not reveal himself to those in the glade.

Where go you, little one? she asked.

He saw Arya rise from her mother's side, make her way through the gathered elves, and then, like a forest sprite, glide underneath the trees beyond. *I walk between the candle and the dark,* he replied, and followed Arya.

Eragon tracked Arya by her delicate scent of crushed pine needles, by the feathery touch of her foot upon the ground, and by the disturbance of her wake in the air. He found her standing alone on the edge of a clearing, poised like a wild creature as she watched the constellations turn in the sky above.

As Eragon emerged in the open, Arya looked at him, and he felt as if she saw him for the first time. Her eyes widened, and she whispered, "Is that you, Eragon?"

"Aye."

"What have they done to you?"

"I know not."

He went to her, and together they wandered the dense woods, which echoed with fragments of music and voices from the festivities. Changed as he was, Eragon was acutely conscious of Arya's presence, of the whisper of her clothes over her skin, of the soft, pale exposure of her neck, and of her eyelashes, which were coated with a layer of oil that made them glisten and curl like black petals wet with rain.

They stopped on the bank of a narrow stream so clear, it was invisible in the faint light. The only thing that betrayed its presence was the throaty gurgle of water pouring over rocks. Around them, the thick pines formed a cave with their branches, hiding Eragon and Arya from the world and muffling the cool, still air. The hollow seemed ageless, as if it were removed from the world and protected by some magic against the withering breath of time.

In that secret place, Eragon felt suddenly close to Arya, and all his passion for her sprang to the fore of his mind. He was so intoxicated with the strength and vitality coursing through his veins— as well as the untamed magic that filled the forest—he ignored caution and said, "How tall the trees, how bright the stars . . . and how beautiful you are, O Arya Svit-kona." Under normal circumstances, he would have considered his deed the height of folly, but in that fey, madcap night, it seemed perfectly sane.

She stiffened. "Eragon . . ."

He ignored her warning. "Arya, I'll do anything to win your hand. I would follow you to the ends of the earth. I would build a palace for you with nothing but my bare hands. I would—"

"Will you stop pursuing me? Can you promise me that?" When he hesitated, she stepped closer and said, low and gentle, "Eragon, this cannot be. You are young and I am old, and that shall never change."

"Do you feel nothing for me?"

"My feelings for you," she said, "are those of a friend and nothing more. I am grateful to you for rescuing me from Gil'ead, and I find your company pleasant. That is all. . . . Relinquish this quest of yours—it will only bring you heartache—and find someone your own age to spend the long years with."

His eyes brimmed with tears. "How can you be so cruel?"

"I am not cruel, but kind. You and I are not meant for each other."

In desperation, he suggested, "You could give me your memories, and then I would have the same amount of experience and knowledge as you."

"It would be an abomination." Arya lifted her chin, her face grave and solemn and brushed with silver from the glimmering stars. A hint of steel entered her voice: "Hear me well, Eragon. This cannot, nor ever shall be. And until you master yourself, our friendship must cease to exist, for your emotions do nothing but distract us from our duty." She bowed to him. "Goodbye, Eragon Shadeslayer." Then she strode past and vanished into Du Weldenvarden.

Now the tears spilled down Eragon's cheeks and dropped to the moss below, where they lay unabsorbed, like pearls strewn across a blanket of emerald velvet. Numb, Eragon sat upon a rotting log and buried his face in his hands, weeping that his affection for Arya was doomed to remain unrequited, and weeping that he had driven her further away.

Within moments, Saphira joined him. *Oh, little one.* She nuzzled him. *Why did you have to inflict this upon yourself? You knew what would happen if you tried to woo Arya again.*

I couldn't stop myself. He wrapped his arms around his belly and rocked back and forth on the log, reduced to hiccuping sobs by the strength of his misery. Putting one warm wing over him, Saphira drew him close to her side, like a mother falcon with her offspring. He curled up against her and remained huddled there as night passed into day and the Agaetí Blödhren came to an end.

✦   ✦   ✦

LANDFALL

Roran stood upon the poop deck of the *Red Boar*, his arms crossed over his chest and his feet planted wide apart to steady himself on the rolling barge. The salty wind ruffled his hair and tugged at his thick beard and tickled the hairs on his bare forearms.

Beside him, Clovis manned the tiller. The weathered sailor pointed toward the coastline at a seagull-covered rock silhouetted on the crest of a rolling hill that extended into the ocean. "Teirm be right on the far side of that peak."

Roran squinted into the afternoon sun, which reflected off the ocean in a blindingly bright band. "We'll stop here for now, then."

"You don't want to go on into the city yet?"

"Not all of us at once. Call over Torson and Flint and have them run the barges up on that shore. It looks like a good place to camp."

Clovis grimaced. "Arrgh. I was hoping t' get a hot meal tonight." Roran understood; the fresh food from Narda had long since been eaten, leaving them with naught but salt pork, salted herring, salted cabbage, sea biscuits the villagers had made from their purchased flour, pickled vegetables, and the occasional fresh meat when the villagers slaughtered one of their few remaining animals or managed to catch game when they landed.

Clovis's rough voice echoed over the water as he shouted to the skippers of the other two barges. When they drew near, he ordered them to pull ashore, much to their vociferous displeasure. They and the other sailors had counted on reaching Teirm that day and lavishing their pay on the city's delights.

After the barges were beached, Roran walked among the villagers and helped them by pitching tents here and there, unloading equipment, fetching water from a nearby stream, and otherwise lending his assistance until everyone was settled. He paused to give Morn and Tara a word of encouragement, for they appeared despondent, and received a guarded response in turn. The tavern owner and his wife had been aloof to him ever since they left Palancar Valley. On the whole, the villagers were in better condition than when they arrived at Narda due to the rest they had garnered on the barges, but constant worry and exposure to the harsh elements had prevented them from recuperating as well as Roran hoped.

"Stronghammer, will you sup at our tent tonight?" asked Thane, coming up to Roran.

Roran declined with as much grace as he could and turned to find himself confronted by Felda, whose husband, Byrd, had been murdered by Sloan. She bobbed a quick curtsy, then said, "May I speak with you, Roran Garrowsson?"

He smiled at her. "Always, Felda. You know that."

"Thank you." With a furtive expression, she fingered the tassels that edged her shawl and glanced toward her tent. "I would ask a favor of you. It's about Mandel—" Roran nodded; he had chosen her eldest son to accompany him into Narda on that fateful trip when he killed the two guards. Mandel had performed admirably then, as well as in the weeks since while he crewed the *Edeline* and learned what he could about piloting the barges. "He's become quite friendly with the sailors on our barge and he's started playing dice with those lawless men. Not for money—we have none—but for small things. Things we need."

"Have you asked him to stop?"

Felda twisted the tassels. "I fear that, since his father died, he no longer respects me as he once did. He has grown wild and willful."

We have all grown wild, thought Roran. "And what would you have me do about it?" he asked gently.

"You have ever dealt generously with Mandel. He admires you. If you talk with him, he will listen."

Roran considered the request, then said, "Very well, I will do what I can." Felda sagged with relief. "Tell me, though, what has he lost at dice?"

"Food mostly." Felda hesitated and then added, "But I know he once risked my grandmother's bracelet for a rabbit those men snared."

Roran frowned. "Put your heart at ease, Felda. I will tend to the matter as soon as I can."

"Thank you." Felda curtsied again, then slipped away between the makeshift tents, leaving Roran to mull over what she had said.

Roran absently scratched his beard as he walked. The problem with Mandel and the sailors was a problem that cut both ways; Roran had noticed that during the trip from Narda, one of Torson's men, Frewin, had become close to Odele—a young friend of Katrina. *They could cause trouble when we leave Clovis.*

Taking care not to attract undue attention, Roran went through the camp and gathered the villagers he trusted the most and had them accompany him to Horst's tent, where he said, "The five we agreed upon will leave now, before it gets much later. Horst will take my place while I'm gone. Remember that your most important task is to ensure Clovis doesn't leave with the barges or damage them in any way. They may be our only means to reach Surda."

"That, and make sure we aren't discovered," commented Orval.

"Exactly. If none of us have returned by nightfall day after tomorrow, assume we were captured. Take the barges and set sail for Surda, but don't stop in Kuasta to buy provisions; the Empire will probably be lying in wait there. You'll have to find food elsewhere."

While his companions readied themselves, Roran went to Clovis's cabin on the *Red Boar*. "Just the five of you be going?" demanded Clovis after Roran explained their plan.

"That's right." Roran let his iron gaze bore into Clovis until the man fidgeted with unease. "And when I get back, I expect you, these barges, and every one of your men to still be here."

"You dare impugn my honor after how I've kept our bargain?"

"I impugn nothing, only tell you what I expect. Too much is at stake. If you commit treachery now, you condemn our entire village to death."

"That I know," muttered Clovis, avoiding his eyes.

"My people will defend themselves during my absence. So long as breath remains in their lungs, they'll not be taken, tricked, or abandoned. And if misfortune *were* to befall them, I'd avenge them even if I had to walk a thousand leagues and fight Galbatorix himself. Heed my words, Master Clovis, for I speak the truth."

"We're not so fond of the Empire as you seem to believe," protested Clovis. "I wouldn't do them a favor more than the next man."

Roran smiled with grim amusement. "Men will do anything to protect their families and homes."

As Roran lifted the door latch, Clovis asked, "And what will you do once you reach Surda?"

"We will—"

"Not we: *you*. What will you do? I've watched you, Roran. I've listened to you. An' you seem a good enough sort, even if I don't care for how you dealt with me. But I cannot fit it in my head, you dropping that hammer of yours and taking up the plow again, just because you've arrived in Surda."

Roran gripped the latch until his knuckles turned white. "When I have delivered the village to Surda," he said in a voice as empty as a blackened desert, "then I shall go hunting."

"Ah. After that redheaded lass of yours? I heard some talk of that, but I didn't put—"

The door slammed behind Roran as he left the cabin. He let his anger burn hot and fast for a moment—enjoying the freedom of the emotion—before he began to subdue his unruly passions. He marched to Felda's tent, where Mandel was throwing a hunting knife at a stump.

Felda's right; someone has to talk some sense into him. "You're wasting your time," said Roran.

Mandel whirled around with surprise. "Why do you say that?"

"In a real fight, you're more likely to put out your own eye than injure your enemy. If you don't know the exact distance between you and your target . . ." Roran shrugged. "You might as well throw rocks."

He watched with detached interest as the younger man bristled with pride. "Gunnar told me about a man he knew in Cithrí who could hit a flying crow with his knife eight times out of ten."

"And the other two times you get killed. It's usually a bad idea to throw away your weapon in battle." Roran waved a hand, forestalling Mandel's objections. "Get your kit together and meet me on the hill past the stream in fifteen minutes. I've decided you should come with us to Teirm."

"Yes, sir!" With an enthusiastic grin, Mandel dove into the tent and began packing.

As Roran left, he encountered Felda, her youngest daughter balanced on one hip. Felda glanced between him and Mandel's activity in the tent, and her expression tightened. "Keep him safe, Stronghammer." She set her daughter on the ground and then bustled about, helping to gather the items Mandel would need.

Roran was the first to arrive at the designated hill. He squatted on a white boulder and watched the sea while he readied himself for the task ahead. When Loring, Gertrude, Birgit, and Nolfavrell, Birgit's son, arrived, Roran jumped off the boulder and said, "We have to wait for Mandel; he'll be joining us."

"What for?" demanded Loring.

Birgit frowned as well. "I thought we agreed no one else should accompany us. Especially not Mandel, since he was seen in Narda. It's dangerous enough having you and Gertrude along, and Mandel only increases the odds that someone will recognize us."

"I'll risk it." Roran met each of their eyes in turn. "He needs to come." In the end, they listened to him, and, with Mandel, the six of them headed south, toward Teirm.

TEIRM

In that area, the coastline was composed of low, rolling hills verdant with lush grass and occasional briars, willows, and poplars. The soft, muddy ground gave under their feet and made walking difficult. To their right lay the glittering sea. To their left ran the purple outline of the Spine. The ranks of snowcapped mountains were laced with clouds and mist.

As Roran's company wended past the properties surrounding Teirm—some freehold farms, others massive estates—they made every effort to go undetected. When they encountered the road that connected Narda to Teirm, they darted across it and continued farther east, toward the mountains, for several more miles before turning south again. Once they were confident they had circumnavigated the city, they angled back toward the ocean until they found the southern road in.

During his time on the *Red Boar*, it had occurred to Roran that officials in Narda might have deduced that whoever killed the two guards was among the men who left upon Clovis's barges. If so, messengers would have warned Teirm's soldiers to watch for anyone matching the villagers' descriptions. And if the Ra'zac had visited Narda, then the soldiers would also know that they were looking not just for a handful of murderers but Roran Stronghammer and the refugees from Carvahall. Teirm could be one huge trap. Yet they could not bypass the city, for the villagers needed supplies and a new mode of transportation.

Roran had decided that their best precaution against capture was to send no one into Teirm who had been seen in Narda, except for Gertrude and himself—Gertrude because only she understood the ingredients for her medicines, and Roran because, though he was the most likely to be recognized, he trusted no one else to do what was required. He knew he possessed the will to act when others hesitated, like the time he slew the guards. The rest of the group was chosen to minimize suspicion. Loring was old but a tough fighter and an excellent liar. Birgit had proven herself canny and strong, and her son, Nolfavrell, had already killed a soldier in combat, despite his tender age. Hopefully, they would appear as nothing more than an extended family traveling together. *That is, if Mandel doesn't throw the scheme awry*, thought Roran.

It was also Roran's idea to enter Teirm from the south, and thus make it seem even more unlikely that they had come from Narda.

Evening was nigh when Teirm came into view, white and ghostly in the gloaming. Roran stopped to inspect what lay before them. The walled city stood alone upon the edge of a large bay, self-contained and impregnable to any conceivable attack. Torches glowed between the merlons on the battlements, where soldiers with bows patrolled their endless circuits. Above the walls rose a citadel, and then a faceted lighthouse, which swept its hazy beam across the dark waters.

"It's so big," said Nolfavrell.

Loring bobbed his head without taking his eyes off Teirm. "Aye, that it is."

Roran's attention was caught by a ship moored at one of the stone piers jutting from the city. The three-masted vessel was larger than any he had seen in Narda, with a high forecastle, two banks of oarlocks, and twelve powerful ballistae mounted along each side of the deck for shooting javelins. The magnificent craft appeared equally suited for either commerce or war. Even more importantly, Roran thought that it might—*might*—be able to hold the entire village.

"That's what we need," he said, pointing.

Birgit uttered a sour grunt. "We'd have to sell ourselves into slavery to afford passage on that monster."

Clovis had warned them that Teirm's portcullis closed at sunset, so they quickened their pace to avoid spending the night in the countryside. As they neared the pale walls, the road filled with a double stream of people hurrying to and from Teirm.

Roran had not anticipated so much traffic, but he soon realized that it could help shield his party from unwanted attention. Beckoning to Mandel, Roran said, "Drop back a ways and follow someone else through the gate, so the guards don't think you're with us. We'll wait for you on the other side. If they ask, you've come here seeking employment as a seaman."

"Yes, sir."

As Mandel fell behind, Roran hunched one shoulder, allowed a limp to creep into his walk, and began to rehearse the story Loring had concocted to explain their presence at Teirm. He stepped off the road and ducked his head as a man drove a pair of lumbering oxen past, grateful for the shadows that concealed his features.

The gate loomed ahead, washed in uncertain orange from the torches placed in sconces on each side of the entrance. Underneath stood a pair of soldiers with Galbatorix's twisting flame stitched onto the front of their crimson tunics. Neither of the armed men so much as glanced at Roran and his companions as they shuffled underneath the spiked portcullis and through the short tunnel beyond.

Roran squared his shoulders and felt some of his tension ease. He and the others clustered by the corner of a house, where Loring murmured, "So far, so good."

When Mandel rejoined them, they set out to find an inexpensive hostel where they could let a room. As they walked, Roran studied the layout of the city with its fortified houses—which grew progressively higher toward the citadel—and the gridlike arrangement of streets. Those north to south radiated from the citadel like a starburst, while those east to west curved gently across and formed a spiderweb pattern, creating numerous places where barriers could be erected and soldiers stationed.

If Carvahall had been built like this, he thought, *no one could have defeated us but the king himself.*

By dusk they had acquired lodging at the Green Chestnut, an exceedingly vile tavern with atrocious ale and flea-infested beds. Its sole advantage was that it cost next to nothing. They went to sleep without dinner to save their precious coin, and huddled together to prevent their purses from being filched by one of the tavern's other guests.

The next day, Roran and his companions left the Green Chestnut before dawn to search for provisions and transportation.

Gertrude said, "I have heard tell of a remarkable herbalist, Angela by name, who lives here and is supposed to work the most amazing cures, perhaps even a touch of magic. I would go see her, for if anyone has what I seek, it would be she."

"You shouldn't go alone," said Roran. He looked at Mandel. "Accompany Gertrude, help her with her purchases, and do your best to protect her if you are attacked. Your nerve may be tested at times, but do nothing to cause alarm, unless you would betray your friends and family."

Mandel touched his forelock and nodded his obedience. He and Gertrude departed at right angles down a cross street, while Roran and the rest resumed their hunt.

Roran had the patience of a stalking predator, but even he began to thrum with restlessness when morning and afternoon slipped by and they still had not found a ship to carry them to Surda. He learned that the three-masted ship, the *Dragon Wing*, was newly built and about to be launched on her maiden voyage; that they had no chance of hiring it from the Blackmoor Shipping Company unless they could pay a roomful of the dwarves' red gold; and indeed, that the villagers lacked the coin to engage even the meanest vessel. Nor would taking Clovis's barges solve their problems, because it still left unanswered the question of what they would eat on their trek.

"It would be hard," said Birgit, "very hard, to steal goods from this place, what with all the soldiers and how close together the houses are and the watchmen at the gate. If we tried to cart that much stuff out of Teirm, they'd want to know what we were doing."

Roran nodded. *That too.*

Roran had suggested to Horst that if the villagers were forced to flee Teirm with naught but their remaining supplies, they could raid for their food. However, Roran knew that such an act would mean they had become as monstrous as those he hated. He had no stomach for it. It was one thing to fight and kill those who served Galbatorix—or even to steal Clovis's barges, since Clovis had other means of supporting himself—but it was quite another to take provisions from innocent farmers who struggled to survive as much as the villagers had in Palancar Valley. That would be murder.

Those hard facts weighed upon Roran like stones. Their venture had always been tenuous at best, sustained in equal parts by fear, desperation, optimism, and last-minute improvisation. Now he feared that he had driven the villagers into the den of their enemies and bound them in place with a chain forged of their own poverty. *I could escape alone and continue my search for Katrina, but what victory would that be if I left my village to be enslaved by the Empire? Whatever our fate in Teirm, I will stand firm with those who trusted me enough to forsake their homes upon my word.*

To relieve their hunger, they stopped at a bakery and bought a loaf of fresh rye bread, as well as a small pot of honey to slather it with. While he paid for the items, Loring mentioned to the baker's assistant that they were in the market for ships, equipment, and food.

At a tap on his shoulder, Roran turned. A man with coarse black hair and a thick slab of belly said, "Pardon me for overhearing your parley with the young master, but if it's ships and such you be after, and at a fair price, then I should guess you'd want to attend the auction."

"What auction is this?" asked Roran.

"Ah, it's a sad story, it is, but all too common nowadays. One of our merchants, Jeod—Jeod Longshanks, as we call him out of hearing—has had the most abominable run of bad luck. In less than a year, he lost four of his ships, an' when he tried to send his goods over land, the caravan was ambushed and destroyed by some thieving outlaws. His investors forced him to declare bankruptcy, and now they're going to sell his property to recoup their losses. I don't know 'bout food, but you'd be sure to find most everything else you're looking to buy at the auction."

A faint ember of hope kindled in Roran's breast. "When will the auction be held?"

"Why, it's posted on every message board throughout the city. Day after tomorrow, to be sure."

That explained to Roran why they had not learned of the auction before; they had done their best to avoid the message boards, on the off chance that someone would recognize Roran from the portrait on his reward poster.

"Thank you much," he said to the man. "You may have saved us a great deal of trouble."

"My pleasure, so it is."

Once Roran and his companions filed out of the shop, they huddled together on the edge of the street. He said, "Do you think we should look into this?"

"It's all we *have* to look into," growled Loring.

"Birgit?"

"You needn't ask me; it's obvious. We cannot wait until the day after tomorrow, though."

"No. I say we meet with this Jeod and see if we can strike a bargain with him before the auction opens. Are we agreed?"

They were, and so they set out for Jeod's house, armed with directions from a passerby. The house—or rather, mansion—was set on the west side of Teirm, close to the citadel, among scores of other opulent buildings embellished with fine scrollwork, wrought-iron gates, statues, and gushing fountains. Roran could scarcely comprehend such riches; it amazed him how different the lives of these people were from his own.

Roran knocked on the front door to Jeod's mansion, which stood next to an abandoned shop. After a moment, the door was pulled open by a plump butler garnished with overly shiny teeth. He eyed the four strangers upon his doorstep with disapproval, then flashed his glazed smile and asked, "How may I help you, sirs and madam?"

"We would talk with Jeod, if he is free."

"Have you an appointment?"

Roran thought the butler knew perfectly well that they did not. "Our stay in Teirm is too brief for us to arrange a proper meeting."

"Ah, well, then I regret to say that your time would have been better spent elsewhere. My master has many matters to tend. He cannot devote himself to every group of ragged tramps that bangs on his door, asking for handouts," said the butler. He exposed even more of his glassy teeth and began to withdraw inside.

"Wait!" cried Roran. "It's not handouts we want; we have a business proposition for Jeod."

The butler lifted one eyebrow. "Is that so?"

"Aye, it is. Please ask him if he will hear us. We've traveled more leagues than you'd care to know, and it's imperative we see Jeod today."

"May I inquire as to the nature of your proposition?"

"It's confidential."

"Very well, sir," said the butler. "I will convey your offer, but I warn you that Jeod is occupied at the moment, and I doubt he will wish to bother himself. By what name shall I announce you, sir?"

"You may call me Stronghammer." The butler's mouth twitched as if amused by the name, then slipped behind the door and closed it.

"If his head were any larger, 'e couldn't fit in the privy," muttered

Loring out the side of his mouth. Nolfavrell uttered a bark of laughter at the insult.

Birgit said, "Let's hope the servant doesn't imitate the master."

A minute later, the door reopened and the butler announced, with a rather brittle expression, "Jeod has agreed to meet you in the study." He moved to the side and gestured with one arm for them to proceed. "This way." After they trooped into the sumptuous entryway, the butler swept past them and down a polished wood hallway to one door among many, which he opened and ushered them through.

JEOD LONGSHANKS

If Roran had known how to read, he might have been more impressed by the treasure trove of books that lined the study walls. As it was, he reserved his attention for the tall man with graying hair who stood behind an oval writing desk. The man—who Roran assumed was Jeod—looked about as tired as Roran felt. His face was lined, careworn, and sad, and when he turned toward them, a nasty scar gleamed white from his scalp to his left temple. To Roran, it bespoke steel in the man. Long and buried, perhaps, but steel nevertheless.

"Do sit," said Jeod. "I won't stand on ceremony in my own house." He watched them with curious eyes as they settled in the soft leather armchairs. "May I offer you pastries and a glass of apricot brandy? I cannot talk for long, but I see you've been on the road for many a week, and I well remember how dusty my throat was after such journeys."

Loring grinned. "Aye. A touch of brandy would be welcome indeed. You're most generous, sir."

"Only a glass of milk for my boy," said Birgit.

"Of course, madam." Jeod rang for the butler, delivered his instructions, then leaned back in his chair. "I am at a disadvantage. I believe you have my name, but I don't have yours."

"Stronghammer, at your service," said Roran.

"Mardra, at your service," said Birgit.

"Kell, at your service," said Nolfavrell.

"And I'd be Wally, at your service," finished Loring.

"And I at yours," responded Jeod. "Now, Rolf mentioned that you wished to do business with me. It's only fair that you know I'm in no position to buy or sell goods, nor have I gold for investing, nor proud ships to carry wool and food, gems and spices across the restless sea. What, then, can I do for you?"

Roran rested his elbows on his knees, then knitted his fingers together and stared between them as he marshaled his thoughts. *A slip of the tongue could kill us here,* he reminded himself. "To put it simply, sir, we represent a certain group of people who—for various reasons—must purchase a large amount of supplies with very little money. We know that your belongings will be auctioned off day after tomorrow to repay your debts, and we would like to offer a bid now on those items we need. We would have waited until the auction, but circumstances press us and we cannot tarry another two days. If we are to strike a bargain, it must be tonight or tomorrow, no later."

"What manner of supplies do you need?" asked Jeod.

"Food and whatever else is required to outfit a ship or other vessel for a long voyage at sea."

A spark of interest gleamed in Jeod's weary face. "Do you have a certain ship in mind? For I know every craft that's plied these waters in the last twenty years."

"We've yet to decide."

Jeod accepted that without question. "I understand now why you thought to come to me, but I fear you labor under a misapprehension." He spread his gray hands, indicating the room. "Everything you see here no longer belongs to me, but to my creditors. I have no authority to sell my possessions, and if I did so without permission, I would likely be imprisoned for cheating my creditors out of the money I owe them."

He paused as Rolf backed into the study, carrying a large silver tray dotted with pastries, cut-crystal goblets, a glass of milk, and a decanter of brandy. The butler placed the tray on a padded footstool and then proceeded to serve the refreshments. Roran took his goblet and sipped the mellow brandy, wondering how soon courtesy would allow the four of them to excuse themselves and resume their quest.

When Rolf left the room, Jeod drained his goblet with a single draught, then said, "I may be of no use to you, but I do know a number of people in my profession who might . . . *might* . . . be able to help. If you can give me a bit more detail about what you want to buy, then I'd have a better idea of who to recommend."

Roran saw no harm in that, so he began to recite a list of items the villagers *had* to have, things they might need, and things they wanted but would never be able to afford unless fortune smiled greatly upon them. Now and then Birgit or Loring mentioned something Roran had forgotten—like lamp oil—and Jeod would glance at them for a moment before returning his hooded gaze to Roran, where it remained with growing intensity. Jeod's interest concerned Roran; it was as if the merchant knew, or suspected, what he was hiding.

"It seems to me," said Jeod at the completion of Roran's inventory, "that this would be enough provisions to transport several hundred people to Feinster or Aroughs . . . or beyond. Admittedly, I've been rather occupied for the past few weeks, but I've heard of no such host in this area, nor can I imagine where one might have come from."

His face blank, Roran met Jeod's stare and said nothing. On the inside, he seethed with self-contempt for allowing Jeod to amass enough information to reach that conclusion.

Jeod shrugged. "Well, be as it may, that's your own concern. I'd suggest that you see Galton on Market Street about your food and old Hamill by the docks for all else. They're both honest men and will treat you true and fair." Reaching over, he plucked a pastry from the tray, took a bite, and then, when he finished chewing, asked Nolfavrell, "So, young Kell, have you enjoyed your stay in Teirm?"

"Yes, sir," said Nolfavrell, and grinned. "I've never seen anything quite so large, sir."

"Is that so?"

"Yes, sir. I—"

Feeling that they were in dangerous territory, Roran interrupted: "I'm curious, sir, as to the nature of the shop next to your house. It seems odd to have such a humble store among all these grand buildings."

For the first time, a smile, if only a small one, brightened Jeod's expression, erasing years from his appearance. "Well, it was owned by a woman who was a bit odd herself: Angela the herbalist, one of the best healers I've ever met. She tended that store for twenty-some years and then, only a few months ago, up and sold it and left for parts unknown." He sighed. "It's a pity, for she made an interesting neighbor."

"That's who Gertrude wanted to meet, isn't it?" asked Nolfavrell, and looked up at his mother.

Roran suppressed a snarl and flashed a warning glance strong enough to make Nolfavrell quail in his chair. The name would mean nothing to Jeod, but unless Nolfavrell guarded his tongue better, he was liable to blurt out something far more damaging. *Time to go*, thought Roran. He put down his goblet.

It was then that he saw the name *did* mean something to Jeod. The merchant's eyes widened with surprise, and he gripped the arms of his chair until the tips of his fingers turned bone white. "It can't be!" Jeod focused on Roran, studying his face as if trying to see past the beard, and then breathed, "Roran . . . Roran Garrowsson."

AN UNEXPECTED ALLY

Roran had already pulled his hammer from his belt and was halfway out of the chair when he heard his father's name. It was the only thing that kept him from leaping across the room and knocking Jeod unconscious. *How does he know who Garrow is?* Beside him, Loring and Birgit jumped to their feet, drawing knives from within their sleeves, and even Nolfavrell readied himself to fight with a dagger in hand.

"It *is* Roran, isn't it?" Jeod asked quietly. He showed no alarm at their weapons.

"How did you guess?"

"Because Brom brought Eragon here, and you look like your cousin. When I saw your poster with Eragon's, I realized that the Empire must have tried to capture you and that you had escaped. Although," Jeod's gaze drifted to the other three, "in all my imaginings, I never suspected that you took the rest of Carvahall with you."

Stunned, Roran dropped back into his chair and placed the hammer across his knees, ready for use. "Eragon was here?"

"Aye. And Saphira too."

"Saphira?"

Again, surprise crossed Jeod's face. "You don't know, then?"

"Know what?"

Jeod considered him for a long minute. "I think the time has come to drop our pretenses, Roran Garrowsson, and talk openly and without deception. I can answer many of the questions you must have—such as why the Empire is pursuing you—but in return, I need to know the reason you came to Teirm . . . the *real* reason."

"An' why should we trust you, Longshanks?" demanded Loring. "You could be working for Galbatorix, you could."

"I was Brom's friend for over twenty years, before he was a story-teller in Carvahall," said Jeod, "and I did my best to help him and Eragon when they were under my roof. But since neither of them are here to vouch for me, I place my life in your hands, to do with as you wish. I could shout for help, but I won't. Nor will I fight you. All I ask is that you tell me your story and hear my own. Then you can decide for yourself what course of action is proper. You're in no immediate danger, so what harm is there in talking?"

Birgit caught Roran's eye with a flick of her chin. "He could just be trying to save his hide."

"Maybe," replied Roran, "but we have to find out whatever it is he knows." Hooking an arm underneath his chair, he dragged it across the room, placed the back of the chair against the door, and then sat in it, so that no one could burst in and catch them un-awares. He jabbed his hammer at Jeod. "All right. You want to talk? Then let us talk, you and I."

"It would be best if you go first."

"If I do, and we're not satisfied by your answers afterward, we'll have to kill you," warned Roran.

Jeod folded his arms. "So be it."

Despite himself, Roran was impressed by the merchant's forti-tude; Jeod appeared unconcerned by his fate, if a bit grim about the mouth. "So be it," Roran echoed.

Roran had relived the events since the Ra'zac's arrival in Carvahall often enough, but never before had he described them in detail to another person. As he did, it struck him how much had happened to him and the other villagers in such a short time and how easy it had been for the Empire to destroy their lives in Palancar Valley. Resuscitating old terrors was painful for Roran, but he at least had the pleasure of seeing Jeod exhibit unfeigned astonishment as he heard about how the villagers had rousted the soldiers and Ra'zac from their camp, the siege of Carvahall thereafter, Sloan's treachery, Katrina's kidnapping, how Roran had convinced the villagers to flee, and the hardships of their journey to Teirm.

"By the Lost Kings!" exclaimed Jeod. "That's the most extraordinary tale. Extraordinary! To think you've managed to thwart Galbatorix and that right now the entire village of Carvahall is hiding outside one of the Empire's largest cities and the king doesn't even know it. . . ." He shook his head with admiration.

"Aye, that's our position," growled Loring, "and it's precarious at best, so you'd better explain well and good why we should *risk* letting you live."

"It places me in as much—"

Jeod stopped as someone rattled the latch behind Roran's chair, trying to open the door, followed by pounding on the oak planks. In the hallway, a woman cried, "Jeod! Let me in, Jeod! You can't hide in that cave of yours."

"May I?" murmured Jeod.

Roran clicked his fingers at Nolfavrell, and the boy tossed his dagger to Roran, who slipped around the writing desk and pressed the flat of the blade against Jeod's throat. "Make her leave."

Raising his voice, Jeod said, "I can't talk now; I'm in the middle of a meeting."

"Liar! You don't have any business. You're bankrupt! Come out and face me, you coward! Are you a man or not that you won't even look your wife in the eye?" She paused for a second, as if expecting a response, then her screeches increased in volume: "Coward! You're a gutless rat, a filthy, yellow-bellied sheep-biter without the common sense to run a meat stall, much less a shipping company. My father would have never lost so much money!"

Roran winced as the insults continued. *I can't restrain Jeod if she goes on much longer.*

"Be still, woman!" commanded Jeod, and silence ensued. "Our

fortunes might be about to change for the better if you but have the sense to restrain your tongue and not rail on like a fishmonger's wife."

Her answer was cold: "I shall wait upon your pleasure in the dining room, dear husband, and unless you choose to attend me by the evening meal and explain yourself, then I shall leave this accursed house, never to return." The sound of her footsteps retreated into the distance.

When he was sure that she was gone, Roran lifted the dagger from Jeod's neck and returned the weapon to Nolfavrell before reseating himself in the chair pushed against the door.

Jeod rubbed his neck and then, with a wry expression, said, "If we don't reach an understanding, you had better kill me; it'd be easier than explaining to Helen that I shouted at her for naught."

"You have my sympathy, Longshanks," said Loring.

"It's not her fault . . . not really. She just doesn't understand why so much misfortune has befallen us." Jeod sighed. "Perhaps it's my fault for not daring to tell her."

"Tell her what?" piped Nolfavrell.

"That I'm an agent for the Varden." Jeod paused at their dumbfounded expressions. "Perhaps I should start from the beginning. Roran, have you heard rumors in the past few months of the existence of a new Rider who opposes Galbatorix?"

"Mutterings here and there, yes, but nothing I'd give credence to."

Jeod hesitated. "I don't know how else to say this, Roran . . . but there is a new Rider in Alagaësia, and it's your cousin, Eragon. The stone he found in the Spine was actually a dragon egg I helped the Varden steal from Galbatorix years ago. The dragon hatched for Eragon and he named her Saphira. That is why the Ra'zac first came to Palancar Valley. They returned because Eragon has become a formidable enemy of the Empire and Galbatorix hoped that by capturing you, they could bring Eragon to bay."

Roran threw back his head and howled with laughter until tears gathered at the corners of his eyes and his stomach hurt from the convulsions. Loring, Birgit, and Nolfavrell looked at him with something akin to fear, but Roran cared not for their opinions. He laughed at the absurdity of Jeod's assertion. He laughed at the terrible possibility that Jeod had told the truth.

Taking rasping breaths, Roran gradually returned to normal, despite an occasional outburst of humorless chuckles. He wiped his face on his sleeve and then regarded Jeod, a hard smile upon his lips. "It fits the facts; I'll give you that. But so do a half dozen other explanations I've thought of."

Birgit said, "If Eragon's stone was a dragon egg, then where did it come from?"

"Ah," replied Jeod, "now there's an affair I'm well acquainted with. . . ."

Comfortable in his chair, Roran listened with disbelief as Jeod spun a fantastic story of how Brom—grumpy old Brom!—had once been a Rider and had supposedly helped establish the Varden, how Jeod had discovered a secret passageway into Urû'baen, how the Varden arranged to filch the last three dragon eggs from Galbatorix, and how only one egg was saved after Brom fought and killed Morzan of the Forsworn. As if that were not preposterous enough, Jeod went on to describe an agreement between the Varden, dwarves, and elves that the egg should be ferried between Du Weldenvarden and the Beor Mountains, which was why the egg and its couriers were near the edge of the great forest when they were ambushed by a Shade.

A *Shade*—ha! thought Roran.

Skeptical as he was, Roran attended with redoubled interest when Jeod began to talk of Eragon finding the egg and raising the dragon Saphira in the forest by Garrow's farm. Roran had been occupied at the time—preparing to leave for Dempton's mill in Therinsford—but he remembered how distracted Eragon had been, how he spent every moment he could outdoors, doing who knows what. . . .

As Jeod explained how and why Garrow died, rage filled Roran that Eragon had dared keep the dragon secret when it so obviously put everyone in danger. *It's his fault my father died!*

"What was he thinking?" burst out Roran.

He hated how Jeod looked at him with calm understanding. "I doubt Eragon knew himself. Riders and their dragons are bound together so closely, it's often hard to differentiate one from the other. Eragon could have no more harmed Saphira than he could have sawed off his own leg."

"He could have," muttered Roran. "Because of him, I've had to do things just as painful, and I know—he could have."

"You've a right to feel as you do," said Jeod, "but don't forget that the reason Eragon left Palancar Valley was to protect you and all who remained. I believe it was an extremely hard choice for him to make. From his point of view, he sacrificed himself to ensure your safety and to avenge your father. And while leaving may not have had the desired effect, things would have certainly turned out far worse if Eragon had stayed."

Roran said nothing more until Jeod mentioned that the reason Brom and Eragon had visited Teirm was to see if they could use the city's shipping manifests to locate the Ra'zac's lair. "And did they?" cried Roran, bolting upright.

"We did indeed."

"Well, where are they, then? For goodness' sake, man, say it; you know how important this is to me!"

"It seemed apparent from the records—and I later had a message from the Varden that Eragon's own account confirmed this—that the Ra'zac's den is in the formation known as Helgrind, by Dras-Leona."

Roran gripped his hammer with excitement. *It's a long way to Dras-Leona, but Teirm has access to the only open pass between here and the southern end of the Spine. If I can get everyone safely heading down the coast, then I could go to this Helgrind, rescue Katrina if she's there, and follow the Jiet River down to Surda.*

Something of Roran's thoughts much have revealed themselves on his face, because Jeod said, "It can't be done, Roran."

"What?"

"No one man can take Helgrind. It's a solid, bare, black mountain of stone that's impossible to climb. Consider the Ra'zac's foul steeds; it seems likely they would have an eyrie near the top of Helgrind rather than bed near the ground, where they are most vulnerable. How, then, would you reach them? And if you could, do you really believe that you could defeat both Ra'zac and their two steeds, if not more? I have no doubt you are a fearsome warrior—after all, you and Eragon share blood—but these are foes beyond any normal human."

Roran shook his head. "I can't abandon Katrina. It may be futile, but I must try to free her, even if it costs me my life."

"It won't do Katrina any good if you get yourself killed," admonished Jeod. "If I may offer a bit of advice: try to reach Surda as you've planned. Once there, I'm sure you can enlist Eragon's help. Even the Ra'zac cannot match a Rider and dragon in open combat."

In his mind's eye, Roran saw the huge gray-skinned beasts the Ra'zac rode upon. He was loath to acknowledge it, but he knew that such creatures were beyond his ability to kill, no matter the strength of his motivation. The instant he accepted that truth, Roran finally believed Jeod's tale—for if he did not, Katrina was forever lost to him.

Eragon, he thought. *Eragon! By the blood I've spilled and the gore on my hands, I swear upon my father's grave I'll have you atone for what you've done by storming Helgrind with me. If you created this mess, then I'll have you clean it up.*

Roran motioned to Jeod. "Continue your account. Let us hear the rest of this sorry play before the day grows much older."

Then Jeod spoke of Brom's death; of Murtagh, son of Morzan; of capture and escape in Gil'ead; of a desperate flight to save an elf; of Urgals and dwarves and a great battle in a place called Farthen Dûr, where Eragon defeated a Shade. And Jeod told them how the Varden left the Beor Mountains for Surda and how Eragon was even now deep within Du Weldenvarden, learning the elves' mysterious secrets of magic and warfare, but would soon return.

When the merchant fell silent, Roran gathered at the far end of the study with Loring, Birgit, and Nolfavrell and asked their thoughts. Lowering his voice, Loring said, "I can't tell whether he's lying or not, but any man who can weave a yarn like that at knife-point deserves to live. A new Rider! And Eragon to boot!" He shook his head.

"Birgit?" asked Roran.

"I don't know. It's so outlandish. . . ." She hesitated. "But it must be true. Another Rider is the only thing that would spur the Empire to pursue us so fiercely."

"Aye," agreed Loring. His eyes were bright with excitement. "We've been entangled in far more *momentous* events than we realized. A new Rider. Just think about it! The old order is about to be washed away, I tell you. . . . You were right all along, Roran."

"Nolfavrell?"

The boy looked solemn at being asked. He bit his lip, then said, "Jeod seems honest enough. I *think* we can trust him."

"Right, then," said Roran. He strode back to Jeod, planted his knuckles on the edge of the desk, and said, "Two last questions, Longshanks. What do Brom and Eragon look like? And how did you recognize Gertrude's name?"

"I knew of Gertrude because Brom mentioned that he left a letter for you in her care. As for what they looked like: Brom stood a bit shorter than me. He had a thick beard, a hooked nose, and he carried a carved staff with him. And I dare say he was rather irritable at times." Roran nodded; that was Brom. "Eragon was . . . young. Brown hair, brown eyes, with a scar on his wrist, and he never stopped asking questions." Roran nodded again; that was his cousin.

Roran stuck his hammer back under his belt. Birgit, Loring, and Nolfavrell sheathed their blades. Then Roran pulled his chair away from the door, and the four of them resumed their seats like civilized beings. "What now, Jeod?" asked Roran. "Can you help us? I know you're in a difficult situation, but we . . . we are desperate and have no one else to turn to. As an agent of the Varden, can you guarantee us the Varden's protection? We are willing to serve them if they'll shield us from Galbatorix's wrath."

"The Varden," said Jeod, "would be more than happy to have you. More than happy. I suspect you already guessed that. As for help . . ." He ran a hand down his long face and stared past Loring at the rows of books on the shelves. "I've been aware for almost a year that my true identity—as well as that of many other merchants here and elsewhere who have assisted the Varden—was betrayed to the Empire. Because of that, I haven't dared flee to Surda. If I tried, the Empire would arrest me, and then who knows what horrors I'd be in for? I've had to watch the gradual destruction of my business without being able to take any action to oppose or escape it. What's worse, now that I cannot ship anything to the Varden and they dare not send envoys to me, I feared that Lord Risthart would have me clapped in irons and dragged off to the dungeons, since I'm of no further interest to the Empire. I've expected it every day since I declared bankruptcy."

"Perhaps," suggested Birgit, "they want you to flee so they can capture whoever else you bring with you."

Jeod smiled. "Perhaps. But now that you are here, I have a means to leave that they never anticipated."

"Then you have a plan?" asked Loring.

Glee crossed Jeod's face. "Oh yes, I have a plan. Did the four of you see the ship *Dragon Wing* moored at port?"

Roran thought back to the vessel. "Aye."

"The *Dragon Wing* is owned by the Blackmoor Shipping Company, a front for the Empire. They handle supplies for the army, which has mobilized to an alarming degree recently, conscripting soldiers among the peasants and commandeering horses, asses, and oxen." Jeod raised an eyebrow. "I'm not sure what it indicates, but it's possible Galbatorix means to march on Surda. In any case, the *Dragon Wing* is to sail for Feinster within the week. She's the finest ship ever built, from a new design by master shipwright Kinnell."

"And you want to pirate her," concluded Roran.

501

"I do. Not only to spite the Empire or because the *Dragon Wing* is reputed to be the fastest square-rigged ship of her tonnage, but because she's already fully provisioned for a long voyage. And since her cargo is food, we'd have enough for the whole village."

Loring uttered a strained cackle. "I 'ope you can sail her yourself, Longshanks, 'cause not one of us knows how to handle anything larger than a barge."

"A few men from the crews of my ships are still in Teirm. They're in the same position I am, unable to fight or flee. I'm confident they'll jump at a chance to get to Surda. They can teach you what to do on the *Dragon Wing*. It won't be easy, but I don't see much choice in the matter."

Roran grinned. The plan was to his liking: swift, decisive, and unexpected.

"You mentioned," said Birgit, "that in the past year none of your ships—nor those from other merchants who serve the Varden—have reached their destination. Why, then, should this mission succeed when so many have failed?"

Jeod was quick to answer: "Because surprise is on our side. The law requires merchant ships to submit their itinerary for approval with the port authority at least two weeks before departure. It takes a great deal of time to prepare a ship for launch, so if we leave without warning, it could be a week or more before Galbatorix can launch intercept vessels. If luck is with us, we won't see so much as the topmast of our pursuers. So," continued Jeod, "if you are willing to attempt this enterprise, this is what we must do. . . ."

ESCAPE

fter they considered Jeod's proposal from every possible angle and agreed to abide by it—with a few modifications—Roran sent Nolfavrell to fetch Gertrude and Mandel from the Green Chestnut, for Jeod had offered their entire party his hospitality.

"Now, if you will excuse me," said Jeod, rising, "I must go reveal to my wife that which I should never have hidden from her and ask if she'll accompany me to Surda. You may take your pick of rooms on the second floor. Rolf will summon you when supper is ready." With long, slow steps, he departed the study.

"Is it wise to let him tell that ogress?" asked Loring.

Roran shrugged. "Wise or not, we can't stop him. And I don't think he'll be at peace until he does."

Instead of going to a room, Roran wandered through the mansion, unconsciously evading the servants as he pondered the things Jeod had said. He stopped at a bay window open to the stables at the rear of the house and filled his lungs with the brisk and smoky air, heavy with the familiar smell of manure.

"Do you hate him?"

He started and turned to see Birgit silhouetted in the doorway. She pulled her shawl tight around her shoulders as she approached.

"Who?" he asked, knowing full well.

"Eragon. Do you hate him?"

Roran looked at the darkening sky. "I don't know. I hate him for causing the death of my father, but he's still family and for that I love him. . . . I suppose that if I didn't need Eragon to save Katrina, I would have nothing to do with him for a long while yet."

"As I need and hate you, Stronghammer."

He snorted with grim amusement. "Aye, we're joined at the hip, aren't we? You have to help me find Eragon in order to avenge Quimby on the Ra'zac."

"And to have my vengeance on you afterward."

"That too." Roran stared into her unwavering eyes for a moment, acknowledging the bond between them. He found it strangely comforting to know that they shared the same drive, the same angry fire that quickened their steps when others faltered. In her, he recognized a kindred spirit.

Returning through the house, Roran stopped by the dining room as he heard the cadence of Jeod's voice. Curious, he fit his eye to a crack by the middle door hinge. Jeod stood opposite a slight, blond woman, who Roran assumed was Helen.

"If what you say is true, how can you expect me to trust you?"

"I cannot," answered Jeod.

"Yet you ask me to become a fugitive for you?"

"You once offered to leave your family and wander the land with me. You begged me to spirit you away from Teirm."

"Once. I thought you were terribly dashing then, what with your sword and your scar."

"I still have those," he said softly. "I made many mistakes with you, Helen; I understand that now. But I still love you and want you to be safe. I have no future here. If I stay, I'll only bring grief to your family. You can return to your father or you can come with me. Do what will make you the happiest. However, I beg you to give me a second chance, to have the courage to leave this place and shed the bitter memories of our life here. We can start anew in Surda."

She was quiet for a long time. "That young man who was here, is he really a Rider?"

"He is. The winds of change are blowing, Helen. The Varden are about to attack, the dwarves are gathering, and even the elves stir in their ancient haunts. War approaches, and if we're fortunate, so does Galbatorix's downfall."

"Are you important among the Varden?"

"They owe me some consideration for my part in acquiring Saphira's egg."

"Then you would have a position with them in Surda?"

"I imagine so." He put his hands on her shoulders, and she did not draw away.

She whispered, "Jeod, Jeod, don't press me. I cannot decide yet."

"Will you think about it?"

She shivered. "Oh yes. I'll think about it."

Roran's heart pained him as he left. *Katrina*.

That night at dinner, Roran noticed Helen's eyes were often upon him, studying and measuring—comparing him, he was sure, to Eragon.

After the meal, Roran beckoned to Mandel and led him out into the courtyard behind the house.

"What is it, sir?" asked Mandel.

"I wished to talk with you in private."

"About what?"

Roran fingered the pitted blade of his hammer and reflected on how much he felt like Garrow when his father gave a lecture on responsibility; Roran could even feel the same phrases rising in his throat. *And so one generation passes to the next*, he thought. "You've become quite friendly with the sailors as of late."

"They're not our enemies," objected Mandel.

"Everyone is an enemy at this point. Clovis and his men could turn on us in an instant. It wouldn't be a problem, though, if being with them hadn't caused you to neglect your duties." Mandel stiffened and color bloomed in his cheeks, but he did not lower himself in Roran's esteem by denying the charge. Pleased, Roran asked, "What is the most important thing we can do right now, Mandel?"

"Protect our families."

"Aye. And what else?"

Mandel hesitated, uncertain, then confessed, "I don't know."

"Help one another. It's the only way any of us are going to survive. I was especially disappointed to learn that you've gambled food with the sailors, since that endangers the entire village. Your time would be far better spent hunting than playing games of dice or learning to throw knives. With your father gone, it's fallen upon *you* to care for your mother and siblings. They rely on you. Am I clear?"

"Very clear, sir," replied Mandel with a choked voice.

"Will this ever happen again?"

"Never again, sir."

"Good. Now I didn't bring you here just to chastise you. You show promise, which is why I'm giving you a task that I would trust to no one else but myself."

"Yes, sir!"

"Tomorrow morning I need you to return to camp and deliver a message to Horst. Jeod believes the Empire has spies watching this house, so it's vital that you make sure you aren't followed. Wait until you're out of the city, then lose whoever is trailing you in the countryside. Kill him if you have to. When you find Horst, tell him to . . ." As Roran outlined his instructions, he watched Mandel's expression change from surprise, to shock, and then to awe.

"What if Clovis objects?" asked Mandel.

"That night, break the tillers on the barges so they can't be steered. It's a dirty trick, but it could be disastrous if Clovis or any of his men arrive at Teirm before you."

"I won't let that happen," vowed Mandel.

Roran smiled. "Good." Satisfied that he had resolved the matter of Mandel's behavior and that the young man would do everything possible to get the message to Horst, Roran went back inside and bade their host good night before heading off to sleep.

With the exception of Mandel, Roran and his companions confined themselves to the mansion throughout the following day, taking advantage of the delay to rest, hone their weapons, and review their stratagems.

From dawn till dusk, they saw some of Helen as she bustled from one room to the next, more of Rolf with his teeth like varnished pearls, and none of Jeod, for the gray-pated merchant had left to walk the city and—seemingly by accident—meet with the few men of the sea whom he trusted for their expedition.

Upon his return, he told Roran, "We can count on five more hands. I only hope it's enough." Jeod remained in his study for the rest of the evening, drawing up various legal documents and otherwise tending to his affairs.

Three hours before dawn, Roran, Loring, Birgit, Gertrude, and Nolfavrell roused themselves and, fighting back prodigious yawns, congregated in the mansion's entryway, where they muffled themselves in long cloaks to obscure their faces. A rapier hung at Jeod's side when he joined them, and Roran thought the narrow sword somehow completed the rangy man, as if it reminded Jeod who he really was.

Jeod lit an oil lantern and held it up before them. "Are we ready?" he asked. They nodded. Then Jeod unlatched the door and they filed outside to the empty cobblestone street. Behind them, Jeod lingered in the entryway, casting a longing gaze toward the stairs on the right, but Helen did not appear. With a shudder, Jeod left his home and closed the door.

Roran put a hand on his arm. "What's done is done."

"I know."

They trotted through the dark city, slowing to a quick walk whenever they encountered watchmen or a fellow creature of the night, most of whom darted away at the sight of them. Once they heard footsteps on top of a nearby building. "The design of the city," explained Jeod, "makes it easy for thieves to climb from one roof to another."

They slowed to a walk again when they arrived at Teirm's eastern gate. Because the gate opened to the harbor, it was closed only four hours each night in order to minimize the disruption to commerce. Indeed, despite the time, several men were already moving through the gate.

Even though Jeod had warned them it might happen, Roran still felt a surge of fear when the guards lowered their pikes and asked what their business was. He wet his mouth and tried not to fidget while the elder soldier examined a scroll that Jeod handed to him. After a long minute, the guard nodded and returned the parchment. "You can pass."

Once they were on the wharf and out of earshot of the city wall, Jeod said, "It's a good thing he couldn't read."

The six of them waited on the damp planking until, one by one, Jeod's men emerged from the gray mist that lay upon the shore. They were grim and silent, with braided hair that hung to the middle of their backs, tar-smeared hands, and an assortment of scars even Roran respected. He liked what he saw, and he could tell they approved of him as well. They did not, however, take to Birgit.

One of the sailors, a large brute of a man, jerked a thumb at her and accused Jeod, "You didn't say there'd be a woman along for the fightin'. How am I supposed to concentrate with some backwoods tramp getting in m' way?"

"Don't talk about her like that," said Nolfavrell between clenched teeth.

"An' her runt too?"

In a calm voice, Jeod said, "Birgit has fought the Ra'zac. And her son has already killed one of Galbatorix's best soldiers. Can you claim as much, Uthar?"

"It's not proper," said another man. "I wouldn't feel safe with a woman at my side; they do naught but bring bad luck. A lady shouldn't—"

Whatever he was going to say was lost, for at that instant, Birgit did a very unladylike thing. Stepping forward, she kicked Uthar between his legs and then grabbed the second man and pressed her knife against his throat. She held him for a moment, so everyone could see what she had done, then released her captive. Uthar rolled on the boards by her feet, holding himself and muttering a stream of curses.

"Does anyone else have an objection?" demanded Birgit. Beside her, Nolfavrell stared with openmouthed amazement at his mother.

Roran pulled his hood lower to conceal his grin. *Good thing they haven't noticed Gertrude*, he thought.

When no one else challenged Birgit, Jeod asked, "Did you bring what I wanted?" Each sailor reached inside his vest and divulged a weighted club and several lengths of rope.

Thus armed, they worked their way down the harbor toward the *Dragon Wing*, doing their best to escape detection. Jeod kept his lantern shuttered the whole while. Near the dock, they hid behind a warehouse and watched the two lights carried by sentries bob around the deck of the ship. The gangway had been pulled away for the night.

"Remember," whispered Jeod, "the most important thing is to keep the alarm from being sounded until we're ready to leave."

"Two men above, two men below, right?" asked Roran.

Uthar replied, "That be the custom."

Roran and Uthar stripped to their breeches, tied the rope and clubs around their waists—Roran left his hammer behind—and then ran farther down the wharf, out of the sentries' sight, where they lowered themselves into the frigid water.

"Garr, I hate when I have to do this," said Uthar.

"You've done it before?"

"Four times now. Don't stop moving or you'll freeze."

Clinging to the slimy piles underneath the wharf, they swam back up the way they had come until they reached the stone pier that led to the *Dragon Wing*, and then turned right. Uthar put his lips to Roran's ear. "I'll take the starboard anchor." Roran nodded his agreement.

They both dove under the black water, and there they separated. Uthar swam like a frog under the bow of the ship, while Roran went straight to the port anchor and clung to its thick chain. He untied the club from his waist and fit it between his teeth—as much to stop them from chattering as to free his hands—and prepared to wait. The rough metal sapped the warmth from his arms as fast as ice.

Not three minutes later, Roran heard the scuff of Birgit's boots above him as she walked to the end of the pier, opposite the middle of the *Dragon Wing*, and then the faint sound of her voice as she engaged the sentries in conversation. Hopefully, she would keep their attention away from the bow.

Now!

Roran pulled himself hand over hand along the chain. His right shoulder burned where the Ra'zac had bit him, but he pressed on. From the porthole where the anchor chain entered the ship, he clambered up the ridges that supported the painted figurehead, over the railing, and onto the deck. Uthar was already there, dripping and panting.

Clubs in hand, they padded toward the aft of the ship, using whatever cover they could find. They stopped not ten feet behind the sentries. The two men leaned on the railing, bandying words with Birgit.

In a flash, Roran and Uthar burst into the open and struck the sentries on the head before they could draw their sabers. Below, Birgit waved for Jeod and the rest of their group, and between them they raised the gangway and slid one end across to the ship, where Uthar lashed it to the railing.

As Nolfavrell ran aboard, Roran tossed his rope to the boy and said, "Tie and gag these two."

Then everyone but Gertrude descended belowdecks to hunt for the remaining sentries. They found four additional men—the purser, the bosun, the ship's cook, and the ship's cook's assistant—all of whom were trundled out of bed, knocked on the head if they resisted, and then securely trussed. In this, Birgit again proved her worth, capturing two men herself.

Jeod had the unhappy prisoners placed in a line on the deck so they could be watched at all times, then declared, "We have much to do, and little time. Roran, Uthar is captain on the *Dragon Wing*. You and the others will take your orders from him."

For the next two hours, the ship was a frenzy of activity. The sailors tended to the rigging and sails, while Roran and those from Carvahall worked to empty the hold of extraneous supplies, such as bales of raw wool. These they lowered overboard to prevent anyone on the wharf from hearing a splash. If the entire village was to fit on the *Dragon Wing*, they needed to clear as much space as possible.

Roran was in the midst of fitting a cable around a barrel when he heard the hoarse cry, "Someone's coming!" Everyone on deck, except Jeod and Uthar, dropped to their bellies and reached for their weapons. The two men who remained standing paced the ship as if they were sentries. Roran's heart pounded while he lay motionless, wondering what was about to happen. He held his breath as Jeod addressed the intruder . . . then footsteps echoed on the gangway.

It was Helen.

She wore a plain dress, her hair was bound under a kerchief, and she carried a burlap sack over one shoulder. She spoke not a word, but stowed her gear in the main cabin and returned to stand by Jeod. Roran thought he had never seen a happier man.

The sky above the distant mountains of the Spine had just

begun to brighten when one of the sailors in the rigging pointed north and whistled to indicate he had spotted the villagers.

Roran moved even faster. What time they had was now gone. He rushed up on deck and peered at the dark line of people advancing down the coast. This part of their plan depended on the fact that, unlike other coastal cities, Teirm's outer wall had not been left open to the sea, but rather completely enclosed the bulk of the city in order to ward off frequent pirate attacks. This meant that the buildings skirting the harbor were left exposed—and that the villagers could walk right up to the *Dragon Wing*.

"Hurry now, hurry!" said Jeod.

At Uthar's command, the sailors brought out armfuls of javelins for the great bows on deck, as well as casks of foul-smelling tar, which they knocked open and used to paint the upper half of the javelins. They then drew and loaded the ballistae on the starboard side; it took two men per bow to pull out the sinew cord until it caught on its hook.

The villagers were two-thirds of the way to the ship before the soldiers patrolling the battlements of Teirm spotted them and trumpeted the alarm. Even before that first note faded, Uthar bellowed, "Light and fire 'em!"

Dashing open Jeod's lantern, Nolfavrell ran from one ballista to the next, holding the flame to the javelins until the tar ignited. The instant a missile caught, the man behind the bow pulled the release line and the javelin vanished with a heavy *thunk*. In all, twelve blazing bolts shot from the *Dragon Wing* and pierced the ships and buildings along the bay like roaring, red-hot meteors from the heavens above.

"Draw and reload!" shouted Uthar.

The creak of bending wood filled the air as every man hauled back on the twisted cords. Javelins were slotted in place. Once again, Nolfavrell made his run. Roran could feel the vibration in his feet as the ballista in front of him sent its deadly projectile winging on its way.

The fire quickly spread along the waterfront, forming an impenetrable barrier that prevented soldiers from reaching the *Dragon Wing* though Teirm's east gate. Roran had counted on the pillar of smoke to hide the ship from the archers on the battlements, but it was a near thing; a flight of arrows tugged at the rigging, and one dart embedded itself in the deck by Gertrude before the soldiers lost sight of the ship.

From the bow, Uthar shouted, "Pick your targets at will!"

The villagers were running pell-mell down the beach now. They reached the north end of the wharf, and a handful of them stumbled and fell as the soldiers in Teirm redirected their aim. Children screamed in terror. Then the villagers regained momentum. They pounded down the planks, past a warehouse engulfed in flame and along the pier. The panting mob charged onto the ship in a confused mass of jostling bodies.

Birgit and Gertrude guided the stream of people to the fore and aft hatches. In a few minutes, the various levels of the ship were packed to their limit, from the cargo hold to the captain's cabin. Those who could not fit below remained huddled on deck, holding Fisk's shields over their heads.

As Roran had asked in his message, all able-bodied men from Carvahall clustered around the mainmast, waiting for instructions. Roran saw Mandel among them and tossed him a proud salute.

Then Uthar pointed at a sailor and barked, "You there, Bonden! Get those swabs to the capstans and weigh anchors, then down to the oars. Double time!" To the rest of the men at the ballistae, he ordered, "Half of you leave off and take the port ballistae. Drive away any boarding parties."

Roran was one of those who switched sides. As he prepared the ballistae, a few laggards staggered out of the acrid smoke and onto the ship. Beside him, Jeod and Helen hoisted the six prisoners one by one onto the gangway and rolled them onto the pier.

Before Roran quite knew it, anchors had been raised, the gangway was cut loose, and a drum pounded beneath his feet, setting the tempo for the oarsmen. Ever so slowly, the *Dragon Wing* turned to starboard—toward the open sea—and then, with gathering speed, pulled away from the dock.

Roran accompanied Jeod to the quarterdeck, where they watched the crimson inferno devour everything flammable between Teirm and the ocean. Through the filter of smoke, the sun appeared a flat, bloated, bloody orange disk as it rose over the city.

How many have I killed now? wondered Roran.

Echoing his thoughts, Jeod observed, "This will harm a great many innocent people."

Guilt made Roran respond with more force than he intended: "Would you rather be in Lord Risthart's prisons? I doubt many will be injured in the blaze, and those that aren't won't face death, like we will if the Empire catches us."

"You needn't lecture me, Roran. I know the arguments well enough. We did what we had to. Just don't ask me to take pleasure in the suffering we've caused to ensure our own safety."

By noon the oars had been stowed and the *Dragon Wing* sailed under her own power, propelled by favorable winds from the north. The gusts of air caused the rigging overhead to emit a low hum.

The ship was miserably overcrowded, but Roran was confident that with some careful planning they could make it to Surda with a minimum of discomfort. The worst inconvenience was that of limited rations; if they were to avoid starvation, food would have to be dispensed in miserly portions. And in such cramped quarters, disease was an all too likely possibility.

After Uthar gave a brief speech about the importance of discipline on a ship, the villagers applied themselves to the tasks that required their immediate attention, such as tending to their wounded, unpacking their meager belongings, and deciding upon the most efficient sleeping arrangement for each deck. They also had to choose people to fill the various positions on the *Dragon Wing*: who would cook, who would train as sailors under Uthar's men, and so forth.

Roran was helping Elain hang a hammock when he became embroiled in a heated dispute between Odele, her family, and Frewin, who had apparently deserted Torson's crew to stay with Odele. The two of them wanted to marry, which Odele's parents vehemently opposed on the grounds that the young sailor lacked a family of his own, a respectable profession, and the means to provide even a modicum of comfort for their daughter. Roran thought it best if the enamored couple remained together—it seemed impractical to try and separate them while they remained confined to the same ship—but Odele's parents refused to give his arguments credence.

Frustrated, Roran said, "What would you do, then? You can't lock her away, and I believe Frewin has proved his devotion more than—"

"Ra'zac!"

The cry came from the crow's nest.

Without a second thought, Roran yanked his hammer from his belt, whirled about, and scrambled up the ladder through the fore hatchway, barking his shin on the way. He sprinted toward the knot of people on the quarterdeck, coming to a halt beside Horst.

The smith pointed.

One of the Ra'zac's dread steeds drifted like a tattered shadow above the edge of the coastline, a Ra'zac on its back. Seeing the two monsters exposed in daylight in no way diminished the creeping horror they inspired in Roran. He shuddered as the winged creature uttered its terrifying shriek, and then the Ra'zac's insectile voice drifted across the water, faint but distinct: *"You shall not essscape!"*

Roran looked at the ballistae, but they could not turn far

515

enough to aim at the Ra'zac or its mount. "Does anyone have a bow?"

"I do," said Baldor. He dropped to one knee and began to string his weapon. "Don't let them see me." Everyone on the quarterdeck gathered in a tight circle around Baldor, shielding him with their bodies from the Ra'zac's malevolent gaze.

"Why don't they attack?" growled Horst.

Puzzled, Roran searched for an explanation but found none. It was Jeod who suggested, "Perhaps it's too bright for them. The Ra'zac hunt at night, and so far as I know they do not willingly venture forth from their lairs while the sun is yet in the sky."

"It's not just that," said Gertrude slowly. "I think they're afraid of the ocean."

"Afraid of the ocean?" scoffed Horst.

"Watch them; they don't fly more than a yard over the water at any given time."

"She's right," said Roran. *At last, a weakness I can use against them!*

A few seconds later, Baldor said, "Ready!"

At his word, the ranks of people who stood before him jumped aside, clearing the path for his arrow. Baldor sprang to his feet and, in a single motion, pulled the feather to his cheek and loosed the reed shaft.

It was a heroic shot. The Ra'zac was at the extreme edge of a longbow's range—far beyond any mark Roran had seen an archer hit—and yet Baldor's aim was true. His arrow struck the flying creature on the right flank, and the beast gave a scream of pain so great that the glass on the deck was shattered and the stones on the shore were riven in shards. Roran clapped his hands over his ears to protect them from the hideous blast. Still screaming, the monster veered inland and dropped behind a line of misty hills.

"Did you kill it?" asked Jeod, his face pale.

"I fear not," replied Baldor. "It was naught but a flesh wound."

Loring, who had just arrived, observed with satisfaction, "Aye. But at least you hurt him, and I'd wager they'll think twice about bothering us again."

Gloom settled over Roran. "Save your triumph for later, Loring. This was no victory."

"Why not?" demanded Horst.

"Because now the Empire knows exactly where we are." The quarterdeck fell silent as they grasped the implications of what he had said.

✦   ✦   ✦

CHILD'S PLAY

"**A**nd this," said Trianna, "is the latest pattern we've invented."

Nasuada took the black veil from the sorceress and ran it through her hands, marveling at its quality. No human could throw lace that fine. She gazed with satisfaction at the rows of boxes on her desk, which contained samples of the many designs Du Vrangr Gata now produced. "You've done well," she said. "Far better than I had hoped. Tell your spellcasters how pleased I am with their work. It means much to the Varden."

Trianna inclined her head at the praise. "I will convey your message to them, Lady Nasuada."

"Have they yet—"

A disturbance at the doors to her quarters interrupted Nasuada. She heard her guards swear and raise their voices, then a yelp of pain. The sound of metal clashing on metal rang in the hallway. Nasuada backed away from the door in alarm, drawing her dagger from its sheath.

"Run, Lady!" said Trianna. The sorceress placed herself in front of Nasuada and pushed back her sleeves, baring her white arms in preparation to work magic. "Take the servants' entrance."

Before Nasuada could move, the doors burst open and a small figure tackled her legs, knocking her to the floor. Even as Nasuada fell, a silvery object flashed through the space she had just occupied, burying itself in the far wall with a dull *thud*.

Then the four guards entered, and all was confusion as Nasuada felt them drag her assailant off her. When Nasuada managed to stand, she saw Elva hanging in their grip.

"What is the meaning of this?" demanded Nasuada.

The black-haired girl smiled, then doubled over and retched on the braided rug. Afterward, she fixed her violet eyes on Nasuada and—in her terrible, knowing voice—she said, "Have your magician examine the wall, O Daughter of Ajihad, and see if I have not fulfilled my promise to you."

Nasuada nodded to Trianna, who glided to the splintered hole in the wall and muttered a spell. She returned holding a metal dart. "This was buried in the wood."

"But where did it come from?" asked Nasuada, bewildered.

Trianna gestured toward the open window overlooking the city of Aberon. "Somewhere out there, I guess."

Nasuada returned her attention to the waiting child. "What do you know about this, Elva?"

The girl's horrible smile widened. "It was an assassin."

"Who sent him?"

"An assassin trained by Galbatorix himself in the dark uses of magic." Her burning eyes grew half-lidded, as if she were in a trance. "The man hates you. He's coming for you. He would have killed you if I hadn't stopped him." She lurched forward and retched again, spewing half-digested food across the floor. Nasuada gagged with revulsion. "And he's about to suffer great pain."

"Why is that?"

"Because I will tell you he stays in the hostel on Fane Street, in the last room, on the top floor. You had better hurry, or he'll get away . . . away." She groaned like a wounded beast and clutched her belly. "Hurry, before Eragon's spell forces me to stop you from hurting him. You'll be sorry, then!"

Trianna was already moving as Nasuada said, "Tell Jörmundur what's happened, then take your strongest magicians and hunt down this man. Capture him if you can. Kill him if you can't." After the sorceress left, Nasuada looked at her men and saw that their legs were bleeding from numerous small cuts. She realized what it must have cost Elva to hurt them. "Go," she told them. "Find a healer who can mend your injuries."

The warriors shook their heads, and their captain said, "No, Ma'am. We will stay by your side until we know it's safe again."

"As you see fit, Captain."

The men barricaded the windows—which worsened the already sweltering heat that plagued Borromeo Castle—then everyone retreated to her inner chambers for further protection.

Nasuada paced, her heart pounding with delayed shock as she contemplated how close she had come to being killed. *What would become of the Varden if I died?* she wondered. *Who would succeed me?* Dismay gripped her; she had made no arrangements for the Varden in the event of her own demise, an oversight that now seemed a monumental failing. *I won't allow the Varden to be thrown into chaos because I failed to take precautions!*

She halted. "I am in your debt, Elva."

"Now and forever."

Nasuada faltered, disconcerted as she often was by the girl's responses, then continued: "I apologize for not ordering my guards to let you pass, night or day. I should have anticipated an event like this."

"You should have," agreed Elva in a mocking tone.

Smoothing the front of her dress, Nasuada resumed pacing, as much to escape the sight of Elva's stone-white, dragon-marked face as to disperse her own nervous energy. "How did you escape your rooms unaccompanied?"

"I told my caretaker, Greta, what she wanted to hear."

"That's all?"

Elva blinked. "It made her very happy."

"And what of Angela?"

"She left on an errand this morning."

"Well, be as that may, you have my gratitude for saving my life. Ask me any boon you want and I shall grant it if it's within my power."

Elva glanced around the ornate bedroom, then said, "Do you have any food? I'm hungry."

PREMONITION OF WAR

Two hours later, Trianna returned, leading a pair of warriors who carried a limp body between them. At Trianna's word, the men dropped the corpse on the floor. Then the sorceress said, "We found the assassin where Elva said we would. Drail was his name."

Motivated by a morbid curiosity, Nasuada examined the face of the man who had tried to kill her. The assassin was short, bearded, and plain-looking, no different from countless other men in the city. She felt a certain connection to him, as if his attempt on her life and the fact that she had arranged his death in return linked them in the most intimate manner possible. "How was he killed?" she asked. "I see no marks on his body."

"He committed suicide with magic when we overwhelmed his defenses and entered his mind, but before we could take control of his actions."

"Were you able to learn anything of use before he died?"

"We were. Drail was part of a network of agents based here in Surda who are loyal to Galbatorix. They are called the Black Hand. They spy on us, sabotage our war efforts, and—best we could determine in our brief glimpse into Drail's memories—are responsible for dozens of murders throughout the Varden. Apparently, they've been waiting for a good chance to kill you ever since we arrived from Farthen Dûr."

"Why hasn't this Black Hand assassinated King Orrin yet?"

Trianna shrugged. "I can't say. It may be that Galbatorix considers you to be more of a threat than Orrin. If that's the case, then once the Black Hand realizes you are protected from their attacks"—here her gaze darted toward Elva—"Orrin won't live another month unless he is guarded by magicians day and night. Or perhaps Galbatorix has abstained from such direct action because he wanted the Black Hand to remain unnoticed. Surda has always existed at his tolerance. Now that it's become a threat . . ."

"Can you protect Orrin as well?" asked Nasuada, turning to Elva. Her violet eyes seemed to glow. "Maybe if he asks nicely."

Nasuada's thoughts raced as she considered how to thwart this new menace. "Can all of Galbatorix's agents use magic?"

"Drail's mind was confused, so it's hard to tell," said Trianna, "but I'd guess a fair number of them can."

Magic, cursed Nasuada to herself. The greatest danger the Varden faced from magicians—or any person trained in the use of their mind—was not assassination, but rather espionage. Magicians could spy on people's thoughts and glean information that could be used to destroy the Varden. That was precisely why Nasuada and the entire command structure of the Varden had been taught to know when someone was touching their minds and how to shield themselves from such attentions. Nasuada suspected that Orrin and Hrothgar relied upon similar precautions within their own governments.

However, since it was impractical for everyone privy to potentially damaging information to master that skill, one of Du Vrangr Gata's many responsibilities was to hunt for anyone who was siphoning off facts as they appeared in people's minds. The cost of such vigilance was that Du Vrangr Gata ended up spying on the Varden as much as on their enemies, a fact that Nasuada made sure to conceal from the bulk of her followers, for it would only sow hatred, distrust, and dissent. She disliked the practice but saw no alternative.

What she had learned about the Black Hand hardened Nasuada's conviction that, somehow, magicians had to be governed.

"Why," she asked, "didn't you discover this sooner? I can understand that you might miss a lone assassin, but an entire network of spellcasters dedicated to our destruction? Explain yourself, Trianna."

The sorceress's eyes flashed with anger at the accusation. "Because here, unlike in Farthen Dûr, we cannot examine everyone's minds for duplicity. There are just too many people for us magicians to keep track of. *That* is why we didn't know about the Black Hand until now, Lady Nasuada."

Nasuada paused, then inclined her head. "Understood. Did you discover the identities of any other members of the Black Hand?"

"A few."

"Good. Use them to ferret out the rest of the agents. I want you to destroy this organization for me, Trianna. Eradicate them as you would an infestation of vermin. I'll give you however many men you need."

The sorceress bowed. "As you wish, Lady Nasuada."

At a knock on the door, the guards drew their swords and positioned themselves on either side of the entranceway, then their captain yanked open the door without warning. A young page stood outside, a fist raised to knock again. He stared with astonishment at the body on the floor, then snapped to attention as the captain asked, "What is it, boy?"

"I have a message for Lady Nasuada from King Orrin."

"Then speak and be quick about it," said Nasuada.

The page took a moment to compose himself. "King Orrin requests that you attend him directly in his council chambers, for he has received reports from the Empire that demand your immediate attention."

"Is that all?"

"Yes, Ma'am."

"I must attend to this. Trianna, you have your orders. Captain, will you leave one of your men to dispose of Drail?"

"Aye, Ma'am."

"Also, please have him locate Farica, my handmaid. She will see to it that my study is cleaned."

"And what of me?" asked Elva, tilting her head.

"You," said Nasuada, "shall accompany me. That is, if you feel strong enough to do so."

The girl threw back her head, and from her small, round mouth emanated a cold laugh. "I'm strong enough, Nasuada. Are you?"

Ignoring the question, Nasuada swept forth into the hallway with her guards clustered around her. The stones of the castle exuded an earthy smell in the heat. Behind her, she heard the patter of Elva's footsteps and was perversely pleased that the ghastly child had to hurry to keep pace with the adults' longer stride.

The guards remained behind in the vestibule to the council chambers while Nasuada and Elva proceeded inside. The chambers were bare to the point of severity, reflecting the militant nature of Surda's existence. The country's kings had devoted their resources to protecting their people and overthrowing Galbatorix, not to decorating Borromeo Castle with idle riches as the dwarves had done with Tronjheim.

In the main room lay a rough-hewn table twelve feet long, upon which a map of Alagaësia was staked open with daggers at the four corners. As was custom, Orrin sat at the head of the table, while his various advisers—many of whom, Nasuada knew, vehemently opposed her—occupied the chairs farther down. The Council of Elders was also present. Nasuada noticed the concern on Jörmundur's face as he looked at her and deduced that Trianna had indeed told him about Drail.

"Sire, you asked for me?"

Orrin rose. "That I did. We have now—" He stopped in midword as he noticed Elva. "Ah, yes, Shining Brow. I have not had the opportunity to grant you audience before, though accounts of your feats have reached my ear and, I must confess, I have been most curious to meet you. Have you found the quarters I arranged for you satisfactory?"

"They are quite nice, Sire. Thank you." At the sound of her eerie voice, the voice of an adult, everyone at the table flinched.

Irwin, the prime minister, bolted upright and pointed a quivering finger at Elva. "Why have you brought this . . . this *abomination* here?"

"You forget your manners, sir," replied Nasuada, though she understood his sentiment.

Orrin frowned. "Yes, do restrain yourself, Irwin. However, his point is valid, Nasuada; we cannot have this child present at our deliberations."

"The Empire," she said, "has just tried to assassinate me." The room echoed with cries of surprise. "If it were not for Elva's swift action, I would be dead. As a result, I have taken her into my confidence; where I go, she goes." *Let them wonder what it is exactly Elva can do.*

"This is indeed distressing news!" exclaimed the king. "Have you caught the blackguard responsible?"

Seeing the eager expressions of his advisers, Nasuada hesitated. "It would be best to wait until I can give you an account in private, Sire."

Orrin appeared put out by her response, but he did not pursue the issue. "Very well. But sit, sit! We have just received the most troubling report." After Nasuada took her place opposite him—Elva lurking behind her—he continued: "It seems that our spies in Gil'ead have been deceived as to the status of Galbatorix's army."

"How so?"

"They believe the army to be *in* Gil'ead, whereas we have here a missive from one of our men in Urû'baen, who says that he witnessed a great host march south past the capital a week and a half ago. It was night, so he could not be sure of their numbers, but he was certain that the host was far larger than the sixteen thousand that form the core of Galbatorix's troops. There may have been as many as a hundred thousand soldiers, or more."

A hundred thousand! A cold pit of fear settled in Nasuada's stomach. "Can we trust your source?"

"His intelligence has always been reliable."

"I don't understand," said Nasuada. "How could Galbatorix move that many men without our knowing of it before? The supply trains alone would be miles long. It's been obvious the army was mobilizing, but the Empire was nowhere near ready to deploy."

Falberd spoke then, slapping a heavy hand on the table for emphasis: "We were outfoxed. Our spies must have been deceived with magic to think the army was still in their barracks in Gil'ead."

Nasuada felt the blood drain from her face. "The only person strong enough to sustain an illusion of that size and duration—"

"Is Galbatorix himself," completed Orrin. "That was our conclusion. It means that Galbatorix has finally abandoned his lair in favor of open combat. Even as we speak, the black foe approaches."

Irwin leaned forward. "The question now is how we should respond. We must confront this threat, of course, but in what manner? Where, when, and how? Our own forces aren't prepared for a campaign of this magnitude, while yours, Lady Nasuada—the Varden—are already accustomed to the fierce clamor of war."

"What do you mean to imply?" *That we should die for you?*

"I but made an observation. Take it how you will."

Then Orrin said, "Alone, we will be crushed against an army so large. We must have allies, and above all else we must have Eragon, especially if we are to confront Galbatorix. Nasuada, will you send for him?"

"I would if I could, but until Arya returns, I have no way to contact the elves or to summon Eragon."

"In that case," said Orrin in a heavy voice, "we must hope that she arrives before it is too late. I do not suppose we can expect the elves' assistance in this affair. While a dragon may traverse the leagues between Aberon and Ellesméra with the speed of a falcon, it would be impossible for the elves to marshal themselves and cross that same distance before the Empire reaches us. That leaves only the dwarves. I know that you have been friends with Hrothgar for many years; will you send him a plea for help on our behalf? The dwarves have always promised they would fight when the time came."

Nasuada nodded. "Du Vrangr Gata has an arrangement with certain dwarf magicians that allows us to transfer messages instantaneously. I will convey your—*our*—request. And I will ask Hrothgar to send an emissary to Ceris to inform the elves of the situation so that they are forewarned, if nothing else."

"Good. We are quite a ways from Farthen Dûr, but if we can delay the Empire for even a week, the dwarves might be able to get here in time."

The discussion that followed was an exceedingly grim one. Various tactics existed for defeating a larger—although not necessarily superior—force, but no one at the table could imagine how they might defeat Galbatorix, especially when Eragon was still so powerless compared to the ancient king. The only ploy that might succeed would be to surround Eragon with as many magicians, dwarf and human, as possible, and then attempt to force Galbatorix to confront them alone. *The problem with that plan,* thought Nasuada, *is that Galbatorix overcame far more formidable enemies during his destruction of the Riders, and his strength has only grown since.* She was certain that this had occurred to everyone else as well. *If we but had the elves' spellweavers to swell our ranks, then victory might be within our reach. Without them . . . If we cannot overthrow Galbatorix, the only avenue left may be to flee Alagaësia across the sundering sea and find a new land in which to build a life for ourselves. There we could wait until Galbatorix is no more. Even he cannot endure forever. The only certainty is that, eventually, all things shall pass.*

They moved on then from tactics to logistics, and here the debate became far more acrimonious as the Council of Elders argued with Orrin's advisers over the distribution of responsibilities between the Varden and Surda: who should pay for this or that, provide rations for laborers who worked for both groups, manage the provisions for their respective warriors, and how numerous other related subjects should be dealt with.

In the midst of the verbal fray, Orrin pulled a scroll from his belt and said to Nasuada, "On the matter of finances, would you be so kind as to explain a rather curious item that was brought to my attention?"

"I'll do my best, Sire."

"I hold in my hand a complaint from the weavers' guild, which asserts that weavers throughout Surda have lost a good share of their profits because the textile market has been inundated with extraordinarily cheap lace—lace they swear originates with the Varden." A pained look crossed his face. "It seems foolish to even ask, but does their claim have basis in fact, and if so, why would the Varden do such a thing?"

Nasuada made no attempt to hide her smile. "If you remember, Sire, when you refused to lend the Varden more gold, you advised me to find another way for us to support ourselves."

"So I did. What of it?" asked Orrin, narrowing his eyes.

"Well, it struck me that while lace takes a long time to make by hand, which is why it's so expensive, lace is quite easy to produce using magic due to the small amount of energy involved. You of all people, as a natural philosopher, should appreciate that. By selling our lace here and in the Empire, we have been able to fully fund our efforts. The Varden no longer want for food or shelter."

Few things in her life pleased Nasuada so much as Orrin's incredulous expression at that instant. The scroll frozen halfway between his chin and the table, his slightly parted mouth, and the quizzical frown upon his brow conspired to give him the stunned appearance of a man who had just seen something he did not understand. She savored the sight.

"*Lace?*" he sputtered.

"Yes, Sire."

"You can't fight Galbatorix with *lace*!"

"Why not, Sire?"

He struggled for a moment, then growled, "Because . . . because it's not respectable, that's why. What bard would compose an epic about our deeds and write about *lace*?"

"We do not fight in order to have epics written in our praise."

"Then blast epics! How am I supposed to answer the weavers' guild? By selling your lace so cheaply, you hurt people's livelihoods and undermine our economy. It won't do. It won't do at all."

Letting her smile become sweet and warm, Nasuada said in her friendliest tone, "Oh dear. If it's too much of a burden for your treasury, the Varden would be more than willing to offer you a loan in return for the kindness you've shown us . . . at a suitable rate of interest, of course."

The Council of Elders managed to maintain their decorum, but behind Nasuada, Elva uttered a quick laugh of amusement.

❖   ❖   ❖

RED BLADE, WHITE BLADE

The moment the sun appeared over the tree-lined horizon, Eragon deepened his breathing, willed his heart to quicken, and opened his eyes as he returned to full awareness. He had not been asleep, for he had not slept since his transformation. When he felt weary and lay himself down to rest, he entered a state that was unto a waking dream. There he beheld many wondrous visions and walked among the gray shades of his memories, yet all the while remained aware of his surroundings.

He watched the sunrise and thoughts of Arya filled his mind, as they had every hour since the Agaetí Blödhren two days before. The morning after the celebration, he had gone looking for her in Tialdarí Hall—intending to try and make amends for his behavior—only to discover that she had already left for Surda. *When will I see her again?* he wondered. In the clear light of day, he had realized just how much the elves' and dragons' magic had dulled his wits during the Agaetí Blödhren. *I may have acted a fool, but it wasn't entirely my fault. I was no more responsible for my conduct than if I were drunk.*

Still, he had meant every word he said to Arya—even if normally he would not have revealed so much of himself. Her rejection cut Eragon to the quick. Freed of the enchantments that had clouded his mind, he was forced to admit that she was probably right, that the difference between their ages was too great to overcome. It was a difficult thing for him to accept, and once he had, the knowledge only increased his anguish.

Eragon had heard the expression "heartbroken" before. Until

then, he always considered it a fanciful description, not an actual physical symptom. But now he felt a deep ache in his chest—like that of a sore muscle—and each beat of his heart pained him.

His only comfort was Saphira. In those two days, she had never criticized what he had done, nor did she leave his side for more than a few minutes at a time, lending him the support of her companionship. She talked to him a great deal as well, doing her best to draw him out of his shell of silence.

To keep himself from brooding over Arya, Eragon took Orik's puzzle ring from his nightstand and rolled it between his fingers, marveling at how keen his senses had become. He could feel every flaw in the twisted metal. As he studied the ring, he perceived a pattern in the arrangement of the gold bands, a pattern that had escaped him before. Trusting his instinct, he manipulated the bands in the sequence suggested by his observation. To his delight, the eight pieces fit together perfectly, forming a solid whole. He slid the ring onto the fourth finger of his right hand, admiring how the woven bands caught the light.

You could not do that before, observed Saphira from the bowl in the floor where she slept.

I can see many things that were once hidden to me.

Eragon went to the wash closet and performed his morning ablutions, including removing the stubble from his cheeks with a spell. Despite the fact that he now closely resembled an elf, he had retained the ability to grow a beard.

Orik was waiting for them when Eragon and Saphira arrived at the sparring field. His eyes brightened as Eragon lifted his hand and displayed the completed puzzle ring. "You solved it, then!"

"It took me longer than I expected," said Eragon, "but yes. Are you here to practice as well?"

"Eh. I already got in a bit o' ax work with an elf who took a rather fiendish delight in cracking me over the head. No . . . I came to watch you fight."

"You've seen me fight before," pointed out Eragon.

"Not for a while, I haven't."

"You mean you're curious to see how I've changed." Orik shrugged in response.

Vanir approached from across the field. He cried, "Are you ready, Shadeslayer?" The elf's condescending demeanor had lessened since their last duel before the Agaetí Blödhren, but not by much.

"I'm ready."

Eragon and Vanir squared off against each other in an open area of the field. Emptying his mind, Eragon grasped and drew Zar'roc as fast as he could. To his surprise, the sword felt as if it weighed no more than a willow wand. Without the expected resistance, Eragon's arm snapped straight, tearing the sword from his hand and sending it whirling twenty yards to his right, where it buried itself in the trunk of a pine tree.

"Can you not even hold on to your blade, Rider?" demanded Vanir.

"I apologize, Vanir-vodhr," gasped Eragon. He clutched his elbow, rubbing the bruised joint to lessen the pain. "I misjudged my strength."

"See that it does not happen again." Going to the tree, Vanir gripped Zar'roc's hilt and tried to pull the sword free. The weapon remained motionless. Vanir's eyebrows met as he frowned at the unyielding crimson blade, as if he suspected some form of trickery. Bracing himself, the elf heaved backward and, with the crack of wood, yanked Zar'roc out of the pine.

Eragon accepted the sword from Vanir and hefted Zar'roc, troubled by how light it was. *Something's wrong*, he thought.

"Take your place!"

This time it was Vanir who initiated the fight. In a single bound, he crossed the distance between them and thrust his blade toward Eragon's right shoulder. To Eragon, it seemed as if the elf moved slower than usual, as if Vanir's reflexes had been reduced to the level of a human's. It was easy for Eragon to deflect Vanir's sword, blue sparks flying from the metal as their blades grated against one another.

Vanir landed with an astonished expression. He struck again, and Eragon evaded the sword by leaning back, like a tree swaying in the wind. In quick succession, Vanir rained a score of heavy blows upon Eragon, each of which Eragon dodged or blocked, using Zar'roc's sheath as often as the sword to foil Vanir's onslaught.

Eragon soon realized that the spectral dragon from the Agaetí Blödhren had done more than alter his appearance; it had also granted him the elves' physical abilities. In strength and speed, Eragon now matched even the most athletic elf.

Fired by that knowledge and a desire to test his limits, Eragon jumped as high as he could. Zar'roc flashed crimson in the sunlight as he flew skyward, soaring more than ten feet above the ground before he flipped like an acrobat and came down behind Vanir, facing the direction from which he had started.

A fierce laugh erupted from Eragon. No more was he helpless before elves, Shades, and other creatures of magic. No more would he suffer the elves' contempt. No more would he have to rely on Saphira or Arya to rescue him from enemies like Durza.

He charged Vanir, and the field rang with a furious din as they strove against each other, raging back and forth upon the trampled grass. The force of their blows created gusts of wind that whipped their hair into tangled disarray. Overhead, the trees shook and dropped their needles. The duel lasted long into the morning, for even with Eragon's newfound skill, Vanir was still a formidable opponent. But in the end, Eragon would not be denied. Playing Zar'roc in a circle, he darted past Vanir's guard and struck him upon the upper arm, breaking the bone.

Vanir dropped his blade, his face turning white with shock. "How swift is your sword," he said, and Eragon recognized the famous line from *The Lay of Umhodan*.

"By the gods!" exclaimed Orik. "That was the best swordsmanship I've ever seen, and I was there when you fought Arya in Farthen Dûr."

Then Vanir did what Eragon had never expected: the elf twisted his uninjured hand in the gesture of fealty, placed it upon his sternum, and bowed. "I beg your pardon for my earlier behavior, Eragon-elda. I thought that you had consigned my race to the void, and out of my fear I acted most shamefully. However, it seems that your race no longer endangers our cause." In a grudging voice, he added: "You are now worthy of the title Rider."

Eragon bowed in return. "You honor me. I'm sorry that I injured you so badly. Will you allow me to heal your arm?"

"No, I shall let nature tend to it at her own pace, as a memento that I once crossed blades with Eragon Shadeslayer. You needn't fear that it will disrupt our sparring tomorrow; I am equally good with my left hand."

They both bowed again, and then Vanir departed.

Orik slapped a hand on his thigh and said, "Now we have a chance at victory, a real chance! I can feel it in my bones. Bones like stone, they say. Ah, this'll please Hrothgar and Nasuada to no end."

Eragon kept his peace and concentrated on removing the block from Zar'roc's edges, but he said to Saphira, *If brawn were all that was required to depose Galbatorix, the elves would have done it long ago.* Still, he could not help being pleased by his heightened prowess, as well as by his long-awaited reprieve from the torment of his back. Without the constant bursts of pain, it was as if a haze had been lifted from his mind, allowing him to think clearly once again.

A few minutes remained before they were supposed to meet with Oromis and Glaedr, so Eragon took his bow and quiver from where they hung on Saphira's back and walked to the range where elves practiced archery. Since the elves' bows were much more powerful than his, their padded targets were both too small and too far away for him. He had to shoot from halfway down the range.

Taking his place, Eragon nocked an arrow and slowly pulled back the string, delighted by how easy it had become. He aimed, released the arrow, and held his position, waiting to see if he would hit his mark. Like a maddened hornet, the dart buzzed toward the target and buried itself in the center. He grinned. Again and again, he fired at the target, his speed increasing with his confidence until he loosed thirty arrows in a minute.

At the thirty-first arrow, he pulled on the string slightly harder than he had ever done—or was capable of doing—before. With an explosive report, the yew bow broke in half underneath his left hand, scratching his fingers and discharging a burst of splinters from the back of the bow. His hand went numb from the jolt.

Eragon stared at the remains of his weapon, dismayed by the loss. Garrow had made it as a birthday present for him over three years ago. Since then, hardly a week went by when Eragon had not used his bow. It had helped him to provide food for his family on numerous occasions when they would have otherwise gone hungry. With it, he had killed his first deer. With it, he had killed his first Urgal. And through it, he had first used magic. Losing his bow was like losing an old friend who could be relied upon in even the worst situation.

Saphira sniffed the two pieces of wood dangling from his grip and said, *It seems you need a new stick thrower.* He grunted—in no mood to talk—and stomped out to retrieve his arrows.

From the open field, he and Saphira flew to the white Crags of Tel'naeír and presented themselves to Oromis, who was seated on a stool in front of his hut, gazing out over the cliff with his farseeing eyes. He said, "Have you entirely recovered, Eragon, from the potent magic of the Blood-oath Celebration?"

"I have, Master."

A long silence followed as Oromis drank from a cup of blackberry tea and resumed contemplating the ancient forest. Eragon waited without complaint; he was used to such pauses when dealing with the old Rider. At length, Oromis said, "Glaedr explained to me, as best he could, what was done to you during the celebration. Such a thing has never before occurred in the history of the Riders. . . . Once again, the dragons have proved themselves capable of far more than we imagined." He sipped his tea. "Glaedr was uncertain exactly what changes you would experience, so I would like you to describe the full extent of your transformation, including your appearance."

Eragon quickly summarized how he had been altered, detailing the increased sensitivity of his sight, smell, hearing, and touch, and ending with an account of his clash with Vanir.

"And how," asked Oromis, "do you feel about this? Do you resent that your body was manipulated without your permission?"

"No, no! Not at all. I might have resented it before the battle of Farthen Dûr, but now I'm just grateful that my back doesn't hurt anymore. I would have willingly submitted myself to far greater changes in order to escape Durza's curse. No, my only response is gratitude."

Oromis nodded. "I am glad that you are wise enough to take that position, for your gift is worth more than all the gold in the world. With it, I believe that our feet are at last set upon the correct path." Again, he sipped his tea. "Let us proceed. Saphira, Glaedr expects you at the Stone of Broken Eggs. Eragon, you will begin today with the third level of Rimgar, if you can. I would know everything you are capable of."

Eragon started toward the square of tamped earth where they usually performed the Dance of Snake and Crane, then hesitated when the silver-haired elf remained behind. "Master, won't you join me?"

A sad smile graced Oromis's face. "Not today, Eragon. The spells required by the Blood-oath Celebration exacted a heavy toll from me. That and my . . . condition. It took the last of my strength to come sit outside."

"I am sorry, Master." *Does he resent that the dragons didn't choose to heal him as well?* wondered Eragon. He immediately discounted the thought; Oromis would never be so petty.

"Do not be. It is no fault of yours that I am crippled."

As Eragon struggled to complete the third level of the Rimgar, it became obvious that he still lacked the elves' balance and flexibility, two attributes that even the elves had to work to acquire. In a way, he welcomed those limitations, for if he were perfect, what would be left for him to accomplish?

The following weeks were difficult for Eragon. On one hand, he made enormous progress with his training, mastering subject after subject that had once confounded him. He still found Oromis's lessons challenging, but he no longer felt as if he were drowning in a sea of his own inadequacy. It was easier for Eragon to read and write, and his increased strength meant that he could now cast elven spells that required so much energy, they would kill any normal human. His strength also made him aware of how weak Oromis was compared to other elves.

And yet, despite those accomplishments, Eragon experienced a growing sense of discontent. No matter how hard he tried to forget Arya, every day that passed increased his yearning, an agony made worse by knowing that she did not want to see or talk with him. But more than that, it seemed to him as if an ominous storm was gathering beyond the edge of the horizon, a storm that threatened to break at any moment and sweep across the land, devastating everything in its path.

Saphira shared his unease. She said, *The world is stretched thin, Eragon. Soon it will snap and madness will burst forth. What you feel is what we dragons feel and what the elves feel—the inexorable march of grim fate as the end of our age approaches. Weep for those who will die in the chaos that shall consume Alagaësia. And hope that we may win a brighter future by the strength of your sword and shield and my fangs and talons.*

Visions Near and Far

The day came when Eragon went to the glade beyond Oromis's hut, seated himself on the polished white stump in the center of the mossy hollow, and—when he opened his mind to observe the creatures around him—sensed not just the birds, beasts, and insects but also the plants of the forest.

The plants possessed a different type of consciousness than animals: slow, deliberate, and decentralized, but in their own way just as cognizant of their surroundings as Eragon himself was. The faint pulse of the plants' awareness bathed the galaxy of stars that wheeled behind his eyes—each bright spark representing a life—in a soft, omnipresent glow. Even the most barren soil teemed with organisms; the land itself was alive and sentient.

Intelligent life, he concluded, existed everywhere.

As Eragon immersed himself in the thoughts and feelings of the beings around him, he was able to attain a state of inner peace so profound that, during that time, he ceased to exist as an individual. He allowed himself to become a nonentity, a void, a receptacle for the voices of the world. Nothing escaped his attention, for his attention was focused on nothing.

He *was* the forest and its inhabitants.

Is that what a god feels like? wondered Eragon when he returned to himself.

He left the glade, sought out Oromis in his hut, and knelt before the elf, saying, "Master, I have done as you told me to. I listened until I heard no more."

Oromis paused in his writing and, with a thoughtful expression, looked at Eragon. "Tell me." For an hour and a half, Eragon waxed eloquent about every aspect of the plants and animals that populated the glade, until Oromis raised his hand and said, "I am convinced; you heard all there was to hear. But did you understand it all?"

"No, Master."

"That is as it should be. Comprehension will come with age. . . . Well done, Eragon-finiarel. Well done indeed. If you were my student in Ilirea, before Galbatorix rose to power, you would have just graduated from your apprenticeship and would be considered a full member of our order and accorded the same rights and privileges as even the oldest Riders." Oromis pushed himself up out of his chair and then remained standing in place, swaying. "Lend me your shoulder, Eragon, and help me outside. My limbs betray my will."

Hurrying to his master's side, Eragon supported the elf's slight weight as Oromis hobbled to the brook that rushed headlong toward the edge of the Crags of Tel'naeír. "Now that you have reached this stage in your education, I can teach you one of the greatest secrets of magic, a secret that even Galbatorix may not know. It is your best hope of matching his power." The elf's gaze sharpened. "What is the cost of magic, Eragon?"

"Energy. A spell costs the same amount of energy as it would to complete the task through mundane means."

Oromis nodded. "And where does the energy come from?"

"The spellcaster's body."

"Does it have to?"

Eragon's mind raced as he considered the awesome implications of Oromis's question. "You mean it can come from other sources?"

"That is exactly what happens whenever Saphira assists you with a spell."

"Yes, but she and I share a unique connection," protested Eragon. "Our bond is the reason I can draw upon her strength. To do that with someone else, I would have to enter . . ." He trailed off as he realized what Oromis was driving at.

"You would have to enter the consciousness of the being—or beings—who was going to provide the energy," said Oromis, completing Eragon's thought. "Today you proved that you can do just that with even the smallest form of life. Now . . ." He stopped and pressed a hand against his chest as he coughed, then continued, "I want you to extract a sphere of water from the stream, using only the energy you can glean from the forest around you."

"Yes, Master."

As Eragon reached out to the nearby plants and animals, he felt Oromis's mind brush against his own, the elf watching and judging his progress. Frowning with concentration, Eragon endeavored to eke the needed force from the environment and hold it within himself until he was ready to release the magic. . . .

"Eragon! Do not take it from me! I am weak enough as is."

Startled, Eragon realized that he had included Oromis in his search. "I'm sorry, Master," he said, chastised. He resumed the process, careful to avoid draining the elf's vitality, and when he was ready, commanded, "Up!"

Silent as the night, a sphere of water a foot wide rose from the brook until it floated at eye level across from Eragon. And while Eragon experienced the usual strain that results from intense effort, the spell itself caused him no fatigue.

The sphere was only in the air for a moment when a wave of death rolled through the smaller creatures Eragon was in contact with. A line of ants keeled over motionless. A baby mouse gasped and entered the void as it lost the strength to keep its heart beating. Countless plants withered and crumbled and became inert as dust.

Eragon flinched, horrified by what he had caused. Given his new respect for the sanctity of life, he found the crime appalling. What made it worse was that he was intimately linked with each being as it ceased to exist; it was as if he himself were dying over and over. He severed the flow of magic—letting the sphere of water splash across the ground—and then whirled on Oromis and growled, "You knew that would happen!"

540

An expression of profound sorrow engulfed the ancient Rider. "It was necessary," he replied.

"Necessary that so many had to die?"

"Necessary that you understand the terrible price of using this type of magic. Mere words cannot convey the feeling of having those whose minds you share die. You had to experience it for yourself."

"I won't do that again," vowed Eragon.

"Nor will you have to. If you are disciplined, you can choose to draw the power only from plants and animals that can withstand the loss. It's impractical in battle, but you may do so in your lessons." Oromis gestured at him, and, still simmering, Eragon allowed the elf to lean on him as they returned to the hut. "You see why this technique was not taught to younger riders. If it were to become known to a spellweaver of evil disposition, he or she could wreak vast amounts of destruction, especially since it would be difficult to stop anyone with access to so much power." Once they were back inside, the elf sighed, lowered himself into his chair, and pressed the tips of his fingers together.

Eragon sat as well. "Since it's possible to absorb energy from"— he waved his hand—"from *life*, is it also possible to absorb it directly from light or fire or from any of the other forms of energy?"

"Ah, Eragon, if it were, we could destroy Galbatorix in an instant. We can exchange energy with other living beings, we can use that energy to move our bodies or to fuel a spell, and we can even store that energy in certain objects for later use, but we cannot assimilate the fundamental forces of nature. Reason says that it can be done, but no one has managed to devise a spell that allows it."

Nine days later, Eragon presented himself to Oromis and said, "Master, it struck me last night that neither you nor the hundreds of elven scrolls I've read have mentioned your religion. What do elves believe?"

A long sigh was Oromis's first answer. Then: "We believe that the world behaves according to certain inviolable rules and that, by

541

persistent effort, we can discover those rules and use them to predict events when circumstances repeat."

Eragon blinked. That did not tell him what he wanted to know. "But who, or what, do you worship?"

"Nothing."

"You worship the concept of nothing?"

"No, Eragon. We do not worship at all."

The thought was so alien, it took Eragon several moments to grasp what Oromis meant. The villagers of Carvahall lacked a single overriding doctrine, but they did share a collection of superstitions and rituals, most of which concerned warding off bad luck. During the course of his training, it had dawned upon Eragon that many of the phenomena that the villagers attributed to supernatural sources were in fact natural processes, such as when he learned in his meditations that maggots hatched from fly eggs instead of spontaneously arising from the dirt, as he had thought before. Nor did it make sense for him to put out an offering of food to keep sprites from turning the milk sour when he knew that sour milk was actually caused by a proliferation of tiny organisms in the liquid. Still, Eragon remained convinced that otherworldly forces influenced the world in mysterious ways, a belief that his exposure to the dwarves' religion had bolstered. He said, "Where do you think the world came from, then, if it wasn't created by the gods?"

"Which gods, Eragon?"

"Your gods, the dwarf gods, our gods . . . someone must have created it."

Oromis raised an eyebrow. "I would not necessarily agree with you. But be as that may, I cannot prove that gods do *not* exist. Nor can I prove that the world and everything in it was not created by an entity or entities in the distant past. But I can tell you that in the millennia we elves have studied nature, we have never witnessed an instance where the rules that govern the world have been broken. That is, we have never seen a miracle. Many events have defied our ability to explain, but we are convinced that we failed

542

because we are still woefully ignorant about the universe and not because a deity altered the workings of nature."

"A god wouldn't have to alter nature to accomplish his will," asserted Eragon. "He could do it within the system that already exists. . . . He could use magic to affect events."

Oromis smiled. "Very true. But ask yourself this, Eragon: If gods exist, have they been good custodians of Alagaësia? Death, sickness, poverty, tyranny, and countless other miseries stalk the land. If this is the handiwork of divine beings, then they are to be rebelled against and overthrown, not given obeisance, obedience, and reverence."

"The dwarves believe—"

"Exactly! The dwarves *believe*. When it comes to certain matters, they rely upon faith rather than reason. They have even been known to ignore proven facts that contradict their dogma."

"Like what?" demanded Eragon.

"Dwarf priests use coral as proof that stone is alive and can grow, which also corroborates their story that Helzvog formed the race of dwarves out of granite. But we elves discovered that coral is actually an exoskeleton secreted by minuscule animals that live inside it. Any magician can sense the animals if he opens his mind. We explained this to the dwarves, but they refused to listen, saying that the life we felt resides in every kind of stone, although their priests are the only ones who are supposed to be able to detect the life in landlocked stones."

For a long time, Eragon stared out the window, turning Oromis's words over in his mind. "You don't believe in an afterlife, then."

"From what Glaedr said, you already knew that."

"And you don't put stock in gods."

"We give credence only to that which we can prove exists. Since we cannot find evidence that gods, miracles, and other supernatural things are real, we do not trouble ourselves about them. If that were to change, if Helzvog were to reveal himself to us, then we would accept the new information and revise our position."

"It seems a cold world without something . . . more."

"On the contrary," said Oromis, "it is a better world. A place where we are responsible for our own actions, where we can be kind to one another because we want to and because it is the right thing to do instead of being frightened into behaving by the threat of divine punishment. I won't tell you what to believe, Eragon. It is far better to be taught to think critically and then be allowed to make your own decisions than to have someone else's notions thrust upon you. You asked after our religion, and I have answered you true. Make of it what you will."

Their discussion—coupled with his previous worries—left Eragon so disturbed that he had difficulty concentrating on his studies in the following days, even when Oromis began to show him how to sing to plants, which Eragon had been eager to learn.

Eragon recognized that his own experiences had already led him to adopt a more skeptical attitude; in principle, he agreed with much of what Oromis had said. The problem he struggled with, though, was that if the elves were right, it meant that nearly all the humans and dwarves were deluded, something Eragon found difficult to accept. *That many people can't be mistaken*, he insisted to himself.

When he asked Saphira about it, she said, *It matters little to me, Eragon. Dragons have never believed in higher powers. Why should we when deer and other prey consider us to be a higher power?* He laughed at that. *Only do not ignore reality in order to comfort yourself, for once you do, you make it easy for others to deceive you.*

That night, Eragon's uncertainties burst forth in his waking dreams, which raged like a wounded bear through his mind, tearing disparate images from his memories and mixing them into such a clamor, he felt as if he were transported back into the confusion of the battle under Farthen Dûr. *He saw Garrow lying dead in Horst's house, then Brom dead in the lonely sandstone cave, and then the face of Angela the herbalist, who whispered, "Beware, Argetlam, betrayal is clear. And it will come from within your family. Beware, Shadeslayer!"*

Then the crimson sky was torn apart and Eragon again beheld the two armies from his premonition in the Beor Mountains. The banks of warriors collided upon an orange and yellow field, accompanied by the harsh screams of gore-crows and the whistle of black arrows. The earth itself seemed to burn: green flames belched from scorched holes that dotted the ground, charring the mangled corpses left in the armies' wake. He heard the roar of a gigantic beast from above that rapidly app—

Eragon jolted upright in bed and scrabbled at the dwarf necklace, which burned at his throat. Using his tunic to protect his hand, he pulled the silver hammer away from his skin and then sat and waited in the dark, his heart thudding from the surprise. He felt his strength ebb as Gannel's spell thwarted whoever was trying to scry him and Saphira. Once again, he wondered if Galbatorix himself was behind the spell, or if it was one of the king's pet magicians.

Eragon frowned and released the hammer as the metal grew cold again. *Something's wrong. I know that much, and I've known it for a while, as has Saphira.* Too uneasy to resume the trancelike state that had replaced sleep for him, he crept from their bedroom without waking Saphira and climbed the spiral staircase to the study. There he unshuttered a white lantern and read one of Analísia's epics until sunrise in an attempt to calm himself.

Just as Eragon put away the scroll, Blagden flew through the open portal in the eastern wall and, with a flutter of wings, landed on the corner of the carved writing desk. The white raven fixed his beady eyes on Eragon and croaked, *"Wyrda!"*

Eragon inclined his head. "And may the stars watch over you, Master Blagden."

The raven hopped closer. He cocked his head to the side and uttered a barking cough, as if he were clearing his throat, then recited in his hoarse voice:

By beak and bone,
Mine blackened stone
Sees rooks and crooks
And bloody brooks!

"What does that mean?" asked Eragon.

Blagden shrugged and repeated the verse. When Eragon still pressed him for an explanation, the bird ruffled his feathers, appearing displeased, and cackled, "Son and father alike, both as blind as bats."

"Wait!" exclaimed Eragon, jolting upright. "Do you know my father? Who is he?"

Blagden cackled again. This time he seemed to be laughing.

While two may share two,
And one of two is certainly one,
One might be two.

"A name, Blagden. Give me a name!" When the raven remained silent, Eragon reached out with his mind, intending to wrench the information from the bird's memories.

Blagden was too wily, however. He deflected Eragon's probe with a flick of his thoughts. Shrieking *"Wyrda!"* he darted forward, plucked a bright glass stopper from an inkwell, and sped away with his trophy clutched in his beak. He dove out of sight before Eragon could cast a spell to bring him back.

Eragon's stomach knotted as he tried to decipher Blagden's two riddles. The last thing he had expected was to hear his father mentioned in Ellesméra. Finally, he muttered, "That's it." *I'll find Blagden later and wring the truth out of him. But right now . . . I would have to be a half-wit to ignore these portents.* He jumped to his feet and ran down the stairs, waking Saphira with his mind and telling her what had transpired during the night. Retrieving his shaving mirror from the wash closet, Eragon sat between Saphira's two front paws so that she could look over his head and see what he saw.

Arya won't appreciate it if we intrude on her privacy, warned Saphira.

I have to know if she's safe.

Saphira accepted that without argument. *How will you find her?*

You said that after her imprisonment, she erected wards that—like your necklace—prevent anyone from scrying her.

If I can scry the people she's with, I might be able to figure out how Arya is. Concentrating on an image of Nasuada, Eragon passed his hand over the mirror and murmured the traditional phrase, "Dream stare."

The mirror shimmered and turned white, except for nine people clustered around an invisible table. Of them, Eragon was familiar with Nasuada and the Council of Elders. But he could not identify a strange girl hooded in black who lurked behind Nasuada. This puzzled him, for a magician could only scry things that he had already seen, and Eragon was certain he had never laid eyes upon the girl before. He forgot about her, though, as he noticed that the men, and even Nasuada, were armed for battle.

Let us hear their words, suggested Saphira.

The instant Eragon made the needed alteration to the spell, Nasuada's voice emanated from the mirror: ". . . and confusion will destroy us. Our warriors can afford but one commander during this conflict. Decide who it is to be, Orrin, and quickly too."

Eragon heard a disembodied sigh. "As you wish; the position is yours."

"But, sir, she is untried!"

"Enough, Irwin," ordered the king. "She has more experience in war than anyone in Surda. And the Varden are the only force to have defeated one of Galbatorix's armies. If Nasuada were a Surdan general—which would be peculiar indeed, I admit—you would not hesitate to nominate her for the post. I shall be happy to deal with questions of authority if they arise afterward, for they will mean I'm still on my feet and not lying in a grave. As it is, we are so outnumbered I fear we are doomed unless Hrothgar can reach us before the end of the week. Now, where is that blasted scroll on the supply train? . . . Ah, thank you, Arya. Three more days without—"

After that the discussion turned to a shortage of bowstrings, which Eragon could glean nothing useful from, so he ended the spell. The mirror cleared, and he found himself staring at his own face.

She lives, he murmured. His relief was overshadowed, though, by the larger meaning of what they had heard.

Saphira looked at him. *We are needed.*

Aye. Why hasn't Oromis told us about this? He must know of it.

Maybe he wanted to avoid disrupting our training.

Troubled, Eragon wondered what else of import was happening in Alagaësia that he was unaware of. *Roran.* With a pang of guilt, Eragon realized that it had been weeks since he last thought of his cousin, and even longer since he scryed him on the way to Ellesméra.

At Eragon's command, the mirror revealed two figures standing against a pure white background. It took Eragon a long moment to recognize the man on the right as Roran. He was garbed in travel-worn clothes, a hammer was stuck under his belt, a thick beard obscured his face, and he bore a haunted expression that bespoke desperation. To the left was Jeod. The men surged up and down, accompanied by the thunderous crash of waves, which masked anything they said. After a while, Roran turned and walked along what Eragon assumed was the deck of a ship, bringing dozens of other villagers into view.

Where are they, and why is Jeod with them? demanded Eragon, bewildered.

Diverting the magic, he scryed in quick succession Teirm—shocked to see that the city's wharfs had been destroyed—Therinsford, Garrow's old farm, and then Carvahall, whereupon Eragon uttered a wounded cry.

The village was gone.

Every building, including Horst's magnificent house, had been burned to the ground. Carvahall no longer existed except as a sooty blot beside the Anora River. The sole remaining inhabitants were four gray wolves that loped through the wreckage.

The mirror dropped from Eragon's hand and shattered across the floor. He leaned against Saphira, tears burning in his eyes as he grieved anew for his lost home. Saphira hummed deep in her chest and brushed his arm with the side of her jaw, enveloping him in a warm blanket of sympathy. *Take comfort, little one. At least your friends are still alive.*

He shuddered and felt a hard core of determination coalesce in his belly. *We have remained sequestered from the world for far too long. It's high time we leave Ellesméra and confront our fate, whatever it may be. For now, Roran must fend for himself, but the Varden . . . the Varden we can help.*

Is it time to fight, Eragon? asked Saphira, an odd note of formality in her voice.

He knew what she meant: Was it time to challenge the Empire head-on, time to kill and rampage to the limit of their considerable abilities, time to unleash every ounce of their rage until Galbatorix lay dead before them? Was it time to commit themselves to a campaign that could take decades to resolve?

It is time.

GIFTS

Eragon packed his belongings in less than five minutes. He took the saddle Oromis had given them, strapped it onto Saphira, then slung his bags over her back and buckled them down.

Saphira tossed her head, nostrils flared, and said, *I will wait for you at the field.* With a roar, she launched herself from the tree house, unfolding her blue wings in midair, and flew off, skimming the forest canopy.

Quick as an elf, Eragon ran to Tialdarí Hall, where he found Orik sitting in his usual corner, playing a game of Runes. The dwarf greeted him with a hearty slap on the arm. "Eragon! What brings you here at this time of the morn? I thought you'd be off banging swords with Vanir."

"Saphira and I are leaving," said Eragon.

Orik stopped with his mouth open, then narrowed his eyes, going serious. "You've had news?"

"I'll tell you about it later. Do you want to come?"

"To Surda?"

"Aye."

A wide smile broke across Orik's hairy face. "You'd have to clap me in irons before I'd stay behind. I've done nothing in Ellesméra but grow fat and lazy. A bit of excitement will do me good. When do we leave?"

"As soon as possible. Gather your things and meet us at the sparring grounds. Can you scrounge up a week's worth of provisions for the two of us?"

"A week's? But that won't—"

"We're flying on Saphira."

The skin above Orik's beard turned pale. "We dwarves don't do well with heights, Eragon. We don't do well at all. It'd be better if we could ride horses, like we did coming here."

Eragon shook his head. "That would take too long. Besides, it's easy to ride Saphira. She'll catch you if you fall." Orik grunted, appearing both queasy and unconvinced. Leaving the hall, Eragon sped through the sylvan city until he rejoined Saphira, and then they flew to the Crags of Tel'naeír.

Oromis was sitting upon Glaedr's right forearm when they landed in the clearing. The dragon's scales gilded the landscape with countless chips of golden light. Neither elf nor dragon stirred. Descending from Saphira's back, Eragon bowed. "Master Glaedr. Master Oromis."

Glaedr said, *You have taken it upon yourself to return to the Varden, have you not?*

We have, replied Saphira.

Eragon's sense of betrayal overcame his self-restraint. "Why did you hide the truth from us? Are you so determined to keep us here that you must resort to such underhand trickery? The Varden are about to be attacked and you didn't even mention it!"

Calm as ever, Oromis asked, "Do you wish to hear why?"

Very much, Master, said Saphira before Eragon could respond. In private, she scolded him, growling, *Be polite!*

"We withheld the tidings for two reasons. Chief among them was that we ourselves did not know until nine days past that the Varden were threatened, and the true size, location, and movements of the Empire's troops remained concealed from us until three days after that, when Lord Däthedr pierced the spells Galbatorix used to deceive our scrying."

"That still doesn't explain why you said nothing of this." Eragon scowled. "Not only that, but once you discovered that the Varden were in danger, why didn't Islanzadí rouse the elves to fight? Are we not allies?"

"She *has* roused the elves, Eragon. The forest echoes with the ring of hammers, the tramp of armored boots, and the grief of those who are about to be parted. For the first time in a century, our race is set to emerge from Du Weldenvarden and challenge our greatest foe. The time has come for elves to once more walk openly in Alagaësia." Gently, Oromis added, "You have been distracted of late, Eragon, and I understand why. Now you must look beyond yourself. The world demands your attention."

Shamefaced, all Eragon could say was, "I am sorry, Master." He remembered Blagden's words and allowed himself a bitter smile. "I'm as blind as a bat."

"Hardly, Eragon. You have done well, considering the enormous responsibilities we have asked you to shoulder." Oromis looked at him gravely. "We expect to receive a missive from Nasuada in the next few days, requesting assistance from Islanzadí and that you rejoin the Varden. I intended to inform you of the Varden's predicament then, when you would still have enough time to reach Surda before swords are drawn. If I told you earlier, you would have been honor-bound to abandon your training and rush to the defense of your liegelord. That is why I and Islanzadí held our tongues."

"My training won't matter if the Varden are destroyed."

"No. But you may be the only person who can prevent them from being destroyed, for a chance exists—slim but terrible—that Galbatorix will be present at this battle. It is far too late for our warriors to assist the Varden, which means that if Galbatorix is indeed there, you shall confront him alone, without the protection of our spellweavers. Under those circumstances, it seemed vital that your training continue for as long as possible."

In an instant, Eragon's anger melted away and was replaced with a cold, hard, and brutally practical mind-set as he understood the necessity for Oromis's silence. Personal feelings were irrelevant in a situation as dire as theirs. With a flat voice, he said, "You were right. My oath of fealty compels me to ensure the safety of Nasuada and the Varden. However, I'm not ready to confront Galbatorix. Not yet, at least."

"My suggestion," said Oromis, "is that if Galbatorix reveals himself, do everything you can to distract him from the Varden until the battle is decided for good or for ill and avoid directly fighting him. Before you go, I ask but one thing: that you and Saphira vow that—once events permit—you will return here to complete your training, for you still have much to learn."

We shall return, pledged Saphira, binding herself in the ancient language.

"We shall return," repeated Eragon, and sealed their fate.

Appearing satisfied, Oromis reached behind himself and produced an embroidered red pouch that he tugged open. "In anticipation of your departure, I gathered together three gifts for you, Eragon." From the pouch, he withdrew a silver bottle. "First, some faelnirv I augmented with my own enchantments. This potion can sustain you when all else fails, and you may find its properties useful in other circumstances as well. Drink it sparingly, for I only had time to prepare a few mouthfuls."

He handed the bottle to Eragon, then removed a long black-and-blue sword belt from the pouch. The belt felt unusually thick and heavy to Eragon when he ran it through his hands. It was made of cloth threads woven together in an interlocking pattern that depicted a coiling Lianí Vine. At Oromis's instruction, Eragon pulled at a tassel at the end of the belt and gasped as a strip in its center slid back to expose twelve diamonds, each an inch across. Four diamonds were white, four were black, and the remainder were red, blue, yellow, and brown. They glittered cold and brilliant, like ice in the dawn, casting a rainbow of multicolored specks onto Eragon's hands.

"Master . . ." Eragon shook his head, at a loss for words for several breaths. "Is it safe to give this to me?"

"Guard it well so that none are tempted to steal it. This is the belt of Beloth the Wise—who you read of in your history of the Year of Darkness—and is one of the great treasures of the Riders. These are the most perfect gems the Riders could find. Some we traded for with the dwarves. Others we won in battle or mined ourselves. The stones have no magic of their own, but you may use them as repositories for your power and draw upon that reserve when in need. This, in addition to the ruby set in Zar'roc's pommel, will allow you to amass a store of energy so that you do not become unduly exhausted casting spells in battle, or even when confronting enemy magicians."

Last, Oromis brought out a thin scroll protected inside a wooden tube that was decorated with a bas-relief sculpture of the Menoa tree. Unfurling the scroll, Eragon saw the poem he had recited at the Agaetí Blödhren. It was lettered in Oromis's finest calligraphy and illustrated with the elf's detailed ink paintings. Plants and animals twined together inside the outline of the first glyph of each quatrain, while delicate scrollwork traced the columns of words and framed the images.

"I thought," said Oromis, "that you would appreciate a copy for yourself."

Eragon stood with twelve priceless diamonds in one hand and Oromis's scroll in the other, and he knew that it was the scroll he deemed the most precious. Eragon bowed and, reduced to the simplest language by the depth of his gratitude, said, "Thank you, Master."

Then Oromis surprised Eragon by initiating the elves' traditional greeting and thereby indicating his respect for Eragon: "May good fortune rule over you."

"May the stars watch over you."

"And may peace live in your heart," finished the silver-haired elf. He repeated the exchange with Saphira. "Now go and fly as fast as the north wind, knowing that you—Saphira Brightscales and Eragon Shadeslayer—carry the blessing of Oromis, last scion of

House Thrándurin, he who is both the Mourning Sage and the Cripple Who Is Whole."

And mine as well, added Glaedr. Extending his neck, he touched the tip of his nose to Saphira's, his gold eyes glittering like swirling pools of embers. *Remember to keep your heart safe, Saphira.* She hummed in response.

They parted with solemn farewells. Saphira soared over the tangled forest and Oromis and Glaedr dwindled behind them, lonely on the crags. Despite the hardships of his stay in Ellesméra, Eragon would miss being among the elves, for with them he had found the closest thing to a home since fleeing Palancar Valley.

I leave here a changed man, he thought, and closed his eyes, clinging to Saphira.

Before going to meet with Orik, they made one more stop: Tialdarí Hall. Saphira landed in the enclosed gardens, careful not to damage any of the plants with her tail or claws. Without waiting for her to crouch, Eragon leaped straight to the ground, a drop that would have injured him before.

A male elf came out, touched his lips with his first two fingers, and asked if he could help them. When Eragon replied that he sought an audience with Islanzadí, the elf said, "Please wait here, Silver Hand."

Not five minutes later, the queen herself emerged from the wooded depths of Tialdarí Hall, her crimson tunic like a drop of blood among the white-robed elf lords and ladies who accompanied her. After the appropriate forms of address were observed, she said, "Oromis informed me of your intention to leave us. I am displeased by this, but one cannot resist the will of fate."

"No, Your Majesty. . . . Your Majesty, we came to pay our respects before departing. You have been most considerate of us, and we thank you and your House for clothing, lodging, and feeding us. We are in your debt."

"Never in our debt, Rider. We but repaid a little of what we owe you and the dragons for our miserable failure in the Fall. I am gratified, though, that you appreciate our hospitality." She paused. "When you arrive in Surda, convey my royal salutations to Lady Nasuada and King Orrin and inform them that our warriors will soon attack the northern half of the Empire. If fortune smiles upon us, we shall catch Galbatorix off guard and, given time, divide his forces."

"As you wish."

"Also, know that I have dispatched twelve of our finest spell-weavers to Surda. If you are still alive when they arrive, they will place themselves under your command and do their best to shield you from danger both night and day."

"Thank you, Your Majesty."

Islanzadí extended a hand and one of the elf lords handed her a shallow, unadorned wooden box. "Oromis had his gifts for you, and I have mine. Let them remind you of your time spent with us under the dusky pines." She opened the box, revealing a long, dark bow with reflexed limbs and curled tips nestled on a bed of velvet. Silver fittings chased with dogwood leaves decorated the ears and grip of the bow. Beside it lay a quiver of new arrows fletched with white swan feathers. "Now that you share our strength, it seems only proper that you should have one of our bows. I sang it myself from a yew tree. The string will never break. And so long as you use these arrows, you will be hard-pressed to miss your target, even if the wind should gust during your shot."

Once again, Eragon was overwhelmed by the elves' generosity. He bowed. "What can I say, my Lady? You honor me that you saw fit to give me the labor of your own hands."

Islanzadí nodded, as if agreeing with him, then stepped past him and said, "Saphira, I brought you no gifts because I could think of nothing you might need or want, but if there is aught of ours you desire, name it and it shall be yours."

Dragons, said Saphira, *do not require possessions to be happy. What use have we for riches when our hides are more glorious than any treasure hoard in existence? No, I am content with the kindness that you have shown Eragon.*

Then Islanzadí bade them a safe journey. Sweeping around, her red cape billowing from her shoulders, she made to leave the gardens, only to stop at the edge of the pleasance and say, "And, Eragon?"

"Yes, Your Majesty?"

"When you meet with Arya, please express my affection to her and tell her that she is sorely missed in Ellesméra." The words were stiff and formal. Without waiting for a reply, she strode away and disappeared among the shadowed boles that guarded the interior of Tialdarí Hall, followed by the elf lords and ladies.

It took Saphira less than a minute to fly to the sparring field, where Orik sat on his bulging pack, tossing his war ax from one hand to the other and scowling ferociously. "About time you got here," he grumbled. He stood and slipped the ax back under his belt. Eragon apologized for the delay, then tied Orik's pack onto the back of his saddle. The dwarf eyed Saphira's shoulder, which loomed high above him. "And how, by Morgothal's black beard, am I supposed to get up there? A cliff has more handholds than you, Saphira."

Here, she said. She lay flat on her belly and pushed her right hind leg out as far as she could, forming a knobby ramp. Pulling himself onto her shin with a loud *huff,* Orik crawled up her leg on hands and knees. A small jet of flame burst from Saphira's nostrils as she snorted. *Hurry up—that tickles!*

Orik paused on the ledge of her haunches, then placed one foot on either side of Saphira's spine and carefully walked his way up her back toward the saddle. He tapped one of the ivory spikes between his legs and said, "There be as good a way to lose your manhood as ever I've seen."

Eragon grinned. "Don't slip." When Orik lowered himself onto the front of the saddle, Eragon mounted Saphira and sat behind the dwarf. To hold Orik in place when Saphira turned or inverted, Eragon loosened the thongs that were meant to secure his arms and had Orik put his legs through them.

As Saphira rose to her full height, Orik swayed, then clutched the spike in front of him. "Garr! Eragon, don't let me open my eyes until we're in the air, else I fear I'll be sick. This is unnatural, it is. Dwarves aren't meant to ride dragons. It's never been done before."

"Never?"

Orik shook his head without answering.

Clusters of elves drifted out of Du Weldenvarden, gathered along the edge of the field, and with solemn expressions watched Saphira lift her translucent wings in preparation to take off.

Eragon tightened his grip as he felt her mighty thews bunch underneath his legs. With a rush of acceleration, Saphira launched herself into the azure sky, flapping swift and hard to rise above the giant trees. She wheeled over the vast forest—spiraling upward as she gained altitude—and then aimed herself south, toward the Hadarac Desert.

Though the wind was loud in Eragon's ears, he heard an elf woman in Ellesméra raise her clear voice in song, as he had when they first arrived. She sang:

Away, away, you shall fly away,
O'er the peaks and vales
To the lands beyond.
Away, away, you shall fly away,
And never return to me. . . .

✦ ✦ ✦

THE MAW OF THE OCEAN

The obsidian seas heaved underneath the *Dragon Wing*, propelling the ship high in the air. There it teetered on the precipitous crest of a foam-capped swell before pitching forward and racing down the face of the wave into the black trough below. Billows of stinging mist drove through the frigid air as the wind groaned and howled like a monstrous spirit.

Roran clung to the starboard rigging at the waist of the ship and retched over the gunwale; nothing came up but sour bile. He had prided himself that his stomach never bothered him while on Clovis's barges, but the storm they raced before was so violent that even Uthar's men—seasoned tars each and every one—had difficulty keeping their whisky down.

It felt like a boulder of ice clouted Roran between the shoulder blades as a wave struck the ship crossways, drenching the deck before draining through the scuppers and pouring back into the frothing, furrowed, furious ocean from whence it came. Roran wiped the salty water from his eyes with fingers as clumsy as frozen lumps of wood, and squinted toward the inky horizon to the aft.

Maybe this will shake them off our scent. Three black-sailed sloops had pursued them ever since they passed the Iron Cliffs and rounded what Jeod dubbed Edur Carthungavë and Uthar identified as Rathbar's Spur. "The tailbone of the Spine, that's what it be," Uthar said, grinning. The sloops were faster than the *Dragon Wing*, weighed down with villagers as it was, and had quickly gained upon the merchant ship until they were close enough to exchange volleys of arrows. Worst of all, it seemed that the lead sloop carried a magician, for its arrows were uncannily accurate, splitting ropes, destroying ballistae, and clogging the blocks. From their attacks, Roran deduced that the Empire no longer cared about capturing him and only wanted to stop him from finding sanctuary with the Varden. He had just been preparing the villagers to repel boarding parties when the clouds above ripened to a bruised purple, heavy with rain, and a ravening tempest blew in from the northwest. At the present, Uthar had the *Dragon Wing* tacked crossways to the wind, heading toward the Southern Isles, where he hoped to elude the sloops among the shoals and coves of Beirland.

A sheet of horizontal lightning flickered between two bulbous thunderheads, and the world became a tableau of pale marble before darkness reigned once more. Every blinding flash imprinted a motionless scene upon Roran's eyes that lingered, pulsing, long after the brazen bolts vanished.

Then came another round of forked lightning, and Roran saw—as if in a series of monochrome paintings—the mizzen topmast twist, crack, and topple into the thrashing sea, port amidships. Grabbing a lifeline, Roran pulled himself to the quarterdeck and, in unison with Bonden, hacked through the cables that still connected the topmast to the *Dragon Wing* and dragged the stern low in the water. The ropes writhed like snakes as they were cut.

Afterward, Roran sank to the deck, his right arm hooked through the gunwale to hold himself in place as the ship dropped twenty . . . thirty . . . feet between waves. A swell washed over him, leaching the warmth from his bones. Shivers racked his body.

Don't let me die here, he pleaded, though whom he addressed, he knew not. *Not in these cruel waves. My task is yet unfinished.* During that long night, he clung to his memories of Katrina, drawing solace from them when he grew weary and hope threatened to desert him.

*　　*　　*

The storm lasted two full days and broke during the wee hours of the night. The following morning brought with it a pale green dawn, clear skies, and three black sails riding the northern horizon. To the southwest, the hazy outline of Beirland lay underneath a shelf of clouds gathered about the ridged mountain that dominated the island.

Roran, Jeod, and Uthar met in a small fore cabin—since the captain's stateroom was given over to the infirm—where Uthar unrolled sea charts on the table and tapped a point above Beirland. "This'd be where we are now," he said. He reached for a larger map of Alagaësia's coastline and tapped the mouth of the Jiet River. "An' this'd be our destination, since food won't last us to Reavstone. How we get there, though, without being overtaken is beyond me. Without our mizzen topgallant, those accursed sloops will catch us by noon tomorrow, evening if we manage the sails well."

"Can we replace the mast?" asked Jeod. "Vessels of this size carry spars to make just such repairs."

Uthar shrugged. "We could, provided we had a proper ship's carpenter among us. Seeing as we don't, I'd rather not let inexperienced hands mount a spar, only to have it crash down on deck and perhaps injure somebody."

Roran said, "If it weren't for the magician or magicians, I'd say we should stand and fight, since we far outnumber the crews of the sloops. As it is, I'm chary of battle. It seems unlikely that we could prevail, considering how many ships sent to help the Varden have disappeared."

Grunting, Uthar drew a circle around their current position. "This'd be how far we can sail by tomorrow evening, assuming the wind stays with us. We could make landfall somewhere on Beirland or Nía if we wanted, but I can't see how that'd help us. We'd be trapped. The soldiers on those sloops or the Ra'zac or Galbatorix himself could hunt us at his leisure."

Roran scowled as he considered their options; a fight with the sloops appeared inevitable.

For several minutes, the cabin was silent except for the slap of waves against the hull. Then Jeod placed his finger on the map between Beirland and Nía, looked at Uthar, and asked, "What about the Boar's Eye?"

To Roran's amazement, the scarred sailor actually blanched. "I'd not risk that, Master Jeod, not on my life. I'd rather face the sloops an' die in the open sea than go to that doomed place. There has consumed twice as many ships as in Galbatorix's fleet."

"I seem to recall reading," said Jeod, leaning back in his chair, "that the passage is perfectly safe at high tide and low tide. Is that not so?"

With great and evident reluctance, Uthar admitted, "Aye. But the Eye is so wide, it requires the most precise timing to cross without being destroyed. We'd be hard-pressed to accomplish that with the sloops near on our tail."

"If we could, though," pressed Jeod, "if we could time it right, the sloops would be wrecked or—if their nerve failed them—forced to circumvent Nía. It would give us time to find a place to hide along Beirland."

"If, if . . . You'd send us to the crushing deep, you would."

"Come now, Uthar, your fear is unreasoning. What I propose is dangerous, I admit, but no more than fleeing Teirm was. Or do you doubt your ability to sail the gap? Are you not man enough to do it?"

Uthar crossed his bare arms. "You've never seen the Eye, have you, sir?"

"I can't say I have."

"It's not that I'm not man enough, but that the Eye far exceeds the strength of men; it puts to shame our biggest ships, our grandest buildings, an' anything else you'd care to name. Tempting it would be like trying to outrun an avalanche; you might succeed, but then you just as well might be ground into dust."

"What," asked Roran, "is this Boar's Eye?"

"The all-devouring maw of the ocean," proclaimed Uthar.

In a milder tone, Jeod said, "It's a whirlpool, Roran. The Eye forms as the result of tidal currents that collide between Beirland and Nía. When the tide waxes, the Eye rotates north to west. When the tide wanes, it rotates north to east."

"That doesn't sound so dangerous."

Uthar shook his head, queue whipping the sides of his windburned neck, and laughed. "Not so dangerous, he says! Ha!"

"What you fail to comprehend," continued Jeod, "is the size of the vortex. On average, the center of the Eye is a league in diameter, while the arms of the pool can be anywhere from ten to fifteen miles across. Ships unlucky enough to be snared by the Eye are borne down to the floor of the ocean and dashed against the jagged rocks therein. Remnants of the vessels are often found as flotsam on the beaches of the two islands."

"Would anyone expect us to take this route?" Roran queried.

"No, an' for good reason," growled Uthar. Jeod shook his head at the same time.

"Is it even possible for us to cross the Eye?"

"It'd be a blasted fool thing to do."

Roran nodded. "I know it's not something you want to risk, Uthar, but our options are limited. I'm no seaman, so I must rely upon your judgment: Can we cross the Eye?"

The captain hesitated. "Maybe, maybe not. You'd have t' be stark raving mad to go nearer'n five miles of that monster."

Pulling out his hammer, Roran banged it on the table, leaving a dent a half-inch deep. "Then I'm stark raving mad!" He held Uthar's gaze until the sailor shifted with discomfort. "Must I remind you, we've only gotten this far by doing what quibbling worrywarts said couldn't, or shouldn't, be done? We of Carvahall dared to abandon our homes and cross the Spine. Jeod dared to imagine we could steal the *Dragon Wing*. What will you dare, Uthar? If we can brave the Eye and live to tell the tale, you shall be hailed as one of the greatest mariners in history. Now answer me and answer me well and true: Can this be done?"

Uthar drew a hand over his face. When he spoke, it was in a low voice, as if Roran's outburst had caused him to abandon all bluster. "I don't know, Stronghammer. . . . If we wait for the Eye to subside, the sloops may be so close to us that if we escape, they'd escape. An' if the wind should falter, we'd be caught in the current, unable to break free."

"As captain, are you willing to attempt it? Neither Jeod nor I can command the *Dragon Wing* in your place."

Long did Uthar stare down at the charts, one hand clasped over the other. He drew a line or two from their position and worked a table of figures that Roran could make nothing of. At last he said, "I fear we sail to our doom, but aye, I'll do my best to see us through."

Satisfied, Roran put away his hammer. "So be it."

RUNNING THE BOAR'S EYE

The sloops continued to draw closer to the *Dragon Wing* over the course of the day. Roran watched their progress whenever he could, concerned that they would get near enough to attack before the *Dragon Wing* reached the Eye. Still, Uthar seemed able to outrun them, at least for a little while longer.

At Uthar's orders, Roran and the other villagers worked to tidy up the ship after the storm and prepare for the ordeal that was to come. Their work ended at nightfall, when they extinguished every light on board in an attempt to confuse their pursuers as to the *Dragon Wing*'s heading. The ruse succeeded in part, for when the sun rose, Roran saw that the sloops had fallen back to the northwest another mile or so, though they soon made up the lost distance.

Late that morning, Roran climbed the mainmast and pulled himself up into the crow's nest a hundred and thirty feet above the deck, so high that the men below appeared no larger than his little finger. The water and sky seemed to rock perilously about him as the *Dragon Wing* heeled from side to side.

Taking out the spyglass he had brought with him, Roran put it to his eye and adjusted it until the sloops came into focus not four miles astern and approaching faster than he would have liked. *They must have realized what we intend to do*, he thought. Sweeping the glass around, he searched the ocean for any sign of the Boar's Eye. He stopped as he descried a great disk of foam the size of an island, gyrating from north to east. *We're late,* he thought, a pit in his stomach. High tide had already passed and the Boar's Eye was gathering in speed and strength as the ocean withdrew from land. Roran trained the glass over the edge of the crow's nest and saw that the knotted rope Uthar had tied to the starboard side of the stern—to detect when they entered the pull of the whirlpool—now floated alongside the *Dragon Wing* instead of trailing behind as was usual. The one thing in their favor was that they were sailing with the Eye's current and not against it. If it had been the other way around, they would have had no choice but to wait until the tide turned.

Below, Roran heard Uthar shout for the villagers to man the oars. A moment later, the *Dragon Wing* sprouted two rows of poles along each side, making the ship look like nothing more than a giant water strider. At the beat of an ox-hide drum, accompanied by Bonden's rhythmic chant as he set the tempo, the oars arched forward, dipped into the sea of green, and swept back across the surface of the water, leaving white streaks of bubbles in their wake. The *Dragon Wing* accelerated quickly, now moving faster than the sloops, which were still outside the Eye's influence.

Roran watched with horrified fascination the play that unfolded around him. The essential plot element, the crux upon which the outcome depended, was time. Though they were late, was the *Dragon Wing*, with its oars and sails combined, fast enough to traverse the Eye? And could the sloops—which had deployed their own oars now—narrow the gap between them and the *Dragon Wing* enough to ensure their own survival? He could not tell. The pounding drum measured out the minutes; Roran was acutely aware of each moment as it trickled by.

He was surprised when an arm reached over the edge of the basket and Baldor's face appeared, looking up at him. "Give me a hand, won't you? I feel like I'm about to fall."

Bracing himself, Roran helped Baldor into the basket. Baldor handed Roran a biscuit and a dried apple and said, "Thought you might like some lunch." With a nod of thanks, Roran tore into the biscuit and resumed gazing through the spyglass. When Baldor asked, "Can you see the Eye?" Roran passed him the glass and concentrated on eating.

Over the next half hour, the foam disk increased the speed of its revolutions until it spun like a top. The water around the foam bulged and began to rise, while the foam itself sank from view into the bottom of a gigantic pit that continued to deepen and enlarge. The air over the vortex filled with a cyclone of twisting mist, and from the ebony throat of the abyss came a tortured howl like the cries of an injured wolf.

The speed with which the Boar's Eye formed amazed Roran. "You'd better go tell Uthar," he said.

Baldor climbed out of the nest. "Tie yourself to the mast or you may get thrown off."

"I will."

Roran left his arms free when he secured himself, making sure that, if needed, he could reach his belt knife to cut himself free. Anxiety filled him as he surveyed the situation. The *Dragon Wing* was but a mile past the median of the Eye, the sloops were but two miles behind her, and the Eye itself was quickly building toward its full fury. Worse, disrupted by the whirlpool, the wind sputtered and gasped, blowing first from one direction and then the other. The sails billowed for a moment, then fell slack, then filled again as the confused wind swirled about the ship.

Perhaps Uthar was right, thought Roran. *Perhaps I've gone too far and pitted myself against an opponent that cannot be overcome by sheer determination. Perhaps I am sending the villagers to their deaths.* The forces of nature were immune to intimidation.

The gaping center of the Boar's Eye was now almost nine and a half miles in circumference, and how many fathoms deep no one could say, except for those who had been trapped within it. The sides of the Eye slanted inward at a forty-five-degree angle; they were striated with shallow grooves, like wet clay being molded on a potter's wheel. The bass howl grew louder, until it seemed to Roran that the entire world must crumble to pieces from the intensity of the vibrations. A glorious rainbow emerged from the mist over the whirling chasm.

The current moved faster than ever, driving the *Dragon Wing* at a breakneck pace as it whipped around the rim of the whirlpool and making it more and more unlikely that the ship could break free at the Eye's southern edge. So prodigious was her velocity, the *Dragon Wing* tilted far to the starboard, suspending Roran out over the rushing water.

Despite the *Dragon Wing*'s progress, the sloops continued to gain on her. The enemy ships sailed abreast less than a mile away, their oars moving in perfect accord, two fins of water flying from each prow as they plowed the ocean. Roran could not help but admire the sight.

He tucked the spyglass away in his shirt; he had no need of it now. The sloops were close enough for the naked eye, while the whirlpool was increasingly obscured by the clouds of white vapor thrown off the lip of the funnel. As it was pulled into the deep, the vapor formed a spiral lens over the gulf, mimicking the whirlpool's appearance.

Then the *Dragon Wing* tacked port, diverging from the current in Uthar's bid for the open sea. The keel chattered across the puckered water, and the ship's speed dropped in half as the *Dragon Wing* fought the deadly embrace of the Boar's Eye. A shudder ran up the mast, jarring Roran's teeth, and the crow's nest swung in the new direction, making him giddy with vertigo.

Fear gripped Roran when they continued to slow. He slashed off his bindings and—with reckless disregard for his own safety—swung himself over the edge of the basket, grabbed the ropes underneath, and shinnied down the rigging so quickly that he lost his grip once and fell several feet before he could catch himself. He jumped to the deck, ran to the fore hatchway, and descended to the first bank of oars, where he joined Baldor and Albriech on an oak pole.

They said not a word, but labored to the sound of their own desperate breathing, the frenzied beat of the drum, Bonden's hoarse shouts, and the roar of the Boar's Eye. Roran could feel the mighty whirlpool resisting with every stroke of the oar.

And yet their efforts could not keep the *Dragon Wing* from coming to a virtual standstill. *We're not going to make it,* thought Roran. His back and legs burned from the exertion. His lungs stabbed. Between the drumbeats, he heard Uthar ordering the hands above deck to trim the sails to take full advantage of the fickle wind.

Two places ahead of Roran, Darmmen and Hamund surrendered their oar to Thane and Ridley, then lay in the middle of the aisle, their limbs trembling. Less than a minute later, someone else collapsed farther down the gallery and was immediately replaced by Birgit and another woman.

If we survive, thought Roran, *it'll only be because we have enough people to sustain this pace however long is necessary.*

It seemed an eternity that he worked the oar in the murky, smoky room, first pushing, then pulling, doing his best to ignore the pain mounting within his body. His neck ached from hunching underneath the low ceiling. The dark wood of the pole was streaked with blood where his skin had blistered and torn. He ripped off his shirt—dropping the spyglass to the floor—wrapped the cloth around the oar, and continued rowing.

At last Roran could do no more. His legs gave way and he fell on his side, slipping across the aisle because he was so sweaty. Orval took his place. Roran lay still until his breath returned, then pushed himself onto his hands and knees and crawled to the hatchway.

Like a fever-mad drunk, he pulled himself up the ladder, swaying with the motion of the ship and often slumping against the wall to rest. When he came out on deck, he took a brief moment to appreciate the fresh air, then staggered aft to the helm, his legs threatening to cramp with every step.

"How goes it?" he gasped to Uthar, who manned the wheel.

Uthar shook his head.

Peering over the gunwale, Roran espied the three sloops perhaps a half mile away and slightly more to the west, closer to the center of the Eye. The sloops appeared motionless in relation to the *Dragon Wing*.

At first, as Roran watched, the positions of the four ships remained unchanged. Then he sensed a shift in the *Dragon Wing's* speed, as if the ship had crossed some crucial point and the forces restraining her had diminished. It was a subtle difference and amounted to little more than a few additional feet per minute—but it was enough that the distance between the *Dragon Wing* and the sloops began to increase. With every stroke of the oars, the *Dragon Wing* gained momentum.

The sloops, however, could not overcome the whirlpool's dreadful strength. Their oars gradually slowed until, one by one, the ships drifted backward and were drawn toward the veil of mist, beyond which waited the gyrating walls of ebony water and the gnashing rocks at the bottom of the ocean floor.

They can't keep rowing, realized Roran. *Their crews are too small and they're too tired.* He could not help but feel a pang of sympathy for the fate of the men on the sloops.

At that precise instant, an arrow sprang from the nearest sloop and burst into green flame as it raced toward the *Dragon Wing*. The dart must have been sustained by magic to have flown so far. It struck the mizzen sail and exploded into globules of liquid fire that stuck to whatever they touched. Within seconds, twenty small fires burned along the mizzenmast, the mizzen sail, and the deck below.

"We can't put it out," shouted one of the sailors with a panicked expression.

"Chop off whatever's burning an' throw it overboard!" roared Uthar in reply.

Unsheathing his belt knife, Roran set to work excising a dollop of green fire from the boards by his feet. Several tense minutes elapsed before the unnatural blazes were removed and it became clear that the conflagrations would not spread to the rest of the ship.

Once the cry of "All clear!" was sounded, Uthar relaxed his grip on the steering wheel. "If that was the best their magician can do, then I'd say we have nothing more to fear of him."

"We're going to get out of the Eye, aren't we?" asked Roran, eager to confirm his hope.

Uthar squared his shoulders and flashed a quick grin, both proud and disbelieving. "Not quite this cycle, but we'll be close. We won't make real progress away from that gaping monster until the tide slacks off. Go tell Bonden to lower the tempo a bit; I don't want them fainting at the oars if'n I can help it."

And so it was. Roran took another shift rowing and, by the time he returned to the deck, the whirlpool was subsiding. The vortex's ghastly howl faded into the usual noise of the wind; the water assumed a calm, flat quality that betrayed no hint of the habitual violence visited upon that location; and the contorted fog that had writhed above the abyss melted under the warm rays of the sun, leaving the air as clear as oiled glass. Of the Boar's Eye itself—as Roran saw when he retrieved the spyglass from among the rowers—nothing remained but the selfsame disk of yellow foam rotating upon the water.

And in the center of the foam, he thought he could discern, just barely, three broken masts and a black sail floating round and round and round in an endless circle. But it might have been his imagination.

Leastways, that's what he told himself.

Elain came up beside him, one hand resting on her swollen belly. In a small voice, she said, "We were lucky, Roran, more lucky than we had reason to expect."

"Aye," he agreed.

✦ ✦ ✦

TO ABERON

Underneath Saphira, the pathless forest stretched wide to each white horizon, fading as it did from the deepest green to a hazy, washed-out purple. Martins, rooks, and other woodland birds flitted above the gnarled pines, uttering shrieks of alarm when they beheld Saphira. She flew low to the canopy in order to protect her two passengers from the arctic temperatures in the upper reaches of the sky.

Except for when Saphira fled the Ra'zac into the Spine, this was the first time she and Eragon had had the opportunity to fly together over a great stretch of distance without having to stop or hold back for companions on the ground. Saphira was especially pleased with the trip, and she delighted in showing Eragon how Glaedr's tutelage had enhanced her strength and endurance.

After his initial discomfort abated, Orik said to Eragon, "I doubt I could ever be comfortable in the air, but I can understand why you and Saphira enjoy it so. Flying makes you feel free and unfettered, like a fierce-eyed hawk hunting his prey! It sets my heart a-pounding, it does."

To reduce the tedium of the journey, Orik played a game of riddles with Saphira. Eragon excused himself from the contest as he had never been particularly adept at riddles; the twist of thought necessary to solve them always seemed to escape him. In this, Saphira far exceeded him. As most dragons are, she was fascinated by puzzles and found them quite easy to unravel.

Orik said, "The only riddles I know are in Dwarvish. I will do mine best to translate them, but the results may be rough and unwieldy." Then he asked:

Tall I am young.
Short I am old.
While with life I do glow,
Urûr's breath is my foe.

Not fair, growled Saphira. *I know little of your gods.* Eragon had no need to repeat her words, for Orik had granted permission for her to project them directly into his mind.

Orik laughed. "Do you give up?"

Never. For a few minutes, the only sound was the sweep of her wings, until she asked, *Is it a candle?*

"Right you are."

A puff of hot smoke floated back into Orik's and Eragon's faces as she snorted. *I do poorly with such riddles. I've not been inside a house since the day I hatched, and I find enigmas difficult that deal with domestic subjects.* Next she offered:

What herb cures all ailments?

This proved a terrible poser for Orik. He grumbled and groaned and gnashed his teeth in frustration. Behind him, Eragon could not help but grin, for he saw the answer plain in Saphira's mind. Finally, Orik said, "Well, what is it? You have bested me with this."

By the black raven's crime, and by this rhyme,
the answer would be thyme.

Now it was Orik's turn to cry, "Not fair! This is not mine native tongue. You cannot expect me to grasp such wordplay!"

Fair is fair. It was a proper riddle.

Eragon watched the muscles at the back of Orik's neck bunch and knot as the dwarf jutted his head forward. "If *that* is your stance, O Irontooth, then I'd have you solve this riddle that every dwarf child knows."

I am named Morgothal's Forge and Helzvog's Womb.
I veil Nordvig's Daughter and bring gray death,
And make the world anew with Helzvog's Blood.
What be I?

And so they went, exchanging riddles of increasing difficulty while Du Weldenvarden sped past below. Gaps in the thatched branches often revealed patches of silver, sections of the many rivers that threaded the forest. Around Saphira, the clouds billowed in a fantastic architecture: vaulting arches, domes, and columns; crenelated ramparts; towers the size of mountains; and ridges and valleys suffused with a glowing light that made Eragon feel as if they flew through a dream.

So fast was Saphira that, when dusk arrived, they had already left Du Weldenvarden behind and entered the auburn fields that separated the great forest from the Hadarac Desert. They made their camp among the grass and hunkered round their small fire, utterly alone upon the flat face of the earth. They were grim-faced and said little, for words only emphasized their insignificance in that bare and empty land.

Eragon took advantage of their stop to store some of his energy in the ruby that adorned Zar'roc's pommel. The gem absorbed all the power he gave it, as well as Saphira's when she lent her strength. It would, concluded Eragon, be a number of days before they could saturate both the ruby and the twelve diamonds concealed within the belt of Beloth the Wise.

Weary from the exercise, he wrapped himself in blankets, lay beside Saphira, and drifted into his waking sleep, where his night phantasms played out against the sea of stars above.

* * *

Soon after they resumed their journey the following morning, the rippling grass gave way to tan scrub, which grew ever more scarce until, in turn, it was replaced by sunbaked ground bare of all but the most hardy plants. Reddish gold dunes appeared. From his vantage on Saphira, they looked to Eragon like lines of waves forever sailing toward a distant shore.

As the sun began its descent, he noticed a cluster of mountains in the distant east and knew he beheld Du Fells Nángoröth, where the wild dragons had gone to mate, to raise their young, and eventually to die. *We must visit there someday*, said Saphira, following his gaze.

Aye.

That night, Eragon felt their solitude even more keenly than before, for they were camped in the emptiest region of the Hadarac Desert, where so little moisture existed in the air that his lips soon cracked, though he smeared them with nalgask every few minutes. He sensed little life in the ground, only a handful of miserable plants interspersed with a few insects and lizards.

As he had when they fled Gil'ead through the desert, Eragon drew water from the soil to replenish their waterskins, and before he allowed the water to drain away, he scryed Nasuada in the pool's reflection to see if the Varden had been attacked yet. To his relief, they had not.

On the third day since leaving Ellesméra, the wind rose up behind them and wafted Saphira farther than she could have flown on her own, carrying them entirely out of the Hadarac Desert.

Near the edge of the waste, they passed over a number of horse-mounted nomads who were garbed in flowing robes to ward against the heat. The men shouted in their rough tongue and shook their swords and spears at Saphira, though none of them dared loose an arrow at her.

Eragon, Saphira, and Orik bivouacked for the night at the

southernmost end of Silverwood Forest, which lay along Lake Tüdosten and was named so because it was composed almost entirely of beeches, willows, and trembling poplars. In contrast to the endless twilight that lay beneath the brooding pines of Du Weldenvarden, Silverwood was filled with bright sunshine, larks, and the gentle rustling of green leaves. The trees seemed young and happy to Eragon, and he was glad to be there. And though all signs of the desert had vanished, the weather remained far warmer than he was accustomed to at that time of year. It felt more like summer than spring.

From there they flew straight to Aberon, the capital of Surda, guided by directions Eragon gleaned from the memories of birds they encountered. Saphira made no attempt to conceal herself along the way, and they often heard cries of amazement and alarm from the villages she swept over.

It was late afternoon when they arrived at Aberon, a low, walled city centered around a bluff in an otherwise flat landscape. Borromeo Castle occupied the top of the bluff. The rambling citadel was protected by three concentric layers of walls, numerous towers, and, Eragon noted, hundreds of ballistae made for shooting down a dragon. The rich amber light from the low sun cast Aberon's buildings in sharp relief and illuminated a plume of dust rising from the city's western gate, where a line of soldiers sought entrance.

As Saphira descended toward the inner ward of the castle, she brought Eragon into contact with the combined thoughts of the people in the capital. The noise overwhelmed him at first—how was he supposed to listen for foes and still function at the same time?—until he realized that, as usual, he was concentrating too much on specifics. All he had to do was sense people's general intentions. He broadened his focus, and the individual voices clamoring for his attention subsided into a continuum of the emotions surrounding him. It was like a sheet of water that lay draped over the nearby landscape, undulating with the rise and fall of people's feelings and spiking whenever someone was racked by extremes of passion.

Thus, Eragon was aware of the alarm that gripped the people below as word of Saphira spread. *Careful,* he told her. *We don't want them to attack us.*

Dirt billowed into the air with each beat of Saphira's powerful wings as she settled in the middle of the courtyard, sinking her claws into the bare ground to steady herself. The horses tethered in the yard neighed with fear, creating such an uproar that Eragon finally inserted himself in their minds and calmed them with words from the ancient language.

Eragon dismounted after Orik, eyeing the many soldiers that lined the parapets and the drawn ballistae they manned. He did not fear the weapons, but he had no desire to become engaged in a fight with his allies.

A group of twelve men, some soldiers, hurried out of the keep toward Saphira. They were led by a tall man with the same dark skin as Nasuada, only the third person Eragon had met with such a complexion. Halting ten paces away, the man bowed—as did his followers—then said, "Welcome, Rider. I am Dahwar, son of Kedar. I am King Orrin's seneschal."

Eragon inclined his head. "And I, Eragon Shadeslayer, son of none."

"And I, Orik, Thrifk's son."

And I, Saphira, daughter of Vervada, said Saphira, using Eragon as her mouthpiece.

Dahwar bowed again. "I apologize that no one of higher rank than myself is present to greet guests as noble as you, but King Orrin, Lady Nasuada, and all the Varden have long since marched to confront Galbatorix's army." Eragon nodded. He had expected as much. "They left orders that if you came here seeking them, you should join them directly, for your prowess is needed if we are to prevail."

"Can you show us on a map how to find them?" asked Eragon.

"Of course, sir. While I have that fetched, would you care to step out of the heat and partake of some refreshments?"

Eragon shook his head. "We have no time to waste. Besides, it is not I who needs to see the map but Saphira, and I doubt she would fit in your halls."

That seemed to catch the seneschal off guard. He blinked and ran his eyes over Saphira, then said, "Quite right, sir. In either case, our hospitality is yours. If there is aught you and your companions desire, you have but to ask."

For the first time, Eragon realized that he could issue commands and expect them to be followed. "We need a week's worth of provisions. For me, only fruit, vegetables, flour, cheese, bread—things like that. We also need our waterskins refilled." He was impressed that Dahwar did not question his avoidance of meat. Orik added his requests then for jerky, bacon, and other such products.

Snapping his fingers, Dahwar sent two servants running back into the keep to collect the supplies. While everyone in the ward waited for the men to return, he asked, "May I assume by your presence here, Shadeslayer, that you completed your training with the elves?"

"My training shall never end so long as I'm alive."

"I see." Then, after a moment, Dahwar said, "Please excuse my impertinence, sir, for I am ignorant of the ways of the Riders, but are you not human? I was told you were."

"That he is," growled Orik. "He was ... changed. And you should be glad he was, or our predicament would be far worse than it is." Dahwar was tactful enough not to pursue the subject, but from his thoughts Eragon concluded that the seneschal would have paid a handsome price for further details—any information about Eragon or Saphira was valuable in Orrin's government.

The food, water, and map were soon brought by two wide-eyed pages. At Eragon's word, they deposited the items beside Saphira, looking terribly frightened as they did, then retreated behind

Dahwar. Kneeling on the ground, Dahwar unrolled the map—which depicted Surda and the neighboring lands—and drew a line northwest from Aberon to Cithrí. He said, "Last I heard, King Orrin and Lady Nasuada stopped here for provender. They did not intend to stay, however, because the Empire is advancing south along the Jiet River and they wished to be in place to confront Galbatorix's army when it arrives. The Varden could be anywhere between Cithrí and the Jiet River. This is only my humble opinion, but I would say the best place to look for them would be the Burning Plains."

"The Burning Plains?"

Dahwar smiled. "You may know them by their old name, then, the name the elves use: Du Völlar Eldrvarya."

"Ah, yes." Now Eragon remembered. He had read about them in one of the histories Oromis assigned him. The plains—which contained huge deposits of peat—lay along the eastern side of the Jiet River where Surda's border crossed it and had been the site of a skirmish between the Riders and the Forsworn. During the fight, the dragons inadvertently lit the peat with the flames from their mouths and the fire had burrowed underground, where it remained smoldering ever since. The land had been rendered uninhabitable by the noxious fumes that poured out of the glowing vents in the charred earth.

A shiver crawled down Eragon's left side as he recalled his premonition: banks of warriors colliding upon an orange and yellow field, accompanied by the harsh screams of gore-crows and the whistle of black arrows. He shivered again. *Fate is converging upon us*, he said to Saphira. Then, gesturing at the map: *Have you seen enough?*

I have.

In short order, he and Orik packed the supplies, remounted Saphira, and from her back thanked Dahwar for his service. As Saphira was about to take off again, Eragon frowned; a note of discord had entered the minds he was monitoring. "Dahwar, two grooms in the stables have gotten into an argument and one of them, Tathal, intends to commit murder. You can stop him, though, if you send men right away."

Dahwar widened his eyes in an expression of astonishment, and even Orik twisted round to look at Eragon. The seneschal asked, "How do you know this, Shadeslayer?"

Eragon merely said, "Because I am a Rider."

Then Saphira unfurled her wings, and everyone on the ground ran back to avoid being battered by the rush of air as she flapped downward and soared into the sky. As Borromeo Castle dwindled behind them, Orik said, "Can you hear my thoughts, Eragon?"

"Do you want me to try? I haven't, you know."

"Try."

Frowning, Eragon concentrated his attention on the dwarf's consciousness and was surprised to find Orik's mind well protected behind thick mental barriers. He could sense Orik's presence, but not his thoughts and feelings. "Nothing."

Orik grinned. "Good. I wanted to make sure I hadn't forgotten my old lessons."

By unspoken consent, they did not stop for the night, but rather forged onward through the blackened sky. Of the moon and stars they saw no sign, no flash or pale gleam to breach the oppressive gloom. The dead hours bloated and sagged and, it seemed to Eragon, clung to each second as if reluctant to surrender to the past.

When the sun finally returned—bringing with it its welcome light—Saphira landed by the edge of a small lake so Eragon and Orik could stretch their legs, relieve themselves, and eat breakfast without the constant movement they experienced on her back.

They had just taken off again when a long, low brown cloud appeared on the edge of the horizon, like a smudge of walnut ink on a sheet of white paper. The cloud grew wider and wider as Saphira approached it, until by late morning it obscured the entire land beneath a pall of foul vapors.

They had reached the Burning Plains of Alagaësia.

THE BURNING PLAINS

Eragon coughed as Saphira descended through the layers of smoke, angling toward the Jiet River, which was hidden behind the haze. He blinked and wiped back tears. The fumes made his eyes smart.

Closer to the ground, the air cleared, giving Eragon an unobstructed view of their destination. The rippling veil of black and crimson smoke filtered the sun's rays in such a way that everything below was bathed in a lurid orange. Occasional rents in the besmirched sky allowed pale bars of light to strike the ground, where they remained, like pillars of translucent glass, until they were truncated by the shifting clouds.

The Jiet River lay before them, as thick and turgid as a gorged snake, its crosshatched surface reflecting the same ghastly hue that pervaded the Burning Plains. Even when a splotch of undiluted light happened to fall upon the river, the water appeared chalky white, opaque and opalescent—almost as if it were the milk of some fearsome beast—and seemed to glow with an eerie luminescence all its own.

Two armies were arrayed along the eastern banks of the oozing waterway. To the south were the Varden and the men of Surda, entrenched behind multiple layers of defense, where they displayed a fine panoply of woven standards, ranks of proud tents, and the picketed horses of King Orrin's cavalry. Strong as they were, their numbers paled in comparison to the size of the force assembled in the north. Galbatorix's army was so large, it measured three miles across on its leading edge and how many in length it was impossible to tell, for the individual men melded into a shadowy mass in the distance.

Between the mortal foes was an empty span of perhaps two miles. This land, and the land that the armies camped on, was pocked with countless ragged orifices in which danced green tongues of fire. From those sickly torches billowed plumes of smoke that dimmed the sun. Every scrap of vegetation had been scorched from the parched soil, except for growths of black, orange, and chartreuse lichen that, from the air, gave the earth a scabbed and infected appearance.

It was the most forbidding vista Eragon had clapped eyes upon.

Saphira emerged over the no-man's-land that separated the grim armies, and now she twisted and dove toward the Varden as fast as she dared, for so long as they remained exposed to the Empire, they were vulnerable to attacks from enemy magicians. Eragon extended his awareness as far as he could in every direction, hunting for hostile minds that could feel his probing touch and would react to it—the minds of magicians and those trained to fend off magicians.

What he felt instead was the sudden panic that overwhelmed the Varden's sentinels, many of whom, he realized, had never before seen Saphira. Fear made them ignore their common sense, and they released a flock of barbed arrows that arched up to intercept her.

Raising his right hand, Eragon cried, "Letta orya thorna!" The arrows froze in place. With a flick of his wrist and the word "Gánga," he redirected them, sending the darts boring toward the no-man's-land, where they could bury themselves in the barren soil without causing harm. He missed one arrow, though, which was fired a few seconds after the first volley.

Eragon leaned as far to his right as he could and, faster than any normal human, plucked the arrow from the air as Saphira flew past it.

Only a hundred feet above the ground, Saphira flared her wings to slow her steep descent before alighting first on her hind legs and then her front legs as she came to a running stop among the Varden's tents.

"Werg," growled Orik, loosening the thongs that held his legs in place. "I'd rather fight a dozen Kull than experience such a fall again." He let himself hang off one side of the saddle, then dropped to Saphira's foreleg below and, from there, to the ground.

Even as Eragon dismounted, dozens of warriors with awestruck expressions gathered around Saphira. From within their midst strode a big bear of a man whom Eragon recognized: Fredric, the Varden's weapon master from Farthen Dûr, still garbed in his hairy ox-hide armor. "Come on, you slack-jawed louts!" roared Fredric. "Don't stand here gawking; get back to your posts or I'll have the lot of you chalked up for extra watches!" At his command, the men began to disperse with many a grumbled word and backward glance. Then Fredric drew nearer and, Eragon could tell, was startled by the change in Eragon's countenance. The bearded man did his best to conceal the reaction by touching his brow and saying, "Welcome, Shadeslayer. You've arrived just in time. . . . I can't tell you how ashamed I am you were attacked. The honor of every man here has been blackened by this mistake. Were the three of you hurt?"

"No."

Relief spread across Fredric's face. "Well, there's that to be grateful for. I've had the men responsible pulled from duty. They'll each be whipped and reduced in rank. . . . Will that punishment satisfy you, Rider?"

"I want to see them," said Eragon.

Sudden concern emanated from Fredric; it was obvious he feared that Eragon wanted to enact some terrible and unnatural retribution on the sentinels. Fredric did not voice his concern, however, but said, "If you'd follow me, then, sir."

He led them through the camp to a striped command tent where twenty or so miserable-looking men were divesting themselves of their arms and armor under the watchful eye of a dozen guards. At the sight of Eragon and Saphira, the prisoners all went down on one knee and remained there, gazing at the ground. "Hail, Shade-slayer!" they cried.

Eragon said nothing, but walked along the line of men while he studied their minds, his boots sinking through the crust of the baked earth with an ominous crunch. At last he said, "You should be proud that you reacted so quickly to our appearance. If Galbatorix attacks, that's exactly what you should do, though I doubt arrows would prove any more effective against him than they were against Saphira and me." The sentinels glanced at him with disbelief, their upturned faces tinted the color of tarnished brass by the variegated light. "I only ask that, in the future, you take a mo-ment to identify your target before shooting. Next time I might be too distracted to stop your missiles. Am I understood?"

"Yes, Shadeslayer!" they shouted.

Stopping before the second-to-last man in the line, Eragon held out the arrow he had snared from Saphira's back. "I believe this is yours, Harwin."

With an expression of wonder, Harwin accepted the arrow from Eragon. "So it is! It has the white band I always paint on my shafts so I can find them later. Thank you, Shadeslayer."

Eragon nodded and then said to Fredric so all could hear, "These are good and true men, and I want no misfortune to befall them be-cause of this event."

"I will see to it personally," said Fredric, and smiled.

"Now, can you take us to Lady Nasuada?"

"Yes, sir."

As he left the sentinels, Eragon knew that his kindness had earned him their undying loyalty, and that tidings of his deed would spread throughout the Varden.

The path Fredric took through the tents brought Eragon into close contact with more minds than he had ever touched before. Hundreds of thoughts, images, and sensations pressed against his consciousness. Despite his effort to keep them at a distance, he could not help absorbing random details of people's lives. Some revelations he found shocking, some meaningless, others touching or, conversely, disgusting, and many embarrassing. A few people perceived the world so differently, their minds leaped out at him on account of that very difference.

How easy it is to view these men as nothing more than objects that I and a few others can manipulate at will. Yet they each possess hopes and dreams, potential for what they might achieve and memories of what they have already accomplished. And they all feel pain.

A handful of the minds he touched were aware of the contact and recoiled from it, hiding their inner life behind defenses of varying strength. At first Eragon was concerned—imagining that he had discovered a great many enemies who had infiltrated the Varden—but then he realized from his quick glimpse that they were the individual members of Du Vrangr Gata.

Saphira said, *They must be scared out of their wits, thinking that they're about to be assaulted by some strange magician.*

I can't convince them otherwise while they block me like this.

You should meet them in person, and soon too, before they decide to band together and attack.

Aye, although I don't think they pose a threat to us. . . . Du Vrangr Gata—their very name betrays their ignorance. Properly, in the ancient language, it should be Du Gata Vrangr.

Their trip ended near the back of the Varden, at a large red pavilion flying a pennant embroidered with a black shield and two parallel swords slanting underneath. Fredric pulled back the flap and Eragon and Orik entered the pavilion. Behind them, Saphira pushed her head through the opening and peered over their shoulders.

A broad table occupied the center of the furnished tent. Nasuada stood at one end, leaning on her hands, studying a slew of maps and scrolls. Eragon's stomach clenched as he saw Arya opposite her. Both women were armored as men for battle.

Nasuada turned her almond-shaped face toward him. "Eragon?" she whispered.

He was unprepared for how glad he was to see her. With a broad grin, he twisted his hand over his sternum in the elves' gesture of fealty and bowed. "At your service."

"Eragon!" This time Nasuada sounded delighted and relieved. Arya, too, appeared pleased. "How did you get our message so quickly?"

"I didn't; I learned about Galbatorix's army from my scrying and left Ellesméra the same day." He smiled at her again. "It's good to be back with the Varden."

While he spoke, Nasuada studied him with a wondering expression. "What has happened to you, Eragon?"

Arya must not have told her, said Saphira.

And so Eragon gave a full account of what had befallen Saphira and him since they left Nasuada in Farthen Dûr so long ago. Much of what he said, he sensed that she had already heard, either from the dwarves or from Arya, but she let him speak without interrupting. Eragon had to be circumspect about his training. He had given his word not to reveal Oromis's existence without permission, and most of his lessons were not to be shared with outsiders, but he did his best to give Nasuada a good idea of his skills and their attendant risks. Of the Agaetí Blödhren, he merely said, ". . . and during the celebration, the dragons worked upon me the change you see, giving me the physical abilities of an elf and healing my back."

"Your scar is gone, then?" asked Nasuada. He nodded. A few more sentences served to end his narrative, briefly mentioning the reason they had left Du Weldenvarden and then summarizing their journey thence. She shook her head. "What a tale. You and Saphira have experienced so much since you left Farthen Dûr."

"As have you." He gestured at the tent. "It's amazing what you've accomplished. It must have taken an enormous amount of work to get the Varden to Surda. . . . Has the Council of Elders caused you much trouble?"

586

"A bit, but nothing extraordinary. They seem to have resigned themselves to my leadership." Her mail clinking together, Nasuada seated herself in a large, high-backed chair and turned to Orik, who had yet to speak. She welcomed him and asked if he had aught to add to Eragon's tale. Orik shrugged and provided a few anecdotes from their stay in Ellesméra, though Eragon suspected that the dwarf kept his true observations a secret for his king.

When he finished, Nasuada said, "I am heartened to know that if we can weather this onslaught, we shall have the elves by our side. Did any of you happen to see Hrothgar's warriors during your flight from Aberon? We are counting on their reinforcements."

No, answered Saphira through Eragon. *But then, it was dark and I was often above or between clouds. I could have easily missed a camp under those conditions. In any case, I doubt we would have crossed paths, for I flew straight from Aberon, and it seems likely the dwarves would choose a different route—perhaps following established roads— rather than march through the wilderness.*

"What," asked Eragon, "is the situation here?"

Nasuada sighed and then told of how she and Orrin had learned about Galbatorix's army and the desperate measures they had resorted to since in order to reach the Burning Plains before the king's soldiers. She finished by saying, "The Empire arrived three days ago. Since then, we've exchanged two messages. First they asked for our surrender, which we refused, and now we wait for their reply."

"How many of them are there?" growled Orik. "It looked a mighty number from Saphira's back."

"Aye. We estimate Galbatorix mustered as many as a hundred thousand soldiers."

Eragon could not contain himself: "A hundred thousand! Where did they come from? It seems impossible that he could find more than a handful of people willing to serve him."

"They were conscripted. We can only hope that the men who were torn from their homes won't be eager to fight. If we can frighten them badly enough, they may break ranks and flee. Our

587

numbers are greater than in Farthen Dûr, for King Orrin has joined forces with us and we have received a veritable flood of volunteers since we began to spread the word about you, Eragon, although we are still far weaker than the Empire."

Then Saphira asked, and Eragon was forced to repeat the dreadful question: *What do you think our chances of victory are?*

"That," said Nasuada, putting emphasis on the word, "depends a great deal upon you and Eragon, and the number of magicians seeded throughout their troops. If you can find and destroy those magicians, then our enemies shall be left unprotected and you can slay them at will. Outright victory, I think, is unlikely at this point, but we might be able to hold them at bay until their supplies run low or until Islanzadí can come to our assistance. That is . . . if Galbatorix doesn't fly into battle himself. In that case, I fear retreat will be our only option."

Just then, Eragon felt a strange mind approaching, one that knew he was watching and yet did not shrink from the contact. One that felt cold and hard, calculating. Alert for danger, Eragon turned his gaze toward the rear of the pavilion, where he saw the same black-haired girl who had appeared when he scryed Nasuada from Ellesméra. The girl stared at him with violet eyes, then said, "Welcome, Shadeslayer. Welcome, Saphira."

Eragon shivered at the sound of her voice, the voice of an adult. He wet his dry mouth and asked, "Who are you?"

Without answering, the girl brushed back her glossy bangs and exposed a silvery white mark on her forehead, exactly like Eragon's gedwëy ignasia. He knew then whom he faced.

No one moved as Eragon went to the girl, accompanied by Saphira, who extended her neck farther into the pavilion. Dropping to one knee, Eragon took the girl's right hand in his own; her skin burned as if with fever. She did not resist him, but merely left her hand limp in his grip. In the ancient language—and also with his mind, so that she would understand—Eragon said, "I am sorry. Can you forgive me for what I did to you?"

The girl's eyes softened, and she leaned forward and kissed Eragon upon the brow. "I forgive you," she whispered, for the first time sounding her age. "How could I not? You and Saphira created who I am, and I know you meant no harm. I forgive you, but I shall let this knowledge torture your conscience: You have condemned me to be aware of all the suffering around me. Even now your spell drives me to rush to the aid of a man not three tents away who just cut his hand, to help the young flag carrier who broke his left index finger in the spokes of a wagon wheel, and to help countless others who have been or are about to be hurt. It costs me dearly to resist those urges, and even more if I consciously cause someone discomfort, as I do by saying this. . . . I cannot even sleep at night for the strength of my compulsion. *That* is your legacy, O Rider." By the end, her voice had regained its bitter, mocking edge.

Saphira interposed herself between them and, with her snout, touched the girl in the center of her mark. *Peace, Changeling. You have much anger in your heart.*

"You don't have to live like this forever," said Eragon. "The elves taught me how to undo a spell, and I believe I can free you of this curse. It won't be easy, but it can be done."

For a moment, the girl seemed to lose her formidable self-control. A small gasp escaped her lips, her hand trembled against Eragon's, and her eyes glistened with a film of tears. Then just as quickly, she hid her true emotions behind a mask of cynical amusement. "Well, we shall see. Either way, you shouldn't try until after this battle."

"I could save you a great deal of pain."

"It wouldn't do to exhaust you when our survival may depend on your talents. I do not deceive myself; you are more important than me." A sly grin crossed her face. "Besides, if you remove your spell now, I won't be able to help any of the Varden if they are threatened. You wouldn't want Nasuada to die because of that, would you?"

"No," admitted Eragon. He paused for a long time, considering the issue, then said, "Very well, I will wait. But I swear to you: If we win this fight, I shall right this wrong."

The girl tilted her head to one side. "I will hold you to your word, Rider."

Rising from her chair, Nasuada said, "Elva was the one who saved me from an assassin in Aberon."

"Did she? In that case, I am in your debt . . . Elva . . . for protecting my liegelord."

"Come now," said Nasuada. "I must introduce the three of you to Orrin and his nobles. Have you met the king before, Orik?"

The dwarf shook his head. "I've never been this far west."

As they left the pavilion—Nasuada in the lead, with Elva by her side—Eragon tried to position himself so he could talk with Arya, but when he neared her, she quickened her pace until she was level with Nasuada. Arya never even looked at him while she walked, a slight that caused him more anguish than any physical wound he had endured. Elva glanced back at him, and he knew that she was aware of his distress.

They soon arrived at another large pavilion, this one white and yellow—although it was difficult to determine the exact hue of the colors, given the garish orange that glazed everything on the Burning Plains. Once they were granted entrance, Eragon was astonished to find the tent crammed with an eccentric collection of beakers, alembics, retorts, and other instruments of natural philosophy. *Who would bother toting all this onto a battlefield?* he wondered, bewildered.

"Eragon," said Nasuada, "I would like you to meet Orrin, son of Larkin and monarch of the realm of Surda."

From the depths of the tangled piles of glass emerged a rather tall, handsome man with shoulder-length hair held back by the gold coronet resting upon his head. His mind, like Nasuada's, was protected behind walls of iron; it was obvious he had received extensive training in that skill. Orrin seemed pleasant enough to

Eragon from their discussion, if a bit green and untried when it came to commanding men in war and more than a little odd in the head. On the whole, Eragon trusted Nasuada's leadership more.

After fending off scores of questions from Orrin about his stay among the elves, Eragon found himself smiling and nodding politely as one earl after another paraded past, each of whom insisted on shaking his hand, telling him what an honor it was to meet a Rider, and inviting him to their respective estates. Eragon dutifully memorized their many names and titles—as he knew Oromis would expect—and did his best to maintain a calm demeanor, despite his growing frustration.

We're about to engage one of the largest armies in history, and here we are, stuck exchanging pleasantries.

Patience, counseled Saphira. *There aren't that many more. . . . Besides, look at it this way: if we win, they'll owe us an entire year of free dinners, what with all their promises.*

He stifled a chuckle. *I think it would dismay them to know what it takes to feed you. Not to mention that you could empty their cellars of beer and wine in a single night.*

I would never, she sniffed, then relented. *Maybe in two nights.*

When at last they won free of Orrin's pavilion, Eragon asked Nasuada, "What shall I do now? How can I serve you?"

Nasuada eyed him with a curious expression. "How do *you* think you can best serve me, Eragon? You know your own abilities far better than I do." Even Arya watched him now, waiting to hear his response.

Eragon gazed up at the bloody sky while he pondered her question. "I shall take control of Du Vrangr Gata, as they once asked me to, and organize them underneath me so I can lead them into battle. Working together will give us the best chance of foiling Galbatorix's magicians."

"That seems an excellent idea."

Is there a place, asked Saphira, *where Eragon can leave his bags? I don't want to carry them or this saddle any longer than I have to.*

When Eragon repeated her question, Nasuada said, "Of course. You may leave them in my pavilion, and I will arrange to have a tent erected for you, Eragon, where you can keep them permanently. I suggest, though, that you don your armor before parting with your bags. You might need it at any moment. . . . That reminds me: we have your armor with us, Saphira. I shall have it unpacked and brought to you."

"And what of me, Lady?" asked Orik.

"We have several knurlan with us from Dûrgrimst Ingeitum who have lent their expertise to the construction of our earthen defenses. You may take command of them if you wish."

Orik seemed heartened by the prospect of seeing fellow dwarves, especially ones from his own clan. He clapped his fist to his chest and said, "I think I will at that. If you'll excuse me, I'll see to it at once." Without a backward glance, he trundled off through the camp, heading north toward the breastwork.

Returning to her pavilion with the four who remained, Nasuada said to Eragon, "Report to me once you have settled matters with Du Vrangr Gata." Then she pushed aside the entrance flap to the pavilion and disappeared with Elva through the dark opening.

As Arya started to follow, Eragon reached toward her and, in the ancient language, said, "Wait." The elf paused and looked at him, betraying nothing. He held her gaze without wavering, staring deep into her eyes, which reflected the strange light around them. "Arya, I won't apologize for how I feel about you. However, I wanted you to know that I *am* sorry for how I acted during the Blood-oath Celebration. I wasn't myself that night; otherwise, I would have never been so forward with you."

"And you won't do it again?"

He suppressed a humorless laugh. "It wouldn't get me anywhere if I did, now would it?" When she remained silent, he said, "No matter. I don't want to trouble you, even if you—" He bit off the end of his sentence before he made a remark he knew he would regret.

Arya's expression softened. "I'm not trying to hurt you, Eragon. You must understand that."

"I understand," he said, but without conviction.

An awkward pause stretched between them. "Your flight went well, I trust?"

"Well enough."

"You encountered no difficulty in the desert?"

"Should we have?"

"No. I only wondered." Then, in an even gentler voice, Arya asked, "What of you, Eragon? How have you been since the celebration? I heard what you said to Nasuada, but you mentioned nothing other than your back."

"I . . ." He tried to lie—not wanting her to know how much he had missed her—but the ancient language stopped the words dead in his mouth and rendered him mute. Finally, he resorted to a technique of the elves: telling only part of the truth in order to create an impression opposite the whole truth. "I'm better than before," he said, meaning, in his mind, the condition of his back.

Despite his subterfuge, Arya appeared unconvinced. She did not press him on the subject, though, but rather said, "I am glad." Nasuada's voice emanated from inside the pavilion, and Arya glanced toward it before facing him again. "I am needed elsewhere, Eragon. . . . We are both needed elsewhere. A battle is about to take place." Lifting the canvas flap, she stepped halfway into the gloomy tent, then hesitated and added, "Take care, Eragon Shadeslayer."

Then she was gone.

Dismay rooted Eragon in place. He had accomplished what he wanted to, but it seemed to have changed nothing between him and Arya. He balled his hands into fists and hunched his shoulders and glared at the ground without seeing it, simmering with frustration.

He started when Saphira nosed him on the shoulder. *Come on, little one*, she said gently. *You can't stay here forever, and this saddle is beginning to itch.*

Going to her side, Eragon pulled on her neck strap, muttering under his breath when it caught in the buckle. He almost hoped the leather would break. Undoing the rest of the straps, he let the saddle and everything tied to it fall to the ground in a jumbled heap. *It feels good to have that off,* said Saphira, rolling her massive shoulders.

Digging his armor out of the saddlebags, Eragon outfitted himself in the bright dress of war. First he pulled his hauberk over his elven tunic, then strapped his chased greaves to his legs and his inlaid bracers to his forearms. On his head went his padded leather cap, followed by his coif of tempered steel and then his gold and silver helm. Last of all, he replaced his regular gloves with his mail-backed gauntlets.

Zar'roc he hung on his left hip using the belt of Beloth the Wise. Across his back, he placed the quiver of white swan feathers Islanzadí had given him. The quiver, he was pleased to find, could also hold the bow the elf queen had sung for him, even when it was strung.

After depositing his and Orik's belongings into the pavilion, Eragon and Saphira set out together to find Trianna, the current leader of Du Vrangr Gata. They had gone no more than a few paces when Eragon sensed a nearby mind that was shielded from his view. Assuming that it was one of the Varden's magicians, they veered toward it.

Twelve yards from their starting point, they came upon a small green tent with a donkey picketed in front. To the left of the tent, a blackened iron cauldron hung from a metal tripod placed over one of the malodorous flames birthed deep within the earth. Cords were strung about the cauldron, over which were draped night-shade, hemlock, rhododendron, savin, bark of the yew tree, and numerous mushrooms, such as death cap and spotted cort, all of which Eragon recognized from Oromis's lessons on poison. And standing next to the cauldron, wielding a long wood paddle with which she stirred the brew, was Angela the herbalist. At her feet sat Solembum.

The werecat uttered a mournful meow, and Angela looked up from her task, her corkscrew hair forming a billowing thundercloud around her glistening face. She frowned, and her expression became positively ghoulish, for it was lit from beneath by the flickering green flame. "So you've returned, eh!"

"We have," said Eragon.

"Is that all you have to say for yourself? Have you seen Elva yet? Have you seen what you did to that poor girl?"

"Aye."

"*Aye!*" cried Angela. "How inarticulate can a person be? All this time in Ellesméra being tutored by the elves, and *aye* is the best you can manage? Let me tell you something, blockhead: anyone who is stupid enough to do what you did deserves—"

Eragon clasped his hands behind his back and waited as Angela informed him, in many explicit, detailed, and highly inventive terms, exactly how great a blockhead he was; what kind of ancestors he must possess to be such a monumental blockhead—she even went so far as to insinuate that one of his grandparents had mated with an Urgal—and the quite hideous punishments he ought to receive for his idiocy. If anyone else had insulted him in that manner, Eragon would have challenged them to a duel, but he tolerated her spleen because he knew he could not judge her behavior by the same standards as he did others, and because he knew her outrage was justified; he had made a dreadful mistake.

When she finally paused for breath, he said, "You're quite right, and I'm going to try to remove the spell once the battle is decided."

Angela blinked three times, one right after the other, and her mouth remained open for a moment in a small "O" before she clamped it shut. With a glare of suspicion, she asked, "You're not saying that just to placate me, are you?"

"I would never."

"And you really intend to undo your curse? I thought such things were irrevocable."

"The elves have discovered many uses of magic."

"Ah . . . Well, then, that's settled, isn't it?" She flashed him a wide smile and then strode past him to pat Saphira on her jowls. "It's good to see you again, Saphira. You've grown."

Well met indeed, Angela.

As Angela returned to stirring her concoction, Eragon said, "That was an impressive tirade you gave."

"Thank you. I worked on it for several weeks. It's a pity you didn't get to hear the ending; it's *memorable*. I could finish it for you if you want."

"No, that's all right. I can imagine what it's like." Glancing at her out of the corner of his eye, Eragon then said, "You don't seem surprised by how I've changed."

The herbalist shrugged. "I have my sources. It's an improvement, in my opinion. You were a bit . . . oh, how shall I say it? . . . *unfinished* before."

"That I was." He gestured at the hanging plants. "What do you plan to do with these?"

"Oh, it's just a little project of mine—an experiment, if you will."

"Mmm." Examining the pattern of colors on a dried mushroom that dangled before him, Eragon asked, "Did you ever figure out if toads exist or not?"

"As a matter of fact, I did! It seems that all toads are frogs, but not all frogs are toads. So in that sense, toads don't really exist, which means that I was right all along." She stopped her patter abruptly, leaned to the side, grabbed a mug from a bench next to her, and offered it to Eragon. "Here, have a cup of tea."

Eragon glanced at the deadly plants surrounding them and then back at Angela's open face before he accepted the mug. Under his breath—so the herbalist would not hear—he muttered three spells to detect poison. Only once he ascertained that the tea was free of contamination did he dare drink. The tea was delicious, though he could not identify the ingredients.

At that moment, Solembum padded over to Saphira and began to arch his back and rub himself up against her leg, just as any normal cat would. Twisting her neck, Saphira bent down and with the tip of her nose brushed the werecat the length of his spine. She said, *I met someone in Ellesméra who knows you.*

Solembum stopped rubbing and cocked his head. *Is that so?*

Yes. Her name was Quickpaw and The Dream Dancer and also Maud.

Solembum's golden eyes widened. A deep, throaty purr rumbled in his chest, and he rubbed against Saphira with renewed vigor.

"So," said Angela, "I assume you already spoke with Nasuada, Arya, and King Orrin." He nodded. "And what did you think of dear old Orrin?"

Eragon chose his words with care, for he was aware that they *were* talking about a king. "Well . . . he seems to have a great many interests."

"Yes, he's as balmy as a moonstruck fool on Midsummer Night Eve. But then everyone is, in one way or another."

Amused by her forthrightness, Eragon said, "He must be crazy to have carted so much glass all the way from Aberon."

Angela raised an eyebrow. "What's this now?"

"Haven't you seen the inside of his tent?"

"Unlike some people," she sniffed, "I don't ingratiate myself with every monarch I meet." So he described for her the mass of instruments Orrin had brought to the Burning Plains. Angela abandoned her stirring as he spoke and listened with great interest. The instant he finished, she began bustling around the cauldron, gathering the plants off the lines—often using tongs to do so—and saying, "I think I had best pay Orrin a visit. The two of you will have to tell me about your trip to Ellesméra at a later time. . . . Well, go on, both of you. Be gone!"

Eragon shook his head as the short little woman drove him and Saphira away from her tent, and he still holding the cup of tea. *Talking with her is always . . .*

Different? suggested Saphira.

Exactly.

THE CLOUDS OF WAR

From there it took them almost half an hour to locate Trianna's tent, which apparently served as the unofficial headquarters of Du Vrangr Gata. They had difficulty finding the tent because few people knew of its existence, and even fewer could tell them where it lay because the tent was hidden behind a spur of rock that served to conceal it from the gaze of enemy magicians in Galbatorix's army.

As Eragon and Saphira approached the black tent, the entrance was thrust open and Trianna strode out, her arms bare to the elbow in preparation to use magic. Behind her clustered a group of determined if frightened-looking spellcasters, many of whom Eragon had seen during the battle in Farthen Dûr, either fighting or healing the wounded.

Eragon watched as Trianna and the others reacted with the now-expected surprise at his altered appearance. Lowering her arms, Trianna said, "Shadeslayer, Saphira. You should have told us sooner that you were here. We've been preparing to confront and battle what we thought was a mighty foe."

"I didn't mean to upset you," said Eragon, "but we had to report to Nasuada and King Orrin immediately after we landed."

"And why have you graced us with your presence now? You never deigned to visit us before, we who are more your brethren than any in the Varden."

"I have come to take command of Du Vrangr Gata." The assembled spellcasters muttered with surprise at his announcement, and Trianna stiffened. Eragon felt several magicians probe his consciousness in an attempt to divine his true intentions. Instead of guarding himself—which would blind him to impending attacks—Eragon retaliated by jabbing the minds of the would-be invaders hard enough that they retreated behind their own barriers. As he did, Eragon had the satisfaction of seeing two men and a woman flinch and avert their gazes.

"By whose order?" demanded Trianna.

"By Nasuada's."

"Ah," said the sorceress with a triumphant smile, "but Nasuada has no direct authority over us. We help the Varden of our own free will."

Her resistance puzzled Eragon. "I'm sure Nasuada would be surprised to hear that, after everything she, and her father, have done for Du Vrangr Gata. It might give her the impression that you no longer wanted the support and protection of the Varden." He let the threat hang in the air for a moment. "Besides, I seem to remember you were willing to give me this post before. Why not now?"

Trianna lifted an eyebrow. "You refused my offer, Shadeslayer . . . or have you forgotten?" Composed as she was, a trace of defensiveness colored her response, and Eragon suspected she knew her position was untenable. She seemed more mature to him than when they last met, and he had to remind himself of the hardships she must have endured since: marching across Alagaësia to Surda, supervising the magicians of Du Vrangr Gata, and preparing for war.

"We could not accept then. It was the wrong time."

Abruptly changing tack, she asked, "Why does Nasuada believe you should command us anyway? Surely you and Saphira would be more useful elsewhere."

"Nasuada wants me to lead you, Du Vrangr Gata, in the coming battle, and so I shall." Eragon thought it best not to mention that it was his idea.

A dark scowl gave Trianna a fierce appearance. She pointed at the cluster of spellcasters behind her. "We have devoted our lives to the study of our art. You have been casting spells for less than two years. What makes you more qualified for this task than any of us? . . . No matter. Tell me: What is your strategy? How do you plan to employ us?"

"My plan is simple," he said. "The lot of you will join minds and search for enemy spellcasters. When you find one, I'll add my strength to yours, and together we can crush the spellcaster's resistance. Then we can slay the troops that previously were protected by his or her wards."

"And what will you be doing the rest of the time?"

"Fighting alongside Saphira."

After an awkward silence, one of the men behind Trianna said, "It's a good plan." He quailed as Trianna cast an angry glare at him.

She slowly faced Eragon again. "Ever since the Twins died, I have led Du Vrangr Gata. Under my guidance, they have provided the means to fund the Varden's war effort, ferreted out the Black Hand—Galbatorix's network of spies that tried to assassinate Nasuada—as well as performing innumerable other services. I do not boast when I say these are no mean accomplishments. And I'm certain I can continue to produce such results. . . . Why, then, does Nasuada want to depose me? How have I displeased her?"

Everything became clear to Eragon, then. *She has grown accustomed to power and doesn't want to surrender it. But more than that, she thinks that my replacing her is a criticism of her leadership.*

You need to resolve this debate, and quickly too, said Saphira. *Our time grows short.*

Eragon racked his brain for a way to establish his authority in Du Vrangr Gata without further alienating Trianna. At last he said, "I didn't come here to stir up trouble. I came to ask for your help." He spoke to the entire congregation but looked only at the sorceress. "I am strong, yes. Saphira and I could probably defeat any number of Galbatorix's pet magicians. But we cannot protect everyone in

601

the Varden. We cannot *be* everywhere. And if the Empire's battle-mages join forces against us, then even we will be hard-pressed to survive. . . . We cannot fight this battle alone. You are quite right, Trianna—you have done well with Du Vrangr Gata, and I'm not here to usurp your authority. It's only that—as a magician—I need to work with Du Vrangr Gata, and—as a Rider—I may also need to give you orders, orders that I have to know will be obeyed without question. The chain of command must be established. That said, you will retain the greater part of your autonomy. Most times I'll be too busy to devote my attention to Du Vrangr Gata. Nor do I intend to ignore your counsel, for I'm aware that you have far more experience than I. . . . So I ask again, will you help us, for the good of the Varden?"

Trianna paused, then bowed. "Of course, Shadeslayer—for the good of the Varden. It will be an honor to have you lead Du Vrangr Gata."

"Then let us begin."

Over the next few hours, Eragon talked with every one of the assembled magicians, although a fair number were absent, being occupied with one task or another to help the Varden. He did his best to acquaint himself with their knowledge of magic. He learned that the majority of men and women in Du Vrangr Gata had been introduced to their craft by a relative, and usually in profound secrecy to avoid attracting attention from those who feared magic—and, of course, Galbatorix himself. Only a handful had received proper apprenticeships. As a result, most of the spellcasters knew little about the ancient language—none could truly speak it fluently—their beliefs about magic were often distorted by religious superstitions, and they were ignorant of numerous applications of gramarye.

No wonder the Twins were so desperate to extract your vocabulary of the ancient language when they tested you in Farthen Dûr, observed Saphira. *With it they could have easily conquered these lesser magicians.*

They're all we have to work with, though.

True. I hope you can see now I was right about Trianna. She places her own desires before the good of the many.

You were right, he agreed. *But I don't condemn her for it. Trianna deals with the world in the best way she can, as do we all. I understand that, even if I don't approve, and understanding—as Oromis said—breeds empathy.*

A bit more than a third of the spellcasters specialized as healers. Those Eragon sent on their way after giving them a quintet of new spells to memorize, enchantments that would allow them to treat a greater range of injuries. The remaining spellcasters Eragon worked with to establish a clear chain of command—he appointed Trianna his lieutenant and let her ensure that his orders were carried out—and to weld their disparate personalities into a cohesive fighting unit. Trying to convince magicians to cooperate, he discovered, was like trying to get a pack of dogs to share a meat bone. Nor did it help that they were in evident awe of him, for he could find no way of using his influence to smooth relations among the contentious magicians.

In order to gain a better idea of their exact proficiency, Eragon had them cast a series of spells. As he watched them struggle with enchantments that he now considered simple, Eragon became aware of just how far his own powers had advanced. To Saphira, he marveled, *And to think I once had trouble lifting a pebble in the air.*

And to think, she replied, *Galbatorix has had over a century to hone his talent.*

The sun was low in the west, intensifying the fermented orange light until the Varden's camp, the livid Jiet River, and the entirety of the Burning Plains glowed in the mad, marbled effulgence, as if in a scene from a lunatic's dreams. The sun was no more than a finger's breadth above the horizon when a runner arrived at the tent. He told Eragon that Nasuada ordered him to attend her at once. "An' I think you'd better hurry, Shadeslayer, if you don't mind me saying so."

After extracting a promise from Du Vrangr Gata that they would be ready and willing when he called upon them for assistance,

603

Eragon ran alongside Saphira through the rows of gray tents toward Nasuada's pavilion. A harsh tumult above them caused Eragon to lift his eyes from the treacherous ground long enough to glance overhead.

What he saw was a giant flock of birds wheeling between the two armies. He spotted eagles, hawks, and falcons, along with countless greedy crows and their larger, dagger-beaked, blue-backed, rapacious cousin, the raven. Each bird shrieked for blood to wet its throat and enough hot meat to fill its belly and sate its hunger. By experience and instinct, they knew that whenever armies appeared in Alagaësia, they could expect to feast on acres of carrion.

The clouds of war are gathering, observed Eragon.

NAR GARZHVOG

Eragon entered the pavilion, Saphira pushing her head through after him. He was met by a steely rasp as Jörmundur and a half-dozen of Nasuada's commanders drew their swords at the intruders. The men lowered their weapons as Nasuada said, "Come here, Eragon."

"What is your bidding?" Eragon asked.

"Our scouts report that a company of some hundred Kull approach from the northeast."

Eragon frowned. He had not expected to encounter Urgals in this battle, since Durza no longer controlled them and so many had been killed in Farthen Dûr. But if they had come, they had come. He felt his bloodlust rise and allowed himself a savage grin as he contemplated destroying Urgals with his new strength. Clapping his hand to Zar'roc's hilt, he said, "It will be a pleasure to eliminate them. Saphira and I can handle it by ourselves, if you want."

Nasuada watched his face carefully as she said, "We can't do that, Eragon. They're flying a white flag, and they have asked to talk with me."

Eragon gaped at her. "Surely you don't intend to grant them an audience?"

"I will offer them the same courtesies I would to any foe who arrives under the banner of truce."

"They're brutes, though. Monsters! It's folly to allow them into the camp. . . . Nasuada, I have seen the atrocities Urgals commit.

They relish pain and suffering and deserve no more mercy than a rabid dog. There is no need for you to waste time over what is surely a trap. Just give the word and I and every last one of your warriors will be more than willing to kill these foul creatures for you."

"In this," said Jörmundur, "I agree with Eragon. If you won't listen to us, Nasuada, at least listen to him."

First Nasuada said to Eragon in a murmur low enough that no one else could hear, "Your training is indeed unfinished if you are so blinded." Then she raised her voice, and in it Eragon heard the same adamantine notes of command that her father had possessed: "You all forget that I fought in Farthen Dûr, the same as you, and that I saw the savagery of the Urgals. . . . However, I also saw our own men commit acts just as heinous. I shall not denigrate what we have endured at the Urgals' hands, but neither shall I ignore potential allies when we are so greatly outnumbered by the Empire."

"My Lady, it's too dangerous for you to meet with a Kull."

"Too dangerous?" Nasuada raised an eyebrow. "While I am protected by Eragon, Saphira, Elva, and all the warriors around me? I think not."

Eragon gritted his teeth with frustration. *Say something, Saphira. You can convince her to abandon this harebrained scheme.*

No, I won't. Your mind is clouded on this issue.

You can't agree with her! exclaimed Eragon, aghast. *You were there in Yazuac with me; you know what the Urgals did to the villagers. And what about when we left Teirm, my capture at Gil'ead, and Farthen Dûr? Every time we've encountered Urgals, they've tried to kill us or worse. They're nothing more than vicious animals.*

The elves believed the same thing about dragons during Du Fyrn Skulblaka.

At Nasuada's behest, her guards tied back the front and side panels of the pavilion, leaving it open for all to see and allowing Saphira to crouch low next to Eragon. Then Nasuada seated herself in her high-backed chair, and Jörmundur and the other commanders arranged themselves in two parallel rows so that anyone who sought an audience with her had to walk between them. Eragon stood at her right hand, Elva by her left.

Less than five minutes later, a great roar of anger erupted from the eastern edge of the camp. The storm of jeers and insults grew louder and louder until a single Kull entered their view, walking toward Nasuada while a mob of the Varden peppered him with taunts. The Urgal—or ram, as Eragon remembered they were called—held his head high and bared his yellow fangs, but did not otherwise react to the abuse directed at him. He was a magnificent specimen, eight and a half feet tall, with strong, proud—if grotesque—features, thick horns that spiraled all the way around, and a fantastic musculature that made it seem he could kill a bear with a single blow. His only clothing was a knotted loincloth, a few plates of crude iron armor held together with scraps of mail, and a curved metal disk nestled between his two horns to protect the top of his head. His long black hair was in a queue.

Eragon felt his lips tighten in a grimace of hate; he had to struggle to keep from drawing Zar'roc and attacking. Yet despite himself, he could not help but admire the Urgal's courage in confronting an entire army of enemies alone and unarmed. To his surprise, he found the Kull's mind strongly shielded.

When the Urgal stopped before the eaves of the pavilion, not daring to come any closer, Nasuada had her guards shout for quiet to settle the crowd. Everyone looked at the Urgal, wondering what he would do next.

The Urgal lifted his bulging arms toward the sky, inhaled a mighty breath, and then opened his maw and bellowed at Nasuada. In an instant, a thicket of swords pointed at the Kull, but he paid them no attention and continued his ululation until his lungs were empty. Then he looked at Nasuada, ignoring the hundreds of people who, it was obvious, longed to kill him, and growled in a thick, guttural accent, "What treachery is this, Lady Nightstalker? I was promised safe passage. Do humans break their word so easily?"

Leaning toward her, one of Nasuada's commanders said, "Let us punish him, Mistress, for his insolence. Once we have taught him the meaning of respect, *then* you can hear his message, whatever it is."

Eragon longed to remain silent, but he knew his duty to Nasuada and the Varden, so he bent down and said in Nasuada's ear, "Don't take offense. This is how they greet their war chiefs. The proper response is to then butt heads, but I don't think you want to try that."

"Did the elves teach you this?" she murmured, never taking her eyes off the waiting Kull.

"Aye."

"What else did they teach you of the Urgals?"

"A great deal," he admitted reluctantly.

Then Nasuada said to the Kull and also to her men beyond, "The Varden are not liars like Galbatorix and the Empire. Speak your mind; you need fear no danger while we hold council under the conditions of truce."

The Urgal grunted and raised his bony chin higher, baring his throat; Eragon recognized it as a gesture of friendship. To lower one's head was a threat in their race, for it meant that an Urgal intended to ram you with his horns. "I am Nar Garzhvog of the Bolvek tribe. I speak for my people." It seemed as if he chewed on each word before spitting it out. "Urgals are hated more than any other race. Elves, dwarves, humans all hunt us, burn us, and drive us from our halls."

"Not without good reason," pointed out Nasuada.

Garzhvog nodded. "Not without reason. Our people love war. Yet how often are we attacked just because you find us as ugly as we find you? We have thrived since the fall of the Riders. Our tribes are now so large, the harsh land we live in can no longer feed us."

"So you made a pact with Galbatorix."

"Aye, Lady Nightstalker. He promised us good land if we killed his enemies. He tricked us, though. His flame-haired shaman, Durza, bent the minds of our war chiefs and forced our tribes to work together, as is not our way. When we learned this in the dwarves' hollow mountain, the Herndall, the dams who rule us, sent my brood mate to Galbatorix to ask why he used us so." Garzhvog shook his ponderous head. "She did not return. Our finest rams died for Galbatorix, then he abandoned us like a broken sword. He is *drajl* and snake-tongued and a lack-horned betrayer. Lady Nightstalker, we are fewer now, but we will fight with you if you let us."

"What is the price?" asked Nasuada. "Your Herndall must want something in return."

"Blood. Galbatorix's blood. And if the Empire falls, we ask that you give us land, land for breeding and growing, land to avoid more battles in the future."

Eragon guessed Nasuada's decision by the set of her face, even before she spoke. So apparently did Jörmundur, for he leaned toward her and said in an undertone, "Nasuada, you can't do this. It goes against nature."

"Nature can't help us defeat the Empire. We *need* allies."

"The men will desert before they'll fight with Urgals."

"That can be worked around. Eragon, will they keep their word?"

"Only so long as we share a common enemy."

With a sharp nod, Nasuada again lifted her voice: "Very well, Nar Garzhvog. You and your warriors may bivouac along the eastern flank of our army, away from the main body, and we shall discuss the terms of our pact."

"Ahgrat ukmar," growled the Kull, clapping his fists to his brow. "You are a wise Herndall, Lady Nightstalker."

"Why do you call me that?"

"Herndall?"

"No, Nightstalker."

Garzhvog made a *ruk-ruk* sound in his throat that Eragon interpreted as laughter. "Nightstalker is the name we gave your sire because of how he hunted us in the dark tunnels under the dwarf mountain and because of the color of his hide. As his cub, you are worthy of the same name." With that he turned on his heel and strode out of the camp.

Standing, Nasuada proclaimed, "Anyone who attacks the Urgals shall be punished as if he attacked a fellow human. See that word of this is posted in every company."

No sooner had she finished than Eragon noticed King Orrin approaching at a quick pace, his cape flapping around him. When he was close enough, he cried, "Nasuada! Is it true you met with an Urgal? What do you mean by it, and why wasn't I alerted sooner? I don't—"

He was interrupted as a sentry emerged from the ranks of gray tents, shouting, "A horseman approaches from the Empire!"

In an instant, King Orrin forgot his argument and joined Nasuada as she hurried toward the vanguard of the army, followed by at least a hundred people. Rather than stay among the crowd, Eragon pulled himself onto Saphira and let her carry him to their destination.

When Saphira halted at the ramparts, trenches, and rows of sharpened poles that protected the Varden's leading edge, Eragon saw a lone soldier riding at a furious clip across the bleak no-man's-land. Above him, the birds of prey swooped low to discover if the first course of their feast had arrived.

The soldier reined in his black stallion some thirty yards from the breastwork, keeping as much distance as possible between him and the Varden. He shouted, "By refusing King Galbatorix's generous terms of surrender, you choose death as your fate. No more shall we negotiate. The hand of friendship has turned into the fist of war! If any of you still hold regard for your rightful sovereign, the all-knowing, all-powerful King Galbatorix, then flee! None may stand before us once we set forth to cleanse Alagaësia of every miscreant, traitor, and subversive. And though it pains our lord—for he knows that most of these rebellious acts are instigated by bitter and misguided leaders—we shall gently chastise the unlawful territory known as Surda and return it to the benevolent rule of King

Galbatorix, he who sacrifices himself day and night for the good of his people. So flee, I say, or suffer the doom of your herald."

With that the soldier untied a canvas sack and flourished a severed head. He threw it into the air and watched it fall among the Varden, then turned his stallion, dug in his spurs, and galloped back toward the dark mass of Galbatorix's army.

"Shall I kill him?" asked Eragon.

Nasuada shook her head. "We will have our due soon enough. I won't violate the sanctity of envoys, even if the Empire has."

"As you—" He yelped with surprise and clutched Saphira's neck to keep from falling as she reared above the ramparts, planting her front legs upon the chartreuse bank. Opening her jaws, Saphira uttered a long, deep roar, much like Garzhvog had done, only this roar was a defiant challenge to their enemies, a warning of the wrath they had roused, and a clarion call to all who hated Galbatorix.

The sound of her trumpeting voice frightened the stallion so badly, he jinked to the right, slipped on the heated ground, and fell on his side. The soldier was thrown free of the horse and landed in a gout of fire that erupted at that very instant. He uttered a single cry so horrible, it made Eragon's scalp prickle, then was silent and still forevermore.

The birds began to descend.

The Varden cheered Saphira's accomplishment. Even Nasuada allowed herself a small smile. Then she clapped her hands and said, "They will attack at dawn, I think. Eragon, gather Du Vrangr Gata and prepare yourself for action. I will have orders for you within the hour." Taking Orrin by the shoulder, she guided him back toward the center of the compound, saying, "Sire, there are decisions we must make. I have a certain plan, but it will require . . ."

Let them come, said Saphira. The tip of her tail twitched like that of a cat stalking a rabbit. *They will all burn.*

WITCH'S BREW

Night had fallen on the Burning Plains. The roof of opaque smoke covered the moon and stars, plunging the land into profound darkness that was broken only by the sullen glow of the sporadic peat fires, and by the thousands of torches each army lit. From Eragon's position near the fore of the Varden, the Empire looked a dense nest of uncertain orange lights as large as any city.

As Eragon buckled the last piece of Saphira's armor onto her tail, he closed his eyes to maintain better contact with the magicians from Du Vrangr Gata. He had to learn to locate them at a moment's notice; his life would depend on communicating with them in a quick and timely manner. In turn, the magicians had to learn to recognize the touch of his mind so they did not block him when he needed their assistance.

Eragon smiled and said, "Hello, Orik." He opened his eyes to see Orik clambering up the low knuckle of rock where he and Saphira sat. The dwarf, who was fully armored, carried his Urgal-horn bow in his left hand.

Hunkering beside Eragon, Orik wiped his brow and shook his head. "How'd you know it was me? I was shielding myself."

Every consciousness feels different, explained Saphira. *Just like no two voices sound exactly the same.*

"Ah."

Eragon asked, "What brings you here?"

Orik shrugged. "It struck me you might appreciate a spot of company in this grim night. Especially since Arya's otherwise engaged and you don't have Murtagh with you for this battle."

And I wish I did, thought Eragon. Murtagh had been the only human who matched Eragon's skill with a sword, at least before the Agaetí Blödhren. Sparring with him had been one of Eragon's few pleasures during their time together. *I would have enjoyed fighting with you again, old friend.*

Remembering how Murtagh was killed—dragged underground by Urgals in Farthen Dûr—forced Eragon to confront a sobering truth: No matter how great a warrior you were, as often as not, pure chance dictated who lived and who died in war.

Orik must have sensed his mood, for he clapped Eragon on the shoulder and said, "You'll be fine. Just imagine how the soldiers out there feel, knowing they have to face *you* before long!"

Gratitude made Eragon smile again. "I'm glad you came."

The tip of Orik's nose reddened, and he glanced down, rolling his bow between gnarled hands. "Ah, well," he grumbled, "Hrothgar wouldn't much like it if I let something happen to you. Besides, we're foster brothers now, eh?"

Through Eragon, Saphira asked, *What about the other dwarves? Aren't they under your command?*

A twinkle sprang into Orik's eyes. "Why, yes, so they are. And they'll be joining us before long. Seeing as Eragon's a member of Dûrgrimst Ingeitum, it's only right we fight the Empire together. That way, the two of you won't be so vulnerable; you can concentrate on finding Galbatorix's magicians instead of defending yourselves from constant attacks."

"A good idea. Thank you." Orik grunted an acknowledgment. Then Eragon asked, "What do you think about Nasuada and the Urgals?"

"She made the right choice."

"You agree with her!"

"I do. I don't like it any more than you, but I do."

Silence enveloped them after that. Eragon sat against Saphira and stared out at the Empire, trying to prevent his growing anxiety from overwhelming him. Minutes dragged by. To him, the interminable waiting before a battle was as stressful as the actual fighting. He oiled Saphira's saddle, polished rust off his hauberk, and then resumed familiarizing himself with the minds of Du Vrangr Gata, anything to pass the time.

Over an hour later, he paused as he sensed two beings approaching from across the no-man's-land. *Angela? Solembum?* Puzzled and alarmed, he woke Orik—who had dozed off—and told him what he had discovered.

The dwarf frowned and drew his war ax from his belt. "I've only met the herbalist a few times, but she didn't seem like the sort who would betray us. She's been welcome among the Varden for decades."

"We should still find out what she was doing," said Eragon.

Together they picked their way through the camp to intercept the duo as they approached the fortifications. Angela soon trotted into the light, Solembum at her heels. The witch was muffled in a dark, full-length cloak that allowed her to blend into the mottled landscape. Displaying a surprising amount of alacrity, strength, and flexibility, she clambered over the many rows of breastwork the dwarves had engineered, swinging from pole to pole, leaping over trenches, and finally running helter-skelter down the steep face of the last rampart to stop, panting, by Saphira.

Throwing back the hood of her cloak, Angela flashed them a bright smile. "A welcoming committee! How thoughtful of you." As she spoke, the werecat shivered along his length, fur rippling. Then his outline blurred as if seen through cloudy water, resolving once more into the nude figure of a shaggy-haired boy. Angela dipped her hand into a leather purse at her belt and passed a child's tunic and breeches back to Solembum, along with the small black dagger he fought with.

"What were you doing out there?" asked Orik, peering at them with a suspicious gaze.

"Oh, this and that."

"I think you better tell us," said Eragon.

Her face hardened. "Is that so? Don't you trust Solembum and me?" The werecat bared his pointed teeth.

"Not really," admitted Eragon, but with a small smile.

"That's good," said Angela. She patted him on the cheek. "You'll live longer. If you must know, then, I was doing my best to help defeat the Empire, only my methods don't involve yelling and running around with a sword."

"And what exactly are your methods?" growled Orik.

Angela paused to roll up her cloak into a tight bundle, which she stored in her purse. "I'd rather not say; I want it to be a surprise. You won't have to wait long to find out. It'll start in a few hours."

Orik tugged on his beard. "What will start? If you can't give us a straight answer, we'll have to take you to Nasuada. Maybe she can wring some sense out of you."

"It's no use dragging me off to Nasuada," said Angela. "She gave me permission to cross lines."

"So you say," challenged Orik, ever more belligerent.

"And so I say," announced Nasuada, walking up to them from behind, as Eragon knew she would. He also sensed that she was accompanied by four Kull, one of whom was Garzhvog. Scowling, he turned to face them, making no attempt to hide his anger at the Urgals' presence.

"My Lady," muttered Eragon.

Orik was not as composed; he jumped back with a mighty oath, grasping his war ax. He quickly realized that they were not under attack and gave Nasuada a terse greeting. But his hand never left the haft of his weapon and his eyes never left the hulking Urgals. Angela seemed to have no such inhibitions. She paid Nasuada the respect due to her, then addressed the Urgals in their own harsh language, to which they answered with evident delight.

Nasuada drew Eragon off to the side so they could have a measure of privacy. There, she said, "I need you to put aside your feelings for a moment and judge what I am about to tell you with logic and reason. Can you do that?" He nodded, stiff-faced. "Good. I'm doing everything I can to ensure we don't lose tomorrow. It doesn't matter, though, how well we fight, or how well I lead the Varden, or even if we rout the Empire if *you*," she poked him in the chest, "are killed. Do you understand?" He nodded again. "There's nothing I can do to protect you if Galbatorix reveals himself; if he does, you will face him alone. Du Vrangr Gata poses no more of a threat to him than they do to you, and I'll not have them eradicated without reason."

"I have always known," said Eragon, "that I would face Galbatorix alone but for Saphira."

A sad smile touched Nasuada's lips. She looked very tired in the flickering torchlight. "Well, there's no reason to invent trouble where none exists. It's possible Galbatorix isn't even here." She did not seem to believe her own words, though. "In any case, I can at least keep you from dying from a sword in the gut. I heard what the dwarves intend to do, and I thought I could improve upon the concept. I asked Garzhvog and three of his rams to be your guards, so long as they agreed—which they have—to let you examine their minds for treachery."

Eragon went rigid. "You can't expect me to fight with those *monsters*. Besides, I already accepted the dwarves' offer to defend Saphira and me. They would take it poorly if I rejected them in favor of Urgals."

"Then they can both guard you," retorted Nasuada. She searched his face for a long time, looking for what he could not tell. "Oh, Eragon. I'd hoped you could see past your hate. What else would you do in my position?" She sighed when he remained silent. "If anyone has cause to hold a grudge against the Urgals, it is I. They killed my father. Yet I cannot allow that to interfere with deciding what's best for the Varden. . . . At least ask Saphira's opinion before you say yea or nay. I can order you to accept the Urgals' protection, but I would rather not."

You're being foolish, observed Saphira without prompting.

616

Foolish to not want Kull watching my back?

No, foolish to refuse help, no matter where it comes from, in our present situation. Think. You know what Oromis would do, and you know what he would say. Don't you trust his judgment?

He can't be right about everything, said Eragon.

That's no argument. . . . Search yourself, Eragon, and tell me whether I speak the truth. You know the correct path. I would be disappointed if you could not bring yourself to embrace it.

Saphira and Nasuada's cajoling only made Eragon more reluctant to agree. Still, he knew he had no choice. "All right, I'll let them guard me, but only if I find nothing suspicious in their minds. Will you promise that, after this battle, you won't make me work with an Urgal again?"

Nasuada shook her head. "I can't do that, not when it might hurt the Varden." She paused and said, "Oh, and Eragon?"

"Yes, my Lady?"

"In the event of my death, I have chosen you as my successor. If that should happen, I suggest you rely upon Jörmundur's advice—he has more experience than the other members of the Council of Elders—and I would expect you to place the welfare of those underneath you before all else. Am I clear, Eragon?"

Her announcement caught him by surprise. Nothing meant more to her than the Varden. Offering it to him was the greatest act of trust she could make. Her confidence humbled and touched him; he bowed his head. "I would strive to be as good a leader as you and Ajihad have been. You honor me, Nasuada."

"Yes, I do." Turning away from him, she rejoined the others.

Still overwhelmed by Nasuada's revelation, and finding his anger tempered by it, Eragon slowly walked back to Saphira. He studied Garzhvog and the other Urgals, trying to gauge their mood, but their features were so different from those he was accustomed to, he could discern nothing more than the broadest of emotions. Nor could he find any empathy within himself for the Urgals. To him, they were feral beasts that would kill him as soon as not and were incapable of love, kindness, or even true intelligence. In short, they were lesser beings.

Deep within his mind, Saphira whispered, *I'm sure Galbatorix is of the same opinion.*

And for good reason, he growled, intending to shock her. Suppressing his revulsion, he said out loud, "Nar Garzhvog, I am told that the four of you agreed to allow me within your minds."

"That is so, Firesword. Lady Nightstalker told us what was required. We are honored to have the chance to battle alongside such a mighty warrior, and one who has done so much for us."

"What do you mean? I have killed scores of your kin." Unbidden, excerpts from one of Oromis's scrolls rose in Eragon's memory. He remembered reading that Urgals, both male and female, determined their rank in society through combat, and that it was this practice, above all else, that had led to so many conflicts between Urgals and other races. Which meant, he realized, that if they admired his feats in battle, then they may have accorded him the same status as one of their war chiefs.

"By killing Durza, you freed us from his control. We are in your debt, Firesword. None of our rams will challenge you, and if you visit our halls, you and the dragon, Flametongue, will be welcomed as no outsiders ever before."

Of all the responses Eragon had expected, gratitude was the last, and it was the one he was least prepared to deal with. Unable to think of anything else, he said, "I won't forget." He switched his gaze to the other Urgals, then returned it to Garzhvog and his yellow eyes. "Are you ready?"

"Aye, Rider."

As Eragon reached toward Garzhvog's consciousness, it reminded him of how the Twins invaded his mind when he first entered Farthen Dûr. That observation was swept away as he immersed himself in the Urgal's identity. The very nature of his search—looking for malevolent intent perhaps hidden somewhere in Garzhvog's past—meant Eragon had to examine years of memories. Unlike the Twins, Eragon avoided causing deliberate pain, but he was not overly gentle. He could feel Garzhvog flinch with occasional pangs of discomfort. Like dwarves and elves, the mind of an Urgal possessed different elements than a human mind. Its structure emphasized rigidity and hierarchy—a result of the tribes the Urgals organized themselves into—but it felt rough and raw, brutal and cunning: the mind of a wild animal.

Though he made no effort to learn more about Garzhvog as an individual, Eragon could not help absorbing pieces of the Urgal's life. Garzhvog did not resist. Indeed, he seemed eager to share his experiences, to convince Eragon that Urgals were not his born enemies. *We cannot afford to have another Rider rise up who seeks to destroy us*, said Garzhvog. *Look well, O Firesword, and see if we are truly the monsters you call us. . . .*

So many images and sensations flashed between them, Eragon almost lost track: Garzhvog's childhood with the other members of his brood in a ramshackle village built deep in the heart of the Spine; his dam brushing his hair with an antler comb and singing a soft song; learning to hunt deer and other prey with his bare hands; growing larger and larger until it was apparent that the old blood still flowed in his veins and he would stand over eight feet tall, making him a Kull; the dozens of challenges he made, accepted, and won; venturing out of the village to gain renown, so he might mate, and gradually learning to hate, distrust, and fear—yes, *fear*— a world that had condemned his race; fighting in Farthen Dûr; discovering they had been manipulated by Durza; and realizing that their only hope of a better life was to put aside old differences, befriend the Varden, and see Galbatorix overthrown. Nowhere was there evidence that Garzhvog lied.

Eragon could not understand what he had seen. Tearing himself from Garzhvog's mind, he dove into each of the three remaining Urgals. Their memories confirmed the facts presented by Garzhvog. They made no attempt to conceal that they had killed humans, but it had been done at the command of Durza when the sorcerer controlled them, or when fighting humans over food or land. *We did what we had to in order to care for our families*, they said.

When he finished, Eragon stood before Garzhvog and knew the Urgal's bloodline was as regal as any prince's. He knew that, though uneducated, Garzhvog was a brilliant commander and as great a thinker and philosopher as Oromis himself. *He's certainly brighter than me*, admitted Eragon to Saphira. Baring his throat as a sign of respect, he said out loud, "Nar Garzhvog," and for the first time, he was aware of the lofty origins of the title *nar*. "I am proud to have you at my side. You may tell the Herndall that so long as the Urgals remain true to their word and do not turn against the Varden, I shall not oppose you." Eragon doubted that he would ever *like* an Urgal, but the iron certitude of his prejudice only a few minutes before now seemed ignorant, and he could not retain it in good conscience.

Saphira flicked him on the arm with her barbed tongue, making the mail clink together. *It takes courage to admit you were wrong.*

Only if you are afraid of looking foolish, and I would have looked far more foolish if I persisted with an erroneous belief.

Why, little one, you just said something wise. Despite her teasing, he could sense her warm pride in what he had accomplished.

"Again, we are in your debt, Firesword," said Garzhvog. He and the other Urgals pressed their fists against their jutting brows.

Eragon could tell that Nasuada wanted to know the details of what had just transpired but that she restrained herself. "Good. Now that this is settled, I must be off. Eragon, you'll receive my signal from Trianna when the time has arrived." With that she strode away into the darkness.

As Eragon settled against Saphira, Orik sidled up to him. "It's lucky we dwarves are going to be here, eh? We'll watch the Kull like hawks, we will. We won't let them catch you while your back is turned. The moment they attack, we'll cut their legs out from under them."

"I thought you agreed with Nasuada's accepting the Urgals' offer."

"That doesn't mean I trust them or want to be right alongside them, now does it?" Eragon smiled and did not bother to argue; it would be impossible to convince Orik that the Urgals were not rapacious killers when he himself had refused to consider the possibility until sharing an Urgal's memories.

The night lay heavy around them as they waited for dawn. Orik removed a whetstone from his pocket and proceeded to hone the edge of his curved ax. Once they arrived, the six other dwarves did the same, and the rasp of metal on stone filled the air with a grating chorus. The Kull sat back to back, chanting death songs under their breaths. Eragon spent the time casting wards about himself, Saphira, Nasuada, Orik, and even Arya. He knew that it was dangerous to protect so many, but he could not bear it if they were harmed. When he finished, he transferred what power he dared into the diamonds embedded within the belt of Beloth the Wise.

Eragon watched with interest as Angela clad herself in green and black armor and then, taking out a carved-wood case, assembled her staff-sword from two separate handles that attached in the middle and two blades of watered steel that threaded into the ends of the resulting pole. She twirled the completed weapon around her head a few times before seeming satisfied that it would hold up to the shock of battle.

The dwarves eyed her with disapproval, and Eragon heard one grumble, ". . . blasphemy that any but Dûrgrimst Quan should wield the hûthvír."

After that the only sound was the discordant music of the dwarves honing their blades.

It was near dawn when the cries began. Eragon and Saphira noticed them first because of their heightened senses, but the agonized screams were soon loud enough for the others to hear. Rising to his feet, Orik looked out toward the Empire, where the cacophony originated. "What manner of creatures are they torturing to extract such fearsome howls? The sound chills the marrow in my bones, it does."

"I told you that you wouldn't have to wait very long," said Angela. Her former cheer had deserted her; she looked pale, drawn, and gray in the face, as if she were ill.

From his post by Saphira, Eragon asked, "*You* did this?"

"Aye. I poisoned their stew, their bread, their drink—anything I could get my hands on. Some will die now, others will die later as the various toxins take their toll. I slipped the officers nightshade and other such poisons so they will hallucinate in battle." She tried to smile, but without much success. "Not a very honorable way to fight, I suppose, but I'd rather do this than be killed. Confusion to our enemies and all that."

"Only a coward or a thief uses poison!" exclaimed Orik. "What glory is there in defeating a sick opponent?" The screams intensified even as he spoke.

Angela gave an unpleasant laugh. "Glory? If you want glory, there are thousands more troops I didn't poison. I'm sure you will have your fill of *glory* by the end of today."

"Is this why you needed the equipment in Orrin's tent?" asked Eragon. He found her deed repugnant but did not pretend to know whether it was good or evil. It was necessary. Angela had poisoned the soldiers for the same reason Nasuada had accepted the Urgals' offer of friendship—because it might be their only hope of survival.

"That's right."

The soldiers' wails increased in number until Eragon longed to plug his ears and block out the sound. It made him wince and fidget, and it put his teeth on edge. He forced himself to listen, though. This was the cost of resisting the Empire. It would be wrong to ignore it. So he sat with his hands clenched into fists and his jaw forming painful knots while the Burning Plains echoed with the disembodied voices of dying men.

THE STORM BREAKS

The first horizontal rays of dawn already streaked across the land when Trianna said to Eragon, *It is time*. A surge of energy erased Eragon's sleepiness. Jumping to his feet, he shouted the word to everyone around him, even as he clambered into Saphira's saddle, pulling his new bow from its quiver. The Kull and dwarves surrounded Saphira, and together they hurried down the breastwork until they reached the opening that had been cleared during the night.

The Varden poured through the gap, quiet as they could be. Rank upon rank of warriors marched past, their armor and weapons padded with rags so no sound would alert the Empire of their approach. Saphira joined the procession when Nasuada appeared on a roan charger in the midst of the men, Arya and Trianna by her side. The five of them acknowledged each other with quick glances, nothing more.

During the night, the mephitic vapors had accumulated low to the ground, and now the dim morning light gilded the turgid clouds, turning them opaque. Thus, the Varden managed to cross three-quarters of the no-man's-land before they were seen by the Empire's sentries. As the alarm horns rang out before them, Nasuada shouted, "Now, Eragon! Tell Orrin to strike. To me, men of the Varden! Fight to win back your homes. Fight to guard your wives and children! Fight to overthrow Galbatorix! Attack and bathe your blades in the blood of our enemies! Charge!" She spurred her horse forward, and with a great bellow, the men followed, shaking their weapons above their heads.

Eragon conveyed Nasuada's order to Barden, the spellcaster who rode with King Orrin. A moment later, he heard the drumming of hooves as Orrin and his cavalry—accompanied by the rest of the Kull, who could run as fast as horses—galloped out of the east. They charged into the Empire's flank, pinning the soldiers against the Jiet River and distracting them long enough for the Varden to cross the remainder of the distance between them without opposition.

The two armies collided with a deafening roar. Pikes clashed against spears, hammers against shields, swords against helms, and above it all whirled the hungry gore-crows uttering their harsh croaks, driven into a frenzy by the smell of fresh meat below.

Eragon's heart leaped within his chest. *I must now kill or be killed.* Almost immediately he felt his wards drawing upon his strength as they deflected attacks from Arya, Orik, Nasuada, and Saphira.

Saphira held back from the leading edge of the battle, for they would be too exposed to Galbatorix's magicians at the front. Taking a deep breath, Eragon began to search for those magicians with his mind, firing arrows all the while.

Du Vrangr Gata found the first enemy spellcaster. The instant he was alerted, Eragon reached out to the woman who made the discovery, and from there to the foe she grappled with. Bringing the full power of his will to bear, Eragon demolished the magician's resistance, took control of his consciousness—doing his best to ignore the man's terror—determined which troops the man was guarding, and slew the man with one of the twelve words of death. Without pause, Eragon located the minds of each of the now-unprotected soldiers and killed them as well. The Varden cheered as the knot of men went limp.

The ease with which he slew them amazed Eragon. The soldiers had had no chance to escape or fight back. *How different from Farthen Dûr*, he thought. Though he marveled at the perfection of his skills, the deaths sickened him. But there was no time to dwell on it.

Recovering from the Varden's initial assault, the Empire began to man their engines of war: catapults that cast round missiles of hard-baked ceramic, trebuchets armed with barrels of liquid fire, and ballistae that bombarded the attackers with a hail of arrows six feet long. The ceramic balls and the liquid fire caused terrific damage when they landed. One ball exploded against the ground not ten yards from Saphira. As Eragon ducked behind his shield, a jagged fragment spun toward his head, only to be stopped dead in the air by one of his wards. He blinked at the sudden loss of energy.

The engines soon stalled the Varden's advance, sowing mayhem wherever they aimed. *They have to be destroyed if we're going to last long enough to wear down the Empire,* realized Eragon. It would be easy for Saphira to dismantle the machines, but she dared not fly among the soldiers for fear of an attack by magic.

Breaking through the Varden lines, eight soldiers stormed toward Saphira, jabbing at her with pikes. Before Eragon could draw Zar'roc, the dwarves and Kull eliminated the entire group.

"A good fight!" roared Garzhvog.

"A good fight!" agreed Orik with a bloody grin.

Eragon did not use spells against the engines; they would be protected against any conceivable enchantment. *Unless . . .* Extending himself, he found the mind of a soldier who tended one of the catapults. Though he was sure the soldier was defended by some magician, Eragon was able to gain dominance over him and direct his actions from afar. He guided the man up to the weapon, which was being loaded, then had him use his sword to hack at the skein of twisted rope that powered the machine. The rope was too thick to sever before the soldier was dragged away by his comrades, but the damage was already done. With a mighty *crack*, the partially wound skein broke, sending the arm of the catapult flying backward and injuring several men. His lips curled in a grim smile, Eragon proceeded to the next catapult and, in short order, disabled the remainder of the engines.

Returning to himself, Eragon became aware of dozens of the Varden collapsing around Saphira; one of Du Vrangr Gata had been overwhelmed. He uttered a dreadful curse and flung himself back along the trail of magic as he searched for the man who cast the fatal spell, entrusting the welfare of his body to Saphira and his guards.

For over an hour, Eragon hunted Galbatorix's magicians, but to little avail, for they were wily and cunning and did not directly attack him. Their reticence puzzled Eragon until he tore from the mind of one spellcaster—moments before he committed suicide—the thought, . . . *ordered not to kill you or the dragon . . . not to kill you or the dragon.*

That answers my question, he said to Saphira, *but* why *does Galbatorix still want us alive? We've made it clear we support the Varden.*

Before she could respond, Nasuada appeared before them, her face streaked with filth and gore, her shield covered with dents, blood sheeting down her left leg from a wound on her thigh. "Eragon," she gasped. "I need you, both of you, to fight, to show yourselves and embolden the men . . . to frighten the soldiers."

Her condition shocked Eragon. "Let me heal you first," he cried, afraid she might faint. *I should have put more wards around her.*

"No! I can wait, but we are lost unless you stem the tide of soldiers." Her eyes were glazed and empty, blank holes in her face. "We need . . . a Rider." She swayed in her saddle.

Eragon saluted her with Zar'roc. "You have one, my Lady."

"Go," she said, "and may what gods there are watch over you."

Eragon was too high on Saphira's back to strike his enemies below, so he dismounted and positioned himself by her right paw. To Orik and Garzhvog, he said, "Protect Saphira's left side. And whatever you do, don't get in our way."

"You will be overrun, Fireword."

626

"No," said Eragon, "I won't. Now take your places!" As they did, he put his hand on Saphira's leg and looked her in one clear-cut sapphire eye. *Shall we dance, friend of my heart?*

We shall, little one.

Then he and she merged their identities to a greater degree than ever before, vanquishing all differences between them to become a single entity. They bellowed, leaped forward, and forged a path to the front line. Once there, Eragon could not tell from whose mouth emanated the ravenous jet of flame that consumed a dozen soldiers, cooking them in their mail, nor whose arm it was that brought Zar'roc down in an arc, cleaving a soldier's helm in half.

The metallic scent of blood clogged the air, and curtains of smoke wafted over the Burning Plains, alternately concealing and revealing the knots, clumps, ranks, and battalions of thrashing bodies. Overhead, the carrion birds waited for their meal and the sun climbed in the firmament toward noon.

From the minds of those around them, Eragon and Saphira caught glimpses of how they appeared. Saphira was always noticed first: a great ravening creature with claws and fangs dyed red, who slew all in her path with swipes of her paws and lashes of her tail and with billowing waves of flame that engulfed entire platoons of soldiers. Her brilliant scales glittered like stars and nearly blinded her foes with their reflected light. Next they saw Eragon running alongside Saphira. He moved faster than the soldiers could react and, with strength beyond men, splintered shields with a single blow, rent armor, and clove the swords of those who opposed him. Shot and dart cast at him fell to the pestilent ground ten feet away, stopped by his wards.

It was harder for Eragon—and, by extension, Saphira—to fight his own race than it had been to fight the Urgals in Farthen Dûr. Every time he saw a frightened face or looked into a soldier's mind, he thought, *This could be me.* But he and Saphira could afford no mercy; if a soldier stood before them, he died.

Three times they sallied forth and three times Eragon and

Saphira slew every man in the Empire's first few ranks before retreating to the main body of the Varden to avoid being surrounded. By the end of their last attack, Eragon had to reduce or eliminate certain wards around Arya, Orik, Nasuada, Saphira, and himself in order to keep the spells from exhausting him too quickly. For though his strength was great, so too were the demands of battle.

Ready? he asked Saphira after a brief respite. She growled an affirmative.

A cloud of arrows whistled toward Eragon the instant he dove back into combat. Fast as an elf, he dodged the bulk of them—since his magic no longer protected him from such missiles—caught twelve on his shield, and stumbled as one struck his belly and one his side. Neither shaft pierced his armor, but they knocked the wind out of him and left bruises the size of apples. *Don't stop! You've dealt with worse pain than this before,* he told himself.

Rushing a cluster of eight soldiers, Eragon darted from one to the next, knocking aside their pikes and jabbing Zar'roc like a deadly bolt of lightning. The fighting had dulled his reflexes, though, and one soldier managed to drive his pike through Eragon's hauberk, slicing his left triceps.

The soldiers cringed as Saphira roared.

Eragon took advantage of the distraction to fortify himself with energy stored within the ruby in Zar'roc's pommel and then to kill the three remaining soldiers.

Sweeping her tail over him, Saphira knocked a score of men out of his way. In the lull that followed, Eragon looked over at his throbbing arm and said, "Waíse heill." He also healed his bruises, relying upon Zar'roc's ruby, as well as the diamonds in the belt of Beloth the Wise.

Then the two of them pressed onward.

Eragon and Saphira choked the Burning Plains with mountains of their enemies, and yet the Empire never faltered or fell back. For every man they killed, another stepped forth to take his place. A sense of hopelessness engulfed Eragon as the mass of soldiers gradually forced the Varden to retreat toward their own camp. He saw his despair mirrored in the faces of Nasuada, Arya, King Orrin, and even Angela when he passed them in battle.

All our training and we still can't stop the Empire, raged Eragon. *There are just too many soldiers! We can't keep this up forever. And Zar'roc and the belt are almost depleted.*

You can draw energy from your surroundings if you have to.

I won't, not unless I kill another of Galbatorix's magicians and can take it from the soldiers. Otherwise, I'll just be hurting the rest of the Varden, since there are no plants or animals here I can use to support us.

As the long hours dragged by, Eragon grew sore and weary and—stripped of many of his arcane defenses—accumulated dozens of minor injuries. His left arm went numb from the countless blows that hammered his mangled shield. A scratch on his forehead kept blinding him with rivulets of hot, sweat-mixed blood. He thought one of his fingers might be broken.

Saphira fared no better. The soldiers' armor tore the inside of her mouth, dozens of swords and arrows cut her unprotected wings, and a javelin punctured one of her own plates of armor, wounding her in the shoulder. Eragon saw the spear coming and tried to deflect it with a spell but was too slow. Whenever Saphira moved, she splattered the ground with hundreds of drops of blood.

Beside them, three of Orik's warriors fell, and two of the Kull.

And the sun began its descent toward evening.

As Eragon and Saphira prepared for their seventh and final assault, a trumpet sounded in the east, loud and clear, and King Orrin shouted, "The dwarves are here! The dwarves are here!"

Dwarves? Eragon blinked and glanced around, confused. He saw nothing but soldiers. Then a jolt of excitement raced through him as he understood. *The dwarves!* He climbed onto Saphira and she jumped into the air, hanging for a moment on her tattered wings as they surveyed the battlefield.

It was true—a great host marched out of the east toward the

Burning Plains. At its head strode King Hrothgar, clad in gold mail, his jeweled helm upon his brow, and Volund, his ancient war hammer, gripped in his iron fist. The dwarf king raised Volund in greeting when he saw Eragon and Saphira.

Eragon howled at the top of his lungs and returned the gesture, brandishing Zar'roc in the air. A surge of renewed vigor made him forget his wounds and feel fierce and determined again. Saphira added her voice to his, and the Varden looked to her with hope, while the Empire's soldiers hesitated with fear.

"What did you see?" cried Orik as Saphira dropped back to earth. "Is it Hrothgar? How many warriors did he bring?"

Ecstatic with relief, Eragon stood in his stirrups and shouted, "Take heart, King Hrothgar is here! And it looks like every single dwarf is behind him! We'll crush the Empire!" After the men stopped cheering, he added, "Now take your swords and remind these flea-bitten cowards why they should fear us. Charge!"

Just as Saphira leaped toward the soldiers, Eragon heard a second cry, this one from the west: "A ship! A ship is coming up the Jiet River!"

"Blast it," he snarled. *We can't let a ship land if it's bringing reinforcements for the Empire.* Contacting Trianna, he said, *Tell Nasuada that Saphira and I will take care of this. We'll sink the ship if it's from Galbatorix.*

As you wish, Argetlam, replied the sorceress.

Without hesitation, Saphira took flight, circling high over the trampled, smoking plain. As the relentless clamor of combat faded from his ears, Eragon took a deep breath, feeling his mind clear. Below, he was surprised by how scattered both armies had become. The Empire and the Varden had disintegrated into a series of smaller groups contending against one another over the entire breadth and width of the Burning Plains. It was into this confused tumult that the dwarves inserted themselves, catching the Empire from the side—as Orrin had done earlier with his cavalry.

Eragon lost sight of the battle when Saphira turned to her left and soared through the clouds in the direction of the Jiet River. A gust of wind blew the peat smoke out of their way and unveiled a large three-masted ship riding upon the orange water, rowing against the current with two banks of oars. The ship was scarred and damaged and flew no colors to declare its allegiance. Nevertheless, Eragon readied himself to destroy the vessel. As Saphira dove toward it, he lifted Zar'roc overhead and loosed his savage war cry.

✦　✦　✦

CONVERGENCE

Roran stood at the prow of the *Dragon Wing* and listened to the oars swish through the water. He had just finished a stint rowing and a cold, jagged ache permeated his right shoulder. *Will I always have to deal with this reminder of the Ra'zac?* He wiped the sweat from his face and ignored the discomfort, concentrating instead on the river ahead, which was obscured by a bank of sooty clouds.

Elain joined him at the railing. She rested a hand on her swollen belly. "The water looks evil," she said. "Perhaps we should have stayed in Dauth, rather than drag ourselves in search of more trouble."

He feared she spoke the truth. After the Boar's Eye, they had sailed east from the Southern Isles back to the coast and then up the mouth of the Jiet River to Surda's port city of Dauth. By the time they made landfall, their stores were exhausted and the villagers sickly.

Roran had every intention of staying in Dauth, especially after they received an enthusiastic welcome from its governor, Lady Alarice. But that was before he was told about Galbatorix's army. If the Varden were defeated, he would never see Katrina again. So, with the help of Jeod, he convinced Horst and many of the other villagers that if they wanted to live in Surda, safe from the Empire, they had to row up the Jiet River and assist the Varden. It was a difficult task, but in the end Roran prevailed. And once they told

Lady Alarice about their quest, she gave them all the supplies they wanted.

Since then, Roran often wondered if he made the right choice. By now everyone hated living on the *Dragon Wing*. People were tense and short-tempered, a situation only aggravated by the knowledge they were sailing toward a battle. *Was it all selfishness on my part?* wondered Roran. *Did I really do this for the benefit of the villagers, or only because it will bring me one step closer to finding Katrina?*

"Perhaps we should have," he said to Elain.

Together they watched as a thick layer of smoke gathered overhead, darkening the sky, obscuring the sun, and filtering the remaining light so that everything below was colored a nauseating hue of orange. It produced an eerie twilight the likes of which Roran had never imagined. The sailors on deck looked about fearfully and muttered charms of protection, pulling out stone amulets to ward off the evil eye.

"Listen," said Elain. She tilted her head. "What is that?"

Roran strained his ears and caught the faint ring of metal striking metal. "That," he said, "is the sound of our destiny." Twisting, he shouted back over his shoulder, "Captain, there's fighting just ahead!"

"Man the ballistae!" roared Uthar. "Double-time on those oars, Bonden. An' every able-bodied man jack among you better be ready or you'll be using your guts for pillows!"

Roran remained where he was as the *Dragon Wing* exploded with activity. Despite the increase in noise, he could still hear swords and shields clanging together in the distance. The screams of men were audible now, as were the roars of some giant beast.

He glanced over as Jeod joined them at the prow. The merchant's face was pale. "Have you ever been in battle before?" asked Roran.

The knob in Jeod's throat bobbed as he swallowed and shook his head. "I got into plenty of fights along with Brom, but never anything of this scale."

"A first for both of us, then."

The bank of smoke thinned on the right, providing them with a glimpse of a dark land that belched forth fire and putrid orange vapor and was covered with masses of struggling men. It was impossible to tell who was the Empire and who was the Varden, but it was apparent to Roran that the battle could tip in either direction given the right nudge. *We can provide that nudge.*

Then a voice echoed over the water as a man shouted, "A ship! A ship is coming up the Jiet River!"

"You should go belowdecks," said Roran to Elain. "It won't be safe for you here." She nodded and hurried to the fore hatchway, where she climbed down the ladder, closing the opening behind her. A moment later, Horst bounded up to the prow and handed Roran one of Fisk's shields.

"Thought you might need that," said Horst.

"Thanks. I—"

Roran stopped as the air around them vibrated, as if from a mighty concussion. *Thud.* His teeth jarred together. *Thud.* His ears hurt from the pressure. Close upon the heels of the second impact came a third—*thud*—and with it a raw-throated yell that Roran recognized, for he had heard it many times in his childhood. He looked up and beheld a gigantic sapphire dragon diving out of the shifting clouds. And on the dragon's back, at the juncture between its neck and shoulders, sat his cousin, Eragon.

It was not the Eragon he remembered, but rather as if an artist had taken his cousin's base features and enhanced them, streamlined them, making them both more noble and more feline. This Eragon was garbed like a prince, in fine cloth and armor—though tarnished by the grime of war—and in his right hand he wielded a blade of iridescent red. This Eragon, Roran knew, could kill without hesitation. This Eragon was powerful and implacable. . . . This Eragon could slay the Ra'zac and their mounts and help him to rescue Katrina.

Flaring its translucent wings, the dragon pulled up sharply and hung before the ship. Then Eragon met Roran's eyes.

Until that moment, Roran had not completely believed Jeod's story about Eragon and Brom. Now, as he stared at his cousin, a wave of confused emotions washed over him. *Eragon is a Rider!* It seemed inconceivable that the slight, moody, overeager boy he grew up with had turned into this fearsome warrior. Seeing him alive again filled Roran with unexpected joy. Yet, at the same time, a terrible, familiar anger welled up inside him over Eragon's role in Garrow's death and the siege of Carvahall. In those few seconds, Roran knew not whether he loved or hated Eragon.

He stiffened with alarm as a vast and alien being touched his mind. From that consciousness emanated Eragon's voice: *Roran?*

"Aye."

Think your answers and I'll hear them. Is everyone from Carvahall with you?

Just about.

How did you . . . No, we can't go into it; there's no time. Stay where you are until the battle is decided. Better yet, go back farther down the river, where the Empire can't attack you.

We have to talk, Eragon. You have much to answer for.

Eragon hesitated with a troubled expression, then said, *I know. But not now, later.* With no visible prompting, the dragon veered away from the ship and flew off to the east, vanishing in the haze over the Burning Plains.

In an awed voice, Horst said, "A Rider! A real Rider! I never thought I'd see the day, much less that it would be Eragon." He shook his head. "I guess you told us the truth, eh, Longshanks?" Jeod grinned in response, looking like a delighted child.

Their words sounded muted to Roran as he stared at the deck, feeling like he was about to explode with tension. A host of unanswerable questions assailed him. He forced himself to ignore them. *I can't think about Eragon now. We have to fight. The Varden must defeat the Empire.*

A rising tide of fury consumed him. He had experienced this before, a berserk frenzy that allowed him to overcome nearly any obstacle, to move objects he could not shift ordinarily, to face an enemy in combat and feel no fear. It gripped him now, a fever in his veins, quickening his breath and setting his heart a-pounding.

He pushed himself off the railing, ran the length of the ship to the quarterdeck, where Uthar stood by the wheel, and said, "Ground the ship."

"What?"

"Ground the ship, I say! Stay here with the rest of the soldiers and use the ballistae to wreak what havoc you can, keep the *Dragon Wing* from being boarded, and guard our families with your lives. Understand?"

Uthar stared at him with flat eyes, and Roran feared he would not accept the orders. Then the scarred sailor grunted and said, "Aye, aye, Stronghammer."

Horst's heavy tread preceded his arrival at the quarterdeck. "What do you intend to do, Roran?"

"Do?" Roran laughed and spun widdershins to stand toe to toe with the smith. "Do? Why, I intend to alter the fate of Alagaësia!"

✦ ✦ ✦

ELDEST

ragon barely noticed as Saphira carried him back into the swirling confusion of the battle. He had known that Roran was at sea, but it never occurred to him that Roran might be heading for Surda, nor that they would reunite in this manner. And Roran's eyes! His eyes seemed to bore into Eragon, questioning, relieved, enraged . . . *accusing*. In them, Eragon saw that his cousin had learned of Eragon's role in Garrow's death and had not yet forgiven him.

It was only when a sword bounced off his greaves that Eragon returned his attention to his surroundings. He unleashed a hoarse shout and slashed downward, cutting away the soldier who struck him. Cursing himself for being so careless, Eragon reached out to Trianna and said, *No one on that ship is an enemy. Spread the word that they're not to be attacked. Ask Nasuada if, as a favor to us, she can send a herald to explain the situation to them and see that they stay away from the fighting.*

As you wish, Argetlam.

From the western flank of the battle, where she alighted, Saphira traversed the Burning Plains in a few giant leaps, stopping before Hrothgar and his dwarves. Dismounting, Eragon went to the king, who said, "Hail, Argetlam! Hail, Saphira! The elves seem to have done more for you than they promised." Beside him stood Orik.

"No, sir, it was the dragons."

"Really? I must hear your adventures once our bloody work here is done. I'm glad you accepted my offer to become Dûrgrimst Ingeitum. It is an honor to have you as mine kin."

"And you mine."

Hrothgar laughed, then turned to Saphira and said, "I still haven't forgotten your vow to mend Isidar Mithrim, dragon. Even now, our artisans are assembling the star sapphire in the center of Tronjheim. I look forward to seeing it whole once again."

She bowed her head. *As I promised, so it shall be.*

After Eragon repeated her words, Hrothgar reached out with a gnarled finger and tapped one of the metal plates on her side. "I see you wear our armor. I hope it has served you well."

Very well, King Hrothgar, said Saphira through Eragon. *It has saved me many an injury.*

Hrothgar straightened and lifted Volund, a twinkle in his deep-set eyes. "Well then, shall we march out and test it once again in the forge of war?" He looked back at his warriors and shouted, "Akh sartos oen dûrgrimst!"

"Vor Hrothgarz korda! Vor Hrothgarz korda!"

Eragon looked at Orik, who translated with a mighty yell, "By Hrothgar's hammer!" Joining the chant, Eragon ran with the dwarf king toward the crimson ranks of soldiers, Saphira by his side.

Now at last, with the help of the dwarves, the battle turned in favor of the Varden. Together they pushed back the Empire, dividing them, crushing them, forcing Galbatorix's vast army to abandon positions they had held since morn. Their efforts were helped by the fact that more of Angela's poisons had taken effect. Many of the Empire's officers behaved irrationally, giving orders that made it easier for the Varden to penetrate deeper into the army, sowing chaos as they went. The soldiers seemed to realize that fortune no longer smiled upon them, for hundreds surrendered, or defected outright and turned on their former comrades, or threw down their weapons and fled.

And the day passed into the late afternoon.

Eragon was in the midst of fighting two soldiers when a flaming javelin roared past overhead and buried itself in one of the Empire's command tents twenty yards away, igniting the fabric. Dispatching his opponents, Eragon glanced back and saw dozens of fiery missiles arcing out from the ship on the Jiet River. *What are you playing at, Roran?* wondered Eragon before charging the next batch of soldiers.

Soon afterward, a horn echoed from the rear of the Empire's army, then another and another. Someone began to pound a sonorous drum, the peals of which stilled the field as everyone looked about for the source of the beat. Even as Eragon watched, an ominous figure detached itself from the horizon in the north and rose up in the lurid sky over the Burning Plains. The gore-crows scattered before the barbed black shadow, which balanced motionless upon the thermals. At first Eragon thought it a Lethrblaka, one of the Ra'zac's mounts. Then a ray of light escaped the clouds and struck the figure crossways from the west.

A red dragon floated above them, glowing and sparkling in the sunbeam like a bed of blood-red coals. His wing membranes were the color of wine held before a lantern. His claws and teeth and the spikes along his spine were white as snow. In his vermilion eyes there gleamed a terrible glee. On his back was fixed a saddle, and in that saddle sat a man garbed in polished steel armor and armed with a hand-and-a-half sword.

Dread clutched at Eragon. *Galbatorix managed to get another dragon to hatch!*

Then the man in steel raised his left hand and a shaft of crackling ruby energy sprang from his palm and smote Hrothgar on the breast. The dwarf spellcasters cried out with agony as the energy from their bodies was consumed trying to block the attack. They collapsed, dead, then Hrothgar clutched his heart and toppled to the ground. The dwarves gave a great groan of despair as they saw their king fall.

"No!" cried Eragon, and Saphira roared in protest. He glared with hate at the enemy Rider. *I'll kill you for that.*

Eragon knew that, as they were, he and Saphira were too tired to confront such a mighty opponent. Glancing around, Eragon spotted a horse lying in the mud, a spear through its side. The stallion was still alive. Eragon put his hand on its neck and murmured, *Sleep, brother.* Then he transferred the horse's remaining vitality into himself and Saphira. It was not enough energy to restore all their strength, but it soothed their aching muscles and stopped their limbs from shaking.

Rejuvenated, Eragon leaped onto Saphira, shouting, "Orik, take command of your kinsmen!" Across the field, he saw Arya gaze at him with concern. He put her out of his mind as he tightened the saddle straps around his legs. Then Saphira launched herself toward the red dragon, pumping her wings at a furious rate to gain the necessary speed.

I hope you remember your lessons with Glaedr, he said. He tightened his grip on his shield.

Saphira did not answer him but roared out with her thoughts at the other dragon, *Traitor! Egg breaker, oath breaker, murderer!* Then as one, she and Eragon assaulted the minds of the pair, seeking to overwhelm their defenses. The consciousness of the Rider felt strange to Eragon, as if it contained multitudes; scores of distinct voices whispered in the caverns of his mind, like imprisoned spirits begging for release.

The instant they made contact, the Rider retaliated with a blast of pure force greater than any even Oromis was capable of summoning. Eragon retreated deep behind his own barriers, frantically reciting a scrap of doggerel Oromis taught him to use in such predicaments:

> *Under a cold and empty winter sky*
> *Stood a wee, small man with a silver sword.*
> *He jumped and stabbed in a fevered frenzy,*
> *Fighting the shadows massed before him. . . .*

The siege on Eragon's mind abated as Saphira and the red dragon crashed together, two incandescent meteors colliding head-on.

They grappled, kicking each other's bellies with their hind legs. Their talons produced hideous screeches as they grated against Saphira's armor and the red dragon's flat scales. The red dragon was smaller than Saphira, but thicker in his legs and shoulders. He managed to kick her off for a moment, then they closed again, each struggling to get their jaws around the other's neck.

It was all Eragon could do to keep hold of Zar'roc as the dragons tumbled toward the ground, battering one another with terrible blows from their feet and tails. No more than fifty yards above the Burning Plains, Saphira and the red dragon disengaged, struggling to regain altitude. Once she halted her descent, Saphira reared her head, like a snake about to strike, and loosed a thick torrent of fire.

It never reached its destination; twelve feet from the red dragon, the fire bifurcated and passed harmlessly on either side. *Blast it*, thought Eragon. Even as the red dragon opened its maw to retaliate, Eragon cried, "Skölir nosu fra brisingr!" He was just in time. The conflagration swirled around them but did not even scorch Saphira's scales.

Now Saphira and the red dragon raced up through the striated smoke into the clear, chill sky beyond, darting back and forth as they tried to climb above their opponent. The red dragon nipped Saphira's tail, and she and Eragon yelped with shared pain. Panting from the effort, Saphira executed a tight backward loop, ending up behind the dragon, who then pivoted to the left and tried to spiral up and over Saphira.

While the dragons dueled with increasingly complex acrobatics, Eragon became aware of a disturbance on the Burning Plains: the spellcasters of Du Vrangr Gata were beset by two new magicians from the Empire. These magicians were far more powerful than those who had preceded them. They had already killed one of Du Vrangr Gata and were battering past the barriers of a second. Eragon heard Trianna scream with her mind, *Shadeslayer! You have to help us! We can't stop them. They'll kill all the Varden. Help us, it's the—*

Her voice was lost to him as the Rider stabbed at his consciousness. "This must end," spat Eragon between clenched teeth as he strove to withstand the onslaught. Over Saphira's neck, he saw the red dragon dive toward them, angling beneath Saphira. Eragon dared not open his mind enough to talk with Saphira, so he said out loud, "Catch me!" With two strokes of Zar'roc, he severed the straps around his legs and jumped off Saphira's back.

This is insane, thought Eragon. He laughed with giddy exhilaration as the feeling of weightlessness took hold of him. The rush of air tore off his helm and made his eyes water and sting. Releasing his shield, Eragon spread out his arms and legs, as Oromis had taught him, in order to stabilize his flight. Below, the steel-clad Rider noticed Eragon's action. The red dragon shied to Eragon's left but could not evade him. Eragon lashed out with Zar'roc as the dragon's flank flashed by, and he felt the blade sink into the creature's hamstring before his momentum carried him past.

The dragon roared in agony.

The impact of the blow sent Eragon spinning up, down, and around. By the time he managed to stop his rotation, he had plummeted through the cloud cover and was heading toward a swift and fatal landing on the Burning Plains. He could stop himself with magic if he had to, but it would drain his last reserves of energy. He glanced over both his shoulders. *Come on, Saphira, where are you?*

As if in answer, she dropped out of the foul smoke, her wings pressed tight against her body. She swooped underneath him and opened her wings a bit to slow her fall. Careful not to impale himself on one of her spikes, Eragon maneuvered himself back into the saddle, welcoming the return of gravity as she pulled out of the dive.

Never do that to me again, she snapped.

He surveyed the steaming blood that laced Zar'roc's blade. *It worked, didn't it?*

His satisfaction disappeared as he realized that his stunt had placed Saphira at the mercy of the red dragon. He hurtled at her from above, harrying her this way and that as he forced her toward the ground. Saphira tried to maneuver out from under him, but every time she did, he dove at her, biting and buffeting her with his wings in order to make her change course.

The dragons twisted and lunged until their tongues lolled out of their mouths, their tails drooped, and they gave up flapping and merely glided.

His mind once again closed to all contact, friendly or not, Eragon said out loud, "Land, Saphira; it's no good. I'll fight him on the ground."

With a grunt of weary resignation, Saphira descended to the nearest flat open area, a small stone plateau set along the western edge of the Jiet River. The water had turned red from the blood pouring into it from the battle. Eragon jumped off Saphira once she alighted on the plateau and tested his footing. It was smooth and hard, with nothing to trip on. He nodded, pleased.

A few seconds later, the red dragon rushed by overhead and settled on the opposite side of the plateau. He held his left hind leg off the ground to avoid aggravating his wound: a long gash that nearly severed the muscle. The dragon trembled his entire length, like an injured dog. He tried to hop forward, then stopped and snarled at Eragon.

The enemy Rider unbuckled his legs and slid down the uninjured side of his dragon. Then he walked around the dragon and examined his leg. Eragon let him; he knew how much pain it would cause the man to see the damage inflicted on his bonded partner. He waited too long, though, for the Rider muttered a few indecipherable words, and within the span of three seconds the dragon's injury was healed.

Eragon shivered with fear. *How could he do that so quickly, and with such a short spell?* Still, whoever he might be, the new Rider certainly was not Galbatorix, whose dragon was black.

Eragon clung to that knowledge as he stepped forward to

confront the Rider. As they met in the center of the plateau, Saphira and the red dragon circled in the background.

The Rider grasped his sword with both hands and swung it over his head toward Eragon, who lifted Zar'roc to defend himself. Their blades collided with a burst of crimson sparks. Then Eragon shoved back his opponent and started a complex series of blows. He stabbed and parried, dancing on light feet as he forced the steel-clad Rider to retreat toward the edge of the plateau.

When they reached the edge, the Rider held his ground, fending off Eragon's attacks, no matter how clever. *It's as if he can anticipate my every move*, thought Eragon, frustrated. If he were rested, it would have been easy for him to defeat the Rider, but as it was, he could make no headway. The Rider did not have the speed and strength of an elf, but his technical skill was better than Vanir's and as good as Eragon's.

Eragon felt a touch of panic when his initial surge of energy began to subside and he had accomplished nothing more than a slight scratch across the Rider's gleaming breastplate. The last reserves of power stored in Zar'roc's ruby and the belt of Beloth the Wise were only enough to maintain his exertions for another minute. Then the Rider took a step forward. Then another. And before Eragon knew it, they had returned to the center of the plateau, where they stood facing each other, exchanging blows.

Zar'roc grew so heavy in his hand, Eragon could barely lift it. His shoulder burned, he gasped for breath, and sweat poured off his face. Not even his desire to avenge Hrothgar could help him to overcome his exhaustion.

At last Eragon slipped and fell. Determined not to be killed lying down, he rolled back onto his feet and stabbed at the Rider, who knocked aside Zar'roc with a lazy flick of his wrist.

The way the Rider flourished his sword afterward—spinning it in a quick circle by his side—suddenly seemed familiar to Eragon, as did all his preceding swordsmanship. He stared with growing horror at his enemy's hand-and-a-half sword, then back up at the eye slits of his mirrored helm, and shouted, "I know you!"

He threw himself at the Rider, trapping both swords between their bodies, hooked his fingers underneath the helm, and ripped it off. And there in the center of the plateau, on the edge of the Burning Plains of Alagaësia, stood Murtagh.

INHERITANCE

Murtagh grinned. Then he said, "Thrysta vindr," and a hard
ball of air coalesced between them and struck Eragon in the
middle of his chest, tossing him twenty feet across the
plateau.

Eragon heard Saphira growl as he landed on his back. His vision
flashed red and white, then he curled into a ball and waited for the
pain to recede. Any delight he felt in Murtagh's reappearance was
overwhelmed by the macabre circumstances of their meeting. A
unstable mixture of shock, confusion, and anger boiled within him.

Lowering his sword, Murtagh pointed at Eragon with his steel-
encased hand, curling every finger but his index into a spiny fist.
"You never would give up."

A chill crept along Eragon's spine, for he recognized the scene
from his premonition while rafting the Az Ragni to Hedarth: *A
man sprawled in the clotted mud with a dented helm and bloody mail—
his face concealed behind an upthrown arm. An armored hand entered
Eragon's view and pointed at the downed man with all the authority of
fate itself.* Past and future had converged. Now Eragon's doom
would be decided.

Pushing himself to his feet, he coughed and said, "Murtagh . . .
how can you be alive? I watched the Urgals drag you underground.
I tried to scry you but saw only darkness."

Murtagh uttered a mirthless laugh. "You saw nothing, just as I
saw nothing the times I tried to scry you during my days in
Urû'baen."

"You *died*, though!" shouted Eragon, almost incoherent. "You died under Farthen Dûr. Arya found your bloody clothes in the tunnels."

A shadow darkened Murtagh's face. "No, I did not die. It was the Twins' doing, Eragon. They took control of a group of Urgals and arranged the ambush in order to kill Ajihad and capture me. Then they ensorcelled me so I could not escape and spirited me off to Urû'baen."

Eragon shook his head, unable to comprehend what had happened. "But why did you agree to serve Galbatorix? You told me you hated him. You told me—"

"Agree!" Murtagh laughed again, and this time his outburst contained an edge of madness. "I did not *agree*. First Galbatorix punished me for spiting his years of protection during my upbringing in Urû'baen, for defying his will and running away. Then he extracted everything I knew about you, Saphira, and the Varden."

"You betrayed us! I was mourning you, and you betrayed us!"

"I had no choice."

"Ajihad was right to lock you up. He should have let you rot in your cell, then none of this—"

"I had no choice!" snarled Murtagh. "And after Thorn hatched for me, Galbatorix forced both of us to swear loyalty to him in the ancient language. We cannot disobey him now."

Pity and disgust welled inside of Eragon. "You have become your father."

A strange gleam leaped into Murtagh's eyes. "No, not my father. I'm stronger than Morzan ever was. Galbatorix taught me things about magic you've never even dreamed of. . . . Spells so powerful, the elves dare not utter them, cowards that they are. Words in the ancient language that were lost until Galbatorix discovered them. Ways to manipulate energy . . . Secrets, terrible secrets, that can destroy your enemies and fulfill all your desires."

Eragon thought back to some of Oromis's lessons and retorted, "Things that should remain secrets."

"If you knew, you would not say that. Brom was a dabbler, nothing more. And the elves, bah! All they can do is hide in their forest and wait to be conquered." Murtagh ran his eyes over Eragon. "You look like an elf now. Did Islanzadí do that to you?" When Eragon remained silent, Murtagh smiled and shrugged. "No matter. I'll learn the truth soon enough." He stopped, frowned, then looked to the east.

Following his gaze, Eragon saw the Twins standing at the front of the Empire, casting balls of energy into the midst of the Varden and the dwarves. The curtains of smoke made it difficult to tell, but Eragon was sure the hairless magicians were grinning and laughing as they slaughtered the men with whom they once pledged solemn friendship. What the Twins failed to notice—and what was clearly visible to Eragon and Murtagh from their vantage point—was that Roran was crawling toward them from the side.

Eragon's heart skipped a beat as he recognized his cousin. *You fool! Get away from them! You'll be killed.*

Just as he opened his mouth to cast a spell that would transport Roran out of danger—no matter the cost—Murtagh said, "Wait. I want to see what he'll do."

"Why?"

A bleak smile crossed Murtagh's face. "The Twins enjoyed tormenting me when I was their captive."

Eragon glanced at him, suspicious. "You won't hurt him? You won't warn the Twins?"

"Vel eïnradhin iet ai Shur'tugal." *Upon my word as a Rider.*

Together they watched as Roran hid behind a mound of bodies. Eragon stiffened as the Twins looked toward the pile. For a moment, it seemed they had spotted him, then they turned away and Roran jumped up. He swung his hammer and bashed one of the Twins in the head, cracking open his skull. The remaining Twin fell to the ground, convulsing, and emitted a wordless scream until he too met his end under Roran's hammer. Then Roran planted his foot upon the corpses of his foes, lifted his hammer over his head, and bellowed his victory.

"What now?" demanded Eragon, turning away from the battle-field. "Are you here to kill me?"

"Of course not. Galbatorix wants you alive."

"What for?"

Murtagh's lips quirked. "You don't know? Ha! There's a fine jest. It's not because of you; it's because of *her*." He jabbed a finger at Saphira. "The dragon inside Galbatorix's last egg, the last dragon egg in the world, is male. Saphira is the only female dragon in existence. If she breeds, she will be the mother of her entire race. Do you see now? Galbatorix doesn't want to eradicate the dragons. He wants to use Saphira to rebuild the Riders. He can't kill you, either of you, if his vision is to become reality. . . . And what a vision it is, Eragon. You should hear him describe it, then you might not think so badly of him. Is it evil that he wants to unite Alagaësia under a single banner, eliminate the need for war, and restore the Riders?"

"He's the one who destroyed the Riders in the first place!"

"And for good reason," asserted Murtagh. "They were old, fat, and corrupt. The elves controlled them and used them to subjugate humans. They had to be removed so that we could start anew."

A furious scowl contorted Eragon's features. He paced back and forth across the plateau, his breathing heavy, then gestured at the battle and said, "How can you justify causing so much suffering on the basis of a madman's ravings? Galbatorix has done nothing but burn and slaughter and amass power for himself. He lies. He murders. He manipulates. You *know* this! It's why you refused to work for him in the first place." Eragon paused, then adopted a gentler tone: "I can understand that you were compelled to act against your will and that you aren't responsible for killing Hrothgar. You can try to escape, though. I'm sure that Arya and I could devise a way to neutralize the bonds Galbatorix has laid upon you. . . . Join me, Murtagh. You could do so much for the Varden. With us, you would be praised and admired, instead of cursed, feared, and hated."

For a moment, as Murtagh gazed down at his notched sword, Eragon hoped he would accept. Then Murtagh said in a low voice,

"You cannot help me, Eragon. No one but Galbatorix can release us from our oaths, and he will never do that. . . . He knows our true names, Eragon. . . . We are his slaves forever."

Though he wanted to, Eragon could not deny the sympathy he felt for Murtagh's plight. With the utmost gravity, he said, "Then let us kill the two of you."

"Kill us! Why should we allow that?"

Eragon chose his words with care: "It would free you from Galbatorix's control. And it would save the lives of hundreds, if not thousands, of people. Isn't that a noble enough cause to sacrifice yourself for?"

Murtagh shook his head. "Maybe for you, but life is still too sweet for me to part with it so easily. No stranger's life is more important than Thorn's or my own."

As much as he hated it—hated the entire situation, in fact— Eragon knew then what had to be done. Renewing his attack on Murtagh's mind, he leaped forward, both feet leaving the ground as he lunged toward Murtagh, intending to stab him through the heart.

"Letta!" barked Murtagh.

Eragon dropped back to the ground as invisible bands clamped around his arms and legs, immobilizing him. To his right, Saphira discharged a jet of rippling fire and sprang at Murtagh like a cat pouncing on a mouse.

"Rïsa!" commanded Murtagh, extending a clawlike hand as if to catch her.

Saphira yelped with surprise as Murtagh's incantation stopped her in midair and held her in place, floating several feet above the plateau. No matter how much she wriggled, she could not touch the ground, nor could she fly any higher.

How can he still be human and have the strength to do that? wondered Eragon. *Even with my new abilities, such a task would leave me gasping for air and unable to walk.* Relying upon his experience counteracting Oromis's spells, Eragon said, "Brakka du vanyalí sem huildar Saphira un eka!"

Murtagh made no attempt to stop him, only gave him a flat stare, as if he found Eragon's resistance a pointless inconvenience. Baring his teeth, Eragon redoubled his efforts. His hands went cold, his bones ached, and his pulse slowed as the magic sapped his energy. Without being asked, Saphira joined forces with him, granting him access to the formidable resources of her body.

Five seconds passed. . . .

Twenty seconds . . . A thick vein pulsed on Murtagh's neck.

A minute . . .

A minute and a half . . . Involuntary tremors racked Eragon. His quadriceps and hamstrings fluttered, and his legs would have given way if he were free to move.

Two minutes passed. . . .

At last Eragon was forced to release the magic, else he risked falling unconscious and passing into the void. He sagged, utterly spent.

He had been afraid before, but only because he thought he might fail. Now he was afraid because he did not know what Murtagh was capable of.

"You cannot hope to compete with me," said Murtagh. "No one can, except for Galbatorix." Walking up to Eragon, he pointed his sword at Eragon's neck, pricking his skin. Eragon resisted the impulse to flinch. "It would be so easy to take you back to Urû'baen."

Eragon gazed deep into his eyes. "Don't. Let me go."

"You just tried to kill me."

"And you would have done the same in my position." When Murtagh remained silent and expressionless, Eragon said, "We were friends once. We fought together. Galbatorix can't have twisted you so much that you've forgotten. . . . If you do this, Murtagh, you'll be lost forever."

A long minute passed where the only sound was the hue and cry of the clashing armies. Blood trickled down Eragon's neck from where the sword point cut him. Saphira lashed her tail with helpless rage.

Finally, Murtagh said, "I was ordered to try and capture you and

Saphira." He paused. "I have tried. . . . Make sure we don't cross paths again. Galbatorix will have me swear additional oaths in the ancient language that will prevent me from showing you such mercy when next we meet." He lowered his sword.

"You're doing the right thing," said Eragon. He tried to step back but was still held in place.

"Perhaps. But before I let you go . . ." Reaching out, Murtagh pried Zar'roc from Eragon's fist and unbuckled Zar'roc's red sheath from the belt of Beloth the Wise. "If I have become my father, then I will have my father's blade. Thorn is my dragon, and a thorn he shall be to all our enemies. It is only right, then, that I should also wield the sword *Misery*. Misery and Thorn, a fit match. Besides, Zar'roc should have gone to Morzan's eldest son, not his youngest. It is mine by right of birth."

A cold pit formed in Eragon's stomach. *It can't be.*

A cruel smile appeared on Murtagh's face. "I never told you my mother's name, did I? And you never told me yours. I'll say it now: Selena. Selena was my mother and your mother. Morzan was our father. The Twins figured out the connection while they were digging around in your head. Galbatorix was quite interested to learn that particular piece of information."

"You're lying!" cried Eragon. He could not bear the thought of being Morzan's son. *Did Brom know? Does Oromis know? . . . Why didn't they tell me?* He remembered, then, Angela predicting that someone in his family would betray him. *She was right.*

Murtagh merely shook his head and repeated his words in the ancient language, then put his lips to Eragon's ear and whispered, "You and I, we are the same, Eragon. Mirror images of one another. You can't deny it."

"You're wrong," growled Eragon, struggling against the spell. "We're nothing alike. I don't have a scar on my back anymore."

Murtagh recoiled as if he had been stung, his face going hard and cold. He lifted Zar'roc and held it upright before his chest. "So be it. I take my inheritance from you, brother. Farewell."

Then he retrieved his helm from the ground and pulled himself onto Thorn. Not once did he look at Eragon as the dragon crouched, raised its wings, and flew off the plateau and into the north. Only after Thorn vanished below the horizon did the web of magic release Eragon and Saphira.

Saphira's talons clicked on the stone as she landed. She crawled over to Eragon and touched him on the arm with her snout. *Are you all right, little one?*

I'm fine. But he was not, and she knew it.

Walking to the edge of the plateau, Eragon surveyed the Burning Plains and the aftermath of the battle, for the battle *was* over. With the death of the Twins, the Varden and dwarves regained lost ground and were able to rout the formations of confused soldiers, herding them into the river or chasing them back from whence they came.

Though the bulk of their forces remained intact, the Empire had sounded the retreat, no doubt to regroup and prepare for a second attempt to invade Surda. In their wake, they left piles of tangled corpses from both sides of the conflict, enough men and dwarves to populate an entire city. Thick black smoke roiled off the bodies that had fallen into the peat fires.

Now that the fighting had subsided, the hawks and eagles, the crows and ravens, descended like a shroud over the field.

Eragon closed his eyes, tears leaking from under the lids.

They had won, but he had lost.

REUNION

ragon and Saphira picked their way between the corpses that littered the Burning Plains, moving slowly on account of their wounds and their exhaustion. They encountered other survivors staggering through the scorched battlefield, hollow-eyed men who looked without truly seeing, their gazes focused somewhere in the distance.

Now that his bloodlust had subsided, Eragon felt nothing but sorrow. The fighting seemed so pointless to him. *What a tragedy that so many must die to thwart a single madman.* He paused to sidestep a thicket of arrows planted in the mud and noticed the gash on Saphira's tail where Thorn had bitten her, as well as her other injuries. *Here, lend me your strength; I'll heal you.*

Tend to those in mortal danger first.

Are you sure?

Quite sure, little one.

Acquiescing, he bent down and mended a soldier's torn neck before moving on to one of the Varden. He made no distinction between friend and foe, treating both to the limit of his abilities.

Eragon was so preoccupied with his thoughts, he paid little attention to his work. He wished he could repudiate Murtagh's claim, but everything Murtagh had said about his mother—*their* mother—coincided with the few things Eragon knew about her: Selena left Carvahall twenty-some years ago, returned once to give birth to Eragon, and was never seen again. His mind darted back to when

654

he and Murtagh first arrived in Farthen Dûr. Murtagh had discussed how his mother had vanished from Morzan's castle while Morzan was hunting Brom, Jeod, and Saphira's egg. *After Morzan threw Zar'roc at Murtagh and nearly killed him, Mother must have hidden her pregnancy and then gone back to Carvahall in order to protect me from Morzan and Galbatorix.*

It heartened Eragon to know that Selena had cared for him so deeply. It also grieved him to know she was dead and they would never meet, for he had nurtured the hope, faint as it was, that his parents might still be alive. He no longer harbored any desire to be acquainted with his father, but he bitterly resented that he had been deprived of the chance to have a relationship with his mother.

Ever since he was old enough to understand that he was a fosterling, Eragon had wondered who his father was and why his mother left him to be raised by her brother, Garrow, and his wife, Marian. Those answers had been thrust upon him from such an unexpected source, and in such an unpropitious setting, it was more than he could make sense of at the moment. It would take months, if not years, to come to terms with the revelation.

Eragon always assumed he would be glad to learn the identity of his father. Now that he had, the knowledge revolted him. When he was younger, he often entertained himself by imagining that his father was someone grand and important, though Eragon knew the opposite was far more likely. Still, it never occurred to him, even in his most extravagant daydreams, that he might be the son of a Rider, much less one of the Forsworn.

It turned a daydream into a nightmare.

I was sired by a monster. . . . My father was the one who betrayed the Riders to Galbatorix. It left Eragon feeling sullied.

But no . . . As he healed a man's broken spine, a new way of viewing the situation occurred to him, one that restored a measure of his self-confidence: *Morzan may be my parent, but he is not my father. Garrow was my father. He raised me. He taught me how to live well and honorably, with integrity. I am who I am because of him. Even*

Brom and Oromis are more my father than Morzan. And Roran is my brother, not Murtagh.

Eragon nodded, determined to maintain that outlook. Until then, he had refused to completely accept Garrow as his father. And even though Garrow was dead, doing so relieved Eragon, gave him a sense of closure, and helped to ameliorate his distress over Morzan.

You have grown wise, observed Saphira.

Wise? He shook his head. *No, I've just learned how to think. That much, at least, Oromis gave me.* Eragon wiped a layer of dirt off the face of a fallen banner boy, making sure he really was dead, then straightened, wincing as his muscles spasmed in protest. *You realize, don't you, that Brom must have known about this. Why else would he choose to hide in Carvahall while he waited for you to hatch? . . . He wanted to keep an eye upon his enemy's son.* It unsettled him to think that Brom might have considered him a threat. *And he was right too. Look what ended up happening to me!*

Saphira ruffled his hair with a gust of her hot breath. *Just remember, whatever Brom's reasons, he always tried to protect us from danger. He died saving you from the Ra'zac.*

I know. . . . Do you think he didn't tell me about this because he was afraid I might emulate Morzan, like Murtagh has?

Of course not.

He looked at her, curious. *How can you be so certain?* She lifted her head high above him and refused to meet his eyes or to answer. *Have it your way, then.* Kneeling by one of King Orrin's men, who had an arrow through the gut, Eragon grabbed his arms to stop him from writhing. "Easy now."

"Water," groaned the man. "For pity's sake, water. My throat is as dry as sand. Please, Shadeslayer." Sweat beaded his face.

Eragon smiled, trying to comfort him. "I can give you a drink now, but it'd be better if you wait until after I heal you. Can you wait? If you do, I promise you can have all the water you want."

"You promise, Shadeslayer?"

"I promise."

The man visibly struggled against another wave of agony before saying, "If I must."

With the aid of magic, Eragon drew out the shaft, then he and Saphira worked to repair the man's innards, using some of the warrior's own energy to fuel the spell. It took several minutes. Afterward, the man examined his belly, pressing his hands against the flawless skin, then gazed at Eragon, tears brimming in his eyes. "I . . . Shadeslayer, you . . ."

Eragon handed him his waterskin. "Here, keep it. You have greater need of it than I."

A hundred yards beyond, Eragon and Saphira breached an acrid wall of smoke. There they came upon Orik and ten other dwarves—some women—arrayed around the body of Hrothgar, who lay upon four shields, resplendent in his golden mail. The dwarves tore at their hair, beat their breasts, and wailed their lamentations to the sky. Eragon bowed his head and murmured, "Stydja unin mor'ranr, Hrothgar Könungr."

After a time, Orik noticed them and rose, his face red from crying and his beard torn free of its usual braid. He staggered over to Eragon and, without preempt, asked, "Did you kill the coward responsible for this?"

"He escaped." Eragon could not bring himself to explain that the Rider was Murtagh.

Orik stamped his fist into his hand. "Barzûln!"

"But I swear to you upon every stone in Alagaësia that, as one of Dûrgrimst Ingeitum, I'll do everything I can to avenge Hrothgar's death."

"Aye, you're the only one besides the elves strong enough to bring this foul murderer to justice. And when you find him . . . grind his bones to dust, Eragon. Pull his teeth and fill his veins with molten lead; make him suffer for every minute of Hrothgar's life that he stole."

"Wasn't it a good death? Wouldn't Hrothgar have wanted to die in battle, with Volund in his hand?"

"In battle, yes, facing an honest foe who dared stand and fight like a man. Not brought low by a magician's trickery. . . ." Shaking his head, Orik looked back at Hrothgar, then crossed his arms and tucked his chin against his collarbone. He took several ragged breaths. "When my parents died of the pox, Hrothgar gave me a life again. He took me into his hall. He made me his heir. Losing him . . ." Orik pinched the bridge of his nose between his thumb and forefinger, covering his face. "Losing him is like losing my father again."

The grief in his voice was so clear, Eragon felt as if he shared the dwarf's sorrow. "I understand," he said.

"I know you do, Eragon. . . . I know you do." After a moment, Orik wiped his eyes and gestured at the ten dwarves. "Before anything else is done, we have to return Hrothgar to Farthen Dûr so he can be entombed with his predecessors. Dûrgrimst Ingeitum must choose a new grimstborith, and then the thirteen clan chiefs—including the ones you see here—will select our next king from among themselves. What happens next, I know not. This tragedy will embolden some clans and turn others against our cause. . . ." He shook his head again.

Eragon put his hand on Orik's shoulder. "Don't worry about that now. You have but to ask, and my arm and my will are at your service. . . . If you want, come to my tent and we can share a cask of mead and toast Hrothgar's memory."

"I'd like that. But not yet. Not until we finish pleading with the gods to grant Hrothgar safe passage to the afterlife." Leaving Eragon, Orik returned to the circle of dwarves and added his voice to their keening.

Continuing on through the Burning Plains, Saphira said, *Hrothgar was a great king.*

Aye, and a good person. Eragon sighed. *We should find Arya and Nasuada. I couldn't even heal a scratch right now, and they need to know about Murtagh.*

Agreed.

They angled south toward the Varden's encampment, but before they traveled more than a few yards, Eragon saw Roran approaching from the Jiet River. Trepidation filled him. Roran stopped directly in front of them, planted his feet wide apart, and stared at Eragon, working his jaw up and down as if he wanted to talk but was unable to get the words past his teeth.

Then he punched Eragon on the chin.

It would have been easy for Eragon to avoid the blow, but he allowed it to land, rolling away from it a bit so Roran did not break his knuckles.

It still hurt.

Wincing, Eragon faced his cousin. "I guess I deserved that."

"That you did. We have to talk."

"Now?"

"It can't wait. The Ra'zac captured Katrina, and I need your help to rescue her. They've had her ever since we left Carvahall."

So that's it. In an instant, Eragon realized why Roran appeared so grim and haunted, and why he had brought the entire village to Surda. *Brom was right, Galbatorix sent the Ra'zac back to Palancar Valley.* Eragon frowned, torn between his responsibility to Roran and his duty to report to Nasuada. "There's something I need to do first, and then we can talk. All right? You can accompany me if you want. . . ."

"I'll come."

As they traversed the pockmarked land, Eragon kept glancing at Roran out of the corner of his eye. Finally, he said in a low voice, "I missed you."

Roran faltered, then responded with a curt nod. A few steps later, he asked, "This is Saphira, right? Jeod said that was her name."

"Aye."

Saphira peered at Roran with one of her glittering eyes. He bore her scrutiny without turning away, which was more than most people could do. *I have always wanted to meet Eragon's nest-mate.*

"She speaks!" exclaimed Roran when Eragon repeated her words.

This time Saphira addressed him directly: *What? Did you think I was as mute as a rock lizard?*

Roran blinked. "I beg your pardon. I didn't know that dragons

659

were so intelligent." A grim smile twisted his lips. "First Ra'zac and magicians, now dwarves, Riders, and talking dragons. It seems the whole world has gone mad."

"It does seem that way."

"I saw you fight that other Rider. Did you wound him? Is that why he fled?"

"Wait. You'll hear."

When they reached the pavilion Eragon was searching for, he swept back the flap and ducked inside, followed by Roran and Saphira, who pushed her head and neck in after them. In the center of the tent, Nasuada sat on the edge of the table, letting a maid remove her twisted armor while she carried on a heated discussion with Arya. The cut on her thigh had been healed.

Nasuada stopped in the middle of her sentence as she spotted the new arrivals. Running toward them, she threw her arms around Eragon and cried, "Where were you? We thought you were dead, or worse."

"Not quite."

"The candle still burns," murmured Arya.

Stepping back, Nasuada said, "We couldn't see what happened to you and Saphira after you landed on the plateau. When the red dragon left and you didn't appear, Arya tried to contact you but felt nothing, so we assumed . . ." She trailed off. "We were just debating the best way to transport Du Vrangr Gata and an entire company of warriors across the river."

"I'm sorry. I didn't mean to worry you. I was just so tired after the fight, I forgot to lower my barriers." Then Eragon brought Roran forward. "Nasuada, I would like to introduce my cousin, Roran. Ajihad may have mentioned him to you before. Roran, Lady Nasuada, leader of the Varden and my liegelord. And this is Arya Svit-kona, the elves' ambassador." Roran bowed to each of them in turn.

"It is an honor to meet Eragon's cousin," said Nasuada.

"Indeed," added Arya.

After they finished exchanging greetings, Eragon explained that the entire village of Carvahall had arrived on the *Dragon Wing*, and that Roran was the one responsible for killing the Twins.

Nasuada lifted a dark eyebrow. "The Varden are in your debt, Roran, for stopping their rampage. Who knows how much damage the Twins would have caused before Eragon or Arya could have confronted them? You helped us to win this battle. I won't forget that. Our supplies are limited, but I will see that everyone on your ship is clothed and fed, and that your sick are treated."

Roran bowed even lower. "Thank you, Lady Nasuada."

"If I weren't so pressed for time, I would insist upon knowing how and why you and your village evaded Galbatorix's men, traveled to Surda, and then found us. Even just the bare facts of your trek make an extraordinary tale. I still intend to learn the specifics—especially since I suspect it concerns Eragon—but I must deal with other, more urgent matters at the moment."

"Of course, Lady Nasuada."

"You may go, then."

"Please," said Eragon, "let him stay. He should be here for this."

Nasuada gave him a quizzical look. "Very well. If you want. But enough of this dawdling. Jump to the meat of the matter and tell us about the Rider!"

Eragon began with a quick history of the three remaining dragon eggs—two of which had now hatched—as well as Morzan and Murtagh, so that Roran would understand the significance of his news. Then he proceeded to describe his and Saphira's fight with Thorn and the mysterious Rider, paying special attention to his extraordinary powers. "As soon as he spun his sword around, I realized we *had* dueled before, so I threw myself at him and tore off his helm." Eragon paused.

"It was Murtagh, wasn't it?" asked Nasuada quietly.

"How . . . ?"

She sighed. "If the Twins survived, it only made sense that Murtagh had as well. Did he tell you what really happened that day in Farthen Dûr?" So Eragon recounted how the Twins betrayed the Varden, recruited the Urgals, and kidnapped Murtagh. A tear rolled down Nasuada's cheek. "It's a pity that this befell Murtagh when he has already endured so much hardship. I enjoyed his company in Tronjheim and believed he was our ally, despite his upbringing. I find it hard to think of him as our enemy." Turning to Roran, she said, "It seems I am also personally in your debt for slaying the traitors who murdered my father."

Fathers, mothers, brothers, cousins, thought Eragon. *It all comes down to family.* Summoning his courage, he completed his report with Murtagh's theft of Zar'roc and then his final, terrible secret.

"It can't be," whispered Nasuada.

Eragon saw shock and revulsion cross Roran's face before he managed to conceal his reactions. That, more than anything else, hurt Eragon.

"Could Murtagh have been lying?" asked Arya.

"I don't see how. When I questioned him, he told me the same thing in the ancient language."

A long, uncomfortable silence filled the pavilion.

Then Arya said, "No one else can know about this. The Varden are demoralized enough by the presence of a new Rider. And they'll be even more upset when they learn it's Murtagh, whom they fought alongside and came to trust in Farthen Dûr. If word spreads that Eragon Shadeslayer is Morzan's son, the men will grow disillusioned and few people will want to join us. Not even King Orrin should be told."

Nasuada rubbed her temples. "I fear you're right. A new Rider . . ." She shook her head. "I knew it was possible for this to occur, but I didn't really believe it would, since Galbatorix's remaining eggs had gone so long without hatching."

"It has a certain symmetry," said Eragon.

"Our task is doubly hard now. We may have held our own today, but the Empire still far outnumbers us, and now we face not one but two Riders, both of whom are stronger than you, Eragon. Do you think you could defeat Murtagh with the help of the elves' spellcasters?"

"Maybe. But I doubt he'd be foolish enough to fight them and me together."

For several minutes, they discussed the effect Murtagh could have on their campaign and strategies to minimize or eliminate it. At last Nasuada said, "Enough. We cannot decide this when we are bloody and tired and our minds are clouded from fighting. Go, rest, and we shall take this up again tomorrow."

As Eragon turned to leave, Arya approached and looked him straight in the eye. "Do not allow this to trouble you overmuch, Eragon-elda. You are not your father, nor your brother. Their shame is not yours."

"Aye," agreed Nasuada. "Nor imagine that it has lowered our opinion of you." She reached out and cupped his face. "I know you, Eragon. You have a good heart. The name of your father cannot change that."

Warmth blossomed inside Eragon. He looked from one woman to the next, then twisted his hand over his chest, overwhelmed by their friendship. "Thank you."

Once they were back out in the open, Eragon put his hands on his hips and took a deep breath of the smoky air. It was late in the day, and the garish orange of noon had subsided into a dusky gold light that suffused the camp and battlefield, giving it a strange beauty. "So now you know," he said.

Roran shrugged. "Blood always tells."

"Don't say that," growled Eragon. "Don't ever say that."

Roran studied him for several seconds. "You're right; it was an ugly thought. I didn't mean it." He scratched his beard and squinted at the bloated sun resting upon the horizon. "Nasuada wasn't what I expected."

That forced a tired chuckle out of Eragon. "The one you were expecting was her father, Ajihad. Still, she's as good a leader as he was, if not better."

"Her skin, is it dyed?"

"No, that's the way she is."

Just then, Eragon felt Jeod, Horst, and a score of other men from

Carvahall hurrying toward them. The villagers slowed as they rounded a tent and glimpsed Saphira. "Horst!" exclaimed Eragon. Stepping forward, he grasped the smith in a bear hug. "It's good to see you again!"

Horst gaped at Eragon, then a delighted grin spread across his face. "Blast if it isn't good to see you as well, Eragon. You've filled out since you left."

"You mean since I ran away."

Meeting the villagers was a strange experience for Eragon. Hardship had altered some of the men so much, he barely recognized them. And they treated him differently than before, with a mixture of awe and reverence. It reminded him of a dream, where everything familiar is rendered alien. He was disconcerted by how out of place he felt among them.

When Eragon came to Jeod, he paused. "You know about Brom?"

"Ajihad sent me a message, but I'd like to hear what happened directly from you."

Eragon nodded, grave. "As soon as I have the chance, we'll sit down together and have a long talk."

Then Jeod moved on to Saphira and bowed to her. "I waited my entire life to see a dragon, and now I have seen two in the same day. I am indeed lucky. However, *you* are the dragon I wanted to meet."

Bending her neck, Saphira touched Jeod on the brow. He shivered at the contact. *Give him my thanks for helping to rescue me from Galbatorix. Otherwise, I would still be languishing in the king's treasury. He was Brom's friend, and so he is our friend.*

After Eragon repeated her words, Jeod said, "Atra esterní ono thelduin, Saphira Bjartskular," surprising them with his knowledge of the ancient language.

"Where did you go?" Horst asked Roran. "We looked high and low for you after you took off in pursuit of those two magicians."

"Never mind that now. Return to the ship and have everyone disembark; the Varden are sending us food and shelter. We can sleep on solid ground tonight!" The men cheered.

Eragon watched with interest as Roran issued his commands. When at last Jeod and the villagers departed, Eragon said, "They trust you. Even Horst obeys you without question. Do you speak for all of Carvahall now?"

"I do."

Heavy darkness was advancing upon the Burning Plains by the time they found the small two-man tent the Varden had assigned Eragon. Since Saphira could not fit her head through the opening, she curled up on the ground beside and prepared to keep watch.

As soon as I get my strength back, I'll see to your wounds, promised Eragon.

I know. Don't stay up too late talking.

Inside the tent, Eragon found an oil lantern that he lit with steel and flint. He could see perfectly well without it, but Roran needed the light.

They sat opposite each other: Eragon on the bedding laid out along one side of the tent, Roran on a folding stool he found leaning in a corner. Eragon was uncertain how to begin, so he remained silent and stared at the lamp's dancing flame.

Neither of them moved.

After uncounted minutes, Roran said, "Tell me how my father died."

"Our father." Eragon remained calm as Roran's expression hardened. In a gentle voice, he said, "I have as much right to call him that as you. Look within yourself; you know it to be true."

"Fine. Our father, how did he die?"

Eragon had recounted the story upon several occasions. But this time he hid nothing. Instead of just listing the events, he described what he had thought and felt ever since he had found Saphira's egg, trying to make Roran understand *why* he did what he did. He had never been so anxious before.

"I was wrong to hide Saphira from the rest of the family," Eragon concluded, "but I was afraid you might insist on killing her, and I didn't realize how much danger she put us in. If I had . . . After Garrow died, I decided to leave in order to track down the Ra'zac, as well as to avoid putting Carvahall in any more danger." A humorless laugh escaped him. "It didn't work, but if I had remained, the soldiers would have come far sooner. And then who knows? Galbatorix might have even visited Palancar Valley himself. I may be the reason Garrow—Father—died, but that was never my intention, nor that you and everyone else in Carvahall should suffer because of my choices. . . ." He gestured helplessly. "I did the best I could, Roran."

"And the rest of it—Brom being a Rider, rescuing Arya at Gil'ead, and killing a Shade at the dwarves' capital—all that happened?"

"Aye." As quickly as he could, Eragon summarized what had taken place since he and Saphira set forth with Brom, including their sojourn to Ellesméra and his own transformation during the Agaetí Blödhren.

Leaning forward, Roran rested his elbows on his knees, clasped his hands, and gazed at the dirt between them. It was impossible for Eragon to read his emotions without reaching into his consciousness, which he refused to do, knowing it would be a terrible mistake to invade Roran's privacy.

Roran was silent for so long, Eragon began to wonder if he would ever respond. Then: "You have made mistakes, but they are no greater than my own. Garrow died because you kept Saphira secret. Many more have died because I refused to give myself up to the Empire. . . . We are equally guilty." He looked up, then slowly extended his right hand. "Brother?"

"Brother," said Eragon.

He gripped Roran's forearm, and they pulled each other into a rough embrace, wrestling to and fro as they used to do at home. When they separated, Eragon had to wipe his eyes with the heel of his hand. "Galbatorix should surrender now that we're together again," he joked. "Who can stand against the two of us?" He lowered himself back onto the bedding. "Now you tell me, how did the Ra'zac capture Katrina?"

All happiness vanished from Roran's face. He began to speak in a low monotone, and Eragon listened with growing amazement as he wove an epic of attacks, sieges, and betrayal, of leaving Carvahall, crossing the Spine, and razing the docks of Teirm, of sailing through a monstrous whirlpool.

When at last he finished, Eragon said, "You are a greater man than I. I couldn't have done half those things. Fight, yes, but not convince everyone to follow me."

"I had no choice. When they took Katrina—" Roran's voice broke. "I could either give up and die, or I could try to escape Galbatorix's trap, no matter the cost." He fixed his burning eyes on Eragon. "I have lied and burned and slaughtered to get here. I no longer have to worry about protecting everyone from Carvahall; the Varden will see to that. Now I have only one goal in life, to find and rescue Katrina, if she's not already dead. Will you help me, Eragon?"

Reaching over, Eragon grabbed his saddlebags from the corner of the tent—where the Varden had deposited them—and removed a wooden bowl and the silver flask of enchanted faelnirv Oromis had given him. He took a small sip of the liqueur to revitalize himself and gasped as it raced down his throat, making his nerves tingle with cold fire. Then he poured faelnirv into the bowl until it formed a shallow pool the width of his hand.

"Watch." Gathering up his burst of new energy, Eragon said, "Draumr kópa."

The liqueur shimmered and turned black. After a few seconds, a thin key of light appeared in the center of the bowl, revealing Katrina. She lay slumped against an invisible wall, her hands suspended above her with invisible manacles and her copper hair splayed like a fan across her back.

"She's alive!" Roran hunched over the bowl, grasping at it as if he thought he could dive through the faelnirv and join Katrina. His hope and determination melded with a look of such tender affection, Eragon knew that only death could stop Roran from trying to free her.

Unable to sustain the spell any longer, Eragon let the image fade away. He leaned against the wall of the tent for support. "Aye," he said wearily, "she's alive. And chances are, she's imprisoned in Helgrind, in the Ra'zac's lair." Eragon grasped Roran by the shoulders. "The answer to your question, brother, is yes. I will travel to Dras-Leona with you. I will help you rescue Katrina. And then, together, you and I shall kill the Ra'zac and avenge our father."

END OF BOOK TWO

THE STORY WILL CONTINUE IN

BOOK THREE OF INHERITANCE

PRONUNCIATION GUIDE

AND

GLOSSARY

On the Origin of Names:

To the casual observer, the various names an intrepid traveler will encounter throughout Alagaësia might seem but a random collection of labels with no inherent integrity, culture, or history. However, as with any land that has been repeatedly colonized by different cultures—and in this case, different races—Alagaësia quickly accumulated layers of names from the elves, dwarves, humans, and even Urgals. Thus, we can have Palancar Valley (a human name), the Anora River and Ristvak'baen (elven names), and Utgard Mountain (a dwarf name) all within a few square miles of each other.

While this is of great historical interest, practically it often leads to confusion as to the correct pronunciation. Unfortunately, there are no set rules for the neophyte. Each name must be learned upon its own terms, unless you can immediately place its language of origin. The matter grows even more confusing when you realize that in many places the spelling and pronunciation of foreign words were altered by the resident population to conform to their own language. The Anora River is a prime example. Originally *anora* was spelled *äenora*, which means *broad* in the ancient language. In their writings, the humans simplified the word to *anora*, and this, combined with a vowel shift wherein *äe* (ay-eh) was said as the easier *a* (uh), created the name as it appears in Eragon's time.

To spare readers as much difficulty as possible, the following list is provided, with the understanding that these are only rough guidelines to the actual pronunciation. The enthusiast is encouraged to study the source languages in order to master their true intricacies.

Pronunciation:

Aiedail—AY-uh-dale
Ajihad—AH-zhi-hod
Alagaësia—al-uh-GAY-zee-uh
Arya—AR-ee-uh
Carvahall—CAR-vuh-hall
Dras-Leona—DRAHS lee-OH-nuh
Du Weldenvarden—doo WELL-den-VAR-den
Ellesméra—el-uhs-MEER-uh
Eragon—EHR-uh-gahn

Farthen Dûr—FAR-then DURE (*dure* rhymes with *lure*)
Galbatorix—gal-buh-TOR-icks
Gil'ead—GILL-ee-id
Glaedr—GLAY-dur
Hrothgar—HROTH-gar
Islanzadí—iss-lan-ZAH-dee
Jeod—JODE (rhymes with *code*)
Murtagh—MUR-tag (*mur* rhymes with *purr*)
Nasuada—Na-soo-AH-dah
Nolfavrell—NOLL-fah-vrel (*noll* rhymes with *toll*)
Oromis—OR-uh-miss
Ra'zac—RAA-zack
Saphira—suh-FEAR-uh
Shruikan—SHREW-kin
Sílthrim—SEAL-thrim (*síl* is a hard sound to transcribe; it's made by
    flicking the tip of the tongue off the roof of the mouth.)
Teirm—TEERM
Trianna—TREE-ah-nuh
Tronjheim—TRONJ-heem
Urû'baen—OO-roo-bane
Vrael—VRAIL
Yazuac—YAA-zoo-ack
Zar'roc—ZAR-rock

THE ANCIENT LANGUAGE:

adurna—water
Agaetí Blödhren—Blood-oath Celebration
Aiedail—The Morning Star
Argetlam—Silver Hand
Atra esterní ono thelduin/Mor'ranr lífa unin hjarta onr/Un du evarínya
    ono varda.—May good fortune rule over you/Peace live in your
    heart/And the stars watch over you.
Atra guliä un ilian tauthr ono un atra ono waíse skölir fra rauthr.—
    May luck and happiness follow you and may you be a shield from
    misfortune.
Atra nosu waíse vardo fra eld hórnya.—Let us be warded from listeners.

Bjartskular—Brightscales
blöthr—halt; stop
Brakka du vanyalí sem huildar Saphira un eka!—Reduce the magic that
    holds Saphira and me!
brisingr—fire
Dagshelgr—Hallowed Day
draumr kópa—dream stare
Du Fells Nángoröth—The Blasted Mountains
Du Fyrn Skulblaka—The Dragon War
Du Völlar Eldrvarya—The Burning Plains
Du Vrangr Gata—The Wandering Path
Du Weldenvarden—The Guarding Forest
dvergar—dwarves
ebrithil—master
edur—a tor or prominence
Eka fricai un Shur'tugal.—I am a Rider and friend.
elda—a gender-neutral honorific of great praise
Eyddr eyreya onr!—Empty your ears!
fairth—a picture taken by magical means
finiarel—an honorific for a young man of great promise
Fricai Andlát—death friend (a poisonous mushroom)
Gala O Wyrda brunhvitr/Abr Berundal vandr-fódhr/Burthro
    laufsblädar ekar undir/Eom kona dauthleikr . . .—Sing O white-
    browed Fate/Of ill-marked Berundal/Born under oaken leaves/
    To mortal woman . . .
gánga aptr—to go backward
gánga fram—to go forward
Gath sem oro un lam iet.—Unite that arrow with my hand.
gedwëy ignasia—shining palm
Gëuloth du knífr.—Dull the knife.
haldthin—thornapple
Helgrind—The Gates of Death
hlaupa—run
hljödhr—silent
jierda—break; hit
kodthr—catch

Kvetha Fricai.—Greetings, Friend.

lethrblaka—a bat; the Ra'zac's mounts (literally, leather-flapper)

letta—stop

Letta orya thorna!—Stop those arrows!

Liduen Kvaedhí—Poetic Script

Losna kalfya iet.—Release my calves.

malthinae—to bind or hold in place; confine

nalgask—a mixture of beeswax and hazelnut oil used to moisten the skin

Osthato Chetowä—the Mourning Sage

Reisa du adurna.—Raise/Lift the water.

rïsa—rise

Sé mor'ranr ono finna.—May you find peace.

Sé onr sverdar sitja hvass!—May your swords stay sharp!

Sé orúm thornessa hávr sharjalví lífs.—May this serpent have life's
  movement.

skölir—shield

Skölir nosu fra brisingr!—Shield us from fire!

sköliro—shielded

skulblaka—dragon (literally, scale-flapper)

Stydja unin mor'ranr, Hrothgar Könungr.—Rest in peace, King
  Hrothgar.

svit-kona—a formal honorific for an elf woman of great wisdom

thrysta—thrust; compress

Thrysta vindr.—Compress the air.

Togira Ikonoka—the Cripple Who Is Whole

the Varden—the Warders

Vel eïnradhin iet ai Shur'tugal.—Upon my word as a Rider.

Vinr Älfakyn—Elf Friend

vodhr—a male honorific of middling praise

vor—a male honorific for a close friend

Waíse heill.—Be healed.

Wiol ono.—For you.

wyrda—fate

Wyrdfell—elven name for the Forsworn

yawë—a bond of trust

zar'roc—misery

The Dwarf Language:

Akh sartos oen dûrgrimst!—For family and clan!

Ascûdgamln—fists of steel

Astim Hefthyn—Sight Guard (inscription on a necklace given to Eragon)

Az Ragni—The River

Az Sweldn rak Anhûin—The Tears of Anhûin

Azt jok jordn rast.—Then you may pass.

barzûl—to curse someone with ill fate

Barzûl knurlar!—Curse them!

barzûln—to curse someone with multiple misfortunes

Beor—cave bear (elf word)

dûrgrimst—clan (literally, our hall/home)

eta—no

Etzil nithgech!—Stop there!

Farthen Dûr—Our Father

Feldûnost—frostbeard (a species of goat native to the Beor Mountains)

Formv Hrethcarach . . . formv Jurgencarmeitder nos eta goroth bahst Tarnag, dûr encestí rak kythn! Jok is warrev az barzûlegûr dûr dûrgrimst, Az Sweldn rak Anhûin, môgh tor rak Jurgenvren? Né ûdim etal os rast knurlar. Knurlag ana . . .—This Shadeslayer . . . this Dragon Rider has no place in Tarnag, our holiest of cities! Do you forget the curse our clan, The Tears of Anhûin, bears from the Dragon War? We will not let him pass. He is . . .

grimstborith—clan chief

grimstcarvlorss—arranger of the house

Gûntera Arûna—Gûntera Bless

Hert dûrgrimst? Fild rastn?—What clan? Who passes?

hírna—likeness; statue

hûthvir—double-bladed staff weapon used by Dûrgrimst Quan

Ignh az voth!—Bring the food!

Ilf gauhnith.—A peculiar dwarf expression that means "It is safe and good." Commonly uttered by the host of a meal, it is a holdover from days when poisoning of guests was prevalent among the clans.

Ingeitum—fire workers; smiths

Isidar Mithrim—Star Rose

Jok is frekk dûrgrimstvren?—Do you want a clan war?

knurl—stone; rock

knurla—dwarf (literally, one of stone)

Knurlag qana qirânû Dûrgrimst Ingeitum! Qarzûl ana Hrothgar oen volfild—He was made a member of Clan Ingeitum! Cursed is Hrothgar and all who—

knurlagn—men

Knurlhiem—Stonehead

Knurlnien—Heart of Stone

Nagra—giant boar, native to the Beor Mountains

oeí—yes; affirmative

Orik Thrifkz menthiv oen Hrethcarach Eragon rak Dûrgrimst Ingeitum. Wharn, az vanyali-carharûg Arya. Né oc Ûndinz grimstbelardn.—Orik, Thrifk's son, and Shadeslayer Eragon of Clan Ingeitum. Also, the elf-courier Arya. We are Ûndin's hall-guests.

Os il dom qirânû carn dûr thargen, zeitmen, oen grimst vor formv edaris rak skilfz. Narho is belgond . . .—Let our flesh, honor, and hall be made as one by this blood of mine. I do pledge . . .

otho—faith

Ragni Hefthyn—River Guard

Shrrg—giant wolf, native to the Beor Mountains

Smer voth.—Serve the food.

Tronjheim—Helm of Giants

Urzhad—cave bear

vanyali—elf (The dwarves borrowed this word from the ancient language, wherein it means *magic*.)

Vor Hrothgarz korda!—By Hrothgar's hammer!

vrron—enough

werg—an exclamation of disgust (the dwarves' equivalent of *ugh*)

THE URGAL LANGUAGE:

Ahgrat ukmar.—It is done.

drajl—spawn of maggots

nar—a gender-neutral title of great respect

ACKNOWLEDGMENTS

Kvetha Fricäya.

As with many authors who undertake an epic the length of the Inheritance trilogy, I have found that the creation of *Eragon*, and now *Eldest*, has become my own personal quest, one that has proven every bit as transforming as Eragon's.

When first I conceived *Eragon*, I was fifteen—not quite a boy and not yet a man—just out of high school, unsure of what path to take in life, and addicted to the potent magic of the fantasy literature that adorned my shelves. The process of writing *Eragon*, marketing it across the world, and now finally completing *Eldest* has swept me into adulthood. I am twenty-one now and, to my continual astonishment, have already published two novels. Stranger things have occurred, I'm sure, but never to me.

Eragon's journey has been my own: plucked from a sheltered rural upbringing and forced to rove the land in a desperate race against time; enduring intense and arduous training; achieving success against all expectations; dealing with the consequences of fame; and eventually finding a measure of peace.

Just as in fiction when the determined and well-meaning protagonist—who really isn't all that bright, now is he?—is helped along his way by a host of wiser characters, so too have I been guided by a number of stupendously talented people. They are:

At home: Mom, for listening whenever I need to talk about a problem with the story or characters and for giving me the courage to throw out twelve pages and rewrite Eragon's entrance into Ellesméra (painful); Dad, as always, for his incisive editing; and my dear sister, Angela, for deigning to reprise her role as a witch and for her contributions to her doppelgänger's dialogue.

At Writers House: my agent, the great and mighty Comma Master, Simon Lipskar, who makes all things possible (Mervyn Peake!); and his brave assistant Daniel Lazar, who keeps the Comma Master from being buried alive underneath a pile of unsolicited manuscripts, many of which I fear are the result of *Eragon*.

At Knopf: my editor, Michelle Frey, who has gone above and beyond the call of duty in performing her job and has made *Eldest* so much better than it would have been otherwise; publicity director Judith Haut, for once again proving that no feat of promotion is beyond her reach (hear her roar!); Isabel Warren-Lynch, art director nonpareil who, with *Eldest*, has exceeded her previous accomplishments; John Jude Palencar, for a cover painting that I like even better than the one for *Eragon*; copy chief Artie Bennett, who has done a splendiferous job of checking all the obscure words in this trilogy and probably knows more than I do about the ancient language, although his Urgal is a mite weak; Chip Gibson, grand master of the children's division at Random House; Nancy Hinkel, publishing director extraordinaire; Joan DeMayo, director of sales (much applause, cheers, and bowing!) and her team; Daisy Kline, who with her team designed the wonderful and eye-catching marketing materials; Linda Palladino, Rebecca Price, and Timothy Terhune, production; a bow of thanks to Pam White and her team, who have helped to spread *Eragon* to the four corners of the world; Melissa Nelson, design; Alison Kolani, copy editing; Michele Burke, Michelle Frey's dedicated, hardworking assistant; and everyone else at Knopf who has supported me.

At Listening Library: Gerard Doyle, who brings the world of Alagaësia to life; Taro Meyer for getting the pronunciation of my languages just right; Jacob Bronstein for pulling all the threads together; and Tim Ditlow, publisher of Listening Library.

Thank you all.

One more volume to go and we shall reach the end of this tale. One more manuscript of heartache, ecstasy, and perseverance. . . . One more codex of dreams.

Stay with me, if it please you, and let us see where this winding path will carry us, both in this world and in Alagaësia.

Sé onr sverdar sitja hvass!

Christopher Paolini
August 23, 2005

Read on for a sneak peek at

BRISINGR

INHERITANCE

BOOK THREE

Coming 20.09.08

www.brisingr.co.uk

LIGHT AND SHADOW

(An Excerpt from the Third Chapter of
the Third Book of the Inheritance trilogy)

Saphira kneaded the soil beneath her feet. Let us be off! Leaving their bags and supplies hanging from the branch of a juniper tree, Eragon and Roran clambered onto Saphira's back. They wasted, no time saddling her; she had worn her tack through the night. The molded leather was warm, almost hot, underneath Eragon. He clutched the neck spike in front of him— to steady himself during sudden changes in direction—while Roran hooked one thick arm around Eragon's waist and brandished his hammer with the other.

A piece of shale cracked under Saphira's weight as she settled into a low crouch and then, in a single giddy bound, leaped up to the rim of the gulch, where she balanced for a moment before un-folding her massive wings. The thin membranes thrummed as Saphira raised them toward the sky. Vertical, they looked like two translucent blue sails.

"Not so tight," grunted Eragon.

"Sorry," said Roran. He loosened his embrace.

Further speech became impossible as Saphira jumped again. When she reached the pinnacle of her jump, she brought her wings down with a mighty whoosh, driving the three of them even higher. With each subsequent flap, they climbed closer to the flat, narrow clouds that extended east to west.

As Saphira angled toward Helgrind, Eragon glanced to his left and discovered that, because of their elevation, he could see a broad swath of Leona Lake some miles distant. A thick layer of mist, gray and ghostly in the pre-dawn glow, emanated from the water, as if witchfire burned upon the surface of the liquid. Eragon tried, but even with his hawklike vision, he could not make out the far shore, nor the southern reaches of the Spine beyond, which he regretted. He had not laid eyes upon the mountain range of his childhood since leaving Palancar Valley.

To the north stood Dras-Leona, a huge, rambling mass that appeared as a blocky silhouette against the wall of mist that edged its western flank. The one building Eragon could identify was the cathedral where the Ra'zac had attacked him; its flanged spire loomed above the rest of the city, like a barbed spearhead.

And somewhere in the landscape that rushed past below, Eragon knew, were the remnants of the campsite where the Ra'zac had mortally wounded Brom. He allowed all of his anger and grief over the events of that day—as well as Garrow's murder and the destruction of their farm—to surge forth and give him the courage, nay, the *desire*, to face the Ra'zac in combat.

Eragon, said Saphira. *Today we need not guard our minds and keep our thoughts secret from one another, do we?*

Not unless another magician should appear.

A fan of golden light flared into existence as the top of the sun crested the horizon. In an instant, the full spectrum of colors enlivened the previously drab world: the mist glowed white, the water became a rich blue, the daubed-mud wall that encircled the center of Dras-Leona revealed its dingy yellow sides, the trees cloaked themselves in every shade of green, and the soil blushed red and orange. Helgrind, however, remained as it always was—black.

The mountain of stone rapidly grew larger as they approached. Even from the air, it was intimidating.

Diving toward the base of Helgrind, Saphira tilted so far to her left, Eragon and Roran would have fallen if they had not already strapped their legs to the saddle. Then she whipped around the apron of scree and over the altar where the priests of Helgrind observed their ceremonies. The lip of Eragon's helm caught the wind from her passage and produced a howl that almost deafened him.

"Well?" shouted Roran. He could not see in front of them.

"The slaves are gone!"

A great weight seemed to press Eragon into his seat as Saphira pulled out of her dive and spiraled up around Helgrind, searching for an entrance to the Ra'zac's hideout.

Not even a hole big enough for a woodrat, she declared. She slowed and hung in place before a ridge that connected the third lowest of the four peaks to the prominence above. The jagged buttress magnified the boom produced by each stroke of her wings until it was as loud as a thunderclap. Eragon's eyes watered as the air pulsed against his skin.

A web of white veins adorned the backside of the crags and pillars, where hoarfrost had collected in the cracks that furrowed the rock. Nothing else disturbed the gloom of Helgrind's inky, windswept ramparts. No trees grew there among the slanting stones, nor shrubs, nor grass, nor moss, nor lichen, nor did eagles dare nest upon the tower's broken ledges. True to its name, Helgrind was a place of death, and stood cloaked in the razor-sharp, sawtoothed folds of its scarps and clefts like a bony specter risen to haunt the earth.

Casting his mind outward, Eragon confirmed the presence of one of the slaves, as well as the two people whom he had discovered imprisoned within Helgrind the previous day, but to his concern, he could not locate the Ra'zac or the Lethrblaka. *If they aren't here, then where?* he wondered. Searching again, he noticed something that had eluded him before: a single flower, a gentian, blooming not fifty feet in front of them where, by all rights, there ought to be solid rock. *How does it get enough light to live?*

Saphira answered his question by perching on a crumbling spur several feet to the right. As she did, she lost her balance for a moment and flared her wings to steady herself. Instead of brushing against the bulk of Helgrind, the tip of her right wing dipped into the rock and then back out again.

1195

Saphira, did you see that!

I did.

Leaning forward, Saphira pushed the tip of her snout toward the sheer rock, paused an inch or two away—as if waiting for a trap to spring—then continued her advance. Scale by scale, Saphira's head slid into Helgrind, until all that was visible of her to Eragon was a neck, torso, and wings.

It's an illusion! exclaimed Saphira.

With a surge of her mighty thews, she abandoned the spur and flung the rest of her body after her head. It required every bit of Eragon's self-control not to cover his face in a desperate bid to protect himself as the crag rushed toward him.

An instant later, he found himself looking at a broad, vaulted cave suffused with the warm glow of morning. Saphira's scales refracted the light, casting thousands of shifting blue flecks across the rock. Twisting around, Eragon saw no wall behind them, only the mouth of the cave and a sweeping view of the landscape beyond.

Eragon grimaced. It had never occurred to him that Galbatorix might have hidden the Ra'zac's lair with magic. *Idiot! I have to do better,* he thought. Underestimating the king was a sure way to get them all killed.

Roran swore and said, "Warn me before you do something like that again."

Hunching forward, Eragon unbuckled his legs from the saddle as he studied their surroundings, alert for any danger.

The opening to the cave was an irregular oval, perhaps fifty feet high and sixty feet wide. From there, the chamber expanded to twice that size before ending a good bowshot away in a pile of thick stone slabs that leaned against each other in a confusion of uncertain angles. A mat of powder-gray scratches defaced the floor, evidence of the many times the Lethrblaka had taken off, landed, and walked about thereon. Like mysterious keyholes, five low tunnels pierced the sides of the cave, as did a lancet passageway large enough to accommodate Saphira. Eragon examined the tunnels carefully, but they were pitch-black and appeared vacant, a fact he confirmed with quick thrusts of his mind. Strange, disjointed murmurs echoed from within Helgrind's innards, suggesting unknown *things* scurrying about in the dark, and endlessly dripping water. Adding to the chorus of whispers was the steady rise and fall of Saphira's breathing, which was overloud in the confines of the bare chamber.

The most distinctive feature of the cavern, however, was the mixture of odors that pervaded it. The smell of cold stone dominated, but underneath it, Eragon discerned whiffs of damp and mold and something far worse: the sickly-sweet fetor of rotting meat.

Undoing the last few straps, Eragon swung his right leg over Saphira's spine, so he was sitting sidesaddle, and prepared to jump off her back. Roran did the same on the opposite side.

Before he released his hold, Eragon heard, amid the many rustlings that teased his ear, a score of simultaneous clicks, as if someone had struck the rock with a collection of hammers. The sound repeated itself a half-second later.

He looked in the direction of the noise, as did Saphira.

A huge, twisted shape hurtled out of the lancet passageway. Eyes black, bulging, rimless. A beak seven feet long. Batlike wings. The torso naked, hairless, rippling with muscle. Claws like iron spikes.

Saphira lurched as she tried to evade the Lethrblaka, but to no avail. The creature crashed into her right side with what felt to Eragon like the strength and fury of an avalanche.

What exactly happened next, he knew not, for the impact sent him tumbling through space without so much as a half-formed thought in his jumbled brain. His blind flight ended as abruptly as it began when something hard and flat rammed against the back of him, and he dropped to the floor, banging his head a second time.

That last collision drove the remaining air clean out of Eragon's lungs. Stunned, he lay curled on his side, gasping and struggling to regain a semblance of control over his unresponsive limbs.

Eragon! cried Saphira.

BRISINGR

INHERITANCE
BOOK THREE

Christopher Paolini

Following the colossal battle against the Empire's warriors, Eragon and Saphira narrowly escaped with their lives. But more awaits the Rider and his dragon, as Eragon finds himself bound by promises he may not be able to keep, including his oath to cousin Roran to help rescue his beloved Katrina. When unrest claims the rebels and danger strikes, Eragon must make choices that take him across the Empire and beyond, choices that may lead to unimagined sacrifice.

Conflict, action, adventure and one devastating death await readers as Eragon battles on behalf of the Varden while Galbatorix ruthlessly attempts to crush and twist him to his own purposes. Can he become a leader who can unite the rebel forces and defeat the King?

978 0 385 60791 9
www.rbooks.co.uk

ABOUT THE AUTHOR

Christopher Paolini's abiding love of fantasy and science fiction inspired him to begin writing his debut novel, *Eragon*, when he graduated from high school at fifteen after being home-schooled all his life. He became a *New York Times* bestselling author at nineteen. Christopher lives in Montana, where the dramatic landscape feeds his vision of Alagaësia.

You can find out more about Christopher, *Eragon*, *Eldest*, *Brisingr* and *Inheritance* at www.alagaesia.com and www.eragon.co.uk

THE BELGARIAD
by David Eddings

Long ago, the sorcerer Belgarath fought the evil God Torak over an object of immense power – the Orb of Aldur. But now Torak is stirring again. And Garion, a young farm boy, is plunged into a quest of unparalleled magic and danger . . .

A magnificent fantasy epic set against a history of seven thousand years of struggles between Gods and Kings and men.

Book One: **PAWN OF PROPHECY**
Book Two: **QUEEN OF SORCERY**
Book Three: **MAGICIAN'S GAMBIT**
Book Four: **CASTLE OF WIZARDRY**
Book Five: **ENCHANTERS' END GAME**

www.**kidsatrandomhouse**.co.uk